Hold the Dream
To Be the Best

Barbara Taylor Bradford

Diamond Books
an imprint of HarperCollins*Publishers*,
77–85 Fulham Palace Road,
Hammersmith, London W6 8JB

This Diamond Books Omnibus edition first published 1993
9 8 7 6 5 4 3 2 1

Hold the Dream © Barbara Taylor Bradford 1985
To Be the Best © Barbara Taylor Bradford 1988

ISBN 1 85813 283 5 (UK)
ISBN Diamond Books 0 261 66168 X (international edition)

Photoset in Linotron Ehrhardt by Rowland Phototypesetting Ltd,
Bury St Edmunds, Suffolk

Printed in Great Britain by Mackays of Chatham Ltd

Contents

For Bob – who makes everything possible
for me, with my love.

Hold the Dream

Contents

'She possessed, in the highest degree,
all the qualities which were required in a
great Prince.'

> GIOVANNI SCARAMELLI,
> Venetian Ambassador
> to the Court of Elizabeth Tudor
> Queen of England

'I would have you know that this kingdom
of mine is not so scant of men but there be
a rogue or two among them.'

> ELIZABETH TUDOR, Queen of England

Family Tree (Emma Harte)

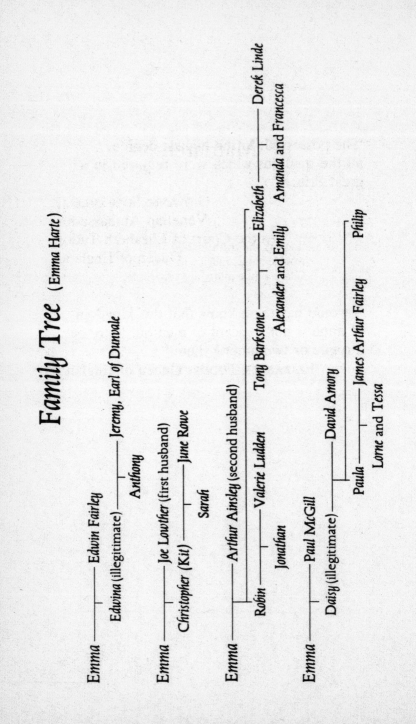

Emma ———— Edwin Fairley
            |
          Edwina (illegitimate) ———— Jeremy, Earl of Dunvale
                                        |
                                     Anthony

Emma ———— Joe Lowther (first husband)
            |
          Christopher (Kit) ———— June Rowe
                                   |
                                 Sarah

Emma ———— Arthur Ainsley (second husband)
            |
     ┌──────┴──────────────┐
   Robin ———— Valerie Ludden   Elizabeth ———— Tony Barkstone / Derek Linde
     | |
  Jonathan   Alexander and Emily / Amanda and Francesca

Emma ———— Paul McGill
            |
          Daisy (illegitimate) ———— David Amory
                                      |
                                    Paula ———— Jim Arthur Fairley
                                               James Arthur Fairley
                                                 |
                                              Philip
                                      Lorne and Tessa

Matriarch

'I speak the truth, not so much as I
would, but as much as I dare; and
I dare a little more, as I grow older.'

MONTAIGNE

1

Emma Harte was almost eighty years old.

She did not look it, for she had always carried her years lightly. Certainly Emma felt like a much younger woman as she sat at her desk in the upstairs parlour of Pennistone Royal on this bright April morning of 1969.

Her posture was erect in the chair, and her alert green eyes, wise and shrewd under the wrinkled lids, missed nothing. The burnished red-gold hair had turned to shining silver long ago, but it was impeccably coiffed in the latest style, and the widow's peak was as dramatic as ever above her oval face. If this was now lined and scored by the years, her excellent bone structure had retained its clarity and her skin held the translucency of her youth. And so, though her great beauty had been blurred by the passage of time, she was still arresting, and her appearance, as always, was stylish.

For the busy working day stretching ahead of her she had chosen to wear a woollen dress of tailored simplicity in the powder-blue shade she so often favoured, and which was so flattering to her. A frothy white lace collar added just the right touch of softness and femininity at her throat, and there were discreet diamond studs on her ears. Otherwise she wore no jewellery, except for a gold watch and her rings.

After her bout with bronchial pneumonia the previous year she was in blooming health, had no infirmities to speak of, and she was filled with the restless vigour and drive that had marked her younger days.

That's my problem, not knowing where to direct all this damned energy, she mused, putting down her pen, leaning back in the chair. She smiled and thought: The devil usually finds work for idle hands, so I'd *better* come up with a new project soon before I get into mischief. Her smile widened. Most people thought she had more than enough to keep her fully occupied, since she continued to control her vast business enterprises which stretched half way round the world. Indeed, they did need her constant supervision; yet, for the most part, they offered her little challenge these days. Emma had always thrived on challenge, and it was this she sorely missed. Playing watchdog was not particularly exciting to her way of thinking. It did not fire her imagination, bring a tingle to her blood, or get her adrenalin flowing in the same way that wheeling and dealing did. Pitting her wits against business adversaries, and striving for power and supremacy in the international market place, had become such second nature to her over the years they were now essential to her well-being.

Restlessly she rose, crossed the floor in swift light steps, and opened one of the soaring leaded windows. She took a deep breath, peered out. The sky was a faultless blue, without a single cloud, and radiant with spring sunshine. New buds, tenderly green, sprouted on the skeletal branches, and under the great oak at the edge of the lawn a mass of daffodils, randomly planted, tossed yellow-bright heads under the fluttering breeze.

'I wandered lonely as a cloud that floats on high o'er vale and hill, when all at once I saw a crowd, a host of golden daffodils,' she recited aloud, then thought: Good heavens, I learned that Wordsworth poem at the village school in Fairley. So long ago, and to think that I've remembered it all these years.

Raising her hand, she closed the window, and the great McGill emerald on the third finger of her left hand flashed as the clear Northern light struck the stone. Its brilliance caught her attention. She had worn this ring for forty-four years, ever since that day, in May of 1925, when Paul McGill had placed it on her finger. He had thrown away her wedding ring, symbol of her disastrous marriage to Arthur Ainsley, then slipped on the massive square-cut emerald. 'We might not have had the benefit of clergy,' Paul had said that memorable day. 'But as far as I'm concerned, you are my wife. From this day forward until death do us part.'

The previous morning their child had been born. Their adored Daisy, conceived in love and raised with love. Her favourite of all her children, just as Paula, Daisy's daughter, was her favourite grandchild, heiress to her enormous retailing empire and half of the colossal McGill fortune which Emma had inherited after Paul's death in 1939. And Paula had given birth to twins four weeks ago, had presented her with her first great-grandchildren, who tomorrow would be christened at the ancient church in Fairley village.

Emma pursed her lips, suddenly wondering if she had made a mistake in acquiescing to this wish of Paula's husband, Jim Fairley. Jim was a traditionalist, and thus wanted his children to be christened at the font where all of the Fairleys had been baptized, and all of the Hartes for that matter, herself included.

Oh well, she thought, I can't very well renege at this late date, and perhaps it *is* only fitting. She had wreaked her revenge on the Fairleys, the vendetta she had waged against them for most of her life was finally at an end, and the two families had been united through Paula's marriage with James Arthur Fairley, the last of the old line. It was a new beginning.

But when Blackie O'Neill had heard of the choice of church he had raised a snowy brow and chuckled and made a remark about the cynic turning into a sentimentalist in her old age, an accusation he was frequently levelling at her of late. Maybe Blackie was right in this assumption. On the other hand, the past no longer troubled her as it once had. The past had been buried with the dead. Only the future concerned her now. And Paula and Jim and their children were that future.

Emma's thoughts centred on Fairley village as she returned to her desk, put on her glasses and stared at the memorandum in front of her. It was from her grandson Alexander, who, with her son Kit, ran her mills, and it was bluntly to the point, in Alexander's inimitable fashion. The Fairley mill was in serious trouble. It had been failing to break even for the longest time and was now deeply in the red. A crucial decision hovered over her head ... to close the mill or keep it running at a considerable loss. Emma, ever the pragmatist, knew deep in her bones that the wisest move would be to close down the Fairley operation, yet she balked at this drastic measure, not wanting to bring hardship to the village of her birth. She had asked Alexander to find an alternative, a workable solution, hoped that he had done so. She would soon know. He was due to arrive for a meeting with her imminently.

One possibility which might enable them to resolve the situation at the Fairley mill had occurred to Emma, but she wanted to give Alexander his head, an opportunity to handle this problem himself. Testing him, she admitted, as I'm constantly testing all of my grandchildren. And why not? That was her prerogative, wasn't it? Everything she owned had been hard won, built on a life rooted in single-mindedness of purpose and the most gruelling work and dogged determination and relentlessness and terrible sacrifice. Nothing had ever been handed to her on a plate. Her mighty empire was entirely of her own making, and, since it was hers and hers alone, she could dispose of it as she wished.

And so with calm deliberation and judiciousness and selectivity she had chosen her heirs one year ago, bypassing four of her five children in favour of her grandchildren in the new will she had drawn; yet she continued to scrutinize the third generation, forever evaluating their worth, seeking weaknesses in them whilst inwardly praying to find none.

They have lived up to my expectations, she reassured herself, then thought with a swift stab of dismay: No, that's not strictly true. There is *one* of whom I am not really sure, *one* whom I don't think I can trust.

Emma unlocked the top drawer of her desk, took out a sheet of paper, and studied the names of her grandchildren, which she had listed only last night when she had experienced her first feelings of uneasiness. Is there a joker in this pack, as I suspect? she asked herself worriedly, squinting at the names. And if there is, how on earth will I handle it?

Her eyes remained riveted to one name. She shook her head, with sadness, pondering.

Treachery had long ceased to surprise Emma, for her natural astuteness and psychological insight had been sharply honed during a long, frequently hard, and always extraordinary life. In fact, relatively few things surprised her anymore, and, with her special brand of cynicism, she had come to expect the worst from people, including family. Yet she *had* been taken aback last year when she had discovered through Gaye Sloane, her secretary, that her four eldest children were wilfully plotting against her. Spurred on by their avariciousness and vaunting ambition, they had endeavoured to wrest her empire away from her in the most underhanded way, seriously underestimating her in the process. Her initial shock, and the pain of betrayal, had been swiftly replaced by an anger of icy ferocity, and she had made her moves with speed and consummate skill and resourcefulness, which was her way when facing any opponent. And she had pushed sentiment and emotions aside, had not allowed feelings to obscure intelligence, for it was her superior intelligence which had inevitably saved her in disastrous situations in the past.

If she had outwitted the inept plotters, had left them floundering stupidly in disarray, she had also finally come to the bitter, and chilling, realization that blood was not thicker than water. It had struck her, and most forcibly, that ties of the blood and of the flesh did not come into play when vast amounts of money and, more importantly, great power, were at stake. People thought nothing of killing to attain even the smallest portions of both. Despite her overriding disgust and disillusionment with her children, she had been very sure of *their* children, *their* devotion to her. Now one of them was causing her to re-evaluate her judgement and question her trust.

She turned the name over in her mind . . . Perhaps she was wrong; she hoped she was wrong. She had nothing to go on really – except gut instinct and her prescience. But, like her intelligence, both had served her well throughout her life.

Always when she faced this kind of dilemma, Emma's instinctive attitude was to wait – and watch. Once again she decided to play for time. By doing thus she could conceal her real feelings, whilst gambling that things would sort themselves out to her advantage, thereby dispensing with the need for harsh action. But I will dole out the rope, she added inwardly. Experience had taught her that when lots of freely proffered rope fell into unwitting hands it invariably formed a noose.

Emma considered the manifold possibilities if this should happen, and a hard grimness settled over her face and her eyes darkened. She did not relish picking up the sword again, to defend herself and her interests, not to mention her other heirs.

History does have a way of repeating itself, she thought wearily, especially in my life. But I refuse to anticipate. That's surely borrowing trouble. Purposefully, she put the list back in the drawer, locked it, and pocketed the key.

Emma Harte had the enviable knack of shelving unsolvable problems in order to concentrate on priorities, and so she was enabled to subdue the nagging – and disturbing – suspicion that a grandchild of hers was untrustworthy, and therefore a potential adversary. Current business was the immediate imperative, and she gave her attention to her appointments for the rest of the day, each of which was with three of the six grandchildren who worked for her.

Alexander would come first.

Emma glanced at her watch. He was due to arrive in fifteen minutes, at ten-thirty. He would be on time, if not indeed early. Her lips twitched in amusement. Alexander had become something of a demon about punctuality, he had even chided *her* last week when she had kept him waiting, and he was forever at odds with his mother, who suffered from a chronic disregard for the clock. Her amused smile fled, was replaced by a cold and disapproving tightness around her mouth as she contemplated her second daughter.

Elizabeth was beginning to push her patience to the limits – gallivanting around the world in the most scandalous manner, marrying and divorcing haphazardly, and with such increasing frequency it was appalling. Her daughter's inconsistency and instability had ceased to baffle her, for she had long understood that Elizabeth had inherited most of her father's worst traits. Arthur Ainsley had been a weak, selfish and self-indulgent man; these flaws were paramount in his daughter, and following his pattern, the beautiful, wild and wilful Elizabeth flouted all the rules, and had remained untamed. And dreadfully unhappy, Emma acknowledged to herself. The woman has become a tragic spectacle, to be pitied, perhaps, rather than condemned.

She wondered where her daughter was at the moment, then instantly dropped the thought. It was of no consequence, she supposed, since they were barely on speaking terms after the matter of the will. Surprisingly, even Alexander

16

had been treated to a degree of cold-shouldering by his adoring mother because he had been favoured in her place. But Elizabeth had not been able to cope with Alexander's cool indifference to her feelings, and her hysterical tantrums and the rivers of tears had abruptly ceased when she realized she was wasting her time. She had capitulated in the face of his aloofness, disapproval, and thinly-veiled contempt. Her son's good opinion of her, and his love, were vital, apparently, and she had made her peace with him, mended her ways. But not for long, Emma thought acidly. *She* soon fell back into her bad habits. And it's certainly no thanks to that foolish and skittish woman that Alexander has turned out so well.

Emma experienced a little rush of warmth mingled with gratification as she contemplated her grandson. Alexander had become the man he was because of his strength of character and his integrity. He was solid, hardworking, dependable. If he did not have his cousin Paula's brilliance, and lacked her vision in business, he was, nonetheless, sound of judgement. His conservative streak was balanced by a degree of flexibility, and he displayed a genuine willingness to weigh the pros and cons of any given situation, and, when necessary, make compromises. Alexander had the ability to keep everything in its proper perspective, and this was reassuring to Emma, who was a born realist herself.

This past year Alexander had proved himself deserving of her faith in him, and she had no regrets about making him the chief heir to Harte Enterprises by leaving him fifty-two per cent of her shares in this privately-held company. Whilst he continued to supervise the mills, she deemed it essential for him to have a true understanding of every aspect of the holding corporation, and she had been training him assiduously, preparing him for the day when he took over the reins from her.

Harte Enterprises controlled her woollen mills, clothing factories, real estate, the General Retail Trading Company, and the Yorkshire Consolidated Newspaper Company, and it was worth many millions of pounds. She had long recognized that Alexander might never increase its worth by much, because of his tendency to be cautious; but, for the same reason, neither would he ruin it through rash decisions and reckless speculation. He would keep it on the steady course she had so carefully charted, following the guidelines and principles she had set down years ago. This was the way she wanted it, had planned it, in point of fact.

Emma drew her appointment book towards her, and checked the time of her lunch with Emily, Alexander's sister.

Emily was due to arrive at one o'clock.

When she had phoned earlier in the week Emily had sounded somewhat enigmatic when she had said she had a serious problem to discuss. There was no mystery, as far as Emma was concerned. She knew what Emily's problem was, had known about it for a long time. She was only surprised her granddaughter had not asked to discuss it before now. She lifted her head and stared into space reflectively, turning the matter over in her mind, and then she frowned. Two weeks ago she had come to a decision about Emily, and she was convinced it was the right one. But would Emily agree? Yes, she answered herself. The girl will see the sense in it, I'm positive of that. Emma brought her eyes back to the open page of the diary.

Paula would stop by at the end of the afternoon.

She and Paula were to discuss the Cross project. Now, if that is skilfully handled by Paula, and she brings the negotiations to a favourable conclusion, then I'll have the challenge I'm looking for, Emma thought. Her mouth settled into its familiar resolute lines as she turned her attention to the balance sheets of the Aire Communications Company, owned by the Crosses. The figures were disastrous – and damning. But its financial problems aside, the company was weighted down with serious afflictions of such enormity they boggled the mind. According to Paula, these could be surmounted and solved, and she had evolved a plan so simple yet so masterful in its premise, Emma had been both intrigued and impressed.

'Let's buy the company, Grandy,' Paula had said to her a few weeks ago. 'I realize Aire looks like a catastrophe, and actually it is, but only because of its bad management, and its present structure. It's a hodgepodge. Too diversified. And they have too many divisions. Those that make a good profit can never get properly ahead and really flourish because they're burdened by the divisions which are in the red, and which they have to support.' Paula had then walked her through the plan, step by step, and Emma had instantly understood how Aire Communications could be turned round and in no time at all. She had instructed her granddaughter to start negotiating immediately.

How she would love to get her hands on that little enterprise. And perhaps she would, and very soon too, if her reading of the situation was as accurate as she thought. Emma was convinced that no one was better equipped to deal with John Cross and his son, Sebastian, than Paula, who had developed into a tough and shrewd negotiator. She no longer equivocated when Emma hurled her into touchy business situations that required nimble thinking and business acumen, which she possessed in good measure. And of late her self-confidence had grown.

Emma glanced at her watch again, then curbed the impulse to telephone Paula at the store in Leeds, to give her a few last-minute tips about John Cross and how to deal with him effectively. Paula had proved she had come into her own, and Emma did not want her to think she was forever breathing down her neck.

The telephone rang. Emma reached for it. 'Hello?'

'It's me, Aunt Emma. Shane. How are you?'

'Why Shane, how lovely to hear your voice. And I'm fine, thanks. You sound pretty good yourself. I'm looking forward to seeing you tomorrow, at the christening.' As she spoke, she took off her glasses and laid them on the desk, relaxed in the chair.

'I was hoping to see you before then, Aunt Emma. How would you like to go out on the town tonight, with two fun-loving bachelors?'

Emma laughed gaily. 'And who's the *other* fun-loving bachelor?'

'Grandfather, of course, who else?'

'Fun-loving! He's getting to be an old stick-in-the-mud, if you ask me.'

'I wouldn't be saying that, mavourneen,' Blackie boomed into the phone, having taken it away from his grandson. 'I bet I could still give *you* a run for your money, if I got half the chance.'

'I'm sure you could, darling.' Emma smiled into the phone, her heart warming to him. 'However, I'm afraid you won't get that chance tonight. I can't accept your invitation, Blackie dear. Some of the family are arriving later, and I ought to be here.'

'No,' Blackie interjected peremptorily. 'You can see *them* tomorrow. Ah now, don't be refusin' me, darlin',' he cajoled. 'Apart from wanting the pleasure of your lovely company, I need your advice on an important business matter.'

'*Oh!*' Emma was mildly taken aback by this statement. Blackie had retired and left the running of his companies to his son, Bryan, and to Shane. Not unnaturally, her curiosity was piqued, and she said, 'What kind of business?'

'I don't want to be discussing it on the telephone, Emma,' Blackie said in a softly chiding tone. 'It's not something that's so cut and dried it can be settled in the matter of a few minutes. We have to be going back and forth, you know, dissecting it a bit, and I think we should be doing it over a nice drop of Irish and a fine meal.'

Emma laughed under her breath, wondering how important this so-called business matter really was, but found herself conceding, 'I suppose I can let them fend for themselves. To tell you the truth, I wasn't much looking forward to tonight. Even though Daisy and David will be here, the prospect of a family gathering isn't particularly exciting. So I accept. And where are you and your dashing grandson planning to take me? Out on the town in Leeds isn't too exciting.'

Laughingly, Blackie concurred and said, 'But don't worry, we'll cook up something, and I promise you won't be bored.'

'What time then?'

'Shane will pick you up around six. Is that all right, me darlin' girl?'

'It's perfect.'

'Good. Good. Until later then. Oh, and Emma?'

'Yes, Blackie?'

'Have you given any more thought to me little proposition?'

'Yes, and I have serious doubts about it working.'

'Oh, so you're still me Doubting Emma after all these years, I can see. Well, we'll discuss that tonight, too, and maybe I can be convincing you yet.'

'Perhaps,' she murmured softly as he hung up.

Emma sat back, contemplating Blackie O'Neill. *Doubting Emma.* A faint smile flickered in her eyes. When had he first called her that? Was it 1904 or 1905? She was no longer sure, but it had been thereabouts, and Blackie had been her dearest, closest friend for all of those sixty-five years. For a whole lifetime. Always there when she needed him, loyal, devoted, supportive and loving. They had been through most of life's exigencies together, had shared each other's terrible losses and defeats, pain and anguish; had celebrated each other's triumphs and joys. Of their contemporaries, there were only the two of them left, and they were closer than ever, inseparable really. She did not know what she would do if anything happened to him. She resolutely squashed this unacceptable thought before it took hold. Blackie was an old war horse, just as she herself was an old war horse, and even though he was eighty-three there was a great deal of surging life and vitality left in him. But no one lasts indefinitely, she thought, experiencing a twinge of anxiousness, whilst acknowledging the inevitable. At their grand ages mortality was a given, one which could not be argued with, and impending death was an old, if unwelcome, familiar.

There was a knock on the door.

Emma glanced at it, adopted her normal expression of cool inscrutability, and called, 'Come in.'

The door swung open and Alexander entered. He was tall, lean and trim in build, with his mother's dark good looks, her large, light-blue eyes; but his somewhat serious, saturnine face made him appear older than his twenty-five years, gave him a dignified air. He wore a well-cut dark grey worsted suit, a white shirt and a burgundy silk tie, all of which reflected, and reinforced, his rather sober personality.

'Good morning, Grandmother,' he said, striding towards her. Reaching the desk, he added, 'I must say, you're looking pretty nifty today.'

'Morning, Alexander, and thank you for the compliment. Mind you, flattery's not going to get you anywhere with me,' she responded crisply. Nonetheless, her eyes danced and she regarded her grandson fondly.

Alexander kissed her on the cheek, seated himself opposite, and protested, 'I'm not trying to flatter you, Grandy, honestly I'm not. You do look absolutely spiffing. That colour really suits you and the dress is very chic.'

Emma nodded impatiently, waved her hand in airy dismissal, and fixed her grandson with a keen and penetrating stare. 'What have you come up with?'

'The *only* solution to the Fairley problem,' Alexander began, understanding she wanted to curtail the small talk and plunge into business. His grandmother loathed procrastination, unless it suited her own ends; then she could elevate procrastination to an art. But she scarcely tolerated it in others, so he rushed on. 'We have to change our product. By that I mean we have to stop manufacturing the expensive woollens and worsted cloths that hardly anybody is buying, and start weaving blends. Man-made fibres, such as nylon and polyester, blended with wool. Those are our best bets.'

'And you think this move will get us out of the red and into the black?' Emma asked, her stare intensifying.

'Yes, I do, Grandy,' he replied, sounding sure of himself. 'One of our chief problems at Fairley has been trying to compete with the man-made fibre goods on the market today. Nobody wants pure wool anymore, except the Savile Row boys, and they're not a big enough market for the Fairley output. Look, either we produce the blends or shut up shop – which you don't want to do. It's as simple as that.'

'Can we make the changeover easily?'

Alexander nodded emphatically. 'We can. By manufacturing cheaper goods we can capture the more popular-priced markets here and abroad, and do volume sales. Of course, it *is* a question of sales and getting a real foothold in those new markets. But I'm sure we can pull it off.' He reached into his inside breast pocket, pulled out a sheet of paper. 'I've analysed every aspect of the plan, and I'm certain I've not overlooked one thing. Here it is.'

Emma took it from him, reached for her glasses, studied the closely-typed sheet. She recognized immediately that he had done his homework with his usual diligence. He had refined the idea she herself had toyed with, although she had no intention of revealing this, not wishing to undermine him, or diminish his efforts. She looked up, removed her spectacles and gave him the benefit of a warm, congratulatory smile.

'Well done, Sandy!' she exclaimed, reverting to the affectionate diminutive of his childhood. 'You've put a lot of sound thinking into this, and I'm delighted, really delighted.'

'That's a relief,' he said, a smile breaking through. Reserved of nature though he was, Alexander was always completely relaxed and outgoing with Emma, who was the one person he truly loved, and now he confessed, 'I've really bashed my brains out on this one, Grandy, played around with all manner of convoluted ideas, I don't mind telling you. Still, I kept coming back to my original plan for creating the new blends.' He leaned closer to the desk, and gave her one of her own penetrating stares. 'But, knowing you, I have a feeling you'd already thought of the solution before you threw the problem at me.'

Emma was tickled at his perceptiveness, but she stifled the laugh that bubbled in her throat. She looked into his candid blue eyes and slowly shook her head. 'No, I didn't,' she lied. Then observing his disbelief, she added, 'But I suppose I would have. Eventually.'

'You're damned right you would,' he acknowledged. He shifted slightly in the chair and crossed his legs, wondering how to break the bit of bad news to her. He decided to jump in with both feet. 'There is one other thing, though, Grandmother.' He hesitated, worry suddenly clouding his face. 'I'm afraid we'll have to cut down on our running costs at the mill. Really tighten our belts out there at Fairley, if we want to operate more efficiently – and profitably. I hate to tell you this, but a number of men will have to be laid off.' There was a slight pause, before he finished gloomily, 'Permanently laid off.'

Emma's face tightened in aggravation. '*Oh dear.*' She nodded slowly, as if confirming something to herself. 'Well, I sort of expected that, Alexander. If you have to do it, you have to do it. I presume you'll be letting the older men go, those who are near retirement age?' she asked, one brow lifting questioningly.

'Yes. I think that's the fairest thing.'

'See to it that they get a special bonus, severance pay, whatever you want to call it. And naturally their pensions will become effective immediately. No penny pinching, and waiting it out until they actually reach retirement age. I won't have any of that nonsense, Sandy.'

'Yes, of course. I second-guessed you on that one. I'm preparing a list of names, and details of our financial obligations to the men. I'll get it to you next week, if that's all right with you.' He sat back, waiting.

Emma made no response. She pushed herself up and walked slowly to the oriel window, where she stood looking down into the magnificent gardens of Pennistone Royal. Concern edged on to her wrinkled face as she ruminated on the mill at Fairley. Her life had been bound up with it in so many different ways. Her father had worked there, and her brother, Frank, when he was only a small boy and should have been at school. Frank had been a bobbin ligger, slaving from early morning until nightfall, hardly able to drag his weary little legs home at the end of the long day, sickly pale from exhaustion and lack of fresh air and sunshine.

Adam Fairley, Jim's great-grandfather and the Squire of Fairley, had been the owner of the mill then. How she had hated him as a girl; for the best part of her life really. With the wisdom of great age, she knew Adam had not been the tyrant she had believed him to be. But he had been negligent, and that in itself was a crime in her eyes. His monumental negligence and his selfish preoccupation with his personal problems and his all-consuming love for Olivia Wainright had caused grievous trouble for others less fortunate. Yes, Adam Fairley had been guilty of abdicating his duties in the most careless and callous fashion, and without so much as a glance at those poor souls who toiled in his mills. The workers who made his cushioned life of ease and privilege possible, who were dependent on him, and were, in a very real sense, his responsibility. Half a century ago, she commented silently. I may understand something of the man now, but I'll never forget what he did. Never.

She glanced down at her small but strong hands, soft and well cared for, the nails manicured to expensive perfection. But once those hands had been red and chapped and sore from scrubbing and polishing and washing and cooking for the Fairleys, when she had been bound in service to them as a child. Lifting one hand, she touched her face, and remembered with stunning clarity Murgatroyd's sharp blows on her cheek. The detestable Murgatroyd, Adam Fairley's butler, who had been permitted by the squire to rule that pernicious and secretive doomed house with a cruelty that bordered on savagery. Despite his harshness and his unremitting persecution of her, Murgatroyd had never frightened her. It was that monstrous house which had filled her with a nameless terror and from which she had wanted always to flee.

Then, one day, *she* had owned that great mausoleum of a place – Fairley's Folly, the villagers had called it – and she had known at once that she would never live in it, would never play the role of the grand lady of the manor. And with a flash of sudden and intense vision she had understood exactly what she must do. She must obliterate it from the face of the earth as if it had never existed. And so she had torn it down, brick by brick by brick, until not a trace of it was left, and she could still recall to this very day the grim satisfaction she had experienced when she had finally razed it to the ground.

Now, across the span of four decades, she heard an echo of her own voice saying to Blackie: 'And destroy this garden. Demolish it completely. I don't want a rosebud, one single leaf left growing.' Blackie had done exactly as she had instructed, uprooting that walled rose garden where Edwin Fairley had so inhumanly and shamefully repudiated her and their child, which she had been carrying. Miraculously, in the space of a few days, the garden, too, had disappeared as if it had never been there at all, and only then had she felt free of the Fairleys at last.

At this time in her life, Emma had acquired the mill. She had done her utmost to give the men proper living wages and overtime and all manner of fringe benefits, and she had kept the village going for years, often at great financial cost to herself. The workers were part of her in a way, for it was from their class that she herself came, and they held a favoured and unique place in her affections. The thought of letting a single one of them go distressed her, yet she had no choice, it seemed. Better, surely, to operate at half her work capacity and keep the mill rolling, than to close it completely.

Half turning she said, 'By the way, Alexander, have you discussed any of this with Kit?'

'Uncle Kit,' Alexander exclaimed, his startled tone reflecting the expression flicking on to his face. 'No, I haven't,' he admitted. 'For one thing, he hasn't been around. And for another, he doesn't seem interested in any of the mills, Fairley least of all. He hasn't appeared to give a damn since you dumped him out of your will.'

'That's a crude way of putting it, I must say!' Emma snapped, and returned to her desk with a show of briskness. 'I didn't *dump* him, as you call it. I passed him over. For his daughter, remember. As I did your mother for you and Emily, and your Uncle Robin for Jonathan. And you know the reasons why, so I won't bother elucidating on them again. Also, let's not forget that my will doesn't come into effect until I die. Which won't be for a long time, if I have anything to do with it.'

'Or me either,' Alexander cried swiftly, as always dismayed by her talk of dying.

Emma smiled at him, fully aware of his devotion to her, his genuine concern for her well being. She continued, in that business-like tone, 'Well, so much for Kit. *Mmmm.* Of course, I realized he was being a bit derelict in his duties; on the other hand, I did think he made an *occasional* visit, if only for appearances' sake.'

'Oh yes, he does do that. But he's so morose and uncommunicative he might as well not be there,' Alexander explained, adding, as an afterthought, 'I can't begin to guess what he does with his time these days.'

'Not much, if I know my eldest son. He never was blessed with much imagination,' Emma shot back sardonically, the suggestion of a disdainful smirk playing on her mouth. She made a mental note to talk to Kit's daughter, Sarah, about her father's present mood. Morose indeed, Emma thought, with disgust. He brought his troubles on entirely by himself. No, not true. Robin gave him a helping hand, and Elizabeth and Edwina, his cohorts in the plot against me. Aware that Alexander was waiting expectantly, Emma finished, 'Anyway, since Kit's not around, he's not going to hamper you – as he has so often in the past. Your way is clear. Put this plan into operation immediately. You have my blessing.'

'Thanks, Grandy.' He leaned forward, said with earnestness, 'We *are* doing the right thing.'

'Yes, I know that.'

'And don't worry about the men who are to be retired. They will be all right, really they will.'

She glanced at him quickly, her eyes narrowed under the hooded lids. She thought: I am so glad it's not Alexander whom I suspect of treachery and duplicity. That I could not bear. It would kill me. She said, 'It pleases me that you've always been so involved with the Fairley mill, and on such a personal basis, Sandy. You *care*, and that's important to me. And I appreciate your understanding . . . I mean of my involvement with that particular mill.' She smiled wryly and shook her head. 'The past, you know, is always with us, always reaching out to claim part of us, and I learned a very long time ago that we cannot escape it.'

'Yes,' he said laconically, but the look in his eyes expressed so much more.

Emma said, 'I've decided to go to the Fairley mill next week. I'll be the one to explain the changes we're going to make. Tell them about the retirements myself, in my own words. It's only proper.'

'Yes, it is, Grandy. And they'll be thrilled to see you. They all worship you, but then you know that.'

'Humph!' she snorted. 'Don't be so foolish, Alexander. And don't exaggerate. You know I can't abide exaggeration.'

Alexander swallowed a smile, remained silent, watching her closely as she sorted through some of the papers on the desk, her head bent. She had spoken swiftly, crossly even, but there had been a curious gruffness in her voice, and he knew that she had been touched by his words. He was amused by her mild chastisement. It was a hoot. Her whole life had been an extraordinary exaggeration, for God's sake. Why she was *larger* than life.

'Are you still here?' Emma said, glancing up, frowning and feigning annoyance. 'I thought you'd be half way to the office by now, with all you've got to do today. Get along with you!'

Alexander laughed, jumped up and went around the desk. He hugged her to him, and kissed the crown of her silvery head. 'There's nobody like you in this entire world, Emma Harte,' he said gently. 'Nobody like you at all.'

2

'Nobody in this world but Emma Harte would have come up with such a preposterous proposition,' Sebastian Cross cried indignantly, glaring, his face turning choleric.

'She didn't come up with it, I did,' Paula replied in her coldest voice, returning his angry look with a steady unblinking gaze.

'Tommy rot! It's your grandmother talking, not you!'

Paula felt herself stiffening in the chair, and she suppressed the swift denial that sprang to her lips. Self-control was essential in all business dealings, and particularly with this odious man. She would not permit him to put her down, nor bait her with his inference that her grandmother was manipulating this negotiation from afar.

'Think what you will,' she said, after a slight pause. 'But regardless of whomever formulated the deal, that's it, as I've outlined it. It's a take it or leave it situation.'

'Then we'll leave it, thank you very much,' Sebastian shot back, filled with rancorous hatred for her and her strange yet compelling beauty, her money and her power. His dark eyes blazed, as he added, 'Who the hell needs you or your grandmother.'

'Now, now, Sebastian, let's not be too hasty,' John Cross soothed. 'And please, do calm down.' He threw his son a cautionary look, then turned to Paula, his whole manner unexpectedly conciliatory. 'You must make allowances for my son. Naturally he's rather upset. After all, your proposal came as something of a shock to him. He is very committed to Aire Communications, as I have always been, and he has no desire to leave the company. Neither do I. In short, we both expect, indeed fully intend, to continue in our present positions. I as chairman of the board, and Sebastian as managing director. Harte Enterprises would have to agree to that.'

'I don't believe that is possible, Mr Cross,' Paula said.

'Forget it, Dad,' Sebastian almost shouted. 'We'll go elsewhere for the money.'

'You've nowhere else to go,' Paula could not help retorting icily, reaching for her briefcase on the conference room table. She stood up, announced with finality, 'Since we seem to have reached an impasse, there's obviously nothing more to say. I think I'd better leave.'

John Cross sprang to his feet, took her arm. 'Please,' he said quietly. 'Please sit down. Let's talk a little more about this.'

Paula hesitated, staring at him. Throughout their relatively short meeting, whilst his son had blustered and snarled, John Cross had adopted a stance of inflexibility, displayed a quiet but firm resoluteness to make the deal on *his* terms, despite their original understanding. Now, for the first time, she detected a sign of wavering on his part. And whether he was aware of it or not, the preceding months of tension and anxiety had taken their toll. The troubles of his floundering company were much in evidence, clearly imprinted on his gaunt and weary face, and there was a quiet desperation behind the bloodshot eyes which held a hint of new panic. He knows I'm right about everything, she thought, carefully assessing him yet again, but he just won't admit it. The fool. She instantly corrected herself. The man standing before her had built up Aire Communications from nothing, so she could hardly characterize him as a fool. Misguided, yes; and, regrettably, he suffered from the serious malady of paternal blindness. He had long invested his son with qualities Sebastian did not possess, nor was ever likely to possess, and therein lay his downfall.

'All right,' she said at last, seating herself tentatively on the edge of the chair. 'I'll stay for a few minutes to hear what you have to say. But very frankly, I meant it when I said we'd reached an impasse.'

'That's not strictly true, in my opinion,' he responded, smiling faintly, and his relief at her continuing presence in his board room was barely concealed as he took a cigarette and lit it. 'Your proposition *is* a bit preposterous, you know. We want new financing. We don't want to be taken over and thrown out of our own company. No, no, that's not what we had in mind when we came to you,' he finished, shaking his head several times for added emphasis.

Paula gazed at him in amazement. She gave him a curious smile. 'You've just pin-pointed the crux of the matter. *You* came to *us*, remember. We didn't seek you out. And you certainly knew enough about Harte Enterprises, and how we operate, to understand that we never invest in companies that are in trouble. We take those over, reorganize them, and put them under new management. Our management. In other words, we get them running smoothly, efficiently, and on a profitable basis. We're not interested in financing other people's continuing disasters. It doesn't pay.'

John Cross winced at this unmistakable thrust, but resisted the parry. Instead

25

he said, 'Quite so, quite so. I've been thinking ... Maybe we can arrive at a workable compromise –'

'*Dad!* Don't!' Sebastian exploded irately, moving violently in his chair.

His father held up one hand, and frowned at him. 'Hear me out, Sebastian. Now, Paula, here's what I think we might do, how we might make a deal after all. Harte Enterprises could buy fifty-two per cent of Aire Communications' shares. That gives you the control you insist you must have. You put in your management, reorganize as you wish, but you must let us stay with –'

'Dad! What are you saying? Are you crazy?' Sebastian bellowed, his flushed face darkening considerably. 'Where would that leave *us*? I'll tell you where. Out in the bloody cold, for Christ's sake.'

'Sebastian! *Please*,' John Cross shouted back, finally losing his composure, his exasperation running high. 'Let me finish for once in my life.'

'Just a minute, Mr Cross,' Paula cut in rapidly, her irritation echoing in her voice. 'Before you go any further, I must point out, *yet again*, that we wouldn't be interested. It must be a *full* buy out. One hundred per cent or nothing. And I told you this right from the –'

'That's the old monster talking again, Dad,' Sebastian interrupted derisively, his mouth contorted into an ugly line. 'Emma Harte! Jesus Christ, the only heart she's got is in her name. Don't deal with them, Dad. They're vultures, both of them, and this one learned well at the knee of the master, that's patently bloody obvious. She wants to swallow us up, in the same way her grandmother has swallowed up companies over the years. I told you, we don't need *them*.'

Paula chose to ignore this unruly and vindictive outburst, deeming it unworthy of a response. She focused all of her attention on John Cross. She was appalled at his deviousness and enraged, but controlling herself, she said as evenly as possible, 'I started to say, that I quite clearly recall mentioning the full buy out to you, Mr Cross, long before today's meeting. I find it hard to believe you've forgotten the protracted conversations we've had about that very matter.' She gave him a hard stare, wondering if he thought she was stupid.

John Cross coloured under her sharp scrutiny. He remembered her initial statements only too well. But he had hoped to get Harte Enterprises interested in the company, whet Emma Harte's appetite, then structure the deal to suit himself. He had been elated when he had realized it was Paula who would do the negotiating. He had believed he could manipulate her, and the situation, to his advantage. His plan had somehow misfired. Maybe Sebastian was right. Yes, Emma Harte was undoubtedly working behind the scenes; all of this had her unmistakable stamp to it. An unreasonable anger surged through him, and he exclaimed heatedly, 'Look here, you're not being fair.'

'*Fair*,' Paula repeated. She smiled thinly, added in a clipped tone, 'The issues of fair or unfair just won't play in this instance.' She held him with her startlingly blue eyes. 'I'm surprised to hear *you* use that word. I told you, at the outset of today's meeting, that Harte Enterprises is prepared to pay you two million pounds for Aire Communications. That's more than *fair*. It's downright generous. Your company is in an unholy mess. It could go belly up at any moment.' She shrugged. 'Well, I suppose that's your affair, Mr Cross, not mine.' She leaned forward, grasped the handle of her briefcase. 'We seem to have nothing further to say to each other.'

The senior Cross said, 'If, and I am saying *if*, we do decide to accept your offer, can my son and I remain with the company?'

She shook her head.

John Cross thought rapidly, came to an unpalatable but necessary decision. 'I would be willing to step aside. After all, I am near retirement age.' He stubbed out his cigarette, fixed his pale eyes on her. 'However,' he went on firmly, 'you must reconsider your decision regarding Sebastian. No one knows this company like my son. Why, he would be invaluable to you. I must insist that he be appointed to the new board of directors and that he be given a contract for five years as special consultant. I would have to have your guarantee on that, and in writing, before we can proceed any further.'

'No,' she said. 'There is no place in Aire Communications for your son if we take the company over.'

The older man was silent.

Sebastian looked pointedly at his father, his expression at once both baleful and condemning. John Cross dropped his eyes, unable to meet that accusatory gaze, toyed with his gold pen, said nothing at all. Sebastian leapt up angrily, seething, and strode across the board room. He stood looking out of the window, his body rigid, and he cursed Paula Fairley under his breath.

Paula's glance followed Sebastian. She felt the malignancy and alertness in him, but intuitively so, for she could not see his face. It was turned into the shadows cast by the window and the buildings outside. Involuntarily she shivered and brought her eyes back to his father. They regarded each other alertly, each wondering which one of them would make the next move. Neither did.

Paula saw a thin, grey-haired man in his early sixties, a self-made man who had pulled himself up by his bootstraps, and who, in the process, had acquired a distinguished air and a degree of superficial polish. He was also a frightened man. His company was sinking like a torpedoed battleship with a gaping hole in its bow, yet seemingly he was prepared to spurn the life belt she had thrown him because of his love for his son. The son who had so badly mismanaged Aire Communications that he had brought it to its present weakened and crippled state. She noticed a muscle twitching in the elder Cross's face and glanced away.

John Cross, for his part, sat facing a young woman of great elegance in her grooming and her dress. She wore a magenta wool suit, magnificently cut and tailored, obviously a pricey piece of *haute couture*, with a man-tailored shirt of white silk. There was an absence of jewellery, except for a simple watch and a plain gold wedding band. He knew that Paula McGill Amory Fairley was only in her mid-twenties, yet she gave the impression of being so much older with her inbred caution, her cool authoritative manner. She reminded him of her famous grandmother, even though her colouring was so different. The glossy black hair, cut in a straight bob that grazed her jawline, the blue eyes flicked with violet, and the ivory complexion were unquestionably striking; but whereas Emma's fabled russet-golden tints had always suggested softness and beguiling femininity, Paula's beauty was somewhat austere, at least to suit his taste in women. Neither were her features quite as perfect as Emma's had once been. Still, they did share the same aura of presence, and she had apparently inherited the old lady's steely toughness as well as that uncommon widow's peak, those sharp eyes that penetrated with a keen intelligence. His heart sank as he continued to study that palely beautiful but obdurate face.

He would never win with her. As this unpleasant realization sank in he did another volte-face, made yet another decision, and this one was final. He would seek financing from another source and insist that the deal include Sebastian. He must ensure his boy's future with the company – one which had been built up expressly for him. That was the only thing he could do; the right and proper thing to do. Yes, he must protect his son above all else, otherwise what had his life been about?

John Cross was the one who broke the prolonged silence. 'We are dead-locked, Paula. I have to pass.' He lifted his hands in a helpless gesture, then let them fall on to the conference table limply. 'Thank you for your time. And please tell your grandmother that her terms are too harsh for my palate.'

Paula laughed softly as they both rose. 'They're my terms, Mr Cross, but I won't labour the point.' Being a courteous young woman she thrust out her hand. 'I wish you lots of luck,' she said with studied politeness.

'Thank you,' he said, his voice equally as civil as hers but not quite as steady. 'Let me escort you to the lift.'

As they passed the window, Paula said, 'Goodbye, Sebastian.'

He swivelled his dark head, nodded curtly, and she was so startled by the naked hatred etched on his cold and bitter face she hardly heard his muttered response. She had recognized a most dangerous enemy.

3

Paula was blazing mad.

Walking rapidly down the Headrow, one of the main thoroughfares in Leeds, she soon put distance between herself and the Aire Communications building. Her mind was racing. Although she had felt the sharp thrust of Sebastian Cross's vindictive and combative personality, had readily acknowledged that he detested her and had become her arch enemy, her thoughts now centred on his father, and with good reason. Having more or less agreed to her terms right from the start, John Cross had ultimately reneged, and, moreover, in the most treacherous and despicable way.

It did not require much analysis on her part to understand why he had done so. It was apparent that he did not want to lose face in front of his domineering son, whose presence had unnerved him, made him defensive and, very possibly, more reckless than he had ever been in his entire life. Yet surely his honour and integrity were important to him too, took precedence over everything else? And what about retaining his son's respect? She laughed hollowly at herself for entertaining such ridiculous thoughts. A young man of Sebastian's perfidious nature had never made the acquaintance of those particular qualities. During the meeting, when she had understood that John Cross was not to be trusted, she had been momentarily astonished. He enjoyed a good reputation in Yorkshire's business community, had always been considered honourable if not necessarily the wisest of men. That he would go back on his word was inconceivable to her.

Her pace accelerated, and so did her anger, as she recalled the energy and thought and time she had expended on Aire Communications. Her grandmother was going to be as infuriated as she was. Emma Harte would not tolerate being played for a fool; neither could she abide anyone who did not deal from a straight deck. Grandy would handle the situation in one of two ways. She would either shrug disdainfully and turn away in disgust, or she would treat Mr Cross to a tongue lashing the likes of which he had never heard before. Her grandmother had an intractable sense of honour, never went back on her handshake or her word, both of which were as good as a written contract, as the whole world knew.

The thought of Emma Harte putting the duplicitous John Cross firmly in his place brought a flicker of a smile to Paula's violet-blue eyes. He deserved that if nothing else. But in reality he was facing much worse than Emma's acid tongue and her virulent condemnation. He was looking disaster right in the eye. Bankruptcy. Total ruin. Obliteration. She knew he was convinced that he could easily find another conglomerate or company to refinance Aire. She also knew he was absolutely wrong in this foolish belief. She had her ear to the ground, and the word was out. Nobody wanted to touch Aire Communications. Not even those ruthless and rapacious asset strippers who bought companies, plundered them, and then tossed to one side the empty shells which were left.

It suddenly occurred to Paula, as she cut down Albion Street, that, unbelievable though it was, John Cross had no real conception of what was about to happen to him or his company. She thought then of those he would take down with him, and of the many employees at Aire who would be thrown out of work. We could have saved him, more importantly saved *them*, she muttered under her breath. The man is unconscionable. Ever since she could remember, her grandmother had instilled a sense of responsibility in her, and this was one of the mandatory rules in Emma's special code of ethics.

'Great wealth and power bring enormous responsibilities, and don't you ever forget that,' Grandy had told her time and time again. 'We must always look after those who work for us, and with us, because they help to make all this possible. And they rely on us, just as we rely on them in other ways,' she had constantly pointed out. Paula was well aware that there were those magnates and industrialists who were jealous of Emma Harte, and who, as adversaries, misguidedly saw her as a hard, ruthless, driven and power-hungry woman. Yet even they did not have the temerity to deny that she was eminently fair. That was something every Harte employee knew from first-hand experience, hence their extraordinary loyalty and devotion to her grandmother, and their love for her.

Paula stopped abruptly, and took several deep breaths. She must get rid of the anger boiling inside her. It was exhausting, took too much of her precious energy – energy which could be directed elsewhere and to much better purpose. And besides, rage blocked reasonable and intelligent thought. She started to walk again, but now her step was slower and more regulated, and by the time she reached Commercial Street she had managed to calm herself considerably.

She dawdled a little bit, stopping to glance in shop windows, until finally she was drawing to a standstill in front of E. Harte, her grandmother's huge department store at the end of the street. She smiled at the uniformed doorman, whom she had known since childhood. 'Hello, Alfred,' she said, smiling.

''Ello, Miss Paula,' he responded with a benevolent grin, touching his cap. 'It's a right beautiful day. Yes, luvely, it is that, Miss Paula. Let's 'ope t'weather 'olds til termorrer, for yer bairns' baptisms.'

'Yes, let's hope so, Alfred.'

He grinned again and pushed open the door for her. She thanked him, hurried through the perfumery department and took the lift to her office on the fourth floor. Her secretary, Agnes, looked up as she walked in, and exclaimed, with a small frown, 'Oh dear, Mrs Fairley, you've just missed Mr O'Neill. Shane O'Neill, that is, and only by a few minutes too. What a shame. He waited for quite a while, then had to rush off to an appointment.'

'*Oh.*' Paula stopped dead in her tracks, taken aback, but she recovered herself, and asked quickly, 'Did he say why he dropped in? Or leave a message?'

'I gathered he was passing the store and decided to say hello on the spur of the moment. No message though, other than to tell you he would be coming to the christening.'

'I see. Anything else, Agnes?'

'Mr Fairley phoned from London. You can't call him back, he was on his way to a luncheon at the Savoy Hotel. He'll be arriving on schedule, at six, with your parents. The other messages are on your desk. Nothing vital.' Agnes hesitated, then asked, 'How did your meeting go at Aire?'

Paula made a sour face. 'Not good, Agnes. In fact I'd venture to say that it went extremely badly.'

'I am sorry, Mrs Fairley. I know the amount of work you put in on those dreadful balance sheets, and then the hours you devoted to the contracts.' Agnes Fuller, prematurely grey at thirty-eight, plain of feature and with a severe expression that actually betrayed the kindest of hearts, had worked her way up through the ranks of the Leeds store. She had been flattered yet apprehensive when Paula had promoted her to private secretary. After all, Paula was the heiress apparent, and Emma Harte's favourite; also, there were those in the store who thought she was cold, remote, unyielding and something of a snob who lacked Emma's extraordinary common touch. But Agnes had soon discovered that Paula had none of the characteristics so unkindly attributed to her by detractors. She was reserved of nature – even a little shy – cautious and prudent, and a veritable work horse, and these traits had, very simply, been misconstrued. Over the past three years, Agnes had come to love the younger woman, was admiring of her, and considered her to be a brilliant executive who was a warm and caring person and a considerate employer.

As she peered at her young boss through her bifocals, Agnes noticed that Paula was paler than usual, and drawn. She gave her a look of sympathy mingled with regret. 'It's all very annoying,' she clucked in commiseration, shaking her head. 'And I hope you're not going to let it bother you, particularly this weekend.'

'No, I won't, I promise you that,' Paula reassured. 'As my grandmother always says, you win a few, lose a few. We lost this one –' She did not finish, and a reflective expression settled on her face. 'But, come to think of it, perhaps that's just as well.' There was a thoughtful pause, before she finished, 'Excuse me, Agnes, I'll see you shortly.'

Paula went into her office and sat down at the huge antique partners' desk which dominated the room. After taking the Aire Communications papers out of her briefcase, she picked up a red pen and wrote *dead* in capitals across the front of the bulging folder. She rose, went to the filing cabinet and slipped it inside, then returned to her desk. The deal *was* dead as far as she was concerned. The negotiations had ended in a fiasco, and, in consequence, she had lost all interest in Aire Communications.

More than any other of the Harte offspring, Paula had inherited an unusual number of Emma's characteristics, and those she had not been born with she had acquired by osmosis, from years of working at Emma's side. Chief amongst these was the ability to admit any kind of mistake with openness and candour, and then put it behind her philosophically. Like Emma, she would invariably say: It didn't work. Perhaps my judgement was flawed. But let's go on from here. We mustn't look back.

And this was exactly what she said to herself now. In her mind, Aire Communications was already a thing of the past. If she had gravely misjudged John Cross and wasted a great deal of time and effort on him, she had no intention of compounding these errors by dwelling on them unnecessarily. She wondered whether she ought to give her grandmother a ring, to explain what had happened, then decided against it. Grandy was seeing both Alexander and Emily this morning, and was bound to be busy. Later, she would drive out to Pennistone Royal, as arranged, and apprise her of the situation. Grandy is going to be disappointed, of course, she thought, sorting through the sheaf of messages. But that won't last long, and I'll soon find another project for her.

Picking up the telephone, Paula returned all of her business calls, signed the stack of letters Agnes had typed, and then sat back in the chair, glancing at her personal messages.

Her mother had called. *Nothing important. Don't bother to call back. Will see you tonight*, Agnes had scribbled, then added one of her inimitable postscripts. *Mrs Amory sounded marvellous, elated about tomorrow. We had a lovely chat. She's got a new hairstyle, and is wearing a grey Christian Dior suit for the event.*

Paula smiled at Agnes's comments, then scanned the message from her cousin, Sarah Lowther. Apparently she was fighting a cold and might not be well enough to attend the christening. *But she didn't sound at all sick*, Agnes had written cryptically. How strange, Paula thought, frowning and re-reading the slip of paper. Sarah obviously doesn't want to come. I wonder why? Since she could not hazard a guess, she turned to the last message. Miranda O'Neill was at the Leeds office of O'Neill Hotels International. *Please call her back before lunch*, Agnes had instructed.

Paula immediately dialled Miranda's private number. The line was busy, as it usually was when she was in the city. Like her grandfather, Miranda had what the poet Dylan Thomas had called 'the beautiful gift of the gab'. She could easily be talking for the next hour. Automatically, Paula's thoughts turned to Miranda's brother, Shane, and instantly she saw his vivid laughing face in her mind's eye. She was terribly disappointed she had missed him earlier. Such a visit had become a rarity. For years he had made it a habit to drop in on her both in Leeds and London, and when these unexpected visits had ceased abruptly she had been hurt and baffled.

Shane O'Neill, son of Bryan, grandson of Blackie, had been Paula's closest friend since childhood. They had grown up with each other, had spent all of their school holidays together, and they had been inseparable for most of their lives, so much so that Emma had nicknamed Paula the Shadow. As her mind lingered on Shane, she realized she had not set eyes on him for many, many months. He was constantly travelling these days, dashing off to Spain and the Caribbean, where a number of the O'Neill hotels were located, and when he was in England, and if she chanced to run into him, he had a preoccupied air and a distant manner. She exhaled softly, slowly. How odd it was that their closeness should end with such finality, as it had two years ago. It still puzzled her. When she had eventually tackled Shane, had asked him what had happened between them, he had looked at her in the most peculiar way, and denied that anything had. He had blamed business and his time-consuming schedule for his absence from her life. Perhaps he had simply outgrown her. Childhood friendships often did change radically; very frequently they deteriorated to such an extent they could never be reinstated. Regrettably, she thought. And I do miss him. I wish I'd been here this morning.

The buzz of the telephone cut into her thoughts. She reached for it. Agnes said, 'It's Miss O'Neill, Mrs Fairley.'

'Thanks, Agnes, put her through, please.'

A split second later Miranda's lilting voice flowed over the wire. 'Hello, Paula. I thought I'd better call you again, since my phone's been busy for ages.'

'That's par for the course,' Paula said with an affectionate laugh. 'When did you get in from London?'

'Last night. I drove up with Shane. And for the last time, I don't mind telling you. He's a maniac in a car. The tyres sizzled the roads. I thought we'd end up in a ditch. I'll never know how I got here safe and sound. I was so shaken up, and white, when we arrived at the house, Mummy knew immediately what had happened. She's forbidden me to drive with him again. She gave him quite a piece of her mind, and –'

'I'll bet,' Paula broke in, with another laugh. 'Your mother thinks the sun shines out of Shane. He can't do anything wrong in her eyes.'

'Well, he's in the dog house at the moment, my dear. She really told him off, and so did Dad.'

'Shane came to see me today, Miranda.'

'Hey, that's good news. Like you, I can't understand why he's so aloof with you these days, but then he's a strange one, that big brother of mine. Too much of the Celt in him, perhaps. Anyway, what did he have to say?'

'Nothing, Miranda, since I wasn't here. I was out at a meeting.'

'Too bad. Still, he's coming to the christening. I know *you* had your doubts, but he told me he was definitely going to go. He even offered to drive me.' Miranda groaned in mock horror at this idea. 'I declined. I was going to go with Grandpops, but naturally he's escorting Aunt Emma. So I'll toddle over by myself. Listen, Paula, apart from wanting to say hello, I was wondering if you'd like to have lunch? I've got to come over to the store to pick up a package for my mother. I could meet you in the Birdcage in half an hour. What do you think?'

'That's a nice suggestion, Merry. I'll see you there at noon.'

'It's a date,' Miranda said. 'Bye.'

'Bye.' As she began clearing her desk of papers, Paula was suddenly glad Miranda had suggested lunch. Her friend was a delight to be with, and a very special girl, with her naturalness, her sweetness, her gaiety and effervescence. She had a joyous, carefree disposition, and laughter sprang readily to her lips, undoubtedly the reason why her nickname Mirry had soon turned into Merry when she was small.

Paula smiled to herself, wondering what Miranda was wearing today, what surprise was in store for her. The twenty-three-year-old girl had a penchant for creating the most outlandish outfits – costumes really – but they were put together with imagination and style, and she certainly carried them off with élan. They would have looked perfectly ridiculous on anyone else, but somehow they were exactly right on Miranda O'Neill. Apart from suiting her tall, some-what boyish figure, they were an adjunct to her fey and whimsical personality. Or so it seemed to Paula, who considered Merry to be an original, the one genuine free spirit she knew. Her grandmother was equally fond of Miranda, and said that Blackie's granddaughter was the best tonic in the world for all of them, because she chased their blues away. 'There's not a bad bone in that girl's body,' Emma had remarked to Paula recently. 'And now that she's grown up she reminds me a lot of her grandmother. There's a good deal of Laura Spencer in Merry – Laura's true goodness for one thing. Also, there's a wise head on those young shoulders, and I'm pleased you two have become such good friends. Every woman needs a close and trusted friend of the same sex. I should know. I never really had one after Laura died.'

Remembering these words of Emma's, Paula thought: But she always had Blackie, and she still has him; whereas I've lost Shane. Funny, though, that Miranda and I drew closer together once Shane had dropped out . . .

There was a knock and Agnes poked her head around the door. 'These proofs just came up from the advertising department. Can you give them your okay?'

'Yes, come in, Agnes.'

'They're the advertisements for the spring fashion sales,' Agnes explained, handing them to her.

After studying the newspaper advertisements for a few seconds, Paula initialled the proofs, gave them back to her secretary and stood up. 'I'm going out on to the floor for a while. Could you phone the Birdcage, Agnes, and tell them I'll need my usual table, please. At noon.'

'Right away,' Agnes said as they went out together.

When Emma Harte had first opened the café on the second floor of the Leeds store, she had called it the Elizabethan Gazebo, and had decorated it in the style of an English country garden. Such things as handpainted wallpaper depicting pastoral scenes, panels of white trellis, artificial topiary animals, and antique birdcages combined to create a most enchanting little setting.

Over the years, as she refurbished the café, the name changed to match the theme, or vice versa. But always a garden or outdoor motif prevailed, often with an international flavour, as Emma had given rein to her imagination and fantasies with flair and not a little wit. After a trip to the Bosphorus, with Paul McGill, she had been inspired to create the effect of a courtyard in a Seraglio. Mosaic tiles, silver wallpaper painted with peacocks, potted palms and a splashing fountain were combined in the new design. She had called the café Turkish Delight, and had been delighted herself to witness its instantaneous popularity as a smart gathering place, not only for women shoppers but local businessmen who came in for lunch. Several years later, Emma decided a more homespun motif was in order. Highland Fling was the name she chose, and the setting took on the appearance of a Scottish castle yard, featuring rustic furniture and colourful tartans. Eventually this ambiance gave way to one which suggested an Oriental teahouse and drew its inspiration from the elegant decorative elements of the Far East. The café was renamed the China Doll. Then came the Balalaika, redolent of nineteenth-century Russia; after that it was transformed into Riviera Terrace, and in 1960 Emma redid the café yet again. This time she used a sophisticated theme based on the skyline of New York City, lining the walls with giant-sized photographic murals of Manhattan. The decor suggested a big-city roof garden and she called it Skyscrapers. But by the late summer of 1968 Emma had grown tired of this decorative mood, and, as the café needed a complete overhaul at this time, she gave the project to Paula, asking her to create something different.

Paula knew everything there was to know about all of the stores in the Harte chain, and she remembered the photographs she had seen of the original Elizabethan Gazebo. She went into the archives, dug out the original plans and sketches, and was instantly struck by the uniqueness and beauty of the antique birdcages. Since she was aware they were stored in packing cases in the basement, she had them brought up and unwrapped. And so the current theme and the latest name were born.

Paula had the wooden and brass birdcages repainted or repolished and, after finding more to add to the collection, she featured them throughout the restaurant. They stood out beautifully against a background of lime-green wallpaper over-patterned with a sharp white trellis design; white wicker chairs and matching tables with glass tops reiterated the outdoor mood. Paula loved all growing things, was, in fact, a gifted gardener, and so her final, masterful touch was a lush assortment of small trees, flowering shrubs and plants. It was the many pots of hydrangeas and azaleas that gave the Birdcage its cachet, and this real garden within the heart of the store bloomed in all seasons under her personal supervision. Emma had recognized at once that it was an evocation of her own first design and as such a little tribute to her, and she was flattered.

A few minutes after twelve, on this Friday morning, Paula hurried into the Birdcage and as always she was struck by the refreshing sight of the flowers and foliage, one which appeared to cheer everyone up. Moving between the tables, where morning shoppers were settling down to lunch, Paula saw that Miranda O'Neill had already arrived. Her burnished copper hair, cascading in a glorious mass of waves and curls around her heart-shaped face, seemed to catch and hold all the light, was like a shining beacon at the far side of the room. Miranda glanced up from the menu she was perusing, saw Paula, and waved.

'Sorry I kept you waiting,' Paula apologized when she reached the table. 'I was delayed in the Designer Salon. We've been having the most awful trouble with the new lighting, and I wanted to check on it again. It's still not right I'm afraid.' She bent down and kissed her friend, slipped into the next chair.

Miranda grinned a little impishly, and said, 'Oh dear, the trials and tribulations of running a store! I'll swap jobs with you any day. Doing public relations for a chain of hotels can be the pits at times.'

'If I remember correctly, you really badgered your father for that job.'

'That's true. But I wouldn't have, if I'd known what I was letting myself in for,' Miranda grumbled, making a long face. But she then had the good grace to laugh, and admitted, 'I suppose I enjoy it really. It's only occasionally that I feel the pressure. But right now I'm in Dad's good books. He's very happy with my latest campaign, and he even went so far as to say I'd been innovative the other day. That's praise indeed from him. He's not given to paying me compliments, as you know. He even said that if I behave myself he's going to send me to Barbados in a few weeks, to look over the hotel we've just bought there. By the time we've remodelled it and redecorated, it'll be super deluxe and as elegant as the Sandy Lane. We all believe it's going to be an important addition to our chain.'

'That's marvellous, Merry. Really exciting for you. Now, shall we order? I don't want to rush you, but I have to leave the store early today.'

'No problem, I'm a bit pushed myself.' Miranda glanced at the menu again, said, 'I'll have the plaice and chips, I think.'

'Good idea. I'll join you.' Paula caught the attention of the waitress, ordered, and then turned to Miranda, looking her over quickly, at once captivated by her outfit. Today she was wearing a rather theatrically-styled jerkin with a wide, flaring collar and three quarter sleeves, and it was laced up the front over a white silk shirt with longer sleeves. There was a twinkle in Paula's eyes as she said, 'You look like a female Robin Hood, in all that Sherwood Green suede, Merry. The only things that are missing are a quiver of arrows and a perky little felt hat with a sweeping feather.'

Miranda broke into laughter. 'Don't think I don't have the hat! I *do*. But I didn't dare wear it to lunch, in case you'd think I was bonkers. Everyone else does.' She swivelled in the chair to reveal her legs, which were encased in tight green-suede pants and matching boots that came up above her knees. 'When Shane saw me this morning he said I looked like the Principal Boy in a pantomime. I went the whole hog with this outfit, I'm afraid. *Is* it too theatrical?'

'Not really. And you could have worn the hat. I for one happen to like you in your fanciful costumes.'

Miranda looked pleased. 'Coming from the elegant you that's a real compliment.' Leaning closer, she hurried on, 'Are you and Jim busy tonight? I was wondering if I could invite you out to dinner?'

'I'd love you to join us tonight, if you won't be bored. Grandy's having a family dinner at Pennistone Royal.'

'I'm not sure that that's still on, Paula. *Your* grandmamma has a hot date with *my* grandfather.' Miranda's laugh held a hint of mischief, which was reflected in her eyes, as she said, 'Can you imagine, and at their ages!'

Paula was thrown by this statement. 'Oh you must be mistaken. I'm certain Grandy intends to be there.'

'I'm not wrong, honestly I'm not. I heard Shane talking to my father a little while ago. Grandfather *is* taking Aunt Emma out to dinner. But I was only teasing when I said they had a hot date, since Shane's going with them.'

'Then Grandy must have changed her plans,' Paula said, dreading the thought of the dinner without her grandmother's presence. 'I expect my mother will play hostess in her place, since I can't imagine Grandy actually cancelling it without talking to me first.'

'No, I don't think she would do that.' Leaning forward again, her manner still teasing, Miranda said, 'When my grandfather and your grandmother get together, they're incorrigible. I told him the other day that it was about time he made an honest woman out of Aunt Emma and married her.'

'If anyone's incorrigible, it's you, Merry! And what did Uncle Blackie say to that?'

'He chuckled, and told me he'd only been waiting for my approval, and now that he had it he was going to pop the question. 'Course, I knew he was only kidding me in return. But to tell you the truth, I don't think it's such a bad idea, do you?'

Paula merely smiled. She said, 'Anyway, getting back to the family dinner, you're very welcome. Come around seven-thirty for drinks. Dinner's at eight-thirty.'

'You are a darling, Paula. Thank you. You've just rescued me from a boring evening with Ma and Pa. All they do these days is talk about the baby.'

'I'm not sure your evening with us will be much more stimulating. My mother has become something of a doting grandma. All *she* does is rave about the twins. I can't seem to shut her up.'

'But I adore Aunt Daisy. She's such a lovely woman, and not a bit like the rest of you –' Miranda stopped, horrified at her words. Her pale, freckled face flamed to scarlet.

'And what's that supposed to mean?' Paula demanded, a dark brow arching as she pretended to be insulted, but the amusement touching her mouth betrayed her.

'I didn't mean it the way it came out,' Miranda exclaimed in embarrassment. 'I wasn't referring to you or Aunt Emma, or your cousins, but to your aunts and uncles actually. I am sorry, though. It was rather rude of me.'

'Don't apologize, I happen to agree with you.' Paula fell silent thinking specifically of her Aunt Edwina, the Dowager Countess of Dunvale, who was due to arrive from Ireland later that day. It was because of Edwina that she and Jim had had their first truly serious quarrel. Some weeks ago, to her utter astonishment and disbelief, Jim had decided that Edwina must be invited to the christening. When Paula had objected, and strenuously so, and had reminded him that Edwina was no favourite of Grandy's, he had brushed aside her protestations and told her she was being silly. And then *he* had reminded *her* that Emma wanted bygones to be bygones, sought peace within the family. 'Well, you'd better not invite Edwina until I've mentioned it to Grandy,' Paula cautioned, and he had acquiesced to this suggestion, at least. When she had told her grandmother about it, Emma had appeared off-hand, indifferent even, and had told her to accept the situation gracefully, to let him invite Edwina, and to put a good face on it if she accepted. But there had been a strange look in Grandy's eyes, and Paula suspected that Emma had been disappointed in Jim. As she had herself, but she had overcome this feeling, loving him as much as she did; and she had excused Jim, too, because he had no family of his own to invite to his children's christening, and Edwina *was* half Fairley. If only Edwina weren't so hostile to Emma and to her.

Miranda, studying her friend, saw that she looked troubled, and ventured, 'You're awfully pensive all of a sudden, Paula. Is something wrong?'

'No, no, of course not.' Paula forced a smile, and changing the subject, she asked, 'How's your mother?'

'Her health's much better, thanks. Also, I think she's finally recovered from the shock of getting pregnant at forty-five and giving birth to a change-of-life baby. And little Laura is simply adorable. I love to watch Grandfather playing with her. He's quite infatuated, and of course he's thrilled they called her Laura, after my grandmother. They almost gave me that name, you know.'

'No, I didn't, Merry.'

'Yes. Then they changed their minds, I suppose. But I wouldn't have minded being named for my grandmother, and I certainly wish I'd known her. She must have been a remarkable woman. Everyone loved her so, especially Aunt Emma.'

'Yes, and Grandy told me, only the other day, that she's never stopped missing Laura since the day she died.'

'We're all muddled up, aren't we Paula?'

'What do you mean?'

'The Hartes and the O'Neills. And the Fairleys, for that matter. Our lives are inextricably linked . . . we can't really escape each other, can we?'

'No, I don't suppose we can.'

Miranda reached over and squeezed Paula's hand. 'I'm glad we can't. I think it's rather nice to have you and Aunt Emma and Aunt Daisy for a second family.' Her huge hazel eyes, sparkling with tiny prisms of gold, overflowed with warmth and affection.

Paula returned the pressure of her hand. 'And it's nice for me to have the O'Neills.'

The arrival of the waitress with the tray of food interrupted this exchange, and for the next fifteen minutes or so the two young women talked mostly about Paula's babies, the christening the next day, and the reception Emma was giving after the church ceremony. But then Miranda, quite suddenly, adopted a serious tone, when she said, 'There's something very important I'd like to discuss with you.'

Paula, at once noticing the change in her friend's demeanour, asked swiftly, 'Do you have problems?'

'Not at all. But I do have an idea I'd like to throw at you, to get your reaction.'

'What kind of idea, Merry?' she asked curiously.

'You and I doing business together.'

'Oh.' This was the last thing Paula expected, and after her initial exclamation she was startled into momentary silence.

Miranda grinned, and not giving her a chance to comment further or brush the idea to one side, she rushed on: 'I had a flash of inspiration last week, when I was going over the blue-prints for the new hotel we're building in Marbella. The architect has planned a galleria of shops, and it struck me immediately that we must include a boutique. Naturally, I thought of Harte's, then I realized one boutique wouldn't interest you. So I took the idea a step further . . . Harte boutiques in all of our hotels. There's the new one we're doing over in Barbados, we're about to remodel the Torremolinos hotel, and eventually the entire chain will get a revamp. We could have a boutique in each one, and Harte's could run them.' Miranda sat back and searched Paula's face for a clue to her feelings, but it was unreadable. She asked eagerly, 'Well, what do you think?'

'I'm not sure,' Paula said. 'Have you discussed this with Uncle Bryan?'

'Yes, and Dad liked the idea. He was very gung ho actually, and told me to talk to you.' Miranda gazed at her friend expectantly and crossed her fingers. '*Would* you be willing to go into the venture with us?'

'I think we might be. I'd have to talk to my grandmother, of course.' This was uttered with Paula's usual caution, but she could not conceal the interest quickening on her face. With a small rush of excitement, she thought: It could be the perfect project for Grandy. The one I've been looking for, and it would certainly take the sting out of the Cross fiasco. Straightening up, Paula said in a more positive voice, 'Give me some additional details, Merry,' and she listened attentively as the other girl talked. Within minutes she began to recognize the endless possibilities and advantages inherent in Miranda O'Neill's idea.

4

Emma sat up with an abrupt jolt.

I don't believe it. I almost dozed off, she thought with exasperation. Only old ladies do that in the middle of the day. She began to laugh. Well, she *was* an old lady, even though she was loath to admit that to anyone, least of all herself.

Shifting her position on the sofa, she stretched, then straightened her skirt, and immediately became aware of the heat from the blazing fire. The room was stifling, even for her – she who had always suffered from the cold and rarely ever felt warm enough. No wonder she had become so drowsy.

With a burst of energy she propelled herself up and off the sofa, and hurried to the windows. She opened one of them and took several deep breaths, fanning herself with her hand. The crisp air felt good, and the breeze brushing against her face soon refreshed her, and she stood there for a moment or two until she was cooler, before turning away and retracing her steps.

Her pace was slower, and she looked around as she skirted the two large plump sofas in the centre of the floor. She nodded with pleasure, thinking how lovely the room appeared at this moment, washed as it was in the golden sunlight now streaming in through the many windows. But then it always did look beautiful to her, and she would rather be here than anywhere else on this earth.

Is it age, I wonder, that makes us cleave to the best-known spaces in our lives, and the well-loved and familiar things? Is it the memories of the years gone by, and of those we cared so much about, which bind us to those places and make them so special in our deepest hearts? She believed that this was true – at least for her. She felt safe, and comforted, when she was in surroundings where so many episodes of her long and colourful life had been played out.

Such a place was Pennistone Royal, this ancient, historic and rambling house on the outskirts of Ripon, which she had purchased in 1932. In particular she favoured this room – the upstairs parlour – where she had spent so many endless happy hours over the years. She had often wondered how it had come to be called the upstairs parlour, for there was nothing parlour-like about it at all. This struck her once again as her glance took in the impressive architectural details and the splendid furnishings.

By the very nature of its dimensions the room had a singular grandeur, with its high, Jacobean ceiling decorated with elaborate plasterwork, its tall leaded windows flanking the unique oriel window, and the carved fireplace of bleached oak. Yet for all its imposing detail, and despite its size, Emma had introduced a mellow charm and great comfort, plus a subtle understated elegance that had taken time, much patience, superb taste and a vast amount of money to create.

Being confident of her original choices, Emma had never felt it necessary to change anything, so the room had remained the same for over thirty years. She knew, for instance, that no other paintings could ever surpass the fine portraits of a young nobleman and his wife by Sir Joshua Reynolds, or the priceless Turner landscape. The three oils were in perfect harmony with her graceful Georgian antiques, collected so lovingly and with infinite care. And such things as the Savonnerie carpet, faded now to a delicate beauty, and her Rose Medallion china in the Chippendale cabinet, were matchless touches that added to the room's graciousness and style. Even the walls were always repainted in their original primrose, for to her discerning eye this pale and delicate colour made the most restful backdrop for the art and the rich patinas of the dark woods, and it introduced the cheerful sunny aspect she preferred.

This morning, the spring-like mood of the setting, created by the airy colour scheme and the brightly-patterned chintz on the sofas, was reinforced by porcelain bowls brimming with jonquils, tulips and hyacinth, which spilled their lively yellows, reds, pinks and mauves on to some of the darkly-gleaming surfaces, and their fragrant scents were aromatic on the still and gentle air.

Emma moved forward, then paused again in front of the fireplace. She never tired of looking at the Turner which hung above the mantelpiece, dominating the soaring chimney wall with its misty greens and blues. The landscape was bucolic, evocative, and a superb example of Turner's poetic and visionary interpretations of the pastoral scene.

It's definitely the light, she decided for the hundredth time, as always fascinated by the luminous sky in the painting. In Emma's opinion, no one had ever been able to capture light on canvas in quite the same manner as Turner. The clear cool light in this masterpiece was forever associated in her mind with the Northern skies under which she had grown up, and had lived for most of her life, and which she would love always. She believed them to be unique because of their clarity, and a radiance that seemed unearthly at times.

Her eye now caught the carriage clock on the mantelpiece. It was almost one. She had better pull herself together, and very smartly, since Emily was due momentarily, and everyone had to be on their toes when the volatile, whirlwind Emily was around. Most especially old ladies, she added inwardly, chuckling softly again.

Hurrying briskly into the adjoining bedroom she sat down at her dressing table. After dabbing her nose with powder, she renewed her pink lipstick and ran a comb through her hair. There, that does it. Passable, she added under her breath, peering into the glass. No, more than passable. I really do look pretty nifty today, as Alexander said.

She swung her head and stared at Paul's photograph standing on one corner of the dressing table, and she began to speak to him in her mind. This was an old habit of hers and one which had become something of a ritual.

I wonder what you would think of me, if you could see me now? Would you recognize your glorious Emma, as you used to call me? Would you think that I have grown old gracefully, as I believe I have?

Picking up the photograph, she sat holding it with both hands, gazing down into his face. After all these years she still remembered every facet of him, and with a poignant vividness, as if she had seen him only yesterday. She blew a mote of dust off the glass. How handsome he looked in his white tie and tails. This was the last picture taken of him. In New York. On February the third, 1939. She recalled the date so easily. It had been his fifty-ninth birthday, and she had invited a group of their friends for drinks at their lavish Fifth Avenue apartment, and then they had gone to the Metropolitan Opera to hear Risë Stevens and Ezio Pinza sing *Mignon*. Afterwards, Paul had taken them to Delmonico's for his birthday dinner, and it had been a wonderful evening, marred only at its outset by Daniel Nelson's talk of impending war, and Paul's equally bleak assessment of the world situation. Paul's mood had been gay later, at dinner. But it was the last carefree evening they ever spent together.

She touched the white wings of his hair with a fingertip, and half smiled to herself. The twins who were being baptized tomorrow were *his* first great-grandchildren too, a continuation of his bloodline. Upon his death, the McGill dynasty had passed into her hands for safekeeping, and she had guarded it well and faithfully, just as she had preserved and multiplied his great fortune, which she had solemnly vowed she would.

Sixteen years, she thought. We only had sixteen years together. Not very much time really, in the span of a life ... particularly a long life like mine.

Without thinking, she spoke aloud: 'If only you had lived longer. If only we could have shared our later years, grown old together. How wonderful that would have been.' Her eyes misted over and she felt a tightening in her throat. Why you foolish, foolish old woman, she admonished herself silently. Weeping now for something gone so far beyond tears. With a swift and darting movement she returned the photograph to its given place.

'Grandma ... are you alone?' Emily asked in a tentative voice from the doorway.

Startled, Emma jumped, and turned in the chair. Her face lit up. 'Oh hello, Emily dear. I didn't hear you come through the parlour. And of course I'm alone.'

Emily ran to her, gave her a resounding kiss, and then looked down at her curiously. She said, with a funny little smile, 'I could have sworn I heard you talking to someone, Gran.'

'I was. I was talking to him.' She inclined her head at the photograph, and added dryly, 'And if you think I'm getting senile, you can forget it. I've talked to that photograph for thirty years.'

'Gosh, Grandy, you're the last person I'd ever think of as being senile!' Emily was quick to reassure, meaning every word. 'Mummy maybe, but never you.'

Emma fixed her coolly probing eyes on her granddaughter. 'Where is your mother, Emily. Do you know?'

'Haiti. Basking in the sun. At least I *think* that's where she's gone.'

'*Haiti*.' Emma sat up in the chair, surprise registering, and then she let out a small whoop of a laugh. 'Isn't that the place they practise voodoo. I hope she isn't having a wax doll made called Emma Harte, into which she can stick pins and wish me ill as she does.'

Emily also laughed, shaking her head. 'Honestly, Gran, you are a card. Mummy wouldn't think of anything like *that*. I doubt she's ever heard of voodoo. Besides, I'm sure she's far too preoccupied. With the Frenchman.'

'*Oh*. So, she's done another bolt, has she? And with a Frenchman this time. Well, I must say, your mother is getting to be a regular United Nations.'

'Yes, she does seem to have developed a fondness for foreign gentlemen, Grandy.' Emily's green eyes brimmed with laughter as she stood rocking on her heels, regarding her grandmother with delight, enjoying their bit of repartee. There was no one like her Gran when it came to the caustic jab which got right to the heart of the matter.

Emma said, 'Knowing your mother, he undoubtedly has an uncertain character, not to mention a dubious title. What's this one's name?'

'Marc Deboyne. You might have read about him. He's always in the gossip columns. And you're right on target, regarding his character. But he doesn't have a title, dubious or otherwise.'

'That's a relief. I'm sick to death of all these counts and princes and barons with unpronounceable names, grandiose ideas and empty wallets, whom your mother unfailingly collects. *And* invariably marries. Deboyne *is* a playboy though, isn't he?'

'I'd categorize him as IWT, Gran.'

'What on earth does that mean, dear?' Emma asked, her brows lifting, expressing her puzzlement.

'International White Trash.'

Emma guffawed. 'That's a new one on me. And whilst I get the implication, explain further, please, Emily.'

'It's a term for men with murky backgrounds, even questionable back-grounds, who have social aspirations which they can only hope to fulfil in another country. I mean a country not their own. You know, where inconsistencies won't be spotted. It could be an Englishman in Paris, a Russian in New York, or, as in this instance, a frog in London.' Emily made a disagreeable face. 'Marc Deboyne has been flitting around Mayfair's fashionable drawing rooms for years, and I'm surprised Mummy got involved with him. He's so *transparent*. He must have managed to dupe her somehow. Personally, I think he stinks, Gran.'

Emma frowned. 'Have you met him then?'

'Yes, and before Mummy too.' She stopped short, deciding not to mention that Deboyne had made a pass at her first. That would really be inflammatory to her Gran. She finished, 'He's quite ghastly.'

Emma sighed, and wondered how much this one was going to cost her daughter. For cost her he would. That type of man always came expensive – frequently emotionally, but *always* financially. Dismally she thought of the million pounds she had given Elizabeth last year. Cold cash, too. Most of it had probably been frittered away by now. Still, what that foolish woman did with the money was no concern of hers. She had only been interested in buying Elizabeth off, and in so doing, protecting Alexander, Emily, and the fifteen-year-old twin girls. Emma said, with some asperity, 'Your mother is impossible. *Impossible*. Where are her brains, for God's sake? Don't bother to answer that, Emily. In the meantime, out of curiosity, whatever happened to the current husband? That lovely Italian.'

Emily stared at her in disbelief. 'Grandy!' she shrieked. 'What a switch! You always said you thought he was a gigolo. In fact, you were usually quite unkind about him, and I was certain you detested him.'

'I changed my mind,' Emma replied loftily. 'As it turned out he wasn't a fortune hunter, and he was nice to the twins.' She stood up. 'Let's go into the parlour and have a drink before lunch.' She tucked her arm through Emily's companionably, and steered her across the floor. She asked again, 'So, where is Gianni what's-his-name?'

'He's around. He's moved out of Mummy's flat, of course. But he's still in London. He's got himself a job with some Italian importing company, antiques, I believe. He often telephones me to ask about Amanda and Francesca. He's rather attached to them I think.'

'I see.' Emma disentangled her arm and lowered herself on to one of the sofas. 'I'd like a gin and tonic, Emily, instead of the usual sherry. Do the honours, please, dear.'

'Yes, Grandy. I think I'll have one myself.' Always in a tearing hurry, Emily dashed across the room to the Georgian table which held a silver tray of bottles and Baccarat crystal glasses. Emma's eyes followed her. In the red wool suit and frilly lilac blouse Emily reminded her of an iridescent humming-bird, so small, so swift, so brilliantly plumed, and so full of life. She's a good girl, Emma thought. Thank God she hasn't turned out like her mother.

Mixing the drinks deftly, Emily said, over her shoulder, 'Talking of my baby half sisters, Gran, are you going to let them stay at Harrogate College?'

'For the moment. But I fully intend to pack them off to finishing school in

Switzerland this September. In the meantime, they seem to be happy at the college. Of course, I realize that's because of my proximity. I suppose I spoil them, letting them come home so much.' Emma paused, remembering the fuss and bother and upset the previous year, when her two youngest grandchildren had tearfully begged to come and live with her. Emma had finally succumbed under their constant pressuring, although her acquiescence had been conditional. For their part, they had had to agree to attend the nearby boarding school Emma had selected. The girls had been thrilled, their mother delighted to be rid of them, Emma relieved that she had averted a nasty family contretemps from developing further.

Leaning back against the cushions, she let out a tiny sigh. 'Anyway, spoil them or not, I do feel those two need mothering, and a chance to lead a normal family life. They've had little enough of either with your mother.'

'That's true,' Emily agreed, carrying the drinks over to the seating arrangement in front of the fire. 'I feel a bit sorry for them myself. I suppose Alexander and I got the best of Mummy, I mean her better years. The girls have had a rough time of it . . . all those husbands. It seems to me that ever since she left their father, our mother has been on a downward slide. Oh well, what can you do? . . .' Emily's young breathy voice petered out sadly. She shrugged in resignation, and her whole demeanour reflected her disenchantment. 'There's not much you or I *can* do about *your* daughter, *my* mother, Grandy. She's not likely to change.'

Emily now looked across at her grandmother, her blonde brows meeting in a frown. She said in a fretful tone, 'The trouble with poor Mummy is that she suffers from the most terrible insecurity about herself, her looks, her figure, her personality . . . well, just about everything.'

'Oh, do you think so,' Emma exclaimed in astonishment at this remark. Her face changed and there was a glint of malice in her flinty green eyes as she remarked, with immense coldness, 'I can't *imagine* why.' She lifted her glass. 'Cheers.'

'Cheers, Gran darling.'

Emma settled into a corner of the vast sofa, and, squinting in the sunlight, she focused on the attractive twenty-two-year-old Emily. The girl had a special place in her affections, for apart from being open and uncomplicated, she had a very lovable personality, one that was sunny, cheerful, and perennially optimistic, and she was a dynamic girl, filled with enthusiasm for life and her work. If Emily's pink-and-cream blonde prettiness had the porcelain fragility of a Dresden shepherdess, it was, nevertheless, deceptive, belying an extraordinary drive that had the velocity and power of an express train running at full speed. Emma knew there were those in the family, specifically her sons, who thought Emily was scatterbrained and flippant. This secretly amused Emma, since she was fully aware that Emily purposely chose to give this fraudulent impression. In no way did it reflect her basic seriousness and diligence. Emma had long ago decided that her sons really disliked their niece because she was far too blunt and opinionated – and truthful – for their comfort. Emma had been witness to more than one scene when the intrepid Emily had made Kit and Robin squirm.

Emma looked into the clear green eyes, a reflection of her own as they had once been, saw the expectancy flickering in them, then noted the confident smile etched on Emily's mouth. Emily had obviously convinced herself she was going to get her own way. *Oh dear.* Taking a deep breath, Emma said, with a faint laugh, 'For someone with a serious problem, you certainly don't look very troubled, dear. You're positively glowing this morning.'

Emily nodded, and admitted, 'I don't think my problem's all that serious, Grandy. I mean, it doesn't seem to be today.'

'I'm glad to hear that. You sounded as if you had the burdens of the world on your shoulders, when you spoke to me on Tuesday morning.'

'Did I really,' Emily laughed. 'I suppose things seem so much brighter when I'm with you. Perhaps that's because I know you can always solve any problem, and I just know you'll –' She broke off when Emma held up a silencing hand.

Emma said: 'I've known for some time that you want to go back to Paris, to work in the store there. That *is* what you want to discuss, isn't it? That is your *problem?*'

'Yes, Gran,' Emily said, her eyes shining with eagerness.

Emma put down her drink on the butler's tray table, and leaned forward, her expression suddenly serious. She said carefully, 'I'm afraid I can't let you go to Paris. I'm very sorry to disappoint you, Emily, but you will have to stay here.'

The happy smile vanished, and Emily's face dropped. 'But why, Grandy?' she asked in a crushed voice. 'I thought you were pleased with the way I handled things in Paris all last summer and through the autumn.'

'I was. Very pleased, in fact, and proud of you. Your performance has nothing to do with my decision. No, that's not strictly true. One of the reasons I've formulated new plans for you is because of the way you performed over there.' Emma's eyes did not leave her granddaughter's face as she explained carefully, 'Plans for your future. Which, in my considered opinion, is with Harte Enterprises.'

'*Harte Enterprises!*' Emily cried, her voice rising incredulously. She froze on the sofa, staring at her grandmother dumbfounded. 'Where would I fit in *there?* Alexander, Sarah and Jonathan are working in that company, and I'd just be a spare wheel! A dogsbody, with nothing to do. Anyway, I've always worked for *you.* In the stores. I love retailing, and you know that, Gran. I'd just hate, positively hate and detest, being pushed into that organization,' Emily protested with uncommon fierceness, flushing bright pink. Breathlessly, she rushed on, 'I really mean it. You've always said it's important to enjoy one's work. Well, I certainly wouldn't enjoy working at Harte Enterprises. Oh please let me go to Paris. I really love that store, and I want to continue to help you get it properly on its feet. Please change your mind. Please, oh *please*, Gran darling. I'll just be miserable if you don't,' she wailed, and her face was as woebegone as her voice as she clenched her hands together in her lap.

Emma made an irritated clucking noise, and shook her head reprovingly. 'Now, now, Emily, don't be so dramatic,' she exclaimed with unusual sharpness. 'And do stop trying to cajole me. I know all about your wheedling. Sometimes it works, other times, like right now, I am quite impervious to it. And incidentally, the Paris store *is* on its feet, thanks, in no small measure, to you. So you're not needed there any more. Very frankly, I need you here.'

This remark, although uttered mildly, caused Emily to sit up swiftly, and she frowned, further taken aback. '*You* need me, Grandy. What for? What do you mean?' Emily's eyes widened and filled with worry. She wondered if her grandmother had a serious problem within Harte Enterprises. Hardly. Her health? That seemed unlikely too. But obviously something was amiss.

'What's wrong, Grandma?' she asked, giving words to her spiralling anxiety, all ideas about Paris swept completely out of her head.

'There is nothing *wrong*, dear,' Emma said with a bright smile, detecting the girl's concern. 'Before I explain my reasons for wanting you here, I would like to clarify my remark about your future. Naturally I realize you like working at the stores, but you can't get much further at Harte's. Paula and your Uncle David have the real power there these days, and Paula will inherit all of my shares one day. Paula respects your ability, and she would love to keep you by her side, but Emily, you'd always be a salaried employee, with no financial interest whatsoever. I do –'

'I know that,' Emily interjected. 'But –'

'Don't interrupt me,' Emma snapped, cutting her off. 'As you learned last spring, I have left you sixteen per cent of Harte Enterprises, and that's a huge interest, since the company is so very rich. And solid. As solid as the Bank of England, in my opinion. Your wealth, your future security, will come from your shares in Harte Enterprises, and I have felt for the longest time that you must have a hand in running it. After all, it will belong, in part, to you one day.'

Emma could not fail to miss the worried expression now settling on Emily's face and she reached across the table and squeezed her arm affectionately. 'Don't look so distressed. I'm not implying that I lack confidence in your brother. You must know that I don't. Alexander will guide, and guard, Harte Enterprises with all of his strength and ability, and with great devotion, I've no fear. Nevertheless, I want *you* to be active there, along with Sandy and your cousins. I really believe that you must direct that considerable energy of yours, and your many talents into the company in which you have such a major stake, and from which you will reap so many benefits.'

Emily was quiet, mulling over her grandmother's words, and after a longish pause, she said slowly, 'Yes, I see what you mean, and I know you have my interests at heart, but there's nothing about the company that appeals to me. Anyway, Sarah has always enjoyed running the clothing end, and she'd resent it if you shoved me in there with her. As for Jonathan, he'd really get on that high horse of his, if you foist me on *him*. He considers the real estate division to be his little kingdom, and his alone. He'd be in revolt if I started poking around there. So what would I do at HE? The only thing I understand is retailing.' Her voice faltered, for she was on the verge of tears, and she looked away swiftly, staring out of the window, her expression exceedingly glum.

The prospect of leaving the Harte chain of stores, and Paula, whom she worshipped, was depressing and distressing to Emily. And she *would* have to leave. That had already been decided, she had the good sense to recognize. Her opinion wasn't being sought. She was being *told* what to do, told what was expected of her, and her grandmother's authority was unassailable. Besides, that cold and stubborn look was now engraved on her grandmother's face, and it was a look they were all familiar with, one which left nothing to the imagination. It said, in no uncertain language, that Emma Harte would have her own way no matter what. Emily felt the prick of tears behind her eyes, as she contemplated her miserable future. Mortified, she blinked them back and swallowed, endeavouring to hold on to her diminishing composure. Tears, emotion, and any other sign of weakness in business were anathema to her grandmother.

Emma, observing the girl closely, saw how troubled and upset she was growing, and realized immediately that she must allay Emily's worries. Adopting her most sympathetic manner, Emma said, 'Don't take this so hard, dear. It's not half as bad as you imagine. And I certainly had no intention of putting you in either of the divisions run by your cousins. That wouldn't be fair to any of you. Nor am I considering making you Sandy's assistant – if that idea has entered your agile little brain. No, no, nothing like that. When I said I needed you here, I did mean *here*. In Yorkshire. I would like you to work at General Retail Trading, and learn everything there is to know about that division of Harte Enterprises. You see, Emily, I want you to run it for me eventually.'

For a moment Emily thought she had misheard. She was so surprised she was speechless. She gaped at her grandmother, and then finally managed to ask, 'Are you serious?'

'Really, Emily, that's a stupid question. Do you honestly think *I* would joke about my *business?*'

'No, Grandy.' Emily bit her lip, trying to digest her grandmother's words. The General Retail Trading Company, known within the family as Genret, was one of Harte Enterprises' most important assets, and an enormous money maker. As the implications behind her grandmother's announcement began to sink in, she was assaulted by a mixture of emotions: she was flattered, overwhelmed, worried and scared all at once. But these feelings were almost instantaneously overshadowed by genuine bafflement.

Sitting forward with a jerk, she asked in a puzzled voice, 'But why do you suddenly need *me?* You have Leonard Harvey. He's been running Genret for years, and brilliantly. Or so you've always said.'

'And I meant what I said.' Emma picked up her drink, took a sip, sat nursing it in her hands. 'However, Len reminded me several weeks ago that he will be retiring in three years. I'd hoped he would stay on, but he insists on going when it's time. He wants a chance to enjoy life, do a few of the things he's always wanted to do, like take a trip around the world, for one thing.' Emma laughed softly. 'I can certainly understand his point of view. That man's worked for me for over thirty-five years, and I don't remember him ever taking a day off, except for his annual summer holidays in August. Naturally, I'd no option but to agree, albeit reluctantly.'

Emma put down her drink, rose, and went to stand with her back to the fireplace. She stared down at Emily, and continued matter-of-factly: 'Len brought up his retirement because he thought it was high time I started to think about his successor. It occurred to me at once that here was the perfect opening for you. I've been wracking my brains for months, wondering how to get you situated within Harte Enterprises, in a division you would enjoy. I believe I've found it, Emily, and I'm also convinced Genret could well use your special talents.'

Emily said nothing. She, who had an opinion about everything which she usually had no qualms expressing, was now oddly at a loss for words.

Emma stood waiting, giving Emily a chance to catch her breath and marshal her thoughts. She understood perfectly the girl's unprecedented reticence. She had just dropped a bombshell on her. But as the silence grew, Emma, always in a hurry to settle matters and move on, announced peremptorily, 'I need you to start working at Genret immediately. Len wants to begin his training programme at once. Three years may seem like a long time to you, but it isn't really. Genret is a large company, and you will have a great deal to absorb and understand. So, what do you say?'

Still Emily was mute, and Emma threw her a sharper look. Then she scowled at her. 'Come along, dear, you must have some comment to make. I can't believe that the cat's got *your* tongue permanently.'

Pulling herself together, Emily gave her grandmother an uncertain smile. 'Are you sure? Really sure about me going into Genret?'

'I wouldn't have suggested it, if I'd had any doubts,' Emma retorted crossly.

'But what about the group at Genret?' Emily asked quickly. 'I mean, will they sit still for it? For me?'

'I *am* Genret, Emily. Or had you forgotten that?'

'No, no, of course I hadn't, Grandmother. What I meant was, will Len and the top management team accept me? I know you can appoint anybody you want, since it's your company, but surely Len must have a protégé, somebody he would like to follow in his footsteps, who knows the inner workings of Genret.'

'He doesn't. Furthermore, he thinks you're the ideal choice. And he's not just pandering to me. Len's too shrewd and outspoken to fall into that trap. And, whilst he realizes I would *like* a member of the family inside Genret once he goes, he would tell me point blank if there was no suitable candidate. He would insist we look outside the family. It just so happens that he thinks you're ideally suited to head up a wholesale supply company. For several reasons, all of them excellent. Your experience with the stores, your considerable knowledge of retailing, not to mention merchandise, plus your natural business abilities. That you also happen to be my granddaughter is simply fortuitous. It didn't influence him one iota, I can assure you of that. Besides, you're a quick study, Emily, and you've learned a lot in the last five years.'

'I'm glad to have Len's vote of confidence, as well as yours, Grandy.' Emily started to relax, and as her depression also began to lift, she discovered she was excited about the sudden turn of events. She asked, 'And Alexander? Have you discussed it with him?'

'Naturally. He thinks you'll be marvellous.'

'What does Paula say?'

'She's delighted too. She's going to miss you at the stores, but she recognizes the good sense behind my plans for you.'

'Then it's settled!' Emily beamed, and allowed her natural enthusiasm to surface. 'Genret is a big responsibility, but now that I've recovered from my initial surprise, I'm looking forward to it, I really am. I'll try very hard, and I'll do my best not to let you down.'

'I know you will, dear.' Emma returned her smile, delighted to finally witness

Emily's eagerness and her excitement. Not that she had had any doubts about her offer being accepted. Emily was far too clever to thwart her, *or* to pass up the opportunity to head a division. Besides, Emily loved a challenge. This last thought prompted Emma to add, 'I'm quite certain you'll enjoy this new venture as much as you did your sojourn in Paris last year. It's going to be equally as challenging, and ultimately very rewarding.'

'Yes, I know it will be.' With a sudden flush of embarrassment, Emily recalled her outburst of earlier. Looking extremely shame-faced, she apologized, 'I'm sorry I behaved in such a childish way, when you said I couldn't go back to Paris, Grandy. It was ridiculous of me to act like that.'

'I understand. You were disappointed. In any case, you'll be going to Paris quite a lot for Genret, and travelling all over the world on your buying trips. That's certainly something to look forward to, Emily.'

'Oh it is, Grandy. And thank you for your faith in me, and for this wonderful opportunity.' Emily jumped up and hugged Emma tightly. With a happy little laugh, she said, 'Oh Grandy, you're such an inspiration! You make everything seem possible – and attainable. And exciting as well. Do you know what? I feel like rushing down to the Genret offices in Leeds right now, and getting stuck into the work with Len immediately.'

'Len and Genret have managed to exist without you until now, Emily, so I think they'll survive for another few days,' Emma replied, her mouth twitching with hidden laughter. 'In the meantime, I have a much better idea. I think you should come downstairs with me, and have lunch instead. I don't know about you, but I'm famished.'

5

Emma sat at the table in her splendidly-appointed Adam dining room, sipping a cup of coffee after lunch, smiling and nodding occasionally, enjoying Emily's natural *joie de vivre* and bubbling enthusiasm for everything. Earlier, when they had been eating, Emily had bombarded her with questions about Genret. Each one had been probing and not without a certain shrewdness, and this had pleased Emma.

Now, the twenty-two-year-old was entertaining her with titbits of gossip about the family, and, as usual, Emma found her pithy comments hilarious. Robin and Kit were most often the butts of her barbed wit, and she had already managed to get in a few sharp digs about her uncles.

But here her sarcasm stopped, for she never made astringent or unkind remarks about anyone else. Although Emily tended to be something of a chatter-box, she was not malicious, nor was she a talebearer intent on stirring up trouble. In point of fact, she was anything but this, and Emma was well aware that her granddaughter's predilection for chattering was harmless enough, especially since she knew herself to be the girl's only confidante. To Emma's considerable relief, Emily was not only discreet but extremely close-mouthed with everyone else in the family, and even Paula and Alexander, with whom she was on very intimate terms, were no exceptions to this rule.

Unexpectedly, Emily veered away from her discourse on the family, and launched into glowing descriptions of the outfits she had chosen for the fifteen-year-old twins to wear the next day. Recently Emily had elected to play a motherly big-sister role with Amanda and Francesca, and Emma had assigned to her the task of selecting their clothes and looking after similar details.

But it was not very long before Emma found her attention straying, her mind forever preoccupied with business, and specifically Paula's meeting with the Crosses. She could not help speculating on the outcome, wondering how Paula had fared. If the negotiations had gone well she was facing a fair amount of work. Not that this troubled Emma unduly. She had always thrived on honest-to-goodness toil, and still did, and Paula had laid out foolproof plans for the takeover.

Emma and Paula wanted Aire Communications for its three most important assets: its magazine division, its local radio stations, its huge, modern building on the Headrow. Following Paula's advice, she fully intended to make Aire Communications a subsidiary of the Yorkshire Consolidated Newspaper Company. Once she had relocated the entire staff of Aire in the offices of the *Yorkshire Morning Gazette*, her newspaper headquartered in Leeds, she would sell the Aire Communications building. This would enable her to cut down on Aire's staggering overheads, and at the same time she would cleverly recoup part of the purchase price, possibly a good half of her two-million-pound investment. Yes, that building's worth at least a million, Emma reflected, whatever Jonathan says to the contrary. She would have to have a little talk with her grandson tomorrow, a very serious talk. He was dragging his feet with his second evaluation of Aire's prime bit of real estate. She had asked him for it days ago and he had not yet responded. Once again she wondered why, and her mouth tightened.

'Grandy, you're not listening to me!' Emily shook her arm impatiently.

'Oh sorry, dear. You were saying you'd chosen navy-blue dresses and coats for the twins. I'm sure they're very smart, you have such good –'

'Goodness, Gran, that was five minutes ago,' Emily interjected. 'I was already on to another subject. Aunt Edwina to be precise.'

'Now why on earth is *she* suddenly so interesting to *you*?'

'She's not really. I think she's an old sourpuss and a crashing bore,' Emily said in her typical blunt fashion. 'However, I'm positive we're going to be in for a rocky ride with her this weekend. I bet she's going to give us all an earful.'

'What about?' Emma asked, sounding slightly baffled.

'The divorce,' Emily said succinctly.

This reply brought Emma upright in her chair, and she stared hard at Emily. 'So, you've heard about *that* have you?' Surprise immediately gave way to humour, and Emma chuckled and shook her head. 'Is there anything you *don't* know about this family of ours?'

'Not much,' said Emily, grinning at her. 'But I don't pry, Gran. You know that. Everyone just tells me things automatically. It must be my sympathetic nature.' Her grin widened. 'And then I tell you. Never secrets, though. I don't break a confidence. Ever.'

'I should hope not, dear. Remember what I've always said . . . a still tongue and a wise head. Anyway, who mentioned Anthony's divorce?'

'Jim. He came to see me last weekend. He wanted my opinion about something, my advice really. He brought up the divorce in passing. It was Aunt Edwina who told him. Apparently she's terribly upset . . . scandal touching the sacred name of the Dunvales and all that silly nonsense. As if anybody *cares* about divorce these days. But she'll harp on about it for the next few days, you mark my words.'

'I doubt it, since Anthony will be here himself. In fact, he's already here.'

'In this house?' It was Emily's turn to be astonished.

'No. He's staying with your Uncle Randolph up at Middleham. Actually, he's going to be there for the next week.' A wicked gleam entered Emma's eyes, and she could not resist teasing, 'Obviously there are *some* things you don't know, Emily. Our young earl is staying with the Hartes because he's courting Sally. Very seriously courting her.' Emma was unable to hold back a laugh as she observed the expression on Emily's face.

Emily was so dumbfounded by this piece of news her jaw had dropped. But it took less than a second for her to recover, and she retorted, 'And I bet Aunt Edwina doesn't know either! Otherwise she would have scuttled that relationship ages ago. And she'll still try.'

'She can do nothing,' Emma snapped, her face hardening. 'Anthony is not only of age, he's thirty-three. He doesn't have to answer to his mother, or anyone else for that matter, and I told him so last night. He has my blessing. Frankly, I'm glad he's going to marry Sally. She's a fine girl and quite lovely, and it's a perfect match in my opinion.'

'I second that, about Sally being a lovely person. But then I'm prejudiced. So are you – even more so, because she looks so much like your mother. And Edwina's going to be prejudiced too, in the other direction.' Emily stopped, thinking of her aunt's reaction, which would be violent, and she cried excitedly, 'Oh my God! I can't wait to see Aunt Edwina's face when she finds out he's involved with Sally Harte. She's going to be absolutely furious, Grandma. She has such grand ideas about everything. And after all, Sally's only a generation removed from the working class.'

'And what do you think Edwina is?'

'A countess,' Emily giggled gleefully, 'and a Fairley to boot! She's never been the same since she discovered her father was Sir Edwin Fairley, and a KC, no less. She's an even bigger snob now than she was before. It's a pity you ever told her the truth about you and old Edwin, Gran.'

'I'm inclined to agree with you.'

Emma averted her face, looked out of the window, focused her thoughts on her eldest grandchild, son of her own first born child. Anthony Standish was the only offspring of Edwina's marriage with the Earl of Dunvale, and as such he was her whole life. Because Emma had been estranged from Edwina for years, she had not really come to know Anthony until he was eighteen. That was in 1951, when her brother Winston had affected a reconciliation between her and her daughter. More like an armed truce, Emma said inwardly, but at least the boy and I took to each other immediately, and thankfully we have continued to be close. She was extremely fond of Anthony, who, despite his reserved nature and gentle manner, had an inner strength and a toughness of mind that Emma had recognized instantly and privately applauded. Upon his father's death, he had inherited the latter's title and lands in Ireland. For the most part, Anthony lived at Clonloughlin, his estate in County Cork, but whenever he had the occasion to be in England he never failed to visit her. It was on one of these trips to Yorkshire, six months ago, that he had become re-acquainted with Sally, Winston's granddaughter, who was his cousin. According to Anthony they had fallen in love at once. 'It was a *coup de foudre*, Grandmother,' he had confided shyly last night. 'And as soon as my divorce from Min is final I intend to marry Sally.' Emma, delighted at this news, had indicated her pleasure, and assured him of her full support.

Shifting in the chair, Emma glanced at Emily, and said, 'I wouldn't worry your head about Anthony. He can take care of himself. I told him not to hide his relationship with Sally any more, from his mother, that is, and to behave naturally at the christening. We might as well get this out in the open once and for all.'

'Edwina will make trouble, Grandma. Big, big trouble,' Emily warned, rolling her eyes at the ceiling.

'If she knows what's good for her she won't,' Emma replied, her voice murderously soft. 'Now, on to other things. You said Jim wanted your advice. What about?'

'The gift he's bought for Paula. It's a strand of pearls, and he wasn't sure she'd like them. But they're beautiful, and I told him she'd be thrilled.'

'That's nice.' Emma glanced at her watch, feeling restless. 'I'll have another quick cup of coffee, and then I'd better go up and do a little paperwork until Paula arrives.'

'I'll get the coffee for you,' Emily volunteered, taking Emma's cup to the sideboard. Returning with it, she said, 'I had dinner with T. B. when I was in London on Tuesday. He sends his love.'

Emma's face softened considerably. She had always cared for Tony Barkstone, Elizabeth's first husband and father of Emily and Alexander. They had remained good friends over the years, and she asked, with a warm smile, 'How is he?'

'In good form. He's as sweet as always, and he seems happy. No, content might be a better word. Or perhaps *accepting* is even better. Yes, that's it. He's accepting.' Emily sighed heavily.

And a little too dramatically, in Emma's opinion. But then Emily was a romantic girl and Emma knew that she had long harboured the desire for her parents to be reunited. A most unlikely event, as far as Emma was concerned. Looking at Emily thoughtfully, Emma's brow lifted quizzically, and she murmured, 'Accepting is a peculiar word to use about your father's life, isn't it, dear?'

'Not really. I think T. B. *is* accepting – of his new family. But I don't believe my father has been really happy since he split with Mummy. To tell you the truth, Gran, I think he's still in love with her.' She confided this in an intense tone, giving Emma a long and knowing look.

'Oh phooey!'

51

'Well, she *was* his grand passion, that I know for a fact – because he once told me so. I believe he's carrying a torch for her.'

'That's a bit farfetched, Emily, they've been divorced for donkey's years.'

'Even so, he could have remained shackled to her emotionally.' Emily tilted her blonde head to one side and wrinkled her nose. 'Unrequited love, and all that. Why are you looking so sceptical, Grandma? Don't you believe that's possible?'

'Possible. Not very practical. And I'm quite certain your father has more common sense than to yearn after Elizabeth. He had *her* pegged years ago.'

'I hope you're right. I'm sure that being in love with someone who doesn't care in return is most unsatisfactory, not to mention painful. Very impractical in the long run, as you just said.' A faraway expression flickered in Emily's wide green eyes, and she said, almost inaudibly, 'If only Sarah would recognize that.'

As quiet as her voice had been Emma had heard her. She put down her coffee cup with a loud clatter and gaped at Emily, frowning. '*Our Sarah.* Is she in love with someone who doesn't love her?'

'Oh gosh, Gran, I shouldn't have mentioned Sarah. It's really none of my business,' Emily muttered, her face flushing and filling with chagrin. 'Please don't say anything to her will you? She'd be ever so upset.'

'Of course I won't say anything. I never do, do I? Who's she carrying a torch for? That's what you implied, you know.'

Emily hesitated. She was suddenly tempted to fib. But she had never lied to her grandmother in her whole life. Still, perhaps in this instance she ought to resort to a white lie.

Emma pressed, 'Who is it?'

There was a moment of silence. Emily swallowed, and knowing herself to be trapped, she mumbled, 'Shane.'

'I'll be damned.' Emma leaned back and focused her keen old eyes on her granddaughter, 'Well, well, well,' she said, and a slow smile spread across her face.

Emily shot up in her chair, her eyes flaring open, and she cried, 'Oh Grandy, don't look like that! *Please* don't look like that!'

'And how am I looking?'

'Gratified. And ever so conspiratorial. I know you and Uncle Blackie have long had hopes that one of us, or one of the Harte girls, would marry Shane O'Neill, and unite our families. But he's not interested in any of us, except for –' Emily bit off the rest of her sentence abruptly, instantly wishing she could also bite off her tongue. This time she really had said far too much. She jumped up and went to the Hepplewhite sideboard, where she hovered over the silver bowl of fruit. 'I think I'll have a banana,' she said, attempting nonchalance. 'Would you like one too, Gran dear?'

'I certainly wouldn't, thank you very much.' Emma swung her head and studied her granddaughter's back. 'Except for *whom*, Emily?'

'No one, Gran.' Emily wondered how to extricate herself, and adroitly, without arousing her grandmother's suspicions further. She sauntered back to her chair, flopped down, and attacked the banana with her dessert knife and fork, her head studiously bent.

Emma watched her, knowing that Emily was avoiding her eyes. And avoiding answering.

'I know you were about to tell me who Shane *is* interested in, Emily. If anyone knows, it's you.' She laughed lightly, endeavouring to be casual. 'You've always been my conduit for information about everyone in the family. And *out* of it for that matter. So come along, finish your sentence.'

Emily, who was still cutting the skin off the banana with painstaking care, finally lifted her head. Her face was a picture of innocence as she said, 'I wasn't about to reveal a thing, really I wasn't. I'm not in Shane's confidence – I don't know anything about his love life. What I was going to say, before, is that he isn't interested in any of us, except for a one night stand.'

'Really, Emily!'

'Sorry.' Emily dropped her eyes, then coyly looked up at Emma through her long lashes. 'Have I shocked you, Grandma?'

'At my age I'm shock resistant, my girl,' Emma replied tartly. 'But I am rather surprised by your remark about Shane. It wasn't very nice. Extremely unkind, in fact.' A new thought struck Emma, and she gave her granddaughter a fierce stare. 'Has he ever suggested anything of the sort –'

'No, no, of course not,' Emily burst out peremptorily before Emma could finish. And then she was swift to qualify her previous statement about Shane. 'It's just a *feeling* I have about him,' she mumbled, hating herself for maligning Shane, who was the nicest person imaginable. 'I didn't mean any harm, Grandy, honestly I didn't. Besides, who can blame him for being a bit of a lady killer, when women fall at his feet like ninepins. That's hardly his fault.'

'True,' Emma acknowledged. 'But getting back to Sarah, I hope this crush she has on him is going to pass soon. I can't bear to think that she's miserable. How does she *really* feel, dear?'

'I don't know, Gran,' Emily replied in all truthfulness. 'She's only discussed Shane with me once, ages ago, and I think she's regretted mentioning him ever since. But I know she's smitten with him, just through my own observation. She always blushes furiously whenever his name comes up, and she gets all self-conscious and sort of dopey when he's around.' Emily levelled her gaze at Emma, and it was direct and candid, as she added, 'No, she'll never say anything to anyone about her feelings. Sarah's basically much too secretive to confide.'

This last comment further surprised Emma, but she decided not to pursue it for the moment. Conscious of the girl's stricken expression, she hastened to say, 'You don't have to be apprehensive about me, darling. Have no fear, I won't mention Shane to Sarah . . . I wouldn't dream of embarrassing her. And she'll come to her senses, if she hasn't already.' Emma's eyes rested on the bowl of spring hyacinths in the centre of the table, and she ruminated briefly on all that had been said. When she raised her head she smiled kindly at Emily. 'I don't want you to think I'm questioning your powers of observation, or your judgement, but you do have a tendency to be overly imaginative at times. You could be wrong about Sarah. Perhaps she has forgotten Shane by now, in view of his lack of interest in her. She *does* have her feet on the ground, you know.'

'Yes, Gran,' Emily said, although she did not agree with her grandmother's assessment of her cousin. Sarah might look as if her feet were firmly planted on the ground but her head was most definitely in the clouds. Emily bit her lip, and she wished more fervently than before that she had never mentioned Sarah in the first place. Embarking on this kind of conversation with her canny grandmother had been a horrible mistake. The trouble was, she was constantly doing it. Emma had always been the most dominant and important person in her young life, and confiding everything in her was a childhood habit which was difficult, if not impossible, to break. But Emily was thankful for one thing – she had caught herself in the nick of time, had managed not to reveal the truth about Shane to Grandy, who doted on him as if he were one of her own.

The realization that she had protected him made Emily feel better, for she liked and admired Blackie's grandson. She smiled to herself as she toyed with the banana in front of her, filled with sudden self-congratulation. For once she had been rather clever, side-stepping Grandy's probing so skilfully. And thankfully Shane O'Neill's secret was still safe. It would always be safe with her. Poor Shane, she thought with a twinge of sadness, what a terrible burden he has to carry. Stifling a sigh, Emily finally said, 'I don't think I want any more of this,' and she pushed her dessert plate away, making a face.

Emma, anxious to bring the lunch to an end, nodded quickly, and said, 'I'd better get back to my desk. What are your plans for this afternoon? You've finished at the Harrogate store, haven't you?'

'Yes, Grandy. I completed the stock inventories you wanted, and selected the clothing for the sales,' Emily explained, relieved that Emma had apparently now dismissed Shane and Sarah Lowther from her mind. 'I'm going to potter around in my room. Hilda asked one of the maids to unpack my suitcases when I arrived, but I prefer to arrange my things myself.'

'Suitcases in the plural, Emily? How many did you bring?'

'Ten, Gran.'

'For the *weekend*?'

Emily cleared her throat and gave her grandmother one of her most engaging and persuasive smiles. 'Not exactly. I thought I'd stay with you for a while, if that's all right with you. It is, isn't it?'

'Well, yes, I suppose so,' Emma answered slowly, wondering what this unexpected move on Emily's part was all about. 'But what about your flat in Headingley?' she thought to ask with a small frown.

'I want to get rid of it. I have for some time, actually. I decided to sell it, or rather that you should ask Jonathan to do so. Anyway, last night I packed a lot of my clothes and other things, because I'd convinced myself you'd be sending me to Paris next week. Now that I'm not going, I might as well stay here at Pennistone Royal. I'll be company for you, Gran. You won't be so lonely.'

I'm not lonely, Emma thought, but said, 'I'm probably being dense, but you seemed awfully taken with that flat when I bought it for you last November. Don't you like it anymore, Emily?'

'It's a very nice flat, really it is, but –. Well, to be honest, Gran darling, I have felt rather isolated there by myself. I'd much rather be *here*. With you.' Emily flashed her beguiling smile again. 'For one thing, it's a lot more fun. And exciting.'

'Personally, I find it pretty dull here. Pretty dull indeed,' Emma muttered and stood up, headed for the dining room door. Over her shoulder she said,

'But you're quite welcome, Emily,' and she hoped she had not sounded too grudging. First the twins, and now Emily, she sighed under her breath. Suddenly they're all moving in on me. And just when I thought I was going to get some peace and quiet for once in my life.

As she walked briskly across the vast Stone Hall and mounted the staircase, with Emily trailing in her wake, Emma had another thought: maybe she would take Blackie up on his little proposition after all.

Paula talked and Emma listened.

They sat together in the upstairs parlour, facing each other across the Georgian silver tea service which Hilda had brought up a few minutes after Paula had arrived.

Emma had poured tea for them both, but she had hardly touched her own cup. She sat so still on the sofa she might have turned to stone, and the familiar mask of inscrutability had dropped down over her face as she concentrated on Paula's words, absorbing each one.

Paula spoke well, recounting the meeting at Aire Communications with precision and careful attention to the smallest detail, and her narration was so graphically descriptive Emma felt as though she had been present herself. Several times she experienced a spurt of anger or annoyance, but not an eyelash flickered, not a muscle moved in her blank, impenetrable face, and not once did she interrupt the flow of words.

Long before Paula came to the retelling of the final scene in the boardroom, Emma's mind, so agile and astute, leaped ahead. She knew without having to be told that John Cross had reneged on the deal. For a moment she was as startled as Paula had been earlier in the day, but when this initial reaction passed with some swiftness she realized she was not so surprised after all. And she came to the conclusion that she knew John Cross better than she had believed. Years ago she had spotted him for what he was, an egotist, puffed-up with his own self-importance, a foolish man with immeasurable weaknesses. At this time in his life he was between a rock and a hard place, dealing from fear and desperation and propelled by increasing panic, and it was patently clear that he would be capable of just about anything. Even a dishonourable action, for apparently he was a man without scruples. And then there was that disreputable son of his, goading him on. A pretty pair indeed, she thought disdainfully.

Paula came to the end of her story at last, and finished with a tiny regretful sigh, 'And there you have it, Grandy. I'm sorry it ended in a debacle. I did my best. More than my best.'

'You certainly did,' Emma said, looking her fully in the face, proud of her, thinking how she had progressed. A year ago Paula would have blamed herself for the breakdown in the talks. 'You've nothing to reproach yourself for, and just chalk this one up to experience and learn from it.'

'Yes, Grandy, I will.' Paula regarded her closely. 'What are you going to do now?' she asked, continuing to study that impassive face in an effort to gauge her grandmother's feelings about the Cross situation.

'Why nothing. Nothing at all.'

Although she was not altogether surprised by this statement, Paula neverthe-less felt bound to say, and a bit heatedly, 'I thought that might be your attitude, but I can't help wishing you'd give John Cross a piece of your mind, tell him what you think of him. Look at all the effort we put into this deal. He's not only wasted our valuable time, but played us for a couple of fools.'

'Played himself for a fool,' Emma corrected, her voice low and without a trace of emotion. 'Very frankly, I wouldn't waste my breath, or the tuppence, on a phone call to him. There's not much to be gained from flogging a dead horse. Besides, I wouldn't give him the satisfaction of knowing I'm put out. There's another thing . . . indifference is a mightily powerful weapon, and so I prefer to ignore Mr Cross. I don't know what his game is, but I won't be a party to it.' The look Emma gave Paula was full of shrewdness and her eyes narrowed. 'It strikes me that he might be using our offer to jack up the price with another company. He won't succeed, he won't have any takers.' A cynical smile glanced across her face, and she laughed quietly to herself. 'He'll come crawling back to you, of course. On his hands and knees. And very soon. Then what will *you* do, Paula? That's more to the point.' Settling back against the cushions she let her eyes rest with intentness on her granddaughter.

Paula opened her mouth to speak, then closed it swiftly. For a split second she hesitated over her answer. She asked herself how Grandy would act in these particular circumstances and then dismissed the question. She knew exactly what *her* course of action was going to be.

In a resolute tone, Paula said, 'I shall tell him to go to hell. Politely. I know I could hammer him down, get Aire Communications at a much lower figure, because when he does come back to us, and I agree that he will, he'll be choking. He'll accept any terms I offer. However, I don't want to do business with that man. I don't trust him.'

'Good girl!' Emma was pleased with this reply and showed it, then went on, 'My sentiments exactly. I've told you many times that it's not particularly impor-tant to like those with whom we do business. But there should always be an element of trust between both parties in any transaction, otherwise it's begging for problems. I concur with what you think about Cross and that son of his. Their behaviour was appalling, unconscionable. I wouldn't touch them with a ten-foot barge pole myself.'

Despite these condemning words and the stern expression lingering on Emma's face, her overall reaction had been so understated, so mild, Paula was still a trifle puzzled. 'I thought you'd be much more annoyed than you are, Grandy, unless you're not showing it. And you don't seem very disappointed either,' she said.

'My initial anger soon changed to disgust. As for being disappointed, well, of course I am in some ways. But even that is being replaced by an enormous sense of relief. As much as I wanted Aire Communications, now, quite sud-denly, I'm glad things turned out the way they did.'

'I am too.' There was the slightest hesitation on Paula's part before she remarked quietly, 'Sebastian Cross has become my enemy, Grandmother.'

'So what!' Emma exclaimed in a dismissive tone. 'If he's your first, he's surely not going to be your last.' As she spoke Emma became aware of the concern reflected in the lovely, deep-violet eyes fastened on hers, and she sucked in her breath quickly. Making an enemy troubles Paula, she thought, and she reached out and squeezed the girl's arm, adopted a gentler tone. 'As unpleasant as it may be, you're bound to make enemies, as I myself did. Very frequently it happens through no fault of ours, that's the sad part.' Emma let out a tiny sigh. 'So many people are jealous and envious by nature, and *you* will always be vulnerable to that kind, and a target, because you have so much. Wealth and power through me, not to mention your looks, your brains and your immense capacity for work. All very enviable attributes. You must learn to ignore the backbiting, darling, rise above it. As I have always done. And forget Sebastian Cross. He's the least of your worries.'

'Yes, you're right on all counts, as usual, Grandmother,' Paula said and pushed away the dismaying memory of those hard eyes which had filled with loathing for her that morning. She felt a shiver trickle through her. Sebastian Cross would do her harm if he could. This unexpected thought immediately seemed silly, farfetched and overly imaginative, and Paula laughed silently at herself, and dismissed such an idea.

Rising, she crossed to the fireplace and stood warming her back for a moment or two. Her eyes swept around the lovely old room. It looked so peaceful, so gentle in the late afternoon sunlight filtering in through the many windows, with every beautiful object in its given place, the fire crackling merrily in the huge grate, the old carriage clock ticking away on the mantelpiece as it had for as long as she could remember. She had loved the upstairs parlour all of her life, had found comfort and tranquillity here. It was a room abundant with graciousness and harmony, where nothing ever changed, and it was this timelessness which made it seem so far removed from the outside world and all its ugliness. It's a very civilized room, she said to herself, created by a very civilized and extraordinary woman. She looked across at Emma, relaxed on the sofa and so pretty in the pale blue dress, and her eyes became tender. Paula thought: she is an old woman now, in her eightieth year, yet she never seems old to me. She could easily be my age with her vigour and strength and zest and enthusiasm. And she is my best friend.

For the first time since she had arrived, Paula smiled. 'So much for my wheeling and dealing ... skirmishing might be a better way to describe it, Grandy.'

'And so much for my new project. Now that that's flown out of the window, I'll have to find another one, or take up knitting.'

Paula could not help grinning. 'That'll be the day,' she retorted, merriment swamping her face. Stepping back to the sofa, she sat down, lifted her cup and took a sip of tea, then remarked casually, 'I had lunch with Miranda O'Neill today, and –'

'Oh dear, that reminds me, I'm afraid I won't be here for dinner this evening. I'm going out with Blackie and Shane.'

'Yes, so Merry told me.'

'My God, can't I take a breath around here without everyone knowing!' Emma paused, scanned Paula's face. 'Well, you don't seem too upset, so I presume you don't mind that I'm trotting off and leaving you to cope with Edwina. Don't worry, she'll behave.'

'I'm not concerned. I was at first, but I decided she's Jim's problem. He invited her, so he can entertain her. In any case, Mummy's always pretty good with Edwina. She knows how to appropriately squelch her, in the nicest possible way too.' Paula put down her cup and saucer, leaned closer. 'Listen, Grandy dear, Merry has had an idea, one that might appeal to you. It could be just the project you're looking for.'

'Oh, has she. Well then, tell me about it.'

Paula did so, but as she came to the end of her little recital she made a small moue with her mouth, and finished lamely, 'I can tell you're not enthusiastic. Don't you think it's a good idea?'

Emma laughed at her crestfallen expression. 'Yes, I do. However I'm not interested in taking it on as a *personal* project. Still, that doesn't mean you shouldn't pursue the idea and develop it further with Merry. It could be good for the stores. Come back to me when you have it refined. Perhaps we *will* open the boutiques.'

'I'll set up a meeting with her for next week –' Paula stopped, peered at Emma. 'Out of curiosity, *why* don't you think it's a project for you?'

'There's no challenge to it. I like tougher nuts to crack.'

'Oh Lord! And where on earth am I going to find such a thing for you?'

'I might find my own project, you know.' Emma's green eyes twinkled, and she shook her head. 'You're constantly trying to mother me these days. I do wish you'd stop.'

Paula joined in Emma's laughter and admitted, 'Yes, I am doing that lately, aren't I. Sorry, Gran.' She glanced at the clock, swung her eyes back to Emma, said: 'I think I'd be much better off going home and mothering my babies. If I hurry I'll get back in time to help the nurse bathe them.'

'Yes, why don't you do that, darling. These early years are the most precious, the best really. Don't sacrifice them.'

Paula stood up and slipped into the magenta jacket, found her handbag, came to kiss Emma. 'Have a lovely time tonight, and give Uncle Blackie and Shane my love.'

'I will. And if I don't see you later, I'll talk to you in the morning.'

Paula was halfway across the room when Emma called, 'Oh, Paula, what time do you expect Jim and your parents?'

'Around six. Jim said he'd be landing at Leeds-Bradford airport at five.'

'So he's flying them up in that dreadful little plane of his, is he?' Emma pursed her lips in annoyance and gave Paula the benefit of a reproving stare. 'I thought I'd told the two of you I don't like you flitting around in that pile of junk.'

'You did indeed, but Jim has a mind of his own, as you well know. And flying is one of his main hobbies. But perhaps you'd better mention it to him again.'

'I certainly will,' Emma said, and waved her out of the room.

6

They all said that he was a true Celt.

And Shane Desmond Ingham O'Neill had himself come to believe that the heritage of his ancestors was buried deep in his bones, that their ancient blood flowed through his veins, and this filled him with an immense satisfaction and the most profound pride.

When he was accused by some members of his family of being extravagant, impetuous, talkative and vain, he would simply nod, as if relishing their criticisms as compliments.

But Shane often wanted to retort that he was also energetic, intelligent and creative; to point out that these, too, had been traits of those early Britons.

It was as a very small boy that Shane O'Neill had been made aware of his exceptional nature. At first he had been self-conscious, then confused, puzzled and hurt. He saw himself as being different, set apart from others, and this had disturbed him. He wanted to be ordinary; they made him feel freakish. He had detested it when he had overheard adults describe him as *fey* and *overly emotional* and *mystical*.

Then, when he was sixteen and had more of an understanding of the things they said about him, he sought further illumination in the only way he knew – through books. If he *was* 'a curious throwback to the Celts', as they said he was, then he must educate himself about these ancient people whom he apparently so resembled. He had turned to the volumes of history which depicted the early Britons in all their splendour and glory, and the time of the great High Kings and the legendary Arthur of Camelot had become as real to him, and as alive, as the present.

In the years that followed his interest in history had never waned, and it was a continuing hobby. Like his Celtic forebears he venerated words and their power, for filled with a recklessness and gaiety though he was, he was also a man of intellectual vigour. And perhaps it was this extraordinary mingling of contrasts – his mass of contradictions – that made him so unusual. If his angers and enmities were deep rooted, so his loves and loyalties were immovable and everlasting. And that theatricality, constantly attributed to the Celt in him, existed easily alongside his introspection and his rare, almost tender, understanding of nature and its beauty.

At twenty-seven there was a dazzle to Shane O'Neill, an intense glamour that sprang not so much from his remarkable looks as from his character and personality. He could devastate any woman in a room; equally, he could captivate his male friends with an incisive discussion on politics, a ribald joke, a humorous story filled with wit and self-mockery. He could entertain with a song in his splendid baritone, whether he was rendering a rollicking sea shanty or a sentimental ballad, and poetry flew with swiftness from his tongue. Yet he could be hard-headed, objective, outspoken and honest almost to the point of cruelty, and he was ambitious and driven, by his own admission. Greatness, and greatness for its own sake in particular, appealed strongly to him. And *he* appealed to everyone who crossed his path. Not that Shane was without enemies, but even they never denied the existence of his potent charm. Some of these traits had been passed on from his paternal Irish grandfather, that other larger-than-life Celt, whose physique and physical presence he had inherited. Yet there was also much of his mother's ancestry in him.

Now on this crisp Friday afternoon, Shane O'Neill stood with his horse, aptly called War Lord, high on the moors overlooking the town of Middleham and the ruined castle below. It was still proud and stately despite its shattered battlements, roofless halls and ghostly chambers, all deserted now except for the numerous small birds nesting in the folds of the ancient stone amongst the daffodils, snowdrops and celandines blooming in the crannies at this time of year.

With his vivid imagination, it was never hard for Shane to visualize how it had once been centuries ago when Warwick and Gareth Ingham, an ancestor on his mother's side, had lived within that stout fortress, spinning their convoluted schemes. Instantly, in his mind's eye, he saw the panoply unfolding as it had in a bygone age . . . glittering occasions of state, princely banquets, other scenes of royal magnificence and of pomp and ceremony, and for a few seconds he was transported into the historical past.

Then he blinked, expunging these images, and lifted his head, tore his eyes away from the ruined battlements, and gazed out at the spectacular vista spread before him. He always felt the same thrill when he stood on this spot. To Shane there was an austerity and an aloofness to the vast and empty moors, and a most singular majesty dwelt within this landscape. The rolling moors swept up and away like a great unfurled banner of green and gold and umber and ochre, flaring out to meet the rim of the endless sky, that incredible blaze of blue shimmering with silvered sunlight at this hour. It was a beauty of such magnitude and stunning clarity Shane found it almost unendurable to look at, and his response, as always, was intensely emotional. Here was the one spot on this earth where he felt he truly belonged, and when he was away from it he was filled with a sense of deprivation, yearned to return. Once again he was about to exile himself, but like all of his other exiles, this, too, was self-imposed.

Shane O'Neill sighed heavily as he felt the old sadness, the melancholy, trickling through him. He leaned his head against the stallion's neck and squeezed his eyes shut, and he willed the pain of longing for her to pass. How could he live here, under the same sky, knowing she was so close yet so far beyond his reach. So he must go . . . go far away and leave this place he loved, leave the woman he loved beyond reason because she could never be his. It was the only way he could survive as a man.

Abruptly he turned, and swung himself into the saddle, determined to pull himself out of the black mood which had so unexpectedly engulfed him. He spurred War Lord forward, taking the wild moorland at a flat out gallop.

Half way along the road he passed a couple of stable lads out exercising two magnificent thoroughbreds and he returned their cheery greetings with a friendly nod, then branched off at the Swine Cross, making for Allington Hall, Randolph Harte's house. In Middleham, a town famous for a dozen or more of the greatest racing stables in England, Allington Hall was considered to be one of the finest, and Randolph a trainer of some renown. Randolph was Blackie O'Neill's trainer, and permitted Shane to stable War Lord, Feudal Baron, and his filly, Celtic Maiden, at Allington alongside his grandfather's string of race horses.

By the time he reached the huge iron gates of Allington Hall, Shane had managed to partially subdue his nagging heartache and lift himself out of his depression. He took several deep breaths, and brought a neutral expression to his face as he turned at the end of the gravel driveway and headed in the direction of the stables at the back of the house. To Shane's surprise, the yard was deserted, but as he clattered across the cobblestones a stable lad appeared, and a moment later Randolph Harte walked out of the stalls and waved to him.

Tall, heavy-set, and bluff in manner, Randolph had a voice to match his build, and he boomed, 'Hello, Shane. I was hoping to see you. I'd like to talk to you, if you can spare me a minute.'

Dismounting, Shane called back, 'It *will* have to be a minute, Randolph. I have an important dinner date tonight and I'm running late.' He handed the reins of War Lord to the lad, who led the horse off to the Rubbing House to be rubbed down. Shane strode over to Randolph, grasped his outstretched hand, and said, 'Nothing wrong, I hope?'

'No, no,' Randolph said quickly, steering him across the yard to the back entrance of the house. 'But let's go inside for a few minutes.' He looked up at Shane, who at six feet four was several inches taller, and grinned. 'Surely you can make it *five* minutes, old chap? The lady, whoever she is, will no doubt be perfectly happy to wait for *you*.'

Shane also grinned. 'The lady in question is Aunt Emma, and we both know *she* doesn't like to be kept waiting.'

'Only too true,' Randolph said, opening the door and ushering Shane inside. 'Now, have you time for a cup of tea, or would you prefer a drink?'

'Scotch, thanks, Randolph.' Shane walked over to the fireplace and stood with his back to it, glancing around the room, feeling suddenly relaxed and at ease for the first time that afternoon. He had known and loved this study all of his life, and it was his favourite room at the Hall. Its ambiance was wholly masculine, this mood reflected in the huge Georgian desk in front of the window, the Chippendale cabinet, the dark wine-coloured leather Chesterfield and armchairs, the circular rent table littered with such magazines as *Country Life* and *Horse and Hounds*, along with racing sheets from the daily papers. A stranger entering this room would have no trouble guessing the chief interest and occupation of the owner. It was redolent of the Turf and the Sport of Kings. The dark green walls were hung with eighteenth-century sporting prints by Stubbs; framed photographs of the winning race horses Randolph had trained graced a dark mahogany chest; and cups and trophies abounded. There was the gleam of brass around the fireplace, in the horse brasses hanging there, and in the Victorian fender. On the mantelpiece, Randolph's pipe rack and tobacco jar nestled between small bronzes of two thoroughbreds and a pair of silver candlesticks. The study had a comfortable lived-in look, was even a bit shabby in spots, but to Shane the scuffed carpet and the cracked leather on the chairs only added to the mellow feeling of warmth and friendliness.

Randolph brought their drinks, the two men clinked glasses and Shane turned to sit in one of the leather arm chairs.

'Whoah! Not there. The spring's going,' Randolph exclaimed.

'It's been going for years,' Shane laughed, but seated himself in the other chair.

'Well, it's finally gone. I keep meaning to have the damn thing sent to the upholsterers, but I always forget.'

Shane put his glass on the edge of the brass fender and searched his pockets for his cigarettes. He lit one, said, 'What did you want to talk to me about?'

'Emerald Bow. What do you think Blackie would say if I entered her in the Grand National next year?'

A surprised look flashed across Shane's face and he sat up straighter. 'He'd be thrilled, surely you know that. But would she have a chance? I know she's a fine mare, but the Aintree course . . . Jaysus! as Blackie would say.'

Randolph nodded, stood up, took a pipe and began to pack it with tobacco. 'Yes, it *is* a demanding course, the supreme test for a man and his horse. But I really do think Emerald Bow has a chance of winning the greatest steeplechase in the world. The breeding is there, and the stamina. She's done extremely well lately, won a few point-to-points, and most impressively.' Randolph paused to light his pipe, then remarked, with a twinkle, 'I believe that *that* lady has hidden charms. But, seriously, she is turning out to be one of the best jumpers I've ever trained.'

'Oh my God, this is wonderful news!' Shane cried, excitement running through him. 'It's always been Grandfather's dream to win the National. Which jockey, Randolph?'

'Steve Larner. He's a tough sod, just what we need to take Emerald Bow around Aintree. If anyone can negotiate her over Beecher's Brook *twice* it's Steve. He's a brilliant horseman.'

'Why haven't you mentioned it to Grandfather?'

'I wanted to get your reaction first. You're the closest to him.'

'You know he always takes your advice. You're his trusted trainer, and the best in the business, as far as we're concerned.'

'Thanks, Shane. Appreciate the confidence. But to be honest, old chap, I've never seen Blackie fuss over any of his horses the way he does that mare. He'd like to keep her wrapped in cotton wool, if you ask me. He was out here last week, and he was treating her as if she was his great lady love.'

A grin tugged at Shane's mouth. 'Don't forget, she *was* a gift from his favourite lady. And talking of Emma, did I hear a hint of annoyance when you mentioned her earlier?'

'Not really. I was a bit irritated with her last night, but . . .' Randolph broke off, and smiled genially. 'Well, I never harbour a grudge where she's concerned, and she *is* the matriarch of our clan, and she's so good to us all. It's just that she can be so bloody bossy. She makes me feel this high.' He held his hand six inches off the ground, and grinned. 'Anyway, getting back to Emerald Bow, I'd intended to mention it to Blackie tomorrow. What do you think about my timing? Should I wait until next week perhaps?'

'No, tell him tomorrow, Randolph. It'll make his day, and Aunt Emma will be delighted.' Shane finished his drink and stood up. 'I don't mind telling you,

I for one am thrilled about this decision of yours. Now, I'm afraid I really have to leave. I want to stop by the stables for a second, to say goodbye to my horses.' Shane smiled a trifle ruefully. 'I'm going away again, Randolph. I'm leaving Monday morning.'

'But you just got back!' Randolph exclaimed. 'Where are you off to this time?'

'Jamaica, then Barbados, where we've recently bought a new hotel,' Shane explained as they left the study together. 'I've a great deal of work there, and I'll be gone for quite a few months.' He fell silent as they crossed the stable yard, and Randolph made no further comment either.

Shane went into the stalls, where he spent a few moments with each of his horses, fondling them, murmuring to them affectionately.

Randolph hung back, watching him intently, and suddenly he experienced a stab of pity for the younger man, although he was not certain what engendered this feeling in him. Unless it was something to do with Shane's demeanour at this moment, the look of infinite sadness in his black eyes. Randolph had retained a soft spot for Shane O'Neill since he had been a child, and had once even hoped that he might take a fancy to Sally or Vivienne. But the boy had always been patently uninterested in his two daughters, had remained slightly aloof from them. It was his son, Winston, who was Shane's closest friend and boon companion. A few eyebrows had been raised two years ago when Winston and Shane had bought a broken down old manor, Beck House, in nearby West Tanfield, remodelled it and moved in together. But Randolph had never questioned the sexual predilections of his son or Shane. He had no need to do so. He knew them both to be the most notorious womanizers, forever chasing skirts up and down the countryside. When his wife, Georgina, had been alive she had often had to comfort more than one broken-hearted young woman, who showed up at the Hall in search of Winston or Shane. Thankfully this no longer happened. *He* wouldn't have known how to cope with such situations. He presumed that if there were any disgruntled young ladies they beat a track directly to Beck House. Randolph smiled inwardly. Those two were a couple of scallywags, but he did love them both very dearly.

Shane finally took leave of his horses and walked slowly back to Randolph standing at the entrance to the stalls. As always, and especially when he had not seen him for a while, Randolph was struck by Shane's unique good looks. He's a handsome son-of-a-gun, Randolph commented silently. Blackie must have looked exactly like Shane fifty years ago.

Putting his arm around the older man's shoulder, Shane said, 'Thanks for everything, Randolph.'

'Oh lad, it's a pleasure. And don't worry about the horses. They'll be well cared for, but then you should know that by now. Oh and Shane, please ask Winston to call me later.'

'I will.'

Randolph's eyes followed Shane O'Neill as he strode off to his car, and there was a thoughtful look on his face. There goes one unhappy young man, he muttered under his breath, shaking his head in bafflement. He has everything anybody could ever want. Health, looks, position, great wealth. He tries to conceal it, but I'm convinced he's miserable inside. And I'm damned if I know the reason why.

Beck House, so called because a pretty little stream ran through the grounds, stood at the bottom of a small hill, at the edge of the village of West Tanfield, about half way between Allington Hall and Pennistone Royal.

Situated in a dell, shaded at the rear by a number of huge old oaks and sycamores, the manor dated back to the late Elizabethan period. It was a charming house, low and rambling, made of local stone supposedly from Fountains Abbey, and it had a half-timbered front facade, tall chimneys and many leaded windows.

Winston and Shane had originally bought the old manor with the intention of selling it once they had rebuilt the ruined parts, remodelled the old-fashioned kitchen and bathrooms, added garages, and cleared away the wilderness which covered the neglected grounds. However, they had devoted so much time and energy and loving care on the house, had become so attached to the manor during the renovations, they had finally decided to keep it for themselves. They were the same age, had been at Oxford together, and had been close since their salad days. They enjoyed sharing the house, which they used mainly at weekends, since they both maintained flats in the Leeds area to be near their respective offices.

Winston Harte was the only grandson of Emma's brother Winston, and her great-nephew, and he had worked for the Yorkshire Consolidated Newspaper Company since he had come down from Oxford. He did not have a specific job, nor a title. Emma called him her 'minister without portfolio', which, translated, meant trouble-shooter to most people. He was, in a sense, her ambassador-at-large within the company, and her eyes and ears and very frequently her voice as well. His word on most things was the final word and he answered only to Emma. Behind his back the other executives called him 'God', and Winston knew this and generally smiled to himself knowingly. He was well aware who 'God' was at Consolidated. It was his Aunt Emma. She was the law, and he respected and honoured her; she had his complete devotion.

Young Winston, as he was still sometimes called in the family, had always been close to his namesake, and his grandfather had instilled in him a great sense of loyalty and duty to Emma, to whom the Hartes owed everything they had. His grandfather had worshipped her until the day he had died at the beginning of the sixties, and it was from him that Winston had learned so much about his aunt's early life, the hard times she had had, the struggles she had experienced as she had climbed the ladder to success. He knew only too well that her brilliant career had been hard won, built on tremendous sacrifices. Because he had been reared on so many fantastic, and often moving, stories about the now-legendary Emma, Winston believed that in certain ways he understood her far better than her own children. And there was nothing he would not do for her.

Winston's grandfather had left him all of his shares in the newspaper company, whilst his Uncle Frank, Emma's younger brother, had left his interest to his widow, Natalie. But it was Emma, with her fifty-two per cent, who controlled the company as she always had. These days, however, she ran it with Winston's help. She consulted with him on every facet of management and policy, frequently deferred to his wishes if they were sound, constantly took his advice. They had a tranquil working relationship and a most special and loving friendship which gave them both a great deal of satisfaction and pleasure.

The newspaper company was very actively on Winston's mind as he drove slowly into the grounds of Beck House. Even so, as preoccupied as he was, he noticed that the little beck was swollen from the heavy rains which had fallen earlier that week. He made a mental note to mention this to Shane. The banks would probably need reinforcing again, otherwise the lawns would be flooded in no time at all, as they had been the previous spring. O'Neill Construction will definitely have to come out here next week, Winston decided, as he pulled the Jaguar up to the front door, parked, took his briefcase and alighted. He went around to the boot of the car to get his suitcase.

Winston was slender, light in build, and about five foot nine, and it was easy to see at a glance that he was a Harte. In point of fact, Winston bore a strong look of Emma. He had her fine, chiselled features and her colouring, which was reflected in his russet-gold hair and vivid green eyes. He was the only member of the family, other than Paula, who had Emma's dramatic widow's peak, and which, his grandfather had once told him, they had all inherited from Big Jack Harte's mother, Esther Harte.

Winston glanced up, squinting at the sky as he approached the short flight of steps leading into the house. Dark clouds had rumbled in from the East Coast and they presaged rain. There was a hint of thunder in the air since the wind had dropped, and a sudden bolt of lightning streaked the tops of the leafy spring trees with a flash of searing white. As he inserted the key large drops of rain splashed on to his hand. Damn, he muttered, thinking of the beck. If there's a storm, we're going to be in serious trouble.

Dimly, from behind the huge carved door, he heard the telephone ringing, but by the time he had let himself inside the house it had stopped. Winston stared at it, fully expecting it to ring again, but when it didn't he shrugged, deposited his suitcase at the foot of the staircase and walked rapidly through the hall. He went into his study at the back of the manor, sat down at his desk, and read the note from Shane telling him to call his father. He threw the note into the wastepaper basket and glanced vaguely at his mail, mostly bills from the village shops and a number of invitations for cocktail parties and dinners from his country neighbours. Putting these on one side, he leaned back in his chair, propped his feet on the desk and closed his eyes, bringing all of his concentration to bear on the matter at hand.

Winston had a problem, and it gave him cause for serious reflection at this moment. Yesterday, during a meeting with Jim Fairley at the London office, he had detected a real and genuine discontent in the other man. Oddly enough, Winston discovered he was not terribly surprised. Months ago he had begun to realize that Jim loathed administration, and in the last few hours, driving back from London, he had come to the conclusion that Jim wanted to be relieved of his position as managing director. Intuitively, Winston felt that Jim was floundering and was truly out of his depth. Jim was very much a working newspaperman, who loved the hurly burly of the news room, the excitement of being at the centre of world events, the challenge of putting out two daily papers. After Emma had promoted him a year ago, upon his engagement to Paula, Jim had continued to act as managing editor of the *Yorkshire Morning Gazette* and the *Yorkshire Evening Standard*. Essentially, by holding down the old job along with the new one, Jim was wearing two hats. Only that of the newspaperman fitted him, in Winston's opinion.

Maybe he ought to resign, Winston thought. It's better that Jim does one job brilliantly, rather than screw up on two. He snapped his eyes open, swung his legs to the floor purposefully and pulled the chair up to the desk. He sat staring into space, thinking about Jim. He admired Fairley's extraordinary ability as a journalist, and he liked the man personally, even though he knew Jim was weak in many respects. He wanted to please everybody and that was hardly possible. And one thing was certain: Winston had never been able to comprehend Paula's fascination with Fairley. They were as different as chalk and cheese. She was far too strong for a man like Jim, but then, that relationship was none of his business really, and anyway perhaps he was prejudiced, considering the circumstances. She was a blind fool. He scowled, chastising himself for thinking badly of her, for he did care for Paula and they were good friends.

Winston now reached for the phone to ring Emma and confide his problem in her, then changed his mind at once. There was no point worrying her at the beginning of her very busy weekend of social activities which had been planned for weeks. Far better to wait until Monday morning and consult with her then.

All of a sudden he felt like kicking himself. How stupid he had been. He should have challenged Jim yesterday, asked him point blank if he wanted to step down. And if he did, who would they appoint in his place? There was no one qualified to take on such heavy responsibilities, at least not inside the company. That was the crux of the problem, his chief concern. At the bottom of him, Winston had the most awful feeling that his aunt might lumber him with the job. He did not want it. He liked things exactly the way they were.

It so happened that Winston Harte, unlike other members of Emma's family, was not particularly ambitious. He did not crave power. He was not crippled by avarice. In fact, he had more money than he knew what to do with. Grandfather Winston, with Emma's guidance, advice and help, had acquired an immense fortune, had thus ensured that neither his widow, Charlotte, nor his offspring would ever want for anything.

Young Winston was dedicated, hard working, and he thrived in the world of newspapers, where he was in his element. But he also enjoyed living. Long ago he had made a decision and it was one he had never veered away from: *He* was not going to sacrifice personal happiness and a tranquil private life for a big business career. Treadmills were decidedly not for him. He would always work diligently at his job, for he was not a parasite, but he also wanted a wife, a family, and a gracious style of living. Like his father, Randolph, Winston was very much at ease in the role of country gentleman. The pastoral scene held a special appeal for him, gave him a sense of renewal. His weekends away from the city were precious, and recharged his batteries. He found horse riding, point-to-point meetings, village cricket, antiquing and pottering around in the grounds of Beck House therapeutic and immensely satisfying. In short, Winston

Harte preferred a quiet, leisurely existence, and he was determined to have it. Battles in board rooms made him irritable, and he found them endlessly boring. That was why Paula continued to surprise him. And it was becoming increasingly apparent to Winston that she was indeed cast in the same mould as her grandmother. Both women relished corporate skirmishing. It seemed to him that business, power, and winning hands-down over a business adversary were narcotics to them. When Emma had wanted him to be Paula's back-up in the negotiations with Aire, he had swiftly demurred, suggested she send Paula in alone. His aunt had readily agreed, much to his considerable relief.

Oh what the hell, he thought, becoming impatient with himself. I'm not going to spend the entire weekend worrying about Jim Fairley's intentions. I'll thrash it out with him next week, once the plans for taking over Aire Communications have been put into operation. Pushing business matters to the back of his mind, he rang his father at Allington Hall and chatted with him for a good twenty minutes. He then dialled Allison Ridley, his current girlfriend. He felt a rush of warmth when he heard her voice, and she sounded equally pleased to hear his. He confirmed that he and Shane would be at her dinner party the following evening, made plans with her for Sunday, and finally dashed upstairs to change.

Ten minutes later, wearing comfortable corduroys, a heavy wool sweater, Wellington boots and an old raincoat, Winston meandered through the dining room and out on to the flagged terrace overlooking the fish pond. The sky had brightened after the brief shower. The trees and shrubs and lawns appeared to shimmer with dewy greenness in the lovely late afternoon light which brought a soft incandescent glow to the fading blue of the sky. The scent of rain and damp grass and wet earth and growing things pervaded the air, and it was a smell Winston loved. He stood on the terrace for a moment, inhaling and exhaling, relaxing and shedding the rest of his business worries, then ran lightly down the steps into the gardens. He hurried in the direction of the beck, wanting to satisfy himself that the condition of the banks had not deteriorated after the recent shower.

7

Edwina had arrived.

Emma was aware that her eldest daughter was sitting downstairs in the library, having a drink and recovering from her journey from Manchester Airport. In the last few minutes first Hilda, then Emily, had been up to see her, to pass on this news.

Well, there's no time like the present, Emma murmured, as she finished dressing in readiness for her dinner date with Blackie and Shane. Putting off the inevitable is not only foolish, it frays the nerves. There's a time bomb ticking inside Edwina, and I'd better defuse it before the weekend begins.

Nodding to herself, glad she had stopped wavering, Emma fastened a pearl choker around her throat, glanced at herself in the mirror, picked up her evening bag and sable jacket, and hurried out.

She descended the long winding staircase at a slower pace, thinking about the things she would say, how she would handle Edwina. Emma had an aversion to confrontation and conflict, preferred to move in roundabout ways, and often with stealth, to accomplish her ends. Accommodation and compromise had been, and still were, her strong suits, both in business and personal matters. But now, as she approached the library, she recognized there was only one thing she could do: tackle Edwina head on.

Her quick, light step faltered as she walked through the vast Stone Hall, and dismay flew to the surface as she thought of doing battle. But Anthony's happiness was at stake, and therefore Edwina had to be dealt with before she made serious trouble for him, for everyone, in fact. Emma took a deep breath, then continued across the hall, her step now ringing with new determination, her manner resolute.

The library door was partially open, and Emma paused for a moment before going in, one hand resting on the door jamb as she observed Edwina sitting in the wing chair in front of the fire. Only one lamp had been turned on and the light in the rest of the room was gloomy. Suddenly a log spurted and flared up the chimney, the lambent flames illuminating the shadowed face, bringing it into sharper focus. Emma blinked, momentarily startled. From this distance her daughter was the spitting image of Adele Fairley ... the same silvery blonde hair, the delicate yet clearly defined profile, the shoulders hunched in concentration. How often had she seen Adele sitting like that, beside the fire in her bedroom at Fairley Hall, staring into the distance, lost in her thoughts. But Adele had not lived to see her thirty-eighth year and Edwina was sixty-three and her beauty had never been as ethereal and as heart-stopping as Adele's once was. So Emma knew this image was part illusion; still, the resemblance was there, had been there since Edwina's birth, and she had always been more of a Fairley than a Harte in many respects.

Clearing her throat, Emma said, 'Good evening, Edwina,' and bustled forward with briskness, not wanting her to know she had been watching her from the doorway.

Her daughter started in surprise and swung her head, straightening up in the chair as she did. 'Hello, Mother,' she replied in a formal voice that rang with coldness.

Emma paid no attention to the tone, accustomed to it by now. It had not changed much over the years. She deposited her jacket and bag on a chair, then proceeded to the fireplace, turning on several lamps as she walked past them. 'I see you have a drink,' she began, seating herself in the other wing chair. 'Does it need refreshing?'

'Not at the moment, thank you.'

'How are you?' Emma asked pleasantly.

'I'm all right. I suppose.' Edwina eyed her mother. 'There's no need to ask how you are. You're positively blooming.'

Emma smiled faintly. Sitting back, she crossed her legs, and said, 'I'm afraid I won't be here for dinner after all. I have to go out. A last minute –'

'Business as usual, I've no doubt,' Edwina sniffed scornfully, giving her an unfriendly look.

Emma winced, but suppressed her annoyance. Edwina's rudeness and sneering manner were generally inflammatory to Emma, but tonight she was determined to overlook her daughter's unwarranted attitude towards her. You don't catch flies with vinegar, she thought dryly; and so she would continue to be pleasant and diplomatic, no matter what. Studying Edwina's face, she at once noticed the tiredness of the drooping mouth, the weary lines around her silver-grey eyes which swam with sadness. Edwina had lost weight, and she seemed nervous, anxious even, and certainly the Dowager Countess of Dunvale, usually filled with her own importance, was not quite so smug this evening. It was apparent she was besieged by troubles.

Emma felt a stab of pity for her, and this was such an unprecedented feeling, and so unexpected, she was a little amazed at herself. Poor Edwina. She is truly miserable, and frightened, but she does bring it on herself I'm afraid, Emma thought. If only I could make her see this, get her to change her ways. Then becoming aware that she was being looked over as carefully as she was scrutinizing, Emma said, 'You're staring at me, Edwina. Is there something wrong with my appearance?'

'The frock, Mother,' Edwina replied without a moment's hesitation. 'It's a little young for you, isn't it?'

Emma stiffened, and wondered if her charitable feelings had been misplaced. Edwina was intent on being obnoxious. Then she relaxed and laughed a gay, dismissive laugh, resolved not to let Edwina get her goat. When she spoke her voice was even. 'I like red,' she said. 'It's lively. What colour would you like me to wear? *Black?* I'm not dead yet you know, and whilst we're on the subject of clothes, why do you insist on wearing those awful lumpy tweeds?' Not waiting for a reply, she added, 'You have a lovely figure, Edwina. You should show it off more.'

Edwina let this small compliment slide by her. And she asked herself why she had ever accepted Jim Fairley's invitation, or agreed to stay here at Pennistone Royal. She must be insane, to expose herself to her mother in this way.

Emma compressed her lips, her eyes narrowing as they weighed Edwina speculatively. She said, with the utmost care, 'I'd like to talk to you about Anthony.'

This statement jolted Edwina out of her introspection, and swinging to face Emma, she exclaimed, 'Oh no, Mother! When Emily said you'd be coming down to see me, I suspected as much. However, I refuse to discuss my son with *you*. You're manipulative and controlling.'

'And you, Edwina, are beginning to sound like a broken record,' Emma remarked. 'I'm tired of hearing that accusation from you. I'm also fed up with your continual sniping. It's impossible to have a decent conversation with you about anything. You're defensive and hostile.'

Strong as these words were, Emma's tone had been mild, and her face was devoid of emotion as she pushed herself up and out of the chair. She went to the William and Mary chest in the corner, poured herself a small glass of sherry, then resumed her position in front of the fire. She sat holding her drink, a reflective light in her eyes. After a long moment, she said, 'I am an

69

old woman. A very old woman really. Although I realize there will never be total peace in this family of mine, I would like a bit of tranquillity for the rest of my life, if that's possible. And so I'm prepared to forget a lot of the things you've said and done, Edwina, because I've come to the conclusion it's about time you and I buried the hatchet. I think we should try to be friends.'

Edwina gaped at her in astonishment, wondering if she was dreaming. She had hardly expected to hear these words from her mother. She finally managed, 'Why *me*? Why not any of the others? Or are you planning to give the same little speech to *them* this weekend?'

'I don't believe they've been invited. And if they had, I would hope they'd have enough sense not to come. I don't have much time for any of them.'

'And you do for me?' Edwina asked incredulously, mentally thrown off balance by her mother's conciliatory gesture.

'Let's put it this way, I think you were the least guilty in that ridiculous plot against me last year. I know now that you were coerced to a certain extent. You never were very devious, avaricious or venal, Edwina. Also, I *do* regret our estrangement over the years. We should have made up long ago, I see that now.' Emma genuinely meant this, but she was also motivated by another reason. *Anthony*. Emma was convinced that only by winning Edwina over to her side could she hope to influence her, get her to adopt a more reasonable attitude towards her son. So she said again, 'I do think we should give it a try. What do we have to lose? And if we can't be real friends, perhaps we can have an amicable relationship at the very least.'

'I don't think so, Mother.'

Emma exhaled wearily. 'I am saddened for you, Edwina, I really am. You threw away one of the most important things in your life, but –'

'What was that?'

'My love for you.'

'Oh come off it, Mother,' Edwina said with a sneer, looking down her nose at Emma. 'You never loved me.'

'Yes, I did.'

'I don't believe this conversation!' Edwina exclaimed, shifting in her chair. She took a gulp of her Scotch, then brought the glass down on the Georgian side table with a bang. 'You're incredible, Mother. You sit there making these extraordinary statements and expecting me to swallow them whole. That's the joke of the century. I might be stupid, but I'm not that stupid.' She leaned forward, staring hard at Emma, her eyes like chips of grey ice. 'What about you? My God, it was *you* who threw *me* away when I was a baby.'

Emma brought herself up in the chair with enormous dignity and her face was formidable, her eyes steely as she said, '*I did not*. And don't you ever dare say that to me again. *Ever*, do you hear? You know that I put you in your Aunt Freda's care because I had to work like a drudge to support you. But we've gone through this enough times in the past, and you'll think what you want, I suppose. In the meantime, I have no intention of being side tracked from what I have to say to you, just because you have the need to dredge up all your old grudges against me.'

Edwina opened her mouth, but Emma shook her head. 'No, let me finish,' she insisted, her green eyes holding Edwina's sharply. 'I don't want you to make the same mistake twice in your life. I don't want you to throw Anthony's love away, as you did mine. And you're in grave danger of doing so.' She sat back, hoping her words would sink in, would have some effect.

'I have never heard anything quite so ridiculous,' Edwina snorted, assuming a haughty expression.

'It's the truth, nevertheless.'

'What do you know about my relationship with my son!'

'A great deal. But despite his love for you, which is considerable, you are hell bent on driving a wedge between the two of you. Why, only last night, he told me how concerned he is about your relationship, and he looked pretty damn worried to me.'

Edwina lifted her head swiftly. 'So he *is* here. When I phoned him at his London club last night they said he'd already left. I couldn't imagine where he was. I had no idea he was coming to the christening. Is he here?'

This was asked with anxiousness, and Emma saw the eager light flickering in her daughter's eyes. She said, 'No, he's not.'

'Where is he staying?'

Emma chose to ignore this question for the moment. She said, 'Anthony can't understand why you're so opposed to his divorce. It seems you're making his life miserable, badgering him night and day to reconcile with Min. He is baffled and distressed, Edwina.'

'So is poor Min! She's heartbroken, and she can't comprehend *him*, or his behaviour. Neither can I. He's upsetting our lives in the most disturbing way, creating havoc. I'm almost as distraught as she is.'

'Well, that's understandable. No one likes divorce, nor the pain it involves. However, you must think of Anthony before anyone else. From what he tells me, he's been very unhappy for –'

'Not *that* unhappy, Mother,' Edwina interrupted, her voice snippy and high-pitched with tension. 'He and Min do have a *lot* in common, whatever he might have told *you*. Naturally, he's disappointed she hasn't had a child. On the other hand, they've only been married six years. She could still get pregnant. Min is perfect for him. And don't look at me like that, Mother, so very superior and knowing. It just so happens that I *know* my son better than you do. Anthony might have strength of character, as you're so fond of pointing out to me whenever you get the opportunity. Nonetheless, he does have certain weaknesses.'

Edwina stopped, uncertain about continuing, then decided her mother might as well know the truth. 'Sex, for one thing,' she announced flatly, staring Emma down with a show of defiance. 'He'll go for a pretty face every time. He got himself into the most awful scrapes with women before he married Min.' Edwina shook her head, and bit her lip, muttering in a low voice, 'I don't know how much Min actually knows, but *I'm* aware that in the last couple of years Anthony has had several affairs, and as usual with the wrong sort of women.'

Emma was not unduly surprised by this bit of information, nor was she particularly interested, and she did not rise to the bait. Instead she gave Edwina a curious look, asked, 'What exactly do you *mean* by the wrong sort of women?'

'You know very well what I mean, Mother. Unsuitable females with no background or breeding. A man in Anthony's position, a peer of the realm with enormous responsibilities, should have a wife who comes from the aristocracy, his own class, who understands his way of life.'

Stifling her amusement at Edwina's hidebound snobbery, Emma said, 'Oh for God's sake, stop talking like a Victorian dowager. We're living in the twenty-first century – well almost. Your views are outdated, my dear.'

'I might have known *you'd* say something like that,' Edwina replied in a snooty voice. 'I must admit, you constantly surprise me, Mother. For a woman of your immense wealth and power you are awfully careless about certain things. Background is one of them.'

Emma chuckled and sipped her sherry and her eyes twinkled over the rim of the glass. 'People who live in glass houses shouldn't throw stones,' she said, and chuckled again.

Edwina's face coloured, and then wrinkling her nose in a gesture of distaste, she said, 'I dread to think of who he'll end up with, if this divorce ever goes through.'

'Oh it's going through all right,' Emma said in her softest tone. 'I think you would be wise to accept that. *Immediately*. It's a fact of life you cannot change.'

'We'll see about that. Min has to agree before he can do anything.'

'But, my dear Edwina, she has agreed.'

Edwina was shocked and she stared at her mother through horrified eyes, trying to grasp these words. For a split-second she was disbelieving, and then with a sinking heart she acknowledged that her mother spoke the truth. Whatever else she was, Emma Harte was not a liar. Furthermore, her information was always reliable, deadly accurate. Edwina finally stammered, 'But ... but ...' Her voice let her down, and she was unable to continue. She reached for her glass with a shaking hand, and then put it back on the table without drinking from it. Slowly she said, 'But Min didn't say anything to me last night when we had dinner. How very strange. We've always been close. Why, she's been like a daughter to me. I wonder why she didn't confide in me, she always has in the past.' Edwina's face was a picture of dismay as she pondered Min's extraordinary behaviour, and her very perplexing reticence.

For the first time, with a sudden flash of insight, Emma understood why her daughter was so frantic. She was obviously on intimate terms with Min, happy in the relationship. Yes, she was comfortable, secure and safe with her daughter-in-law. Anthony, in upsetting the matrimonial applecart, had put his mother's world in jeopardy, or at least so Edwina believed. She was petrified of change, of a new woman in her son's life, who may not accept her quite as readily as Min had, who might even alienate her son from her.

Leaning towards Edwina, Emma said with more gentleness than usual, 'Perhaps Min was afraid to tell you, afraid of distressing you further. Look here, you mustn't feel threatened by this divorce. It's not going to change your life that much, and I'm sure Anthony won't object if you remain friendly with Min.' She attempted a light laugh. 'And after all, Anthony is getting a divorce from Min, not from you, Edwina. He would never do anything to hurt you,' she placated.

'He already has. His behaviour is unforgivable.' Edwina's voice was harsh and unrelenting and her face flooded with bitterness.

Emma drew back, and the irritation she had been suppressing suddenly rose up in her. Her mouth curved down in a tight line, and her eyes turned cold. 'You're a selfish woman, Edwina,' she admonished. 'You're not thinking of Anthony, you're only concerned with yourself. You claim your son is the centre of your life, well, if he is, you have a damn poor way of showing it. He needs your love and support at a difficult time like this, not your animosity.' Emma threw her a condemning stare. 'I don't understand you. There's far too much resentment and hostility in you, for everyone, not only me. I can't imagine why. You've had a good life, your marriage was happy, at least I presume it was. I know Jeremy adored you, and I always thought you loved him.' Her glance remained fixed on Edwina. 'I hope to God you *did* love him, for your own sake. Yet despite all the wonderful things life has given you, you are filled with an all-consuming anger. Please turn away from it, put this bitterness out of your heart once and for all.'

Edwina remained engulfed in silence, her expression as obdurate as ever, and Emma went on, 'Trust your son, trust his judgement. I certainly do. You're knocking your head against a brick wall, fighting this divorce. You can't possibly win. In fact, you'll end up the loser. You'll drive Anthony away forever.' She searched her daughter's face, seeking a sign of softening on her part, but it was still closed and unyielding.

Sighing to herself, Emma thought: I give up. I'll never get through to her. And then she felt compelled to make one last stab at convincing her to change her views. She cautioned gravely, 'You'll end up a lonely old woman. I can't believe you would want that to happen. And if you think I have an axe to grind, remember I have nothing to gain. Very genuinely, Edwina, I simply want to prevent you from making the most terrible mistake.'

Although Edwina was unresponsive, sat huddled in the chair, avoiding her mother's penetrating eyes, she had been listening attentively for the last few minutes, and digesting Emma's words. They had struck home, Emma's belief to the contrary. Now, in the inner recesses of Edwina's mind, something stirred. It was a dim awareness that she had been wrong. Suddenly, discomfort with herself overwhelmed her, and she felt guilty about Anthony. She *had* been selfish, more selfish than she had realized until this moment. It was true that she loved Min like the daughter she had never had, and she dreaded the thought of losing her. But she dreaded losing her son more. And that had already begun to happen.

Edwina did not have much insight, nor was she a clever woman, but she was not without a certain intelligence, and this now told her that Anthony had turned to his grandmother in desperation, had confided in Emma instead of her. Resentment and jealousy, her worst traits, flared within her at the thought of this betrayal on her son's part. And then, with a wisdom uncommon for her, she put aside these feelings. Anthony had not really been treacherous or disloyal. *It was all her fault.* She was driving him away from her, as her mother had pointed out. Emma was being sincere in trying to bridge the rift rapidly developing between herself and her son. Emma did want them to remain close, that seemed obvious, if she considered her words dispassionately and with fairness. This admission astonished Edwina, and against her volition she experienced a feeling of gratitude to her mother for making this effort on her behalf.

Edwina spoke slowly, in a muted voice. 'It's been a shock, the divorce, I mean. But you're right, Mother. I must think of Anthony first. Yes, it's *his* happiness that counts.'

For the first time in her life, Edwina found herself turning to Emma for help. Her anger and bitterness now somewhat diffused, she asked softly, 'What do you think I should do, Mother? He must be very angry with me.'

Believing that her attempts to drill some common sense into Edwina had had no effect whatsoever, Emma was a bit taken aback by this unanticipated reversal. Rapidly regrouping her thoughts, she said, 'No, he's not angry. Hurt perhaps, worried even. He loves you very much, you know, and the last thing he wants is a permanent split between you.' Emma half smiled. 'You asked me what you should do. Why, Edwina, I think you should tell him exactly what you've just told me . . . that his happiness is the most important thing to you, and that he has your blessing, whatever he plans to do with his life.'

'I will,' Edwina cried. 'I must.' She gazed at Emma, for once without rancour, and added, 'There's something else.' She swallowed, finished in a strangled voice, 'Thank you, Mother. Thank you for trying to help.'

Emma nodded and glanced away. Her face was calm but she was filling with uneasiness. I have to tell her about Sally, she thought. If I avoid revealing his involvement with the girl, holy hell will break loose tomorrow. Everything I've accomplished in the last half hour will be swept away by Edwina's wrath when she sees them together. This way, she'll have time to sleep on her rage, perhaps put it behind her. When she's calm she'll surely recognize she cannot live her son's life for him.

Gathering her strength, Emma said, 'I have something further to say to you, Edwina, and I want you to hear me out before you make any comment.'

Edwina frowned. 'What is it?' she asked nervously, clasping her hands together in her lap. Emma was silent, but her face was readable for a change. It telegraphed trouble to Edwina. Steeling herself for what she somehow knew would be a body blow, she nodded for her mother to proceed.

Emma said, 'Anthony is in love with another woman. It's Sally . . . Sally Harte. Now, Edwina, I –'

'Oh no!' Edwina cried, aghast. Her face had paled and she gripped the arms of the chair to steady herself.

'*I asked you to hear me out*. You just said your son's happiness was the only thing that matters. I trust you really meant that. He intends to marry Sally when he is free to do so, and you are –'

Again Edwina interrupted. 'And you said you had no axe to grind!'

'I don't,' Emma declared. 'And if you think I've encouraged them, you're mistaken. I *was* aware he'd taken her out several times, when he's been in Yorkshire, I don't deny that. But I hadn't paid much attention. Anyway, it seems they are seriously involved. Also, Anthony came to *announce* his plans to me, not ask my permission to marry my great-niece. Furthermore, I gather he took the same stance with Randolph, told him he was going to marry his daughter, and without so much as a by your leave. Randolph can be old-fashioned at times, and his nose was considerably out of joint when we spoke late last night. But I soon put *him* straight.'

Moving to the edge of the chair, the fuming Edwina let her furious glance roam over Emma. She examined that old and wrinkled face minutely, looking for signs of duplicity and cunning. But they were absent, and the hooded green eyes were clear, guileless. Then without warning, a vivid picture of Sally Harte flew into Edwina's twisting mind. They had run into each other nine months ago, at the exhibition of Sally's paintings at the Royal Academy. She had sought Edwina out actually, and had been charming, very friendly. At the time Edwina had thought that Sally had grown up to become one of the most beautiful women she had ever laid eyes on. A Harte though, through and through, with her grandfather Winston's arresting looks, his carefree blue eyes, his dark windblown hair.

Edwina snuffed out the disturbing image of Sally Harte and concentrated her attention on the old woman sitting opposite her, who in turn was observing her acutely and with sternness. Always ready and willing to brand her mother a manipulator, a schemer who contrived to control them and run all of their lives, Edwina decided that in this instance Emma Harte had indeed been an innocent bystander. As much as she wanted to blame her for this . . . this disaster, she could not. She had the most dreadful conviction that it was her son's doing, and his alone. Anthony would be unable to resist that lovely, laughing, bewitching face, which she had been so struck by herself. It was his pattern, after all . . . falling for beautiful features and a shapely figure. Yes, once again, Anthony had managed to get himself involved with the wrong sort of woman, and all because of sex.

With a little shiver, Edwina drew herself up, and said in a clipped voice, 'Well, Mother, I must admit you've convinced me that you've not been a party to this unfortunate relationship. I give you the benefit of the doubt.'

'Thanks a lot,' Emma said.

'Nonetheless,' Edwina continued purposefully, her face set, 'I must voice my disapproval of this match, or I should say mis-match, to my son. Sally is not cut out to be his wife. She is most *unsuitable*. For one thing, she is dedicated to her career. Her painting will always come first with her. Consequently, she most certainly won't fit into his life at Clonloughlin, a life that revolves around the estate, the local gentry and their country pursuits. He is making a terrible mistake, one he will live to regret for the rest of his life. So, therefore, I intend to put a stop to this *affair* at once.'

How could I have ever given birth to such a pig-headed fool? Emma asked herself. She stood up and said, with great firmness, her manner conclusive, 'I must leave. Shane will be here any minute. But before I go I have two statements to make, and I want you to listen most carefully. The first concerns Sally. You cannot point a finger at her, since she is beyond reproach and her reputation is impeccable in every sense. As for her career, well, she can just as easily paint at Clonloughlin as she can here. I might also remind you, silly snob that you are, that she is not only accepted by those ridiculous nit wits in so-called high society, whom you have the desire to kowtow to constantly, but is assiduously courted by them. Thank God *she* has more sense than you, and hasn't fallen for all that worthless, high falutin clap trap.'

'As usual, you're being insulting, Mother,' Edwina snapped.

Emma shook her silvered head disbelievingly, her lips pursing. Trust Edwina to interrupt a serious conversation because her sensibilities were offended. She said with a small, very cold smile, 'Old people believe that age gives them the licence to say exactly what they think, without being concerned that they may be giving offence. I *don't* mince my words these days, Edwina. I speak the truth. And I will continue to do so until the day I die. Anything else is a waste of time. But getting back to Sally, I would like to remind you that she is an artist of some repute, also, in case you'd forgotten, she is an heiress in her own right, since my brother Winston left his grandchildren a great fortune. Mind you, I'll give you your due, I know money isn't particularly interesting to you, or Anthony, for that matter. Still, that doesn't change the facts, and you're making yourself look ridiculous by saying she is unsuitable. Poppycock! Sally is ideal for him. And let's not dismiss their feelings for each other. They are in love, Edwina, and that's the most important consideration of all.'

'Love? Sex, you mean,' Edwina began, and then stopped, seeing the look of disapproval in Emma's eyes. 'Well, you are correct about one thing, Mother, money doesn't matter to the Dunvale family,' Edwina finished, looking as if she had just smelled something rotten.

Emma said with cool authority, 'Anthony is his own man, and for that I will be eternally grateful. *He will do as he wishes*. And if this relationship is a mistake, then it will be his own mistake to make. Not yours, not mine. Anthony is a man of thirty-three, not a snot-nosed boy in short pants. It would behove you to stop treating him as such.'

Abruptly Emma swung away from Edwina and crossed to the desk in front of the window. She stood behind it, regarding her daughter intently. 'And so, my dear Edwina, if you do speak to Anthony, I suggest you restrict your conversation to motherly words of love and concern for his well being. And I want you to restrain yourself when he mentions Sally, as no doubt he will. I don't believe he will tolerate any criticism of her, or his future plans.'

A horn hooted outside the window, startling both women. Emma glanced over her shoulder, saw Shane getting out of his bright red Ferrari. Turning back to Edwina she lifted the address book off the desk and waved it at her. 'You will find Randolph's number in here. Anthony is staying at Allington Hall. Take my advice, call your son and make up with him.' Emma paused, added with finality, 'Before it is too late.'

Edwina sat rigidly in the chair and not one word passed her white and trembling mouth.

Emma gave her only a cursory glance as she passed the chair, picked up the jacket and evening bag, and left the library. Closing the door quietly behind her she reassured herself she had tried her very best to solve this troublesome family problem and make friends with Edwina at the same time. But she and Edwina did not matter. They would live with their armed truce as they had always done. Only Anthony and Sally were important in the scheme of things.

Emma threw back her shoulders and drew herself to her full height, striking out across the Stone Hall to the front door. And she hoped against hope that Edwina would come to her senses about her son and give him her blessing.

8

Blackie O'Neill had a plan.

Now, this plan vastly entertained him whenever he thought about it, which had been frequently in the last few days. He was mostly amused because he had never come up with a plan in his entire life.

It had always been Emma who had had a plan. When she had been a little snippet of a girl in patched clothes and worn-out button boots there had been her Plan with a capital P. That had been a plan so grand it had left no room for doubt, and when she had set it finally in motion it had carried her away from Fairley and out into the wide world to seek her fame and fortune. Later she had devised innumerable other plans – for her first shop, her second and her third; then she had created plans to acquire the Gregson Warehouse, the Fairley mills, and yet another for the creation of the Lady Hamilton line of fashions with David Kallinski. And of course there had been her Building Plan, which she tended to pronounce as if this, too, were capitalized. He had been very much a part of that most grandiose plan of all, drawing the architectural blueprints and building her enormous store in Knightsbridge. And this great edifice still stood and it was a proud testament to her most extraordinary achievements.

Yes, his Emma had lived with one kind of plan or another for as long as he had known her, and each one had been put into operation with determination and carried through with consummate skill in her inimitable way. And with every success she would give him a tiny smile of cold triumph and say, 'You see, I told you it would work.' He would throw back his head and roar, and congratulate her, and insist they celebrate, and her face would soften and he knew that she was giddy with excitement inside, even if she did not really want to show it.

But *he* had never made a plan before.

In fact, almost everything that had happened to Blackie O'Neill in his long life had been by sheer happenstance.

When he had first come over from Ireland as a young spalpeen, to work on the Leeds canals with his Uncle Pat, he had never imagined in his wildest fantasies that he would become a millionaire many times over. Oh, he had boasted that he was going to be a rich 'toff' to young Emma, when she had been a servant at Fairley Hall, but at that time it had seemed unlikely ever to come true. It had been something of an idle boast, and he had laughed at himself in secret. His boasting had proved not to be so idle after all.

Over the years, Emma had often teased him and said that he had the luck of the Irish, and this was true in many respects. He had had to work hard; on the other hand, he had also carried Lady Luck in his breast pocket, and great and good fortune had continually blessed him. There had been times of terrible sadness in his personal life, and sorrow too. For one thing, he had lost his lovely Laura far too young, but she had given him his son, and he considered Bryan to be his best bit of luck of all. As a child Bryan had been warm and loving, and they had stayed close, enjoyed a unique relationship to this day. Bryan had a shrewd, sharp brain, was inspired and fearless in business, a genius really, and together they had parlayed O'Neill Construction into one of the biggest and most important building companies in Europe. When Bryan's wife, Geraldine, had inherited two hotels from her father, Leonard Ingham, it was Bryan who had had the foresight and brains to hang on to them. Those little hotels in Scarborough and Bridlington, catering to family holidaymakers, had become the nucleus for the great O'Neill chain, which was now an international concern, and a public company trading on the London Stock Exchange.

But had Blackie planned all this? No, never. It had simply come about by chance, through the most marvellous serendipity. Of course he had been smart enough to recognize *his* train when it had come rolling through *his* station, and he had jumped on it with alacrity, and he had used every opportunity that presented itself to his advantage. In so doing, he had, like Emma, created an empire, and founded a dynasty of his own.

These thoughts ran through Blackie's head as he dressed for dinner, and he chuckled to himself from time to time as he contemplated *his* first Plan, also with a capital P. Not unnaturally, it involved Emma, with whom he spent a great deal of time these days. *He had decided to take her on a trip around the world.* When he had first suggested this a few weeks ago, she had looked at him askance, scoffed at the idea, and told him *she* was far too busy and preoccupied with her affairs to go gallivanting off on a holiday in foreign parts. His smooth Irish tongue and persuasive manner had seemingly had no effect. Nevertheless, he had made up his mind to get his own way. After a great deal of thought, and pacing the floor wracking his brains, he had devised a plan – and the key to it was Australia. Blackie knew that Emma secretly itched to go to Sydney, to see her grandson Philip McGill Amory, who was being trained to take over the vast McGill holdings. He was also aware that Emma had balked at the thought of the long and exhausting trip to the other side of the world, and she was still vacillating about going.

So he would take her, and they would travel in style.

Naturally she would be unable to resist his invitation when he explained how comfortable, luxurious, leisurely and effortless their journey would be. First they would fly to New York and spend a week there, before going to San Francisco for another week. Once they were rested and refreshed they would hop over to Hong Kong and the Far East, and slowly head to their final destination in easy stages.

And he fully intended to make sure she had a little fun on their peregrinations. Blackie could no longer count the times he had asked himself if Emma had ever really had any honest-to-goodness fun in her life. Perhaps becoming one of the richest women in the world had been her way of enjoying herself. On the other hand, he was not sure how much pleasure she had derived from this consuming, back-breaking endeavour. In any event, he was planning all sorts of entertaining diversions, and young Philip was the tempting morsel he would dangle in front of her nose, and if he was not mistaken the trip would prove to be irresistible to her.

Blackie knotted his blue silk tie and stood away from the mirror, eyeing it critically.

It's sober enough, I am thinking, he muttered, knowing Emma would make a sarcastic remark if he wore one of his gaudier numbers. Long, long ago Laura had curbed, at least to some extent, his exotic taste for colourful brocade waistcoats, elaborately-tailored suits and flashy jewellery; Emma had cured him completely. Well, almost. Occasionally Blackie could not resist the temptation to indulge himself in a few jazzy silk ties and handkerchiefs and ascots in florid patterns and brilliant colours, but he made certain never to wear them when he was seeing Emma. He reached for his dark blue jacket and put it on, smoothed the edge of his pristine white collar, and nodded at his reflection. I might be an old codger, but sure an' I feel like a young spalpeen tonight, he thought with another chuckle.

Snowy-haired though he was, Blackie's bright black eyes were still as merry and mischievous as they had been when he was a young man in his prime, and his bulk and size were undiminished by age. He was in remarkable health and looked more like a man in his seventies than one who was eighty-three. His mind was alert, agile and unimpaired, and senility was a foreign word to him, in much the same way as it was to Emma.

Pausing in the middle of the bedroom he dwelled momentarily on the evening ahead, the business matter he would discuss with Emma. He was glad Shane and he had decided to broach the subject to her. Once that was out of the way, and when they were alone, he would move gently into the conversation about the trip. It won't be easy, he told himself, you know she's the stubborn one. When he had first met Emma he had recognized at once that she had the most pertinacious will it had ever been his misfortune to encounter, and it had only grown more inflexible over the years.

A scene flashed, transporting him back to the past. 1906. A bitter cold January day. Emma sitting next to him on the tramcar going to Armley, looking impossibly beautiful in a new black wool coat and the green-and-black scarf and tam-o'-shanter he had given her for Christmas. The green tones in the tartan bringing out the green depths in her eyes, the black showing off the flawlessness of her alabaster skin.

What a pallor her face had held that Sunday, nonetheless, it had not marred her loveliness, he ruminated, remembering every detail of that afternoon so clearly. She had been seventeen and carrying Edwina, and oh how rigid she had been in her obstinacy. It had taken all of his powers of persuasion to manoeuvre her on to that tram. She had not wanted to go to Armley, nor to make the acquaintance of his dear friend, Laura Spencer. Still, when the two girls had met they had taken to each other instantly, and were the closest of loving friends until the day poor Laura died. Yes, Emma's terrible burdens had eased, once she had moved into Laura's snug little house, and he had experienced an enormous sense of relief, knowing Laura would mother her, watch over her. And he had won that day, as he fully intended to win with her now, sixty-three years later.

Opening the top drawer of the bureau at the other side of the room, he took out a small black leather jewel box, stared at it thoughtfully, and then slipped it in his pocket. Humming to himself he strode out and went downstairs.

Blackie O'Neill still lived in the grand mansion he had built for himself in Harrogate in 1919. A handsome wide staircase, so beautifully designed it appeared to float, curved down into a charming circular entrance hall of lovely dimensions, where walls painted a rich apricot acted as a counterpoint to the crisp black-and-white marble floor. The square marble slabs had been set down at an angle, so that they became diamond shapes, and they led the eye to the niches on either side of the front door. White marble statues, of the Greek goddesses Artemis and Hecate, graced these niches and were highlighted by hidden spots. An elegant Sheraton console, inlaid with exotic fruitwoods, stood against one wall underneath a gilt Georgian mirror, and was flanked on either side by Sheraton chairs upholstered in apricot velvet. Illuminating the hall was a huge antique crystal-and-bronze-dore chandelier which dropped down from the domed ceiling, and the setting had elegance without the slightest hint of ostentation.

Crossing the hall, Blackie went into the drawing room. Here a log fire burned cheerily in the Adam fireplace, and the silk-shaded lamps cast rafts of warming light on to the cool green walls, on the sofas and chairs covered in darker green silk. Splendid paintings, and Sheraton and Hepplewhite antiques, added to the graciousness of the room, which exemplified Blackie's sense of style and colour and perspective in furniture and design.

He fussed with the bottle of champagne in the silver wine cooler, turning it several times, shifting the ice around, then he took a cigar from the humidor and went over to his favourite chair to wait. He had no sooner trimmed the cigar, and lighted it, than he heard them in the hall. He put the cigar in the ashtray, and rose.

'There you are, mavourneen,' he cried, hurrying to meet Emma as she came into the room. There was a wide smile on his ruddy face as he exclaimed, 'You're a sight for sore eyes.' He hugged her tightly to his broad chest, held her away and looked down at her. He smiled again, admiration shining in his eyes. 'And aren't you my bonny colleen tonight.'

Emma smiled back at him, love and warmth overflowing in her. 'Thank you, Blackie dear. And I must admit, you don't look so bad yourself. That's a beautiful suit.' Her eyes twinkled merrily as she ran a hand down his arm expertly. 'Mmmm. Very nice cloth. It feels like a bit of my best worsted.'

'It is, it is,' Blackie said, and winked at Shane who was standing behind Emma. 'Would I be wearing anything else now. But come, me darlin', and sit here, and let me get you a glass of champagne.'

Emma allowed him to guide her across the room to the sofa. She sat down, and a brow lifted. 'Are we celebrating something?'

'No, no, not really. Unless it's reaching our grand old ages and being in such good health.' He squeezed her shoulder affectionately, added, 'Also, I know you prefer wine to the stronger stuff.' He glanced at Shane. 'Would you do the honours, me boy? And make mine a drop of me good Irish.'

'Right you are, Grandfather.'

Blackie seated himself in the chair facing Emma, picked up his cigar and puffed on it reflectively for a moment, then said to her, 'And I expect you've had a busy day as usual. I'm beginning to wonder if you'll ever retire . . . as you're constantly threatening to do.'

'I don't suppose I ever will,' Emma laughed. 'You know very well I plan to go with my boots on.'

Blackie shot her a chastising look. 'Don't talk to *me* about dying. I've no intention of doing that for a long time.' He chuckled softly. 'I've a lot more damage to do yet.'

Emma laughed with him, and so did Shane, who carried their drinks over to them. He fetched his own, and they clinked glasses and toasted each other. Shane took a swallow of his Scotch, and said, 'Would you both excuse me for a few minutes. I have to phone Winston.'

Emma said, 'I hope you have better luck than I did. I was trying to get him for ages, earlier. First the line was busy, then there was no answer.'

Shane frowned. 'Perhaps he'd slipped down to the village. Any message, Aunt Emma?'

'Tell him that we didn't – ' Changing her mind, she broke off and shook her head. 'Never mind, Shane. It's not important. I'll be seeing him tomorrow, and I'm sure we'll have a chance to chat at some point then.'

When they were alone, Blackie reached across and took Emma's hand in his, and stared deeply into her face. 'It's grand to see you, me darlin'. I've missed you.'

Emma's eyes danced. 'Get along with you, you silly old thing. You just saw me the day before yesterday,' she exclaimed, amusement surfacing. 'Don't tell me you've forgotten our dinner at Pennistone.'

'Of course I haven't. But it seems like a long time to me, caring about you the way I do.' He patted her hand affectionately and sat back in his chair, giving her the fondest of looks. 'And I meant it when I said you looked bonny, Emma. You're a real bobby dazzler in that dress, it's very flattering on you, me darlin' girl.'

'Some girl! But thank you, I'm glad you like it,' she answered with a smile of real pleasure. 'My friend Ginette Spanier, at Balmain's, picked it out for me and had it shipped over from Paris last week. Mind you, Edwina was rather scathing earlier. She told me it was too young for me, the colour, you know.'

Blackie's expression altered radically. 'She was just being catty, Emma. Edwina's got a chip on her shoulder the size of that old oak tree out yonder in my garden. *She'll* never change.' He noticed the look of pain flit across Emma's face, and he frowned with concern for her, cursing her daughter under his breath. Edwina had always been troublesome. But then so had most of the others, and there were a couple of Emma's children whom he could quite cheerfully strangle with his bare hands. He cried heatedly, 'I hope she's not been giving you a hard time!'

'No, not really.'

She sounded unusually hesitant, and Blackie spotted this immediately, and shook his marvellous white, leonine head, and exhaled in exasperation. 'I'll never understand Jim. I don't know what prompted him to invite her. It was stupid on his part, if you ask me.'

'Yes, and Paula was upset too, but I decided not to intervene. I thought it would look petty. But . . .' Emma shrugged, and, since she confided most things in Blackie these days, she told him about her conversation with Edwina, her attempts to reason with her daughter.

Blackie listened carefully, occasionally nodding, and when she had finished he said, in a low voice, 'Well, I'm happy for Sally, if this is what she wants. She's a lovely lass, and Anthony is a nice chap. Down-to-earth, and not a bit stuck up, which is more than I can say for that mother of his.' He paused. Recollections swamped him. Slowly, he added, 'She was most peculiar when she was growing up, and never very nice to you, Emma. Always slighting you, if I remember correctly, and believe me, I do. I haven't forgotten how she used to show her preference for Joe Lowther, making it so bloody obvious too. She was a little bitch, and she hasn't changed. Please promise me you'll let this matter about Anthony rest. I don't want you getting agitated because of Edwina. She's not worth it.'

'Yes, you're right, and I promise.' She smiled faintly. 'Let's forget about Edwina. Where are you taking me to dinner? Shane was most mysterious when we were driving over here.'

'Was he now, mavourneen.' Blackie grinned from ear to ear. 'To tell you the truth, Emma, I couldn't think of a nice enough place, so I told Mrs Padgett to prepare dinner for us here. I know you like her home cooking, and she's rustled up a lovely bit of spring lamb. I told her to make new potatoes, brussel sprouts and Yorkshire pudding, all your favourites. Now, me darlin', how does that sound to you?'

'Delicious, and I'm glad we're not going out. It's much cosier here, and I do feel a bit tired.'

His black eyes narrowed under his bushy brows as he examined her alertly. 'Ah,' he said softly, 'so you're finally admitting it. I do wish you wouldn't push yourself so hard. There's no need for it any more, you know.'

Dismissing this comment with an easy smile, Emma leaned closer to him, and no longer able to suppress her curiosity, she asked eagerly, 'What do you want my advice about? You sounded cagey on the phone this morning.'

'I didn't mean to, darlin'.' He sipped his whiskey, puffed away for a moment, and continued, 'But I'd prefer to wait until Shane comes back, if you don't mind, since it concerns him.'

'What concerns me?' Shane asked from the doorway. He strolled into the room, his drink in his hand.

'The business matter I want to discuss with Emma.'

'I'll say it concerns me!' Shane exclaimed rather forcefully. 'It was my idea in the first place.' Seating himself on the sofa next to Emma, he settled against the cushions, crossed his legs and turned to her. 'Winston's sorry he missed your calls. He was out in the garden earlier, worrying about the beck flooding. It's dangerously near to it apparently.' His eyes swivelled to his grandfather. 'I just rang Derek and asked him to get a couple of our men over to Beck House tomorrow, to check things out.'

'Aye, that's a good idea. But they'll have to shore up those banks a lot better than they did last year,' Blackie remarked pointedly. 'Now, if you'd both listened to me, it would have been done right in the first place. Let me explain a couple of things.' He commenced to do so, not giving Shane a chance to respond. And then for the next couple of minutes they discussed various methods of reinforcement. They sounded for all the world like a couple of builders about to embark on a major construction project, and Blackie was most vociferous in his opinions, which tickled Emma. He was still a bricklayer at heart.

But she soon lost interest in their somewhat technical conversation. She had become extremely conscious of Shane's presence next to her. His bulk did more than fill the sofa, it commandeered it. For the first time in years she began to regard him through newly perceptive and objective eyes, not as an old family friend, but as a younger woman – a stranger – might. How marvellous looking he was tonight, dressed in an impeccably tailored grey suit and a pale-blue voile shirt with a silver-grey silk tie. He had inherited his grand-father's large frame, his broad sweeping back and powerful shoulders, along with Blackie's wavy black hair and those sparkling eyes so like jet. His complexion was dark too, but *his* light mahogany tan came from winter sun, garnered on the ski slopes of Switzerland or a lazy Caribbean beach, and not from toiling long hours as a navvy out in the open as his grandfather had once done.

His appearance was much like Blackie's had been at his age. The face is different, though, she thought, sneaking another surreptitious look at him, but he does have Blackie's distinctive cleft in his chin, the same dimples when he smiles. And that long upper lip betrays his Celtic origins. I bet he's broken many a heart already, she added silently with an inward smile of amusement. Then she experienced a tiny pang of sadness for Sarah. Easy to understand why the girl had a crush on him. He was a splendid young man who exuded virility and manliness, and there was a unique warmth and gentleness in him. That was the most devastating of combinations, and she knew only too well about men like Shane O'Neill. She had loved such a man herself, had had her heart broken by him once when she had been young and vulnerable and very much in love. But *he* had repaired *her* broken heart, had given her immeasurable happiness and fulfilment in the end. Yes, Paul McGill had had the same kind of potency and fatal charm such as Shane O'Neill possessed in some abundance.

Blackie said, 'Daydreaming, Emma darlin'?'

She shifted her position on the sofa and smiled lightly. 'No. I'm patiently waiting for you two to finish discussing that damn beck, so we can get down to brass tacks about the business you want my advice on.'

'Why yes, of course, it's wasting time we are,' he admitted, his manner more genial than ever. In fact, conviviality seemed to spill out of Blackie tonight, and he beamed first at Emma, then at Shane. 'Now, me boy,' he said, 'please top up Emma's glass with a drop more of that bubbly, and give me a refill, and we'll settle in for a nice little chat.'

And this they did, after Shane had attended to their drinks.

It was Shane who began, concentrating his attention entirely on Emma, his tone as sober as his face had become. He spoke rapidly, but clearly, as he generally did in business, plunging in without preamble. Emma appreciated his directness, and she, in turn, gave him all of her attention.

Shane said: 'We've been wanting to build, or acquire, a hotel in New York for several years. Dad and I have both spent a great deal of time scouting out possibilities. Recently we found the ideal place. It's a residential hotel in the East Sixties. Old-fashioned, of course, and the interiors are in need of consider-able remodelling – rebuilding actually. That's what we'll do – most likely. You see, we tendered a bid, it has been accepted, and we're buying the hotel. The papers are currently being drawn up.'

'Congratulations, Shane, and you too, Blackie!' Emma looked from one to the other, her face bathed in genuine delight. 'But how can I be of help to you? Why do you need to talk to me? I don't know a blessed thing about hotels, except whether or not they're comfortable and efficient.'

'But you do know New York City, Emma,' Blackie countered, leaning forward with intentness. 'That's *why* we need you.'

'I'm not sure that I follow you –'

'We need you to steer us in the right direction to the best people,' Shane cut in, wanting to get to the crux of the matter. He pinned her with his bright black eyes. 'It seems to me that you've made that city your own in so many different ways, so you must know what makes it tick. Or rather what makes its business and commerce tick.' His generous mouth curved up into the cheekiest of grins. 'We want to pick your brains, and use your connections,' he finished, regarding her carefully, his cheekiness still very much in evidence.

Amusement flickered in Emma's eyes. She had always liked Shane's style, his directness, his boyish impudence. She stifled a laugh, said, 'I see. Do continue.'

'Right,' Shane replied, all seriousness again. 'Look, we're a foreign corporation, and in my opinion that city's as tight as drum. We can't go in cold ... well, we could, but we'd have a tough time. I'm sure we'd be resented. We need advisers – the proper advisers – and some good connections. Political connections for one thing. And we'll need help with the unions, with any number of things. I'm sure you of all people understand what I'm talking about, Aunt Emma. So, where do we go? Who do we go to?'

Emma's mind had been working with its usual swiftness and acuity, and she saw the sense in Shane's words. He had analysed the situation most shrewdly. She told him this, went on without hesitation, 'It *would* be unwise of you to start operating in New York without the most influential backing and support. You'll need everybody in your corner, and the only way you'll get them in it is through friends. Good friends with clout. I think I can help.'

'I knew if anybody could, it would be you. Thanks, Aunt Emma,' Shane said, and she saw him visibly relaxing.

'Yes, we're very grateful, me darlin',' Blackie added, pushing himself up out of the chair. He took his drink to the console behind the sofa, plopped in extra ice, added more water to his whiskey, and said, 'Well, go on, Shane, as Emma asked.' He touched her shoulder lightly, lovingly. Emma glanced behind her, questions on her face. Blackie chuckled. 'Oh yes, there's more,' he said, and ambled back to his chair by the fireside.

Shane said: 'We have a solid, well-established law firm representing us in the purchase of the hotel – they're specialists in real estate. However, I feel we are going to need additional representation for other business matters. I'd like to find a really prestigious law firm that has political savvy and a few gilt-edged connections. Any suggestions about that?'

There was a moment of thoughtfulness, before Emma said, 'Yes, of course. I could send you to my lawyers, and to any number of people who would be of use to you. But I've been thinking hard whilst I've been listening, and I believe there is one person who would be of more assistance to you than me and my lawyers and my friends put together. His name is Ross Nelson. He's a banker – head of a private bank, in fact. He has the very best connections in New York, throughout the States, for that matter. I'm sure he'll be able to recommend the law firm most qualified for your purposes, and assist you in a variety of other ways.'

'But will he do it?' Shane asked, doubt echoing.

'He will if *I* ask him,' she said, giving Shane the benefit of a reassuring smile. 'I can telephone him on Monday, and explain everything. I hope I'll be able to enlist his help immediately. Would you like me to do that?'

'Yes, I would. *We* would.' He swung his head to Blackie. 'Wouldn't we, Grandfather?'

'Anything you say, my boy. This is your deal.' Blackie tapped ash from his cigar, looked across at Emma. 'That name Nelson rings a bell. Have I met him?'

'Why yes, I think you did once. It was some years ago, Blackie. Ross was over in England with his great-uncle, Daniel P. Nelson. Dan was a close friend and associate of Paul's, if you recall. He's the fellow who wanted me to send Daisy over to the States during the war, to stay with him and his wife, Alicia. But as you know, I never wanted Daisy to be evacuated. Anyway, the Nelsons only had one child, Richard. The boy was killed in the Pacific. Dan was never quite the same after that. He made Ross his heir, after his wife, of course. Ross inherited controlling interest in the bank in Wall Street when Dan died, and God knows what else. Not millions. *Zillions*, I think. Daniel P. Nelson was one of the richest men in America, had tremendous power.'

Shane was impressed and this showed in his face. He asked quickly, 'How old a man is Ross Nelson?'

'Oh he must be in his late thirties, early forties, not much more.'

'Are you sure he won't mind helping us? I'd hate to think he would regard your request as an imposition. That kind of situation can create difficulties,' Shane remarked. He was intrigued with Nelson, wanted to know more about him. He reached for his drink and took a swallow, observing Emma out of the corner of his eye.

Emma laughed quietly. 'He owes me a few favours. And he won't think I'm imposing, I can assure you of that.' She gave Shane a shrewd look through her narrowed green eyes. 'Mind you, I know Ross, and he's going to expect something in return. Business, I'm sure, in one form or another. Actually, you might consider doing some of your investment banking with him, and let his bank handle your affairs on that side of the Atlantic. You could do worse.' There was a cynical edge to her voice, as she finished, 'There are two things you must remember, Shane . . . one hand always washes the other, and there's never anything free in this world. Especially in business.'

Shane met her cool, concentrated gaze steadily. 'I understand,' he said softly. 'And I learned long ago that anything for nothing is usually not worth having. As for Ross Nelson, I'll know how to show my appreciation, you have no worries there.'

Blackie, who had been following this exchange with considerable interest, slapped his knee and laughed uproariously. 'Ah, Emma, it's a spry one I've got me here.' He shook his head and his benevolent smile expressed his love and pride. 'There are no flies on you, my boy, I'm glad to see, and it won't be the same without you.' A hint of sadness crept on to his face, wiping away the laughter. 'I know it's important and necessary, but I hate to see you go away again, and so quickly. It pains me, it truly does.'

Emma put down her glass and stared at Shane. 'When *are* you leaving, Shane?'

'I fly to New York on Monday morning. I'll be staying there for a good six months, maybe longer. I'll be supervising the rebuilding of the hotel in Manhattan, and trotting down to the Caribbean every few weeks to check on our hotels in the islands.'

'*Six months,*' she repeated in surprise. 'That *is* a long time. We shall miss you.' But perhaps it's just as well he won't be around for a while, she added under her breath, thinking of her granddaughter Sarah Lowther. Out of sight, out of mind. Or so she hoped.

Shane cut into her thoughts, when he said, 'I shall miss you too, Aunt Emma, and Grandfather, everyone in fact. But I'll be back almost before you can say Jack Robinson.' He leaned into Emma and squeezed her arm. 'And keep an eye on this lovable old scoundrel here. He's very dear to me.'

'And to me too, Shane. Of course I'll look after him.'

'Ah, and won't we be taking care of each other now,' Blackie announced, sounding extremely pleased with himself all of a sudden, thinking of his Plan with a capital P. 'But then we've been doing that for half a century or more, and it's a difficult habit to break, sure an' it is.'

'I can imagine.' Shane laughed, marvelling at the two of them. What an extraordinary pair they were, and the love and friendship they felt for each other was a most enviable thing. Sighing under his breath, he reached for his Scotch, peered into the amber liquid, reflecting. After a swallow he turned to Emma. 'But getting back to Ross Nelson, what kind of a chap is he?'

'Unusual in many ways,' Emma said slowly, staring into space, as if visualizing Ross Nelson in her mind's eye. 'Ross is deceptive. He has a certain charm, and he appears to be very friendly. On the surface. I've always thought there was an innate coldness in him, and a curious kind of calculation, as if he stands apart from himself, watching the effect he has on people. There's a terrific ego there, and especially when it comes to women. He's something of a ladies' man, and has just been divorced for the second time. Not that this is significant: on the other hand, it's frequently struck me that he might be unscrupulous . . . in his private life.'

She paused, brought her eyes to meet Shane's, and added, 'But that has nothing to do with you or me. As far as business is concerned, I deem Ross to be trustworthy. You have no cause to worry in that respect. But be warned, he's clever, razor sharp, and he has the *need* to get his own way – that monumental ego rears up constantly.'

'Quite a picture you've painted, Aunt Emma. Obviously I'll have to have my wits about me.'

'That's always wise, Shane, whoever you're dealing with.' She smiled faintly. 'On the other hand, you're going to Ross for advice, not pitting yourself against him in a business deal. You'll be able to handle Ross Nelson very nicely. In fact, I think you'll get along with him just fine. Don't forget, he owes me a few favours, so he'll bend over backwards to be cooperative and helpful.'

'I know your judgement is never flawed, always spot on,' Shane replied. He rose, walked around the sofa to fix himself another drink, thinking of the characterization she had drawn in her thumbnail sketch. He was anxious to meet the man. It was obvious that Nelson was going to be invaluable. And he was impatient to get the ball rolling with the New York hotel. He needed to submerge himself in business, to take his mind off troubling personal matters. Ross Nelson might possibly be a pain in the neck in his private life, but who cared about his philandering. As long as he was smart, shrewd, trustworthy, and willing to help, that was all that mattered.

Blackie's eyes flicked briefly to his grandson, and then settled on Emma. 'I'm not so sure I like the sound of this Ross Nelson fellow,' he began.

Emma cut him off with a laugh. 'My money's on Shane. He's a grown lad who knows how to take care of himself very well. Very well indeed, Blackie. I'll even go as far as to say that Ross Nelson might have met his match in Shane.' This observation seemed to entertain her, and she continued to laugh.

Shane grinned, but made no comment.

He was looking forward to meeting Mr Ross Nelson more than ever. The banker would add spice to the New York venture.

9

They sat in front of the blazing fire in the library – just the two of them.

Blackie nursed a snifter of aged Napoleon cognac, and Emma sipped a cup of tea with lemon. He had poured her a small glass of Bonnie Prince Charlie, her favourite Drambuie liqueur, but it remained untouched on the Sheraton side table next to her chair.

They were quiet, lost in their diverse thoughts, relaxing after Mrs Padgett's fine dinner. Shane had left, and, as much as they both loved him in their individual ways, they were content to have this time alone together.

The firelight flickered and danced across the bleached-pine panelled walls which had taken on a mellow amber cast in the warm roseate glow emanating from the hearth. In the garden beyond the French doors, the towering old oak creaked and rustled and swayed under the force of the wind that had turned into a roaring gale in the last hour. The door and the windows rattled, and the rain was flung against the glass in an unrelenting stream, beating a steady staccato rhythm, and it was difficult to see out through this curtain of falling water. But in the fine old room all was warmth, cosiness and comfort. The logs crackled and hissed and spurted from time to time, and the grandfather clock, an ancient sentinel in the corner, ticked away in unison.

His eyes had been focused on her for a while.

In repose, as it was now, Emma's face was gentle, the firm jaw and determined chin and stern mouth softer, less forbidding in the flattering light. Her hair held the lustre of the purest silver, and she seemed, to him, to be a lovely dainty doll, sitting there so sedately, perfectly groomed and dressed as always, elegance and refinement apparent in every line of her slender body.

She had not changed really.

Oh, he was aware that when the flames blazed more brightly, he would notice the wrinkles and the hooded lids and the faint brown speckles of age on her hands. But he knew, deep in his soul, that she was still the same girl inside.

She would always be his wild young colleen of the moors, that little starveling creature he had come across early one morning in 1904, when she had been tramping so bravely to Fairley Hall to scrub and clean in order to earn a few miserable coppers to help her impoverished family. His destination had been the same place, for Squire Adam Fairley had hired him to do bricklaying at the Hall, and then he had stupidly gone and lost himself in the mist on those bleak and empty Godforsaken hills . . . so long ago . . . but not so long to him. He had never forgotten that day.

Blackie's gaze lingered on Emma.

He had loved this woman from the first moment he had met her and all the days of his life thereafter. He had been eighteen, that day on the lonely moors, and she had been a fourteen-year-old waif, all skin and bones and huge emerald eyes, and she had touched his heart like no one else before or after, and bound him to her forever without even trying.

Once he had asked her to marry him.

She, believing it was out of kindness and friendship, and the goodness of his heart, had refused him. She had thanked him sweetly, her face wet with tears, and explained that she and the child she was carrying, by another man, would only be burdens to him. And she would not inflict such a terrible load on her dearest friend Blackie, she had said.

Eventually, he had married Laura Spencer, and he had loved her well and true. And yet he had never stopped loving his bonny mavourneen, even though at times he was hard pressed to explain that unique love to himself, or articulate it to her, or anyone else for that matter.

There was a time when he had half expected Emma to marry David Kallinski, but once again she had turned down a splendid, upright young man. Later, she had confided the reason to him. She had not wanted to create trouble between David and his family, who were Jewish. Although Mrs Kallinski was motherly towards her, Emma said she had long realized that as a gentile she would not be considered appropriate as a daughter-in-law by Janessa Kallinski, who was Orthodox and expected her son to marry in the Faith.

Then one day, Joe Lowther had come riding by, metaphorically speaking, and to Blackie's astonishment – and not inconsiderable bewilderment – Emma had plunged into holy matrimony with Joe. He had never been able to fully comprehend their union. In his opinion, it was difficult, if not downright impossible, to hitch a race horse and a cart horse to the same wagon. But Joe had been a kindly man, if plodding and dull and not particularly brilliant or engaging. Still, he and Blackie had liked each other well enough and had gone off to fight a war together. And he had seen Joe Lowther killed in the muddy trenches of the bloody, battle-torn Somme, and had wept real tears for him, for Joe had been too young a man to die. And he had never been able to talk about Joe's ghastly death, to tell her that he had seen Joe blown to smithereens. Only years later did he learn from Emma that she had married Joe, who adored her, to protect herself and her baby daughter Edwina from the Fairleys, after Gerald Fairley had attempted to rape her one night at her little shop in Armley. 'It wasn't as calculating as it sounds,' she had gone on. 'I liked Joe, cared for him, and because he was a good man I felt honour-bound to be a good wife.' And she had been devoted, *he* knew that.

The second time he had wanted to marry Emma he had truly believed his timing was perfect, that he had every chance of being accepted, and he was buoyed up with soaring hopes and anticipation. It was a short while after the First World War when they were both widowed. In the end, though, uncertain of her true feelings for him, and filled with sudden nervousness about Emma's astonishing achievements in comparison to his own, he had lost his nerve, and his tongue, and so he had not spoken up. Regrettably. And she had unexpectedly gone off and married Arthur Ainsley, a man not good enough to lick her boots, and had suffered all kinds of pain and humiliation at Ainsley's hands. Finally, in the 1920s, as he was biding his time and waiting for the propitious moment, Paul McGill had come back to England to claim her at last for himself.

And he had lost his chance again.

Now it was too late for them to marry. Yet, in a sense, they had something akin to marriage and just as good, to his way of thinking ... this friendship, this closeness, this total understanding. Yes, all were of immense and incalculable value. And Emma and he were perfectly attuned to each other in the twilight of their days, and what did the rest mean, or matter, at this stage in the game of life?

But he still had that ring ...

Much to his own surprise, Blackie had kept the engagement ring he had bought for Emma so long ago. There had never been another woman to give it to – at least, not one he cared enough about; and for a reason he could not fathom, he had never wanted to sell it.

Tonight the ring had burned a hole in his pocket all through drinks and dinner, in much the same way his Plan with a capital P burned a hole in his head. Putting down his drink, he leaned closer to the hearth, lifted the poker and shoved the logs around in the grate, wondering if it was finally the right time to give it to her. Why not?

He heard the rustle of silk and a sigh that was hardly audible.

'Did I startle you, Emma?'

'No, Blackie.'

'I have something for you.'

'You do? What is it?'

He reached into his pocket and brought out the box, sat holding it in his large hands.

Emma asked curiously, 'Is it my birthday present?' and she gave him a warm little smile of obvious pleasure, laughter sparkling in her eyes.

'Oh no, indeed it's not. I intend to give you *that* on your birthday at the ...' He curbed himself. The elaborate party he and Daisy were planning was very hush-hush and meant to be a big surprise for Emma. 'You'll get your birthday gift at the end of the month, on the very day you're eighty,' he improvised adroitly. 'No, this is something I bought for you . . .' He had to laugh, as he added, 'Fifty years ago, believe it or not.'

She threw him a startled look. 'Fifty years! But why didn't you give it to me before now?'

'Ah, Emma, thereby hangs a long tale,' he said, and fell silent as memories came unbidden.

How beautiful she had looked that night, with her red hair piled high on her head in an elaborate plaited coil, wearing a superb white velvet gown, cut low and off the shoulders. Pinned to one of the small sleeves was the emerald bow he had had made for her thirtieth birthday, an exquisite replica of the cheap little green-glass brooch he had given her when she was fifteen. She had been touched and delighted that he had not forgotten his old promise, made to her in the kitchen of Fairley Hall. But on that particular Christmas night, in all her elegant finery, with McGill's magnificent emeralds blazing on her ears, he had thought his emerald bow, costly though it had been, looked like a trumpery bauble in comparison to those earrings . . .

Growing impatient, Emma frowned and exclaimed, 'Well, are you going to tell me the tale or not?'

He pushed the past to one side, flashed her a smile. 'Do you remember that first party I gave here? It was Christmas . . .'

'Boxing Day night!' Emma cried, her face lighting up. 'You had just completed this house, finished furnishing it with all the lovely Sheraton and Hepplewhite pieces you'd scoured the country to find. And you were so proud of what you'd created all by yourself. Of course I remember the party, and very clearly. It was 1919.'

Blackie nodded, glanced down at the box, continuing to finger it. He raised his head. Unabashed love shone on his craggy, wrinkled face, giving it a more youthful appearance. 'I'd bought this for you earlier that week. I'd travelled down to London to choose it, gone to the finest jeweller, too. It was in the pocket of my tuxedo. I'd intended to give it to you at the party.'

'But you never did . . . why not? What ever made you change your mind, Blackie?' She looked at him oddly, through eyes awash with perplexity.

'I'd decided to have a talk first – with Winston. Why, it was here, in this very room, as a matter of fact.' He looked about him, as if seeing that ancient scene being re-enacted in the shadows; seeing the ghost of Winston, as he had been as a young man, lurking there. He cleared his throat. 'Your brother and I talked about you, and . . .'

'What *about* me?'

'We discussed you and your business ventures. I was worried to death about you, Emma, distressed because of the way you had plunged into the commodities market, and recklessly, or so I thought. I was concerned about your rapid expansion of the stores in the North, your determination to keep on building, acquiring other holdings. I believed you were over-extending yourself, gambling . . .'

'I've always been a gambler,' she murmured softly. 'In a way, that's the secret of my success . . . being willing to take chances . . .' She left the rest unsaid. He surely knew it all by now.

'Aye,' he agreed. 'Maybe it is. Anyway, Winston explained that you'd stopped the commodities lark, after making a fortune speculating, and he told me you were not in over your head. Just the opposite. He told me you were a millionairess. And as he talked, and ever so proudly, I began to realize that you were a far, far bigger success than I'd ever dreamed, that you'd surpassed me, outstripped David Kallinski, left us both behind in business. It suddenly seemed to me that you were quite beyond my reach. That's why I never gave you this ring . . . You see Emma, I was going to ask you to marry me that night.'

'Oh Blackie, Blackie darling,' was all she could manage to say, so stupefied was she. Tears pricked the back of Emma's eyes as a variety of emotions seized her with some force. Her love and friendship for him rose up in her to mingle with a terrible sadness and a sense of regret for Blackie, as she envisioned the pain he must have suffered then and afterwards, perhaps. He had wanted her, and he had not said a word. That was his tragedy. At the party in 1919 she had believed Paul McGill was lost to her forever. How vulnerable and susceptible she would have been to her one true friend Blackie in her heartbreak, loneliness and despair. And if he had been more courageous how different their lives would have turned out. Her thoughts ran on endlessly. Why had she never suspected that he cared for her in that way . . . that he had marriage on his mind? She must have been blind or dense or too involved with business.

The silence between them drifted.

Blackie sat unmoving in the chair, staring into the fire, saying not a word, remembering so much himself. It's odd, he thought suddenly, how things which happened to me when I was a young man have an extraordinary vividness these days. More so than events of last week, or even yesterday. I suspect that's part of growing old.

Emma was the first to rouse herself.

She said, in a small, pained voice, 'Were you trying to tell me, a few minutes ago, that my *success* put you *off*? Prevented you from proposing?' She studied that dear, familiar face with infinite compassion, thinking of the years he had wasted, the happiness he had let slip through his fingers, and all because of his love for her. A love unuttered.

Blackie nodded. 'Aye, I suppose I am, mavourneen. I decided, there and then, that you could never be weaned away from your business because it was very much a part of you, *was* you, really. In any event, I lost my confidence. After all, I wasn't half as rich and successful as you in those days. I didn't think you'd have me. My nerve failed me. Yes, that's precisely what happened.'

A deep sigh trickled out of Emma, and slowly she shook her head. 'How foolish you were, my dearest, dearest friend.'

Blackie gaped at her, his jaw slack with astonishment. 'Are you saying that you would have married me, Emma Harte?' he asked, unable to keep the shock and incredulity out of his voice.

'Yes, I believe I would, Blackie O'Neill.'

Now it was Blackie who began to shake his head, and he did so in wonderment, trying to absorb her words. For a few minutes he could not speak as old emotions took hold of him, surprising him with the strength of their impact.

At last he said, 'It does me good to hear that, even so long afterwards.' His voice took on a quavering treble, as he added, 'Perhaps it's just as well we

91

didn't marry, Emma. I'd have been left high and dry, not to mention broken-hearted, when Paul swept you off your feet again.'

'How can you say such a thing! What kind of woman do you think I am!' she cried, her indignation flaring as she jerked herself up in the chair and glared at him with such unprecedented ferocity he flinched. 'I would never have hurt *you*! I've always loved you, cared about your well being, and you know it. Apologize at once,' she spluttered angrily, and added, as an afterthought, 'or I'll never speak to you again!'

He was so startled by her vehemence he was speechless for a few seconds. Slowly a shame-faced look crept on to his face. He said in a most tender and placating voice, 'It's sorry I am, Emma, I take back those words. I believe you. I don't think you would have left me for Paul. And that's not my ego talking. I know you . . . better than anyone does. No, you wouldn't have betrayed me, you wouldn't have given him the time of day if you'd been married to me. It's not in you to be cruel to someone you love, and then there's your morality and your loyalty and goodness and sense of responsibility. Those would have worked in my favour. Besides –' He gave her a boyish grin that brought his dimples out. '*I* would have made you happy.'

'Yes, Blackie, I believe you would.'

This was said rapidly, and there was a sudden urgency in her manner as she leaned forward anxiously, needing to clarify the past, to make him under-stand the reasons which had motivated her and Paul, quite aside from their great love. 'Don't forget,' she began, intent on jogging his memory. 'My marriage to Arthur Ainsley was on the rocks long before Paul McGill returned to this country. I was on the verge of divorce when Paul showed up. Besides, and this is most important, Blackie, Paul wouldn't have intruded, wouldn't have sought me out, if I'd been happily married. It was only because Frank had told him I was miserable, and separated from Ainsley, that he arrived on my doorstep.'

She paused, settled back in the chair, and clasped her hands tightly in her lap. 'I *know* I would not have seen hide nor hair of Paul ever again, *if* my life had been on an even keel. He told me that himself. He came searching for me because he was aware I was unhappy – and also available. He most certainly wouldn't have done that if I'd been married to *you*. Have you forgotten how much he liked and respected you?'

'No, I haven't. And you're correct in what you say . . . Yes, Paul was a fine and honourable man. I always had a lot of time for him.'

Blackie now rose.

'Well,' he said, 'that's all water under an old and decrepit bridge, my girl. There's no point rehashing our troubles of half a century ago. And maybe it was meant to be . . .' he lifted his hands and shoulders in a brief shrug '. . . exactly the way it is. But I would like you to have the ring. It's always been yours, you know.'

He bent over her. She looked up at him, and then at the black leather box in his hands. He lifted the lid, turned the box to her.

Emma gasped.

The ring was exquisite, throwing off the most brilliant prisms of light, and sparkling with life and fire against the black velvet. The central diamond was round and multi-faceted, and very large, at least twenty carats, and it was surrounded by smaller stones which were equally as lovely and superbly cut, and these formed a circle at the base of the mounting.

Even Emma, accustomed to magnificent jewellery, was awestruck and she found herself blinking, truly taken aback by its size and beauty. 'It's stunning, Blackie,' she said a bit breathlessly. 'One of the most beautiful rings I've ever seen.'

His joy at her words was evident. 'It's an old setting, of course, the original, and perhaps it's even a bit outdated. But I didn't want to have it reset. Here, slip it on, mavourneen.'

She shook her head. 'No, you do it, my fine black Irishman.' She offered him her left hand. 'Put it on the third finger, next to my wedding ring.'

He did so.

Emma held out her small, strong hand, her head on one side, admiring the ring glittering so brightly in the fire's glow. And then she glanced up at him, her expression unmistakably mischievous. 'Are we finally engaged to be married then?' she teased in a flirtatious voice, and offered him a smile that was decidedly coy.

Blackie laughed, with delight, hugely amused. He'd always enjoyed her sense of humour.

Bending closer to her, he kissed her cheek. 'Let's just say we're engaged to be – to be the dearest and closest friends and companions for the rest of the time we have on this earth.'

'Oh Blackie, that's such a lovely thing to say, and thank you for my beautiful ring.' She caught his hand and held on to it and pressed it tightly and looked up at him again, and then she smiled that incomparable smile that filled her face with radiance. 'My dear old friend, you're so very very special to me,' she said.

'As you are to me, my Emma.'

He stepped away from her chair as if heading to his own, and then he paused and swung his white head. 'I hope you're going to wear the ring,' he remarked off-handedly but his glance remained riveted intently on hers. 'I sincerely hope you're not going to put it away in that safe of yours.'

'Certainly *not*. How could you think such a thing. I'm never going to take it off . . . ever again.'

He touched her shoulder and returned to his seat, smiling to himself. 'I'm glad I gave you your ring, me darlin'. I've thought about doing so many times, and I've often wondered what you'd say. I know I'm always accusing *you* of being a sentimentalist in your old age, but I do believe *I've* become a sentimental old man myself.'

'And tell me, Blackie O'Neill, what's wrong with sentiment? It's a pity there isn't more of it in this world,' she said, her eyes unexpectedly moist. 'It might be a better place to live in, for one thing.'

'Aye,' was all he said.

After a short while, Blackie cleared his throat, and remarked, 'Now, what about that little proposition of mine, Emma? This morning you said you were doubtful that it would work, but I can't agree.'

'Do you know,' she exclaimed brightly in an enthusiastic voice, 'I was thinking about it again this afternoon. Emily's moved in with me, and it suddenly struck me that the only way I'll get a bit of peace and quiet is to accept your generous invitation.'

'Then you'll come with me! Ah, me darlin', this news warms the cockles of me heart, sure an' it does.' He beamed at her, happiness and excitement welling inside him. He lifted his brandy balloon high. 'Come along, take a sip of your Bonnie Prince Charlie, Emma. This calls for a toast, it does indeed.'

She held up her hand instead. 'Wait a minute! I didn't actually say *yes*. I can't accept – at least not just yet. I *am* seriously thinking about the trip, but you'll have to give me a few more weeks to settle things, to adjust to the idea of being absent for several months.'

Biting down on his disappointment, he said, 'All right, I'll be patient. However, I will have to start making the arrangements soon, so please don't delay your answer for too long.'

'I'll let you know as quickly as possible. I promise.'

He sipped his cognac, savouring it, and slowly a sly gleam entered his eyes. He was wrapped in thought for a minute or two longer, said finally, 'By the way, Emma, I've recently made a plan, as no doubt *you'll* be surprised to hear. I think of it as my Plan with a capital P, since it happens to be the first plan *I've* ever made.' He was unable to contain himself, and let out a throaty chortle and his eyes became merry and teasing. 'Do you remember that first plan of *yours?*'

'Goodness me, I'd forgotten all about *that*.'

'I never did. And I even recall the day you confided it in me. Such a small slip of a thing you were, too, and I was most impressed. Anyway, if you've got a few minutes, I'd like to tell you about mine. It's a most marvellous plan, me darlin', even though I say so myself. And I'll bet my last quid it's going to intrigue you, sure an' I know it will.'

Amusement touched her mouth. 'I'd love to hear about your plan, Blackie dear.'

He sat back expansively, nodding to himself, and began: 'Well, it's like this. There is this woman I know, and she's the most stubborn creature I've met in all my born days. It just so happens that this stubborn, contrary, maddening but quite adorable woman has a grandson living in Australia. I know she wants to go and see him, and I thought it would be a wonderful treat for her, if I took her out there to see him myself. And so I've made a very *special* plan, and this is how it goes . . .'

Emily had fallen asleep on one of the huge sofas in the upstairs parlour.

To Emma, standing over her, she looked small and defenceless and innocent, wrapped in a white towelling robe and curled up in a ball against the pile of cushions. A feeling of infinite tenderness swept through Emma, and she bent down and gently moved a strand of pale blonde hair away from Emily's eyes, and brushed her lips against the girl's smooth young cheek. She straightened up, wondering whether to awaken her or not, decided to get ready for bed herself first, and tiptoed into the adjoining bedroom.

Emma hung up her sable jacket, took off her pearl choker and matching earrings and placed them on the dressing table. After removing her watch and the McGill emerald, she started to pull off Blackie's ring, then stopped and looked down at it. This ring had lain in a vault waiting for her for fifty years, and she had promised Blackie she would never take it off. She pushed the ring back on her finger, next to Paul's platinum wedding band, and finished undressing. She had just put on her nightgown when there was a tap on the door and Emily's smiling face appeared around it.

'There you are, Grandy. I waited up for you.'

'So I noticed, darling. But you didn't have to, you know.'

'I wanted to, Gran. But to be honest, I didn't think you'd be as late as this. It's turned *twelve thirty*!'

'I'm well aware of the time, Emily. And look here, if you're going to live with me, you mustn't start monitoring my comings and goings. And I don't need mothering either. I get enough of that from Paula at the store,' Emma remarked evenly, putting on her silk dressing gown and knotting the belt.

Emily giggled and skipped into the room, obviously wide awake and full of her usual *joie de vivre*. 'It's not role reversal, if that's what you're thinking. I'm *not* trying to mother you. I was merely commenting on the time.'

'Just bear in mind what I said.'

'I will, Grandma.' Emily hovered near the dressing table. She saw the jewellery strewn across it and her eyes darted to Emma's hand. She noticed the diamond at once, which shone with brilliance in the bright light from the lamps. 'Aren't you going to show me Blackie's ring?' she asked.

Emma's brows shot up. 'And how did *you* know about the ring?' The words had no sooner left her mouth than she wondered why she had even bothered to ask Emily, of all people, such a question.

'Merry and I were Blackie's conspirators,' Emily explained. 'About two weeks ago he asked *her* to ask *me* to check your ring size. He thought your fingers might have shrunk.'

'Did he indeed! I'll have to have a few strong words with him tomorrow. Does he think I've turned into a shrivelled up old crone,' Emma exclaimed pithily.

Emily could not keep the laughter out of her voice as she said, 'Nobody would think that about you, Gran, least of all Blackie. You're still beautiful.'

'No, I'm not. I *am* an old woman,' Emma stated flatly. 'But thank you for being nice, Emily. Of course,' she added with a laugh, 'everyone knows *you're* prejudiced.' She held out her left hand. 'Well, how do you like it?'

Emily took hold of Emma's hand, her bright green eyes huge, and as round as saucers, her excitement apparent on her expressive, mobile face. 'Gosh, Gran, I'd no idea it was going to be so big, and such a beauty! It's fabulous!' She scrutinized the ring more closely, and with an expert's eye, lifted her head and nodded knowingly. 'It's a perfect diamond, Gran. I bet it cost a fortune . . .' Her voice trailed off and she hesitated, then asked in an uncertain tone, 'Does this mean you and Blackie are going to get married?'

Emma burst out laughing and extracted her hand. 'Of course not, you silly goose. Whatever will you think of next.' She touched Emily's face lovingly, 'You're such a romantic girl,' she murmured, sighing softly. 'No, it wouldn't be appropriate. Not at our ages. As Blackie said, we're engaged to be the best of friends for the rest of our lives.' Emma now became aware of the undisguised curiosity and interest lingering on Emily's face, and before she could stop herself she said, 'I'll tell you the story about the ring, if you like.'

'Oh yes, I'd love to hear it, Grandy. Let's go to the parlour, though. I have a thermos of hot chocolate waiting for you. Come along.' She took hold of her grandmother's arm possessively, and shepherded her next door, not realizing she was fussing and bustling like a mother hen. Emma merely smiled, allowed herself to be bullied, secretly amused.

After filling two mugs with chocolate and giving one to Emma, Emily curled up on the sofa she had so recently vacated, tucked her feet under her and gleefully snuggled down into the cushions. Lifting her mug she took a sip and cried with delight, 'This is such fun, it's like being back at boarding school and having midnight feasts.'

Emma's mouth twitched. 'Don't get carried away, Emily,' she laughed. 'We won't be doing this every night. I'm usually in bed by this time. And talking of bed, it's getting *very* late. I'd better tell you the story quickly, so that we can go to sleep. We have a hectic day tomorrow.'

'Yes, Gran.' Emily gave her grandmother her rapt attention.

When the old story was finally told, Emily said, 'Oh Grandma, that's so lovely and touching, and a little sad in a way. And imagine him keeping the ring all these years. Gosh, that's real devotion.' A wistful look swept across her delicately pretty face and she shook her head. 'And you're *sceptical* about unrequited love! This should prove you're absolutely wrong.'

Emma smiled indulgently, made no comment.

Brightening, Emily rushed on in her breathy voice, 'Just think, if you'd married Blackie instead of Awful Arthur all those years ago, your children would have been very different – it's all a matter of genes, you know. I wonder if the oldies would have been any nicer?' Emily tilted her head and pursed her lips, lost in thought, her mind racing. Several things occurred to her all at once, and she burst out, 'What about your grandchildren? Paula, for instance. And *me*. Goodness, Grandy, I might not have been *me* at all. I could have been someone altogether different . . .'

Emma cut in, 'But I would have loved you just as much, Emily, and Paula too.'

'Oh yes, of course you would, I know that. But your family would have been very –'

'Now you're speculating about things we'll never know. And it's all *much* too complicated for me, especially at this hour,' Emma said with a dismissive yet kindly smile. 'But speaking of my family, what happened here this evening? How was the dinner party?'

Instantly Emily's face underwent a change, became serious as she sat up abruptly, swung her feet to the floor, and leaned closer to Emma. Her manner was confiding as she said, 'You're not going to believe this, but Edwina's behaviour was quite extraordinary –'

'In what way?' Emma asked sharply, dreading the worst.

Seeing the apprehensive expression settling on her grandmother's face, Emily shook her head with some vehemence. 'Don't look like that. It was *all right*. Edwina was nice . . . so nice I couldn't get over it, and neither could Paula. The Dowager Countess was charm personified. Well, that's not strictly true.'

Emily made a moue. 'You know I have a tendency to exaggerate.' Emily wrinkled her nose, went on, 'She was sort of . . . *cautious* with Paula and me. She doesn't really like us. She was polite, though, and pleasant to everyone else. I can't imagine what you said to her earlier, Grandma, but it certainly had a drastic effect on her.' Emily searched Emma's face and probed, 'You must have given her an awful lecture. You *did*, didn't you?' A blonde brow lifted quizzically.

Emma said nothing.

Emily volunteered, 'I think Aunt Edwina had been crying before she came down for drinks. Her eyes were puffy and red, and so was her nose. She didn't want a drink. She asked me for aspirins and a glass of water. We'd only been alone together for a couple of minutes when Paula and Jim arrived with Aunt Daisy and Uncle David. Edwina attached herself to Daisy immediately – it's funny, she seems to have a thing about Daisy. Anyway, she didn't say much to anyone else, not even Jim, during cocktails.' Emily's shoulders hunched in a small off-handed shrug. 'I thought she seemed ever so subdued, and she was certainly abstemious. You know how incorrigible she and Mummy are, always tippling. They never know when they've had enough. Edwina didn't touch a drop all night, though, not even wine with dinner.' Flopping back against the cushions, regarding Emma more closely, she pressed, 'What actually *did* you say to her, Gran?'

'Now, Emily, don't be so nosy. That's a private matter between Edwina and me. Anyway, it's not important. What matters is that my words penetrated. Perhaps I drilled some sense into her after all.'

'Oh I'm sure that's true,' Emily agreed. 'And there's something else – you'll never guess what she did before we went in to dinner.'

'No, I'm certain I won't. So you might as well tell me, Emily.'

'She asked Aunt Daisy if she could invite Anthony over for coffee later, and then went to telephone him at Uncle Randolph's.'

Emma stiffened, asked with a frown, 'Did he come?'

'Oh yes.' Emily grinned. 'With cousin Sally. Oh Gran, they're so much in love, and super together.'

'Sally came with him! How did Edwina treat her?'

'With cordiality. *My* eyes were popping, I can tell you that, and I wouldn't have missed that little scene for all the tea in China. Of course Edwina was falling all over Anthony. She was a bit *too* obsequious, if you ask me, you know Uriah Heepish, but then she's always fawned over her son.' She gave Emma a huge smile, and finished, 'In a nutshell, Grandma, the dinner was a roaring success.'

Emma was flabbergasted and temporarily rendered speechless. 'Well,' she said at last, 'this is one for the books. I never expected Edwina to do such a *volte-face*.' Privately she congratulated herself. Her dire warnings had frightened Edwina into behaving like a normal person seemingly. This is a major victory, she thought, and hoped that her daughter would not have a change of heart. Edwina *was* unpredictable. There was no telling what she might do in a moment of pique. Now, don't go begging for trouble, Emma cautioned herself. Relax.

Smiling brightly, filled with an enormous sense of relief, Emma propelled herself to her feet. 'On that rather surprising but pleasant note I think I'll get off to bed, darling girl.' She leaned over and kissed Emily. 'It looks as if everyone is going to behave with decorum tomorrow. Well, let's hope so. Goodnight, Emily.'

Emily rose and hugged her tightly. 'I do love you so much, Gran. And goodnight, sleep tight.' She picked up the tray. 'I suppose I'd better do the same. I've got to collect the twins from Harrogate College tomorrow, and I've *thousands* of other chores.' She sucked in her breath. '*Phew!*' she exhaled, 'I never seem to have a minute to spare.'

Emma swallowed a smile and disappeared into her bedroom before Emily decided to regale her with those chores she had planned for the following morning.

'Oh Grandy.' Emily called after her, 'I'm glad you're not upset about the Aire Communications deal collapsing.'

Emma came back to the doorway. 'I'd venture to say that it's their loss, our gain.'

'Yes, so Paula indicated when she mentioned it earlier.' Emily glided to the door, and muttered with a degree of terseness, 'Sebastian Cross is simply dreadful. I thought Jonathan might make headway with him. Apparently he didn't, and if Jonathan couldn't succeed, then nobody could.'

Emma stood perfectly still, said with the utmost care, 'What are you chattering on about, Emily?'

Emily stopped in her tracks, swung to face Emma. 'The Aire deal. You asked Jonathan to talk to Sebastian, didn't you?'

'No,' Emma replied in the quietest of voices.

'Oh,' Emily said, looking confused.

'What makes you think I propelled Jonathan into those particular negotiations?' As she spoke Emma steadied herself against the door jamb, her astute eyes glinting darkly as they rested with fixity on her grandchild. All of her senses were alerted, and she remarked tersely, 'Obviously *something* did.'

'Well, yes,' Emily began, and scowled. 'On Tuesday, when I had dinner with Daddy in London, I saw the two of them in the bar of Les Ambassadeurs when we were leaving. We'd had an early dinner, you see, and Daddy was in a frightful stew about being late for a business meeting. He was in such a hurry I didn't get a chance to go over and speak to Jonathan.'

'I see.' Emma was thoughtful for a moment, asked, 'Why did you suggest Jonathan would be able to influence young Cross?'

'Because of their old friendship . . . they were at Eton together. But then you know that, Gran. You once took me there with you, when you went to visit Jonathan at half-term. Don't you remember?'

'Yes. Naturally I also remember that Jonathan went to Eton. What I hadn't realized was that Cross was a pupil there as well, or that Jonathan and he had been friends in those days. I had –'

'I think they're still friends actually,' Emily interrupted.

This bit of information chilled Emma to the bone, but she attempted a smile. 'He probably wanted to surprise me. He might have realized the negotiations were going to be touchy and was endeavouring to smooth the way for Paula,' she said, trying to convince herself this was the truth. But her intuition told her it was not. Emma gripped the door jamb more tightly, and, adopting a meticulously casual tone, asked, 'Did Jonathan see you in Les Ambassadeurs, Emily?'

Emily shook her head. 'He was in deep conversation with Cross.' She pondered, asked swiftly, 'Why? Is it important?'

'Not really. Did you mention this to Paula?'

'I didn't get an opportunity. She had just started to tell me about the Aire fiasco, as she called it, and Cross being horrid to her, when Hilda announced dinner.' Emily bit her inner lip, frowning, beginning to wonder precisely what her grandmother was leading up to with her questions.

Emma nodded, as though to herself, remarked in that same lightly casual voice, 'I'd prefer you not to say anything about this to Paula. I wouldn't want her to think he was interfering, queering her pitch. Unintentionally, of course. And don't bother to bring it up with Jonathan either. I'll talk to him, find out what his aim was, if indeed he had an aim. It might have been a strictly social evening you know, in view of their friendship.'

'Yes, Grandy, whatever you say.'

Emily stood rooted to the spot, studying her grandmother closely, filling with alarm. Emma's face had paled as they had been talking and she noticed that the happy light in her eyes had fled. They were uncommonly dull, lifeless for once. Emily put down the tray hurriedly, and flew across the room. She grasped Emma's arm, exclaimed with concern, 'Are you all right, Gran darling?'

Emma made no response. Her mind was working with that razor-sharp precision and vivid intelligence which were so integral to her great genius. Assessing and analysing with her rare brand of shrewdness and perception, she suddenly saw things with a clarity that shocked. For a split-second she recoiled from the truth. I'm making assumptions, she thought, but then her ingrained pragmatism reminded her that she was rarely wrong. The truth was staring her in the face.

Becoming conscious of Emily's hand clutching her arm, her worry and anxiousness apparent, Emma dragged herself out of her disturbing thoughts. She patted the girl's hand, brought a smile to her face that was convincing, reassuring in its certitude.

'I'm just tired,' Emma said in a contained voice and smiled again. But she felt as though something cold had touched her heart.

10

The medieval church at the top of the hill in Fairley village was filled to capacity, almost bursting at the seams.

Family and friends occupied the front pews and the villagers were crowded in closely behind, for they had turned out in full force to honour Emma Harte at the baptism of her great-grandchildren. And after the ceremony they would troop across the road to the parish hall to partake of the special celebration tea, which Emma had instructed Alexander to arrange.

All was peace and serenity within the ancient grey stone walls. Sunshine pouring in through the stained-glass windows threw rainbow arcs of dancing, jewelled light across the sombre stone floor and the dark wood pews. Masses of spring flowers were banked around the altar and on the altar steps. The mingled scents of hyacinths, narcissi, freesia, imported mimosa and lilac filled the air, diminishing the peculiar musty smell of mildew and dust and old wood that was so prevalent in the church. It was the odour of antiquity, and one Emma had detested since childhood: she had automatically chosen the most fragrant of flowers for this occasion in an attempt to counteract it.

She sat in the front pew, proud and dignified, wearing a midnight-blue wool-crepe dress and loose matching coat. A small velvet beret of the same deep blue was perched at a jaunty angle on her immaculate silver hair, and she wore the McGill emeralds and a long rope of matchless pearls. Blackie was seated to her left, handsome in a dark suit, whilst Daisy sat with her husband, David Amory, to Emma's right. Edwina was wedged in between David and Sarah Lowther, her posture rigid, her expression rather prim, as usual.

Emma had been somewhat taken aback to find Sarah standing on the porch steps when they had arrived. No one had expected to see her, since she was supposed to have a bad cold. They had spoken briefly at the back of the church before taking their seats, and Emma had been immediately struck by her granddaughter's healthy appearance. In her opinion, Sarah had either made a miraculous recovery overnight, or had not been sick in the first place. It was more than likely she had toyed with the idea of not coming in order to avoid Shane. Emma could not hold that against her. She understood, had a good idea how Sarah probably felt. But, she thought, I'll say this for Sarah. She's a cool customer. Sarah had not blinked an eyelash nor displayed the slightest sign of self-consciousness when Shane had greeted them earlier.

Now Emma sneaked a look at him.

He was sitting with his parents in a pew across the nave, his face in profile. Suddenly, as if he knew he was being observed, he turned his head slightly to the right and caught Emma's eye, half smiled and then gave her a conspiratorial wink. Emma returned his smile, swung her eyes back to the altar.

Paula and Jim were standing at the carved stone font which dated back to 1574, and were surrounded by the godparents of their children, totalling six in all. The vicar, the Reverend Geoffrey Huntley, having christened the boy Lorne McGill Harte Fairley, was now preparing to baptize the girl, who was to be named Tessa. Like her twin she would bear the same additional middle names.

Emily, one of Tessa's godmothers, was holding the baby in her arms, and standing on Emma's left were Anthony, and Vivienne Harte, who were the other godparents. Vivienne's elder sister, Sally, was godmother to Lorne and cradled him, flanked on either side by his godfathers, Alexander and Winston.

What an attractive group of young people they are, Emma said inwardly, her eyes lighting up with pleasure, and she saw in her mind, for a brief instant, their antecedents . . . her own parents, her brother Winston, Arthur Ainsley, Paul McGill, Adele and Adam Fairley. How miraculous it was that she and

Blackie were still alive and were able to be here today to witness this event, to share in the joyfulness of the occasion.

She shifted her eyes to Paula and Jim.

They do look well together, she thought. He so tall and broad and fair, and the living embodiment of his great-grandfather, Adam; Paula so slender and willowy and dark, and so dramatic looking with her vivid McGill colouring. And Paula's inbred elegance was most apparent in the way she held herself, and in her clothes. She had chosen a tailored wool suit of a deep violet tone, and wore it with a lighter coloured violet satin blouse and a satin pillbox of the same tone. The violet echoed her eyes. She's still too thin, Emma thought, but she has such an extraordinary radiance this afternoon.

Her love for her granddaughter and her pride in the girl were emotions most paramount in Emma at this moment, and her face relaxed into softer lines as she continued to regard Paula. The young woman standing up there at the font had given her nothing but happiness and comfort since the day she had been born, in much the same way her mother, Daisy, had done, and continued to do.

Emma closed her eyes. Paul would have been as proud of Paula as she was, for the girl had all the qualities he had most admired: Honour, integrity, honesty, fairness and an intelligence that frequently startled with its brilliance. Although she had gentle manners, and was inclined to shyness, Paula possessed a certain cool poise, and she had inherited her grandfather's great sense of fun, as had Daisy. Yes, she's a McGill all right, Emma remarked under her breath. But she's a Harte as well. Thank God she has my toughness and astuteness, my indomitability and stamina. She's going to need all of those in the years to come, with what I'm leaving her, with what she has inherited from her grandfather. I hope she never thinks of her inheritance as a terrible burden. It *is* an enormous responsibility, of course . . .

Baby Tessa started to shriek, her piercing wails echoing throughout the church. Emma opened her eyes and blinked. She leaned forward, peered at the scene at the font. Everyone wore expressions of concern. The vicar was holding the baby, sprinkling the holy water on her forehead, christening her now in the name of the Father, the Son and the Holy Ghost. When he had finished he handed the child back to Emily, obviously with some relief. Emily began to rock her, trying to calm and soothe the infant to no avail.

Emma chuckled quietly, knowing it was the shock of the cold water on her forehead which had made Tessa cry. The child was protesting – and most vociferously. I can see it already, she thought, little Tessa McGill Harte Fairley is going to be the rebellious one in *that* family.

Daisy, also smiling, took hold of her mother's arm and squeezed it. She whispered, 'It sounds to me as if Tessa is a chip off the old block, Mummy.'

Emma turned her head to look into her favourite daughter's wide clear blue eyes. 'Yes,' Emma whispered back, 'she's always been the livelier of the two. Another maverick in the brood?' She arched a silver brow most eloquently. Daisy simply nodded in answer, her fine eyes dancing with happiness and some amusement.

Within minutes the ceremony was over and they were slowly filing up the aisle. Emma, her arm tucked through Blackie's, smiled and nodded graciously, but she did not pause to speak to anyone.

Before long the entire family, their friends and the villagers were assembled on the porch, congratulating the parents and chatting amongst themselves.

Several of the local residents came up to Emma, stood talking to her for a few minutes, but very shortly she excused herself and drew Blackie away from the crowd. She said, 'I'll slip away now and I'll be back before anyone notices my absence. Then we can get off to Pennistone Royal.'

'All right, Emma. Are you sure I can't go with you?'

'No. But thanks anyway, Blackie. I won't be a minute.'

As Emma edged away from the busy porch, Milson, Blackie's chauffeur, hurried towards her carrying a basket of flowers. She took it from him, smiled, and murmured her thanks.

She went through the lych-gate leading into the graveyard adjoining the church.

Her feet knew the way by heart, and they led her down the flagged path to the far corner, a bit secluded and bosky and shaded by an old elm tree growing by the side of the moss-covered stone wall. Lying in that corner, beneath the headstones she herself had chosen years before, were her parents, John and Elizabeth Harte. Next to them were her two brothers, Winston and Frank. She took bunches of flowers from the basket and placed one on each of the four graves. Straightening up, she rested her hand on her mother's headstone and stared out towards the bleak moors, a smudged dark line against the periwinkle blue sky filled with scudding white clouds and intermittent sunshine. It was a lovely day, surprisingly warm, balmy even, after the thunderstorms of yesterday. A perfect day to go climbing to the Top of the World. She strained her eyes, but that spot was too far away in the distance to see, and obscured by the soaring fells. She sighed, remembering. Her eyes swept from headstone to headstone, name to name. I've carried each one of you in my heart all the days of my life, she said silently. I've never forgotten any of you. Then unexpectedly the queerest thought entered her mind – she would not be coming back here again to visit these graves.

Emma turned away at last.

Her steps carried her along the same flagged path that curved through the cemetery, and she did not stop until she reached a wide plot of ground at the other side, in the gloomy shadows of the church. This large private plot was encircled by iron railings which set it apart, told everyone that it was special and exclusive. She pushed open the small gate and found herself amongst generations of Fairleys. She glanced at the graves, and finally her eyes came to rest on Adam Fairley's headstone made of white marble. On either side of him were his two wives – Adele, the first, and Olivia, the second. Those two beautiful sisters who had loved and married the same man, and who had, in their own ways, been good to her when she had been a young girl. She had never forgotten their kindness to her, but it was on the middle grave that her gaze lingered for a moment longer.

Well, Adam Fairley, she thought, I won. In the end it was I who triumphed. There is nothing left that your family owns in the village, except this plot of land where you are buried. Everything else belongs to me, and even the church operates mostly through my largesse. Your great-great-grandchildren have just been christened and they bear both of our names, but it is from *me* that they will inherit great wealth and power and position. These thoughts were not rancorous, ran through her mind in a matter of fact way, for she had lost all hatred for the Fairleys, and it was not in her nature to gloat, especially when standing next to a man's last resting place.

Slowly she walked back to the church, and the smile on her serene face was one of gentleness and peace.

Coming through the lych-gate, Emma saw Blackie standing to one side, away from the large group of people, talking to her two youngest grandchildren, Amanda and Francesca.

Blackie chuckled as she came to a standstill by his side. 'You might know *these* two would see you do your disappearing act! I had to forcibly restrain them from running after you. Well, almost.'

'We wanted to look at the graves, too, Grandy,' Amanda explained. 'We love cemeteries.'

Emma gave her a look of mock horror. 'How morbid.'

'No, it isn't, it's interesting,' Francesca chirped up. 'We like to read the tombstones, and we try to guess what the people were like, what kind of lives they led. It's like reading a book.'

'Is it now?' Emma laughed, and the look she gave the fifteen-year-old was affectionate. 'I think we should go back to the house,' Emma continued. 'Did Emily tell you we're having a champagne tea this afternoon?'

'Yes, but she said we couldn't have any champagne. We can, though, can't we, Gran?' Amanda asked.

'Just one glass each, I don't want you both getting tiddly.'

'Oh thank you, Gran,' Amanda said, and Francesca linked her arm in Emma's, and announced, 'We'll come with you. Uncle Blackie's car is much nicer than Emily's old Jag.'

'That's not a very nice attitude, Francesca. You came with Emily, and you will drive back with her. Besides, Uncle Blackie and I have things to discuss.'

But they did not really have anything very special or important to talk about. Emma simply wanted to be alone with her dear old friend, to relax before the reception, to catch her breath before she was engulfed by her large and unorthodox clan.

At one point, as they were driving along, Blackie looked at her and said, 'It was a grand christening, Emma. Very beautiful. But you had such a strange look on your face when the vicar was baptizing Lorne, I couldn't help wondering what was going through your mind.'

Emma half turned to face him. 'I was thinking about another christening . . . the one you performed when you baptized Edwina with Armley tap water in Laura's kitchen sink.' Her eyes held his for the longest moment. 'I couldn't help dwelling on the past. You know, Edwin Fairley wouldn't have been permitted to marry me when I was pregnant, even if he had wanted to, and so Edwina could never have been christened here at Fairley. That really struck home today.'

'Yes,' he said in agreement, 'it would have been denied her, no matter what.'

Emma nodded. 'And so, as I thought of everything that has gone before in my long life, it suddenly occurred to me that this occasion today was a most compelling example of ironic reversal. And that Adam Fairley, more than anyone else, would have appreciated the poetic justice of it all.'

She paused, smiled faintly. 'The wheel of fortune truly has come full circle.'

11

Jim Fairley, orphaned at the age of ten and raised by his widowed grandfather, had always been lonely as a child.

In consequence, he thoroughly enjoyed being a part of Emma Harte's huge family, one which had become his own when he married Paula in 1968. In a way, being flung head first into this extraordinary clan was something of a novelty to him; also, as yet, he remained unscathed by them and thus had kept an open mind about their individual characters, had not attempted to do a tally of their attributes or their faults. And he had held himself apart from the complex animosities and alliances, feuds and friendships that flourished around Emma.

Because Jim rarely thought ill of anyone, he was frequently startled when Paula came down hard on one of her aunts or uncles, and at times he even wondered if she exaggerated when she listed their imperfections, the terrible wrongs they had done her grandmother. But then she was fiercely protective of her beloved Grandy, whom she doted on. Jim was secretly amused by his wife's attitude, since he believed no one was better equipped to take care of herself than Emma Harte.

A short while ago Jim had decided that Paula's warnings about the Countess of Dunvale were written in water. So far this weekend Edwina had behaved impeccably – as he had fully expected she would. If she was somewhat reserved with Paula she was at least civil, and he had even managed to make Edwina laugh on their way back from church. She was still in an amiable mood, as he could now see.

His aunt was chatting with her son, Anthony, and Sally Harte, near the fireplace and her usually stiff, tight-lipped expression had all but vanished. For once she appeared to be relatively at ease. Poor old thing, she's not so bad, he thought, as charitable about others as always, and swung his eyes to the painting to Edwina's left. This hung over the white marble fireplace and it was one of his favourites.

Jim stood at the entrance to the Peach Drawing Room. Pennistone Royal, that lovely mixture of Renaissance and Jacobean design, boasted two formal reception rooms. Paula had chosen this one for the christening party.

He was glad that she had.

He thought it was the loveliest spot in the entire house, with its cream and peach colour scheme and exquisite paintings. Although Emma had depleted

104

her renowned collection of Impressionists by selling some of them off last year, she had retained the two Monets and the three Sisleys that graced these walls. In his opinion it was the works of art that gave the tranquil and elegant Regency room its great beauty.

Jim gazed at the Sisley for a second or two longer, admiring it from this vantage point. He had never coveted anything material in his whole life, but he longed to own this painting. Of course he never would. It would always hang in this house, as Emma had decreed in her will. One day it would be Paula's property, and therefore he would never be deprived of it, could gaze at the landscape whenever he wished. That was why his intense desire for personal possession of it constantly startled him. He had never felt so strongly about anything, except perhaps his wife. His eyes sought Paula without success. The room had filled up during the ten minutes he had been absent with the photographer, who was setting up his equipment in the Grey Drawing Room. It was just possible she was hidden from view.

He went in rapidly.

At six foot one, well built but trim of figure and with long legs, James Arthur Fairley cut quite a swathe, especially since he was something of a clothes horse, was never anything but faultlessly dressed right down to his handmade shoes. Like his great-grandfather before him, he had a weakness for elegant clothes and a penchant for wearing them with a bit of a dash. Fair of colouring, with light brown hair, he had a pleasant rather sensitive face and soulful greyish-blue eyes. Born and bred a gentleman, he had a natural self-confidence and handled himself easily, and with aplomb, in any given situation. He had a certain quiet charm and a ready smile for everyone.

This flashed as he strode into the centre of the room, glanced about, looking for Paula.

Since he could not find her he took a glass of champagne from a passing waiter, and made a move in his father-in-law's direction. Edwina spotted him and hurried over, cutting him off before he reached David Amory. She at once launched into a rave about the church ceremony, and then engaged him in a conversation that centred on Fairley village. As he listened patiently, Jim realized yet again, and with a recurrence of his initial surprise, that being a Fairley was of tremendous importance to her. Ever since their first meeting, she had continued to ply him with questions about his grandfather, his grandmother and her father, the long-dead Earl of Carlesmoor, and was inquisitive about his own parents who had been tragically killed in a plane crash in 1948.

On the various occasions he had been with his half great-aunt, for that was what she actually was, he had detected a sense of embarrassment in her because of her illegitimacy, and he had always felt slightly sorry for her. This was one of the reasons he tried to be kind, to include her in those family celebrations about which he had something to say. His mother-in-law had a nice way with Edwina, but apart from this, Jim recognized that Edwina was drawn to Daisy because they had both been born on the wrong side of the blanket. Emma's first child strongly identified with her youngest because of this similarity in their births. But their illegitimacy was the only thing they had in common. The two women were the antithesis of each other. His mother-in-law had the sweetest nature, was a compassionate and considerate woman, and a lady in the truest sense of that word. There was no 'side' to Daisy Amory, and he liked her for her relaxed attitude towards life, her gaiety and her sense of humour. Sadly, his Aunt Edwina was inflexible and sour, tense and standoffish, a dyed-in-the-wool snob, whose basic values were quite alien to him. Yet there was something indefinable in her that touched him, filled him with a curious sympathy for her. Perhaps this was because they shared the same blood. Paula constantly said that blood was *not* thicker than water, but he tended to disagree. He was sure of one thing. His relationship with Edwina, slender and tenuous though it was, annoyed Paula to the point of anger. He found this to be most unreasonable on her part, and he fervently wished she could be less emotional about his aunt. In his opinion, Edwina was a harmless old lady.

'I'm so sorry, Aunt Edwina, I missed that,' Jim said with an apologetic smile, giving her his undivided attention again.

'I was saying that it was a pity my mother had Fairley Hall torn down.' Edwina gave him a long and careful look through her narrowed silvery eyes. 'The house was very old, and by rights it really ought to have been preserved as a landmark in Yorkshire. And just think, if it were still standing, you could have lived there with Paula.'

Jim missed the inherent criticism of her mother in these words. He laughed and shook his head. 'I don't think so. I didn't like the look of Fairley Hall from the photographs I've seen. According to Grandfather it was a hodge podge of architectural styles and a bit of a monstrosity. He never liked it himself, and personally I think Grandy did the right thing.'

Daisy, who had been hovering close by, caught the tail end of their conversation, and exclaimed, 'I second that, Jim. Besides, Mother put the land it stood on to very good use, by turning it into a park for the villagers. It's a charming spot for them during the warm weather. It was very generous of her.' She glanced across at the Vicar of Fairley who was talking to her husband, and explained, 'And the reason Reverend Huntley is beaming right now is because Mother has just given him a large cheque for the church restoration fund. She keeps that village going in more ways than one.' Having rebutted Edwina, squelched her in the pleasantest way, Daisy gave her half-sister a warm smile. 'I haven't complimented you, Edwina dear. You look lovely, and that's a very smart suit you're wearing.'

'Oh,' Edwina said, startled by these kind words. She hardly ever received compliments, and she preened a little, and a sparkle entered her pale eyes as she automatically reached up and patted her hair. Then remembering her manners, she rushed on, 'Thank you very much, Daisy. You look beautiful yourself, but then you always do. As for my suit, it's by Hardy Amies. I wasn't sure it was right for me, but he persuaded me it was.'

The two women discussed clothes for a few seconds, then Daisy exclaimed, 'You'll have to excuse me, I'm afraid. I can see Mother trying to catch my eye.'

Left alone with Jim again, Edwina began to enumerate the delights of her home in Ireland. 'I do wish you could see Clonloughlin at this time of year, Jim. It's perfectly beautiful, everything's so green. Why don't you and Paula make plans to come over for a weekend soon? You've never seen it, and we'd love to have you. It's only a hop, skip and a jump in that plane of yours.'

'Thank you, Edwina, perhaps we will.' As he spoke Jim knew Paula would never agree. He decided to cover himself, added, 'However, I don't think I'll be able to drag her away from the babies for some time yet.'

'Yes, I do understand,' Edwina murmured, wondering if she had been rebuffed, and to cover her confusion, she went on talking nonstop.

Jim, listening politely and trying to be attentive, wished he could make his escape. Because of his height he towered above Edwina, who was quite small, and now he glanced over her silvery blonde head, looking around, wondering what had happened to Paula. Most of their guests had arrived. *She* was noticeably absent.

Sarah Lowther had just walked in on the arm of her cousin, Jonathan Ainsley. Bryan and Geraldine O'Neill were talking to Alexander Barkstone and his girl friend. Blackie was standing by the window, engaged in an animated conversation with Randolph Harte, and he appeared to be excited about something, was beckoning to his granddaughter. Miranda floated over to join them, a vision in one of her crazy costumes, her freckled face brimming with laughter, her bright auburn hair gleaming like a copper helmet in the sunshine pouring through the tall windows.

Jim shifted slightly on his feet, surveying the room at large. Emma was perched on the arm of a sofa, being attentive to her brothers' widows, Charlotte and Natalie. These two genteel-looking ladies gave the impression of frailty and great age in comparison to Emma, who exuded vitality and happiness this afternoon. He studied her face for a moment. He had revered and respected this remarkable woman all the years he had worked for her; since his marriage to her granddaughter he had come to know a different side of her, had grown to love her. Emma had such an understanding heart, was kind and generous, and the most fair minded person he had ever met. What a fool his grandfather had been to let her escape. But he supposed things were difficult in those days. Stupid class differences, he thought, and sighed under his breath. Then, quite suddenly, he wished that Edwin Fairley had lived long enough to witness this day ... to see the Fairleys and the Hartes united at last through matrimony. Their blood was mingled now. He and Paula had started a new blood line.

He became aware that Edwina had stopped her ceaseless chattering and was staring up at him. He said quickly, 'Let me give you a refill, Aunt Edwina, then I think I'd better go and look for Paula. I can't imagine what's happened to her.'

'No more champagne at the moment, thank you, Jim,' Edwina said with the faintest of smiles. She was determined to remain cool and collected and keep a clear head this afternoon. Too much wine would have an adverse effect on her, make her lose her self-possession. That she could not afford. She said, 'Before you disappear, there is one thing I'd like to ask of you. I've been wondering if you would be kind enough to invite me to your house in Harrogate. I know it belonged to your grandfather.' She hesitated, nervously cleared her throat, finished, 'I'd love to see where he ... where my father lived for so many years of his life.'

'Of course, you must come over for drinks,' Jim said, understanding this need in her. He hoped Paula would not fly into one of her tempers when he told her he had acquiesced to his aunt's request. He began to edge away when

Emily, with Amanda and Francesca in tow, breezed up to them, cutting off his escape route.

Smiling brightly, Emily grabbed his arm, glanced at Edwina and cried, 'Hello, you two. Isn't this the most amazing bun fight. I think it's going to be a super party.'

Jim smiled at her indulgently. He was extremely fond of young Emily. 'Have you seen my wife anywhere?' he asked.

'She went upstairs with the nursemaid and the babies, muttering something about changing them. I guess they wet themselves rather thoroughly.' Emily giggled and rolled her eyes in an exaggerated fashion. 'Just be glad they didn't get that elegant Kilgour and French suit of yours drenched with their wee w –'

'Really, Emily,' Edwina sniffed reprovingly, 'don't be so vulgar.' She gave her niece a cold and disapproving look.

Emily, blithely unconcerned, giggled again. 'Babies do do that, you know. They're like puppies. They can't control their bladders. And I *wasn't* being vulgar, Aunt Edwina, merely stating a fact of life.'

Jim could not resist laughing, recognizing that Emily was purposely being provocative. He threw her a warning frown, glanced at his aunt, praying she would not pounce on Emily.

Edwina was obviously annoyed. Fortunately, before she could think of a suitably chilly response, Winston hove in view, made a beeline for them, greeted everyone and positioned himself between Emily and Amanda.

He turned to Jim, and said, 'Sorry to bring up business on such a festive occasion, but I'm afraid I have no alternative. I'd like to get together with you first thing on Monday, to discuss a couple of matters. Will you have time to see me?'

'Of course,' Jim said, giving Winston a puzzled look. Concern edged into his eyes and he frowned. 'Anything serious?'

'No, no, and the only reason I mentioned it now was to make sure you'd keep an hour free for me. I have to go to Doncaster and Sheffield that day, and the rest of the week is impossible. I'm really jammed.'

'Then let's make a definite date, Winston. Say about ten thirty? I'll have the first edition out on the streets by then.'

'That's fine,' said Winston.

With this matter settled, Jim said, 'Your father seems very pleased with himself, and so does Blackie. Look at them both. They're behaving like a couple of kids with a new toy. What's all the excitement about?'

Winston glanced over his shoulder and laughed. 'My father wants to run Emerald Bow in the National next year, and Blackie's tickled to death about it. I think Aunt Emma's just as thrilled.'

'So I can see,' Jim said.

'Gosh, what marvellous news, Winston,' Emily exclaimed.

'I hope Grandma invites us all to go to Aintree next March.' The conversation now centred around the Grand National and the possibility of Emerald Bow winning the steeplechase. All kinds of opinions were voiced, and even the fifteen-year-old twins had something to say.

But not Edwina. She was silent.

She sipped the last drop of champagne in her glass, eyed Winston with an oblique surreptitiousness. She did not particularly like him. But then she had never had much time for the Hartes. All they had was pots and pots of money. And looks. She could not deny that they were a good looking family – each and every one of them. Suddenly, with a small start of surprise, she saw how closely Winston resembled her mother. She had always been aware they shared certain physical characteristics, yet had never realized how pointed and strong these were. Why, Winston Harte is a younger, male replica of *her*, Edwina muttered to herself. More so than any of her children or grandchildren. The same features, so clearly defined they might have been cut by a chisel; that red hair shot through with gold; those quick intelligent eyes of an unnatural green. Even his small hands holding the glass are like *hers*. My God, it's uncanny, Edwina thought, and looked away quickly, wondering why this revelation disturbed her.

Jim, who had been listening with interest to Winston talking about Steve Larner, the jockey, interrupted him when he exclaimed, 'There's Paula at last.' His face filled with pleasure and he waved to her. 'I'll see you all a little later.' He squeezed Edwina's arm reassuringly and dashed across the room.

Paula watched him hurrying to her, a happy expectant smile playing around her mouth. Her heart tightened. She loved Jim very much and she was so lucky to have found him. He was the dearest, sweetest man, and fine and honourable and good. She would have to try harder with Edwina . . . she wanted so much to please her husband.

Jim caught Paula's hands in his as he came to a standstill by her side. He smiled down into her face. 'You were gone such a long time,' he said. 'I missed you.'

'The babies, darling, they needed me.' Her sparkling bright eyes rested on him lovingly. 'I hope you're not going to turn out to be one of those jealous fathers I keep hearing about.'

'Not on your life. I adore those little moppets.' He leaned into her, pulled her closer and lowered his voice to a hoarse whisper. 'But I also adore *you*. Listen, darling, let's sneak away tonight and have a quiet dinner. Just the two of us. Your parents won't mind. They can have dinner with Emma.'

'Well . . .'

'I won't take no for an answer, my pet.' He bent over her and whispered in her ear, gripped her hands all that more tightly as he did so.

Paula blushed at his words, then laughed a light sweet laugh. 'You're positively wicked. A regular devil.' Looking at him archly, she teased flirtatiously, 'I'll have you know I'm a married woman, sir. What you propose is most indecent. Quite improper, I'd say.'

'Do you really think so?' He laughed, and then he winked, '*I* think my ideas are very *exciting*.'

'Mummy's heading this way,' Paula said laughing and adroitly changing the subject. 'And she's looking very determined about something.'

'Say yes,' Jim demanded. 'To everything.'

'*Yes. Yes. Yes.*'

Daisy looked from one to the other fondly and shook her head. 'Sorry to break up you two love birds, but Mother is champing at the bit. She wants to get the photography out of the way as soon as possible now. I'm rounding everyone up. So come along, let's start assembling in the Grey Drawing Room. Oh, and by the way, Jim dear, I've suggested that Edwina be included in one of the family group portraits, and my mother has agreed.'

'How very nice of you, Daisy,' Jim exclaimed with warmth and sincerity, thinking how typical it was of her to be thoughtful, and caring about another person's feelings. That Daisy had shown such consideration for Edwina was doubly commendable.

Emma Harte had never missed a trick in her entire life.

This afternoon was no exception. Her eyes were everywhere, and from her position near the fireplace she had an overall view of the room, and everyone in it. In much the same way that Jim Fairley held himself apart and took in everything, so Emma herself played the observer much of the time these days.

However, unlike Jim, who only saw things on the surface and, moreover, believed exactly what he saw, Emma had an almost frightening perception, one that pierced any facade to comprehend what actually lay behind it. She understood that nothing was ever the way it seemed, and so she was acutely conscious of the undercurrents in the room – the rivalries, the conflicts, the bad blood that existed between some of those present.

A sardonic smile touched her lips. As usual, cliques had formed. It was easy to see who was allied to whom. And she could read them all like an open book.

Edwina was the one who had surprised her the most, in that she had obviously had the intelligence to accept the inevitable. Her eldest daughter was giving off an aura of cordiality, sitting on the sofa near the window, chatting with Sally. On the other hand, Emma had noticed that she was assiduously avoiding any real contact with the other Hartes in the drawing room.

Randolph, Sally's father, and his two other children, Vivienne and Winston, were most decidedly *persona non grata* with Edwina, and her intense dislike of them was barely concealed behind the stiff and chilly smiles she had given them earlier. Edwina was also cold-shouldering Blackie, although there was nothing new about that. Once, last year, Edwina had referred to him as the grand seigneur, meaning it disparagingly, her voice ringing with sarcasm.

Emma smiled inwardly. She had rather liked the description then: she did so now. It was apt.

Blackie was indeed behaving like the grand patrician gentleman, strolling around as if he had territorial rights, his manner distinctly proprietary, being gracious and charming, playing the genial host to the limit. And why not? He was her greatest friend, and her escort after all, and this was her house, and she was the hostess at this gathering. He had stood at her side during the toasts and the cutting of the christening cake, and after Randolph had finished speaking he had made a toast himself. To her. He had called her the youngest and most beautiful great-grandmother in the world. Now he had paused, was hovering over Paula, who in turn hovered over her babies. Daisy joined them, her serenity and sincerity and goodness a beacon in this room.

Emma shifted her eyes to the far corner, where they settled on her grandson, Alexander.

Always reserved, Alexander seemed particularly so with Jonathan and Sarah, whom he had briefly acknowledged when he had arrived. Since then he had consistently and carefully ignored them. He had attached himself to Bryan and Geraldine O'Neill at the commencement of the reception, returned to sit with them after the photographs had been taken. She did not understand why he was being cool and distant with Sarah and Jonathan. Could they have had a disagreement? Even a falling out? Or was he simply bored by the company of his cousins, with whom he worked at Harte Enterprises? She turned these possibilities over and then let them go. She would know soon enough if there were any real problems between these three. She wished Alexander would make up his mind about that nice Marguerite Reynolds. He had kept that poor girl dangling for too long. Now where was *she* hiding herself?

Emma scanned the room. Ah yes, there she was, near the door, laughing with Merry O'Neill and Amanda. Good God, was that child drinking another glass of champagne. Her *third*? Emily is supposed to be looking after those sisters of hers, and she's not even in the room, Emma thought, and took a step forward, making for Amanda, then stopped in her tracks. Emily had just returned with Winston and Shane, had spotted Amanda and was about to chastise her little sister, who wore a guilty expression. Emma nodded to herself, amused at the little scene being enacted. Emily, for all her youth and gay disposition, could be very tough when she wanted to be.

Shane had detached himself from Winston and Emily, and was prowling across the floor. Her eyes followed him. He came to a stop next to David, drew Paula's father to one side, began speaking to him intently. Shane is not himself today, Emma decided. He has a remote air. It occurred to her he might be suffering from ennui at this family function of hers, not to mention preoccupation with his impending trip to New York.

As for Sarah, her auburn-haired granddaughter appeared to be patently uninterested in Shane. Did Emily exaggerate? No, definitely not. Sarah, clinging to Jonathan like a barnacle to a hull, was, by her very actions, proving to Emma that she did indeed care greatly. If Shane no longer mattered to her she would not be huddled in a corner staying out of his way. Was Jonathan a handy convenience? Or had he and Sarah formed some kind of special alliance lately? If so, why? They had never been particularly close in the past.

Emma gave Jonathan a long hard stare, studying that bland and smiling face, noting his insouciant manner. How disarming he could be. He's clever, she thought, but not quite as clever as he believes he is. He has acquired the knack of dissembling, most likely from me. And because I'm better at dissimulation than he is, he doesn't deceive me one little bit. I have no hard evidence of his treachery, nothing concrete with which I can nail him, and yet I know he's up to no good.

When Emma had first arrived at Fairley church, Jonathan had rushed over to her, and told her he would see her on Monday morning, would bring her his new evaluation of the Aire Communications building. She had merely nodded, kept her face inscrutable. But she had immediately wondered why he suddenly thought the evaluation of the building's worth was no longer urgent, that it could now wait until Monday. She had been stressing its urgency to him for some time. Emma had not had to think very hard to come up with the answer. Jonathan knew the evaluation was no longer pressing because he was aware that the Aire deal had collapsed. Neither she nor Paula had mentioned the failure of those negotiations, so he could only have acquired his information from Sebastian Cross, and in the last twenty-four hours.

This conversation at the church, coupled with Emily's revelation of the night before, had convinced Emma that Jonathan was somehow involved with the Crosses, in cahoots with them. But to what purpose?

She did not know. But she would soon find out. She had no intention of confronting Jonathan on Monday morning. It was not her way to show her hand when that hand could be doling out rope, forming a noose. Instead she would go to London next week and start digging. Discreetly. Jonathan's behaviour today had only served to underscore the nagging suspicion that he was not trustworthy, a feeling that she had harboured for weeks. Without realizing it, he had alerted her further. If he were really smart he would have acted as though the Aire deal were still alive. He had made a small slip – but it was a fatal one in her eyes.

Jonathan happened to turn around at this moment. His glance met hers. He smiled broadly and loped across the room to her.

'Goodness, Grandy, why are you standing here all alone?' he asked showing concern for her. Not waiting for a reply he went on, 'Do you want anything? A glass of champagne, or a cup of tea maybe? And do come and sit down. You must be tired.' He took hold of her arm affectionately, and his posture was loving.

'I don't want anything, thank you,' Emma said. 'And I'm not a bit tired. In fact, I never felt better.' She gave him a smile as fraudulently sweet as his had been. Extracting her arm ever so gently, she remarked, 'I've been enjoying myself, standing here watching everyone. You'd be surprised what people reveal about themselves when they believe they're unobserved.' Her eyes were riveted to his face.

She waited.

He squirmed under her unflinching gaze, returned it, managed to keep his expression open and candid. But he laughed too quickly and too loudly as he said, 'You are a card, Grandy.'

And possibly you're the joker in the pack, Emma thought coldly. She said, 'What's wrong with Sarah? She's being rather aloof with everyone, apart from you, of course.'

'She's not feeling well,' he answered with swiftness. 'Fighting a bad cold.'

'She looks as fit as a fiddle to me,' Emma observed dryly, throwing a rapid glance in Sarah's direction.

Emma suddenly stepped back, moved away from Jonathan, and levelled her direct stare on him again. 'Did you come up here together? And when did you arrive in Yorkshire?'

'No, we came separately. Sarah by train last night. I drove up this morning.' This was said steadily enough, and he smiled down at her.

Emma saw the faintest flicker of deceit in his light eyes. She studied his face briefly. Arthur Ainsley's weak mouth, she thought. She said, 'I'm glad Sarah has you to look after her today, Jonathan. It's most kind of you.'

He said nothing, changed the subject by remarking, 'Are you sure you don't want to sit down, Grandmother?'

'I suppose I might as well.'

He steered her across the room towards Charlotte and Natalie, and Emma smothered a laugh. So that's where he thinks I belong, with the old ladies, she thought with some acerbity.

He saw her settled on the sofa, spoke briefly to his great-aunts, and disappeared, heading back to Sarah.

Emma watched him go, filled with sadness and disappointment. Too bad about Jonathan, she thought with resignation. He surely doesn't realize it, but he's as transparent as water. Just like his father. She had always seen right through Robin, and had been several jumps ahead of *him* all of his life, usually to his perpetual irritation and discomfort. Sighing, Emma pushed herself into the cushions and accepted a cup of tea offered by one of the waiters, then turned to her sisters-in-law. Natalie, Frank's widow, was unusually garrulous this afternoon, and she soon dominated the conversation, caught up in an endless recital about her only child, Rosamund, who lived in Italy with her diplomat husband. Charlotte and Emma listened, eyeing each other with amusement from time to time, but Emma's interest rapidly waned. She soon fell into her myriad thoughts.

Emma would never know what prompted her to suddenly put down her cup of tea, stand up, and swing around at the precise moment that she did. And later, when she thought about it in private, she was to wish she had remained seated.

But she did go through these motions, and found Shane O'Neill in her direct line of vision. He did not see her. He stood alone, leaning against the wall in the shadow of a tall Regency cabinet. There was an expression of such unadulterated love and aching yearning on his handsome face Emma had to stifle a gasp of surprise. His face was naked, utterly vulnerable, and it revealed the strongest and most powerful emotions a man could feel for a woman.

And it was Paula whom Shane was staring at with such concentrated intensity and longing.

Oh my God, Emma thought, dismay flooding through her. Her heart missed a beat. How well she knew that look on a man's face. It signified passion and desire, the overwhelming urgency to possess absolutely. And forever.

But her granddaughter was oblivious to him. She was bending over the nursemaid who sat cradling Tessa, adjusting the child's christening robe, cooing to her. Paula's face was tender with a mother's love and she was completely absorbed in the baby.

Emma was so shocked by what she saw she could not move. She was rooted to the spot, staring at him transfixed, unable to tear her eyes away from Shane, who undoubtedly believed he was safe from prying eyes. Emma reached out blindly and gripped the back of the sofa, filled with a terrible shaking sensation.

To her immense relief the expression on Shane's face was fleeting. In a flash it vanished, was replaced by a studied expression of assumed nonchalance, one she knew so well. He moved out of the shadows without noticing her, and mingled with the crowd again. Distantly she heard his vibrant, throaty laugh, and then Randolph's voice in response to something he had said.

Endeavouring to marshal her thoughts, Emma shifted her stance, turned to face the room. Had anyone else witnessed this intensely private moment of

Shane's when his guard was down? Where was Jim? Emma's quick alert eyes darted from side to side, came to rest on Emily, who stood motionless a few yards away, staring back at her appalled, anxiety clouding her pretty young face.

Emma frowned. She pinned Emily with a knowing look, then motioned to the door with a brief nod of her head. Emma went out of the drawing room slowly. She was filled with sorrow, and her heart ached for Shane O'Neill. And as she crossed the Stone Hall everything became crystal clear to her, and her sorrow deepened immeasurably.

Upon entering the library, Emma sat down heavily on the nearest chair. She was surprised her legs had carried her this far. She felt weak at the knees.

Emily came in a split second later, closed the door firmly behind her, and leaned against it speechlessly.

To Emma she looked as if she had seen a ghost. She was unnaturally pale and her face was tight, very strained.

Emma said, 'You saw it then? The way Shane was gazing at Paula?'

'Yes,' Emily whispered.

'He's very much in love with her,' Emma said, her voice husky. Her throat tightened. She paused, got a grip on herself, 'But then you knew that *before* today, Emily. In fact, you almost let it slip out yesterday. But you managed to stop yourself just in time. That is correct, isn't it?'

'Yes, Gran.'

'Don't look so scared, Emily. And come here and sit with me. I must talk to you about this. It's most disturbing.'

Emily ran across the room and took the adjoining chair. She gazed deeply into Emma's troubled face, which looked oddly fatigued and weary all of a sudden. She said, 'I'm truly sorry you had to find out. I never wanted you to know, Grandma. I knew it would pain you.'

'Yes, that's true, it does. But now that I do know, I've a couple of questions. First of all, how did you find out that Shane was in love with Paula in the first place?'

'Because I've seen that look on his face before. It was at Paula's wedding in London last year . . . when he thought no one was watching him. Much the same kind of situation as today. He was tucked away in a corner, at the reception at Claridge's, and his eyes never left her. And then there's his behaviour . . . let's face it, Grandy, he's been distant and peculiar with her for the longest time. Actually, to be honest, he's dropped her like a ton of bricks. Obviously he can't bear to be around her, knowing she's married to someone else.'

Emily bit her lip nervously. 'I suspect that's also one of the reasons he spends so much time abroad. I know he has to travel because of their hotel chain, but Merry recently said something to me about Shane constantly jumping on planes at the slightest excuse. She said he seemed to have ants in his pants these days.'

'I see,' Emma said. 'So Shane has never confided in you?'

'God no! He *wouldn't*. He's too proud.'

'Yes,' Emma said, 'I know what you mean.' She was reflective for a moment, then said almost to herself, 'That seems to be a family characteristic. And it's false pride, too. What a waste of time *that* is. So very foolish in the long run.

114

It serves no good purpose.' She looked away, staring into the distance absently, seeing so much, understanding.

Emily patted her hand in her old-fashioned, motherly way, and urged, 'Try not to worry, Gran. I know you love Shane like one of your own grandchildren, but there's nothing you can do about this.'

'I'm aware of that, darling. But getting back to the incident in the drawing room, do you think anyone else saw what we saw? Jim, for instance?'

'Jim had gone outside a few minutes before, Gran. I spoke to him as he followed Anthony and Sally out on to the terrace. Then Miranda joined them, and the twins.' Emily chewed her inner lip again. '*Sarah*. She has been sneaking looks at Shane all afternoon. She might have caught it, I'm just not sure.'

'I certainly hope she didn't!' Emma exclaimed worriedly.

'So do I.' Emily took a deep breath, volunteered in a low voice, 'There was one person who noticed . . .'

'Who?' Emma demanded, looking at her swiftly.

'Winston.'

'Well, thank God for small mercies. I'm glad it wasn't anyone else. Go and fetch him to me, Emily, and don't discuss a thing. Not in there. Too many nosy parkers around.'

'Yes, Grandmother.' Emily flew out of the room.

Emma rose and went to the windows, staring out at her beautiful gardens. How peaceful they look in the radiant sunlight . . . next door in the drawing room there is a young man who has everything except the woman he loves and who may never know genuine peace in his whole life because of that. Unless his love for Paula ceases to exist. Emma doubted this would happen. The kind of love she had seen etched on his face was everlasting. Its depth and intensity chilled her to the bone. She was absolutely convinced that a man like Shane O'Neill would not be content to worship from afar. His emotions could easily propel him to take more overt action in time. He might try to fight for Paula one day, in the future. And even if Paula was not interested in Shane, the situation still spelled trouble, in Emma's opinion. Triangles were not only uncomfortable, they were explosive.

Emma let out a tiny sigh. She had no answers, no solutions, and speculating was surely a big waste of time.

Her thoughts settled on Paula. She prayed her granddaughter would be happy with Jim Fairley for the rest of her life. If she was not, Shane might indeed make headway with her. Yet this first year of the marriage had been idyllic. On the other hand, there were things she herself had noticed, and which had given her food for thought and cause to wonder about Jim. Instinctively, she knew that he was no match for Paula when it came to inherent strength of character. Paula was inordinately stubborn, and she had a will of iron. And she was so much cleverer than Jim – on every level.

Emma admired Jim professionally – he was a brilliant newspaperman. Also, she was fond of him personally. It was difficult not to be. On the other hand, Emma had recognized for some time that his judgement was flawed in many areas, and most especially when it came to his assessment of people. He was not terribly discriminating. He liked everyone; furthermore, he wanted everyone to be happy, and all of the time, no less. He hated controversy and upset, bent over backward to keep the peace – and very often that was to his own detriment. In Emma's mind, one of Jim's main problems was his overwhelming need to be liked in return, to be popular with every member of the family, his friends, and those in his employment. This trait in him both dismayed and irritated Emma. It was lonely at the top. And it was generally not very wise to be overly familiar with employees. That quickly led to trouble. Loath though she was to admit it, Jim was simply not of the same calibre as Paula. Would he hold up over the years? Every marriage had its problems, its stresses, its emotional upheavals. If Jim caved in because of his lack of stamina and endurance under pressure, what would happen to that marriage? To Paula? To their children? She hated to contemplate the future in this dismal way, and instantly pushed all negative thoughts out of her mind. They did love each other very much, and perhaps their love would overcome any differences they may have.

Winston said, 'You wanted to see me Aunt Emma?' He sounded both nervous and concerned.

'Yes,' Emma said, pivoting. She walked over to a grouping of chairs, motioned Winston and Emily to join her.

They sat down opposite her, waiting.

Winston had been mystified when Emily had dragged him out of the drawing room, whispering that Emma had sent her to get him. He knew at once, from the girl's anxious demeanour, that something was wrong. Now his worried air intensified as he puffed rapidly on his cigarette. Out of the corner of his eye he saw that Emily's face was stark above her yellow suit, its bony pallor more pronounced.

Getting right to the point, Emma said, 'A few minutes ago I saw Shane looking at Paula in such a way that it left no doubt in my mind about his feelings for her. Emily tells me you also noticed.'

'Yes, I did,' Winston said, at once, realizing there was no point in denying it, or lying. He braced himself, wondering what she would say next. He studied her face which was severe and grave.

'Shane is in love with Paula,' Emma announced in a clipped tone.

'Yes. And desperately so,' Winston replied, shaking his head. He had wondered for a long time when this would come out in the open, and now that it had he decided it was wisest to be completely candid with Emma. In a way, he felt relieved that she finally knew. It had been a heavy burden for him to carry alone.

Desperately, Emma repeated under her breath. And her heart sank. Winston was underscoring her own suspicions, confirming her conclusions. She said slowly, 'Has Shane discussed his feelings for her with you, Winston?'

'No, Aunt Emma, he hasn't. He's a very private man, and discreet. But I've picked up a few things lately, and I've known about his emotional involvement with Paula for a while now . . . through my own observations. After all, we do share the same house at weekends. To be honest, I have a feeling Shane *thinks* I know, but he's never brought the matter up. As I said, he's extremely discreet.'

Emma sat back, pursing her lips, her eyes more reflective than before. After a short silence, she said, 'They've been as close as two peas in a pod all of their lives, Winston. How could he have let her slip through his fingers?'

'I can only hazard a guess,' Winston muttered, eyeing her closely. He stubbed

116

out his cigarette, the gesture filled with sudden anger. 'It's because they grew up together . . . I mean, I don't think he could see the wood for the trees, see what was under his nose. I'm positive Shane only realized the depth of his feelings for her when she became engaged to Jim. And they got married so quickly after their engagement was announced, Shane hardly had time to catch his breath. Or act. It all went very fast, as you know.'

Winston now lifted his shoulders in a weary shrug, and glanced away, thinking of Shane's abject misery. It had grown more intense and acute – and more noticeable – lately. He was glad Shane was going to the States – for Shane's own sake. He turned back to Emma, finished, 'That's my analysis of what happened, for what it's worth, Aunt Emma. I truly believe that it took another man in the picture to make Shane understand how much he loved Paula.'

'Yes, I think you're correct, Winston,' Emma said.

'Do you think Paula ever knew, or knows, that he cares about her in that way?' Emily asked Winston in a hushed voice, touching his arm lightly, looking up at him.

'I honestly can't answer that, Emily. But I –'

Emma interrupted with great firmness, 'I'm sure she didn't and doesn't have an inkling, dear.' She cleared her throat, continued in that same clear strong voice, 'This is a most tragic state of affairs for Shane, but there's nothing anyone can do, least of all me. Not any more. Also, it's really none of my business. Nor is it anyone else's, for that matter. The last thing I want is for Shane or Paula to become topics for the gossip mongers in this family, and we all know there are a few who would love to tittle-tattle, perhaps blow this matter out of proportion. I have implicit faith in the both of you, and in your discretion and loyalty. However, I must ask you both to promise me faithfully that you will never mention what you saw this afternoon to anyone, ever. Is that clearly understood?'

'Of course I promise, Grandma,' Emily cried in a shocked voice, looking at Emma aghast. 'You must know I would never talk about Paula, or do anything to hurt her. I feel the same way about Shane.'

'I wasn't doubting you, Emily. I simply felt compelled to stress the importance of your absolute silence on this matter.' She directed her attention at Winston.

He said, 'I promise, Aunt Emma. I care about Paula and Shane as much as Emily does. And I tend to agree with you about the gossips in our family. There's also a lot of free-floating jealousy about Paula. Shane too, in many ways. They're very special people, so obviously they'll always be targets. My lips are sealed, Aunt Emma. Please don't worry about *me*.'

'Thank you,' Emma said, and made a mental note of Winston's astute comments. She smiled thinly. 'I would prefer it if we ourselves never referred to this matter again. I believe it would be best forgotten by the three of us. Shane is going away for six months. Let's hope he will forget Paula –'

'He'll never let go of her!' Winston cut in fiercely, heatedly. 'It's not in his nature to –' Angrily he clamped his mouth shut, regretting that he had opened it in the first place.

But he had said enough for Emma to get a clear picture. Yes, she thought, that's what I'm afraid of, too. She said, as steadily as possible, 'Perhaps he *will* always care for her, Winston. But he's a young man, and virile. He has normal appetites and desires, I've no doubt. Let us hope that he'll eventually find someone who'll meet his needs, and come up to his standards, a woman who can help him to forget Paula. I sincerely hope he makes a rewarding life for himself, finds fulfilment and happiness.'

'I don't know about that,' Winston muttered, changing his mind yet again. He ought to be truthful with Emma. He owed her that, after all. He threw his aunt a gloom-filled glance. And then, because he had always been able to say anything to her without a shred of embarrassment, he added, in a blunt fashion, 'I'm sure he'll continue to have his brief, hit-and-run affairs, his sexual entanglements. He couldn't avoid them, not the way women throw themselves at him. Shane's no saint, you know. And he's hardly the type to lead a celibate life. After all, Aunt Emma, you don't have to be in love with a woman to sleep with her.'

'Quite,' Emma said, lifting a brow, glancing at Emily.

Winston noticed this, but Emily was a big girl. She knew what was what. Undeterred, he plunged on, 'I suppose you won't want to hear this, but I'm going to say it anyway. In my opinion, Shane O'Neill will never love anyone but Paula. You said a few minutes ago that this was a tragic thing for Shane. And it is. But it's also tragic for Paula, *I* think. She'd have been far better off and happier with a man like Shane than with Jim Fairley.'

Winston's harsh tone, not to mention his condemning words, brought Emma up with a start. She looked at him swiftly, in astonishment, noticing the grim expression ringing his mouth, the angry glint in his eyes. Why, he bears a grudge against Jim, she thought, that's what his suppressed rage and resentment are all about. Winston is against Jim Fairley because he won Paula, cut Shane out.

Emma nodded, made no comment whatsoever.

Emily, her face puckering up, said quietly, 'Poor Shane. Life's so unfair.'

'Come now, darling, you're only seeing Shane's side of this situation.' Emma clucked gently, reprovingly. 'Perhaps Paula doesn't think life is unfair. I'm sure she's happy with Jim. I know she loves him. And besides, Emily, whoever told you life is fair? It's most *unfair*, and it has always been damned hard, in my experience. How we cope with life, react to our hardships and suffering, and overcome them, that's what really counts in the end. We must all be strong, learn from our troubles, grow in stature and character. We can't ever let adversity get us down, Emily. Now, let us end this discussion. Run along the two of you. I want to be alone for a few minutes.'

Winston went over and kissed her. So did Emily. They left together in silence.

Emma sat by herself for a while.

She felt weary, bone tired. It seemed to her that she solved one problem only to encounter another. But then her life had never been any different. Dear, dear Shane, she murmured under her breath. My heart goes out to you. Life has dealt you a bad hand in this particular instance. But you'll survive. We all do.

Quite unexpectedly tears came into her eyes and trickled down her cheeks. She searched her pockets for a handkerchief and dabbed at her wrinkled old face. She felt like weeping buckets of tears. But that was not her way, giving in like that. And tears solved nothing. She blew her nose, pocketed her handkerchief, and stood up, smoothing down her dress as she did.

Emma walked over to the windows again, taking a few deep breaths, drawing on her great strength, her will power. And slowly she pulled herself together. Her thoughts came back to Shane. Perhaps Winston was right in his assessment. Maybe Shane hadn't realized how he truly felt about Paula until it was too late. Then again, maybe he had believed he had all the time in the world to claim her for his own. We all think that time is endless when we're young, she sighed to herself. The years ahead seem to stretch out forever and indefinitely. But they don't ... they disappear in a flash, in the wink of an eye. Blackie edged into her mind. She wondered what he would have to say about this situation. She decided, at once, not to tell him. It would upset him, cause him too much grief.

Last night Blackie had said that life was too damned short for dilly-dallying. There was a great deal of truth and wisdom in his words. Especially when it came to a couple of old warriors like themselves. Emma made another sudden decision. She was going to accept Blackie's invitation to go on that trip around the world after all. No more dilly-dallying for her.

Turning away from the window, Emma walked briskly across the floor and left the library. She went into the drawing room purposefully, seeking Blackie, picturing his expression when she told him to put his Plan with a capital P into operation immediately. And this she fully intended to do the minute she found him in the crowded room.

12

'Do you think all families are like ours?'

'What do you mean – *exactly*?' Winston asked, turning to face Emily.

'We've always got a drama of one kind or another erupting. It seems to me there's never been a minute's peace for as long as I can remember. If it's not the awful aunts and uncles being beastly and scratching everyone's eyes out, it's our generation quarrelling and creating the most dreadful upsets. To tell you the truth, I feel as though I'm on a battlefield half the time, and I don't think I'm a very good combatant.'

Winston chuckled at her mournful tone, which reflected her dire expression. 'You manage all right, Emily. You're a good little scrapper – so I've noticed.'

The two of them sat together on an old stone garden seat at the bottom on the rolling lawns that sloped away from the wide terrace which fronted the Peach Drawing Room. Behind them, Pennistone Royal soared up into a sky of deepening blue, awesome in its grandeur and majestic beauty, the many windows glittering in the sunshine of late afternoon.

Now Winston said more thoughtfully, 'But to answer your question, I don't suppose other families are *quite* like ours. After all, how many have an Emma Harte as the matriarch?'

Emily drew away, looking up at him, a small frown puckering her smooth brow. Her eyes held his gravely as she said, 'Don't blame Grandma for the dramatics that are being endlessly enacted. I think she's an innocent bystander, poor thing. I really get angry when I think of the heartache some members of this family cause her.'

Winston exclaimed, 'I wasn't being critical of her, if that's what you think. Or suggesting for one minute that she's responsible for these situations, Emily. I agree with you – she's not at fault. I was merely pointing out that as the most remarkable woman of our time, and an original, there's bound to be controversy surrounding her. Look, she's had a very complex and complicated life, and one she's certainly lived to the fullest. She has shoals of children and grand-children, and if you include all of us Hartes, which you must, her family is *huge*. Bigger than most. And don't forget her other close attachments – the O'Neill and Kallinski clans. Add up the numbers – and you've got an army, more or less.'

'Everything you say is true, Winston. Still, I do get awfully fed up with the infighting and bickering. I just wish we could all live peacefully together, and get *on* with it, for God's sake.'

'Yes . . . but there's another thing you must take into consideration, Emily. Immense wealth and power are vested in her, and in this family, so obviously there are going to be jealousies and competitiveness and all kinds of machina-tions. It strikes me that intrigues are inescapable, given the nature of people . . . they *can* be rotten, Emily. Selfish, greedy, self-serving and ruthless. I've discovered that some people will stop at nothing when their own interests are at stake.'

'Don't I know it!' Emily stared down into the murky depths of the pond, looking troubled. Finally she lifted her head, swung her eyes to Winston. 'When I mentioned dramas a few minutes ago, naturally I was referring to Shane. But, I must admit, I sensed things this afternoon, you know, *undercurrents*. As usual, the room was divided into camps. There was a lot of manoeuvring going on.'

'And who was doing what to whom?' Winston asked with some alertness, his curiosity aroused.

'Jonathan and Sarah are as thick as thieves, for one thing. That's very strange, because I know she never used to like him. I can't put my finger on it, yet I can't help feeling they're concocting something. Alexander is probably suspicious of that new liaison. Didn't you notice how he's steered clear of them today?'

'Now that you mention it, yes. Personally, I've never had much time for Jonathan Ainsley. He was a bully as a child, and like all bullies he's basically a coward. He projects a lot of charm these days, but I don't expect he's changed much over the years, not *inside*. I haven't forgotten the time he hit me over the head with a cricket bat. The nasty little bugger. He could have done me real damage.'

'I know he could, and he was always horrid to me when we were growing up. I still believe it was Master Jonathan who cut the tyres on that bicycle Grandy gave me when I was ten, even though he denied it when she challenged him. He came up with some sort of plausible alibi about his whereabouts that day, but I just *know* it was a total fib.' Emily scowled. 'As for Sarah, well, she's been a loner, and secretive, all of her life.'

'You know what they say – still waters run deep and the devil's at the bottom,' Winston remarked.

He bent down, picked up a pebble and idly threw it into the pond, watching the ripples eddying out from the pool's centre. 'There have been occasions when I've thought that Sarah has the hots for Shane.'

Emily started in surprise. 'You're not the only one,' she admitted quietly. 'Well, fat chance she's got . . .' She stopped, added swiftly, 'That sounded mean, and I didn't intend to be catty, Winston. I don't dislike Sarah. She can be very sweet, and I feel sorry for her really. Carrying a torch for a man like Shane O'Neill must be positively awful. Even heartbreaking, perhaps. She and I have never been all that close, but . . . well, I always thought she was true blue – until today. Now I'm not sure any more.'

'She might have been using Jonathan as a shield, and that's all. It was pretty obvious she was trying to disappear into the woodwork, because of Shane's presence, I've no doubt.'

'Maybe you're right.' Changing the subject, Emily remarked, 'Jim's very taken with Edwina and with Anthony, by the look of it. He's been glued to our young earl for the last hour or so. Maybe titles impress him. Anyway, what do you think about Anthony and Sally getting together?'

'Anthony's decent enough, but my father's not so happy about Sally's involvement with him, mostly because of Edwina. If Sally does marry him, we're going to have that old battleaxe slap bang in our midst. Not a very pleasing prospect. She hates the Hartes for some reason.'

'It's because Grandma is a Harte!' Emily exclaimed. 'Edwina has always looked down her nose at her mother. What a stupid woman she is, I really can't bear her.' Emily looked away, pondering. After a short silence, she said in a casual tone, 'You don't like Jim Fairley, do you?'

Winston shook his head vehemently. 'No, no, you're wrong there. I *do* like him, and I certainly have a high regard for his professional abilities. It's just that –' Winston shrugged, made a face, '– well, I know Paula better than most people. Despite that quiet facade, she's very strong, as *you* know. She's also ambitious, driven, a work horse, and a brilliant businesswoman to boot. She's quite extraordinary for her age, and the older she gets the more like Emma she'll become, you mark my words. Actually she's been brought up and groomed to be exactly that – the next Emma Harte. By Emma Harte herself. So, because of this, and the differences in their personalities, I can't help thinking she and Jim are ill suited. But then I'm prejudiced I suppose . . . in Shane's favour. He's my best friend, and one hell of a man. But then –'

Emily broke in peremptorily, 'There's something I want to tell you about Jim, Winston. I believe he's got a lot more depth and strength than some people realize. Paula told me that he used to have the most terrible and agonizing fear of flying, because his parents were killed in a plane crash when he was a small boy. And that's why he took up flying and bought his own plane. He became a pilot to conquer his fear. I know Gran hates him tootling around in his little tin bird, as she calls it, but it's obviously important for him to do so, perhaps even essential to his well being.'

Winston looked surprised. He said, 'Then I've got to hand it to him, it takes guts and courage to overcome that kind of paralysing fear. I'm glad you told me, Emily. Anyway, I was about to say that I could be wrong about Paula and Jim. I'm not infallible. Maybe those two will make it together. I certainly don't wish any unhappiness on Paula, of whom I'm very fond. Or on Jim for that matter.'

He paused, gave Emily a cheeky grin, and finished, 'Besides, nobody knows what really goes on between two people, or what happens in the privacy of the bedroom. Jim could have hidden charms, you know.' He winked at her suggestively.

Emily could not help laughing. 'You are wicked, Winston.' Her eyes filled with mischief. 'You should have seen Grandy's face when you were rattling on about Shane and his hit-and-run affairs and sexual entanglements. It was a picture. And she kept giving me the most surreptitious and concerned glances, as if I wasn't supposed to know about sex.'

'And of course you *are* the lady of great experience, eh, Tiddler?'

Emily adopted a haughty expression and drew herself up on the bench. 'Have you forgotten that I'm now twenty-two years of age? *I* know exactly how many beans make five.'

They grinned at each other. She saw that Winston was highly amused.

Emily went on, 'Do you know, you haven't called me Tiddler since I was just that – a very little girl.'

'And you were, too. The tiniest of little tots for your age.'

'But I did sprout suddenly. I'll have you know I'm now five foot five inches tall, Winston Harte!'

'And a very grown up young woman, I'll wager,' he teased. 'We had fun as kids, though, didn't we, Tiddler? Do you remember that day we decided to play at being Early Britons, and I dubbed you Queen Boadicea?'

'How could I forget!' Emily shrieked. Her face flooded with merriment. 'You painted me blue. *All over.*'

'Not quite, since you insisted on keeping your knickers on, and your liberty bodice. You *were* a modest little thing, as I recall.'

'No, I wasn't! It was the dead of winter, and freezing in Grandy's garage. Besides, why would I be bashful *then*? I didn't have anything to show off when I was five years old.'

Winston gave her an appraising look, one full of speculation, seeing her through the eyes of a grown man. 'But you do now –' He left the rest of his sentence unfinished, feeling self-conscious all of a sudden. Then he became intensely aware of her close proximity as he breathed in the scent of her floral perfume, the lemony tang of her newly-washed hair. Her face, at this moment upturned to his, was trusting, and it had lost its earlier pallor. She looked more like herself, so very pretty and delicate, and as sweet as a summer rose, dewy and fresh and innocent.

Winston cleared his throat, and could not resist drawing her closer to him, wanting and needing that closeness. He said tenderly, in a newly-gentle voice, 'It's a good thing you were a modest child, Emily. If you hadn't kept some of your clothes on, I *would* have painted you all over, and probably killed you in the process.'

122

'How were we to know, at our ages, that skin can't breathe through paint. It wasn't really your fault, Winston. I was just as bad, and after all I painted parts of you.' Emily relaxed against him. She was as conscious of Winston as he was of her, and she longed to prolong this unanticipated and unexpected moment of real physical contact.

He let out a deep chuckle. 'I'll never forget Aunt Emma's terrible fury when she found us in the garage. I thought she was going to give me the whipping of my life. Do you know, every time I smell turpentine I think of that day, of those gruesome turpentine baths she and Hilda gave us. I swear to God she scrubbed me twice as hard as she did you. Extra punishment for me, of course, the irresponsible ten-year-old boy, who should have known better. I was raw for days.'

Emily squeezed his arm. 'We were always getting into trouble, weren't we? You were the ring leader, I the devoted follower, faithfully trailing after you, doing your bidding. I did adore you so, Winston.'

He nodded, looking down into a pair of sparkling eyes that were extraordinary reflections of his own.

Winston caught his breath. He saw something flashing in those green depths, an intensity of feeling, the self-same adoration she had had for him when she had been a child. Unexpectedly his heart began to clatter, and before he could stop himself he bent forward and kissed her on the mouth.

Instantly Emily's arms went around his neck, and she returned his kiss so fervently he was momentarily taken aback. He gripped her tighter, and kissed her again, and then again, and with increasing passion. He felt an overwhelming desire for her flowing through him, rising in him. My God, he was suddenly as hard as a rock. He wanted Emily, and with every part of himself. His whole body was throbbing for her, and he was stunned, thrown off balance by this discovery.

Eventually they loosened their grip on each other and pulled apart breathlessly.

They stared at each other in amazement.

Emily's face was flushed, her eyes startlingly bright, and he saw, with sudden clarity, the love burning in them. Love for him. He touched her cheek and found it was red hot under his caress, burning like her eyes burned. Impatiently he dragged her into his arms again, and his mouth sought hers roughly. They kissed with mounting passion. Their tongues met tantalizingly. He probed her mouth, devoured it. They pressed closer, their bodies cleaving.

Vaguely, dimly, at the back of his swimming mind, Winston remembered how he had always had the urge to undress her when they had been children. In a rush he recalled the long-forgotten games they had played in the attics here ... secret, intimate, exciting games when he had experienced his first arousals. He thought of how his clumsy boy's hands had explored her little girl's body ... he wanted to explore it again with the sure hands of the experienced man he now was, to touch every part of her, woman that she now was, to plunge into her, to possess her completely. His erection was enormous and he thought he was going to explode. He struggled for control, knowing he ought to curtail their love-making at once, but he found he was unwilling to release her from his arms. He gave in to his feelings, kissing her face, her neck, her hair, touching her breasts, taut under the flimsy silk blouse.

It was Emily who finally broke the spell which held them enraptured with each other. She extricated herself from his forceful embrace, but ever so gently and with reluctance. She gazed up at him. Her expression was one of stupefaction.

'Oh Winston,' she whispered, and reached out to touch his sensual, trembling mouth with two fingers. She let them rest there for a moment, as if gentling him.

Winston was speechless.

He sat rigidly on the bench, waiting for his excitement to subside. Emily was motionless at his side, looking up into his face. His eyes bored into her, telegraphing so much to her.

At last he managed, in a strangled voice thick with emotion, 'Emily, I . . .'

'Please,' she whispered quaveringly, 'don't say anything. At least not now.' She glanced away, biting her inner lip, giving him a few moments to steady himself, to regain his composure. Then she stood up, held out her hand. 'Come on,' she said, 'we'd better go inside. It's getting ever so late.'

He said nothing, simply rose; and they walked up the steps in silence, holding hands tightly, each conscious of the other, whilst lost within themselves.

Emily was filled with euphoria.

He has noticed me again, she thought, her heart soaring. At last. Since I was sixteen I've been waiting for him to see me as a woman. I want him. I've never stopped wanting him since we were children. Oh Winston, please feel the same way as I do. Take me for yourself. I've always belonged to you. You made sure of that when I was a child.

Winston, for his part, was awash with all manner of conflicting emotions and turbulent feelings.

He was not only astonished at himself, but at Emily as well – staggered really. They had fallen into each other's arms a moment ago with such ardour and passion he knew that if they had been in more suitable surroundings they would have made love. Nothing would have stopped them. And they had come together without premeditation.

Self-analysis and self-appraisal now edged into his whirling thoughts, cooling him down considerably. He came to his senses, asking himself how this could have happened. She was his cousin, after all. Well, his third cousin. And he had known her for his entire life, although he had paid little attention to her over the past ten years. And inevitably he asked himself finally how he could feel so strongly about Emily when he was in love with Allison Ridley.

This thought nagged at him, and maddeningly so as they mounted the long flight of steps. But when they stepped out on to the circular driveway he let the thought go free as he saw Shane's red Ferrari hurtling around the corner. It slowed to a standstill with a screeching of brakes.

Shane rolled down the window and poked his head out, grinning at them. 'Where have you two been?' he asked. 'I've been looking all over for you, to say goodbye.'

'Emily was feeling a bit bilious in that packed room, so we came out for a breath of fresh air,' Winston ad-libbed quickly. 'Where are you off to in such a tearing hurry, and at this early hour?'

'Like Emily, I was beginning to feel oppressed indoors. I thought I'd take a drive. To Harrogate. I have to say a few farewells . . . to a couple of chums.'

Winston's eyes narrowed imperceptibly. He's going to see Dorothea Mallet, he thought. Some good that'll do him. He said, 'Don't be late for Allison's dinner party. Eight sharp.'

'I'll be there on time, don't worry.'

Emily asked, 'Will you be around tomorrow, Shane?'

'I don't think so, Emily.' He opened the car door and got out. He took hold of her, hugged her tightly. 'I'll see you in six months, or so. Unless you come to New York first.' He smiled at her fondly. 'Aunt Emma just told me you're going to work for Genret. Congratulations, little one.'

'Thank you, Shane, I'm excited about it.' She stood on tiptoe and kissed his cheek. 'And perhaps I will get over to the States on my travels for Genret. You'll have to show me the town, you know!'

'That's a date,' he laughed. 'Take care of yourself, Emily.'

'And you too, Shane.'

'See you later, Winston,' Shane said, and got back into the car.

'Yes,' Winston answered laconically. He looked at Emily oddly as Shane drove off. 'You didn't tell me about Genret.' This was said fretfully, and he felt so unexpectedly gloomy that he was surprised at himself.

She said, 'I haven't had a chance, Winston.'

'Does it mean you'll be doing a great deal of travelling?' he probed, scowling at her.

'Eventually. Why?' Emily lifted a brow quizzically, secretly delighted by his reaction.

'Oh, I just wondered,' he muttered. He realized, with a small shock, that he did not relish the idea of her roaming the world by herself, trotting off on buying trips for Genret.

They fell silent again as they continued up the drive to the house, but just before they went inside, Emily ventured, in a hesitant voice, 'Is it serious? With you and Allison, I mean?'

'No, of course not,' Winston exclaimed swiftly, then asked himself why he had told such a bare-faced lie. He was on the verge of proposing to Allison.

Emily's face brightened. She said, 'I'm sorry you're busy tonight. I'd hoped you'd stay and have dinner with us.'

'I'm afraid I'm stuck.' Winston grimaced to himself, discovering, to his further astonishment, that he was no longer looking forward to the dinner party. He smiled with some wryness, then took hold of Emily's arm as she pushed open the back door, and swung her to face him. 'What are you doing tomorrow?'

'I have to take the girls back to Harrogate College after Sunday lunch here. I'm free in the evening,' she volunteered, and returned his steady gaze unblinkingly. Expectancy illuminated her face.

'How would you like to cook supper for a lonely bachelor? I could come over to your flat in Headingley, Emily,' he suggested.

The smile slipped off her face and she shook her head. 'It's not possible,

Winston. I've just moved in here with Grandy. Yesterday, actually. I'm getting rid of the flat. Otherwise I'd have loved to cook for you.'

Winston stood staring down at her, his hands resting on her shoulders. He was swamped with mixed emotions. He was positive she wanted him. He certainly wanted her. Urgently. Allison loomed up between them. Oh what the hell, he thought, making a decision he hoped he would have no reason to regret later.

Tilting her chin, he kissed her quickly on the mouth. He said, with a wide grin, 'Then we're neighbours. Come over to Beck House tomorrow night, and *I'll* cook for *you*. We'll have a nice evening, I promise. What do you say?'

'I think it's a super idea, Winston,' she said, filling with happiness and excitement. 'What time shall I come over?'

'As soon as you possibly can, darling.'

13

The room was in total darkness.

Not even the merest sliver of light penetrated the tightly drawn curtains, and the lamps had been doused. He craved the darkness. It was like a balm to him. The darkness brought anonymity. He liked it that way. He could not bear to make love in the light anymore.

He lay absolutely still, with his eyes closed, flat on his back, his long legs stretched out in front of him, his arms resting by his sides inertly. His shoulder barely touched hers. He could hear her breathing softly, in unison with himself.

It was not working between the two of them.

And it would not work, he knew that, and he wondered why he was here at all. He really ought to leave. Make a graceful exit. Immediately. He swallowed, fighting back the nausea, wishing he had not downed two glasses of whiskey on top of all that champagne. His head was swimming and he was dizzy, but he was not drunk. In a way, he regretted he was not.

She murmured his name, meltingly, pleadingly, repeating it several times, her fingers brushing up and down his arm.

He was motionless, saying nothing, endeavouring to find the energy to get up and dress and leave. He felt enervated, lethargic. The ghastly afternoon, with its extreme tensions and painful moments, plus the effort he had exerted to conceal his raw emotions, had vitiated him, undermined his stamina.

Now he felt an imperceptible movement close to him, but still he did not open his eyes.

She touched one of his nipples, tentatively at first, then more insistently, pinching it between her fingertips. Absently, he moved her hand away, without bothering to explain that his nipples were not as sensitive as she obviously believed they were. But he had told her that before, hadn't he? Her hand rested on his chest for a moment, then fluttered on to his stomach, making gentle circular movements, creeping down in the direction of his crotch. He knew

126

what she had in mind, what she was about to do next, but he lacked the will to stop her, or to tell her he was leaving in a moment.

She began to stroke him. He hardly paid attention, drifting off into his thoughts. Vaguely he heard the rustle of sheets. She had slithered down the bed and was crouched over him. Her long hair brushed his thighs, and then her warm lips encircled him, enclosed him fully. She was a versatile lover. Despite his buzzing head, his queasy stomach and his lack of interest in her, slowly, steadily, with infinite care, and painstaking deliberation, she managed to arouse him. And in doing so she took him by surprise. When finally she lifted her head and moved her lips higher, on to his stomach, trailed them up over his chest to settle on his mouth, he found himself responding automatically. He returned her fervent kisses, his excitement mounting.

With suddenness, abruptness, he moved rapidly, holding her tightly against him, rolling them both over so that he was lying on top of her. His hands went into the cloud of dark hair and he held her head in his hands, kissing her more deeply and thoroughly, their tongues grazing. He squeezed his eyes tightly shut, not wanting to look into her face pressed so close to his. His fingers left her hair, moved down to fondle her full, voluptuous breasts, her hardening nipples; he pushed his hands under her shoulder blades, then her buttocks, lifting her body, fitting it into the curve of his. He was hard enough to slide into her swiftly, easily, expertly. Together they found a rhythm, rising and falling, their movements growing swifter, more frenzied, gaining in momentum. Her legs went high around his back so that he could shaft deeper and deeper into the warmth of her.

The darkness ... the blackness ... welcoming him ... enveloping him. He was falling ... falling into that endless, bottomless, velvet pit. Paula. Paula. Paula. I love you. Take me. Take all of me. All of my essence. Brilliantly clear images of her exquisite face flashed behind his eyes, were trapped beneath his lids. Paula, my darling, he cried silently, oh Paula ...

'Shane! You're hurting me.'

He heard the voice as if from a long distance, and it was like a knife slashing at his viscera.

It brought him down. Brought him back to this room. And back to her. And it killed the mood he had so carefully created for himself, and only for himself. His fantasy shattered around him.

He fell against her body and lay perfectly still. He was deflated, flaccid, all of his vitality draining away.

At last he said, in a low mumble, 'I'm sorry if I hurt you, Dorothea. It seems I don't know my own strength.' Perhaps you do, he added sardonically under his breath. Or rather, your want of it. Instantly he was embarrassed by his lack of staying power, his inability to bring the act of love to its proper culmination for them both. Act of sex, you mean, he thought, and he shuddered. Revulsion trickled through him, for himself, for her, although she was hardly to blame.

Dorothea said, 'Your watch strap was cutting into my back. But I suppose I shouldn't have said anything just then. You were on the edge, the verge of –'

He covered her mouth with his hand, gently but firmly, in order to stop the flow of words. He did not want to hear her apology. He did not say one single word, just lay against her for the longest moment, his heart slamming against his rib cage, his throat tight with a strangling sensation. Thankfully she, too, was silent. Finally, he lifted himself off her body, touched her shoulder lightly, and left the rumpled bed.

Shane went into the bathroom, locked the door and leaned against it, filled with considerable relief. He fumbled for the switch, snapped on the light, blinked rapidly in the sudden intense glare. The room swam in front of him, and the white-tiled floor appeared to tilt upward to hit him between the eyes. The vertigo and the nausea returned.

He stumbled to the wash basin, leaned over it, and vomited. Blindly he searched for the tap with one hand, and turned it on so that the sound of running water would drown out his retching. He retched and retched until he thought he had nothing left in his insides. When the nausea mercifully subsided he wiped his mouth with the flannel and drank several glasses of cold water, braced himself against the sink, staring down, his eyes closed.

Eventually Shane lifted his head and saw himself in the mirror and he did not like what he saw. His eyes were red-rimmed and bloodshot, his face puffy and congested, and his tousled black hair stood on end. He noticed a smudge of bright red lipstick on the side of his mouth and took the damp flannel and scrubbed at it furiously, angrily. But his anger was directed solely at himself. It had nothing to do with Dorothea. This was not her fault. He was entirely to blame.

He could no longer make love to her successfully, or to any other woman, for that matter. Something always happened to bring him back to reality, and when he realized it was not Paula in his arms, as he had fantasized, he fell apart, could not reach fulfilment. Sometimes, stupefied by drink, his vision and his senses blurred, he could somehow manage, but even these rare occasions were becoming rarer.

He stared at his face in the mirror and without warning he was struck by panic and fear.

Was it always going to be like this? For the rest of his life? Would he never have a happy sexual relationship again? Was he doomed to lead an arid existence without a woman? Would he have to resort to celibacy to save face? To stave off that dreadful moment of embarrassment such as the one which had just occurred in Dorothea's bed?

He was not impotent. He knew he was not afflicted in that way. It was a simple matter really – if his partner intruded into his thoughts, made her presence felt, no longer remained anonymous, then he lost his erection. Try though he did, he could not hold it long enough to satisfy her or himself. The woman he idolized impinged, edged in between them, rendering him weak and ineffectual, he who had always been considered a good lover. What would he *do*, for Christ's sake? *How* would be cure himself? *Was* there a cure? Did he *need* to see a doctor?

The silence in the room pressed in on him. He had no ready answers for himself in his awful predicament.

His anguish flared. God damn it! God damn it to hell! he blasphemed silently, and unexpectedly his eyes filled with tears of helplessness, frustration and rage, startling him. And then instantaneously he was shocked and mortified by this shameful loss of control. For a split second he wanted to smash his fist into the mirror, to shatter that tearful image of himself staring out to mock him. He wanted to smash those finely-tuned, crystalline images of Paula. Damn *her*. Destroy those indelible imprints of her that were stamped so strongly on his tormented, aching brain they seemed to control his life, affected everything he did. At times he felt hopelessly victimized by the vibrant inner vision of her face, the sound of her laughter and her gentle voice that echoed endlessly in his head. But all were locked so securely in his imagination he could not eradicate them, no matter how hard he tried.

But he did not move. He kept his hand clenched at his side, the knuckles white, protruding sharply. Then he closed his eyes convulsively, no longer able to look at himself in this moment of weakness. He leaned against the wall to steady himself, was immobilized like this until he grew calmer, got a grip on himself. Swinging around, he stepped into the shower stall, turned on the taps, let the water sluice down over him. And slowly, but with an iron-clad determination, he emptied his heart and his mind, threw out every vestige of emotion, all feeling.

Minutes later he emerged from the steaming shower, took a bath sheet and dried himself vigorously. He found a fresh towel, tied it around his waist, then searched the cupboard under the sink for the toilet kit he had left there weeks ago. He cleaned his teeth, ran the electric razor over his chin to remove his faint five o'clock shadow, splashed cologne on his face, and combed his damp hair.

He was refreshed, looked more like himself . . . coolly contained, smoothly in control once more. He stared at his reflection a fraction longer, wondering about himself. He was a strapping, healthy young man of twenty-seven, stood six foot three and had a muscular body that was strong and powerful. He had an equally powerful brain to go with his splendid physique. And yet . . . he was so fragile really. The mind is a peculiar thing, he thought, it has such a delicate balance. And who can explain the logic of the heart.

Turning away, he took a deep breath, prepared himself for the inevitable scene with Dorothea. Today he had come to her against his own volition – he could not wait to leave her.

He opened the bathroom door, blinked as he walked back into the shadow-filled bedroom, adjusting his eyes to the darkness. The room was silent, and he wondered if she had fallen asleep, prayed that she had. He groped around for his clothes on the chair where he had discarded them earlier, pulled on his underpants and socks, dispensed with the towel. He slipped on his shirt, buttoned it quickly, dragged his trousers up over his legs and zipped them.

At this moment the bedside lamp flared into life, flooding the room with chilly brightness.

'You're not leaving!' Dorothea exploded. She sounded aghast, furious.

He pivoted.

He could not look at her. Unable to meet her gaze, which he knew would be hurt and condemning, he stared at the far wall.

'I have to go,' he said after a short pause. He sat down on the chair and began to put on his shoes. He could feel her eyes on him.

'You've got a nerve!' she cried, sitting up violently, rattling the headboard as she did. She pulled the sheet around her body with an angry gesture. 'You stroll in here unannounced, help yourself to my booze, bed me, fumble *that*, and leave me high and dry whilst you disappear into the bathroom for half an hour.' She glared at him, added in the same harsh, accusatory tone, 'Then you creep back in here, and calmly proceed to dress in the dark as if you owe me nothing. You were obviously going to *sneak off* to your blasted dinner party!'

He winced. Sighing under his breath, he stood up, and walked over to the bed. He sat down on the edge, took hold of her hand, wanting to be nice, to part with her in a friendly manner. She snatched her hand away, and pressed it to her trembling mouth, attempting to quell the tears glittering in her dark eyes.

Shane said, in his gentlest voice, 'Come on, don't get upset. I told you last week about the dinner tonight. And I reminded you about it when I first arrived this afternoon. It didn't seem to bother you a few hours ago, you were very welcoming.'

'Well, it bothers me now,' she gasped, choking on her words. 'I didn't think you'd leave me, not on your last evening in Yorkshire. Especially after we'd spent several hours in bed together. I thought we'd be having supper, we usually do, and that you would be sleeping here tonight, Shane.'

He was silent. He glanced away uncomfortably.

She misconstrued his reticence. 'I'm sorry I spoiled it for you, Shane. At the last minute, I mean,' she whispered, her voice softer, more cajoling. She adopted a most winning and conciliatory demeanour. 'Please say you forgive me. I love you so much. I can't bear it when you're angry.'

'I'm not angry, and there's nothing to forgive,' he muttered, striving for patience whilst longing to be gone. 'Don't start flagellating yourself, or donning a hair shirt. Look, it doesn't matter, honestly it doesn't, Dorothea.'

She caught something strange in his voice. She was not sure what it was exactly, but it riled her, nevertheless. 'It matters to me,' she snapped, her sweetness immediately evaporating. When there was no response from him, she cried heatedly, 'This afternoon finally *proves* it to me.'

'Proves what?' he asked, sounding bored.

'That you can't make it with *me* – because there's another woman. You're in love with someone else, Shane, and I think you're a bastard for using me the way you have.'

Stunned that she had unwittingly stumbled on the truth, but trying to hide this, he stood up at once, his movements jerky. He edged away from the bed. 'I haven't used you,' he protested, his mouth tightening. He glanced at the door.

'I haven't used you,' she mimicked, her tone mocking, hard, her lip curling down with derision. 'Of course you have. *And*, by the way, I think your friend Winston Harte is as big a bastard as you are, for not inviting me to the dinner party tonight.'

'He's not giving it – Allison Ridley is, and she doesn't know you, or know about our relationship. You and I always agreed we would lead our own lives, with our own friends, and not become a special twosome,' he exclaimed, his voice rising. 'There've never been any strings attached to our relationship . . . that's the way *you* wanted it, if I'm not mistaken.'

Shane took a breath, curbed his increasing annoyance. 'Besides, you've never

130

been interested in my chums before today,' he reminded her with a cool indifference now, wishing she would not colour everything with emotion.

'I've changed my mind. Please take me with you, Shane. I want to come. I really do. This *is* your last night. Please, darling,' she begged, offering him a wistfully-sweet smile, but it faltered in the face of his chilly expression, his rigid stance.

'You know that's not possible, not at this late hour. Anyway, it's a seated dinner. Look, don't try to make *me* wear a hair shirt –' He moved wearily towards the door.

'I know *I'm* not welcome in *your* precious little clique!' she yelled, further losing her control. 'My God, you all make me want to puke! The O'Neills, the Hartes, the Kallinskis . . . what a tight, toffy-nosed group you are. No outsiders permitted to join *your* exclusive club, to become part of *your* charmed circle. No room for us common folk amongst your snooty lot. Anybody would think you're royalty the way you all behave, what with your airs and graces and pretensions. And your stinking money,' she scoffed irately, her face ringed with bitterness. 'You're just a bunch of rotten snobs – the lot of you. And bloody incestuous if you ask me, huddling together in the rarified air of your posh compounds, shutting out the rest of the world. It's sick!'

Flabbergasted at her violence, he looked at her icily and with spiralling disdain. He was appalled at her words, her venom, but immediately held himself in check, deciding not to be provoked into retaliating.

There was an unpleasant silence.

'I've got to go. I'm extremely late.' This was said evenly enough, but Shane was seething inside. He strode across the room, his blood boiling at her insults, threw his tie around his neck, picked up his jacket, slung it over his shoulder.

'I'm sorry we're parting on such a bad note,' he said, giving her a glance of condemnation, 'but there seems to be nothing more to say.' He shrugged. 'I had hoped we could remain friends, at the very least.'

'*Friends!*' she repeated shrilly, her temper blazing. 'You must be crazy. Go on, get out! Go to your lady love. No doubt *she'll* be at your precious dinner!' She laughed hysterically through her blinding tears, then brushed her eyes, made an effort to cling to her last ounce of composure, without success. She swallowed a sob, cried, 'I must admit, I'm curious about one thing! What makes you come crawling back into *my* bed all the time, hot and bothered and raring to go, when someone else has a claim on your heart? Is she a crown princess from one of the clans? A young lady of such refinement – so chaste and virginal – you wouldn't dream of sullying her? What's wrong, Shane, don't you have the guts to sleep with *her* until you're well and truly married and have the blessings of your families? Or could it be that *she's* not interested in *you?* Don't your fatal charms have any effect on *her?* Are you less than irresistible –' She bit off the end of her sentence when she saw the look of intense pain fly across his face, understanding that somehow she had struck the mark, albeit inadvertently.

'Shane, I'm sorry,' she apologized at once, instantly contrite. She was genuinely concerned, afraid she had gone too far this time.

She leapt out of bed, struggled into her robe. 'Shane, forgive me! I didn't mean it, didn't mean to be cruel, to hurt you. I love you, Shane. I have since

the first day we met. Please, please forgive me. And forget what I just said.'
She started to weep.

He did not answer. Nor did he look at her again.

He left. The door slammed with finality behind him.

Shane hurried across the hall, let himself out of her flat, and ran down the stairs at breakneck speed. His head was pounding, and his stomach lurched as the nausea rose in him again.

He sprinted across the lawn, wrenched open the door of his car and jumped in with agility. He drove off with a roar, his hands tightly gripping the wheel, his face set in angry lines, a muscle throbbing on his temple.

When he reached the Stray, the stretch of breezy open common ground in the centre of Harrogate, he slowed down and parked.

Shane sat smoking for a few minutes, pulling himself together, calming his frazzled nerves, a remote look in his troubled black eyes. He stubbed out the cigarette impatiently, suddenly hating the taste of the nicotine. His head ached, reverberated with Dorothea Mallet's vituperative words. Her attitude had been extreme, uncalled for under the circumstances, but then that was her usual pattern. She had displayed her jealousy before, and by now he ought to be accustomed to her tantrums, her temperamental outbursts.

Quite unexpectedly it struck him that he had no reason whatsoever to chastise himself about his behaviour towards her. He had always been considerate and kind to Dorothea. He was a decent man, and he had integrity and honour; furthermore, he would never willingly hurt her or any woman.

He considered the lousy things she had said. In particular her comment about another woman in his life had been like a punch in his stomach. But she was obviously stabbing in the dark, conjecturing, since she could not possibly know he loved Paula. No one knew. It was his secret.

Shane's heart tightened as reality hit him in the face with some force. There was no chance that Paula would ever be his. She was most obviously very much in love with Jim Fairley. He had seen it written all over her face earlier in the day. Not only that, she was a mother now . . . *they were a family*. She had been transparently delighted to see him at the christening, yet despite her loving warmth she had been preoccupied with her husband and her babies.

He squeezed his eyes tightly shut, his face twisting in a grimace of mental anguish. His love for her was a hopeless love without a future. It had nowhere to go. He had known this for the longest time, and yet a faint hope that something might happen to change things had lingered in his mind. Of course it would not. He must put Paula Fairley out of his heart, obliterate her from his consciousness, as he had decided on the moors yesterday. It was not going to be easy, he was well aware. On the other hand, it was imperative that he make the effort, draw on his inner reserves for strength. He had to make his sojourn in New York a new beginning . . . it was his chance to make some sort of worthwhile life for himself. His resolve intensified.

At last Shane opened his eyes, swung his head and gazed out of the window, shaking off the memories of Paula . . . his dearest love. And a married woman, a mother, he reminded himself.

Blinking, he became conscious of his surroundings.

He noticed the daffodils blowing in the breeze that had lately sprung up –

rafts of stinging yellow against the verdant green of the grass. I ought to have bought flowers for Allison, he thought absently, remembering the dinner party. He glanced at the clock on the dashboard. It read seven thirty. The shops were closed . . . and he was going to be late. But if he kept his foot down on the accelerator he would make it in half an hour.

He switched on the radio, twiddled the knob to the BBC's classical station. The strains of the Pachelbel Canon filled the car as he swung it out on to the main road.

Within minutes the Ferrari was hurtling in the direction of the ancient cathedral town of Ripon where Allison Ridley lived. He gunned the engine forward, concentrating on the road ahead.

14

There was something of the actor in Shane O'Neill.

It was a talent inherited from Blackie, and he was able to fall back on that skill whenever it suited him. It did now.

He pushed open the front door of Holly Tree Cottage, took several deep breaths, donned a mask of geniality, and headed down the stone-flagged passageway.

He paused at the entrance to the living room, drew his inbred self-assurance around him, and stepped over the threshold.

At this instant he became what they expected him to be – a man without the slightest care, and one who held the world in his arms.

Laughter sprang readily to his lips, a sparkle entered his brilliant eyes, and he exuded ebullience and bonhomie, strolling forward at a leisurely pace to join his closest male friends – Winston Harte, Alexander Barkstone, and Michael Kallinski. Allison and her women guests were nowhere in sight, and these three stood huddled in front of the window, next to the refectory table set up as a bar for the evening.

Meandering across the floor, Shane glanced about with interest, struck at once by the beauty of this main room in the cottage, which was really two dwellings knocked into one. He remembered that Allison had recently finished decorating it, and she had done wonders with the place. The low, beamed ceiling and wide stone fireplace – both Tudor – gave the setting its real character, but the colourful cretonnes covering the sofas and chairs, the old pine furniture, and Sally Harte's dreamlike watercolours on the whitewashed walls contributed much to its intrinsic charm. It was a rustic country room, free of pretensions and fussiness, yet eminently comfortable and cosy, the kind he liked. He made a mental note to congratulate Allison the minute he saw her.

As soon as Shane drew to a standstill in front of his friends the banter started.

They joshed him unmercifully about being late, and made innumerable innuendos about the real reason behind his tardiness. He took it all with good humour, laughed good-naturedly, and shot back a few missiles of his own. The strain and tension eased out of his aching muscles and he started to relax at last, feeling comfortable and at home with the three men. And within minutes he was responding fully to their warmth, affection and friendship, and to the carefree mood, the jollity that prevailed here this evening.

At one moment he took a cigarette, brought his lighter to its tip, and as he did he thought fleetingly of Dorothea's virulent condemnation of his set, their world. Well, she had been correct in one sense – they were extremely clannish, he had to admit that. If they clung together, it was because they had been brought up with each other, had always been close and intimately involved on every level. Blackie, Emma and David Kallinski, Michael's grandfather, had seen to that. *They* had been through a lot together in the early days at the turn of the century, sharing their terrible struggles and later triumphs, and it was from them that the unbreakable bonds of friendship sprang. That extraordinary trio, founders of three powerful Yorkshire dynasties, had been tight most of their lives, from the day they had met in fact, and devoted thereafter, right up to David's untimely death in the early sixties. Because their children and grandchildren had been thrown together since birth, and in the ensuing years, it was only natural that a large number of them remained staunchly loyal, the dearest of friends and constant companions.

What the hell, Shane thought, filling with a spurt of impatience with himself. Why do I worry about *her* opinions of *us*? This is the way we are, the way we live; and what's more, we genuinely care about each other and deeply so. And we've always been there for each other in times of trouble and grief – just as our grandparents were before we were born.

Winston, misunderstanding Shane's sudden silence, said to the others, 'Okay, chaps, let's give him a breather. What would you like, Shane? A Scotch?'

'No, thanks. Just soda water, please.'

'What's the matter with you tonight?' Winston asked, as he filled the glass. 'It's not like an Irishman to be imbibing this innocuous stuff.'

Shane grinned as he took the drink. 'Too much champagne earlier. But I must say, none of you seem the worse for wear and you were *all* knocking it back like sailors on shore leave.' Looking at Michael, he went on, 'I assume your parents are still in Hong Kong, since they weren't with you at the christening.'

'Yes. They get back in two weeks, and then I leave for New York. I hope we can get together, Shane. Where will you be staying?'

'At Aunt Emma's Fifth Avenue flat, until I find a place of my own. And I'll be bloody furious if you don't phone me.' Shane now glanced past Winston. Valentine Stone, Michael's girl friend, was coming back into the room from the garden, followed by Marguerite Reynolds and a blonde girl. He guessed she was Allison's American friend and the reason for the dinner party. He waved to them, then took Michael's arm. 'Do I notice a ring on Valentine's finger?'

'Yes, but it's on her right hand, not her left, you idiot!' Michael Kallinski made a face, chuckled. 'You'll be the first to know when I decide to take that ghastly step, Shane.'

Alexander cut in, 'Just listen to the man . . . we all know she's got you where she wants you, Mike.'

'You've got room to talk,' Michael shot back. 'Marguerite has you pinioned down in the same position, flat on your back in a stranglehold, gasping for air.'

They all laughed.

Alexander flushed, retorted, 'Don't be too sure.' He hesitated, then volunteered, 'One thing is certain though, Grandmother likes Maggie, approves of her. *She* thinks I should pop the question now, before some other fellow steals her away from under my nose. Some confidence Emma Harte has in her grandson, I must say.' Alexander shook his head, took refuge in his usual reserved shell, observing Maggie out of the corner of his eye. She looked stunning tonight in a scarlet pants suit, her light brown hair swept up in an old-fashioned pompadour. Perhaps he *should* take his grandmother's advice.

Shane, who had flinched inside at Alexander's words, said in a low voice, 'Don't let her escape. Aunt Emma's right, she's quite a catch, Sandy, and such a nice girl.'

Michael added, 'And the world *is* full of predatory males, as we all know, Alexander. You'd better do what E. H. says before it's too late.'

Shane swung to Winston. 'And where's *your* lady love hiding herself?'

'What?' Winston asked, pulling himself away from thoughts of Emily. He frowned. 'What are you talking about?'

'*Allison*. Where is she?' Shane stared at him, and went on, 'I haven't said hello to my hostess yet.'

'Oh! Yes, Allison. She dashed off to the kitchen just before you arrived,' Winston said quickly, trying to cover his lapse. 'She'll be back in a second. She went to see if the two local girls she hired for the evening are coping. In the meantime, I'd better take you over to the guest of honour, and introduce you, otherwise Allison'll have my guts for garters.' Winston gave Shane a knowing wink. 'Allison's friend lives in New York. If you behave yourself tonight she might even agree to go out with you.'

'I won't have time for women. I'll be far too busy with the hotel. Stop trying to fix me up, Winston,' Shane remonstrated, then thought to ask, 'Anyway, what makes you think I'd be interested?'

'Because she's rather nice,' Winston replied.

Shane made no comment, followed his friend down the long room to the fireplace where the three women stood chatting.

The tall, slender blonde watched them approaching, trying not to give the appearance of doing so, instantly struck by Shane O'Neill's undeniable presence even from this distance. In fact she had been aware of him the minute she had returned to the living room. Allison had told her who and what he was ... the young scion of a famous Yorkshire family, the most eligible of bachelors, and one who had been born with a golden spoon in his mouth, the money to buy himself the world if he wanted. He also had the looks to take him wherever he wanted. And right into *any* woman's bed, if he so wished, she decided. Allison had not exaggerated.

Shane kissed Valentine and Marguerite, and Winston said, 'Skye, I'd like you to meet Shane O'Neill. Shane, this is Skye Smith from New York.'

They shook hands, exchanged greetings.

Shane said pleasantly, with a friendly smile, 'I hear this is your first trip to Yorkshire. Are you enjoying it?'

'I'm loving every minute. It's so beautiful ... the Dales are breathtaking. Allison's whizzed me all over this past week, buying antiques, so I've seen a lot of your glorious countryside.'

'Allison's the expert, so I'm sure she helped you find some really interesting things. You're in the same business, Winston tells me,' Shane remarked.

'Yes, I have a small antique shop on Lexington Avenue, in the Sixties. And fortunately a lot of good customers who are hungry for English antiques and silver.' She laughed lightly. 'I've bought up half of Yorkshire, and now I'm worrying about storing everything I'm having shipped home next week. My shop's going to be bursting at the seams.'

Valentine said, 'Allison told me you came across some beautiful old Victorian silver in Richmond. Surely you won't have a problem selling those pieces. And immediately.'

'No, I won't,' Skye said, and gave them a detailed description of every item of silver now in her possession. Winston excused himself, and ambled off. Shane lolled against the fireplace, bored with the subject of antiques and only vaguely listening to the women's chatter. He studied the American girl. She was charming; certainly she was good looking, personable, and obviously very bright. Still, he had known at once that she was not his type. Cool, pristine blondes who looked like Scandinavian ice maidens had never appealed to him much. He preferred dark exotic women. Like Paula. He crushed the thought of her.

After a polite interval had elapsed, he said, 'I really ought to go and find Allison. Please excuse me.' With a brief nod he disappeared, went down the narrow hall, making for the kitchen. But as he passed the small intimate dining room he spotted Allison through the open door. She was surveying the table intently.

'There you are, Miss Ridley!' he exclaimed, striding inside, pulling her to him, enveloping her in a bear hug. 'Congratulations. The cottage looks lovely. Now, why are you hiding from me? I've begun to think you're punishing me for being so late.'

'Not you, Shane darling. You can do anything – I'd never be angry with you.'

'You'd better not let Winston hear you say things like that. You'll make him jealous.'

The merriment left Allison's face, and she said in a tight voice, 'I'm not so sure . . .'

Shane threw her a questioning look. 'What's that supposed to mean?'

Allison shrugged, bent over the table, and moved a small silver bird closer to its companion, averting her head.

Shane's face was a study in perplexity as he waited for her to finish fiddling with the table decorations, to respond to his question. When she did not, he took her arm gently, turned her to him. He immediately perceived she was upset.

'Hey, what's wrong?' he murmured softly, staring down into her bleak face.

'Nothing. Really and truly . . .' she began and broke off, wavering. Finally, she said in a great rush of words, 'Oh I'm not going to lie to *you*, Shane. Winston's been funny with me since he arrived tonight. Not himself. Dis-

136

tracted.' Her light grey eyes searched his face. 'Did something happen this afternoon . . . something that might have upset him?'

Shane shook his head. 'Not that I know of, Allison.'

'I think it must have. If it didn't, then his odd behaviour must have something to do with me, with us. Perhaps he's lost interest in me.'

'I'm sure you're wrong.'

'I'm *not*, Shane. I know Winston almost as well as you do. Generally he is sunny tempered, and he's warm and affectionate. We've been getting on wonderfully these last few months. So much so, I had the feeling he might propose soon. He's been sending out signals . . . he told me how much his father liked me, and, perhaps more importantly, Emma Harte. When he arrived earlier I noticed a change in him . . . he was different, preoccupied. He got here late, when he'd promised to come before the other guests to help me move the refectory table and do a few other things – and you know he's never late. That didn't matter, of course. But he was cool, even a bit brusque, and naturally I was taken aback. He did soften during drinks, after Alexander and Maggie had arrived, but frankly he *is* distant. It's not like him in the least – being so moody, I mean.'

Shane was more baffled than ever. He ran the events of the afternoon through his head, wondering if something had occurred which had disturbed Winston. But nothing untoward had happened to his knowledge, and Winston had seemed untroubled to him.

He said, 'Listen, maybe it *is* something to do with business. That seems to be the most plausible explanation to me. Yes, it must be a business worry.' He offered her a reassuring smile. 'I'm convinced his attitude has nothing to do with your relationship. And he's certainly not lost interest in *you*. How could you think that?'

She looked at him for the longest moment, and smiled regretfully. 'A woman senses these things.'

Shane exclaimed, 'You're reading this the wrong way, imagining the worst.' He took her hand, tucked it through his arm and walked her to the door. 'Come on, let's go back to the sitting room and I'll buy you a good stiff drink. I could use one myself.' His eyes were warm with affection. 'You'll see, Winston will be his old self with you.'

'You sound more certain of that than I feel,' she replied softly. But she brought a carefree expression to her face as she returned to her guests, clinging to Shane's arm, thankful to have his support.

Later in the evening, when they were at dinner, Shane decided that Allison had been right in one respect: Winston was not entirely himself.

He sat at the head of the table, and although he was pleasant and charming, played the good host to the hilt, Shane detected an abstracted look flickering behind his eyes, recognized the forced note in his laughter, the falseness behind his joviality.

To distract everyone's attention, and wanting to give Winston breathing space, Shane became the life and soul of the dinner party. He was gregarious, outgoing, witty and amusing. He was particularly attentive to Allison, on whose right he sat, was pleased that she responded in a positive way, and appeared to be more relaxed and at ease as the evening progressed.

But it was she who brought the meal finally to an end when, after dessert, she said, 'Let's have coffee and liqueurs in the sitting room, shall we?'

'That's a splendid idea,' Winston exclaimed, smiling at her more warmly than he had since his arrival. He was the first to rise, and ushered Allison and the other women out of the dining room. Shane followed with Michael and Alexander at his heels.

Winston went immediately to the refectory table, where he began to pour different liqueurs for the women guests. Shane strolled over to him, and striving to be casual, said, 'Make mine a Bonnie Prince Charlie, please.'

'Since when have you been drinking that awful stuff?' Winston asked, looking up. He grinned, turned back to his task of pouring white *crème de menthe* over the crushed ice he had spooned into a goblet.

'Don't sound so disapproving. You used to like it as much as I did when we were kids, gulping it down wholesale when Aunt Emma wasn't looking.'

'Yes, and if I remember correctly, we both used to get bloody sick on it. But okay, if that's what you want.' Winston filled a glass with the liqueur, handed it to Shane with another grin, finished pouring cognacs for Michael, Alexander, and himself.

Shane stood watching him. At last he asked in a low voice, 'Are you okay?'

Winston lifted his head sharply. 'Of course I am. Why do you ask?'

'You've seemed a bit out of it tonight.'

'It's been a long day, hectic. I am a bit weary, I'm afraid. Do me a favour, toddle over to Skye and ask her if she's changed her mind about an after-dinner drink, whilst I dutifully dispense these to the others. Allison will be back in a minute with the coffee.' Winston picked up the tray and walked across the room, whistling under his breath.

Shane's eyes followed him, narrowing thoughtfully. Winston seemed normal enough now, and perhaps he had spoken the truth when he had claimed fatigue. Shane sauntered over to Skye Smith who sat on the wide stone hearth by herself. 'You're not drinking. Try this,' he said in a commanding tone, handing her the glass.

She took it, sniffed it delicately, looked up at him questioningly.

'It's a Bonnie Prince Charlie,' Shane explained.

'What's that?'

He laughed. 'Drambuie. Go on take a sip, it won't poison you.'

She did as he said, and nodded her approval. 'It has an unusual taste. I like it. Thank you, Shane.'

'Don't move. I'll be right back.' He returned a moment later with a Drambuie for himself, sat down next to her, and clinked her glass with his. 'Cheers.'

'Cheers.' Skye glanced at him out of the corner of her eye. He *was* handsome. Perhaps too handsome. Men who looked like Shane O'Neill terrified her. They were usually untrustworthy . . . too much temptation fell into their paths.

Shane savoured his drink for a minute, then put his glass on the hearth, asked: 'Do you mind if I smoke a cigar?'

'No, not at all. And tell me something – why is Drambuie called Bonnie Prince Charlie?'

'Because when Bonnie Prince Charlie went to Scotland, in 1745, trying to regain the throne of his ancestors, he was aided by a Mackinnon of Skye. In gratitude, Prince Charlie gave the man his own recipe for his personal liqueur. Ever since then the secret for its preparation has remained with the Mackinnons, and Drambuie gets its nickname from the legend. And speaking of the Isle of Skye, is that how you spell your name . . . sky with an *e* at the end?'

'Yes, but my name is really Schuyler. It's Dutch. A family name. I have a feeling my Mom thought plain old Smith needed jazzing up a bit.' She smiled at him slowly.

'It's a very pretty name. It suits you,' he said with a show of gallantry.

'Why thank you kindly, sir.'

They fell silent.

Skye Smith was trying to decide whether she could suggest he call her in New York without appearing forward. She was not interested in him as a lover, on the other hand she had found herself drawn to him during dinner, almost against her will. He was entertaining, good company, and a delightful man, if a little vain and too sure of himself. But perhaps they could be friends.

Shane was still dwelling on Winston, discreetly observing him. He lounged on a sofa at the other side of the room, nursing his brandy, looking relaxed. Whatever problem had been bothering him earlier had apparently been resolved, or dismissed as unimportant. He was laughing suddenly and in a natural manner, and teasing Allison. Shane noticed that her face was radiant. So much for all that, he thought, it was a storm about nothing. He filled with relief. He was going away tomorrow and he did not like to think he was leaving when his dearest friend had troubles.

Skye finally spoke, interrupting Shane's contemplations. She said, 'I hope this doesn't sound pushy or anything like that, but if I can be of help in New York, do feel free to call me.' She added quickly, wanting to sound more businesslike, 'The shop is listed under Brandt-Smith Antiques.'

'That's very kind of you. I will,' Shane said, and startled himself with his ready acquiescence to her suggestion. He puffed on his cigar for a second, then feeling the need to explain, he went on, 'I don't know many people in New York. Just a couple of lawyers who work for our company. Oh, and I have an introduction to a man called Ross Nelson. A banker.'

'Oh,' she exclaimed.

Shane glanced at her, saw the surprise in her eyes. Or was it shock that had registered? 'So you know Ross,' he said, his curiosity flaring.

'No. No, I don't,' she replied too swiftly. 'I've heard of him, read about him in the newspapers, but that's all.'

Shane nodded, and for a reason he could not fathom, he immediately changed the subject. But as they talked about other things he could not help thinking that Skye Smith was much better acquainted with the notorious Mr Nelson than she wanted him to believe. And he asked himself why she had felt the need to lie about this.

Shane O'Neill left Yorkshire the following morning.

It was dawn. The mist had rolled down from the moors and the higher fells to spread across the meadows like a mantle of grey lace, partially obscuring the trees and the drystone walls and the cottages nestling in the folds of the fields. And all were inchoate images, spectral and illusory under the remote and bitter sky. Dew dripped from the overhanging branches, glistened on the white wildflowers gleaming in the hedgerows, ran in little rivulets down the grassy banks at the sides of the lane. Nothing stirred in the drifting vaporous mists and there was an unearthly quiescence, an unmoving stillness lying over the whole of the countryside and it was a dreamlike landscape . . . the landscape of his childhood dreams.

Gradually, from behind the rim of the dim horizon, the early sun began to rise, its streaming corridors of slanting light piercing outward to illuminate the bowl of that cold and fading sky with a sudden breathtaking radiance. And through the tops of the leafy domes of trees, caught in the distant shimmer of sunlight like a mirage, glittered the chimneys of Pennistone Royal. House of his childhood dreams . . . but there was another house in his childhood dreams . . . a villa by the sea where they had laughed and played and dreamed away the careless carefree days of their childhood summers . . . where nothing had ever changed . . . and time had been an eternity.

And she was always there . . . with him . . . at that villa high on the cliffs above the sunlit sea . . . laughter in her eyes the colour of the summer sky and gentleness in her smile that had truly been only for him . . . dreamlike land-scapes . . . dreamlike houses . . . dreamlike child of his childhood dreams . . . locked in his heart and mind for all of time . . . haunting him always . . . dim shadows on his Celtic soul.

He was going away now . . . so far away . . . leaving them behind . . . but he never left them behind . . . he carried them with him wherever he went . . . and they would never change . . . they were his childhood dreams . . . Paula and Pennistone Royal and the villa by the sunlit sea . . .

The car sped on, down the narrow winding country lanes, past the great iron gates of Pennistone Royal, on through the village of the same name, out now on to the main road. Shane glimpsed the familiar signs flying by . . . South Stainley, Ripley, Harrogate, Alwoodley.

He slowed down as he roared into Leeds, although there was no traffic, no one abroad, deserted as it was at this hour and without a sign of life. Grey, grimy, vital Leeds, great industrial city of the North, the seat of Emma's power and his grandfather's and David Kallinski's family.

Circling City Square, where the statue of the Black Prince dominated, he drove on, down the short hill near City Station, heading towards the M1, the road leading south to London. Shane picked up speed the moment he rolled on to the motorway, and he did not reduce it until he was nosing the car over the county boundary . . . leaving Yorkshire behind.

15

The garden was her magical place.

It never failed to give Paula a sense of accomplishment and satisfaction and it was therapeutic when she was frustrated or needed a release from the stresses and tensions of business.

When she began to plan a garden, whether large or small, she gave free rein to her imagination, and every plot of ground that fell into her sure and talented hands was miraculously transformed, became a breathtaking testament to her instinctive understanding of nature.

In fact, she was an inspired gardener. Flowers, plants, trees and shrubs were woven into a tapestry of living colour and design by her, one that stunned the eye with its compelling beauty. Yet despite her careful planning, none of her gardens ever looked in the least contrived.

Indeed there was a genuine old-world air about them, for she planted them with an abundance of old-fashioned flowers and shrubs, that were typically English in character. The garden she now called her own, and which she had been working on for almost a year, was beginning to take on this particular look.

But for once she was hardly aware of the garden.

She stood poised at the edge of the terrace, gazing down the long green stretch of lawn, yet not really seeing it, an abstracted expression on her face. She was thinking of Jim. Their quarrel of last night had been dreadful, and although they had eventually made up – in bed where they usually managed to put aside their mutual anger – she was still shaken. They had quarrelled about Edwina. Again. And in the end he had won, since she was hopelessly weak where he was concerned, loving him the way she did. And so she had finally agreed to entertain Edwina tonight, to show her the house and the grounds, offer her cocktails before they went out to dinner. But Paula wished now that she had been more resolute with him. In the early hours of the morning, after he had made love to her, he had cajoled, teased and laughed her into agreeing to do as he wished. He had cleverly twisted her around his little finger, and she resented it suddenly.

Sighing, she walked purposefully over to the rockery she was creating, trying to shake off the remnants of the violent quarrel. I refuse to harbour a grudge, she told herself firmly. I've got to let go of my anger before he comes home tonight. She knelt down, continuing the work that she had started earlier that day, hell bent on bringing order to that intractable pile of stone, filled with the intense desire to make this rockery as beautiful as the one at Grandy's seaside house.

As usually happened, Paula soon lost herself entirely in gardening, concentrating totally on the work, allowing the tranquillity of nature to lap over her until she was enfolded by its soothing gentleness, at peace within herself.

It was as a child that Paula had discovered her love of the earth and all growing things. She had been eight years old.

The same year Emma had bought a house to use during her grandchildren's spring and summer holidays from school. It was called Heron's Nest and it stood on the high cliffs at Scarborough, overlooking the pale sands and the lead-coloured bay beyond, a piece of Victorian gingerbread with its intricately-wrought wood portico, wide porch, large sunny rooms, and sprawling garden that was a veritable wilderness when Emma had first taken title to the property.

Aside from wanting a place where she could spend the holidays with her young brood and enjoy their company, Emma had had another valid reason for purchasing Heron's Nest. She had long felt the urgent need to have her grandchildren under her complete control and influence for uninterrupted periods. Her objective was simple. She wanted to teach them a few of the essentials of life, the practicalities of everyday living, and to make sure that they understood the true value of money. Emma had for years found it intolerable that most of her children had grown accustomed to living in luxury without giving one thought to the cost of their pampered existences, and that they were overly dependent on armies of servants to take care of even their simplest needs.

And so, in her inimitable way, she had devised a scheme when she had decided that her grandchildren must be brought up to be less spoiled, more self-reliant, and certainly down-to-earth where matters of money were concerned. 'There's an old Yorkshire saying and it goes like this –' she had remarked to her investment banker, Henry Rossiter, one day, '– from clogs to clogs in three generations. Well, you can be damned sure that that's not going to hold true for my lot!' Immediately afterwards she had signed the cheque for the house.

Heron's Nest was the answer to many things, in her mind. And it would become her school. To this end, Emma had seen fit to engage only one maid, a local woman from the town who would come every day. And she had told the rather jolly, plump Mrs Bonnyface that her main task would be to take care of the seaside villa when the family were not in residence. Emma had gone on to outline her rather unorthodox plans, had explained how she fully intended to run the house herself – with the help of her numerous grandchildren. Whatever Mrs Bonnyface had thought of this unusual state of affairs, she had never said. She had accepted Emma's scheme and with enthusiasm, and had obviously felt privileged to work for the famous Mrs Harte, if her general demeanour was anything to judge by.

Being clever and a dissembler of the highest order, Emma had not confided her intentions or motives in anyone else, least of all her grandchildren. Only after she had made the acquisition and hired Mrs Bonnyface, had she told them about Heron's Nest, but she had given glowing details, cloaked it with such an aura of glamour they had been agog with excitement. They regarded the whole idea of a house by the sea as a great adventure, since they would be alone with Emma and far away from their parents.

Emma had realized almost immediately that the regime she had instituted had come as something of a shock, and she had smiled inwardly as she had watched them floundering around with mops and buckets, carpet sweepers and brooms, furniture polish and dusters, and unmanageable ironing boards. There had been huge disasters in the kitchen . . . demolished frying pans, pots charred to cinders, and vile, unpalatable meals. They had grumbled about burned fingers, blisters, headaches, housemaid's knee, and other minor ailments, real and imaginary, some of which had sounded extremely farfetched to Emma.

But it was Jonathan who had come up with the most inventive and imaginative excuse for wriggling out of his allocated chores, on the day he had told her that he had strained his Achilles tendons mowing the lawn, and was far too crippled to do any more work for days. Emma had been both startled and impressed by his cleverness. She had nodded most sympathetically. And to prove to this canny little boy that she was so much smarter than he believed she was, she had explained to him, and in diabolically graphic terms, exactly how strained Achilles tendons were treated. 'And so, since you're in such dreadful agony, I'd better drive you down to the doctor's surgery so that he can get to work on you immediately,' she had said, reaching for her handbag and the car keys. Jonathan had swiftly suggested they wait for a few hours, just in case the pain went away. Seemingly it did. He had made a stunningly rapid recovery, apparently not relishing the prospect of spending the remainder of the spring uncomfortably encased in a plaster of Paris cast reaching from the tips of his toes to his waist. Or of being left behind with Mrs Bonnyface when his cousins returned to their respective schools and his grandmother to Pennistone Royal.

During those first few weeks at the holiday house in Scarborough they soon settled down to a steady routine. The girls quickly began to show a certain proficiency in their housework and cooking, and the boys readily learned to cope with the heavier household work, weeding the garden and mowing the lawns. Not one of them was ever permitted to shirk his or her duties. Emma was not the type to stand any nonsense for long, and she was relatively strict, showed no favouritism whatsoever.

'I've never heard of anyone dying from scrubbing a floor or polishing the silver,' she was fond of saying if one of them dared to complain or invent an imaginary illness as Jonathan had done. The recalcitrant child who had screwed up enough nerve to protest or fib would instantly blanche under her steely green gaze, remembering Jonathan's narrow escape.

And when the time came for them all to pack up and leave the seaside house Emma had congratulated herself, had admitted that they had been real troopers indeed. They had put on good faces and had truly pulled together to please her. As far as she was concerned, the experiment had proved to be an unconditional success. Every year thereafter, when the harsh Yorkshire winters gave way to the warmer weather, she had gathered them up and carted them off to Scarborough.

Eventually the Harte cousins and the O'Neill and Kallinski grandchildren became regular visitors. Even they were given their fair share of chores, and they had had no choice but to pitch in cheerfully when they arrived to spend July and August by the sea. They quickly came to understand that they would not be invited back if they did not comply with Emma's wishes and pull their weight.

The children had called Emma 'The General' behind her back, and indeed they had often felt as though they were living in an army camp because of her stringent rules and regulations. On the other hand, they had truly enjoyed themselves during those happy, carefree years, and they had ended up having such enormous fun together that even the chores were regarded as games. Much to their parents' astonishment, and Emma's immense satisfaction, each one had come to so look forward to those sojourns in the little seaside town they vociferously declined any other holiday invitations. They had insisted on returning to Heron's Nest the minute Emma opened up the house.

Despite her own terrible addiction to work and little else, Emma had been shrewd enough to recognize that her 'small band of brigands', as she called them, needed plenty of opportunities to let off steam and lots of pleasurable pursuits to fill the long summer days. 'All work and no play makes Jack a dull boy, you know,' she would constantly repeat to Mrs Bonnyface, and then proceed to invent exciting projects in which she and the children could participate together.

She took them on interesting expeditions up and down the coast, to Whitby, Robin Hood's Bay and Flamborough Head, and gave them numerous other rewards for their strenuous endeavours. There were visits to the local picture house and the town's little theatre; they went for leisurely picnics on the cliffs; sailed in the bay and had swimming parties on the beach. Frequently they went fishing with the local fishermen and were thrilled when they were allowed to keep some of the catch. On those propitious days they would return in triumph to Heron's Nest, where they would cook their small and meagre fish for Emma's supper, and she had eaten them as if they had been prepared by the French chef at the Ritz. When the weather was overcast and the seas rough, Emma had organized egg-and-spoon races and treasure hunts in the garden, and, since she truly understood the acquisitive nature of children, she made certain that the treasure was extra special and worth finding. And she had always provided more than enough items for each child, had usually dropped blatant clues to those who were coming up empty-handed and wearing tearful or disappointed expressions. On rainy days when they had to stay indoors they had played charades or put on their own plays.

One year the boys formed their own band. They called themselves The Herons, and Shane and Winston were the chief instigators and organizers. Shane appointed himself the band leader. He was also the piano player and the vocalist. Alexander sat at the drums and cymbals, Philip blew the flute, Jonathan scraped the violin and Michael Kallinski warbled the harmonica. But it was Winston who thought he was the most important and talented member of the ensemble. He adopted the trumpet as his own and fervently insisted he was the new Bix Beiderbecke, inspired no doubt by a film Emma had taken them to see called *Young Man With A Horn*. Sarah wondered out loud where he had learned to play and Emma smiled thinly and said that he hadn't, and that was the trouble. And at times she thought her eardrums would burst when the cacophony of sound filled the house during practice times, which seemed eternal and never ending to her.

Eventually, when they believed themselves to be polished enough to perform before a live audience, The Herons invited Emma and the girls to a concert in the garden. Emma watched them in amazement, secretly amused by their elaborate and endless preparations. They put out deck chairs, set up a small stage made of planks balanced on bricks, and rolled out the piano to stand next to it. And they took great pains dressing themselves in what they called their 'rig-outs' – their new white cricket flannels worn with brilliant scarlet satin shirts, made, no doubt, at one of the Kallinski factories, Emma decided. Purple satin kerchiefs were tied around their necks and debonair straw boaters were rakishly angled on top of their heads.

Having caught a glimpse of them assembling on the stage, from her bedroom window, Emma immediately changed into a silk afternoon dress and hurried down the corridor to the girls' rooms. She insisted they wear their best cotton frocks in honour of the auspicious occasion, and they had all trooped out just after four o'clock dressed in their finery, curiosity and expectancy written on their pretty young faces.

As Emma listened to The Herons give their renditions of current popular songs and a couple of old ballads, she found herself enjoying the concert, and was rather surprised to discover that they really weren't such bad musicians after all. At the end of their recital she praised the boys, laughing with merriment as she showed her delight in them. The boys laughed too, and taking her lavish accolades to heart they had gone on playing relentlessly all that summer, much to the horror of the girls. Whenever they heard them rehearsing they made snide remarks, sniggered loudly and declared that The Herons stank to high heaven.

Shane, like Winston, was exceptionally vain about his musical accomplishments, and most especially his voice. He soon made certain that the critical young females were suitably intimidated. One night all of them found a foul-smelling object in their beds, ranging from frogs and dead fish with glassy eyes, to raw onions and bags of sulphur. Shane's retaliatory measure worked. After that dreadful night of changing sheets, opening the windows wide and shaking Emma's good perfumes all over their rooms, none of the girls dared to use the word stinking for the rest of the holidays. At least certainly not in reference to The Herons.

And slowly but very deliberately over these years, Emma had striven to instil in every child the importance of the team spirit, playing the game, being a good sport and abiding by the rules. Duty and responsibility were words forever on her lips, for she was resolute in her determination to arm each and every one of them with sound principles, and the proper precepts for the future when they became adults. She taught them the meaning of honour, integrity, honesty and truthfulness, amongst so many other things. But her frequently strong and tough pronouncements were always spoken with an underlying kindness, and she gave them a great deal of love and understanding, not to mention genuine friendship. And it was a friendship most of them were never to forget for the rest of their lives. Deep in her heart, Emma regretted that she had neglected her own children at certain times in her life, when they were in their formative years and growing up. She wanted her grandchildren to benefit from the mistakes she had made in the past, and if some of this washed off on her great-nephews and nieces, and the grandchildren of her closest friends, then so much the better.

But of all the years they had spent in the tall old villa on the cliffs, that very first spring of 1952 had been the most special and memorable to Paula, and it would live in her heart and her mind always. That particular year she became aware of her affinity with nature and her overwhelming desire – the need in her really – to make things grow.

One blustery Saturday in April she wandered out into the garden with little Emily whom Emma had put in her charge that day. Paula glanced around, her eager young eyes keenly observing, newly perceptive. The undergrowth had been cut away, the hedges neatly trimmed, and the lawns mowed to such perfection by the boys they resembled bolts of smooth emerald velvet rolled out to touch the perimeters of the high stone walls. The piece of land behind the house was now uncommonly immaculate – and totally lacking in character.

She was amazed at herself when she unexpectedly realized how the garden *could* look if it was correctly planted. The eight-year-old girl had a vision, saw reflected in her child's imagination an array of textures and shapes and great bursts of colour . . . luscious pinks and mauves, blazing reds and blues, brilliant yellows, warm ambers, oranges and golds, and cool clear whites. She instantly envisioned dazzling mixtures of flowers and shrubs . . . plump bushes of rhododendrons with their delicately-formed petals and dark polished leaves . . . pale peonies, wax-like in their perfection . . . splayed branches of azaleas laden down with heavy bright blossoms . . . masses of stately foxgloves brushing up against merry tulips and daffodils . . . and hugging cosily to the ground, dainty beds of pansies, primroses and violets, and the icy little snowdrop scattered randomly under the trees.

And as she saw all this in her mind's eye, she knew what she must do. She must create the most beautiful garden – a garden for her Grandy. And it would be filled with every flower imaginable, except roses, of course. For some unknown reason her grandmother hated roses, detested the smell of them, said they made her feel nauseous, and she could not stand to have them in her houses or her gardens. She rushed into the house, bursting with excitement, her young face flushed, her eyes sparkling.

Paula raided her money box, hurriedly breaking it open with her embroidery scissors.

As the pennies and threepenny bits and half crowns and shillings came tumbling out, Emily cried fretfully, 'You'll get into trouble when Grandma finds out you've smashed your new money box and stolen the money.'

Paula shook her head. 'No I won't. And I'm not stealing it. All this is mine. I saved it from my weekly pocket money.' Armed with her precious hoard, and with Emily trotting faithfully after her, she walked purposefully into the town.

As it turned out, Emily became something of a nuisance in Scarborough and Paula soon began to regret bringing her along. Emily wanted to stop for mussels and winkles at the shellfish stand, then for lemonade at a nearby café, claiming she was hungry and thirsty, and in a burst of wilfulness she stamped her foot.

Paula gave her a stern look. 'How can you be hungry? We've just had lunch. And you ate more than anybody. You're growing more like a fat little porky pig every day.' She hurried on, leaving Emily trailing behind, pouting.

'You're mean!' Emily yelled and she increased her pace, endeavouring to keep up with her cousin's longer strides.

Paula glanced back over her shoulder, and said, 'I think you must have a tape worm.'

This was announced so suddenly and so fiercely Emily stopped dead in her tracks. After a moment's shocked silence, she began to run after Paula as fast as her little legs would carry her. 'What a horrid thing to say!' Emily shouted at the top of her lungs. She was terrified by Paula's words, and the mere thought of some huge worm growing inside her propelled her forward, and with urgency. 'I don't have a worm! I don't!' She caught her breath, and gasped, '*Do* I, Paula? Oh please, please tell me I don't. Can Grandma fish It out of me?'

'Oh don't be so silly!' Paula snapped with growing irritation, intent on her purpose, anxious to find a flower shop selling bulbs and plants.

'I don't feel well, Paula. I'm going to be sick!'

'It's all that bread-and-butter pudding.'

'No, it isn't,' Emily wailed. 'It's thinking about my worm. I feel awful. I'm going to throw up,' the child threatened. Emily turned ashen, and her huge eyes swam with tears.

Paula was instantly filled with chagrin. She did love little Emily and she was rarely unkind to her. She put her arm around the five-year-old's heaving shoulders and stroked her soft blonde hair. 'There, there, don't cry, Emily. I'm sure you don't have a tape worm, really I am. Cross my heart and hope to die.'

Eventually Emily stopped crying and searched the pocket of her cardigan for a handkerchief. She blew her nose loudly, then put her hand trustingly in Paula's and trotted along next to her quietly, tamed and subdued as they walked along the sea front past the many quaint old shops. At last she plucked up her courage and ventured timidly, in a whisper, 'But just suppose I do have It? What will I do about my –'

'I forbid you to discuss your nasty worm, you horrid little girl!' Paula exclaimed, her impatience returning. 'You know what, Emily Barkstone, you're a pest. A *terrible* pest. I may send you to Coventry, if you don't shut up.'

Emily was crushed. 'But you always say I'm your *favourite*. Do you mean I'm your favourite pest?' Emily asked, hurrying to stay in step, gazing longingly at her older cousin, whom she worshipped.

Paula started to laugh. She pulled Emily into her arms and hugged the small round child. 'Yes, you're my favourite pest, Apple Dumpling. And because I know you're going to be a good girl and stop behaving like a spoiled baby, I'm going to tell you a very, very special secret.'

Emily was so flattered her tears ceased, and her green eyes widened. 'What kind of secret?'

'I'm going to make a garden for Grandy, a most beautiful garden. That's why we came to Scarborough, to buy the seeds and the things I need. But you mustn't say anything to her. It's a big, big secret.'

'I promise, I promise!' Emily was excited.

For the next half hour, as the two little girls roamed from florist to florist, Paula kept Emily completely enthralled. She was articulate as she spoke about the wonderful things she was going to plant in her garden. She described the colours and the petals and the leaves and the scents of the flowers in detail, and Emily was so utterly enchanted and delighted to be part of such a grown-up enterprise she soon forgot about the tape worm. Slowly, and with painstaking care, Paula finally settled on her grandmother's favourite flowers and made her purchases. They left the last flower shop with a bag brimming with bulbs and packets of seeds and gardening catalogues.

When they reached the top of the street, Emily looked up at Paula and smiled with great sweetness, her round little face dimpling. 'Can we go to the winkle stand now then?'

'Emily! You're being a pest again! You'd better behave yourself.'

Emily paid no attention to this remonstration. 'I've got a better idea. Let's go to the Grand for tea. I'd like that. We can have cream puffs and cucumber sandwiches and scones with strawberry jam and clotted cream and –'

'I don't have any money left,' Paula announced with firmness, hoping to demolish this idea immediately.

'Scribble on the bill like Grandma does,' Emily suggested.

'We're not going to the Grand, and that's final. So shut up. And look, Emily, stop dawdling . . . it's getting late. We'd better hurry now.'

By the time the two little girls arrived at Heron's Nest they had become firm friends again. Emily immediately volunteered to help, wishing to ingratiate herself with her cousin, as always seeking Paula's approbation and her love. She crouched on the ground, offering unsolicited advice in her piping child's voice. After watching Paula for a while, Emily said, 'I bet you've got green fingers, if anybody does, Paula.'

'It's a green thumb,' Paula corrected, without looking up, intent on her work. And she continued digging into the rich soil, planting her first flowers with supreme self-confidence, never doubting for a moment that they would flourish and grow. She was gathering up the garden tools when Emily startled her as she leapt up and let out a wild scream of terror.

'Oh! Oh!' Emily screeched, jumping up and down and brushing her skirt in a frantic fashion. 'Oh! Oh!'

'What's wrong with you, you silly thing? You'll have Grandy out here in a minute and then the garden won't be a surprise.'

'It was a worm! Look, there near your foot! It was crawling on my skirt. Ugh! All slimy and wriggly.' Emily had gone as white as chalk and she was trembling.

Paula was struck by her second inspired idea that day, and she cleverly seized the opportunity. She grabbed the trowel and jabbed at the worm, cutting it in half. She piled soil over it and gave Emily a cheerful and triumphant grin. 'It must have been your tape worm. I expect It left you of its own accord. And I've killed It, so now everything's all right.'

Paula picked up the small box of tools and beckoning Emily to follow, she hurried up the garden path to the potting shed. She stopped suddenly, and after a minute's rapid thought, she said, 'But you'd better not mention anything about It to Grandy, or she might make you take some medicine just to be sure you don't get another.'

Emily shuddered at the very idea.

148

Later that same summer, when Paula and Emily came back to the villa by the sea, they could hardly contain themselves when they saw the garden in full bloom. A profusion of flowers had sprouted up during their absence, and the many different species Paula had selected splashed the dark earth with their brilliant paintbox hues.

Emma was touched when, on their first day at Heron's Nest, the two girls led her through the garden, showing her everything that Paula had planted, looking up at her expectantly, watching her face for her reactions. Emily told her all about their trip into Scarborough although she was careful to omit any mention of worms. Emma had been aware of the little expedition on that Saturday in the spring, but she pretended to be surprised. She praised them both for being so clever, and, recognizing Paula's potential as a budding horticulturist, she had encouraged her to pursue her hobby.

And so Paula's long and passionate love affair with gardening began that year. She had not stopped planting, weeding, pruning and hoeing since then.

With Emma's approval she had cultivated vegetable and herb gardens on her grandmother's Yorkshire estate, and eventually she had created the now famous Rhododendron Walk. The Walk took her years to plan, plant and grow, and it was another example of her determination to excel at whatever she did, and in this instance it was a rather spectacular example at that.

But of all the gardens Paula had created, the one at Heron's Nest remained the dearest.

She was reminded of it this afternoon, seventeen years after she had started it, as she stood up and stretched. She pulled off her gardening gloves, placed them on the wheelbarrow, stepped back to regard the rockery.

Finally it's beginning to take shape, she thought. Making Edwin Fairley's garden beautiful was giving her as much pleasure as her first garden had done.

After Edwin Fairley's death, Jim had inherited his house in Harrogate called Long Meadow. It was here that Paula had come to live as a bride almost a year ago. Although the house was sound and in good repair, it was badly in need of remodelling as well as redecorating. Conversely, Edwin Fairley had seen to it that his gardener had tended the grounds religiously. Nevertheless, they were bereft of colour since little replenishing had been done as flowers and flowering shrubs had died. Paula had seen these deficiencies the moment it became hers, and had itched to start working on it. However, the house took precedence; yet somehow she managed to cope with both at the same time, bringing wholly new aspects and fresh dimensions to both.

Glancing at the herbaceous borders she decided that her dogged toil over the last eleven months *had* been worthwhile. The garden was her private world, and here she found escape and emotional enrichment as her business and personal problems fled.

Well, for a short while. For the last hour or so she had not given one thought to their quarrel of the night before. Now the memory of their heated words edged back. The problem was that Jim could be so stubborn. But then, so could she, and very often to her own annoyance. We both have to be more flexible, she thought, otherwise we're always going to be at loggerheads about certain matters. The funny thing was they hadn't really had any disagreements before their marriage, and no serious quarrels until the problem of Edwina had arisen. They had certainly locked horns about her. She loathed her aunt; Jim was much taken with her. Therein lay the problem.

Quite unexpectedly, Paula remembered something her grandmother had said to her last year, words spoken with love immediately prior to her wedding. They echoed with great clarity in her mind.

'Love is a handful of seeds, marriage the garden,' Emma had said softly. 'And like your gardens, Paula, marriage requires total commitment, hard work, and a great deal of love and care. Be ruthless with the weeds. Pull them out before they take hold. Bring the same dedication to your marriage that you do to your gardens and everything will be all right. Remember that a marriage has to be constantly replenished too, if you want it to flourish . . .'

Such wise words, Paula thought, turning them over in her mind. She leaned back in the chair and closed her eyes. Their quarrel was a weed, wasn't it? So she must uproot it. At once. Yes, she must toss it aside before it took hold. The only way to do that was to dismiss their differences about Edwina.

Paula opened her eyes and smiled to herself. She felt better all of a sudden. She pulled off her muddy Wellington boots, and put on her shoes, and went into the house. She loved Jim. He loved her. Surely that was all that really mattered. Her heart felt lighter as she flew up the stairs to the nursery and their children.

16

Nora, the nursemaid who looked after the Fairley twins, sat sewing in a rocking chair in the nursery. As Paula's smiling face appeared around the door, she brought her finger to her lips and made a soft shushing sound.

Paula immediately nodded her understanding, mouthed silently, 'I'll be back in a while. I'm going to take a bath.'

After luxuriating in a hot tub for fifteen minutes, Paula felt rejuvenated. But as she dried herself vigorously she had to admit that although the warm water had eased her tired body, this lovely sense of well being sprang from the decision she had just made in the garden to be more understanding about Jim's feelings for Edwina. Yes, it was the only attitude she could take, she saw that clearer than ever. To adopt any other stance would be utterly self-defeating. She would simply rise above it all, as Grandy would do in similar circumstances. Her grandmother was too big a woman to succumb to pettiness, and she would try her level best to act exactly in the same way.

Paula put on a towelling robe and went back into the bedroom. This was spacious, with a high ceiling and a bay window overlooking the gardens, and it bore no resemblance to the way it had looked when Edwin Fairley had been alive. The first day Paula had seen the room her heart sank as she had stood staring in horror at the dark blue flocked wallpaper and the heavy, ponderous mahogany furniture crammed into the space. The bedroom had reflected the rest of the Victorian house, which was a dubious monument to a bygone age. All of the rooms had been old-fashioned, dark, lifeless and depressing. The house had oppressed her with its gloomy, shadow-filled rooms and antiquated furniture and ornate festooned draperies and ugly lamps. She had wondered dismally how she could ever live at Long Meadow with any degree of comfort or happiness, or bring up children in such a bleak and dreary ambiance.

But Jim had insisted they move in, and he had refused point blank to take even one look at the lovely old farmhouse which Winston had found for her at West Tanfield. And so she had been obliged to acquiesce to keep the peace, but only with the understanding that Jim allowed her *carte blanche* to renovate and redecorate the entire house. Fortunately he had agreed, and this she had done immediately, before he had a chance to change his mind, or tried to persuade her to live in the midst of the hopeless muddle of nondescript furnishings which his grandfather had so assiduously accumulated during his lifetime. The refurbishing of the house had been her parents' wedding gift to them, and her mother had helped her create a totally new look, and with such efficiency, boldness and speed even Emma had been surprised, and somewhat amused by their ruthlessness. They threw out everything except a few good pieces of furniture, including Edwin's desk, a Venetian mirror and a French Provincial armoire of light oak, as well as several relatively valuable oil paintings. The pale pastel colours she and Daisy had selected for the rooms instantly brought an airy lightness to the house and opened it up to introduce a feeling of great spaciousness and freedom. Pretty fabrics, porcelain and jade lamps, and the charming country antiques her mother had found added charm, liveliness, understated elegance and comfort.

The dark blue bedroom was transformed into a bower of yellow, white, peach and pale green, with these clear colours repeated throughout in the floral wallpaper and matching fabrics and in the Chinese lamps. Although Jim had voiced the opinion that the white carpeting was rather impractical, he had afterwards acknowledged that the room was lovely and in perfect taste. And to Paula's relief he had liked the rest of the house.

Their bedroom looked sunny and restful this afternoon as she padded across the floor to the dressing table which took pride of place in the wide and curving bay window. She sat down, and, after brushing her hair, she applied her makeup in readiness for the evening ahead. Her thoughts lingered on her grandmother. How lovely she had looked at the christening, and she had been so charming and gracious, so alive with energy and spirit, everyone had paled in comparison. Jim had said the same things about her grandmother over dinner on Saturday night at the Red Lion in South Stainley, where they had gone to dine alone. And then he had lapsed into one of his strange silences for a few minutes and she had known he was thinking of his grandfather.

Paula put down her lipstick, and swivelled in the chair, and sat staring into space, remembering the night Jim had first brought her to this house to meet Sir Edwin Fairley KC.

The scene played for her again, vividly alive in her mind.

He had been dozing in front of the fire in the small, pine-panelled library, and he had roused himself when they arrived, had walked across the floor, smiling warmly, his hand outstretched, a frail, white-haired old man, and lovely in his gentleness and courtesy. When he had been only a few feet away from her his step had faltered as he had seen her more clearly in the dimming light. Shock struck his face and he had looked as if he had seen a ghost as Jim had introduced them. And of course he had. He had seen a reflection of Emma Harte in *her*, although she and Jim had not understood this at that time. But he must have dismissed the resemblance as mere coincidence because he had recovered himself almost immediately. And then during drinks he had asked her what she did, and she had said she worked for her grandmother, Emma Harte, as Jim did, but that she was employed at the stores. He had started violently in the chair and stifled a gasp, and stared at her more intently. His eyes were suddenly alive with burgeoning interest and an unveiled and avid curiosity. He had asked her about her parents, and her life, and she had answered him frankly, and he had smiled and nodded and patted her hand and told her she was a lovely young woman, that he approved of this match. She had met him several times after that first occasion, and he had never been anything but welcoming, obviously overjoyed to see her. After she and Jim had broken up he had apparently been disconsolate, and extremely distressed as their rift had widened, Jim had told her.

Sir Edwin had died before they were reconciled. And then married, with Emma's blessing.

She had asked her grandmother innumerable questions about Edwin, once *their* old story was out in the open and no longer relegated to the closet along with the other skeletons Emma had hidden there.

Emma, who had hitherto glossed over certain aspects of her early life, had suddenly been quite willing to talk, and she had been surprisingly candid. She had told Paula how she had become involved with Edwin when she had been a servant at Fairley Hall, how they had drawn together after both of their mothers had died. She spoke of the moors and the Top of the World and the cave where they had sheltered from the raging storm and where Edwin had seduced her. 'Oh, but Edwin Fairley wasn't a bad person,' Grandy had said to her only a few weeks ago, when they had been discussing things again. 'Just terribly, *terribly* weak, and afraid of his father, and hidebound to his class. Naturally. That was the way it was in those days. We're going back over sixty years, you know. Still, I've often wished that he hadn't been so cowardly, that he had made some sort of effort to help me when I was carrying his child. Then perhaps I wouldn't have hated him so much.'

Emma had shrugged. 'But there you are, that's the way it happened. I survived, didn't I. I was sixteen and about to have an illegitimate child, and because I didn't want to bring shame to my father, I ran away to Leeds. To Blackie. He was my only friend in my dreadful predicament. And Laura, of course, though Blackie wasn't married to my lovely Laura at the time. I had the baby, obviously. You know the rest.'

Paula had asked her why she had called the child Edwina. 'A peculiar, rather unfortunate, slip of the tongue,' Emma had replied with a dry laugh. 'When I wasn't thinking. Or rather, perhaps I should say when I was thinking about Edwin.'

'But how on earth did you manage, Grandma?' Paula had next asked, her eyes full and her heart aching as she had pictured the young Emma's awful ordeal, one she had had to face alone and penniless and without her family.

'Ah well, I had a couple of things going for me,' Emma had remarked with an odd smile. 'And they pulled me through.' Paula had quietly insisted she elaborate further, and Emma had said, 'Well, let's see. I had my strength of character, my physical stamina, a few brains, not such bad looks, and most importantly an implacable will to succeed. Plus, a hell of a lot of courage, now that I think about it. But that's enough of my life story today.' And at this point Emma had brought the conversation to an abrupt halt.

Now Paula thought: Edwin Fairley was not only weak, he was unconscionable in the way he treated her. She shifted her thoughts to her grandmother and was overwhelmed with pride, and enormous love for her. Emma Harte had been strong, and because of her great strength and her immense courage she had conquered the whole damned world. She had stood tall, and she still stood tall. Edwina suddenly flashed through her mind. That child born a Fairley had caused Emma nothing but heartache from the day she had been born. And that's one of the reasons I can't bear being near her, Paula muttered. Why doesn't Jim understand? she asked herself, and squashed this question instantly. Edwina had caused *her* problems recently, but only because she herself had allowed that to happen. Edwina is insignificant in the scheme of things. Grandy said so weeks ago, and as usual she is absolutely right.

The clock struck the half hour and Paula glanced at it, saw that it was four-thirty. She had no more time to waste, she realized, pulling herself away from her reflections. Jumping up she went to her clothes closet, found a pair of grey flannel trousers and a white silk shirt, dressed in them swiftly. And her step had a ring of decisiveness as she walked across the upstairs hall and into the nursery.

Nora peered out of the tiny kitchen, once a large cupboard that Paula had had remodelled into a nursery pantry. She was holding a baby's milk bottle and said, 'I was about to feed them, Mrs Fairley.'

'Then I'm just in time to help you, Nora.' Paula bent over the cot nearest to her. Tessa was now wide awake, gazing up at her through eyes as stunningly green as her great-grandmother's, and she suddenly began to gurgle and kick her little fat legs in the air. Paula picked up her daughter, holding her tightly, kissing the child's fuzzy head and soft downy cheek, her heart clenching with love and she held Tessa for a second longer before returning her to the cot. Immediately the baby girl began to cry.

Paula glanced down at Tessa and there was joyful laughter in her voice as she said, 'Well, my goodness, aren't you the rumbustious little one, Miss Fairley. But we don't play favourites in this family. I have to give your brother a few kisses too, you know, and a little bit of attention as well.'

Almost as if she had understood the baby girl stopped her wailing.

Paula stepped over to the other cot to see Lorne staring at her solemnly. She lifted him out, hugging him as fiercely as she had his sister, experiencing the same profound emotions of protectiveness and tender love.

'Oh you darling,' she whispered against his cheek, so warm, and wet with slaver, 'Your father is right, you're a little poppet.' She kissed Lorne, held him away from her, and shook her head, grinning broadly at him. 'But you're always so serious, Lorne. You remind me of a little old man. Goodness me, you have such ancient worldly eyes, and you gaze at me as if there's nothing you don't know.'

Paula walked over to the small loveseat in front of the windows and sat down. She bounced Lorne up and down on her knees and the baby seemed to enjoy this, since he at once started to chortle and waved his clenched fists as if he was happy and glad to be alive.

'I'll feed Lorne, since I have him, Nora, and you can take care of his more vocal sister,' Paula said.

'Yes, Mrs Fairley.' Nora smiled at her, glanced over at Tessa's cot. 'She is a little minx, I must admit. She certainly wants to make sure we all know she's here.'

Paula and Nora chatted desultorily about the babies and matters pertaining to their care as they fed the twins. At one moment Paula explained that she had adjusted her timetable and office hours again, so that she could fit in with the schedule the twins were currently following and went on: 'So I'll be home early every day, to help you feed and bathe them. But I won't be able to spend bath time with you tonight, I'm afraid, Nora. We're having guests for drinks, before we go out to dinner.'

'Yes, I understand, Mrs Fairley.' Nora brought Tessa upright in her arms. She laid the baby against her shoulder and patted her back. The little girl burped loudly, and several times.

This brought a smile to Paula's face.

Nora said, 'Isn't she a pickle! She'll find a way to make herself heard, no matter what. But she's a good baby, so is Lorne.'

Paula nodded. 'Let's be thankful for that. But, you know, both my mother and my grandmother seem to think that Tessa's going to be the maverick in the family.' She smiled to herself, mulling this over and leaned back against the cushions, concentrating on Lorne.

Paula cherished these quiet times with her children, away from the bustle and frantic pace of her hectic working life. All was peace and gentleness in the large yet cosy nursery, with its white-painted walls and furniture, blue-and-pink accents and nursery-rhyme paintings hanging on the walls. Golden sunlight filtered in through the filmy curtains blowing gently in the light breeze and there were the mingled smells of babies and talcum powder and boiled milk and freshly-ironed clothes permeating the air. She looked down at her son, so contentedly sucking on his bottle, and she stroked his small fair head. How lucky I am, she mused. I have so much to be thankful for . . . these adorable healthy beautiful babies . . . Grandy and my parents . . . a job that excites me, and, most important of all, the most wonderful husband. Quite suddenly she couldn't wait for Jim to get home from the newspaper so that she could tell him how much she loved him and how much she regretted their ridiculous quarrels about their aunt.

'I'm glad everything's gone well on your first day, Emily, but don't overdo it this week. You sound awfully tired,' Paula said. 'Please try and pace yourself properly.' She sat back in the chair, dragging the telephone across the white wicker desk as she did.

'Oh yes, I will, don't worry,' Emily exclaimed, her voice rising slightly as it came over the wire. 'Grandy's already told me to keep regular office hours, not to try and gulp everything down all at once. But it's so exciting here at Genret, Paula, and I've so much to absorb and learn. Len Harvey is a super person, we're going to get on fine together. He says we'll probably go to Hong Kong next month. On a buying trip. We may even go into Mainland China. Something to do with purchasing pigs' bristles or whiskers.'

Paula's laugh rang out. 'What on earth are you talking about?'

'*Brushes*. Made of pig's bristles. They're the best, so I understand. Paula . . . it's quite amazing here. I hadn't realized how much merchandise we bought abroad. Genret is the biggest importing company in England. Well, *one* of the biggest. We stock everything . . . false eyelashes, wigs, cosmetics, silks and satins, pots and pans –'

'Not to mention pigs' whiskers,' Paula teased. 'Yes, I knew that, Emily, and I think this job is going to be marvellous for you. A lot of responsibility – but I know you can handle it. To tell you the truth, Apple Dumpling, I miss you already, and this is only your first day over there.'

'I feel the same way. I shall miss working with you, too. Still, it's not as if we're disappearing from each other's lives. What made you call me Apple Dumping just then? You haven't for years.'

Paula smiled into the phone. 'I've been gardening today, making a rockery, and I kept thinking about the first garden I planted . . . at Heron's Nest. Do you remember that day I took you into Scarborough –'

'How could I ever forget it. I've been terrified of worms ever since,' Emily cut in with a light laugh. 'And I *was* an apple dumpling then, wasn't I? More like a roly-poly butterball.'

'But not any more, little one. Listen, would you like to join us for dinner tonight? We're going to the Granby . . . at least I think that's where Jim's decided to take us.'

'I'd love to, but I can't, I'm afraid. Anyway, who's *us*?'

'Sally, Anthony and Aunt Edwina.'

'Oh God, I don't envy you, Paula,' Emily groaned. 'I would come if I could, just to give *you* moral support. However –' she broke off and giggled. 'I have a rather special date.'

'*Oh!* Who with?'

'My secret lover.'

'And who's that?' Paula asked quickly, her curiosity aroused.

'If I told you he'd no longer be my secret lover, now would he?' Emily replied mysteriously. 'He's someone extra special and gorgeous, and when the time comes – if it comes, that is – you'll be the first to know.' Laughter shaded her voice.

'Have I met him?' Paula probed, as usual feeling protective of Emily.

'I refuse to say one more word about him.' Wanting to change the subject, Emily asked in a more sober tone, 'By the way, why did Grandy go to London this afternoon?'

'She said something about pulling a new wardrobe together, for her trip with Blackie to far-flung places. Why do you ask?'

'That's what she said to me, but I just wondered if there was another reason. She always tells *you* everything.'

'What other reason *could* there be?' Paula asked, sounding baffled.

'Well . . . she popped in to see me a little while ago, and she looked as if she was on the war path. You know that expression she gets on her face when she's about to do battle. *Implacable* is the best way to describe it, I suppose.'

Paula was thoughtful at the other end of the phone. She stared out at the garden, a frown marring her smooth brow. 'I'm sure she doesn't have any business in London, Emily,' she said after a short pause, and laughed dismissively. 'Besides, you ought to know by now that Grandy always looks implacable. It's become her normal expression. Also, she was probably in a hurry when you saw her. Mummy and Daddy were driving back with her, and she wouldn't have wanted to keep them waiting in the car. I know the clothes are preoccupying her. She told me yesterday that they're going to be hitting a lot of different climates, and that they'll be gone for three months. Let's face it, Emily, she has quite a task ahead of her selecting the appropriate things.'

'Perhaps you're right,' Emily conceded slowly, not entirely convinced. 'She's very excited by the trip, Paula. She's done nothing but talk about it to me all weekend.'

'It'll do her good, since it's the first real holiday she's had in years. And she can't wait to see Philip, and visit Dunoon. She always had such wonderful times there with my grandfather. And listen, Dumpling darling, talking of my baby brother, I'm going to have to hang up. When he telephoned from Sydney yesterday I promised I'd write to him today, and tell him all about the christening. I must get the letter out of the way before Jim gets home.'

'I understand. Thanks for ringing, Paula, and I'll see you later in the week. Give Philip my love. Bye.'

Paula murmured her goodbye, replaced the receiver, and immediately started her letter to Philip. Her young brother was recuperating from a bout of pneumonia, and she and her parents and her grandmother had all agreed it was unfair and unnecessary to drag him from Australia just for one day. As she wrote, Paula relived the weekend, filling the letter with details about the church ceremony, the reception afterwards, along with news of the entire family and their mutual friends, especially the O'Neills and the Kallinskis.

She stopped after three pages in her small neat script and looked up, thinking about Philip. They had always been close and were good friends, and she missed him. She was aware that Philip missed her too, and their parents and Grandy, and that he was sometimes awfully homesick for England. On the other hand, Dunoon, their sheep station at Coonamble in New South Wales, had fired his imagination since his childhood, and she believed it now held his complete affection. Also, running their vast Australian holdings, which their grandfather, Paul McGill, had left Emma, was a tremendous challenge. She knew Philip more than relished his job. He had settled down at last in this past year, and had started to make a full and complete life for himself out there, and she was glad of that. She finished the letter, addressed and sealed the envelope, then stood up, walked to the far end of the room. She bent down and picked up several blossoms which had dropped off a bright pink azalea, laid them in an ashtray on a ceramic drum table and then glanced around, wondering whether to serve drinks in here or in the drawing room.

Although Paula thought of this favourite room as her very own private spot in the house, it had fallen into general use lately. She often found Jim reading here, and most of their guests automatically gravitated to it. In actuality the room was a conservatory, typical of those built on to Victorian mansions in the second half of the nineteenth century, after Joseph Paxton had pioneered the use of iron girders as supports for glass houses. Paula considered the large conservatory, like the garden, one of the few real assets at Long Meadow. It was Gothic in design, and she had filled it with tropical green plants, small trees, and exotic orchids, plus a lovely array of small and colourful flowering shrubs. The fir green carpeting, and the green-and-white ivy print she had chosen for the wicker furniture and skirted tables produced a cool restful ambiance, and the conservatory appeared to flow out into the grounds beyond the glass walls. Since Paula's redecoration it provided an extra sitting room as well as a study for her in the refreshing environment of a garden that grew the year round.

Turning around, her eyes fell on one of her prized hydrangeas and she was concerned to see that it had developed discoloured edges. She continued to examine it thoughtfully until the shrilling telephone forced her to return to her desk. She answered it with a bright 'Hello?'

'And how's the little mother?' Miranda O'Neill asked in her lovely, lilting voice.

'I'm fine, Merry, how're you, lovey?'

'Exhausted, if you want to know the truth. I've had my nose to the grindstone all day, and I was in the office most of yesterday, developing my idea for the Harte boutiques in our hotels. I believe I've formulated some really workable plans. I want to show them to my father tomorrow, and then I thought we might get together later in the week, if you have time.'

'Of course I do, and I must say you've been awfully fast, and extremely diligent.'

'Thanks. Aunt Emma was most enthusiastic when I spoke to her on Saturday, and I didn't want to lose any time. As your grandmother always says, time is money. Besides, if we're going to do it, the areas for the boutiques must be included in the new architectural blueprints, and those will be on the drawing board soon.'

'I realize there's a time element involved here, because of your building and remodelling programme, Merry. So let's meet on Wednesday. About two o'clock?'

'That's perfect for me, and let's do it in my office.' Miranda chuckled, said, 'Isn't it fabulous news about Aunt Emma going off on a world tour with Grandpops? We're all thrilled at home.'

'So are we . . . it'll do them both good.'

Merry said: 'You should have seen him this morning. I couldn't believe it when he showed up at the office bright and early. There he was behind his desk, where he hadn't been for months, making phone calls, hustling and bustling, and driving that poor old secretary of his crazy. He kept saying to her, "First Class, *First Class*, and all the way, Gertie! This has to be a deluxe trip." Aunt Emma agreeing to go with him has given him a new lease on life, not that he really needed one, actually, since he's always so *up*, and bubbly. But do you know, he got quite miffed with me when I mentioned my idea about the boutiques. He actually bellowed at me to keep Emma out of it, said that he didn't want my piddling bit of business interfering with his plan with a capital P. It took me ages to calm him down.'

'How did you manage to do that?' Paula asked, laughing under her breath, trying to envisage Blackie in a rage which was rather difficult to do.

'When I finally got a word in edgeways, I said Aunt Emma wasn't involved, that you were, and that *we* could cope very well without *either* of them. Then he beamed and said I was his clever darling girl, but just to be sure to keep out of his way for the next few days, because he was very preoccupied and extremely busy. Anybody would think they were going off on a honeymoon.'

'Well, he did give her the ring, you know, Merry.'

'Isn't it *sweet*. They're a couple of lovely old dears, aren't they?'

Paula burst out laughing. 'I'd hardly characterize *my* grandmother and *your* grandfather as a couple of *old dears*. Blackie and Emma are more like fire-crackers, in my opinion. And weren't you the one who told me only the other day that they were incorrigible when they got together?' Paula reminded Miranda.

Merry had the good grace to laugh with Paula, and she admitted, 'That's true, I did, and you're right. And by the way, talking of Aunt Emma, I don't know what to buy her for her eightieth birthday. I've been wracking my brains for days. Any suggestions?'

'You've got to be joking! We all have the same problem. Mummy and Daddy were discussing it with me over lunch today. And Emily's been nagging me to think of something she can get. Frankly, I'm at a loss, like you and everyone else.'

'Well, let's compare notes again on Wednesday,' Merry said. 'I'd better go, Paula. My father's waiting for me. We have to go over some of my rough drafts for the press release – about the acquisition of the hotel in New York. I hope to God he likes *one* of the versions, otherwise I'm going to be at my desk until midnight. Not that that would be anything unusual,' Miranda grumbled. 'I seem to have become a work horse lately. No wonder I don't have any private life these days.'

'I just told Emily to take it easy at Genret. And you'd better do the same, Merry,' Paula cautioned.

'Listen who's talking!' Miranda said, and laughed hollowly.

17

Since the conservatory opened directly off the marble-floored entrance hall, Paula heard Jim's footsteps the moment he entered the house. She was standing near the fading hydrangea plant, holding the discoloured leaf in her hand, and she turned, expectancy and warmth filling her face.

'Hello, darling,' she said, as he came down the two steps, and moved swiftly towards him, her eagerness to see him most apparent.

'Hello,' he replied.

They met in the centre of the room. He gave her a light kiss, then lowered himself into a chair without saying another word.

Paula stood staring down at him, puzzlement in her eyes. He had sounded so apathetic and the kiss was so perfunctory she knew he was not himself. She said instantly, 'Is there something the matter, Jim?'

He shook his head. 'Just tired,' he said, smiling that bland, dismissive smile she had come to know so well. 'There was an accident on the Harrogate road, quite a pile up of cars because of it, and it slowed the traffic. We crawled along for miles. Frustrating . . . exhausting, actually.'

'How awful. I'm sorry. That's all you needed. Let me fix you a drink,' she suggested, not entirely satisfied with this explanation but making up her mind not to press too hard for the moment.

'That's a good idea,' he exclaimed in a stronger tone. 'Thanks, a gin-and-tonic should hit the spot.'

'I'll just go for some ice,' she said, and made to leave the conservatory.

'Ring for Meg. She can bring it.' He frowned. 'The bell's not broken again, is it?'

'No, but it'll be quicker if I go,' Paula said, pausing with one foot on the step, glancing over her shoulder.

'I wonder, sometimes, why we have a maid,' he said with a hint of irritation, looking up, levelling his pale greyish-blue eyes on her.

She stared back at him, detecting criticism in his tone and manner, but she remarked with evenness, 'She's awfully busy right now, and anyway Grandy brought us up not to be overly dependent on servants, as I've told you so many times.' Not waiting for a response she hurried out, but she heard his pained sigh as she went into the hall. Maybe it *is* only weariness, a hard day at the paper, the difficult drive home, plus the hectic weekend, Paula thought, endeavouring to persuade herself these were the real reasons for his peculiar mood. He wasn't often moody, at least not exactly like this. As she pushed open the kitchen door she noticed she was still holding the leaf. It was mangled in her hand. Relax, she instructed herself, his moodiness means nothing. He'll be more like himself after a drink.

Meg said, 'Do you think I've made enough canapés, Mrs Fairley?' She indicated the silver tray, pausing in her work.

'Yes, that's plenty, Meg, and they look delicious. Thank you. Could you fill the ice bucket please?' Whilst the maid busied herself at the refrigerator Paula threw the leaf in the rubbish bin and washed her hands at the kitchen sink.

Jim had risen in her absence and he was standing looking out into the garden when Paula went back to the conservatory with the ice. His face was in profile, nonetheless she could not fail to miss the morose curve of his mouth, and when he swung around his eyes were vague.

Questions flew to her tongue, but she bit them back and hurried to the skirted table which held bottles and a tray of glasses. Pouring his gin-and-tonic, she said without turning around, 'I thought we'd have drinks in here later, or do you prefer the drawing room?'

'Wherever you wish,' he replied in an uninterested voice.

Striving for a normal manner, she continued steadily, 'Did you book at the Granby after all, Jim?'

'Yes. We have a table reserved for eight thirty. Anthony called earlier today and said they wouldn't be able to get here until seven fifteen. That gives us an hour to relax.'

'Yes.' Anxiety was rising in her. He *was* strange, there were no two ways about it, and she wondered if their quarrel of the previous evening still lingered in the back of his mind, rankled perhaps. But why would it? He had won, and anyway he had been chatty and pleasant at breakfast. But she resolved to get to the root of whatever was bothering him. She also decided to have a vodka-and-tonic, even though she hardly ever drank hard liquor.

Jim seemed to visibly cheer up as he sipped his drink. He lit a cigarette, asked casually, 'Heard from anybody today?'

'Emily, Merry O'Neill. And Grandy, of course. She rang me just after you left this morning to let me know she was going to London for a few days.' Paula now looked directly at him, took a deep breath. 'Why are we making small talk, Jim, when you're troubled? I know something's wrong. Please tell me what it is, darling.'

He was silent.

She leaned forward intently, her unwavering eyes holding his. 'Look, I want to know what's bothering you,' she insisted.

Jim sighed heavily. 'I suppose there's no point putting it off . . . I had a bit of a set-to with Winston today, and –'

Paula laughed with relief. 'Is that all! Well, you've had clashes with him before, and they always blow over. So will this –'

'I've resigned,' Jim announced flatly.

She looked at him uncomprehendingly, totally at a loss for words. Slowly she put down her drink. Her dark brows drew together in a frown. '*Resigned?*'

'As managing director of the company, that is,' he added quickly. 'Effective immediately.'

Thunderstruck, she continued to gape at him. She found her voice and it rose slightly as she asked, 'But *why*? And why didn't you mention it to me, tell me what was on your mind? I simply don't understand . . .' She did not finish her sentence, sat tensely in the chair.

'There was nothing to discuss. You see, I didn't know I was going to resign – until I did.'

'Jim, this is perfectly ridiculous,' she said, attempting a laugh. 'Just because you had a little row with Winston doesn't mean you have to do something as drastic as this . . . after all, Grandy has the final word, you know that. She appointed you, she'll reinstate you at once. She'll put Winston straight, deal with him. Look, I'll speak to her tomorrow, ring her first thing in the morning.' She gave him an encouraging smile, but it faltered as he held up his hand with an abrupt movement that was uncharacteristic.

'I'm afraid you're misunderstanding me. Winston didn't force me to resign, or anything like that, if that's what you're thinking. I did so of my own accord. I wanted to, and rather badly, although I must admit, in all truthfulness, that

I didn't realize this until the opportunity presented itself. So I certainly don't want to be reinstated.'

'But why not, for heaven's sake?' she cried, her perplexity and concern mounting, rising to the surface to cloud her face.

'Because I don't like the job. Never have. When Winston came to see me this morning, he asked me point blank if I wished to continue as managing director, and as he was speaking I knew – really *knew*, Paula – that I didn't. I've never been particularly good at administrative work, or interested in it, and I told Winston so, and he said he'd sensed this for some time. He pointed out that perhaps it would be better if I stuck to journalism, ran the papers but not the company. I thoroughly agree with him, so I stepped down. That's all there is to it, actually,' he shrugged, smiled faintly.

'*All there is to it*,' she echoed incredulously. She was aghast at what he had done, and at his attitude. 'I don't believe I'm hearing *you* say these things. You're acting as if it didn't matter, as if this wasn't serious, when it's terribly serious. And you're being so cavalier, so dismissive, I'm absolutely staggered.'

'Don't get so het up. Frankly, *I'm* filled with relief.'

'Relief should be the last thing on your mind,' she said in a small dismayed voice. 'What about duty? Responsibility? Grandy showed a great deal of faith in you, put her trust in you when she appointed you managing director last year. *I* think you've let her down, and rather badly.'

'I'm sorry you feel that way, Paula, because I must disagree with you. I haven't let Grandy down,' he protested. 'I'm still going to be managing editor in charge of two of the most important newspapers in the Consolidated group. I'll be doing what I do best, being a newspaperman, and a damned good one at that.' He sat back, crossed his legs, and returned her penetrating stare with an unblinking gaze. His expression was adamant.

'And who's going to run the company, now that you've stepped down?'

'Winston, of course.'

'You know very well he doesn't want that job.'

'Neither do I.'

Paula's lips drew together in aggravation. Another thought struck her and she exclaimed fiercely, 'I hope this sudden and rather extraordinary decision of yours doesn't mean that Grandy will have to cancel her trip with Blackie. She really needs that holiday. What did she say? I presume you've told her.'

'Naturally I've told her. Winston and I walked over to the store at lunch time for a meeting with her. Your grandmother accepted my resignation, Winston's agreed to take the job, and he didn't seem very perturbed about the idea either. Grandy isn't going to cancel her holiday, rest assured of that.' He leaned forward and clasped her hand in his. 'Come on, relax. You're the one who's more upset than anyone. Grandy and Winston respect my decision. They didn't quibble. In fact, there was very little discussion . . . it was rather cut and dried, actually.'

'You've simply misunderstood their reactions,' she murmured filled with misery.

Jim laughed. 'Now *you're* being ridiculous, Paula. I know them both very well and I can assure you that everything is all right.'

Paula could think of no easy reply to this statement. She was astonished at his lack of insight, and his assumption that things were on an even keel showed extremely flawed judgement on his part. Jim obviously had no conception of what made her grandmother and Winston tick. *She* didn't have to think twice to know that they had accepted the situation because they had had no alternative. They would pull together to keep the company running smoothly. That's *our* way she thought. We do our duty, accept responsibility, no matter how difficult that is. Things were far from *all right*, as he so glibly put it.

Jim was watching her, trying to ascertain what she was thinking but her violet eyes were veiled, unreadable. He said anxiously, 'Please try to see my point of view, understand my feelings about the situation. Your grandmother and Winston do. And don't let's argue about my resignation. Since it's a *fait accompli* this is all rather silly, wouldn't you say?'

Paula said nothing. She leaned back in her chair, extracted her hand quietly, and reached for her drink. She took a quick sip. There was a protracted silence before she said, 'Jim, I do wish you'd reconsider . . . there are other things involved here. Grandy was going to tell you this herself later in the week, but I know she won't mind if *I* tell you *now*. She's going to change her will. At the moment her shares in the newspaper company are part of the assets of Harte Enterprises, which as you know my cousins are to inherit. But she's decided to leave the newspaper shares to the twins – our children – so I know it's important to her that you're totally involved with the newspaper company and on every level. I don't care what she said to you this morning, I'm absolutely convinced she's terribly disappointed deep down because you've chosen to step away from the managerial side –'

Jim's brief laugh stopped her short. She looked at him, searched his face, wondering if she had imagined the edge to that laugh.

He said patiently in a soft, smooth voice, 'Paula, whether I'm managing director, managing editor or both, or neither, for that matter, your grandmother will still change her will. She'll leave those shares to our children no matter what and for several good reasons.'

'What reasons?'

'They're Fairleys, for one thing, and then there's her guilt.'

Paula blinked, for a second not understanding what he was getting at, then quite suddenly she had a flash of insight, and she stared at him intently. She hoped she had misunderstood the implication behind his words. She took a deep breath to steady herself, and asked very slowly, 'Her guilt about *what* exactly?'

'Wresting the *Yorkshire Morning Gazette* away from my grandfather, grabbing control of the company,' he said off-handedly, lighting a cigarette.

'You make it sound as if she stole it!' Paula tersely exclaimed. 'You know very well that your grandfather ran that newspaper into the ground, and that certainly had nothing to do with Grandy. You've said often enough that he was a brilliant barrister but a lousy businessman. Surely I don't have to remind you that the other shareholders begged Grandy to take over. She bailed them out – and your grandfather, for that matter. He made a lot of money on his shares.'

'Yes, you're correct – especially about him mismanaging the paper, but I suppose he would have muddled through, limped along somehow and retained control, if your grandmother hadn't swooped down and scooped it up.' He gulped some of his drink, drew on his cigarette.

'The paper would have gone bankrupt! Then where would your grandfather have been?' She glared at him. 'In a mess, that's where!'

'Look here, Paula, don't sound so shocked. I'm only reminding you of the facts. We both know that Grandy ruined the Fairleys.' He gave her an easy lopsided smile. 'We're both adults, so we'd be rather silly if we tried to sweep all that under the rug, just because you and I are married. What happened did *actually* happen, you know. You and I are not going to change it, and it's certainly nonsensical for us to quarrel about it now, so long after the event.'

Paula recoiled, gaping at him. Dismay had lodged like a rock in the pit of her stomach and she was shaking inside. As his words echoed in her head, her patience evaporated, the tension of the last few weeks rose up in her, and something snapped all of a sudden. 'She no more ruined the Fairleys than I did! It just so happens that Adam Fairley and that eldest son of his, Gerald, did it all by themselves. Whether you want to believe it or not, your great-grandfather and great-uncle were negligent, stupid, self-indulgent and very poor businessmen. And besides, even if she had ruined them, I for one wouldn't blame her. I'd applaud her for settling the score. The Fairleys treated my grandmother abominably. And as for your sainted grandfather, what he did to her was . . . was unspeakable!' she gasped. 'Unconscionable, do you hear! Fine upstanding young man Edwin was, wasn't he? Getting her pregnant at sixteen and then leaving her to fend for herself. He didn't even lift a finger to help her. As for –'

'I know all that –' Jim began, wondering how to placate her, stop this flow of angry words.

She cut him off peremptorily. 'What you don't know perhaps is that your great-uncle Gerald tried to rape her, and believe you me, no woman ever forgets the man who has attempted *rape* on her! So don't start presenting a case for the Fairleys to me. And how dare you point a finger at my grandmother, after all she's done for you! Could it be that you're trying to gloss over your abdication of your duty to her –' Paula stopped herself from saying any more. Her emotions were running high and she was so furious she was shaking like a leaf.

A sudden chill settled in the room.

They stared at each other. Both of them were appalled. Paula's face was so white her deep blue eyes seemed more startling than ever, and Jim's face was taut with shock.

His distress prevented him from speaking for a few seconds. He was stunned by her outburst and dismayed that she had chosen to totally misconstrue his words, uttered idly, and rather carelessly, he now had to admit.

He finally exclaimed with great fervency, 'Paula, please believe me, I wasn't making a case for the Fairleys, or pointing a finger at Emma. How can you possibly think I would do anything like that. I've always respected and honoured her, since the first day I worked for her. And I've grown to love her since we've been married. She's a wonderful woman, and I'm the first to appreciate everything she's done for me.'

'That's nice to know.'

Jim caught his breath, cringed at her sarcastic tone. 'Please, Paula, don't look at me like that. You've misunderstood me completely.'

She did not reply, averted her face, stared at the mass of plants lining the glass walls of the conservatory.

Jim jumped up. He grabbed her hands and pulled her out of the chair, took her in his arms. 'Darling, please listen to me. I love you. The past doesn't matter, Grandy's the first person to say so. I was wrong to even bring it up. What *they* all did to each other half a century ago has nothing to do with *us*. Somehow we've gone off the rails because of this . . . this discussion about my resignation. Everything has been blown out of proportion. You're overly upset about nothing. Please, please calm yourself.' As he spoke he led her to a loveseat and pressed her down, seated himself next to her, and took her hand, looked deeply into her face.

He said, 'Look, I agree with you, Paula, what my grandfather did *was* unspeakable. And he knew that himself. He lived with a guilty conscience for the rest of his life. In fact, his actions as a young man *ruined* his life in many ways. He confided that in me before he died. He never stopped regretting losing Emma and their child, nor did he stop loving her, and at the end all he wanted was your grandmother's forgiveness. When he was dying he implored me to go to Emma and beg her forgiveness for everything the Fairleys had done to her, himself most of all. Don't you remember I told you this? I spoke to Grandy about it the night she announced our engagement.'

'Yes,' Paula said.

'I repeated everything to Grandy – his last words just before he slipped away. He said, "Jim, it will be an unquiet grave I lie in if Emma does not forgive me. Implore her to do so, Jim, so that my tortured soul can rest in peace." And when I told Emma she wept a little, and she said, "I think perhaps your grandfather suffered more than I did, after all." And Paula, Emma forgave him. She forgave all of the Fairleys. Why can't you?'

She lifted her head sharply, startled by the question. 'Oh Jim, I –' There was a short pause before she finished, 'There's nothing for *me* to forgive. I think *you've* misunderstood *me*.'

'Perhaps. But you were so angry, shouting at me, going on about the Fairleys . . .'

'Yes, I did lose my temper, but you riled me when you said Grandy had guilty feelings. I know her, and far better than you, Jim, and I'm convinced she doesn't feel guilty about anything.'

'Then I was wrong,' he said with a weak smile. 'I apologize.' He was relieved she sounded more normal.

'You're wrong about something else too.'

'What's that?'

'The past. You just said that the past doesn't matter, but I can't agree with you. The past is always coming back to haunt us, and we can never escape it. It makes prisoners of us all. Grandy might give lip service to the idea that the past is no longer important, but she doesn't really believe this. She's often said to me that the past is immutable and it most certainly is, in my opinion.'

'The sins of the fathers and all that – is that what you mean?' he asked quietly.

164

'Yes.'

Jim exhaled, shook his head.

Paula looked at him carefully. 'I have a question. You might not like it, but I feel compelled to ask it.' She waited, watching him closely.

He stared back at her. 'Paula, I'm your husband, and I love you, and there should never be anything but complete honesty and directness between us. Obviously you can ask me anything. What's the question?'

She took a breath, plunged. 'Do you resent Grandy? I mean because she's the owner of the *Gazette* and not you? If your grandfather had managed to retain control you would have inherited the paper.'

Jim's jaw dropped in astonishment and he gaped at her, then he laughed. 'If I had any resentment – or bitterness or jealousy – I'd hardly be resigning as managing director. I'd be scheming to get the paper for myself – at least, to get as much power as I possibly could. And I'd have been dropping hints to you long ago to influence Grandy to leave the newspaper shares to our children . . . so I could get absolute control through their holdings. With that kind of clout at my fingertips I would be kingpin in the company, after Emma was dead. Actually, it would be mine in a manner of speaking, since I would be handling their business affairs until they came of age.' He shook his head, still laughing. 'Now wouldn't I have done that?'

'Yes, I suppose so,' Paula admitted in a drained voice, feeling suddenly debilitated.

Jim said, 'Paula, surely you realize by now that I'm not money hungry, nor particularly ambitious for power. I like running the papers, being managing editor, I admit that, but I don't want to be involved in business and administration.'

'Not even when you know that the newspaper company will be your children's one day?'

'I trust Winston. He'll do a good job. After all, he does have rather a big stake in the Consolidated group when you consider that he and the Hartes own half the company. He controls forty-eight per cent of the shares, don't forget.'

Paula knew there was no point arguing with him any further about his resignation, at least not now. She stood up. 'I think I've got to go outside . . . I need some fresh air.'

Jim also rose, looking at her with concern. 'Are you all right? You're awfully pale.'

'Yes, really. Why don't you spend a few minutes with the babies before you change? I'll be up in a short while – I just need to take a stroll around the garden.'

He caught her arm as she moved towards the door, swung her to face him. 'Friends again, darling?' he asked softly.

'Yes, of course,' she reassured him, conscious of the anxiety reflected in his eyes and recognizing the plea in his voice.

Paula walked slowly through the garden, circumvented the plantation of trees and took the narrow path leading to the second lawn that sloped down towards the grove of laburnum trees and the pond.

She was considerably shaken by their quarrel and her senses were swimming. She sat down on the steps of the white-painted summerhouse, relieved to be alone, to regain her equilibrium. She deplored the fact that she had lost control, flown into a temper, and her only excuse was the extreme provocation. Jim's remark that her grandmother was guilt-ridden about the Fairleys had been so inflammatory it had made her blood boil. The suggestion was ridiculous. Just as his resignation was ludicrous.

Although she was desperately troubled by that impulsive and irresponsible move on his part, her dismay about it had been jostled to one side by the impact of their collision. This last row was a lot more serious than one of their quarrels about Edwina. It had struck an important fundamental in any marriage – trust; and it raised questions in her mind about Jim, his innermost feelings for her grandmother and his loyalty to Emma. Her head was teeming with questions. Did he bear a grudge against Emma Harte because she now owned everything the Fairleys had once owned? Perhaps subconsciously, without really understanding that he did? It struck her, and very sharply, that this was not beyond the realms of possibility. After all, he had been the one to launch into the past, not she, and if the past didn't matter, as he had claimed, then why had he brought it up in the first place?

Were resentment and bitterness at the root of his statement after all? She trembled at this thought. Those were the most dangerous emotions in the world, for like cancer they gnawed away at a person's insides, and they were destructive, coloured everything a person did. Yet when she had asked Jim bluntly if he resented Grandy he had obviously been flabbergasted by the idea, and his answer had been immediate, direct, and totally without guile. He had been genuine, she had seen that instantly. She had always found Jim relatively easy to read. He was not a devious man, quite the reverse really, in that he was not constitutionally cut out to dissemble.

Paula leaned against the railings and closed her eyes, her mind working at its rapid and most intelligent best, assessing and analysing. She had always believed she knew Jim inside out, but did she really? Perhaps it was arrogant of her to think she had such great insight into him. After all, how well did anyone know another person when one got right down to it? There had been times when she had found those who were closest to her, with whom she had grown up, difficult and even impossible to comprehend on occasions. If members of her immediate family and her oldest friends were frequently baffling, how could she possibly understand a man she had known for a brief two years, a man who might easily be termed a stranger even though he was her husband? She had come to realize that people could not always be taken on face value ... most people were highly complex. Sometimes they themselves did not recognize what motivated them to do the things they did. How well did James Arthur Fairley actually know himself? And, come to think of it, how well did he know *her*?

These nagging questions hung in the air, and she finally let go of them, sighing, understanding that she had no ready answers for herself. She opened her eyes and looked down at her hands, so relaxed, curled in her lap. The tension had gone, and now that her anger had all but dissipated entirely she was able to think objectively and with a cool head. She acknowledged that she had leapt down Jim's throat. Of course he had been awfully provocative, but that was no doubt unintentional on his part. They were both at fault, and if he had a few imperfections then most assuredly so did she. They were both human. As he had defended himself against her strong verbal onslaught she had heard the ring of truth and sincerity in his voice, had noted the genuine love written all over his face. It suddenly seemed inconceivable to her that Jim could harbour ill feelings for her grandmother. Furthermore, she owed it to her husband to believe that he did not. Yes, she must trust him, give him the benefit of the doubt. If she was not capable of doing that then their relationship would be threatened. Besides, he had made a very salient point, one she could not now ignore. He had said he would hardly be resigning as managing director if he was embittered and felt that the *Gazette* was his by rights, that instead he would be making sure he grabbed all the power for himself. She could not deny that his words made sense. Anybody who was goaded on by resentment to get even, to win, would hardly be quitting the arena. He would be planning the *coup-de-grâce*.

Thoughts of his resignation intruded more sharply, but she clamped down on them with resoluteness. Wisely, she decided she had better shelve that sensitive issue for the time being. It was hardly the time to start tackling him about that again when their guests were due to arrive shortly. And especially since Edwina was one of those guests. She most certainly wasn't going to let *her* see a chink in the armour.

Jim stood at the window where, from this angle, he could see Paula sitting on the steps of the summerhouse. His eyes remained riveted on her and he wished she would come back inside. It was imperative that he smooth things over between them.

He had not meant any harm when he had mentioned that old worn out story about Emma Harte ruining the Fairleys. But he had been tactless, no use denying it, and a bloody fool for not realizing that Paula would react fiercely. Jim exhaled wearily. She had overreacted in his opinion; after all, facts were facts and quite inescapable. But then his wife was irrational about her grand-mother, worshipping her the way she did. She wielded a club on anyone who dared to even hint that Emma was less than perfect. Not that he ever said a wrong word about her . . . he had no reason to criticize or condemn Emma Harte. Just the opposite, actually.

Paula's revelation about Gerald Fairley attempting to rape the young Emma edged to the front of his mind. It was undoubtedly true, and the very idea of it was so repellent to him he shivered involuntarily. On the rare occasions Gerald's name had cropped up in conversation, he had divined a look of immense distaste and contempt on his grandfather's face, and now he under-stood why. Jim shook his head wonderingly, thinking how entangled the lives of the Fairleys and the Hartes had been at the turn of the century; still the actions of his antecedents were hardly his fault or his responsibility. He had not known any of them, except for his grandfather, and so they were shadowy figures at best, and anyway the present was the only thing that mattered, that counted for anything.

This thought brought his eyes back to the window. He moved the curtain slightly. Paula was a motionless figure on the steps of the old summerhouse, lost in her contemplations. Once she had returned to the bedroom to change her clothes, he would sit her down, talk to her, do his damnedest to make up to her, apologize again if necessary. He was beginning to loathe these quarrels, which had become so frequent of late.

He ran his hand through his fair hair absently, a meditative look settling on his finely-drawn, rather sensitive face. Paula could be right – maybe Emma was not in the least troubled by her past deeds. Now that he considered it objectively, in a rational manner, it suddenly struck him that she was far too pragmatic a woman to worry about matters that could not be altered. And yet he could not dismiss the sense of guilt he had detected in her from time to time. Perhaps her guilt was centred solely on him, had nothing to do with those long-dead Fairleys. There was no question in his mind that Emma worried about him. This was the reason he had not been in the least surprised when Paula had mentioned the will, since he had always expected Emma to change it, to favour his children. He did not crave the shares for himself, nor could Emma leave him her interest in the papers without causing a stink in the family. And so Emma, being fair minded and scrupulous, was doing her level best to make amends, to make things right and proper in the only way she knew how. She was giving Lorne and Tessa their birthright . . . the inheritance he himself would have willed to his children if his family had retained control of the newspaper.

Jim was completely convinced that genuine emotion motivated Emma. She had once loved his grandfather, and, in consequence, she cared deeply about him. There was not the slightest doubt in his mind about that. He might even have been her grandson if circumstances had been slightly different.

Yes, Grandy had shown her true feelings for him in an infinite variety of ways – he had hard evidence. He ran all of the instances through his head . . . she had given him the job as managing editor when there had been other candidates just as well qualified; she had ended her vendetta against the Fairleys because of him; she had blessed his marriage to her favourite grandchild. In fact, Emma Harte was always bending over backward to please him, and she was on his side – her actions more than proved this. Grandy had persuaded Paula to live here at Long Meadow because he so wished it. She had acknowledged that the twins must be christened at Fairley church and, moreover, she had not objected when he had invited Edwina. It was only ever Paula who made a fuss about that unfortunate woman who had never done anybody any harm.

Jim shifted his stance impatiently, wondering how long Paula intended to sit out there. He glanced at his watch with irritation. If she did not come in within the next few minutes he would go out and talk to her in the garden. He did want to make sure she understood one thing . . . Emma was not disappointed in him. That morning, when he had told her he wanted to resign, Grandy had agreed, said that she appreciated his honesty. 'If that's what you want, then that's what you must do,' Emma had said with a little smile. 'I'd be the last person to stop you.' Emma was compassionate and full of humanity, and she loved him in her own way. And he was loyal to her, devoted. There was a special bond between them. It was never mentioned but it existed, nevertheless.

Much to his relief Jim now saw Paula walking up the path. Thank God she was coming back to the house. His tension lessened, even though it was impossible from this distance to gauge her state of mind, or ascertain what her attitude would be. But then he always had trouble doing that. It seemed to him that she constantly had him on the edge, kept him guessing. She was temperamental, even difficult at times, but no woman had captivated him, ensnared him as she had. And she had done so without even trying. There was enormous chemistry between them and their sexual attraction for each other was so strong it was overpowering. Paula was so intense, so serious, so complex she often left him floundering and baffled. Yet he found her depth and sincerity gratifying; equally he was thrilled by her passion, her desire for him in bed. The women he had been involved with before her had often complained about his sex drive. They seemed to think it was abnormal, were unable to cope, balked at his staying power. But not Paula ... she never complained, always welcomed him with open arms, as ready as he to abandon herself to their lovemaking, and he could never get enough of her. He knew she felt the same.

Paula was the best thing in the world that had ever happened to him, and he was struck by this realization more and more every day. How lucky he had been to meet her on that plane journey from Paris.

He thought back to it now, remembering clearly every little detail of their first meeting. Her name had sounded familiar and her lovely face had touched a chord in his memory, but he had not been able to place her. But later that night, restless, unable to sleep, haunted by her, everything had suddenly clicked into place. It had dawned on him that she was the daughter of David Amory, who ran the Harte stores, and that she was therefore the granddaughter of Emma Harte, his employer. He had been at once intimidated and dismayed, had not closed his eyes all night, worrying about the situation and the ramifications it involved.

The following morning, confused, disturbed and ambivalent, he had wavered, had wondered whether to cancel their dinner date planned for that evening. In the end he had been unable to resist seeing her again, had gone to the Mirabelle in a troubled state. He had been keyed up, anxious, and his heart had been in his mouth. After one of the waiters had made a remark about her grandmother, he had seen his chance. He had the perfect opening gambit, had asked her who her prestigious grandparent was, and Paula had told him without hesitation. She had made light of this, had made it easy for him, and surprisingly her relationship to Emma Harte had suddenly not mattered. His extraordinary feelings for Paula swept everything to one side, and he had fallen in love with her over dinner at the Mirabelle, had made up his mind to marry her – even if Emma sacked him and disinherited her heiress.

Jim recalled the night, a month after their first date, when he had finally succeeded in getting Paula into bed. Unexpectedly, erotic images of them together began to dance around in his head, made the heat rush through him. He knew what he was going to do the minute she walked in, knew how to put everything right between them. Words and long explanations were meaningless, inconsequential, now that he thought about it. Actions counted. Yes, his was the best way, the only way to demolish the residue of their quarrel completely.

Now, as Paula entered the bedroom, Jim saw that she was calmer, that her colour was perfectly normal. He went to her, took her hands in his. 'I can't bear these awful rows,' he said.

'Neither can I.'

Without saying anything else, he took her face between his hands and kissed her, his mouth working sensually on hers. His passion soared. He was at full arousal. His arms went around her and he brought her closer, so that she was positioned into the curve of his body. His hands slid down her back on to her buttocks, and he pressed her into him with impatience. She must understand the extent of his excitement, understand that he intended to possess her immediately.

Paula accepted his kisses, and then quickly but gently pushed him away. 'Jim, please. They'll be here in a few minutes. We don't have time –'

He silenced her with another kiss, then breaking away from her, he led her to the bed. He pushed her down on to it purposefully, lay next to her, wrapped his long legs around her. In a voice thickened by desire, he said against her neck, 'I must have you. *Now*. Quickly, before they arrive. We do have time. And you know we always make up, once we've made love. Come on, take your clothes off for me, darling.'

Paula started to protest, not wanting this, wary of him, sensing she was being manipulated again. But he was already fumbling with the buttons on her shirt and so she swallowed her words. It was far easier if she was compliant, as she had so quickly come to realize in the last year. Jim believed that sex solved every one of their problems. But of course it did not.

18

At six thirty the following morning Paula left Long Meadow for the office, looking coolly elegant in a smartly tailored black linen suit and a crisp white silk shirt.

After a restless night of tossing and turning and worrying, she had risen earlier than usual. Only Nora had been astir at that hour, preparing the babies' bottles, and after she had showered and dressed Paula had spent fifteen tranquil minutes with her and the twins in the nursery, before going downstairs to the kitchen. As she had drunk a quick cup of tea she had scribbled a note to Jim, explaining that she was facing a hectic day at the store and wanted to get a head start.

This was only partially true. Paula had the most urgent need to unscramble her jumbled thoughts and take stock of the situation. She could only do that when she was alone – and the only time she was not surrounded by people was either when she was gardening or driving.

As she pointed the car down the gravel driveway she realized she was relieved to be escaping from the house. It seemed more suffocating than ever to her today. Although she enjoyed the grounds and the conservatory, Long Meadow would never really be her favourite place, despite the more attractive ambiance she and her mother had created. As Grandy had said, 'You've both done your best but you can't make a silk purse out of a sow's ear.'

And whatever Jim believed, the house *was* oppressive. Her grandmother felt the same way as she did, and rarely came, preferring instead to have them over to Pennistone Royal. This aside, it was extremely difficult to run efficiently. It was poorly designed, had endless staircases, winding corridors and dark landings. Meg and the daily char, Mrs Coe, were constantly complaining, and even Nora, who was younger than they, had taken to grumbling about her aching legs lately. Jim made light of their complaints. He loved Long Meadow, and she knew he would not consider moving, so there was no point in dreaming about another house, one which was more practical and suitable for their needs.

He was selfish.

So jolted was Paula by this unexpected thought she stiffened and gripped the steering wheel tighter. She stared ahead at the road, her eyes momentarily glazed by her troubles. What an unkind and disloyal thing to think, she chided herself. But try though she did to convince herself she was wrong about Jim, she did not succeed. It was the truth. For months she had tried to ignore this unfortunate and dismaying characteristic in him, had made perpetual excuses for him. Suddenly this was no longer possible. She had to stop deluding herself about Jim, look at the facts unflinchingly, accept that he only ever did what he *wanted* to do. He was deceptive in that he gave the impression of trying to please, especially with colleagues and friends, and when small irrelevant matters were involved. Then he bent over backward to be obliging. When it came to major issues he dug his feet in and always strove to get his own way, regardless of anyone else's wishes. That was the dichotomy in his nature and it had begun to worry her.

Paula sighed to herself. They were both stubborn, but at least she was not inflexible. With a start, Paula recognized that Jim was absolutely rigid. This trait had been staring her glaringly in the face for months, yet she had been reluctant, perhaps even afraid, to acknowledge it.

She began to scrutinize the pattern of their life together for the past year, and now discovered that she could remember innumerable examples of that ingrained rigidity. There had been his refusal point blank to accept a new plane from Grandy, not to mention the fuss about their wedding plans. He had been adamant when her grandmother had asked him to get rid of his rickety old four-seater plane, and suggested he buy a more up-to-date jet at her expense. Being conscious of his pride, Grandy had handled it diplomatically, had pointed out that she felt she should have a company plane at her immediate disposal, and who better to select the best piece of equipment and make the purchase than he. But he would not budge from his position, and Emma had thrown up her hands in exasperation at his intractability.

Almost immediately afterwards he had told her parents and Grandy that he wanted to have their marriage ceremony at Fairley Church. They had all three been staggered by this suggestion, and so had she. Apart from the fact that the village church was far too small to accommodate some three hundred guests, her parents and Emma had wanted the wedding to be held in London, to be followed by a reception at Claridge's Hotel. It had been especially important to her grandmother that she have a lovely, elegant and glamorous wedding. It was her mother who had scotched Jim's idea. Daisy had told him that the marriage arrangements were hardly his concern, since they were always the prerogative of the bride's parents. Clever clever Daisy. She had won by simply pointing out the correct etiquette, the proper form. In this instance he had had no option but to back down.

But he had made a swift recovery, and the next battle had been about Long Meadow. Jim had been the winner that time, but in a sense by default. She had only agreed to live there to keep the peace, and also because her grand-mother had told her to be accommodating. 'Jim's ego and his masculinity are on the line,' her grandmother had remarked. 'I agree the house is a monstrosity, but he has a genuine need to be the provider, to give you a home on his own terms. You'd better accept the situation for now.'

For this same reason she and Grandy had gone along with his wish to have the twins christened at Fairley Church, even though Emma had initially balked at this idea, had hardly been overjoyed to trek all the way to Fairley, of all places. She rarely went *there* these days.

Paula slowed down and stopped at a traffic light, mulling over this first year of marriage. People said it was the most difficult year and perhaps it *was* inevitable that there would be a few unpleasant revelations. Whizzing up the short hill, she cruised past the Stray and turned on to the main road to Leeds. I suppose I might as well accept that the honeymoon is now definitely *over*, she muttered under her breath, then laughed ironically. He had even been contrary about their actual honeymoon, had whisked her off to the Lake District instead of to the sunny South of France. Wanting to please him, in love and feeling euphoric, she had accepted his decision, even though France had been more appealing to her. They had been greeted by inclement weather and thunder-storms when they had reached Windermere, and had spent a week shivering in front of the fire in their hotel suite, or in bed making love.

Her thoughts automatically settled on their sex life. She was in love with Jim, and wanted him physically, had normal desires and a healthy attitude about sex. But lately it was growing more and more apparent to her that Jim was abnormally driven. His marathons were becoming tiring, even tedious. There were other things in a marriage as well as sex. He was insatiable, and endless, mindless sex was not particularly fulfilling to her. Sometimes she found herself wishing he had more finesse, a better understanding of a woman's body – *her* body, *her* needs. Loath though she was to admit it, she knew deep within herself that Jim was just as selfish in bed as he was out of it, always pleasing himself, never giving a thought to her. It was growing harder and harder for her to cope with his need to make love all the time. Her work was demanding and she craved sleep, but he was seemingly tireless.

Sudden anger flared in Paula as she considered the way he used sex as an antidote for their rows. Her resentment was increasing, because it was manipulative. It seemed incredible to her that he believed their problems evap-orated into thin air once they were locked in a tight embrace. Of course that didn't happen, their difficulties were still there afterwards. And naturally they remained unsolved.

Oh God, if only he would *talk* to me, Paula thought. He should communicate. Instead he retreats behind his charm and his jokes, and whenever I try to explain my feelings he laughs me off. Yes, Jim had a childish tendency to pretend their differences did not exist. She could never get him to open up, try though she did. It occurred to her that she had reached an impasse. She had come to a turning point in her marriage. And after only one year, she said to herself wonderingly. Had she made a terrible mistake? Was divorce the only solution?

Horror trickled through her at the mere idea of breaking up, and was quickly replaced by a rush of panic. Beads of sweat broke out on her forehead, and she began to tremble inside. Slowing the car to a crawl she pulled into the first side road she saw and parked. Leaning forward, she rested her head on the steering wheel and closed her eyes. Divorce was unthinkable. She was stunned that it had even crossed her mind a moment ago. She loved him . . . truly, truly loved him. And in spite of their problems they were compatible in so many important ways. And there were the twins . . . Lorne and Tessa needed a father, needed Jim as much as she needed him.

Instantly, it struck her that she had been unfair to her husband, adding to his faults, mentally compiling lists of grudges against him when he was not present to defend himself. He was a nice man, a good man, and he had so many lovely qualities. She owed it to him to be scrupulously honest with herself about his manifold attributes.

Silently she began to tick them off in her head. He understood about her work. He appreciated her desire to be out there in the marketplace. Certainly he never interfered with her career; he did not grumble about her preoccupation with the stores, the late hours she kept. At least he's an enlightened man in that respect, she acknowledged swiftly, and he allows me to be myself. He's not threatened by me either. Furthermore, he was obviously cut out to be a marvellous father, that was already evident. There was no question that he adored her, was devoted to her. Jim would never be a philanderer who played around with other women. He was strictly a one-woman man and totally geared to his family, and family life, and she was thankful of that.

Straightening up, Paula smoothed her hair into place. I've got to make a go of this relationship, she told herself. It's vitally important to me, and I know it's essential to Jim. She remembered something her grandmother had once said . . . that it was always the woman who made a marriage work. Paula believed this. Her grandmother was wise and experienced, she had lived it all, seen it all. No one knew better about marriage than Emma Harte.

Paula resolved to be as understanding of Jim as she possibly could. She would put extra effort and time into their relationship. She would be loving and tolerant. It would be immature of her if she did not. After all, everybody had faults, and you didn't stop loving a man simply because he had a few imperfections. You loved him in spite of them.

Turning the ignition key, Paula started the car and backed out of the side road. Her mind began to revolve around her grandmother and Jim's resignation as she sped down the road heading in the direction of Alwoodley. Convinced though she was that Jim had totally misjudged Emma's reaction to his decision, she nevertheless hoped that her grandmother was not angry with him. She did not want Grandy to think badly of Jim.

Less than half an hour later Paula sat behind her desk in her office at the Harte store in Leeds, talking to her grandmother whom she had reached at the flat in Belgrave Square.

'I'm sorry to wake you up,' Paula apologized, although she strongly suspected she had not done so.

Emma's warm and vibrant voice flowed over the wire and confirmed this, as she said, 'I was having my morning tea and waiting for your call. You want to talk to me about Jim, his resignation, don't you?'

'Yes, Gran. I was a bit floored last night when he told me what he'd done, and naturally rather upset. I feel he's let you down, and at the worst time, when you're about to go away. I can't help thinking that you must be disappointed in him.'

'A little,' Emma said. 'However, I decided not to persuade Jim to retain the managing directorship . . . not under the circumstances. His heart's not in the job, Paula, and that's not good. It's better he steps down.'

'Yes,' Paula agreed quietly. 'What about Winston? Is he frightfully annoyed?'

'Well, he was at first, and I thought for a moment he was going to explode when I told him he would have to take on the job. But he agreed, almost at once. There's no one else, as you well know.'

'I feel awful about this situation, Grandy. There's not much I can say, except that I'm sorry. Jim shouldn't have done this in my opinion. I think it was irresponsible. *He* doesn't agree with me, of course.' There was a fractional pause, and then Paula added, 'I'm not trying to make excuses for him, Gran, but I've come to realize that Jim isn't like *us*, you know as far as duty is concerned. We've all done jobs we haven't really liked during the years we've all worked for you. Those jobs never killed us, and we learned a lot from the experience. I know I shouldn't make comparisons, but last night when Jim was talking I kept thinking of little Emily – her example. She's been a brick, the way she's gone into Genret and with the best will in the world.'

'That's true,' Emma agreed, then added swiftly, in a kinder tone, 'You mustn't be too hard on Jim, Paula dear. People do have their limitations, and remember, he wasn't brought up in the same way as you and your cousins. Anyway, let's be grateful for his talent as a managing editor. He's brilliant, the best in the business, and that's why I gave him the job years ago. Now, if he'd resigned from that position we *would* have a major tragedy on our hands.'

'I realize that. He does love the newspaper business, and that's why he's been so successful as a journalist.' Paula was beginning to feel easier in her mind, and she went on, 'I have to defend Jim in one respect . . . he's been honest with you, and we must give him credit for that. He's as straight as a die, Grandy.'

'You don't have to tell me, Paula. Jim's not duplicitous. Far from it, and I told him yesterday morning that I appreciated his truthfulness. Half-hearted, unenthusiastic executives spell disaster to me.'

'Then you're not too angry with him?' Paula asked, clutching the phone tensely, holding her breath.

'That was only a passing feeling yesterday. It quickly dissipated,' Emma said. 'We can't let emotions take charge of us in business, we must always deal from intelligence, but then I've told you that all of your life. Sorry to keep repeating myself.'

'That's all right, and I must admit I'm relieved you're taking this so well, Grandma. He'd never *intentionally* do anything to hurt or upset you.'

Brushing this remark aside, considering it unimportant, Emma said, 'I want you to relax, Paula. This is not really your problem. Anyway, we do have everything under control. Actually, when I was talking to Winston after Jim had left, it occurred to me – and rather forcibly – that things are not going to be much *different* at Consolidated. Winston was sitting there, grousing away, going on and on *ad infinitum* about being overworked, listing his present duties, demanding to know how I expected him to cope with everything. And as he talked his head off I began to realize that he's actually been carrying the administrative and business load at Consolidated for the longest time. He's been functioning as managing director without knowing it. I told him so, told him he was now getting the title to go with his tremendous responsibilities, plus a large raise in salary. You know Winston has a great sense of humour, and he began to laugh. He said, "Damn it, Aunt Emma, we both think we're so smart, so why haven't we realized before today how brilliant *I* am?" So, darling, you don't have to be concerned about me, Consolidated, or Winston either.'

'I'm glad to hear that, Grandy. Look, can I ask you something? It's about the shares in Consolidated. Why are you changing your will and leaving your interest to the twins?'

'What a funny question. I thought I'd made it clear, thought that you'd understood me. Surely it's obvious – I'm leaving my shares in the newspaper company to the twins because they are *your* children, Paula. What other reason could there be?' Emma murmured, sounding extremely perplexed.

'None, I just wondered, that's all,' Paula answered. 'However, it struck me the other day that your decision might have something to do with Jim. You know, because he's a Fairley. I mean, if his grandfather had hung on to the *Gazette* it would have been his today, wouldn't it?'

Emma burst into peals of laughter. 'I very much doubt that,' she gasped. Immediately recovering herself, she said, 'Edwin Fairley would have lost the paper eventually, as I've told you before. Besides, the Fairleys owned only the *Yorkshire Morning Gazette*, none of the other papers in the Consolidated chain. You know I acquired those myself, and with the help of my brothers.' Her incredulous laughter reverberated down the wire again. 'You can't possibly think that I feel *guilty* about the Fairleys,' she spluttered, obviously highly entertained by this idea.

'Of course I don't,' Paula exclaimed heatedly, wishing she had never brought the subject up, realizing that she had been right, and Jim wrong, all along.

'I should hope not, my darling girl,' Emma said, stifling her merriment. 'I've always admitted that I gave the Fairleys a few nudges, and very sharp ones at that, as they waltzed down the path to folly which they had chosen for themselves. But I can assure you that I never once lost a wink of sleep about any of my actions. I was delighted I was able to turn the tables on them, come out the big winner. So don't think for one minute that I'm troubled by any guilty feelings about a lot of dead Fairleys, or Jim for that matter. And if he has suggested such a thing to you, you can tell him from me that he's wrong, quite wrong.'

'Oh no, he didn't bring it up,' Paula lied smoothly, knowing such an admission would annoy her grandmother. 'It was merely a thought that flitted through my active brain.'

Emma chuckled under her breath at Paula's hurried response, uncertain of its veracity. She said, 'I hope you feel better now that we've cleared the air about Jim's resignation.'

'Yes, Gran, you always help me to get everything in its right perspective.'

19

Ten days later Emma could not conceive how she had managed to do all that she had since she had been in London. But she had worked miracles, accomplished more in that brief span of time than in the last six months. Or so it seemed to her this afternoon as she glanced at her check list on the yellow legal pad.

She had reviewed her various business enterprises, to be certain everything was in perfect order and to reassure herself that there would be no snags during her long absence. She had met with her solicitors several times, and with her banker Henry Rossiter, and she and Henry had even been able to spend a couple of pleasant social evenings together. There had been long sessions with Winston and Alexander respectively; she had conferred with Sarah, approved all of the designs for the 1970 Spring Collection of Lady Hamilton clothes and had gone over the new advertising campaign with her. And as she had worked late at the store, rushed hither and yon, switching mental gears as she went from one meeting to the next, she had found time to pull together that all-important wardrobe for her round-the-world trip with Blackie.

Emma felt settled in her mind about everything – except Jonathan. He was her enemy. She did not know the reason why, nor could she prove it. Nonetheless, Emma was filled with the growing conviction that he was the one grandchild she could not trust.

Opening the folder on her desk, her shrewd eyes scanned the report from private investigators she had engaged to check on Jonathan's activities in his business and personal life. They had turned up nothing untoward, but this did not convince her that he was innocent of any wrongdoing. The firm of Graves and Saunderson would have to dig deeper, look farther afield. She was positive there was something – somewhere.

All of her life Emma Harte had been able to see through everyone, had the gift of second-guessing her family and friends and adversaries alike. It was almost as if she had a demon telling her things. She also possessed that highly sensitive built-in antenna which born survivors are usually blessed with, a sort of sixth sense that enabled her to pick up vibrations – both good and bad, but especially bad. And then of course there was her gut instinct which she had come to trust, to rely on without questioning it, knowing it would never mislead her. For some time now, all of her faculties of acute perception had combined to alert her to trouble brewing, yet so far she had not put her hand on anything concrete. Still, it was there, as if hovering in the dark, and just beyond her reach.

Her gaze now settled on the few brief paragraphs about Sebastian Cross. They were good friends, he and Jonathan, real intimates, in fact, but that was the extent of it. When she had first learned of their close relationship, which dated back to their school days at Eton, she had wondered whether or not there was a homosexual involvement here. But apparently not, quite to the contrary, according to Mr Graves. She closed the folder with a decisive slap. There was no point in reading it over and over again. That was a waste of time. Besides, she had gone through it with a small-tooth comb already, searching for one single clue, a small lead, and had come up empty-handed. Emma slipped the folder in the desk and locked the drawer, not wanting to dwell any longer on the possibility of treachery.

A dismal feeling trickled through her. It had been painful and sad for her to resort to these awful and chilling measures – to put detectives on one of her own kin. But she had not known what else to do. And she had only ever taken such a dreadful step – spied on someone – once in her life before, and then, like now, it had been repugnant, had gone against her nature. Some forty years ago she had seen fit to have the activities of her second husband monitored . . . to protect herself and her children. She was suddenly struck by the bitter irony of the present situation. Her second husband, Arthur Ainsley, had been Jonathan's grandfather.

Sitting back in the chair, Emma wrestled with another pressing problem – whether or not to discuss her suspicions about Jonathan with Alexander and Paula. Maybe it would be wisest to confide in them. What if something happened to her when she was abroad? What if she fell sick? Or dropped dead? She did not think there was much chance of either. She was in good health and she felt strong and vital, and certainly she was more energetic than ever. On the other hand, she *would* be eighty years old in a couple of days. Perhaps, to be on the safe side, she ought to tell them. They were her chief heirs. Her empire would be under their control one day in the future . . .

There was a knock on the door and as she said, 'Come in', Gaye Sloane's face appeared around it. 'Do you need anything else, Mrs Harte?' her private secretary asked.

Emma shook her head. 'No, Gaye, thanks very much. I'm waiting for Paula. We're going out to dinner. But there's no need for you to hang around. You might as well get off.'

'Thanks, Mrs Harte, I will. See you tomorrow, and good night.'

'Good night, Gaye dear.'

Ten minutes later Paula walked in, and Emma looked up from the papers on her desk, her face softening. 'Paula, you look awfully tired!' she exclaimed, her worry resounding audibly. 'You've got dark shadows and you're very pale. Are you sure you're all right?'

'Yes,' Paula reassured her, and gave her a small rueful smile as she flopped down into the chair opposite the desk. 'It's been one of those beastly days. Interminable problems with the French Week planned for July.'

'What kind of problems?' Emma asked, straightening up and then leaning over the desk, resting her chin in her hands.

'People problems mostly. You know, temperaments, ruffled feathers, noses out of joint. But I've managed to get things moving smoothly again. I really miss Emily, though, Grandy. She was always so good at pulling our special events together, and she was certainly a soothing influence on everybody.'

'That's part of Emily's talent, I've always thought. I know she used to make the store managers tremble in their boots, but she usually had them eating out of her hand in the long run, charming them all the way. Perhaps you ought to consider getting an assistant – someone to replace Emily.' Emma's brows lifted. 'Why not?'

'Oh I don't know –' Paula shrugged. 'I think I can cope, anyway, let's not worry about that now. The French Week is finally under control and I don't foresee any more major difficulties cropping up. God forbid! In the meantime, did you get a chance to look at the boutique plans? And did you speak to Merry?'

'Yes, I did. This afternoon. I spent an hour poring over the plans and then I phoned her, told her you both had my blessing. You were right, Paula, the scheme is excellent, and we should do very well with the boutiques.'

'Oh I'm so glad you agree, Grandy.' Paula looked pleased as she added, 'Merry worked so hard, and *she* deserves all the credit, not I. Incidentally, I mentioned our new venture to Emily yesterday. Since she's going to Hong Kong early next month, I thought she might keep her eyes open for special merchandise for the boutiques. You know, straw hats and bags, sandals, pretty shawls, summer jewellery, *anything* really that would be suitable for holiday and resort wear.'

Emma nodded her approval. 'Very good thought, and Emily does have a penchant for spotting fashionable goods.' She paused, placed a pile of papers in a blue folder, then glanced up, gave her granddaughter a careful look. 'Did Emily tell you anything special? I mean, confide anything in you?'

Paula began to laugh. 'I suppose you're referring to her new boyfriend. I must admit, she's being awfully cagey with me, and that's not like Emily. We've always shared our secrets, as you well know. However, she hasn't shared a thing about her new love, other than to drop hints that he's gorgeous, and special. She calls him her mysterious lover, no, *secret* lover. Mind you, I'm sure he's not *actually* her *lover*,' Paula suddenly thought to add, being protective of Emily, not wanting her grandmother to get the wrong impression about the young girl's morals. 'You know how she tends to exaggerate.'

Emma bit back a smile, filling with understanding. 'You don't have to defend Emily to me, Paula dear. I know she's not promiscuous . . . she hasn't followed in her mother's footsteps, that's one thing I'm absolutely certain of. However, he *is* her lover.'

Paula said, very startled, 'How do you know that?'

'Why I got it from the horse's mouth,' Emma announced, mischief sparking her tired eyes with sudden life. She sat back and grinned at Paula.

'You're looking like the cat that's swallowed the canary, Grandy,' Paula laughed. 'Which horse?'

'*Emily*. She told me all about him herself. And the so-called secret lover is no longer a *secret*, neither is he very mysterious.' Emma's mouth twitched with amusement as she watched Paula, noted the surprised expression settling on her face.

'Oh,' was all Paula could manage.

Emma's light laugh rang out. 'Emily came to see me the night before last, and she was rather blunt – in her usual fashion. She said, "Gran, I'm terribly in love, and it's very serious. I'm sleeping with him, but I don't want you to worry. I won't get pregnant. I'm taking birth control pills." That didn't surprise me, after all she was always a rather practical girl ... Emily does have her head screwed on the right way, like you. In fact, Elizabeth could take a few lessons from the two of you. Well, I *was* taken aback, I don't mind admitting *that*, but not shocked, though I suspect Emily had anticipated that I would be. I wonder occasionally if that girl thinks I'm the Virgin Mary. Anyway, she was very honest, endearingly so.' Emma paused, then smiled her very special smile that filled her face with radiance. 'Our little Emily has stars in her eyes right now, darling. She's genuinely in love. Very much so.'

'But who *is* he?' Paula pressed. 'You said he's not mysterious, so it must be somebody I know.'

'Oh yes, it is.' Emma chuckled and her eyes twinkled brightly. She was suddenly enjoying herself, enjoying teasing Paula, glad to turn away from the unpleasantness surrounding Jonathan, which she found so appalling.

'Come on, don't be so mean,' Paula admonished, smiling herself, picking up on her grandmother's gaiety which was infectious. 'Tell me his *name*, for heaven's sake! I'm dying to know.'

'Winston.'

'*Winston*,' Paula gasped, and her violet eyes widened. 'I don't believe it!'

'Oh but you must, because it's absolutely true. Don't look so shocked, darling. Winston's very eligible, and let's face it, he has lots of charm, a lot going for him. He's also rather good looking. He's a lot like me, you know.'

Paula hooted with laughter, tickled by this small show of personal vanity on her grandmother's part. She said, 'Yes, Grandma, I have noticed the resemblance from time to time.' She then continued, 'The *only* reason I'm thunderstruck is because this news is so unexpected. And rather startling, I mean, Winston and Emily ... goodness me, when did they become romantically entangled? When did all this start?' Paula's black brows drew together in a sudden frown. 'Oh dear, what about nice Allison Ridley?'

'Yes, nice Allison indeed. That part is sad – I always rather liked that young woman. But I'm afraid it's off with her. Winston spoke to me yesterday about Allison, explained that he went to see her, told her as kindly and as gently as possible that it's over between them. As to the first part of your question, I believe Emily and Winston realized the depth of their feelings for each other on the day of the christening. Winston asked me if I minded about his involvement with Emily and I told him I didn't, that I was delighted.' Emma once again leaned across the desk, the expression of deeply-felt happiness flashing on her face. She confided, 'I had a business meeting with Winston this morning, and after we'd finished, he brought out the ring he's bought for Emily. It's an emerald.' Emma paused, then announced, 'Winston asked my permission to marry Emily. I gave it, and they're going to announce their engagement this week, before I leave for New York.'

'Oh Gran, this is going a bit fast isn't it?' Paula asked softly, and with a hint of concern, staring at Emma.

'I wouldn't say that, dear,' Emma remarked. 'They're hardly strangers, Paula. They grew up together, and I should think they know each other pretty well by now. They won't have any unpleasant surprises about each other after they're married. Of course the wedding can't take place until *next* summer, what with my trip to Australia and their travelling. But frankly, I'm relieved to know Emily has someone to look after her . . . I won't be around forever, you know. Yes, I find it most satisfying that those two are settling down together, most satisfying indeed. It gives me a lovely warm feeling here.' She patted her chest, continuing to smile.

'If you're happy and Emily is happy then I am too,' Paula said. 'And come to think of it, she and Winston were extremely close when they were little . . . they're admirably suited. Shouldn't I call her, Gran, to congratulate her?' Paula half rose, made to reach for the telephone on Emma's desk.

Emma said, 'I don't think you'll find her at Belgrave Square. She was going to the theatre with Winston, and she's probably left the flat by now.' Glancing at her watch, Emma nodded. 'Yes, it's already turned seven. You'll have to ring her late tonight. In the meantime, I really think I've got to get out of this place, I've been here since eight this morning. I've had it – and you look as if you have too.' Emma stood up, frowning at Paula as she did. 'Are you sure you're quite well?'

Paula summoned a smile. 'Never better, Gran,' she fibbed, not wanting to worry her grandmother.

Privately Emma thought that Paula looked completely exhausted, worn down. She had never seen the girl like this and it concerned her. But she made no further comment, and turning away she picked up her handbag. Her mouth tightened imperceptibly. She had a sneaking suspicion that for all his easy grace and lighthearted charm and boyish manner, Jim Fairley was a difficult man. But she would not pry, nor would she try to live her granddaughter's life for her.

As they left the office, Emma said, 'I've booked a table at Cunningham's – I hope you fancy fish.'

'Yes, and I'm not very hungry anyway, Gran.'

Later, over dinner at the Mayfair oyster bar and fish restaurant, Paula's appearance underwent a change, one which pleased Emma. Her alabaster complexion took on a soft shell-pink cast, and her eyes lost their haunted expression as she visibly relaxed. By the time coffee was served Paula seemed so much more like her normal self, Emma made a decision: She would take Paula into her confidence. Before they left Cunningham's this evening she would make brief mention of her suspicions about Jonathan, but casually so, and in passing. She felt it was necessary to warn Paula; on the other hand she did not wish to alarm her unduly. And tomorrow, when she had dinner with Alexander, she would apprise *him* of the situation. In one sense it was more important that he was alerted, put on his guard, since Jonathan Ainsley worked for Harte Enterprises.

20

It was the thirtieth of April and today she was eighty years old.

She awakened early, as was usual, and as she lay in her bed, shaking off the residues of sleep, she thought: Today is a special day, isn't it? And then instantly she remembered why this day was different from others. *It was her birthday.*

Emma had an aversion to lying in bed once she was awake, and she pushed herself up and brought her feet to the floor, half smiling to herself as she padded across the carpet to the windows. *She had made it.* She had never imagined she would live so long. Why, she was eleven years older than this century. In 1889, in that small cottage in Top Fold in Fairley village, her mother Elizabeth Harte had brought her into the world.

Drawing the draperies, she peered out. Her smile widened. It was a gorgeous day, full of sunshine and a startling brilliance. The sky was a crystalline blue and cloudless, and the trees below her in Belgrave Square were full blown and brightly green, their heavily-laden branches undulating with shimmering light under the breeze. She had been born on such a day as this, a balmy spring day, her mother had once told her, a day that was unusually warm for this time of year, especially in the cool Northern climes of Yorkshire.

Emma stretched. She felt alert and refreshed after a good night's rest, and as vigorous as she had ever been. Full of piss and vinegar, she thought, and immediately an image of her brother Winston flashed into her mind. That had been his favourite expression to describe her, when she had been revved up and bubbling over with enthusiasm, energy and drive. She wished he was still alive, and her younger brother, Frank. Sudden sadness streamed through her, but it was fleeting. Today was not a day for feeling sorry for herself, for missing those whom she had so dearly loved and who had departed this world. Today was a day for positive thoughts. A day for celebration. A day for looking to the future, concentrating on the younger generation . . . her grandchildren.

If all of her children except Daisy were lost to her, at least she had the immense satisfaction of knowing that their offspring would carry her bright banner forward, continue the great dynasty she had created, preserve her mighty business empire.

She stopped abruptly, paused in her progress across the room, and asked herself if it was a ferocious personal vanity that had fostered the dynastic impulse in her. *A desire for immortality perhaps?* She was not certain. But she did comprehend one thing – to produce a dynasty such as she had done, it

181

was absolutely necessary to view ambition on the grandest of scales, to imbue it in others.

Emma laughed out loud. It was just conceivable that she had always envisioned herself as being larger than life, different, and so truly indomitable she was not mortal at all. Egotism, she thought, and once more her rippling laughter filled the silent bedroom. Her enemies had frequently labelled her the total and supreme egotist. But why not? It was the truth, indeed it was. And without her enormous ego surely she would never have done the things she had done, accomplished all that she had. That ego, that belief in herself, had given her courage and self-confidence, had propelled her forward and upward, right to the top. To the glittering pinnacle of success.

Well, she didn't have time to waste this morning, contemplating her motives, analysing the internal forces that had driven her all the days of her life. She had done what she felt had to be done, and, very simply, that was that. She walked purposefully into the bathroom to prepare herself for the day facing her, shoving to one side these thoughts, deeming them unimportant.

An hour later, after she had bathed, dressed and breakfasted, Emma hurried downstairs to the second floor of her maisonette. She looked fresh and vitally alive, dressed in a crisply tailored light-wool dress in a shade of delphinium blue. She wore splendid jewellery with it – sapphire earrings and a matching brooch pinned on to one shoulder, a double strand of pearls, Paul's wedding ring and Blackie's large diamond. Not one hair of her immaculate, gleaming silver head was out of place, her makeup was perfect, and the bounce in her step belied her great age.

Emma still lived in Belgrave Square in the elegant, beautifully appointed mansion which Paul McGill had purchased for them in the late summer of 1925, soon after the birth of their daughter Daisy. At the time, catering to Emma's fear of vicious gossip, her reluctance to flaunt their relationship and her overwhelming need to be discreet and circumspect, he had had the house remodelled into two flats. And he had spared no expense in the process. The noted architect he had engaged had designed small bachelor quarters on the ground floor for Paul; the three floors which soared above were transformed into the luxurious triplex flat for Emma, Daisy, the nanny, and the rest of the staff. To the outside observer, the bachelor apartment and the large airy flat spanning three floors were entirely separate, were two distinct, self-contained dwellings, each having its own entrance. However, the two were ingeniously linked by a private interior elevator, which ran between the small hall in Paul's bachelor quarters to the larger and more elegant foyer in Emma's flat on the next floor. Because of this lift, the dwellings operated efficiently as one house.

During the war years, immediately following Paul's crippling accident and tragic suicide in Australia in 1939, Emma had closed up his bachelor flat. Unable to enter it without breaking down with uncontrollable grief and searing despair, she had turned her back on these rooms, ignoring them except for having them regularly cleaned. In 1948, when she was finally able to confront his possessions, she had had some of the rooms modernized and redecorated. Since then she had utilized the smaller downstairs flat as guest quarters for visiting friends or her grandchildren.

Parker, her butler, was busy sorting the morning post when Emma walked into her study. This was a pleasant, airy room of medium size, comfortably furnished with country antiques.

'Happy birthday, Mrs Harte,' said Parker, looking up and smiling. 'Quite a heavy post this morning, madam.'

'Oh my goodness, I see what you mean!' Emma exclaimed. The butler had stacked a staggering amount of mail on the chintz-covered sofa, and was methodically opening envelopes with a paper knife, removing the birthday cards, and throwing the envelopes into the wastepaper basket.

Emma joined him in this task, but soon she had to keep breaking off to answer the phone, and then, not long afterwards, the door bell began ringing as flowers and gifts arrived in a steady and continuing stream. Parker and Mrs Ramsey, the housekeeper, had their hands full, and Emma was left alone to cope with the post.

At about eleven thirty, when the activity was at its height Daisy McGill Amory walked in, unexpected and unannounced.

Emma's youngest daughter would be forty-four in May, but she did not look her age. She had a slender figure, softly curling black hair that framed her tranquil, unlined face, and luminous blue eyes that mirrored her lovely disposition and gentle nature. Unlike her daughter Paula, who favoured a hard-edged chic and was extremely fashion conscious, Daisy was more like Emma in her taste in clothes. She always chose soft, rather feminine outfits, and this morning she wore a simple lilac wool suit and a matching blouse with a frilly jabot which fell down the front, gold jewellery, and black patent pumps and handbag.

'Happy happy birthday, Mother,' Daisy said from the doorway, her expression loving, her eyes awash with tenderness.

Emma looked up from the pile of envelopes and broke into smiles. She was delighted to see Daisy, welcomed her calm presence. Springing up from behind the desk, Emma went to greet her with affection and warmth.

'This is from us . . . David and I do hope you like it, Mummy.' She laughed. 'You're awfully hard to buy for, you know. You *do* have everything.' She thrust a package at Emma.

'Thank you, Daisy, and since you have the best taste in the world I'm sure it's going to be something quite lovely.'

Sinking on to the sofa, Emma began to unwrap Daisy's gift. 'All this fuss! And at my age!'

Daisy knew that her mother was enjoying every minute, despite her protestations. She joined her on the sofa and said, 'But Mummy, that's just the point. This is an important day . . . you must sit back, relax, and savour every minute of it.'

'Perhaps you're right. But it certainly looks as if I'll never get to the store this morning.'

Daisy stared at her, her bright blue eyes aghast. 'You can't go to work this morning, darling, it –'

'Why ever not?' Emma interrupted. 'I *always* go to work.'

'Not today you're not! It wouldn't be appropriate.' Daisy shook her head vigorously. 'Besides,' she paused, glanced at her watch and went on, 'in a short while I'm going to take you off to lunch.'

'But I –'

'No buts, my darling Mamma,' Daisy said, her tone amused yet firm. 'I'm not your daughter, *and* Paul McGill's, for nothing. I can be just as tough as he *was*, and as you *are*, when I want to be. And this is one of those days when I'm putting my foot down. *Hard*. We haven't had lunch together for the longest time, and in a few days you'll be leaving with Uncle Blackie – and you'll be gone for months, from what *I* hear. Please don't disappoint me, I've been so looking forward to it, and I've already reserved a table at the Mirabelle.'

Emma smiled at Daisy, her favourite, her best-loved child. She had always found it hard to refuse her anything. 'All right,' she said, relenting. 'We'll have lunch together, and then I'll go to the store this afternoon. Oh Daisy, this is lovely!' Emma now exclaimed, staring at the solid gold, handmade evening bag she held in her hands. 'Why, darling, it's simply beautiful.' Her pleasure was apparent as she turned the bag around, opening it, looked inside, closed it. After examining it for a few seconds longer, she returned it to its protective black leather case, leaned over and kissed her daughter. 'Thank you, Daisy, this is stunning. And perfect for my trip, since it'll go with all my evening clothes.'

Daisy nodded, pleased and relieved that the gift was a success. 'That's what David and I thought, and we really racked our brains to come up with an unusual present. Are you sure you like the style? If you don't, Asprey's will be happy to send a salesperson over with two or three others for you to look at.'

'No, no, I don't want to see anything else, I like this one,' Emma assured her. 'Actually, I shall carry it tonight.'

The phone rang. 'Shall I get that for you, Mummy?'

'Would you, darling, please?'

Daisy leaned over the desk, took the phone, answered crisply. There was a brief exchange of pleasantries and after a moment Daisy said, 'I'll see if she can come to the phone. It's a little hectic here this morning. Just a minute, please.' Depressing the hold button, Daisy glanced at her mother. 'It's Elizabeth. She's back in London. Do you want to speak to her? I think perhaps you should.'

'Of course I'll speak to her.' Emma crossed to the desk. If she was surprised she did not show it, and she said steadily, 'Hello, Elizabeth.' Sitting down, she leaned back in the chair and cradled the receiver on her shoulder, toying with the pen in the onyx inkstand.

'Thank you,' she responded shortly, 'yes, it *is* a grand age, but I don't feel eighty. More like fifty-eight! And I'm as fit as a fiddle.' There was another pause. Emma focused her eyes on the wall opposite. They narrowed slightly and suddenly she cut in peremptorily, 'I think Winston was simply being courteous when he asked my permission. It wasn't really necessary. I don't think I have to remind you that Emily is of age. She can do anything she wants. And *no*, I didn't speak to Tony. I thought it was up to Emily to break the news to her father.'

Emma fell silent as her middle daughter talked incessantly at the other end of the phone. She looked across at Daisy, and made a face, rolled her eyes heavenward. Her patience began to dwindle and she interrupted again. 'I thought you phoned to wish me a happy birthday, Elizabeth, not to complain about Emily's engagement.'

An ironic smile flitted across Emma's face as she listened to Elizabeth's protests that she was not complaining.

'I'm glad to hear you say so,' Emma said into the receiver, 'because that would be a waste of breath. Now, how was your trip to Haiti? And how's your new boyfriend – Marc Deboyne?'

Elizabeth gurgled ecstatically into Emma's ear for a few more minutes, and finally Emma brought their conversation to a close with a brisk, 'Well, I'm glad you're happy, and thank you for calling, and for the birthday present. I'm sure it will arrive here any minute. Goodbye, Elizabeth.' She hung up.

Daisy asked, 'Is she upset about Emily and Winston?'

Emma laughed with some acerbity. 'Of course not. She's just making appropriate noises because she wasn't informed first, before me. You know Elizabeth as well as I do, she's very self-involved. But it was nice of her to ring up for my birthday.' Emma walked back to the couch and sat down. She gave Daisy an odd look, and half shrugged. 'Edwina phoned earlier, and so did Robin and Kit . . . I must say, I was very surprised to hear from my sons. I haven't heard a peep out of them, since that debacle over the will last year. Then today they're as nice as pie, and tell me they've sent me gifts too. Can you believe it?'

'Perhaps they're sorry, Mother, regret their plotting –'

'I doubt it!' Emma exclaimed softly. 'I'm far too cynical to think that either of *them* would have a change of heart. No, I'm sure their wives were behind the calls. June and Valerie have always been decent women. I can't imagine how they've managed to put up with my sons all these years. Kit plots. Robin schemes. Oh well –' Emma reached out now and took Daisy's hand in hers. 'There's something I've been meaning to ask you, darling. It's about this house . . . are you sure you don't want it?'

Daisy was startled, and she said in a surprised voice, 'But you've left this house to Sarah, haven't you?'

'Yes. However, I only bequeathed it to her because you indicated that you weren't interested in owning it, when we discussed the matter last year. But it should be yours or your children's. After all, your father did buy it for *us*.'

'I know, and I've always adored this house. It holds so many special memories for me . . . of my years growing up, of Daddy and you, and the lovely times the three of us had here. It is a little big though, and –'

Emma held up a silencing hand. 'Not if you think of it as two flats rather than one house. He did that for me, as you know. I did so want to keep up appearances . . .' Emma broke off and started to laugh. 'Goodness, Daisy, how times have *changed*. People think nothing of living together quite openly these days. Anyway, getting back to the disposition of this house, I thought you might want to reconsider. You have grandchildren now. Philip's bound to marry one day and in the not too distant future, I expect. He'll have children, he may even want to send them to school in England. Two self-contained flats under one unifying roof is awfully useful.'

'I'm not sure what to say, Mother. Your points are well taken, though.'

'Think about it. I can always change my will.'

'But you've left me so much . . . more than I'll ever need. It seems greedy, accepting this house.'

185

'That's a load of codswallop, Daisy. By rights it should be yours. If you decline, then I think that perhaps I'd better leave it to Paula or Philip.'

'But what about Sarah?'

'She's not a McGill.'

Daisy pursed her lips thoughtfully. 'All right, I'll do as you say – think about it. Look here, Mother, I know a woman of your immense wealth has to have her affairs in proper order at all times, but to tell you the truth, I do hate these discussions about your will and your death. They really make my stomach churn. Your death is certainly something I can't bear to think about, never mind discuss in this offhanded way. I get very upset.'

Emma looked at Daisy, said nothing. She squeezed her hand, sat back, continuing to stare at her intently.

Daisy took a deep breath, exhaled, forced a weak smile. 'Sorry, I didn't mean to speak to you so harshly. However, I do especially dislike talking about such things today, of *all* days. It's your birthday, remember.'

'I understand.' There was a tiny silence, and eventually Emma said in the quietest voice, 'I have been a good mother to you, haven't I, Daisy darling?'

'How could you ever think otherwise!' Daisy cried, her face ringed with concern. Her large and brilliant eyes of the deepest cornflower blue widened considerably, unexpectedly filled. 'You've been the most wonderful mother anyone could ever have wished for, always so loving and understanding.' Daisy returned Emma's steadfast gaze unblinkingly, and as she looked deeply into that wrinkled face her heart clenched with the most profound love for this remarkable woman who had borne her. She knew that the forbidding demeanour and the permanently stern expression were only surface characteristics, camouflage for a vast reservoir of emotion, and compassion. Emma Harte was a complex, many-faceted person, and contrary to what some believed, she was much more vulnerable and sensitive than most.

Daisy's gentle face underwent another change as her adoration and loyalty to her mother rose up in her. 'You're so very special, Mummy.' Daisy stopped, searched Emma's face, and shook her head wonderingly. 'You're the most honourable and loving person I've ever known. I've been so very lucky to have you all these years. Really blessed.'

Emma was deeply moved. 'Thank you, Daisy, for saying those beautiful things.' She looked into the distance, then murmured in a saddened voice, 'I've failed miserably with your half brothers and half sisters. I couldn't bear to think that I'd also failed with you. Or that I'd ever let you down in any way, not given you my best and dearest love.'

'You've given me everything . . . why, I couldn't begin to tell you what I owe you. And I don't believe you've failed the others. Not in the slightest. Didn't my father say once that each of us is the author of our own lives? That we are responsible for what we are? For the deeds, both good and bad, that we do?'

'He did.'

'Then *believe* it, Mother. It's true!'

'If you say so, darling.'

Emma fell into momentary silence, reflecting on her daughter's words. She was proud of Daisy, or the woman she had become. For all her sweetness, her soft manners and her intrinsic charm, Daisy had a strong, even tough, inner core and immense resilience and fortitude. Emma knew that when she chose to be, her Daisy was as immovable as a mountain and unwavering in her resoluteness. This was especially true if her convictions and principles were involved. Daisy, so young looking, was also inordinately youthful in her attitudes. She had a gaiety, a joyousness about life that was infectious, and she was of that rare breed of women who are liked by their own sex as well as by men. In fact, Emma was well aware that most people found it difficult, if not indeed impossible, to dislike Daisy. She was so full of integrity, so honourable, so beyond reproach, yet so truly human and caring, she towered above everyone. If her half brothers and half sisters were jealous of her, even resented her slightly, they were nevertheless rendered helpless under the force of her warm personality and extraordinary sincerity. It was her goodness, purity, and sense of fair play that also kept them off balance and at bay. She was the conscience of the family.

'You've got a faraway look on your face, Mother. Are you daydreaming? You seem so intense all of a sudden, what are you thinking about?' Daisy leaned closer to Emma, searching her face, and touching her cheek lightly.

'Oh nothing much.' Emma shook off her introspection, gave Daisy's clothes an appraising glance. 'Perhaps I ought to go and change, since we're going to the Mirabelle for lunch.'

'You don't have to, darling. Don't bother struggling into something else.'

'All right, I won't. But what about tonight. Blackie tells me he's wearing a dinner jacket. You don't think he actually wants me to wear a *long* frock, do you? I mean, after all, we're only going to be eight.'

Oh my God, Daisy thought, wait until she finds out it's closer to sixty. She wondered if her mother would be annoyed with them for giving the surprise party. Clearing her throat, praying that she sounded offhand, Daisy remarked, 'But Uncle Blackie wants this to be a festive evening, extra special. As he said to me the other day, "How often is your mother going to be eighty?" So naturally I agreed with him that we should dress. Still, you don't have to be that grand, wearing a long frock, I mean. I've decided on a peacock-blue faille cocktail dress myself. Look, I'd wear one of those lovely chiffons of yours, if I were you.'

'That's a relief. I have the green chiffon, it'll do quite nicely. Oh dear, there's the door bell *again*! I do hope it's not more flowers. This place is beginning to resemble a funeral parlour.'

'Mother! What an awful analogy!'

Daisy sprang up, moved swiftly across the floor, said over her shoulder, 'Perhaps it's the gift Elizabeth sent, or the ones from Kit and Robin. I'll go and ask Parker.'

Before Emma had a chance to blink, Daisy returned. 'It *is* a gift, Mother.' She glanced into the foyer, nodded, then took up a position near the fireplace, standing under the portrait in oils of Paul McGill.

Emma, acute as ever, peered at her suspiciously. 'What's going on? You looked exactly like your father did when he had something up his sleeve.' Her eyes strayed to Paul's portrait and then back to Daisy. There was no doubt whose daughter she was. Her likeness to him was more pronounced than ever

187

today . . . the same bright blue eyes, the black hair, the cleft in the chin. 'Come on, what are you hiding?'

Daisy looked expectantly at the door and beckoned.

On cue, Amanda and Francesca walked in, doing their level best to be sedate and grown up. They came to a halt in the centre of the floor, focused on Emma.

'Happy birthday to you, dear Grandma, happy birthday to you,' they chorused, sounding enthusiastic if slightly off-key.

Sarah, Emily and Paula had followed them into the study, stood behind their young cousins. They echoed, 'Happy birthday, Grandma,' gazing at her lovingly.

'Good heavens, what's all this!' Emma cried, truly taken by surprise. She gaped at her granddaughters, then addressing the twins, asked, 'And what are *you* two doing here? It's not half term, is it?'

Daisy cut in, '*I* took them out of school for a couple of days, Mother. They're staying with me and David. After all, it *is* your birthday.'

'I knew somebody was cooking up *something*,' Emma said, giving Daisy a sharp penetrating look. 'To tell you the truth, I thought you and Blackie were conniving together, Daisy. I suspected that you'd planned some sort of celebration for tonight.'

Daisy managed to keep her face neutral. But before she got the opportunity to say anything, Emily came forward purposefully. She handed a beautifully-wrapped package to Francesca, and touched Amanda's shoulder lightly. 'You haven't forgotten your speech have you?'

'Course not,' Amanda hissed back indignantly, reached for Francesca's hand and gave her twin a little tug, drew them both nearer to Emma.

Taking a deep breath, the fifteen-year-old said carefully, enunciating each word clearly, 'Grandy, this gift is from all your grandchildren – from Philip, Anthony, Alexander, Jonathan, Paula, Sarah, Emily, Francesca and me. Each one of us has contributed to it, so that we could present you with something special on this your eightieth birthday. We give it to you with our very dearest love always.'

Amanda went to Emma, bent down and kissed her; Francesca followed suit, then handed her the present.

'Thank you, girls,' Emma said to the twins. 'And your little speech was very nicely rendered, Amanda. Well done.' She looked over at their sister and cousins. 'My thanks to *all* of you.'

Emma sat for a moment without moving, holding the present on her lap. She let her eyes rest on each one of her elder granddaughters who were grouped together, and she smiled at them individually, nodding to herself, thinking how pretty and charming they looked. Tears welled unexpectedly, and she blinked them back, glanced down at the package, endeavouring to conceal her emotional reaction to this unexpected family scene. To her astonishment her hands shook as she untied the purple ribbon and lifted the object from its box.

The gift was a clock in the shape of an egg, made of the most translucent blue enamel she had ever set eyes on. A miniature cockerel, enamelled and delicately worked, was mounted on top of the egg, heavily jewelled with diamonds, rubies and sapphires. Emma marvelled at the design and craftsmanship, which were exquisite, and she recognized the clock for the precious work of art it truly was.

'It's by Fabergé, isn't it?' she managed at last, her voice hardly audible.

'Yes,' Emily said. 'Actually, Gran, it's an Imperial Easter egg which Fabergé made for the Empress Marie Fedorovna of Russia. Her son, Nicholas II, the last Tsar, ordered it for her.'

'How on earth did you manage to find something as rare and valuable as this?' Emma asked, awed. As an art collector of discernment she was aware that such pieces by Fabergé were becoming increasingly scarce.

'Paula heard about the clock through Henry Rossiter,' Emily volunteered. 'He had learned it was going to be auctioned last week at Sotherby's.'

'And Henry went to the auction for you?'

'No, Grandy. We all went *en masse*, except for the twins, who were at school, of course. Henry did come with us, though. Paula had called us, and we got together for a confab. We each agreed at once that we should try to buy the clock for you – as a collective gift from us. It was terribly exciting!'

'We almost lost it several times, but we just kept on going, topping other bids. And suddenly we had it. We were so thrilled, Grandma!'

'And so am I, my darlings.' Her eyes encompassed them all.

Parker suddenly appeared, also on cue from Daisy, bringing in a tray of glasses brimming with sparkling champagne. When each of them had a drink they clustered around Emma, wished her a happy birthday again, and toasted her health.

Once things had calmed down, Emma turned to Daisy and said, 'Are we really going to lunch at the Mirabelle? Or was that a ruse to prevent me from going to the store?'

Daisy grinned. 'Of course we're going to lunch – all of us who are present, in fact. Anthony, Alexander, Jonathan and David will be joining us. So, you can forget about going to work today, Mother.'

Emma was about to assert herself on this point, but she recognized the look on Daisy's face. Since it forbade argument, she held her tongue.

It was dusk.

Emma walked across the entrance foyer, so bosky and still at this hour, her step light as she entered her study.

She was dressed for the dinner party Blackie was giving at the Ritz, wearing a short dress made of layers and layers of pale and dark green chiffon, simply cut with long floating Mandarin sleeves. The magnificent McGill emeralds, blazing at her throat, on her ears, arms and hand, looked stunning against the mingled greens of the delicate fabric, the fire, depth and brilliance of the gems intensified by the repetition of their colour.

Yes, it was a good choice, Emma decided, as she passed the one mirror in the room and caught a fleeting glimpse of herself. She did not stop, but continued across the floor, the only sound the swishing of her dress as she moved with her usual briskness.

When she reached the console where some of her many birthday presents were stacked, she picked up the Imperial Easter egg and carried it back to the drawing room.

Placing it on an antique occasional table near the fireplace, she stood back, admiring it again. It was undoubtedly one of the loveliest things she had ever been given, and she could not wait to show it to Blackie.

The sharp trilling of the bell made her start, and in rapid succession she heard Parker's footsteps resounding in the foyer, the front door banging and muffled voices.

A moment later Blackie was striding into the room, splendidly attired in a superbly-cut tuxedo, the wide grin on his face competing with the sparkle in his black eyes, and he was obviously buoyed up with excitement.

'Happy birthday, me darlin',' he boomed, and drawing to a standstill he swept her up into his arms. Then he released his grip, stepped away and caught her hands in his, looked down into her face, repeating the gestures practised on her for years. 'You look bonnier than ever tonight, Emma,' he said, beaming, and bent to kiss her.

'Thank you, Blackie.' Emma returned his smile, and moved towards the sofa. 'Did you tell Parker what you wanted to drink?'

'Sure and I did. My usual.' He lowered himself into the chair opposite her, his large frame filling it completely. 'I don't want you to think I've come empty handed – your birthday present is outside. I'll go and get it –'

The butler's discreet knock interrupted him, and Parker came in with a tumbler of neat Irish whiskey for Blackie and a goblet of white wine for Emma.

As soon as they were alone, Blackie raised his glass. 'Here's to you, mavourneen. And may we celebrate many, many more of our birthdays together.'

'I know we will,' Emma laughed. 'And here's to our trip, Blackie dear.'

'To the trip.' After only one sip, Blackie sprang up. 'Don't move,' he instructed, 'and when I tell you to close your eyes, I want you to do just that, and no cheating, mind you.'

She sat waiting for him to come back, guessed he had enlisted Parker's help when she heard the low murmur of the butler's voice, Blackie's response, then the sound of paper being ripped.

'Close your eyes,' Blackie ordered from the doorway several seconds later. 'Remember what I said, no peeking, Emma!'

'I won't,' she reassured him, laughter bringing a lilt to her voice. She sat perfectly still, her hands clasped in her lap, and she suddenly felt like a young girl again; like the little starveling girl who had received her first real present wrapped in silver paper and tied with silver ribbon. It had been from him – had been that cheap little green glass brooch which she had cherished all of her life. She still had it tucked away in her jewel case, alongside the fine replica he had eventually had made in emeralds. And once, long ago, that bit of green glass had been her most treasured and valuable possession.

'Now!' Blackie cried.

Slowly Emma opened her eyes, and as she looked at the painting he was holding in front of her she instantly recognized the work of her great-niece, Sally Harte. Emma gasped in astonished delight, and then she filled with a swift and piercing pain of poignant nostalgia as haunting memories rippled through her. Her throat tightened. She focused her eyes, took in every detail, every brushstroke, and she could only gaze at the painting's evocative beauty, unable to say a word.

'Oh Blackie,' she said at last, 'it's perfectly lovely . . . the moors above Fairley. My moors, where we first met.'

'Look a bit closer, me darlin'.'

'I don't have to, I can see it's the Top of the World.' She raised her eyes and shook her head in wonderment. 'What a truly meaningful gift this is, my dear old friend. The painting is extraordinary. Why I feel as though I can reach out and pick a bunch of that heather, as I used to do for my mother.' She let one finger rest lightly against the canvas, barely touching it. 'I can hear the tinkle of this little beck, here in the corner, and the sound of its crystal water tumbling down over the polished stones. It's so . . . so real, I can even smell the scent of bilberry and bracken and the heather. Oh Blackie darling . . .'

Emma looked up at him and smiled her incomparable smile, then swiftly brought her gaze back to the painting. 'It's a real Yorkshire sky, isn't it? So full of clarity and shimmering radiance. What immense talent that girl has, and only Turner and Van Gogh have ever been able to capture the true quality of light on canvas in such a way. Yes, Sally has surpassed herself with this.'

Gratification and pleasure shone on his craggy, expressive face. 'I took Sally over there myself, showed her the exact spot. And she kept going back, time and time again. She wanted perfection for you, Emma, as I did, and I think she got the painting just right in the end.'

'She most certainly did. Thank you, thank you so much for thinking of such an unusual present.'

Blackie said softly, 'I had her write this on the back. In paint.' He turned the painting around, indicated the neat lettering. 'You won't be able to read what it says without your glasses, so I shall tell you what I asked her to put. It says, "To Emma Harte on reaching her eightieth birthday with love from her life-long friend, Blackie O'Neill." Then there's the date underneath.'

For the second time that day, Emma was greatly moved. She could not speak, and she turned away quickly so that he would not see her misty eyes. She sat down, took a sip of her drink, composed herself, and finally murmured, 'That's lovely, just lovely, darling.'

After propping the painting against a console table, and making sure it was in her direct line of vision, he returned to his seat and lifted his own glass. 'And it *is* a lifetime, too, Emma. Sixty-six years to be precise.' He nodded at the painting. 'Aye, the Top of the World – your mother's name for Ramsden Crags. I'll never forget the day you found me lost on the moors, and we came up out of the Ghyll and I saw the Crags for the first time.'

Emma followed the direction of his eyes. Over six decades dropped away and she saw herself as she had been at fourteen. A poor little servant girl . . . trudging across the moors at dawn in her broken-down button boots and the old patched coat Cook had given her. That coat had been a treasured item too, even though it had been small and tight and threadbare. It had hardly protected her from the rain and snow and bitter North wind.

Now she stared fully at Blackie, seeing him as he was tonight, but remembering how he had looked in his rough, drab workman's clothes and his cheap cloth cap worn at such a cheeky angle, carrying his sack of tools slung over his broad shoulder. *Disreputable*, Cook had called the dirty old burlap bag that contained *his* most treasured possessions – his hammers and trowels and mortar board.

Emma said slowly: 'Who would have thought that we would both live to such great ages ... that we would acquire so much in our lifetimes ... immense power, immeasurable wealth ... that we would become what we are today.'

Blackie gave her an odd look, then chuckled, at the amazement ringing in her voice. 'I for one never doubted our rosy futures,' he announced, his voice underscored by a bubbling merriment. 'I told you I was going to be a toff, a real millionaire, and that you would be a grand lady. Mind you, me darlin', I'll be confessing to you now that I never suspected you'd be quite as *grand* as you are.'

They both smiled, their wise old eyes holding, secure in their love and friendship, revelling in the knowledge that they truly understood each other, and as no other person alive did. So many years ... so many experiences shared welded them. The bonds between them were like steel, and so strong they were unbreakable.

The silence drifted for a while.

Eventually Blackie roused himself. 'Now, mavourneen mine, tell me about your busy day.'

'One thing surprised me, Blackie. *They* called. *The plotters*. I was startled to hear from my sons and Elizabeth, I don't mind telling you. She's back in London of course. No doubt with the French boyfriend. Edwina gave me a ring this morning, and she was pleasant, believe it or not. Perhaps *she's* mended her ways finally. And I had two other most wonderful calls ... they really touched me.' Her eyes lit up. 'Philip rang from Sydney, and your Shane from New York. Wasn't that nice?' He nodded, smiling, and she continued, 'It seems that your grandson and mine are planning birthday parties for me when we arrive in their cities, so be prepared. As for my day, well you can see for yourself what it's brought.' Emma waved her hand around, her eyes sweeping the room. 'Flowers, cards and so many gifts. And I had lunch with Daisy, David and my grandchildren at the Mirabelle.'

She proceeded to recount every detail of the luncheon party, then told him how they had whisked her away from the restaurant at three thirty and taken her to her store in Knightsbridge. Marched by her grandchildren into her boardroom, she had been greeted by her top executives who were anxiously awaiting her arrival at the special reception they had arranged for her.

When she had finished this somewhat breathless recital, Emma rose and picked up the Imperial Easter egg, said confidingly, 'This is what my grandchildren gave me, and like your painting it is a most meaningful gift. I shall treasure them both always.'

'So you had a lovely day – I'm glad. That's the way it should always be.' Blackie stood up. 'Come along, I think we'd better be on our way. We're meeting in Bryan's suite at the Ritz for a drop of bubbly before we go down to dinner.'

Ten minutes later when they arrived at the Ritz Hotel in Piccadilly, Blackie ushered Emma up the steps. He paused briefly at the reception desk, asked the young man behind it to announce his arrival to his son, Mr Bryan O'Neill, and gave the number of the suite.

'Of course, Mr O'Neill.' The young assistant manager smiled at Emma. 'Good evening, Mrs Harte.'

Emma acknowledged his greeting pleasantly, and after Blackie had expressed his thanks they proceeded along the lobby unaware how striking they looked and of the heads turned to watch them.

Emma remained silent as they rode up in the lift, and Blackie stole several surreptitious looks at her, wondering if she had any inkling about the party which had been planned with such secrecy. He could not hazard a guess. Her face, as always, was inscrutable. He believed Emma would not be angry, despite Daisy's prediction that her mother might easily react adversely. He knew his Emma, understood that she was like a child at times. She enjoyed surprises and gifts and special occasions, particularly when those occasions revolved around her.

That's because of the deprivations of her youth, he said to himself. In those days she had had nothing, nothing of any real value. No, that wasn't strictly true. She had had her startling looks, her brains, her stamina and her extraordinary health, and her enormous courage. Not to mention that terrible pride of hers. Oh that pride, and oh the shame she had experienced because of that pride and because she was poor. 'But poverty's not a crime, even though people who're better off always try to make you feel like a criminal,' she had once cried to him, her anger bringing a fierce dark gleam to her young eyes. Ah yes, he remembered everything ... Emma had had more than her fair share of pain and sorrow and grief in her life. But she would not suffer again, nor ever be deprived again, and there would be no more pain. They were both far too old for tragedies ... tragedies were for the young.

Finally they drew to a stop in front of the door to the suite. Blackie smiled inwardly. The phone call from reception had been the alert signal for Bryan and Daisy to keep the guests absolutely quiet. Obviously they had succeeded admirably. A pin dropping would have sounded like a gun going off in the silence permeating the corridor.

Giving Emma a final rapid glance, Blackie raised his hand and rapped. The door was opened almost at once by Daisy. 'There you are, Mother, Uncle Blackie. We've been waiting for you. Do come in.'

Blackie propelled Emma forward and stepped inside after her.

'*Happy birthday!*' fifty-eight people shrieked in unison.

That Emma was thunderstruck was immediately evident to everyone present. She stared at the crowd made up of relatives and friends who had gathered together to celebrate her birthday, her expression startled, and she coloured slightly, the blush rising from her neck to suffuse her face. Her eyes immediately swivelled to Blackie's, and she whispered, 'You devil! Why didn't you give me a hint, some warning at least?'

He grinned, gratified that the secret had obviously been well and truly kept. 'I didn't dare. Daisy said she'd kill me. And don't start telling me you're annoyed, because I can see from your face that you're not!'

'That's true,' she admitted and finally permitted herself to smile.

She swung her head, faced the packed room, and was momentarily rooted to the spot. The lingering smile slowly grew wider and wider as she noted the familiar faces smiling back at her in welcome.

Her two sons, Kit Lowther and Robin Ainsley, were there with their wives, June and Valerie; her daughters Edwina and Elizabeth flanked a distinguished-looking man who was outrageously handsome. She supposed this was the notorious Marc Deboyne – International White Trash, Emily had so succinctly labelled him. Still, he did have a rather fascinating smile and a glamorous aura. Elizabeth always went for the pretty ones, of course. Well, *she* was hardly the one to criticize. The men who had tenanted her life had had their fair share of good looks.

Daisy had slipped across the room, stood with her arm linked through David's, and he, in turn, was positioned next to her sisters-in-law, the two old ladies, Charlotte and Natalie, who were dressed to the nines and dripping with jewels. Paula and Jim hovered next to them; Winston was shepherding Emily, Amanda and Francesca, and was apparently enjoying his role of protector. Emma's eyes automatically dropped to Emily's left hand and she winked at her granddaughter when she spotted the glittering emerald engagement ring.

She stared beyond them into the adjoining suite, saw Sarah, Jonathan, Alexander and his girl friend Maggie Reynolds crowded together in the entrance. On their left was the entire Kallinski family, and edging up to them were Bryan, Geraldine and Merry O'Neill. Positioned next to the latter were the rest of the Hartes. Randolph's beaming face peered out at her, just visible above the shoulders of his two daughters, Vivienne and Sally. Anthony, her grandson, smiled back at her from Sally's side.

Henry Rossiter was leaning against the fireplace at the far end of the second suite. He looks better than ever, Emma thought, and eyed his current girl friend, the noted model Jennifer Glenn. She was at least forty years younger. That's one way to ensure a heart attack, dear Henry, Emma thought to herself, her eyes amused. Gaye Sloane, her private secretary, graced Henry's right, and the remainder of the guests were made up of old friends, as well as close business associates such as Len Harvey, who ran Genret, and his wife Monica.

Emma's initial stunned surprise had completely dissipated in the few minutes she had stood motionless surveying the gathering. Now she was again totally in command of herself, all those present, and this occasion. Looking autocratic, proud, dignified, and supremely elegant she took a step forward and inclined her head.

'Well,' she exclaimed, her strong clear voice ringing out as she broke the silence at last, 'I never realized I knew so many people who were capable of keeping a secret. At least, from *me*.' Their laughter rippled around her as she glided forward into their midst, accepting their affectionate greetings and good wishes with a graciousness that few could match.

Blackie edged over to Daisy, stood watching Emma circulating, dispensing her inimitable charm. And by the ladleful, he muttered under his breath. A huge grin suddenly illuminated his face and his eyes crinkled with humour. He exclaimed to Daisy, 'And you worried yourself to death, thinking she was going to be upset! Just *look* at her . . . she's in her element, handling them all with aplomb and behaving as if she's Royalty.'

194

21

An hour later, at eight o'clock, Blackie escorted Emma into the private dining room farther along the corridor where the birthday celebration dinner was to be held.

Bending towards her, he whispered, 'Daisy didn't want anybody's feelings to be hurt, nor did she wish to be accused of favouritism, so none of your children or grandchildren will be sitting at our table.'

'That was smart of her,' Emma murmured, her mouth twitching with hidden laughter. Well, Daisy *was* the one true diplomat in the family; on the other hand, she knew her sons would not exactly be clamouring to sit with her. Emma was still astonished that they had deigned to come at all. Elizabeth's presence did not surprise her. It was just conceivable that her daughter wanted to make friends again, since she always had her eye on the main chance. No doubt she thought she could ingratiate herself, probably with the hopes of extracting more money. Her other motivations would be a desire to see her children and show off her new boyfriend. As for Edwina, she was currying favour with Anthony, who would have disapproved if his mother had declined the invitation.

Slowly she and Blackie crossed to the main table, which was flanked on either side by two other tables. All were arranged in a semi-circle around the small dance floor, and at the opposite side of this square of polished parquet a band was already playing a selection of popular music.

Emma's all-encompassing glance took in everything. In the flickering candle-light emanating from the five round tables, the room resembled a charming summer garden, with masses of flowers banked on every side, and small colour-ful bouquets decorating the tables. The latter were covered in shell-pink table-cloths and gleamed brightly with the sparkle of crystal, silver and fine china.

Nodding with pleasure and smiling with approval, Emma turned to Blackie as they came to a standstill, and said, 'What a lovely setting Daisy has created . . . it's so very festive.'

Blackie beamed. 'Yes, she worked hard with the banqueting manager, and supervised everything herself.' He pulled out a chair for her, but remained standing himself.

Once she was seated Emma squinted at the place cards on either side of her, and said, 'I see you're on my right, Henry on my left, but who else will be joining us?'

'Charlotte and Natalie of course, Len and Monica Harvey, and Henry's girlfriend Jennifer. We've also got Mark and Ronnie Kallinski and their wives with us, which makes twelve altogether.'

'Oh I *am* glad some of the Kallinskis will be sitting with us. I couldn't help thinking of David tonight, wishing he were here. Although Ronnie doesn't look as much like David as Mark, he does remind me of his father. He has many of his mannerisms. Don't you agree?'

'I do indeed, me darlin'. Ah, here comes Randolph with his mother and his aunt.'

Emma half turned, welcomed Charlotte and Natalie, and with his usual flourish and show of old-world gallantry, Blackie ushered Emma's sisters-in-law to their seats.

Randolph, bluff and hearty as always, squeezed Emma's shoulder and boomed, 'I'm sitting at Bryan's table, over there. But I'll be back, Aunt Emma.' He winked at her. 'I intend to claim at least one dance.'

Laughing, Emma said, 'A foxtrot, Randolph, nothing more energetic than that.'

'You're on.'

His mother leaned over to Emma and confided, 'Emily's the best thing that has happened to that grandson of mine. I couldn't be more delighted about the engagement.'

'Oh so am I, Charlotte, and that was a sweet gesture of yours, giving Emily the strand of pearls as an engagement present. I remember when Winston gave them to you.'

Charlotte beamed. 'Yes, when we became engaged in 1919. Now, about the wedding. I do hope they'll get married in Yorkshire, Emma. Elizabeth was talking to me earlier, and she seems to think the wedding should be in London.'

'Does she now,' Emma said with dryness. 'I wouldn't worry about it for one moment. Elizabeth's always had grand ideas, and usually they're self-serving. Under the circumstances, I think it's for Emily and Winston to decide, and they've indicated to me that they want to get married in Ripon Cathedral. I think that's a lovely idea, and then we can have the reception at the house.'

The three women talked about Emily's wedding, planned for the following summer, for a few minutes longer and then Emma started to tell them about her impending trip with Blackie and the places they would visit on their journey to Australia.

Blackie continued to direct traffic, and within a few minutes the room had filled up, everyone was seated, and the waiters were gliding between the five tables, filling glasses with white wine. There was a feeling of conviviality and gaiety in the air. Laughter reverberated, the cacophony of voices rose to a crescendo, the hubbub of noise balanced by the strains of the light music playing in the background.

Emma, her mind as razor-sharp as always, her eyes everywhere, soon discerned that her family and friends were enjoying themselves wholeheartedly, appeared to be having the best of times. After the first course of smoked salmon had been served, some of the younger guests immediately took to the dance floor, and Emma watched them, filled with pride, thinking how attractive they looked . . . the girls in their pretty dresses, the young men in their smart dinner jackets. They whirled around the dance floor, their clear young faces shining with happiness, their eyes bright with hope and limitless expectations for the future, their lives ahead of them, offering so much.

Jonathan's bland and smiling face came into her line of vision as he guided young Amanda around the perimeters of the floor, and for a split second she wondered if she had been wrong about him. She clamped down on this thought, not wanting to dwell on problems tonight, and swung her eyes to his father.

Robin was dancing with his half sister, Daisy, and oozing charm. Dark, exotic-looking Robin, once her favourite son, the dashing Member of Parliament, currently politically secure after a few rocky rides. Well, he *was* shrewd and smart when it came to his own career. He had always been the dyed-in-the-wool politician, the consummate deal maker, and, she had to admit, popular in the Labour Party, not to mention with his constituents in Leeds.

Blackie cut into her thoughts when he touched her arm lightly, pushed back his chair, and said, 'Come on, Emma, you owe me the first dance.'

He led her proudly on to the floor, took her in his arms, and they glided away, smoothly in step to the strains of the Cole Porter medley the band had begun to play.

Blackie was well aware that they cut quite a swathe together, and towering above Emma as he did, he was conscious that they were the centre of attraction, knew that all eyes were on them. He caught sight of Kit scrutinizing them and he inclined his head, smiled, and peered around, seeking Robin. There he was, swinging Daisy across the floor, so smooth, so sleek . . . and so slippery. Blackie despised her sons for their treachery towards Emma, and now he wondered if either of them had enough sense to realize how foolish they had been, pitting themselves against this brilliant woman, trying to outsmart her. They had had as much chance as a snowball in hell. Of course she had won hands down. She always won.

Emma whispered against his chest, 'Everybody's looking at us, talking about us, Blackie.'

'Nothing's changed much then.'

Emma simply smiled and they finished their dance in silence.

The evening continued to progress without a hitch. Everyone ate the delicious food, partook of the excellent wines, talked, joked, laughed and danced, and with a carefreeness that surprised Emma. It seemed to her that for once there were no undercurrents. It was as if an unspoken truce had been automatically declared between the various factions, as if animosities, rivalries, hatreds and jealousies had been temporarily buried. Tomorrow they might well be at each other's throats, but tonight they were friendly, and apparently at ease with each other. Perhaps this was only on the surface, but nonetheless it pleased her to see them behaving with a decorum that befitted the occasion.

Emma, too, was enjoying herself, but as the hours sped by she realizing the evening was inducing mixed emotions in her. Memories came unbidden . . . memories that were both joyous and heartrending. Bits of her life kept rushing back to her, and even the location had a profound effect on her at one moment. The Ritz Hotel was so bound up with Paul and their early years together, for here they had snatched shreds of happiness during the First World War before he had gone back to the trenches in France. For a second or two Paul McGill dominated her mind, and she sank back into herself, looking inward, her eyes momentarily glazed as she drifted into the past. But then she heard Daisy's vivid laughter at the next table, and looked up sharply as the present intruded forcefully. She shook off the wistfulness that had briefly enveloped her, sternly reminded herself that she had recently resolved to look only to the future.

Blackie, who had become conscious of her periodic lapses into silence, drew her into conversation, and had her laughing in a matter of minutes. Suddenly, he interrupted himself in the middle of a story he was recounting and exclaimed, 'Brace yourself, me love, here comes Randolph to claim his dance.'

'Then dance I shall,' Emma said, and allowed herself to be swept off by her beaming nephew. They had circled the floor once when Jonathan cut in, who in turn had to give way to Winston after only a few minutes. Anthony was the next to steal his grandmother away, and soon Alexander was tapping his cousin on the shoulder, so that he could complete the waltz with her.

When the music stopped Alexander did not release her, but stood looking down at her as they lingered in the middle of the floor, an unreadable expression in his eyes.

Emma searched his face inquiringly. 'What is it Sandy? You look as if you're about to say something important.'

'I am, Grandy.' He bent closer and whispered.

'Of course,' Emma said, smiling. She whispered something back to him as he escorted her to her table.

Sitting down, Emma turned to Blackie, fanned herself with her hand. 'Phew! That was a *marathon*. To tell you the truth, I think I'm getting too old to be gallivanting around dance floors.'

'What, a spring chicken like you? *Never*. Anyway, you seem to be thoroughly enjoying yourself,' Blackie laughed.

'I am, darling. It's a lovely party, and everyone's so very friendly with each other.' When he did not answer, she stared hard at him. 'They really are, you know.'

'Aye,' he said at last, laconic, very noncommittal, 'perhaps you're right.' But Blackie was not so certain she *was* right, found her children's unexpected chumminess suspect. On the other hand, they were behaving themselves, and that was all that mattered to him. In a few days the two of them would be winging their way to New York, and when Emma was gone from their midst her family could start murdering each other for all he cared.

Suddenly the din ceased and everyone glanced at each other as the wall candelabras and ceiling chandelier were dimmed. There was a deafening drum roll. A waiter came forward pushing a trolley on which there reposed an enormous birthday cake topped with eighty candles flickering brightly in the muted light. The moment the waiter came to a halt in the middle of the dance floor the band struck up the 'Happy Birthday' refrain, and the majority of the guests followed Blackie's lead as he began to sing, joining in exuberantly. When the music finished Blackie assisted Emma to her feet and walked her over to the cake, and together they blew out the candles. Emma picked up the knife and cut the first slice, and smiling and nodding to the guests she returned with Blackie to their table.

Champagne was poured, the cake passed around by the waiters, and once each person had been served, Daisy rose and tapped her glass with a spoon. 'Can I have your attention! *Please!*' Conversation ceased and all eyes settled on her.

'Thank you,' Daisy said, 'and thank you very much for coming tonight, to celebrate my mother's birthday. Blackie and I are delighted you managed to keep our secret. We knew from Mother's face when she arrived that she was truly surprised.'

Daisy gave them her warmest smile, continued: 'In the past few weeks Blackie and I have been approached by various members of the family, and friends, who wanted to say a few words, to pay tribute to Emma Harte this evening. It was quite a dilemma for us – knowing who to choose, and inevitably we realized that the great lady we are honouring would soon become impatient if she had to sit through a lot of speeches. Especially since she herself would be the subject of those speeches. It was Blackie who came up with the best solution, but before I announce the first speaker, I would like my mother and all of you to know that we had requests from the following.'

Daisy picked up a piece of paper, glanced at it, lifted her head and focused her eyes on Emma. 'All of your grandchildren wanted to propose a toast to you, Mother, to be the representative of the third generation. Robin and Elizabeth both wished to say something on behalf of us, your children. Henry, Jim, Len and Bryan all asked to be the one to offer you the very best wishes of your many friends and business associates.'

Emma inclined her head graciously, looking first to her right, then to her left, acknowledging those whom Daisy had mentioned.

Daisy proceeded, 'As I told you, Blackie solved our little problem, and most appropriately, in my opinion. Now I would like to introduce our first speaker – Mr Ronald Kallinski.'

Ronnie rose. He was a man of dominating presence, tall, slender, with a saturnine face and black wavy hair tinged with grey. He had inherited the eyes of his father and his grandmother Janessa Kallinski. These were of the brightest blue and seemed all that more startling because he had a weatherbeaten complexion.

'Daisy, Emma, Blackie, ladies and gentlemen,' he began, his generous smile revealing flashing white teeth. Ronnie had a considerable amount of charm and savoir faire, and as chairman of the board of Kallinski Industries, he was used to public speaking. 'There are many of Emma's friends and business associates present, however I feel certain that they will not be offended if I term this evening a gathering of the clans. Three clans to be precise . . . the Hartes, the O'Neills and the Kallinskis. Well over half a century ago three young people became bosom friends. Emma, Blackie and David, my father. From what I've been told, this friendship apparently seemed startling, even peculiar to many people, who could not understand what a Gentile, an Irish Catholic and a Jew could possibly have in common. But those three young people knew. They recognized their own likeness in each other, saw qualities that *were* common denominators. They were warm, loving, outgoing and filled with hope. They shared ambition, drive, a determination to succeed at all costs, yet without sacrificing honour, honesty or integrity. And they believed in charity to others. The trio were soon bound together by bonds of love and respect, and they remained loyal, and devoted throughout their lives, until my father's death a few years ago.'

Ronnie shifted his stance slightly as he paused for breath. 'Some of you may not know this,' he remarked after a moment, 'but the trio dubbed themselves the Three Musketeers, and when Blackie asked me to speak to you tonight, to pay homage to Emma, he said I would be standing in for that third Musketeer who is no longer with us. *My father.*'

After a quick sip of water, Ronnie levelled his eyes at the main table. 'Emma Harte is the most remarkable of women, and her attributes are manifold. So it is hard, if not downright impossible, to know which one to single out as being extra special. However, if David Kallinski were present tonight I know that he would choose to speak to you about the immense and extraordinary *courage* of Emma Harte. This quality first manifested itself to the Kallinski family in 1905 when Emma was sixteen. Let me tell you about this. One day, as she wandered in the North Street area of Leeds seeking work, she came across a group of ruffians attacking a middle-aged man. He was in need of help, since he had fallen to the ground and lay huddled near a wall trying to protect himself as they continued to stone him. Without giving a thought to her condition – Emma was pregnant at the time – this young girl on the deserted street instantly rushed to his aid. She was fearless as she drove the attackers away. After helping the man to his feet and checking his injuries, she retrieved his scattered packages and insisted on escorting him to his home in the Leylands. The name of that man was Abraham Kallinski. He was my grandfather. As Emma guided him to the safety of his simple abode, she asked Abraham why the ruffians had been stoning him. Abraham told her: *Because I am a Jew*. The young Emma was baffled by this statement, and Abraham went on to explain to her that the Jews in Leeds were persecuted because their religion, dietary laws and customs appeared foreign to the local people. He told her of the terrible brutalities the Jews suffered at the hands of marauding bands of hooligans who entered the Leylands, which was a ghetto, and attacked them and their homes. Emma was disgusted and outraged to hear such things. And she at once condemned these persecutors as cruel, stupid and ignorant.'

Ronnie Kallinski nodded to himself, then looked directly at Emma, his face reflecting his love and admiration for her. He said slowly, 'From that day to the present, this most extraordinary woman has fought stupidity, ignorance, and every kind of inequity, has always condemned the wicked traits she recognized in some at such a tender age. She has continued to loathe religious and ethnic prejudice, any kind of prejudice, in fact. Her courage has never diminished. It has only grown in strength. She has remained consistent in her belief in justice, truth and fair play.'

Henry Rossiter began to clap, and others followed suit, and Ronnie eventually had to call out for them to be quiet.

'My father once told me that Emma, Blackie and he had helped to create a city's greatness as they had lifted themselves out of the grinding poverty of their youth, but that it was Emma most of all who had put her indelible stamp on the city of Leeds. Indeed he spoke the truth, and her contributions to industry and her philanthropy are renowned. However, I would like to add a comment of my own, and it is this: Emma has also put her inimitable imprimatur on each one of us present . . . not only on every member of the three closely-knit clans, but on her friends and business associates. We must be proud of that, for we are better people for knowing her, for being part of her circle. Emma Harte honours us with her devoted friendship, her love and depth of understanding. And she does us the greatest honour by her presence tonight. And so, in my late father's name, and in the name of all the Kallinskis absent and present, I ask you to raise your glasses to Emma Harte. A woman of outstanding courage and indomitability who has never been defeated, and who has always stood tall . . . so tall she towers above all of us.'

Ronnie raised his glass. 'To Emma Harte.'

After the toast had been repeated, Ronnie said: 'And now Blackie will say a few words.'

Blackie pushed himself to his feet. 'Thank you, Ronnie. David could not have said it better, and your own tribute to Emma was fitting and most moving. As Daisy told you, we knew Emma would not sit still for a lot of laudatory talk. Also, since I'm aware she regards the shortest of speeches as humbug, I'm going to be brief.' Blackie chuckled. 'Well, as brief as I can be. Obviously on this special occasion of Emma's eightieth birthday I do feel the need to say a few kind words about her.'

As Blackie launched himself into a recital about her strength of character, her ability to conquer against all odds, and her great business achievements, Emma sat back. She was only partially listening. During Ronnie's speech, she had begun to ruminate on her early beginnings. She thought of the place she had started out from, the great distance she had travelled and she marvelled at herself, wondering how she had accomplished all that she had, and for the most part entirely by herself.

But after a short while she became aware that many pairs of eyes were on her as well as Blackie, and she roused herself from her reflections. Her old friend was moving away from bygone eras, talking of the present. And Emma's thoughts instantly settled on her life as it was today.

Well, she thought, whatever my life has been about my grandchildren are proof positive to me that it has been worthwhile. Quite unexpectedly, as she experienced a flash of clarity, everything became clear to Emma. So clear she was startled for a moment. And she knew what she must do tonight, what her course of action must be.

Blackie was drawing to a close. 'It has been the greatest privilege of my life to be her friend. So please join in my toast to Emma, which comes from my heart.' Blackie leaned forward, grasped hold of his glass.

Lifting it high, Blackie smiled down at her. 'Emma, you truly are a woman of substance in the finest sense of that phrase. May you long be with us. To you, Emma.'

Emma felt the heat rush to her face as the roomful of smiling friends and relatives toasted her and her throat tightened with sudden emotion.

Once everyone was seated, Blackie, who had continued to stand, said: 'I give you our guest of honour, Emma Harte.'

Emma rose, stepped around her chair and pushed it under the table. She stood with her hands resting on its back, her eyes slowing roving around the room, her glance touching each one of them briefly.

Finally, she said, 'Thank you for joining me on my birthday, and for the lovely gifts and flowers you sent me today. I was very touched. I must also express my thanks to Blackie and Daisy, for giving this party, and for being such wonderful hosts.'

She let her gaze linger on Ronnie Kallinski, her eyes very bright, glittering with moisture under the wrinkled lids. 'I am so glad you and your family are here with me tonight, Ronnie. And I thank you for your eloquent words, for standing in for your father. David is sorely missed.' She turned her attention to Blackie. 'You said some beautiful things about me too ... thank you, Blackie.'

Then in a crisper tone Emma said, 'As many of you know, Emily and Winston are to be married next year. However, they did want me to formally announce their engagement to you all this evening. It seems that romance is in the air in the Harte clan. Alexander also asked me to announce his engagement to Marguerite Reynolds. So, let us drink to the future happiness of these four young people.'

The toast was given amidst a ripple of excited whispers, exclamations.

Emma stood waiting, gripping the back of the chair more tightly than ever. Her expression was benign but her narrowed green eyes were watchful. She knew exactly what she would say, even though she had decided to make this announcement only ten minutes before.

Paula, scrutinizing Emma, took note of the friendly expression on her face. But her grandmother did not fool her for one moment. She recognized that implacable glint in her eyes. It signalled something ... Emma was about to drop one of her bombshells. Paula instantly tensed, wondering what this could be. She could not hazard a guess. Her eyes remained riveted on Emma. How imperious Grandy looks at this moment, she thought, standing there so erect and proud, totally in command of herself, and this audience.

Emma moved slightly and in the soft light emanating from the many candles the emeralds blazed more brilliantly, and there was a shimmer, a luminosity about Emma at this moment. Power, Paula thought. My grandmother exudes immense power.

A hush had fallen over everyone and, like Paula, they stared at Emma, filled with unexpected anticipation.

Finally Emma spoke. Her voice rang out clear and strong, dominating the room. 'In everybody's life there comes a time when it is appropriate to step aside, to permit younger voices to be heard, greater visions to be perceived. *Tonight is that time for me.*' Emma paused, letting her words sink in.

There was a collective gasp.

'*I am going.* And going willingly. It struck me tonight that I've earned the right to rest these tired old bones at last, to relax for the first time in my life, and who knows I might even get around to having a little fun.'

Her light laugh reverberated as she scanned their faces. Their shock was unconcealed. 'How surprised you're looking,' she remarked, almost offhandedly. 'Well, perhaps I've even surprised myself. But I came to a decision during the speeches. As I sat there listening to my life being recounted it suddenly occurred to me that now is the right time for me to retire. And to retire gracefully. Everyone knows that Blackie and I are about to leave on a trip around the world. I am happy to announce to you that I've decided to spend the rest of the days left to me on this earth with my oldest, dearest and most trusted friend.'

Half turning, Emma lifted one hand and let it rest easily on Blackie's broad shoulder. She said, in a more confiding tone, 'Blackie said to me the other day, "Grow old with me, the best is yet to be," and you know, he might just be right.'

No one moved or spoke. Each guest continued to regard her intently, understanding that this slender, silver-haired woman who wielded enormous power had something more to say to them.

Emma stepped away from her chair and walked with swiftness to one of the other tables. She came to a halt next to Alexander, who jumped up immediately. His eyes were brilliant in his white face. Recognizing that he too was reeling from shock, she touched his arm lightly, as if to reassure him.

Glancing around at the expectant faces, Emma said briskly, 'My grandson Alexander has just become the head of Harte Enterprises.' She thrust out her hand. He took it, staring at her speechlessly. 'Congratulations, Alexander.' He stammered his thanks.

Moving at a dignified pace to the table diagonally opposite, Emma was aware of the tension and the sheathed excitement permeating the air. She drew to a standstill next to Paula. Pushing back her chair, Paula was on her feet as speedily as Alexander had been.

Taking the young woman's hand in hers, Emma held on to it tightly. How icy it is, she thought absently, and squeezed it, endeavouring to impart some of her own great strength to Paula, who had begun to tremble.

Once again, Emma's piercing green gaze swept the entire room. 'The Harte department store chain will, as of tonight, be run by my granddaughter, Paula McGill Amory Fairley.'

She pivoted to face Paula and gazed long and hard into her violet eyes. And then Emma smiled her incomparable smile that filled her face with radiance.

'I charge you to hold my dream,' Emma said.

Heiress

'Passions spin the plot; We are betrayed
by what is false within.'

GEORGE MEREDITH

'I am not made or unmade by the things which
happen to me but by my reactions to them.
That is all God cares about.'

ST JOHN OF THE CROSS

22

She had been alone for two weeks and had drawn strength and a sense of renewal from her solitude.

But now on this warm and pleasant Sunday Paula suddenly experienced a little spurt of pleasure at the thought of seeing Emily. Her cousin was driving over from Pennistone Royal for tea, and she was really looking forward to her company.

After she had finished setting the wrought-iron table on the terrace, Paula hurried down the steps and on to the lawn, to check on the twins. Lorne and Tessa lay in the double pram, sleeping peacefully in the shade. They looked so contented she could not help smiling before turning away and going back to the terrace to wait for Emily.

It was one of those afternoons in the middle of September which frequently occur in Yorkshire and rival the most beautiful days in midsummer. The arc of the sky was a light periwinkle blue, clear and radiant, with a few scattered cotton-ball clouds scudding intermittently across the sun which had blazed down since the late morning. The gardens at Long Meadow were riotous with colour and the warm air was filled with the pervasive scents of the flowers and shrubs.

Paula stretched out on the garden chaise, basking in the golden light, thinking of nothing very special as she relaxed. The tranquillity soothed her, was like a balm after her particularly hectic week, during which she had been on the go nonstop. They had been holding their annual Autumn Fashion Fair for five days; models had paraded through the Birdcage at lunch time wearing the latest ready-to-wear winter styles; every afternoon at three o'clock there had been a fashion show of designer clothes in the couture salon. Fashion aside, Harte's had had other special events during the past week, including the opening of a cookery school in the basement; daily appearances by a famous makeup artist in the cosmetic department; on Thursday evening there had been a cocktail party for the unveiling of the new art gallery in the store and the exhibition of oils and watercolours by Sally Harte. The *vernissage* had been a huge success and most of Sally's paintings of the Yorkshire Dales and the Lake District had already been sold. Whilst coping with these in-store promotions, Paula had had to handle her normal work load and it seemed to her now that every department had needed her complete attention. Much to her dismay, two buyers had resigned on Tuesday and she had had to start interviewing replacements immediately; she had also found it necessary to dismiss the jewellery buyer for incompetence late on Friday and this had proved to be a most unpleasant scene. But continuing daily problems and constant activity of this nature were par for the course, part of the daily routine of a large and successful department store such as theirs. Still, Paula knew she had been pushing herself harder than ever since Jim had been abroad, rising at five in the morning to get to the store by six-thirty so that she could leave early on most days in order to arrive home in time to bath the twins.

She had eaten dinner alone every night, had not done any socializing whatsoever, and, apart from Sally Harte, the only other people she had seen were her staff at the house, her business colleagues, the few friends who had attended the art gallery opening. During these two weeks of solitude in her private life Paula had come to realize more fully how vital it was for her to have these stretches of absolute peace and rest at the end of each frantic day. Working as intensely as she did, in a job that required her total concentration, frequently left her frazzled. It was essential for her well being to have periods entirely alone so that she could recoup her sapped strength. She had the need to think, to review her schedule, to plan ahead as she pottered around in the garden, played with the babies, read or simply listened to classical music in the cool greenness of the conservatory.

With a wry smile Paula had to admit that even if she had wanted to gad about, lead a gay life during Jim's absence in Canada, there was no one available to play with. Winston had flown off a week ago to join Jim in Toronto where they were attending a world conference of newspaper editors, publishers and proprietors. But the real reason for Winston's trip was to start negotiations with a Canadian papermill which was up for sale. He hoped to acquire it for the Yorkshire Consolidated Newspaper Company. Miranda O'Neill was in Barbados for the opening of their new hotel and the launching of the Harte boutique. Sarah was with her, acting as fashion adviser, supervising the interior displays and the dressing of the windows. Alexander was taking a holiday in the South of France with Maggie Reynolds, and they were staying at Emma's house in Cap Martin. Until last night Emily had been in Paris on a buying trip for Genret.

Jonathan was the only member of the family who was not travelling somewhere, but *their* paths rarely crossed. This was the chief reason Paula had been surprised when he had dropped in to see her at the store on Wednesday. Before she had even asked him what he was doing in Yorkshire, he had volunteered, and rather defensively she thought, that he was in Leeds on real estate business for Harte Enterprises. He had wasted an hour of her precious time chatting about absolutely nothing, although he had asked her, and several times during the course of their aimless conversation, when Grandy was returning from Australia. She had said she had no idea, which was the truth, and had been non-committal about matters in general. Cautious by nature, Paula had never been overly-fond of Jonathan Ainsley, always wary of him. This feeling had only intensified since Emma had alerted her to him, confided her worries about his loyalty.

After her grandmother's unexpected retirement and her departure on her world tour – almost five months ago – she and Alexander had met in London to discuss the situation in general. They had agreed they should continue to confer regularly once a month, in order to review matters pertaining to the business empires they were running, had even acknowledged they might well need each other as a sounding board.

At their first get-together they had come to the conclusion that Emily should be told about Emma's suspicions regarding Jonathan. They had invited her to lunch the following day, and had taken her into their confidence, had suggested that she attend their monthly brainstorming sessions. All three had concurred that they must watch Jonathan like a hawk. By mutual agreement they had also made the decision to exclude Sarah from their confabs, feeling that her sudden closeness to Jonathan was suspicious. Paula, Emily and Alexander had thus become the self-appointed triumvirate who were resolved in their determination to run Emma's companies in the way she wanted, whilst guarding her great legacy.

The French doors leading to the drawing room were open and dimly, in the background, Paula heard the grandfather clock in the hall striking four. She roused herself and went inside, hurrying through into the kitchen. She put the babies' bottles in a pan of water to be warmed up later, loaded the tray with sandwiches, scones, strawberry jam, and a cream cake, then went to the cupboard for the tea caddy. Ten minutes later, as she completed her tasks, she heard a car in the driveway and looked out of the window to see Emily alighting from her battered white Jaguar.

Emily bounced into the kitchen with her usual *joie de vivre*, wearing a happy grin. She ran to Paula and hugged her. 'Sorry I'm late,' Emily said as they drew apart, 'but that pile of old junk has been acting up all the way from Pennistone Royal. I really think I'll have to splurge and buy myself a new car.'

Paula laughed. 'You're not late, and I think you're right about the Jag, it *has* seen better days. Anyway welcome back, Emily.'

'It's good to be home, although I did enjoy Paris. It's still my favourite city.' Emily perched on the edge of a kitchen chair as Paula hovered near the stove. 'Have you heard from anybody? Grandy to be specific?'

'Yes.' Paula swung around, the kettle in her hand. 'She rang me up at midnight on Thursday. She wanted to hear about the *vernissage* and how the opening of the art gallery went – you know that's been her pet project for the last year. She said she and Blackie were going to Coonamble with Philip for four or five days. She sends you her love.'

'I'm beginning to think she'll never come back. Did Gran indicate what their plans were?'

'Yes she did, as a matter of fact. She and Blackie intend to leave Sydney in the middle of October, wend their way back to New York before returning here sometime in late November. She promised to be home in time for Christmas at Pennistone Royal.'

'My God, that's a long way off! I can't wait to see her. It's not the same without Grandma is it?'

'No.' Paula stared at Emily, scowled. 'You've got a face like a wet week, Emily. Do you have problems with Genret?'

Emily shook her head negatively. 'No, no, everything's fine. I miss Gran, that's all, and even though she *has* retired, it's awfully reassuring to know she's in the background. And right now she seems so far away, sitting over there at the other side of the world.'

'I know what you mean,' Paula said slowly, having sorely missed Emma's presence herself. She dreaded to think what it would be like, how they would manage, when her grandmother was gone from them forever. She instantly squashed this morbid and distressing thought, and forced a bright smile.

'Come on, Emily, let's go out to the terrace. I thought we'd have tea in the garden, it's such a gorgeous day. But we have to feed the babies first. Nora asked to change her day off this week, and Meg is never here on Sundays, so I've been coping alone today. I've enjoyed it actually.'

Emily followed her outside to the terrace. She ran down the steps to the pram. 'They're both wide awake,' she called over her shoulder, and began making cooing noises to the twins, leaning into the pram and touching their downy cheeks.

'Upsidaisy,' Paula murmured, lifting Lorne into her arms, 'time for your bottle, little boy.'

Emily scooped up Tessa and the two young women returned to sit at the table on the terrace. Half an hour later, after the children had been slowly fed, dutifully burped and then returned to their perambulator, Paula went inside. Not long after she came back carrying the tea tray.

As she poured, she said, 'Any news from Winston?'

'Yes, he phoned me last night. He's gone up to Vancouver. He's already in negotiations with the directors of that paper mill, and he thinks he's going to make the deal. There are a few more details to iron out, but he says they'll be able to conclude everything in a matter of days. He was very optimistic, and the mill will be a wonderful acquisition for Consolidated. Anyway, he's going to stop off in New York to spend a few days with Shane. Apparently *he's* in Barbados for the opening of the hotel, and won't be in New York until the middle of this coming week.'

'I'm glad to hear the deal is going through!' Paula exclaimed. 'When I spoke to Jim a few days ago he sounded uncertain about its outcome, and said Winston was down in the dumps. Obviously he was wrong, or things have changed radically overnight.' She sipped her tea and continued, 'Talking of Barbados . . . Sarah flew out there ten days ago to help Merry supervise the unpacking of the Lady Hamilton clothes and get the merchandise on the racks. I expect they're all having a whale of a time –'

Emily exclaimed, 'Sarah went to Barbados! Why ever was that necessary?' She banged the cup down with such an angry clatter Paula was taken aback.

She threw Emily a baffled look. 'Goodness, you *do* sound fierce. Sarah seemed to think it was her *duty* to go out there. In fact, she was hell bent on going. Since she *is* running our fashion division, and since the boutiques are mostly stocking Lady Hamilton beach clothes and resort wear I suppose she has a point. Besides I couldn't very well interfere. She doesn't have to answer to me . . . only to your brother. You know Sarah, she considers herself her own boss.'

'Oh well.' Emily shrugged, trying to act as if Sarah was of no consequence. But her fertile brain whirled and two and two suddenly made more than four. She was convinced the only interest Sarah Lowther had in Barbados and the Harte boutique was Shane O'Neill. Sarah must have found out from Miranda that he was going to be in the Caribbean for the opening of the hotel. Sarah was probably making a fool of herself at this very moment – throwing herself at Shane.

Emily, changing the subject, said with a rueful smile, 'Poor Alexander. I called him yesterday before I left Paris and found out that Mummy's descended on him with Marc Deboyne in tow. She's installed them at Grandy's villa, claims she has a right to be there and to visit with her darling daughters. Sandy says she's being a pain in the neck. Very bossy. I think Amanda and Francesca are anxious to fly home immediately. They haven't had much time for Mummy, not for ages.'

'Oh what a shame he's having to cope with problems on holiday – he was so looking forward to going away. Won't your little sisters have to be back here very soon anyway?'

'Yes. They're due at Harrogate College on the last day of this month. I'm glad Gran agreed to let them stay there for another term before packing them off to Switzerland. I don't think those two relish the idea of being far away from her, and –' Emily stopped, cocked her bright blonde head, listening. 'Isn't that the phone?'

'Yes. I'll be back in a second.' Paula dashed through the drawing room into the hall to answer it, snatching at the receiver.

Before she had a chance to say a word, the caller was exclaiming, 'Jim? Is that you?'

'Oh hello, Auntie Edwina,' she said, surprised. 'It's Paula. Jim's not here. He's in Canada on business.'

'*Canada*. Oh my God!'

Instantly recognizing the anxiety in the high-pitched voice, Paula asked, 'Is there something wrong?'

Edwina began to babble so hysterically Paula was unable to make sense of her aunt's words. She was incoherent, obviously distraught. Paula listened for a few seconds longer, filling with increasing alarm. Finally she cut in. 'Aunt Edwina, I can't understand a thing you're saying. Please speak a little more clearly, and slower.'

Paula heard Edwina sucking in her breath. There was a drawn-out moment of silence.

'It's poor Min,' Edwina gasped at last. 'Anthony's wife ... she's ... she's ... *dead*. She's been found ... drowned ...' Though she had choked on these words, Edwina managed to add, 'In the lake at Clonloughlin. And ... and ...' Edwina was unable to continue and began to weep.

Paula went cold from head to toe. Innumerable questions leapt into her mind. How had she drowned? Accident? Suicide? And why had Min been at Clonloughlin in the first place when she and Anthony were estranged? Aware suddenly that her aunt's sobbing had lessened, if only a fraction, Paula said sympathetically, 'I'm so sorry, so very sorry. This must be a terrible shock for you.'

Edwina gasped, 'It's not only Min. It's poor Anthony. Paula – the police are here. They're questioning Anthony again. Oh my poor boy! I don't know what to do! I wish I could talk to Jim. It's also a pity Mother isn't in England. She'd know how to handle this ghastly mess. Oh dear God, what am I going to do?'

Paula stiffened. Her mind worked swiftly, striving to comprehend what Edwina was intimating. 'What do you mean about the police? You're not trying to tell me they think Anthony is somehow involved in Min's death are you?'

There was an awful stillness at Edwina's end. Her voice was a terrified whisper when she spoke. '*Yes*,' she said.

211

Paula sat down heavily on the hall chair. She felt prickles of goose flesh on her arms and her heartbeat accelerated against her rib cage. Horror was trickling through her but instantly this gave way to a burst of anger. 'How ridiculous! Your local police force must be bonkers. Anthony under suspicion of murd –' Paula bit off the remainder of the word, reluctant to say it. Again she exclaimed, 'This is *preposterous*.'

'They think he ki –' Edwina faltered, for like Paula she was unable to voice the unthinkable.

Striving to take hold of herself, Paula said in her firmest manner, 'Aunt Edwina, please start at the beginning and tell me everything. Grandy and Jim may not be here, but I am, and I will do everything I can to help, but you must be absolutely honest with me so that I can make the proper decisions.'

'Yes. Yes. All right.' Edwina sounded slightly calmer, and although she stumbled a few times she was able to give Paula the essential details about the discovery of Min's body early that morning, the arrival of the police, who had been summoned by Anthony, their departure and their subsequent return two hours ago. After poking around the estate they had ensconced themselves with Anthony in the library at Clonloughlin and were still with him.

When Edwina finished, Paula said, 'It sounds very cut and dried to me. Min obviously had an accident.' She hesitated. 'Look,' she went on, 'I think this is merely routine . . . I mean the police coming back this afternoon.'

'No! No!' Edwina cried. 'It isn't routine. Min's been creating problems lately. She changed her mind several weeks ago – about the divorce. She refused to go ahead with it. Other things have been happening. Dreadful things.' Then Edwina added rapidly, in a voice so quiet Paula had to strain to hear, 'That's why the police are here.'

'You'd better tell me everything,' Paula said as steadily as she could, even though her sense of dread was mounting by the second.

Edwina gulped. 'Yes, I think I must. The trouble started a month ago actually. Min came down here – she's been living in Waterford – and started to make a nuisance of herself, caused the most horrendous scenes. Sometimes she was really sloshed, reeling from drink. She and Anthony had fierce quarrels and there were some unfortunate scenes in front of the staff, the estate workers, and even a nasty confrontation one afternoon in the village, when she accosted Anthony. All the rows, the violence, have inevitably caused gossip, and Sally Harte's presence here earlier this summer hasn't done anything to help the situation. You know what people are like in a small place, Paula. Gossip is their way of life. There's been an awful lot of talk – distressing talk – about *the other woman*.'

Paula groaned inwardly. 'Let's go back for a moment. What did you mean when you referred to *violence*?'

'Oh violent words mostly. Shouting and screaming on Min's part, but Anthony did become enraged last weekend when she showed up on Saturday. At dinner time. He had guests. I was there. They had a fight, a verbal fight that is, and she hit Anthony with a golf club. He pushed her away from him, a natural reaction, I suppose. She fell though, in the hall. Min wasn't really hurt, but she pretended she was. She was overly dramatic about it, screamed something about Anthony wanting her –'

'Yes, Aunt Edwina, go on,' Paula encouraged as the silence lengthened.

There was a sound of harsh breathing before Edwina told Paula, with a sob, 'Min shouted something about Anthony wanting her dead and buried and that she wouldn't be surprised if she was found murdered. And very soon. Several people heard her say this. I did myself.'

'Oh my God!' Paula's heart sank and her apprehension spiralled into genuine fear. She did not think for a single moment that her cousin had killed his wife, but it was suddenly apparent to her why the police harboured suspicions about Anthony. Her mind momentarily floundered, then rallied, as she told herself she had to come to grips with this dilemma. But where to begin? Who to enlist?

Paula said in a strong, calm voice that belied her inner nervousness, 'All the gossip, the scenes are meaningless in the long run. The police need hard evidence before they can do anything – arrest Anthony, accuse him of killing her. When did she drown? What about an alibi? Surely Anthony has one.'

'They're not sure about the time of death . . . at least that's what they say. I think they're doing an autopsy,' Edwina went on miserably. 'Alibi? No, that's the terrible part, Anthony doesn't have one.'

'Where was he yesterday? *Last night?* Those must be the crucial hours.'

'Last night,' Edwina repeated as if she was confused. Then she said quickly, 'Yes, yes, I see what you mean. Min arrived at Clonloughlin at about five o'clock yesterday. I saw her driving up – from my bedroom window in the Dower House. I phoned Anthony to warn him. He was annoyed. He told me he was going to hop into his old land rover and drive out to the lake – in the hopes of avoiding her.'

'And he did that? Went out to the lake?' Paula asked.

'Yes. But she must have seen him driving off in that direction or she simply second guessed where he had gone . . . it was one of his favourite spots. She followed him out there. And –'

'They had a quarrel at the lake?' Paula cut in.

'Oh no. He never even spoke to her!' Edwina cried. 'You see, he saw her mini in the distance – the land is flat around the far side of the lake. He simply got back into the land rover and was going to return to the house the long way around. But he hadn't driven very far when the land rover conked out. Anthony left it parked and started to walk home. He wanted to avoid Min . . . don't you understand?'

'Yes. And he left the land rover near the lake, is that what you're saying?' Paula demanded, wondering if this was incriminating or not.

'Of course he left it there, it wouldn't start,' Edwina was saying, her high-pitched voice trembling again.

'Please don't cry, Aunt Edwina,' Paula pleaded. 'It's essential that you control yourself. *Please.*'

'Yes. Yes. I'll try.' she sniffed.

Paula heard her blowing her nose and then her aunt resumed, 'You don't know Clonloughlin, Paula, it's vast. It took Anthony an hour to walk back. He had to go up the hill, through the wood and several fields to get to the road that cuts across the estate and leads to the village. He –'

'Road!' Paula exclaimed, seizing on this fact immediately. 'Didn't he see anyone?'

213

'No, he didn't. At least he never mentioned that. Anyway Anthony got back to the house around six-thirty. He phoned me, told me about the land rover breaking down. Then he said he would change for dinner, see me later. I went up to the house around seven. We had drinks and ate, but Anthony was very nervous, not himself. You see, he thought Min would show up and start behaving offensively again.'

'But she didn't, did she?'

'No, we were alone all evening. As I said, Anthony was out of sorts and he walked me back to the Dower House around nine-thirty, perhaps nine-forty-five, then he returned to Clonloughlin.'

'And who found Min's body?'

'The estate manager. He was driving past the lake very early this morning and saw the land rover, also the mini. Then he found –' Edwina broke down, sobbing as if her heart would break.

Paula tried to soothe her aunt, reassure her, and said, 'Please, Aunt Edwina, be brave. I'm sure everything is going to be all right.' She prayed she was right.

'But I'm frightened for him,' Edwina mumbled in a tear-filled tone, 'truly frightened –'

'Now listen to me and please do as I tell you,' Paula instructed peremptorily, taking charge. 'Don't make any more phone calls, and if you receive any, hang up as quickly as possible. I want you to keep this line open. I shall ring you back very shortly. I presume you're calling from the Dower House?'

'Yes.' Edwina hesitated, asked, 'But what are you going to do?'

'I think I'd better get my mother over there to stay with you for the next few days. You shouldn't be alone at a time like this. I assume there's going to be an inquest. The main thing is I don't want you to worry. Fretting won't help anyone. I know it won't be easy, but you *must* try. I'll ring you back within the hour.'

'Th-th-th-thank you, P-P-Paula,' Edwina stammered.

They said goodbye and hung up. Paula immediately lifted the phone and dialled her parents' flat in London. The line was busy. She flung the receiver back into the cradle with impatience and leapt up, realizing she had better go and talk to Emily.

As Paula raced through the drawing room she almost fell over an occasional table in her haste. Righting it, she stumbled out on to the terrace, blinking as she came out in the bright sunlight.

Having heard the crash Emily swung her head and grinned. 'You are a clumsy clot –' She stopped, her eyes opening widely. 'What's happened?' Emily asked. 'You're as white as a sheet.'

Paula leaned against a chair. 'We have some trouble, really *serious* trouble, Emily. I'm going to have to deal with it – and you'll have to help me. Please come inside. I must reach my mother. It'll save time if you listen whilst I explain everything to her.'

23

'You don't think he could have done it, do you?'

Paula lifted her head sharply. 'Of course not!' She stared at Emily, who sat opposite her on the sofa in the conservatory. Her stare intensified and she frowned, 'Why, do you?'

Without hesitation, Emily exclaimed, 'No. I don't think he would be capable of it.' There was a pause, and Emily bit her lip. She said in a rush, 'On the other hand, you said something –'

'*I* did? What do you mean? When?'

'Oh not today, Paula, months ago, when you and Alexander took me to lunch just after Gran left. You know the day we discussed Jonathan. We also spoke about Sarah. You made an interesting remark and it's stuck in my mind ever since. You said we never *really* know about other people, not even those who are closest to us, and that we know very little about what goes on in people's private lives. I was struck by the essential truth in your words at the time, and let's face it, we don't know Anthony all that well. We've never spent a lot of time with him.'

'You're right. But I've got to go with my gut instinct on this, Emily, I just know he didn't have anything to do with Min's death. Admittedly the circumstances *sound* peculiar, but no . . .' Paula shook her head vehemently, 'I don't believe he killed her. I'm convinced it was an accident. Or suicide. Look here, Emily, Grandy is the shrewdest person we know, and she is brilliant at reading people, spotting character flaws. She thinks the world of Anthony and –'

'Even the nicest people can commit murder,' Emily interrupted quietly. 'If they're under pressure, pushed hard enough. What about crimes of passion, for instance?'

'We must presume Anthony's innocence! That is British law, after all – innocent until proven guilty.'

'Please don't think I was implying that he *did* kill her, because I wasn't. I was just speculating that's all. To be honest, I'm inclined to go along with you on the suicide theory. Still, I hope she didn't kill herself. Think how hard that would be on Sally and Anthony – having to live with the knowledge that Min took her own life because of them.'

'Yes, that had crossed my mind earlier. It would affect them in the worst way,' Paula said, her eyes darkening with worry. She glanced at her watch. 'I wish my mother would call back. I hope she's not having a problem getting a plane to Ireland.'

Emily also checked her watch. 'She's only had fifteen minutes, Paula. Give her a chance. In the meantime, let's go over your list again, check your plan.'

'Right,' Paula replied, aware positive action would help to subdue her nagging anxiety. Lifting the pad, she scanned it, said, '*One*. We get Mummy over to Ireland as soon as possible, so that she can hold the fort. She's already working on that so –' Paula picked up her pen, ticked it off, '– *Two*. My father has to put a call through to Philip at Coonamble between nine and ten tonight, to alert Philip. God forbid Grandy reads about this trouble in the papers first. Daddy understands he must do this once Mother is on the plane.' Again this item was checked off, and she went on reading aloud: '*Three*. Put a lid on this mess as far as the newspapers are concerned. I'll call Sam Fellowes at the *Yorkshire Morning Gazette* and Pete Smythe on our evening paper. Actually, I'll have to call all of the papers in our chain. I can't control the national press but I can certainly make sure those we own don't carry a single line. *Four*. Talk to Henry Rossiter about legal advice. We might have to send John Crawford. As the family lawyer he would represent Anthony if necessary. *Five*. Get hold of Winston, Jim, or both, to let them know what's happened.' She lifted her eyes. 'Maybe you can make *that* phone call, Emily, but not until *we* have everything under control. I don't want either of them flying back here. *Six*. Ring Edwina to reassure her and talk to Anthony, tell him what we've done. *Seven*. Locate Sally Harte. You can do that as well.'

'Okay.' Emily peered through the door of the conservatory and out into the hall. The telephone was in her direct line of vision. 'I think you should work at your desk here, and I'll use the phone in the hall. That way we can see each other, talk easily between calls.'

'Good idea. Look, I had better speak to Fellowes and get that out of the way.'

'Yes, and I'll start trying to find Sally. Did she tell you on Thursday where exactly she was going in the Lake District?'

'No, and I didn't think to ask, but Uncle Randolph will know. Don't mention a thing about this – not yet,' Paula warned.

'Not on your life. He'd go into a flat spin.' Emily jumped up. 'If the other line rings while you're talking to Fellowes I'll pick it up. It'll probably be your mother.'

As Emily ran out, Paula lifted the receiver and dialled the editor's private line at the *Yorkshire Morning Gazette*. He answered on the second ring, and Paula quickly cut through the usual pleasantries. 'Sam, I'm calling about a family matter. My cousin, the Earl of Dunvale, has had a terrible tragedy. His wife has been drowned in the lake on his estate in Ireland.'

'That is indeed tragic,' Fellowes said. 'I'll get one of my top writers on to the obituary immediately.'

'No, no, Sam. The reason I'm calling is to let you know I don't want anything in the paper. I'm pretty sure the wire services will be carrying something later tonight, or tomorrow. In any event, I want the story killed. No obituary either.'

'But why not?' he demanded. 'If the story's on the wires, the national press will be running it. We'll look ridiculous if we don't mention –'

'*Sam*,' Paula cut in quietly, 'you should know by now that Emma Harte does not wish to read anything – *anything at all* – about *her* family in *her* newspapers.'

'I know that,' he snapped. 'But surely this is different. How's it going to look if every paper in the country but ours has it? What kind of newspaper are we anyway? I definitely do not like suppressing news.'

'Then perhaps you're working on the wrong newspaper, Sam. Because believe you me, Emma Harte makes the rules around here, and you'd better respect them.'

'I'm going to call Jim and Winston in Canada. *They* run the papers, and it seems to me that it's their decision – about what we print and what we don't print.'

'In their absence, and in the absence of my grandmother, it is my decision and mine alone. *I* have told you what to do. *No* story. *No* obituary.'

'If you say so,' he said, his anger ill-concealed.

'I *do* say so. Thank you, Sam, and goodbye.'

Paula hung up, bristling. She pulled her address book towards her, looking up Pete Smythe's home number, since the evening paper was closed on Sundays. She hoped she would not get the same arguments from Smythe. She was about to dial when Emily flew down the steps, and she swung around in the chair. 'Was that my mother?'

'Yes, or rather, Uncle David. Aer Lingus has a flight out early this evening, but he doesn't think Auntie Daisy will make the airport in time. So he's arranged for your mother to be flown over by private plane. Uncle David's going to phone Edwina right now, to let her know Auntie Daisy's virtually on her way. Your mother's packing. She'll call before she leaves the flat.'

'That's a relief. Did you speak to Uncle Randolph?'

'No, he was out. But Vivienne told me Sally's due back in Middleham shortly. It's been raining in the Lake District, so she packed her painting gear and is driving home. I told Vivienne to have her call here the minute she arrives.'

'Was she curious?'

'Not really. I said you wanted to speak to Sally, and got off the phone quickly.'

'I dread having to tell her about this –' Paula murmured, her face grim, her eyes reflecting her deep concern.

'Yes, it's going to be awful for her, but she'll *have* to be told. In person, I think, don't you?'

'*Absolutely*. Well, let's not waste time. We'd better get on, Emily.'

'What shall I do next?'

'Could you bring the babies into the house, please? You can park the pram in here for a while. I must call those other editors.'

'Yes, do it, and I'll be back in a jiffy.'

Paula reached Pete Smythe, editor of the *Yorkshire Evening Standard* at his home in Knaresborough. She repeated the story she had told Sam Fellowes. After sympathizing with her about the accident, Pete concurred with her decision and gave her no arguments.

'I wouldn't have run anything anyway, Paula,' Pete told her, 'I know how Mrs Harte feels. She'd skin me alive if a single line appeared about any of you, regardless of the circumstances.'

'Sam Fellowes was a bit difficult,' Paula volunteered. 'I hope I'm not going to meet any similar resistance from our other editors.'

'You won't – Sam's a special case. Not the easiest person to deal with. If you want I'll make the calls to our Doncaster, Sheffield, Bradford and Darlington papers.'

'Oh would you, Pete? That'd be marvellous. I really appreciate your help.

Thanks a lot.' The phone shrilled the moment Paula had put it down. It was her mother.

'Hello, darling,' Daisy said with her usual calm control. 'I'm about to leave. I'm taking a cab to the airport, so that your father can be here at the flat, just in case you need him. He spoke to Edwina a few minutes ago. She's relieved I'm on my way. He said she sounded less agitated. The police have left. Anthony's with her. They're waiting for your call.'

'I know. I'll ring them when we hang up. Thanks for going over to Ireland, Mother. You're the only one who can handle this. Edwina does trust you, and you'll deal with everyone diplomatically, which is more than she could manage.'

'Heavens, Paula, I don't mind. We are a family and we must stick together. But what an appalling situation. I can't understand the police over there . . . it seems very straight-forward to me. Your father agrees. Anyway talking about it endlessly won't solve a thing. I must rush. Goodbye, dear.'

'Bye, Mummy, and have a safe journey. We'll speak tomorrow.'

Emily was pushing the pram down the two low steps into the conservatory when Paula glanced up from her pad. 'I'm going to make a fast call to Henry, and then I'll talk to Ireland.' As she dialled Henry's number Paula quickly gave Emily details about her conversations with Pete Smythe and her mother.

It was Henry Rossiter's housekeeper who answered at his Gloucestershire house. Paula spoke to her briefly, replaced the receiver, said to Emily, 'I just missed him. He's driving back to London. Apparently he should be arriving around eight-thirty. Do you think I should call Gran's solicitors or wait to speak to Henry?'

'I'm not sure . . . what do you think Grandy would *do*?' She answered herself instantly. 'She'd talk to Henry first.'

'That's my feeling,' Paula agreed, her hand resting on the telephone. She took a deep breath, preparing herself to make the call to Edwina at Clonlough-lin. Picking up the receiver, she instantly put it back in the cradle, swung around. 'Sally may be in touch any minute. You'll have to talk to her, Emily, so let's decide what you'll say.'

The two young women stared at each other worriedly for the longest moment.

Finally Paula said, 'It seems to me that the wisest thing would be to tell her that *I* have a problem, that I want to see her, talk to her, and will she please drive over immediately.'

'She'll want to know what's wrong on the phone!' Emily cried, her eyes flaring. 'I know I said we should tell her face to face, but now I'm wondering what explanation to give.'

'You'll manage. Wriggle out of it, don't say anything concrete. You're very good at being evasive, Emily.'

'I *am*?' Emily gave Paula a doubtful stare. 'If you say so.' She shrugged, then ran over to the pram as Tessa began wailing.

Paula sprung up and followed her cousin. 'They're probably *both* damp and need changing. Let's take them upstairs anyway, and maybe you could then start preparing their bottles.'

'Nora would be off today, wouldn't she?' Emily moaned.

'It's always the way,' Paula murmured, rocking her baby daughter in her arms, making soft hushing sounds.

'Dower house, Clonloughlin,' a quiet male voice announced when Paula got through to Ireland fifteen minutes later.

She gave her name, asked to speak to the Earl, and a split second later Anthony was on the line.

'*Paula* . . . hello. Thanks for everything, for taking charge the way you have. I'm very grateful. My mother was panicked earlier, quite at her wits' end, and she fell apart when the police came back.'

'I realize that, and it was nothing, really. I'm glad to help in any way I can. How are you feeling?'

'Fine. Very fine,' he asserted. 'I'm holding up pretty well under the circumstances. This is extremely unpleasant, of course, but I know it's going to be all right.'

'Yes,' Paula said, thinking he did not sound fine. Not in the least. His voice was weary, drained. Hoping she sounded more positive than she felt, she added, 'Everything will be over and done with in the next twenty-four hours, you'll see. Try not to worry in the meantime. I'd like to know what's been happening, but first I must tell you that Emily spoke to Sally a few minutes ago. She's coming over here. She thinks *I* have some sort of crisis. We thought it was wiser not to tell her about this on the telephone.'

'I'm relieved to hear you've contacted her, Paula, I've been worried about Sally. I didn't know where to reach her in the Lake District. When we spoke on Friday Sally said she'd call me on Monday or Tuesday. Perhaps you would ask her to ring me, once you've explained this dreadful situation.'

'Of course. What are the latest developments? I know from my mother that the police have left . . . obviously they haven't charged you –'

'How could they!' he interrupted heatedly. 'I haven't done anything *wrong*, Paula! I wasn't involved in Min's death –' His voice cracked and there was a pause as he struggled for control. After a moment he spoke more steadily, apologized, 'Sorry for breaking down. It's been such a terrible shock. Min and I have been having bitter quarrels, and she *was* being impossible, but I didn't wish anything like this to happen.' He lapsed into silence.

Paula heard his harsh breathing as he tried to compose himself. She said gently, 'You must be strong. We'll get you through this safely, Anthony, I promise.'

Eventually he said, 'You've been awfully good, Paula, awfully helpful. Well' – he sighed, added wearily, ' – they've established the time of death. The local doctor did an examination. He thinks it was between ten-thirty and midnight.'

Paula's mouth went dry. From what Edwina had said, Anthony had taken her back to the Dower House around nine forty-five, then returned home. To go to bed? If so it was most unlikely that he had an alibi for his whereabouts during those key hours. But she made no comment, not wanting to alarm him further. 'Your mother said something about an autopsy.'

'Oh yes. I hope that'll be tomorrow. The inquest and Coroner's Court will be on Wednesday or Thursday. Everything's so tediously slow here.' There was another heavy sigh, then dropping his voice, Anthony confided, 'It's that damnable land rover. I'm not certain the police believe me – about it breaking down in the afternoon.'

'Yes,' Paula acknowledged. 'But are you sure no one saw the land rover out there in the late afternoon, when it really *did* break down? Perhaps one of the estate workers? That would prove to the police that you're speaking the truth.'

'No-one has come forward, and it's very deserted in that area of the estate – miles away from the house. I doubt anyone was around. However, there has been *one* positive development. A bit of news. The police have information that should exonerate me. They've been interviewing everyone here for the past few hours ... the staff, the estate workers. Bridget – my housekeeper – told them that she saw me in the house between eleven and midnight.'

'Why didn't you tell me this before! Then you have an alibi!' Paula was flooded with relief.

'Yes, I do. I only hope the police believe her story.'

'Why wouldn't they?' she demanded, tensing.

'Don't misunderstand me, Paula, I've no reason to think they don't believe her, but Bridget has worked at Clonloughlin all of her life. Her mother was the housekeeper here before her, and she and I – well, we sort of grew up together. I'm praying the police don't get the idea she's lying to protect me. Mind you, she's unshakable in her story.'

Puzzled, Paula asked nervously, 'Why didn't *you* mention this to the police before? If you were with her last night after your mother left, surely –'

'I wasn't with her,' Anthony interjected. 'Actually, I didn't even see her. Bridget suffers from migraines, and apparently she had one all last evening. She was cleaning the kitchen after dinner when the migraine became unbearable. She passed the library on her way upstairs to her room. The light was on, the door was open, and she glanced in, saw me reading. However, she didn't call out to me because of her blinding pain. She ran upstairs, found her pills, and returned to the kitchen. She made herself a pot of tea, rested in the chair for half an hour, finished her work, set the dining room table for breakfast, and just after midnight she went to bed. Again she glanced through the open library door. I was by then working on the estate books, doing the accounting, and not wishing to interrupt me, she simply went on up to bed without even saying goodnight. It was her day off today and she wasn't here when the police first came.'

'Oh Anthony, this is the best news I've heard today!'

'I think it is. Still, she is the only person who saw me during those crucial hours. The two maids who work here had already gone home to the village – they come in daily. So ... there's no one to corroborate her story, and it's well known around these parts that she's devoted to me, and is extraordinarily loyal to our family. The police might – and remember I'm only saying *might* – doubt her word, think she and I concocted the alibi.'

Paula's heart plummeted, her relief of a moment ago evaporating entirely. 'Oh God, don't say that.'

'I have to look at the worst, view this situation objectively,' Anthony said. 'On the other hand, I don't see how the police can dismiss her, say she's lying without being absolutely certain that she *is* making it up, and I know she'll stick to her guns.'

Pulling herself upright in the chair, Paula said slowly, 'Yes, that's true. However, when I talk to Henry Rossiter later, about getting legal advice, I'm also going to suggest we retain a criminal lawyer.'

'Hang on a minute!' Anthony exclaimed. 'That's jumping the gun isn't it!' He sounded aghast at this idea. 'I haven't done anything *wrong*, I've told you that, Paula. *A criminal lawyer*. Christ, that's going to make me look as guilty as hell.'

'Of course it isn't,' Paula shot back sternly, determined to stand her ground. 'And let's wait to hear what Henry has to say. I trust his judgement, as Grandy has for many years. He won't steer us in the wrong direction. Please, Anthony, don't make swift decisions out of hand.'

'Very well, get Henry's opinion,' he agreed, although somewhat grudgingly.

After they had concluded their conversation Paula sat at her desk in the conservatory. She ran a hand through her hair, rubbed her eyes, stretched. Then eyeing the pad in front of her on the desk she dragged her thoughts back to her list. Three people still had to be called . . . Jim, Winston, Henry Rossiter. Looking at her watch she saw that it was now seven-thirty. Henry would not be available for another hour at least, and obviously Emily had not had a chance to reach Jim or Winston in Canada, since she was preparing the babies' bottles in the nursery. Paula went to join her there.

Once they were settled comfortably, each cradling a child, Paula recounted her conversation with Anthony.

Emily listened carefully as she adjusted the feeding bottle, glancing at Paula several times, nodding her understanding.

'That's the gist of it then . . . Bridget has given Anthony an alibi.'

A silence fell between them as they concentrated on the babies. Then very quietly, but in a voice of steel, Paula said, 'No grandson of Emma Harte's is going to be in the dock standing trial for murder. *I promise you that*.'

24

'I hope you really *do* understand why we had to lie to you, Sally,' Paula said gently.

'Yes. And it's just as well that you did.' Sally Harte swallowed and cleared her throat nervously. Her voice shook as she added, 'I don't think I could have driven over here without having an accident if Emily had told me the truth on the phone.'

Paula nodded, continued to survey her cousin intently, filled with anxiousness for her.

For the last fifteen minutes, all through Paula's account of the events in Ireland, Sally had managed to cling to her self-control. Paula admired her for taking the terrible news without flinching. I ought to have known she would be brave, Paula thought. She always was stoical even as a child. The Harte backbone, her grandmother called it. Yet despite this extraordinary show of strength, Paula knew Sally was shattered. It showed in her cornflower eyes, now so devastated, and in her lovely face which was stark with shock.

Sally was holding herself so rigidly in the chair she looked as if she had been paralysed by Paula's recital, and leaning forward Paula took hold of Sally's hand. She was alarmed at its deathly coldness, said, 'Sally, you're frozen! Let me get you a brandy, or make you a cup of tea. You need something to warm you up.'

'No, no, really. Thanks anyway.' Sally attempted to bring a smile to her face without success, and as she continued to meet Paula's worried gaze her eyes suddenly filled. 'Anthony must be under the most dreadful strain,' she began unsteadily and stopped. Now the tears came, spilling out of her wide blue eyes, rolling down her ashen cheeks. Still she did not stir, nor did she utter a sound.

Paula got up and went and knelt in front of Sally, encircling her cousin with her arms. 'Oh darling, it's going to be all right.' Paula murmured with the utmost gentleness, full of compassion. 'Don't fight the tears. It's much better to cry really, to get the pain out, and crying does help a bit. It's a release.'

Sally clung to Paula, heaving with silent, wracking sobs, and Paula stroked her black hair, gentled her, and eventually the awful quiet heaving lessened. Soon Sally straightened up, brushing her wet face with her strong painter's hands.

'I'm sorry,' she gasped, her voice strangling in her throat. She strove hard to get a hold of herself, blinking the tears away. 'I love him so much, Paula. I can hardly stand it, knowing what he's going through . . . he's so *alone* over there. I'm sure Aunt Edwina is no help at all. She's probably blaming all this on me.' She shook her head desperately. 'Oh God!' She pressed her hands to her contorted face which expressed her anguished thoughts. 'He needs me . . .'

Paula, who had returned to her chair, stiffened at these words. She held her breath, willing herself to be silent. She knew what must be said, but she was also aware that it would be wiser and kinder to wait until Sally had calmed herself further.

Emily, hovering in the doorway of the drawing room, flashed Paula a warning look and began to move her head violently from side to side. Silently Emily mouthed, *'Don't let her go over there.'*

Paula nodded, motioned for Emily to come into the room. This she did at once, seating herself in a nearby chair. In a half whisper, Emily said to Paula, 'No luck, I'm afraid. There's no reply from Jim's room or Winston's either. I've left messages for them to call here the minute they get back to their hotels.'

Although Emily had spoken softly, Sally had heard her, and at the mention of her brother's name her hands fell away from her face. She jerked her head, looked directly at Emily. 'I wish Winston were here. I feel so . . . *helpless* . . .'

'I wish he were here too,' Emily replied and patted Sally's arm in her motherly way. 'But you're not helpless, since you've got us. It's going to be fine, honestly it is. Paula's been super, and she's in full control, on top of everything. Try not to worry.'

'I'll do my best.' Sally's eyes swivelled to Paula. 'I haven't thanked you – you've been wonderful. So have you, Emily, and I'm very grateful to you both.'

Discerning that Sally was a little more composed, Paula said, 'There is one thing I must say to you – please don't go to Ireland to be with Anthony. I know you're sick at heart, dreadfully concerned about him, but you really mustn't go over there. You can't do anything constructive, and, very frankly, your presence would be highly inflammatory.'

Sally was startled. 'I've no intention of going to *Clonloughlin*! I know there's been a lot of nasty gossip, Anthony told me about *that* weeks ago – he tells me everything. Obviously I don't want to add fuel to the fire. But Paula, I do think I ought to go to Ireland, either to Waterford or, better still, Dublin. I'll go tomorrow. I can leave in the morning, from Manchester Airport, and be there in several hours. At least I'll be closer to him than I am here in Yorkshire –'

'No!' Paula exclaimed with unusual sharpness. 'You can't go. You're staying here – even if I have to put you under lock and key!'

Sally began, 'But I –'

'*I'm not going to let you go to Ireland.*' Paula threw her cousin a stern look and her mouth settled into resolute lines.

Sally stared back at Paula defiantly, and her pellucid blue eyes filled with stubbornness. Asserting herself, she said with equal firmness, 'I understand your reasoning. On the other hand, what harm is there in my being in Dublin?' When Paula remained silent Sally went on, 'It's hundreds of miles away from Clonloughlin.' She stopped again, frowned. 'If I'm in Dublin, Anthony will at least know I'm within easy reach, and we can be together once the inquest is over,' she finished shakily, sounding less sure of herself. The trembling started anew, and Sally clenched her hands together in her lap, striving to curb this, and then her eyes unexpectedly welled. 'He needs me, Paula. Don't you understand that? Understand that I have to be with him?'

Paula commanded: 'Now listen to me, and listen very, very carefully. You cannot help Anthony in any way whatsoever in this trying situation. In fact, you could easily do him irrevocable damage by showing up in Ireland. If Anthony were suspected of murder, you could be his motive. In Grandy's absence I am in charge in this family, and you'd better understand that I'm making *all* the rules. Therefore, Sally, I must insist that you stay here.'

Sally had shrunk back in the chair, momentarily stunned by Paula's vehemence. She had not realized how formidable her cousin could be.

Paula and Emily were watching Sally and now they exchanged knowing glances. It was Emily who broke the silence. She touched Sally's arm, said, 'Please take Paula's advice, Sal.'

Emotionally, Sally had the desire to be with Anthony because she believed he needed her during this dreadful time; intellectually, she was beginning to accept that going to him would be the wrong move to make. Paula *was* right in everything she had been saying. Listen to your head, not your heart, she cautioned herself.

'I'll stay here,' Sally whispered finally, leaning back in the chair, passing her hands over the aching muscles in her face.

Paula let out a sigh of relief. 'Thank God for that. Are you feeling up to ringing Anthony now? He's anxious to speak to you and you'll set his mind at rest, once he knows how well you're coping.'

Sally jumped up. 'Yes, yes, I must talk to him at once.'

'Why don't you go to my bedroom where it's quiet – private,' Paula suggested kindly.

223

'Thanks, I will.' Sally paused at the door, swung her head. She stared at Paula. 'You're the most daunting person I know,' she said and disappeared down the hall.

Paula gazed after her, then looked at Emily speechlessly.

Emily said, 'I'd better get to the phone too – don't you want to reach Henry Rossiter? It's well past eight-thirty, you know.'

Together they sat on the terrace, enjoying the gentle stillness of the gardens, cloaked now by a dark-blue sky peppered with brightly twinkling stars. It was a clear night, cloudless, with a full moon, and its silvered rim was just visible above the tops of the distant trees swaying and rustling under the soft evening breeze.

'I don't know about you, but I'm wiped out,' Emily said, breaking the long silence at last, peering across at Paula in the dusky, shadowy light.

Paula turned her face, and quite suddenly it was clearly illuminated in the bright glow emanating from the lamps in the drawing room immediately behind them. Emily noticed at once that the stern veil had been lifted, and a lovely softness dwelt there again and there was warmth in her cousin's expression.

Finally Paula answered. 'Yes, I'm a bit done in too, I must admit. But at least all the important phone calls are out of the way.' She lifted the goblet of white wine and took a long swallow. 'This *was* a good idea of yours Emily. Sitting waiting for Jim or Winston to ring us was getting awfully wearisome and frustrating.'

'Yes it was. I wonder if your father has managed to get hold of Philip yet? It must be nine-thirty by now.'

Squinting at her watch, Paula nodded. 'Almost. We have to give him time to get through to Australia. He'll be in touch soon.' Paula cleared her throat, continued, 'I do wish Sally had stayed longer. Do you think she was really all right when she left?'

'She was certainly calmer when she came downstairs, but awfully subdued.'

'Well, that's understandable.'

Emily made no response. Shifting her position in her chair, she picked up her drink, sipped it. 'Did you notice anything different about Sally?' There was a moment's hesitation on Emily's part before she added, 'I don't mean when she left, but in general.'

'She's put on weight.'

Emily's fingers tightened around her glass and dropping her voice, she whispered, 'I have a horrible feeling . . . well, I might as well say it, I think Sally's pregnant.'

Paula sighed. Her worst fears had been confirmed. 'That's what I was afraid you'd say Emily. Actually, so do I.'

'Oh bloody hell!' Emily exploded, her voice rising. 'That's all we need. I'm surprised you didn't spot her condition at the *vernissage*. Or did you?'

'No, I didn't. Mind you, she was wearing a sort of loose, tenty dress. Anyway I was harassed, surrounded by people. But when she walked in tonight I was struck by her heaviness, especially across her bustline. Still, I was so concerned about the news I had to break I didn't dwell on her figure. I noticed her weight gain when she was standing near the fireplace, just before she left. It was most pronounced.'

'That's when it occurred to me. Oh my God, Paula, the balloon's going to go up when Uncle Randolph finds out!' Emily groaned loudly. 'I can't help wishing Gran were here.'

'So do I, but she isn't, and I don't want her dragged back needlessly. We'll have to cope the best way we can.' Paula rubbed her weary face and exhaled heavily. 'Oh God, what a ghastly mess this is, and poor Sally . . .' She shook her head sadly. 'I do feel sorry for her . . .' Paula left the rest of her sentence unfinished, sat staring into the shadows, filled with terrible misgivings about the situation in Ireland.

Emily said suddenly, 'Well, if she is pregnant there's no problem. At least they'll be able to get married now that –'

'Emily!' Paula swung her head, glared at her cousin horror struck. '*Don't say it,*' she warned.

'Oh sorry,' Emily apologized swiftly, but could not resist adding with her typical unnerving bluntness, 'Nevertheless, it *is* true.'

Paula gave her a withering look.

Lifting the wine bottle out of the ice bucket, Emily refilled their glasses, and remarked, 'I don't think I'd better mention the possibility of Sally being pregnant to Winston.'

'Don't you dare! In fact, we're not going to say anything to anyone, not even Grandy. I don't want *her* to have that kind of worry. As for the rest of the family . . . you know how gossipy they're inclined to be. To even hint that Sally's pregnant would be like throwing a can of petrol on a bonfire. Besides, let's face it, Emily, we don't *know* that she is expecting. She might have merely gained weight lately.'

'Yes,' Emily said, 'there is that possibility, and we don't want to give certain people room to talk.' She fell silent, sank back into the chair, gazing out at the garden. It had acquired a magical almost ethereal quality and the trees had turned to shimmering silver in the moonlight which now bathed everything in its extraordinary radiance. 'It's so peaceful, so beautiful,' Emily murmured. 'I could sit here forever. But I suppose I ought to drive over to Pennistone Royal to get my clothes for the office tomorrow, if I'm going to stay here with you tonight. I told Hilda what to pack for me, and she'll have my suitcase ready, so I won't be very long.'

Paula roused herself from her own reverie. 'Perhaps you should pop back there, but take my car, Emily. The Jag *is* ready for the scrap heap, and I don't want you stranded in the middle of nowhere.' Paula stood up. 'I'll look in on the babies, and then start supper. Do you really want bubble and squeak?' she asked, reaching for the ice bucket and moving into the drawing room.

'Yes, it's sort of *comforting*, it takes me back to the summers at Heron's Nest. We always had bubble and squeak on Sunday nights with Gran when we were little. Oh for the good old days. Besides, you've a lot of left-over vegetables in your 'fridge. We might as well use them up. And I'm ravenous.'

Paula looked over her shoulder and shook her head wonderingly. 'Doesn't anything ever affect your appetite, Apple Dumpling?'

Emily, following her inside, grinned somewhat self-consciously. 'I suppose not, Beanstalk,' she shot back, using Paula's childhood nickname. 'But listen, I'm going to scoot. I'll be back as quickly as I can, and if Winston happens to ring give him lots of love from me.'

As was usual on Sunday night, Harrogate was deserted and virtually free of traffic, and within minutes Emily was on the main Ripon road, speeding steadily along towards Pennistone Royal.

Since Paula had said she could take either of the two cars in the garage, Emily had elected to drive Jim's Aston Martin. For a while she concentrated on getting the feel of the powerful piece of machinery under her hands, enjoying its smoothness and the sense of security she felt in the well-built and beautifully designed car. It was certainly a pleasant change from her rackety Jaguar which was so decrepit it was practically useless and probably unsafe.

Emily had clung to the old Jag for sentimental reasons in a way, inasmuch as it had once belonged to Winston. He had sold it to her four years ago and, until their fraternal relationship had blossomed into a love affair, driving his car had somehow seemed to bring him closer to her. It no longer held any significance because Winston himself was completely hers now that they were engaged. And the Jaguar had become a nuisance really, always breaking down at the most inopportune times. Grandy had been after her to get rid of it for ages and she decided she had better do so next week. She wondered what car to buy. An Aston Martin perhaps? Why not, it was a solid car, constructed like a tank. Emily began to ponder cars, but after a short while her thoughts not unnaturally turned to events in Ireland.

The land rover breaking down was a rotten piece of luck for Anthony, Emily thought. If it hadn't he would be totally in the clear. This would be an open-and-shut case. Pity he didn't go back for it before dinner, but no doubt he was trying to avoid Min. That poor woman . . . dying like that . . . drowning is the worst death . . . terrifying.

Emily shivered involuntarily as she contemplated the accident, endeavoured to push away the image of cold black water eddying and swirling, dragging Min down into its murky depths. Emily swallowed, held the steering wheel more tightly. She had inherited her grandmother's fear of water, and like Emma she was a poor swimmer, assiduously avoided boats, the sea, lakes and even the most innocuous of swimming pools. All terrified her.

In an effort to dispel the vivid mental picture of Min Standish's death, she turned on the car radio, twiddled the knob, but unable to find the station she liked she instantly switched it off. Through the car window she noticed the sign post which indicated she was approaching Ripley, and slowed down as she went through the small village, picking up speed as she left it behind, heading for South Stainley.

Unexpectedly, Emily felt her face tensing as a thought so distressing suddenly flashed through her mind, and she swerved, caught in the grip of apprehension. Righting the car immediately, she brought her full attention to the road, telling herself she would have an accident if she didn't concentrate.

Nonetheless, the thought would not go away. It was a question really, and it hovered over her in the most maddening way, and she wondered why it had not reared up before now. Finally she faced it head on: What *had* Min actually been *doing* out at the lake for some *five hours* before she drowned?

All through those summers they had spent at Heron's Nest, Emma Harte had instilled many things in her grandchildren. Chief amongst these was the importance of analysing a problem down to the last detail, examining every single aspect of it. Now Emily's brain began to turn with rapidity in the way it had been trained by Emma.

One possible answer to the question struck her instantly – Min had not spent five hours at the lake, because she had not been there in the afternoon. It had been late at night when she had gone there for the first time yesterday. Oh my God, Emily thought, shuddering uncontrollably, that would mean Anthony is lying. That can't be so, and even if he *was* responsible for her death, why didn't he remove the land rover? Why did he leave it at the lake?

Start at the beginning, Emily instructed herself. Think it through logically, and first of all work on the premise that he *could* be lying. She ran a possible sequence of events through her head.

Anthony has dinner with Edwina. He takes her home to the Dower House after-wards. He returns to Clonloughlin House around ten. Min arrives unexpectedly soon after. They quarrel. He rushes out, jumps into the land rover and drives off. Min follows, accosts him at the lake. They row again, she becomes violent, following her pattern of the past few weeks. He fends her off. They struggle. He accidentally kills her. He dumps the body in the lake so that it will look like an accident. Then the land rover won't start, or it conks out. He has no alternative but to walk back to the house.

It could have happened that way, Emily told herself reluctantly. But *if* it did, why didn't he return to the lake later to get the land rover? The last thing he would do is leave it there.

Her mind raced as she took her original thought to its conclusion.

Anthony decides it's risky trying to tow the land rover by himself late at night. He resolves to remove it early the next morning. But the estate manager is up and about at the crack of dawn and finds it first. Anthony concocts a plausible story with Edwina about Min arriving in the afternoon, explains the land rover broke down at that time. He cleverly bluffs his way through, counting on everyone to conclude, as I myself did, that only an innocent man would leave such damning evidence at the scene. On the other hand, Anthony does have an alibi for those crucial hours late at night. The housekeeper saw him. But is Bridget to be believed?

Was Anthony's story a huge pack of lies? Was this an immensely daring and brilliant bluff?

As Emily passed through Pennistone village and turned into the gates of her grandmother's estate she told herself that a man would have to be awfully cold-blooded and ruthless, would have to have nerves of steel to carry off such a scheme so successfully. Was Anthony such a man? *No.* How do you know that, Emily Barkstone? Only a few hours ago you told Paula that neither of you knew him all that *well*.

Appalled at her thoughts, Emily did her best to shake them off as she parked and climbed out of the car.

Hilda, her grandmother's housekeeper, was coming out of the door leading to the kitchen and the servants' quarters at the back of the house.

A broad smile flew on to Hilda's face at the sight of her. 'There you are, Miss Emily,' she said, and peered through her glasses worriedly. She clucked, 'You're looking a bit poorly. You'd best come to the kitchen for a cup of tea.'

'Thanks, Hilda, but I have to get back to Miss Paula's immediately. I'm fine, honestly, just a bit tired.' Emily managed to produce a smile, then glanced around, looking for her suitcase.

'Your overnight bag's here,' Hilda said, producing it from behind one of the heavy Tudor hall chairs. She carried it to her saying, 'What terrible news, just awful. It gave me a right turn, that it did. I had to sit down and have a drop of brandy after your phone call. His poor lordship . . . oh deary me what a tragedy for him. But then life's so unpredictable, isn't it.' She nodded, her face mournful, then took hold of Emily's arm with a show of affection. Accompanying her across the hall, she said, 'Does Mrs Harte know yet? Have you spoken to her?'

'No, Hilda. Mr David is trying to reach Mr Philip in Australia. Don't worry, Grandma will be all right.'

'Oh I've no doubts about that, none at all, Miss Emily. But it does seem so unfair. Just when she gets a chance for a little rest, a nice holiday, a dreadful thing like this accident has to happen. Your poor grandmother's life has been full of troubles . . . I'd hoped that by now she'd be free of them.'

'Yes, Hilda, I second that. But you said it yourself – unexpected things happen and we can't control life.'

Emily began edging her way to the front door, looking about her as she did, savouring the beauty of the Stone Hall, but also suddenly acutely conscious of its normality. It was filled with lovely warm light, the fire in the huge hearth blazed as it always did through the autumn and winter, and pots of gold and bronze chrysanthemums were clustered in the well of the great staircase. Yes, this hall looked exactly the way it had all of her life, even to the brass urn filled with copper beech on the refectory table.

Its unchanging appearance engendered an enormous sense of security in Emily, and she felt Emma's presence so powerfully, so forcefully at this precise moment she was reassured, and her fears began to ebb away. Her grandmother was a brilliant woman with a shrewd and penetrating understanding of people. She loved and trusted Anthony . . . not because he was her grandson but because of his character and his qualities as a man.

Swinging around, Emily gave Hilda a dimpling smile and although her green eyes were serious her voice was strong as she said, 'Don't worry, Hilda, Gran will take this in her stride. And thanks for packing my bag.'

'It was no trouble, Miss Emily, and you drive carefully, do you hear.'

Taking her leave of Hilda, Emily ran outside to the Aston Martin, threw her bag on the back seat and within seconds she had reversed the car and was spinning down the driveway, heading back the way she had come.

On her return trip to Harrogate she kept a firm hold on the positive feelings she had experienced at Pennistone Royal, and she kept telling herself that Anthony had been truthful and that Min's death was an accident.

228

In fact Emily had so brainwashed herself she was in exceptionally good spirits when she drove into the garage at Long Meadow. Although she had made the journey to Pennistone and back in record time, it had taken her a good hour, and she was beginning to feel faint with hunger. She was looking forward to a pleasant supper and her mouth watered as she thought of cold lamb, bubble and squeak and a glass of icy white wine.

But all such thoughts were swept out of her head as she went into the kitchen. She could not fail to see the disarray at once. Food lay abandoned on the counter top. The lamb was only half carved, the bubble and squeak had congealed in the frying pan on top of the stove and cupboard doors swung open.

Paula sat inertly at the kitchen table and there was such a stricken look on her face Emily's worries sprang to life.

'What is it?' she cried from the doorway. 'Something awful's happened at Clonloughlin. They haven't arrested –'

'No, no, nothing like that,' Paula assured her, lifting her eyes. 'I haven't even heard a peep out of them.' Her voice was exhausted.

'Then what is it?' Emily demanded, joining her at the table, scanning her troubled face.

Paula exhaled, remained mute.

Emily suspected her cousin had been crying, and leaning forward she took hold of her slender, tapering hand and patted it. 'Please tell me,' she said softly.

'I've had a terrible row with Jim. He phoned a little while ago and he was so snotty with me I can't get over it.'

'But *why?*'

'*Sam Fellowes*. He ignored my warning and called Jim. He left three urgent messages at the hotel in Toronto. When Jim got in he rang him back, and Fellowes told him about the accident, and my instructions not to run a story, or an obituary. Fellowes said I'd treated him in a most rude and high-handed manner, that I'd even threatened to give him the sack. Jim was obviously furious, yelled at me, *chastised* me. He thinks I handled things most undiplomatically. He said he'd had to spend twenty minutes placating Fellowes, and had finally convinced him not to resign.' Paula reached for a handkerchief and blew her nose.

'I can't believe it!' Emily was aghast. 'Surely Jim apologized once he understood your reasons for putting a lid on the story, when you explained about Anthony being under suspicion.'

'Oh he did ease off a bit,' Paula told her morosely, 'but his nose was definitely out of joint. And no, he didn't apologize. He was more concerned about whether he could get a flight to Ireland tomorrow. He thinks he should be with Edwina and Anthony to give them moral support.'

Emily made a disagreeable face. 'He would.' She shook her head slowly. 'What's wrong with Jim? Has he forgotten Grandy's rule about the family not being mentioned in our newspapers?'

'No. At the outset of our conversation he said this was different, that since reports of Min's death would probably appear in the nationals, we'd look ridiculous if we didn't carry an obituary. Once he was fully aware of the facts he sort of calmed down, but he still insisted I had handled Fellowes in the wrong way.'

'What the hell did he expect you to do?'

Paula smiled thinly. 'He said I should have told Fellowes not to run anything in the early editions, but to have the obituary prepared, and then to hold it until either Winston or he had been contacted in Canada. He told me it was their decision – his and Winston's – not *mine*.'

Emily's jaw dropped and she gave Paula a hard and baffled stare. 'Doesn't he *know* that you have Grandy's power of attorney, and Winston's, to act on their behalf in an emergency?'

'I didn't see any reason to say anything before he left,' Paula murmured. 'I didn't want to hurt his feelings. I'd have had to break the news that I'm the trustee, with Winston and Alexander, of our children's shares in Consolidated, not him.' When Emily said nothing, Paula insisted, 'How could I tell him *that*, Emily?'

'Well, you should have,' Emily retorted crossly.

'Perhaps,' Paula admitted, ignoring her tone.

I bet she still hasn't told him, Emily thought, but said, 'Is Jim *really* going to rush to Ireland?'

'I'm not certain. He was anxious to talk to Winston. Jim had been trying to reach him in Vancouver before he called here.'

'You mean we were the *last* on his list and after all the urgent messages I left?' Emily was flabbergasted.

Paula nodded. The two cousins exchanged long, very knowing looks, remembering their grandmother's strictest rule, one that had been drilled into them continually. Emma had told them to always check with at least one member of the family in any emergency before acting, to resist talking to strangers, to be supportive of each other, and most importantly to close ranks to protect the family.

Paula said hesitantly, 'I suppose he thought there was something wrong at the paper –'

'He might not have been brought up by Grandy, but he sure as hell knows her rules!' Emily exploded. 'He ought to have called us *first*, then he would have had the facts. It might have prevented the row you two had if nothing else.' She sat back jerkily, her annoyance with Jim apparent.

'That's true. Oh, never mind, Emily, it doesn't matter. Look, I should have told you this the moment you arrived . . . Winston rang.' Paula gave her a smile, determined to forget about Jim's unreasonable behaviour.

'When?' Emily asked eagerly, then added pithily, 'I bet *he* didn't have long dialogues with the whole world first!'

Paula laughed for the first time in hours. 'You're absolutely right, darling. And he reached me just a few minutes after I'd hung up on Jim.'

'Tell me everything Winston said, and please don't miss out on one single word.'

Paula looked across at Emily with fond indulgence, her expression warm and caring. 'Winston had been having lunch with the chairman of the board of the paper mill, at the latter's home. When he finally got back to the hotel late this afternoon, afternoon in Canada that is, he found a pile of messages.

230

Sam Fellowes had called – *naturally* – so had Sally, Jim and you. Since you'd left *this* number, and since Fellowes had said it was urgent they speak, Winston immediately suspected there was some sort of crisis at the paper. Naturally he wanted to talk to me or you before anyone else. Grandy's golden rule is not something any of *us* is likely to forget. Winston was really thrown off balance when I told him Min was dead, and he was particularly concerned about Sally. "Keep that sister of mine as far away from Clonloughlin as you can," he repeated quite a few times. I set his mind at rest, of course, and he was awfully relieved I'd been tough with her. He asked a lot of pertinent questions, which I was able to answer, and he said I'd done the right things, and that between the two of us we'd made all the right moves, too. He was also glad you're staying here tonight.'

'Does he plan to fly home?' Emily asked.

'No, not unless the situation at Clonloughlin changes – for the worse. He reminded me that we'd all been trained in the same army camp by the same general, and pointed out that he couldn't contribute anything more than you or I could, and so therefore he intended to go about his business in a normal manner.'

'He's right of course.' Emily paused for a fraction of a second, before asking, 'Did you say anything about the row, Jim's attitude towards you?'

'Only in passing, Emily. I didn't want to make a big thing about it, but I'm afraid Winston was fit to be tied. He was very down on Jim. He also said Fellowes was a fool, that his job had been in the balance for a long time. And then he sort of wondered aloud why Jim hadn't spoken to me before calling Fellowes back.' Paula shrugged. 'I told him his guess was as good as mine. In any event, he's going to talk to Jim about Fellowes, and also about going to Ireland. He thinks Jim should stay in Canada, but I got the feeling Winston wouldn't interfere if Jim insisted on leaving for Dublin tomorrow. That's about it, but he asked for you, of course, and he sends his love.'

'I do wish I hadn't missed him. I was longing to talk to him,' Emily said a little wistfully.

'Oh you can do that, any time after midnight – our time,' Paula immediately volunteered. 'Winston's not going out this evening. He told me he would order something up to the suite, and he indicated he was going to ring Sally and Jim, and I suspect he's going to give Sam Fellowes an earful.'

'I'm sure he is, and I'll give him a buzz a bit later.' Emily rose, slipped out of her cardigan and hung it on the back of the chair. 'What about your father . . . did he reach Philip?'

'Yes, about an hour ago, only a few minutes after you'd left for Pennistone. It was breakfast time at Dunoon and Grandy was up, having her morning tea and toast with Philip. She knows. Daddy spoke to her as well.' Paula eyed Emily carefully. 'What do you bet we'll hear from her before very long?'

'Everything I have,' Emily laughed. 'It's a certainty Grandy'll ring us as soon as she's had time to think up a few penetrating questions which are bound to catch us off guard.'

Paula could not help laughing with Emily. 'That's a bit naughty.'

'Well, you know as well as I do that Emma Harte is always testing her grandchildren, to see if they're on their toes. Why should tonight be any different?'

Throwing her a thoughtful glance, Paula said, 'I don't suppose it is, and let's be thankful she brought us up the way she did . . . at least we're capable of handling any emergency.'

'Yes,' Emily agreed. 'And in the meantime, I'm going to revive the bubble and squeak and make us a lovely supper.'

25

'I'm beginning to think that Jim and I are always going to be at cross purposes, Daddy,' Paula said.

David Amory, who was standing at the bar cabinet in the drawing room of his Regent's Park flat, swung around. The remark had startled him in as much as he had caught a most discernible hint of irritation in his daughter's voice. A dark brow lifted. 'In what sense, darling?'

'He sees things quite differently than I do. Of course, that's all right, because everyone has their own vision of the world, of life, and each of us handles problems, people and situations in our individual way, as best we can. But Jim will never admit he's wrong about anything, and he's continually accusing me of over-reacting.'

David made no response. A wry smile flickered and his cool intelligent eyes held his daughter's for a split second before he turned back to the bar and refilled their glasses. Carrying them over to the seating arrangement in front of the tall windows, he handed her the vodka and tonic, seated himself opposite her.

Settling back in the chair, David took a swallow of his scotch and soda, and asked, 'Does he think you've reacted too strongly to the mess in Ireland? Is that it?'

'Yes.'

David nodded thoughtfully. 'Do *you* think you have?'

'No, I don't.'

'Good girl. I've always rather admired your decisiveness, your unwavering attitude, and you're one of the few women I know who isn't forever changing her mind. So stick to your guns, and don't let Jim upset you, especially when you're certain you've made the proper moves. We can't please everyone in life, Paula, and so the important thing is to be true to oneself. That's *your* priority.'

'I know it is.' Paula leaned forward, said now with some intensity, 'I have enough common sense to admit it when I'm wrong, but in this instance I'm convinced I was wise to take the precautions I did, to clap a lid on everything, to cover us for *any* eventuality. It may be a status quo in Ireland, and the national papers may have treated the story in a routine way – so far. But that doesn't mean we're out of the woods yet.'

'Naturally we're not, and we won't be until after the autopsy and the inquest.'

David gazed down into his drink reflectively. 'I didn't particularly like the wire service story that ran today in some of the papers . . . about the police investigating the mysterious circumstances surrounding Min's death. On the other hand, there was no mention of Anthony. Thank God for the rather stringent libel laws in this country.' He looked up, frowned. 'I'm just praying that none of the more sensational dailies don't blow the investigation out of proportion. Well –' He gave her a kindly smile, finished, 'We're just going to have to sit this one out, darling. And getting back to Jim, I don't wish to sound critical, but if you ask me he's the one who has over-reacted. It was quite unnecessary for him to fly to Ireland. Your mother is coping nicely.'

'Yes she is, and I'm proud of her.'

Reaching for a cigarette and lighting it, David remarked, 'For what it's worth, you did exactly what Grandy would have done had she been here. Throughout the twenty-seven years I've known her, Emma has constantly told me she doesn't like unpleasant surprises, and that in her lexicon prevention is infinitely better than any kind of cure. Jim may not concur with your decisions, your actions, but Grandy, Henry and I do, and we've all told you so in the last twenty-four hours.'

'You've been very supportive, and when Gran called me again this afternoon, just before I left Leeds, she reiterated her confidence in me and in all of us, actually.'

'So you said – and that's the reason she's decided not to come back. Look Paula, this may sound silly, when we're under such a great deal of tension, but please do try to relax. *I* certainly shall. And don't worry about Jim's attitude. Whilst I'm fully aware you want his approval, you'd be wise to recognize you're not going to get it, because he doesn't understand –' David stopped short, regretting this slip, not wishing to criticize his son-in-law. He had long been disappointed in Jim, but he had managed to keep his feelings to himself thus far. He had not even voiced them to Daisy.

Paula, quick as ever, said, 'Were you going to say he doesn't understand my reasoning, or that he doesn't understand me?'

There was an awkward silence.

Paula stared at her father. David met her questioning gaze unblinkingly. He was convinced Jim Fairley did not have the slightest conception of his daughter's character nor her business ethos, but electing to go with the lesser of two evils, he said, 'Your reasoning.'

She nodded. 'I've known that for some time now. Jim can be very naive, which is especially surprising to me, since he's a newspaperman accustomed to seeing so many of the worst aspects of people, of life. Yet his judgement is way off more often than not, and it seems to me that he looks at the world through rose-coloured glasses.' She let out a tiny sigh. 'And to be honest, I'm also starting to think he doesn't understand the first thing about me, or the way my mind works, or why I do the things I do.'

David was conscious of the misery in her tone and he looked across at her, filling with concern at the sight of her forlorn expression and her confirmation of his own suspicions about Jim. 'You can tell me to mind my own business if you want – but look here, Paula, is your marriage in trouble?'

233

'No, I don't think so, even though we do have our differences. I love Jim very much, Daddy.'

'I'm sure you do and that he feels the same way, but love isn't always enough, Paula. You've got to be able to live with someone twenty-four hours a day, year in and year out, and comfortably so on that continuing basis. And you can only do that if there is true understanding between the two of you.'

'Yes,' she agreed with a faint, hesitant smile, wondering whether to pour out her troubles to her father. She decided against it. Tonight was not the right moment. Adopting a more confident tone, she assured him, 'We'll work it out, I'm certain of that, because we really do care for each other. Please don't worry, and don't say anything to Mummy, will you? Promise?'

'I promise, and I'm not going to pry, but I do want you to remember that you can confide in me any time you wish, darling. I love you very much and naturally your happiness is important to me.' David drained his glass, continued, 'As it is to your mother too. However, you're right, she'd be disturbed if she thought your relationship with Jim was anything less than perfect.'

'You've been so happy with Mummy, haven't you, Daddy?'

'Yes. *Very*. Mind you, we've had our ups and downs.' David chuckled, noticing the look of genuine astonishment registering in Paula's eyes. 'It's nice to know you were never aware of our rough patches, and we *did* have a few. But then any marriage worth its salt is never all sweetness and light. There's a marvellous line in *David Copperfield* which I've always been partial to, and it's very apt when I think of my marriage to Daisy . . . *the strongest steel goes through the hottest fire*. Yes, my dear, we had our troubles just like most people do. Nevertheless, we overcame them.'

Paula, still surprised at his revelation said, '*Troubles*. Were they really serious?'

Shaking his head and chuckling again, David told her, 'Now, when I look back, they were very piddling, but when we were suffering through them they seemed quite monumental. Which is why I'm inclined to agree with you when you say you'll work things out with Jim. I'm sure you will, and the marriage will be all that much better. But if it isn't –' He gave her a long hard stare. 'Then don't be afraid to let go, to end it whilst you're still young and can find someone else. And don't fall into the trap of staying together for the children's sake if the marriage *is* seriously damaged. That kind of reasoning is cockeyed in my opinion. In the long run, everyone's miserably unhappy, including the children. Self-sacrifice of that nature is for martyrs, and *they* usually end up being a pain in the rear end,' he finished, deciding he had said enough, if not far too much perhaps. Still, Paula was strong, sound of judgement, and determined to lead her own life. He knew she would brook no interference. And neither he nor anyone else would have much, if any, influence on her decisions. Not now or in the future.

'Thanks, Daddy, for being such a good friend,' Paula said, 'and for not pontificating as some fathers would. I see you've finished your drink, and I don't really want mine, so let's go to dinner shall we?'

'Splendid idea.' He glanced at the clock on the mantelpiece. 'Why yes, we ought to get a move on. I have a table for eight-thirty at Ziegi's.'

They went out into the hall together and as David helped her on with her coat he bent and kissed the top of her head, making a sudden gesture of affection. She pivoted to face him, stood on tiptoe to kiss his cheek in return. 'You're truly special, Daddy.'

His eyes, usually so cool and appraising, filled with great warmth. 'So are you, Daughter.'

Out on the street, David found a taxi at once, and after whizzing across town to Charles Street in Mayfair, they were being seated in the upstairs dining room of the famous club fifteen minutes after leaving the flat.

David brushed aside Paula's announcement that she was not very hungry, as he had so often done when she was a child. He took matters into his own hands, ordered Colchester oysters, steak Diane and pureed vegetables for them both, perused the impressive wine list with a knowledgeable eye, finally selected a vintage Mouton Rothschild, then insisted Paula share half a bottle of champagne with him whilst they waited for the meal.

By unspoken agreement neither mentioned the difficult situation at Clonloughlin, wanting a respite from their worry. For a while Paula did most of the talking, discussing matters pertaining to the stores, of which her father was now chairman of the board since Emma's retirement. Paula had stepped into his shoes automatically, held the title of managing director, and in consequence it was she who bore the brunt of running the chain on a day-to-day basis.

He was content to sit back and listen, enjoying her company, her wit and her charm, not to mention her indisputably brilliant mind. But then his daughter had always intrigued him. When she had been growing up she had seemed, at times, more like Emma's child than Daisy's and his, in that Emma had made Paula her very own. He had vaguely resented this, but had never been able to combat Emma's influence over her. Then when she was ten or thereabouts he began to understand that the child loved the three of them equally, played no one as a favourite, for with a wisdom that was remarkable, almost frightening, in one so young, she had made this perfectly clear to him, her mother and Emma. David was amused when some members of the family implied that Emma had brainwashed Paula to such an extent she had turned her into a clone. He knew his daughter had far too strong and stubborn a mind to follow the leader blindly, to permit herself to become something she was not, to accept indoctrination without question. The truth was much simpler. Emma had indeed trained Paula in her ways, but his daughter was already so much like Emma this had hardly been necessary. The similarities of their characters aside, they had always been on the same wave length and over the years this had become so finely tuned they appeared to read each other's thoughts, and frequently finished sentences for each other, much to everyone's amazement, including his own. But of all the qualities they shared, the one which truly impressed David was their ability to bring the most intense concentration and single-mindedness to the matter at hand. He was aware of the amount of mental and physical energy this took, and he considered it a great virtue in both women, a mark of their extraordinary genius. For genius it was.

Sometimes David had to remind himself that Paula was not yet twenty-five, as he did at this moment, struck as he was by her maturity and her keen understanding of complex business matters. As he absorbed her words he observed her closely, noting for the second time in the last hour her elegance and refinement. He never thought of Paula as being beautiful, and she was not, at least not in the accepted sense, because of her somewhat angular features, broad forehead and strong jawline. Rather, she was arrestingly attractive with her vividness of colouring, her translucent complexion and her superb grooming. Yes, it's her immense elegance, he thought, that's undoubtedly what draws all eyes to her. For the half hour they had been in Ziegi's he had not failed to miss the discreet glances directed at them from time to time. He wondered, with a small flicker of amusement, if they thought she was his young mistress.

Detecting the laughter playing around his eyes, Paula abandoned the point she was making and leaned forward. 'What's so funny, Daddy?'

He flashed a wide grin. 'I'm the envy of the men in this room . . . they most probably think you're my girlfriend.'

She shrugged, smiled, eyeing him objectively. If the other diners did harbour such a thought it was not so far fetched really. At fifty-one her father was a good-looking man whom women found attractive and appealing. He had a strong, well-bred face, fine clear eyes, and a head of dark wavy hair tinged at the sides with grey that did nothing to age him. He was athletically inclined, skied and played squash in winter, took to the tennis courts in summer, and in consequence he was in excellent physical shape. Fastidious about his appearance, he was always beautifully dressed, a characteristic she knew she had inherited from him.

David was saying, 'You do look lovely tonight, Paula. The dress has great style. Black has always suited you, of course. Still, few women could carry it off as well as you do. It is rather severe, and –'

'Don't you like it?'

'Very much so.' He studied the Egyptian-style gold collar that encircled her long neck and partially filled out the squared neckline of the long-sleeved wool dress. Nefertiti, he said under his breath. Aloud he remarked, 'I've never seen you wearing the collar before. It's beautiful, rather striking, in fact. Is it new? A gift from Jim?'

Paula smiled mischievously, dropped her voice. 'Don't tell anyone, but it's a piece of costume jewellery. From Harte's. I'm sure it's not even brass, and it'll probably turn colour in no time at all. But when I saw it I knew it was perfect for this dress. It gives it a bit of a dash, wouldn't you say?'

'I would indeed.' He made a mental note to talk to the jewellery buyer tomorrow, decided to have the collar copied for Paula for her Christmas gift. He was usually at a loss to know what to give her for anniversaries and special occasions. She was not overly fond of jewels or other baubles and because of her highly individual taste it was difficult to shop for her successfully.

As the dinner progressed David and Paula touched on many topics of mutual interest, but eventually Paula brought the conversation back to business. Slowly, but with her usual self-assurance, she began to outline an idea she had for the stores.

David sat up straighter in the chair, listening alertly, intrigued by her concept, which showed an intuitive understanding of the buying public. And like so many really clever ideas it was rooted in simplicity. He wondered why no other retailer had ever thought of it.

Paula said, 'You've got a peculiar look on your face. Don't you think it will work?'

'On the contrary, I think it will be a tremendous hit. Expand on it further for me please, Paula.'

She did so, finished, 'But it would have to be a completely self-contained shop within the store.'

'You'd need a whole floor?'

'Not necessarily. Half a floor should work very well. I thought there could be three separate salons. One selling suits, plus shirts and blouses, another for coats and dresses, and a third salon offering shoes, boots and handbags. The key, of course, is having the individual salons adjoining each other, so that a woman can coordinate a complete outfit quickly and easily without having to trundle up and down to other floors searching for different items. It will save mistakes, not to mention time, for the shopper. And with an imaginative advertising campaign and some clever promotion I think we can do tremendous business.' She sat back, watching him through keenly attentive eyes.

'It's excellent. Yes, I'm enthusiastic. Any ideas about a name for this total shop of yours?'

'There are several very obvious ones, Daddy, such as *Working Woman* or *Career Woman*. However, I've already dismissed those as being far too prosaic. We need a name that expresses exactly what we are about. We must put over the concept that we are selling clothes – good, well-designed clothes – to working women with business and professional careers, that we are offering a special service since we're making their task of putting a wardrobe together so much easier.'

'What about *Career Cachet*?' David suggested.

'Not bad.' Paula frowned. 'Is it too much in the other direction? Too fancy perhaps?' she asked, thinking aloud, and before he had a chance to reply went on, 'I thought of *Career Club* when I was driving to London this afternoon. But I'm not sure if that says what I want to say. Well, right now the name doesn't really matter. The main thing is to get the career shop into work. So . . . do I have your blessing?'

'Naturally you do, although you don't really need it.' David's eyes twinkled as he reminded her, 'The Harte chain is yours, Paula, lock, stock and barrel, and you *are* managing director.'

'But you're the chairman of the board,' she shot back. 'And therefore you're still my boss.'

'You always did have to have the last word, didn't you?' he murmured, and could not help thinking: as Emma always does.

'Sorry I'm late getting back,' Paula apologized as she hurried into the executive offices at the Knightsbridge store on Wednesday afternoon at five minutes to three.

'How was your meeting with Henry Rossiter?' Gaye asked, rising, following Paula into the palatial Georgian-style office that bore Emma's inimitable stamp.

'No problems. We spent most of the time reviewing Grandy's other holdings. We hardly touched on the Irish mess, gave it only a few minutes after our

237

business session. When we were having lunch, actually. Any further news from over there, by the way?' Paula threw her handbag on a chair, sat down behind the huge partners' desk that had once been her grandmother's.

'Yes. Your mother rang again. She wanted you to know she won't stay on after the inquest in Cork tomorrow as she had planned. She's decided to fly back to London immediately,' Gaye explained, taking the chair opposite the desk.

'I'm glad she's changed her mind. Once the inquest is out of the way we'll be able to breathe a little easier . . . I sincerely hope.'

'Since the police haven't made any moves I'm positive the hearing will be quite routine,' Gaye volunteered in a quiet tone.

'Let us pray.' Paula attempted a smile, then noticing Gaye's gloomy demeanour for the first time, she asked, '*You're* not looking too happy. What's been happening since I walked out of here at eleven o'clock?'

Gaye cleared her throat. 'Sorry to greet you with problems, Paula . . . but I'm afraid that's all we've got this afternoon.'

'Par for the course this week, or so it seems. All right Gaye, let's have the bad news.'

'I'll start with what I feel are the real priorities,' Gaye said, lifting her head. 'Dale Stevens rang you about twenty minutes ago. Not from Texas though. He's in New York. At the Pierre Hotel. He sounded odd, worried, in my opinion. Certainly he wasn't his usual ebullient self.'

Trouble at Sitex, Paula thought. Stifling her apprehension, she said, 'Did he give you any indication why he wanted to speak to me?'

Gaye shook her head. 'But he did ask me when you plan to visit Harte's in New York. I said probably not before November, and this seemed to upset him. He sort of bit back a four-letter word and asked, "Are you sure she won't be over in the States earlier than that?" I said you wouldn't, not unless there was something urgent that needed your attention. I was fishing when I made that remark, but he didn't rise to the bait.'

'I'd better ring him back.' Paula reached for the phone.

Gaye said, 'He's not there. He went to a meeting. The message was to call him at six our time.'

'That's *all* he said?'

'Not one word more. Very cagey, our Mr Stevens was. I can tell from your expression that you're worried, think the worst, suspect that there's something amiss at Sitex Oil. I have to agree. He did sound awfully tense, even morose.'

'As you said before, that's very unusual. Dale's always so relaxed and cheerful. But there's no use speculating. Okay. Sitex at six. What's next?'

'Winston checked in from Vancouver over lunch time. *He* was also anxiety ridden. He has unexpected problems with the Canadian paper mill. They erupted late yesterday, after you and he had already spoken. The negotiations have stalled. He's withdrawing the offer today, as you both agreed he should if any difficulties developed. He's going to give them twenty-four hours, and if it's not back on the tracks by then he's flying to New York on Friday. He doesn't want you to bother ringing him. He said he'd be in touch – either way. But he doesn't hold out much hope of making the deal. He has a feeling it's kaput.'

'Damnation, that *is* annoying! It would have been such a good acquisition for Consolidated. We'll just have to hope he can turn the situation around. Go on, Gaye.'

'Sally Harte's disappeared,' Gaye murmured, giving Paula a sympathetic look.

'The fool! The silly little fool!' Paula cried sitting bolt upright. 'I told her not to go rushing off to Ireland, and I bet that's exactly where she's gone. Who called? Uncle Randolph?'

'No, Emily. Your Uncle Randolph spoke to her a couple of hours ago. Emily was on her way out when she received the call. She's on her way to town right now. As you know, she has a meeting at the London office of Genret tomorrow. Anyway, apparently your Uncle Randolph is in quite a rage, although Emily says she did her best to calm him down. Emily thinks Vivienne is hiding something, knows where Sally's gone but won't talk. She suggested you tackle Vivienne when you have a moment.'

Paula groaned. 'I do so love Emily's advice. Why the hell didn't she speak to Vivienne when she was still in Yorkshire! This is all I need today.'

'I did ask Emily to take a minute to talk to Vivienne before setting off, but she demurred, explained that it wouldn't do any good. She said, "Tell Paula I'm not as daunting as she is," and she hung up before I could say another word.'

'I see.' The two women exchanged concerned glances. Paula looked away, focusing on the fireplace, her face reflective, and then her mouth curved down in a stern and resolute line and her eyes narrowed.

Watching her closely, Gaye could not help thinking how much Paula resembled her grandmother at this moment and she thought: I hope to God she really is as strong as Emma Harte – as we have all come to believe.

Paula brought her gaze back to her assistant. 'I'll get to Vivienne later. Wherever Sally is, I can't very well remove her bodily, or force her to do as I say. Right now, business comes first. Anything else?'

'John Cross telephoned. He's in London. He asked for an appointment. Tomorrow morning, if convenient.'

'*Oh!*' Paula exclaimed, but she was not as surprised as she appeared to be. She had been expecting to hear from the head of Aire Communications for weeks. She and her grandmother had agreed he would come crawling back eventually.

Gaye stared at her, trying to fathom her expression which was quite unreadable. 'Cross left a number, Paula,' she said at last, breaking the silence. 'What do you want to do? You've a fairly clear calendar tomorrow.'

Pursing her lips and shaking her head, Paula admitted, 'To be truthful, I'm not sure . . . there doesn't seem to be much point in seeing him. I've nothing to say to that particular gentleman. I'll let you know before the end of the day.'

'Your cousin Sarah's back from Barbados, and she wants to see you. At four o'clock today. She says she has to come over to the store to see the ready-to-wear buyer, and could pop up for a few minutes. She was rather insistent.'

'She's back sooner than I expected. I'd better see her. It can't be anything important, so it shouldn't take very long. Sarah most likely wants to tell me about the opening of the boutique and the new hotel this past weekend. Is that all of it, Gaye?'

'It's enough, isn't it?' Gaye replied dourly.

Paula sat back, surveying her. 'Do you really like being my assistant? Or would you prefer to be my secretary after all? I can demote you, Gaye, if that's what you want. I aim to please in all things,' Paula teased, and laughed in spite of her many worries.

Gaye had the good grace to laugh too. 'Sorry I sounded so glum. And I'm relishing the new job, honestly I am. Besides, Sheila would be hurt and affronted if she was relegated to being the junior secretary again. She's so proud she works for you personally. She's very efficient, isn't she?'

'Yes, thanks to your assiduous training over the last few years.'

The telephone rang. Paula glared at it, shook her head.

Lifting the receiver, Gaye said crisply: 'Mrs Fairley's office.' There was a slight pause before she added, 'She's right here.' Handing her the phone, Gaye mouthed, 'It's okay – it's only Alexander.' Gaye hurried out of the room.

'How do you like being back at the old grindstone?' Paula said into the phone.

'Bloody awful after two weeks of sunshine and indolence in the South of France. But it's a relief in one sense – I don't have to cope with my mother,' Alexander answered in a sarcastic voice, rushed on, 'Can you have supper with me tonight? There's a few things I'd like to discuss with you.'

'*Serious?*'

'No. Interesting, though.'

'Why don't you tell me now?' Paula pressed, her curiosity flaring.

'Too involved. Also, I'm due to start a meeting in exactly ten minutes. Since you and I are both in town and alone, I thought it was a good opportunity to get together. Fancy dining at the White Elephant?'

'That sounds like a nice change. Thanks for the invitation, and I'd love to see you, as long as we can make it around nine. I have to work late.'

'Who doesn't, and nine's fine. I'll pick you up at Belgrave Square shall I? Around eight-thirty?'

'Perfect. Oh, and Sandy, you'd better make the reservation for three. Your sister's on her way up to London, and I'm sure Emily'll insist on joining us.'

'Too true. Miss Nosey Parker has to be in on everything,' he responded with a dry laugh. 'See you later.'

Paula rose and walked over to stand with her back to the fireplace. The weather had turned cold in the last few days and as soon as there was the slightest hint of an autumn nip in the air the fire was automatically lit every morning as it had been for years. Paula was glad that Emma's long tradition continued unchanged. She suddenly felt chilled to the bone and the bright blaze was warming, also brought a cheerful aspect to the handsome room.

She scowled to herself as her thoughts settled on Dale Stevens. It was not unusual for him to be in constant contact with her, since she was her grand-mother's representative at Sitex. Emma, who with forty-two per cent of the stock was the largest single stockholder, had always been a power in the oil company and a member of the board. Now that she filled this role Dale con-ferred with her several times a month. On the other hand, this afternoon's call had apparently not been routine. Gaye had discerned a troubled note in his voice, and she trusted Gaye's judgement. After all, it had been the redoubtable Sloane who had discovered the plot against Grandy last year. Dale is probably having trouble with the Harry Marriott faction on the board, Paula suddenly thought. He had been her grandfather's partner when Paul McGill had founded Sydney-Texas Oil in the twenties, and he had always been difficult. Emma had managed to get him kicked upstairs as chairman of the board in January of 1968, and had manipulated the board to do her will. They had voted with her, and had hired Dale Stevens, Emma's protégé, as the new president. Still, some of the board members who were Marriott's cronies resented Dale, and Paula decided that they were most likely creating an untenable situation for him.

Damn, she cursed under her breath. I wish I could reach him before six. Paula glanced at her watch. It was three-thirty. Two and a half hours to wait. Well, at least she had time to sign her letters, go over the inter-office memos piled on her desk, and speak to Vivienne Harte before Sarah Lowther appeared on the scene.

Returning to her desk, Paula flipped through the memos, saw that some of them raised questions which were too complicated to deal with quickly, and these she placed on one side. After signing the morning's correspondence, she put through a call to Allington Hall in Middleham.

'Hello, Vivienne,' Paula said when her cousin answered. 'How are you?'

'Oh, Paula! Hello. I'm pretty good, and you?'

'Worried, Vivienne. I just heard that –'

'If you're phoning about Sally I won't tell you where she is! *I promised her.* Daddy can't get it out of me, and neither will you.'

Paula said with firmness, 'Now, Vivienne, I'm sure Sally wouldn't be upset if you told me. I'm the –'

'Oh yes she would,' Vivienne interrupted heatedly. 'She doesn't want anybody to know where she's gone. Not even you. Please don't badger me, put me in this terrible position.'

'You *can* tell me . . . Listen, I won't say a thing to your father, or another soul, not even Winston when he calls me later. You must know I won't break my word.'

'No, I don't know that . . . you're expecting *me* to break *mine*,' Vivienne retorted. 'My poor sister is like a wounded bird, worn out too, and she needs to have a little peace and quiet. Daddy hasn't stopped ranting and raving at her since Sunday night.'

'I'm sorry to hear that. Look here, you don't have to tell me where she is, but would you agree to tell me where she's *not*?'

'What do you mean?' Vivienne asked warily.

'If I name a place where Sally has *not* gone, will you tell me? All you have to say is *no.*'

Vivienne laughed hollowly. 'You're trying to trap me, Paula. If I'm silent when I hear a particular name you'll know immediately that's where she's staying.' Vivienne laughed again, her incredulity echoing down the wire. 'Do you think I'm daft? Or green? I haven't fallen off a banana boat, you know.'

'I need to know where your sister is hiding herself,' Paula snapped, growing exasperated, 'and for a variety of reasons which I don't propose to go into with you.'

'Don't talk to me as if I'm a little kid. I'm nineteen,' Vivienne cried, her own temper flaring.

Paula sighed. 'Let's not argue, Viv, and I can only add this . . . if Sally's gone dashing off to Ireland she's a bigger fool than I thought, because she will only be creating problems for herself, and for Anthony.'

'Sally's hardly a *fool*! Obviously she wouldn't be stupid enough to go to Ireland –' Vivienne stopped abruptly.

Success, Paula thought with a faint smile. Her ruse had worked. She said, 'If Sally happens to phone you, tell her I'm having dinner with Alexander and Emily at the White Elephant tonight. Just in case she wants to join us.'

'I've got to go, Paula,' Vivienne said hurriedly after a short pause. 'Daddy needs me in the stables. So I'll say goodbye now.'

'Tell Sally to get in touch with me if she needs anything. Goodbye, Vivienne dear.'

Paula stared at the phone for a long moment, reflecting on their conversation. Well, Sally was not in Ireland. More than likely she was not in London either, since it was not her favourite place. Could she still be in Yorkshire? If so, where? A phrase Vivienne had used echoed into her mind. She had referred to her sister as a *wounded bird*. A figure of speech to describe Sally's state? Or had it perhaps been an unconscious association in the girl's mind? Wounded birds tried to get back to their nests . . . Heron's Nest? *Of course*. Sally loved Scarborough and many of her paintings were of the spots where they had spent so much time as children. That's where *I* would go if I wanted to hide, Paula said to herself. It's accessible, comfortable, the larder is always fully stocked, and old Mrs Bonnyface has a set of keys.

Lifting the receiver, Paula started to dial Heron's Nest and then changed her mind. It would be infinitely kinder to leave Sally alone for the time being. Whether she was in Scarborough or not was irrelevant really. The important thing was that she was nowhere near Clonloughlin, and this knowledge now eased Paula's anxiety about Sally Harte, of whom she was extremely fond.

'Paula?'

'Yes, Gaye?' Paula asked leaning closer to the intercom.

'Sarah's arrived.'

'Have her come in, Gaye, please.'

A moment later Sarah Lowther was walking across the floor, the expression on her pale freckled face as purposeful as her step. She wore a bottle-green gabardine suit so beautifully cut it did wonders for her somewhat plumpish figure. Also, the colour was a flattering contrast to her russet-red hair which framed her face in luxuriant waves and softened her broad but not unattractive features.

'Hello, Paula,' she said briskly, coming to a halt in the centre of the room. 'You're looking well. Thinner than ever. I don't know how you do it . . . it's a struggle for me to lose an ounce.'

Paula half smiled, and brushing aside the personal comment, said 'Welcome back, Sarah.' She stepped around the desk, kissed her cousin on the cheek. 'Let's sit over there by the fire,' she went on. 'Would you like a cup of tea?'

'No, thanks anyway.' Sarah turned smartly on her high heels and moved in the direction of the sofa. Seating herself in the corner nearest the fireplace, she leaned back, crossed her legs and smoothed her skirt. She let her eyes rove over Paula, admiring the simplicity and elegance of the deep purple wool dress. It was a marvel, and as head of the fashion division of Harte Enterprises Sarah knew it was by Yves Saint-Laurent. Biting back the compliment which had sprung to her lips, she said, 'Jonathan tells me the Irish lot are killing each other off . . . I'm surprised Grandmother hasn't hot-footed it back here.'

'That's not a very nice thing to say about Anthony, Sarah,' Paula gently reproved, seating herself in a chair, frowning. 'Min's death was an accident, and *why* should Gran come back? The whole thing's going to be over and done with by tomorrow at this time.'

Sarah gave Paula an odd look, raised an auburn brow. 'Let's hope you're right.'

'Tell me about the opening of the new hotel and our first boutique,' Paula said, neatly changing the subject.

Sarah remained silent.

Paula insisted, 'Come on, I'm longing to hear all about it.'

'It went off well,' Sarah said at last. 'But then why wouldn't it? I've worked very hard for months to ensure that it would. To tell you the truth, the whole trip was a hard grind. I was on my feet twenty-four hours a day. Miranda was tied up with the hotel, so I had to really buckle down, supervise the unpacking and pressing of the dresses, get the windows dressed, create eye-catching interior displays,' she grumbled. 'But the merchandise I selected turned out to be perfect, even though I do say so myself. My Lady Hamilton dresses and resort wear appealed to everyone. They said the colours were fantastic, the fabrics superior, the designs bang on. We were jammed the day we opened, so we should do record business right through the season.'

'Oh I am pleased,' Paula said with enthusiasm, deciding to ignore Sarah's remarks about her contribution to the boutique which, in all truth, had been negligible. She asked, 'How's Merry?'

'All right, I suppose. I didn't see much of her. The O'Neills invited a plane load of celebrities to the hotel's gala opening weekend. So naturally she was busy rubbing noses with the famous.'

Paula's back went up at this remark, which she deemed bitchy and uncalled for, but she wisely let it pass. 'Did Shane fly down from New York?'

'Yes.'

'And?'

'And *what*?' Sarah asked, her voice turning huffy all of a sudden. She gave Paula a challenging stare and her face settled in cold lines.

Instantly struck by the dislike in Sarah's expression, Paula recoiled in surprise. Thrown though she was, she managed to say, 'Surely you saw something of Shane and Uncle Bryan? Merry may have been rushed off her feet as head of public relations, but I can't believe the O'Neills ignored you. After all they're family, and they're not like that.'

'Oh yes, I was invited to the gala evenings. But I was generally too exhausted to enjoy them. I didn't have much fun at all. That side of it was a complete bust.'

Sarah glanced into the fire, remembering her mortifying weekend of embarrassment, acute disappointment. Shane had been cruel, ignoring her much of the time. And when he had deigned to notice her he had been offhand, patently uninterested in her as a woman. He wouldn't have treated Paula in such a rotten way, she thought miserably, sinking back into herself. An image of his face leapt out at her from the flames, his expression one of immense passion and love. She blinked, wanting to expunge this from her mind. That look had not been for her, but for Paula . . . that terrible day of the christening . . . she would never forget that look or that occasion. It was only then she had realized, to her horror and distress, that Shane O'Neill loved Paula Fairley. That's the real reason he has no time for me, she said silently. Damn Paula. I detest her. Jealousy rose up in Sarah so unexpectedly and with such force she kept her face averted, willing the emotion to go away, feeling faint and sick inside.

'Well, I'm sorry you didn't have a good time,' Paula murmured, attempting to be gracious yet asking herself what she had done to engender such sudden dislike in Sarah. Paula sat back and her eyes narrowed thoughtfully. She had no reason to think that Sarah was lying about the gala weekend, but somehow she did. She considered Sarah's self-congratulatory remarks, her pleased tone when she had spoken of her hard work. How she exaggerated.

Paula could not resist adding, 'So the work was gruelling – that's retailing, you know, Sarah. And let's face it, *you* were the one who insisted on going to Barbados. If I –'

'And it's a jolly good thing I did, isn't it?' Sarah interjected peremptorily, tearing her gaze from the fire, swinging her head to glare at Paula. 'Somebody had to be there to organize things. We'd have been in a nice mess if we'd relied on Merry, in view of her abdication of her duties. Or if we'd left things to chance as you wanted us to do.'

Paula was further astonished by this criticism and the belligerence underlying the comment. Unwilling to let Sarah get away with it, she said with some sharpness, 'That's most unfair of you. I had no intention of leaving anything to chance. I had intended to fly out there myself, until you made such a song and dance about going. Anyway, you don't have to worry about the other boutiques. I've hired Melanie Redfern from Harvey Nichols. She starts next week. She will be in charge of the Harte shops in all the O'Neill hotels, and she'll be working closely with me. And Merry, of course.'

'I see.' Sarah shifted her position and cleared her throat. 'Actually, the main reason I came to see you today is to make you an offer.'

'An *offer*?' Paula stiffened, wondering what Sarah was about to spring on her.

'Yes. I'd like to buy the boutiques for my division. There won't be any problem about money. We have stacks of spare cash. You see, in view of my considerable involvement with the boutiques, I'd like to have them under my aegis, make them part of Lady Hamilton Clothes. So just name your price – I'll meet it.'

Flabbergasted though she was at Sarah's ridiculous proposition, Paula retorted swiftly. 'Even if I wanted to, I couldn't do that, as you well know. The boutiques belong to the Harte department store chain.'

Sarah stared Paula down. Her expression hardened. 'So what – I'm offering you an easy way to make a fast profit. And a big one. That should please you, since your eyes are eternally glued to the bottom of a balance sheet.'

'I'd like to remind you that the Harte chain is a public company,' Paula exclaimed, thinking that her cousin had taken leave of her senses. 'I do have shareholders and a board of directors to answer to, in case this has escaped your notice.'

Sarah smiled narrowly. 'Don't talk to me about the board at Harte's. We all know about the board, my dear. It consists of Grandmother, you, your parents, Alexander and a handful of old codgers who'll do anything you say. If you wanted to, you could easily sell me the boutiques. It's your decision. Don't expect me to believe otherwise. That board will acquiesce to your wishes no matter what, as they always did what Grandmother wanted in the past. She had them in her pocket, and so do you.'

Paula fixed a pair of immensely cold eyes on her cousin, and her voice was equally icy, as she said, 'Harte's have invested a great deal of money in the new shops, and I have personally devoted an incredible amount of time and effort to the project for many months. I therefore have no intention of selling them to you, or to anyone else, even if the board sanctioned such a sale, which believe me, they wouldn't, not at this stage. You see Sarah, I want the boutiques for Harte's, they're part of our growth and expansion programme. Also, I –'

'*Your* effort!' Sarah cried, seizing on this particular point. 'That's a laugh. I've worked much harder than you, and I selected all of the merchandise. Under the circumstances, it's only fair that –'

'Stop right there!' Paula warned, her face revealing her growing annoyance and impatience. 'I'm not sitting still for this nonsense, Sarah. Why you're bloody preposterous. You walk in here, commence to criticize me, then try to take credit for the success of the Barbados shop . . . and at the moment that's a moot point. Only time will tell us how successful it really is. But getting back to *your* efforts, I think you have a real nerve. It just so happens that Emily has done a lot more for us than you. She purchased every single accessory, which was no mean feat, and I recall that *I* picked out every bit of beach wear. Furthermore, Merry and I selected all of the clothing from your company – not *you*. I'll concede that you made the best lines available at Lady Hamilton, and designed the special evening wear, and perhaps you have worked conscientiously for the past ten days. However, your contribution to the first boutique was minor, very *minor* indeed.'

Paula rose and walked over to her desk, and sat down behind it. She finished quietly, 'As for trying to buy the boutiques from Harte's –' She shook her head wonderingly. 'I can only add that that's the most foolish thing I've ever heard, especially coming from you, when you of all people know how Grandy has structured things. Look, if you want to get involved in a new project, maybe we can put our heads together –' Paula stopped, immediately regretted her conciliatory gesture. Sarah's coldness was more pronounced than ever.

Sarah stood up without saying a thing. She made a beeline for the desk, stood facing Paula.

In a soft and uncommonly steady tone, Sarah said, 'Grandmother might have other ideas about the boutiques. She may well like the idea of selling them to me – has that occurred to you?' Not giving Paula a chance to reply, she continued in her oddly calm way, 'Grandy's not dead yet, and if I know her, I bet she hasn't signed over her seventy per cent of the shares in Harte's to you. Oh no, she's hanging on to those, I'm *quite* certain, wily as *she* is. And so, as far as I'm concerned, she's still the boss lady around here. I want you to understand one thing . . . I'm not letting the matter rest here. With you. Oh no, not by a long shot. I fully intend to telex Grandy. *Today*, Paula. I shall apprise her of our meeting, my offer and your rejection of it. We'll see who really runs Harte stores, won't we?'

Paula gave her a regretful look through saddened eyes. 'Send a telex. Send ten if you wish. You won't accomplish anything –'

'You're not the only grandchild Emma Harte has,' Sarah cut in, her voice biting. 'Although anyone would think it, the way you behave.'

'Sarah, don't let's quarrel like this. You're being childish, and you've always known Harte's is a public –' Paula's sentence was left dangling in mid air. Sarah had walked out. The door closed softly behind her.

Paula stared after her, shaking her head again, not yet fully recovered from her astonishment, Sarah's preposterous proposition and irrational attitude. She sighed under her breath. Only two weeks ago she had remarked to Emily that tranquillity had reigned supreme since their grandmother's departure in May.

I spoke too soon, Paula now thought, and she discovered that the most disturbing part of the meeting had been Sarah's blatant dislike of her. As Paula continued to contemplate her cousin's unexpected hostility she asked herself if it signalled the beginning of open warfare.

26

Emily was awed.

'Just look at this evening gown. It's absolutely exquisite,' she said in hushed tones, lifting the garment out of the large box lined with layers and layers of tissue paper.

Alexander, lolling on the bed in one of the guest rooms in Emma's Belgrave Square flat, nodded in agreement. 'It also looks as if it's in perfect condition.' A fond smile glanced across his serious face as Emily glided into the middle of the floor and held it against herself, carefully.

The gown was a long slender sheath of turquoise silk, entirely encrusted with thousands of tiny bugle beads in shades of pale blue and emerald green. Emily moved slightly and the dress undulated, the beads instantly changing colour as they caught and held the light. The effect was dazzling.

Cocking his head to one side, continuing to regard his sister intently, Alexander said, 'You know, it contains all the colours of a summer sea in the South of France, and it certainly matches your eyes, Emily. What a pity you can't keep it, have it for yourself. It's not a bit outdated.'

'Oh I know, and I'd love it, but it's far too valuable really. Anyway, I couldn't do that to Paula. She needs the dress for her fashion exhibition next January.'

'Has she found a name for that yet?'

'She's considering calling it Fashion Fantasia, with the subheading Fifty Years of Elegance and Style. I rather like it, don't you?'

'Yes.' He watched Emily as she expertly folded the gown into the box and covered it with the tissue, remarking, 'Imagine Gran keeping the evening dress all these years. It's easily forty-five years old, and it really pongs of moth balls.' He curled his nose in distaste, then added, 'But I bet our Gran looked smashing in it, with her red-gold hair and green eyes.'

Emily lifted her blonde head. 'To say the least, and you're right about its age. Just before Gran left she said we'd find it in one of her cedar closets on the top floor, along with the other clothes. Gran told us she'd first worn it at the supper dance she gave Uncle Frank and Aunt Natalie when they got engaged.' Emily put the lid on to the box, patted it down, glanced over at her brother. 'Do you know, there's even a pair of emerald satin slippers from Pinet to go with it, and they're in mint condition too. They look as if they've been worn once or twice and that's all.'

'Yes, everything's been so carefully preserved,' Alexander observed, thinking of his canny grandmother's sense of thrift which was legendary. Swinging his legs off the bed, he ambled over to the long metal clothes rack positioned near the window, ran his hand along the rack. Peering at the labels on the suits, dresses and evening gowns, he read out loud, 'Chanel, Vionet, Balenciaga, Molyneaux . . . these are all as good as new, Emily, and they *must* date back to the twenties and thirties.'

'They do, and that's why they're essential for the exhibition. Several other women who are noted for their elegance – Best Dressed List ladies – are loaning similar designer clothes to Paula, and they've all accepted her invitation to come to the cocktail party at the store the night she opens the exhibition to the public.'

Emily now crossed to the dressing table, picked up a typed sheet, made a notation, slipped the sheet into its folder and said, 'Thanks for keeping me company, Sandy, while I checked everything off. Well, let's go downstairs, that's all I have time to do tonight. I promised to help Paula organize the rest of the clothes this weekend, since she's snowed under at the moment.'

'Where is she, by the way?' Alexander asked, following Emily out of the guest room on to the second floor landing. 'Don't tell me she's still at the store.'

'Oh no, she's here,' Emily said over her shoulder, tripping down the staircase. 'After we'd unpacked the clothes and hung them up to be checked for any minor repairs, she went to change her dress. She's probably popped into the old nursery.'

Alexander pushed open the drawing room door for Emily, stepped inside after her. 'Are the babies here too?' he asked, surprised.

'Yes, and Nora. Paula brought them to town with her on Monday afternoon. Oh look, Sandy, good old Parker's put out a bottle of white wine for us. Shall we have a glass now?' She rushed over to the console.

'Why not? Thanks, Emily.' He took a chair near the fireplace, crossed his long legs and lit a cigarette, studying his sister as she poured the wine. Although

247

she was of average height he generally thought of her as being small, perhaps because she was so delicately made, so daintily proportioned. He nodded to himself. Emily had turned into a very pretty young woman in the last few years. How mean he and his male cousins had been to little Emily when they were children, teasing her about her enormous appetite and her totally spherical body, calling her Apple Dumpling. She was no longer anything like a dumpling – tonight she resembled a pert china doll in the flattering pink wool dress. Some china doll, he added under his breath, ruminating on her tremendous physical and mental energy, wondering, as he so often did, where it came from. Their grandmother. Certainly it was not something she had inherited from their parents. Their mother was an indolent, bored, spoiled socialite without a serious thought in her head. Their father was a has-been who had never really made it in the first place, forever the failure. Poor Dad, he thought, he's without doubt the nicest, kindest chap I know. Alexander reminded himself to ring his father tomorrow to make a date for lunch or dinner. They didn't really see enough of each other these days.

'Gosh, Sandy, I didn't notice your lovely tan when we were upstairs,' Emily remarked, bringing him the glass of wine, scrutinizing him closely. She flopped on to the chair opposite. 'You really look super. You should sit in the sun more often.'

'What, and let Harte Enterprises go to rack and ruin? Not on your life.' He raised his glass. '*Santé.*'

'Cheers,' said Emily, and after taking a sip, she asked, 'Where's old Mag?'

'She went to Scotland this morning to look at a shooting lodge that's going up for sale. The owner wants the real estate firm she works for to handle it, so Maggie's about to be given the grand tour. If she likes it, it'll go on their books. God knows who'll buy it, though. Who on earth wants a shooting lodge in this day and age I ask you?'

'A rich American,' Emily suggested. 'Have you set a date for your wedding?'

'June . . . possibly.'

'That's not fair!' Emily wailed, her eyes flashing. 'You know Winston and I are getting married in June. You'd better make sure Maggie checks with me before you set a firm date.'

'We could have a double wedding,' he said, and burst out laughing at her expression. 'Why are you looking at me like that?'

'If you don't know then I'm not going to tell you,' she retorted huffily. 'On the other hand, perhaps I should.'

'Forget that I said it. Anyway, I wasn't really serious.'

'Yes, you were, and I *shall* tell you,' Emily announced. 'There are three good reasons. One . . . every bride wants to be the centre of attraction on *her* special day and she certainly can't be if there's *another bride loitering around.* Two . . . Gran would have a fit because she'd consider it icky, bad form. Three . . . we can't disappoint our grandmother who's looking forward to giving *two* big super-duper extra special weddings with all the trimmings next summer.'

'You've convinced me, Emily – a double wedding is out of the question,' he replied in a teasing voice. He sobered almost at once, drew on his cigarette, quickly stubbed it out, his gestures unexpectedly nervous.

Emily, forever the acute observer, exclaimed, 'Is something the matter?'

'Paula might have managed to nip one scandal in the bud – over in Ireland – but I'm afraid we have another one about to explode. It's –'

'*Scandal*,' Paula repeated quietly, entering the room. She closed the door behind her and stood staring at Alexander and Emily with a worried expression.

'Paula,' Alexander said, rising and going to greet her affectionately. 'Let me get you a glass of wine, and then we'll have a little pow-pow before we go to the White Elephant.'

Paula sat down on the sofa and her gaze followed him across the room. With a scowl she asked him, 'What kind of scandal, Sandy?'

He brought her the drink, returned to the chair. 'It's Mother again – I'm sorry to have to tell you both.' His concerned eyes swung from Paula to Emily. 'She rang me this morning from Paris sounding quite hysterical. Apparently Gianni Raviolli –'

'Don't be mean,' Emily remonstrated. 'How many times do I have to tell you his name's Ravello and Gianni's very sweet.'

'– Has started divorce proceedings,' Alexander continued in a stronger tone, after throwing a chastising frown in Emily's direction, 'and she's on the verge of nervous collapse, or so she says –'

'What the hell does she expect,' Emily broke in again. '*She's* the one who did a bolt with the detestable Frog.'

'If you keep interrupting me, we're never going to get to dinner,' Alexander pointed out, sternly wagging a finger at his sister. 'In any event, our Mother's distressed because of Gianni's intractability. You see, even though she's given him the evidence, he refuses to name Marc Deboyne.'

'*Why?*' Emily asked, her curiosity piqued.

Paula said, 'Who *is* he naming? Obviously that's at the root of your mother's upset.'

Alexander gave her a sharp look. 'Smart girl, that's it exactly.' There was a slight pause before he went on with the utmost quiet, 'It seems he's going to cite a number of . . . Ministers of the Crown as the co-respondents. Darling Mummy must've gone through the Cabinet like a dose of salts.'

'You've got to be joking,' Paula cried, staring at him in astonishment and alarm.

'I wish I were,' Alexander said, his gloominess mounting as he thought of the consequences of his mother's adultery, the embarrassment to the family, particularly his grandmother. *She would be mortified.*

Emily was all agog. Her eyes widened and she shrieked, 'Uncle Robin's cronies I'll wager!' Groaning theatrically she rolled her eyes at the ceiling. 'I can just see the banner headline in the *Daily Mirror* – Italian count cites entire British Government in society divorce. Or what about this one in the *News of the World* – Socialite lays all her eggs in Government basket. The papers are going to have a field day with this one!' She leered at them wickedly.

Paula's mouth twitched involuntarily and she could not help laughing despite her annoyance with her aunt and the seriousness of the situation. 'Stop it, Emily, you're impossible.' Paula attempted to swallow her rising laughter, which she knew partially sprang from her nervousness tonight.

Alexander, who was not amused, glared at both women. 'It's not funny, you know . . .' He broke off, shaking his head, suddenly at a loss for words. He had been seething ever since his mother had telephoned him that morning. Like Emma, he was constantly maddened by her outrageous behaviour, and being conservative her morals were offensive to him.

In a rush, Emily said, 'I'd love to know who Mummy's lovers were.' A speculative gleam flashed across her face and she wrinkled her nose. 'No, I can't picture the beauteous Elizabeth in bed with Fat Dabs.'

'Fat Dabs?' Paula echoed in perplexity.

'Really, Emily!' Alexander exploded.

Quite undaunted by Alexander's reprimand, and adopting an exaggerated Yorkshire accent, Emily informed Paula, 'Aye, Fat Dabs. That's wot t'lads at Genret call our 'Arold from 'Uddersfield.' Another thought instantly occurred to Emily, and, reverting to her normal cultivated tone, she pointed out, 'Robin's going to have apoplexy. Let's not forget that our charming uncle, Member of Parliament for South-East Leeds, is also one of Harold Wilson's Cabinet Ministers. He's expecting to be appointed Chancellor of the Exchequer, you know, if Labour gets in again at the next election. Gosh, Sandy, you're right, there's going to be a huge scandal . . . shades of Profumo, do you think? We'll never be able to nip this one in the bud.'

'I'm not going to worry myself about Uncle Robin's precious political career,' Alexander retorted with acerbity. 'Oh no, not at all. Besides, he's such an opportunist he'll find a way to get mileage out of this, if I'm not mistaken. Anyway, it's probably all his fault. You put your finger on it, Emily, I'm sure Mother met the gentleman in question through him. She was constantly dashing over to his fancy parties in Eaton Square.' He shot Paula a worried glance. 'Once the divorce papers are filed with the law courts the press will be on to it in no time, and Emily's not too far off the mark about those banner headlines.'

Paula sat reflecting, said at last, 'How much? To buy him off?'

'Not sure,' Alexander said.

Emily cried, 'Oh I don't think he wants anything.'

Paula pinned her cousin with her cool knowing gaze. 'I'm surprised at your naïveté, Emily. We've been raised by a woman who has continually told us that everyone has a price, and that it's only ever a question of how much. Of course he wants money – *then* he'll do the gentlemanly thing and name Marc Deboyne.'

Emily protested with fierceness, 'I know him better than either of you and I don't think he's like that.'

'Gran is also fond of saying that the price isn't necessarily money,' Alexander was quick to remind them. 'And now that I think about it, I'm inclined to agree with you, Emily. I honestly don't believe he wants lots of cash. But he does want something. *Revenge.* I'm certain he still loves our mother – although God knows why in view of her treatment of him – and he's badly hurt. So . . . he has the need to strike back, hurt her in return and the only way he knows is to embarrass her publicly.'

'Maybe,' Paula admitted, seeing the sense in Alexander's theory. 'Apparently he has all the evidence he needs?' This came out sounding like a question.

'Oh yes,' Alexander told her, 'Mother was quite clear that he has the goods on her. He's not making idle threats.'

'Are you sure she didn't tell you who the ministers were?' Emily probed with her usual inquisitiveness.

Alexander looked at her pityingly. 'Come *on*, she may be a foolish, misguided woman, but deep down she's quite crafty. Of course she didn't volunteer any names.'

Paula said, 'Did your mother tell you what she wanted you to do, Sandy?'

'Yes, she wants me to go and see Gianni, to persuade him to name Marc Deboyne in the suit. She seems to believe I can influence him, but she's up a bloody gum tree there. I don't know him that well, and anyway, it's Emily he likes the most.'

'Oh no,' Emily shrieked, 'not me!'

Alexander and Paula exchanged conspiratorial looks, and Paula said, 'You might be the best person to deal with him, darling.'

Emily moaned, fell back in the chair. She found the idea of talking to Gianni about her mother's infidelity quite repugnant. On the other hand, she liked the man, and Alexander might be tactless with him. She said firmly, as she straightened up, 'I simply refuse to offer Gianni money, and that's flat!'

'What will your approach be?' Alexander asked, filling with profound relief that she'd apparently agreed to take on this unpleasant task.

'I shall –' Emily thought hard and her face brightened. She said, 'Why I shall appeal to his better nature, explain that he will be hurting Amanda and Francesca more than Mummy, and he's very fond of the girls. He wouldn't want them to suffer.'

Paula said with a degree of hesitation, 'Very well ... Handle it that way – however, you'd better have something up your sleeve, just in case his better nature fails him.'

'You do sound cynical at times,' Emily declared, pursing her lips reprovingly. 'I will not insult that poor betrayed man by offering him money.'

Paying no attention to Emily's irate manner Paula shrugged, said, 'You could always offer him a job – if he's adamant, if he insists on naming half the damned Government.'

'A job? Where? Who with?'

'With Harte's, Emily. I've been looking for someone to run Trade Winds, the new antique accessory shop I'm planning to open in the near future. Since Gianni's an expert in that area perhaps he'd prefer working for the family rather than that antique importing company where he's currently employed. We'd be killing several birds with one stone in a sense – ensuring he's on *our* side, if not your mother's especially, and he wouldn't really be under our feet since he'd have to do a lot of travelling. Also, I might get myself a good man for Trade Winds. And he'll certainly earn more at Harte's.'

'What a marvellous solution!' Alexander exclaimed, immediately cheering up, relaxing in his chair.

Emily bit her lip. 'I shall only mention the job at Harte's if he's difficult,' she warned, convinced that Gianni was not an opportunist. She added quickly, 'I *know* he won't be, that he'll do the right thing. I just do.'

'We'll see,' Paula murmured.

Alexander stood up, strode across the room. 'Now that we've dealt with Mother's love life there's another matter I must discuss.' He paused at the door. 'Won't be a minute ... I left my briefcase in the hall when I arrived.'

In his absence, Emily leaned towards Paula, confided, 'Gianni really is a lovely person, you just don't know him very well.'

'I'm sure he is, under normal circumstances. But it's wiser to be prepared for the worst.'

Emily said nothing, and a moment later Alexander returned, sat down, took a folder out of his briefcase. He handed it to Paula.

'What's this?' she asked, taking it from him.

'A report from Mr Graves of Graves and Sanderson. But there's no need to read it now.'

'Is it about Jonathan?' Paula ventured, turning the folder over, fingering it, her breath catching in her throat with apprehension.

'No. The report concerns Sebastian Cross.

'*Oh.*' Paula put one hand to her mouth, remembering that day in the boardroom at Aire, wondering why she had a sudden sense of foreboding.

Alexander explained, 'I think it'll be quicker if I give you the information in a few short sentences. The report *is* rather long, tedious in parts, which is why I suggest you peruse it at your leisure.'

'Hurry up then, tell us, Sandy,' Emily ordered. 'We ought to be leaving for dinner in a few minutes. I'm starved.'

'Mr Graves has been digging for months, trying to find something on Sebastian, as you're both aware,' Alexander commenced. 'His inquiries were business-oriented at first, since he was following Grandy's instructions. When he came up empty-handed yet again, he decided to investigate Sebastian's private life. After a number of false leads, interviews with different people in London, he went up to Yorkshire. And he stumbled on some information that's not very pleasant, I don't mind telling you. Knowing that a lot of the chaps from Aire Communications congregate at Polly's Bar in Leeds he started hanging around there. One lunchtime he struck up a conversation with a young chap who'd once worked at Aire. Graves and the fellow eventually became very chummy, got to meeting for drinks regularly over a three week period. One night Tommy Charwood – that's the fellow's name – told Graves that Sebastian was a nasty piece of work, said he'd like to get him in a dark alley one night and give him the thrashing of his life.' Alexander stopped to light a cigarette, then continued, 'When Graves asked the reason, Tommy Charwood told him that he'd been courting a girl who had also worked at Aire, and that Sebastian had taken her away from him. Now, it seems that the girl, Alice Peele –'

'I've met Alice –' Paula interjected quickly, her face quickening with interest. 'She's in public relations, and she once came to see me about a job at Harte's.'

'What's she like?' Alexander asked curiously.

'Talented in her field, rather pleasant. I remember her quite distinctly because she was well turned out and very striking. Tall, dark, with an unusually pretty face.'

Alexander cleared his throat, pinned his grave eyes on Paula. 'I'm not too sure how pretty she is these days. According to Tommy Charwood, Sebastian Cross beat her up a number of times. And so badly the last time, Alice Peele had to see a plastic surgeon. Charwood told Graves that she would have been disfigured for life without the prompt emergency treatment she received at

Leeds General Infirmary. You see, Cross beat her with such a vengeance her jaw was broken, also one cheekbone, and her face was a bloody pulp.'

'Oh my God!' Paula cried. 'How appalling, what a horrible thing to happen.'

Emily had also blanched. Shuddering, she looked across at Paula, then whispered, 'Your instincts were right about Sebastian Cross.' Emily swallowed, turned to her brother. 'Didn't the girl bring charges? Go to the police? Prosecute?'

'No, seemingly not. Charwood told Graves that she was terrified of Cross. Her father had wanted to go to the police, but Alice begged him not to do so, insisted it would only stir up more trouble. That's when Mr Peele confided in Tommy, whom he'd remained friendly with. Tommy tried to talk Peele into going to Leeds CID – he knows a number of detectives on the force – but Peele kept wavering. In the end he decided against it. About a month after this last terrible beating, John Cross paid a visit to the Peele family, offered Mr Peele money. Peele, who sounds like the salt of the earth, threw the money in John Cross's face. As soon as Alice was sufficiently recovered, he shipped her off to live with her married brother in Gibraltar. The brother's in the Royal Navy, helicopters I think, and is stationed permanently in Gib. Tommy Charwood believes she's still out there.'

'What a ghastly story,' Paula said, continuing to shiver. 'I'm not surprised Alice Peele is terrified of Cross . . .' She faltered, stopped, turned away, filled with revulsion for the man.

Emily gasped, 'He must be a maniac! That girl's family should have prosecuted him, regardless of what *she* said.'

Alexander nodded, and his expression, reflecting Paula's, was one of immense distaste. He said with harshness, 'And that's not all . . . Charwood gave Graves some additional information, after our wily private eye ingratiated himself further. Charwood swears Sebastian is into *drugs*, quite aside from being a heavy drinker, and is a congenital gambler who has suffered some big losses at the tables. At Crockford's, and God knows where else.'

'And this is the man who is Jonathan Ainsley's best friend,' Paula said. 'This is just awful.'

'Yes, it is,' Alexander concurred. 'And whilst the information about Cross doesn't really do *us* any good, it does reflect rather badly on Jonathan, in that he's Cross's bosom chum. Wouldn't you say?'

Paula nodded.

Emily looked from Paula to her brother. 'Do you think Jonathan's also on drugs? That he gambles?'

'He'd better not be on drugs,' Alexander snapped. 'Not if he wants to continue running the real estate division of Harte Enterprises. Let's not forget he handles a great deal of money, and also has to make some very important decisions at times.' Alexander stood up, walked over to the console, poured a glass of wine, muttered, 'I'm going to have to monitor *everything* he does from now on – watch him even more closely than before. I simply can't afford to have him make any mistakes whatsoever. As for gambling –' Alexander shrugged, shook his head. 'I can't hazard a guess about that. But he might be playing the tables, and that's another reason why I'm going to take a bigger interest in the real estate division. As I said, there's an awful lot of cash going through that company.'

'Presumably you've instructed Mr Graves to keep at it, Sandy. To dig deeper?' Paula said.

'Naturally.'

'Oddly enough,' Paula went on thoughtfully, 'John Cross rang the store today. He wanted an appointment.'

'Are you going to see him?' Alexander asked, returning to the chair.

'I don't know – probably not. Gaye tried to reach him at his hotel late this afternoon but he'd gone out. I expect he'll phone again in the morning.'

'In one sense, I'd be curious to know what he has to say. He can't possibly imagine we'd be interested in Aire. Not now, after he's sold the building, which was the main asset of the company.'

Paula lifted her shoulders in a shrug, and instantly changed the subject. She said, 'Sarah came to see me this afternoon.' She proceeded to recount the meeting, not missing out on a single detail. When she had finished she sat back, waiting for their reactions.

Emily had been all eyes and ears throughout Paula's recital. She exclaimed, 'I'd like to hear Miranda's version of the weekend, not to mention the whole ten days Sarah spent in Barbados. I have a feeling their stories will vary considerably. Sarah was always rather good at taking the credit when it wasn't due her.'

'Yes, I know.' Paula immediately thought of their childhood days at Heron's Nest. She and Emily had been aware of Sarah's craftiness even then. Their cousin had forever tried to curry favour with their grandmother, paint herself in the best possible light, frequently at their expense.

Alexander spoke up. 'Sarah's not stupid. She knows you can't sell the boutiques, not without first going to the board. She's also well aware that she can't spend the fashion division's money willy-nilly unless she has my permission. Therefore she must have convinced herself she can bypass us, succeed in her aims by going to Grandy directly. I'm certain she sent the telex, as she threatened to do.'

'I am too,' Emily muttered, condemning Sarah under her breath. Paula had far too many worries and problems to contend with at the moment, without Sarah creating difficulties.

'I won't argue with either of you.' Paula smiled faintly. 'However, I can assure you that the telex ended up in the wastepaper basket. What Sarah doesn't know is that Grandy really came to believe in the boutiques before she left in May. At the last minute she suddenly saw them as a clever means to expand and in a relatively easy way for our organization. She's convinced the boutiques will increase the value of the Harte shares, and of course they will, so she has no more intention of selling off the boutiques than I do.'

'Yes, but you just said Sarah doesn't realize that,' Emily pointed out quietly. 'And anyway, I've always thought she was infuriated because you got the Harte chain and not her. After all, she *is* the eldest granddaughter, and she has quite an opinion of herself as a businesswoman.'

'Emily's taken the words out of my mouth,' Alexander said, turning swiftly to Paula. 'Sarah's visit this afternoon may have been a nasty little exercise –

one specifically designed to upset you, Paula, to unnerve you, throw you off balance.' As he was speaking another thought struck him. 'I say, could this be the beginning of the guerrilla war we've talked about, and have been antici-pating?'

'That had crossed my mind earlier,' Paula told him.

'If it is, what does Sarah hope to gain, Sandy?' Emily demanded.

'The satisfaction of knowing Paula's aggravated, under additional pressure. Also, a person who has been thrown off balance is not always thinking clearly or coolly, and frequently concentration is damaged.' Alexander gave them both a very pointed look. 'Sarah's been hand-in-glove with Jonathan for a long time. She bears watching as closely as he does.'

Paula stood up. 'Enough of *them*, for tonight at least. Let's go to dinner. It's been a difficult day, and a terrible week so far.' She sighed wearily. 'I'm not going to burden either of you with my problems at Sitex Oil, but I've had those to cope with today as well. I think I've just run out of steam. I need a little light relief, such as an amusing evening at the White Elephant.'

'Are they serious problems?' Alexander asked as the three of them went out into the entrance foyer to get their coats. He squeezed Paula's shoulder affectionately. 'Can I be of help?'

Paula gave him a grateful smile. 'Thanks, Sandy, it's sweet of you to offer. I've got things under control –' She hesitated before adding, 'Dale Stevens was determined to resign as president this afternoon. I spent over an hour on the phone with him, convinced him to stay on. He has a number of enemies on the board, unmitigated troublemakers who try to tie his hands whenever they can.' She shook her head ruefully. 'What I should have said a moment ago is that he's agreed to stay on as president until the end of the year. All I've done really is buy myself a little time.'

27

'John Crawford offered to explain the procedure in a coroner's court,' Daisy said, looking from Edwina to Anthony. 'He feels it will help us to be more relaxed about the inquest.'

Anthony said, 'It certainly would, Aunty Daisy.' He stood up. 'I'll go and fetch Bridget. I think she ought to hear what your family solicitor has to say. Excuse me, I won't be a moment.'

As he left the library, Daisy rose and joined Edwina on the sofa. She took her half-sister's hand in hers and squeezed it, looking deeply into her careworn face. 'Try not to worry, Edwina. In a few hours this tragedy will be behind us. We must go on, you know, endeavour to get on with our lives as best we can.'

'Yes, Daisy, and thank you for your concern. I'll be all right,' Edwina mur-mured in a tired voice. The last few days of anxiety and strain had taken their toll, and she looked exhausted, near total collapse. The black dress she had chosen to wear, stark and unrelieved by jewellery or any accent colour, did nothing to enhance her appearance. It appeared to drain what bit of colour she had from her face, emphasizing her pallor more than ever. She looked ill, and her age showed pronouncedly this morning.

Gratitude suddenly flickered in Edwina's silvery-grey eyes as she added quietly, 'I don't know what I would have done without you and Jim. Where is he, Daisy?'

'Right now he's on the phone to Paula, and I believe he has a few calls to make to people on the paper. But he'll join us as soon as he's finished. It's not really essential for him to be briefed. He knows the inner workings of a coroner's court since he used to cover inquests in his early days as a reporter.'

'Oh yes, of course, he would understand about those things.' Edwina shifted her glance to the clock on the mantelpiece at the other side of the handsome panelled room. 'It's almost eight-thirty. We'll have to leave soon to drive into Cork. It'll take us well over an hour, perhaps an hour and a half, you know.'

Detecting the nervousness and panic in Edwina's voice, Daisy said reassuringly, 'We've plenty of time. The inquest is set for eleven, and this session with John won't take very long. He said he could cover the important points in about ten minutes. After that we can start out, drive in at a leisurely pace. Do stay calm, my dear.'

'I'm fine, really. Just a little tired. I didn't sleep very well.'

'I don't think any of us did,' Daisy said with a slight smile. 'I'm going to have another cup of coffee. Would you like one?'

'No, thank you, Daisy.' Edwina sat rigidly on the sofa, twisting her hands in her lap, her chest tight with apprehension. For four days and nights she had lived with this terrible fear for her son. She could not wait to go to the county court, to get the inquest over and done with, so that the cloud surrounding him would be lifted finally. Only then would she be able to relax. She would willingly give her life for Anthony. He was the only person that mattered to her, and once the inquiry into the cause of Min's death was over, she would support him in anything he wished to do. Even if that meant accepting Sally Harte, of whom she did not approve. Until the day she died she would regret her passive role in the trouble that had developed between Min and Anthony in the past few weeks. Anthony had asked her to intercede, to reason with her, insisting she could influence his estranged wife to proceed with the divorce as originally agreed. And perhaps she could have, but she would never know, for she had refused. Now poor Min was dead. *She would still be alive if I had spoken to her*, Edwina thought for the umpteenth time. The pain in her heart intensified. Her guilt soared.

Daisy brought her cup of coffee and sat down in the chair opposite. She said, 'Have you decided what you want to do? Will you come to London for a few days' rest after the funeral?'

'Perhaps I should get away from here,' Edwina began and stopped, looking at the door as Anthony came in with Bridget O'Donnell, the housekeeper at Clonloughlin.

'M'lady, Mrs Amory,' Bridget said, inclining her head, taking the chair Anthony indicated.

Daisy, always gracious, smiled at her. 'As you know, Mr Crawford is our solicitor and he came over to help in any way he can. He is going to explain a few things to us, Bridget, as I'm sure Lord Dunvale has told you. However, I just want to add that there's nothing to be alarmed about.'

'Oh I'm not worried, Mrs Amory, not at all,' Bridget answered quickly, in a clipped tone that partially obscured the lilting burr, meeting Daisy's gaze unblinkingly. 'It's a very simple matter, telling the truth. And that's what I aim to do.' A small smug smile flicked across her narrow pale mouth and she sat back, crossed her legs. Her red hair gleamed in the sunlight, its fiery hue contrasting markedly with her icy cold blue eyes.

Daisy's opinion that Bridget O'Donnell was a cool customer, calculating and sure of herself, was reaffirmed. She did not particularly like this woman, who she guessed was about thirty-five or thereabouts, even though she did not look it.

Glancing away, Daisy turned to Anthony, but before she had a chance to say anything the door opened to admit John Crawford, the son of Emma's solicitor of many years and now a senior partner in the firm of Crawford, Creighton, Phipps and Crawford. Of medium height and build, he was nevertheless ramrod straight and had a military bearing which combined with his forceful personality to give him an aura of presence. At forty-six he had sandy hair peppered with grey, bright informed brown eyes in a pleasant face that was oddly bland, and did nothing to reveal a razor-sharp legal brain of great brilliance.

'Good morning. Sorry to keep you waiting,' he said briskly, striding forward to join them at the windowed end of the long book-filled room. Daisy offered him coffee but he declined. He remained standing behind a chair, his hands resting lightly on its back. He looked completely relaxed and untroubled, and as he always did with his clients, he endeavoured to convey a feeling of supreme confidence whatever his private thoughts and opinions were.

Crawford said, 'I realize this is going to be quite an ordeal for you this morning, and so I thought I might help if I gave you a run down on the manner in which a coroner's court is conducted. Understanding something about the proceedings may lessen everyone's nervousness, I hope.' His eyes swept over the four of them. 'Feel free to ask any questions as I go along. Since none of you have attended an inquest before, let me first say that the coroner's court is conducted in a rather *informal* way. However –' He paused, looked at them keenly, and speaking slowly, as if to give added emphasis to his words, went on, 'I must stress that the informality in no way lessens its *importance*. It is one of the *highest* courts in the land, and it is ruled by the *law of evidence*. Any questions?' A sandy brow lifted. 'All right, on to the next –'

'Excuse me, John,' Daisy said, 'could you please clarify what you mean by *informal*. I don't quite understand.'

'Ah yes, of course. By informal I mean that the coroner is not wearing robes. He is dressed in a business suit, also the manner of speaking is less formal than other courts. The coroner chats informally with the interested parties before evidence is given on the witness stand under oath.'

'Thank you, John. One other question. The coroner is usually a solicitor, a barrister, or a doctor with legal training, isn't he?'

'That is quite correct, Daisy. The coroner is not a judge, even though he is in fact making the ruling. He also has a very wide latitude in his conduct of an inquiry. If there are no other questions, I shall continue. I now come to a most important point, and it is this. The coroner will accept *hearsay* in this court, which is not common practice in other courts of law under British justice, where hearsay is *inadmissible* evidence.'

Anthony leaned forward. 'What does that mean?' He shook his head. 'It can't mean what I think it does!' he went on to exclaim, his voice more high-pitched than normal.

'Yes, Lord Dunvale, it does. A coroner will listen to something a person has heard but does not know to be true ... rumour, gossip, if you will.'

'I see,' Anthony said in a more composed voice, even though he was experiencing inner alarm at the thought of the gossip which had been rife in the village for months.

Edwina and Daisy exchanged worried glances. Neither said one word.

John Crawford, aware of their uneasiness, cleared his throat, continued, 'Let me qualify hearsay more fully, as it applies in the coroner's court. In this instance, hearsay might be words spoken by the deceased, immediately prior to his or her death, to a member of the family, a friend, a doctor or a solicitor. A witness might say that the deceased has threatened to commit suicide on one or numerous occasions. Or may venture the opinion that said deceased was depressed. The coroner will take note of these points. Perhaps another example would be useful, a good illustration – a policeman could pass the opinion to the coroner that he believes the deceased has committed suicide based on the evidence he has gathered. Or then again, a policeman might say his findings lead him to believe that death was accidental. The coroner does take such opinions into account. I would also like to stress that hearsay of this nature *does* have a bearing on the case and indeed on the rest of the questions posed by the coroner.'

'Do the police question any of the witnesses?' Anthony asked.

'No, no. Never. That is not permissible in a coroner's court. Only the coroner is empowered to ask the questions.' Crawford swung around as the door opened.

Michael Lamont, the estate manager at Clonloughlin, entered swiftly, closed the door behind him. Tall and heavy-set, he had a shock of dark curly hair and a merry weather-beaten face that matched a jovial manner. As he hurried across the floor he apologized profusely.

Anthony said quickly, 'I'll fill you in later, Michael. John's been explaining the procedure ... the way in which an inquest is conducted.'

Nodding his understanding, Lamont sat down next to Edwina on the sofa, acknowledged the other women with a quick smile. He said, 'I did attend an inquest once before, so I'm vaguely aware of the form.'

'Good, good,' Crawford exclaimed with a brief nod. 'I shall get on with this as quickly as possible. There may or may not be a jury of six or eight people. Either way, the coroner imposes his will, if necessary talks the jury around to his way of thinking and what he feels is right. But it *is* the coroner who decides and pronounces the verdict – of misadventure, suicide, accidental death, natural causes or –' He paused, added quietly, ' – or murder.'

There was a deathly silence as this word hung in the air.

It was Anthony who broke it. 'What if the coroner is uncertain? What if he can't decide whether it was suicide, an accident, or murder?'

'Ah yes, well, in that instance the coroner would have to leave an open verdict ... he might pronounce that a person or persons unknown could be responsible for the death of the deceased and that they could be brought to justice at a later date.'

Edwina, watching her son intently, gasped and turned ashen. Michael Lamont reached out and took her hand, whispered something to her.

Crawford glanced at them, then brought his attention back to Anthony. 'The pathologist's report, the findings of his post-mortem, usually clarify cause of death and without any question of doubt.'

'I understand,' Anthony said in a low voice.

Crawford announced, 'I've covered the most important points, I believe. I would like to add that I am most confident that the inquest will progress in a normal manner.' His eyes rested on Michael Lamont. 'You will probably be the first witness, since you were the one who found Lady Dunvale's body. The Clonloughlin police sergeant will give evidence after you. Then we will hear medical testimony – from the local doctor who did the initial examination and from the pathologist who conducted the second examination and performed the post-mortem. Does anyone need further clarification on any specific point?'

'Yes,' Anthony said. 'Just a couple – I presume I will be questioned. But what about my mother? And Bridget?'

'I see no reason for Lady Dunvale to be called to the witness stand, since she really cannot contribute anything. You will have to give evidence, and, most probably, so will Miss O'Donnell. It's very likely that the coroner will chat to all of you in an informal way, before the main witnesses are called, as I explained earlier. Nothing to worry about.' Crawford glanced at his watch. 'I suggest we leave here in the next ten minutes or so.' Turning to Daisy who had risen, he asked, 'Where's Jim? Perhaps you ought to let him know we're going to leave shortly to drive into Cork.'

'Yes,' Daisy said. 'I'll tell him right away. I've got to go upstairs for my things.'

Fifteen minutes later the small group left Clonloughlin House.

Edwina, Anthony, Bridget O'Donnell and Michael Lamont travelled in the first car, with Michael at the wheel.

Jim Fairley drove the second car, and followed closely behind. He was accompanied by Daisy and John Crawford. No one spoke for the first ten minutes or so. Finally, Jim said, 'Explaining the formalities was a good idea, John.' He glanced out of the corner of his eye at Crawford, who sat next to him on the front seat, swung his eyes back to the road, went on to remark, 'I'm sure it helped my aunt. She's a bundle of nerves. Anthony seems calm enough, though. Rather self-contained, totally in control. But he looks dreadful. This ghastly mess has aged him quite a lot.'

'Yes,' Crawford said laconically. He rolled down the window, peered over his shoulder at Daisy, said, 'Do you mind if I smoke?'

'No, not at all.' Daisy leaned forward, resting her hand on the back of the front seat, and addressed Jim. 'How was Paula?'

'She's fine and sends her love.' Jim's grip on the steering wheel tightened as he wondered whether to repeat Paula's final comments, which she had voiced with such anxiety he himself had become alarmed. Uncertain of what to do he remarked, 'She kept insisting we phone her immediately the inquest is over, as if we wouldn't have done that anyway.'

'She'll be anxious to get in touch with Mother at once,' Daisy murmured. She settled back in the corner, smoothed the skirt of her understated and restrained dark grey suit, thinking of Emma sitting in suspense at their sheep station in Australia, worrying about the outcome and about her grandson Anthony. The fact that her mother was under such strain worried Daisy. After all, she *was* eighty. Reassuring herself that Emma Harte was invincible, was really taking this in her stride as she kept insisting when she telephoned, Daisy attempted to relax. Eventually she said, 'Have you decided what you're going to do, Jim?'

'Yes, I'll stay on here, for the funeral tomorrow. I think they'll appreciate the support and it's the least I can do. I'll fly back on Saturday. I hope to persuade Anthony to come with me. He has to get away from this place for a while.'

'Of course,' Daisy said. 'And I'm sure he'll want to see Sally.' She swung her eyes to John Crawford. 'I assume the inquest will be over in a couple of hours ... David has arranged for his friend's private jet to be at Cork Airport at noon, waiting for us. You will be coming back to London with me, won't you, John?'

'Yes, thanks a lot. I appreciate the ride. And yes, all being well we should be through in a couple of hours. I just hope we don't have to recess for lunch. In the event that this happens the inquest will unfortunately drag on into the afternoon.'

Jim said, 'You don't have any reason to believe it won't be routine, do you?'

'No, not really,' Crawford replied, but there was a strange hesitancy in his voice.

Jim picked this up at once. 'You don't sound as confident as you did last night, John. Is there something Daisy and I ought to know?'

'No, no, of course not,' Crawford murmured.

This response did nothing to convince Jim. He decided to plunge in, confide Emily's worries, which Paula had relayed to him during their phone conversation earlier. He said, 'Paula's a bit anxious. Emily's raised something ... apparently she woke Paula during the night, and told her that ever since Sunday she has been concerned ... about those five or six hours Min spent at the lake, after she arrived in the afternoon and before she died late at night. Emily thinks –'

'I don't understand why those hours are important,' Daisy interjected.

John Crawford pondered for a second, elected to be honest and swung around in the front seat to face Daisy. 'I must now confess that I myself have been troubled about the self same thing, my dear. And if *I* find that elapse of time strange, not to mention young Emily, don't you think an experienced coroner will ask himself what the deceased was doing for that extraordinary length of time.'

'Yes.' Daisy frowned. 'But *why* do those hours matter anyway? Look, maybe she went away and came back again.'

'Or maybe she was ncver at Clonloughlin in the afternoon,' Crawford said softly. 'That possibility might easily occur to the coroner, as it has to me, and probably to young Emily too. Don't you see, Daisy, those unexplained hours raise questions . . . in regard to Lord Dunvale's story about the time his wife arrived, a story which, I might add, is only corroborated by his mother.'

'You mean the coroner could think Anthony is lying, that Min came there late at night.' Daisy caught her breath. 'Oh good Lord, yes, I see what you mean! The coroner might jump to the conclusion that Anthony was also at the lake late at night –' She broke off, and began to tremble, feeling suddenly nervous for the first time since her arrival in Ireland.

'Perhaps. But Daisy, my dear, I do say *perhaps*. It would ease my mind considerably if we had a witness who saw the late Lady Dunvale driving into the grounds of Clonloughlin in the afternoon, or leaving around that time. Unfortunately, we apparently don't have such a witness.' Crawford threw Daisy a sympathetic look. He had adored her for years, wanted always to protect her. 'Please don't distress yourself needlessly, my dear. I haven't mentioned my worries to you before, for the simple reason I knew I would upset you if I did.' Giving her a reassuring and confident smile, he finished, 'The post-mortem is usually the key in this type of case. It *will* prove conclusively how she died.' Crawford gave Jim a pointed look. 'I'm quite certain the pathologist will pro- nounce it death by accidental drowning.' As long as he had found water in her lungs, Crawford added to himself, praying that the pathologist had done so. If he hadn't, they were in trouble. The gravest trouble imaginable. Lack of water in the deceased's lungs would prove she had died before her body entered the water. In which case a murder charge would be levelled at somebody . . . or persons unknown.

Jim, understanding that John wished to allay his mother-in-law's nervous- ness, said in a strong firm voice, 'I agree with you wholeheartedly, John. I'm sure Min's death was accidental. Now, Daisy, stay calm and cool, as you have been all through this ordeal. Edwina will fall to pieces if she detects the slightest sign of distress in you.'

Daisy said, 'I'm all right, you've nothing to be concerned about, and I agree, I think we should all three of us be as positive as possible. Anthony and Edwina are going to find the inquest exceedingly trying, no matter what, so we must be supportive and cheerful.'

Once again, Daisy McGill Amory settled back into the corner of the seat, and for the rest of the journey into Cork she remained silent, left the talking to Jim and John Crawford. She had her own troubling thoughts to preoccupy her.

Mr Liam O'Connor, a local solicitor, was the coroner presiding at the judicial inquiry into the cause of death in the case of Minerva Gwendolyn Standish, the late Countess of Dunvale.

The inquest was being held in the small Coroner's Court within the County Law Courts in the city of Cork, county seat of Cork County.

A jury of six people sat to his right. They were all local residents of the city who had been passing the courts that morning, and had been gathered together by an official of the coroner's court. This was the custom under British law in regard to inquests. Whatever their engagements planned for that day, they had had no option but to do as bidden and enter the Coroner's Court to be sworn in as jurors.

The coroner said, 'And now Lord Dunvale, before I hear testimony from Police Sergeant McNamara, the pathologist, and others present, perhaps you could give the court some idea of the deceased's state of mind, prior to her tragic death. You may speak from where you are sitting. You do not have to stand in the witness box at this moment.'

Anthony said in a clear and remarkably strong voice, 'My wife and I were separated and were about to divorce. In consequence of this, she had moved out of Clonloughlin House and was living in Waterford. Lately she had been in the habit of visiting Clonloughlin, and in the past month I began to realize that her disposition had changed radically. She was somewhat irrational, even quite violent both verbally and physically. I became increasingly concerned about her mental stability.'

The coroner nodded. 'Did the deceased ever mention suicide? Did she ever threaten to take her own life during these spells of irrationality?'

'No, she did not,' Anthony replied in an even firmer tone. 'Furthermore, I would like to state categorically that I do not believe my wife would kill herself whatever her state of mind. She was not a suicidal type of person. I am convinced her death was an accident.'

The coroner asked for further details about the deceased's behaviour, and as Anthony answered, Daisy watched the coroner closely, listening with great attentiveness. Liam O'Connor was a small, spry man, with a deeply lined face. His expression was somewhat dour, but she noticed that he had wise and kindly eyes and a reflective manner, and these characteristics filled Daisy with a degree of relief. She was confident Liam O'Connor would brook no nonsense in his court, that he would stick to the letter of the law most scrupulously, yet she also sensed he would be eminently fair.

As the coroner continued his informal questioning of Anthony, Daisy stole a surreptitious look at Edwina. Her tension was so acute Daisy feared she would collapse any minute. She reached for Edwina's hand, held on to it tightly, wanting to give her strength and confidence.

'Thank you, Lord Dunvale,' the coroner was saying. 'Lady Dunvale, I wonder if you have anything you can add pertaining to your daughter-in-law's unusual behaviour immediately before her death?'

Edwina was evidently surprised to hear her name mentioned and she started in her seat, literally gaped at the coroner speechlessly. She began to shake.

Daisy tightened her grip on her hand, whispered, 'Edwina, don't be afraid. And do answer the coroner, my dear.'

Clearing her throat numerous times, Edwina finally spoke in a low voice that trembled excessively. 'Min . . . my daughter-in-law, that is, was . . . *was* distressed in recent weeks. Yes, that is quite true.' Edwina stopped abruptly, choking on her words, and tears sprang into her eyes as she thought of the dead young woman, whom she had loved like a daughter. There was a long and painful hesitation before Edwina whispered, 'I'm afraid she was – was – drinking heavily lately. At least she arrived at Clonloughlin in an inebriated state numerous times over the last month. Bridget, er . . . er . . . Miss O'Donnell, my son's . . . Lord Dunvale's housekeeper –' Edwina stopped again, glanced at Bridget, then resumed, 'Quite recently Miss O'Donnell had to put my daughter-in-law to bed in a guest room at Clonloughlin. I remember the occasion very clearly. Miss O'Donnell told me she was afraid Lady Dunvale would have an accident if she was allowed to drive back to Waterford in her . . . debilitated condition.'

Edwina swallowed. Her mouth had gone dry and she was unable to continue. Also, the effort to speak coherently and to hang on to a semblance of control had depleted her. She fell back against the seat, her face chalky and filmed with perspiration.

'Thank you, Lady Dunvale,' the coroner said, sounding sympathetic. He put on his glasses, referred to the papers in front of him, looked up, removed his spectacles and surveyed those gathered before him. 'Miss O'Donnell, would you give me a few more details about the particular occasion to which Lady Dunvale has just referred, please?'

'Yes, sir, indeed I will.' Bridget leaned forward slightly, and in her usual clipped, precise way she confirmed Edwina's story and also the various incidents of irrationality referred to by Anthony.

Listening to her, Daisy thought that never had a better witness been heard. The woman was quite remarkable, especially in her attention to the smallest detail, and she obviously had a prodigious if not indeed photographic memory.

'And did the deceased ever suggest to *you*, Miss O'Donnell, that she might do anything at all to harm herself?' The coroner steepled his fingers, peered out over them, fixing his keen eyes on the housekeeper.

Apparently Bridget O'Donnell did not have to think twice about this question. 'Oh yes, sir, her ladyship did. Not once, but several times lately.'

There were audible gasps in the courtroom.

Anthony, stiffening in his chair, exclaimed, 'That can't be so –' He made to rise, but was restrained by John Crawford, who hushed him into silence, aware of the stern eyes of the coroner.

The latter motioned for silence in the court, and the hurried whisperings which had broken out ceased. 'Please recount those incidents, Miss O'Donnell,' he ordered.

'Yes, sir,' she said without hesitation, but she did cast a swift glance at Anthony before continuing.

Daisy, whose eyes had not left Bridget's face, thought she saw an apology signalled to him silently, but she was not sure.

Bridget O'Donnell, directing herself to the coroner, said, 'The late Lady Dunvale was a changed woman in the last few weeks of her life, as his lordship mentioned. She was hysterical in my presence on numerous occasions, and privately she said to me that she had nothing to live for, that she wished she were dead. The last time she threatened to put an end to her life was about a week before her death. She drove to Clonloughlin one afternoon, but I was the only person who saw her. His lordship was out on the estate with Mr Lamont, and the Dowager Countess was in Dublin. In any event, sir, her ladyship was very despondent, and she repeated over and over again that she wanted to escape the misery and unhappiness of her life by – by dying. She cried uncontrollably that afternoon, and although I tried to calm her, give her sympathy, she was beyond help really. At one moment, when I tried to soothe her by putting my arm around her, comforting her, she struck me across the face. The minute she had done this she seemed to come to her senses, and apologized over and over again. I made a pot of tea and we sat and talked in the kitchen for a while. It was then that her ladyship confided in me about something else. She told me that the greatest tragedy of her life was that she had not had any children.' Bridget paused, took a breath, resumed: 'Lady Dunvale began to weep again, but quietly, sort of desperately, and added that she was barren, that she couldn't bear children. Again I attempted to comfort her ladyship. I told her she was a young woman, had a lot to live for, and that she could make a new life for herself. This helped to calm her, and I thought she seemed more hopeful about things when she left a little later.'

Bridget sat back. She glanced down at her hands. Raising her eyes she stared at the coroner, and enunciated in the clearest voice, 'I think her ladyship did take her life, sir, because of the failure of her marriage and because she knew she could never have children.'

The coroner inclined his head, brought his gaze back to the papers spread before him.

The court was deathly quiet. No one stirred and not one single whisper was heard.

Daisy, glancing around discreetly, saw that the jurors wore thoughtful expressions and there was no doubt in her mind that everyone had been affected by Bridget O'Donnell's story. In its full context it left little to the imagination regarding the late woman's mental state, her unhappiness and despair. Stealing a quick look at Anthony she was struck by his extreme pallor and a pulse beating rapidly on his temple. His face was devastated.

The coroner's voice brought an end to the extraordinary stillness. Glancing at Michael Lamont, he said, 'Since you are employed by Lord Dunvale to run the estate at Clonloughlin, Mr Lamont, you obviously came into contact with the deceased in the last few weeks. Do you have anything to add to Miss O'Donnell's comments?'

Lamont cleared his throat, said in a subdued tone, 'Not really, sir. I never heard her ladyship mention suicide, and I would be inclined to agree with Lord Dunvale that she was not the sort of woman to harm herself. However –' There was a moment's hesitation before he added, 'I can attest to her ladyship's despondency ... Miss O'Donnell is correct in that assertion. I spoke to Lady Dunvale about two weeks ago, and she *was* in a very depressed state.' He cleared his throat nervously. 'She had also been drinking. Quite heavily, I thought that day. But what struck me the most was the deep, deep depression. She seemed burdened down by it. But that is all I can tell you. Lady Dunvale did not indicate why she was depressed, nor did I refer to it.' Another pause, and then he finished softly, 'I didn't think it was my place to intrude on her ladyship's privacy. As an employee of Lord Dunvale's that would have been a presumption on my part.'

'Thank you, Mr Lamont.' The coroner swivelled in his seat, focused his attention on the police sergeant. 'Sergeant McNamara, can you shed any light on the disposition and mental state of Lady Dunvale?'

'Well, Sir, I'm afraid that I can't be telling you anything I've observed personally,' McNamara began, rubbing his chin, and shaking his head somewhat mournfully. 'I haven't had the occasion to speak to her ladyship in the past few weeks. Mind you, Sir, I knew she'd been visiting Clonloughlin House. Oh yes, that she had. I'd seen her little red car going through the village. And there has been talk in the village about her very weird behaviour from time to time in recent weeks, which sort of confirms the things Miss O'Donnell and Lord Dunvale have said about her stability not being what it usually was.'

'Have you formed any opinion about the cause of death?' the coroner asked.

'Well now, Sir, I've had several opinions,' McNamara said, straightening up a trifle importantly. 'At first I believed her ladyship's death was an accident. Then later I must admit I thought of suicide. I've also wondered if foul play was involved, since her ladyship did die in mysterious circumstances.' McNamara pulled out a notebook, opened it.

'You will be able to elaborate on your findings, from the witness stand a little later in the proceedings, Sergeant McNamara,' the coroner said.

'Yes, Sir,' the police sergeant replied, closing the notebook with a slap.

The coroner sat back, clasped his hands together, and directed his next words to the entire court. He said, 'It is the duty and burden of this court to establish the manner, cause and circumstances of the death of Minerva Gwendolyn Standish, the Countess of Dunvale. After hearing the evidence, the court must decide if death was from natural or unnatural causes, whether it was an accident, suicide, or a murder committed by persons known or unknown.'

Anthony was now called to the stand, and was asked to recall, to the best of his ability, the events of the previous Saturday. Speaking quietly, Anthony told the court: 'Late that afternoon my mother telephoned me from the Dower House. She had seen my wife's car entering the grounds and driving up to the main house. In view of the distressing scenes between my wife and myself in the preceding weeks I decided to leave Clonloughlin House. I thought that once she realized I was not at home my wife would leave, that we would therefore avoid any further unpleasantness and disturbances. I drove out to the lake in my land rover. I had not been there very long when I saw my wife's red Austin mini approaching in the distance. I was standing under a tree near the lake and I went back to the land rover, intending to drive away. It would not start, the battery seemed to be dead, so I set out to walk back to Clonloughlin House, taking the long way around the estate to avoid my wife. I spoke to my mother on the telephone once I got home, and she arrived to have dinner with me a little later. Around nine-thirty I walked my mother back to the Dower House, returned home and spent several hours working on the estate account books in the library. I then went to bed. I did not know my wife had remained on the estate at Clonloughlin until I was awakened the following morning by Mr Lamont, who told me he had found my wife's – ' Anthony's voice trembled, as he finished, 'my wife's body in the lake.' He stopped again, took a deep breath and his eyes were moist and despairing when he said with overwhelming sadness. 'I should have waited at the lake – spoken to my wife. She might still be alive if I had.'

After thanking Anthony, the coroner asked Bridget O'Donnell to take the oath, to give her evidence. He commenced to question her about her activities on the day of the death.

'No, sir, I did not see Lady Dunvale's car that afternoon, nor did I know his lordship had left the house,' Bridget said. 'I was making dinner in the kitchen. Later on I served his lordship and the Dowager Countess, and after dinner I worked between the kitchen and the dining room for half an hour, clearing up.' She then spoke about her migraine, told how she had walked past the library around eleven o'clock on her way upstairs to get her pills, had noticed the earl at his desk in the library, and had seen him again around midnight when she had retired for the night.

'I was up very early on Sunday morning, sir,' Bridget O'Donnell continued. 'After drinking a cup of tea in the kitchen I drove to Waterford to attend first mass with my sister. I stayed in Waterford for lunch, and in the middle of the afternoon I returned to Clonloughlin village to see my mother. It was only then that I learned of her ladyship's death, and naturally I drove back to the estate, where I was interviewed by Sergeant McNamara.'

The next person to take the witness stand was the estate manager. Michael Lamont also said that he had not seen Lady Dunvale on Saturday afternoon, and explained his movements the following morning. 'I too was up and about quite early last Sunday. I was driving to my office at Clonloughlin House to retrieve some papers I had left there, which I needed to work on that day. I saw his lordship's land rover parked near the lake, and I got out to investigate.' Lamont swallowed. 'I thought Lord Dunvale was in the vicinity. When I realized he wasn't, I turned around to go back into my jeep. It was then that I saw her ladyship's car at the far side of the lake. Before I reached the Austin mini I saw a body floating in the lake.' Lamont suddenly looked discomfited, and he bit his underlip, appeared upset. Gaining control of himself almost immediately, he went on, 'I jumped out of the jeep for a closer look. The body, or rather a piece of clothing, had caught on a large log near the edge of the lake. I saw at once that it was Lady Dunvale in the lake. I went immediately to Clonloughlin House to inform the earl.'

'And after you informed Lord Dunvale, you telephoned the police presumably?'

'That is correct, sir, and Sergeant McNamara arrived promptly, and we, that is Lord Dunvale and myself, accompanied the sergeant to the lake.'

The coroner now called on Sergeant McNamara to report his findings. After confirming the details of Lamont's story, McNamara launched into a recital of the investigation he had conducted on the Sunday morning after the discovery of the body.

'Mr Lamont and I retrieved the body, his lordship being too distressed by far to help. I then removed the deceased to Doctor Brennan's surgery in the village, for examination and to establish possible time of death. From there I put through a phone call to forensic in Cork, knowing there would have to be a post-mortem, and to arrange for immediate transportation of the body to the forensic laboratory in Cork. I went back to Clonloughlin House, where I took a statement from his lordship, the Dowager Countess and Mr Lamont. I then searched the area around the lake, also Lady Dunvale's Austin. There was a silver hip flask, empty, but smelling of whiskey, in the glove compartment. Her handbag was on the seat and its contents did not look as if they had been tampered with. There was a considerable amount of money in the wallet. In the afternoon I thought I'd better return this to the estate. You see, Sir, it was like this . . . I was baffled . . . and about several things. Doctor Brennan had told me he believed death had occurred around eleven-thirty at night. I couldn't help wondering what her ladyship had been doing *out at the lake alone for five hours or more*. There was something else odd. I couldn't imagine how anybody could accidentally *fall* into the lake. There is no high ground, in fact the land is rather flat, and to get into Clonloughlin Lake a person would have to *walk* or *wade* into it. It was during this second search that I found an empty whiskey bottle thrown into a clump of bushes. Now that got me to thinking, it did indeed, Sir. I asked meself if death had really been accidental, as everyone was thinking. The more I pondered the more I came around to thinking it could have been suicide, perhaps even murder.' Sergeant McNamara nodded to himself. 'Yes, I must admit I did wonder if her ladyship had been the victim of foul play.'

'Foul play by whom, Sergeant McNamara?' The coroner stared intently at the police officer, his face more dolorous than ever.

'By persons unknown, Sir. A tramp, a stray gypsy, perhaps a stranger in the parts, up to no good, who her ladyship might have surprised out there in that lonely, deserted spot. But there were no signs of any kind of struggle, or a scuffle. No trampled bushes, no marks in the grass near the lake, marks like a body being dragged would cause for instance. No, no, nothing like that at all, Sir. The Mini was carefully parked, and as I said her handbag was lying there on the seat.' McNamara rubbed the side of his large red nose. 'Nor am I suggesting that Lord Dunvale had anything to do with his wife's death. Miss O'Donnell's statement that he was in the library at the time the deceased drowned removes any suspicion about his lordship. I had to interrogate him a second time on Sunday afternoon, mind you, Sir. That was in my line of duty.' McNamara gave Anthony a careful look, as if to exonerate himself in his eyes. 'Anyway, it's those five or six hours. What her ladyship was doing out there during that long period remains the greatest mystery to me, Sir.'

The coroner pondered, said thoughtfully, 'Of course, Sergeant McNamara, Lady Dunvale could have left the grounds of Clonloughlin House, driven back to Waterford and returned to Clonloughlin later – on the evening in question, perhaps hoping to speak to the earl at that time.'

'Oh yes, Sir, that is true. Very true, indeed it is. *But she didn't*. I made inquiries in the village, sure and I did, and not one solitary soul saw her during those *mysterious* five hours. And she would have had to drive through the village to get to the main road leading to Waterford.'

Daisy, who had been holding herself very still, hardly dared to breathe. She looked worriedly at John Crawford, who gave her a reassuring smile. But she guessed he was as concerned as she was at this moment. Drat Sergeant McNamara, she thought.

'Thank you, Sergeant McNamara.' The coroner nodded his dismissal and called the village doctor, Patrick Brennan, to give evidence.

Doctor Brennan's testimony was brief. 'I examined the body of the deceased late on Sunday morning, after receiving a telephone call from Sergeant McNamara, and the arrival of said body at my surgery. I saw at once that rigor mortis was present throughout the entire body. I established death to be in the proximity of eleven-thirty to midnight.'

'Were there any visible marks on the body of the deceased?' the coroner said.

'Nothing other than a diagonal bruise on the deceased's left cheek, which could have been caused by the log mentioned by Mr Lamont.'

The coroner thanked the doctor and summoned the Cork pathologist, Doctor Stephen Kenmarr.

Daisy moved to the edge of her seat, scrutinizing the pathologist intently. His would be the most crucial testimony, as she and the rest of the family were aware. She felt the tension of the Dunvales and Jim enveloping her as though this were a palpable thing. The court was deathly quiet once again, so quiet, in fact, Daisy could hear her own heart thudding.

Doctor Stephen Kenmarr was as precise a witness as Bridget O'Donnell had been. He got straight to the point.

'I concur with Doctor Brennan's theory about the abrasion on the deceased's left cheek. It could have been caused by an object in the lake, which the deceased struck when entering the water, most probably the aforementioned log. On Lady Dunvale's left cheek and cheekbone was an area of ecchymosis, that is, a dark bruise, reddish-blue in colour. I determined that it was a fresh ecchymosis, and not an old one, because of its colour. For the benefit of the laymen present, a bruise changes colour in stages, goes from reddish blue or dark purple to brown, then paler brown, lightens to a yellowish green and yellow in its last healing stages. Therefore, because of its dark colour, I knew the abrasion was recent. I found no traumatic wounds to the skull or other injuries to the head area of the body. There were no outward visible marks on any area of the body, no sign of a struggle, or any evidence to suggest that the deceased had been attacked physically in a violent manner, or killed prior to the body entering the water. After the external examination I performed an autopsy on the deceased.'

Kenmarr paused, peered at his sheaf of notes. He said, 'I discovered that the deceased's bloodstream contained a large amount of alcohol and barbiturates. The lungs held a quantity of water. I therefore concluded that death was by drowning due to the excessive amount of water taken into the lungs. Death occurred at approximately eleven-forty in the evening.'

'Thank you, Doctor Kenmarr,' the coroner said. He slipped on his glasses and looked down at the papers before him. After a few minutes he settled back in his chair and, turning to his right, he addressed the six jurors.

'From testimony we have heard in this court today we must all be fully and most sadly cognizant of the fact that the deceased was a troubled woman who was under severe mental strain, whose normal stable disposition had been affected by acute depression, owing to the failure of her marriage, and her inability to bear children.' He leaned forward. 'I put great store in the testimony of Miss Bridget O'Donnell, a clear, coherent and unemotional witness, who was perhaps far more able to see the deceased in an objective light than her husband. Miss O'Donnell was most convincing, and I trust her judgement when she says that the deceased was, only days before her death, in a frame of mind that could induce her to do harm to herself. We have heard the testimony of Doctor Kenmarr, the pathologist. He has told us there were no signs of a struggle, nor any visible marks on the body, other than the abrasion, which he has explained was recent, caused by the log. We have heard his toxicology report, his findings of alcohol and barbiturates in the bloodstream. The excessive amount of water in the lungs proved conclusively to Doctor Kenmarr that death was by drowning.'

The coroner's direct gaze rested for a split second on each juror. He resumed, 'Sergeant McNamara has drawn our attention to the curious elapse of time between the deceased's arrival at the lake and her death some five hours later. Sergeant McNamara referred to them as *mysterious hours* – but are they really? Let us now try to reconstruct those crucial hours when the deceased was alone at the lake – and we must presume she did remain there, since no one saw her leave the grounds of Clonloughlin House or pass through the village. Let us also consider the deceased herself – a troubled, depressed woman who was in a state of irrationality, that irrationality obviously inflamed by alcohol. She may well have been drinking before her arrival, but undoubtedly she consumed a large quantity of alcohol after she arrived. It was found in her bloodstream, and Sergeant McNamara testified that he not only discovered an empty *flask* smelling of *whiskey*, but an empty *whiskey bottle* thrown into the bushes. We have the deceased sitting at the lake, drinking, possibly hoping, indeed perhaps *expecting*, her husband to return to the lake within a short span of time. Let us not forget that his land rover was parked on the other side of the water, and was quite visible to her. Is it not then within the realm of possibility that she did indeed remain there? That she hoped to discuss her problems with him, to find some surcease from her pain? Let me propose the following to you ... hours pass ... it grows dark ... as she continues to linger, could not the alcohol have blurred her sense of time? Or even rendered her unconscious. Then again, could it not have induced in her the conviction that her husband would indeed come back to retrieve the land rover? But finally, in the end, realizing her hopes were groundless, could she not have come to a most terrible and tragic decision? The decision to put an end to her life? We have been told she was unusually despondent, filled with a feeling of hopelessness about her future, and by *two* witnesses. It is quite conceivable to me that the deceased swallowed barbiturates at this most dreadful moment in time, either in a misguided attempt to ease her mental anguish – or perhaps to numb her sense before walking into that lake. Yes, I believe that the events on that evening could have progressed in exactly this way and as I have so outlined to you. There is no other feasible explanation. Medical testimony has ruled out the possibility of foul play – murder. Sergeant McNamara has pointed out that it would be difficult for a person to accidentally fall into the lake at Clonloughlin even if a person was in a drunken stupor, befuddled and disoriented by alcohol, because of the nature of the topography of the area. There is no high ground surrounding that particular body of water.' There was a split second's pause, before the coroner finished, 'And so, after giving due consideration to all of the evidence presented today, I must draw the conclusion that this is a clear case of suicide.' The coroner scanned the jurors for one final time. 'Are there any questions?'

The jurors turned to each other, spoke together in low tones for a few seconds, and finally a clean-cut young man addressed the coroner with the apparent approval of the others. 'We are all in agreement, sir. We believe as you do and that it happened the way you say.'

Straightening himself up to his full height in the chair, the coroner now addressed the entire court.

'As coroner presiding in this Coroner's Court of the County of Cork I must now pronounce a verdict that Minerva Gwendolyn Standish, the Countess of Dunvale, did die by her own hand whilst the balance of her mind was disturbed, and whilst she was under the influence of alcohol and barbiturates.'

There was a moment of complete silence and then a buzz began, rippling through the court. Daisy patted Edwina's hand, leaned forward and glanced at John Crawford, who smiled very faintly and nodded. Daisy's eyes rested momentarily on Anthony, who sat as unmoving as a statue on the seat. He looked stricken, disbelieving. Daisy filled with sadness and pity for him. He had so wanted Min's death to be proven an accident.

Daisy rose and helped the weeping Edwina to her feet, escorted her out into the corridor. Bridget O'Donnell caught up with them.

'I'm sorry, your ladyship,' Bridget murmured.

Edwina turned, stared at her, shook her head vehemently without speaking.

Bridget went on, 'I had to say what I said about Lady Dunvale because –' There was the merest fraction of a pause before she finished sullenly, 'Because it was the truth.'

Daisy, observing her, thought: Oh no, it wasn't. Startled at herself, she wondered what had prompted her to assume such a thing, and instantly dismissed the curious idea that Bridget O'Donnell had been lying. But the thought was to recur often and the housekeeper's testimony would trouble Daisy for the longest time.

Edwina swayed against her, and Daisy turned her attention to her half-sister. 'Come, Edwina dear, sit down,' she murmured with great gentleness and led her to a bench.

Bridget rushed to help. 'I'll go and fetch you a drink of water, your ladyship.'

'No!' Edwina exclaimed. 'I don't want you to get me anything.'

The sharpness of Edwina's tone seemed to stun Bridget, and she stepped back uncertainly. 'But your ladyship –' she began and faltered.

Ignoring her, Edwina opened her handbag and took out a compact, patted her red nose and tear-stained face with the powder puff. Bridget continued to gape at Edwina, her icy blue eyes filling with perplexity and then she edged nearer to the door leading into the coroner's court. When she saw Michael Lamont emerging she hurried to his side.

'Are you all right now, Edwina?' Daisy asked, bending over the other woman, filled with concern.

Edwina made no response. She rose and looked Daisy fully in the face. To Daisy it seemed as though an immense change had been wrought in her during

270

the passing of only a few seconds. A veil of dignity had fallen over Edwina's face and her bearing was suddenly regal, almost imperious.

Finally she spoke, and her voice was clear, unusually strong. 'I have just remembered who I am – I am Emma Harte's daughter and my son is her grandson, and therefore we are made of sterner stuff than most people might think. It's about time I made them realize that, and I also think it's time that I stopped feeling sorry for myself.'

A warm smile swept across Daisy's astonished face. She reached out and grasped Edwina's arm. 'Welcome to the family,' she said.

28

Miranda O'Neill was laughing with such merriment tears sprang into her eyes.

Recovering herself after a few seconds, she flicked the tears away with her fingertips. 'Honestly, Paula, I've never heard such a load of nonsense in my life.'

Paula said, 'You're confirming my suspicions . . . I thought Sarah was lying to me.'

Searching her handbag for a tissue, Merry blew her nose, said, 'Lying is rather a strong word – let's just say that she fudged the facts. Or, to use one of Grandpop's favourite phrases, she bent the truth to suit her purpose.'

'So what really happened in Barbados?' Paula probed. 'She made it sound as if she worked like a galley slave.'

'Oh rubbish! She had lots of help from the two local girls I'd engaged and the young woman who's going to manage the boutique for us.' Merry stood up, drifted over to the sofa positioned near the window in Paula's office at the Leeds store.

Watching her progress across the room Paula decided she had not seen Miranda looking so well for a long time. She had caught the sun in the Caribbean and her freckled face, usually so pale, had a soft tan that was most flattering to her, gave her an extra-special glow. She wore a full-skirted wool dress of an unusual ginger shade that enhanced the colour of her burnished copper hair, and her tawny eyes seemed more golden than hazel today. Paula could not help thinking of the autumn foliage in her garden at Long Meadow. Merry's natural colouring and the clothes she had chosen echoed its russet hues perfectly.

Draping herself on the sofa, Miranda explained: 'The minute Sarah arrived she was obviously in that take charge mood of hers, very superior, bossy, even demanding. I volunteered to help in any way I could, but she practically ordered me out of the shop, said she could manage, thank you very much. Frankly, I was taken aback since she's not really involved with us in the boutiques. But I decided to let her have her way.' The auburn brows met in a deep frown and her expressive face signalled her irritation. 'She didn't want me around, Paula, that's the long and short of it. I *was* rather busy with other things in the hotel,

271

but not too busy to check in several times a day by phone. And I went down every evening to see how the boutique was shaping up.' Miranda's wide-set eyes rested on Paula, grew quizzical. 'Surely you knew I'd be on top of things?'

'Naturally I did, silly. I'm only mentioning it because Sarah made such a fuss about the hard work she *said* she'd done. She also told me that she hadn't enjoyed herself, implied that the O'Neills ostracized her.'

'Now that *is* a downright lie!' Miranda exclaimed, her annoyance more apparent than ever. 'Both my father and Shane paid numerous visits to the shop, and she was invited to every single one of our special events.' Miranda glanced at her hands thoughtfully, nodded to herself and looked up at Paula. 'Well, perhaps she didn't have any fun actually. She was certainly bizarre in the way she behaved. She seemed to think it was Shane's duty to be her permanent escort, to drag her around with him wherever he went, *and* to pay constant court to her. Shane was awfully pleasant and patient under the circumstances – after all he was preoccupied with the hotel. We were all *working*, for God's sake.'

'I know you were,' Paula answered. 'And I didn't really pay attention to the things she said . . . but I must admit I was a bit thunderstruck at first. And why would she lie to me? Surely she knew I'd find out from you what actually transpired.'

'Sarah's strange, lives in her own world.' Miranda leaned forward, gave Paula a knowing stare. 'Consider some of the rotten little things she did when we were children. And she's always been full of her own importance. Smug. Self-satisfied. Look, I don't think she merits this long discussion, do you? Let's –'

'There's something I haven't told you. The real reason she came to see me two weeks ago was to make me an offer . . . she wanted to buy the boutiques.' Paula sat back, waiting for Merry's reaction, aware that she would be angrier than ever. But she had to be told.

'What a bloody cheek! *Our boutiques!* I've never heard of anything so outrageous in my life . . . where was her head? I mean, you're a public company. I presume you sent *her* on her merry way and with a few choice words ringing in her ears. I hope you did!'

'Yes, of course. But she wasn't taking my *no* for an answer. She threatened to telex Grandy in Australia.'

'And did she?'

'No. She telephoned her at Dunoon. Can you imagine, bothering Gran like that? Anyway, Grandy made short shrift of her.' Paula's mouth worked with sudden amusement as she thought of her recent conversation with her grandmother. 'When Sarah told Gran that she thought she should be allowed to buy the boutiques for her division, because of all her hard work, effort, brilliance, etcetera, Gran told me she said, "Oh really Sarah, so that's what you think, is it? Well, remember what thought did – followed a muck cart and thought it was a wedding." Then Grandy told her that her suggestion was ill-conceived, ridiculous, and out of the question. She added that it would *always* be out of the question, advised Sarah never to dare to mention such a thing again.'

'There's nobody quite as pithy and scathing as Aunt Emma when she wants to be,' Miranda said, and leaned back. 'I assume dear Sarah got the message?'

'I haven't heard a whisper from her since.'

'Well, that doesn't mean anything, she's busy with the summer line right now.' A look of comprehension flitted on to Miranda's face. 'What you've just told me probably explains something – Sarah was awfully funny with me when I went up to Lady Hamilton Clothes the other day. I can't say she was rude, because she's always well mannered, but she was unusually standoffish, even for her. Not to digress, but it's a lovely line by the way, and I hope you'll see it when you're in London next week. We ought to place our order soon, Paula.'

'Yes, I know, and Gaye has made an appointment for me to go to the showroom. And whatever else she is, Sarah is a marvellous designer. The Lady Hamilton Collection has never been anything but stunning.'

'Yes,' Miranda said, thinking how generous and fair-minded Paula was, and she constantly strived to find something positive in everyone. 'Incidentally, Allison Ridley was at the fashion show, and *she* was strange with me as well, treated me as if I had a social disease.'

'Probably because of Winston and Emily.'

'What's that got to do with *me*?'

'You're very close to Emily, and I hear that Allison's extremely cut up about Winston. Quite broken hearted, according to Michael Kallinski, who came in to see me yesterday. He told me she and Sarah have become very thick lately, and no doubt Allison regards you as a member of the enemy camp. Anyway, Michael said Allison's thinking of moving to New York. *Permanently*.'

Miranda was surprised. 'Well, well, well . . . maybe she's contemplating going into partnership with that friend of hers – Skye Smith.'

There was such a disparaging note in Merry's voice Paula glanced at her quickly. 'Don't you like Skye Smith?'

'Not particularly,' Merry answered, as usual being completely open and honest with her dearest friend. 'I have to admit that she has been very nice to Shane since he's been in New York. She's given a few dinner parties for him and has introduced him to some of her friends, and he seems to like her. But –' Merry's voice trailed off, and she made a face. 'She's too good to be true, in my opinion, so sweet all the time, too sweet if the truth be known. She acts as if butter wouldn't melt in her mouth, plays the innocent, but I can't help feeling she's quite experienced – where men are concerned. I said so to Shane, but he just laughed, thought it was very amusing. Winston tended to agree with me. I'm sure he's told you that Shane had a small dinner party for us both at Twenty One when we were in New York last week. Well, it was actually for Winston – to celebrate the deal he made with the Canadian paper mill.'

'I thought he hadn't missed out one detail,' Paula said slowly, 'but obviously he did, since he made no mention of Skye Smith.'

'Oh,' Merry said, thinking this omission was odd. She hurried on, 'But Skye *was* there. With Shane. And I had a chance to get to know her a bit better, observe her more closely. I came away from that dinner with the most peculiar feeling. I think she has something to hide – you know, about her past.'

'What a strange thing for you to think, Merry.'

'Isn't it,' Merry agreed. 'And don't ask me *why* I think it, because I can't offer you a proper explanation. Instinct, perhaps, intuition on my part.' Merry gave a tiny shrug. 'Still, on the plane coming back to London with Winston, he and I had a long discussion about her, and we both decided she has a devious nature. He's not very keen on her anymore, even though he quite liked her when he and Shane first met her at Allison's in the spring.'

'Is it serious? I mean between Shane and her?' Paula was surprised how tight her voice sounded and as her stomach lurched she realized that the idea of Skye and her old friend being involved troubled her. Her eyes did not leave Merry's face.

'I sincerely hope it isn't! I don't like the idea of *her* being around on a permanent basis. Winston thinks it's only platonic, and he ought to know. By the way, talking of Winston, how's Sally?'

'Oh she's much better. Anthony came over from Ireland about ten days ago and went immediately to Heron's Nest, where Sally's been staying. I spoke to them on the phone yesterday, and they're benefiting from the peace and quiet, are glad to be alone together. Actually Anthony's coming to see me this afternoon.'

'What an awful time you must have had because of his wife's death. I would have to be out of the country, wouldn't I? I wish I'd been here, to give you moral support, Paula.'

'Oh Merry, that's sweet of you. But fortunately Emily was back from Paris, and she and I managed to keep each other going. We got through it, which is the main thing.'

'Yes. But you do look tired,' Merry ventured, using the mildest word she could find. From the moment she had arrived at the store she had been struck by Paula's white, drained face, the dark shadows. Her friend looked quite ill to her. 'Can't you take a few days off? Get away somewhere for a rest?'

'You've got to be joking! Look at this desk.'

Merry made no further comment, deciding it would be wiser not to voice her worries about Paula's health. She averted her face to conceal her anxiety. Her eyes fell on the collection of family photographs on Emma's large mahogany side table. A number of familiar faces gazed back at her – her grandparents, Blackie and Laura on their wedding day, her father as a baby lying on a fur rug, she and Shane when they were toddlers, her parents on the day of their marriage, and Emma's children in various stages of growing up.

Reaching for the largest photograph of the handsome man in an officer's uniform, she studied it for a moment, then remarked, 'Your mother looks a lot like Paul McGill. Yes, Aunt Daisy has her father's eyes. But then, so do you.' Glad she had found a way to change the subject, she added, 'But the frame's dented, Paula. You ought to get it fixed for Aunt Emma. It's such a shame. Why this is a really lovely piece of silver. An antique.' Merry held up the frame, pointed to the damage.

'Grandy doesn't want it repaired,' Paula told her with a faint half smile. 'When I said the same thing a couple of years ago, she laughed and told me the *dent* was part of her memories.'

'What did she mean?' Merry asked.

'My grandfather didn't return to England after the end of the First World War. He stayed in Australia. The story is a bit involved, but one day, in a moment of rage and frustration, Gran threw his picture across the room – that particular picture in that very frame. The glass shattered, the frame was dented, but she kept it nevertheless. She told me that ever since then, whenever she looked at his photograph, she reminded herself to trust love. She thinks that if she had trusted Paul when he disappeared – *trusted his love for her* – she would have had absolute faith in him, would have waited for him to come back. She believes she would have saved herself the terrible years of heartache she suffered during her dreadfully unhappy marriage to Arthur Ainsley.'

'But Paul and she did get back together in the end, had years of happiness,' Merry said softly, her expression suddenly disconsolate.

'You do sound unhappy, Merry. Love problems yourself? None of your old boyfriends around, is that it?' Paula looked sympathetic.

Merry nodded. 'No new ones either. I seem to have nothing but bad luck in that department these days. Most of the men I've gone out with in the last few months can't seem to see beyond the O'Neill money, my looks and my so-called sexuality. I'm getting more leery by the minute.' Merry grimaced. '*I'll* probably end up being an old maid. Emily's lucky, snagging Winston the way she did. At least she knows he's in love with *her* and not her bank balance. Especially since he's got a pretty hefty one of his own.'

'Oh Merry, not every man is after money –' Paula began and stopped, recognizing there was a grain of truth in Merry's statement. Being an heiress *did* have its manifold disadvantages, although money was only one of them.

Miranda was silent. After a moment she said, '*Perhaps*. The trouble is that the men *I* meet are simply not able to see beyond their noses, past the externals, to the person I am, to the real me. I'm not a fairy tale princess, for heaven's sake. I work jolly hard and carry quite a load of responsibility at O'Neill Hotels International. And I have very real values, as you're aware. Shane and I were brought up to understand the value of a pound note, just as you were. And my father and grandfather, aside from all they instilled, Aunt Emma certainly drilled enough sense into me during those summers at Heron's Nest.'

Paula said, 'Yes, I understand what you're trying to say. People do have funny ideas about us, don't they? But nothing is ever the way it seems – to outsiders anyway.'

Walking over to Paula's desk, Merry sat down in the chair opposite, her sadness mirrored in her tawny eyes. Her face became more downcast. 'I'll tell you something else, Paula, I'd much prefer to marry a man I've known all my life, who loves me for *myself*, for what I am as a person, and not for what he *imagines* me to be. The other day I came to the conclusion that I don't want to get seriously involved with a fascinating stranger. To hell with fascinating strangers, they spell trouble and are frequently full of nasty surprises. If it's not the money, then it's the power they crave. Then there are the sex maniacs, the chaps who're only interested in hopping into bed.' She smiled wryly. 'As Shane keeps saying, sex is easy to come by but love is hard to find. That brother of mine happens to be right in this instance.'

Anthony said, 'It's awfully good of you to spend all this time with me this afternoon, Paula. I really appreciate it, and I'd just like to say again that you've been wonderful through this most difficult period. I can't tha –'

Paula held up her hand. 'If you say thank you to me once more I'll turf you out of my office.' She lifted the teapot and poured him a second cup of tea. 'I'm glad to be of help when I can, and let's not lose sight of the fact that you're a member of this family.' She gave him a small but warm smile. 'Besides,' she added quickly, 'I'm not all that busy this afternoon,' resorting to the white lie in order to make him feel better. 'Now, to answer your question, I think Grandy *would* be upset – very upset actually – if you and Sally got married before she returns from Australia.'

'You do really,' he murmured, his face crestfallen. He lit a cigarette, sat back in the chair and crossed his legs. He stared past her into space, focusing on the painting above the antique chest on the far wall. He seemed momentarily distracted, as if trying to work something out in his head. 'And when do you think she will be getting back, in fact?' he asked eventually, bringing his attention back to Paula again.

'She promised me she'd be home in time to have our traditional family Christmas at Pennistone Royal –' Paula stopped in mid-sentence, struck by a sudden, and appealing, idea. Leaning forward over the butler's tray table between them, she exclaimed, 'That's when you should marry Sally. At Christmas. Gran will love it, and you can stay with her at Pennistone Royal through the holidays.'

He made no response.

Paula said in a rush, 'It's a marvellous idea, Anthony. Why are you hesitating?'

Still he was mute, and as she watched him closely Paula saw a pained look cross his sensitive face, which was grey and lined with fatigue. His eyes became anxious, even alarmed. He has eyes like Jim, like Aunt Edwina. Fairley eyes, Paula thought idly. She pushed aside this inconsequential observation, and wanting to pin him down, said, 'Yes, Christmas *would* be perfect, ideal. Do say yes. We can try and reach Grandy in Sydney. No, it's too late now,' she muttered, thinking aloud about the time difference, glancing at her watch. It was four o'clock. Two in the morning in Australia. 'Well, we can send her a telex,' she announced decisively.

'I suppose Christmas will be all right,' Anthony said slowly, reluctantly. 'It *will* have to be a quiet wedding, Paula. Very quiet. Because by then –' His voice wavered slightly, became a low mumble as he told her, 'Sally's pregnant, and her condition will be noticeable by then.'

Aware at once of his discomfort, Paula adopted a cheerful, matter-of-fact tone. 'I imagine Sally will be about six months along in December, so we'll have to make her a really lovely wedding dress that conceals her awkward figure.'

Startled, Anthony said, '*You knew?*'

'No, guessed. Both Emily and I thought she had put on weight when we saw her in September, and we came to the conclusion she might be expecting. Don't worry, no one else knows, except Winston.'

'Her father and Vivienne are also aware –'

'I'm talking about the rest of the family, Anthony. And as you said it should be quiet . . . only a handful of people. The Hartes, of course, Gran, Jim and myself, your mother, and Emily. She'd be hurt if she didn't come.'

'Yes,' he said. 'I'm very fond of Emily, and she was such a help . . .' He stopped, swallowed. 'Under the circumstances, do you think it's indecent – my getting married again? I mean, so soon after Min's death?'

'No, of course I don't.'

Anthony looked at Paula uncertainly.

She looked back, her gaze direct and penetrating.

She saw a man under great strain, and this showed in his haggard face, was echoed by his bleak manner, and the apathy she had divined in him the moment he had arrived. That he had aged in the past few weeks was transparent. He was not the same person he had been at her grandmother's birthday celebration. His fair colouring and very blond, rather English good looks had been most pronounced, and he had appeared more striking than ever in the well-tailored tuxedo, which he had worn with the same kind of panache Jim possessed. That night he had laughed a lot, been so carefree and gay, unusually outgoing, charming them all. Now he was a shattered wreck.

Paula made a snap decision. She leaned forward, pinning him down with her eyes. 'Listen to me, Anthony. You were unhappily married to Min, separated from her and about to divorce. You've been devastated by her death, the circumstances of it, and understandably so. However, it was not your fault. You must put it out of your mind, otherwise it's going to come between you and your happiness with Sally, affect your future, perhaps even ruin your life.' Recognizing she had spoken harshly, she softened her tone. 'You must think about Sally and the baby from this moment on . . . they are your priorities.'

'Oh yes, what you say is true,' he acknowledged. 'I'm not a hypocrite. Please don't think I'm mourning excessively for her.' A quiver entered his voice when he said, 'But I never wished her dead, Paula. That she had to die in such a terrible way is more than I –'

Paula stood up, joined him on the sofa. She took his hand, looked into his face, her own filled with immense compassion. 'I know, I know, Anthony. And please believe me, I'm not being cold hearted, not in the least. And whatever *you* think, you *weren't* responsible. My grandmother, *our grandmother*, says we are each one of us responsible for our own lives, that we write our own scripts and then live them out to the bitter end. That *is* true, you know. Min was responsible for herself, her life, not you. Try and draw strength and courage from Grandy's philosophy.'

'Yes,' he said. 'But it *is* hard, so very hard.'

Paula was more convinced than ever that her cousin was in grave emotional trouble, and she racked her brain, wondering what to say, how to jostle him out of his present troubled state. She was not insensitive to his feelings. But she also knew that if he allowed Min's death to dominate his life he was cutting off his chance of making that brand new life with Sally.

Speaking so quietly, so gently that her voice was hardly audible, Paula said, 'It may be difficult for you to believe me when I say that I can comprehend your feelings, but truly I can. You must put this tragedy behind you. If you don't it will cripple you. You will also be committing a terrible sin – against your own child.' Purposely she stopped with suddenness, abruptness, sat waiting, watching him.

He blinked, his eyes wide with shock. 'What on earth do you mean by that?'

he managed in a strangled voice. 'I don't understand . . . *committing a sin against my own child,*' he repeated. He was horrified.

'Yes. If you permit Min's memory, her suicide, to haunt you, to fill you with guilt, you will not be able to love that child as you should – with all your heart and soul and mind. Because Min will be there, creating a wedge between you, and, let me add, between you and Sally. Also, remember that you and Sally created this baby out of your love for each other . . . it didn't ask to be born . . . it's an innocent little thing. Don't cheat it because of *your* problems. He or she is going to need the very best of you, Anthony. To give the child anything less . . . well, yes, that would be a sin.'

He stared at her for the longest moment, blinking, striving to curb his emotions so dangerously near the surface. He leapt up, strode to the window, stood peering absently into the street below. But he saw only the death mask of Min's face as it had looked when they had brought her back from the lake. He closed his eyes convulsively, needing to expunge the image. Anthony groped for his handkerchief, blew his nose, ruminated on Paula's words. And then Sally's voice echoed in his throbbing head. *Life is for the living,* she had said last night. *We can't change what has happened. We can't spend the rest of our lives flagellating ourselves. If we do then Min will have won. And won from the grave.* The things Sally had said had been rooted in fundamental truths, he might as well admit it. Something else occurred to him, brought his head up with a swift jerk. The woman Min had become in the last few years bore no resemblance to the girl he had fallen in love with. Min had turned sour, bitter and vindictive, and her bitterness and resentment had only served to erode his love. Sally had not broken up his marriage, as Min had so violently asserted. Only bad marriages could be shattered by another person. Those unions that were strong remained inviolate against all outside forces. Now he thought: it was Min who broke up our marriage. For a split second he believed this was a sudden revelation, but then acknowledged that he had always been aware of this in the back of his mind. He had been so busy blaming himself he had not let this fact rise to the surface. The pain in his chest began to ease, and slowly he gathered his self possession to him. Eventually he turned and went back to the sofa and Paula.

Anthony's pellucid eyes held hers, and it was his turn to reach out, to take her hand in his. He said, 'You're a very special woman, Paula. Wise, and so very compassionate, such a good and loving person. Thank you for bringing me to my senses. I shall give Sally and our child every ounce of love that I have. They will have the very best of me. I promise you that.'

After Anthony had left, Paula plunged into her work with a vengeance. She was still hard at it when Agnes poked her head around the door at six-thirty.

'How late are we going to be here tonight, Mrs Fairley?'

Paula raised her eyes, put down her pen and sat back in the chair. 'Come in, Agnes.' She rubbed her aching face, picked up the cup of tea, and, realizing it had gone cold hours before, immediately put it down with a grimace. 'I'll be about another half hour, that's all, but you can leave if you want.'

'Oh no, I wouldn't dream,' Agnes said. Conscious of Paula's drawn white face, she eyed the cup, volunteered, 'Let me make you a nice cup of hot tea, Mrs Fairley. You look dead beat.'

'Yes, thanks a lot, Agnes. No, wait a minute, let's have a drink. I could use one tonight, and I'm sure you could too.'

'That'll be very nice, Mrs Fairley. But what have we got?'

Paula let out her first genuine laugh that day. 'Sorry,' she apologized, observing the hurt and baffled expression on her secretary's face. 'You did sound droll just then. And you're right, what *do* we have . . . very little that's palatable, I suspect. There was a bottle of sherry in the coat closet. Why don't you see if it's still there.'

Agnes hurried to the walk-in closet and Paula started to shuffle her papers, slipping items into the different coloured folders spread before her, quickly bringing order to her desk.

A second later Agnes emerged from the closet, smiling triumphantly. 'Bristol Cream, Mrs Fairley.' She held up the bottle with a flourish.

'Oh good, let's have a glass, and we can kill two birds with one stone, go over a few final things since it's Saturday tomorrow. I've decided not to come in, Agnes. I want to spend the day with my babies. And you don't have to be here either, you know.'

'Thank you, Mrs Fairley.' Agnes beamed at her.

Ten minutes later, between sips of sherry, Paula had reduced the pile of folders on her desk. Most of them now sat on the floor at Agnes's feet.

'You can send these last three to Gaye Sloane in London. The blue folder contains all the final details for the career clothes shop. Incidentally, I've decided to use the name Emily came up with, after all. I think it's the best . . . *The Total Woman* says exactly what I want it to say. Do you like it?'

'I do, very much. I told Miss Emily so the other day. She was, well, sort of taking a poll around the executive offices, asking the other secretaries and typists what they thought.'

'Was she now,' Paula murmured, smiling to herself as she thought affectionately of Emily, her busy little bee forever trying to be of help. 'The red folder has all the information for the fashion exhibition in January, and this green one has my notes for Trade Winds, plus a list of merchants we'll be buying from in Hong Kong, India and Japan. Do you have your pad?' Paula nodded as Agnes lifted it up. 'Drop a line to Gaye and ask her to make duplicates of the lists. Also, send a memo to –'

The private phone on Paula's desk began to ring and Agnes, rising and reaching over, answered it. 'Yes, just a minute please,' she said, depressing the hold button. She handed the receiver to Paula. 'It's Mr Stevens calling from Odessa, Texas.'

'Hello, Dale,' Paula said. 'How are –'

He cut her off abruptly. 'Paula, I'm sorry, but I have bad news.'

'What's wrong, Dale?'

'The worst, I'm afraid. One of our oil tankers is in trouble. It was loading crude oil off the coast of Texas this morning, Galveston, and there was an explosion in the engine room. A very bad explosion.'

Gripping the phone tightly, striving to hear him through the abnormally bad static, Paula said, with rising apprehension, 'No casualties, I hope, Dale?'

There was a moment of silence. 'Yes, I'm afraid we've lost six of the crew ... four other crew members badly injured –'

'Oh Dale this is horrendous!' Paula exclaimed. 'How did it happen, for God's sake?'

'We don't know. We're investigating. Blaze ripped through the vessel. It's under control now. She's not gone down. I stress *not* gone down . . .'

There was a bad echo on the line and Paula cried, 'I'm having difficulty hearing you.'

'I'm here,' he shouted back. 'Static sure is high today. I said we don't know what caused the explosion, but there'll be an inquiry. We've lost one and a quarter million gallons of crude, and we're facing a massive clean up job. The crude's drifting into Galveston Bay already. Seabirds and wildlife threatened by it, also the shrimp breeding grounds. God knows how much oil spill will wash ashore.'

'This is a disaster,' Paula said unsteadily.

'I can't hear *you*, Paula,' Dale Stevens bellowed.

'I said it's a catastrophe. We're going to have everybody on our backs from ecology people to – I dread to think who else. The families of the crew members – those poor people must be taken care of, Dale, as I'm sure you know without me telling you. Small comfort financial compensation will be. Listen, do you want me to fly over? I don't know what I could do, though, except give you moral support.'

'No, no, Paula, there's hardly any point in that. I'm handling everything. I've been in touch with the insurance company. It's going to cost us millions of dollars to do a concentrated clean up.'

'How much?'

'Don't know. Depends on the spill, the damage it does. It could be anywhere between five to ten million dollars to do a proper job.'

Paula caught her breath, aghast at the figure, then said, 'To hell with what it costs. We have to do it. Stay in touch, Dale. I want to know how such an explosion could possibly happen. We've had such a good safety record.'

'Nobody's immune. That's the oil business. I'll call you tomorrow, perhaps even later tonight if I have any further news.' The line was clearer now, his voice coming over as if he was speaking from around the corner.

'I'll be home all evening,' Paula said. 'And Dale, do everything you can for those bereaved families.'

'It's already in the works.'

'This is going to be a stain on our record.'

'I know, honey. I'm going to have to hang up. Situation is pressing here.'

'Dale, one more thing . . . you haven't told me which tanker it was.'

'Sorry, Paula, but it's the *Emeremm III*. I'm very sorry, honey.'

Paula put down the phone and fell back against the chair, feeling sick inside. Her face was grim.

Agnes said worriedly, 'I got the gist of your conversation, Mrs Fairley. One of the Sitex oil tankers sank.' This assertion came out sounding more like a question.

Paula shook her head, gave her secretary the details, then explained, 'The *Emeremm III* was named for my grandmother. She once owned a company called Emeremm and my grandfather loved the name – it's a contraction of emeralds and Emma. His favourite stone and his favourite lady.' She attempted a smile unsuccessfully. 'It was he who launched the first Emeremm, and then the *Emeremm II*. Ever since then it's been a tradition to have a vessel in the Sitex fleet bearing that name . . . that very special name.'

'I am sorry, Mrs Fairley,' Agnes sympathized. 'I know how proud you are of the company's safety record. This is just awful.'

'Thank you, Agnes,' Paula murmured. 'It's a dreadful blow, especially since there has been loss of lives.' Pulling herself together, she exhaled, drew her pad towards her. 'I'd better draft a telex to my grandmother.' As she picked up her pen Paula shivered, felt a quiver run up her spine. Although she was not superstitious by nature she had a strange presentiment that disaster loomed. The explosion in the *Emeremm III* was a bad omen.

29

'Didn't you enjoy yourself, Winston?' Emily asked, squinting at him in the muted glow emanating from the dying fire in the living room at Beck House.

Winston put down his brandy balloon and gaped at her, genuine astonishment invading his face. He shook his head in wonderment. 'Paula sits there looking as if she's at death's door, hardly opening her mouth all night. Jim manages to get stewed to the gills between cocktails and the main course. My sister is so pregnant she seems about ready to drop *triplets* right there at the dinner table. Merry doesn't stop bemoaning the fact that she's on the shelf at twenty-three because all of the men she's grown up with are otherwise involved. Alexander is in a raging snit because of your mother's sexual antics with half the bloody government. Maggie Reynolds bores me senseless, droning on about some dilapidated shooting lodge in the Outer Hebrides, and you ask a question like that. Oh yes, Emily, I enjoyed myself thoroughly. I had a wonderful time. It was one of the most exciting, entertaining evenings of my life.' He began to laugh, suddenly seeing the humorous side.

Emily laughed with him. She snuggled into the corner of the sofa, tucked her feet under her and said, 'But Anthony was on good form.'

'Amazingly so. Well, he seems to have *his* feet on the ground these days and is coping extremely well.'

'Thanks to Paula. She told me she had a long talk with him a few weeks ago, sort of gave him a lecture, advised him to put the past behind him and get on with his life.'

'She's very good at that,' Winston muttered, swirling the cognac around in his glass, his face thoughtful.

'What do you mean?'

'Giving advice. Mind you, she's usually right about everything she says. If only she'd take some of her own advice.'

Emily's face sobered instantly. 'Yes.'

Winston leaned back against the cushions, put his feet up on the coffee table, and let himself drift into his thoughts. The evening at Long Meadow had been a disaster and he had been relieved to escape with Emily relatively early, to come back here to the comfort and tranquillity of Beck House. But one dreary dinner party was meaningless, of no consequence. What troubled him was Paula's physical appearance and her state of mind. For some weeks now, since his return from Vancouver via New York, he had been vaguely conscious of her misery. The last few hours had confirmed his feelings. She was an unhappy woman. He was convinced her marriage to Jim was at the root of her pain.

Emily said, 'You're very quiet, Winston, you're worrying about Paula, aren't you?'

'I'm afraid so, darling. Apart from the fact that she looked so dreadful tonight, she spoke in monosyllables. I know she's a bit reserved at times, not a chatterbox like you, but she's normally much more communicative, especially with the family group.'

'It's not the work that's getting her down,' Emily exclaimed, 'she's used to pressure, long hours, carrying tremendous responsibilities. Anyway, she has the stamina of a bull – like Grandma.'

'I'm aware of that, Emily. I know Paula almost as well as you do. I meant it just now when I said she looks as if she's at death's door; however I realize she's not actually physically ill. She's emotionally disturbed at the moment.' He swung his feet to the floor, searched the pocket of his robe for the packet of cigarettes. 'There are a lot of problems in that marriage. Want to bet?' he asked, lighting a cigarette.

'Oh you're so right, Winston. I've tried to bring the subject up several times lately, but she just gives me funny looks and retreats into herself, or talks about something else.'

'But you two have always been so close. Hasn't she said anything at all?' he asked, his voice rising an octave, registering his surprise.

'No, not really. I told you before, she was upset on that awful Sunday in September. You know, because of Jim's attitude, the way he spoke to her in regard to her problems with Sam Fellowes. And I knew she'd been crying when I got back from Pennistone Royal. The weekend Jim returned from Ireland, when the three of us were in London, she murmured something about Jim being irritable, even irascible with her. I started to probe a bit, and she sort of . . . shrugged it off, became as uncommunicative as she was tonight. But I've noticed that tendency a lot in the last few months, and she *is* burying herself in work. That's all she does actually, except for spending any free time she has with the babies. She adores the twins. Actually, *I* think they've become her whole life, aside from business of course.'

'That's no good. Aunt Emma's going to be miffed, not too thrilled, when she gets back next month – seeing Paula like this.' Winston shifted his position on the sofa, immediately saw the concern ringing Emily's face. He took her hand, 'Hey, poppet, come on, don't look so miserable. It'll all work out. Life has a funny way of taking care of itself.'

'I suppose so,' Emily murmured, wondering if it would, deciding that it wouldn't, because of Paula's basic nature. She would cling to her marriage no matter what, because of the children and her extraordinary sense of duty to them, as well as her determination not to be defeated.

'Would you like me to talk to Paula,' Winston ventured. 'I could –'

'God no!' Emily cried fiercely, sitting up with a jerk. 'She'd resent it, consider it an intrusion into her privacy, and anyway, you'd only get a flea in your ear for your trouble.'

Winston sighed. 'I suspect that's true. Listen, if you want my opinion, I think she and Jim ought to get a divorce.'

'She'd never do that! She thinks as I do about divorce.'

'*Oh*. And how's that?' he asked, pricking up his ears. He gave her a long hard stare.

'Well,' Emily said slowly, 'we sort of disapprove really. I mean after all, we've had a lovely example with my mother. She's had so many husbands and so many divorces I've lost count.'

'Your mother's the exception to the rule, Emily.'

Ignoring this comment, Emily hurried on, 'Paula believes that if there are problems in a marriage they've got to be worked out. She says that people can't keep getting divorced at the drop of a hat, just because they meet a few snags along the way, that this is no solution. She thinks marriage requires a great deal of effort –'

'It takes two to tango, you know.'

A reflective look washed over Emily's face as she nodded, said, 'You're implying Jim might not make the effort . . . Is that actually what you mean?'

Winston hesitated. 'Perhaps. But I could be wrong, and anyway who really knows about other people's private lives. That's why this conversation should be terminated right now. It's rather futile, Dumpling.'

'Yes,' she said. 'Winston, don't call me Dumpling. I'm very *svelte* these days.'

He laughed. 'I meant it affectionately, not critically, you silly goose.' He put down his drink, moved over to her side of the sofa. Putting his arm around her, he whispered against her cheek, 'So I'm stuck with you for the rest of my life it seems, in view of your opinions about divorce.'

'Yes,' she whispered back, 'we're stuck with each other. Thank God!'

'I second that.' He pulled away slightly, looked down into Emily's innocent young face. How pretty she was, and there *was* an innocence about her and she was very young, and yet she had a depth of wisdom that at times took him by surprise. He said softly, 'I could never be happy with anyone else, Dumpling, not now after I've had you.'

'Why?' She returned his gaze through flirtatious eyes.

'Always fishing, aren't you?'

'Tell me why . . .'

'Because I know you so thoroughly and understand you, my love, and because we're so compatible sexually.'

'Are you really sure we are?' she teased.

'Now that you mention it . . . well, perhaps we ought to give it another try.' He smiled, loving her with his eyes. Standing up, he held out his hand. 'Let's go to bed, darling, and experiment some more, just to make quite certain.' He led her upstairs.

'It's a good thing you put central heating in this house, otherwise we'd be freezing. It's very cold tonight,' Emily said half an hour later, wrapping part of the sheet around herself.

'Oh, I don't know about that, I think we're pretty hot stuff together.' Winston winked, pushing a pillow behind his head and reaching for the glass of brandy he had brought upstairs with him. He offered it to Emily. 'Like a sip?'

'No thanks, I don't want any more. It gives me heart palpitations.'

'Oh damn! And I thought I was the one who caused those.' He grinned, asked, 'Shall I light the fire anyway?'

'Aren't we going to sleep?'

'That wasn't part of my present plan,' he said, leering at her. 'Are you tired already?'

She shook her head, laughing, and her gaze followed him as he leapt out of bed, pulled on his dressing gown and strode to the fireplace directly opposite the old-fashioned four poster. He struck a match, ignited the paper and wood already arranged in the grate, then worked the pair of old bellows to get the blaze properly going. Emily liked watching Winston doing things. He was so clever and competent with his hands, forever repairing things in the house and on the grounds. She thought of the little bridge he had built across the pond at Heron's Nest when they were children. It had been charming, and a master-piece of intricate design and clever engineering. Yes, he had been excellent at carpentry. She still had the small jewellery box he had made for her tenth birthday, so prettily painted and lined inside with red velvet. But he had given up his woodworking for music when he and Shane had formed The Herons.

Smiling to herself, she said suddenly, 'Winston, whatever happened to your trumpet?'

He was in a crouching position in front of the fire and he swung his head, taken aback by this question which had come out of the blue. 'Whatever made you think of my trumpet, for God's sake?'

'I was lying here remembering ... you know, remembering bits of our childhood.'

'Funnily enough, Sally came across it a few weeks ago, when she was poking around in one of the cupboards at Heron's Nest.' He returned to the bed, threw off his robe and climbed in next to her. 'Wasn't I awful in those days? Really fancied myself on the old horn, thought I was the bee's knees.'

'*I* thought you were *wonderful*. Not the trumpet though ... you did stink. Gosh, I bet it was *you* who put the dead fish in *my* bed!' She thumped him on the arm. 'You rotten thing. I'll never forget that fishy smell. Ugh!' He grabbed her, wrestled her back against the pillows, pinned her down with his hands. 'You deserved it, you were a precocious little wretch.' He bent into her, kissed her on the mouth, let his tongue linger on hers. As he drew away finally, he whispered, 'If I'd had any sense I should have put myself in your bed –'

'You'd never have dared, Winston Harte, so don't pretend you would! Grandma had eyes in the back of her head.'

'She still does,' he quipped. He moved away from her, amusement dancing in his eyes. He picked up the brandy balloon, nursed it in both hands, then savoured a mouthful. He felt so good, was enjoying this friendly bit of idle banter with Emily, this relaxed break in their arduous but exciting lovemaking. He always did with her. She was so easy to be with afterwards. There was never any tension between them when their passion was spent, only during their loving. Then her intensity, her endless desire for him inflamed and thrilled him. He reached for her hand lying on top of the sheet, held on to it tightly, thinking of his narrow escape. He knew now that it would never have worked with Allison Ridley. He hadn't loved her, not really, not in the way he loved Emily.

Winston closed his eyes, reliving that special Sunday night in April, when she had driven over to have the supper he was supposedly going to cook. He never did cook it. The moment Emily had arrived they had looked knowingly and longingly into each other's eyes. And they had ended up, a fast ten minutes later, in the middle of this bed, where he had proceeded to surprise himself by making love to her three times in quick succession. His cousin, third cousin he corrected himself, had astonished him with her lack of inhibitions, her willingness to give pleasure and receive it, her unstinting generosity and joyousness in bed. At eleven-thirty, wrapped in bath towels, sitting in front of the living room fire, they had made an al fresco picnic of the odds and ends in his bachelor refrigerator, washing everything down with a bottle of Shane's vintage champagne. It had been the most wonderful evening . . .

Emily said, 'Winston, please don't get cross with me, but there's something I want to tell you. It's really important.'

Dragging himself away from his erotic meanderings about her, he lifted his lids, glanced out of the corner of his eye. 'Why should I get angry. Go on, tell me, Dumps.'

'That's even worse than Dumpling,' she groused, pulling a face, pretending to be annoyed. 'Why is it that the English have this ridiculous predilection for silly nicknames?'

'Because nicknames are pet names, and they express warmth, affection, familiarity, intimacy, caring. Are you going to tell me this *really important thing*, or not, Dumps?'

'Yes, I am.' She pushed herself up and half turned to face him, propping herself on her elbow, staring into his face intently. 'It's about Min's death . . . the inquest.'

'Oh no, Emily, not again!' He groaned and rolled his eyes in an exaggerated fashion. 'You've driven Paula crazy, now you're starting on me.'

'Please listen to me, just for a minute.'

'Okay, but you'd better make it quick. I think I've got myself into quite a state again.'

'Winston, you're insatiable.'

'Only with you, my sweet seductive passionate little thing.'

'I'm not so little,' she countered. 'Listen – Sally told me Anthony is still unconvinced that Min killed herself. He thinks it was an accident, and I –'

'This is a terrible waste of time, darling,' Winston interjected impatiently, wanting her desperately. 'Aunt Daisy and Jim have each given us detailed accounts of the inquest. It couldn't have been an accident from what I understand. No chance.'

'I agree. I mean about it *not* being an accident. However, *I* don't believe it was suicide either.'

Winston laughed disbelievingly. 'Are you trying to tell me you think it was murder? Oh come on, Emily.'

'I'm afraid I *do* think so, Winston.'

'*Then who did it?* Certainly you can't possibly harbour the idea that it was poor old Anthony, who wouldn't say boo to a goose?'

'No. And I don't *know* who. But her death bothers me a lot . . . I can't seem to forget it. You see Winston, it's those five hours. They've always seemed odd to me, and even that Irish policeman called them mysterious, Aunty Daisy told me so. I happen to agree with him, they are, and they're also most peculiar.'

'You've missed your calling, poppet. You should have been a mystery writer,' he retorted, chortling. 'Maybe she just passed out from the booze.'

'Laugh if you want, Winston, but I bet it'll come out one day, you wait and see,' Emily shot back. Her voice was grave.

Winston sat up, paying attention. For as long as he could remember he had always thought Emily was exceptional – bright, smart, clever, and a lot shrewder than some of the family realized. This belief had been considerably reinforced since he had become seriously involved with her. She made sense in so many ways, and he had grown accustomed to listening to her, trusting her judgement. Certainly it was she who had pushed him to go after the Canadian paper mill, insisted he persist when the talks had faltered. Lately, even some of her drive and ambition had washed off on him, and she had convinced him it was his duty to make a bigger contribution to the newspaper chain. So much so, he had actually abandoned the idea of leading the life of a country gentleman.

For all these reasons he had to take her seriously now. Slowly, he said, 'You say you don't know who could have killed her, and that is a tough nut, I admit. On the other hand, you've obviously thought a great deal about Min's death, so you must have some theories about what *might* have happened. Tell me, I'm all ears. Honestly, Dumps, I'm not laughing at you anymore.'

Emily gave him a small gratified smile. 'Nothing will ever convince *me* that Min hung around the lake for all that length of time. I think she left, *went to see someone*, where she proceeded to get horribly drunk. Whoever she was with probably helped her along, might also have given her the pills – you know, Winston, to dull her senses. Then, once she was out cold, unconscious, she was put in the lake to make it look like suicide or an accident.'

'Look, I'm not ridiculing you, honestly I'm not, but this is a bit far fetched. Besides, from all the accounts we've heard, she never left the estate.'

'I know, but that's a presumption. And she *might* have. She could have *walked* somewhere, left her Mini at the lake.'

'Oh Emily, Emily.' He shook his head, looking at her helplessly. 'This doesn't make any sense. Who would want to kill Min? And why? What was the motive? I have lots of questions, and I could shoot lots of holes in your theory. I'm sure Paula did. What did she say?'

'She more or less said the same thing as you . . . then she told me to forget it, that the case was closed, that everyone had come out of it relatively unscathed. She used some terrible cliché like "let sleeping dogs lie", and brushed me off. But what about Anthony and Sally having to live with the knowledge that Min killed herself because of them? And there's another thing, Winston, think of Min. If she was murdered in cold blood, which I think she was, the person who did it should be brought to justice.'

Winston was silent, mulling over her words. He said quietly, 'Oh darling, don't be a crusader. There's nothing you can do really, and Paula's right, the case *is* closed, finished with. You'd only be opening a tin of worms, putting Sally and Anthony through more unpleasantness. I could talk to you for hours about this matter, Dumps, but –' He sighed. 'I just don't have the inclination or the strength at the moment.'

Emily bit her lip. 'I'm sorry. I shouldn't have brought it up tonight.'

'Well, let's face it, darling, you did pick a most inopportune time.' He touched her cheek lightly with one finger traced a line down on to her neck, ran it diagonally across her bare chest to the edge of the sheet tucked around her. 'Emily, in case you didn't realize it, I do have other things on my mind.'

She smiled winningly shoving aside her worry about the inquest. 'I said I was sorry. Let's drop it.'

'Your wish is my command.' He turned, put the brandy glass on the side table, then swivelled his head quickly, 'I'd prefer you not to mention any of this . . . your theory . . . to Sally.'

'Of course I won't. I'm not a dunce.'

'Far from it. Come here. I want you.' He switched off the lamp.

Emily did the same, slithered across the bed, nestled into his arms opened to her, wrapped her legs around his body, fitting herself into him.

He said, 'See what's happened. Your lurid murder theory has rendered me incapable of performing my duty as a devoted fiancé.' He stroked her hair which simmered brightly gold in the firelight blazing up the chimney.

'Not for long, if I know you,' she murmured, pulling his head down to hers, seeking his mouth, kissing him passionately.

Responding to her ardent kisses, he ran his hand over her body, touching her breasts, her stomach, her inner thigh, enjoying the feel of her silky skin. He brought his hand up swiftly, cupped one breast, lowered his mouth, let it linger around the nipple. Her hand went into his hair and he felt her strong fingers on the nape of his neck, heard the faint moan in her throat as the tip of his tongue touched the tip of her hardened nipple.

Emily held herself very still, her breathing strangled as Winston moved down and away from her breast. He began to kiss her stomach, and his hand stroked down her outer thigh again, then her inner thigh, his touch sensuous, thrilling her. He knew exactly how to arouse her. But then he always had. He had acquired more expertise, more finesse, had a better understanding of a woman's body since their childhood days. His hand fluttered between her thighs, then probed, enveloped her fully. In a swift, sudden movement that momentarily startled her he pulled his hand away, dragged himself on top of her. He slipped his hands under her back, lifting her forward as he went into her and took possession of her. His mouth found hers, they locked together, her body arching to his. Emily gripped his shoulder blades, let herself be carried along by his rhythmic movements and the growing momentum of their bodies rising and falling in unison.

Some time later, as they lay exhausted in each other's arms, Emily said with a small smile, 'I wonder who passed around that nasty and most erroneous story about Englishmen being terrible lovers?'

There was a contented sigh from Winston, followed by a deep chuckle. 'Foreigners, who else,' he said.

<h1 style="text-align:center">30</h1>

It was a blustery day.

The leaves swirled around her feet as Paula walked down the path and across the lawn to the wheelbarrow, which she had left there yesterday. The sun came out from behind the bank of leaden clouds that piled the bitter sky with sombre grey, its brilliance shafting through the autumn foliage. Suddenly the trees shimmered in the refulgence of light as they fluttered in the wind and they looked as if they had been draped with shreds of gold and copper.

She stopped in her tracks and lifted her head, her eyes scanning the garden. How beautiful it is, even in November, she thought. Her glance travelled the length of the lawn and this too looked as if it had been spread with a cloth of gold or perhaps an ancient tapestry woven with skeins of russet and copper, burnt ochre and chrome yellow.

Moving forward, she reached for the rake and began to scrape the leaves towards her, making a large heap, working doggedly, glad to be out of the house for a short while. Her mind was numb from worry and fatigue, and she hoped that an hour in the garden would revive her, enable her to shake off the sense of desperation which was slowly turning into a feeling of depression, an unfamiliar state of being for her. She stopped after only a few minutes, leaned the rake against the wheelbarrow and took off her gardening gloves. She tightened her scarf, pulled her wool cap over her ears and turned up the collar of her old tweed coat, feeling the bite of the northern wind. There was a nip of frost in the air, a hint of snow. She slipped on her gloves, started raking again, then stopped to shovel the leaves into the wheelbarrow. About half an hour had passed when she heard the crunch of footsteps behind her on the path. She went on raking, knowing it was Jim.

'Morning, darling,' he called, endeavouring to sound cheerful. 'You're out here bright and early.'

Not wanting to look at him until she had arranged a neutral expression on her face, she continued to rake, said, 'I thought I ought to clear up some of the leaves before I left for London. Anyway the fresh air and the exercise do me good.'

His footsteps finally stopped. 'Yes, I suppose so, but you don't have to kill yourself. Fred can do it tomorrow. That's what he's paid for.'

'It's too much for one gardener.' Paula straightened up, swung around, planted the rake in the ground and leaned her weight on it, her eyes finally meeting his.

His smile was sheepish, embarrassed. 'You're angry with me.'

'No, I'm not, Jim.'

'You should be. I got awfully drunk last night.'

'It doesn't happen often,' she said, then asked herself why she was making excuses for him, giving him a way out. He had been intoxicated a number of times in the last few weeks, but last night his condition and his behaviour at his own dinner party had been inexcusable.

Relief flooded across his face and he stepped closer, eyeing her nervously. He placed his hands on top of hers on the rake. 'Come on, let's really make up,' he said shakily. 'After all, what's one drink too many amongst friends.' When she was silent he leaned forward and kissed her on the cheek. 'I apologize. It won't happen again.'

'It's all right, really it is.' She pushed a smile on to her face. 'It was a pretty ghastly evening anyway. Everyone was acting strangely, and I'm not a bit surprised Winston and Emily left early.'

'Those two have better fish to fry.' He laughed, the nervousness echoing noticeably. 'I say, I hope I didn't insult Winston, or anyone else for that matter.' He seemed concerned, contrite.

'No, you didn't. You were very cordial if very drunk.'

'I'm paying for my bacchanalia this morning, if that's any consolation. I feel lousy.' He hunched into his overcoat, stuck his hands in his pocket, shivering. 'It's bloody cold out here. I don't know how you can stand it.'

She said nothing, examined his face closely. He was pale, a little drawn around the eyes. The wind whipped his hair and as it blew about in the sunshine it was shot through with silvery-gold. He lifted his hand and brushed it away from his forehead, squinting at her in the brilliant light. 'Well, darling, I think I'll push off. Just came out to tell you how sorry I am about last night, give you a hug and a kiss, wish you bon voyage.'

Paula frowned, asked in a surprised tone, 'Where are you going?'

'Yeadon.'

'Surely you're not going flying in this awful wind and with that hangover.'

'The hangover will evaporate once I'm up there –' he said, raising his head to the sky, ' – in the bright blue yonder.' He dropped his eyes to hers, half smiled. 'It's nice of you to worry about me, comforting really, but please don't, I'll be fine. I phoned the airport a little while ago and they told me the weather forecast is good. The wind is supposed to drop in an hour.'

'Jim, please don't go to Yeadon, at least not yet, not until I've left for London. Let's go inside and have a cup of coffee. I'm going to be in New York for two or three weeks and I don't want to leave with things the way they are between us. I must talk to you.'

'*I* must be a bit dense,' he remarked lightly, but his eyes narrowed, turned wary. 'I'm not really following you. What do you want to talk about?'

'About us, Jim. Our marriage, our problems, this awful strain between us.'

'*Strain?*' He looked at her blankly. 'There isn't any that I know of . . . we're both tired, that's all. And *if* we have problems, they're unimportant ones, very normal, actually. We both work hard and we're under a great deal of pressure, and there's been that dreadful fuss in Ireland to plague us. So . . . it's not unnatural that there are tensions at times. But they'll pass, Paula. They generally blow over. I know –'

289

'Why do you always do this?' she cried, her eyes blazing. 'You're like an ostrich, sticking your head in the sand. We have *problems*, Jim, and I for one can't continue like this.'

'Hey, steady on, don't get so excited,' he said, smiling weakly. He sought a way to placate her. He was growing weary of her constant attempts to discuss and dissect their marriage, to delve into areas that were best left alone. He wondered how to forestall this impromptu chat. He wanted to flee immediately, to go flying, to lose himself up there for a while. Only then, as he soared higher and higher above the clouds, did he feel free, at peace and able to escape his mundane worries, his internal strife. Yes, those were the very best moments of his life ... *and* being with his children ... *and* making love to her.

Leaning forward, he took hold of Paula's arm. 'Oh come on, darling, don't let's quarrel like this immediately before you go off on a trip. Everything's fine. I love you. You love me, and that's all that counts. Being away for a while will do you good. You'll come home refreshed, and we'll work out our little differences.' He grinned, looking suddenly boyish. 'They'll probably have worked themselves out before you even return.'

'I don't think so, not unless you start talking to me, discussing our difficulties in an intelligent and mature manner. That's one of the problems – perhaps the worst – this perpetual reluctance on your part to engage in a little verbal give and take.'

'If we have problems, Paula, as you insist, it's because of your tendency to over-react to every situation, to blow small, inconsequential incidents out of proportion. And there's another thing, you're too sensitive by far.'

She gaped at him. 'Oh Jim, don't try to throw the blame on me. Why won't you admit you have trouble communicating with me?'

'Because I don't ... that's something in your imagination. In any event, making love is the best way two people can communicate, and we have no problems in that area, none whatsoever.'

'I think we do,' she whispered so softly he barely heard her.

It was Jim's turn to look astonished. 'How can you say that! We're ideally matched sexually. You know you like it as much as I do.'

Paula winced, recognizing once more that he had no comprehension of what she was as a person, or any idea what she was getting at. 'I have normal desires, Jim, after all I'm a young woman, and I do love you. But sometimes you're –' She stopped, seeking the right expression, knowing she was treading on dangerous and sensitive ground.

'I'm what?' he pressed, leaning into her, fixing her with his light transparent eyes, his interest fully engaged.

'You're a little too ... overenthusiastic, that's the best way to put it, I think. I'm frequently exhausted when I get home from the office and not up to midnight marathons in bed.' She hesitated, meeting his gaze directly, asking herself if she had been wise to embark on such a touchy subject. She now wished she had not responded initially.

He said slowly, 'I've been telling you for months that you're working too hard these days. You're just going to have to slow down. It's not necessary for you to be on this foolish treadmill. My God, you're going to be one of the richest women in the world one day.'

Irritated though she was by this last statement, she said as steadily as she could, 'I work because I enjoy it, and because I have a great sense of responsibility, not only to Grandy because of the legacy she's leaving me, but to our employees.'

'Nevertheless, if you didn't work as obsessively as you do, you wouldn't be so tired all the time.' He blinked, shading his eyes against the sun with his hand. Another thought flickered in the back of his mind. He asked, and with sudden urgency, 'Are you saying that I don't satisfy you in bed?'

She shook her head. 'No, I'm not.' There was a brief hesitation, then, against her better judgement, she added, 'But my needs are a little different from yours, Jim. Women are not made exactly the same way as men physically. Women . . . we . . . *I* need to be led into . . . well, into the final act, and gradually. You see, it's . . .' she did not finish, noticing the change in his expression. He looked as if some basic truth had just dawned on him.

In point of fact, Jim was not certain whether he was annoyed or amused. So that's it, he thought. *Sex.* The root of all evil, or so they say. He gave her a quick glance, his eyes roving over her. 'Paula . . . darling . . . I'm sorry, especially if I've been selfish, thinking only of myself. I didn't realize, really I didn't. Actually, it's your fault in one sense – because of the way you make me feel. Perhaps I'm inclined to get carried away by my own desires and drives. I'll be different in the future, I promise you.' He gave a little laugh, 'I must admit I've never been much of a man for the . . . er . . . er . . . the preliminaries in bed. They've always struck me as being rather unmanly. However, I will try to help you along, be less impatient, wait for you to be –' He cleared his throat. 'I believe *ready for me* is the correct phrase.'

Paula felt the colour flooding her face. His voice had been slightly sarcastic with a patronizing undertone, and she was mortified. *Help me along*, she thought, he makes me sound like a cripple. All I want is a little understanding in every area of our marriage. Unfortunately he had seized on their sex life, sidetracking her, and she regretted rising to the bait. And there was another thing. Why were they standing out here having such a vital and serious talk? In the middle of the garden, for God's sake. Because he would feel pinned down indoors, she answered herself. He doesn't want to talk. If the truth be known he wishes he could wriggle out of it yet again, slide off to go flying or occupy himself with one of his other hobbies. He's only humouring me. Paula shivered, feeling chilled now that the sun had dipped behind the clouds in the darkening sky that presaged rain.

'You're cold,' he observed, swiftly taking her arm. 'Maybe we should go indoors after all.' He smiled a slow and somewhat suggestive smile. 'I have a wonderful idea, darling. Why don't we hop into bed right now. I'll prove to you that I can be the most considerate lover in the world and –'

'Jim, how can you!' she exclaimed, shaking his hand off, drawing away from him, glaring. 'You think sex solves all of our differences!'

'You just implied we have sexual problems. I'd like to show you that that isn't true.'

'I did not imply any such thing. I said I wasn't up to making love endlessly.' She almost added *mindlessly*, but managed to restrain herself.

He said, 'Come on,' and hurried her up the garden path.

She did not protest, allowed herself to be led into the house. He turned to her in the hall, remarked quietly, 'I'll get us two mugs of coffee.'

'Thanks, I'm freezing.' She shrugged out of her coat. 'I'll be in the study.' She knew her voice was clipped, but she couldn't help it. Her exasperation was running high. He said nothing, disappeared in the direction of the kitchen, and she pushed open the door to his private domain. Here a log fire blazed cheerfully in the grate, throwing off tremendous heat in the small room, one of the more cosy areas in Long Meadow.

Seating herself in a wing chair in front of the fire, she tried to relax, but when he came in a moment later carrying the mugs of coffee she noticed at once that his face was cold and closed. Her heart sank.

'All right,' he said briskly, handing her one of the mugs and taking the other wing chair, 'let's talk.'

Although his tone did little to encourage her, she said, 'Jim, I do love you, and I want our marriage to work . . . but very frankly, I don't think that it is. Not at the moment anyway.'

'What's wrong with it?' he demanded.

She saw the bafflement on his face, and wondered if he was genuinely puzzled or faking it. 'There's that lack of communication I've just mentioned,' she began. 'Every time I try to broach something that troubles me, you reject me out of hand, turn away from me, behave as if my thoughts and feelings don't matter.' She gazed at him miserably. 'Yet I know you love me. On the other hand, I feel shut out. It's as if you've built a wall around yourself. I can't seem to reach you anymore. And whenever something flares up between us, your solution is to make love. You think once we've done so all of our difficulties will disappear but they don't, they're still there afterwards.'

He sighed. 'I'm sorry. Unfortunately I wasn't brought up surrounded by a huge family like you were. I was a solitary little boy, with only my grandfather – an old man – for company. Perhaps I do have trouble articulating things to you . . . but I did think I listened to what you have to say. As far as sex is concerned, it's the only way I know *how* to patch things up between us. I thought you enjoyed it as much as I do, but if I'm forcing myself on you then –'

'Jim, no! Stop right there!' she exclaimed. 'You're misunderstanding me. Of course I want a normal sexual relationship with you, you're my husband, and I do desire you. But I can't bear it when you use sex to manipulate me. It's exploitative and unfair.'

He sucked in his breath in amazement. 'You see, there you go *again*! Exaggerating, imagining things. I never *manipulate* you.'

Paula swallowed. She decided to take a different approach, wanting to force him into being honest with her if she could. 'I probably sound as if I'm criticizing you, and I'm not. I'm only pointing out a few things that disturb me a bit. Look – I'm sure I can be annoying at times. So . . . fair's fair. It's your turn, air your views about me. Ventilate your feelings, and let's have an intelligent exchange like two mature adults.'

Jim began to laugh. 'Oh Paula you're so intense, so irate this morning. Quite frankly, I think you're being rather silly, creating a situation where one doesn't exist. As for my views about you, why darling, I can only say that I think you're wonderful and that I love you. If I've any complaints or criticisms . . . well . . . they're very minor ones, of no consequence.'

'They are to me. Tell me what they are, Jim. *Please.*'

With obvious reluctance, he said slowly, 'I do think you tend to be hard on yourself, where your work is concerned. Your hours are crippling and they don't have to be. Just because your grandmother worked like a drudge all of her life doesn't mean that you have to do the same. Also, it seems to me that you're taking on too many unnecessary projects.'

Ignoring the remark about Emma, she said, 'Do you mean the new departments at Harte's, and the fashion exhibition?'

'Yes. After all, Harte's is a thriving success, and it has been for donkey's years. You don't need to –'

'Jim,' she interjected impatiently, 'the secret of retailing *is* constant change and growth. We need innovation and on a continuing basis, and we have to meet the public's buying needs, second-guess new trends, have the vision to know exactly when and how to expand for the future. No business can stand still, particularly a department store chain.'

'If you say so, darling, you know best.' Privately he believed she was absolutely wrong, killing herself with work the way she did, but he did not have the interest, energy or desire to engage in a long discussion about her business. That would be pointless since she always did as she wished. Instead he felt the pressing need to curtail any further carping and probing into their relationship on her part. He was bored to death already, growing more anxious than ever to leave. He glanced at the clock surreptitiously.

Paula noticed, said swiftly, 'This is so important, Jim. We're beginning to make a good start. I think we ought to continue, thrash –'

'And *I* think you have to relax, Paula, learn to curb this compulsion of yours to turn minor problems into stupendous dramas. If you want my opinion, this discussion is really rather stupid. I can't imagine why you thought it was necessary in the first place, and especially *today* when you're leaving for almost a month. We're very happy together, yet you insist on borrowing trouble by trying to convince me we're not.'

'Oh Jim, I only want to save –'

'Hush, darling. Hush,' he said softly, smiling engagingly, taking her hand in his. 'When I look around at our friends and acquaintances I know we have the most marvellous of marriages. We're very lucky, Paula, and I congratulate myself every day, knowing how compatible we are.'

Dismay lodged in her stomach like a heavy stone. Observing the stubbornness settling on his face she acknowledged there was no reason to continue. She was talking to a brick wall.

Jim said, 'You *are* looking thoughtful all of a sudden. And do you know something, you think too much and far too hard.' He laughed lightly, dismissively, taking the sting out of his words. 'Analysing every tiny thing the way you are prone to do isn't very smart. I discovered that years ago. Whenever one puts something under a microscope, seeking flaws, one inevitably finds them. There's nothing wrong with our relationship, Paula. Do try to take it easy, darling.' He bent forward, kissed her on the cheek, then rose purposefully. 'Now that we've had our chat, settled matters, I'll be going, if you don't mind.'

He squeezed her shoulder. 'Drive carefully and phone me tonight before you go to sleep.' He winked. 'That's always when I miss you the most.'

Paula sat staring at him, stupefied, unable to speak. Finally she managed a nod. When he turned away her eyes followed him. There was a void in her heart as she watched him walk across the room.

The study door clicked behind him. She heard the echo of his footsteps crossing the hall, the front door slamming, and a few seconds later the sound of his car as he revved the engine. She sat very still in the chair for a long time after he had left, filled with despair and an overwhelming sense of defeat.

Finally she roused herself from her troubled thoughts, pushed herself up out of the chair and left the room. Slowly, wearily, she climbed the stairs to the nursery and her children. They had always been the joy of her existence. They were her whole existence now.

31

Paula looked from Dale Stevens to Ross Nelson. 'My grandmother would never consider selling her stock in Sitex Oil. Never.'

Ross Nelson smiled, his expression sanguine. '*Never* is a word I've learned to distrust. It has a way of coming back to haunt one, and that's why I hardly ever use it.'

'I understand the point you're trying to make,' Paula said, 'but, nevertheless, I know what my grandmother's feelings are about Sitex, and she wouldn't be interested in your proposal. She promised my grandfather –' Paula cut herself short, shrugged off-handedly. 'However, that's another story, and this conversation is really a waste of time – Dale's, yours and mine.'

Dale Stevens said, 'Maybe you ought to broach it to Emma when she gets back from Australia next month, test the water, see what she has to say. She might like the idea. Times have changed, and let's not lose sight of the fact that she stands to make millions if she sells out.'

'I don't think money comes into play here,' Paula answered.

'Harry Marriott and his cronies on the board are a tough bunch, Paula,' Dale remarked, giving her a pointed look, levelling his alert dark eyes at her. 'They've wanted Emma out for years, resent her influence, and the situation can only worsen, get harder for you in the future. When she's no longer around you'll find yourself –'

'My grandmother's not dead yet,' Paula interjected, meeting his fixed stare with a cool glance. 'And I refuse to speculate about the future and eventualities that are a long way off. I deal with business the only way I know how – on a day to day basis. I'm certainly not going to seek out trouble, and I'd like to remind you that Marriott is a very old man. He won't last for ever, and, therefore, neither will his influence.'

'There's that nephew of his,' Dale pointed out quietly. 'Marriott Watson's a nasty son of a bitch, a troublemaker.'

'Oh don't talk to me about nephews,' Paula began and stopped, biting her inner lip. She turned to Ross, remembering that he was the nephew of Daniel P. Nelson and his heir. She laughed lightly, and apologized, 'Sorry, Ross, I didn't mean to sound disparaging about nephews in general. I wasn't getting at you.'

He laughed with her and there was a hint of humour surfacing in his hazel eyes. 'Don't worry, I don't take offence that easily.' He leaned forward, his face growing serious. 'What Dale is trying to say is that those members of the board who have strained under Emma's yoke are going to be awfully rough with you, for the simple reason that you're a –'

Paula held up her hand. 'You don't have to say it, Ross, I know the reason – I'm a *woman* and a young one at that. I realize they've only listened to my grandmother all these years because they've had no option. She *is* the single largest stockholder, and my grandfather *was* the founder of the company, and obviously certain people have always hated her because of her enormous power, and, of course, because she is a woman.' Paula paused. 'Still, Emma Harte has managed, and managed very well indeed. She has always outsmarted that board, and so will I. I'm not without intelligence and inventiveness – I'll find a way to make them listen, take notice of me.'

Ross and Dale were silent, exchanged knowing glances.

Ross spoke first. 'I wouldn't want you to think I'm bigoted, a male chauvinist pig like some of those idiots on the board of Sitex, but despite the inroads women have been making in business lately, of which I totally approve I might add, I'm afraid we have to face the facts. It's still a man's –'

Paula broke into laughter, instantly cutting him off. 'I know it's still a man's world, you don't have to rub it in. And it always will be until the day women can go into the men's room.'

Ross Nelson's smile was slow, amused. He appreciated her sense of humour as well as her inherent toughness and courage. She was one hell of a woman. His eyes lingered on her appraisingly. He was strongly attracted to her, fascinated by her self-control, her sharp mind, her extraordinary self-confidence. He wanted her for himself. He wondered what approach to take, the best tactics to use, how long it would take him to get her into his bed. He fully intended to do that – and the sooner the better.

He disengaged his eyes from hers, conscious of the prolonged silence. He said, with a strangled laugh, 'Not all deals are made in the men's room, Paula.'

'Most of them are,' she shot back, throwing him that challenging look again. 'Or the equivalent of the men's room,' she added, making a moue with her mouth.

This further inflamed him, and he could only grin, suddenly feeling asinine, like an inexperienced schoolboy. He had the compelling urge to fasten his mouth on hers and he would have done so if Dale had not been present.

Dale coughed behind his hand, said quickly, 'Marriott Watson has been gunning for me for a long time, Paula, because I'm Emma's protégé. Don't think he won't make strong moves against me when I'm no longer under her protection. He can't wait.'

'I'm well aware of that,' Paula replied, her tone as sober as his. 'But right now you do have her protection, and mine, for what it's worth. Also, let's not overlook those board members who are on our side. Together we wield a lot of power. In September you promised me you'd stay on as president until Christmas. Last month you agreed to continue until your contract runs out, in spite of the present harassment from certain quarters within the company. You're not changing your mind, reneging on me, are you?'

'No, honey, no way. I'll be right in there with you, fighting the good fight,' Dale insisted with firmness. 'However, I would like you to mention Ross's idea to Emma when she's back in England.'

'I've every intention of doing so, and she has a right to know. Don't be concerned, she'll get a full report of this meeting.' She swung her head to face Ross. 'She *will* ask me who your client is, Ross. Naturally she'll want to know who's interested in buying her stock. You haven't given me the name yet.' She sat back in the chair, eyeing him speculatively.

Ross Nelson, in full control again, shook his head. 'I can't tell you, Paula. At least not yet. Once you express a genuine interest in selling the Sitex stock I will, of course, do so at once. Until then the name must remain confidential. At the specific request of our client. And I would like to repeat what I said at the outset of this meeting – that the interested party has been a client of the bank for a long time and is highly respected.'

Paula was amused at his insistence on secrecy but she kept her face neutral. 'It's obviously another oil company, and I doubt that it's one of the really huge ones like Getty or Standard. It must be a medium-sized company – a company such as International Petroleum perhaps?' There was a shrewd glint in her knowing violet eyes.

Ross was impressed. His admiration for her went up another notch. She had stabbed in the dark most probably, but hit the bull's eye nonetheless. 'No, it isn't International Petroleum,' he lied smoothly. 'And please don't start a guessing game, because it won't do you any good.' He flashed her one of his deep warm smiles. 'The name cannot be revealed until our client gives permission, and it may interest you to know that not even Dale has an inkling of who it is.'

But you haven't denied it's an oil company, Paula thought. She said, 'Then I suppose I may never know, since my grandmother won't be interested in selling.' Paula crossed her legs, adopting a more relaxed posture, wondering if Ross had told her the truth when he had denied it was International Petroleum. She was not sure, neither was she sure of her feelings about the man himself. Her attitude towards him had always been ambivalent. She had never been able to decide whether she liked him or not. On the surface Ross Nelson was charming, courteous, sure of himself, forever ready to oblige. A handsome man in his late thirties, he was about five feet nine, well built, fair of colouring with an open almost guileless face and the friendliest of smiles that flashed relentlessly to reveal his big white perfect teeth. His appearance was sleek and polished, his clothes impeccable, as were his manners.

And yet all of this was deceptive, or so it seemed to Paula. She could not help thinking that there was something concealed and predatory about him. Quietly observing Ross now, it suddenly struck her that the beautiful clothes and the insouciance he projected were mere facades to camouflage unpleasant characteristics that only came to light behind the closed doors of the bank's board room. As Emma had divined before her, Paula scented a cold and calculating ruthlessness in him, a grim hardness behind the charm, the smiles, and the golden boy image.

Dale and Ross had been chatting about the explosion in the engine room of the *Emeremm III*, and Paula gave the two men her entire attention.

Dale was saying, 'Of course sabotage crossed my mind, Ross, but it's been ruled out. There was that recent inquiry and nothing untoward was discovered. Nothing at all. Anyway, who would do such a thing?' He shook his head rapidly, frowned. 'No, no, it was definitely an accident, even though we haven't been able to discover exactly what caused the explosion.'

Paula thought: the disaster to the *Emeremm III* was a harbinger of bad luck, but she said, 'So it remains a mystery it seems, and a terrible stain on our safety record.'

''Fraid so, honey.' Dale's grin was rueful and his brown eyes crinkled at the corners in his leathery, weatherbeaten face. 'Hate to keep repeating myself, but the oil game is a high risk business in more ways than one. However, the *Emeremm III* is a sturdy vessel and I just heard this morning that she's seaworthy again and back in the fleet.'

'Well, that's a bit of good news!' Paula exclaimed, looking pleased, giving Dale a warm smile. The president of Sitex was a man she liked and trusted and whom she never had any qualms about. He was smart, tough, exceedingly ambitious for himself, but he was honest, and exactly what he seemed, not given to dissembling or craftiness. Studying him surreptitiously, she thought that even his clothes reflected the man himself, were good but conservative, lacked the expensive elegance of the other man's. She asked herself then what this wily, hard-grinding, fifty-three-year-old Texan who had risen the hard way could possibly have in common with the smooth Eastern Seaboard banker sitting next to him. The latter reeked of the old guard, pots and pots of inherited money and a privileged heritage. Yet close friends they were. Ross Nelson had introduced Dale Stevens to Emma two years ago, and it was through the investment banker that Dale was now president of the oil company.

Watching *her* watching *him*, Dale suddenly said, 'I hope you don't think I lack confidence in you, because that's not true, honey.'

'But I am an unknown quantity, right?' she retorted swiftly, and continued in the same mild voice, 'I understand your motives, Dale, and I can't say I blame you. You're looking to the future, and you've decided that things will operate much more smoothly at Sitex if our big block of preferred stock is controlled by someone else, someone whom you believe *might* be better equipped to handle the disruptive faction on the Sitex board.'

Continuing to scrutinize her closely, forever conscious of her astuteness and perception, and never one to underestimate this clever young woman, Dale decided to be truthful. 'Yes,' he said, giving her a direct and open look, 'that's part of my reasoning, I admit that. But it's not all of it. In one sense I'm also thinking of you, your heavy burdens. It seems to me that you have your hands full with the Harte chain and your considerable business interests in England and Australia. And of course, you *are* based in England, honey.'

Paula said pithily, 'Telephones work, telex machines transmit, planes fly.'

'But Sitex is still an additional pressure for you,' he said, paying no attention to her sarcastic tone. 'And do you really need it?' Dale shook his head, as if making up her mind for her. 'I don't think you do, and if it were me, why I'd persuade Emma to sell out and make a huge profit. You could reinvest the millions you make from the stock in something else – something that's less of a headache.'

She said nothing.

'I concur with Dale,' Ross stated, his tone flat. He cleared his throat. 'Obviously I've long been aware of the difficulties at Sitex, not only through Dale, but because of Emma's confidences over the last few years. And so, when the bank's client professed an interest in buying up Sitex stock, I immediately thought of Emma's vast holdings in the company. I spoke to Dale and he agreed we should raise the matter with you immediately. The bank's client has already invested in Sitex's common stock. And with your forty-two per cent –' He stopped, offered her one of his perpetual all-embracing smiles. 'Why, Paula, that would give our client real clout.'

'*Anybody* who owns that forty-two per cent has *clout*,' Paula said crisply. 'Whether it's us or your client is quite beside the point. You know as well as I do that it's the actual stock, not the owner of it, that counts. And anyway, your client's common stock doesn't come into play since it's not voting stock and has no power attached to it. Obviously this client of yours – whether an individual or a company – needs my grandmother's stock to give him, or them, a voice in the running of the company. *Control* is what they're after. I understand everything perfectly.'

Neither man responded, both acknowledging to themselves that there was no point in making denials and in so doing looking foolish.

Paula stood up, and adopting her most gracious manner, went on, 'I'm afraid I have to bring our informal little get-together to a close, gentlemen. I think we've covered as much ground as we can today. I will talk to my grandmother in December, and I'm sure you'll be hearing from her personally. And it really is up to her – her decision.' Paula laughed softly, murmured, 'And who knows, she might surprise even me and decide to sell after all.'

Dale and Ross had risen when she had, and as Paula walked them to the door, Dale said, 'I'm flying back to Odessa tonight, but just give me a holler if you need me, or need anything at all. In any event I'll be calling you next week to touch base.'

'Thanks, Dale, I appreciate that,' Paula said, taking his outstretched hand.

'Are you sure you won't join us for lunch?' Ross asked.

'Thank you again, but I can't. I have a date with the fashion director of Harte's USA, and since we're going to be planning the French Designer Week promotion over lunch it's not possible for me to cancel.'

'Our loss,' he said, sounding disappointed, keeping his eyes focused on her, still clasping her hand tightly in his. 'Unlike Dale, *I'm* not flying off anywhere, Paula. I'm staying right here in little old Manhattan. Let me know if *I* can help you with anything – anything whatsoever. And I hope I can take you to dinner one evening this week.'

Extracting her hand, Paula said, 'How kind of you, Ross. I'm afraid I'm rather busy this week. Every night actually.' This was untrue but she had no desire to see him socially.

'Not next week I sincerely hope!' He leaned into her, squeezed her arm. 'I'll call you on Monday and I won't take no for an answer,' he warned with a hearty laugh.

Once they had left, Paula walked slowly across the room to the desk, a great slab of glass supported by a simple base of polished steel. It was the dramatic focal point in Emma's highly dramatic office at Harte Enterprises, where Paula always based herself when she was in New York. The room was furnished with modern pieces and washed throughout with a melange of misty greys and blues. The soft muted colours were enlivened by some of Emma's priceless French Impressionist paintings, while sculpture by Henry Moore and Brancusi, and rare temple heads from Angkor Wat, were displayed on black marble pedestals around the room. All made a strong definitive statement, and evidenced Emma's great love of art.

Seating herself at the desk, Paula placed her elbows on it, cupped her face in her hands, thinking about the meeting she had just finished. At the back of her mind a germ of an idea flickered, began to take shape, and as it did a slow smile spread across her face. Quite unwittingly Ross Nelson and Dale Stevens had shown her a way to resolve some of her problems at Sitex, if not, in fact, all of them. But not now, she thought. Later, when I really need to make everyone keep in step to the beat of *my* drum.

As she straightened up she laughed out loud. It was not a very nice idea, indeed it was rather diabolical – Machiavellian – but it would be effective, and it bore Emma Harte's inimitable stamp. Still laughing quietly, she thought: I must be growing more like Grandy every day. The possibility that this was true pleased her. In a sense it helped to alleviate some of the depression and frustration she had been experiencing since her abortive attempt to talk to Jim before she had left England.

If her marriage was in a shambles, her personal life grounded in aridity, then she was going to make certain she had a fruitful career, her own successes in business to compensate for her other losses. Work had been Emma's strong citadel when *her* private life had been wrecked, and so it would become Paula's, sustaining her at all times. With her business to occupy her thoughts, and her abiding love for her children to give her emotional nourishment, she would survive, and survive well, perhaps even with style as her grandmother had done. Her thoughts jumped to Jim, but they were neither rancorous nor condemning. She felt only a terrible sadness for him. He did not know what he had lost, and that was the pity, the tragedy of it all.

Shane O'Neill was in a quandary this afternoon.

He strode up Park Avenue at a rapid pace dodging in and out between the other pedestrians, his thoughts twisting and turning at a similar accelerated rate. He was unable to make up his mind about Paula. Should he phone her or not? The knowledge that she was in New York, sitting only a few blocks away from him at this very moment, had so unnerved him he couldn't imagine what being in her presence would do to him. And if he did call her he would have no alternative but to see her, invite her out, take her to lunch or dinner, at the very least have drinks with her.

Earlier that day, when he had been talking to their London office, he had been taken aback when his father had mentioned in passing that Paula had flown to New York yesterday. 'Merry and I had supper with her in London on Sunday night,' his father had gone on to explain before reverting to their discussion about current business matters. And before they had hung up, his father had exclaimed, 'Oh Shane, just a minute, here comes Merry now. She wants to say hello to you.'

But Merry had given him more than a greeting. She had issued instructions. 'Please ring Paula,' Merry had urged. 'I gave her your numbers the other night, but I know she won't call you. She'd be too intimidated.' When he asked her for clarification, his sister had told him that Paula had long been acutely conscious of his aloofness, as she had herself. 'She'll be scared of being rebuffed,' Merry had pointed out. 'So it's really up to you. Be nice, Shane, she's such an old friend. And she doesn't look very well.' This last statement had been announced in a grave and worried voice, and Merry had rushed on, 'She seems weighted down, troubled, morose even, and that's not the Paula *we* know. Please take her out, give her a good time. Have some fun together, Shane, make her laugh again, like you used to do when we were all children.' His sister's comments had alarmed him; he had pressed for more information about Paula's state of mind and health. Merry had not really been able to enlighten him any further, and before they had said goodbye he had faithfully promised his sister he would get in touch with Paula.

But he was wavering again. Whilst he longed to see her, he knew that by succumbing to his yearning he would only be inflicting punishment on himself. She was another man's wife. Lost to him forever. To spend time with her would open up all the old wounds . . . wounds which had not exactly healed but *had* scabbed over at least, and were therefore much less painful. It will be unsettling, he thought, reflecting on the life he had built for himself in New York over the past eight months. It was not an exciting life; rather it was dull and uneventful, with no great highs but no debilitating lows either. He was neither happy nor sad, in limbo in a sense, but he did have peace and quiet. There were no women around any more. Two sorties in that direction had foundered miserably and rendered him helpless, despairing. And he had decided, yet again, that celibacy was infinitely preferable to disastrous scenes in the bedroom which ended in embarrassment, left him shaken and filled with mortification at his own inadequacies. And so he scrupulously avoided all female entanglements, and spent most of his time working. More often than not he remained at the new offices of O'Neill Hotels International until eight or nine at night, and then went home to a dreary supper in front of the television set. From time to time he made a date with Ross Nelson or with one of the other two men he had become friendly with; occasionally he took Skye Smith to a movie or the theatre and then on to dinner afterwards. But for the most part he led a solitary existence, with books and music as his sole companions. He was not happy, but there was no pain to deal with. He was dead inside.

As all of this ran through his head Shane had a sudden change of heart. He really ought to see Paula, if only for appearances' sake. Should any of his other childhood friends happen to visit the city, he would wine and dine them automatically. To avoid Paula would look peculiar, pointed actually, especially to Emma and his grandfather, who would undoubtedly ask him about her when they passed through New York next month. Besides that, Merry had said Paula was not looking well. Yes, he had better invite her to dinner, just to satisfy himself she was really all right. But she's not your responsibility, he cautioned himself, thinking of Jim Fairley. *Her husband.* Unexpectedly, a savage feeling of jealousy seized him, and he had to make a strenuous effort to fling this emotion off as he crossed Fifty-Ninth Street and continued on up Park, making for the mid-sixties.

In a few minutes he would be arriving at the site of their new hotel. The construction company had almost finished rebuilding the old-fashioned interiors and momentarily he would be surrounded by the crews, the foremen, the architects and the interior designers. All would be demanding his attention. I must make a decision about Paula. *Now.* No more procrastinating. Oh, to hell with Jim Fairley! She's my oldest and dearest friend. I grew up with her. Of course I'm going to see her. No, you can't. It will be too hurtful. Once again Shane reversed himself.

And he was paralysed into inaction by the knowledge that he was vulnerable to her. If he so much as set eyes on the only woman he loved he would be exposing himself to pain and suffering from which he might never fully recover.

Skye Smith looked at Ross Nelson nervously, and her voice quavered slightly as she said, 'But your divorce has been final for weeks now. I don't understand. I always thought we were going to get married.'

'I'm afraid that has been wishful thinking on your part, Skye,' Ross said, endeavouring to keep his voice level, to be courteous if nothing else.

'But what about Jennifer?'

'What about her?'

'*She's your child, Ross!*'

For a moment he said nothing. He had been furious when he had arrived home from Wall Street ten minutes earlier to find Skye Smith, his former mistress, sitting in his living room so coolly composed and obviously determined to fight with him yet again. He was growing exasperated with her and the constant pressuring. The moment she left he was going to fire his housekeeper for being stupid enough to allow her into the apartment.

Skye sat twisting her hands together, her face white, her eyes filled with mute appeal.

Ross Nelson stared at her, his implacability increasing as he noted her agitation. Her apparent distress did nothing to engender sympathy or compassion in him. It only served to annoy him further. 'You say she's my child. But is she really?' he asked cruelly. 'I've never been too sure . . . about her paternity.'

Skye gasped, drew back on the sofa. 'How can you say that! You know you're her father. She's the spitting image of you, Ross, and there's the blood test. And anyway you kept me virtually under lock and key for four years. I never so much as looked at another man.'

He smiled ironically. 'But you're looking at one these days, and very lovingly so, aren't you, Skye? Shane O'Neill to be precise. And since you're sleeping with him I suggest you use your considerable sexual wiles to ensnare him. You'd better lead *him* by the nose to the altar, and as quickly as possible.'

'I'm not sleeping with him,' she protested fiercely, her apathy dropping away, her eyes flashing angrily with sudden life.

'Do you really expect me to believe *that*,' he exclaimed with a cynical laugh. 'I know everything there is to know about you, Skye, and then some.' His eyes hardened as they swept over her and his mouth lifted at the corner in a scornful smile. 'You can't resist tall husky handsome studs, they've always been your terrible weakness, my dear. As we both know only too well. You'd be wise to marry one of them while you still have your beautiful blonde looks and that extraordinarily athletic sexual ability. Shane's definitely the most likely prospect. He's getting it from you in bed, so why don't you get him to make it legal, while the romance is still in that first euphoric flush. He's your type, no two ways about it. He's also a rich man, and he's certainly available.'

'Ross, I'm telling you the truth. I'm not having an affair with Shane O'Neill,' she insisted.

Ross laughed in her face, reached for the silver cigarette box on the antique Chinese coffee table, slowly put a flame to the cigarette he held between his fingers.

Skye's eyes rested on him. She wondered why she had ever let herself become embroiled with him, and so foolishly, years ago, asked herself why it was her misfortune to love this man in the way in which she did. The trouble was he knew exactly how she felt, and that was why he had lately begun to cool towards her. Ross only wanted the things in life which he could not possess, and especially women who showed no interest in him whatsoever. He's perverse, she thought, but oh God how I love him. She knew she had to make him believe her about Shane for the child's sake as well as her own. Suddenly realizing that the only way to convince him was to be open and explicit, she said quietly. 'All right, I admit it. I did go to bed with Shane. *Once*. It was when I discovered you'd taken Denise Hodgson to South America with you, when I found out about your affair with her. Retaliation, I suppose. But it didn't work between us. We never made love. And we've never been near each other since, not in that way, Ross. We're friends, that's all. Chums.'

'*Chums*,' Ross spluttered, shaking his head. 'Come on, Skye, it's me you're talking to, remember. I haven't known you for five years not to understand exactly how you can make a man feel, especially in the beginning, when he's not yet slept with you.' He laughed derisively. 'Didn't work between you, eh?' he muttered, his expression one of total disbelief.

Skye swallowed, knowing she had to continue talking, give him a full explanation if she was to make any headway, ingratiate herself with him again, somehow win him back. 'Yes, that's correct, I promise you, Ross. Shane and I are simply good friends.' She swallowed again. 'He couldn't . . . well, the night we went to bed . . . he wasn't able to . . . you know, do anything.'

Ross slapped his knee, raucous laughter rippling through him. 'Do you expect me to believe Shane O'Neill couldn't get it up with you? Oh no, Skye, I'll never accept that one from you.'

'But it's the truth,' she whispered, remembering so clearly that miserable night, Shane's dreadful embarrassment, her own confusion. 'It's the God's truth.' She leaned across the coffee table, finished in a much stronger tone, 'I swear it on Jennifer's head, on my child – on our child.'

His laughter ceased and his eyes narrowed, observed her thoughtfully. Instantly he knew she was not lying, not when she brought the child into it. He said, 'So . . . Shane's got a little problem has he?'

She nodded. 'With me at least.' She hesitated. 'I have a feeling he's in love with someone.'

'I wonder who that could be, who the woman in question is? Do you know?'

'That's a silly thing to ask. How could I possibly know. He hasn't confided anything. Don't you see, Ross, that's why he's not available as a husband for me.'

'Neither am I.'

'Why?'

'I have no desire to get married again,' he said almost chattily, 'not with my track record. I've had enough of grasping wives and the divorce court. Besides I'm paying too much alimony as it is. Hundreds of thousands of dollars a year. But if I *were* ever demented enough to take that suicidal plunge I can assure you my bride would have to be a rich one.'

'Oh come off it! Money doesn't interest you, Ross,' she scoffed. 'You couldn't spend your millions if you lived to be a hundred.'

He said nothing.

Skye said slowly, her face growing soft, almost tender, 'We've had so much together. We have a child, and I love you very much.'

'You don't seem to understand – I don't love you.'

She flinched, but kept her hurt to herself. He had a penchant for being cruel, and his moods changed like the wind. In five minutes he might easily do a turn about and sweep her off to bed. That had happened so many times before. A thought came to her, and she stood up, went and sat down next to him on the other sofa, laid her hand on his knee. She drew closer, whispered, 'You don't really mean that, Ross darling, you know it's not true. You do love me. There's a special kind of magic between us, and there always has been.' She smiled into his cold face, her eyes enticing. 'Let's go to bed. I'll show you just how strong the bonds are between us.'

He lifted her hand from his knee and placed it in her lap. 'I didn't think you were a masochist, that you'd want a repetition of your misadventure with Shane O'Neill. It must be very humiliating for a woman like you to realize that her sexual expertise has lost its power.'

She pulled away from him, gaping, and her eyes filled with tears.

Wanting to be rid of her, he went in for the kill, said in the quietest but hardest of voices, 'You see, Skye, you don't turn me on any more.'

Rising, she blundered across the room to the window, flicking the tears off her cheeks, trying to stem their flow, her shoulders heaving. She knew she had lost him. Her life was in shreds.

Ross also rose and crossed to the small Regency writing table. He opened the drawer, took out his chequebook, picked up the pen and wrote. As he ripped the cheque out of the book she turned around, stood staring at him, puzzlement replacing the anguish on her strained face.

'What are you doing?' she asked, beginning to tremble.

'This is for you, for the child,' he said, pushing himself up out of the chair, walking to her. 'I will make arrangements with my accountants for you to receive the same amount every month. It should be more than enough.' He stopped in front of her, held out the cheque.

Skye shook her head wildly. 'I don't want it, Ross. *I* can support *our* child. I'm not interested in your money, and I never have been. It's only you I want. As a husband, as a father for Jennifer.'

'That's too high a price for me.' He tried to force the cheque into her hands but she refused to take it, balling her fists, backing away from him.

He shrugged, turned, walked back to the sofas in front of the fireplace. He opened her handbag, slipped the cheque inside, then carried her bag to her, put it in her hands. 'I think it's time for you to leave, Skye. I'm expecting guests. It's over between us. There's nothing more to say.'

Lifting her head, she gathered some of her shattered pride around her, and she was surprisingly cool and steady as she said, 'Oh yes, there *is* something more to say, Ross, and it's this . . .' She paused, looked deeply into his face. 'Things are *not* over between us and they never will be, whether we see each other again or not. And one day you're going to need me. I don't know for what reason, or why, but need me you will.' She opened her bag, took out the cheque and tore it in half without looking at it. She let it flutter to the floor. And then she pivoted and walked away from him without a backward glance, her pace measured and controlled.

Ross picked up the torn cheque and pocketed it, his face expressionless. He would write another one tomorrow and mail it to her. He ambled over to the window and parted the curtain, looked down on to Park Avenue. In a few minutes she would leave the building and cross the street as she always did, heading in the direction of Lexington. He sighed. It was a pity about the child. His face softened a fraction. There was no way he could have his three-year-old daughter without the mother, and the mother he neither wanted nor needed. She was far too troublesome in far too many ways. He felt a sudden twinge about Shane and the manner in which he had manoeuvred him, had tried to throw Skye into his arms. Funny coincidence, he thought, the way Skye and Shane were introduced in Yorkshire and then a week later he phoned me at the bank with an introduction from Emma Harte. The minute he had met Shane he had thought of Skye, realizing he might have found a solution to his problems with her. He had manipulated Skye, had augmented the beginning of the affair, if one could call it that. Oh well, they say all's fair in love and war. Skye's unexpected revelation about Shane's impotency *had* surprised him though. Shocked him. Shane O'Neill of all people. Poor son of a bitch, Ross muttered, wondering for the second time what woman had so got her hooks into O'Neill he couldn't perform with anyone else.

Ross pressed his face to the glass, saw Skye hurrying across Park, lingering on the centre island, waiting for the lights to change. She was wearing the mink coat he had given her. He supposed he had loved her once. Now she bored him. He let the curtain drop, and she was instantly dismissed as he turned his mind to his present plans.

Moving towards the fireplace, Ross Nelson stood for a few minutes with his hand on the mantelshelf, staring into space, lost in his reverie, pondering Paula

Fairley. He had known her for years, paid little attention to her in the past. But this morning, in her office, he had been intrigued by her. He had to have her. He was going to have her. Nobody, nothing, would stop him. Now there is a powder keg of suppressed sexuality, he decided. He had spotted that at once. It was apparent in the way she held her body, from the hunger he had detected in those unusual violet-tinted eyes, so long-lashed and seductive. He would put the match to the powder keg, explode it, then lie back and let the flames of her sexuality consume them both. He began to realize that just thinking about her excited him inordinately, in a way he had not been excited for some time, jaded as he had become. He itched to get his hands on that slender body, so willowy and graceful, yet curiously boyish except for the beautiful breasts. He closed his eyes, holding his breath, recalling how taut and firm they had looked under the white silk shirt she had been wearing. He lusted for her right now, this very minute. Her image was suddenly so vividly alive in his mind he snapped his eyes open swiftly, lowered himself on to the sofa, knowing he must dispel the tantalizing picture of them in bed together. He would have a miserable evening if he did not do so immediately.

But Ross Nelson discovered she was difficult to forget, so potent was her sexual appeal to him. And then of course there was her money. He began to contemplate her great fortune, Emma's fortune, which she would inherit one day. To his astonishment the idea of matrimony was suddenly most appealing after all. There was a husband in the background somewhere, wasn't there? He would soon dispense with Fairley. Once he had bedded Paula she would be his completely. They always were, particularly those who came inexperienced and breathless with anticipation into his arms. He felt the old familiar ache in his groin. To take his mind off sex he endeavoured to concentrate on Paula Fairley's huge fortune. The ache only intensified. He crossed his legs, growing uncomfortably hot. He began to laugh at himself. How fortunate it was that he had not indulged himself in his erotic imaginings about Paula earlier. Otherwise he would have been forced to take Skye to bed – for one last time.

He glanced at the phone on the writing desk, wondering why it had not yet rung. He had been expecting to hear from Paula the moment he had arrived home.

32

'Where on earth did those ghastly vermilion roses come from, Ann?' Paula asked, staring through the open door of the drawing room and then turning to look at her grandmother's American housekeeper.

Ann Donovan, standing next to Paula in the large entrance foyer of Emma's Fifth Avenue apartment, shook her head. 'I don't know, Miss Paula. I left the card on the console, next to the vase.'

She followed Paula into the room, continuing, 'I wasn't sure where to put them, to be honest, the bouquet is so huge. I even wondered if I ought to leave them out here. In all the years I've worked for Mrs Harte we've never had roses in the apartment. Don't you like them either?'

'They don't really bother me, Ann, at least not in the way they disturb my grandmother. I'm just not accustomed to seeing roses around, that's all. I never plant them, or buy them for that matter.' She wrinkled her nose, indicating her distaste, remarked off-handedly, 'And that colour, it's such a violent red, and the whole arrangement is overwhelming. Very pretentious.'

She reached for the envelope, ripped it open, looked at the card. It had been signed by Ross Nelson. His writing was small, neat, cramped almost, and he was inviting her to his country house for the weekend. What a cheek he's got, Paula thought. And what makes him think I'd want to spend the weekend with him. I hope *he's* not going to become a pest. She tore up the card, dropped it into a nearby ashtray, said to the housekeeper, 'I really can't stand the roses, Ann, would you mind taking them out to the back, please?'

'No, of course not, Miss Paula.' Ann picked up the offending vase and headed out of the drawing room, saying over her shoulder, 'You received some other flowers – not very long ago. I popped them in the den.'

'*Oh*. Well, I suppose I'd better go and look at them,' Paula murmured, walking out after the housekeeper who was already hurrying across the foyer in the direction of her own rooms.

Paula's face lit up the minute she saw the lovely little basket of African violets in the centre of the mahogany coffee table near the fireplace. She bent over them, touched the glossy dark green leaves, then the velvet-textured petals of the deep purple flowers. How delicate, how tender they are, she thought and picked up the envelope. It was blank and she wondered who the violets were from as she opened it. She stiffened in surprise. The name *Shane* was scrawled across the front of the card in his familiar bold handwriting. There was no message, simply his first name.

Still holding the card, Paula sat down on the nearest chair, frowning to herself, not quite certain what to make of the flowers. For the first time in almost two years he had done something sweet and thoughtful, the kind of thing he used to do in the past. And she was at a loss, not sure how to deal with it. She pondered. Was the basket of violets a signal that he wanted to be friends with her again? Or merely a polite gesture, one made out of a sense of family obligation and duty? Certainly sending her flowers was a way of saying welcome to New York without him actually having to speak to her.

Paula glanced into the fire, her expression abstracted. She was positive that Merry would have told him she was in the city, after all they were brother and sister and business colleagues, and they chatted back and forth across the Atlantic on a weekly, sometimes daily, basis. Perhaps her friend had put pressure on Shane to make an effort, to be nice to her. His aloofness and remoteness still perplexed Paula. How many times had she asked herself what she had done to hurt or upset him, and how many times had the answer been a negative one. She had done nothing wrong. Yet he continued to hold himself apart, barely acknowledging her existence. And when he did do so, she knew it was because he had no alternative, considering the long and intimate involvement of their two families.

Pulling her eyes away from the fire, Paula stared at the card again and for the longest time. The simple signature without one other word was not very encouraging. In a way it was intimidating. If only he had suggested that she phone him, or hinted that they might get together before she returned to England.

Damn, she muttered under her breath, and suddenly stood up abruptly, unexpectedly filled with anger with him. Shane O'Neill had been her dearest friend for as long as she could remember, since she could first walk and talk. They had grown up together ... shared so much ... become so very close over those formative and meaningful years ... their lives had been so deeply intertwined. And then he had dropped her, turned away from her, and without any kind of proper explanation. It was not logical.

I've had enough of this. I'm sick and tired of people behaving as if *my* feelings don't matter, she thought, still bridling with anger. She rushed out of the den to find her briefcase. It was on a bench in the foyer where she had left it when she had walked in from the office. Grabbing it, she sped back to the den and sat down at the desk. Snapping open the locks, she pulled out her address book, turned to Shane's New York numbers, then sat back in the chair, eyeing the phone.

I'm going to have it out with him once and for all, she decided, whether it's tonight, next week, or the very day I leave. I don't care when it is, as long as I pin him down finally. I want to know why he ended our long friendship so cruelly. *I'm entitled to an explanation.* She reached for the receiver, then let her hand fall away, realizing it would be prudent to calm herself first. Yes, it *would* be most unwise to confront him now. She had not seen Shane since April. He had just sent her flowers. Therefore it would appear odd, even irrational, if she tackled him about their relationship out of the blue. Also, she abhorred telephone confrontations, preferred to look people right in the eye when she was thrashing out something of crucial importance, needing to observe their reactions. I ought to have insisted on a frank talk long ago, she added under her breath. I've been spineless. It suddenly occurred to her that she was not so much angry with Shane as she was with herself. She should never have permitted the breach to continue as she had. Her annoyance began to dissipate.

Sitting up straighter, she lifted the receiver, then hesitated. How would she begin the conversation? You are befuddled, really jet-lagged tonight, she told herself with a rueful smile. Obviously you'll thank him for the flowers. What else? It's the perfect opening gambit. She dialled his apartment. The phone rang and rang. There was no reply. Disappointed, she replaced the receiver. Then something his father had said to her on Sunday night flashed through her mind. Uncle Bryan had made a remark about Shane being as addicted to work as she was these days. Paula looked at her watch. It was a few minutes before seven. Could he still be at the office? Miranda had given her two numbers for O'Neill Hotels International, and one of them was Shane's private line.

Once again she dialled.

The phone was picked up on the second ring. 'Hello,' a very masculine voice said.

'Shane?'

There was a pause before he answered. 'Hello, Paula,' he finally said.

'Why Shane, how clever of you to recognize my voice and at once,' she exclaimed with assumed flippancy. 'I'm so glad I caught you. I just got back here and found your violets. They're lovely, so springlike, and it was such a dear thought. Thank you.'

'I'm glad you like them,' he said.

His neutral, unenthusiastic tone was so off-putting it chilled her, but nevertheless, she hurried on, 'It's been ages since we've seen each other, at least eight months, and now here we both are, far away from Yorkshire, a couple of Tykes in New York City. The least we can do is get together –' She stopped, then taking a deep breath said, very rapidly, '– for dinner.'

There was an even longer pause at his end of the phone. 'I ... er ... well ... I'm not sure when I could do that actually. When were you thinking of, Paula? Which night?'

'Tonight seems as good a time as any,' she said determinedly. 'If you're not already busy, that is.'

'I am a bit, I'm afraid. I'd planned to work late. I have an awful lot of paperwork to catch up with this week.'

'You've got to eat sometime,' she pointed out in her most persuasive voice. She laughed gaily. 'Remember what Grandy was forever saying to Mrs Bonnyface at Heron's Nest. All work and no play, etcetera. And you never used to argue with that sentiment.'

He was silent.

Softly she said, 'I'm so sorry, I shouldn't be pushing you like this. I know what it's like to be overburdened by work. Perhaps another night. I'm going to be here for about three weeks. I'll leave it up to you, call me if you have a free evening. Thanks again for the flowers, Shane. 'Bye.' She hung up immediately, not giving him an opportunity to respond.

Pushing herself out of the chair, Paula walked over to the coffee table, picked up the card and threw it into the fire, watched it burn. He had been cold, unbending, only marginally civil.

Why? Why? Why?

What ever had she done to Shane O'Neill to make him behave in such an unfriendly and unkind manner? She ran her hand through her hair distractedly, then shrugged as she returned to the desk. I am a stupid fool, she thought. He's probably heavily involved with Skye Smith and can't be bothered to entertain a childhood friend, especially one he no longer cares about. He might even be living with her. Merry and Winston think their relationship is platonic, but how can they really know. They're always saying he's close mouthed. Funny, though, he never was with me, nor I with him, for that matter. We never had secrets, we told each other everything.

The phone shrilled. She glanced at it, picked it up. Before she said hello he spoke.

'I couldn't make it for at least an hour, maybe a bit longer,' Shane said hurriedly, sounding breathless. 'I'll have to go back to my flat to change, and it's turned seven already.'

'You know you don't have to bother doing that for me, of all people, for heaven's sake,' she exclaimed softly, surprised but gratified that he had rung back. 'After all, we're family.' She laughed under her breath. He was vain about his appearance, but she didn't mind. She rather liked that trait in him. 'Anyway,' she went on, 'you can freshen up here if you want, and listen, we don't have to go to a fancy restaurant, a simple place will do nicely.'

'All right. I'll be there around seven thirty,' he said. 'See you then.' He hung up as swiftly as she had done a few minutes before.

Paula sat back, staring at the phone. She felt curiously light headed and wondered why.

Shane O'Neill sighed heavily, crushed out the cigarette he had lit before calling Paula.

Reaching for the phone again, he dialled a small French bistro he liked, made a reservation for nine o'clock and then stood up. Hurriedly rolling down his sleeves, he fastened the buttons on the cuffs, knotted his tie which he had loosened earlier, then walked over to the closet to get his jacket and overcoat.

You're a bloody fool, he chastised himself, allowing her to get to you in the way she did. You threw your resolve not to see her out of the window and all because she sounded so wistful when she said goodbye. And disappointed. And lonely. Desperately lonely. He had lived in that solitary and isolated state far too long not to detect it in her immediately. Besides, he knew and understood Paula much better than anyone else did, and he had always been able to accurately gauge her moods. Even when she was putting up a front. Like her grandmother she was adroit at doing that, and exceptionally deceptive. She could don that inscrutable expression at will, affect a gaiety when she spoke that did nothing to betray her real feelings. Except to him, of course. She had adopted a fraudulent lightness with him a few moments ago, he was well aware. Her laughter and flippancy had been forced. So his sister *had* been right. Paula was troubled, disturbed. But about what exactly? Business? Her marriage? Well, he wasn't going to contemplate *that* relationship.

Slipping into his sports jacket, he pulled his overcoat off the hanger and left the offices, locking the door behind him. Several seconds later, stepping out of the building on to Park Avenue, he was relieved to see that the traffic had eased. He spotted a cab, hailed it, jumped in and gave the address on Fifth Avenue. Settling back, he fished around in his pocket for cigarettes and his lighter.

As he smoked, a sardonic smile struck his wide Celtic mouth. You're putting a noose around your neck, O'Neill, he warned himself. But then you knew that when you sent her the flowers. You expected her to call you when she received them, be honest, you did. You simply lobbed the ball over into her court. Yes, this was the truth – and yet only partially so.

That afternoon, on his way back to the office from the hotel site, he had noticed the violets as he had passed the flower shop, instantly thinking of her eyes. And then, as he had hovered uncertainly outside, gazing through the window, he had been transported back in time ... back to the house by the sea ... and she had been there in that dreamlike villa high on the soaring cliffs ... dreamlike child of his childhood dreams ... the tender young girl with the garden hoe ...

He had gone in and bought the violets, knowing how much she would love them, not giving it a second thought, swept along by the tide of his nostalgia. Only later had he questioned his motives.

Oh what the hell, it's too late now, he thought, impatiently stubbing out his cigarette. I've invited her out. I've got to go through with it. After all, I'm a grown man, I'm well able to handle the situation. Besides, I'm simply taking her to dinner. Surely there is no harm in that.

33

Some ten minutes later Shane was alighting on Fifth Avenue at Seventy-Seventh Street.

Since he had lived in Emma's apartment for the first three months he had been in New York the doorman on duty knew him, and they exchanged greetings before the man turned to the intercom to announce him.

Riding up in the elevator to the tenth floor, Shane discovered he had a tight knot of apprehension – or was it anticipation? – in his chest. He cautioned himself to watch his step with Paula, took a firm grip on his emotions and arranged a pleasant smile on his face. When he reached the duplex he hesitated for a split second before ringing the bell. As he lifted his hand to do so the door suddenly opened and he found himself staring into Ann Donovan's pleasant Irish face.

'Good evening, Mr O'Neill,' she said, stepping back to let him enter. 'It's nice to see you.'

'Hello, Ann, it's nice to see you too.' He walked in, closed the door behind him, shrugged out of his overcoat. 'You're looking well.'

Ann took his coat. 'Thank you, and so are you, Mr O'Neill.' She turned to the coat closet, and added, 'Miss Paula's waiting for you in the den.'

But she wasn't. She was walking across the spacious hall towards him, a bright smile of welcome on her face.

The impact of seeing her hit him in the pit of his stomach, and the shock sped down to his legs. For a moment he was rooted to the spot, unable to move or speak. He recovered himself swiftly, stepped forward, the smile on his face growing wider.

'Paula!' he exclaimed, and he was surprised that his voice was steady and perfectly normal.

'You got here in record time, Shane,' Paula said, 'it's just seven thirty.'

'Not much traffic tonight.' His eyes were riveted on her as she drew to a standstill in front of him.

Paula looked up at him, her eyes glowing.

He bent forward to kiss her proffered cheek, took hold of her arm with one hand, drawing her closer, then he let his hand fall away quickly, afraid of even the merest close contact with her.

She began to laugh, staring at him.

'What is it?'

'You've grown a moustache!' She eyed it critically, her head on one side.

'Oh. Yes . . .' His hand went to his mouth automatically. 'Of course, you haven't seen it.'

'How could I. I haven't set eyes on you since April.'

'Don't you like it?'

'Yes . . . I think so,' she said haltingly, then linked her arm through his, led him into the den, continuing to talk. '*You* certainly look as fit as a fiddle. My God, that tan! And all *I* hear is how hard you're working in New York. I bet if the truth were known you're really leading an idle life on the golden sandy beaches of the Caribbean.'

'Fat chance of that. The old man's a slave driver.'

He was glad when she let go of his arm finally and moved away from him, putting distance between them. She walked over to the small chest at the far side of the room. He hovered near the coffee table, watching her as she plopped ice into the glass. He noticed that she poured scotch, added soda, without asking him what he wanted. But why would she ask? She knew what he drank. He caught sight of the basket of violets and smiled and then suddenly she was beside him, offering the drink.

He took it, thanked her, asked, 'Aren't you having anything?'

'Yes, a glass of white wine. It's over there. I'd just poured it when you arrived.' As she spoke she sat down in the armchair near the fireplace, lifted the goblet. 'Cheers, Shane.'

'Cheers.' He lowered himself into the chair opposite, relieved to be sitting down. He still felt shaken, unsteady, and so extremely conscious of her he was slightly alarmed. You'd better be careful, he thought, and put down his glass on the end table. He lit a cigarette to hide his nervousness, and discovered, as he puffed on it, that he was unexpectedly tongue-tied. He glanced around, admiring the room as he usually did. He felt comfortable here. Emma had used a mixture of light and dark greens, a colourful floral chintz on the sofa and chairs, and some rather handsome English Regency antiques. The ambience gave him a sense of home, evoked nostalgic feelings in him. He said, at last, 'I practically lived in this den when I was staying here.'

'Funny you should say that, so do I.' Paula leaned back in the chair, crossed her long legs. 'It reminds me of the upstairs parlour at Pennistone Royal, although it's smaller of course, but it's cosy, warm and lived in.'

'Yes.' He cleared his throat. 'I've booked a table at Le Veau D'Or. Have you ever been there?'

'No, I haven't.'

'I think you'll like it – like the atmosphere. It's a small French bistro, very lively and gay, and the food's excellent. I took Aunt Emma and Grandpops there one night, when they were in New York. They really enjoyed themselves.'

'It sounds lovely. And talking of our grandparents, they'll be here again in a few weeks, on their way back to England, won't they? Are you coming home with them? For Christmas?'

'No, afraid not, Paula. Dad wants me to go down to Barbados for the holidays. It's a big season for the hotel.'

'Everybody'll be disappointed not to see you in Yorkshire,' Paula murmured, looking across at him, trying to get used to the moustache. It changed his appearance, made him seem different, a bit older than his twenty-eight years, and more dashing. If that was possible. He had always been the kind of man people looked at twice, because of his height and build, his dark good looks, the sense of presence he exuded.

'You're staring at me,' he said. A black brow arched and his expression was questioning.

'I could say the same about you.'

'You've lost weight,' he began, stopped, reached for his drink.

Paula's brow wrinkled worriedly. 'Yes, I have. And I haven't been dieting, you know I never do that. Am I too thin?'

'Yes, a little. What you need is fattening up, my girl, and since we're on the subject, you also –'

'You've been saying that to me all of your life, and *mine*,' she interrupted, pursing her lips. 'At least for as long as I can remember.'

'True enough. I started to say you also look tired, in need of a good rest, a holiday.' He brought his drink to his mouth, his gaze levelled at her over the rim of the glass, studying her. After taking a swallow, he set it on the table, leaned forward avidly. 'You've done a good job with the makeup, but then you always do. However, cosmetics don't fool me. Your face is gaunt and you've got faint purple smudges under your eyes,' he remarked with his usual unnerving forthrightness. 'No wonder my sister and Winston are worried about you.'

This comment took Paula by surprise, and she exclaimed rapidly, 'I didn't know they were. Neither of them has said anything to me!'

'I'm sure they haven't. In fact I don't suppose anybody has – they're all afraid of you, afraid of upsetting you. But not me, Beanstalk, we've always been blunt with each other, and honest. That'll never change, I hope.'

'So do I.' She could not help thinking about his behaviour lately, the break he had created in their relationship. He had been less than honest with her about that, she was quite sure. She wondered whether to take him to task about it, then decided not to do so. Another time would be more appropriate perhaps. She did not want to put him on the defensive, create trouble on their first evening. She wanted to relax with him, enjoy his company. She had truly missed Shane, now wanted him back in her life on the old footing, needed to rekindle their childhood friendship. It was vital to her. And so she said, 'It's lovely to see you and I'm so glad we're having dinner together, Shane. It'll be like old times.'

She gave him such a warm and loving smile and there was such eagerness in her fine, intelligent eyes, his heart missed a beat. He smiled back at her. 'It already is,' he said, and realized that this was the truth. His tension slipped away and he began to laugh. 'I'm not very nice, or very gallant, am I? Picking on you the minute I arrive. And despite what I've just said, you do look lovely, Paula, and as elegant as always.'

His eyes swept over her approvingly, took in the scarlet silk shirt and the white wool trousers. A smile of amusement tugged at the corner of his mouth. 'Now, if you'd only thought to add a purple kerchief, you'd look absolutely bang on, perfectly smashing.'

Perplexity flashed on to her face. She glanced down at her shirt and then started to laugh with him. 'The Herons! It never occurred to me when I was dressing, but of course, these were your colours.'

He nodded, his black eyes merry, and then he stood up. He took his glass to the chest, added more soda water and ice to dilute the scotch. She had fixed the drink exactly right, the way he liked it, but he wanted to be especially careful tonight. Returning to the fireplace, he said in a more sober voice, 'Winston told me Sally stayed at Heron's Nest during all that fuss in Ireland, and I understand everything's back to normal. But how is Sally *really?*'

'She's marvellous. Very well. Anthony is living at Allington Hall for the moment. I expect you know she's pregnant.'

'Yes, Winston told me —' He broke off, looked at her alertly. 'No wonder you're done in, worn out – all *you've* had to cope with.' He was suddenly sympathetic, and it showed on his face.

'I managed.' Wanting to keep the conversation lighthearted, and long weary of family problems, Paula changed the subject by launching into a recital about Emma, Blackie and their travels. She regaled Shane with snippets she remembered from her grandmother's long letters, titbits chosen at random from their weekly phone conversations. She spiced up her stories with comments of her own, peals of laughter and merriment punctuating these small asides as she warmed to her subject.

Shane's laughter echoed hers, and he nodded from time to time, listening attentively, content to sit back and let her do the talking. It gave him a chance to observe her more closely, to fully enjoy her. The familiar vivacity was there, spilling out of her, and she was humorous, pithy, and gentle by turn, displaying her love for Emma and his grandfather with every word she uttered.

If her gaiety had been forced, fraudulent, on the telephone earlier, it no longer was. He had to acknowledge that she was her natural self, open, outgoing, the girl he had grown up with and whom he knew as well as he knew himself. There was an easiness between them now, after the first few strained moments, and he felt as though he had seen her only yesterday. The rift he had created in their friendship might never have happened.

As he continued to listen to her soft musical voice, a tranquillity settled over Shane. He was at peace with himself, and in a way he had not been for the longest time. But then he was generally at peace when he was with Paula. They never played silly games. There were no false barriers, no affectations, no phoney attitudes. They were entirely themselves, and they were completely attuned to each other as they had been since they were children.

He studied her face quite openly, no longer bothering to hide his interest in her. Its angularity and gauntness had been softened by the warm light from the lamp behind her. It was mobile, expressive, and it articulated much about her thoughts and feelings. There were those who said Paula was not beautiful. She was to him. Her colouring was startling in its vividness, exotic really. The shiny black hair coming to a dramatic widow's peak above her smooth wide brow, the translucent ivory complexion unstained by colour, the violet eyes set wide apart, large and thickly lashed – all these features combined to create a unique kind of beauty. If he had to equate her with any of the flowers she loved to grow, he would have had to liken her to an orchid or a gardenia – and yet he would never send her either, only ever violets. He thought of her

313

basic nature then ... she *was* retiring, reserved and gentle. But, conversely, she was also intense, ardent, passionate about her likes and dislikes, and quick, intelligent, fair minded and honourable. He smiled to himself. She could be devious when it came to business, but that was a family trait, inherited from the redoubtable E.H. Now, as he pondered Paula, Shane had to admit she was the most complex of women, more complicated than any female he had ever met. Yet he loved that very complexity in her which others might easily find so baffling, even disturbing. Perhaps that was because he knew exactly where she was coming from, knew the elements and forces that had made her all the things she was.

He sat back trying to see her objectively, as another man might. His gaze lingered, then he dropped his eyes. His own emotions were intruding, blinding him, making it impossible to view her with any kind of objectivity. How could he do that? He loved her. Loved her desperately. He would always love her. If he could not have her, and he knew he could not, then he would have no other woman. Second best was worse than nothing at all. Also, without another woman in his life he would not be forced into making comparisons as he yearned for Paula. And he *would* continue to yearn for her. You mustn't think of that, he told himself sharply. She is your oldest, dearest friend. You've missed her. So settle for friendship – if that's all you can have. And enjoy this evening for what it is, not what you think it could be in your imagination.

Paula was saying, 'Anyway, that's all of my news about our indefatigable, globe-trotting grandparents. They're apparently having a whale of a time.'

'Yes, it sounds like it,' Shane agreed. 'And Emma's a much more diligent correspondent than Blackie. All Grandpops does is send each one of us a weekly picture postcard with an obtuse message scribbled on the back. I have three I'll prize forever. One from Hong Kong, showing Chinese junks in an orange sunset, with a single word on the other side – *Cheers*. Another from Bora Bora on which he'd written, *Drinking your health in coconut juice*.' Shane grinned at her. '*That's* a likely story, as we both know.'

Paula giggled, asked, 'And the third card?'

'One from Sydney which said, *Off to the outback today*. What a character he is, and I must say I've enjoyed hearing your news about the two of them, their activities. It brings them closer somehow.'

'Yes, it does, but now it's your turn to do the talking,' Paula announced. 'Tell me all about your life in New York.'

'There's not much to tell, Paula,' he said, thinking of his lonely existence, the barrenness of his life. 'I race between the office and the hotel site six, sometimes seven, days a week, fly down to Jamaica and Barbados about once a month, to make sure the hotels are running smoothly. It's the usual grind, and the truth is, I *do* work like a dog.'

She nodded. 'I thought you were only staying in New York for six months. It's been eight already.'

'Dad and I decided it would be more practical if I remained here until the hotel is finished and open, operating properly. It's a lot more practical than flying backward and forward between New York and London, also the islands are closer. Now Dad has indicated he wants me to stay on in the States indefinitely.'

314

'Well, I can understand his reasoning,' she acknowledged softly. Swirling the drink around, she stared down into the glass, her face thoughtful. The idea of Shane being in New York permanently filled her with sudden and inexplicable anxiety. Then unexpectedly she thought of Skye Smith, experienced the same twinge of discomfort she had felt when Merry had mentioned her name weeks ago.

Before she could stop herself, Paula said, with a faint smile, 'I suppose New York is a wonderful place to be – for a fun-loving bachelor like you, Shane. I bet the girls are falling all over you, queuing up for dates.'

Astonishment crossed his face. 'I'm not interested in other women,' he exclaimed, and halted, recognizing his slip, instantly cursing himself. He decided to let the remark slide by, aware that the less said the better.

Not understanding that he had been referring to her, Paula nodded. 'Oh yes, of course, you have a girlfriend now. Merry mentioned Skye Smith to me.'

Irritated though he was with his sister and her big mouth, he nevertheless managed to grin, relieved that his gaff had gone over Paula's head. 'Oh, Skye Smith's only a friend, whatever Merry has said to you. I'm not involved with her – or anyone else for that matter.' He gave Paula a hard stare. 'I told you, Dad's very practised at cracking the whip these days, and I'm devoting my time to business. I don't enjoy much of a social life. I stay at the offices until all hours, stagger back to my apartment and fall into bed exhausted.'

'It seems we're all on a treadmill these days,' Paula said. Shane had obviously changed a great deal. He and Winston had been a couple of Don Juans, playboys, wild and reckless, according to the family gossip she had heard. But Winston had settled down. Perhaps Shane had done so as well. She was pleased he was not having an affair with Skye. Why did that woman bother her? Probably because Merry had been so scathing about her.

'Penny for your thoughts,' Shane said.

She laughed. 'They're not worth a farthing. Merry told me you have an apartment on Sutton Place South,' she went on, 'what's it like?'

'Not bad actually. I rent it furnished, and the owner's taste is not mine exactly. But it's the penthouse and the views are spectacular, especially at night. The whole of Manhattan is stretched out at my feet, and as far as the eye can see. I find myself sitting and enjoying those glittering vistas for hours on end. This is an exciting city, Paula, and challenging. I also happen to think it's beautiful, and the architecture never ceases to astonish me.'

'I can tell from your voice that you like it here, but sometimes I wonder about the States –' She shook her head, her face growing serious, reflective.

'What do you mean?'

'I can't help thinking that it's a violent country. All those dreadful, mind-boggling assassinations – Martin Luther King, President Kennedy, and then Bobby Kennedy only last year. And this past August the ghastly Manson murders in California.' She shuddered. 'And the hippies and the drugs and the crime and the protests.'

Shane looked across at her, said slowly, 'There's a lot of truth in what you say. But it's a young country in a sense, and still going through its growing pains. Things will be all right here, they'll level off, I guarantee you that. Besides, we have hippies, drugs, crime and protests in England, everywhere in the world. The sixties *have* been turbulent, but we'll soon be in a new decade. Perhaps the seventies will be more tranquil.'

'I hope so. Anyway, I do hope you'll invite me over to see your apartment before I leave.'

'Any time you want. And talking of leaving, I think we'd better make tracks to the restaurant. I don't want to lose the table.'

'Fine, I'll just go and get my things.' She was half way across the room when she stopped, pivoted to him. 'I'm not very thoughtful, am I? I said on the phone you could freshen up here and then immediately forgot all about it. Would you like to use my bathroom?'

'No, no, thanks anyway. The one down here is okay.' Rising, he followed her out.

'See you in a minute then,' she said, running lightly up the stairs.

Shane strode across the foyer to the guest bathroom. He washed his hands and face, combed his curly black hair, stared at himself in the mirror. He wondered whether to shave off his moustache tomorrow morning. No. He liked it. He grimaced at his reflection, wishing he had gone home to change his clothes after all. Oh what the hell, I'm not trying to impress Paula, he thought, and went out.

She stood waiting for him in the foyer.

She had put on a white wool jacket that matched the trousers, and had flung a white mohair cape over her shoulders. She looked impossibly beautiful to him.

He turned to get his overcoat out of the closet, gritted his teeth as the familiar longing for her surged through him. He clamped down on the feeling, knowing that the situation was useless, hopeless. She was married to Jim Fairley and very much in love with him.

All you can be is her friend, as you've always been, Shane reminded himself as they left the apartment and went down in the lift.

Le Veau D'Or was busy, jammed with people, as Shane had known it would be.

Gerard came forward to greet them, smiling, as usual the genial host. He promised them that their table would be ready in ten minutes, suggested they have a drink at the small bar while they waited to be seated.

Shane ushered Paula forward, pulled out a stool for her, and without asking her what she wanted he ordered two *kir royales*. He lit a cigarette, watched the bartender pour the cassis into the large wine goblets, then fill both to the brim with sparkling champagne.

Once they had their drinks, Shane turned to Paula, clinked glasses with her. 'To old friendships,' he said, and looked down at her, his eyes warm.

'Old friendships, Shane.'

'Do you know, the last time I had one of these was at La Reserve in the South of France . . . with you.'

She gave him a quick glance, and a smile of recollection glanced across her mouth. 'I remember . . . you'd been so unkind to Emily, driving the boat at a crazy speed and with such wildness. She was terrified, poor thing. Then to make amends, you dragged us both off, pouring *kir royales* into us with a vengeance.' She shook her head, laughing. 'It was about four years ago, that summer we all went down to Gran's villa at the Cap.'

'But the drinks had no effect, if I remember correctly. My escapade with the speedboat cost me dearly ... an expensive silk scarf was the price I had to pay for my lack of thought and recklessness. Still, it was worth it, just to bring the smile back to Emily's face.'

'She's petrified of water – so is Gran.'

'But you're not afraid of anything, are you?'

'What makes you say that?' She frowned at him.

'You were intrepid as a child, tagging along after me, doing all the things I did. You were such a tomboy, quite fearless, and you never flinched, whatever the obstacle, or its danger.'

'But I trusted you. I knew you wouldn't let anything happen to me, and you never did.'

And I never will, my darling, he thought, filled with love for her. A lump came into his throat, surprising him. He took a long gulp of his drink, momentarily averted his face as he placed the glass on the bar, not wishing her to see his eyes. They would reveal too much.

Paula began to chat about Emily's engagement to Winston, and once more Shane was happy to let her do the talking. It gave him a chance to marshal his feelings, get a hold on them again before they overwhelmed him. Eventually he was able to join in the conversation in a normal way, and they covered a wide range of topics. They gossiped about their mutual friends, discussed the Harte boutiques in the O'Neill hotels, wondered about Emerald Bow's chances at the Grand National. And they were still dissecting the difficulties of the Aintree course and the greatest steeplechase in the world when they were finally seated.

Settling back comfortably on the red banquette, Shane said, 'All I had for lunch was a sandwich at my desk, so I'm ravenous. Knowing you, you're going to say you're not hungry, but I think we should order immediately.'

'But I am hungry,' she protested truthfully. For the first time in months she was looking forward to dinner. Her violet eyes, resting on him, welled with humour. 'However, I'll let you order for both of us. I'll have the same as you – it's safer, don't you think?'

His mouth twitched. 'I believe so. Otherwise you'll want what I have, as you always did when we were kids, end up eating off my plate and leave me starving.' He winked. 'Don't think I've forgotten your bad habits, because I haven't.'

After perusing the menu, Shane motioned to their waiter, selected *saucisson chaud* to be followed by *tripes à la mode de Caen* and asked for a bottle of burgundy.

It was the custom at Le Veau D'Or for appetizers to be placed before the diners, to tide them over while they waited for dinner to be served. Two plates instantly materialized in front of them, and Shane exclaimed, 'Oh good, mussels tonight. They're delicious. Try them, Paula.' Dipping his fork into the mound of shellfish, he continued, 'Will you be going to Texas while you're in the States?'

'I don't think so – gosh, you're right, these are good.' She munched on a

317

forkful of the mussels, before adding, 'I hope I don't have to go to Odessa. I met with Dale Stevens this morning, and fortunately things are relatively quiet at Sitex. Naturally, Harry Marriott is being his usual obstreperous self. That man is singularly without vision. He forever tried to block my grandfather, hated expansion and innovation, and he's constantly trying to do the same with us. He's still grousing about Sitex going into North Sea oil. But it's working extremely well, as you know. The off-shore drilling paid off, and we were one of the first companies to strike oil this year. Once again, Emma Harte has proved that man totally wrong.'

Shane smiled, nodded, went on eating.

Paula said, 'I know Grandy gave you an introduction to Ross Nelson. What do you think of him?'

'Ross is okay. We get on quite well, actually. I suspect he's a bit of a sod when it comes to women, though. As for business,' Shane shrugged, 'he's above board. Very sharp, mind you, but honest. Obviously he's always looking out for the bank, that's only natural. He's been very helpful, useful to me in a variety of ways.' He eyed her. 'And what's your opinion of Mr Nelson?'

'The same as yours, Shane.' Paula told him about the meeting with Dale and Ross earlier in the day, confiding all of the details.

'Emma would never sell her shares in Sitex!' Shane exclaimed, when she had finished. His black brows knitted together. 'I can't imagine how Ross could think that or why he is so keen for you to sell out. He can't make a profit from insider information about stock transactions, trading, it's against the law. And as a private investment banker of his standing and reputation he would be a stickler about legalities, staying within the law, toeing the line drawn by the Securities Exchange Commission. No, financial gain has nothing to do with this, and anyway he's as rich as Croesus. Of course, if Ross helped to steer that kind of deal through for one of the bank's clients, he'd be a big man with that client, now wouldn't he?' Not waiting for a response, Shane rushed on, 'Yes, that's why he's interested in Sitex. From all you've just told me, his client wants control, or so it seems. Then again, if he's such a chum of Dale's, he's probably looking out for his buddy. He's trying to kill two birds with one stone.'

'Yes, I reasoned things out the same way as you earlier, after they'd left. Ross Nelson can pester me as much as he wants – I've no intention of talking Grandy into selling, which is what he hopes I'll do, in my estimation.'

Shane gave her a cool and piercing look. 'You'd better watch old Ross – he's bound to make a pass at you.'

Paula was about to tell him about the roses, the invitation to spend the weekend at Ross's country home, but for a reason she could not immediately fathom she changed her mind. She said, with a dry laugh, 'He wouldn't dare. I'm married. Also, he wouldn't want to upset Gran.'

'Don't be so naïve, Paula,' Shane retorted swiftly. 'Your marital status and your grandmother's displeasure would not influence Ross Nelson. Not one iota. He's bloody unscrupulous, if one is to believe the gossip one hears, and I'm afraid I do.' Shane did not particularly like the idea of the banker hovering anywhere near Paula, and he brought the conversation around to another subject. He began to speak about their New York hotel, and continued to do so through the first course and as they waited for their main dish.

She listened with growing interest, enjoying being at the receiving end of his confidences. Earlier, before Shane had arrived at the apartment, it had crossed Paula's mind that they might feel awkward, perhaps shy with each other, discomfited and restrained even. They had not been alone or spent any time together for ages. But this had not been the case, nor was it now. It *was* like old times, as she had predicted it would be over drinks. It had not taken them long to get back on their former footing. There was warmth and affection flowing between them, and the camaraderie of their youth was much in evidence.

'So I'd like you to come over to the hotel, take a look round,' Shane said, 'whenever you have a spare hour this week. Some of the floors are finished and I can show you a few of the suites. I'd appreciate your opinion about the decorative schemes – I just received the renderings from the interior design firm this afternoon. You have such good taste, I'd like your opinion.'

Paula's face lit up with pleasure. 'Why I'd love to see the hotel. I've heard quite a lot about it from Uncle Bryan and Merry. Actually, tomorrow's an easy day for me. I could meet you there in the late afternoon.' She leaned closer, looked up into his face, hers full of eagerness. 'And perhaps you'd come back with me for dinner at the apartment. Ann told me she wants to cook for you. She said something about your favourite Irish stew. And why not tomorrow evening?'

Because the more I see of you, the more I'll want you, he thought.

He said, 'Thanks a lot, that'll be nice.' He was startled that he had accepted her invitation so readily. Then suddenly, with a small shock, he knew that he intended to spend as much time with her as he could during her sojourn in New York.

He walked her back to the apartment.

It was a clear, bright evening, cool, but not particularly cold for November. After the warmth and noisiness of the bistro the air was refreshing, their companionable silence restful.

They were on Madison Avenue, drawing closer to Seventy-Second Street, when Shane said, 'Would you like to go riding on Sunday?'

'I'd love to,' Paula cried, turning to glance up at him. 'It's ages since I've been on a horse. I don't have my riding togs with me, obviously. But I suppose I could wear jeans.'

'Yes, or you could go to Kauffman's. They're down town and they have everything you'd need.'

'Then that's what I'll do. Where do you ride?'

'In Connecticut – a country town called New Milford. Actually I own a place up there. An old barn. I've been renovating it, remodelling it for the past few months and –'

'Shane O'Neill! How secretive and mean of you! Why didn't you tell me about the barn before?'

'I haven't had a chance so far. We've had such a lot of other things to talk about over dinner. More important things, such as your business affairs, our new hotel.' His laugh was deep, throaty. He went on, 'Would you like to see it?'

'That's a ridiculous question. Of course I would. But I will, won't I? On Sunday, I mean.'

'Yes.'

'If you like I can fix a picnic lunch, and we can take it up with us. What time would we leave on Sunday?' Paula asked.

'You ought to leave fairly early. You see, I'll be there already. I've arranged for a couple of our carpenters to be there on Friday. to work with me. I'm driving up on Thursday night. I plan to spend the weekend at the barn.'

'*Oh*. Then how will I get there on Sunday?'

'No problem, I'll arrange for a car and driver to bring you. Unless –' he paused, exclaimed, 'I have a great idea, Paula. Why don't you drive up with me on Thursday night, stay for the weekend? Surely you can take Friday off.' He gave her a quick look out of the corner of his eye, added in a jocular tone, 'I'll buy you a spade. You can dig to your heart's content, make a garden for me.'

She laughed. 'In this weather! The ground's probably as hard as iron. But I'd love to come up for the weekend, Shane.'

'Terrific.' He smiled to himself.

She linked her arm through his, fell into step with him. They walked on in silence. She was thinking of their childhood days at Heron's Nest and, although she had no way of knowing it, so was he.

34

Paula awakened on Friday morning to the sound of raised masculine voices and raucous laughter echoing outside.

She sat up in bed with a start and rubbed her eyes, blinking in the faint light, for a moment disoriented and wondering where she was. Then she remembered. Of course, she was at Shane's barn in New Milford. Glancing at her small travelling clock on the white wicker bedside table she saw to her surprise that it was almost ten. She found it hard to believe she had overslept and by four hours. Normally she was up and dressed by six o'clock every day.

Bounding out of bed, feeling rested and filled with energy, she padded over to the window, parted the red cotton twill curtains, looked down into the yard. Just below her, two men stood talking near a pile of lumber.

Shane was out of her line of vision, but she knew he was there when she heard him say, 'Listen you guys, keep the noise down, will you please. My lady friend is still asleep. And when I say lady I do mean *lady* – so watch your language.'

Half smiling, she turned away and looked around the bedroom with interest. She had been too tired last night to pay much attention, but now she realized how charming it was, small and quaint, with white walls that stopped at a floor painted bright red. The few pieces of furniture were of white wicker, but it was the brass bed covered with patchwork quilt that dominated the space.

Gliding into the adjoining minuscule of bathroom, Paula took a quick shower, brushed her hair, put on lipstick and mascara, went back into the bedroom. She dressed in a pair of blue jeans, a pink cotton shirt and a heavy purple sweater, then pulled a pair of knee-high red leather boots on over the jeans. After strapping on her watch, she ran downstairs to the kitchen.

This was large, country in feeling, with rustic beams and wall-hung copper utensils, but there was every modern appliance, and it was spotless. It looked to her as if it had just been freshly cleaned. The white cabinets and counter tops, encircling the white walls, gleamed brightly in the sunshine that filtered in through two small windows where blue-and-white checked curtains hung in crisp, starched folds. She peered out. Shane and the men were nowhere in sight.

Paula sniffed. There was a lovely aroma of coffee in the air, and spotting the bubbling percolator, she began opening cupboards, looking for a mug. She found one, filled it, then strolled through into the main living area of the barn.

She came to a halt half way down the long expanse of space, her eyes sweeping around, trying to take in everything at once, knowing this was virtually impossible. She needed days to absorb everything Shane had accomplished here. It had looked lovely last night; this morning, filled with sunlight, it was breathtaking.

Only one room, he had said, as they were driving up from Manhattan. But what a room it was – huge, spectacular in its dimensions, with a high ceiling of exposed rafters intersected by cross beams, a picture window on a long wall, and a gargantuan stone fireplace. A fire already blazed up the chimney, the big logs hissing and spitting in the silence.

She stepped over to the baby grand and sat down on the stool, sipping the coffee, continuing to glance up and down. He had positioned the piano in the exact centre of the room and she understood why. It created a natural demarcation between the seating arrangement next to the fireplace and the dining area near the kitchen. The colour scheme was primarily white, the coolness warmed by dark wood tones. The walls had been whitewashed; two huge Chesterfield sofas and the big armchairs were upholstered in heavy white twill; the draperies matched; there were white area rugs on the polished wood floor. But pictures, prints, books and plants added splashes of livelier colour against the white background.

Shane had told her he had gone antiquing in the area, had stumbled on some genuinely good pieces. Now her eyes rested on two handsome chests she had not really noticed last night, moved on to regard a Coromandel screen that was obviously very old and rare. Its decorative panels made a striking backdrop for the mahogany dining table. I bet that screen cost a fortune, she thought.

A feeling of dismay trickled through her.

It was quite apparent that he had spent a great deal of money on the barn, not to mention time and effort. Shane had explained that most of the basic remodelling had been done by Sonny and Elaine Vickers, from whom he had bought the barn. 'All I did was put in the cantilevered staircase and the plate glass window, and add a few other finishing touches to the basic shell before I furnished,' he had said.

Nevertheless, in the last few minutes something had registered and it troubled her. The place had the look of permanence, had been made into a real home for someone who intended to live in it for a long time. Not only that, he was somewhere outside right now with the carpenters, sawing wood for shelves and cupboards. They were intended for the tiny spare room he had shown her and which he had said he was turning into a den for himself.

Did he plan to stay in America for ever? Was he never coming back to England? And why did that matter to her?

Paula jumped up abruptly and hurried to the fire. She seated herself in an overstuffed armchair and placed the mug on the hearth. Her eyes fell on his cigarettes and lighter and, although she rarely smoked, she took one, lit it, sat smoking, thinking hard about the previous evening. They had arrived at nine o'clock, just as the thunderstorm had hit the area. They had been drenched after making several trips to the car to collect the bag of groceries and their suitcases, and he had insisted she change into dry clothes, immediately shooing her upstairs.

Twenty minutes later she had come back down and had stood hovering on the threshold of this room, admiring it. In her absence he had turned on all the lamps, lit the fire. The baronial expanse seemed more intimate, suffused in a warm and welcoming glow and reverberating with the strains of Bob Dylan's *Blowin' In The Wind*. Wandering over to the fireplace, she had swung around to stand with her back to it, an old habit. At that very moment she had been surprised to see him emerge from the kitchen, carrying two drinks, looking spruced up and fresh in a pristine white shirt and blue jeans.

'You've been quick, doing all this and changing as well,' she had exclaimed. He had given her a cheeky grin. 'Training will out, as they say, and I was trained by a hard-assed general in a tough army camp, remember.' She had retorted in mock reproof, 'Emma Harte hard-assed! That's not a very nice thing to say about my distinguished grandmother.' Handing her the vodka and tonic, Shane had clinked his glass against hers, then asserted, 'Emma would appreciate my description of her, even if you don't.'

They had begun to reminisce about Heron's Nest then, laughing a lot and teasing each other, and later he had brought out a huge platter of smoked salmon and a tray of cheeses. They had sat on the floor, eating off the coffee table in front of the fire, washing down their light supper with ice-cold Pouilly Fumé. And they had talked endlessly, late into the night, and about so many varied things, content to be together, at ease and comfortable in their companionship.

Towards the end of the evening Shane had noticed that she kept rubbing her neck, and in answer to his concerned glance, she had volunteered, 'It's stiff – from sitting long hours at my desk, I've no doubt. It's nothing. Really.' Without saying a word, he had knelt behind her, massaged her shoulders, her nape, and the base of her skull.

Recalling the scene, Paula remembered the pleasure she had felt as Shane's strong hard fingers had kneaded her aching muscles, drawn the tension out of her. She had not wanted him to stop. And later, when he had given her a chaste goodnight peck on the cheek outside her bedroom door, she had felt a compulsion to put her arms around his neck. She had gone in swiftly, closed the door, her cheeks flaming.

Paula sat up in the chair with a jerk. Last night she had been baffled at herself. Now she understood. She had *wanted* Shane to touch her, to kiss her. Face it. Your so-called sisterly feelings towards him aren't very fraternal. Not anymore. *They're sexual. You're sexually attracted to him.*

This last thought so startled and shocked Paula, she leapt to her feet, threw the cigarette into the fire, and almost ran across to the picture window.

She stood staring out at the landscape, hardly aware of its beauty as she tried to calm herself. She *must* put aside these new and extraordinary feelings he had aroused in her. They shook her up, distressed her. And she had no right to be interested in Shane O'Neill – she was married. Besides, she was only his childhood friend, nothing more in his eyes.

Endeavouring to nudge thoughts of him out of her mind she discovered that they refused to budge. They nagged at her, and then the image of Shane as he had looked last night danced before her eyes. He had seemed different, and yet his appearance and manner were exactly the same as they always were. Then it dawned on her. It was she who was different – and she had been looking at him through newly objective, newly perceptive eyes.

Why am I suddenly so aware of Shane? Because he is handsome, virile, amusing and charming? Or because he exudes such sex appeal? But he always has, he hasn't changed. Besides blatant sex appeal makes no impression on me. His sexuality isn't blatant, though. It simply exists as an integral part of him. My God, I must be insane, thinking in this way about Shane. Anyway, I'm not interested in sex. It turns me off. Jim has seen to that.

A little shiver ran through Paula. Jim loomed up in front of her. Merry had an expression she used to describe certain men. She called them, "the wham, bang and the thank you, ma'am chaps". How apt. Paula sighed heavily, blinked in the sunlight as it pierced through the window, a blinding cataract of brilliant light. Her thoughts remained on Jim. Shane's image was demolished.

Yesterday afternoon, around two o'clock, she had telephoned Long Meadow. It had been seven in the evening in England. She had spoken to Jim. But only briefly. He had been pleasant, bland as always, but hurried, on his way out to dinner, he had informed her. He had quickly passed her over to Nora, so that she could chat to the nurse about her babies, get all the news. She missed Lorne and Tessa terribly. When she had asked Nora to put her husband back on the line, Nora had said that he had already left the house. Paula could hardly believe that he had not waited to say goodbye to her. Furious with him, she had hung up. Then the depression had set in. Seemingly Jim had forgotten their confrontation last Sunday – and what it had been about.

My God, that's less than a week ago, she thought, as the picture of them standing in the garden flashed through her head with startling clarity. Something had died in her that day. It would never be reborn. Jim had been dense, dismissive, cavalier in his attitude. And yes, irresponsible and indifferent to her, almost callous, now that she thought about it again. He simply didn't care about her emotions, her thoughts, her needs. Once more she acknowledged that he and she were incompatible. And on every possible level, not only sexually. If sex were their only problem she would be able to cope. His attitude on the phone had only reinforced her sense of despair about him. The last vestiges of her commitment to her marriage had been swept away, and she had turned to the papers on her desk, thankful that she had so much business to occupy her.

My work and the children . . . that's where I shall direct all of my energies from now on, she reminded herself for the umpteenth time. Hurrying back to the hearth, she picked up the mug, headed for the kitchen. It was high time she went outside to find Shane, to wish him good morning and ask about their plans for the rest of the day.

But he was already in the kitchen, pouring himself a mug of coffee. 'So there you are!' he exclaimed. 'I bet my chaps woke you up, rowdy devils!'

Paula gaped at him, instantly conscious of his rough clothing. He was wearing shapeless, baggy corduroys, heavy work boots, a bulky fisherman's sweater and a cloth cap set at a rakish angle on his black curls. She began to laugh, shaking her head.

'What's the matter?' he demanded, frowning, his eyes clouding.

'Your clothes!' she spluttered. 'You look like an Irish navvy!'

'My dear girl, hasn't anybody told you that that's exactly what I am. Just like my grandfather.'

Later in the morning they drove into New Milford.

On their way down the hill, Shane pointed out the farm where his friends Sonny and Elaine Vickers lived, told her in passing that he had invited them over for dinner that night. 'He's a musician, she's a writer. They're lots of fun, you'll like them,' he said, and then went on to discuss the menu with her.

By the time they were parking the car they had agreed on what she would cook – an old fashioned North Country dinner with all the trimmings. They would start with Yorkshire pudding, have a leg of lamb, roast potatoes and brussel sprouts for the main course, finish with an English trifle.

They went to the farm stands and various markets, bought fresh vegetables, fruit and lamb and various other meats for the weekend, and spices, fancy candles and armfuls of bronze and gold chrysanthemums. They staggered down Main Street, their arms laden, laughing and joking, their hilarity high.

On the return journey, Paula realized that she was being her normal self with Shane, as he was with her. But then why wouldn't he be? He couldn't read her mind, and even if he could, there was now nothing unusual to read – except friendly, affectionate thoughts, happy remembrances of their youthful past. Fortunately those strange and disturbing feelings he had evoked in her last night had entirely disappeared in the last few hours. Shane was just her old chum, her good friend, and part of the family. Everything was normal again. She felt weak with the relief.

Once they were back at the barn, Shane unpacked their purchases and put them away, while she arranged the flowers in two large stone pots. As they worked, he said, 'I'm afraid it's another picnic for lunch. Is that okay with you, Beanstalk?'

'Of course. But what about your carpenters? Don't you have to feed them?'

'No. They brought their own sandwiches and they told me they were going to eat at noon, while we were out shopping. But I wonder where they are? They were supposed to start putting up some of the shelves – it's awfully silent.' He began to laugh as the sound of hammering floated down from the upper floor. 'I spoke too soon, it seems. They're obviously hard at it.'

Lunch, eaten in front of the fire in the main room, consisted of ripe brie cheese, thick chunks of French bread, fruit and a bottle of red wine. At one moment Paula looked across at Shane and said, 'Are you planning to live in the States for the rest of your life?'

'Why do you ask that?' He wondered why it mattered to her.

Glancing around, she said, 'This place has the look of a permanent residence, and you've obviously put a lot of care and money into it.'

'Yes, and it's been very therapeutic for me, coming up here whenever I could, working on the place. It's given me something to do at weekends, in my spare time. I don't have many friends, no real social life to speak of. Besides, you know I've always enjoyed rebuilding old places.' He lolled back in the chair, his eyes resting on her thoughtfully. 'Winston and I turned a tidy profit when we sold those old cottages we renovated in Yorkshire, and I know I'll do the same here, when the time comes for me to sell the barn.' He continued to observe her. Was that relief in her eyes, or was he imagining things?

'What's going to happen to Beck House? I mean now that Winston and Emily are getting married?' Paula asked curiously.

'When Winston was in New York he said he and Emily wanted to live there for a while, to see if Emily liked it. If she does, he'll buy me out, if she doesn't –' Shane shrugged. 'There's no problem, we'll probably continue to share it as a weekend place. Or we'll put it up for sale.'

'Winston told me he's asked you to be his best man.'

Shane nodded.

'And I'm going to be Emily's matron of honour.'

'Yes, I know.'

'Won't you be in England before then, Shane?'

There it was again, that peculiar concerned expression in her eyes. He said, 'I've no idea, Paula. As I explained the other day, Dad wants me to spend the Christmas season in Jamaica and Barbados, and I might just have to go to Australia next February or March.'

'Australia!' She sat up straighter on the sofa, looking puzzled.

'Yes. Blackie's taken a shine to Sydney, and several times, when he's spoken to Dad lately, he has urged him to build a hotel there. I spoke to the old man yesterday morning, and he's actually received a letter from Grandpops about that very thing. So – I may have to go over there, scout the place.'

'Blackie's as bad as Grandy. Don't those two ever stop thinking about business?'

'Do you? Or do I, for that matter?' He chuckled. 'We're a couple of chips off a couple of old blocks, wouldn't you say?'

'I suppose so.' She leaned forward, her face suddenly intent. 'Do you think I work too hard?'

'Of course I don't. Anyway, it's your nature to be a worker, Paula. It's also the way you were reared – as I was reared. I don't have much time for parasites.

Frankly, I'd go crazy if I had lots of free time on my hands. I love being out in the marketplace, love the rough and tumble, the wheeling and dealing, and so do you. There's another thing, I get a lot of gratification knowing I'm continuing the family business started by Grandpops, and you have to feel exactly the same way.'

'I do.'

'It's expected of us both . . . duty has been beaten into us since our births, we wouldn't know any other way to live. Look, our respective grandparents devoted their lives to building two great business empires, strove to give us better lives than they had in the beginning, and financial security, and independence and power. How –'

'Jim says the pursuit of power leads to isolation, the death of human values and the death of the soul,' Paula interjected.

This was the first time she had mentioned Jim since she had arrived in New York and Shane was momentarily thrown. He cleared his throat. He had no desire to discuss her husband, but knew he had to make some sort of response. 'And you? Do you agree?'

'No, actually, I don't. Wasn't it Lord Acton who said power corrupts, absolute power corrupts absolutely? That's what Jim was getting at, I think. But to hell with Lord Acton, whoever *he* was. I prefer Emma Harte's philosophy. She says power only corrupts when those who have it will do anything to hang on to it. Grandy says that power can be ennobling, if one understands that power is a tremendous responsibility. And especially to others. I happen to agree with *her*, not Jim. I do feel responsible, Shane. To Gran, to our employees and shareholders. And to myself.'

Shane nodded. 'You're right, and so is Emma. I was going to say, a moment ago, how ungrateful and even unconscionable we would be if we were indifferent to our inheritances, turned away from them. It would be negating Blackie and Emma, and all their superhuman efforts.' He stood up, glanced at the clock. 'It's almost four, and since we're on the subject of responsibility I'd better go and find my chaps, pay them, tell them to knock off.'

Paula also rose, picked up the luncheon tray. 'The day's disappeared! I should start preparing the food for dinner.'

As they went out, Shane looked down at her, flashed his cheeky grin. 'And for your information, Beanstalk, Lord Acton was an English historian, a devout Catholic, a Liberal member of Parliament and close friend of Gladstone's.'

'That's nice to know,' she said, laughing, and walked into the kitchen.

After stacking the dishwasher, Paula peeled the potatoes, cleaned the sprouts, prepared the lamb, smearing it with butter, adding pepper and dried rosemary leaves. Once the trifle was made and had been placed in the refrigerator, she beat flour, eggs and milk into a batter for the Yorkshire pudding, humming happily to herself. Shane poked his head around the door several times during the hour she was working, volunteering to help, but she declined his offer, told him to scoot. She was enjoying herself in much the same way she took pleasure in gardening, using her hands instead of her brain for a change. Therapeutic, she thought, recalling his words about working on the barn.

When she eventually went back into the main room she noticed that he had laid the table for dinner, stacked piles of logs on one end of the hearth, put

Beethoven's *Ninth* on the stereo. But he was nowhere in sight. Paula curled up on the sofa comfortably, listening to the symphony, feeling relaxed and even a little drowsy. She yawned. It's the wine. I'm not used to it at lunch time, she thought, closing her eyes. It had been a lovely day, the nicest she had spent in a long time, and free of tension, verbal fencing. It was a relief to be herself, not to be constantly on the defensive as she so often was with Jim.

Shane made her jump, when he said, 'Now, how about that walk?'

Sitting up, she covered her mouth with her hand, yawning repeatedly. '*Sorry.* I feel so sleepy. Do you mind if we scrap the walk for today?'

He stood near the sofa, hovering over her. 'No. I'm wacked myself, I was up at the crack of dawn.' He did not add that he'd hardly slept, knowing she was in the room opposite his, so near and yet so far removed from him. He had wanted her very much last night, had longed to hold her in his arms. He said, 'Why don't you have a nap?'

'I think I will. But what are you going to do?'

'I've a few more chores, a couple of phone calls to make, and then I'll probably do the same.'

She settled back against the cushions, smiling to herself as he went out, whistling under his breath. As she half dozed she remembered she had not yet tackled him about his behaviour over the last eighteen months. Oh there's plenty of time, all weekend, she thought. I'll do it another day. Something stirred at the back of her mind. It was an incomplete thought and it slid away before she could fully grasp it. She sighed contentedly, felt herself being enveloped by the music and the warmth. Within seconds she was fast asleep.

35

It was one of those evenings which, right from the outset, was destined to be perfect.

A few minutes before seven, Paula came downstairs looking for Shane.

She was dressed in a light wool caftan which Emily had made for her. It was a deep violet colour, simply styled, loose and floating, with unusual butterfly-wing sleeves that buttoned tightly at the wrists. With it she wore a long strand of lavender jade beads, another gift from Emily, who had bought them for her in Hong Kong.

Paula found Shane in the main room. He stood by the huge window, looking out.

She noticed that he had lit the many candles they had scattered around earlier, and set up a bar on one of the small chests.

The fire blazed in the hearth like a huge bonfire, the few lamps he had turned on glowed rosily, and the voice of Ella Fitzgerald singing Cole Porter echoed softly in the background.

Walking forward, Paula said, 'I can see that there's nothing for me to do but sit down and have a drink.'

Shane swung around. His eyes swept over her.

As she drew closer he saw that she had stroked purple shadow on her lids, and because of this and the colour of her dress, those uncanny eyes appeared to be more violet than ever. Shining black hair, brushed back and curling under in a pageboy, framed the pale face, accentuated its translucency. The widow's peak made a sharp indentation on her wide brow. It was dramatic. She was dramatic.

The strain had gone out of her face. He thought she looked more beautiful than she had in years. He said, 'You look nice, Paula.'

'Thank you – so do you.'

He laughed dismissively. 'You mentioned a drink. What would you like?'

'White wine, please.'

Paula remained standing near the hearth, observing him as he opened the bottle.

He wore dark grey slacks, a lighter grey turtle-necked sweater and a black cashmere sports jacket. Studying him, she thought: he's the same old Shane, and yet somehow he's not. He *is* different. Maybe it's the moustache after all. Or is it me? She instantly squashed this possibility.

He brought her the drink. She caught the faint whiff of soap and cologne. He was freshly shaved, his hair well brushed, his nails newly manicured. Paula bit back a smile, remembering how his habit of looking at himself whenever he passed a mirror had driven her grandmother crazy. Emma had even threatened to have all of the mirrors removed from Heron's Nest if he did not curb his vanity. He had been eighteen that particular year and very conscious of his astonishing looks, his husky, athletic build. She suspected he was still most aware of his physical appeal, although he no longer gazed at himself in mirrors. At least, not publicly. Perhaps he had learned to accept his striking appearance. She turned to the fire to hide another smile. He *was* vain, even a little conceited about some of his attributes and accomplishments, and so very sure of himself. Yet there was an inherent sweetness in him, a gentleness, and he was loving to the core with friends and family, and so very kind. How well she knew Shane Desmond Ingham O'Neill.

Shane, pouring himself a scotch and soda, called across to her, 'Don't be surprised if Sonny brings his guitar. He usually does. I may accompany him on the piano – give everyone a treat. We might even have a sing song later.'

'Oh God, shades of The Herons!' Paula laughed. 'You really did stink, you know.'

'On the contrary, I think we were rather good,' he retorted, also laughing. He joined her. 'You and the girls were jealous because we stole the show that summer, were the centre of attraction. And you were envious of our smashing rig-outs. I'm surprised you didn't start a girls' band just to compete with us.'

She laughed again. He touched his glass to hers.

Paula stared up at him towering above her, feeling dwarfed by his six feet four inches, and suddenly weak, defenceless and decidedly female. There definitely was something irresistible about him. The weird feelings he had aroused in her last night began to stir. Her skin tingled. Her heart missed a beat.

Their eyes held.

Paula wanted to look away but his dark and piercing gaze was hypnotic.

Shane broke the contact, swiftly turning, making a show of searching for his cigarettes as he stifled the urge to kiss her. You must be careful, he told himself. He wondered if he had been wrong inviting her for the weekend. He knew he was skating on thin ice. I won't see her again while she's in the States. Inwardly he laughed. He knew he would.

A series of cheery hellos rang out. To his immense relief Sonny and Elaine walked in.

Shane hurried across the room to greet them, a huge grin surfacing. He was glad he had invited them. His tension eased.

After propping the guitar case against a chair, Sonny grasped his hand, embraced him, said, 'Cognac . . . for after dinner.' He handed Shane a bottle wrapped in fancy paper.

Elaine thrust a basket at him. 'And here's some of my freshly baked bread for your breakfast,' she exclaimed as Shane bent to kiss her cheek.

Shane thanked them, put the gifts on a chest, and brought the Vickers over to be introduced to Paula.

The minute she met them, Paula knew she was going to like the couple. Sonny was tall, lean and fair, with a blond beard and merry brown eyes. Elaine, softly pretty and feminine, was one of those women whose genuine sweetness is instantly recognizable. She had an open, friendly face, and her eyes were vividly blue, her short, curly hair prematurely silver.

The three of them sat down, and Shane went to make drinks for the new arrivals. Paula was glad she had chosen the caftan, even though Shane had told her to dress casually. Elaine was wearing black velvet trousers with a Chinese jacket of blue brocade and looked elegant in an understated way.

Smiling at her, Elaine said, 'Shane told us you're Emma Harte's granddaughter, and that you run her business now. I'm crazy about your London store. I can spend all day there –'

'She's not kidding either,' Sonny interrupted, grinning at Paula. 'My wife and your store are going to bankrupt me one day.'

'Oh don't pay any attention to my husband, *he's* the one who's kidding,' Elaine said, and continued to rave about Harte's in Knightsbridge.

But when Shane came back with glasses of wine for Sonny and Elaine, the conversation turned to country matters and local gossip. Paula leaned back in her chair, listening quietly, sipping her drink. As the talk ebbed and flowed between Shane and his friends, she soon became aware of his liking for them, recognized how relaxed he was in their company. But then, so was she. They were easy to be with – warm, outgoing, very real and down-to-earth people. Sonny's wit was as quick as Shane's, although not quite as brilliant and astringent, and the two men were soon bouncing funny lines back and forth. There was a great deal of laughter and jollity in the air, and a festive mood prevailed.

After the first half hour, Paula felt as though she had known this engaging couple for years. Individually each of them drew her out, encouraged her to talk about her work, the stores, and both of them were particularly interested in hearing about her famous grandmother. And she, who was generally reserved with strangers, found herself chatting away. She and Sonny discussed music and his composing, and Paula discovered that he had written several Broadway musicals as well as the background music for numerous Hollywood films.

Elaine, in turn, talked about her writing career and her books. And she did so in a manner that was not only informative but amusing, especially when she recounted funny incidents which had happened to her when she was on promotional tours. She told a good story, and entertainingly so, and there was a great deal of laughter and bonhomie among the four of them.

Occasionally Paula stole surreptitious glances at Shane. He was a wonderful host, constantly up and down, taking care of the drinks, changing the records on the stereo, throwing logs on the fire, and steering the conversation around to different subjects, involving them with each other. And he was obviously delighted with the way the Vickers had warmed to her. He kept smiling across at her, nodding as if in approval, and twice when he passed her chair to do a small chore he squeezed her shoulder affectionately.

Paula had been out to check on the food once, and the second time she rose, Elaine also stood up.

'I'm letting you do all the work,' Elaine said, 'and that's not fair. I'm coming to help you.'

'Things are under control,' Paula protested.

'No, no, I insist.' Elaine followed Paula out to the kitchen, and as she came through the doorway, she exclaimed, 'Everything smells so delicious – my mouth's beginning to water. Now, what can _I_ do?'

'Nothing really.' Paula smiled at her, bent down and took the meat out of the oven, placed it on to a platter. 'Well, there is one thing. Could you cover this with silver foil, please?'

'Consider it done,' Elaine said, tearing off a large piece of the silver paper, tucking it around the leg of lamb. She stood watching Paula, and after a moment, she said, 'It's a lovely evening. I'm so glad you're here. And you certainly cheer Shane up.'

'Do I really?' Paula swung to face Elaine, gave her a curious puzzled look. 'You make it sound as if he's been down in the dumps.'

'We think he has. Sonny and I worry about him a lot. He's so nice, generous, very engaging, and pleasant and charming. Still . . .' She shrugged. 'To be truthful, he's always up here alone, never brings . . . friends, and there are times when he seems despondent, melancholy.' She shrugged again. 'Of course England is a long way off and –'

'Yes, I do think he gets a bit homesick,' Paula volunteered, pivoting, turning her attention to the oven again.

Elaine stared at Paula's back, her brow puckering. 'Oh but I didn't mean it that way –' She stopped abruptly as Shane walked in, swinging the corkscrew in one hand.

He said, 'I think I'd better open the wine, let it breathe for a while.' He proceeded to do so, remarking to Paula, 'I suppose the meat has to stand and bleed for fifteen minutes or so, before I carve it. Well, I might as well hang around, keep you company.'

Elaine slipped out quietly, leaving them alone.

'It was a wonderful dinner,' Elaine said, putting down her dessert fork and spoon, looking across the table at Paula. 'And I'd love to have the recipe for this trifle. It was yummy.'

'And the recipe for the Yorkshire pudding,' Sonny suggested. He flashed his wife a sly but loving grin, added, 'And I know Elaine won't take offence when I tell you that her puddings come out like great lumps of soggy dough.'

Everyone laughed.

Paula said, 'I'll write them out for you tomorrow.' A smile of pleasure tugged at her mouth. 'You're both very good for my ego. I've never had so many compliments about my cooking.'

'That's not true,' Shane exclaimed. 'I've been giving you praise for years. You never pay attention to anything I say, that's your trouble,' he groused, but there was laughter on his face.

'Oh yes I do,' Paula shot back. 'And I always have.'

Chuckling, Shane pushed back his chair. 'I'd better retreat to the kitchen, make the coffee.'

'I'll assist you,' Sonny said, springing up, walking out after him.

Elaine sat back in the chair, studying Paula. How arresting and unusual her looks were. She wondered how old she was. Earlier, Elaine had decided she must be in her late twenties, perhaps even thirty. But now, in the soft candle-light, Paula looked much younger than that; her face held the vulnerability of a little girl's, and she was most appealing. Conscious she was staring rudely, Elaine said, 'You're a beautiful woman, Paula, and so very accomplished. No wonder he's miserable most of the time.'

Paula instantly stiffened, put down her glass unsteadily. 'I'm afraid I'm not following you.'

Elaine blurted out, 'Shane . . . he's crazy about you! It's written all over his face, and reflected in everything he says. What a pity you're so far away in England. That's what I was getting at earlier – when we were in the kitchen.'

Paula was stunned. She managed, 'Oh but Elaine, we're just old friends, childhood friends.'

For a split second Elaine thought Paula was joking, continuing the banter which had punctuated the good talk during dinner. Then she saw the horrified expression on Paula's face. 'Oh my God, I've said the wrong thing obviously. I'm so sorry. I just assumed you and Shane were having . . .' Her voice trailed off miserably.

Paula pushed back her sense of dismay. 'Please don't look so stricken, Elaine. It's all right, really it is. I understand. You've simply mistaken Shane's brotherly affection for me, read it to mean something else, something entirely different. Anybody could make that error.'

There was an awkward silence as the two women regarded each other. Both were at a loss for words.

Elaine cleared her throat. 'Now I've gone and spoiled a lovely evening . . . me and my big mouth.' Her expression was chagrined, apologetic. 'Sonny says my mouth's always open and my foot's always in it. He's right.'

Wanting to make her feel comfortable, Paula murmured softly, 'Oh please, Elaine, don't be embarrassed. I'm not. I like you, and I do want us to be friends. And look here, why wouldn't you jump to conclusions. After all, I am staying here with him, living under the same roof, and we are rather free and easy with each other. But then we grew up together, and we've been around each other all of our lives. There's a certain kind of naturalness between us, and it could easily be misinterpreted. But our relationship is not what you think.' Paula attempted a laugh, glanced down at her hands. 'I've just realized I'm not wearing my rings tonight, and we haven't discussed my personal life, so you couldn't possibly know that I'm married.'

'Oh well, then that explains everything!' Elaine cried, immediately flushing. She shook her head. 'There I go again . . . forgive me, Paula, my apologies. I'm saying all the wrong things tonight. I've probably had far too much to drink.'

Paula summoned another light, dismissive laugh. 'I think we ought to talk about something else, don't you? Shane and Sonny will be back at any moment.'

'Agreed. And please don't say anything to Shane . . . about what I assumed. He'll think I'm a real busy body.'

'Of course I won't say anything,' Paula reassured her. She rose. 'Let's go and sit by the fire.'

As the two of them walked across the floor, Paula slipped her arm through Elaine's companionably, said in a low voice, 'Try not to look so upset, so worried. Shane'll spot that straight away. He's very intuitive. It's the Celt in him, I suppose. When I was little I actually believed he could read my mind . . . he was always second guessing me in the most maddening way.'

Elaine merely smiled at this remark as she lowered herself into a chair. Although she had recovered some of her composure, she was cursing herself under her breath. How stupid she had been to presume they were having an affair. But who wouldn't think that . . . there *was* an intimacy between them, a kind of bonding, and Shane devoured Paula with his eyes, hung on to her every word. It was transparent that he was in love with her, no matter what Paula believed. And who's *she* kidding? Only herself. Well, self-delusion is a very human trait, Elaine thought, and stole a look at Paula, who sat in the chair opposite. Whether she knows it or not, she adores him. And not just as an old friend would . . . it's much more than that, more complex and it runs deeper. Still, perhaps she hasn't realized the extent of her feelings for him. And *I* ought not to have said anything. Elaine chastised herself again.

But a few seconds later, when Shane brought the tray of coffee to the fireplace, Elaine saw Paula's eyes instantly fly to his face, detected curiosity and a new and avid interest glittering in them. Elaine thought: Who knows, maybe I wasn't so foolish . . . maybe I've done them both a big favour by speaking out of turn.

Shane served the coffee. Sonny poured cognac, and ten minutes later he fetched his guitar and began to play. He was a classical guitarist and immensely talented, and the others sat back, captivated by his playing and his music, entranced by the magic he created for them.

Paula was only half listening. She was thankful not to have to make conversation. Her mind was in a turmoil. Elaine had stunned her, and much more than she had permitted the other woman to see. But the shock was receding and she tried to sort out her troubled thoughts.

She was positive that Elaine had simply misunderstood Shane's attitude, his behaviour towards her. On the other hand, what if Elaine was correct? Elaine had asserted that her marriage explained everything – meaning, of course, that it explained Shane's unhappiness, which they had apparently detected. Paula suddenly remembered the incomplete thought she had had that afternoon when she had been dozing on the sofa. She had been dwelling on the past few days, thinking that Shane was his old self, the way he was before her marriage. Something had clicked in her head, but then she had fallen asleep. Now that thought became whole, fully formed. *Shane had changed, had dropped her, the moment her engagement to Jim had been announced.* Why? Because he was jealous. That was the obvious explanation. How stupid she had been not to recognize this before tonight. But why hadn't Shane made it clear to her that he cared for her? When she was still free. Perhaps he had not understood that . . . until it was too late. It all made sense suddenly.

Paula leaned back in the chair, shattered by her conclusions. She closed her eyes, letting the music lap over her. She thought of Shane. He sat only a few feet away from her. What were his thoughts and emotions at this moment? Was he really in love with her? Crazy about her, so Elaine had said. Paula's heart clenched. And what about me? How do I feel about Shane? Am I unconsciously responding to vibrations emanating from him? Or am *I* in love with *him*? . . . Have I always been in love with him without knowing it? She tried to examine her innermost emotions, take stock of her feelings. She floundered.

They left at eleven forty-five.

Shane saw them out.

She knew what she was going to do.

Rising, she walked over to the chest, retrieved the bottle of cognac, carried it back to the fireside. She refilled their brandy balloons, placed the bottle in the centre of the coffee table, threw a couple of logs on to the fire.

Then she sat down on the sofa to wait for him.

A few minutes later she heard his step, glanced around as he came in. She smiled across the room at him.

Shane faltered, surprised to see her sitting there, holding another drink. He frowned. 'Are you planning to stay up all night? I would've thought you'd be half dead by now. It's been a long day, you worked so hard in the kitchen. Shouldn't we go –'

'I just got a second wind!' she cried, cutting him off before he suggested they go to sleep. 'I'm having a nightcap. I've poured one for you. Aren't you going to join me?' When he did not reply she laughed gaily. 'Oh don't be such an old spoil sport, Shane.'

He hesitated fractionally. He was afraid of being alone with her. He had been much too aware of her this evening. His desire for her had flared time and time again. His emotions were near the surface. He had sunk a lot of booze. He suddenly wasn't sure whether he could trust himself with her. This thought instantly annoyed him. He wasn't a callow youth, out on his first date, itching to make a conquest. He was a grown man. And he was with the girl he had known all his life. Yes, he loved her. But she trusted him. He was a gentleman. And he could handle himself. Still, I ought to put an end to the evening now, he thought. He said, 'Well, just one for the road. I'd planned for us to go riding tomorrow morning – bright and early.'

He strolled over to the fireplace, striving to appear off-hand. He reached for the drink she had poured, stepped away from the coffee table, planning to sit in the chair next to the hearth.

Paula patted the sofa. 'No, sit here, Shane, next to me. I want to talk to you.'

He tensed, looked at her alertly, searching her face. Her expression was neutral, placid even. It baffled him. She was usually much more animated. 'Okay.' He sat as far away from her as possible, squashed himself in the opposite corner of the sofa.

'Cheers,' Paula said, leaning closer, knocking her glass against his.

'Cheers.' Their hands accidentally touched as they lifted their glasses. He felt a spark of electricity shoot up his arm. He pushed himself even further into the corner, crossed his legs. 'What do you want to talk to me about?'

'I'd like to ask you a question.'

'Go on then . . .'

'Will you tell me the truth?'

He eyed her, suddenly wary. 'It depends on the question. If I don't like it I might be evasive in my answer.'

She gave him an odd look. 'You and I always told each other the truth when we were children. We never dealt in lies then . . . I'd like it to be like that between us again.'

'But it is!'

'Not really, Shane.' She saw the surprise registering in his eyes. 'Oh yes,' she said, 'it's been like old times this week, I admit, but there has been an estrangement between us for almost two years. Please don't even try to deny that.' There, it was out at last. 'In fact,' she went on quickly, 'you've been cold and distant with me for the longest time. When I asked you about your remoteness, your absence from my life, oh ages ago now, you brushed me off with silly excuses. Pressure of work, travel, you said.' Paula placed her drink on the coffee table and stared hard at him. 'I never really believed you in my heart of hearts, and that brings me to my question.' She paused, her eyes stayed on his face. 'And it's this: what awful thing did I do to you, to drive you out of my life? *You* – my oldest and dearest friend.'

He stared back at her, unable to make any kind of response. If he told her the truth he would reveal himself, his real feelings. If he lied he would hate himself for doing so. Anyway, she was clever. She would spot the lie immediately. He swallowed, put his drink down, looked ahead at the fire, his face reflective. Better to be silent.

Neither of them spoke for a while.

Paula, her eyes fixed on him, knew suddenly what his terrible dilemma was. Oh my darling, she thought, open your heart to me, tell me everything. Her love for Shane flowed through her, sweeping all else aside. She caught her breath in astonishment as she finally acknowledged her feelings. She longed to put her arms around him, to expunge the sadness on his face with her kisses.

The silence lengthened.

Paula said softly, 'I realize how difficult it is for you to answer my question.' There was only the merest hesitation before she finished, 'And so I will do it for you. You dropped me because I became engaged to Jim and then married him shortly afterwards.'

Still he did not dare open his mouth, afraid of giving himself away. So she had guessed. But exactly how *much* had she guessed. He blinked, continuing to focus on the dancing flames. He knew he could not let her see his face until he had wiped it clean of all emotion.

Eventually he half turned to her, said slowly, in a voice that was strangely hoarse, 'Yes, that's the reason I put distance between us, Paula. Perhaps I was wrong to do that. But . . . you see . . . I thought . . . that Jim would resent me, yes, and that you would too. After all, why would either of you want an old chum like me loitering on your doorstep . . .' He left the sentence unfinished.

'Shane . . . you're not telling me the truth . . . you know you're not, and so do I.'

It was the inflection of her voice that caught his attention, prompted him to swing his head. In the bright glow of the firelight the pallor of her face had acquired a curious luminosity, a pearly sheen. The violet eyes had darkened, burned with an unfamiliar look he could not fathom. He noticed a vein pulsing rapidly in her neck. She parted her lips as if to say something, but remained silent. *That expression in her eyes.* Again it struck him with unusual force. His desire for her raged through him. His heart thudded, an internal shaking gripped him. It took all of his self-control to remain seated, to stay away from her. Then he knew what he must do – he must get up, walk out, leave her. But he found he could not move.

They gazed at each other.

Paula saw his love, no longer concealed, leaping out from his brilliantly black eyes. Instantaneously Shane saw her love fully revealed, saw the yearning on her face, the longing and desire that hitherto had been only his to disguise, to withhold.

The shock of recognition transfixed him.

And then with sureness, absolute certainty, they moved at precisely the same moment.

They were in each other's arms. Their mouths met. Her lips were warm and soft and they parted slightly, welcomed him. Their tongues grazed, caressed, lay still. He pushed her down on to the mound of pillows, his left hand holding the nape of her neck, his right smoothing her hair away from her face, stroking her cheek, her long neck. Her hands pressed into his shoulder blades, then moved up into his hair, strong and firm on his scalp. He began to kiss her as he had wanted to kiss her for so long, with passion and force, his mouth hard and demanding on hers, his tongue thrusting, their breath, their saliva, mingling. But unexpectedly his kisses became gentle, tender, as he moved his hand on to her breast. He held it firmly, then slowly stroked it until the nipple sprang up hard under his fingers. His heart was slamming against hers.

They pulled apart at last, their breathing laboured. He looked down into her face. His eyes impaled hers. She reached up, touched his face, traced one finger across the line of his long upper lip under the moustache.

Shane stood up, undressed rapidly, flung his clothes on to the chair. Paula did the same, and they came together on the sofa with urgency, their hands clutching at each other. He took her in his arms and held her tightly against his chest, kissing her face, her hair, her shoulders. Then he pushed himself up on one elbow, bent over her. How well he knew this body. He had watched it grow from infant to child to young woman. But he had never seen it like this – entirely naked, every inch of it exposed to him, waiting for him. He let his hand slide down over her high, firm breasts, on to her flat stomach, along the edge of her outer thigh, then her inner thigh, smoothing, caressing, touching every part of her until they came to rest on that soft black vee of hair that concealed the core of her womanhood. He covered it with his entire hand, moved his body so that he could rest his face against her thigh. His fingers seemed to move of their own accord, gently seeking, probing, learning her. And finally he brought his mouth down to join with his fingers in their tender exploration.

Shane felt her immediately stiffen. He stopped, lifted his head, stared up along the slender stretch of her body, met her widening eyes. She was watching him intently, her expression baffled, alarmed. He smiled. So much for her marriage. His way of loving her, giving her pleasure, was seemingly new, and most transparently so. This sudden insight, the thought of her inexperience, delighted and thrilled him. At least no other man had touched her thus.

Her tenseness increased. She tried to raise herself on her elbows, opened her mouth to speak.

He murmured, 'Be still, let me love you.'

'But you, what about you?' she whispered.

'What's a few more minutes after all the years I've waited for you.'

Paula fell back against the cushions, sighing lightly. She closed her eyes, let her body go limp, allowed him to do as he wished with her. Her senses were beginning to reel, not only from the suddenness with which they had come together, but from his passion and sensuality. The way Shane was kissing and touching every part of her was unfamiliar, erotic. With his knowledge, expertise and sensitivity he knew exactly how to arouse her fully. He excited her as she had never been excited before, and she opened up to him uninhibitedly. Quiver upon quiver ran through her as his mouth and fingers loved her with delicacy, then fervency and always with consummate skill. They seemed to transmit a scorching heat, struck the core of her being with an exquisite sensation that she had never known had existed until this moment. The heat was spreading, searing her body. 'Oh Shane, Shane, please don't stop,' she gasped, unaware that she had spoken.

He could not answer unless he stopped, and he could not stop now. He was being carried along by her mounting excitement. It matched his own. He was aroused as he had never been, and her desire for him was thrilling, a powerful aphrodisiac. He intensified his concentration on her, savouring the warmth of her, bringing her to the pinnacle of ecstacy. He knew that any moment she would spasm. She did and he lifted himself on top of her, joined himself to her with a power and force that made them both cry out. She clung to him, screamed his name. He brought his mouth down hard on hers. She cleaved to him, her body arching. They began to move in unison their mutual passion rising.

Shane opened his eyes. The room was brilliant with light. And he who had so recently craved darkness now wanted that light . . . blinding glittering light.

He wanted to see her face, catch every flicker of emotion that crossed it, needed to know that it truly was she whom he was loving. He pushed himself up, his hands braced on each side of her, and she lifted her lids, staring into his face. He stared back. He began to move again and with rapidity and she followed his lead and not once did his searching eyes leave hers. Suddenly he slowed the rhythm, wanting to prolong their joining.

He suddenly understood that this went far, far beyond mere sexual possession. He was possessing her soul, her heart, her mind, as she was possessing his. She was his dreamlike child of his childhood dreams ... in his arms at last ... truly his at last. She belonged to him now. He held the world in his arms. The pain he had lived with ceased abruptly. His old life fell away ... down ... down ... into a dark void ... a new life was beginning ... he was someone entirely new. He was a complete man ... made whole as he came up ... up into the blinding, blinding light where she waited in the centre of the radiance.

They were mesmerized by each other. Their eyes locked, became wider as their scrutiny intensified. They looked deeper, deeper still, endeavouring to convey the extent and strength of their emotions, and they saw into infinity, saw their own souls and each other's. And everything was made clear.

She is my life, he thought. *And oh the blessed peace of it.*

She thought: *There is only Shane. There only ever has been Shane.*

He started to move against her, slowly at first and then more urgently and without restraint. She matched him, was as unrestrained as he. Their bodies entwined. Their mouths joined. They became one.

As he felt his life's essence flowing through him into her, he cried out, 'I love you, I have always loved you, I will love you until the day I die.'

Shane's bedroom was much larger and more spacious than the one he had given her, but it was warm because the entire barn was centrally heated.

As in her room, a huge brass bed dominated the space. Paula now lay propped up against the mound of snowy pillows, a down comforter tucked around her chest, only her bare shoulders revealed. She sighed, filled with contentment and an extraordinary feeling of inner peace, and of completeness. The physical release she had experienced with Shane was wholly new to her. She had never achieved satisfaction before, and she marvelled at him, at herself, and at their lovemaking. How unselfish and tender he was, and oh how she had responded to his emotion, to his yearning desire for her. And because of his genuine understanding of her, his caring, their loving had been natural, uninhibited, full of exultation and joyousness, a true bonding in every way.

When they finally doused the lights in the main room and crept upstairs carrying their clothes, she had believed their mutual passion was entirely spent. Exhausted, they had lain here in this great bed, their bodies touching, holding hands under the sheet, and they had not stopped talking. And then quite suddenly their desire for each other had flared unexpectedly, and they had made love for the second time with the same urgent need and breathlessness.

Shane had turned on the lamp, thrown back the bedclothes, telling her he must look at her, know that it was really she, must witness the emotions he was evoking in her. The kissing, the touching had been unhurried and voluptuous, and again he had brought her to that blissful state of fulfilment before taking her to him, and had led her into new regions, murmuring what he wanted, showing her how to excite him further, love him as he had loved her. And she had done so willingly, lovingly, taking pleasure from his pleasure. But he had stopped her when he was on the brink, and pulled her on top of him, his body thrusting upward to join with hers. And together they had reached greater heights of rapture than the first time.

Shane had finally switched off the lamp, and wrapped in each other's arms they had tried to sleep but it had eluded them both. They were too keyed up and conscious of each other, needed to prolong their new-found intimacy. And so they had begun to talk in the dark, and then a few minutes ago Shane had gone downstairs to make tea for them.

Paula leaned forward and glanced at the clock on the small campaign chest at his side of the bed. It was nearly four. We made love endlessly, she thought, but not mindlessly. Oh no, not mindlessly at all. She had not realized until tonight how beautiful the sexual union between a man and a woman could be. In fact she had always thought that sex was not what it was cracked up to be. How wrong she had been. But it has to be the right man with the right woman, she said under her breath. She sank into the pillows, another sigh escaping as she waited for Shane to come back.

He did so a moment or two later, carrying a laden tray and singing a popular song at the top of his voice.

'Who do you think you are?' 'A pop star?' she cried, sitting up in bed, grinning at him.

His answer was to gyrate his body at her several times and leer in an exaggerated fashion.

He brought her the mug of tea and the plate of ginger biscuits she had requested, put his own tea and chocolate biscuits on his bedside chest. Continuing to hum the melody, he slipped off his robe, threw it across a nearby chair.

She looked at his broad back, massive shoulders and strong arms, and admiringly so. He was a big, well-built man, and she had seen him in swimming trunks for years. So why did his powerful physique seem so startling to her tonight? Because now she really *knew* him? Because she had learned about his body as he had hers and in the most intimate way?

As he swung around he noticed that she was staring at him.

'What's wrong?' he asked.

'Nothing. I was just thinking I've never seen you so brown.' She giggled. 'But you've got a white bottom.'

'And you too, madame, will have a brown back and a white bottom by this time next week.' He strode over to the bed, unselfconscious in his nakedness, and got in next to her, kissed her cheek. 'If I've got anything to do with it, that is.'

'Oh,' was all she said, gazing at him.

'Yes. I have to go to Barbados on Tuesday. Come with me, Paula.' His eyes appealed.

'Oh Shane, what a lovely idea. Of course I'll come with you.' Her face instantly dropped. 'But I couldn't get away until Wednesday.'

'That's all right.' He turned to get his mug of tea, took a sip. 'It'll give me a chance to do some of my work. Actually, I will have to spend some time every morning in the administrative offices. But we'll have the afternoons . . . and all those beautiful nights.' His smile was suggestive, his dancing black eyes wickedly teasing.

She said, with a small smile, 'I've been dying to go to Barbados – to see the Harte boutique.'

He lifted his brows. 'Ah ha, so that's why you agreed, and so readily. And I thought you were after my body again.'

Paula gave him a light playful punch on his arm. 'Oh you!' She drank her tea. It tasted good, hot and refreshing. And she felt good. No, wonderful. And filled with wonderment. She reached out, took a chocolate biscuit from the plate on his lap, munched it, then took another.

'I wonder what a psychiatrist would make of that?' Shane said.

'Make of what?'

'This constant desire of yours to eat off my plate. You've been doing it all of your life, and perhaps it has some hidden sexual meaning. Do you think it's a form of oral gratification, linked in some way to me and your feelings for me?'

She threw back her head and laughed, enjoying him, being with him. 'I don't know. And I'll try to stop doing it, but childhood habits are hard to break. As a matter of fact, very seriously, I've really got to curb my appetite. I haven't stopped eating since I've been with you. Anyone would think I've been on a starvation diet.'

Shane merely smiled, thought: You have, my darling, in more ways than you know.

They finished their tea and biscuits, continuing to chat about the trip to Barbados, and Shane was delighted she was so obviously thrilled and excited about the prospect of spending five days with him in the sun. At one moment Shane got out of bed, found his cigarettes and opened the window. 'You don't mind if I smoke do you?' he asked, climbing back into bed.

'Not at all.' Paula edged closer to him, so that their legs touched and their shoulders grazed, wanting the closeness of him.

'Happy, darling?' he asked, glancing at her through the corner of his eye.

'Very happy. Are you?'

'As never before.'

There was a short silence, then Paula confessed, 'I've never made love like that before.'

'I know you haven't.'

'Was it that obvious . . . my inexperience?'

He chuckled, squeezed her hand, said nothing.

She said, 'But you're *very* experienced, Shane.' She stole a look at his face. Jealousy, an unfamiliar feeling, trickled through her. 'You've had a lot of women.'

He was not certain if this last remark was a question or a statement. 'You've heard all the gossip about me and my romantic escapades over the years.'

'The stories were all true then?'

'Yes.'

'Why not me, Shane?'

'That's fairly obvious, easy to answer … because of Emma and Blackie, their relationship, the closeness and involvement of our two families. But even if I'd understood my true feelings for you, Paula, I wouldn't have dared come near you, tried to make love to you. I'd have been skinned alive, and you know I would.' He thought of Dorothea Mallet's words, added, 'Before your marriage, you were sort of – well, the crown princess of the three clans. And, therefore, inviolate. A man doesn't sleep with a woman like you, have an affair with her. He proposes marriage. Sadly, regrettably I didn't know that I wanted you desperately, or how I felt about you when you were available, unattached. I was too close to you, I suppose.'

'I understand.' She looked at his face. A feeling of possessiveness came over her, and the jealousy intensified. She asked softly, 'Those other women … did you make love with them the same way you made love with me tonight?'

He was momentarily startled by the question. He was on the verge of lying, not wishing to hurt or upset her, and then knew he should be honest. Opting for the cold truth, he said, 'Yes, sometimes, but not always, not with all of them. You and I made love in the most personal and intimate way there is, Paula. Most of my former girlfriends didn't arouse that kind of desire, that need in me – as you do. Oral sex is … well, *extremely* intimate, as I just said. I've got to be very emotionally committed to want that.' He half smiled. 'It's not something I have ever been able to do indiscriminately, Paula.'

She nodded. 'I think that it probably springs from the urge and the desire and the compulsion to totally possess the other person.'

'Oh yes, yes, it does.' He gave her a penetrating glance.

'Since you've been in New York –' She paused, hating herself for prying, but she could not help it. She cleared her throat. 'Have you had a lot of affairs?'

'No.'

'Why not?'

'Because of you.' Shane drew on his cigarette, exhaled, said, 'My bedroom liaisons have been pretty disastrous ever since the day I understood that I loved you.' He turned his head, looked deeply into her eyes. 'Actually, I've had a lot of trouble in that direction … I've been impotent.'

He saw the surprise and dismay cross her face. She stiffened against him slightly, but she said not one word.

Shane went on, 'I managed to make it occasionally, if the room was dark and my partner did not shatter my fragile fantasy … my fantasy that it was you whom I was with. If I could hold the image of you in my mind, then it was all right. But for the most part it's been bloody difficult.'

Without mentioning names, he told her then about his experience in Harrogate the afternoon of the christening, and recounted other devastating incidents. He felt neither shame nor embarrassment talking to Paula in this most self-revealing manner. He was glad to unburden himself, and as he continued to speak he acknowledged that he was only following his old pattern of confiding in her, sharing his secrets with her as he had when they were children.

Once he had finished, Paula reached up, put her arms around his neck, held him close. 'Oh Shane, Shane darling, I'm so sorry I caused you such pain and heartache.'

He stroked her head, pressed it closer to his shoulder with one hand. 'It was hardly your fault.' He then asked softly, 'When did you discover how you felt about me?'

'I've been very conscious of you since I came to New York. Last night, then again this evening, the strangest feelings began to stir in me. I realized I desired you sexually, wanted you to make love to me, and I to you. Suddenly – when we were talking after Elaine and Sonny left – it dawned on me that I was in love with you.'

He did not speak for a few seconds, then he said, 'I didn't bring you up here to seduce you, Pau –'

'I know that!'

'I just wanted to be with you, spend time with you. I've missed you very much.' There was a short pause. 'I've had a golden rule for years – no married women. I never wanted to take something that belonged to another man.'

'I believe I belong to myself,' she said.

Shane was silent. He was eaten up with curiosity about her marriage, and his jealousy of Jim was rife, but he was reluctant to embark on this subject, afraid of spoiling the mood that presently existed between them.

Paula remarked evenly, 'Surely you know I wouldn't be here with you like this, Shane, if I were happy in my marriage.'

'Jesus, Paula, of course I do! You're not promiscuous. I know you'd never play around just for the sake of it.' He scowled, eyed her closely through his narrowed gaze. 'It's not working then?'

'No. I've tried, Shane, God knows I've tried. I'm not blaming Jim. I think it takes two to create a disaster. I don't hate him, he's not a bad person. We're not right together, that's all there is to it. We're incompatible in every way.' She bit her inner lip. 'I'd like to leave it at that . . . for tonight anyway. All of a sudden I don't want to talk about my marriage.'

'I know, darling, I know.'

For a short while they were silent, lost in their own reflections. But eventually Paula murmured, 'Oh Shane what a mess I've made. If only we could turn the clock back.'

'Ah but that's not possible . . . and time is not so important, you know. And you mustn't think about yesterday or tomorrow, only today. Anyway, time isn't portioned out and then encased in little capsules – time is like a river. The past, the present, the future all flow together to become one long continuing and never-ending stream. We get echoes of the past every day of our lives, and we see images of the future as we live in the present. Time gone and time yet to come is all around us, Paula, and time is a dimension unto itself.'

She looked up into his familiar and well-loved face, and in her mind's eye she saw the man as he had been as a boy, recalled his preoccupation with the Celt in himself and his Celtic forebears and Celtic legend. That old dreamy look born of his mysticism filled his eyes, and his deep introspection was evidenced in his expression and she knew that he was lost somewhere in the far, far distant past. And then he blinked, gave her a funny little lopsided smile, one she remembered so well. The man instantly became that small boy at Heron's Nest and their childhood was all around them, encompassing them, filling this room. And she knew that Shane was correct in the things he had said about time being like a flowing river, and she reached out and touched his arm and told him this.

He said slowly, thoughtfully, 'And there's another thing, Paula. Life has its own intricate pattern – there is a grand design, really. What has already happened in our lives was meant to happen, perhaps to show us the way, lead us to each other. And the future is already here with us, *now*, at this very moment, whether we're aware of it or not.' He put his hand under her chin, lifted her face to his, looked deeply into her eyes. 'And we're not going to think about anything except this weekend. We'll take each day after that as it comes.' He leaned into her, kissed her lightly, drew back. 'Don't look so serious. Life has a way of taking care of itself and I have a feeling that we are going to do just fine together.'

Her throat tightened with a rush of emotion. She clung to him, whispered, 'I love you so much, Shane. How could I have ever not known that!'

'You do now, and that's all that matters, isn't it?'

36

She arrived in Barbados on Wednesday afternoon.

As she walked out of customs, carrying her suit jacket over her arm and clutching her travelling bag, she thought that he had not come to meet her after all. Disappointment replaced anticipation. She looked around seeking a chauffeur or someone wearing the uniform of the Coral Cove Hotel whom he may have sent in his place.

The porter trailing behind her, carrying her large case, asked if she wanted a taxi. She explained she was expecting to be met, then peered again at the blur of people crowding the busy airport entrance.

Paula saw Shane before he saw her.

He came barrelling through the main glass doors, looking anxious. She stood stock still, taut with excitement. Her heart began to clatter unreasonably. She had been with him on Monday night. Two days ago. But seeing him now was a shock. Every detail of his appearance leapt out at her, as though she was observing a total stranger, someone she did not know. His wavy hair, longish and curling down on to his neck, the well-defined brows and the distinctive moustache all appeared blacker and his brilliant eyes were like pieces of onyx in his tan face. Even the cleft in his chin seemed more pronounced. She saw that he wore a beautifully cut cream silk suit, a cream shirt with fine burgundy stripes and a burgundy tie. A silk handkerchief of the same wine colour flared in his breast pocket. His brown loafers gleamed. He was immaculate from head to toe. But he was the same old Shane. It was she who was new. The new Paula who was in love with him. He was the only man she wanted.

Finally he spotted her and pushed through the crowd, purposeful, confident. He was there, towering above her, grinning, his eyes filled with laughter.

She felt weak at the knees.

'Darling,' he said, 'I'm sorry. I cut it fine, as usual.'

She could not speak, just stood there, smiling up at him inanely.

He bent to kiss her cheek, and then took her arm, motioned for the porter to follow them, bustled her outside.

A chauffeur leaning against the hood of a silver-grey Cadillac sprang forward, opened the passenger door, stowed the suitcase in the trunk. Shane tipped the porter, helped her into the car, climbed in after her. He pressed a button. The glass partition behind the driver's seat closed. As the car slid noiselessly away from the kerb he put his arm around her, tilted her face to his. He stared at her, as if he had not seen her for years. She stared back, saw her own reflection mirrored in his glistening black eyes. Her mouth went dry as he bent towards her. And as his tongue slid past her parched lips to touch hers, blood rushed through her. She felt dizzy. His grip on her tightened. Her arms went around his neck. Her hands slipped up into his thick hair. She knew he was terribly excited. But then, so was she.

Shane held her away from him, shaking his head, half laughing. 'I think I'd better exercise a bit of restraint here, otherwise I'll end up making love to you on the back seat and that *would* cause a scandal.' He held her eyes. He seemed unexpectedly amused at them both. 'You do get me hot and bothered, lady.'

'It works both ways, you know.'

Smiling, he lit a cigarette, asked her if she had had a good flight, and then began to talk effortlessly about the island, pointing out interesting landmarks, giving her a brief history of Barbados. For the next half hour or so he talked incessantly, reached out to squeeze her hand from time to time.

'Coral Cove is on the west side of the island,' Shane was saying. 'It's not far from the Sandy Lane Hotel, which we'll be passing in a few seconds. I'll take you there to lunch one day – it's a lovely spot. Anyway, our place is located in the area known as the Platinum Coast, so called because of its sandy white beaches. I hope you're going to like it.'

'Oh Shane, I know I will, but I'd be happy anywhere with you, darling.'

His eyes instantly swivelled to hers. 'Would you really, Paula?'

'Yes, Shane.'

'Love me?'

'Madly.'

'You'd better.'

'And you?'

'I'm crazy about you, darling. So crazily, overwhelmingly in love with you I'll never let you go,' he replied, his voice light. And then he took hold of her hand tightly and his expression and his voice changed. 'I mean that, Paula. I won't let you go. *Never.*'

Startled, she swallowed, not knowing what to say. England and her life there, momentarily forgotten in her euphoria at being with him, loomed hideously. She met his piercing gaze, said haltingly, 'There're a lot of prob –'

He covered her mouth with his large, sunburned hand, shook his head. 'Sorry, darling, I shouldn't have said that. At least, not now.' He gave her his cheeky, boyish grin. 'We're not going to even think about problems, never mind talk about them, for the next few days. There'll be plenty of time for that when we're back in New York.'

And before she could reply the car was slowing down. The chauffeur turned in through iron gates and as the Cadillac swept on she caught a glimpse of the name Coral Cove. A moment later, at the end of the short driveway, they came to a standstill in front of the hotel.

The intense heat hit her as Shane helped her out of the air-conditioned car. She looked around. Coral Cove was larger than she had expected, painted white and pale pink on the outside. She could see it was set in the middle of lush, exotic gardens. Just beyond the edge of the green lawns lay a stretch of silver sand and the turquoise ocean glittering in the sunshine.

'Oh Shane, it's beautiful,' she exclaimed as he looked at her expectantly, his eyes eager.

He nodded, took her elbow. 'I think so – and thanks. But come on, it's bloody hot outside at this time of day.'

He led her through the spacious, airy lobby, washed in white and furnished with rattan pieces and immense tropical plants in ceramic tubs. Ceiling fans whirred pleasantly, creating a gentle breeze and the ambiance was cool, shady, welcoming.

Even though she wanted to stop and look around, Shane would not permit her to linger.

He whisked her smartly up to the suite, and once they were inside he pulled her into his arms roughly, began to kiss her, his hands hard on her body. Paula clung to him, returned his kisses. A loud rapping on the door interrupted this moment of intimacy, forced them apart.

Shane called, 'Come in, Albert,' and hurried forward to take her suitcase from the bellboy.

When they were alone, Shane said, 'All this kissing's going to lead to something else any minute. And since I don't want you to think I'm a sex maniac I'm going to show you around.' He drew her into the centre of the room. 'Listen, I've got a whole programme mapped out for you. Sun and sleep.' The impudent grin flashed, as he went on, 'And Shane. Lots and lots of Shane. Day and night, non-stop. How does that sound to you?'

'Scrumptious,' she said laughing. 'And so is this suite.'

'I knew you'd like this particular one, Paula.'

She glanced about with pleasure, noting the coral and lime accents highlighting the cool whiteness of the room, the handsome wicker furniture, the comfortable sofas covered in a pretty floral fabric.

He had filled the room with masses of flowers. Bowls and bud vases held all manner of exotic blooms that were a blaze of stunning colour. 'Shane . . . the flowers . . . they're beautiful.' She smiled at him, reached out to touch a delicate purple spray. 'Just exquisite. Thank you.'

'Those are miniature orchids . . . wild orchids. But most likely you know that. They grow all over the island. Come on, let me show you the bedroom.'

He propelled her through the open door and she found herself standing in another large white room, this one accented with yellow and pale blue. The furniture was of white-lacquered wood; there was a big bed, curtained in white muslin, which faced out towards the terrace that ran the length of the suite. More flowers abounded here, but something was missing, and as her glance swept from wall to wall she realized that the bedroom, like the living room, looked curiously unoccupied. It had an unlived-in air.

She turned to him. 'Do you have another suite for yourself, Shane?'

'Yes, the adjoining one. I thought it was more discreet.' He smiled wryly. 'Not that anyone will be deceived – hotel staffs are notorious for knowing everything that's going on.' He took a key out of his pocket, opened a door, motioned her to follow him.

His suite was similar to her own, but here his possessions were strewn all over; his briefcase was on a table, a yellow sweater was thrown across the back of a chair; papers and his work littered the small desk; a bottle of scotch, an ice bucket and glasses were arranged on a tray on a white wicker console.

'Then why bother to have another suite, if that's the case,' she asked. 'I mean, our families would never be suspicious of us – we're supposed to be like brother and sister.'

'Then if this is incest, give me incest any time.'

She laughed.

He sobered, added, 'But you never know ... I think it's wiser ... just for appearances' sake, the switchboard, and the hotel register. Let's not borrow trouble unnecessarily. I've instructed the switchboard to monitor all calls. For both of us. That way we won't be taken off guard.' He put his arm around her, walked her through to her suite. 'Don't fret, I've every intention of staying in here with you. All the time. Now, do you want to freshen up, have a drink or a cup of tea? Or would you like to pop down to see the boutique?'

'Oh Shane, let's do that.' She gave him a studiously prim look. 'After all, that's the real reason I came to Barbados.'

'*Rat.*'

The Harte boutique was situated on the far side of the main garden nearest to the hotel. It was the central building in a semi-circle of five shops which looked out on to a grassy lawn. Here a fountain played in the centre. Flower beds added bright splashes of colour around the edge of the smooth clipped lawn.

A feeling of excitement trickled through Paula. There it was, the familiar and distinctive lettering that read *E. Harte*, staring out at her above the bright pink door. The large windows on either side were well-dressed, eye-catching, most professionally done.

She grabbed Shane's arm. 'I know it's only a boutique, and nothing like our large department stores, but I feel so proud, Shane. Here we are – in the Caribbean! Harte's has another branch. I do wish Grandy could see it, she'd be as thrilled as I am.'

'Yes, she would, and I know what you mean. It's a combination of things – pride of ownership, gratification, a sense of tremendous satisfaction. And don't forget, this is *yours*, Paula, as the other boutiques in our hotel chain will be.'

'Merry thought of the idea, Shane, not I.'

'You did all the work.'

'Not according to Sarah.'

'I told you last week to forget Sarah Lowther. She's jealous of you.'

'Because I'm running the stores?'

'Yes. She's a nit-wit. She could never handle Emma's business, and Aunt Emma has always known that. She picked the best man she had . . . you.'

'If anybody else but you had said that, I'd accuse him of being a male chauvinist.'

'Sorry, you know I didn't mean it the way it came out. Just a figure of speech.' He gave her a pointed look. 'There's nothing masculine about you, my darling, let me assure you of that. Come on, let's go inside.'

He pushed open the door to the sound of tinkling bells.

Together they stepped inside and Paula caught her breath. The central area of the boutique was white with lots of chrome fixtures and the floor was made of white ceramic tiles. There was a paucity of clutter but this starkness made an ideal background for showing off the colourful clothes and accessories. A small cantilevered staircase led to an upper floor. It was cooled by the many ceiling fans.

'Oh Shane, you've outdone yourself,' Paula exclaimed.

He gave her a delighted grin, turned to introduce her to Marianna, the manager, and the three assistants who worked for Harte's. Paula chatted to them enthusiastically as she was given a tour. The young women were all pleasant, outgoing, well informed about fashion, and Paula found herself warming to them as they showed her the various displays, gave her a run down on current sales, showed her the latest sales figures.

At the end of an hour, she said to Shane, 'I have to buy a few things. I simply didn't get a chance to pick up everything I needed at the New York store. But look, you don't have to wait. I can meet you back at the hotel.'

'Oh I'm in no hurry,' he said with a nonchalant smile. 'I haven't seen you since Monday night. You're not getting rid of me that easily. Besides, I may have something to say about the things you're going to buy.'

After trying on swim suits and other beachwear, and having received a nod of approval from Shane, Paula began to look at cocktail dresses. She threw a number of casual summer evening outfits over one arm, and then Shane joined her, picked out several items he liked. Handing them to her, he gave her a conspiratorial wink. 'What about these?'

Paula made a face. 'I'm not sure they're really *me*.'

'Yes, they are. Trust my judgement.'

Not wishing to cause a fuss in the shop, she took them from him. As a child and a young girl Paula had always strived to please Shane, to cater to his wishes, and she found this desire surfacing. It overcame her objections to the outfits he had chosen. All of the dresses and evening wear bore the Lady Hamilton label, and as Paula went back into the dressing room she could not help thinking of Sarah again. Shane was correct about her cousin. Instantly she dismissed Sarah from her mind, not wanting to spoil her lighthearted mood by dwelling on unpleasant memories of *their* last encounter. She tried one of the outfits on, and returned to the main area of the boutique.

As she swung around she suddenly liked her reflection in the long mirrored wall. He obviously did. He was nodding emphatically. He told her she looked sensational.

Paula stood in front of the glass, studying the dress. It was short, made of the deepest blue chiffon and was simply styled, with only one shoulder and a rouched effect over the bodice. If it lacked the hard-edged chic she usually favoured, it was flattering, feminine and curiously sexy in the way in which it clung to her body. It was a wholly new look for her, but the colour was glorious.

Shane enthused over a white silk trouser suit he had selected, but told her to forget the short red dress he had pulled off a rack. In the end she bought two of his choices, the blue and the white, and a long yellow shift made of silk jersey trimmed with violet ribbons. He waited patiently as she tried on sandals, settled on several pairs, and then picked up a couple of straw hats and added these to her purchases. After complimenting Marianna on the way she was running the boutique, Paula promised to visit them the following day.

They meandered around the semi-circle of boutiques, window shopping. Paula said, 'Our layout is stunning, Shane. Merry showed me the renderings, but one can never really tell from drawings. Thank you for making our boutique so special.'

'I'm notorious for pleasing those I love and adore,' he said.

Slowly they strolled back to the hotel. Shane could not help smiling as he noticed the way Paula's eyes swung from side to side, scrutinizing the many and varied tropical plants, flowering shrubs and unusual blooms indigenous to the island.

'Well,' he said, 'I'll know where to find you – if you're missing in the next few days. Did you pack a trowel?'

'No, and it's odd, Shane, I have no desire to do any gardening.' This was true and she was surprised at herself. She glanced up at him. 'All I want is to be with you.'

He put his arm around her shoulder, kissed the top of her head. 'So let's go up to the suite, shall we?'

She lay within the circle of his arms.

The bedroom was dusky, shadow filled. The filmy muslin curtains around the bed stirred gently in the soft breeze, and beyond the open louvred doors leading out to the terrace the sky had turned to a deep pavonian blue. The only sounds were the rustling of the palm trees and the faint distant roar of the ocean.

The bosky stillness was soothing after their frantic and impassioned love-making, and she luxuriated in it, and in her own sense of fulfilment. How surprising she was with him. Whenever they made love she felt completely satiated as they drew apart, exhausted, staring in astonishment. But the minute Shane was aroused again, so was she, and her feverishness echoed his. And each time he took her they reached a greater pitch of excitement and the ultimate in gratification.

A tiny sigh of contentment trickled through Paula. She could no longer recognize herself. Only a few days of loving Shane . . . being loved by him . . . and she would never be the same woman again. Shane had somehow helped her to shed her old self. He had recreated her. And in so doing he had made her his.

On Monday and Tuesday she had worked frantically to be able to leave for

Barbados today. She had raced between the apartment, the store and Harte Enterprises, and had worked until three in the morning on Tuesday. He had rarely been out of her mind, and whatever she was doing he insinuated himself into her thoughts. Their relationship had reverted to what it had been when they were growing up. With added dimensions – sexual adoration and a deep abiding love, that of a man for a woman, a woman for a man.

There were no jarring notes or irritating habits to contend with. Shane was a communicator. He venerated the language, verbalized everything that came into his fertile, agile, searching mind. And he never shut her out. He shared, confided, never ever withheld. She did the same. His secrets were her secrets now. Hers had been conveyed to him and in explicit detail. His responses, his thoughts and his understanding were her great consolation. He made her feel whole, and completely female. A total woman.

She stole a look at his face. It was in repose. He drowsed. Her heart filled. What a mixture he was – impetuous, extravagant, and vain in some ways. Yet he was intelligent, tender, loving, thoughtful and passionate in everything he did. There was that strangely fey, mystical side to his nature which she knew sprang from the Celt in him, and he could be melancholy and brooding at times. And yes, he had a terrible temper. In the past they had had their violent quarrels. As a child she had often been the victim of his whims and moods and temperamental outbursts. But Shane was flexible, and he could disarm and enchant her with his self-deprecating humour, his dry wit, and his sweeping natural charm. As a man he was as complex as she was as a woman.

Suddenly she endeavoured to evaluate their relationship as it stood at this moment. It was so unusual she could think of no way to describe it to herself. And then she thought: Shane and I have an intimacy of the heart and mind as well as the body. Together we are complete. I feel more married to Shane than I do to Jim.

She held herself very still, appalled at this thought. Gradually she eased herself back into it, and acknowledged that it was the truth. Her mind swung to Jim.

Why did you marry him? Shane had asked her the other night in New York. *Because I was in love with him*, she had responded. Shane had admitted that she probably had been, but he had also suggested that Jim's fatal attraction might have been his name. *A Fairley was forbidden to you because of Emma's past*, Shane had ventured, and possibly he was right. She *had* believed herself to be in love with Jim, and yet now she understood that her feelings for him had never equalled her tremendous emotional bonding to Shane. She and Jim were totally different; she and Shane were incredibly alike. And she had never known what sex was all about, had never really enjoyed participating until Shane had made love to her. She had told him this. He had said nothing, had simply sighed and held her more tightly in his strong and loving arms.

Her life, her responsibilities, the complications of her business and family intruded. Suddenly the future glared her in the face like a terrible spectre. She was frightened. What was going to happen to them? What would she and Shane do? Release the fear, fling aside these distressing thoughts, she told herself. For God's sake don't dwell on your problems now. You'll spoil the next few days if you do. Enjoy this time with Shane, enjoy being free, unfettered.

She nestled closer to him, slipped her arm across his stomach, let her fingers curl against his side, bent herself into the shape of his body.

Shane stirred, opened his eyes, looked down at her. He smiled to himself, his heart full of love and tenderness for her. His dreamlike child of his childhood dreams had become his dreamlike woman. Except that she was no dream. Paula was reality. His reality. His life. She had extinguished all pain, all hurt, all of the anguish in his heart and mind. And with her he could truly be himself, expose himself, warts and all, and in a way he had never been able to do with any other woman. There had been legions of women until two years ago. Too many really, and of too little quality. Now he belonged to Paula – as he always had in his soul and heart and his imagination. He would belong to her for the rest of his life. She owned him.

She opened her eyes, looked up at him, smiled. He smiled back, bent to kiss her, stroked her rounded breast, moved his hand down to nestle between her thighs. She reached out to touch him, knowing how much he took pleasure from the feel of her hand on him. Within the space of a few minutes they were both aroused, craving each other. Shane rolled on top of her, slipped his arms under her back, took her to him. He began to move against her slowly, looked down into her unnaturally blue eyes, marvelled at the joy that lit her face. He whispered her name, spoke his love for her, his heart leaping at her swift and ardent responses. He closed his eyes, as did she, and they lost themselves in each other and their love.

The jangling telephone bell pierced the silence.

They stopped, startled, snapped open their eyes, gaped at each other. 'Oh Christ!' Shane groaned. He disentangled himself, switched on the light, shot another look at her as she clutched his arm fiercely.

Sitting up, Paula exclaimed, 'Maybe I'd better answer it, since we're in my suite.'

'It's all right, don't look so alarmed. I told you the switchboard's monitoring all of our calls.' He lifted the receiver on the fourth ring. 'Shane O'Neill.' He paused. 'Thanks, Louanne. Put him through.' He covered the mouthpiece with one hand. 'It's my father,' he said.

'Oh.' Paula tugged at the sheet, covered herself.

Shane began to chuckle. 'He can't see you lying here naked, you know.'

She had the good grace to laugh. 'But I feel funny. Exposed.'

'You'd better be – to me.' Shane said, then shouted into the phone, 'Dad! Hello! How are you? What's up?' As he began to listen, he cradled the phone between his ear and his shoulder, lit a cigarette, shuffled himself up against the pillows.

'Well, I have to admit I've been expecting it, Dad, and let's be honest, the idea does have a lot of merit. But look here, I can't go over there right now. Certainly not until January or February. I've got my hands full in New York. You know the hotel's at the most crucial stage. It would be disaster if I left. And I thought you wanted me down here in the islands over the holidays. Jesus, Dad, I can't be in two or three places at once.'

Shane flicked his cigarette ash, relaxed against the pillows, listening once more. 'Oh good,' he interrupted. 'Yes, yes, I agree. And you'll enjoy the trip. Why don't you take Mother with you?'

Paula slipped out of bed, found her dressing gown in the bathroom, slipped it on, returned to the bedroom. She began to pick up their clothes which were scattered all over the floor. We were in a terrible hurry when we first went to bed, she thought, then sat down on a chair, watching him.

Shane, silent again, winked at her, blew her a kiss, then again he interrupted his father. He exclaimed, 'I say, Dad, Paula's just this minute walked in and she wants to say hello.'

Paula shook her head. She felt ridiculously – and irrationally – self-conscious.

Shane put down the phone and his cigarette, leapt out of bed, grabbed her and dragged her to the phone, whispering, 'He doesn't know we've been making passionate love for the last two hours, you silly thing. It's only seven-thirty here. I'm sure he thinks we're having drinks before dinner.'

Paula had no option but to take the phone. 'Hello, Uncle Bryan,' she said in the most normal voice she could summon. Then she fell quiet, listening to Shane's father. 'Oh yes,' she said after a moment, 'I got in this afternoon. The hotel's simply beautiful, so is the boutique, Uncle Bryan. Shane's done a marvellous job. He's very talented. I'm most impressed.' She sat down on the bed, as Bryan commenced to relay his news from London.

Eventually, Paula had a chance to reply: 'Then you'll be seeing Grandy before me. And Uncle Blackie. Do give them both my love. And lots of love to Aunty Geraldine and Merry. See you soon, Uncle Bryan, and have a safe trip. Here's Shane again.'

He took the phone from her and she lolled across the end of the bed. Shane resumed his business conversation with his father, but after only a few minutes, he said, 'All right, Dad, that's it then. I'll be here until Monday morning, after that you can get me in New York. Love to Mother and Merry, kiss little Laura for me, and take care of yourself. And listen, don't forget to give my love to Grandpops and Aunt Emma. Bye, Dad.'

Shane hung up, looked at Paula, rolled his eyes. They burst out laughing. 'Come here, you witch, you,' he exclaimed, dragging her up from the end of the bed, wrapping his arms around her.

She struggled with him, still laughing and rumpling his hair. They rolled over and over on the bed, their merriment accelerating. He gasped, 'My father certainly picks the wrong time to call, doesn't he? Just as we were about to have another few minutes of lovely passion.'

'Few minutes!' she shrieked. 'More like an hour, you mean.'

'Are you complaining or is that a testimonial?' He kissed her ear, chuckled again, mimicked her, saying, 'Shane's done a marvellous job, Uncle Bryan. He's very talented. I'm most impressed.' Reverting to his own voice, he murmured against her neck, 'I sincerely hope Shane's done a marvellous job, that he's talented, and that you're truly impressed, sugar.'

'Oh you!' She beat her fists lightly against his chest. 'You vain conceited impossible gorgeous man!'

He caught her wrists, held them tightly in his hands, peered down into her face. 'But oh how that man loves you, darling.' He released her suddenly, sat up.

Paula did the same. She said, 'Imagine Blackie deciding to buy a hotel in Sydney. I'll bet you anything that that grandmother of mine was goading him on.' She gave him a long look. 'Uncle Bryan wanted you to go to Sydney, didn't he?'

'Yep. Grandfather hasn't actually bought the hotel yet. That's why he wants either Dad or me to fly there immediately, give it the once over. What I said's true, Paula, I can't get away. I'm jammed. And you don't think I'm going anywhere while you're still in New York, do you? It'll do Dad good to get away for a week or two. He said he might fly back to New York with Blackie and Emma early in December. But we'll see. I hope he takes my mother along, they'll have a good time.'

Shane kissed the tip of her nose. 'I'd better go and shower, get dressed, wander downstairs, check up on a few things.'

He sprang off the bed, pulled her to her feet. 'Would you mind meeting me downstairs when you're ready?'

'No, of course not. Where will I find you?'

'How long will it take you to dress?'

'About three-quarters of an hour.'

'By then I'll be waiting for you in the bar off the main lobby. You can't miss it – it's called the Aviary.' He chucked her lightly under the chin. 'I would've called it The Birdcage, but I didn't want to be accused of stealing someone else's idea.'

At Shane's twenty-fourth birthday party, early in June of 1965, Emma had made a comment to Paula. She had said that he had an intense glamour. Paula had not understood exactly what her grandmother had meant four years ago. She did now.

Paula was poised at the entrance to The Aviary, viewing him with unprecedented objectivity. He was at the far end, stood leaning with one elbow on the bar, one foot resting on the brass rail that encircled the base of the bar.

He was wearing black linen trousers, a black voile shirt and a jacket of silver-grey silk. Although he was tieless, he nevertheless looked extremely well dressed, as impeccably groomed as usual. But the aura of glamour her grandmother had spoken about had little to do with his clothes, as Paula was realizing as she continued to study him unobserved. It emanated from his height and build, his natural good looks, and the force of his personality. He was in command of himself – and this room. And he has abundant charisma, Paula thought. That's what it is, and it's the kind that every politician in the world would give his eye teeth to possess.

Shane was talking animatedly to a couple, obviously guests of the hotel, his face alive, expressive. The woman was entranced, hanging on to his every word. But then, seemingly so was the man who accompanied her.

Shane happened to swing his head. He saw Paula, straightened up, excused himself graciously.

The bar was fairly busy and as they walked towards each other Paula was aware that more than one pair of female eyes followed his progress.

'I'm glad you wore the blue dress,' he said, catching hold of her hand when he reached her side. He led her swiftly to a reserved table in the corner. 'It looks wonderful on you. You look wonderful.'

Her radiant smile, her shining eyes conveyed her pleasure and her thanks.

He said, 'I thought we'd have champagne, since it's a celebration.'

'What are we celebrating?'

'Finding each other again.'

'Oh Shane, that's a lovely sentiment.'

A waiter appeared, opened the bottle which already stood on the table in an ice bucket, poured a little into Shane's glass. He tasted it, nodded, 'It's perfect, Danny. Thank you.'

'You're welcome, Mr Shane.' The smiling waiter filled their glasses, quietly moved away.

'To us,' Shane said, raising his glass.

'To us, Shane.' After a few seconds Paula's eyes roamed around the bar discreetly, taking in the decor. 'I can see how this spot acquired its name . . . it looks exactly like the café in the Leeds store.' Her expression was teasing.

'Our birdcages aren't half as nice as yours though.' He grinned at her. 'Mind you, the artist did a good job with the murals. I must admit I do love exotic birds.' His eyes swept over her suggestively.

Paula laughed at the innuendo.

Shane moved in his chair, reached into his pocket for his cigarettes. His shirt was partially open down the front and she suddenly caught the gleam of gold against his suntanned chest. She peered at him. 'Goodness, is that the St Christopher medal I gave you?'

He looked down, fingered it. 'The very same.'

'You haven't been wearing it though – before tonight.'

'I haven't worn it for a couple of years. I found it in the flat on Monday night when I was packing. The catch was broken. I brought it with me, had it repaired in Holetown. They just delivered it back to me half an hour ago.'

'I'm glad you're wearing it again.'

'Do you remember when you gave it to me?'

'When you were twenty. For your birthday eight years ago.'

'And what did I give you when you were twenty?'

'A pair of antique earrings.' She frowned, then laughed lightly. 'Did you think I'd forgotten, Shane O'Neill?'

'I was sure you hadn't forgotten. However, I bet you don't remember what I gave you when you reached the ripe old age of five.'

'Oh yes I do. A bag of blue marbles.'

He sat back, looking pleased. 'Correct. Which you promptly began to lose one by one. You cried so much I had to promise to buy you another bag. But I never did, and so –' He put his hand in his jacket pocket. '– Here's the replacement. Sorry it's taken me so long to fulfil a boyhood promise.' He dropped a small opaque plastic bag in front of her.

Laughing, enjoying his mood and flirting with him, Paula picked it up, opened the bag, dipped into it. 'You are a fool, but a most adorable one –' She stopped. A pair of sapphire-and-diamond earrings, beautifully cut and of superb quality, lay glittering in her hands. 'Oh Shane, they're absolutely exquisite. Thank you, thank you so much.' She kissed his cheek, added, 'But you're awfully extravagant.'

'So I've been told. Like them?'

'Like them! I love them. And most especially because they're from you.' She pulled off the gold studs she was wearing, slipped them into her silk evening purse, took out a small mirror and put on the sapphires. She glanced at herself, admiring the earrings. 'Oh Shane, they *do* look lovely on me, don't they?'

'Almost as lovely as those uncanny eyes of yours.'

She squeezed his hand. She was touched by the unexpected present, overwhelmed really. Her throat tightened. She recalled the gifts he had given her when she had been a child. He had always been uncommonly generous, saving his pocket money for months to be able to buy something special. And he had had a knack of giving her exactly the right thing – like the earrings tonight. For a reason she could not comprehend her eyes filled with tears.

'What's the matter, darling?' he asked gently, leaning across the table.

She shook her head, blinking. 'I don't know, aren't I silly.' She groped in her bag, found a handkerchief, blew her nose, gave him a watery smile.

He watched her silently, waiting for her to compose herself.

'I was thinking of our childhood,' she commenced after a few seconds. 'At the time, it seemed as if it would never end – all those lovely summers at Heron's Nest. But it did come to an end, just as those summers did.' Before she could stop herself, she added, 'As this will come to an end too.'

He put his hand over hers. 'Oh darling, don't be sad.'

'Our days here in the sun, this magic time . . . it's just a brief sojourn really, Shane.'

Squeezing her hand, entwining his fingers with hers, he said slowly, '*You* talk of endings . . . *I* think of beginnings. That's what this is, Paula. A beginning. Remember what I said about time? Well, this *is* the future. It's here. Now. All around us. Part of the flowing river of time.'

She was silent, her eyes resting on him, searching his face.

'I hadn't wanted to get into a discussion about the mess we've found ourselves in, Paula, at least not down here. But perhaps we'd better have a talk. Would you like to do that?'

Paula nodded.

The smile settling on his face was confident, very sure. 'You know how much I love you. I said in the car, earlier today, that I'd never let you go, and I won't, Paula. Our feelings for each other are too strong to be ignored. We're meant to be together for the rest of our lives. Do you agree?'

'Yes,' she whispered.

'Then it's obvious what you're going to have to do. You'll have to get a divorce so that you can marry me. You do want to marry me, don't you?'

'Oh yes, Shane, very much.'

He saw that her face had paled, and that her very bright supernaturally blue eyes had darkened with apprehension. 'Tell me what's troubling you, Paula.'

'You said I was intrepid when I was a child – but as a grown woman I'm not. I'm frightened, Shane.'

'What about?' he asked, his gentleness increasing. 'Come on, let's have it. If anyone can chase your fears away, surely it's me.'

'I'm afraid of losing my children and of losing you.'

'You know that will never happen. The three of us will be with you always.'

Paula took a deep breath, plunged in. She said, 'I don't think Jim will agree to a divorce.'

Shane pulled back slightly, eyeing her askance. 'I can't imagine him taking that attitude. Not once he knows you want to end a bad marriage.'

'You don't know Jim,' she interjected, her voice tense. 'He's stubborn, and he can be difficult. I have a horrible feeling he's going to adopt an inflexible stance. I told you, he doesn't think there's anything wrong with our marriage. He'll use the children as a wedge, and especially if he thinks there's another man.'

'He's *not* going to think there's another man in your life,' Shane said quietly. 'I'll be the only man you're seeing, and nobody is going to be suspicious of *me*.' He attempted to laugh. 'Me, your childhood playmate!' His brows shot up. 'Come on, darling, don't be so gloomy.'

Paula sighed heavily. 'Yes, perhaps I shouldn't anticipate.' She shook her head. 'Poor Jim. I feel sorry for him actually.'

'I know. But you can't build a relationship on pity, Paula. There's no reward in that for either party. You'll start regarding yourself as a martyr and he'll sink under his humiliation. You'll end up genuinely hating each other.'

'I suppose you're right,' she admitted, seeing the truth in his words.

'I *know* I'm right. And look here, don't start feeling guilty either. That's another wasted emotion.' He tightened his grip on her fingers. 'And anyway you don't have one single reason to feel guilty, Paula. You've given your marriage your best efforts, done your damnedest to hold it together, from what you've told me. It simply hasn't worked. And so you must end it – for Jim's sake as well as your own.'

Paula bit her inner lip. Her worry flared. Then she murmured, 'It may take me a while to work everything out, to get things settled properly.'

'I'm aware of that, these emotional situations are never easy. But I'll wait, I'll be a model of patience. I'll be there to give you moral support. And there's another thing, we're both young. We have all the time in the world.'

'Don't tempt providence, Shane!'

Shane shook his head, scoffed lightly, in amusement. 'I'm not, I'm merely stating facts.' Whilst he trusted her judgement, privately concurred with her assessment of Jim, he did not want to burden her further by acknowledging this. Not tonight. Instead he wanted to dispel her gloominess by making light of her worries. And so he produced his most assured smile, adopted his most engaging manner. He exclaimed, 'Let's make a pact – like we used to when we were kids.'

'All right. What kind of pact?'

'Let's agree not to discuss our problems, and they *are* mine as well as yours, for the next few weeks. Two days before you return to England we'll have a long session, thrash things out. Together we'll decide how you're going to proceed. What do you say?'

'Yes, it's a good idea. We mustn't let things get to us, must we? Otherwise we won't enjoy this precious time we have together.'

'That's my girl. Shall we drink to our pact? We've hardly touched this champagne.'

She nodded. He poured. They clinked glasses. Their hands automatically entwined.

His eyes were tender and warm as they rested on her. He said, after a while, 'You must trust me. Trust my love, Paula.'

She looked at him in surprise, remembering how her grandmother had once said that it was important to trust love. As she met Shane O'Neill's dark and steadfast gaze, saw the depth and strength of his feelings for her, Paula's fears slowly began to evaporate. Her depression lifted.

'I do trust your love, and you must trust mine.' A small smile played around her mouth. 'Everything *is* going to be all right. It really is, Shane, because we have each other.'

But Paula was wrong. Her troubles were about to begin.

37

Emma Harte stared hard at Paula, a frown knitting her brow. 'I'm not sure I'm following you,' she said. 'What exactly do you mean when you say Christmas is going to be difficult?'

Paula said quickly, 'Before I explain, I just want you to understand that he's all right actually –'

'Who's all right?'

'Jim, Grandy. I'm afraid he's had an accident. A rather bad accident, and he's –'

'Not in that plane of his?' Emma cried, and straightened up in the chair jerkily, her frown intensifying.

'Yes, he crashed. Two weeks ago. It happened a couple of days after I got back from New York, at the beginning of December,' Paula said in a rush. Wanting to allay her grandmother's worry, she hurried on, 'But he was lucky, in one sense at least, since the plane came down at Yeadon Airport. They were able to pull him out of the plane before it exploded in flames.'

'Oh my God!' Emma's hackles rose as she thought of Jim's narrow escape. He could so easily have been killed, and Paula might have been in the plane with him, might not have survived. Leaning forward, she asked in an urgent voice, 'How badly is he injured?'

'He's broken his right leg and his left shoulder, and his ribs are cracked. He's also badly bruised. But there are no injuries that are permanently disabling or life threatening. Obviously though, those he has sustained are serious enough.'

'No internal damage?'

'None, thank heavens, Grandy. Jim was rushed to Leeds Infirmary immediately, and he stayed there for five days, having all kinds of tests – neurological, what have you. Fortunately the doctors didn't find a thing. Every injury is external.' Paula paused, looked across at her grandmother. Worry ringed her face. She said, 'He's in two casts and his ribs are taped. I've had to hire a male nurse to look after him. You see, Jim can't dress himself and he finds it awkward, almost impossible, to do the most normal things.'

Emma exhaled, still reeling from the news. She exclaimed, 'Why on earth didn't you tell me about this when I was in New York? Or yesterday, when I arrived in London?'

'I didn't want to worry you when you were still on your holiday, and so far away. And last night you were so excited about being back I didn't want to spoil your homecoming and the little supper my mother had planned for you here. I'd intended to mention it on our way in from the airport but –' Paula shrugged, gave her a small apologetic smile. 'I decided it could easily wait until today.'

'I see.' Emma sat back, shaking her head. 'I am sorry, Paula, this is just dreadful, simply dreadful. But we must be thankful it's not any worse, more serious than it is. He's going to be out of action for months, of course.'

'Yes,' Paula murmured. 'The casts have to be on at least six weeks. Then he'll have to have intensive physical therapy. The muscles will atrophy from lack of use. The doctor has explained that Jim won't be able to lift his arm or put weight on his leg until those dead muscles have been built up again. It seems it'll be a good six months before he's back to normal.'

'Broken bones are a lot more serious than people realize,' Emma said quietly. She fixed Paula with a steely glance. 'And how did it happen?'

'The engine stalled. Jim tried to land as best he could, and thankfully he was on the approach to Yeadon airstrip. But – well, he couldn't control the plane. It plunged down, virtually broke in two when it hit the ground. He's been awfully lucky.'

'He has indeed.' Emma's mouth tightened. 'I always knew he'd have an accident in that damned plane one day, Paula. It's worried me to death.' She shook her head again, her dismay apparent. 'Whilst I'm upset and sorry that Jim's been hurt, I can't help feeling he's been somewhat irresponsible.' She gave Paula a long and careful look. Her eyes narrowed. 'He's a married man with two children, and he should not have been taking that kind of risk. Utter foolishness on his part. If only he'd given up that pile of junk when I asked him, this wouldn't have happened.'

'Well, Jim is inclined to be a bit stubborn.'

'That's the understatement of the year,' Emma snapped. 'I don't mean to sound callous or unsympathetic, but it strikes me he was putting himself in unnecessary physical danger. And why *I'll* never know. Perhaps that husband of yours will listen to me *now*. And I insist that we buy a corporate jet if we must have a plane in the family. I will not permit Jim to waltz around the skies in a flimsy light aircraft ever again. Oh no, not under any circumstances.' Emma leaned back in the chair, her face grimly set in its rigid determination.

'Yes, Grandy.' Paula glanced down at her hands, recognizing the implacability in that dear and familiar voice. Her grandmother was furious, and she could not blame her. Jim did lack a sense of responsibility and he had most wilfully ignored everyone's pleas to get a more stable, up-to-date plane.

Suddenly realizing she had sounded harsh, Emma said rapidly, in a softer tone, 'I expect poor Jim is in a lot of pain, isn't he, lovey?'

'Excruciating. The shoulder's driving him crazy. He says he's not sure which

356

is the worst, the persistent nagging ache in the shoulder itself, or the cramp and stiffness from having his arm permanently bent in the cast. It's constricting, you know.' Paula winced, recalling the past ten days, knowing how much he was genuinely suffering. Once her initial shock and fright had subsided, exasperation with him had surfaced, only to be replaced by compassion. Being inherently kind, she was doing her utmost to make him as comfortable as possible. And she had shelved the discussion about a divorce. She would have to wait until he was in better physical condition to talk about her freedom.

Emma said, 'Surely the doctor has given him pain killers.'

'Yes and they help. But he says they make him feel doped up, woozy, a little out of it.'

'I hate pills myself. Still, if they ease the pain he ought to stay on them. I see what you mean about Christmas being difficult, Paula. Oh dear, this is such an added burden for you – on top of all of your work during one of our busiest seasons at the stores. Not only that, we have so many family things planned at Pennistone Royal ... our traditional Christmas Eve with the O'Neills and the Kallinskis, lunch on Christmas Day, and Sally's wedding to Anthony –' Emma cut herself short.

Her green eyes became thoughtful. An idea came to her and she made a snap decision. Taking command in her usual way, she exclaimed, 'Running back and forth between your house and mine is going to become the bane of your life, and transporting Jim hither and yon will prove tiring. I think you'd better move everyone in with me ... Jim, the babies, Nora, and the male nurse. I've plenty of room and, in fact, I'd rather enjoy having you all with me after my eight-month absence.'

'Oh Gran, what a wonderful idea!' Paula cried, swamped with relief. 'And it's a marvellous solution.' A smile broke through as she confided, 'I've been panicky, wondering how I would ever cope.'

Emma laughed quietly, amusement flickering on her mouth. 'You'll always cope, my girl, that's your basic nature. But I don't see why your life shouldn't be made as easy as possible, since you carry enough responsibility to bury three people. Now that I'm back home, I aim to see to it that things run smoothly for you. You've had a rough few months, between business problems and all the family upsets.'

'Thank you, Gran. What a lovely thought, moving into Pennistone Royal, being with *you*. Why ever didn't I think of it?'

'I suspect you've had enough on your plate these past few weeks. I'm sure Jim is not a good patient ... too active a man to be confined in this way. Is he getting around at all?'

'No. Ever since he came home from Leeds Infirmary he's been sleeping in his den, virtually living in it – he can't navigate the stairs, for one thing. He's awfully frustrated being disabled. Even more frustrated because he can't go to the paper. He misses it.'

'I'm sure he does. But he won't be able to go to work for a long time. No use fussing over that. Well, he certainly won't be able to manage the staircase at Pennistone Royal. It's too long and steep. But never mind. Hilda can turn the small parlour next to the dining room into a bedroom for him. Now, Paula, please try not to worry any more. What's done is done, we'll have to make the best of it.'

'You're right, Grandma, and moving in with you is going to make my life so much easier,' Paula said, thinking that being surrounded by people was going to be a real blessing. Jim was becoming fractious because of the pain, his helplessness. He had started to complain about her work more vociferously than ever, forever grumbled about the hours she kept. And he was drinking more than he should.

Rising, Emma now walked across to the fireplace, stood with her back to it, warming herself. She and Paula were having coffee in the charming study of her Belgrave Square flat where they were both staying until they journeyed to Yorkshire the following day.

Paula glanced up at her grandmother, thinking how rested and well she looked this morning after yesterday's transatlantic flight. Emma wore a coral wool dress and pearls. Her silver hair was beautifully styled and immaculate and her makeup perfectly applied. There was a freshness and vitality about her. Paula thought: it doesn't seem possible that she is eighty years old. She looks ten years younger at least.

'You're scrutinizing me very intently,' Emma said. 'What's wrong with my appearance?'

'Nothing, Gran, and I was admiring you really. You're positively blooming this morning.'

'Thank you. I must admit to feeling marvellous. I'm not a bit jet-lagged.' She glanced at her watch. 'It's only ten o'clock. I'd better not ring Blackie just yet. He may still be sleeping. Bryan's driving him back to Harrogate later in the day, you know.'

'So Merry said last night at the airport.'

'It was nice having Bryan and Geraldine in Sydney for a couple of weeks,' Emma now volunteered with a smile of fond recollection. 'And they really enjoyed themselves. However, I was a bit disappointed that it wasn't Shane who came to negotiate the deal on the hotel they've bought.'

'From what Shane said to me, November was a difficult time for him.'

'Yes, Bryan mentioned it.' Flashing Paula a warm and loving glance, Emma continued, 'I'm glad you were able to find time to pop down to Barbados to see our boutique when Shane was there. It did you good, seemingly. You're positively blooming yourself, Paula. You look better than I've seen you for years.'

'I enjoyed the trip, the little rest,' Paula said, keeping her voice very steady. 'I still have traces of my tan, so perhaps that's it.'

Emma nodded. She studied her favourite granddaughter. Paula has become as inscrutable as I am, she thought. I'm actually having difficulty reading her at this moment. Clearing her throat, Emma said, 'So ... you and Shane are good friends again. I *am* happy about that.'

Paula made no comment.

Emma, riddled with curiosity, probed, 'And did he explain what it was all about finally?'

'Pressure of work, his schedule, his travelling, as he's always said, Gran. However, I do think he was afraid of intruding ...' Paula met her grandmother's quizzical gaze with a cool, direct look of complete innocence. She added in a calm voice, 'You know what I mean – intruding on a couple of newlyweds. I think he was simply being diplomatic and considerate.'

'Really,' Emma said. A snowy brow arched. She did not believe his reasons, but she said nothing else, moved in the direction of the desk. Seating herself, she gave her attention to the three different folders Paula had arranged there earlier. Emma opened one, stared at the memorandum on top, but she was not actually reading it. Instead she was contemplating Paula and Shane. Ever since she had heard about their rapprochement, which was no great secret, she had wondered if Shane had finally made an overt move. She had never forgotten that look on his face at the christening. A man who loved a woman the way Shane O'Neill loved her granddaughter would be unable to repress his feelings indefinitely. He would have to come out in the open. One day. He would not be able to help himself. Had he already done so? And if so, what had his reception been? She could not hazard a guess. Shane had been unreadable in New York, as Paula was now. She concentrated on Shane, whom she knew like one of her own, and thought of his nature. He was impetuous, impulsive, passionate. And what of Paula? Of course Paula would have spurned him. Would she? Yes, Emma answered herself. She is happily married. But is she?

Partially raising her eyes, Emma stole a look at Paula, surreptitiously, over the top of her glasses. There was something different about her granddaughter – she had noticed it last night. She seemed more womanly, more feminine than usual. Had there been a radical internal change? Or was it merely her outward appearance? The longer hair, the extra weight, the general air of softness she had acquired? Had a man's influence been at work? Shane's? Or was her current look simply a new style she had formulated for herself. I'm damned if I know, Emma thought. And I refuse to pry. Her life is her own. I will never interfere. I dare not. If she has anything to tell me she will do so . . . eventually.

Paula said, 'I asked Alexander and Emily to prepare those reports for you, Grandy, and I've written one myself. Each folder –'

'So I see,' Emma interrupted, glancing up. 'Are they simply summations of business matters over the past eight months? Or have you included anything I don't already know about?'

'Oh no, Grandy, we've simply recapped everything for you, the matters we telexed you about, or discussed on the phone. There's nothing new at the moment, but I thought you ought to have the reports just to refresh your memory. Later, at your leisure.'

'I don't have to refresh my memory,' Emma exclaimed dryly. 'I forget nothing. Thank you for going to all this trouble, though. I'm sure it goes without saying that I trust the three of you, and I'm very proud of you and your cousins. You've handled yourselves in the most exemplary manner, been extremely diligent, and, I might add, very smart in a number of instances.' Emma's eyes gleamed shrewdly under the hooded lids. 'And how's Gianni what's-his-name working out at Trade Winds?'

Paula could not help grinning at her grandmother's knowing expression. 'He's the best antique expert Harte's has ever had,' she said. 'And he's done a terrific job on his trips to the Orient recently. He's worth every penny we're paying him.'

'I sincerely hope so . . . presumably he's now giving Elizabeth the divorce without causing a scandal?'

'Yes, he is, Gran.'

'Alexander never did explain fully about that fuss and bother with his mother, when he rang me in Australia.' Emma's eyes sharpened. 'Who was Gianni going to cite instead of Marc Deboyne?'

'Oh some cabinet minister, I believe,' Paula said, striving to sound offhand, not wanting to go into the outrageous details. 'Alexander was worried that a well-known politician being involved in the divorce would simply draw additional press attention to the case, to the family.'

'Good thinking.' Leaning over her desk, Emma now remarked, 'Talking of politicians, or rather a politician's son, have you anything to tell me about Jonathan?'

'Not one thing, Gran.' Paula hesitated. 'But Mr Graves of Graves and Sanderson dug up some unpleasant personal information about Sebastian Cross.' Paula grimaced. 'Alexander has the report. I'm sure you don't want to read it – it's rather disgusting. Alexander will explain it to you better than I.'

'I've lived with unpleasantness all of my life, Paula. However, obviously *you* prefer not to dicuss it, so we'll let it go for now. I'll take it up with Alexander when he gets here later. And what about your cousin Sarah? Is she behaving herself?'

'I haven't seen her, but Emily tells me she's very snotty with her, and holding herself aloof. Apparently Sarah's become rather chummy with Allison Ridley, Winston's old girlfriend. Emily thinks that's the reason for Sarah's coldness towards her.'

'I'm rather surprised,' Emma muttered. 'Why would Sarah take umbrage at Emily?' She looked across at Paula, and began to laugh at herself. 'That's a pretty stupid comment on my part, when I think of the terrible things members of this family have done to each other.' She sat back in the chair, went on, 'Would you mind giving me another cup of coffee, please?'

'Of course not. Coming right up, Gran.' After filling the cup, adding milk and sugar, Paula brought the coffee to the desk, hovered. She said slowly, 'Look, this isn't a criticism of Emily, you know how much I love her, but she's got a ridiculous bee in her bonnet about the mess in Ireland. I'd like you to talk to her –'

'Oh she's already mentioned it to me, Paula,' Emma interrupted. 'Last night, when you were on the phone to Long Meadow.' Emma swallowed a smile as she observed Paula's serious expression. 'Murder most foul and all that nonsense, right?'

Paula nodded.

Emma said, 'I gave her a little lecture. I don't believe she'll ever bring it up again. However –' Emma eyed her granddaughter closely. 'You know, your mother mentioned something about Ireland too last night. When you were out of the room. She doesn't believe the housekeeper was telling the truth . . . I mean about Min's craziness and drinking.'

Paula exclaimed fiercely, in irritation, 'Good God, the two of them are incorrigible! Honestly, Grandma, I hope you've nipped their imaginative chatter in the bud. It's a load of tripe, and can only lead to further trouble. Loose tongues are dangerous.'

'Agreed. But whether it's tripe or not is beside the point, Paula. What matters, in reality, is that the case is closed. *Firmly closed*. Min's death was a suicide. That was the coroner's ruling and it's good enough for me. And for John Crawford. Don't worry, neither your mother nor Emily will mention anything about murder in the future. I've seen to that.'

'Thank heavens you have.' Paula came around the desk and hugged Emma tightly, kissed her cheek. 'Oh Gran darling, I'm so glad you're back. I've missed you so much. It's positively awful when you're not here.'

Emma smiled up at her, patted her hand. 'If you've said that once since I stepped off the plane, you've said it a hundred times, darling. But thank you, it's nice to hear. And I've missed you too – all of you. I've enjoyed myself, travelling the world with Blackie, seeing so many, many wonderful things. I've had a little fun for once. He was sweet. And he pampered me in a way I've not been pampered for years. Not since your grandfather died. But no more gallivanting off to foreign parts.'

'I didn't begrudge you the wonderful trip around the world, Gran, please don't think that . . . but you seemed to be so far away most of the time.'

'I was always here in spirit, Paula.'

'Yes, I know. But it's not quite the same as having you here in the flesh!'

'Alexander should be arriving in a few minutes.' Emma glanced at the carriage clock on the mantelpiece. 'Then Emily at noon. I thought we would lunch at one.' Her mouth twitched. 'I suggested to Parker that we have fish and chips – and from the local fish shop. That's the one thing I missed when I was away.'

Paula chortled. 'Oh Gran, you are lovely, and you haven't changed.'

'And it's hardly likely that I will, not at my age.'

'I'll just have time to dash across to Harte's, deal with a few things, and get back for lunch.'

'Yes, do run along, dear. I know what it's like . . . I used to feel exactly the same way when I was your age. I couldn't wait to get to the store.'

'See you later then.' Paula bent to kiss Emma's cheek.

'Yes. Oh and by the way, Paula, I had lunch with Ross Nelson the day before I left New York. I haven't had a chance to tell you – but I scotched that idea about selling my Sitex stock.'

'Good for you. He was getting to be a pest – in more ways than one, if you want the truth.'

Emma pursed her lips, staring at Paula with sudden alertness. 'Was he now,' she said. 'Well, yes, I must admit I did get the feeling he was rather keen on you. Tiresome man. Full of himself, and his so-called fatal charms, wouldn't you say?'

'He's the worst kind of bore. The deadliest really. And so transparent. I'm afraid I can't stand him.'

Paula walked to Harte's in Knightsbridge.

It was a frosty day. The etiolated sky was bloated with snow, but its bleached-out quality made the light seem curiously luminous despite the fugitive sun.

She was hardly conscious of the weather as she hurried along. She was thinking of Shane. She always thought of him. He was rarely out of her mind for very long. Today was the twentieth of December. When she had spoken to him yesterday he had said he would ring her at seven New York time. Noon in London. Immediately afterwards he was taking a plane to Barbados, since it was the height of the season at the Coral Cove Hotel.

Paula sighed under her breath as she cut down a side street, heading for the main thoroughfare. Jim's accident had thrown all of their plans askew.

But this aside, he had nearly been killed and all because of his ingrained pigheadedness. Her mind leapt back to the dreadful weekend two weeks ago. She had arrived in London on Saturday, having taken an overnight flight from the States, and had been driven straight to Yorkshire by her grandmother's chauffeur.

When she got to Long Meadow in the early afternoon her first stop had been the nursery. To her distress the twins and Nora were suffering from streaming colds. At four o'clock, when Jim had walked in from the newspaper, he had muttered he was coming down with it himself, and had retired to bed immediately. She seized the opportunity to vacate their bedroom. That night she had slept in one of the guest rooms, explaining she could not afford to get sick, not with the whole household under siege and a business to run. He had not complained.

On Sunday Jim had been much better, certainly well enough to get up for lunch, eat a hearty meal and drink half a bottle of red wine. She had been aghast when he had insisted on going off to fly that dangerous little plane, had begged him to stay at home. Jim had laughed, told her she was being ridiculous, protested he was neither drunk nor sick. When the phone call had come through from the airport later that afternoon her heart had stopped beating for several seconds, and then she had leapt in the car and rushed to Leeds Infirmary to be with him. At odds with him though she was, and in love with Shane O'Neill, Paula still harboured affectionate feelings for her husband. She had once cared deeply for him, he was the father of her children, and she wished him no harm.

But later, when she could think clearly, she had realized there was no excuse for his behaviour. The crash need not have happened. He had been reckless. At heart Paula doubted his story about the engine stalling. He had been taking pills for his cold; he had demolished half a bottle of wine. If he had not been drugged or drunk exactly, he had hardly been in a fit condition to take the plane up.

When she had telephoned Shane in New Milford, later on that fated Sunday, he had been distressed for her. But he had been understanding of her dilemma, had agreed they could not make their moves until Jim was well enough to cope with her news. She was going to tell him she wanted a divorce.

As she swung into Knightsbridge, she prayed that Jim would agree. The worry that he might fight her nagged at the back of her head constantly.

Don't think about it, don't be so negative, she told herself firmly. All you have to do is get yourself through the next few months. She and Shane had made new plans this past week, changing their business commitments to accommodate each other. They needed to be together as often as they could. In January she would go to New York to be with him. During February and March he would visit Australia to start work on the rebuilding of the hotel the O'Neill chain had just purchased. He would stay with her brother Philip. Shane would come to England in April to see Emerald Bow run in the Grand National, but she would be with him in London before and after the race. At the end of April he would return to New York. They had decided that Jim ought to be on his feet again by then, and once Shane had left for the States she would tackle her husband. In May she would finally tell her grandmother everything, move herself and the twins into Pennistone Royal.

May, Paula repeated under her breath. Such a long way off. No, not really. And anyway, Shane and I have the rest of our lives ahead of us.

Her pace automatically quickened. She ached for the sound of his voice. Thank God for the telephone, she thought, as she went into the staff entrance at Harte's. At least we can talk every day.

38

It snowed heavily for the next four days.

Yorkshire was quickly covered with a mantle of white. The countryside around Pennistone Royal looked particularly picturesque. Drystone walls disappeared under monstrous drifts, trees were weighted down by their laden branches, rivers and streams were glazed over with blue-tinted ice.

But the snowstorm ceased with abruptness on the afternoon of Christmas Eve. Suddenly the blindingly-white landscape had a crystalline beauty as the sun broke through. There was a diamond-bright dazzle to the sky, a sparkling crispness in the air.

By nightfall the fields and the fells and the rolling moors were ethereal under a clear winter moon that coated them with a silvery sheen.

Emma, standing at the window of her bedroom, was momentarily transfixed as she gazed down at her gardens. The snow and the ice had created the most magical effect, enveloping the land in a strange white silence, an overwhelming stillness that seemed like a palpable thing to her. But despite the breathtaking beauty spread before her, Emma knew that beyond the great iron gates of her house, the roads and country lanes were dangerous, very treacherous in this kind of weather.

As she turned away and walked through into the upstairs parlour, she could not help but worry, thinking of her family and friends who were currently driving on those roads. All were courageously braving the icy conditions in order to spend this special evening with her. It had been a tradition for many years, and none of them wanted to miss it. She hoped each one of them would arrive safely and without any mishaps.

Emma already had a full house.

Once they were back in Yorkshire, Paula had lost no time in moving her family into Pennistone Royal. Jim, the babies, the nanny and the male nurse were already ensconced. Emily had brought Amanda and Francesca home from Harrogate College earlier in the week. David and Daisy had taken the train from London yesterday, accompanied by Alexander and his fiancée, Maggie Reynolds. Edwina and Anthony had flown into Manchester Airport from Dublin that morning, had reached the ancient house in time for a late lunch.

Pausing at her desk, Emma picked up the guest list, scanned it quickly. Her sons and their wives had been invited, but she was quite certain they would not come. Well, it did not matter anymore. She was adjusted to their absence from her life. Kit and Robin would avoid her again. She knew why. They were as guilty as hell about their treachery towards her. Elizabeth was not coming either, was remaining in Paris with Marc Deboyne, but at least her daughter had been gracious when she had phoned to decline and to wish her a happy Christmas. I hope this is the last husband *she's* going to have, Emma thought, her glance travelling on down the list.

Her eyes rested briefly on Jonathan's name. He had accepted. So had Sarah. They were driving over from Bramhope together. She could not help wondering about their current chumminess. Were they up to something? Now, Emma Harte, no bad thoughts tonight, she cautioned herself. It instantly struck her that she was unutterably weary of intrigue. It had dogged her all of her life. She was getting too old to pick up the sword again.

A thoughtful look settled on her face as she remained standing at the desk, clutching the guest list. *She was eighty*. She had paid her dues long ago. Her time was now far too precious to indulge in battles. Let them get on with it, she muttered. As I shall get on with my life – what's left of it. All I want is to have peace and quiet and to be with my dear old friend. We'll march on together into the future, Blackie and I . . . a couple of old war horses. She felt as if a great burden had been lifted as she suddenly acknowledged that she *had* abdicated eight months ago. She *was* out of the fray. She was determined to stay out.

Emma finished perusing the list. Blackie, who was spending Christmas with Bryan and Geraldine in Wetherby, was due to arrive with them and Miranda shortly. The entire Kallinski clan had also promised to come early. The Hartes would be out in full force tonight. Randolph, too, had a house full, since his mother, Charlotte, and his Aunt Natalie, were staying at Allington Hall with Sally, Vivienne and himself. Winston was a self-invited guest at Pennistone Royal, had walked in at four o'clock with his suitcase and three large shopping bags top-heavy with gifts. Only Philip and Shane are missing, Emma murmured to herself, putting down the list. But perhaps next year they will be here. We'll all be together. Then the three clans will really be complete.

The clock struck six.

The chimes roused her from her meandering thoughts. She gazed down at the one remaining present that lay on the desk. Earlier all of the others had been taken downstairs to the Stone Hall to be placed under the tree. Sitting down, Emma thought for a moment, then inscribed the card carefully.

There was a knock on the door. 'Cooee, Gran, it's me,' Emily called, floating in on a cloud of perfume.

Emma lifted her head, smiled at her granddaughter. 'And don't you look lovely!' she exclaimed, scrutinizing her intently. 'That's the dress tartan of the Seaforth Highlanders,' Emma remarked, referring to the long taffeta skirt Emily wore, immediately recognizing the plaid. 'My father's old regiment, and Joe's and Blackie's when they were in the First World War. It certainly looks smart with your white silk shirt.'

'Yes, I thought so too.' Emily planted a kiss on Emma's cheek, said quickly, 'You seemed a bit surprised when Winston arrived this afternoon. I could have sworn I'd told you he was coming to stay.'

'No, you didn't. But that's all right.' Sitting back, Emma pursed her lips, gave Emily a pointed look. 'I expect it's too much to ask you to behave yourselves, but *please*, do be discreet if you're bedroom hopping.'

Emily's face flushed. 'How can you think a thing like that, Grandma!'

'Because I was young once, believe it or not, and I know what it's like to be in love. But be careful, dear. After all, we do have a lot of house guests. I wouldn't want your reputation besmirched.'

'In this family! Good God, nobody can afford to throw any stones –' Emily stopped. 'Sorry, I didn't mean to be rude, Grandma.'

'Don't apologize for speaking the truth, Emily. But remember what I've just said.'

Nodding and looking relieved, Emily drifted over to the fireplace, stood observing her grandmother. 'You should always wear dark green velvet. It's very becoming on you, especially with all your emeralds.'

'Goodness me, Emily, you make it sound as if they're dripping from every pore. I'm only wearing Paul's ring and earrings and Blackie's little bow. But thank you for the compliment, and tell me, what's happening downstairs?'

'Amanda and Francesca are finishing trimming the tree, at least the top half which I started earlier. Little monkeys, they haven't helped me one bit today. All they've done is loll around in their room, listening to the Beatles and shrieking their heads off, or alternately swooning and being silly. I routed them out an hour ago and set them to work.'

'Good for you. I'm going to have to take those two in hand during the holidays, put my foot down. There has to be a limit on the time they spend listening to those records. Apart from anything else, the racket was deafening this afternoon. Anyone else down yet?'

'Aunty Daisy, looking gorgeous in a red silk trouser suit and masses of rubies and diamonds –'

'Why do you always exaggerate?' Emma shook her head, faintly reprimanding, but her eyes were fond. 'She doesn't have masses of rubies and diamonds, to my knowledge.'

'Well, a pair of beautiful earrings,' Emily admitted wrinkling her nose. 'She was helping to set up the bar. Jim's there, in the new wheelchair you got for him, having a drink and –'

'He's started a bit early, hasn't he?' Emma exclaimed, a silver brow lifting in surprise.

'What do you mean started early? He hasn't stopped since lunch.'

Emma was dismayed. 'Ought he to be drinking?' she asked. 'He's on pain killers – so Paula told me. That combination can be awfully dangerous.' Her eyes grew flinty with a mixture of concern and annoyance.

Emily nodded. 'I mentioned that to him a few minutes ago, so don't *you* say anything. He told me to mind my own business. He's awfully grouchy, I don't envy Paula one bit.'

'I've noticed his moodiness. Still, we have to make allowances, I suppose. Has Paula come home from the store yet?'

'No, but she should be here any minute.'

'Oh dear, the roads are so bad tonight . . .' Emma's voice faltered.

'Don't fret, Gran, she's a careful driver. Besides, she went over to the Harrogate store this afternoon. However, knowing Paula she'll probably stay until closing time. But at least her driving time has been cut in half.'

'I'll rest easier once she gets here. Well, continue, who else has made an appearance?'

'Maggie. She's sorting the Christmas tree decorations, helping the girls. Alexander and Uncle David are hanging mistletoe. Hilda and Joe are preparing the refectory table for the buffet, and Winston's stacking gifts under the tree.' Emily smirked. 'Oh yes, and Aunt Edwina is making herself useful for once – she's instructing Winston exactly *how* to arrange the packages for the best effect. As if it mattered.'

'At least she's talking to a Harte for a change. That's certainly a step in the right direction.' Emma motioned to Emily. 'Come here, dear, I want to show you something.'

As Emily joined her, Emma lifted the lid of an old leather jewellery case and then handed it to her granddaughter.

Emily gasped, staring down at the beautiful diamond necklace lying on the dark red velvet. It was a glittering lacy web of brilliant, perfectly cut and mounted stones. The diamonds had such fire, such life, such matchless beauty, Emily gasped again. 'This is extraordinary, Grandma, and obviously very old. Where did it come from? I don't think I've ever seen you wear it.'

'No, you haven't, because I never have. I haven't even tried it on since I've owned it.'

'I don't understand,' Emily said, her eyes perplexed.

'I've never wanted to wear it, and I only bought it when it was auctioned because – well, it was a sort of symbol to me. It represented everything I never had when I was a young girl – when I was a maid at Fairley Hall.' Emma took the case back from Emily, lifted out the necklace, held it up to the light. 'Yes, it's superb. Superb. It belonged to Adele Fairley, Jim's great-grandmother. I can still recall the night of a big dinner when I helped Adele to dress, fastened this around her throat. I was very bitter that night. The necklace, you see, represented the grinding toil and drudgery of the villagers, and my father, my brother Frank, and I myself.' Emma shook her head. 'When the Fairleys went down the drain, after Adam died, Gerald put this up for sale.' Her shoulders lifted in a shrug. 'I outbid everyone,' she explained and placed the necklace in its case.

Emily said, 'But why have you never worn it, Grandy?'

'Because it was suddenly meaningless to me once I owned it . . . I preferred the things which had been given to me with love, by those who loved me.'

'What are you going to do with it?' Emily eyed the fancy wrapping paper and silver ribbon on the desk. 'Oh I know! You're going to give it to Paula because she's married to Jim.'

'No, not Paula.'

'Then who?'

'Edwina.'

'*Edwina*. Why her? She's always so awful to you!'

'So what. And just because she behaves badly doesn't mean I have to do the same. Anyway throughout my life I've tried to rise above that sort of thing. Always remember that it is far better to be gracious in difficult situations, Emily, than to sink to the levels of others. Anyway, Paula wouldn't want this. She might bear the name of Fairley, but I don't believe she considers herself to be one, no, not at all. On the other hand, Edwina *does*. The Fairley name is important to her, and I think she, above everyone in the family, would appreciate owning this and –'

'But Gran,' Emily began.

Emma held up her hand. 'Edwina was denied her birthright because she was illegitimate, and I know how much the circumstances of her birth troubled her, perhaps still do. I feel it is only proper that she has something that belonged to them – this kind of family heirloom. *I* don't want it, since it has no meaning for me. Neither am I trying to ingratiate myself with her, or redeem myself in her eyes. I simply want to give it to her, and that's all there is to it. She will enjoy wearing it, of that I feel sure. Now, perhaps you would be kind enough to wrap it for me, Emily.'

'Of course I will. May I sit at the desk? It's easier to work there.'

'Yes.' Emma rose, walked across to the fireplace, stood with her back to it.

Emily glanced at the necklace again, closed the case, began to wrap it, thinking what an extraordinary woman her grandmother was. There was no one like her in the whole world. She was so generous and so very forgiving. Damn Edwina, she thought. I wish *she* would make just one gesture of love towards Gran. That would make *me* feel better.

There was a tap on the door. It opened and Paula looked in, exclaimed, 'Hello, you two! I'm frightfully late, I'm afraid. The Harrogate store was mobbed all day, like bedlam when we closed. Then the roads were ghastly. See you both in a while. I must pop in on the babies and Nora before I change.'

'Thank heaven you got here safely,' Emma was filled with relief at the sight of Paula's smiling face. 'And take your time, dear. Nobody's going anywhere.'

'I will.' Paula closed the door softly.

Emma said to Emily, 'Once you finish wrapping the necklace I think we'd better go downstairs. The O'Neills and the Kallinskis will be arriving any moment.'

'It's finished.' Emily clipped off the end of the silver ribbon, sat back to admire her handiwork. She lifted her dancing green eyes, focused them on her grandmother. 'I bet old Edwina has a heart attack when she opens this later, Gran!' she said, grinning mischievously.

'Really, Emily, sometimes –' Emma shook her head, tried to look disapproving without much success.

The Stone Hall at Pennistone Royal derived its name from the local grey stone which had been used throughout – on the ceiling, the walls, the floor and the fireplace facade. But it was more than an entrance hall, had the overtones of a huge sitting room with its handsome Jacobean and Tudor furniture which partially underscored the architecture of the house.

Dark wood beams criss-crossed the stone ceiling, introduced a touch of warmth, as did the faded Aubusson carpets on the floor, the antique tapestries and oil paintings on the walls. The baronial overtones were further diminished by the blaze of rosy light from the chandelier and wall sconces, and the huge fire crackling up the chimney back. Pots of yellow, pink and purple chrysanthemums and deep-orange amaryllis sparked some of the wood surfaces, and tall brass urns filled with dark green holly, bright with red berries, graced several corners.

But taking pride of place and dominating the hall tonight was a giant Christmas tree. This was nine feet tall, with wide spreading branches and it towered up to touch the edge of the minstrels' gallery at the far end of the hall.

Emma, descending the staircase with Emily, paused half way, stood for a moment admiring the scene. 'Oh, doesn't it look festive!' she cried. Not waiting for a response, she hurried down, glided across the floor to join the throng of family members, her eyes sparkling, her face wreathed in smiles.

'Hello, everyone,' she said. 'And well done. You've obviously worked hard to make the hall look beautiful tonight. Thank you.'

They came to greet her in turn, kissed her, told her she looked wonderful. Winston took the gift she handed him and put it under the tree. Jim, who had trouble manœuvring the wheel chair, could only wave.

Emma hurried over to him, rested her hand on his good shoulder, squeezed it, bent to kiss him. 'How are you feeling?' she asked, her concern for his well being apparent in her expression.

'Bloody awful, but I'll survive.' He gazed up at her through his light silvery eyes, then grimaced. 'What a rotten way to spend Christmas.'

'Yes, I know, dear, and you must be terribly uncomfortable. Can I get you anything?'

'No, thanks. Where's Paula? She should be home by now. It's almost six-thirty.' His voice was unexpectedly querulous, and he scowled at Emma, his mouth twisting into an angry line which he could not manage to conceal. Before she had a chance to answer, he exclaimed, 'I don't know why she had to go to the store today. It's ridiculous the way she works, and it is Christmas Eve. She ought to be here with her family. The babies need her, and furthermore, so do I – crippled as I am in this way. I think she's inconsiderate.'

Emma drew back, amazed at his words, his nasty tone, his sudden burst of petulance. She knew he was not feeling well, but she could not help thinking that he was overdoing it a bit. She said softly, 'It's because it *is* Christmas that she had to be at the stores today, Jim. You know this is her busiest period.'

'She should have left at noon,' he groused, 'come home to me. After all, the circumstances are a little exceptional, wouldn't you say?'

Emma bit back a sharp retort, knowing she must excuse him, blame his irascibility and immaturity on his condition. She said, more quietly than before, '*I* was never an absentee landlord and I doubt that Paula will ever be one either. And as a matter of fact, she just got back. She'll be down in a few minutes. She's changing into a cocktail dress. I see you have a drink and your cigarettes, Jim, so if you'll excuse me I'll go and deal with those two rowdy teenagers.'

Hurrying over to the tree, where Amanda and Francesca stood on two stepladders quarrelling furiously, Emma exclaimed, 'Now, girls, stop that and come down. At once, do you hear!'

'Yes, Grandma,' Amanda said dutifully, quickly doing as she was bidden.

Francesca lingered. She placed a silver bell on the tip of a branch, craning her neck to study it.

Amanda, having reached the bottom of the ladder, took a step back, watching her sister. She shrieked, 'Not there, you clot! It's right next to a silver icicle. You need more colour on that branch. Put the red star you're holding in that spot instead of the bell.'

'Go to hell!' Francesca retorted. 'I'm sick of you tonight. You're a dimwit. And far too *bossy*.'

'That's enough!' Emma snapped. 'Get down, Francesca, and immediately. Otherwise you'll spend this evening in your room.'

'Yes, Grandy,' Francesca mumbled, clattering down the stepladder to join her sister who was standing next to Emma.

'Now upstairs, both of you.' Emma gave them a disapproving glance. 'You look like a couple of street urchins. I want you out of those disgusting jeans and grimy shirts and into more suitable clothes. *Instantly*. And wash your faces and brush your hair. I've never seen you both in such an appalling state. And please don't dress alike. I'm getting sick and tired of this twin-sister act of yours. You're like a music hall turn.'

'Yes, Grandmother,' Amanda murmured meekly.

'What do you want us to wear?' Francesca asked, eyeing Emma boldly, giving her a cheeky grin.

Quite unexpectedly, Emma wanted to laugh, but she controlled herself, said sternly, 'You can put on your red velvet frock, Francesca. And *you*, Amanda, had better wear your blue silk. That should do it. If nothing else, at least I'll be able to distinguish you from each other. Now run along.'

Emily, who had witnessed this little scene, laughed when her half-sisters were out of earshot. 'Thanks, Gran. They've been extremely bolshy these last few days. I almost threatened to send them to Paris to join our mother, but it would've been an idle threat. I wouldn't have the heart to do that to them – as tiresome as they are.'

'They're just trying the two of us on for size, you know, seeing how much they can get away with.' Emma chuckled.

'I know. Would you like a drink?'

'Why not, Emily. Perhaps you can ask Winston or your brother to open a bottle of champagne. I think I'd like a glass. And let's have some music.' Emma swung around as Emily hurried off to fetch the wine, and called across to David Amory, 'Please pop a record on, David dear, one of those selections of Christmas carols. No, not the carols just yet. I rather like that Bing Crosby ... *White Christmas* I believe it's called.'

'Right away, Emma. And it's certainly appropriate this year.'

Emma turned to the box of tree decorations, started to dress the lower branches which were relatively bare and unfinished. She had been working only a few seconds when she felt a hand touch her arm tentatively. She swivelled, found herself face-to-face with Edwina.

'May I help, Mother?'

'Yes, I'd like that,' Emma said, camouflaging her surprise. 'Root around in the other box. Perhaps you'll find something sparkling and pretty for these low branches. It seems to me that the most beautiful ornaments generally end up on the top of the tree.' Emma's eyes roved over her eldest daughter. She nodded. 'Blue has always suited you, Edwina. You look lovely tonight, and that's a beautiful frock.'

'Thank you ... Daisy talked me into buying it.' Edwina hesitated. 'You look very elegant, but then you always do, Mother.' Edwina offered her a smile that was as tentative as her touch had been.

Emma smiled in return, wondering what to make of the unprecedented compliment, then reached for a gold *papier mâché* pear, hooked it on to a branch, frowning to herself. Edwina was certainly most cordial all of a sudden. Still, she had to admit she was pleased at this show of friendliness.

After a moment, Edwina tapped Emma's arm, held out a blue glass star. 'Here you are, Mother, would you like to hang this one? Maybe over there, next to the angel. Or wherever you think it would look right.'

Taking it from her, Emma searched her daughter's face.

For a split second she was transported back in time ... to a Christmas long, long ago. *December of 1915*. Joe Lowther had still been alive. It was the year before he had been killed in the Battle of the Somme. They had lived in the avenue called the Towers in Armley. In her mind's eye the memory flashed so vividly Emma caught her breath. Edwina had been nine-years-old and exceptionally pretty with her long blonde hair, her silvery eyes so like Adele's, her delicate features inherited from Edwin Fairley, her father. But the little girl had believed Joe to be her father and she had adored him. Worshipped him really.

The three of them had stood in front of a giant fir, very similar to this one, and on a snowy Christmas Eve such as this. Dim echoes of their joyous laughter reverberated in Emma's head. But it had been the child and the man who had laughed, shared the delight and fun of dressing the splendid tree. She had been the interloper, unwanted by her daughter. Edwina had spurned her, slighted her every time she had offered that beautiful but disdainful child a pretty bauble to hang on the tree. And she had left the room, her heart almost breaking. She had put on her coat and run down the short avenue to Blackie's and Laura's house, and her dearest Laura had comforted her, helped to take the sting out of the child's spitefulness.

Edwina said, 'Are you feeling all right, Mother?'

Emma blinked. The memory dissolved. 'Yes,' she said, 'Oh yes, I'm fine. I was just remembering something.'

'What were you remembering?'

'Oh a Christmas . . . so long ago now you've surely forgotten it.' Emma smiled faintly. 'But I've never forgotten it – not really.'

'You were thinking about the Christmas of 1915, weren't you?' Edwina moved closer to Emma.

'Yes.'

'Mother . . .' Edwina looked deeply into Emma's old wise eyes. 'I've not forgotten that Christmas either.' She paused, seemed to consider and then reached out and took hold of Emma's hand impulsively. 'Forgive me, Mother, please, please forgive me for that terrible Christmas,' she whispered.

Emma stared back at her daughter in stupefaction. And then she instantly knew what Edwina was trying to say. She wanted to be forgiven for all of her transgressions over the years and not just that particular Christmas. Emma said slowly, 'You were such a little girl, so young. You didn't understand . . . understand how things were in an adult world. You had no conception of pain or heartbreak.'

'Please say you forgive me, Mother,' Edwina begged, her sincerity evident. 'It's become so very important to me.'

'Why of course I forgive you, Edwina. You are my daughter, my first born child. And I told you months ago that I've always loved you. My love has never wavered or changed, though you have doubted me.'

'I don't anymore.' Tears swam in Edwina's pale eyes. 'Can we be friends at last – so late in our lives – do you think?'

'I know we can.' Emma smiled her incomparable smile that always filled her face with radiance. 'Why we already are, my dear,' she said, clasping Edwina's hand tightly.

Jonathan Ainsley was beginning to realize how dangerous the conditions were after he left the main Ripon road and manœuvered his Aston Martin down a narrow side lane, taking a short cut to the village of Pennistone Royal.

'You shouldn't have come this way,' Sarah complained. 'The lane twists and turns too much. We'll have an accident if you're not careful.'

'This is the fastest route,' Jonathan replied. A cold smile touched his mouth. 'I don't want to miss anything tonight, I think it's going to be –' He broke off as he felt the wheels sliding on the ice. The car was going into a skid. He gripped the steering wheel tighter, turning the car into the skid in an effort to avert it, gently pressing his foot on the brake as he did.

Sarah, stiffening with fright, grabbed his arm.

Angrily Jonathan shook off her hand, managed to right the Aston in the nick of time, shouted, 'You'll have us in a bloody ditch!' He slowed his pace to a slow crawl. 'For God's sake don't ever do a thing like that again, Sarah. It's very dangerous.'

'I'm sorry. It *was* a silly reaction. Don't be angry with me. You know I can't bear it when you lose your temper.'

'Okay, okay, let's forget it,' he muttered, pushing his annoyance to one side. The last thing he wanted was to upset Sarah. He needed her too much to incur her disfavour. He peered ahead, watching for new ice patches in the glare of the headlights.

Neither of the cousins spoke for a while.

Sarah shrank into the corner of the seat, pulling her silver fox coat around her, hoping his good humour would soon be restored.

Jonathan concentrated on the road, driving now with the utmost care. The Aston Martin was new, not even paid for yet. A bashed up hood or a damaged fender would be costly. He relaxed a fraction as he hit a clear stretch, but still he did not increase his pace, determined to be cautious. His mind swung to his cousin sitting next to him. He wondered how to persuade Sarah to put up more money, invest another few hundred thousand pounds in the company he secretly owned with Sebastian Cross. Sarah was their partner now. Her money was vital to them. Urgently needed. They had had a lot of bad luck lately. And Sebastian had made some disastrous deals, which negated the good ones he had closed. But they would pull out of it. One good deal would do the trick.

A grimness settled on his face as his duplicitous brain continued to turn at a rapid rate. Maybe he would have to steer one of the deals he was handling for Harte Enterprises into Stonewall Properties, his own company. *Why not?* The thought tickled him. Jonathan Ainsley was aware that he had larceny in his heart, accepted that he was avaricious, greedy for the good things in life, hungry for power. He also knew he was not a good sport, despite his grandmother's efforts to instil in him the importance of playing the game. Who wants to play the game? he now asked himself. He was a bad loser. He didn't care. But he would be damned if he would ever be the loser again. He was going to be the winner . . .

Sarah said, 'We're almost at the end of the lane, Jonny.'

'Yes, I know.' Jonathan began to ponder her. He had been manipulating Sarah for months, playing on her hatred for Paula, feeding her jealousy, envy and bitterness. But she had every reason to be bitter. Just as he did. Paula was the favourite. The Crown Princess. She was getting everything, damn her. And so was Alexander. A small tremor of fury shot through Jonathan. He instantly curbed it, warning himself to stay cool tonight. He had schooled himself not to show his hand to the family, and least of all to his grandmother. Bloody old witch, he thought. My father's right. She's never going to kick the bucket. We *will* have to shoot her in the end. Poor Dad. He was cheated out of his inheritance. But he's a great politician and one of the greatest men in England. He might even be Prime Minister one day. He's so smart. He thought my idea of starting my own business was brilliant. He gave me his blessing. Jonathan wondered if his grandmother suspected him. Never. She was too old, getting senile. Once Emma Harte was dead he would inherit the New York apartment. The bequest to him was in her will. It had to be worth five million dollars at least. And Sarah was to get the Belgrave Square house. I'll make her sell it, invest the cash with me. The mere thought of this enormous amount of money cheered him. He tingled with excitement. His mood became sanguine. He felt much better all of a sudden, and quite up to facing his boring family. He wished he could park and smoke a joint before they reached the house. He did not dare. Sarah would disapprove. She was such a bore. A pain really. Better cater to her. He needed her support, her continuing friendship. Sebastian had recently had the idea of marrying Sarah. Jonathan was not sure that he should encourage this. He despised Sarah, but Sebastian was a strange bird, and the gambling had grown worse – he was growing ever more reckless. Besides, Jonathan did not want to lose control of Sarah, or, more precisely, her money.

At the end of the lane Jonathan drew to a standstill, flicked his lights, then pulled out on to the main road. He said, 'That was a bumpy ride, but like all bumpy rides it was worth it. At least we won't be all that late.'

'Why are you so anxious to get to Grandy's early? What are you afraid of missing?' Sarah asked, filled with curiosity.

'*Family dramas.*' Jonathan chortled. 'And there are bound to be some, with that motley crew in attendance. There'll be our peer of the realm hovering over his pregnant mistress. Christ, Sarah, Anthony's been lucky. He's just missed standing trial for murder, and by the skin of his teeth. I hear Sally Harte's blown up like a helium balloon, got his bun in her oven all right, and for all the world to see.'

'Do you always have to be so crude?' Sarah said with her usual primness.

He glanced at her quickly out of the corner of his eye and, undeterred, said 'And there'll be our two love birds, billing and cooing inanely. I always knew Emily was itching to get into Winston's trousers when we were kids. She's a bloody little sex pot if you ask me, just like her randy mum.'

'Allison Ridley's devastated about Winston,' Sarah remarked as evenly as she could, brushing aside his vulgarity. 'She's moving to New York in a few weeks. I can't say I blame her. Our crowd is too close-knit . . . she'd always be running into Winston.'

'*He's* certainly riding high at the moment, got *his* hands on the newspaper company because of Jim's accident.' Instantly Jonathan saw a way to inflame Sarah, added swiftly, 'That plane crash was a bit odd, don't you think?'

'In what way?'

'It struck me at the time that Jim might have been trying to do himself in – you know, end it all in one dramatic moment.'

Sarah was shocked. 'Jonathan! That's a terrible thing to say! Why would Jim want to kill himself, for heaven's sake?'

'Who wouldn't – being married to the Ice Queen?'

'Yes,' Sarah muttered. 'She is a cold bitch. Probably frigid.'

'Oh, I wouldn't say *that* –' Jonathan stopped, waiting for Sarah to take the bait.

'I thought you hated Paula as much as I do?'

'I haven't changed,' he reassured her.

'But you just implied that she's not cold, Jonny.'

'I heard something about her that leads me to think otherwise –' Again he broke off, wanting to further intrigue Sarah.

'Oh! Tell me the gossip.'

Jonathan sighed. 'I shouldn't have started this conversation with you, Sarah dear. The last thing I want to do is upset you on Christmas Eve.'

Sarah said, 'I won't be upset . . . come on, don't be mean, give me all the dirt on Paula. I'm certainly all ears.'

'No, I'm positive I oughtn't to continue.' He smothered a gleeful laugh, enjoying this cat and mouse game. He always did. It gave him a sense of power.

There was a small silence.

'On the other hand, you're a big girl –' He patted her hand. 'And of course it might *not* be true at all.'

'For God's sake tell me . . . this is driving me crazy,' Sarah cried.

'Paula was in Barbados in November, as you know. But were you aware that Shane O'Neill was there at the same time?'

Sarah tensed. She sucked in her breath, obviously taken aback. 'So what?' she managed after a moment. 'He was down there when *I* went out to supervise the opening of the boutique. His presence on the island doesn't mean a thing.'

'Perhaps not – on the surface. But you were the one who told me you'd seen him ogling her, looking all hot eyed and turned on at the christening.'

'He was!'

'Well, Rodney Robinson, my old school chum from Eton, was in Barbados at the same time as Paula. He was staying at the Sandy Lane Hotel, and he told me he saw her having lunch at the hotel. She was with a man –'

'It may not have been Shane,' Sarah said swiftly. She could hardly bear to think of Shane with her cousin. It made her physically ill.

'It *was* Shane,' Jonathan said steadily. 'Rodney thought he looked familiar. After they'd left, old Rod spoke to the head waiter, asked him if he knew the name of the man with the tall, dark, striking young woman. The head waiter told him it was a Mr O'Neill who owned the Coral Cove Hotel.'

'Having lunch together isn't anything unusual. They've always been close friends,' Sarah protested, willing the pain in her chest to go away.

'Oh I agree, love. Except for one thing. Rodney told me they were looking extremely cosy. Intimate, was his word. In fact, he said Shane was practically getting it off with her at the table.'

'P-p-please,' Sarah stammered, 'y-y-you know I loathe it when you're vulgar.'

'Oh sorry, love.' He patted her hand again. His glee spiralled. 'They were drooling all over each other and in the most disgusting way. So Rodney said. Obviously our Ice Queen isn't so icy after all, nor is she the little Miss Goody Two Shoes she pretends to be. Poor Jim. I'm not surprised he almost plunged to his death.'

Sarah swallowed. She was overwhelmed by jealousy, hardly able to breathe.

Jonathan, aware of her feelings for Shane O'Neill, continued relentlessly, 'Yes, methinks there's something rotten in the state of Denmark, to quote old Will Shakespeare. *Adultery* perhaps? Rocking the House of Fairley.' He chuckled sarcastically.

'They can't be having an affair,' Sarah moaned. 'Paula wouldn't dare. She'd be too scared that Grandy would find out. Anyway, she's in love with Jim.'

'A hundred to one that you're entirely wrong, Sarah, my poppet.'

'I don't think we should talk about this anymore. I *am* getting upset after all. Actually, I feel rather queasy.'

'I do hope you're going to be all right,' Jonathan murmured softly, pretending to be concerned. 'I knew I shouldn't have told you. But you've always been able to twist me around your little finger. Thank God we have each other, Sarah. We'll fight those cousins of ours and to the bitter end. We'll come out on top, you'll see. Sebastian and I have the company really rolling now. You're going to make millions with us, and be as rich and powerful as Paula bloody Fairley.'

There was no response from Sarah, who sat hugging herself, fighting back the tears. She loved Shane so much it was painful hearing these things about him and Paula. She did not doubt Jonathan.

Jonathan said, 'Cheer up, love. And remember one thing – Shane is a Roman Catholic. He'd never marry a divorced woman. And *if* he is involved with the lady he's bound to tire of her soon. He's a real stu –' Jonathan cleared his throat, quickly corrected himself by substituting, 'Ladies man.' He continued, 'And he's still sowing his wild oats. That's what this affair with Paula is – Shane's bound to calm down soon. And *voilà*! You'll be there waiting for him. Rich, too, as you walk to the altar with him. By the way, I've been meaning to tell you, you're looking very beautiful these days, Sarah, since you lost so much weight. Shane won't be able to resist you. I'm going to help you, don't worry. I'm going to make certain you get the man you love.'

'Oh Jonny, you're always so nice to me,' Sarah said, instantly cheering. 'Everything you say is true, I just know it is. *I* will end up with Shane. And I am glad about our real estate company.' She peered at him in the dim light of the car. 'Am I really going to be as wealthy as Paula?'

'Absolutely. I guarantee it. Incidentally, after Christmas Sebastian and I want you to come to our first real board meeting. We'll show you the books, go over our various deals, explain the new ones that are pending. You may have to invest a little more money, but it'll be worth it. Think of the dowry you'll take to Shane. I realize that sounds old fashioned, but don't let's be foolish enough to dismiss money in this instance. Shane O'Neill is bloody ambitious, and he'd never look twice at a poor woman. So ... I'm going to make sure you are loaded, Sarah.'

'What would I do without you?' Sarah sighed, blissful at the prospect of her rosy future. 'I'm feeling tons better now.' She giggled. 'It must be the thought of lauding it over Paula in the not too distant future, and snatching Shane out from under her nose.'

'That's the spirit, Sarah! When should I arrange for us to get together with Sebastian Cross?'

'Any time you like. And of course I'll put up some more money. I trust you, Jonny, you've always been on my side, been my best friend.'

'And as you have been mine, my pet.'

Within minutes Jonathan was turning into the gates of Pennistone Royal. As he parked he noticed the long line up of cars and realized they were probably the last to arrive. Secretly laughing up his sleeve at Sarah's gullibility, he nevertheless managed to keep his face straight as he helped her out of the car, ran around to the boot to collect their gifts for their grandmother.

Puffed-up with self-congratulation at his adroit handling of his cousin, he put his hand under her elbow, arranged a suitably insouciant smile and escorted her inside.

Joe, the houseman, was on duty, and he wished them a happy Christmas as he took their coats. They returned his greeting. Jonathan's sharp, ever-quick eyes darted around as he and Sarah went down the short flight of steps leading into the Stone Hall. The party was in full swing. Everyone was present. The air was filled with the sound of Christmas music playing on the stereo, and the high-pitched buzz of chatter intermingled with bursts of jolly laughter. The fire roared, the giant tree blazed with lights, and the familiar faces which turned to greet them were ringed with happy smiles.

Jonathan smiled back, nodded, but did not stop. He propelled Sarah on a steady course down the hall. He saw Paula sitting on the arm of Blackie's chair, talking to the old man very earnestly, her face tender. If I exaggerated Rodney's story to goad Sarah, I know I wasn't far off the mark, Jonathan commented silently. I bet Shane O'Neill has got her where he wants her. In his bed. Good old Rodney. I owe him one.

Now Jonathan noticed Jim, trapped in the wheelchair, talking to Anthony. They had a strong look of each other. Fairley blood, he thought. He felt the sardonic laughter rising in his throat, almost choking him. He swallowed, made sure his charming smile was intact. As soon as Jim's alone I'll go over and talk to him, sow a few seeds of doubt in his mind about that holier-than-thou wife of his. In the meantime, I'd better find the old dragon, go over and genuflect.

Jonathan's predictions to Sarah to the contrary, there were no dramas at Pennistone Royal that evening.

Emma's traditional Christmas Eve party progressed without a hitch. However, Emily's comment about Edwina being shocked to death when she saw the diamond necklace proved to be no exaggeration.

After the buffet supper had been served and eaten, and before the carol singing began, Emma distributed her generous tokens of her affection to her family and friends. They were thrilled and touched by their presents, recognizing the amount of time she had spent in selecting something extra special for each of them. Even the malcontents were pleased – Jonathan with his gold-and-jade cuff links, Sarah with the pearl-and-jade necklace she had received.

But it was Edwina who was genuinely stunned, momentarily rendered speechless as she gaped in amazement at the Fairley necklace. Observing her closely, Emma thought her daughter was indeed going to keel over from a heart attack. Instead Edwina collapsed in floods of tears.

After she had composed herself, Edwina began to realize that the Fairley heirloom she had been given was a gesture of unselfish love, that of a mother for a daughter, and she was more than thankful she had made the initial move to end her estrangement from her mother earlier. She remained at Emma's side for the rest of the evening.

The happy mood prevailed until midnight. Only Paula felt out of it at times, when her thoughts turned to Shane. She was attentive to Jim and his needs, and chatted with everyone, but she constantly found herself gravitating to the O'Neills, needing to be in the midst of Shane's family. Somehow it seemed to bring him closer.

Next year, she kept thinking. Next year. We'll be together next year.

39

It was a rainy night in the middle of January.

Jim Fairley sat in the Peach Drawing Room, sipping a straight vodka, gazing at his favourite painting, the Sisley he loved so much and longed to possess for himself. So rapt was he in his contemplation of it, he did not realize that Emma had appeared in the doorway of her drawing room.

She stood observing him closely.

Her worry about Jim was increasing daily, and she could not help thinking now that she was watching the slow but steady disintegration of a man. He had changed so radically during her absence abroad and over the last six weeks, he was hardly recognizable as the personable young editor she had first employed. She had tried to talk to him, but her words seemed to flow over him, leaving him untouched. He continued on his downward slide.

He was drinking steadily. Ever since she had chastized him about this a few days after Christmas he had endeavoured to conceal his tippling. Still, she was aware he was consuming great quantities of liquor – day and night.

She thought of his family. Every single one of the Fairleys had been drinkers. His great-grandmother, Adele, had fallen down the staircase at Fairley Hall in a drunken stupor, breaking her neck. The shattered wine glass had been scattered around her body, on that dreadful morning when Annie, the other maid, had found her.

Emma frowned to herself. She wondered if alcoholism was congenital. Jim was not yet an alcoholic, but she was convinced he was well on the way to becoming one. And then there were the pain killers. He had not really persuaded her he had stopped taking pills. And yet she could not for the life of her imagine where he was getting them from. Continuing to study his face in profile, thinking how good looking he was despite the ravages of drink, medication and his physical pain, a phrase Blackie had used recently leapt into her mind. They had been at Allington Hall stables, looking over his string of racehorses. 'The breeding's there, but no stamina,' Blackie had said, referring to one of his thoroughbreds. An appropriate analogy, Emma mused. Loath though she was to condemn Jim, it was apparent to her that he was weak, lacked strength of character. But had she not always suspected this?

Emma cleared her throat, said in a cheerful voice, 'Good evening, Jim.' She walked into the room purposefully.

She had startled him. He swung his head quickly. He gave her a half smile. 'I wondered where you were,' he exclaimed, forcing a conviviality he did not feel. 'I hope you don't mind, but I didn't wait for you.' He glanced at the drink. 'But this *is* my first today, Grandy.'

That's a downright lie, she thought. She said, 'I was delayed on the telephone, but I'll now join you in a cocktail before dinner.'

Pouring herself a glass of white wine, Emma continued, 'I was just speaking to Daisy. She rang from Chamonix. They're so sorry you're not with them. David misses you on the slopes.' She brought her drink, and sat down near the fire. 'Daisy's not much of a skier, as you know, and David is feeling lonely without you, his boon companion. Well, never mind, you'll be able to go with them next year, Jim.'

'I sincerely hope so.' He moved his broken shoulder slightly, gave her a quirky little smile. 'It's a relief to have this in a sling, I can tell you that, and Doctor Hedley's going to take the cast off my leg tomorrow.'

She knew all about this, but faked surprise, not wanting him to know she was constantly consulting with the family doctor about him. 'That's *wonderful* news. You must start therapy immediately, get those muscles in shape again.'

'Try to stop me.' He gave her a long careful look. 'Did Paula call you from New York today?'

Emma's eyes flickered. 'No, she didn't, but I wasn't expecting to hear from her. Surely she told you last night, when she called, that she was flying to Texas today. Sitex business, you know.'

'Oh, that's right. I'd forgotten.'

Emma wondered if he really had, but let the comment pass. 'Emily just told me that Winston's coming to dinner after all. That'll be nice for you, Jim, a little male company should cheer you up. It must be very boring for you – surrounded by women.'

He laughed. 'You're all very attentive, but it'll be nice to see Winston, hear what's happening in the outside world. I feel so cut off, and weary of this inactivity. I hope I can get back to the paper in a couple of weeks. What do you think?'

It struck Emma that this would be a wise move, and she said swiftly, 'I'm all for it. I've always found that work is a wonderful cure for what ails *me*.'

Jim cleared his throat. 'Talking of the newspapers, Emma, there's something I've been meaning to ask you for the longest time.'

'Oh, and what's that, Jim?'

He hesitated briefly, then said in a low voice, 'When I came back from Canada in September, Paula and I had a bit of a quarrel about Sam Fellowes, and the instructions she had given him in my absence, you know, about suppressing the stories dealing with Min's death.'

'Yes, she mentioned something about it – her decision, not your quarrel.' Emma gave him a questioning look.

'Paula told me that she has your power of attorney, and Winston's, to act on your behalf or his, if the need comes up.'

'That's quite true.'

'I couldn't help wondering why you didn't give those powers of attorney to me?'

Emma sat very still, was silent for a second, and said gently, 'Jim, when you resigned as managing director of the Yorkshire Consolidated Newspaper Company you forfeited your right to any power in that company, other than the editorial power you have as managing editor, of course. Since you said you were not interested in the administrative side of the newspapers, it seemed patently obvious to me that those powers of attorney had to rest in the hands of someone who was ready, willing and able to act, to take charge, if the situation arose – *administratively* take control, I mean.'

'I see.'

Watching him closely, she saw his face stiffen in annoyance, his eyes cloud over with resentment. 'You did resign of your own accord, Jim,' she remarked evenly, in that same gentle voice.

'I know.' He took a long swallow of the vodka, placed the drink on the end table, stared into the fire. Finally he swung his eyes to hers. 'Paula is also the trustee of my children's shares in the newspaper company, isn't she?'

'She is.'

'Why, Grandy? Why didn't you make me the trustee for them? I am their father, after all.'

'It's not as simple as it seems, Jim. The shares which I am leaving to Lorne and Tessa are not in a separate trust, but in their overall trust fund into which I have placed many other shares from my different holdings. It seems clear to me that such a giant trust must be managed by one person. It would be ridiculous to have a number of different trusts, have each one handled by a different individual. Far too confusing.'

He nodded, made no comment.

Emma gave him a discerning look, recognizing that he was not only put out, but furious, even though he was doing his best to conceal this emotion from her. Whilst she knew she had no obligation to explain her actions to anyone, she nevertheless wanted to make him feel better about himself.

She said, 'My decision to appoint Paula is no reflection on you, or your ability. She – and she alone – would be the trustee of her children's trust fund whoever she was married to, Jim.'

'I understand,' he murmured, although deep down he did not. He felt he had been passed over. But then he had no one to blame but himself. He suddenly realized he should never have resigned as managing director of the newspaper company.

Ignoring his moody expression, his angry silence, Emma remarked, 'If Emily and Winston have children before I die, and if I created a trust fund for their offsprings which of course I *would*, Winston will be in the same position as you are. So would Sarah's husband, should she marry whilst I'm still alive. I'm not singling you out.'

'I said I understand, and I do, Emma. Thanks for explaining things to me. I appreciate –'

There was a tap on the door, and Hilda came in, said, 'Excuse me, Mrs Harte, but Mr O'Neill is on the phone. He said that if you're busy you can ring him back. He's at Mr Bryan's, in Wetherby.'

'Thank you, Hilda, I'll take it.' She rose, smiled at Jim, 'Excuse me, dear, I won't be a moment.'

He nodded, and the minute he was alone he trundled himself over to the Regency sideboard and filled his glass with vodka, plopped in ice. He put the drink in his left hand which peeped out from the sling, then pushed his chair back to the fireplace with his right.

He drank half the vodka down quickly, so that Emma would not know he had refilled his glass, then sat pondering her words. Suddenly everything was clear to him. Emma was placing all of her power in the hands of her grand-children. She was ensuring it stayed within the family. And absolutely so. He had thought he was family. He was an outsider after all.

Sighing, he lifted his eyes to the Sisley. The painting had always had a hypnotic effect on him. Again he wished it was his as he always did when he gazed on it. He wondered what exactly it was about this particular landscape that so enthralled him. There were other Sisleys in the room, and Monets. All were worth millions.

Suddenly, and with a small stab of acute horror, Jim understood. This paint-ing represented wealth and power to him. That was the reason he coveted it – the *real* reason. That the Sisley was heartstopping, lyrical, a great piece of art which appealed to his sensibilities more than the others, was beside the point. His hand trembled and he put the drink on the table, closed his eyes, blocking out the painting.

I want the money. I want the power. I want it all back . . . all that my great-grandfather and my great-uncle so foolishly squandered or lost, and which Emma Harte took from the Fairleys. Instantly Jim was appalled at these thoughts and at himself. I've had too much to drink. I'm getting maudlin. No, I'm not. I've not had that much vodka today. I've been very careful about my intake.

The trembling seemed to seize his whole body, and he opened his eyes, gripped the sides of his wheelchair to steady himself. The image of Paula flashed through his mind. He had married her because he was madly in love with her. He had. He knew he had. *No.* There was another reason. He had wanted her because she was Emma Harte's granddaughter. Wrong again. Emma Harte's principal heir to her vast fortune.

For a split second James Arthur Fairley saw himself as he truly was. It was his epiphany. And he did not like what he saw in that intense flash of clarity. *It was the truth.* He did love his wife, but he craved her money and her power. He groaned aloud and his eyes filled. This sudden self-revelation was insup-portable. He was not the man he had believed himself to be all of his life. His grandfather had brought him up to be a gentleman, to look to the higher things in life, to be unconcerned about material wealth and position. Edwin Fairley had brainwashed him. Yet secretly he had always longed for the power, the glory and the riches. There was a dichotomy in his nature. That was the true cause of his internal strife. I've deluded myself for years, he thought. I've lived a lie.

He groaned again and ran his hand through his hair. I love Paula for herself, I really do.

The nagging pain in his shoulder intruded and so insistently he winced in agony. It was the rainy weather. His shoulder was like a barometer. He groped around in his pocket for a pill, washed it down with vodka.

'Blackie's so excited,' Emma said from the doorway, hurrying in, laughing gaily. 'He's making such elaborate plans for the Grand National. He's taking *all* of us to Aintree for the steeplechase. It's the first Saturday in April.' Emma sat down, took a sip of her wine. 'And so you'll be able to come with us, Jim. You'll be as fit as a fiddle by then.'

40

'What are we going to do, Shane?' Paula stared at him, her expression troubled.

'We're going to take this one step at a time, get through each day as best we can,' he said confidently. He gave her one of his reassuring smiles. 'And we're going to make it.'

They sat in her office in the Leeds store. It was an afternoon in the middle of April of 1970. Shane had just returned from a quick trip to Spain, where he had been to supervise the remodelling currently in progress at their Marbella hotel.

Now he edged closer to her on the sofa, put his arm around her, held her tightly in his arms. 'Try not to worry so much, darling.'

'I can't help it. The situation hasn't improved – it's just worsened. And everything's dragging on interminably. I'm beginning to think I'll never be free of my problems.'

'Yes, you will.' Moving away, he lifted her face, looked deeply into her eyes. 'We've both got innumerable business pressures right now, a load of responsibilities, and we're just going to have to concentrate on those, keep ourselves busy, knowing that ultimately we'll be together. And when we are it will be for always. Think of the future, Paula, keep your eyes trained on that.'

'I try, I do try, Shane, but –' her voice wavered and stopped. Her eyes filled up.

'Hey, come on, love,' he said. 'No tears. We've got to keep moving ahead, and purposefully so. I keep telling you, time is on our side. We're both young, and we are going to win in the end.'

'Yes.' She brushed her eyes with her fingertips, forced a more cheerful expression on to her face. 'It's just that – oh Shane, I miss you so much.'

'I know, I know, and I miss you too. It's sheer hell being apart. But look here, I *would* have to go to New York next week, and then on to Sydney for two months, even if your situation was straightened out. There's no way I can change those circumstances. And it's not been so bad, has it? We were together in New York for part of January and we've managed to grab some time together these past few weeks. So –'

'I can't help feeling that it's not fair to you. I'm keeping you dangling and –'

His laughter obliterated her words. 'I love you, and only you. I'll wait for you, Paula.' He hugged her fiercely. 'What kind of a man do you think I am, you silly, silly girl. None of this is your fault. It's beyond your control. Life intrudes, that can't be helped. We're just going to have to battle it through.'

'I'm sorry, Shane. I *am* being mournful today, aren't I? Perhaps that's because you'll be leaving in a few days. I feel so desperately alone when you're not in England.'

'But you're *not* alone, Paula. You have me, my love and my support – *always*. I carry you in my heart wherever I go, and you're never out of my thoughts, not for a single moment. We talk on the telephone practically every day, and if you need me urgently I'll come to you as fast as I can. You know I'd be on the first plane out, whether I'm in Australia or the States.' He gazed at her, his black eyes quizzical all of a sudden. 'You *do* know that, don't you?'

'Yes, yes, of course I do.'

'Remember what I said to you in Barbados?'

'That I must trust your love for me.'

'That's right. *As I trust yours for me.* Now, are you going to change your mind and come to dinner at Beck House tonight? It'll do you good, and Emily was so disappointed when you declined her invitation.'

'Perhaps I will, after all.' Paula frowned. 'Do you think she and Winston suspect anything about us?'

'*No.* They believe we've become good friends again, and that's all.'

Paula was not entirely convinced he was correct. However she had no wish to implant troublesome ideas in his mind, and she said, 'I couldn't get there until eight. I want to go home to see Tessa and Lorne, and then I have to go to the nursing home to see Jim.'

'I understand.'

'You really *do*, don't you, Shane?'

'Of course, and I wouldn't expect anything less of you, Paula. You're far too good, and too compassionate a woman, to turn your back on Jim at a time like this. You said over lunch that he was a bit better. What's the general prognosis?'

'The doctor told me yesterday that he could be out of the nursing home in a few weeks, *if* he continued to improve the way he has. He's not as depressed as he was and he's responding well to treatment, to the psychiatric help.' She shook her head and her worry flared up in her. 'But you never know with a nervous breakdown. I mean, some people recover quickly, others take months, and it's not unusual for a person to have relapses.' She hesitated, murmured in a low almost inaudible tone, 'I can't bring myself to say anything to him just yet – about my freedom.'

'I'm aware of that, you don't have to keep repeating yourself,' Shane said rapidly but with gentleness. 'We agreed that we must wait until Jim's back to normal, truly capable of handling things, before you tell him you want a divorce. I'm not reneging on our agreement. What else *can* we do? I'd like to be able to live with myself in the future, and I know you would, too.'

'Yes. Oh Shane, thank you, thank you so much for your understanding, and most of all for your love. I don't know what I'd do without you.'

He took her in his arms and kissed her, and they sat holding each other for a few minutes. Finally he released her. 'I've got to get back to the office. I've a couple of meetings scheduled, and with Dad in London at the international hotel conference I've got my hands full. Then I want to stop off and see Grandpops on my way home to Beck House.'

They rose and she walked him to the door. 'Give my love to Uncle Blackie,' Paula said, looking up at him. She offered him a brighter smile. 'I feel much better – now that I've seen you.'

Shane touched her face lightly. 'You'll be all right, darling, *we'll* be all right. Just so long as we stay cool and keep a positive attitude. We mustn't let anything rattle us or throw us off our course.'

Several hours later, when Shane pushed open the door of the library in his grandfather's house, he found Blackie standing in front of an antique chest. He had a soft yellow duster in his hand and was carefully rubbing away at the silver trophy which was now his pride and joy.

Shane smiled. If his grandfather polished it once a day, he did so at least half a dozen times. Of all the things Blackie owned it had become his proudest and most treasured possession. At the beginning of April, Blackie's eight-year-old mare, Emerald Bow, had run at Aintree and had won the Grand National. Winning the greatest steeplechase in the world had been the fulfilment of Blackie's lifelong dream. Curious though, Shane now thought, that of all the horses he owns it had to be the one Emma gave him which finally won the most coveted prize for him. There has to be something prophetic in that.

Moving forward, Shane said, 'Hello, Grandpops, sorry I'm late.'

Blackie turned around, his face lighting up. The sight of his handsome strapping grandson warmed his heart. 'Shane, me boy!' he cried and ambled across the floor.

The two men embraced. But as his arms went around his grandfather in a bear hug, Shane realized, with a small shock, that Blackie had lost weight since he had last seen him. My God, I can feel his bones through his suit. He's suddenly become so frail, Shane thought with a spurt of worry mingled with sadness. They drew apart and Shane looked into Blackie's face, his eyes scanning it swiftly. The weight loss was evident in the sunken cheeks, the scrawny neck. His shirt collar looked too big for him, and Blackie was unnaturally pale tonight. His ebony black eyes were cloudy, seemed to have a milky film.

'Are you feeling all right, Grandfather?' Shane asked, his scrutiny fixed on the old man.

'Never felt better.'

'That's good to hear,' Shane answered, but he reminded himself that his grandfather usually said this. Not wishing to press him further about his health, Shane eyed the cloth in Blackie's hand. 'If you're not careful you're going to rub a hole in that thing with your constant polishing, and then where will you be?'

Blackie snorted in amusement, followed Shane's glance, which was directed at the trophy. He lumbered over to the chest where it reposed, his pace as slow as before. Putting the cloth down, he rested his hand on top of the symbol of Emerald Bow's great triumph.

'I won't go so far as to say that winning this was the crowning moment of my life, but it was certainly the most thrilling.' Blackie nodded to himself. 'It truly was.'

Shane smiled across the room at his grandfather. 'And mine, too,' he asserted.

'Aye, lad, but you're going to have greater triumphs in your life than I've ever had. That's in the cards, sure and it is.' Stepping up to the small console, Blackie picked up a crystal decanter and poured whiskey in two glasses. 'Let's drink to that foregone conclusion with a drop of me good Irish.'

Shane joined him, took the tumbler, clinked it against Blackie's and said, 'To future triumphs – for us both, Grandpops.'

'Yes indeed. And to Emerald Bow and next year's Grand National. You never know, she could win again.' Blackie shot Shane a knowing look, went over to the fireplace and sat down in his favourite wing chair.

Shane followed him, struck once more by his grandfather's slow gait, which was almost a shuffle, and his fragility. Concern mounted in Shane, but he pressed down on it. Perhaps his grandfather was merely tired this evening. Also, the excitement of the Grand National, winning, and all the partying that had ensued might easily have taken its toll. And after all he was an old man, very old now. He was eighty-four years old.

Blackie sat musing to himself for a second or two, gazing into the flames, an abstracted look in his eyes, then he said to his grandson, 'I don't think I'll ever forget the finish.' Swinging his head, he leaned forward with a burst of energy and eagerness, his glass clasped tightly between his hands, his eyes shining brightly as he relived the race in his mind's eye.

He exclaimed excitedly: 'There they were, Shane, coming to the last fence! Emerald Bow with two other big horses alongside her! *Almost neck and neck.* Steve Larner, tough little sod that he is, going hell for leather. High in the stirrups, pushing her forward, a grim look on his face. Me heart was in me mouth, aye, it was that, Shane. I thought she wasn't going to make it. Sure and I believed one of the other two would beat her to it, if only by a hair's breadth. When Highland Boy went first, sailed up but hit the top of the fence, rolled over and was out of the race, just like that, well, I couldn't believe me eyes. And then King's Gold went the same way, catapulting over and landing on his back. I knew he'd taken it too close to the roots of the fence. Me old eyes were glued on Emerald Bow. And only a fraction of a second after the others had fallen, there she was, me valiant little mare, jumping the fence like a gazelle and finishing two hundred yards in front of the field. Aye, Shane, it was the most spectacular finish I've ever seen, and I've been to a hell of a lot of horse races during my long life.' Blackie's face was flushed, and he fell back against the chair. He was momentarily breathless, but recovered himself in a matter of moments.

'I was there, Grandpops. I saw it all, remember.'

Blackie winked at him. 'Sure you saw it, but I can't help reliving it with you, lad. It gets the blood flowing through me veins again, and you know your father doesn't understand how I feel – not really. It's you, Shane, who has inherited my love of horses, and you've got as good an eye as me when it comes to spotting a thoroughbred.'

Blackie paused, and his eyes danced merrily as another thought struck him. 'Poor Emma, how she suffered that day, in one way and another. Worrying because I was getting overly excited, concerning herself with thoughts of my disappointment if Emerald Bow lost, and she even got hurt in the process. I grabbed hold of her so hard at the finish she was bruised for days, at least so she tells me. Said I'd almost crushed some of her fragile old bones. Still, she did enjoy it, no two ways about that. And she was as excited as I was. As I still am, if the truth be known.'

'And why not, Grandpops, it was a wonderful victory for you, and so well deserved.'

Blackie sat back, took a sip of his whiskey. His face sobered and he became reflective. After a moment he said, 'Randolph was always right about Emerald Bow, you know, from the day Emma gave her to me. He never stopped telling me she had the stamina required for the National. It's a hard race, bloody carnage too, when you consider that out of the forty horses that start, only about eight finish. If that. Thirty fences to jump, and twice over Beecher's Brook. So many horses are injured, and it's exhausting for those that last. The stuffing's knocked out of them by the time they're coming into the final stretch.'

'The National's also a hell of a *fast* race,' Shane volunteered. 'It's over in about ten minutes.'

'Aye, it is, it is.' Blackie peered at Shane. His expression was one of self-congratulation and gratification. 'The party I threw at the Adelphi Hotel after the race was one of the best ever given, so I've been told. It *was* a grand bash, wasn't it?'

'Smashing! And so was the welcome we received when we got back to Middleham on Sunday lunch time. The huge banner congratulating Emerald Bow stretched across the main street, the boys coming out of the pubs when you and Randolph paraded her around the town, and then the luncheon at Allington Hall – memorable, all of it, Grandfather. I was so pleased and proud for you, I wouldn't have missed it for anything.'

'I know you wouldn't, but still, I admit I was a bit worried when you got bogged down with work in Sydney, early in March. I held my breath, I did indeed. I thought you mightn't make it and that would have been a severe blow to me, my boy.' Blackie sighed and a look of true contentment crossed his face. 'It's been a wonderful twelve months when I look back now. The trip around the world with me darlin' Emma, and now this –' He broke off, glanced at the trophy, the smile lingering on his face. 'Imagine *me* winning the greatest race in existence.'

'You're not still talking about the Grand National are you?' Emma exclaimed sharply, walking into the library in her usual brisk way. 'We're never going to hear the end of it, I can see.'

Laughing, Blackie pushed himself, up, went to greet her, kissed her cheek. 'Now, mavourneen, don't spoil me bit of fun.' He held her away from him, and studied her closely. 'Bonny as always, and I see you're wearing my emerald bow.' His face filled with genuine pleasure as he gestured to the brooch pinned on to the white-silk shawl collar of her grey wool dress. 'I notice you haven't had this off since we won. Now if that's not an emblem of the National, I don't know what is, mavourneen.'

Emma laughed, squeezed his arm, turned to Shane as he walked across the floor to join them.

Shane said, 'Hello, Aunt Emma, and Grandfather's right, you do look lovely tonight.' He bent forward, kissed her cheek.

'Thank you, Shane. How was the trip to Spain? I see you're keeping that tan of yours going strong.'

'I try,' he said, grinning. 'And the trip was very successful.'

Returning to the chair by the fire and drawing Emma along with him, Blackie said, 'Shane will get you a drink. What would you like to have, Emma?'

'Sherry, thank you.'

'And where's Emily?' Blackie asked. 'I thought she was coming in for a drink. Is she parking the car?'

'No. She dropped me off and went on her way. She had to get over to Beck House early. She sends you her love, and her apologies. Apparently she's cooking dinner for Shane and Winston tonight.'

'Oh I am disappointed not to see her. I was looking forward to her visit – I've got a soft spot for young Emily. She always gives me a good chuckle, no one quite so pithy and blunt as Emily – except for you, of course.' Blackie reached for a cigar, clipped off the end.

Frowning at him, Emma exclaimed fiercely, 'Should you be smoking that thing? You promised me you were going to cut them out.' He gave a throaty chuckle, grinned at her. 'At my age!' Shrugging, he went on, 'I keep telling you, I'm living on borrowed time. I don't aim to deprive myself of me last few pleasures. *This* –' He waved the cigar under her nose. 'And me drop of whiskey.'

Emma let out a long-suffering sigh, knowing there was no use arguing with him.

Shane carried the glass of sherry over to Emma, sat down on the sofa. His grandfather and she had begun to talk about Emily's wedding, which was to take place in two months. He sat back, lit a cigarette, listened, his mind straying to Paula. He worried about her constantly, and even though he presented a patient and understanding demeanour to her, he was extremely anxious for Jim to make a quick recovery from whatever ailed him. And what did ail Fairley? Booze and pills, Shane thought. He was convinced that this lethal combination had contributed to, if not caused, Jim's recent collapse. Emma, Winston and Emily tended to agree with him, and Paula had confided in January that she thought Jim was an alcoholic.

'Winston tells me you won't be able to be his best man after all,' Emma said, drawing Shane into the conversation. 'We're so disappointed.'

'No more than I am, Aunt Emma. But Dad wants me to go to Sydney again, after I've spent a couple of weeks in New York, and I'll have to remain there through the end of May into June. Nothing much I can do about it – somebody has to supervise the building of the new hotel.'

'Yes, so Winston explained.'

Shane said, 'Michael Kallinski's standing in for me, and I can't think of a better man for the job.'

'I hear his father's not been too well,' Blackie interjected worriedly. 'Have you spoken to Ronnie in the last few days, Emma?'

'Yes, and he's up and about. He's had a bout of pneumonia, but he's feeling much better. This April weather has been most treacherous. So sunny, but the wind has been awfully cold, hasn't it? I've felt nithered to death these last few days.'

'That's nothing new,' Blackie announced, sitting back, contemplating her fondly. 'You suffered from the cold even when you were a slip of a girl. I remember how you used to shiver and complain about being frozen stiff at Fairley Hall.'

The two of them were soon engaged in a discussion about the past, which Shane had noticed they were prone to do quite frequently these days. He listened for a while, but when the clock on the mantelpiece struck he glanced at it, saw that it was six-thirty. Stubbing out his cigarette and downing the last drops of his drink, he stood up. 'I'm going to push off, leave you two lovebirds to your own devices. Don't do anything I wouldn't do, Grandpops.'

'That gives me a lot of rope then,' Blackie retorted, winking broadly.

'Several hundred yards at least,' Shane answered, his tone jocular. He bent over the chair and kissed his grandfather in the tenderest way, touched his shoulder. 'Take it easy, and I'll come and see you tomorrow.'

'Yes, please do, my boy. I'll be looking forward to it, and have a nice evening.'

'Thanks, I will Grandpops.' Shane stepped over to Emma. He thought how pretty she was despite her grand age. After kissing her, he said, 'Keep an eye on this old warrior for me, Aunt Emma. I know he's a handful – but then you've had his number for years.'

The look Emma gave Shane was full of love. 'I will.'

'Humph!' Blackie's eyes travelled from Emma to Shane. 'And don't think I haven't got *her* number. I've always had it!'

Their laughter followed Shane as he walked to the door. He looked back over his shoulder as he went out, saw that they were already contentedly chatting away, retreating into their own private world, sharing their memories. He closed the door softly behind him.

Blackie glanced at the door, leaned forward and said in a conspiratorial whisper, 'Do you think Shane's still leading a wild life and chasing fast women, like he used to do, Emma?'

'No, I don't,' Emma reassured. 'I'm perfectly sure he doesn't have time for that, Blackie dear, not the way he works.'

'Everyone's getting married and he's still single. And at twenty-eight,' Blackie complained, sounding unusually fretful. 'I'd hoped to see him settled down before I died, but it doesn't look as if I will. No chance of bouncing *his* babies on my knee.'

Emma threw him a chastizing look, clucked softly, said, 'Of course there is, you silly old thing. What's got into you tonight? You're the one who's forever telling me you're going to live to be ninety.'

'Ah, I've grave doubts about that, mavourneen.'

Ignoring this comment, Emma hurried on, 'Shane *will* settle down, but only when *he's* good and ready.'

'Aye, I suppose so.' Blackie moved his great white leonine head from side to side. A look of helplessness spread across his face. 'This generation – I don't know, Emma, they baffle me at times. They make such messes of their lives, or so it seems to me.'

Emma froze in her chair, watching him closely, her eyes growing sharper. Was he generalizing or was he referring to anyone in particular? Surely he had not guessed about Shane's feelings for Paula. She said: 'Were we any different? Our generation was just as bad, Blackie dear.'

He was silent.

387

'Think about it – you'll have to agree that I'm correct, you know that.' She smiled and her shrewd green eyes danced. 'Now who made a bigger mess than me at different times in her life?'

He had to laugh. 'That's true. And here I am, going on about Shane, and I haven't even asked you how Paula is faring. Is she all right?'

'Coping, poor girl. She does seem to have her hands full at the moment. However, Jim is on the mend, I think. I sincerely hope he is, for their sakes. She's been worried to death about him, and so have I.'

'I was about to ask you about Jim.' Blackie gave her an odd look and there was a small pause before he asked, 'How long is he going to have to stay in the mental asylum?'

'Psychiatric clinic,' Emma corrected. 'About another month, maybe six weeks.'

'That long! Oh dear, Emma, that is a terrible burden for Paula.' He rubbed his chin, gave her a piercing stare. 'He will get better, won't he?'

'Of course!' Emma said in her most positive voice, but she couldn't help asking herself if he would. Her mind strayed to his family's troubled history.

As if he had read her thoughts, Blackie reflected out loud, 'A funny family – the Fairleys.' He looked at her again and for the longest moment. 'Adele Fairley used to seem a shade demented to me ... the way she wandered around Fairley Hall like an apparition. And then there was the dreadful way she died. Tragic. I can't help thinking that this illness of Jim's might be –'

'I'd prefer not to contemplate something like that, if you don't mind, dear,' Emma said firmly. 'It's all too depressing and worrying for everyone concerned.'

Leaning forward, Emma now smiled her most winning smile, and changed the subject. 'You and I agreed that we wouldn't go gallivanting off again, but I was wondering if you'd like to come and stay with me at my house in the South of France? This summer, Blackie, perhaps in the middle of June, after Emily's wedding, and before Alexander's in July. What do you think?'

'That is a tempting idea. These old bones of mine could use a bit of warming sunshine. Like you, I've been feeling the bite of the Northern wind this past week or so. To tell you the truth, I thought I was coming down with the flu.'

'Aren't you feeling well?' Emma's quick darting glance betrayed her concern for him.

'Oh sure and I am, me darlin'. Don't be fussing over me, Emma, you know I've never been able to stand that.' His wide Celtic mouth curved up in a smile of tenderness. 'Let's face it, we're not spring chickens anymore. We're both very old now.' He chuckled, eyeing her in amusement, his eyes suddenly teasing. 'Two bags of ancient bones, that's what we are, Emma.'

'Speak for yourself,' she retorted, but her expression was as loving as his.

They were interrupted by Mrs Padgett, Blackie's housekeeper, who came in to tell them that dinner was served.

As they walked across the library and out into the lovely circular entrance hall, Emma noticed, as Shane had done earlier, that Blackie's steps were belaboured this evening. She had to slow her own pace so that he could keep up with her, and this troubled her deeply.

During dinner she realized that he was picking at his food, not really eating. He seemed to have no appetite, and he hardly touched his glass of red wine, which was most unusual. But she made no comment, deciding instead that she would take matters into her own hands. Tomorrow she would telephone Doctor Hedley, ask him to drive over to give Blackie a thorough examination.

For a short while Blackie talked about the Grand National, and Emma let him ramble on, knowing how important winning had been to him. But at one moment he unexpectedly dropped this subject when he said, 'It's always seemed strange to me that Shane was never interested in one of your girls, Emma. There was a time, when they were growing up, that I thought he and Paula might end up marrying each other . . . one day.'

Emma held her breath. For a split second she was on the verge of confiding in him, and then instantly changed her mind. It would only distress him if he knew about Shane's love for her granddaughter. Particularly since she had now come to the conclusion that Paula did not reciprocate Shane's feelings. Blackie would not be able to bear the thought of Shane's heartache.

Emma leaned over and patted his hand lying on the table. 'I suppose being together all of their lives makes them feel like brother and sister.'

'Aye, most probably, but it would've been lovely if they'd married, wouldn't it, me darlin'?'

'Oh yes, Blackie, it would have been wonderful.'

As they left the dining room, Mrs Padgett reminded Blackie she was taking the rest of the evening off, and bid them good night. Slowly he and Emma walked back through the hall and went into the library. Emma poured a cognac for him, a liqueur glass of Bonnie Prince Charlie for herself.

They sat in silence for a while, sipping their drinks, lost in their own contemplations, as companionable tonight as they had been all of their lives. But eventually Blackie roused himself. 'Don't you think it would be nice to play some records, Emma? Listen to a few old tunes, the ones we used to love.'

'What a good idea.' Emma rose and went over to the small cabinet that housed the stereo, looked through the stack of records. 'My goodness, I didn't know you still had this . . . that John McCormack selection of old Irish ballads I gave you years ago. Shall I put it on?'

'Aye, why not.' Blackie gave her a small grin as she returned to her chair, boasted, 'I still have a good voice, you know. I'll sing along with the music, if you like.'

'I always did love that rich baritone of yours.'

They listened to the selection and, true to his word, Blackie did sing a few snatches of the old songs now and then, but his voice was feeble and quavering, and so he mostly hummed the melodies.

When the record came to an end, Emma remarked, 'Those songs bring back a lot of memories . . . especially *Danny Boy*. I'll never forget that night I came looking for you, after I'd run away from Fairley Hall. I found you at the Mucky Duck, singing that ballad as if your life depended on it. Oh Blackie, you looked so marvellous, standing there next to the piano, and goodness me, you were *so* theatrical. A real ham.'

He smiled.

Emma's eyes rested on him affectionately, took in the wavy hair, still thick but white as driven snow now, the craggy features, the broad face marked by the signs of age, and suddenly, in her imagination, she saw him as he had been in his youth, as he had looked that night in the pub. Vibrant black curls rippling back from a tanned face, black eyes dancing, white teeth flashing between rosy lips, his superb looks prominently highlighted in the glare from the burning gas lamps.

Leaning forward, Emma asked, 'Do you remember that particular night, Blackie?'

'How could I ever forget it, Emma? We went and sat together in the Saloon Bar and you drank a lemonade. I had a pint of bitter. Ah, such a little snippet of a lass you were . . . and you told me you were pregnant . . . and I asked you to marry me. Perhaps you should have.'

'Yes, perhaps. But I didn't want to burden you . . .' Emma did not finish, and she picked up her liqueur, took a sip.

Blackie settled back in his chair, a faint smile playing around his mouth, and then he nodded to himself, said, 'You do look bonny tonight, Emma. You're the most fetching colleen in the whole country.'

'You're prejudiced,' she murmured, returning his unwavering gaze, his gentle smile.

Blackie sat up a little straighter, peering across at her in the soft dim glow of the muted light in the room. 'I'll never be able to tell you what our holiday has meant to me, Emma. Those eight months with you have made up for all the bad things that ever happened to me in my entire life – the pain, the heartache, the sorrow. And I do thank you, me darlin'.'

'What a lovely thing to say, Blackie. But it is I who should thank you for making your Plan with a capital P.'

'It was a good plan –' Blackie stopped short and grimaced.

Instantly Emma was on her feet, leaning over him. 'What's the matter? Are you ill?'

He shook his head. 'It's nothing . . . just a twinge of indigestion.'

'I'm going to ring the doctor, and then I'm going to get you upstairs to bed.' She turned away from him, made a movement towards the desk near the window.

'No, no.' He tried to restrain her but his hand fell away weakly. 'I won't make it, Emma.'

'Yes, you will,' she insisted. 'I'll help you.'

Blackie shook his head very slowly.

'I *am* going to telephone Doctor Hedley,' Emma announced with a show of her old firmness.

'Sit down here with me, Emma. *Please*,' he begged. 'Just for a minute or two.'

Emma pulled up a hassock, seated herself, took his hand in hers, searched his face. 'What is it, Blackie?'

He squeezed her fingers, then smiled at her. Suddenly his eyes opened very widely. 'All my life,' he whispered hoarsely, 'I've known you all my life. We've been through so much together, Emma.'

'Yes,' she said, 'we have and I don't know what I'd have done without you, Blackie.'

He sighed a very long slow sigh. 'I'm sorry to have to leave you alone. So very sorry, mavourneen.'

Emma could not speak. Tears rushed into her eyes, fell down her wrinkled cheeks, splashed over the white silk collar and the emerald bow, and on to their entwined hands.

Blackie's eyes widened again, and he stared at her more acutely, as if memorizing her face. And then he said in a surprisingly clear voice, 'I've always loved you, me darlin'.'

'And I have always loved you, Blackie.'

A fleeting smile struck his pale mouth. His eyelids fluttered, closed, lay still. His head fell to one side. His hand went slack in her tenacious grip.

'Blackie,' she said. '*Blackie!*'

The silence overwhelmed her.

She held on to his hand tightly, closed her eyes. The tears seeped out from under her old lids, ran down her face in streaming rivulets. She lowered her head and rested it on their clasped hands, drenching them with her tears.

'Goodbye, my dearest friend, goodbye,' she said at last. She continued to weep quietly, unable to stem the tears, and she sat there for a long time, her aching heart full of love for him.

But eventually she lifted her head, let go of his hand and pushed herself up on to her feet. She bent over him, gently smoothed his snow-white hair back from his forehead, and kissed his icy lips. How cold he is, she thought.

Emma's pace was slow and her step faltering as she moved blindly towards his chair near the window, where he had so often sat lately looking out at his garden. She took the small wool blanket patterned with the tartan of the Seaforth Highlanders and brought it to him and covered his legs and tucked it around him.

And then at the same snail's crawl she went to his desk. She lifted the phone and with trembling hands she dialled Beck House.

It was Shane who answered. 'Hello?' he said.

On hearing his strong and vibrant tone her tears began to flow once more. 'It's Blackie,' Emma said through her tears in a voice that shook. 'He's gone . . . please come, Shane.'

Shane arrived within the hour, bringing Paula, Emily and Winston with him.

They found her sitting on the hassock next to Blackie, her hand resting on his knee, her silver head bowed. She did not turn nor did she move at all, merely went on sitting there, staring into the fire.

Shane hurried to her, put his hand on her shoulder lightly, brought his face to hers. 'I'm here, Aunt Emma,' he said in the kindest of voices.

She made no response.

Shane took her hands in his and brought her to her feet slowly, gentleness flowing out of him.

Emma finally lifted her face to look up into his and she began to weep and Shane took her in his arms and held her close, soothing her.

'I miss him already and he's only just died,' Emma said with a small heartbreaking sob. 'Whatever am I going to do without Blackie?'

'Hush, Aunt Emma, hush,' Shane murmured and then he led her over to the sofa, motioning with his eyes to Paula, who stood in the doorway white-faced and trembling. She came and sat with her grandmother, began to comfort her, and Emily joined them.

Shane stepped over to Blackie. His throat was thick with emotion and the sorrow rose in him and tears ran down his cheeks. He gazed at Blackie's face and saw how peaceful it was in death and then he leaned forward and kissed his withered cheek.

'God speed, Grandfather,' he said in a low and saddened voice. 'God speed.'

41

Paula began cautiously, 'It's your birthday in two days, Grandy, and I thought we might have a –'

'Oh dear,' Emma interrupted softly, with a small frown. 'Don't bring that up. Blackie's only been dead a couple of weeks and I'm not in the mood for a celebration.'

'I know, and I wasn't talking about a big party. Just a small dinner here at Pennistone Royal. There would only be me, Emily, Winston and my parents. We thought it would cheer you up.'

'Cheer me up,' Emma repeated hollowly, and then reached out and patted Paula's hand. 'I don't think anything would cheer me right now. But I suppose I have to keep plodding on. All right then . . . just the five of you, though. Please don't invite anyone else. I'm not in much of a mood for people right now. They tire me.'

'I promise I won't invite another solitary single soul,' Paula assured her, pleased that the suggestion had met with success.

'And no presents, Paula. I don't want any presents. As far as I'm concerned reaching eighty-one is cause for lament, not receiving gifts and whooping it up.'

'Don't worry, Grandma, we'll keep it very simple and casual. And it'll be nice for you to have Mummy and Daddy here for a few days.'

'Yes,' Emma murmured. She glanced down at the album on her lap. She had been looking at it when Paula had arrived a short while ago. She stared at the old photographs absently, her thoughts drifting into the past for a few seconds. Then she lifted her head, pushed the album towards Paula, remarked, 'Look at us here – Blackie, Laura and me. We're standing outside my first shop in Armley. That's me – in the tam o'shanter.'

'Yes, I recognize you.' Paula had seen this picture many times before, knew the pages of the album by heart. But wanting to humour her grandmother, she said, 'Let's look at some of the others, and you can tell me a few of your lovely stories about your early days in business. You know how I like hearing them.'

Emma nodded and at once began to talk with sudden animation as they leafed through the book, and for the next twenty minutes the two of them sat side by side in the upstairs parlour, reliving parts of Emma Harte's life.

At one point Emma broke off, peered at Paula and said, 'How long do you think I'm going to live?'

Taken aback at this question, Paula stared at her grandmother askance, filling with sudden alarm. She cleared her throat, said firmly, 'A long time, darling.'

'You're very optimistic,' Emma said and turned away, looked out into space, a faraway expression settling on her face.

Paula exclaimed, 'You're extremely fit for your age, remarkable really, and not a bit forgetful. You have years ahead of you, Grandy, as long as you take care of yourself.'

Emma brought her ancient and wise green gaze to meet Paula's troubled face, and she smiled slowly. 'Yes, yes, you're quite right. I don't know what's got into me today – I'm being morbid, aren't I? Blackie's death has been such a terrible blow to me, but I suppose I must be positive.' She let out a chuckle. 'Anyway, I might be old and a trifle weary these days, but I don't want to leave this world yet.'

'That's the spirit, Grandy.'

Emma did not reply. She rose and walked over to the oriel window, stood looking down at her gardens and the daffodils blowing in the breeze. It's such a beautiful afternoon, she thought. Another perfect spring day . . . just like the day of Blackie's funeral. How eternal the land is, constantly renewing itself. Yes, in death there is always life. Sighing again, Emma returned to the fireplace and sat down in the chair next to it. She said, 'It was lovely of you to come over to see me, Paula dear. But I think I'd like to be by myself for a while, to have a little rest before dinner.'

Paula came to her, kissed her cheek, her heart full of love for Emma. 'All right, Gran, and I'll pop in tomorrow with the babies.'

'That'll be very nice,' Emma answered, and settled back in the chair as her granddaughter left the room. Her mind turned inward. The young don't really understand, she thought. Paula tries, and tries very hard, but she doesn't know what it's like to be the sole survivor, the only one left of one's contemporaries. They've all gone now. They're all dead and buried. My dearest friends, my loved ones. Even my enemies are no longer around to get my goat and spark the will in me to fight. I'm so alone without Blackie. We kept each other going all these years – he and I. Rambling on together into our twilight years. We had so many memories to share, a lifetime of experiences, and so much love and friendship to give each other. Why, my whole life has been lived out with my sweet Irishman. I didn't expect him to go like that. Such a shock. I knew he was old, as I am old, but he seemed so strong, and indomitable, like me. Funny, I always thought I would die first. Whatever will I do? However will I manage without him?

Emma's grief and enormous sense of loss overcame her again, as it had done so frequently in the last two weeks since Blackie's sudden death. Tears came into her eyes and she choked back a sob, brought her hand to her trembling lips. I miss Blackie so much. Such a void without him. There are so many things I didn't tell him and now it's too late. I ought to have told him about

Shane and his love for Paula. I didn't want to upset Blackie. He would have worried. But I do wish I had told him after all.

Emma wiped her damp cheeks with her hand and rested her head against the chair. She was filled with an aching loneliness she could not endure. She closed her eyes and after a few minutes she began to drowse, drifting off into a gentle sleep.

After leaving her grandmother, Paula had gone downstairs in search of Emily. She had found her in the library and now they sat together discussing Emma.

'She's putting up a good front, of course,' Paula said, 'but she's really suffering inside.'

Emily frowned worriedly. 'I agree with you. She's absolutely lost without Blackie. I think all the fight's gone out of her. To tell you the truth, the other day I even wished we *had* found something on Jonathan. At least that might have captured her interest, made her angry enough to lift her out of this resigned mood.'

Paula said, 'She was very busy with the plans for your wedding before Blackie died. Can't you get her involved again?'

'Don't think I haven't tried, because I have. But she seems so distracted, almost absent-minded, which is not like her.'

'You know something, Emily, there's only one thing for it!' Paula leaned forward eagerly. 'Emma Harte has been a work horse all of her life, and her business was her strong citadel in times of grief and sorrow and trouble in the past. We've got to persuade her to come out of retirement . . . get her back in the harness again.'

Emily sat up with a jerk, her face brightening. 'That's the best idea I've heard in weeks. And Grandma used to say she intended to die with her boots on. Oh, let's do it, Paula.' Instantly Emily's face fell, and she bit her inner lip, shaking her blonde head. 'I'm not sure she'll agree. She might not want to intrude on us . . . she can be very funny, you know.'

'We have to make a stab at it – personally I think that it's her only salvation. She'll just fade away and die, if we don't encourage her to be active, come back to work.'

'Agreed, and you can count on me. There's another thing –' Emily hesitated, gave Paula a careful look, then rushed on, 'Why don't you move back in here with Nora and the babies? At least until Jim comes out of the nursing home.'

'Oddly enough, I thought of that when I was with Gran a little while ago. There's nothing like a couple of babies to liven things up, and perhaps having her great-grandchildren with her will give Grandy a new lease of life.'

'Absolutely. And together you and I can jolly Gran out of her despondency, don't you think?'

'Oh God, I hope so, Emily.'

'When do you think you could move in to Pennistone Royal?'

Paula laughed. 'How does tomorrow sound?'

'Terrific. I'll come over and help you if you like.'

'I'd love it, and then on Monday morning I'm going to vacate Grandy's office at the Leeds store, move back into my old one. That evening when we have the dinner for her birthday, you and I can make our proposal to her. I'll alert my parents, and they might be able to add a few words of persuasion.' Paula stood. 'I'd better go, Emily. I want to stop off at the nursing home. I promised Jim I'd come by later today.'

The two cousins left the library and walked across the Stone Hall to the front door.

Emily caught hold of Paula's arm just before they reached the short flight of steps. She said in a low tone, 'Jim's been in there for ten weeks now. How much longer, Paula?'

'Another month to six weeks. If he continues to improve. Otherwise –' She shrugged wearily, added, 'Then it could be longer, of course.'

Emily stared at Paula, said swiftly, 'Look, I hope you don't mind me saying this, but I hope that Jim knows what drink does to him now. I mean, he won't be able to touch a drop ever again and –'

'He knows,' Paula interjected. 'And you can be damned sure *I* know. Thanks for being concerned, Emily. One step at a time right now. That's the only way I can live my life, get through each day without losing my sanity. And very frankly, our grandmother is my priority at the moment.'

'Yes,' Emily said. 'I understand, and she's mine too. You can rely on me to help you any way I can.'

They cajoled, pleaded, challenged and attempted to bully her, using every ruse they knew to get Emma Harte to return to work.

But consistently, and quite categorically, she refused to be budged. Her stance was inflexible. She would shake her head emphatically, repeat over and over again that she had retired and that was that.

Eventually Paula and Emily gave up, at least on the surface. But they were forever dropping pointed remarks and making asides at meal times. They continued to seek her advice, even when they did not really need it, using every opportunity to gain her interest, and induce in her the desire to take an active role in her business once more.

Emma was fully aware of their ploys, and she would smile to herself, touched by their love and concern for her, but she remained resolute in her determination to lead a quiet life at Pennistone Royal.

And then one morning in the middle of May, Emma awakened early. She discovered that she was filled with her old energy and restlessness and drive. This surprised her, and she lay in bed for a while pondering to herself.

'I'm bored silly,' she said to Hilda, when her housekeeper brought up her breakfast tray at eight o'clock.

Placing the tray on Emma's lap, Hilda clucked sympathetically. 'Of course you are, Mrs Harte. You've been such an active woman your entire life, this drifting along, doing nothing, doesn't sit well on you. Perhaps you ought to let Tilson drive you into Leeds today. You could have lunch with Miss Paula or Miss Emily. Getting out of this house would do you the world of good, I just know it.'

'I've got a better idea, Hilda,' Emma said thoughtfully. 'I think I'll start going to the office for a short while every day. I know I don't want to get involved with my business on a day-to-day basis, on the other hand, I would like to keep busy.' Emma shook her head, looking regretful. 'I ought to be helping Emily plan that wedding of hers. I've been awfully neglectful, a selfish old woman, now that I think about it . . . feeling sorry for myself because my old friends are dead.' A look of comprehension flitted across the wrinkled face. 'Why, Hilda, my grandchildren are my friends, aren't they?'

'You can be sure they are, Mrs Harte,' Hilda replied. 'And Miss Emily will be delighted to have your help with her wedding, what with her mother living in Paris and seemingly not all that interested. She's such a lot to do, and time is running out on her. June fifteenth is not so far off, you know, madame.' Hilda beamed. 'I shall go downstairs right now and ask Tilson to bring the car around at ten-thirty. How does that sound?'

'It sounds wonderful, Hilda. Thank you very much.'

It was ten minutes to twelve when Emma Harte walked into her large department store in Leeds. She looked smart in a tailored navy-blue dress and matching coat. Milky pearls encircled her throat. Diamonds glittered in her ears. Her silver hair was perfectly dressed and her makeup artfully applied.

Emma hurried through the cosmetic department on the street level, her step purposeful and brisk, a wide smile ringing her mouth. And as she stopped to greet the various sales assistants she discovered she was almost moved to tears at the genuine welcome she received from them all.

She took the lift to the executive offices, and then hesitated for a moment outside the door leading into her own private suite. She could not help asking herself what Paula and Agnes would say. She turned the knob and stepped inside.

Paula and Agnes were standing next to the latter's desk deep in conversation. Both women automatically glanced at the door as it swung open. They were speechless at the sight of Emma, obviously completely taken by surprise.

'Well,' Emma said, 'I'm back. And I'm here to stay.' She began to laugh at their stunned expressions, and reverting to the vernacular of the North, she added, 'Don't stand there gaping at me like a couple of sucking ducks. Say something.'

Paula grinned with pleasure. 'Welcome, Grandy,' she said, moving forward, catching hold of Emma's arm. 'Come on, your office is waiting for you – it's been ready for weeks.'

It seemed to Emma that the next few months sped by before she hardly had a chance to catch her breath. Every day she arrived at the Leeds store at eleven and stayed until four o'clock. She was soon in the swing of things, and taking a renewed interest in her colossal business empire, although she left the daily running of it to her grandchildren. She strenuously refused to take back the reins, pointing out, yet again, that she had retired the previous year and had no intention of resuming her role as head of her various enterprises. She did agree to be a sounding board whenever they needed one, and she was always available to them, offering astute advice. And she was as smart and as alert and as agile as she had ever been.

And so, whilst she kept a canny eye on the business, she devoted most of her time to planning the two weddings due to take place in June and July. Emily was vastly relieved to have her grandmother's help, as was Maggie Reynolds, Alexander's fiancée. Maggie's mother had been dead for a number of years, and her father, a retired army colonel, had not been in the best of health lately. Nor was he the type of man to embroil himself in such a feminine matter as his daughter's wedding, being gruff and taciturn by nature.

With her inimitable brand of efficiency, and her extraordinary ability to concentrate totally on the matter at hand, Emma ploughed ahead, making elaborate arrangements. She dealt with the invitations, the guest lists, the caterers, the florists, the dress designers and the musicians who were to play at the two receptions. Several times she visited the Dean of Ripon, the Very Reverend Edwin LeGrice, to discuss each marriage ceremony, which he was to personally perform in Ripon Cathedral. Emma spoke to the organist and to the choir master at great length, and she helped the two future brides and their grooms select the appropriate music for their nuptials.

Not even the slightest detail was left to chance. Emma Harte wanted perfection and she aimed to have it, whatever it cost in time, energy and money. Winston said to her one evening, 'Well, Aunt Emma, it's good to have you back in command, playing the general again, *and* cracking your whip like you used to at Heron's Nest. Whatever would we do without you?'

'Manage, I'm sure,' Emma said in her pithy way, but she laughed, pleased by Winston's remark. She wanted to be wanted, enjoyed feeling useful. And they help to keep me young and alive and cheerful, she thought later that same evening, as she was getting ready for bed. She also acknowledged that planning the weddings had helped to take her mind off Blackie's death, had eased her sorrow and her sense of loneliness. Positive action, she muttered under her breath as she slipped on her nightdress. And happy occasions. That's what every old person needs to give them a reason to go on living.

It was with a heart bursting with love and pride and joyousness that Emma watched Emily walk down the great aisle of Ripon Cathedral on the arm of her father Tony Barkstone at noon on June fifteenth.

To Emma, her young granddaughter looked her most beautiful that day. She resembled a delicate Dresden figurine in her wedding gown made of white taffeta. It was styled like an old-fashioned crinoline, the overskirt lifted at the hem, draped and caught with tiny sprigs of forget-me-nots and lily-of-the-valley. A mixture of these same flowers, also made of silk, had been woven into a small coronet which held her flowing veil in place. Her only pieces of jewellery, other than her engagement ring, were the teardrop diamond earrings Emma had given her in 1968, and Great-Aunt Charlotte's string of pearls which had been *her* engagement present from Emma's brother, Winston, immediately after the First World War. Emily's half-sisters Amanda and Francesca were her bridesmaids and were charming in blue taffeta gowns, wearing wreaths of honeysuckle in their hair.

The reception was held in the gardens of Pennistone Royal, and as Emma moved amongst her family, friends and the many guests she kept telling herself how fortunate she was to be here on this most special day in Emily's life and her own. The weather was glorious. The sky was a bright China blue, and the sun brilliant. Emma decided, as she glanced about, that her gardens had never been so stunning in their beauty, the many flowers a vivid blaze of riotous colour against the fresh greenness of the lawns and the trees. That afternoon she had an acute awareness of everything, and she saw nature's loveliness and the people present through eyes that were more penetrating than ever in their perception. The smallest things suddenly took on a new importance and significance, and at one moment Emma knew that she was filled with a contentment she had not hitherto felt.

As she sat drinking her tea, watching the young people dancing, she thought of her hard life, her struggles, the sorrow and pain she had endured, the defeats and losses she had suffered. Quite suddenly they were all quite meaningless. I've been so lucky, she commented to herself. Luckier than most, in fact. I've experienced a great love, had dear and loving friends, achieved enormous success, amassed colossal wealth, and enjoyed good health all of my life. And most important of all, I have grandchildren who love me, care about me now in my old age. Oh yes, I've been lucky to have had all that I've had.

Five weeks later, at the end of July, Emma experienced similar emotions when her grandson was married to Marguerite Reynolds. Maggie made another lovely bride, was elegant and svelte in a simply-styled gown of heavy cream satin. It had a high neck, long tight sleeves and a slender skirt that extended out into a long train. With it Maggie wore a satin pillbox hat encrusted with seed pearls and a veil of Brussels lace. The glorious weather of June held for the July ceremony at Ripon Cathedral and for the reception, which was again held in the grounds of Emma's great old house.

One Sunday, about a week after the second wedding, Emma and Paula went for a walk through the gardens of Pennistone Royal. Emma said suddenly, 'Thank you for chivying me out of my despondency after Blackie died. If you hadn't I might not have been around to witness those two wonderful occasions, to see Emily settled with Winston and Sandy with Maggie.' She winked mischievously at Paula, and added, 'Now, with a little bit of luck, I might still be here to welcome a couple of new great-grandchildren into my family in the not too distant future.'

'You'll be here, Grandma!' Paula exclaimed, returning Emma's smile. 'I'm going to make damned sure of that.'

Emma linked her arm through Paula's as they continued to meander up the Rhododendron Walk. After a short while, Emma said quietly, 'I'm pleased Jim came out of the nursing home in time to attend Alexander's wedding, at least.'

'So am I, Grandy.' Paula turned to Emma, remarked evenly, 'And he's much better. Poor Jim – he's been down at the bottom of the pit. He can only go up from now on.'

'Yes, darling, let's hope so.' There was a slight hesitation on Emma's part before she murmured, 'I've tried to speak to him about the nervous breakdown because I wanted to understand what brought it on. But I'm afraid he's not very forthcoming, is he?'

'No. He doesn't seem able to talk about it, not even with me. I decided it was better not to press him. I'm sure he'll open up later.' Paula sighed. 'In some ways Jim's very introverted, Gran. Doctor Hedley told me that the psychiatrist at the nursing home has been somewhat baffled too. Apparently he hasn't really been able to get to the root of Jim's despondency.'

Emma made no comment and the two of them walked on in silence and finally sat down on the bench at the top of the hill. Emma stared ahead, still thinking of Jim. Her expression changed, became sad as she wondered why he was so bottled up inside and seemingly incapable of unburdening himself to the psychiatrist, a doctor who might well be able to help him.

Paula, watching her grandmother, said, 'What are you thinking about, darling? You look so pensive all of a sudden.'

'Nothing of any great importance,' Emma murmured. 'I'm glad Jim went to my house in the South of France with Daisy and David. I think the holiday will do him a lot of good. The sun, the fresh air, outdoor activities, plenty of good food and rest always seem to work wonders. When he comes back at the end of August he'll be able to go back to the newspaper.' When Paula was silent, Emma glanced at her curiously. 'He will, won't he? You're not hiding something from me, are you, dear?'

'No, no, of course I'm not,' Paula exclaimed, dragging herself out of her own worrying thoughts. 'And like you I'm happy he agreed to take the holiday with my parents.'

'I'm surprised he didn't insist you went with them,' Emma ventured, eyeing her with greater interest.

'I promised Jim I'd join them for a week in the middle of August, if that's all right with you. In fact, I was hoping you'd come too.'

'Oh no, I don't want to start gadding off again. I shall stay here, and keep my eye on those great-grandchildren of mine.' Emma paused, reflected, then remarked as casually as she could manage, 'It'll be nice for me if you'd stay on at Pennistone Royal, Paula. If Jim's agreeable and would like to live here, of course. The house is so big, and it's going to seem rather desolate without little Emily.' Emma burst out laughing. 'I'd better not call her that anymore, had I? After all, she's a married woman now.'

'And very much aware of it,' Paula said, also laughing. 'I'd like us to live here with you, Grandy. I'll talk to Jim when I'm at the Cap.' Paula was on the verge of telling Emma that she also fully intended to talk to Jim about a divorce. She stole a look at her grandmother, and changed her mind. Why worry her. Far better to get everything settled with Jim first.

42

It was a hot afternoon at the end of August.

Emma sat at her desk in her office at the Leeds store, checking a list of sales figures for Paula. Quite suddenly she had the feeling she was not alone. She looked up quickly and glanced at the open door leading into Paula's office, expecting to see her granddaughter standing there.

There was no sign of Paula.

'I'm beginning to imagine things,' Emma said out loud, and then laughed under her breath. I'm also talking to myself, she thought, I hope I'm not getting senile. That state of affairs I couldn't bear.

She put down her pen and stared at the sheet of figures on her desk. She was filled with distaste, found she no longer had any interest in them whatsoever. She peered at her watch. It was almost five. Paula usually slipped out on to one of the floors around this time, and perhaps she had gone to meet Emily in the Rayne-Delman shoe salon. Emily had said something about buying shoes when she had phoned from her office at Genret earlier in the day.

A smile of intense pleasure touched the corners of Emma's implacable mouth, softening its resoluteness. They were having a girls' evening at Pennistone Royal tonight, as they often did on Fridays. Just the three of them and Merry O'Neill.

Emma leaned back in her chair, ruminating on the evening ahead, looking forward to it, and then she blinked in the brilliant light which was streaming in through the windows. How bright the sun is all of a sudden, blinding really, she muttered to herself. Rising, Emma walked over to the sofa and sat down.

She closed her eyes, wanting to shut out that harsh light which was flooding the room. But it seemed to penetrate through the thin skin of her old lids and she lifted them, stared out into that most extraordinary and unnatural radiance. Emma's eyes narrowed as she shaded them with her hand. How very dazzling it is, she thought again. I must tell Paula to get blinds for this office. It's quite unbearable in here on such a sunny day.

To avoid the intense glare Emma turned her head. Her gaze rested on the photograph frames on the table next to the sofa. The silver and the brass and the glass glittered sharply in the luminescence that now washed over her office, and there was a curious lustre to those well-loved faces that stared back at her and so hauntingly. Yes, they *had* been haunting her lately ... Laura and Blackie, her brothers Winston and Frank, and Paul. Oh yes, always her dearest Paul. In the last few days their faces had been so vividly clear in her imagination, their voices so strong and vibrant in her mind. They were as real to her as when they had been alive.

It seemed to Emma that the past had started to acquire a greater and more pronounced reality than the present. She was constantly invaded by memories ... memories of years gone by, and they rushed at her with a force and clarity that stunned. They engulfed her, led her into other regions of time and frequently she felt that time itself had been suspended at some juncture long ago when she had been a young woman. Yes, her dear, dead loved ones had begun to completely tenant her waking moments, encroach on her restless nights. For the past week she had dreamed so many strange dreams and *they* were there with her in those dreams.

Emma reached for Paul's picture, smiling to herself. She held it tightly between her hands, looking down into his face. How often she had picked up this particular photograph in the last forty-eight hours, irresistibly drawn to it, continually magnetized by his smile, his laughing eyes.

The intensity of the coruscating light sharpened so markedly Emma blinked again. Her whole office was glowing with a shimmering iridescence. It was as if thousands of lights had been turned on and were focused on the very centre of the room. She hugged Paul's picture close to her body and gazed wide-eyed into that supernatural light, no longer disturbed by its refulgence. It was glorious and it had an aura of splendour.

But after a few moments of gazing into it she leaned her head against the cushions and closed her eyes. Emma let out a tiny sigh of pleasure. She was filled with happiness, the kind of happiness she had never known before or believed existed. A feeling of warmth began to spread through her body. How lovely it is, she thought. And she, who had suffered from the cold all of her life, was suffused with that warmth and with a peacefulness that was perfection itself. She felt drowsy, enervated, without strength. And yet somehow Emma recognized she was stronger than she had ever been in her whole life. And gradually she became aware of something else. He was here. In this room with her. That was the presence she had felt a few minutes ago.

He walked through the light, coming towards her, growing closer and closer. But he was so young . . . he looked exactly the way he had that night when she had first set eyes on him at the Ritz Hotel during the First World War. He was wearing his army uniform. Major Paul McGill of the Australian Corps. He was standing over her, smiling that engaging smile of his, the blue eyes so wide and clear and spilling his love for her. 'I knew I'd find you here in the office, Emma,' Paul said. 'But it's time for you to stop. Your work on this earth is finished. You have accomplished all you had to accomplish, done everything you had to do. And now you must come with me. I've waited for you for over thirty years. Come, my Emma.' He smiled at her and held out his hand. Emma sighed through her smiles. 'Not yet, Paul,' she said. 'Don't take me yet. Let me see them again . . . Paula and Emily. They'll be here any minute. Let me say goodbye to my girls. Then I'll come with you and willingly so. I want to be with you now. I too know it is time for me to leave.' Paul smiled and moved away from the sofa, stepped into the core of the glorious shining light. 'Paul, wait for me, my darling,' Emma cried. He answered, 'Yes, I'm here. I'll never leave you again. You're safe now, Emma.' She reached out her arms to him, straining towards him.

The photograph fell out of her arms, crashed to the floor, the glass shattering. Emma felt so weak she did not have the strength to pick it up. She did not even have the strength to open her eyes.

Paula and Emily, entering the adjoining office, heard the sudden noise. They looked at each other in panic and ran into their grandmother's office.

Emma lay quite motionless against the cushions. In repose her face was so still, so quiet, they were both unnerved. Paula put a calming hand on Emily's arm and together they approached the sofa. They stood looking down at their grandmother in apprehension.

'She's just having one of her little snoozes,' Emily whispered, instantly filling with relief. She noticed the photograph on the floor, picked it up, returned it to its given place.

But Paula was regarding the still and gentle face more closely. She saw the pinched nose, so white around the nostrils, the pale lips, the chalky pallor of the cheeks. 'No, she's not dozing.' Paula's mouth began to tremble uncontrollably. 'She's dying, Grandy's dying.'

Emily's face paled and she went rigid with fear. Her green eyes, so like Emma's welled, 'No, no, it can't be so. We must call Doctor Hedley immediately.'

Paula's throat tightened and tears sprang into her eyes. She flicked them away with a trembling hand. 'It's too late, Emily. I think she only has a few minutes.' Paula repressed a sob and knelt at Emma's feet, took one of her frail old hands in hers. 'Gran,' she said softly, 'It's me, Paula.'

Emma's lids lifted. Instantly her face lit up. 'I waited for you, darling, and for Emily. Where is she? I can't see her.' Emma's voice was feeble, fading.

'I'm here, Grandma,' Emily gasped, choking on her words. She too knelt down and took Emma's other hand in hers.

Emma saw her, half inclined her head. She closed her eyes but opened them at once. She straightened up with a small burst of energy and stared directly into Paula's tear-stained face. Her voice was very weak yet clear, almost youthful, as she said, 'I asked you to hold my dream . . . but you must also have your own dream, Paula, as well as mine. And you too, Emily. And you must both hold on to your dreams . . . always.' She lay back against the sofa as if exhausted and her eyelids drooped.

Her two granddaughters gazed at her speechlessly, clinging to her hands, seared by their grief, their strangled sobbing the only sound in the room.

All of a sudden Emma opened her eyes for a second time. She smiled at Paula and then at Emily before looking away. She directed her gaze into the far, far distance, as if she saw a place they could not see and someone who was visible only to her.

'Yes,' Emma said. 'I know it is time now.'

Her green eyes stretched, became very bright and shining and they glowed with the purest of inner light. And she smiled her incomparable smile which illuminated her face with radiance, and then her expression became one of rapture and perfect joy as she looked for the last time on her granddaughters. Her eyes closed.

'Gran, Gran we love you so much.' Emily began to weep as if her heart would break.

'She's at peace,' Paula whispered, her mouth twisting in pain and sorrow. Tears were trickling down her face. After a moment she stood up. Leaning over her grandmother, she kissed her on the lips, her tears dripping on to Emma's cheeks. 'You'll always be in my heart, Gran. All the days of my life. And you are the very best part of me.'

Emily had been kissing Emma's small hand over and over and over again, and now she too rose. Paula moved to one side so that her cousin could also bid Emma farewell.

Reaching out, Emily stroked her grandmother's cheek, then she kissed her on the lips. 'As long as I'm alive you'll be alive, Gran. I'll love you always. And I'll never forget you.'

Paula and Emily automatically drew together, put their arms around each other. The two young women clung together for a few minutes, weeping, sharing their grief, endeavouring to comfort each other. Gradually they became a little calmer.

Emily stared at Paula. Tremulously she said, 'I've always been afraid of death. But I'll never be afraid of it again. I'll never forget Grandy's face, the way it looked as she was dying. It was filled with such radiance, such luminosity, and her eyes were brimming with happiness. Whatever it was our grandmother saw, it was something beautiful, Paula.'

Paula's throat constricted. 'Yes,' she said shakily. 'She did see something beautiful, Emily. She saw Paul . . . and Winston and Frank . . . and Laura and Blackie. And she *was* happy because she was going to join them at last.'

43

In death, as in life, Emma Harte was in full command.

After summoning Doctor Hedley to the store, telephoning members of the family, and then accompanying Emma's body to the undertaker's, Paula and Emily finally drove out to Pennistone Royal.

A tearful Hilda greeted them in the Stone Hall.

The housekeeper handed Paula a letter she was clutching. 'Mrs Harte gave this to me a few weeks ago. She asked me to hold it for you, Miss Paula, until her death.' Hilda, who had worked for Emma for over thirty years, burst into tears again. 'It doesn't seem possible that she's gone,' Hilda said, wiping her eyes. 'She looked so well this morning when she left for the store.'

'Yes, she did,' Paula murmured quietly. 'And let's be glad she had her faculties until the end, and that her death was so peaceful, quite beautiful really, Hilda.' Paula and Emily spent the next few minutes comforting the sorrowful housekeeper, and gave her the full details of Emma's passing, which seemed to soothe her.

Finally pulling herself together, Hilda said, 'I know you both must have a lot to do. I'll be in the kitchen if you need anything.'

'Thanks, Hilda,' Paula said. Slowly she walked across the Stone Hall and mounted the great staircase, clasping the letter to her chest. Emily trailed in her wake.

They went into Emma's upstairs parlour where a fire blazed and the lamps glowed. They sat down on the sofa together and it was with shaking hands that Paula opened the sealed envelope and read the four pages covered with Emma's neat yet elegant handwriting. The letter was neither maudlin nor sad, but brisk and matter of fact and it contained Emma's instructions for her funeral. She wanted a short and simple service, only one prayer and two hymns, one of them to be sung by Shane O'Neill. She forbade eulogizing, but suggested that if Paula so wished there could be one. It had to be spoken by Randolph, her nephew, and no one else.

It was the very cheerfulness that brought the tears to Paula's eyes. Swallowing, she passed the letter to Emily. 'These are Grandy's last wishes. She doesn't want the funeral service to be long or drawn out, and it mustn't be overly religious. We must do as she asks, Emily.'

Emily also wept as she read the letter. After mopping her streaming eyes and blowing her nose, she asked in a quavering tone, 'Whatever are we going to do without Grandy, Paula?'

Paula put her arm around Emily and comforted her. After a while she said firmly, but with gentleness, 'We are going to do what she wants us to do, take charge, and bury her the way she requested. And from now on we are going to be strong, and very brave. She wouldn't expect less of us. After all, that's the way she raised us. She taught us to stand tall, as she did throughout her life, and so we *must*. We can't let her down. Not now. *Not ever.*'

'Yes, you're right.' Emily took a deep breath. 'Sorry, I don't mean to be a burden to you. I know it's just as hard for you as it is for me.' Emily frowned and then added, 'Did you notice the date on the letter?'

'Yes. She wrote it a few days after Alexander's wedding – only a month ago.'

'Do you think Grandy knew she was going to die soon?'

'Perhaps, but I can't be sure. Still, they say old people do see death approaching. Blackie going so suddenly shook her up, as you know, and it made her feel vulnerable, even more conscious of her own mortality.' Paula forced a watery smile. 'On the other hand, I'd like to believe that *our* Gran was just being her usual efficient self, thinking of every contingency when she wrote the letter. You know as well as I do that Emma Harte never left one single thing to chance.'

These comments seemed to cheer Emily. 'That's true. And at least Gran died the way she wanted to die – at the office, with her boots on.'

Both young women glanced around as the door opened suddenly.

Winston hurried into the parlour, his face grave, his eyes red-rimmed. 'Sorry I'm late. I've been on the phone for ages,' he said. He kissed his wife, squeezed her shoulder comfortingly, and then bent down and kissed Paula on the cheek. 'You both look as done in as I feel. How about a drink?'

'Thanks, Winston, I'll have a vodka and tonic,' Paula said.

'The same for me, darling,' Emily said.

He brought them their drinks, took a chair next to the fire and lit a cigarette. Paula passed Emma's letter to him, explaining, 'These are Emma's last instructions, her final wishes.'

After reading it, he said, 'Emma's been very explicit and precise. Thank God. It'll save a lot of family discussions and arguments about her funeral, especially with Robin. You know what he's like, so vociferous about everything, too bloody opinionated.'

Paula looked across at him curiously. 'I hardly think he would volunteer an opinion about his mother's funeral – not under the circumstances. Surely he wouldn't dare.'

Winston grimaced. 'He might, knowing him. But her letter spells it out and that's that.'

'And you can be sure Grandy's funeral is going to be exactly the way she herself planned it,' Paula exclaimed.

Winston nodded, asked, 'What did Doctor Hedley say after he examined Aunt Emma?'

'Heart failure,' Emily volunteered. She gulped. 'Gran's poor old heart just gave out, stopped beating.'

Winston drew on his cigarette and looked away, his eyes suddenly swimming. There was a tremor in his voice as he remarked, 'Grandfather Winston always used to tell me that his sister had a heart as big as a paving stone, and Emma did, she surely did.' He sighed softly. 'At least she went peacefully, and for that we must all be grateful.' He brought his eyes back to Paula. 'When is the funeral? Have you decided yet?'

'I'm afraid we can't have it until Tuesday at the earliest. Mainly because of Philip getting here from Australia,' Paula told him. 'Fortunately Pip was in Sydney, not out at the sheep station in Coonamble, when I rang him tonight. He said he'd leave first thing in the morning. Very early. He's chartering a private jet. He thinks it'll be quicker than taking a commercial flight. I also spoke to my mother. Naturally she was as devastated as we are, and she wants to get home as quickly as possible. So she, my father and Jim are flying from Nice directly to Manchester tomorrow morning. Alexander and Maggie will be arriving then, too.'

Emily said, 'I spoke to Mummy in Paris. I told her she didn't have to come until Sunday or Monday. I also talked to Robin and Kit. They're here in Yorkshire, so there's no problem. We managed to contact everyone on our list including Sarah and Jonathan. What about you, Winston?'

'I got hold of Dad at the hotel in London. He'll be on a train in the morning. Vivienne's at Middleham, of course. Sally and Anthony were both at Clonlough-lin. But Aunt Edwina is in Dublin. Anthony told me he'll reach her later this evening. They'll fly over on Sunday. You're going to have a house full, Paula.'

'Yes, I know.'

Winston said reflectively, 'I think Emily and I ought to move in here with you for the next few days. What do –'

Paula interjected. 'Oh yes, please do. I'd appreciate it.'

Clearing his throat, Winston now asked in a muffled tone, 'When are they bringing her body – I mean, bringing Aunt Emma back to Pennistone Royal?'

Paula blinked rapidly as her eyes moistened. 'Tomorrow afternoon. I'm going to take the dress she wanted to wear to the undertaker in Leeds first thing in the morning.' Paula turned her head, pressing back her tears with her fingertips. After a second, she went on, 'Emily and I didn't want to leave her there all alone for the next few days. It may sound silly, but we didn't want – her to be lonely without us. And so her coffin will be brought here, to this house, her home, the one place she truly loved on this earth. We've decided to let the coffin stand in the Stone Hall. She liked the hall so much . . .' Her voice trailed off.

Emily said, with a little burst of anger, 'You wouldn't believe how stupid the undertaker was, Winston! So bureaucratic. He actually tried to argue with us earlier this evening, when we insisted on accompanying Gran to – his place.'

'Oh I know, darling,' Winston murmured sympathetically. 'There's always a lot of stupid red tape. But you got your way, which is the main thing.'

'You can bet your last shilling we did,' Paula asserted. 'By the way, Emily reached Merry just as she was leaving the office, to come to dinner here, and she went to tell Uncle Bryan about Emma. Apparently he was so heartbroken she had to drive him home to Wetherby.'

'I'm sure he was, and is,' Winston replied. 'Aunt Emma was like a mother to Bryan when he was a child growing up.'

'Merry rang us back at the office,' Emily said. 'The O'Neills are popping over at about nine o'clock to be with us.'

'Incidentally, I tried to get hold of Shane. He was due back from Spain this afternoon.' Winston fixed his eyes on Paula. 'But when I rang the London office at six-forty-five there was no reply. I guess I missed him –'

'I caught him there,' Paula interrupted. 'At six. He'd just walked in from the airport. He's on his way to Yorkshire right now – driving. He'll come straight here, and he should arrive about eleven.'

There was a knock on the door and Hilda walked into the parlour. 'Excuse me, Miss Paula,' she said. 'But I'd already prepared the usual cold buffet for tonight, as I always do on Friday. You know, before you rang me about –' The housekeeper stopped, covered her mouth with her hand. She took a breath, and her voice wobbled as she finished, 'About Mrs Harte passing away.' She stared at Paula helplessly, unable to utter another word.

'I'm sorry, Hilda, but I don't feel like eating.' Paula glanced at Emily and Winston. 'Do either of you?' They both shook their heads, and Paula added, 'I think we'd better skip dinner tonight, thanks anyway, Hilda.'

'Oh I understand, Miss Paula,' Hilda made a face. 'I can't eat either. To tell you the truth, I'd choke on the food,' she muttered and disappeared.

'Blunt as ever, Hilda is,' Winston said. 'But I know what she means. I feel the same way.' He rose and went to the console, where he poured himself another scotch and soda. He turned suddenly, looked first at his wife and then at Paula. He said thoughtfully, 'This may seem like a peculiar thing to say, rather far-fetched even, but now that Aunt Emma's dead I feel her presence more acutely than ever. I don't mean because I'm here in this room, which was her favourite, but in general. She's – well, she's just *with* me. I've felt her closeness ever since you called me at our Harrogate office to tell me that she'd died.'

Emily nodded and emphatically so. 'It's not far-fetched, Winston. Paula and I discussed that very thing when we were driving back here tonight.'

For a moment Paula sat silently reflecting and then she said in a quiet voice, 'We all feel her presence because she *is* here with us, Winston. She's all around us. And inside us. She made us what we are, gave us so much of herself that we're full of her.' A sudden and lovely warm smile spread across Paula's tired face. 'Grandy will be with each one of us for all of our days. And so, in a sense, she'll never really be dead. Emma Harte will live on forever through us.'

Emma Harte's funeral was held in Ripon Cathedral, as she had requested. It took place at one o'clock on the Tuesday following her death.

Her entire family was present, along with friends, colleagues, employees and most of the inhabitants of the village of Pennistone Royal, where she had lived for well over thirty years. The cathedral was packed to overflowing and if there were some present who were dry eyed, they were far outnumbered by those who were tearful and sorrowing.

Her coffin was borne down the central nave and through the great chancel to the altar by the six pallbearers she herself had chosen. Three of them were her grandsons: Philip McGill Amory, Alexander Barkstone and Anthony Standish, Earl of Dunvale. The other three were her great-nephew Winston

Harte, Shane O'Neill and Michael Kallinski, the grandsons of her two dear friends from her youth.

Although her coffin was not heavy, the six young men walked at a slow, measured pace, their steps keeping time with the organ music that swelled to the rafters of the ancient cathedral. Finally the pallbearers came to a stop in front of the magnificent altar and it was here that they rested Emma's coffin amidst a profusion of exquisite floral bouquets and wreaths. The central area where the coffin stood was bathed in light from the many flickering candles and the sunlight pouring in through the jewel-coloured stained glass windows.

The family occupied all of the front pews. Paula sat between Jim and her mother. Her father was on Daisy's other side. He, in turn, had Emily on his right side. She was mothering Amanda and Francesca, who cried continuously into their damp handkerchiefs. Although Emily was as distressed as her sisters, she somehow managed to keep a firm grip on herself, endeavouring to comfort the heartbroken teenagers.

Once the pallbearers had been seated with the rest of the mourners, the Dean of Ripon, the Very Reverend Edwin LeGrice, began the short service. He spoke beautifully about Emma, his words eloquent and moving, and when he eventually stepped down from the pulpit ten minutes later, his place was taken by Emma's nephew Randolph Harte.

Randolph gave the sole eulogy. He had difficulty at times, his strong voice cracking with emotion and he choked on some of his sentences, his sorrow and sense of loss rising to the surface frequently. Randolph's words about his aunt were very simple and loving, spoken from the heart and with genuine feeling. His eulogizing of Emma was limited to a recital of her attributes as a human being. He made no mention of her business career as one of the world's greatest merchant princes. Instead he touched on her generosity of spirit, her kind nature, her understanding heart, her great acts of charity, her loyalty as a friend and relative, her extraordinary qualities as a woman of remarkable character and strength and indomitable will.

After the eulogy, which had caused many to weep, the Ripon Cathedral choir rose and gave their beautiful harmonized rendition of *Onward Christian Soldiers*, one of the two hymns Emma had learned as a child, and which she had wanted sung today.

As the choir sat down, the Dean of Ripon returned to the pulpit. He led the mourners in a single prayer, before offering up his own brief prayer for Emma Harte's soul and for her eternal life. When he brought this to a close he asked all of those present to say their own personal and private prayers for Emma during the next few minutes of absolute silence.

Paula, her head bowed, squeezed her eyes tightly shut, but the tears seeped out anyway and dripped on to her clasped hands. The cathedral was perfectly still now, its peacefulness enveloping them all. But occasionally the silent hallowed space echoed with a muffled sob, a small gasp of grief or a strangled cough.

And then suddenly his voice rang out, so true and clear and pure Paula thought her heart was going to burst. She had known Shane was going to sing *Jerusalem*, since this was one of Emma's last wishes, but nevertheless she was startled. She brought her handkerchief up to her face, wondering how she could ever bear this part of the service.

Shane O'Neill stood alone in a far corner of the cathedral and he sang William Blake's old hymn without accompaniment, his rich full baritone echoing to every corner of the church.

As he came to the end of the first verse and commenced the second Paula experienced a sudden and extraordinary feeling of peace and release as the words washed over her. He held her enthralled.

Shane's lilting voice reached out to touch everyone present as he now sang:

> 'Bring me my bow of burning gold!
> Bring me my arrows of desire!
> Bring me my spear! O clouds, unfold!
> Bring me my chariot of fire!
> I will not cease from mental fight,
> Nor shall my sword sleep in my hand
> Till we have built Jerusalem
> In England's green and pleasant land.'

As Shane's voice faded away, Paula unexpectedly understood the need, the significance and the importance of the ritual and ceremony of death. Somehow they were helping her to endure her sorrow. The prayers, brief though they had been, the choir boys and then Shane singing so melodiously, the masses of flowers and the extraordinary beauty of this ancient cathedral had given her a degree of ease from her overwhelming pain. The presence of the Dean, whom she had known for years, was calming, comforting to her. It suddenly struck her that when grief could be shared in this way the burden of the heartbreak became slightly lighter to bear. She knew the service had been a shade more elaborate than her grandmother had intended, but somehow she felt it had been extremely consoling to those who genuinely cared about Emma and mourned her truly. We did her honour, we gave her a wonderful tribute as she leaves this earthly life, Paula thought. It has been our way of saying our loving goodbyes. Paula felt a new strength flowing through her as she lifted her head.

Instantly she became conscious of her mother's terrible anguish. Daisy was sobbing unrestrainedly against David's shoulder. Paula put her hand on her mother's arm, whispered, 'It's all right, Mummy. Draw comfort from knowing that she's safe at last. She's gone to your father, to Paul, and now they're together for all time, for eternity.'

'Yes,' Daisy gasped. 'I know, darling, I know. But I shall miss her so much. She was the best. The very, very best there is in this world.'

The organ music began again and rose to a crescendo as her coffin was lifted by the pallbearers. They brought it back through the chancel and down the nave and out of Ripon Cathedral. Emma's immediate family walked behind her coffin and then they stood outside, watching as it was placed in the hearse and covered with a blanket of flowers for her last journey.

Paula noticed that Edwina was as stricken and tearful as her mother and impulsively she went over, placed her hand on her aunt's arm. 'I'm glad you made your peace with Grandy,' Paula said in a shaky voice. 'Really glad, Aunt Edwina.'

Edwina turned to Paula, her light grey eyes brimming. 'It was too late. I should have done it years ago. I was wrong. So very wrong, Paula dear.'

Paula said, 'She understood. She always understood everything, that was the beauty of Emma Harte. And she was so pleased you and she became friends – overjoyed, if you want to know the truth.'

'That helps a little,' Edwina said softly. 'And you and I, Paula, we must be friends too. Can you forgive me?'

'Yes,' Paula said very simply, and bent forward and kissed Edwina's wet cheek.

A long line of cars followed the cortège out of Ripon and on to Harrogate. They soon left the bucolic Dales behind, passed through the city of Leeds, the seat of Emma's power, and travelled through the grimy industrial valleys of the West Riding. But eventually the procession came up on to the high moorland road that cut through the great Pennine chain of hills.

On this sunlit afternoon in early September those grim and savage Yorkshire moors had lost their blackened and daunting aspects that could so appal the eye. Dark and implacable for most of the year, they now blazed with sudden and glorious splendour. As it always did at the end of the summer, wave upon wave of purple and magenta heather undulated across the great sweep of wild, untenanted moors. It was as if a cloth of royal purple had been rolled out, and it rippled gently under the light breeze. High above floated a resplendent sky that was as blue as speedwells and brilliant with that incredible clarity of light so peculiar to the North of England. The air was pure and bracing. Larks and linnets wheeled and turned with a rush and fluttering of wings and their sweet trillings pierced the silence, and there was the fragrant scent of harebells and wild flowers and heather on the lucent air.

Finally the cortège began its downward descent, leaving the moorland behind, and several hours after its departure from Ripon it progressed slowly into the village of Fairley. The hearse came to a standstill outside the quaint Norman church where eighty-one years ago she had been christened.

Her six young pallbearers, representing the three clans, shouldered her coffin for the last time. Moving at a slow pace and with great care, they carried her through the lychgate into the cemetery, where the vicar, the Reverend Huntley, was waiting at the graveside.

Against the drystone walls and under the blowing trees and along the winding paths stood the villagers of Fairley. They were silent and grieving, the men with their caps in their hands, the women and children holding sprays of wild flowers, and heather, for remembrance, and all had their heads bowed and most of them were weeping quietly. They had come out of love to pay their last respects, to say farewell to this woman who was one of their own, she who had risen so high in the world but had never once forgotten them.

After a brief ceremony under that wide and shimmering sky which she had believed to be unique, Emma Harte was buried in the benign earth which had for so long sheltered her loved ones. Her grave was between those of her mother and Winston, her final resting place overshadowed by the moors she had so loved and wandered over as a child, and where she had never felt lonely or alone in her solitude.

Tycoon

'Cease to ask what the morrow will
bring forth, and set down as gain
each day that Fortune grants.'

HORACE

44

'I still think there's something fishy going on,' Alexander muttered, pacing the floor of Paula's office at the London store.

'So do I,' she agreed, her eyes following him as he progressed up and down between the fireplace and her desk. 'But having suspicions is simply not good enough. We need concrete evidence of some kind before we can make a move against Jonathan. And Sarah perhaps. I'm still not certain whether she is being treacherous or not.'

'Neither am I. But we do need to get the goods on him, you're quite right. Until then our hands are tied.' Alexander rubbed his chin, his expression thoughtful. He came to a stop in front of Paula's desk and levelled his gaze at her. 'My gut instinct tells me that Jonathan's double dealing is staring me in the face, and you can bet it's going to *hit* me in the face one day very soon.' He shook his head. 'And to borrow a phrase of Grandy's, I don't like unpleasant surprises.'

'Who does?' Paula sighed, her worrying growing more acute. She knew Alexander was the most conservative of men and not prone to exaggeration or flights of fancy. Besides, their grandmother had been convinced of Jonathan Ainsley's duplicity until the day of her death five weeks ago. But, like them, Emma had not had the proof. Settling back in her chair, Paula said, 'Whatever it *is* he's doing, he's obviously been very clever about it, since the accountants haven't found anything wrong after checking the books.'

'Naturally he is, and you know he's always been bloody devious. He doesn't let his right hand know what his left is doing, for God's sake. He hasn't changed much over the years.' Alexander gave her a pained look. 'Don Littleton thinks I'm stark raving mad. If I've made him go over the books once, I've had him do it a dozen times.' Alexander lifted his shoulder in a helpless shrug. 'Don and two of the other accountants with his firm put the real estate division under a microscope. There's nothing untoward – not a single thing that seems suspicious. At least, not as far as money matters are concerned.'

Paula leaned forward, rested her elbows on her desk, propped her chin in her hands. 'He wouldn't be stupid enough to *steal*, Sandy, and he's smart. He'd cover his tracks wherever they led. I wish we could think of some way to lure him out into the open, get him to show his hand . . .' Her sentence remained unfinished as she considered this idea, racked her brains for likely possibilities.

Her brother Philip, who sat on the sofa at the other side of the room, had been listening intently for the last fifteen minutes. Finally breaking his silence, he said, 'The only way you'll ever trap our dear cousin is to set him up as a target.'

Alexander pivoted on his heels. 'How?' he asked.

Philip rose and strolled over to join them. Of all of Emma's grandsons, Philip McGill Amory was the most handsome. He was the spitting image of his grandfather and had the McGill colouring that his mother and his sister had inherited. His hair was the same glossy black, his eyes that uncanny blue which bordered on deep violet, and he was as tall, virile and dashing as Paul McGill had been. Although only twenty-four, Philip also happened to be the shrewdest of Emma's grandsons, since he had been blessed with Paul's extraordinary business acumen and financial genius, as well as a great deal of his grandmother's not inconsiderable brilliance. He had been diligently trained by Emma since the age of seventeen and after taking over the vast McGill empire in Australia he had proved himself to be worthy of her trust many times over. He was known as a man to be reckoned with, and one who had a wisdom beyond his years.

Drawing to a stop next to Alexander, he put his hand on his cousin's shoulder and said, 'I'll tell you *how* in a minute, Sandy.' Lowering himself into one of the chairs facing his sister, he remarked, 'That detective Gran hired – Graves – hasn't been able to dig up a thing on Jonathan. However, *I* still believe that it's very probable he has his own company – one that is being run by straw men, and –'

'Don't think I've dismissed that possibility,' Alexander fiercely interrupted, 'because I haven't.'

Philip nodded. 'Okay, so let's start with the assumption that he *does* indeed have a real estate company, and that he's been funnelling deals into it. Big deals that by rights should be going to Harte Enterprises. That in itself is enough to hang him.' Philip sat forward urgently, looked first at his sister and then at Alexander. 'I propose that *we* put the noose around his neck. And I'll tell you how. It's very simple really. We have to get someone to present a deal to Jonathan as head of the real estate division of Harte Enterprises. Now, here's the twist . . . we have to make the deal so attractive, so juicy, he won't be able to resist putting it through his own company. Naturally it must be extremely appealing, and so very big, so tempting, his greed will far outweigh his judgement. If the stakes for himself are high enough he'll act rashly, believe me he will.'

Sitting back, Philip crossed his long legs, glanced from Alexander to Paula and back to Alexander. 'Well, what do you say?'

Alexander now sat down heavily in the other chair, nodded slowly. 'I must admit, it's a smart ploy, and I'll go along with it, providing you can answer a couple of questions.'

'*Shoot.*'

'Philip, let's be practical, where the hell are *we* going to find this tempting deal to dangle like a carrot in front of Jonathan? That's for openers, and secondly, who are *we* going to get to offer it to him?' Alexander smiled narrowly. 'Let's not underestimate our wily cousin . . . he'll spot the holes immediately.'

'Ah, but there won't be any,' Philip replied evenly. 'I have someone who can offer the deal to Jonathan, a close friend who has his own real estate company here in London. So that answers your first question. As far as the deal itself is concerned, I believe my friend may have something up his sleeve that would be most appropriate, and tempting. All I need is your approval, and then I'll talk to him.'

'I suppose it's worth having a go,' Alexander said, fully aware of Philip's inbred shrewdness and discretion. He turned to Paula. 'What do you think?'

Paula said, 'I'm all for it, if you are, Sandy.' She eyed her brother. 'What's the name of your friend?'

'Malcolm Perring. Surely you remember old Malcolm – we were at Wellington together.'

'Vaguely. I think you introduced us once, when I came down to visit you at half term.'

'I did. Anyway, he and I remained relatively close friends after we left school, and he was out in Australia for a year and –'

'Jonathan's bound to smell a rat,' Paula said sharply. 'You and Malcolm were at the same public school, then he was in Australia. Jonathan'll put two and two together.'

'I doubt it,' Philip said, sounding assured and confident. 'Malcolm's been back here for a couple of years. He inherited his brother's real estate company after that poor chap dropped dead of a heart attack at thirty-nine. Besides, Jonathan's not going to ask a lot of personal questions, and Malcolm can be adroit and evasive, believe me, he can.'

'I trust you. I know you wouldn't embroil somebody in our affairs whom you couldn't rely on to be absolutely discreet. And you *will* have to take him into your confidence,' Paula remarked.

'Obviously. But Malcolm *is* reliable . . . true blue, Paula.' Philip chuckled. 'I'm sure he has a deal that is ready to go – Perring and Perring is a huge company, and wouldn't it be ironic if we were able to kill two birds with one stone? Catch Jonathan red-handed and do a bit of smart business for Harte Enterprises at the same time.'

Alexander began to laugh dryly, tickled at the idea. 'Oh how Grandy would love this!'

Paula half smiled. 'Perhaps we should go ahead then, Philip, since Alexander is all for it. And actually it must be his decision – as managing director of Harte Enterprises.'

Alexander exclaimed, 'We don't have anything to lose and, very frankly, I'm relieved we're taking aggressive action. This sitting around waiting for Jonathan Ainsley to tip his hand is most frustrating. I feel we must force him out in the open if we can.'

'I shall talk to Malcolm first thing tomorrow morning.' Philip glanced at his watch. 'If we're going to grab a bite of lunch before we go to John Crawford's office, I think we ought to leave. It's eleven-thirty. We have to be at John's at two-thirty, don't we Paula?'

'Yes.' She stood up, brushed a piece of lint off her black dress. 'I'm not looking forward to this afternoon,' she began and stopped. Her upper lip quivered and her eyes filled with tears. She glanced away quickly. After a moment she managed to compose herself, and she smiled weakly at the two men.

'I'm so sorry,' she said. 'That happens when I least expect it – I think of Gran and just choke up. I can't get used to her not being here. It's just awful, such a gap in my life . . . all of our lives, I suppose.'

'Yes,' Philip agreed. 'Alexander and I feel the same way as you do. In fact, we were discussing it last night at dinner. It's hard to realize that she's not going to suddenly swoop down on us with a bit of unorthodox but frighteningly clever advice, or make one of those blunt or pithy comments of hers.'

Philip walked around the desk and took hold of Paula's shoulders gently, looked down into her white face. 'The reading of the will *is* going to be dreadfully upsetting, Paula, because it emphasizes the reality of her death. But you must be there . . . we all must.' He attempted a bit of levity as he finished, 'Grandy will be mad at us if we're not.'

Paula nodded, smiling faintly at his remark, knowing he wanted to cheer her up. Her sadness did ease slightly. 'I'll tell you one thing – it gets my goat when I think of the leeches who are going to be present later.' She sighed. 'Ah well, there we are, nothing we can do about it and my apologies to the two of you again. I think the less said about this afternoon the better. Now, come on, let's go to lunch. Emily's joining us – I've booked a table at the Ritz.'

'The Ritz!' Philip exclaimed in surprise. 'A bit fancy, isn't it, for a quick snack?'

She tucked her arm through her brother's, glanced up at him and then across at Alexander, a hint of genuine gaiety surfacing. 'Not really. It *was* one of Grandy's favourite places. And I chose it because it has such happy associations for the four of us . . . all those lovely treats she used to give us there when we were children.' Paula laughed, now addressed her brother, 'Besides, you and I might not be here if Emma and Paul hadn't indulged in a bit of romantic dallying at the Ritz over sixty years ago!'

'Correct,' Philip answered with a laugh. 'And in that case I think lunch had better be on Paul McGill! Consider this my treat.'

'Jolly decent of you,' Alexander said as they left Paula's office and went out to the staff lift. Alexander engaged Philip in a few seconds of conversation about his friend Malcolm Perring as they rode down. Satisfied with Philip's answers, confident that his cousin had selected the right man to help them corner Jonathan, he asked, 'By the way, how long are we going to have the pleasure of your company?'

'I'll be here until the end of October, when I'm apparently going to Texas with Paula. So she told me before you arrived. Sitex business. From there, it's back to Sydney for a few weeks, and then I'm coming home again – for Christmas.'

'Oh!' Paula exclaimed. 'You didn't tell me.'

'I only just decided at breakfast this morning. I haven't had a chance to mention it. Mum's so done in at the moment, I think I ought to be here. It'll cheer her up. I've also agreed to go to Chamonix with them in January, and of course they're both delighted about that.'

'And so am I – this is great news.' Alexander beamed. 'Maggie and I have been invited to join Aunty Daisy and Uncle David.' He shot Paula a quick glance. 'Are you going to change your mind, now that Philip's coming along?'

'*No*. When *I* take a vacation I want to lie in the hot sun and bake myself to a crisp dark brown. The ski slopes have never appealed to me, as you both well know. Also, I have to be in New York in January. We're doing a big promotion of French and Italian couture fashions at the store, and I'm opening the Total Woman Shop at our Fifth Avenue branch then.' She gave them a wicked grin as they stepped out of the lift. 'Somebody has to work in this family.'

Laughing, they bustled her outside into Knightsbridge and into a taxicab and headed for the Ritz Hotel.

Emily was already waiting for them at a table in the restaurant. Elegant in a black suit, which was most flattering and showed off her blonde beauty to perfection, she nevertheless wore a mournful expression. Her green eyes were wistful as her cousins and brother sat down with her. 'I'll be glad when today's over,' she muttered to Alexander. 'The thought of hearing the will is so depressing.'

Alexander said, 'Come on, Emily lovey, cheer up. Philip and I have just been through the same recital with Paula.' He squeezed her arm. 'Grandy wouldn't approve. In fact, she'd be bloody furious if she could see us sitting around moping. Remember what she used to say?'

'Which particular thing?' Emily asked pensively.

'The remark she often made when we'd had some sort of failure or disappointment . . . she usually told us to forget yesterday, think of tomorrow and keep forging ahead without looking back. Don't you think that's what we should do, especially today?'

'Yes,' Emily admitted, giving her brother a more cheerful smile.

'Good girl,' Alexander said.

Philip said, 'I'm going to order a bottle of champagne and we're going to drink to the memory of that remarkable woman who gave us life, taught us everything we know and made us what we are.'

He motioned the wine waiter.

After Philip had ordered a bottle of Dom Perignon, and whilst they waited for it to be brought to the table, Paula leaned closer to Emily. She whispered, 'Philip has had a clever idea, thought of a way to possibly flush Jonathan out into the open. Once we've toasted Grandy, he'll tell you about it.'

'I can't wait,' Emily exclaimed. Her glistening green eyes narrowed with sudden shrewdness as she contemplated Jonathan's downfall. 'Now that would be a fitting tribute to Gran – if we can uncover his treachery to her and deal with him as she would have done.'

45

John Crawford, Emma's solicitor, and a senior partner in the firm of Crawford, Creighton, Phipps and Crawford, hurried into the large conference room.

He glanced about and nodded with satisfaction. The twenty-four chairs which were permanent fixtures around the long mahogany table had been rounded out to twenty-nine with the addition of five more. His secretary had rustled these up from other offices within the law firm, and the room could now accommodate himself and the twenty-eight people who were due to arrive any moment.

John strode down the floor, placed the last will and testament of Emma Harte on the table in front of his chair at its head. His eyes rested on it briefly but thoughtfully. It was a bulky document and he was facing a long session. No matter, he thought, and half shrugging he stepped over to the window, parted the curtains and looked down into Upper Grosvenor Street.

A few seconds later he saw a taxi pulling up outside the front door. David Amory alighted, followed by Daisy and Edwina. Even from this distance he could see that Daisy looked drawn, very sad, but she was still as beautiful as ever. He sighed under his breath. No wonder his marriage had failed. It was impossible to be married to one woman whilst worshipping another. He had been in love with Daisy for as long as he could remember. Most of his adult life really. No hope there. She had married young, and she had only ever had eyes for David. How special she was, so sweet and unaffected, and not a bit spoiled by that extraordinary wealth. They were good friends, and spent two days a month working together, since it was Daisy who ran the Emma Harte Foundation, a rich organization devoted to charity. Daisy frequently needed his legal advice on other matters, and sometimes he was lucky, was able to spend a few extra hours with her. He was grateful for these small crumbs of her time, and looked forward with eagerness to their business luncheons.

He swung away from the window at the sound of his secretary's voice as she showed the Amorys and Edwina into the conference room. Smiling, he went to greet them, struck by Edwina's ghastly appearance. Like Daisy, she wore black and in consequence her face looked utterly colourless and drained of life. But this aside, she had become an old woman in the last few weeks. Emma's death had apparently affected her deeply.

He stood chatting to the three of them for a few minutes, and then they took their seats as the others began to arrive in rapid succession. By two-twenty everyone was present except for Jim and Winston. They came hurrying in five minutes later, apologizing, and explaining they had been held up in the traffic on the way from Fleet Street.

At precisely two-thirty John brought the room to order. He said: 'It is a very sad occasion that brings us all together today, but as Emma said to me the last time I saw her at the beginning of August, "No long faces after I'm dead. I've had an extraordinary life, known the best and the worst, and so there hasn't been one dull moment. Sing no sad songs for me." However, before I proceed with the business at hand, I would like to say that I personally mourn a very good and dear friend, who was the most remarkable woman – no, correction, person – I've ever been privileged to know. She will be sorely missed.'

There were a few scattered mutterings of approval at the expression of these sentiments before John said in a more solemn voice: 'This is the Last Will and Testament of Emma Harte Lowther Ainsley, who shall, hereafter, be known simply as Emma Harte throughout the reading of the will.' He cleared his throat, and his tone became more conversational as he said, 'Before her death Mrs Harte told me that members of her immediate family were aware of certain of the contents, since these were revealed to them by her in April of 1968. However, since the will covers the disposal of her entire estate, and because there are other beneficiaries I must read the will in its entirety. Also, that is the law. I must therefore ask you all to bear with me. It is a long document, I'm afraid, and one of some complexity.'

Paula, who sat between Jim and Philip, leaned back in her chair, folded her hands in her lap and directed her attention on the family solicitor. Her face expressionless.

The first five or six pages dealt with Emma's bequests to the staff employed in her various homes, and all were generous, showed Emma's special consideration for each individual and their needs. Paula was genuinely gratified when she heard that Hilda was to receive a substantial pension when she retired, as well as the deed to one of the cottages Emma owned in the village of Pennistone Royal.

Hilda was not present, but Gaye Sloane was, and Emma's former secretary looked across at Paula and gave her a surprised smile of delight, after John had read out the details of Emma's gift to her. Gaye was to receive two hundred thousand pounds and a pair of diamond-and-gold earrings with a matching brooch.

The second portion of the will was concerned with Emma's considerable art collection. John explained, 'In the will drawn in 1968, Emma Harte left all of the art works to her grandson, Philip McGill Amory, with the exception of the paintings hanging at Pennistone Royal. This bequest has been modified.' He swung his eyes to Philip. 'Mrs Harte told me that she discussed this change with you and gave you her reasons for making it, and that you were fully understanding of her motives.'

'Yes,' Philip said, 'Grandmother was seeking my approval and I told her this was not necessary, that she must dispose of her art as she so wished, since it was hers and hers alone. I am totally in accord with her.'

John nodded, glanced down at the document and read out Emma's words: '"In recognition of their many years of devotion, loyalty and friendship, I do give and bequeath to Henry Rossiter the Van Gogh landscape; to Ronald Kallinski the Picasso from the Blue Period; to Bryan O'Neill the Degas ballet dancer, each of which currently hangs in my Belgrave Square residence. To my beloved nephew, Randolph Harte, in appreciation of his love and friendship, I bequeath the four horse paintings by Stubbs and the two Barbara Hepworth sculptures, which are at present housed at Pennistone Royal. All of my other art works, *excluding* those hanging at Pennistone Royal, I give to my grandson, Philip. Also *excluded* from this bequest to Philip is the painting entitled The Top of the World by Sally Harte."'

Philip leaned into Paula and whispered, 'Uncle Randolph and the others are very touched. I'm glad she made those gifts to them, aren't you?'

Paula nodded, gave him a small smile.

John Crawford said, 'Regarding the matter of the Fabergé Imperial Easter Egg –' The solicitor paused to take a sip of water, and went on to explain that Emma wished the Fabergé object of art to be auctioned, the money returned to her grandchildren who had purchased it for her as a gift for her eightieth birthday. Any balance of money left over, should the Imperial Easter Egg bring more than they had paid for it, was to be donated to charity in accordance with Emma's wishes.

Paula's eyes were surreptitiously wandering around the conference room.

She had been aware of the mounting tension for the last fifteen minutes, had noticed the anxiety written on the faces of Robin, Kit and Elizabeth. Edwina, on the other hand, seemed oblivious to the proceedings, sat twisting her hands in her lap. She appeared more dolorous than ever.

As John began, 'I now come to the trust funds Emma Harte created for her children,' Paula could almost feel the anxiousness and nervousness emanating from her two uncles and her aunt. She quickly averted her eyes, trained them on John once again.

Leaning back in his chair, the solicitor said, 'The trusts, which became effective some years ago, have not been rescinded or changed in any way, shape or form by Mrs Harte. They remain intact, and the beneficiaries, Edwina, Kit, Robin and Elizabeth, will continue to receive the income from their trusts.'

John's voice droned on as he elucidated further details of the trusts, and just as she had sensed the apprehension in three of those four earlier, Paula was conscious of their profound relief. Robin and his twin, Elizabeth, were unable to conceal their jubilation. Kit's face was sober, but his eyes betrayed him as they flickered with triumph. Only Edwina was unaccountably distressed, weeping copiously into her handkerchief. Paula realized that her aunt was undoubtedly thinking of Emma, understanding yet again how eminently fair her mother had been.

'I will move on to the trusts which Emma Harte created for her grandchildren,' John announced, and Paula's grave face became very alert. She could not help wondering if Grandy had changed these. It soon became clear that Emma had not. Emily, Sarah, Alexander, Jonathan, Anthony, Francesca and Amanda would continue to benefit from the trust funds which Emma had provided for them in April of 1968. After spelling out the terms of the trust, the solicitor paused, shifted his position in his chair.

His glance rested on Paula, then moved on to regard Anthony. He remarked, 'At this point in the proceedings I must tell you that Emma Harte created three additional trust funds. These are for her great-grandchildren, Lorne and Tessa Fairley, son and daughter of Jim and Paula Fairley, and Jeremy, the Viscount Standish, son of Anthony and Sally Standish, the Earl and Countess of Dunvale. Each trust for these three great-grandchildren is in the amount of one million pounds.'

Picking up the will, John once more launched into a relatively long recitation of Emma's wishes which were couched in her own language. When this section was dispensed with, he moved on briskly, introduced the portion of the will that dealt with the dispersal of Emma's vast business enterprises and the enormous McGill fortune. She had again left the 1968 bequests intact. Alexander received fifty-two per cent of Harte Enterprises and was formally appointed head of this company for life. His sister Emily, as well as Sarah and Jonathan, each received sixteen per cent of the shares respectively. In the event of Alexander's death or disability, Emily would automatically assume control of the company, holding this position for her lifetime.

Paula eyed Jonathan and Sarah, and asked herself if they knew how lucky they had been. Jonathan could hardly conceal his glee, Sarah was smiling smugly, Paula noticed, and her face became closed and cold.

At the mention of her own name Paula gave John her full attention, even though she expected no surprises. She listened as he repeated Emma's words, written by her in 1968. Paula received all of Emma's shares in the Harte Stores which gave her total control of the company.

The entire McGill fortune went to Daisy McGill Amory, with the stipulation that her son, Philip, was to continue as Chief Executive Officer of the McGill Corporation of Australia, a conglomerate that owned the diverse McGill companies. Paula was to remain as her mother's representative in all matters pertaining to Sitex Oil. Upon Daisy's death, the McGill holdings were to be equally divided between Paula and Philip. Daisy inherited Pennistone Royal, all land and property attached to the house, all of its furniture, furnishings and works of art, as well as the McGill emeralds. The house, its contents, the land, and the jewels, were to pass to Paula on her mother's death. Paula received the remainder of her grandmother's considerable emerald collection.

'Mrs Harte's other jewellery is, for the most part, to be divided among her granddaughters. However there are other bequests – to Marguerite Barkstone, Alexander's wife, Sally Harte Standish and Vivienne Harte, her great-nieces, and Rosamund Harte Ellsworthy, her niece,' John told them. 'Emma made the selections for each individual, and these are as follows. "To my dearest granddaughter, Emily Barkstone Harte, I do give and bequeath my sapphire collection, comprising of . . ."' John intoned as he commenced to read from the long list.

It took the solicitor almost an hour to complete the reading of this part of the will, since Emma had owned a huge collection of jewellery, and those who were not beneficiaries became restless. There were rustlings and small muffled sounds as people moved around in their chairs. Cigarettes were lit. Someone poured a glass of water. Edwina blew her nose several times. Robin coughed behind his hand.

John Crawford was perfectly calm, as he always was, and oblivious to the scattered shufflings and odd noises. He read slowly, precisely, and it was obvious to everyone that he had no intention of being hurried. At last he finished, 'That completes the details of the disposal of Mrs Harte's collection of jewellery. I shall now proceed with the portion of the will that covers some of her real estate, mainly the house in Jamaica, British West Indies; the Avenue Foch apartment in Paris; the villa at Cap Martin in the South of France.'

The solicitor explained that the bequests Emma Harte had made in April of 1968 were unchanged. Emily Barkstone Harte was to inherit the Paris apartment, her brother Alexander Barkstone the villa on the Riviera, and Anthony was to get the house in the Caribbean.

At this juncture, John suddenly put the will down. His eyes roved from face to face and then his own face changed perceptibly as he brought himself up in his chair.

He enunciated in a most careful tone, 'It is now my duty to inform you that Emma Harte changed the remainder of her will.'

There were several audible gasps and the majority of those present stiffened in their seats. A number of worried glances were exchanged. Paula felt Philip's hand on her knee and she looked at him swiftly, her dark brows lifting before she brought her eyes back to Crawford. He was turning the page he had just read and perusing the one following.

Paula felt the tension flowing around her as it had earlier and there was a sense of great anticipation mingled with apprehension in the air. Her chest tightened as she clasped her hands together, wondering what bombshells were about to burst. I always knew it deep down, Paula thought. Unconsciously I knew that Gran would have a few surprises up her sleeve. She could hardly wait for John to continue.

The silence in the room was deathly.

Twenty-eight pairs of eyes were fixed unwaveringly on the solicitor.

Finally John looked up. He scanned their faces a second time, noting the expressions on each. Some were fearful or anxious, others avidly curious, a few merely interested. He smiled and read out in a strong voice:

'"I, Emma Harte Lowther Ainsley, hereafter known as Emma Harte, do hereby declare that the codicils attached to my Last Will and Testament on this Twenty-Fifth Day of April in the Year of Our Lord Nineteen Hundred and Sixty-Nine are made whilst I am sound of body and mind. I do further declare and attest that no undue pressure or influence was brought to bear on me by any person or individual to make said changes in my Last Will and Testament and are solely of my own volition and doing."'

There was a brief pause on John's part as he turned the page, then gave his entire attention to the legal document in his hands.

'"Codicil One. I do give and bequeath to Shane Desmond Ingham O'Neill, grandson of my dearest lifelong friend, Blackie O'Neill, the diamond ring given to me by his late and aforementioned grandfather. I also bequeath to Shane O'Neill the painting known as The Top of the World, which I also received from his grandfather. Further, I do give to Shane O'Neill the sum of one million pounds in the form of a trust which I have had created for him. I make these gifts to Shane out of love for him, and in appreciation of his constant love and devotion to me.

'"Codicil Two. I give to Miranda O'Neill, granddaughter of my friend, Blackie O'Neill, the emerald bow brooch, presented to me by her grandfather. I do also make a gift to Miranda O'Neill of all other pieces of jewellery which were given to me by her grandfather during his lifetime. List of said pieces is attached to the end of these codicils. Further, I do give and bequeath to Miranda the sum of five hundred thousand pounds in the form of a trust. I do so in recognition of her affection and love for me and in memory of my dearest friend, Laura Spencer O'Neill, her grandmother.

'"Codicil Three. I do bequeath to my great-nephew, Winston John Harte, grandson of my beloved brother Winston, the property known as Heron's Nest in Scarborough, Yorkshire, and the sum of one million pounds, held in a trust similar to the aforementioned trusts. Also, I bequeath to Winston Harte fifteen per cent of my shares in my new company Consolidated Newspapers International, which he and I formed in March of 1969. I make these bequests to Winston Harte as a gesture of my love, and because of his love, devotion and uncommon loyalty to me over the years and because of his marriage to my granddaughter Emily, for the benefit of them both and any offspring of their marriage."'

At this point John stopped, took a quick sip of water and, aware of the taut atmosphere which now prevailed, he hurried on:

'"Codicil Four. I give to James Arthur Fairley, husband of my granddaughter Paula Fairley, ten per cent of my shares in Consolidated Newspapers International. This is a personal bequest to Jim Fairley and is in no way related to the trusts established for my great-grandchildren, Lorne and Tessa. This bequest is to show my appreciation of his dedication to me and my interests at the Yorkshire Consolidated Newspaper Company, and is also given as an expression of my affection for him.

'"Codicil Five. To my great-niece Vivienne Harte, granddaughter of my dear brother Winston, and to my niece Rosamund Harte Ellsworthy, daughter of my dear brother Frank, I do give and bequeath five hundred thousand pounds each in the form of trust funds which I have had drawn up for them. I do this out of my considerable affection for them both and in memory of my brothers.

'"Codicil Six. I do give and bequeath to my granddaughter Paula McGill Amory Fairley, and my grandson, Philip McGill Amory, my Fifth Avenue apartment in New York and my Belgrave Square house, both properties to be owned jointly by them. I make these gifts to Paula and Philip because the aforementioned residences were bought for me by their grandfather, Paul McGill. After long and careful consideration, I have decided that Paul McGill's grandchildren should rightfully inherit these homes. For this reason I have rescinded the original bequest made in my will drawn in April of 1968.

'"Codicil Seven. I give to my granddaughter Paula McGill Amory Fairley the remainder of my estate, including all motor cars, clothing, furs, and cash in my current cheque accounts. Further, I do give and bequeath to Paula Fairley all assets held in my private company, E.H. Incorporated. Said assets include my personally owned real estate, my personal stocks and shares, and cash balances. Total value of these assets is estimated at six million, eight hundred and ninety five thousand pounds, six shillings and sixpence."'

The solicitor lifted his head, said to the gathering, 'That concludes the reading of the Last Will and Testament Of Emma Harte Lowther Ainsley, except for –'

'Just a minute!' Jonathan exploded. Seething, he jumped up. His eyes were wild, his face as white as bleached bone. 'I'm going to contest this will! I was left the Fifth Avenue apartment in her original will and it's mine by rights. I'm going to –'

'Please be so kind as to sit down, Jonathan,' the solicitor exclaimed coldly, glaring at him. 'I have not finished.'

Bristling, his rage apparent, Jonathan did as he was asked but not without crying, '*Dad!* Don't you have anything to say about this?'

Robin, also infuriated, nevertheless shook his head, motioned for his son to be silent.

Crawford continued: 'I was about to read the final statement made by Mrs Harte at the end of her will. I will now proceed to do so, and I must ask that there be no further unruly outbursts of this nature. This is Mrs Harte's last statement: "I truly believe that I have been right, proper and fair in the disposal of all my worldly goods and possessions. I sincerely hope that my heirs understand why some of them are receiving greater inheritances than others.

'"However, should any of my heirs feel that they have been cheated or passed over for other members of my family, I must state again that this is not the case. Furthermore, should any member of my family contemplate contesting this will, I must caution them most strongly not to do so. Once again I attest that no undue influence, or influence of any kind, was brought to bear on me at any time. No one, other than my solicitor, John Crawford, knew of these changes and codicils which are entirely of my own creation. I must also state that I am not senile, nor is the balance of my mind disturbed. Attached to this document, which is my Last Will and Testament, are four affidavits signed by four doctors. These doctors were hitherto unknown to me before the date of this will, and are therefore uninterested parties. Two general practitioners and two psychiatrists examined me on the morning and afternoon of April Twenty-Fifth of Nineteen Sixty-Nine, prior to this will being drawn on the evening of that same date. The results of their examinations are contained in the affidavits and confirm that I am in excellent physical condition and perfect health, that I am mentally stable, and that none of my faculties are impaired.

'"Therefore, I must now point out that this will is irreversible, irrevocable and absolutely water tight. It cannot be contested in a court of law. I appoint my beloved and devoted daughter, Daisy McGill Amory, as executrix of my estate, and Henry Rossiter of the Rossiter Merchant Bank and John Crawford, of Crawford, Creighton, Phipps and Crawford as the co-executors of my estate."'

John sat back, waiting for the storm to erupt.

It did so instantly.

Everyone began to talk at once. Jonathan was on his feet and almost running down the long stretch of the conference room, looking as if he was about to physically accost John Crawford. Robin had also risen, and so had Kit Lowther and Sarah. These three also bore down on John, their expressions furious, their rage unconcealed as they began to rail at him shrilly.

Jonathan was apoplectic, shouted that the O'Neills had been favoured in his place and that Paula and Philip had stolen his inheritance. Sarah began to weep. Her mother, June, hurried to her, endeavouring to console her, and trying to hide her own considerable embarrassment without success.

Bryan O'Neill leapt to his feet. He went over to Daisy, and as the sole member of his family present, he protested that the O'Neills did not wish to accept Emma's legacies to them, in view of Jonathan's comments.

The brouhaha swirled around Paula. Jim, who had been sitting next to her, turned and said, 'Wasn't that lovely of Grandy to leave me the shares in the newspaper company?'

'Yes, it was,' Paula said, noting his shining eyes, his gratified smile.

Philip, who sat on her left, tapped her on the shoulder and leaned closer. Paula swung her eyes and stared at her brother. They gazed at each other knowingly for a protracted moment. Paula tried to keep her face straight but had difficulty doing so. She compressed her lips to prevent herself from laughing out loud. She murmured, 'Good old Grandy, as usual she thought of everything. What a brilliant stroke of genius that was, attaching those medical affidavits. The malcontents can do nothing – their hands have been firmly tied by Emma Harte.'

Philip nodded. 'Yes, but there will be trouble with them, you mark my words.

424

On the other hand, knowing Jonathan's temperament, this sudden turn of events could easily make him behave in the most irrational way. He might act rashly. And we will probably uncover his treachery to Gran sooner than we think.'

'Let's hope so. Perhaps Grandy realized that too, Philip. I don't doubt her sincerity about leaving the McGill residence to us because we're McGills, but let's not forget how shrewd and wily she was.' Paula could not help smiling. 'You have to agree that Emma Harte has had the last laugh.'

'I would call it a loud guffaw,' Philip replied, chuckling.

Daisy pushed back her chair and came around the table rapidly. She bent over Paula and said, 'Poor John . . . he's being verbally castigated and most unfairly. Mummy's will was her own doing not his. He's only the family solicitor. Can't you put a stop to their disgusting behaviour. The Lowthers and the Ainsleys are getting out of hand.'

'Perhaps Daddy can say something,' Paula muttered.

'No,' Daisy answered firmly. 'Emma Harte made you the head of the family. It's your responsibility, darling. I'm sorry, but that's the way it is.'

Paula nodded and stood up. 'Please, everybody, do be quiet for a moment.'

Her natural reserve made it difficult for Paula to assert herself in a large group such as this, but when none of the rowdy troublemakers paid any attention to her, she leaned forward and banged her clenched fist on the table. She exclaimed fiercely, 'Shut up! All of you! And sit down!'

The Ainsleys and the Lowthers looked at her with antipathy, and although they did not budge from their positions around John Crawford's chair, they did stop quarrelling amongst themselves.

'Thank you,' Paula said, more evenly, but her voice reflected her icy eyes. She drew herself up to her full height and her inbred hauteur and imperiousness reached out to momentarily stun them all.

'How dare you behave in this unconscionable manner!' she reprimanded sternly. 'You're perfectly reprehensible, the lot of you. I think you might show a little respect for Emma Harte. My God, she's only been dead a few weeks and here you are, behaving like vultures, picking over her bones.' Paula's eyes were now riveted on Jonathan and Sarah, who stood together. 'My grandmother knew what she was doing, and I think she has been overly generous to certain members of this family.'

Paula gripped the back of the chair tightly and continued in a tone that was almost threatening, 'Don't any one of you dare to even *think* about contesting Emma Harte's will. Because if you do, I shall fight you to the bitter end – and if it takes every hour of my time and every penny I have.'

The entire gathering stared at her. Most of those present were admiring of her, a few were condemning, but all were mesmerized by the aura of power she conveyed.

Winston edged closer to Emily and touched her arm. He whispered to his wife, 'Just look at her . . . she's Emma Harte personified. I think the legend lives.'

46

Shane and Paula walked across the British Airways terminal at Kennedy Airport, took the escalator to the second level and went into the First Class lounge.

They found a quiet corner.

After helping her off with her wild mink cape, Shane shrugged out of his trenchcoat and threw it on a chair nearby.

'Let's have a drink,' he suggested. 'We have time before your flight.'

'That'll be nice. Thank you, darling.'

Shane smiled down at her, and ambled over to the bar at the other side of the lounge.

Paula watched him. How marvellous he looked. So darkly handsome and commanding, in absolute control. Her expression became soft; her eyes filled with love for him. In the year they had been having their love affair her feelings for him had only grown deeper. He was so much part of her now she felt lost when they separated and only half alive without him. He never ceased to surprise her. Although she had known him all of her life, she had never fully realized how truly dependable he was in every circumstance or emergency. He had a tremendous sense of commitment to her, and to every single thing that was important in his life. His strength of character was almost awesome. He has iron in his soul, she thought.

She gazed at him lovingly as he returned with their drinks. Shane smiled back, handed her the vodka and tonic and took the seat next to her.

He touched his glass to hers, said, 'Here's to next month, Paula, to the beginning of the new year.'

'To 1971,' Paula said.

'It *is* going to be our year, darling. Everything will be worked out with Jim. You'll be free, and just think, you'll be back here in January, not too long, really. We can start making our plans for the future. *Finally.*'

'Won't that be wonderful,' she said, but her luminous eyes darkened with incipient worry.

Shane noticed. He frowned. 'I don't like that look on your face, Paula. What's wrong?'

She shook her head, laughed gaily. 'Nothing. I'll just be glad when I've talked to Jim, settled matters with him. He's so frustrating, refusing to admit anything's wrong, burying his head in the sand. I know you probably think I've been ineffectual in dealing with the situation. However, it's hard to talk to someone who simply will not listen.' She reached out, squeezed his arm. 'Sorry. I'm going over old ground, repeating myself.'

'That's all right. I understand. But you'll tackle him when you get back.' A grin surfaced as Shane added, 'You should get him in a room, lock the door and pocket the key. That way he'll have to hear you out.'

'If necessary that's what I *will* do. I promise. I'm very determined to thrash this out once and for all. Of course, it's not a good time, with Christmas only two weeks away. On the other hand, I suppose there is never a *right* time for discussing divorce . . . emotional situations are always difficult.'

'Yes.' He leaned forward urgently. 'I know it won't be easy, Paula. I wish I could be in England with you, there in the background if you need me, but I have to go to the islands. I've no option. However –' He stopped, stared at her intently. 'I'll fly to London immediately, if you can't cope alone.'

'I know you will, but I'll manage. Really I will, Shane.' There was a small silence and then she said, 'Thank you for this past month. It's been wonderful. And having an uninterrupted period of time with you has worked miracles for me. I feel so much better than I did when I arrived in November . . . in every way.'

'So do I. And look here, Paula, it's been a triumphant month for you, if you think about it. Getting Dale Stevens's contract renewed and defeating Marriott Watson on so many of the issues at Sitex ought to make you feel good. And perhaps your success augurs well for the future. You've had a lot of sadness to deal with.'

'*You* pulled me through, Shane, you truly did. You've been so supportive and consoling. I'm stronger than I ever was because of you, your love and your understanding. And talking of Sitex . . .' Her voice trailed off lamely. She eyed him carefully and wrinkled her nose. 'I know that *you* won't laugh when I tell you this, since you're such a superstitious Celt at heart . . .' Again she stopped. Her eyes did not leave his face.

'I never laugh at you. So go on, tell me.'

Her fine mouth curved up into a light smile and she shook her head, suddenly laughing at herself. 'Well, when I first heard about the explosion in the *Emeremm III* I couldn't help thinking it was a bad omen, a sign of more hideous disasters looming ahead. And in a way I was right. Looking back, these past fourteen months have been fraught with problems . . . Min's death, the trouble in Ireland around the time of the explosion. Grandy's growing suspicions about Jonathan, Sarah's nastiness to me personally, her scheming to get her hands on the Harte boutiques. My marriage falling apart. Aunt Elizabeth's awful behaviour, the fear of scandal because of her divorce and Gianni's attitude. The continuing difficulties with Sitex, the internal fighting in that company, not to mention Jim's plane crash, then his nervous breakdown. The suddenness of Blackie's death, and Grandy going so soon after him, and all that horrendous quarrelling in the family about her will.' She pursed her lips. 'I feel as if someone put a curse on me, or rather, on Emma's family.'

Shane took her hand in his. 'In a sense, you *have* had more than your fair share. But let's be objective. First of all, Blackie was eighty-four and Emma was eighty-one, so it was to be expected that they would die soon. And they did have peaceful deaths, Paula, after long and productive lives. Secondly, you've put an end to the screaming and shouting about her will in certain quarters. You've settled many of the problems at Sitex, and Sarah's scheming against you was nipped in the bud by Emma. Jim has apparently recovered. Anthony and Sally are happily married and have a lovely son. Even your Aunt Elizabeth got off scot free and is seemingly happy with Marc Deboyne. As for your marriage, it was doomed long before the *Emeremm III* exploded.'

He put his arm around her, kissed her cheek, then drew away, looking into her face, so close to his. 'What about adding up the positives? Blackie and Emma were able to celebrate her eightieth birthday together, and they did have a wonderful eight months travelling the world. Emerald Bow won the Grand National which was a triumph for Grandpops. Edwina was reconciled with Emma, who lived long enough to see Emily married to Winston, Alexander to Maggie. There have been many happy occasions, and a lot of good things have happened along with the bad.'

'Oh Shane, you're so right. How silly I must sound.'

'Not at all, and as you said, there's nobody more superstitious than I. Still, I do try to look for the rainbow. There usually is one, you know.' His face changed slightly and he peered at her through dark eyes grown quizzical. 'When you phoned me that night in October, after the reading of Aunt Emma's will, you said she'd made me one of her heirs because she loved me like one of her own, and because of her lifelong friendship with my grandfather. And I know you keep repeating that, but –' He sat back, groped in his pocket for his cigarettes, took one, lit it. He smoked for a second or two, staring into the distance.

Observing him closely, her interest piqued, Paula probed, 'What are you getting at? Leading up to, Shane?'

'I can't help wondering if Emma had other reasons, or more precisely, *one* other reason.'

'Such as what?'

'Maybe Emma knew about us, Paula.'

'Oh Shane, I don't think so!' Paula exclaimed, giving him a curious stare. 'I'm sure she would have mentioned something to me. You know how close I was to Grandy. Anyway, she would have told Blackie, I know she would, and *he* would have certainly brought it up with you. He wouldn't have been able to resist doing so.'

Shane flicked ash into the ashtray. 'I'm not quite as positive as you are. Emma was the smartest person I've ever known. I doubt that she *would* have said anything, under the circumstances. For one thing, she wouldn't have wanted to intrude on my privacy, or yours, and she wouldn't have told Grandpops because she would have been afraid he'd worry. Let's face it, she did leave me the engagement ring. Hoping that *I* might end up giving it to *you* one day?'

Paula said, 'Perhaps she simply thought you were entitled to own the ring, that it was rightfully yours, considering from whom it came. It is very valuable. Besides, she left you the painting which was another gift from your grandfather.'

'True. But Paula, a million pounds in trust for me . . . that's one hell of a hefty present by anybody's standards.'

'Agreed.' Paula smiled at him and her bright blue eyes, flickering with violet lights, filled with tenderness and warmth. 'My grandmother cared for you very much, Shane. She thought of you as another grandson. And look here, what about Merry? Grandy was awfully generous to her, too.'

'Yes.' Shane let out a small sigh. 'I'd love to know the real truth. But I don't suppose I ever shall.' Sudden laughter bubbled in his throat and his eyes danced mischievously. 'I must confess *I* like to think that Emma *did* know about us, and that she approved.'

'Well, that's one thing I can be sure of, Shane. I know she would have given us her blessing. Also –' Paula stopped abruptly when an announcement was made over the loudspeaker. She glanced at him and pulled a face. 'That's it, darling, they're announcing the departure of my flight.' She made a motion to stand up.

Shane restrained her. He took her in his arms and whispered against her hair, 'I love you so much, Paula, remember that in the next couple of weeks.'

'How could I ever forget . . . it's part of my great strength. And I love you too, Shane, and I will for *all* of my life.'

Emily said, 'No, Jim, she hasn't arrived yet. I'm expecting her shortly, though.' Balancing the receiver between her ear and her raised shoulder, Emily zipped up her skirt as she continued to listen to Jim. He was phoning from Yorkshire and had caught her just as she was dressing.

After a few seconds, Emily exclaimed with impatience, 'I *know* the plane has landed. I checked with Heathrow and it *was* on time. It touched down at seven-thirty *exactly*. Paula has to clear customs and then get into town, you know.' Emily glanced at the clock on the bedside table. 'It's only *nine*, for heaven's sake, Jim. Look, I have to go. I'll tell her to ring you back the minute she walks in.'

'I'm about to leave the office, Emily,' Jim said. 'I'm driving up to London. Tell Paula not to bother coming to Yorkshire as she planned. I'll see her at Belgrave Square tonight. And you and Winston as well. Let's have dinner together, make it a *bon voyage* party.'

'Oh yes,' Emily muttered, 'I see what you mean, because Winston's going to Canada tomorrow.'

'Yes . . . and I'm going with him, Emily. I just hung up on him at our London office, and he's delighted that I've decided to tag along.'

'Oh,' Emily said, taken aback. 'Well, yes, it will be company for him, I suppose. I'll see you tonight, Jim. Bye.'

'Goodbye, Emily.'

She dropped the receiver in the cradle and stared at it for a moment. She grimaced, wondering if Winston was really as pleased as Jim thought. She doubted it. Neither of them had much time for Jim Fairley these days.

The phone rang again. Emily picked it up quickly, feeling quite certain it was her husband. 'Yes, Winston?' she said.

Winston laughed. 'How did you know it was me?'

'Because I was speaking to Jim a moment ago. He was looking for Paula. He told me he's going to Toronto with you. Aren't you thrilled to bits?' she asked sarcastically.

'Like hell I am,' Winston said. 'There's really no reason for him to come with me, but I couldn't very well tell him to get lost. He does own ten per cent of the new company, and he's curious about the latest acquisition, wants to look the new newspaper over. You know how odd he is these days, a real fuss pot, and frankly he's getting to be a pain in the arse.'

429

'What a bore for you, Winston.' Emily sighed. 'Look, I hope he doesn't start messing around with the *Toronto Sentinel*. Editorially, I mean. That could delay you. You'd better be back here for Christmas, Winston.'

'I will, don't worry, lovey. As for Jim, well, I shall make short shrift of him if he starts interfering.'

'He suggested we all have dinner tonight. A *bon voyage* party, he called it. I'd prefer to be alone with you, but I suppose we'll have to join them,' Emily said, her tone grudging.

'We've no choice. Anyway, I only rang to tell you about Jim coming to Canada with me. Must dash. I'm about to start a meeting.'

After saying goodbye, Emily took her suit jacket out of the armoire and slipped it on. She hurried down the stairs in the Belgrave Square maisonette, where she and Winston had been staying for the weekend, heading in the direction of the study.

The lime-and-white room with its bright yellow and peach accents was filled with cold December light on this dreary Monday morning. Yet it had a cheerful feeling because of the bowls of fresh flowers, the blazing fire, the many lamps that glowed warmly. Emily noticed that Parker had brought in a tray of coffee and three cups and saucers. Her brother was due to arrive at ten o'clock, soon after Paula was expected.

Seating herself at the desk, Emily telephoned her secretary at Genret's London office and explained she would not be coming in that day. As she hung up she heard Parker greeting Paula in the foyer. She leapt to her feet and ran out to welcome her cousin.

'What a lovely surprise to see your smiling face,' Paula said warmly, rushing to embrace Emily. 'I didn't expect you to be in London, Dumpling. What are you doing here?'

'I'll fill you in shortly.'

Paula turned to the butler, 'Tilson's keeping the luggage in the car, Parker, since he's driving me to Yorkshire later today.'

Emily said, 'Oh, er, Paula, Jim rang a bit ago. He's on his way to London. He wanted you to know that, and suggested you stay here tonight.'

Paula bit back an exclamation of annoyance and murmured, 'I see.' She smiled weakly at the butler. 'Would you please ask Tilson to bring my luggage in after all, Parker.'

'Yes, madam.' Parker went to the front door.

Paula threw her mink cape on a hall chair and stepped after Emily, following her into the study. She closed the door, leaned against it and said heatedly, 'Damn it! Jim knew I was anxious to go *straight* to Yorkshire to see Lorne and Tessa! Did he say why he's suddenly coming up to town?'

'Yes. Winston's going to Toronto tomorrow, to review the situation at the new newspaper. Jim has decided to tag along.'

'Oh no!' Paula cried, her face tightening. She walked over to the fire and sat down heavily on the sofa. Her anger flared inside her. Jim was doing a disappearing act again, as he had in October when he had gone to Ireland to stay with Edwina. Did he have a sixth sense? Did he somehow *know* when she was about to broach the subject of divorce?

Emily stood near the fireplace, scrutinizing her cousin closely. Finally she said, 'You look awfully upset, Paula. Is something wrong?'

Paula hesitated, then confided, 'I don't suppose you'll be surprised, Emily, if I tell you that Jim and I have a lot of personal problems to discuss. And resolve. I'd hoped to get down to brass tacks in the next few days. Now he's leaving. *Again*. Unless I can persuade him to cancel the trip with Winston, I'm going to have to wait until he gets back from Canada to talk to him.'

Emily lowered herself on to the sofa and patted her hand. 'I've known for a long time that things were difficult between the two of you, Paula. And you *should* talk to Jim – about a divorce, if you want my opinion. Winston happens to agree.'

Paula searched Emily's face and with alertness. 'So it's that apparent, is it?'

'Oh no, not to everyone, but certainly to those closest to you.'

'My parents?' Paula asked swiftly, sitting up straighter.

'Your father is aware there is great strain and he's concerned about the situation, but I'm not sure about Aunt Daisy. I mean, I don't think she realizes how bad it is, Paula. She's so nice, always making allowances for everyone.'

Paula sighed wearily. 'Do you think I can persuade him not to go to Canada?'

'No, I definitely don't. Because of those shares Grandy left him, Jim feels very much a part of the new company, and he wants to get his fingers into the pie. He's a bit of a meddler, these days.'

'I know.' Paula rubbed her face, feeling suddenly fatigued. She blinked. 'I hate these overnight transatlantic flights.'

Emily nodded. She took a deep breath, then said, 'You wouldn't be able to go to Yorkshire today anyway, Paula. Alexander needs you here in London. As a matter of fact, he'll be arriving in a few minutes to have a meeting with us.'

'What's happened?' Instantly, a look of comprehension flashed. 'Not Jonathan?'

'Yes, I'm afraid so.'

'Tell me all about it.' Paula stared at Emily anxiously, thoughts of Jim and the divorce momentarily swept to one side.

'Alexander prefers to fill you in, Paula. He asked me to ask you to wait until he gets here. It's rather involved. And that's why I'm in London – because of Jonathan. Alexander wanted me to be here for the meeting with you. Actually, Alexander and I have thrashed the situation to bits for the past two weeks –'

'You mean you've known all this time and you didn't let me know!'

'We wanted to be sure, and get a plan together, also we had to talk to Henry Rossiter and John Crawford. We needed their advice. We're going to have to take drastic steps, Paula.'

'Is it that bad?'

'Pretty serious. However, Sandy and I have it well under control. Sarah is involved to a certain extent.'

'As we thought.' Paula sighed. Her dismay increased.

The door opened quietly and Alexander walked into the study. 'Morning Emily, welcome back, Paula.' He came over to the sofa, kissed them both and took a chair facing them. 'I wouldn't mind a cup of coffee, Emily,' he said to his sister. 'I walked over from Eaton Square and the weather's beastly this morning. I'm frozen.'

'Yes, of course.' Emily lifted the silver pot, poured. 'What about you, Paula?'

'Yes, thanks, I might as well.' Her eyes were penetrating as they rested on Alexander. 'You ought to have let me know.'

'To be honest, I thought about doing so, Paula. Emily and I discussed it at great length, and we finally decided there wasn't much point. You would have worried and you couldn't have contributed very much from New York. Besides, you had your hands full with Sitex. I didn't want to drag you back to London. Furthermore, I only just got to the root of it all at the end of last week. Well, more or less.'

Paula nodded. 'Tell me everything, Sandy.'

'Well, here goes. Philip's plan worked. Malcolm Perring helped me to flush Jonathan out, but I had another source of information. It was this source that enabled me to really nail him. But I'm jumping ahead of myself. I'd better begin at the beginning.'

'Please,' Paula said.

'Malcolm Perring *did* eventually come up with the perfect property deal for Harte Enterprises. He took it to Jonathan – who expressed considerable interest. Then nothing happened. Malcolm kept ringing him over a two week period, and Jonathan stalled. However, in the middle of November, Jonathan invited Malcolm to come over to the office for a meeting. Apparently Jonathan waffled on for a while about it being an excellent deal, but finally he turned it down. He said Harte Enterprises could not handle it at that particular time. He suggested Malcolm take the deal to a man called Stanley Jervis at a new company, Stonewall Properties. He explained that Jervis was an old friend, very reliable, and in the market for big real estate deals.'

'Don't tell me,' Paula muttered, 'Stonewall Properties belongs to Jonathan Ainsley.'

'*Correct*. And get this – Sebastian Cross is his partner.'

'That odious man. Ugh!' Paula shuddered.

'Sarah also has money in the company,' Alexander told her. He shook his head. 'Foolish girl.'

'She's been duped by Jonathan again, just as she was when she was a child,' Paula remarked softly.

'Precisely,' Emily interjected. 'Only this time there are far reaching consequences for her.'

'Yes.' Paula scowled in perplexity, now demanded, 'But how did Malcolm Perring manage to find all this out?'

Alexander answered, 'He didn't. I did. Malcolm Perring went along with Jonathan's idea, since that was the whole purpose of our plan – catching him with his hand in the till, so to speak. Malcolm had two meetings with this Jervis chap, and then suddenly Sebastian Cross was on the scene. He's pretty much up front in the company now, even though Jonathan is obviously hiding behind straw men, his men, since his name doesn't appear anywhere.'

Alexander lit a cigarette, continued, 'Malcolm started negotiations with Cross and Jervis, playing them along, inducing them to believe he was prepared to close the deal with Stonewall. He didn't take to either of them, and suspected that the company was shaky financially. He did a bit of investigating, talked to people around the town, and his suspicions were soon confirmed. As planned, Malcolm began to back off, much to the astonishment of Jervis and Cross. They were scared of losing the deal, and started to boast about the big business transactions they had recently handled. Malcolm brought this information to me. I went through the files in our real estate division late one night, and discovered that *we* could have made all of those deals. Jonathan had passed them over to Stonewall. That clinched it for me, Paula. I knew positively that he was as guilty as hell. Malcolm finally cut off negotiations with Stonewall, explaining that another real estate company had come in with an enormous offer, one which his partners were insisting the firm accept.'

'And they bought it?' Paula asked.

'They had no choice. I was ready to swoop down on Jonathan and then quite unexpectedly some other information fell into my lap. And within forty-eight hours I had enough on Jonathan to hang him.'

'Where did the new information come from?' Paula leaned forward eagerly, riddled with curiosity.

'John Cross.'

'Alexander, you can't be serious!' Paula's astonishment was evident. '*John Cross*,' she repeated and her eyes widened as she drew back, looked at Alexander askance. 'I don't believe it.'

'It's the truth.'

'But why would he confide in you?'

'Actually, Paula, John Cross was looking to confide in *you*. He only got in touch with me because you weren't around. He asked me to come to Leeds to see him . . . he was in St James's Hospital.'

'Oh,' Paula said. 'What was wrong with him? Was he very sick?'

'Poor old man,' he murmured. 'He died, Paula. John Cross died just a few days after I saw him. It was cancer, I'm afraid. He was riddled with it, and obviously in great pain.'

'Oh Sandy, how awful.' Paula pursed her lips. 'Poor man. I wouldn't wish that on anyone. And he wasn't so bad. Weak, a little misguided maybe, and under the thumb of that rotten son of his.'

Alexander cleared his throat. 'I immediately drove to Leeds, and went to see John Cross at the hospital. I was with him for almost four hours. The doctor allowed me to stay that length of time, because – well, he *was* dying. John Cross talked about you for a while. He said he had a great deal of respect for you, Paula, admired your honesty and fairness. He then explained that you'd been very courteous to him in the autumn of 1969 when you saw him in London. I told him I knew about your meeting. He commented about your patience and your kindness to him that day, and said he understood why you hadn't been interested in re-opening negotiations for the acquisition of Aire Communications . . . because his company no longer had any real assets since the building had been sold. That's when he confided that Stonewall Properties had bought the Aire building for five hundred thousand pounds. Apparently his son persuaded him to sell. He insisted that he'd been cheated by them, because the building was worth a million at least. I had to agree with him. John Cross became very upset, and he said this to me, Paula: "Imagine my shock when I discovered six months ago that it was my son who robbed me, who ruined me, ruined any chance for Aire Communications to make a recovery. I was heartbroken that Sebastian could do such a terrible thing to me. My son . . . my only child." He began to weep, and I can't say I blamed him.'

'What a ghastly thing to happen to him . . . so Grandy was always right about Jonathan . . . she was very suspicious of him at the time of the Aire Communications negotiations,' Paula said.

'And with good reason.' Alexander crossed his legs, sat back. 'Mr Cross wanted *you* to know, *us* to know, that Jonathan was Sebastian's partner and that he had been working against Emma Harte for years. He mumbled something about despising family treachery, said he wanted to die with an easy conscience.'

Paula sighed, rubbed her weary face. 'What else did he reveal about Stonewall Properties?'

'Not a lot, at least, nothing I didn't already know through Malcolm. Mr Cross confirmed that Jonathan had been moving deals away from Harte Enterprises and into Stonewall, and he confessed that his son had bled him dry, taken every penny he had. The old man was very bitter when he explained that it was only because of his sister's generosity that he was able to have a private room at St James's, and private doctors. You see, Paula, old Mr Cross was destitute.'

Paula sank back against the cushions and for a reason she would never fully understand her eyes filled with tears. She coughed behind her hand and reached for one of Alexander's cigarettes. 'How sad that he had to end his days in such a frightful way . . . betrayed by his own son.'

Emily announced, 'Sebastian Cross is a bastard. And Jonathan Ainsley is no better, is he, Sandy?'

'No.' Alexander gave Paula a long look. 'John Cross told me something else, and this is the worst part of all. However, because of it, I *am* going to get Jonathan. Really *get* him, Paula. In an effort to bail out Stonewall Properties, which is in grave financial difficulties, Jonathan borrowed a lot of money – against his shares in Harte Enterprises.'

Paula was momentarily dumbfounded and thrown off balance. She gaped at her cousins, then gasped, 'But he's not allowed to do that.'

'Exactly!' Emily cried. 'Don't you see, because he did that we can nail him . . . actually, he's nailed himself to the cross, hasn't he?'

Paula nodded, asked sharply, 'Are you sure there's no mistake?'

'None,' Alexander replied. 'John Cross knew about the loan, don't ask me how, but he did. He wouldn't reveal his source, nor did he realize the true importance of his information to us. He merely wanted to alert us to our cousin's activities. In a funny way, I think he blamed Jonathan for his son's transgressions, although I'm not so sure he's correct there. However, he *was* able to give me the name of the finance company who made the loan to Jonathan. Obviously Jonathan couldn't borrow from a bank – they'd want to know too much.'

'I can't believe he would be so foolhardy,' Paula said. 'He's fully aware he's not permitted to use his shares in Harte Enterprises as collateral, nor can he sell those shares unless it's to another shareholder –'

'That's right,' Alexander interrupted. 'He can only sell them to me, Emily or Sarah. Those are the company laws, which are very precisely spelled out in the articles of incorporation by Grandy. She wanted to ensure that Harte Enterprises remained a private company, a family concern, with no strangers or outsiders involved, and she made damned certain that that was the way it would be.'

'Which finance company did he get involved with?'

'Financial Investment and Loan.'

'Good God, Sandy, they're crooks,' Paula exclaimed, horrified. 'Everyone knows that they're a shady outfit. How could he be so stupid?'

'I told you, he couldn't go to the bank. A bank would want to know everything as far as those shares are concerned, as would a reputable finance company.'

'How much did he borrow and against how many shares?' Paula demanded.

'He put up seven per cent of his shares, just under half of his sixteen per cent, and he raised four million pounds against them. However, the loan company gave him a poor deal. Those shares are worth twice that much, except, of course, that they cannot be sold to anyone – except to one of us. Still, the finance company weren't aware of that at the time they made the loan. They are now.'

Paula experienced a sudden sense of relief and her troubled expression lifted. 'You paid off his note and retrieved the shares, didn't you, Sandy?'

'I did. Last Thursday Emily and I met with the managing director of that dubious little company, along with Henry Rossiter and John Crawford. It was all very troublesome, and there were a lot of strong words, heated arguments and general unpleasantness. We returned again on Friday, all four of us, and I paid them back their four million pounds and they returned the shares. There was some interest due, but Henry and John were adamant, refused to let me pay that. They told the managing director to go after Jonathan. And there you have all the gory details.'

'Where did you and Emily get the four million from? Did you use your own money?'

'No. John Crawford figured out a way for Harte Enterprises to buy the shares back, rather than an individual. As you know, Paula, Grandy drew up a number of legal papers in regard to Harte Enterprises just before she died. I have extraordinary powers, a free hand in many instances, especially if the overall good of the company is involved. John and Henry agreed that this situation with Jonathan was such an instance. However, I told them that Emily and I are perfectly willing to purchase those shares if they decide, at a future date, that this is the proper thing to do.'

'I see.' Paula stood up and walked to the fireplace. A thought struck her. 'Are Sarah's shares involved?'

'No. Stupid she might be, but she would never risk her shares,' Alexander replied.

'What are you going to do about Jonathan and Sarah?' Paula asked, her eyes sharpening.

'I intend to fire them both. At noon today. I've called a meeting. I'd like you to be present, Paula.'

47

There was a sanguine air about Jonathan Ainsley as he walked into Alexander's office at Harte Enterprises.

Being an egotist who was convinced he was smarter and shrewder than anyone else, it never occurred to him that his double dealing might have been uncovered.

'Hello, Alexander,' he said, strolling nonchalantly across the room, shaking his cousin's hand. 'Sarah told me she's been asked to come to this meeting too. What's it all about then?'

Alexander sat down in the chair behind his desk and said, 'There are some important matters I have to discuss. It won't take long.' Alexander's clear blue eyes, so intelligent and honest, rested on Jonathan, but only briefly. He shuffled the papers on his desk, filled with contempt and loathing for the other man.

Walking over to the sofa, Jonathan sat down, lit a cigarette and lolled back against the leather cushions. He glanced at the door as Emily came in, and gave her a warm smile. This was entirely fraudulent, since he disliked Emily. But the feeling in no way matched his virulent hatred for Paula, and that hatred flared when she hove into view, stood in the doorway a split second later.

Rising, he greeted Emily with a degree of cordiality, but his voice turned a shade colder as he said to Paula, 'You're not involved in the day-to-day running of Harte Enterprises, so what are you doing here?'

'Alexander invited me since I have a family matter to talk about.'

'Ah yes, family matters do seem to preoccupy you these days, don't they, Paula?' he said, sardonically. He lowered himself into a chair, muttering, 'Not the will again, I hope.'

'No, not that,' Paula replied, her voice calm, betraying nothing. She followed Emily over to the sofa and sat down. Ever since his bitter outburst at the reading of the will, Jonathan had dropped all pretence with her. He did not bother to conceal his animosity and a minute ago she had seen the antipathy flickering. She had also noted that his anxiety had slipped through the bland facade he was trying so hard to hold in place. Paula looked down at her hands, half smiling to herself. Her presence had unnerved him, try though he might not to show it. After a second or two she lifted her head, studied him surreptitiously, her eyes objective. How attractive his appearance was. So fair of colouring and fine of feature. Yes, he *was* very clean cut, and there were times, such as now, that he had the look of an innocent choir boy. Yet she knew he was a schemer who would stop at nothing to gain his own ends.

Sarah swept in grandly, scanned the room. 'Hello, everyone,' she murmured coolly, and then spoke to Alexander directly: 'I'm in rather a hurry. I have a luncheon date at one o'clock with a very important buyer. I hope this isn't going to take long.'

'No, it won't,' Alexander said. 'I intend to make our meeting as short as possible.'

'Oh good.' Sarah swung away from the desk, looked at Emily and Paula on the sofa, and purposely chose a chair near Jonathan. Sitting back she offered Alexander a sweet smile.

He stared at her for the longest moment. Not an eyelash flickered and his face was suddenly cold and implacable. Sarah's smile slipped and she frowned at him, obviously puzzled by his manner.

'It seems odd to me,' Alexander began, 'that Stonewall Properties has such severe, such grave, financial problems.' He focused on Jonathan. 'Bad management, do you suppose?'

Jonathan felt a tightening of his stomach muscles and all of his senses were alerted for trouble. Secure in the knowledge that he could not be linked to Stonewall, he managed to keep a composed demeanour. He shrugged. 'How would I know. And don't tell me you've dragged us here to discuss another company?'

'Why yes, that is one of the reasons.' Alexander leaned forward, peering at Sarah. 'Were you aware that Stonewall Properties is likely to go belly up in the near future?'

Sarah opened her mouth and closed it swiftly. The disturbing information about the secret company, which she had invested so much money in, had stunned her. She did not doubt its truth, since it came from the reliable Alexander. She was anxious to speak to Jonathan alone, but she dreaded tackling him. He could be so difficult and now it was fear of his wrath that made her hold her tongue.

Alexander continued to regard her unwaveringly. She had paled under his fixed observation and her eyes were suddenly alarmed. He knew Sarah would crack if he increased the pressure.

But he addressed the room at large. 'What really baffles me, though, is how they managed to get into this state. Stonewall have closed an amazing number of genuinely good deals. I can't imagine why they are floundering so badly. Unless, of course, somebody has had a hand in the till.'

Rattled by this remark, Sarah cried, 'Do you think that's possible, and if –'

Jonathan interjected peremptorily, 'Now look here, Alexander, let's forget about the problems at Stonewall and get on with our own business.'

'Oh, but Stonewall *is* our business,' Alexander said in a murderously quiet voice. 'And you know it, since Stonewall Properties is your company, Jonathan.'

There was an involuntary gasp from Sarah and then she shrank back in the chair.

Jonathan laughed dismissively and threw Alexander a look that was both challenging and threatening. 'What bloody nonsense you do talk. I've never heard anything so preposterous.'

'Jonathan, I know everything there is to know about Stonewall. The company is jointly owned by you and Sebastian Cross, and Sarah has invested a great deal of money in it. It's run by Cross and Stanley Jervis, along with a number of straw men put in there by you. Cross and you formed the company in 1968. You've been channelling real estate deals intended for Harte Enterprises into your own company. You've lost us an enormous amount of business, important and highly profitable business, Jonathan, and you queered Grandy's pitch when she was in negotiations with Aire Communications. I'm appalled. You have been disloyal and a traitor to this company. You have betrayed Grandy's trust in you, and therefore I have no alternative but to –'

'Just try to prove it!' Jonathan shouted angrily, leaping to his feet. He slapped both his hands on the edge of Alexander's desk and bent over it, glaring into his cousin's face. 'You'll have the greatest difficulty doing so. There is not one shred of evidence to support or substantiate these ridiculous accusations.'

'You're absolutely wrong. I have all the evidence I need,' Alexander shot back evenly, but his tone was glacial, his look condemning. He patted the file of folders on his desk, which in fact had nothing to do with Stonewall, and said, with a thin smile, 'It's *all* here, Jonathan. Then of course there is your partner in –' Alexander lifted his hands and shrugged '– shall we *say* crime, for want of a better word. Yes, there she sits in stunned silence . . . Sarah Lowther.'

'Now you're trying to bring poor Sarah into this plot of yours,' Jonathan shouted. 'Yes, that's what it is – a plot to discredit us both. You've always been out to get me, Alexander Barkstone, ever since we were kids. And Sarah as well. But you're not going to get away with it. I'll see you in hell first. I shall fight for my rights, and for Sarah's. So just beware,' he threatened.

Alexander leaned back in the chair, and his blue eyes, so cold and hard a second before, instantly changed when he gave Sarah a look of pity. 'Yes, *poor* Sarah indeed,' he remarked softly. 'You've been duped, I'm afraid. Your money has gone down the drain, Sarah, sad for you really, but there's nothing you can do about it now.'

'A-A-Alexander,' Sarah stammered, 'I-I-I don't –'

'Be quiet, and let *me* do all the talking, Sarah dear. He's a crafty devil. He'll trap you into saying the wrong thing.' Jonathan brought his blazing eyes back to the other man. His lip curled. 'You're the biggest bastard alive!'

'All right, that's enough!' Alexander was on his feet behind the desk. 'Don't you dare call *me* a bastard.'

'Cut you to the quick, have I?' Jonathan laughed nastily. 'But that's what you undoubtedly are, and so is that sister of yours. You would do well to remember that it is *your* mother who sleeps around, not mine.'

'You're fired!' Alexander exclaimed, his anger spiralling into pure rage.

'You can't fire me.' Jonathan threw back his head and guffawed. 'I'm a shareholder in this company and –'

'Your holdings in this company have been considerably reduced,' Alexander interrupted in a steadier tone, taking full control of himself. 'By exactly seven per cent.' He lifted the top folder and took out the share certificates, waved them under Jonathan's nose. 'I just retrieved these . . . last Friday. It cost Harte Enterprises exactly four million pounds to pay off your loan to the finance company you borrowed from, but I was happy to do it in order to get these shares back.'

Jonathan had blanched. He stood gaping at Alexander in stupefaction. For once in his life he could think of nothing to say. For a moment he thought he was finished, and then he exclaimed, with a scornful smirk, 'I still own nine per cent of this company. Furthermore, there's no way you can fire me. Under the company laws, a shareholder cannot be fired.'

'Grandy made that ruling in 1968, when she drew her will and divided her one hundred per cent between the four of us. However, *she* still owned her one hundred per cent until the day she died, and therefore she owned the company outright. And as the sole owner of Harte Enterprises, Emma Harte could do anything she wanted, as you well know. And so, just before she went to Australia, Grandy changed all of the company laws. Actually what she did was to reconstruct the company and caused new articles of incorporation to be drawn. Under the new company laws, I, as managing director, chairman of the board and majority shareholder, can do practically anything I wish. I have extraordinary powers. I can buy out a shareholder, if that shareholder is agreeable. I can hire. I can fire.' Alexander leaned over his desk and impaled Jonathan with his eyes. 'And so I am firing *you*.' He looked past Jonathan, fixed his gaze on Sarah. 'You're also fired, Sarah. Your behaviour has been as shoddy as Jonathan's.'

Sarah could not speak. She seemed to have turned to stone in the chair.

'We'll see about all this bloody nonsense,' Jonathan railed. 'I'm going to pay a visit to John Crawford the minute I leave here, and I'm taking Sarah with me. There's –'

'Do go and see him by all means,' Alexander cut in, dropping the share certificates on the desk. He slipped his hands into his trouser pockets and rocked back and forth on his heels. 'He'll be perfectly happy to confirm what I've just told you. As a matter of fact, he does want a word with you anyway. He was with me at the two meetings I had with Financial Investment and Loan, and John was a little bit disturbed about the interest you owe to them. They're a shady bunch, Jonathan. You'd better pay up and smartly.'

Jonathan opened his mouth, and then snapped it shut, glaring at his cousin.

Sarah, having partially recovered, hurried to the desk. She appealed to Alexander tearfully, 'I haven't done anything with my shares ... I haven't done *anything* wrong. Why are you firing me?'

'Because you *have* done something wrong, Sarah. You invested in a company which was in direct competition with the real estate division of Harte Enterprises. You've been disloyal, a traitor like Jonathan. I'm sorry, but as I just told you, I cannot condone your behaviour.'

'But I love Lady Hamilton Clothes,' she gasped, and began to sob.

'You should have thought of that when you threw your lot in with your reckless cousin here,' Alexander answered steadily, quite unmoved by her tears. 'And God in heaven only knows why you ever did.'

Jonathan cried irately: 'I intend to take this matter to another solicitor. I'm not convinced those papers Grandmother drew are quite as legal as you seem to believe.'

'I can assure you that they are ... *very very legal*. John Crawford and Henry Rossiter, as directors of Harte Enterprises, approved them, as did I. Don't try to challenge anything Emma Harte did, because believe you me you won't get anywhere. She outsmarted you.'

Suddenly Jonathan went berserk. He yelled, 'I'll get you for this, you bloody sod!' He swivelled on his heels and shook his fist at Paula, 'And you too, you bitch!'

'*Get out*.' Alexander made a move towards Jonathan. 'Before I personally take you by the scruff of your neck and throw you out.'

Paula jumped to her feet and ran to Alexander, put a restraining hand on his arm.

She stared at Jonathan and Sarah, pressing back her disgust and disdain. She said, very quietly, 'How *could* you? How could you do it to *her*? She who gave you so much, who was so fair and generous. She suspected you, Jonathan, for a long time before she died, and you, Sarah, latterly. And yet she gave you both the benefit of the doubt because she had no real proof. She did not rescind your trust funds, nor did she take back the shares in Harte Enterprises she so generously gave you.' Paula shook her head sorrowfully. 'You are both everything Grandy loathed and despised ... treacherous, devious and dishonest, and liars and cheats besides.'

Neither of them spoke. Jonathan's face was ringed with bitter hatred, and Sarah looked as if she was going to pass out from shock.

Paula's voice took on a new note, one of calm resoluteness as she said, 'I'm afraid I'm not as forgiving as Emma Harte was. She tolerated your fathers long after their treacherous treatment of her. But I will not tolerate either of you. I only have this to add ... neither of you are welcome at family gatherings in the future. Please remember that.'

Sarah, still white and trembling, became hysterical at Paula's words of banishment. She turned on Jonathan and cried accusingly, 'This is all your fault. I should never have listened to you. I've not only lost my money, but Lady Hamilton Clothes and the family as well.' She started to sob anew.

Jonathan ignored her. He leaned closer to Paula, his eyes baleful, his face contorted in a mask of hatred. 'I'll get you for this, Paula Fairley. Sebastian and I will bloody well get you!'

Alexander finally lost his temper completely. He sprang past Paula, grabbed Jonathan's arm roughly, and dragged him to the door. 'I think you'd better leave before I give you the thrashing of your life.'

Struggling out of his cousin's tenacious grip, Jonathan yelled, 'Keep your filthy hands off me, you sneaky sod. And don't think you're immune. Don't forget what I said. We'll get you too, Barkstone. If it takes all my life I'm going to make certain you get yours.' Jonathan flung open the door and stormed out.

Sarah ran to Alexander, who still stood near the doorway. 'What am I going to do?' she wailed, brushing her hands over her wet face.

'I really don't know, Sarah,' Alexander answered in a cold and quiet voice. 'I really don't know.'

She looked at him helplessly, then brought her gaze to Paula and finally to Emily. She knew from their closed faces that her plight was hopeless. Cursing Jonathan under her breath, she found her handbag and left the office as quickly as she could, striving to quell her tears.

Alexander walked across the room, seated himself behind his desk and took a cigarette. He saw that his hands shook as he struck a match and lit it, and he was not surprised. 'That was all rather unpleasant,' he said. 'But no worse than I expected. I have to admit, I couldn't help feeling Sarah was in over her head and without knowing it.'

'Yes,' Paula agreed, and took the chair opposite his desk. She turned and glanced at Emily. 'There was a moment when I actually felt sorry for her, but it passed when I thought of Gran, and the wonderful things she did for them all their lives.'

'I didn't have one ounce of sympathy for Sarah!' Emily cried indignantly. 'She deserved everything she got. As for Jonathan – he's despicable.'

'He'll try and make trouble but he won't succeed,' Alexander announced. 'He'll huff and he'll puff but he'll never blow our house down. All he did was make idle threats.' Alexander grinned. 'I couldn't believe it when he shook his fist at you, just like the villain in a Victorian drama.'

Paula laughed nervously. 'I know what you mean. On the other hand, Sandy, I don't think we should dismiss Jonathan quite so lightly. Not with Sebastian Cross – my enemy – in the background, egging him on to do heaven knows what. I've told you before, I have a very low opinion of Cross.'

Alexander sat back, observing her quietly, musing on her words.

Emily hurried over and stood next to Paula. She said, 'Honestly, Alexander, Paula's right. We've not heard the last of Jonathan Ainsley, Sarah Lowther and Sebastian Cross – not by a long shot.'

Leaning over his desk, Alexander smiled warmly and confidently. 'Forget the three of them, please. There's nothing they can do to us . . . not now or in the future. They're quite powerless.'

Paula was not so sure about this, but she said, 'Spoken like a true grandson of Emma Harte's.' Pushing aside her worry, adopting a positive attitude, she exclaimed, 'And as she would have said, let's get on with it. We've got a lot more to accomplish today. Now, Sandy, who do you have in mind to run Lady Hamilton Clothes?'

'As a matter of fact I was thinking of putting Maggie in there. She has a good business head, and with a bit of help from the two of you . . .' He stopped, looked at his sister and his cousin. 'Well?'

'It's a terrific idea!' Emily cried.

'I second that,' said Paula.

48

The old nursery at Pennistone Royal, slightly shabby though it was, glowed with comfort and warmth. A huge fire crackled in the grate, lamps shone brightly and there was a feeling of gaiety and lightheartedness in the air.

It was early evening on a cold Saturday in January of 1971. Emily, sitting on the window seat observing Paula and her children, was filled with delight as she witnessed the happy scene being enacted in front of her. Paula was so very carefree tonight, and her eyes, which had been unusually troubled of late, sparkled with laughter. There was a new tranquillity in her face, and as always when she was with the children, her demeanour was gentle and loving.

The twins, who would be two years old next month, had already been bathed and were dressed in their night clothes. Paula was holding their hands, and the three of them formed a circle in the centre of the floor.

'All right, ready, set, go!' Paula cried and slowly began to move, taking small steps, leading the children around and around. Their freshly scrubbed faces shone with joy and their smiles were vividly bright, their eyes glowing.

Paula now began to sing: 'Half a pound of tuppenny rice, half a pound of treacle. Mix it up and make it nice. *Pop* goes the weasel!'

As they came to a standstill, Lorne broke free and flopped down on to the floor, giggling and laughing and rolling about. 'Pop!' he shouted loudly. 'Pop! Pop!' He continued to chortle and kick his legs in the air with the abandonment of a frisky puppy.

Tessa, clinging to Paula's hand, stared down at him and then up at her mother. 'Silly,' Tessa said. 'Rorn . . . silly.'

Paula crouched on her haunches and smiled into the solemn little face regarding her so intently. 'Not silly, darling. Lorne is happy. We're all happy after such a lovely day. Try and say Lorne, sweetheart.'

Tessa nodded. 'Rorn,' she repeated, unable as yet to properly pronounce her brother's name.

Paula's heart was bursting with love. She reached out and stroked the child's porcelain cheek with one finger. The green eyes surveying her reminded her of chartreuse liqueur that had only been slightly diluted, so startling was their depth of colour. She took Tessa in her arms and hugged her close, rumpling her burnished red-gold curls. 'Oh you're such a darling, Tess.'

Tessa clung to Paula for a moment longer and then wriggled free. She pushed her face at her mother, craning her neck, and pursing her lips. 'Mama . . . Mama,' she said and made small smacking sounds with her mouth. Paula smiled, leaned into her daughter and kissed her, ruffled her hair again. 'Run and give Aunty Emily a kiss, sweetheart. It's well past your bed time.'

Paula watched Tessa march purposefully across the floor. In her white flannel nightdress and blue robe she looked adorable, resembled a cherub. Turning to Lorne, Paula knelt on the floor and began to tickle him. He squirmed and kicked, enjoying every minute of the game, his peals of laughter slicing through the gentle silence. Finally Paula stopped and lifted him to her. She stroked his flushed cheek and swept back his hair, which was slightly darker red than his sister's, and endeavoured to calm him. 'Mummy's the silly one, Lorne, getting you so excited and just when it's time for bed.'

He cocked his head to one side and looked at her with great interest. 'Me,' he said. 'Mam . . . Mam.' Lorne now held up his face to be kissed, pursing his lips in the way his sister had done. This was a nightly ritual with both children, and Paula took his head between her hands and kissed his cheek, the tip of his nose, and his damp rosy lips. She drew back. 'You're such a good boy, Lorne,' she murmured, straightening the collar of his pyjama jacket, overwhelmed by tenderness for her little boy.

Lorne reached up, touched her face and then flopped against her, grabbing her arms tightly with his small hands, rocking to and fro. Paula held him close, also rocking and smoothing her hand over his copper head shining so brightly in the firelight. But after a few seconds she gently disentangled herself, rose and pulled him up off the floor with her. Taking his hand, she walked him over to Emily and Tessa who were cuddling on the window seat.

'The Sandman's about to arrive, Aunty Emily,' Paula announced, making this sound most important. 'Shall we go into the bedroom to welcome him?'

'What a lovely idea,' Emily said, taking Tessa's hand, helping her down off the seat. 'I haven't seen the Sandman for years.'

Together the four of them went into the adjoining bedroom where a small night light glowed on the table between the two beds.

'Off with your dressing gowns,' Paula instructed. 'And into bed with you both. Quick! We don't want the Sandman to go away because two little poppets dawdle.'

Tessa and Lorne struggled with their belts, and Paula and Emily went to their assistance. The twins scrambled into their beds and Paula pulled up the bedclothes, tucked them in and gave them a kiss in turn.

'Take a seat, Aunty Emily, and be very very quiet or you'll frighten the Sandman away,' Paula cautioned as she pulled up a stool and sat down between the two beds.

'I'll be as quiet as a mouse,' Emily whispered, going along with the game, seating herself on the bottom of Lorne's bed.

Paula gazed at her children. 'Sssh!' she said softly, bringing a finger to her lips.

'Pom,' Tessa said, 'pom . . . Mam.'

'All right, I'll say the Sandman's poem for you, but snuggle down, and close your eyes both of you.'

Each child did as she said. Lorne put his thumb in his mouth and Tessa clutched at the white lamb lying next to her in the bed, and began to suck on its ear.

Paula began to recite in the softest of voices:

'The Sandman has the swiftest wings
And shoes that are made of gold,
He calls on you when the first star sings
When the night is not very old.
He carries a tiny silver spoon
And a bucket made of night,
He fills your eyes with bits of moon
And stardust that's shiny and bright.
He takes you on a ship that sails
Through the land of dreams and joys,
And tells you many wonderous tales
Of dragons and magical toys.
So come now and rest your sleepyhead
And close your eyes very tight,
For should you stay awake instead
The Sandman won't pass by tonight.'

Paula stopped, stood up and went to peer at the twins. Both were already fast asleep. A tender smile flickered on her mouth. They had had an unusually hectic day and were worn out. Gently she kissed each of them and moved the stool out of the way. Emily went to Lorne and Tessa, also bent and kissed them, and the two young women crept out of the bedroom on their tiptoes.

By seven o'clock Paula was beginning to wonder what had happened to Jim. Emily had left over half an hour ago, after having a quick drink with her in the library. She had seated herself at the desk, intending to do some paperwork, but her worries had intruded.

It was the fifth of January. The day she had mentally set aside to have a serious talk with Jim. Her parents and Philip had returned to London three days ago, after spending Christmas at Pennistone Royal. They had already departed for their skiing holiday in Chamonix.

Christmas had been exceptionally quiet. Randolph and Vivienne had accepted an invitation to visit Anthony and Sally at Clonloughlin, and the O'Neills had made a last-minute decision to join Shane in Barbados. Emily and Winston, along with Alexander and Maggie, had come to stay for a few days, and the entire Kallinski clan had driven over on Christmas Eve. But the whole holiday period had been sad and depressing for everyone without Emma. She had always been the catalyst, the mover and the doer, and without her things were not the same.

Paula had somehow struggled through, making a supreme effort for the children and her parents, whilst counting the hours until today. And then Jim had suddenly rushed off to the newspaper this morning before she had had a chance to open her mouth.

Suddenly Paula swung around in the chair and jumped up as she heard the sound of a car on the gravel driveway outside. She stepped up to the window behind her chair, cupped her hands against the glass and peered out. The light over the back door shone brightly, clearly illuminating Jim's Aston Martin.

With a small intake of breath she held herself rigid as her eyes fell on the pair of skis sticking out of one of the back windows. So that was why he was so late. He had gone to Long Meadow first – to collect his skiing gear. He was going to Chamonix after all.

It's now or never, Paula muttered under her breath and flew across the library. Wrenching open the door she stepped out into the Stone Hall, waiting for him, suppressing her exasperation.

Jim came in a moment later and headed in the direction of the main staircase at the other end of the hall.

'I'm in here, Jim,' she exclaimed.

Startled, he pivoted swiftly, stood regarding her with uncertainty.

'Can you spare me a few minutes?' she asked, striving to bring her voice down to a lower pitch, not wanting to alert him or scare him off.

'Why not? I was just going up to change. Had a rather hectic day,' he announced, walking toward her. 'Surprisingly busy for Saturday.'

Not so surprising, she thought, stepping back, opening the door wider.

You've been clearing your desk in readiness for your imminent departure. But she said none of this.

Jim strolled past her into the library, without kissing her or making any gesture of affection. There was a great deal of strain between them and this had lately turned into real coldness.

Paula closed the door firmly, thought of locking it, but changed her mind. She followed him over to the fireplace.

Sitting down in a wing chair, Paula glanced up at him hovering near the fire. 'Dinner's not until eight. You've plenty of time to freshen up. Make yourself comfortable, Jim, let's chat for a while.'

Throwing her an odd look, he nevertheless took the other chair, pulled out his cigarettes and put one in his mouth. After lighting it he smoked in silence for a second, staring ahead at the fire. Then he said, 'How was your day?'

'Fine. I spent it with the children. Emily came over for lunch and stayed all afternoon. Winston had gone to a football match.'

Jim said nothing.

Paula kept her voice very low as she said, 'So you *are* going to Chamonix.'

'Yes.' He did not look at her.

'When are you leaving?'

He cleared his throat. 'I thought I'd drive up to London late tonight, around ten or eleven. The roads will be virtually empty. I can make it in record time. That way I can catch the first flight to Geneva tomorrow.'

Anger rushed through her, but she clamped down on it, knowing that she had to keep a cool head and must not inflame him if she was to accomplish anything. She said, 'Please don't go, Jim. At least not for a few days.'

'*Why?*' Now he swung his head, levelled his silvery-grey eyes on her and a blond brow lifted in surprise. He said, 'You're going to New York.'

'Yes, but not until the eighth or ninth. I told you, when you came back from Canada, that I wanted to discuss our problems. You put me off because it was Christmas and we were expecting guests. You promised you wouldn't go to Chamonix until we had settled things, thrashed out our problems.'

'*Your* problems, not mine, Paula.'

'*Our problems.*'

'I beg to disagree. If there are any problems in our marriage you have created them. For over a year now you've been looking for trouble, insisting we had difficulties when we didn't have any. Also, you are the one who has . . . left the marital bed, not I. You, and you alone, Paula, are the one who has brought about the present untenable situation.' He smiled faintly, eyeing her more closely. 'Because of *you* we only have half a marriage, but I'm prepared to live with it.'

'We have no marriage at all.'

He laughed hollowly. 'We do have two children, though, and I'm prepared to share the same house with you for their sakes. They need us both. And talking of houses, when I come back from Chamonix we are *all* going to move back to Long Meadow. That is *my* house, *my* home, and *my* children are going to be brought up there.'

Paula stared at him aghast. 'You know very well Grandy wanted –'

'This is not your house,' he cut in rapidly. 'It belongs to your mother.'

'You know very well Mummy and Daddy have to live in London so he can go to Harte's every day.'

'That's their problem, not ours.'

'Grandy didn't want Pennistone Royal to be left unoccupied half of the year. It was always a foregone conclusion that I would live here most of the time, that my parents would come for weekends when they could, spend the summer months and special holidays at the house.'

'I have every intention of moving back into Long Meadow. With the children,' he said in a rush. 'You are very welcome. Of course, I can't force you to move in with us –' He broke off, shrugged. 'It's your decision.'

Paula looked at him, biting her inner lip. She said, 'Jim, I want a divorce.'

He said coldly, 'I don't. I will never agree to one. *Never*. Furthermore, I think you should know that if you decide to take such a step I will fight you for custody of Lorne and Tessa. *My* children are going to be with me.'

'Children need their mother,' she began, and shook her head. 'Surely you of all people know that. Naturally, you would have full visiting rights. I would never keep the children away from you, Jim. You would see them whenever you wanted, and they would come and stay with you.'

He smiled narrowly as he snapped, 'You're priceless, do you know that. Quite extraordinary, and the most selfish woman I've ever known. You want it *all*, don't you. Your freedom to do what you want, to live where you want, and the children as well.' His eyes became icy. 'Do you also want to take my job away from me?'

Paula sucked in her breath. 'How can you think a thing like that! Of course I don't. Grandy renewed your contract before she died, and your job is safe for the rest of your life. And you also have the shares in the new company.'

'Ah yes,' he mused softly. 'The new company. I rather like Toronto ... lovely city. I might move there for a few years. That idea had crossed my mind in December. I'd enjoy running the *Toronto Sentinel*. Naturally the children would go with me.'

'No!' she cried, her face paling.

'Oh yes,' he countered. 'But it *is* up to you, Paula. If you persist in this ridiculous idea of getting a divorce, if you break up *my* family, I will settle in Toronto and I have every intention of taking *my* children with me.'

'They're also mine.'

'Yes,' he said, 'they are. And you are *my* wife.' He softened his tone, gave her a warmer look. 'We're a family, Paula. The children need you, I need you.' He reached out, took her hand in his. 'Why can't you stop all this nonsense, put aside your silly and *unfounded* grudges against me, make an effort to patch up our marriage. I'm willing to try.' He flashed her his bland smile. 'Why not start right now – *tonight*.' He tightened his grip on her fingers and leaned closer to her, added in a suggestive tone, 'There's no time like the present, darling. Come on, let's go upstairs and make love. I'll prove to you that all of these differences you're forever talking about are imaginary, exist only in *your head*. Come back to my bed, come back into my arms, Paula.'

She did not dare say a word.

There was a long and painful silence.

Finally Jim murmured, 'All right, not tonight then. Pity. Listen, since I'm going off to Chamonix and you're about to head for New York, let us both take the rest of this month to come to terms with ourselves during our separation. And then, when we're both back home in a few weeks, we'll start afresh. We'll move into Long Meadow and begin again, build a better relationship than we ever had before.'

'There's nothing left between us, Jim, and therefore there is nothing to build on,' she whispered miserably.

He let go of her hand and gazed into the fire. After a short while he said, 'Psychologists call it compulsive repetition.'

Not understanding what he was suddenly talking about, Paula frowned and said, 'I'm not following you.'

Jim turned to face her, and repeated, 'Psychologists call it *compulsive repetition.*'

'What's that supposed to mean?' she asked sharply, wondering if he was attempting to sidetrack her as he so often did.

'It refers to the pattern of behaviour some people adopt – an offspring actually *reliving* the life of a parent or grandparent, repeating that life, mistakes and all, as if he or she is guided by some terrible inner compulsion.'

Paula gaped at him speechlessly. But she quickly found her voice. 'Are you trying to say that I am reliving my grandmother's life?'

'*Exactly.*'

'You're absolutely wrong!' Paula cried. 'I am my *own* person. I am living my *own* life.'

'Think that if you wish, but it's not true. You are compulsively doing everything Emma Harte ever did, and with great precision. You work your fingers to the bone, devote every moment of your time to that wretched business, selfishly flitting around the world, wheeling and dealing and neglecting your duties as a wife and mother. You make everybody toe the line, *your line*, and you lack emotional stability just as she did.'

Paula was furious. 'How dare you! How dare you criticize Grandy! You're making her out to be something she was not, she who was so good to you! You've really got a bloody nerve. Furthermore, I don't neglect my children, and I never neglected you. Our estrangement came about because of the things which are lacking in you, Jim. I'm not emotionally unstable, but it strikes me that you are. I wasn't the one in a –' Paula stopped herself, clenched her hands together in her lap.

'I knew you'd never let me live that down,' he said his face darkening. 'Has it ever occurred to you that you might be responsible for my nervous breakdown?' he challenged.

Paula gasped, 'If anybody's compulsive, you are. You continually want to blame *me* for everything that you yourself do.'

Jim sighed. He glanced away, ruminating for a few seconds, and then he brought his eyes to Paula. He gave her a penetrating stare. 'Why are you so keen to get a divorce?'

'Because our marriage is over. It's ridiculous to continue,' she murmured, adopting a calmer, more reasonable tone. 'It's not fair to the children, to you, or to me, Jim.'

'We were in love,' he mused almost to himself then asked, 'weren't we?'

447

'Yes, we were.' She took a deep breath. 'But being in love doesn't guarantee happiness, Jim. Two people have to be compatible and able to live with each other on a day-to-day basis. Being in love is never enough, I'm afraid. A marriage needs a solid foundation based on genuine friendship.'

'Is there another man?' he demanded. His eyes remained fixed on hers.

Unexpected though the question was, Paula managed to keep her neutral expression in place. Although her heart missed a beat, she said in her most convincing voice, 'No, there isn't, Jim.'

He did not say anything for a few seconds. And then he got up, went and stood over her chair. He gripped her shoulder. 'There had better not be, Paula. Because if there is I will destroy you. I'll counter-sue you for divorce, and I'll have you declared an unfit mother. I'll get custody of my children, never you fear. No judge in England is going to give the children of a broken marriage to a woman who wilfully broke up that marriage and who is neglectful of those children, who travels the world in pursuit of her business interests to the detriment of those children.' He brought his face closer to hers, and tightened his hand on her shoulder. 'Or one who is screwing around with another man.'

Paula managed to throw off his vice-like grip. She leapt to her feet, her face blazing. 'Try it,' she said in a cold voice. 'Just try it. We'll see who wins.'

He stepped away from her and laughed in her face. 'And you don't think you're reliving Emma Harte's life. That's the joke of the century. Just look at you – why you sound exactly like her. And you think the way she did. You, too, believe that money and power make you invulnerable. Sadly, my dear, they don't.' He swung around and walked towards the door.

'Where are you going?' Paula called after him.

Jim stopped in his tracks and turned to face her. 'To London. There's not much point my staying here for dinner. We'll only continue to fight. Frankly, I'm weary of it all.'

Paula ran after him, took his arm, gave him a pleading look, 'But there is no real reason for us to quarrel in this way, Jim,' she said in a shaken voice. 'We can work this out like civilized people, like adults who are mature and intelligent. I know we can.'

'It's really up to you, Paula,' Jim said, also speaking in a more reasonable voice. 'Think about everything I've said and perhaps when I get back from Chamonix you'll have come to your senses.'

49

John Crawford, the family solicitor, had been listening to Paula for over an hour.

He had not interrupted her once, deeming it wiser to let her unburden herself before asking any relevant questions. Also he had discerned, in his astute and insightful way, that she had not discussed her disastrous marriage with anyone else before tonight. Certainly not at great length, and he decided that in a sense talking to him was a catharsis for her. He believed that by talking, opening up, she would feel better.

Paula finally paused for breath. He instantly detected a relaxation in the way she held her body, a sudden slackening of her rigid facial muscles, and relief was mirrored in her startling blue eyes. 'That's about it,' she said, smiling a bit uncertainly. 'I don't think I've missed anything.'

John nodded, continuing to observe her. He recognized she was in total control, calm enough to accept what he was about to say. He cleared his throat. 'I don't want to alarm you, and this is only a suggestion, but perhaps we ought to make the children wards of court.'

Although she was startled, Paula said steadily enough, 'Oh John, surely that's far too drastic a step. It might even be begging for trouble. It's so inflammatory.'

John, who had long harboured a visceral dislike of Jim Fairley, clasped his hands together and brought them up to his face. He looked at her over them, his eyes reflective. 'It seems to me, from the things you've told me, that Jim virtually threatened to take those children out of the country, to Canada to be precise, if you don't do as he wants. Isn't that so, Paula?'

'Yes,' she admitted.

'By making children wards of court one prevents their physical removal from their country of domicile by a disgruntled and angry parent involved in this kind of distressing emotional situation.'

'Yes, John, I know what it means. But Jim believes I will change my mind about getting a divorce. He's not going to suddenly swoop down, grab the children and fly off to Toronto. He would certainly try to ascertain what I'm going to do first. Besides, he's in Chamonix.'

'And you, Paula, are going to the States in a couple of days. He knows that. He could easily try to pull something whilst you're absent. After all, Geneva is only a few hours away.'

'I'm sure he wouldn't –' She stopped abruptly, alertly searching the solicitor's face. 'From your expression you obviously think he might.'

'There is that possibility.' John stood up and walked across the drawing room, poured himself another dry martini from the jug on the bar cart, swung around and apologized, 'I'm sorry, I didn't ask you if you wanted another drink. Do you?'

'No, thanks anyway.'

Returning to his seat, John sat down, continued, 'I'm going to ask you a very blunt question, Paula, a crucial question, and I would like you to think most carefully before you answer.'

She nodded.

He said: 'Do you believe that Jim is mentally stable?'

Without hesitation, Paula replied. 'Oh yes, John, I do. I realize he was in a nursing home an awfully long time after his nervous breakdown, but he's fully recovered now. He's behaving quite normally.' She smiled ruefully. 'If you can call his attitude to me normal, that is. He's stubborn, pigheaded really, but then he always has been. He blinds himself to the truth, to reality. He's convinced our problems are figments of my imagination, as I just told you. However, I'll say it again, I do not believe he is unstable. Upset at the moment, yes, but that's all.'

'Very well, I trust your judgement, and I also understand your reluctance to take steps that would inflame him. However, I think it would be advisable for you to talk to Daisy, alert her to the situation. If Jim should leave Chamonix unexpectedly she must contact me at once.'

'No, not Mummy,' Paula exclaimed. 'I'd prefer not to worry her. Anyway, I've never confided in her, or anyone, to be truthful. Well, actually I have spoken to Emily and my father a few times lately, and they know how bad the marriage is, and, in fact, Emily and Winston have urged me to get a divorce. The point is this . . . Emily and Winston are going off to Chamonix the day after tomorrow. They'll be there for the next two weeks. I'll speak to her before she leaves, explain everything and ask her to ring you if anything untoward happens.'

John's face brightened. 'Good, good. Emily is level-headed and smart. I feel more confident knowing she's going to be staying at the chalet. As your grandmother always said, there're no flies on Emily. So in view of that and because you're against it, I'll drop the idea of having you make the twins wards of court.' He gave her a funny little smile. 'It's crossed my mind that you may think I'm paranoid, but I'm not. Still, I am prudent and fully aware that it's often wiser to take precautions to avert trouble.' He leaned forward intently. 'That's why I suggested the idea in the first place, also it struck me that you were worried about the children yourself, otherwise you wouldn't have brought them to London with you yesterday.'

'Yes, I was a bit concerned,' Paula agreed. 'I was badly shaken up on Saturday night after Jim left. On Sunday morning I decided I ought to have Lorne and Tessa with me. They looked so small and defenceless, so vulnerable, John. They're only babies, and I do love them so much. I even thought of taking them to New York with me, but that would be uprooting them unnecessarily. Nora is quite happy to spend a few weeks in London, and at least the weather's better here than it is in Yorkshire. They'll be fine, and Nora has Parker and Mrs Ramsey as back-up at the London flat.'

'Yes, they're both very reliable. Try not to worry, my dear. I'll keep an eye on things at Belgrave Square. Make sure Nora has my telephone numbers, though, and explain that she must ring me if Jim arrives on the scene.'

'I'll do that tonight.' Paula gazed past John, staring at the dark green damask curtains, her face suddenly thoughtful. She said a little haltingly, 'Jim can't take them away from me, can he, John?'

'Of course not. Don't even contemplate such a thing!' John patted her hand and, wishing to reassure her, said, 'Jim can threaten all kinds of things in an effort to make *you* do as *he* wishes, but threats are meaningless in the long run. Thankfully, we do have courts of law in this land and they are eminently fair, which is more than I can say about the judicial systems in a lot of other countries.'

'Yes,' she murmured, then let out a tiny sigh of weariness. 'He says I want it all, want everything my way.'

John laughed. 'That's like the kettle calling the pot black, Paula. Hasn't it occurred to you that Jim wants it *his* way?' Not waiting for an answer, the solicitor hurried on, 'He's being selfish, expecting you to toe *his* line, regardless of your own feelings, and despite the fact that you have a disastrous marriage.

450

It's already playing havoc with you emotionally, and it will inevitably start affecting the children. The only thing to do with a marriage that has failed so miserably is to end it immediately for everyone's sakes. Stop the flow of blood, in a manner of speaking. I ought to know.'

Paula looked across at him. 'Poor John, you went through hell too, didn't you?'

'To put it mildly, my dear,' he replied. 'However, those troubles are behind me, and Millicent and I are good friends these days, most amicable really.'

'I do hope Jim and I can be friends eventually,' Paula said as if musing aloud. 'I don't hate him, far from it. To be honest, John, I feel rather sad for him . . . because he just cannot face reality.' She lifted her shoulders in a light shrug. 'But look, I came here to talk to you about a plan of action, and I want to say now that I wish to be scrupulously fair with him in every way. I want him to have total access to the twins, and of course there's no question about him staying on at the newspapers.' She scowled at the solicitor. 'I was stunned when he suggested I would take his job away.'

John stared into his glass for a moment, slowly lifted his eyes which were grave and intent. 'I don't want to delude you into thinking we're going to have an easy time with Jim, because we are not. I *know* we're going to have a fight on our hands. It's patently obvious, from what you've said, that he doesn't want to let you go, that he is prepared to put up with the worst kind of marital situation to remain your husband. Understandable perhaps. You are the mother of his children, you are a desirable and accomplished young woman, with immense wealth and power. What man wouldn't want to hang on to you. Also –'

'But Jim isn't interested in my money or my power,' Paula cut in rapidly. 'Why, John, he resents my business, does nothing but complain about my career.'

'Don't be naïve!'

Paula stared at him, her brows drawing together as she sat back, her expression changing to one of total disbelief. She opened her mouth, and then quickly closed it, wanting to hear what else John had to say.

'Of course he cares about your money and your power, Paula,' the solicitor remarked quietly. 'And he always has, in my opinion. Jim is not quite as altruistic as you seem to believe. As your solicitor I feel it is my duty to point this out to you, however unpalatable that might be to you. Jim has apparently been complaining very vociferously about your work, but he knew long before he married you that you were Emma's chief heir. He was also aware that you would not only inherit most of her wealth, but *all* of her tremendous responsibilities as well. He's merely using your career as an excuse to get at you, to hurt you, to punish you. At the same time it enables him to paint a picture of himself as the long-suffering, neglected and injured husband. In other words, he strikes a pose that will gain him sympathy. Please, my dear, do be aware of that for your own sake, and for your own peace of mind.'

'Perhaps you're right,' she conceded, knowing that John Crawford was a shrewd and brilliant lawyer and a man with great psychological insight into people. She leaned forward. 'If Jim *is* interested in money, as you imply,' she shook her head and laughed, 'no, *insist*, then let us give him money. I'm prepared to make a large financial settlement on him. Suggest an amount, John, and let's set a date when we can have a meeting with Jim. He'll be back at the end of the month, as will I, and I would like to put things in motion.'

'I can't come up with an amount tonight, off the top of my head,' John explained. 'That wouldn't be fair to anyone. It requires careful thought.' He took a sip of his martini, put the glass down and stood up. He walked over to the humidor on a side table, and took a cigar, not wanting her to see the cynical smile that had touched his mouth involuntarily. If my assessment of Jim is correct, and I'm sure it is, money will do the trick, John decided. Clipping off the end of the cigar, he strolled back to his chair, contemplating the settlement. It was a good card to have up his sleeve and would be a powerful negotiating weapon if Jim did prove to be intransigent.

Striking a match, John puffed hard on the cigar until it ignited, then told her, 'As far as a meeting is concerned, we can get together any time you wish –' He did not complete his sentence, but began to shake his head in a negative fashion instead.

'What's wrong?' Paula asked, clasping her hands together, experiencing a stab of apprehension.

'Nothing for you to look *so* concerned about, my dear. I think, however, that you're going to have your job cut out for you – getting Jim to meet with me, I mean. He's so dead set against the divorce and obstinate by nature. Maybe it would be better if I simply dropped by for a drink one night when he's in town. On his way back to Yorkshire after the Chamonix trip, perhaps?'

'Yes, that is a good idea,' Paula agreed. 'He did mutter something about seeing me in London in two weeks, before he left Pennistone Royal on Saturday.' Paula pushed herself to the edge of her chair and her face filled with sincerity as she reminded him, 'Don't forget that I want to be fair with Jim about the children, and I am willing to be very generous when it comes to money. It's important to me that Jim is financially secure for the rest of his life.'

'I'll remember everything,' John assured her. 'And whilst you're in New York I'll work on the terms of the divorce and make them most acceptable to Jim, I promise.' He gave her a fond smile. 'Not many women would be as kind as you. He's very lucky.'

'I'm sure *he* doesn't think that right now,' she ventured, rising to her feet. 'Thank you for being so understanding. I feel better after talking to you and much more positive about the future. And now I'm going to leave you in peace to have your dinner. I've taken up far too much of your evening as it is.'

He squeezed her arm affectionately as he escorted her across the drawing room and out into the small foyer. Loving her mother as he did, he considered Paula to be the daughter he had never had. He felt inordinately protective of her sometimes. Shrewd and clever in business though she was, she had had little or no experience with men, had been protected all of her life by Emma Harte and her parents. In many ways the harsher aspects of everyday living were unknown to her, and she might well be an easy target for an unscrupulous man.

As they reached the door, John turned her to face him. He bent forward, kissed her cheek, and with a chuckle, he said, '*You* can take up my time whenever you wish, my dear. It does a crusty old bachelor like me a lot of good to see your beautiful face. I'm only sorry we were meeting to discuss such a sad matter.'

Paula hugged him affectionately. 'You're not a crusty old bachelor,' she declared, smiling at him. 'You're the most wonderful friend – to all of us. Thank you for being that, and for everything, John. I'll speak to you before I leave for New York.'

'Please do, my dear.' He opened the door, then caught her arm as she went outside. 'It's going to be all right, Paula, really it is. Do try not to worry.'

'I will.' She ran down the short flight of steps in front of his house in Chester Street, turned and waved. John lifted his hand in response, went inside and closed the door, pressing back his concern for her.

Paula hurried down the street, making for Belgrave Square which was only a few minutes away. She had meant it when she had told John Crawford she felt relieved after talking to him. But this was not the only reason why her depression of the last forty-eight hours had lifted so unexpectedly. Making a decision, taking positive and constructive action, had worked wonders for her. Paula never vacillated. Like Emma before her, she was expedient by nature, always preferred action and commitment in preference to waiting. In consequence, marking time for the past year because of Jim's plane crash and subsequent sojourn in the mental home, had been unendurable. But she was nothing if not prudent, and she had schooled herself to be patient, had acknowledged months ago that if waiting was debilitating it was infinitely preferable to making rash moves she might live to regret.

But now, as she walked at a brisk pace, she experienced a great sense of release. The act of talking to John, of putting matters in his hands was liberating. She was confident he would work out an equable divorce agreement, and surely Jim would be convinced she was serious, in deadly earnest, when he knew she had taken this final step.

Paula glowed with a new optimism as she crossed Belgrave Square and went into the great mansion purchased so many years before by her grandfather, Paul McGill. She slammed the heavy exterior glass-and-wrought-iron door behind her, climbed the short circular staircase that led up to the front entrance of the maisonette and let herself in with her key.

Slipping off her tweed coat, she hung it in the hall closet and turned as Parker came hurrying out of the back quarters and into the large entrance foyer.

'Oh, Mrs Fairley, I was just wondering whether I ought to telephone you at Mr Crawford's house. Mr O'Neill is in the drawing room. He's been waiting for you for quite a while. I gave him a drink. Would you like anything, madam?'

'No, thank you, Parker.'

Wondering what Uncle Bryan wanted, why he had arrived so unexpectedly and without ringing first, she pushed open the drawing room door and stood stock still on the threshold. Fully expecting to see Bryan she was thrown at the sight of Shane. He stood up, grinning like a Cheshire cat from ear to ear.

'My God!' she cried, 'what are you doing here?' She pushed the door closed with her foot and ran into his arms, her face wreathed in delighted smiles.

Shane kissed her, took her by the shoulders and held her away from him.

'I was so worried about you after those awful phone conversations on Saturday and Sunday I decided to come home. I arrived at London airport about two hours ago.'

'Oh Shane, I'm sorry I worried you ... but it is a wonderful surprise to see you, and several days sooner than I expected.' She drew him over to the sofa and they sat down, continuing to hold hands. Paula said, with a bright little laugh, 'But I'm leaving for New York the day after tomorrow, and you know that –'

'I thought we'd fly back together,' he interjected, his dark eyes roving over her lovingly. 'As a matter of fact, I concocted a rather good plan in the last half hour. I thought I'd sidetrack for a few days, whisk you off to Barbados for the weekend on our way to the States. What do you think?'

'Oh Shane,' Paula began and hesitated, her face sobering. She said gravely, 'I told you Jim asked me if there is another man. And even though I denied it, I don't know that he's entirely convinced. What if someone should see us in Barbados? Or even travelling together? I don't want to do anything that would jeopardize my position and my custody of the children. He would be vindictive, I just know he would.'

Shane said, 'I understand your worry, darling, and I'd taken those points into consideration earlier. Now look, Paula, he's never going to be suspicious of me. It would be like him suspecting your brother Philip, for God's sake. Also, you do own a boutique in Barbados. You've every reason to go there, to check on it. And finally, no one will see us on the plane, and we can lay low once we get to Coral Cove.'

'Nobody will see us?' she repeated questioningly. 'What do you mean?'

'I have another surprise for you, Beanstalk. I finally took delivery of the private jet Dad and I decided to buy for the company. I just whizzed across the Atlantic in it, but let's forget that, and pretend our trip to the Caribbean is really its inaugural flight. Come on, say yes, sweetheart.'

'All right then,' Paula agreed, making a snap decision. Surely it was safe to travel with Shane. He was her childhood friend, after all. The grave expression fled and her violet eyes lit up. 'It's just what I need to give me a lift after the upsetting weekend.'

'Yes, it is.' He beamed at her. 'We have to think of an appropriate name for the jet, you know. Any ideas?'

'No, but I *will* bring a bottle of champagne and break it on the side, wet its bottom so to speak, even if we don't have a name,' she announced, enjoying the sudden and unexpected fun, the joyousness of being with him. Her heart soared with love for him, and she felt the old dizziness, the lightheadedness she experienced when she was with him again after a separation. Shane made all the difference in the world to her. And he made everything seem possible. The residue of her depression fell away so completely it might never have existed.

Shane now pulled her to her feet. 'I told Parker you were going out to dinner. I hope you don't mind me taking you over.' He gave her his boyish grin, and kissed her forehead. His face immediately turned serious. 'I want to know about your meeting with John. We can talk about it over a bottle of good wine and a pleasant meal at the White Elephant.'

50

The chalet was deserted.

Emily realized this as she ran lightly down the stairs and stood poised in the circular entrance hall, her head cocked on one side as she listened for the usual morning sounds. Generally voices and laughter reverberated and the radio was always playing in the background. But all were absent on this Saturday morning late in January.

Swinging to her left, Emily went into the dining room. Her mother was standing near the window, holding a small hand mirror and peering at her face in great concentration.

'Good morning, Mummy,' Emily called in a cheery tone from the doorway and meandered across the floor.

Elizbeth turned with swiftness, smiled and said, 'Oh Emily, there you are, good morning, darling.'

After planting a kiss on her mother's cheek, Emily sat down at the long rustic table and lifted the coffee pot. She asked, 'Where is everybody?'

For a moment Elizabeth did not answer, continuing to examine her face in the bright sunlight pouring in through the window and then, sighing under her breath, she joined her daughter at the table. 'The devoted skiers left ages ago, as they always do. You've just missed Winston. He decided to go skiing at the last minute, and hurried off, hoping to catch up with the others. Apparently you were sleeping so soundly he didn't have the heart to wake you. He asked me to tell you he'll see you at lunch.'

'I just couldn't get up early this morning,' Emily murmured, stirring her coffee, eyeing the croissants longingly. They smelled delicious. Her mouth watered.

'I'm not surprised. It was awfully late when everyone left last night. I'm paying for it myself this morning –' Elizabeth cut herself short, glanced at Emily quickly. 'Do you think I need to have my eyes done?'

Laughing, Emily put the coffee cup down and leaned across the table, staring at her mother's eyes. She was accustomed to such questions and aware that she had to pay the strictest attention when they were asked. She shook her head several times. 'No, of course you don't, your eyes are marvellous.'

'Do you really think so, dear?' Elizabeth lifted the mirror and gazed at herself again.

'For heaven's sake, Mummy, you're a young woman, only fifty –'

'Not so *loud*, darling,' Elizabeth muttered. She placed the mirror on the table and went on, 'I must admit I have been toying with the idea lately. I think my lids look a bit wrinkled. Marc is so conscious of a woman's looks, and being older than he is –'

'I didn't know he was younger than you, Mummy! He certainly doesn't look it.'

This seemed to cheer Elizabeth and her face brightened. 'I'm glad to hear that, Emily, but he *is* younger, I'm afraid.'

'By how many years?' Emily reached for a croissant, no longer able to resist temptation and broke it in half.

'Five.'

'Good heavens, that's nothing. And forget about having facial surgery, Mum, you're a beautiful woman, and don't look a day older than forty.' Emily plunged her knife into the mound of creamy butter, lavishly spread it on a portion of the breakfast roll and added peach jam.

Elizabeth, distracted from her constant preoccupation with herself for a moment, stared at her in disapproval. 'You're not really going to eat that are you, dear? It's loaded with calories.'

Emily grinned. 'Of course I am. I'm ravenous.'

'You know, you must watch your weight, Emily. You've always had a tendency to get plump very quickly ever since you were a child.'

'I'll starve myself when we get home.'

Elizabeth shook her head in exasperation, but knowing it was useless to argue, she remarked, 'Did you notice Marc flirting with that French countess at the party last night?'

'No, I can't say I did. But he flirts with everyone, Mother. He can't help it, and it doesn't mean anything, I'm sure. I wish you'd relax about that man. He's lucky to have you.'

'And I'm most fortunate to have him. He's very good to me, the best husband I've had, if you want to know the truth.'

Emily doubted this and before she could stop herself, she exclaimed, 'What about *Daddy*? He was wonderful to you. It's a pity you ever left *him*.'

'Naturally you're prejudiced about Tony. He *is* your father. But you have no conception of how it was between us, dear. Latterly, I mean. You were only a small child. Anyway, I don't propose to start regurgitating all the details of my first marriage with you, Emily, picking it over and examining it under a microscope.'

'That's very *wise* of you,' Emily said with acerbity and munched on the roll, conscious they were touching on an explosive subject.

Elizabeth gave her daughter a sharp look but she, too, sagely held her tongue. She poured herself another cup of coffee and lit a cigarette, sat observing Emily, thinking how pretty she looked this morning in her emerald green sweater and trousers. They intensified the colour of her eyes. After almost two weeks in the French Alps, her hair was a lighter brighter blonde and her delicate face had the hint of a suntan. Elizabeth was suddenly glad that she and Marc had accepted Daisy's invitation to join them at the chalet they had rented. She had enjoyed being with her children and she had derived a great deal of satisfaction from Marc's attentiveness to them, especially to Amanda and Francesca.

Between bites, Emily said, 'I think I'll go into the town later. I need to buy a few things.'

'That's a good idea,' Elizabeth remarked. 'And perhaps you'll drop me off at the hairdressers, darling.'

Emily burst out laughing. 'You don't need your hair doing, Mummy, you were there yesterday.'

'Now, Emily, let's not get into a long discussion about my hair. *You* paddle your canoe and *I'll* paddle mine.'

'Okay.' Leaning forward, Emily propped her elbows on the table and continued, 'I have a vague remembrance of Amanda and Francesca barging into our room at some ungodly hour this morning and smothering Winston and me with kisses. I assume Alexander dragged them off to Geneva – screaming at the top of their lungs, no doubt.'

Elizabeth nodded. 'They *were* rather obstreperous. Neither of them seem to like the finishing school on Lake Geneva, and I can't imagine why. But they settled down when they knew Daisy was going to Geneva with them. She wanted to do some shopping and decided to go along with Alexander. They're planning to take the girls to lunch at the Hotel Richmond before returning them to the school. I do love that hotel, Emily, and in fact I promised the twins I'd fly up to Geneva from Paris at Easter to spend a few days with them.' Elizabeth had a sudden thought and it brought a warm smile to her face. 'Why don't you and Winston join Marc and me, as my guests at the Richmond? It would be fun, Emily.'

Pleasantly surprised at this unprecedented gesture, Emily said, 'That's a lovely thought, Mother, and very kind of you to invite us. I'll ask Winston and let you know later.' Emily reached out, her hand hovering over another croissant.

'Please don't eat that, darling!'

Looking slightly shamefaced, Emily pulled her hand back. 'Yes, you're right. They are awfully fattening.' Emily rose. 'I think I'd better go upstairs and get ready to go into the town. I know if I sit here chatting to you I'll demolish that entire plate.'

'I'll come up too,' Elizabeth said. 'I want to change.'

Emily groaned. 'You look perfectly gorgeous, Mummy, you don't have to bother . . . you're only going to the hairdressers.'

'One never knows who one might meet,' Elizabeth countered. Glancing at her watch, she added, 'It's not quite eleven. I'll only be half an hour. I promise.'

To Emily's relief her mother was true to her word for once, and a few minutes after eleven-thirty she was turning the key in the ignition and pulling away from the chalet. This was located in a small hamlet on the outskirts of Chamonix, the lovely ancient town that nestled at the foot of Mont Blanc. As Emily swung out on to the main road and cruised along at a steady speed, she could not help admiring the extraordinary scenery which never failed to make her catch her breath.

The Valley of Chamonix, bounded on one side by the Mont Blanc range and on the other by the Aiguilles Rouges chain, was like a natural platform from which to view the highest peak of Europe. And now, as Emily peered ahead at Mont Blanc and the surrounding mountains, she could not help feeling overawed by their grandeur and majesty. Their glittering snow-covered pinnacles thrust up into a high-flung sky that was clear cerulean blue, filled with white puff-ball clouds and brilliant sunshine.

As though reading her daughter's thoughts, Elizabeth exclaimed, 'Impressive, isn't it, Emily! And it's such a glorious day.'

'Yes,' Emily agreed. 'I bet our skiing enthusiasts are happy as larks, enjoying themselves on the slopes.' She glanced at her mother through the corner of her eye. 'By the way, did Marc go with Uncle David and the others?'

'Yes, and Maggie.'

'Oh,' Emily said, surprised. 'I thought she was driving to Geneva with Alexander.'

'She wanted to go skiing instead, make the most of it, I suppose, since they're leaving tomorrow for London.'

'Jan and Peter are travelling back with them, so Jan told me last night,' Emily remarked, referring to the only non-family members who were house guests of her aunt and uncle.

'I tried to persuade them to stay on for a few days longer,' Elizabeth explained. 'I rather like them, and *he's* such a charmer.'

'Peter Coles! Honestly, Mummy, you do have funny tastes. I think he's a crashing bore. So pompous.' Emily giggled. 'But he is especially attentive to you, and I've seen Marc give him more than one filthy look during the ten days they've been here. I do believe the old Frog is as jealous as hell.'

'Please don't refer to Marc as an *old frog*, darling, it's a very unkind description and most inappropriate,' Elizabeth chastized. Then she laughed with sudden gaiety. 'So you think Peter makes Marc jealous. That's nice to know. *Mmmm.*'

'Very.' Emily smiled to herself, realizing how happy this bit of irrelevant information made her mother feel. But maybe it wasn't so irrelevant to her. The poor woman was dotty about Marc Deboyne. That snake in the grass, Emily thought. She detested him, and wouldn't trust him as far as she could throw him.

Elizabeth now launched into a glowing recital about her new husband's manifold qualities and Emily nodded and made small agreeable sounds, as if concurring. But she was only half listening. Her mother was quite irritating when she went on and on about him in this ridiculous way, and Emily was pleased when she saw the town of Chamonix looming immediately ahead.

After leaving the Citroën in the car park, Emily and her mother walked briskly down one of the main boulevards, heading in the direction of the small square where the hairdressing salon was situated. When they arrived at its door, Emily said, 'How long will you be?'

'Oh just about an hour, dear. I'm only having a comb out. Why don't you meet me at that little bistro over there at the other side of the square. We'll have an apéritif before going back to the chalet for lunch.'

'All right. Bye, Mummy.'

Emily sauntered leisurely around the square, glancing in the shop windows. She only had a few things to buy and an hour to waste, so she took her time. After traversing the entire square she continued down the boulevard, making for a boutique that sold highly original *après ski* clothes, and went inside. The

458

sales assistants knew her and she wasted twenty minutes chatting to them and trying on evening tops, none of which she liked enough to buy.

Back on the street, Emily wandered down to the pharmacy, purchased the small items she needed, tucked them in her shoulder bag, and left the shop. Slowly she retraced her steps, remembering she wanted to pick up some picture postcards to send to friends in England.

To her astonishment Emily saw Marc Deboyne coming towards her. He was hurrying, looked deeply preoccupied, and he had obviously not seen her.

As they drew level with each other, Emily said archly, 'Fancy meeting you, Marc. Mummy thinks you've gone skiing.'

Marc Deboyne, caught off guard, was both startled and embarrassed. Quickly recovering his equilibrium, he exclaimed, 'Ah, Emilee, Emilee, my dear,' and caught hold of her arm, squeezed it affectionately. He added, in his Gallic-accented but perfect English, 'I changed my mind. I decided to go for a walk. I have a headache.'

Leaning into him, Emily said pointedly, 'It's not the only thing you have, Marc. You've also got lipstick on the neck of your sweater.'

His smile was indulgent but his eyes reproved, and then he chuckled. 'Emilee, what *are* you implying? It's undoubtedly your mother's lipstick.'

Ignoring this remark, she said, 'Mummy's having her hair done. I'm meeting her at the bistro opposite for a drink. At one o'clock. She'll be disappointed if you don't join us.' Emily's tone was all sweetness. Her eyes were chips of green ice.

'I would not disappoint Elizabeth. I shall meet you there. *Ciao*, Emilee.' He gave an odd little salute and moved on, walking at the same rapid pace.

Emily stared after him, watched him as he crossed the road and cut down a side street. She wondered where he was going. Bastard, she thought. I bet he was having a quickie with that ghastly countess from the party last night, who is no more of a Frenchwoman than I am. Filled with dislike for him, Emily grimaced in distaste and turned on her heels, marching up the street in search of a newspaper shop. She found one within minutes and browsed for a while, flipping through the latest magazines, still endeavouring to pass the time. Finally peeking at her watch she saw that it was almost one o'clock, almost time to meet her mother. Stepping up to the metal rack holding cards of Chamonix, she selected four and went to pay for them.

Putting the cards and the change in her shoulder bag, Emily smiled at the woman behind the counter. '*Merci, madame.*'

The woman started to respond and then stopped abruptly, cocking her head. At that precise moment there was a sudden extraordinary rumbling sound that rent the air around them and increased to thunderous and deafening proportions within the space of a split second.

Emily shouted, 'That sounds like a terrible explosion.'

The woman gaped at her through terrified eyes, screamed back, 'No! Avalanche!' She swung her plump body, grabbed the telephone.

Clutching her bag, Emily ran out into the street.

Shop doors were opening and people were emerging, all of them wearing the same frightened expressions, as were the passers-by.

'*Avalanche!*' a man cried to Emily and pointed in the direction of Mont Blanc as he sped on down the street.

Emily stood transfixed, mesmerized by the sight. Even from this distance she could see that great fractures boomed across the slopes of Mont Blanc and half the mountainside was rumbling down in a tremendous swath that looked to be hundreds and hundreds of feet across. Gargantuan slabs of snow were hurtling forward at gathering speed, gaining momentum as they tumbled on their precipitous downward journey, sweeping aside all that lay in their path. And rising up into the brilliant blue air were enormous billowing clouds of powdered snow that had been pulverized by the turbulence of the slide into millions of tiny snow-smithereens.

Two police cars, their sirens screaming, raced along the street at breakneck speed. Their high-pitched wails broke the hypnotic spell that had momentarily held Emily in its grip. She blinked several times and then the blood seemed to drain out of her. *Winston was up there. Everyone was up there. David. Philip. Jim. Maggie. Jan and Peter Coles.*

She began to shake like a leaf and she could not move. Her legs turned to jelly as the fear rushed through her, swamped her, overwhelmed her. '*Oh my God! Winston!*' Emily cried out loud. '*Winston. Oh God! No!*'

It was as if the sound of her own voice galvanized her. She began to run, racing along the pavement, her head thrust forward, her feet flying over the stones as she ran faster and faster, making for the large cable-car terminal she knew was only a short distance away.

Her heart pounded in her chest, her breathing was laboured as she hurled herself on, blinking again, squeezing back the tears that stung her eyes. *Oh God, let Winston be safe. Please let Winston be safe. And the others. Make them all safe. Oh God, don't let any of them be dead.*

Emily became aware of other running feet, other people pressing around her. Some were outstripping her as they pounded past. They were also making for the terminal, which was now in her line of vision. A man jostled her as he leapt ahead, and she almost tripped and fell. But she recovered her balance and went on running, her fear propelling her.

She thought her heart was bursting when she finally reached the terminal. Only then did Emily slow down and come to a standstill, gasping for breath. She pressed her hand against her heaving chest. Rasping noises emanated from her throat. She leaned against one of the police cars parked near the cable-car depot, and fumbled in her shoulder bag. She found her handkerchief, wiped her sweating face and neck, endeavoured to marshal her swimming senses, willed herself to stay calm.

After a few seconds her breathing was more normal and she straightened up, looked around. Her eyes were frantic as they swept over the crowd that had already gathered in the space of fifteen minutes.

Emily hoped against hope that Winston had finished skiing before the avalanche had struck, prayed that he was somewhere amongst the tourists and townspeople milling around. She threw herself into their midst, her eyes darting from side to side, seeking him, her anxiety paramount. Instant dismay lodged in the pit of her stomach. He was nowhere in sight.

Turning away, Emily pressed her hands to her mouth, choking. Terror seized

460

her, held her in a vice. She stumbled back to the police car, leaned against its hood, her heart clenching. *How could anyone have survived that avalanche? She had seen it hurtling down at such speed and force it would have crushed anything that stood in its way.* Emily closed her eyes. She ought to go and speak to someone, ask about rescue teams, but she had no strength. She closed her eyes. She felt her legs slipping and sliding under her as if she had lost all control of her body.

Suddenly two strong arms gripped her, pulled her upright.

'Emily! Emily! It's me.'

Her eyes flew open as she was spun around rapidly. It was Winston. She grabbed at his ski jacket, weak with relief, and then her face crumpled as she burst into tears.

Winston held her close, supporting her limp body and soothing her at the same time. 'It's all right, it's all right,' he kept repeating over and over again.

'Thank God! Thank God!' Emily gasped. 'I thought you were dead. Oh Winston, thank God you're alive.' She searched his worried face. 'The others?' she began and stopped when she saw his grim expression, the clenched jaw.

'I don't know whether they're safe or not. I hope to God they are. I pray they are,' Winston said, putting his arm around her.

'But you –'

Winston interrupted fiercely, 'I didn't go skiing this morning. When I got here I'd just missed a cable car. I waited around for a while, planning to take the next one, but I got fed up. I had a bit of a hangover and I was beginning to feel queasy. So I left, went in to the town. I bought the English papers, stopped at a café and had a *fernet branca*. By the time I felt better it was too late to go skiing, so I did a bit of shopping. I was actually in the car park, stowing the stuff in the car, when I heard a *whoomp* that sounded like a blast of dynamite. There was an American parked next to me, and he shouted something about an avalanche, that his daughter was on the slopes, and then he ran like hell. I followed him, knowing –' Winston swallowed. 'Knowing that everybody from the chalet, well practically everybody, was up there too.'

An unexpected feeling of hope soared in Emily. She exclaimed, 'Perhaps they decided to ski on that other range.'

Winston shook his head. His face was bleak.

Emily grabbed hold of him. 'Oh Winston!'

He calmed her. 'Come on, Emily, you must be strong, very brave –' He broke off and swung his head as he heard his name being called. He spotted Marc Deboyne and Elizabeth running in their direction and lifted his hand in a wave, looked down at his wife and said, 'Your mother and Marc are coming.'

Elizabeth almost flung herself at Winston and embraced him, crying. 'You're safe, you're safe. I was petrified for you, Winston.' She looked at him through anxious eyes. Her white face was stark, but she was exercising immense control. She hugged Emily, then said, 'What about the others, Winston? Have you seen any of the family, or Jan and Peter?'

'No. You see, I didn't go skiing this morning. I changed my mind.'

There was a sudden flurry of activity in the area. They all turned around. The rescue teams had arrived, professional skiers wearing backpacks and con-

461

trolling a number of German shepherds. With them were additional police, a group of French soldiers and town officials.

'I will go and ask a few questions,' Marc muttered and strode off purposefully.

Winston exclaimed, 'It's stopped! Do you realize the avalanche has stopped.'

Elizabeth stared at him. 'It stopped when Marc and I were running down here. After that deafening noise the silence was awful, deathly.'

Before Winston could reply, Marc was back with them, explaining: 'The teams are going up now. They've got the best equipment in those backpacks. Listening devices, probing rods, and the dogs, of course. Let us be hopeful.'

'*Is* there any hope?' Winston asked in a low intense tone.

Marc hesitated, tempted to lie. But he elected to speak the truth. 'It's doubtful,' he murmured quietly. 'The avalanche must have been travelling at enormous speed, anywhere between one hundred and twenty to two hundred miles per hour . . . and then there is the force, the weight of the snow. And yet –' He attempted an encouraging smile. 'People have been known to live through avalanches and snow slides as bad as this one. It depends where they are on the slopes when it strikes. Those near the bottom would have the best chance, providing they knew to throw away their skis and poles, make swimming motions with their arms. That creates air pockets in front of the face. Even if a person is felled by snow it is vital to keep the arms moving in that manner to provide air around the body. People have lived for days under the snow – because they had those air pockets.'

Emily said worriedly, 'David, Jim and Philip are experienced skiers, but *Maggie* –'

Elizabeth suppressed a cry of fear. She gasped. 'We must have courage and keep our hopes high. Please don't let's talk so mournfully. It makes me nervous. I must continue to believe that they are *all* alive.'

Marc put his arm around her protectively, 'You are right, *chérie*. We must be positive.'

Winston said to Emily, 'I think you ought to take your mother over to one of the nearby cafés. Wait there. There's nothing you can do here.'

'No!' Emily cried heatedly, glaring at him. 'I want to be here with you. Please, Winston.'

'Yes, we must stay here,' Elizabeth insisted. She blew her nose and got a grip on her diminishing composure. Silently she began to pray.

Exactly one hour after the avalanche had struck the rescue teams and the dogs went up in the cable cars.

In just under an hour they returned with the first eight people they had found. Five of them were dead. Three were miraculously alive. Two were young girls. One was a man.

'It's Philip!' Emily screamed and breaking away from Winston and her mother, she began to run towards her cousin.

Philip was being supported by a member of the rescue team. As he limped across to her, Emily saw that one side of his face was scraped and covered with congealed blood, and his bright blue eyes were dazed. But otherwise he looked as if he had escaped with no really serious injuries.

'Philip!' Emily exclaimed, drawing up beside him, 'Thank God you're safe. Are you hurt at all do you think?'

He shook his head. Despite the odd glazed look in his eyes, he recognized her, reached out to her.

A second later, Winston, Elizabeth and Marc were also by his side, asking questions. Philip simply went on shaking his head helplessly, remained mute.

The skier who had found him said in halting English, 'This man, your friend, has been lucky . . . he knew what to do. He did not panic. He discarded his poles . . . the skis . . . did the swimming. Yes, he was most fortunate . . . this man was at the bottom of the slope . . . had completed his run. He was covered with only ten feet of snow . . . the dogs . . . they found him. Now . . . if you please. We go. To the first aid station over there.'

Philip finally spoke. He asked, in hoarse voice, 'Dad? Maggie? The others?'

Winston said. 'No news yet.'

Philip closed his eyes, then opened them quickly, allowed himself to be helped away.

Turning to Emily, Winston said, 'You and your mother had better go along with Philip, lovey. Marc and I will wait here. Once you've ascertained that he has no internal injuries, I want the three of you to go back to the chalet.'

Emily started to protest. Winston cut her off sharply. 'Please, Emily, don't argue. Look after Philip. And somebody *should* be at the chalet . . . when Daisy and Alexander get back from Geneva.'

'Yes,' Emily acquiesced, realizing the sense he made. She kissed him and ran after her mother, who had walked ahead with Philip and the skier.

Winston and Marc stood around for another hour, smoking incessantly, occasionally talking to each other, and striking up conversations with other people who were keeping the same distressing vigil at the terminal.

The rescue teams continued to go up and down in the cable cars. Four more survivors were brought to safety, to be followed by nine who were dead.

At four o'clock one of the rescue teams which had been long and endlessly searching the higher part of the mountain returned. They brought with them five more vacationing skiers who had been trapped by the avalanche. The bad news spread quickly. All were dead.

'We must go over and check,' Winston said, throwing his cigarette on the ground, grinding his toe on the butt. Bracing himself, he swung to Marc. 'Will you come with me?'

'Yes, Winston. No use putting it off.'

The bodies were being laid on stretchers. When he was a few feet away from them, Winston came to a sudden halt. His strength ebbed out of him, but somehow he managed to take several more steps forward after this brief pause.

He felt Marc's strong hand under his armpit, heard the Frenchman say sorrowfully, 'I am so sorry, so very sorry. This is a tragedy for the family.'

Winston found he could not speak.

He gazed down at the five people who lay on the stretchers. Two of them he did not know, but the other three . . . For a moment his mind floundered. It did not seem possible that they were dead. Only a few hours ago they had all been laughing together at breakfast.

Sucking in his breath, and brushing his hand across his brimming eyes, Winston went to identify the bodies of David Amory, Jim Fairley and Maggie Barkstone, fatal victims of the avalanche. And he thought of Daisy and Alexander, driving back from Geneva, and of Paula, who was in New York, and he wondered how he was ever going to break the devastating news to them.

51

Shane O'Neill stood in the kitchen of the barn in New Milford, waiting for the second pot of coffee to brew.

After lighting a cigarette, he reached for the wall phone and dialled the farm. When Elaine Vickers answered, he said cheerily, 'Top of the morning to you.'

'Hi, Shane,' Elaine replied. 'We thought you weren't coming up this weekend when we didn't hear from you last night. But Sonny saw your car earlier this morning, so we knew you'd made it.'

'It was late when we arrived,' Shane explained. 'The farm was in darkness and I thought twice about waking you. Paula didn't get back from Texas until early evening and it was after nine when we left the city. Sorry I didn't ring you before now, but we got off to a slow start this morning.'

Elaine laughed. 'I'll say you did. It's almost noon. But the way you two work you deserve to take it easy occasionally. I hope we're going to see you for dinner tonight,' she went on. 'We've been looking forward to it all week.'

'We'll be over around seven-thirty as planned,' Shane assured her.

Elaine exclaimed, 'Oh Shane, you'll have to excuse me. That was the oven bell. My bread's going to spoil if I don't take it out immediately. See you tonight.'

'Bye, Elaine.' Shane dropped the phone in its cradle, stubbed out his cigarette and went to the sink. He rinsed the two mugs and dried them. He was just about to pour the coffee when the telephone began to ring. Putting down the pot, he picked up the receiver. 'Hello?'

There was no response at the other end of the phone, only the sound of static and a hollow echo. 'Hello? Hello?' Shane said again in a stronger tone.

Finally a muffled voice came down the wire. 'It's me. Winston. I'm phoning from Chamonix. Can you hear me, Shane?'

'I can now. Winston! How –'

Winston cut him off. 'Something terrible has happened here, Shane, and I don't know where Paula is, where to reach her, and I thought I'd better speak to you first anyway.'

Shane gripped the receiver tighter, frowned to himself. 'Actually she's staying here with me for the weekend. What's wrong, Winston?'

464

'There has been a disastrous avalanche on Mont Blanc, at about one o'clock today, the worst in years,' Winston began, his voice sounding more muffled and gruff than ever. 'Some of the family have been killed.' Winston's voice cracked and he was unable to continue.

'Oh Jesus!' Shane steadied himself against the counter, waiting to hear the worst. His heart had begun to thud in his chest and intuitively he knew that Winston was about to impart news that would devastate Paula. He knew it in his bones.

Thousands of miles away, in the dining room of the chalet on the outskirts of Chamonix, Winston Harte stood at the window gazing into the distance. Mont Blanc loomed up into the darkening sky, looked so peaceful now in the twilight after the havoc it had wrought only five hours ago. He got a grip on himself, said in a controlled voice, 'Sorry for breaking down. It's been the worst day of my life. Look, Shane, I'm going to give it to you straight because it's the only way I know how.' Winston took a deep breath and began to speak, relaying the tragic news to his friend.

As he listened Shane felt the shock strike him like a body blow and ten minutes later when Winston finally hung up he was still reeling. He stood with his hand on the phone, staring blankly into the middle of the room. He began to blink as bright sunlight streamed in through the windows. How normal everything seemed here in this kitchen. It was so tranquil. Peaceful. And it was such a pretty day outside. The sky was a bright blue, clear and without a single cloud and the sun was radiant. But over in France the family he had been so close to for his entire life were living with unexpected death and sorrow. How abruptly, how suddenly lives had been changed, almost in the flicker of an eyelash. Oh dear God, Shane thought, how am I going to tell Paula? Where will I find the words?

He heard her step in the hall outside and swung around to face the door, then held himself very still, waiting.

She was laughing as she came in and said in a teasing voice, 'That's the last time I'll ever ask you to make the coffee. You've been on the phone for ages. Who were you talking to, darling?'

Shane took a step towards her. He tried to speak but nothing came out. There was a parched gravelly feeling in his throat and his mouth went dry.

'You've got the oddest look on your face, Shane. What's wrong?' Paula demanded, instantly tensing.

He put his arm around her shoulder and propelled her out of the kitchen and into the big living room, leading her to the fire. She demanded again, and with fierceness, 'Shane, what's happened? Please tell me.'

'I will, I will,' he said hoarsely, pressing her down on the sofa, seating himself next to her. He took her hands in his, held on to them tightly, and looked into that face he had loved all of his life. He saw the worry, the sudden apprehension invading it.

Shane's heart clenched as he said in the softest of voices, 'I just got some very bad news, some dreadful news, Paula darling. From Winston. There was the most hideous accident in Chamonix around one o'clock today. An avalanche on Mont Blanc. Some of the family have been killed.'

Paula gaped at him. Her eyes, opening widely, were pinned on his. He saw the horror mirrored in them and the draining away of all colour from her face. It turned chalky white. *'Who?'* she asked in a strangled whisper.

Shane's grip increased, his fingers biting into her flesh. 'You must be brave, my darling,' he said. 'Very brave. I'm here, I'll help you through this.' He paused, swallowed hard, sought the right phrases, the right words. But there were no such things, he knew that.

Paula, her mind racing, thought of the most dedicated skiers in the group. She cried harshly, 'Not Daddy? *Not my father?'*

Shane's throat constricted. He nodded. 'I'm so sorry. So very sorry, my darling,' he murmured in a dim and shaken voice.

For a moment Paula could not say a word. She continued to stare at Shane, stunned and stupefied, almost uncomprehending, unable to conceive what he was saying – or accept it.

Aware that it would be kinder to tell her everything at once, quickly, and without further delay, he said in the same saddened tone, 'Paula, I don't know how to tell you this, and I'm so sorry, but Jim was also killed. And Maggie. They were on top of the mountain with your father when it happened.'

'No!' she said. 'No!' She wrenched her hands out of his and clapped them over her mouth, looking around the room frenziedly, as if seeking escape, as if trying to run from this new and dreadful knowledge. Her eyes stretched and stretched in her ashen face. She jumped up jerkily and shouted in a frantic voice, 'It can't be so! *No!* It just can't be so! Oh my God! *Philip. My brother.* Was he –'

'He's all right,' Shane exclaimed, also leaping to his feet, wrapping his arms around her. 'Everyone is safe, except for Jan and Peter Coles. They haven't been found yet.'

Paula pulled away from him roughly, staring up into his face. Her violet eyes were black with the pain and horror of it all, and her face twisted in a grimace of grief and anguish and heartbreak. She began to tremble violently but as Shane reached for her once more, wanting to help her, to comfort her, Paula ran into the middle of the room, moving her head from side to side, denying, denying. Suddenly she wrapped her arms around her body and doubled over in agony.

She began to make small but high-pitched mewling noises like a terrified animal in immense pain. It was a keening really and it did not cease. Grief and shock continued to assault her, swept over her like giant tidal waves and engulfed her finally. She slipped to the floor unconscious.

The private jet owned by O'Neill Hotels International sliced through the dark night sky high above the English Channel. It was set on a steady course for London airport where it would soon be landing after a seven-hour flight across the Atlantic.

Shane sat opposite Paula, who was stretched out on one of the banquettes and wrapped in several light woollen travelling rugs. He watched her closely, hardly daring to take his eyes off her. Occasionally he leaned over her, soothed her gently, as he had throughout the long and difficult trip. She tossed about restlessly despite the sedatives she had been given at different intervals since he had told her about the tragedy in Chamonix.

The local doctor in New Milford, instantly summoned by Shane after she had collapsed, had treated her for shock. He had injected her and given Shane a small box of additional sedatives in tablet form. Before leaving the barn he had instructed Shane to administer them during the flight whenever he considered it necessary, but to use his discretion.

Shane had rapidly come to realize that Paula was fighting the tranquillizing drugs, just as she had fought him at times during the night. Twice over the Atlantic she had tried to struggle up off the banquette, her eyes filled with panic and fear. She had vomited once, retching until there was nothing left inside. He had tended to her every need with infinite patience, tenderness and love, helping her in every way he could, murmuring consoling words to her, trying to ease her mental turmoil, ensure her physical comfort.

Now, as he sat observing her, Shane's worry accelerated. She had not broken down or cried once, and this was abnormal for her, she who was such an emotional woman by nature. Nor had she spoken to him and it was this extraordinary and protracted silence plus the wild and febrile look in her eyes that frightened him so much.

He glanced at his watch. They would be on the ground in no time at all. His father and Miranda would be there to meet them with a private ambulance and Paula's London doctor, Harvey Langen. Thank God for Harvey, Shane thought. He'll know what to do, the best way to treat her condition. And then he asked himself how a doctor could treat the overwhelming grief and anguish she was experiencing and he acknowledged miserably that he had no ready answers.

Shane sat in the small study of the Belgrave Square flat with his sister Merry. His expression was morose, his black eyes abstracted as he sipped his third cup of coffee, then drew on his cigarette.

Parker, the butler, had prepared breakfast a short while ago, but none of them had been able to eat a thing, and Shane had been chain-smoking since he had entered this room.

Bryan O'Neill, who had been showing the doctor out, came back in and hurried over to Shane. His hand rested on his son's shoulder, and he said in an optimistic tone, 'You were mistaken, Shane. Harvey says Paula's definitely not in catatonic shock. I tackled him about that, as you asked me to. She is in shock, of course, we're all aware of that, but Harvey believes she'll be pulling out of it later today, or tomorrow at the very latest.'

Shane looked at his father and nodded. 'Oh God, I hope so, Dad. I can't bear to see her like this, suffering so much. If only she would speak to me, say something.'

'She will, Shane, very soon,' Bryan said, squeezing Shane's shoulder affectionately. Sighing, he lowered himself into a chair and continued, 'This kind of catastrophe is devastating and sudden death, sudden loss, is always the hardest to bear because of its very unexpectedness, apart from anything else.'

'If only I knew how to help her,' Shane exclaimed. 'But I'm floundering

467

right now. I haven't been able to get through to her, get a reaction from her, and yet I know she is in the most dreadful agony. I must find a way to ease the burden of her sorrow and pain.'

Miranda said, 'If anyone can help her it's you, Shane. You're the closest to her and perhaps when you come back tonight she'll be out of the shock as Harvey said she would. She'll talk to you then, I just know it. You will be able to console her, let her know that she's not alone, that she has you.'

Shane stared at his sister. 'What do you mean *come back tonight*? I'm not leaving her. I'm going to be right here until she sleeps off the drugs . . . I wouldn't let her wake up alone.'

'I'll stay with you,' Merry announced. '*I* won't permit *you* to be alone.'

Bryan, who had been listening to this exchange between his children, instantly understood so many things that had baffled him in the last year. He said slowly, 'Shane, I didn't know – I didn't realize you were in love with Paula, that you loved her so profoundly.'

'*Love her*,' Shane repeated almost wonderingly, glancing across at his father in astonishment. 'Why, Dad, she's my whole life.'

'Yes,' Bryan said. 'Yes, Shane, I realize that now, seeing you like this. She'll recover, please believe me she will. People have enormous inner strength in times of trouble, and Paula is no exception. In fact she's stronger than most – one of the strongest women I know. There's a lot of Emma in her. Oh yes, she'll pull out of this eventually. In time everything will be all right.'

Shane threw him a dismal look and his eyes reflected his own pain. 'No, it won't,' he said in the bleakest of voices. 'You're wrong, Dad. Quite wrong.'

52

The harsh winter had passed.

The spring came, bringing a new and wondrous greenness to her gardens at Pennistone Royal. And then, before she knew it, the summer was filling the air with its sweet fragrance as the flowers burst into bloom under warming sunlight and skies that were as blue as speedwells and filled with that glorious Northern light.

She was alone now. Entirely alone except for her children. Lorne and Tessa filled every waking moment of her time and she drew consolation and joy from their laughter, their carefree spirits and their childlike pleasures.

The grief that had shattered her at the end of January had been brought under control.

Paula had reached deep inside herself, had drawn on her inner resources for sustenance and strength in her time of loss and pain and trouble. She had had no option really. Too many people were dependent on her.

Her mother and Alexander had returned from Chamonix grief-stricken and crushed by sorrow. They had automatically turned to her, had needed her comfort and her support, her immense fortitude to help them through the difficult period of the funerals and the distressing weeks that followed. They were plunged deeper into mourning as their shock receded and reality took over. Her children had also needed the security of her love and devotion, every bit of attention she could give them now that they were without a father.

And finally her enormous empire required her to be at the helm, guiding its course at all times, and she devoted herself to the great legacy she had inherited from her grandmother, working around the clock to ensure that it remained safe and only increased in importance and wealth. And work had become her strong citadel in the way it had been Emma's in the past.

But as the grief lessened, grew a little easier to bear, her guilt only increased and intensified. And it was the guilt that continued to cripple her now, so many months after the tragedy that had decimated the family.

It was a many-faceted guilt ... survivor guilt that she was alive when her father, Jim and Maggie were dead ... guilt that she and Jim had parted with such animosity the day before he had left for Chamonix ... and, worst of all, guilt that she had been with Shane when those three people she cared about had met their untimely and hideous deaths.

As they had been suffocating under thousands of tons of snow she had been in Shane's arms, transported by passion and the ecstasy of fulfilment. Illogical as it was, she nevertheless felt responsible, blamed herself for their deaths. Intellectually she knew that she was not to blame, that it was wrong to feel this way, but emotionally she could not come to grips with true reality.

And she never wanted to make love again because in her mind the act of love was now associated with death and dying. In consequence, the mere thought of sex appalled her. She was desensitized, without feeling and emotionally and physically frigid, incapable of giving of herself as a woman.

Slowly Paula had come to realize she had nothing to offer Shane O'Neill. He was too virile, too passionate a man to settle for only a small part of her, and since she could not participate in love-making she believed the relationship to be doomed.

And so she sent him away. She knew his heart was broken and she loathed herself for inflicting pain and heartache on him, but she had convinced herself that she was doing the best thing for him, for them both ultimately.

Shane had remained by her side through February, always there when she needed him, giving her his continuing love, and friendship. Sensitive by nature, and knowing her as well as he did, he never made demands on her whatsoever. He shared her grief, her pain and her anguish, was consoling, became kindness itself. But after a month's sojourn in London and Yorkshire, he had had to resume his business activities. He had flown off to Australia to supervise the building of the new O'Neill hotel which Blackie had purchased on his trip with Emma.

Around this period, Paula had conceived the idea of sending her mother to Sydney with Philip, who was returning on the O'Neill private jet with Shane. At first Daisy had demurred, had protested that she must remain in England to be with Paula and the twins, but Paula had persuaded her to go. At the last minute Daisy had hurriedly packed and travelled across the world with the two men. Her mother was still in Australia, trying to pick up the threads of her life without David, acting as Philip's hostess and taking an interest in the McGill holdings. And Paula was aware that her mother was starting to throw off her own pain and function again.

But Shane had returned to England in April and had come again to Yorkshire to see her. Once more, as was his way, he had been understanding of her dilemma. He had explained that he recognized that she needed time to adjust herself to the loss of her father, to whom she had been so close, to the loss of her husband, who though estranged from her was still the father of her children.

'I only wanted my freedom, a divorce from Jim. I never wished him harm, or wanted him to die. He was so young,' she had whispered on the day Shane was setting off for New York with Miranda.

'I know, I know, darling,' Shane had said with gentleness. 'I'm there whenever you need me. I'll wait for you, Paula.'

But she had not wanted him to wait, for she knew deep within herself that she would never be ready. She could never be Shane's wife. In a sense, that part of her life was over and she had adjusted herself to the knowledge that she would live alone with her children, would never share herself or her life with a man. It was not possible any more.

She had not told Shane about the dreadful nights when she awakened from the same terrifying nightmare, the nightmare that she was suffocating and one which constantly haunted her. It was so real she would sit up in bed with a start, her trembling body bathed in sweat as she cried out in terror and fear. And always in the centre of her mind there wobbled the horrifying image of her father and Jim and Maggie being swept away by the avalanche, being buried under that icy snow that had smothered them, snuffed out thcir lives with such suddenness and so pointlessly.

But Shane O'Neill was no fool and it soon became apparent to him that Paula had changed towards him, and she *knew* that he knew. How could he not. She could not help her attitude or her demeanour, nor could she alter the circumstances that had wrought the shift in her emotional balance. Her remoteness, her detachment, her preoccupation with her children and her work combined to stun him initially, and then they eventually told him everything he needed to know.

Sometimes she was lonely, frequently she was sad and sorrowing, and occasionally she was afraid.

She stood alone. Her grandmother and her father, the two people from whom she had received so much support and love, were dead. She was the head of the Harte clan. Everyone looked to her, deferred to her, came to her with their problems both personal and in business. There were times when her responsibilities and burdens were crushing, overwhelming, too much for one woman to bear. But then she would think of Emma and draw strength from the memories of that beloved woman who was so much a part of her and whose blood ran in her veins. And every single day she thanked God for Winston, who was her rock, and for Emily, who was her greatest consolation, her dearest friend and her most loving, loyal and devoted cousin. Without them her life would be very bleak indeed.

The old familiar sadness enveloped Paula on this Saturday morning in August as she strolled slowly up the Rhododendron Walk which she herself had created. It seemed so long ago now – that spring when she had planted these bushes. So much had happened to her in the last few years ... so many losses, so many defeats ... and yet so many triumphs and gains as well. She smiled to herself as she suddenly thought of the children and the happiness and love they gave her. Her sadness lifted slightly and her smile widened. An hour ago Emily had arrived to take them, and Nora, off to Heron's Nest for the next three weeks. They would spend the remainder of August and the first two weeks of September in the old villa by the sea, whilst she herself was in Texas and New York on business. They loved their Aunty Emily, and their older counterparts, Amanda and Francesca, who would be joining them for the holiday in Scarborough. They had been so excited as they had toddled down the steps to the car, clutching their buckets and spades. And they had looked so adorable in their cotton sunsuits and matching sun hats. Little monkeys, she muttered affectionately, recalling the scene which had been enacted in the driveway a short while before. For once they had not been a bit concerned that they would be apart from her. After kissing her hastily they had clambered into the car and had been driven off without so much as giving her a backward glance.

No matter, she thought, as she turned and retraced her steps down the steep walk. They will enjoy the sun and the sea air and have a rare old time with Emily. And I know they are truly in safe hands in my absence.

Paula paused when she came to the lily pond at the bottom of the long sloping lawns. She stood reflecting as Shane edged into her mind.

The last time she had seen him the two of them had sat here on the stone bench near the pond. It had been a very hot sunny day towards the end of June. Almost two months ago. She had been exhausted, careworn on that Saturday, after a debilitating week rushing between the Harte stores in Leeds, Harrogate and Sheffield. He had arrived after lunch, unexpected and unannounced, and they had ended up having a violent quarrel. No, that was not actually true. They had not quarrelled. But he had lost his temper with her and she had simply sat there, letting his anger roll over her, aware that there was nothing else she could do. She had often been subjected to his outbursts as a child, and she had never won with him. It was always better to remain silent, let him rant and rave and get everything off his chest. That Saturday he had been justified. It would be wrong of her not to admit this.

Lowering herself on to the stone bench, Paula stared ahead and it was as if she was watching a piece of film as she sat back, saw herself and Shane as they had been on that stifling June Saturday only a few weeks ago.

'I can't go on like this, Paula,' Shane had exclaimed suddenly in the middle of their conversation. His voice had risen, and to an unnatural level for him these days, as he had burst out, 'I know it's only been five months, and I understand your pain, understand what you're going through. But you don't give me any hope for the future. If you did that, perhaps I *could* go on coping. But without hope a man has nothing. You turned away from me on that ghastly day at the barn, and you're drawing further away as you retreat deeper into yourself.'

'I can't help it,' she had murmured. 'I'm sorry, Shane.'

'But why? For God's sake tell me *why*?'

She had taken a while to reply. Then she had murmured in her quietest voice, 'If only I hadn't been with you ... and I mean *with* you in the most intimate way, then perhaps things would be different now. But Shane, we were making love at seven o'clock on that Saturday morning. It was one o'clock in France, and the moment the avalanche struck. Don't you see, I can't face making love ever again. I just can't. When I envision doing so I fall apart emotionally. I link it to the tragedy, to the awful way Daddy and Jim and Maggie died.'

He had stared at her helplessly, his face tensing. 'I knew it. I knew that was it,' he had finally remarked in a curiously hoarse, choked voice.

There had been a short silence and then she had told him, had spelled out in actual words what she had long believed he knew within himself, understood in his heart of hearts. 'Shane, it's better that we don't see each other again,' she had whispered. 'Not even as friends. I have nothing to offer you, not even friendship right now. Look, it wouldn't be fair to you if we continued in this way. Perhaps one day I will be able to resume our friendship, be your friend, but ...' Her voice had trailed off.

He had stared at her hard, his eyes piercing into hers, and she had seen the shock and hurt, the disbelief, and then the sudden anger reflected on his handsome face.

'I can't believe you're saying this to me!' he had cried heatedly, his face blazing. 'I love you, Paula, and even though you want to deny it at this moment, *you love me*. I know you do. We've had so much, and have so much together. That deep closeness that has grown from childhood affection to the mature abiding love of two adults, and compatibility in every way, and passion. Yes, I understand how you feel about sex because of the last time we made love, but that awful memory of the catastrophe will eventually fade. It has to. It would be abnormal if it didn't go away.'

She had shaken her head, remained mute, her hands clasped in her lap.

'You blame yourself!' he shouted, losing patience with her. 'Now I understand your attitude even more. You actually *blame* yourself and you're punishing yourself! Punishing me! You're so wrong, Paula. So wrong. It wasn't your fault. The avalanche was an Act of God. You didn't cause it to happen. And now you think that by flagellating yourself, leading a chaste life, you'll redeem yourself! *Is that it?*' Not waiting for her response he had rushed on, 'Whatever you do, Paula, you can't bring them back. Accept that. Accept that life is for the living. You have every *right* to be happy. And so do I. So do *we* – together. You need a husband, you need *me*, and Lorne and Tessa need a father. I love the twins. I want to be a loving father to them, an adoring husband to you. You cannot be alone for the rest of your life. It would be a waste, the most terrible and wanton waste.'

He had paused for breath at this point and she had reached out, touched his arm gently. 'Please, Shane, don't upset yourself like this.'

'Upset myself! That's a joke, Paula! Here you are, telling me we must part ... forever, seemingly, and you use a word like *upset*. Jesus Christ, I'm *shattered*, don't you realize that? You are my whole life. I have nothing if I don't have you.'

'Shane,' she had begun, reaching out again.

He had shaken her hand off his arm and leapt to his feet. 'I cannot continue this ridiculous discussion. I have to go. Get away from here. God knows how I'll ever find peace of mind again, but I don't suppose that's your problem, is it, Paula? It's mine.' He had stepped away from her, gazed down at her, his expression one she could not quite read. 'Goodbye, Paula,' he had said in a shaking voice and as he had turned away she had seen the tears glittering in his black eyes.

She had wanted to run after him as he had bounded up the steps to the terrace. But she had restrained herself, knowing that there was no point. She had been cruel to Shane but at least she had told him the truth and perhaps one day he would understand her motives. She hoped that he would come to realize that she had given him his freedom because she could no longer continue to hurt him by dangling the future in front of his nose. It was a future that did not exist.

Now, as she rose and went up the stone steps to the terrace in front of Pennistone Royal, Paula remembered how oddly detached she had felt that day. It had troubled her then and it troubled her now. Was she always going to be like this?

Sighing under her breath, she went in through the open French doors, crossed the Peach Drawing Room and hurried down the length of the Stone Hall. As she ran lightly up the grand staircase, heading for the upstairs parlour, she put all private and personal thoughts to one side. She was driving to London later in the day, taking a plane to Texas on Monday. She was about to do battle at Sitex and her plan of action needed every ounce of her attention, her total concentration.

53

'Anyway, Shane, when John Crawford told me he was going to Australia to spend a month with Daisy and Philip, I was delighted,' Winston said across the luncheon table to his closest friend.

'So am I.' Shane lifted his glass, took a sip of red wine and continued, 'Daisy was looking much better, and she was certainly in brighter spirits when I saw her in Sydney in August. I think she's adjusting to life without David.'

'Daisy's a sensible woman.' Winston eyed Shane and then he laughed quietly. 'I must admit, I've always had a sneaking suspicion that John had a crush on Daisy.' Shrugging lightly, he added, 'Who knows, maybe he can give her a bit of love and companionship. After all, she's still a young woman.'

'Yes.' Shane's face changed. His expression turned morose and brooding as he gazed across the restaurant absently. He was lost in his thoughts, pondering his future, as he so often did of late.

Winston leaned forward and said slowly, carefully, 'Despite Paula's attitude at this moment, she could easily reverse herself, you know. Women are unpredictable creatures at the best of times.'

'Not Paula,' Shane said after a few seconds of consideration. 'She's very strong, and once her mind is made up, it's made up.' He shook his head sadly. 'I'm going to have to do my damnedest to forget her, Winston, and make a fresh start. It won't be easy, but I'm certainly going to give it a try. I can't go around carrying a torch for her for the rest of my life. There's not much to be gained from that.'

'No, there isn't.'

Shane brought out his cigarettes, offered one to Winston. They sat smoking for a few minutes and then Shane said, 'I'm glad you stopped off in New York for a couple of days on your way back to London. It's been a –'

'So am I,' Winston interjected, and chuckled. 'I rather like the idea of flying home in style on that private jet of yours. Not to mention having you for company. And thanks again for delaying your plans, waiting for me. I appreciate it.'

'Yes, and what I started to tell you is that I've appreciated having your company.' Shane pursed his lips, gave Winston a pointed stare. 'As you're aware, I've never talked about women or my love affairs to you, but I needed to confide my feelings for Paula, unburden myself to someone I trust and respect. You've been very patient and helpful. Thanks, Winston.'

Winston sat back, finished his wine, and then puffed on his cigarette, looking thoughtful. Finally he murmured, 'I should have told you this the other night, but you seemed done in after your marathon session on the subject of Paula. Anyway, you weren't really telling me anything I didn't know. I mean about you being in love with Paula. I've known that for the longest time now. So has Emily.'

Shane said, very startled, 'And I thought no one knew. Just goes to show you, doesn't it.'

Winston said softly, 'Emma knew too, Shane.'

'She did!' Shane's astonishment was more pronounced and for a split second he was speechless, then he smiled faintly. 'Funnily enough, I've had the strangest feeling since she died that she was aware of our relationship. But Paula pooh-poohed the idea, dismissed it out of hand.'

'Aunt Emma didn't know you were involved, that's true,' Winston exclaimed rapidly. 'And to tell you the honest truth, neither Emily nor I were too sure about that either. Aunt Emma spotted a look in your eyes when you were observing Paula at the christening two-and-a-half years ago. That's when Emily and I also realized how deeply you felt about Paula.'

'I see.' Leaning across the table, Shane gave Winston a hard and questioning stare, asked, 'Obviously Aunt Emma discussed it with you. What did she say?'

'She was worried about you, Shane. She loved you a lot, you know, like one of us, one of her own. I think it was a disappointment to her that you hadn't spoken up earlier, before Paula married Jim. But she was philosophical about it really, knew she couldn't interfere. However, if she were alive she wouldn't be a bit surprised to know that Paula reciprocates your love for her, that I can guarantee you.'

'*Reciprocated* in the past tense, mate,' Shane muttered, and made a sour face. 'The lady has chosen to walk a solitary path.'

'She might change her mind,' Winston shot back, wanting to cheer him up. 'I keep telling you, women do that half a dozen times a day. Besides, it's only been nine months. Give her a chance, a bit longer to pull herself together. Look, Shane, I have an idea. Don't fly back to London with me this afternoon. Stay here in New York. Paula's been in Texas for a week, and I know she's due back in the city in a couple of days, either tomorrow or Wednesday. See her again, take her out, wine and dine her, talk to her. You can be very persuasive and –'

Shane held up his hand and shook his head with firmness. 'No, Winston, it won't do any good. She made it very clear to me in June that it was over. *Finished*. Besides, I can't delay my return any longer. Dad's due to go out to Sydney later this week. His turn, you know, and with Merry running this hotel, I have to be on the scene at home for a few months. I'll be racing between Leeds and London, but spending more time in Yorkshire, I hope.'

'Emily's looking forward to having you at Beck House at weekends, Shane, as soon as she's back from Scarborough. I hope you're not going to disappoint her, or me for that matter.'

'No. I'll be staying with you at weekends when I can, and thanks a lot. I want to spend some time at your father's stables, talk to him about Emerald Bow, and our racing programme for next year. Grandpops left me the racehorse to race, not to put out to pasture. And I haven't been on a horse for months. I'm itching to get into the saddle, give War Lord and Celtic Maiden a few good workouts.'

'That's great, Shane, it'll be –' Winston stopped, grinned from ear to ear and waved. To Shane, he said, 'Here's that gorgeous sister of yours.'

Shane swung around and his face lit up when he saw Miranda, who was hurrying across the restaurant looking as if she had something of vital importance to tell him. He smiled at her extraordinary costume, for that was all he could call it. She resembled a redheaded gypsy in her colourful patchwork cotton dress and masses of gold chains. Taking over as head of their New York operation had not induced her to change her spectacular style of dressing. Good for you, Merry, Shane thought. Stick to your guns. Be your highly original self, one of the genuine free spirits of this world.

'Hello, you two gorgeous men, and don't get up,' Merry exclaimed as they both made to rise. She flopped down into the empty chair and said, 'Come closer. I've something interesting to tell you.' Giving them both a conspiratorial look, she went on, 'You'll *never* guess who I've just seen. Not in a million years!'

Winston looked amused. 'Then tell us, Merry darling. It'll save a lot of time.'

'Yes, do,' Shane remarked. 'Would you like a glass of this?' He lifted the bottle of wine, showed it to her.

'Thanks, that'll be lovely.' Merry settled back in her chair, waited until her brother had poured the last of the wine into their three glasses, then said, 'I was in the Terrace Café, talking to the *maitre d'* when I spotted them ... talk about the Terrible Trio!'

Both men looked at her blankly.

475

Grinning, Miranda wrinkled her freckled nose and hissed, 'Allison Ridley, Skye Smith and – *Sarah Lowther*. All lunching together and looking very, very chummy, to say the least. Can you believe it!'

'Sarah!' Winston chuckled sardonically. 'Well, well, well, that's very interesting. I wonder what she's doing in New York. Paula and Emily haven't heard anything about her for months, or Jonathan either, for that matter, since he went to the Far East.'

'Don't mention that bastard,' Shane said, scowling. 'He's always been a troublemaker, and as devious as the devil.'

Winston nodded in agreement.

Merry said, 'I suppose I ought to have gone over and spoken to them, but quite frankly I beat a hasty retreat. I wanted to warn you both that a couple of your old girlfriends were floating around our hotel. Thank God they didn't decide to lunch in here – then where would you have been?'

Winston said jokingly, 'Allison would have probably slipped a Mickey Finn in my drink.'

'Skye Smith was *never* a girlfriend of *mine*,' Shane announced, and winked at Merry. 'Not my type.'

'We all know *you* don't like blondes, that you prefer dark exotic beauties like my darling Pau –' Miranda bit off the name and gave her brother an apologetic and concerned look. 'Sorry, Shane, I didn't mean to rub salt in the wound.'

'That's all right, Merry, and I'm a big boy. I might be still licking my wounds but at least I've managed to stem the flow of blood finally.'

'Yes, I know.' Merry took a small swallow of her wine and began to talk about their impending flight to London, making an effort to change the subject. Despite Shane's flippancy, the front he put up, she was aware that he was deeply hurt and still suffering inside. He yearned for Paula. He would all of his life, that was the depressing part. If only Jim had not been so tragically killed, Merry thought. Paula would have eventually been divorced and Shane and she would have married. Now Paula had put herself on a rack. And Shane too. Why is she doing this? Miranda asked herself. I don't understand her anymore.

Shane said, 'Daydreaming suddenly, Merry? You started to say something about the car.'

'Oh yes, sorry,' Merry said, smiling at him. 'I arranged for the limousine to be outside at three o'clock. That gives you plenty of time to get to Kennedy before the rush hour.'

Skye Smith was the first to excuse herself after lunch. She could not wait to escape, and it was with a sigh of relief that she crossed the elegant lobby of the Plaza Towers Hotel, property of the O'Neills, and hurried out into the street.

She peered at her watch. It was just turning off two-thirty, and she had plenty of time to get back to the antique shop for her next appointment at three.

As she strolled towards Park Avenue she thought about Sarah Lowther. She did not particularly like her and she could not help wondering what Allison saw in her. Sarah was the bitchiest woman she had ever met, and not very bright in some ways.

On the other hand, Sarah had inadvertently dropped a gold mine of information on to the table over lunch, and had opened up in such a personal way about her private affairs, Skye was still slightly taken aback.

She smiled cynically as she waited on the corner for the traffic lights to change before crossing Park. *So Paula Fairley was the mystery woman, the love of Shane's life, the lady who had got her clutches into him. And so much so he was incapable of making it with any other woman.*

This news had staggered Skye. When Sarah had discovered that Skye had occasionally dated Shane, the Englishwoman had turned to stone at the luncheon table. Skye had thought for a minute that Sarah was going to scratch her eyes out, so venomous was the look on the redhead's face. It had become patently obvious to Skye that Sarah was madly in love with Shane, and she had quickly assured Allison's friend that they had only ever had a platonic relationship. This had seemed to appease Sarah, and she had relaxed again, confided more dirt about the family, and in particular about Paula. The hatred Sarah harboured for her cousin was frightening. Hell hath no fury like a woman scorned, Skye thought, hurrying along. I ought to know.

She hardly ever saw Shane O'Neill these days. He had become a world traveller as their holdings had increased, and apparently he spent a great deal of time in Australia. He was only in New York on rare fleeting visits since his sister had been made the president of their American hotel corporation. He had called her once, almost a year ago now, and they had had a drink together, but he had seemed preoccupied and restless, and she had decided against pressing him to take her to dinner.

Ross, on the other hand, was always taking Paula Fairley to lunch, especially in the last six months or so. He had let that slip accidentally. When she had teased him about Paula, Ross had said it was strictly business. And at heart she knew there was a great deal of truth in this. Ross had been close to Paula's grandmother, as had his uncle, Daniel P. Nelson. Still, Skye knew Ross as well as she knew herself. Business it might indeed be, but he no doubt hankered after the woman. Paula Fairley was everything Ross craved. Good looking. Young. Rich. Powerful. And available – now that she was a widow. Ross probably had some scheme up his sleeve, a plan to propel Paula Fairley into his bed, and possibly into matrimony. He had once told her that if he ever married again he would make sure his intended bride was wealthy. Yes, Ross would always continue to repeat his old patterns. He desired what he could not have. And after the things Sarah had told her there was no question in her mind that Paula Fairley had held herself apart, had not succumbed to Ross's charms. And why would she with Shane O'Neill in the background – her lover of long standing.

Skye now thought about her dinner date with Ross on Wednesday night and laughed under her breath. They dined once a week since they had become friends again. It had taken her a long time to forgive his shoddy treatment of her, but in the end she had forgiven him. She had done so because of their daughter Jennifer. When Ross had come begging to see their child she had consistently and categorically refused to permit this. The longer she had remained cold and unbending, refused to reverse her decision, the more his need to see his little girl had increased. How typical of him. What he could not have he did persist in chasing and forever tried to attain. She had taken great pleasure in making Ross implore and crawl on his hands and knees to her. And that he had eventually done – well almost.

With reluctance she had finally given in, but only because she had come to understand how much Jennifer loved her father, longed to see him on a continuing basis and to spend time with him. She could not deprive the child because of the man and his character.

The laughter bubbled up in Skye again as she continued walking at a steady pace, heading for her shop on Seventy-Third and Lexington. What fun she would have with Ross at dinner later in the week. She would adroitly drop a few spicy tid-bits about Paula Fairley and Shane O'Neill at the right moment, and then sit back and watch Ross choke on his food. It would drive him crazy when he knew that the sorrowing *widder* was, in reality, the Merry Widow, waltzing to Shane's tune and bestowing her very special favours on him. Although Ross and Shane had done business together in the past, Ross had always been disparaging about Shane behind his back, constantly referring to him as the stud.

Although she was not an unkind woman, Skye Smith was bitter about Ross Nelson. A cold gleam entered her eyes as she contemplated making her former lover squirm. I knew if I waited long enough I'd be able to twist the knife in Ross's back one day, she thought. And he deserves it, after all the pain and humiliation he's inflicted on me. I forgave him for our daughter's sake. But I've never forgotten and I never will.

She did not understand that she wanted Ross for herself.

Ross Nelson's sanguine expression vanished. His light hazel eyes clouded and narrowed slightly as he leaned back in his leather chair and stared harder at Dale Stevens.

Finally Ross cleared his throat and asked, 'Exactly what do you mean when you say Paula changed her mind?'

'She's decided not to sell her Sitex stock,' Dale told him and shrugged. 'We both misread her I guess. And badly.'

'She reneged? Reneged on our deal?' Ross exclaimed in a cold, tight voice. 'And where the hell were you, Dale, when all this was happening?' When Dale did not reply, he continued in a sharper accusatory tone, 'This is one hell of a disaster! I'm going to look like the biggest fool in the world. Milt Jackson is going to have apoplexy when he finds out.'

Dale sighed and crossed his legs, waiting for the banker to cool down.

The two men sat in Ross Nelson's private office in his bank on Wall Street. It was early on Thursday afternoon in the first week of September, the day after Dale had flown up from Texas with Paula.

'What am I going to say to him?' Ross pressed, leaning forward urgently across his huge partner's desk, endeavouring to control his considerable annoyance.

'Tell him the truth. That's all you can do.'

478

'Why didn't you call me after the board meeting yesterday? Give me a chance to collect my thoughts, come up with a reasonable story?' Ross demanded tersely.

'I felt it was better to tell you in person.'

'I just can't believe this,' Ross muttered angrily, shifting his weight in the chair. 'I was certain she was going to sell, convinced of it. I could wring her neck after the merry dance she's led us.'

Dale sighed wearily. 'Nobody was more surprised than I was when she pulled her stunt at the board meeting. But last night, when I could think dispassionately, I began to realize that she simply blinded us – with words, sweet talk, charm, and a lot of dissembling. And you know something, Ross, she *didn't* renege. I had time to analyse the situation last night, and as I ran everything through my head, replayed every meeting we've ever had with her and particularly in the last six months, I suddenly saw things very clearly. Yes, she talked incessantly about her problems, her worries, the burdens of running the Harte chain, and she did keep intimating she wanted to sell her mother's stock. But she never actually came out and said she would do so. In my anxiousness to render Marriott Watson helpless, have International Petroleum take over the company, and in your *own* anxiousness to please Milt Jackson, your valued client, we *assumed* she would unload. If anything, we're at fault, believing we could push her around, get her to do our bidding.'

'She listened to us both so attentively,' Ross exploded. 'She asked for our advice, seemed to be taking it. Not only that, she insisted on knowing who the prospective buyer was, and against my better judgement I told her!' Ross groaned. 'Oh Jesus, what a fool I've been! I should never have arranged those meetings between her, Milt Jackson and us.' The banker reached for a cigarette and lit it nervously. 'Milt thinks Sitex is in the bag. Jesus Christ, he's going to be convinced I misled him, or that I've suddenly developed flawed judgement, in the prime of my life. We've got to come up with a plausible story to tell him.'

'I repeat what I just said, we have to tell him the truth, explain that *she* misled *us*. He'll have to accept it, there's nothing else he *can* do,' Dale insisted.

Ross drew on his cigarette and then stubbed it out. He rose, walked around his desk and began to pace up and down, his hands behind his back as he contemplated the meeting with Milton Jackson, chairman of the board of International Petroleum, and an important client of the bank. Suddenly he stopped in his tracks and fixed his eyes on Dale. 'If this gets out we're going to look like the biggest idiots on Wall Street. Two grown men, seasoned businessmen, shrewd, tough and hard assed, taken by a slip of a girl.' He ran his hand through his blondish hair and grimaced with disgust at himself and Dale. 'Talk about Emma Harte. Paula Fairley puts her to shame. The double-dealing little wretch. I would never have believed it of her. I really thought she was taking our guidance.'

'I had my doubts about that on several occasions,' Dale remarked dryly. 'And then I admit I began to read just my thinking about her, particularly in view of the events over the past year. There was Emma's death, that knocked her for a loop, and then she lost her Daddy and her husband. She was in shock. You witnessed her state with your own eyes. So there she was, all alone, and suddenly I believed it would be a cinch. I genuinely thought she would unload the stock. She indicated she'd be happy to do that, would be relieved to get out of the oil rat race. What a foul up.'

Ross said in a rush, 'I'm going to tell Milt that she *did* in fact renege. To hell with it. Guys renege on deals every day in the street and in the oil business. Why should a woman be any different. More likely to change her mind in my opinion. I can't afford to lose Milt Jackson as a client of this bank, or International Petroleum as a corporate account.'

'Okay,' Dale concurred. 'Basically he's your baby anyway. I don't owe him an explanation.' The oil man brought out a cigar, fiddled with the end, finally struck a match and brought the flame to the cigar. He said, 'You do realize my hands were tied at the board meeting, don't you, Ross? There was nothing I could do.'

'Sure, sure,' Ross mumbled and returned to his chair. 'Tell me exactly what happened on Tuesday.'

'Be happy to, Ross. Paula arrived looking like a demure little nun, wearing a black dress with a white collar and cuffs. She was unusually pale, even for her, and it gave her a waif-like look. She had a sort of innocence about her.'

'Save me the description, God damn it! I'm interested in what she said, not how she looked.'

'Her appearance is important,' Dale replied. Paula had played her role very well. He had realized, as he had sat in the Sitex board room in Odessa, that there was something of the actress in her. 'Don't you understand, Ross, she looked like a little girl, easy to handle, and some of those old buzzards on the board, who don't know her very well – why they were rubbing their hands with glee. Metaphorically speaking, that is. Yes, Marriott Watson's cronies thought they were going to eat her alive.'

'As we did,' Ross muttered softly.

Dale smiled faintly. 'We weren't the only guys who were fooled, Ross, take comfort in that, cold as it is. Before we got down to general business, the North Sea oil situation and the renewal of my contract, Paula asked to make a statement to the board. Naturally, Marriott Watson had no choice but to agree. She said that it was her duty to inform her fellow board members that she was about to sell her mother's stock. The entire block – the entire forty per cent of it. Everyone was taken aback, and that was when Jason Emerson piped up.'

Ross nodded. 'He's still sharp, smart as hell, despite his great age.'

Dale agreed. 'Tough old wild catters like Jason don't change, not in my experience. I sat back, enjoying every minute, thinking it was going our way. It was only later that I began to realize Paula had made good use of the week she had spent in Texas, prior to the board meeting. She had done a lot of lobbying, entertained a number of the directors socially. Especially Jason. He was primed by her, no doubt in my mind about that. Still, he was close to Paul McGill in the thirties, and had remained loyal to Emma for forty years.'

'I know about that,' Ross snapped.

'Jason Emerson asked Paula who she was selling the stock to, and when she intended to sell. She told him, very sweetly, that she was selling all forty per cent to International Petroleum. *Immediately*. I thought that some of the board members were going to have a collective coronary. Holy hell broke loose. I said nothing, pleased at the way she had handled herself. There was a lot of heated talk about International Petroleum and Milt. It's no secret in the oil business that he has that company on a growth and expansion programme and that once he gets a foothold in a company he does his damnedest to swoop down and take it over. Also, certain board members seemed to be aware that Milt has been buying up Sitex's common stock, and that he now holds an enormous amount of it. Only a dunce could fail to miss the implications.'

'If I'm following the script correctly, as I think I am, presumably Jason spoke up again, asked her not to sell to International Petroleum.'

'You've got it, old buddy.' Dale shook his head regretfully. 'Sure as God made little green apples, once the shouting had died down, old Jason started to persuade her to reconsider her decision. It was a bit of real craftiness, I can tell you, Ross. Before I had a chance to jump in with a few comments of my own, the majority of the board were singing his tune. Except Marriott Watson. He looked as if he was about to spit blood. I'm not certain, but he may have deduced that the tough negotiating between Paula and Jason had been set up in advance.'

'And she capitulated of course.'

'Not at first. She said she would reconsider not selling her block of stock, providing she was guaranteed a stronger voice on the board and if certain conditions were met. *Her conditions*. To be precise, the continuation of the North Sea drilling and the renewal of my contract.'

'She blackmailed the board!' Ross shouted.

Dale shook his head very slowly and a gleam of admiration now entered his brown eyes. 'No, Ross, I wouldn't call it blackmail. It was the most brilliant bit of manipulation I've seen in a long time. In one way I've got to take my hat off to her because that's what business is all about – manipulation.'

'That's true,' Ross acknowledged. 'At least you got what *you* wanted, despite everything. Your contract has been renewed again and is secure for two years, Marriott Watson is temporarily muzzled and you have a free hand. But what's your position with Paula now, Dale?'

Dale grinned. 'My position remains the same. I'm president of Sitex Oil, she controls the stock of her mother, who is the largest single stockholder. Paula has more power on the board than she ever had. Naturally I'll continue confiding in her as I always have. I intend to remain friendly. You never know, she still might decide to sell her stock one day. International Petroleum isn't going anywhere.'

'Points well taken.' Ross laughed unexpectedly. 'Business is business. Not every deal works out the way one would wish. There's no point my being immature about this. The bank still handles some of her business in the States. Anyway, if I can't succeed with her in the boardroom maybe I'll get lucky – in the bedroom.'

54

Paula Fairley was late.

Ross Nelson glanced at the carriage clock on the mantelpiece of his living room for the umpteenth time. He was growing impatient. When she had telephoned at six-thirty to say she was delayed he had told her to take her time. But he had expected her to arrive before now.

He strolled across the antique Chinese carpet and hovered in front of the bar contained in the ebony-and-gilt Chinese chest. He poured himself another dry martini, dropped in an olive and walked to the window, looking down on to Park Avenue. His thoughts continued to dwell on Paula.

She was one of the few women he had not been able to fathom. Or coax into his bed. He had desired her for the longest time now. Since the fall of 1969 when he had first become aware of her potent sexuality. She had always managed to keep their relationship on a cool business-like basis. At first he had believed he would win her over. Women generally fell for him. Later he had become annoyed as she continued to be uninterested. But he had kept up his battery on the telephone, constantly invited her out to dinner and bombarded her with flowers. Since he was conceited, and had enjoyed much success with women from all walks of life, Ross convinced himself that Paula would one day be his alone.

After Jim Fairley had been killed in the avalanche, Ross had played the role of a concerned good friend whenever she had been in New York. In the past nine months he had seen more of her than usual, since she had wanted to divest herself of some of Emma Harte's holdings which she had inherited. He had been on hand to help the sorrowing widow handle her business. He had hoped to persuade her to sell the Sitex stock – and seduce her as well. Her grief and curiously distant manner had induced him to hold himself in check. He had bided his time. But he had no intention of doing so any longer. Not now, not after Skye Smith's revelations last night.

He focused on the gossip Skye had relayed about Paula and Shane O'Neill. He had been stunned and disbelieving, had demanded to know the source. Skye had been only too ready to further confide. At the end of the evening he had walked home bridling with anger and riddled with frustration. All these months, as he had held her hand and comforted her, Paula had been sleeping with Shane O'Neill. He knew Skye had not lied. After all, Sarah Lowther, Paula's cousin, had been the one who had spilled the beans.

He was delighted that Dale and his wife had been called back to Texas so unexpectedly. They had planned a foursome for dinner. He relished the idea of being alone with Paula tonight. His way was clear with her. *Finally*. At long last he was going to possess this most elusive of women.

Ross sat down on the sofa, put his martini on the Chinese coffee table and took a cigarette, suppressing the sudden grin that had begun to spread across his face. He had not told Paula that Dale and Jessica had returned to the ranch. Why alert her, give her the opportunity to cancel. But he had given his housekeeper the evening off, and telephoned the restaurant to change the reservation to ten o'clock. That would give him ample time to make his moves.

Thoughts of her slender boyish body, the voluptuous breasts, intruded, brought a sudden flush to his neck. He lifted the glass, downed the rest of the drink, and went to the bar to pour another one. It was his third. He hesitated. Oh what the hell, he muttered. I can handle my liquor. Ross prided himself on his ability to drink gallons and remain a potent lover. His glance fell on the bottle of champagne in the ice bucket and he smiled confidently. After a few glasses of that, and a little of his sweet talking, Paula Fairley would be much more susceptible to his masculine appeal.

Ross Nelson had almost demolished his third martini when the intercom rang. Leaping to his feet, he rushed out into the foyer to answer it, hardly able to contain himself. He told the doorman to send Mrs Fairley up and stood waiting for her.

A few minutes later he was kissing Paula's cool cheek, ushering her across the hall and into the living room.

She paused in the entrance and swung her head, looked up at him, her violet eyes quizzical. 'Haven't Jessica and Dale arrived yet?' she asked before she moved forward.

He gazed after her, watching the fluid movement of her body, the shapely outline of her long legs through the thin silk of the pale grey cocktail dress. He almost salivated with longing. He could hardly wait to remove the dress, to strip her naked and revel in her beauty.

Paula turned to face him, catching him off guard. He blinked rapidly, hurried into the room, explained, with a nervous laugh. 'They had to fly back at the last minute. An illness in the family.' He stepped up to the bar, began to open the bottle of champagne. 'Dale sends his apologies and he told me to tell you he'll phone you tomorrow.'

'I see,' Paula said, seating herself on the sofa. 'I'm disappointed they're not having dinner with us. I did have a few more things to discuss with Dale.' She gave him a small smile. 'Never mind.'

'Yes,' Ross murmured and carried the drink over to her. Seating himself in the chair opposite, he lifted his own glass and grinned at her. 'Well, Paula, congratulations! You've certainly pulled off a coup at Sitex!' ·

'Cheers, Ross,' Paula said, took a sip of the champagne and then eyed him speculatively. 'You're probably annoyed with me, angry that I finally decided to hold on to the Sitex stock. But –'

'Of course not,' he lied blandly, wanting to keep the atmosphere cosy and totally free of conflict. 'It was your choice. Dale and I could only advise you. We only wanted to help you, Paula. As Dale said to me at the bank this afternoon, International Petroleum is not going anywhere. I think Milton Jackson would always be interested in buying you out.'

'I'm sure he would,' Paula responded quietly. 'And I do want to thank you for your concern, all of your help with the Sitex matter, and with my other American business. I'm most appreciative.'

'My pleasure.'

Paula leaned back on the sofa and crossed her legs, trying to hide her surprise at his attitude. She had expected Ross to be furious, knowing how much he valued Milton Jackson as a client of the bank. Dale, she knew, would always give her his support. But Ross Nelson was another kettle of fish. She was relieved that he was being so agreeable. He was always agreeable though, wasn't he? She sighed, realizing she would have to spend the next few hours alone with him. There was no way she could get out of dining with him. She decided to be gracious and get through the evening as best she could.

Ross began to talk about her brother Philip, whom he had met the previous autumn when they had both been in New York. And for the next half hour the banker kept up a steady stream of conversation about the family in general, her grandmother, and Harte Enterprises. In between, he kept refilling her glass, downed another martini and lit endless cigarettes.

At ten to nine, Paula cut him short suddenly, and asked 'Shouldn't we be leaving, Ross? For the restaurant I mean?'

'No, not just yet. I'm afraid I had problems with the reservation at Twenty-One. They couldn't give me a table before nine thirty, ten o'clock. We might as well relax here.'

'Oh all right,' Paula said, but she was irritated. She disliked eating when the evening was almost over.

As he talked, believing he was being entertaining, Ross continued to drink. He also scrutinized Paula intently, admiring her elegance and beauty. The dress she wore was simple, with a draped cowl collar and short sleeves. She wore emerald earrings and, apart from a watch, these were her only pieces of jewellery. She looked stunning and the grey silk moulded her figure in all the right places. Suddenly he was unable to keep his distance.

He rose, strolled to the bar cabinet, topped his glass and joined her on the sofa. He rested his arm on the back, and sipped his drink. His eyes held hers and he smiled a slow warm smile. 'You're looking exceptionally lovely tonight, Paula.'

'Thank you, Ross.' She returned his gaze and her brow puckered. There was something in those hazel eyes of his that instantly alerted her and she drew back slightly, pressed herself closer to the arm of the small sofa.

She felt a sense of panic.

Ross placed his glass on the coffee table and in one swift move he pulled her into his arms, brought his mouth down hard on hers. She struggled with him, tried to push him away, but his grip was firm as he held her tightly. He forced his tongue against her mouth, forced her mouth open and began to suck on her tongue and her lips. Heat ran through him and he moved slightly so that he could grasp her left breast with his right hand. He squeezed it, pinched the nipple, increased the pressure of his fingers.

Paula continued to struggle, tried to disentangle herself from his arms, but he was a big man, and strong, and she had no chance against him. He somehow managed to pull her forward, sliding her body down the sofa into a supine position, and then he fell on top of her, working his tongue on her mouth again. She clamped her teeth shut and moved her head to one side rapidly. He ran his hand over her thigh, lifted her skirt, slid his hand underneath, stroked her upper leg and then worked his fingers against her crotch.

Paula, lying under the weight of Ross Nelson, was in a state of shock. She struggled hard to break free from his tenacious hold on her. He had leapt on her so unexpectedly, taken her totally by surprise, and only a split second after she had noticed the lust burning in his eyes. She was horrified, and revolted by him, and also terribly frightened. She knew she had to escape from him, from his apartment. Quickly. If only she could get her hands up to his face to scratch him. They were trapped under his bulk. She moved her head from side to side again, frantically avoiding his mouth without success. His hands were now ripping at her tights and dimly through the roaring in her head she heard the nylon tear as he tugged at the crotch of the tights. Oh my God. His fingers were against her skin, pushing into her as he slobbered against her face, his mouth slack and wet. Shudders rippled through her. She thought she was going to vomit. He was hurting her, trying to penetrate her with his fingers.

Tears sprang into her eyes, induced by the fear, the shock, the revulsion and the pain as he pushed his hand harder between her legs. He stopped kissing her at last, drew back for breath.

Paula opened her mouth and began to scream.

Ross was jarred from his exploration of her body and he sat up swiftly, looked down into her tearstained face, and clamped one hand over her mouth.

'Shut up,' he hissed. 'You know you like this, you bitch. Don't play the innocent with me. You've been getting it from Shane O'Neill for months. Now it's old Ross's turn.'

He laughed loudly and Paula realized that he was very drunk. She struggled, moving under him violently, easing herself to the edge of the sofa.

To pull her back he had to remove his hand from her mouth. The minute he did she began to scream again. Once more he covered her face with his large hand, wrapped one of his heavy legs around her body, and pinioned her under him. 'You've been playing the grieving widow with me far too long, Paula,' he gasped, his glazed eyes roving over her lasciviously. His lust was mounting by the minute, inflamed by the fight she was putting up. It brought a flushed and congested look to his face. 'Come on, let's go to the bedroom,' he mumbled, his words slurred. 'You know you want to screw me.'

Paula had been waiting for the right moment, and now she endeavoured to nod her head, as if acquiescing to this suggestion. She acknowledged him with her eyes, softening her gaze.

'No more screaming,' he muttered. 'Okay?'

She nodded again.

He took his hand away from her mouth and leaned into her as if to kiss her.

Paula whispered, 'I thought you wanted to go into the bedroom?'

He grinned at her drunkenly. 'That's the idea, baby.'

'What are we waiting for?'

Still grinning he got up off the sofa. Before Paula had a chance to do the same he bent down, took hold of her arms and pulled her to her feet.

She did not dare struggle, knowing his great strength. She would have to pick the right moment to flee. She swallowed as he dragged her to him and nestled his face against her hair. 'You're going to have to tell me everything liddle old Shane did to excite you, baby. Whatever old Shane can do, Ross can do better. And then some, baby.'

Swallowing her disgust and fear, summoning all of her strength, Paula pushed him away from her. Drunk, believing she was playing along with him, Ross was taken by surprise. He lost his balance, staggered back, and flopped down on the sofa.

Paula reached for her solid gold evening bag on the coffee table and swung around.

He was far too fast for her and grabbed her again. They struggled in the middle of the room. She kicked his shin and he yelled in pain, instantly loosened his grip on her. Finally she was able to pull away from him.

Ross snatched at her dress. The cowl collar ripped under his hand.

Paula kicked him again as he took a step towards her, his expression threatening, and then in a swift movement she raised her hand and smashed the heavy gold bag into his face with all her might.

He cried out in pain as the precious metal struck his cheek and backed off, stumbling against the Chinese coffee table immediately behind him. He went sprawling on the floor. 'You bitch!' he screamed, bringing his hands to his bleeding face.

Gasping for breath, shaking and terrified, Paula dashed into the foyer. The Chinese rug skidded under her but she recovered her balance, hitting her face against the edge of the tall cabinet as she did. But ignoring the stab of pain she flew to the door, jerked it open and banged it after her as she ran out. She pressed the button for the lift, cowering against the wall, praying he would not follow her.

Tears rushed to her eyes as she fiddled with the collar of her torn dress. She pushed them back, attempted to compose herself. When the doors rolled open she almost fell into the car, avoided the curious glance of the uniformed operator. She moved further back, retreated into the shadow, opened her bag and took out her compact. She ran the powder puff over her face and then smoothed her hand over her hair, aware of her dishevelled appearance.

Within seconds she was stepping out into the marble lobby of the building, hurrying across it at her fastest pace, and then hailing a cab on Park Avenue.

55

Paula somehow managed to keep a grip on herself until she reached the Fifth Avenue apartment.

After letting herself in quietly, she tiptoed upstairs, not wishing Ann, the housekeeper, to see her in this terrible state.

She slipped into her bedroom, locked the heavy carved-wood door and leaned against it, finally beginning to breathe a little easier. Her body was taut, rigid still with the fear that had swamped her when Ross Nelson had so unexpectedly launched his physical attack on her.

Eventually she found the strength to move forward on her trembling legs, and her hands shook as she unzipped her ruined dress and pulled it up over her head and discarded it. Once she had removed her underwear and her ripped stockings, she stumbled blindly into the bathroom.

Paula stood in the shower stall for ten minutes, soaping herself over and over again, letting the hot steaming water sluice down over her body. She felt battered and unclean, had the urgent need to erase the smell of him, the touch of him.

When at last she stepped out and looked at herself in the mirrored side wall, she saw that her body was bright pink, red in parts as if she had scalded herself, damaged the skin. But at least she felt cleaned of Ross Nelson. Pulling on a towelling robe without bothering to dry herself, she went over to the washbasin and peered at her face in the mirror. Her cheek bone was bruised where she had struck it against the cabinet. It would be black and blue tomorrow.

She continued to stare at herself.

Her blue eyes were dark, almost black, and they held the look of a wild hunted deer, were wide with fright and shock. She squeezed them tightly shut, wanting to forget what had happened to her only a short while ago. But she could not and she lifted her lids. His lustful face danced before her eyes, was reflected in the mirror, as if he was standing behind her in the bathroom. Paula shuddered and gripped the edge of the sink as she remembered how his hands had wandered so roughly over her body, how his horrible wet mouth had slobbered against hers, how his weight had trapped her under him. She had felt as though she was being suffocated.

Anger blazed through her. Ross Nelson had virtually tried to rape her. That he had been dreadfully drunk was no excuse. There was no excuse for that unconscionable behaviour. He was a disgusting specimen of a man. The worst. He was not a man. He was an animal. The shuddering intensified. How violated, how damaged she was feeling!

Nausea rose up in Paula. She began to vomit in the washbasin, retching until she had nothing left inside. The dry heaving continued for a while and then eventually subsided. Lifting her head, she wiped her streaming eyes and her sweating face with the damp flannel, then leaned her head against the cool tiles of the wall. Her head throbbed, her eyes ached and her muscles were sore from struggling with him, fighting him off.

Blocking out the image of him, she closed her eyes, gulping air, calming herself as best she could, and when she was steadier on her legs she moved away from the washbasin and blundered back into the bedroom. She lay down on the bed.

It was only then that Paula Fairley fell apart.

Quite suddenly she was gripped by an internal shaking and then her whole body began to shake as if she had palsy. She pulled the eiderdown up over her. Her teeth began to chatter and she shivered as icy chills swept through her. Clutching at the pillow, she buried her face in it and she began to sob as if her heart was breaking.

Paula cried without restraint for the next hour.

And all of the pain and sorrow she had suppressed since the tragic deaths of her father, Jim, and Maggie broke free at last.

Her terrible grief overwhelmed her, but she let it wash over her, envelope her completely, gave herself up to it, recognizing finally that it had been wrong and foolish of her to bottle it up inside. But she had not known what else to do. She had had to be strong, so very strong for her mother and Alexander and her children. And so she had deliberately buried the grief. It had lain there dormant, yet it had gradually gnawed away at her, eating her alive, rendering her helpless in so many aspects of her life.

As Paula Fairley wept the bitter tears she should have wept nine months ago, and had not, she began to experience a measure of ease, a genuine relief from the searing heartache and anguish that had engulfed her since the avalanche.

When she had no more tears left inside her she lay quietly on the bed, her body limp and exhausted, her eyes red and swollen, wide open, staring up at the ceiling.

Slowly, but with her usual intelligence and analytical powers, she began to sort out her muddled thoughts, sift through the painful memories, examine her emotional and physical frigidity with a new and stunning objectivity.

It was as if the shock of Ross Nelson's violent assault on her had cleared her brain, startled her out of her state of frozen containment. She started to see herself with new objectivity, and she knew with sudden sureness that the burdensome weight of her enormous guilt had crushed all feeling in her, all emotional response to others except her children. *She had no reason to be guilty. She was not to blame for anything. Not one single thing.*

Shane was correct in everything he had said.

How cruel she had been to him, inflicting pain on him because her own pain had blinded her to the truth, to reality. *Shane.* She saw his face in her imagination, transferred it in her imagination to the ceiling. If only he were really here now. She longed to have the comfort and security of his strong arms around her, keeping her safe.

Tears rushed into Paula's eyes. She had sent him away, had been so wilful in her determination to tread her solitary lonely road, believing it to be the only road for her. She wondered if he would ever be able to forgive her.

Ross Nelson's hideous, grinning, drunken face nudged Shane's to one side, obliterated him. Paula shuddered violently and sat up in bed. Fury ripped through her, momentarily, stunning her. *He had tried to rape her.* Never in her entire life had anything quite so disgusting happened to her. But then she had never been exposed to the harsher side of life. She had always been so protected. By Grandy. By her parents. By her large family. And by all that power and wealth. She did not know the streets, the hard world where other women had to live and fight and hold on to their sanity somehow, despite the burdens they had to carry, the punishment certain kinds of men made them endure.

Certainly she had never been exposed to men – not men like Ross Nelson, who were exploitative, pursued their own ends relentlessly. There had only ever been Jim. He had been her first lover and then she had married him. If he had been selfish and self-involved, and he undoubtedly had, if he had been swept along by his own needs, most certainly he had never been violent with her. He had never really forced himself on her, not once in all the time they had been married.

And then there had been Shane . . . theirs had been the grandest of passions, but physical desire had blended in with their deep abiding love, that love which he had said had grown out of their childhood affection and friendship. With Shane there had been a true bonding and on every level.

The brutalizing experience she had suffered at the hands of Ross Nelson had been terrifying. It was the worst kind of violation a man could inflict on a woman – an invasion not only of the body but of the mind and the heart and the soul as well. It had been cruel, painful and humiliating. She realized how lucky she had been to escape before he had committed that final act and a small series of shivers rippled over her and her anger surfaced yet again.

And yet his violence with her *had* shocked her into reality, brought her back to life, released the dam of her grief, destroyed the shell she had so carefully and deliberately built around her. But the carapace had cracked open and she was permitting herself to crawl out of it, to come back into the real world, to live again. Yes, she wanted to start afresh, to move forward, to put the past behind her, to look ahead to the future. Don't look back, forge ahead, Emma had always said to her. And that was what she must now do.

It was dawn when Paula finally fell asleep.

She slept deeply, as if she had been drugged. Not once during the night did she awaken and sit up in sudden fear, crying out in terror as she felt herself being buried alive under tons of cold snow that brought with it icy death.

The nightmare that had haunted her nights for so long had been exorcized, along with so many ghosts, so many troubled memories.

When she arose the following morning, after only a few hours of rest, she discovered she felt lighter, freer. It seemed as if a great weight had been lifted and she recognized then that the guilt she had carried had started to dissolve. That too would disappear entirely . . . one day in the future.

A new strength came into Paula as she dressed to go to the store on Fifth Avenue. And with that strength came a steadiness, a calmness, and a sure and thrusting knowledge that reached deep into her heart. She knew where she must go, what she must do, and as she stood in front of the mirror she nodded to herself. Her way *was* clear. She was about to set out on a new road.

56

He sat on one of the ancient ruined walls of Middleham Castle, daydreaming on this warm Sunday afternoon in September.

The high-flung canopy of the sky was a pewter colour, cloudy and overcast, presaging rain, despite the sun which was valiantly trying to push through. It finally emerged from behind the bank of cumulus and great rafts of brilliant silver light streamed across the heavens.

Shane lifted his head, looked up, was struck at once by the supernatural quality of that blinding light. It seemed to emanate from some hidden source behind those wild implacable hills and it held a shimmering clarity, a pure radiance that was unearthly, made him catch his breath.

His dark brooding eyes swept across the sky and then he glanced away, focused his attention on the ruined arch of Warwick's once-great stronghold, his mind turning inward. He was lonely and alone and yet he knew within his heart that he would find a measure of peace here in Yorkshire. He had made a decision when he had flown home from New York with Winston, at the beginning of this past week.

Shane O'Neill was going to end his long, self-imposed exile at last. There was too much pain in his life now to bring additional pain on himself and that he would surely continue to do if he persisted in exiling himself. When he was not travelling the world he would live here, surrounded by the beauty he had grown up with and which he so dearly loved. It was the one spot in this earth where he felt truly happy.

It would be hard for him at first but he would manage somehow. He was a man, mature, intelligent, and he had always been strong. Somewhere he would find the courage to create a new life for himself without her. And he fully intended to live out that life here.

War Lord was tethered nearby and he whinnied. Shane swung his head, looked about, expecting to see hikers or tourists. But he was still entirely alone. The ruined castle was deserted today and there was little sign of life, except for the occasional call of a kingfisher or a curlew, the *gawk-gawk* cry of a seagull which had flown in from the North Sea. His eyes lifted to the rolling moors, ranged up against the skyline, glorious today as the heather bloomed and rippling below were the lush green slopes of the Dales.

Shane sat there for a long time, feasting his eyes on the landscape, enjoying its stunning beauty. The grandeur and majesty of this place never failed to touch his Celtic soul which was so attuned to nature.

Suddenly he blinked, lifted his hand to shade his eyes. He saw a speck moving across the line of the hills coming steadily down the bridlepath, heading in the direction of the Castle.

When the lone horse and rider drew closer he stiffened on the wall and stared ahead, focusing his vision.

The rider was a young woman. She trotted at a brisk pace, handled the horse beautifully, showing great equestrian skill. Her long dark hair was blowing in the light breeze, streaming out behind a pale intense face.

In the passing of a moment he felt his heart leap and begin to clatter abnormally against his rib cage. The rider was spurring the horse forward. He recognized his own mare, Celtic Maiden, and he knew that girl, so clearly visible in that shimmering Northern light that washed the sky and the hills and the castle walls with its penetrating radiance.

It was his dreamlike child of his childhood dreams . . . riding through the dreamlike landscape of his childhood dreams . . . riding through the sunlight and the shadow . . . drawing nearer . . . nearer . . . nearer . . . raising her hand in greeting. His dreamlike child of his childhood dreams was coming to him . . . at last. But she had grown to womanhood now . . . as he was a man now

. . . she was the dreamlike woman he loved, had always loved, would always love until the day he died.

The thud of the hooves on the rich dark earth drowned out the clattering of his heart. Slowly, disbelievingly, he rose from the wall, his eyes full of questions. But his face was still and without expression.

She swung down out of the saddle lightly, threw the reins over the tree stump where War Lord was tethered, took a step towards him and stopped.

'I thought you were in New York,' Shane heard his voice say. He was surprised he sounded so controlled, so normal.

'I took the overnight flight from Kennedy to Manchester on Friday. Tilson picked me up yesterday and drove me back home . . . to Pennistone Royal.'

'I see.' Shane stepped back involuntarily, sat down on the wall, feeling weak.

She joined him on the old greystone wall and studied him for a long moment. Neither of them spoke.

Finally Shane said, 'What's happened to your face?'

'I fell. It's nothing.'

'What are you doing here?'

'I came looking for you. Randolph told me where you were. I came to ask you something, Shane.'

'Yes?'

'Would you please give me the ring . . . the ring Blackie gave to Emma?'

'You can have it if you want, Paula. She should have left it to you in the first place.'

'No. She meant you to have it. *She* never made mistakes like that. And I wasn't asking you to give me the ring as . . . you know, as a gift.' She hesitated only for the briefest second. 'I want you to give it to me as your future wife.'

He gaped at her.

She smiled at him.

Paula's uncanny violet eyes grew enormous in her pale face. 'I want to spend the rest of my life with you, Shane. If you still want me.'

He was incapable of answering. He put his arms around her and held her close to his shaking heart. And then he began to kiss her hair, her eyes and finally her soft and tender lips. The kiss was deep and passionate yet there was tenderness in it and a depth of feeling that sprang from the recent pain they had both endured.

They sat for a long time on the ruined wall of Middleham Castle, their arms around each other. They did not speak, lost for a while in their own thoughts.

Paula felt safe at last now that she was with him. She would never leave him again. They would be together always until the end of their days. They belonged together, were part of each other.

Shane, his eyes scanning the gaunt bleak silhouette of the castle, was filled with a sense of timelessness that he always experienced here. And then slowly he was enveloped in a new and wondrous peacefulness and he knew it would never leave him now that she was to live with him for the rest of his life.

Paula murmured, 'If only Blackie and Emma knew . . . if only they could see us together.'

He looked into her face and smiled, and then he lifted his eyes to the dark hills, resplendent in that extraordinary supernatural light, his glance sweeping across the sky.

Then the Celt in him rose up and he reached out and touched her face with gentleness. 'Perhaps they can, Paula,' Shane said. 'Perhaps they can.'

To Be the Best

For Bob, who is,
with my love

Contents

PROLOGUE

To be on my team, you've got to be the best.
And to be the best, you've got to have character.

EMMA HARTE, in *A Woman of Substance*

PROLOGUE

Paula left Pennistone Royal just before dawn.

It was still dark as she eased the car out of the tall iron gates and turned left, heading for the moors. But as she came up onto the road which cut through the Pennine Chain of hills the sky was already beginning to change. Its blurred mass of anthracite greys was giving way to amethyst and pink and a cold and fading green; on the far horizon the first rays of the sun shimmered like shards of silver against the dark rim of the moors. It was an eerie hour, neither day nor night, and the silent spacious moors seemed emptier, more remote than ever. And then unexpectedly there was a sudden burst of radiance and that crystalline light so peculiar to the north of England filled the entire sky; day finally broke.

Paula rolled down the window and took a deep breath, then leaned back in the seat, relaxing as she pushed the car forward at a steady speed. The breeze that blew in was cool, but then it was always cool up here on the 'tops', whatever the time of year, and hardly the right place to gauge the weather. She knew it would be a scorching day again, and she was glad she had set out early.

It was the end of August when the heather always blooms in Yorkshire and the wild, untenanted moors were glorious. Grim and daunting for most of the year, they were breathtaking in their beauty this morning, a sea of violet and magenta rippling under the wind, rolling ahead as far as the eye could see. On an impulse Paula stopped the car and got out, glancing around, filling her eyes. The landscape was awesome . . . stunning. She felt her throat tighten with emotion. Grandy's moors, she murmured, thinking of Emma Harte. I love them just as much as she did . . . as my own daughters Tessa and Linnet have grown to love them too.

Paula stood for a moment by the car, savouring her surroundings, looking and listening. She could hear the sharp trilling of the larks as they soared and wheeled high on the clouds and in the distance was the tinkling of water as a little beck rushed down over rocky crags, and on the cool air were the mingled scents of heather and bilberry, wild flowers and bracken. She closed her eyes briefly, remembering so many things, and then she lifted her head and looked up. The inverted bowl of a sky was China blue and filled with white puff-ball clouds and brilliant sunshine. The beginning of a pretty day, she thought, smiling. There is nowhere like the moors when the weather is beautiful, nowhere in the whole world. It was a long time since she had been up here. Too long really. My roots are here, just as Grandy's were, she said under her breath, lingering a moment longer, the memories flooding her fully, carrying her back . . .

Abruptly, Paula turned away, got into her Aston Martin DB 2–4, and drove on, following the winding moorland road for another hour until it finally started its descent into the valley below, and Fairley. Because it was so early, the village still slumbered. The streets were entirely deserted. Paula parked in front of the ancient grey stone church with its square Norman tower and stained-glass windows, then she alighted, went around to the passenger door and opened it. She had wedged the cardboard box on the floor near the seat, and now she lifted the vase of summer flowers out of the box and closed the door with her knee.

Carrying the vase with both hands, she pushed through the lych-gate that led into the cemetery adjoining the church.

Her steps carried her down the flagged path until she came to the far corner, secluded, bosky, infinitely still. Here, near the ancient moss-covered stone wall and shaded by a gnarled old elm tree, was a cluster of graves. For a while she stood staring at one headstone.

Emma Harte was the name engraved upon the dark green marble, and below were the dates *1889–1970*.

Eleven years ago, Paula thought. She died eleven years ago today. Whatever has happened to the time? It has spun away from me so fast . . . it seems only yesterday that she was alive and vigorous, running her business and ordering us all around.

Moving closer to her grandmother's grave, Paula bent down, placed the flowers on it, then straightened and stood motionless with one hand resting on the headstone, staring out towards the distant hills. There was a reflective look in her eyes, and she was lost for a moment in the sweep of her thoughts.

I've got to do something, Grandy, something drastic that you wouldn't like. But I'm certain you'd understand my reason . . . that I want to create something of my own. If you were in my position you'd do exactly the same thing. I know you would. And it'll come out right. It must. There is no room for doubt . . .

The striking of the church clock split the silence like thunder, made Paula start, and brought her out of her reverie with a jolt.

After another moment or two she turned away from Emma's grave and let her eyes roam over the other headstones. They came to rest on David Amory's, then moved on to regard Jim Fairley's: her father . . . her husband . . . who had lain here for ten years. They had both been far too young to die. Sadness struck at her with such sharpness she caught her breath in surprise and her heart filled with an old familiar ache. She steadied herself, and continued along the path, clamping down on the pain and sadness the memories engendered in her. She reminded herself that life was for the living.

Paula broke her rapid pace only once, when she passed the private plot which stood close to the church. Encircled by iron railings, it was filled with the graves of Jim's forebears . . . Adam and Adele . . . Olivia . . . Gerald. So many Fairleys . . . just as there were so many Hartes buried here. Two families whose lives had been entwined for three generations . . . bound together in a bitter feud . . . and in love and hate and revenge and marriage . . . and finally in death. Here they lay, together in their eternal resting place under the shadow of the windswept moors, at peace at last in this benign earth . . .

As they lych-gate clicked behind her, Paula straightened up, threw back her shoulders and hurried to the car, a new determination in her step, a new resoluteness in her expression. There was so much ahead of her, so many challenges, so much she had to accomplish.

She got into the car and settled herself comfortably for the long drive ahead of her.

The tape was on the passenger seat where she had placed it earlier that morning in readiness for the journey. After slipping it into the player in the dashboard, she turned up the volume. The strains of Mozart's *Jupiter* symphony filled the car . . . rich, melodious, so full of spirit and vivacity and, for her at least, a soaring hope. It was one of her favourites. Tessa had bought the tape for her a few weeks ago. It was the latest recording. Herbert von Karajan conducting the Berliner Philharmoniker. Paula shut her eyes, letting the music wash over her, thrilling to the first movement . . . *allegro vivace*. . . it made her feel . . . uplifted.

A moment passed, and then another, and she opened her eyes finally, turned on the ignition and coasted down the hill, making for the Leeds-Bradford road which would lead her onto the M1. She swung onto it thirty minutes later and saw at once that the traffic was light. There were only a few stray cars on the road and no trucks at all. If she was lucky and continued to have a clear run, she would be sitting behind her desk at Harte's in Knightsbridge within four hours.

Picking up speed, Paula roared ahead, her foot hard down on the accelerator, her eyes fixed on the road.

The symphony swelled to a crescendo, fell away, rose again, enveloping her in its beauty, transporting her with its magic. She experienced a surge of real happiness. Her mind was vividly alive.

She increased her speed. The Aston Martin flew forward along the motorway as if it had wings and were airborne. She was enjoying the feel of this superb piece of machinery under her hands, enjoying the sense of control she felt . . . control of the car, of herself, of the future. She had made her plan. *Her master plan*. She intended to execute it as soon as possible. It was watertight. Nothing could possibly go wrong . . .

PART ONE

Lovers & Strangers

Call no man foe, but never love a stranger.

STELLA BENSON

Be not forgetful to entertain strangers: for
thereby some have entertained angels
unawares.

THE BIBLE: HEBREWS

My true-love hath my heart, and I have his,
By just exchange one for the other given:
I hold his dear, and mine he cannot miss,
There never was a better bargain driven.

SIR PHILIP SIDNEY

1

Paula walked into her private office at the London store with her usual briskness and, after removing several folders from her briefcase, sat down at the antique partners' desk in the corner. It was precisely at this moment that she noticed the buff-coloured envelope propped against the antique porcelain lamp.

Marked PERSONAL, it had apparently been hand-delivered, and she recognized the writing at once. She felt a small shiver of pleasure. Eagerly, she reached for the envelope, slit it open with the gold-and-jade paper knife, and took out the folded piece of paper.

The note was boldly penned.

Meet me in Paris. Tonight, it said. You're booked on Flight 902. British Airways. 6. P.M. I'll be waiting impatiently. Usual place. Don't disappoint me.

Paula frowned. The tone was peremptory, commanding, and implicit in his words was the assumption that she would go. Mild irritation at his high-handedness flared and diluted the flush of pleasure she had experienced a second before. Of course she wouldn't go. She couldn't. She must spend the weekend with her children as planned, *wanted* to spend it with them, in fact.

Still clutching the note, she leaned back in the chair and gazed into space, thinking about him. Bossy . . . conceited . . . those were the adjectives which sprang into her head. They were certainly appropriate. A trace of a smile surfaced, flickered on her mouth. She was suddenly amused by the invitation and sorely tempted to accept. Admit it, you'd love to spend the weekend in Paris with *him*. But then you'd love to do a lot of things you constantly pass up, a small voice at the back of her head reminded her. And she smiled again, though this time with wryness, a hint of regret even, knowing that she could never be indulgent with herself. Perish the thought! Duty had to come first. That little rule of Emma Harte's had been inculcated in her since childhood, although sometimes she wished her grandmother had not been so thorough. But Grandy had schooled her well, had taught her that wealth and privilege also meant responsibilities, and that they had to be shouldered without flinching, no matter what the cost to oneself. And since she was now thirty-six, almost thirty-seven, her character was hardly likely to change at this stage in her life.

Paula sat up, slipped the note back into its envelope, sighing under her breath as she did. A romantic interlude in her favourite city with that very special and exceptional man was infinitely appealing but decidedly not possible. No, she would not go to Paris for a weekend of love and intimacy and pleasure. Instead, she would go to her children and be a good mother. Her children needed her. After all, she had not seen them for two weeks. On the other hand, she had not seen him either . . .

'Damn and blast,' she muttered out loud, wishing he had not sent the note. It had thrown her off balance, made her feel unexpectedly restless, and at a moment when she could not afford to have distractions of any kind. The months ahead were going to be extremely complicated, and they would be crucial months.

And so she would phone him later, tell him she was not coming; she must also cancel the airline reservation he had made for her. On second thoughts, perhaps she ought to call British Airways immediately.

As she reached for the telephone it began to ring.

She picked it up swiftly, said, 'Hello?' and glanced at the door as her assistant, Jill, hurried in with a cup of coffee.

'Hello, Paula, it's me,' her cousin Alexander was saying at the other end of the phone. 'I came into the Leeds store looking for you, only to find that on the *one* day I'm up here, *you're* in London.'

'Oh Sandy darling, I *am* sorry to have missed you,' she exclaimed, then covered the mouthpiece, murmured her thanks to Jill, who placed the coffee in front of her, smiled, and disappeared.

Paula went on, 'Were you in Yorkshire last night?'

'Yes. I got in around six-thirty.'

'I was still at the store, Sandy. You should've called me. We could've had dinner.'

'No, we couldn't. You see, I had to get out to Nutton Priory as early as possible. My estate manager's going off on holiday today and we had a lot to go over.' Alexander paused, cleared his throat. 'You were at Grandy's grave this morning . . . those *are* your flowers, aren't they, Paula?'

'Yes,' she said, her voice growing softer. 'I went there very early, before driving to London.'

'I was close on your heels.' He laughed faintly. 'I suppose we just weren't meant to meet up today. Well . . . my loss.'

Paula loved her cousin dearly and thus was sensitive to his moods. She had caught something odd in his voice, a nuance that disturbed her. 'Sandy, do you have some sort of problem?' she asked quickly. 'Do you want to talk to me about anything?'

There was only the slightest hesitation before he exclaimed with a certain firmness, 'No, no, not at all! I merely thought it would be nice for us to lunch together, I haven't seen you for weeks. I realize you've been busy . . . however, I do miss our *tête-à-têtes*, old thing.'

Paula had been listening attentively, straining to catch that peculiar inflection she had noticed a moment ago, but now it was absent. His voice sounded perfectly normal – as controlled as it always was.

She said, 'Yes, I miss them too, Sandy, and it has been a bit hectic for me this summer, what with all the flying to the south of France and back, and staying ahead of the game with the business. And look here, whilst I have you on the phone there's something I've been meaning to say to you for ages.' She took a quick breath, and her voice was a trifle sterner when she continued, 'I'm terribly cross with you, Alexander. You've hardly spent any time with us at Cap Martin this year, and it is *your* house for God's sake. Besides, I do think you –'

'You're not the only person who works for a living!' he shot back tersely, then added, in a rush of words, 'I've had a lot on my plate, too, you know, so please, Paula darling, don't nag. Emily's become quite the expert at that technique. *She's* beginning to get on my nerves.'

'Your sister thinks you don't get enough relaxation. She wants you to take it easy, enjoy life a bit more. And I happen to agree with Emily. Wholeheartedly, I might add.'

Ignoring these comments and her reproachful tone, Alexander said, 'I expect you're going down to the villa this weekend, aren't you?'

'Yes. I'm catching the nine o'clock plane to Nice tomorrow morning, returning early on Monday. Sandy! I've just had a wonderful idea! Why don't you come with me? You'll enjoy it, you know you will, and the children will be so thrilled to see you. So will Emily.'

'I really do have to be at Nutton Priory for the next few days. Honestly I do, Paula. I'd love to join you, but there's far too much that needs my attention on the estate. Look, let's have lunch on Tuesday.' His voice was suddenly eager.

'Oh God, I *can't*,' she groaned. 'I'm taking the Concorde to New York first thing on Tuesday morning, and at the end of the week I'm flying from New York to Sydney. I'll be gone for the whole of September.'

'Oh. I see.'

His disappointment communicated itself to her so acutely, she exclaimed, 'Why don't we make a date now? For October.' As she spoke she opened her engagement book, flipped the pages. 'How about the first Wednesday in the month?'

'I'm sure it's fine, but let me look at my pocket diary. Hold on, Paula.'

There was a clatter as he put down the phone.

Paula lifted her cup, took a sip of the hot coffee.

A moment later, Sandy was back on the line, his voice bright and chipper. 'All free and clear, darling. I'll see you in October then. And I'll be looking forward to it.'

'Oh so will I! And Sandy . . .'

'Yes?'

'Take care of yourself.'

'I will, and you do the same, Paula. My love to everyone at the villa.'

After they had hung up, Paula sat drinking her coffee, frowning, and staring at the telephone, her mind on her cousin.

She felt a pang of genuine regret for having let the summer slide by without putting more pressure on him to come to the Riviera with them. On the other hand, would her insistence have done any real good? Most likely not. After all, Emily had been relentless with him since Easter, using all of her not inconsiderable wiles and doing everything in her power to persuade him to join them at the Villa Faviola. He had flown down twice, but only for brief stays and then only to please his sister. This had been quite evident to both her and Emily.

Still, she could not help feeling guilty now, recognizing that she had neglected Alexander of late. There had been so much to cope with this past year; so many things had encroached on her free time, interfered with her various friendships. Sandy had been a casualty of the merciless work ethic she had adopted for herself. Poor Sandy, she hadn't had time for him, that was the sad truth.

Perhaps that was why he had sounded strange. No, that was not the reason at all. The peculiar inflection in his voice, which she knew she had not imagined, had been tension pure and simple. No, it had been strain. Or anxiety? Yes, that was it. *Anxiety*. And it had alerted her to something . . . to trouble.

As she came to this realization, Paula thought, with a sinking feeling: *Everything's not right with Sandy. I just know it in my bones.*

A curious unease took hold of her. Frowning, she ran things through her mind at the speed of light. There could be nothing amiss at Harte Enterprises. Emily would have known and would have told her. His health was good. He certainly had no financial problems. And even though he was not wooing anyone special – according to Emily, who knew everything about everyone in the family – he did not appear to lack for female companionship whenever he felt the need of it. His social life was not spectacular. But then again, this seemed to be his preference, the manner in which he chose to live his life these days.

He must often be lonely though, she mused, wishing for the hundredth-or-so time that Sandy had remarried.

After Maggie's tragic death in the avalanche at Chamonix he had been grief-stricken and inconsolable for so long. Then slowly he had pulled out of it, had regained his self-possession, and, painstakingly, he had put himself back together. But it was as if he had assembled all of the pieces of himself in a new and wholly different pattern. He had not seemed quite the same ever again.

The avalanche affected us all, Paula reminded herself, thinking in particular of her brother, Philip. He had also been skiing on the mountain that day. But he had been the one family member who had lived . . . the sole survivor. And then there was her mother, who had lost a husband. And *I* lost a father; and my children lost a father. Yes, the avalanche wreaked havoc on the entire family. It damaged us, changed us, irrevocably. Each one of us has been decidedly odd ever since . . .

She began to laugh under her breath. And *me* most of all, she thought, as she endeavoured to shake off that sense of unease she had felt about her cousin a moment ago. Wasn't she being overly imaginative, perhaps? After all, she and Sandy had been close as children, had remained close over the years. If there truly *was* something troubling him, he would have confided it to her on the telephone. I'm being irrational about this, she decided, and made a resolute effort to dismiss her worries about Alexander.

Her gaze came back to the papers on her desk.

The quickest of glances told her there was nothing particularly urgent to be dealt with, and she was relieved. Problems that arose on Fridays usually had a way of impinging on her weekends – and ruining them. This did not matter so much in the winter, but in the summer, when the children were home from their respective schools for a long period, it was distressing for them. They treasured their weekends with her, guarded them jealously, and resented any intrusions on their time, just as she did.

Once she had read the morning's mail and a memorandum from Jill, which detailed suggested structural changes in the Designer Salon, she checked the pile of purchase orders, then reached for the telexes. All had emanated from the New York store and were signed by her American assistant, Madelana O'Shea. They had come in late last night and only one required an answer.

Pulling a yellow pad towards her, Paula began to draft a reply. When this was done, she opened the thickest of the folders she had brought with her from Yorkshire and took out the top sheet of paper. It was the only thing which interested her at this moment. On it were the salient points of her master plan. A single sheet of paper ... but it was the key to so much ... the key to the future.

Within seconds she was so immersed in her work, so busy making additional notes on the pad, that all thoughts of her cousin Sandy fled. But months later Paula was to recall this day only too well. She would remember her uneasiness about him with great clarity, and she would fervently wish she had paid more attention to her intuition. Most of all, she would bitterly regret that she had not pressed him to confide in her. Knowing about his problems would not have enabled her to change the inevitable outcome, but at least she could have revised her travel plans. In so doing she would have been able to help him, simply by being there for him whenever he needed her.

But on this scorching morning in August of 1981, Paula had no way of knowing any of this, and that sense of impending trouble – a foreboding almost – which she had experienced earlier had already been squashed by the force of her will. Also, like her grandmother before her, she had the enviable knack of pushing everything to one side in order to concentrate on her business priorities, and this she now did. Head bent, eyes riveted on the page, she fell deeper and deeper into her concentration, as always so totally absorbed in her work that she was oblivious to everything else.

Twenty minutes later, Paula finally lifted her head, stapled her notes together, and put them in the folder along with the single sheet of paper; she then locked the folder in the centre drawer of her desk for safe-keeping over the weekend. Half smiling to herself, satisfied that she had thought of everything and was prepared for any contingency, she sat holding the key for a split second longer before placing it carefully in her briefcase.

Pushing the chair back, she rose, stretched, walked across the floor, feeling the need to move around. Her body was cramped, her bones stiff from sitting – first in the Aston Martin and then here at her desk. She found herself at the window and parted the curtains, looked down into Knightsbridge below, noticed that the traffic appeared to be more congested than ever this morning, but then Fridays were usually wicked in the summer months.

Turning, Paula stood facing the room, a look of approval washing over her face. From her earliest childhood days she had loved this office, had felt comfortable within its confines. She had seen no reason to change it when she had inherited it from her grandmother, and so she had left everything virtually intact. She had added a few mementoes of her own and photographs of her children, but that was the extent of it.

The office was more like a drawing room in an English country house than a place of business, and this was the real secret of its great charm. The ambiance was intentional. It had been created by Emma Harte some sixty-odd years earlier when she had used valuable Georgian antiques and English oil paintings of great worth instead of more prosaic furnishings. Classic chintz fabrics on the sofas and chairs and at the windows introduced glorious colour against the pine-panelled walls, while antique porcelain lamps and other fine accessories lent their own touches of elegance and distinction. The decorative look aside, the room was spacious and graceful, and it had a beautiful old Adam fireplace which was always in use on cold days. The office never palled on Paula, and she was delighted when people entering it for the first time exclaimed about its beauty.

Like everything else she did, Grandy got this room exactly right, Paula thought, walking across the priceless Savonnerie carpet, drawing to a standstill in front of the carved pine fireplace. She gazed up at the portrait of her grandmother which hung above it, painted when Emma had been a young woman. She still missed her, intensely so at times, but she had long drawn comfort from the feeling that Emma lived on in her . . . in her heart and in her memories.

As she continued to stare at that lovely yet determined face in the portrait, she experienced a feeling of immense pride in Emma's extraordinary achievements. Grandy started out with nothing and created one of the greatest business empires in the world . . . what incredible courage she must have had at my age. *I* must have her kind of courage and strength and determination. *I* must not falter in what *I* have to do . . . my master plan must succeed just as her plan did. Paula's mind raced, leapt forward to the future, and she filled with excitement at the thought of what lay ahead.

She returned to her desk, realizing she must get on with the day's business. She flipped on the intercom. 'Jill . . .'

'Yes, Paula?'

'My things *were* brought up from the car, weren't they?'

'Some time ago, actually, but I didn't want to disturb you. Do you want me to bring everything in now?'

'Please.'

Within seconds Jill's bright auburn head appeared around the door and she hurried through into Paula's office, holding aloft Paula's garment bag in one hand, a suitcase in the other. Jill was tall, well built, an athletic type of young woman, and she appeared to manage these items with the greatest of ease.

'I'll put these in your dressing room,' she said.

'Thanks,' Paula murmured, and when her assistant returned to her office, she went on, 'Sit down for a minute, would you, please, Jill? I'd like to go over a couple of things with you.'

Jill Marton nodded, took the chair on the other side of the desk, sat watching Paula through warm and intelligent brown eyes. Jill had worked for her for over five years and she never ceased to admire her, forever marvelling at her extraordinary energy and stamina. The woman opposite her was a powerhouse – astute, inspired and frequently daring in business. Jill had never worked for anyone like her. Those at the store who had known the legendary Emma said that Paula was a chip off the old block. Jill suspected this was the truth, that the traits she so admired in her boss were inherited from the famous founder of the Harte chain. Yes, it's all in the genes, Jill thought, continuing to observe Paula surreptitiously.

'Ah, here it is . . . your memo about the Designer Salon,' Paula said, picking up the piece of paper she had been searching for on the desk.

Jill sat up straighter in her chair, looked at Paula with alertness. 'I hope it makes sense to you,' she said.

'It does indeed. Your recommendations are excellent. I've nothing to add. You can put the structural alterations into work immediately and make the other changes as well. They'll do wonders for the salon, Jill.'

On hearing this compliment Jill felt vivid colour staining her neck and cheeks, and with a flush of pleasure she took the memo which Paula had slid across the highly-polished surface between them. She said, 'I'm so glad you approve,' and beamed.

Paula returned her smile. 'Send this telex to Madelana later, and here's the morning mail . . . nothing important, as you already know. You can deal with it easily. I've initialled these purchase orders.' She tapped them with a bright-red finger nail, then asked, 'Now, did any of last week's advertisements come up from the art department yet?'

Jill shook her head. 'But they'll be on your desk immediately after lunch. I spoke to Alison Warren earlier, and they're almost ready.'

'Good. And speaking of lunch, did Michael Kallinski confirm? Or let you know where I'm supposed to meet him?'

'He called a bit earlier. He didn't want me to bother you, since you'd just arrived when he rang. That's why I didn't put him through. He's picking you up at twelve-fifteen.'

'Oh.' Paula looked at her watch, rose and walked over to the dressing room, paused at the door, glanced down at her wrinkled cotton slacks. 'In that case, I'd better change. I want to go out onto the floor, check a few things before Michael arrives, and I don't have too much time. Excuse me, Jill.'

'Of course.' Jill scooped up the papers on the desk and headed to her own office. 'Let me know if you need anything.'

'I will,' Paula said, closing the door behind her.

The dressing area had been the filing room in Emma's day, but Paula had revamped it, adding floor-to-ceiling closets with mirrored doors, excellent lighting and a dressing table. She sat down at this, freshened her make-up and brushed her hair, then she slipped out of the shirt, trousers and sandals she had worn for driving from Yorkshire.

Within seconds she was dressed in the clothes she had brought with her in the garment bag: a black silk shantung suit, designed especially for her by Christina Crowther, classically simple, tailored and smart, worn with a white silk camisole, dark, very sheer stockings and high-heeled black patent pumps. The jewellery she added was equally simple but effective: a three-strand pearl choker with a diamond clasp at the front encircled her neck, and large *mabé* pearl studs ringed with diamonds glittered on her ears.

Staring at herself in the mirror, eyeing her reflection critically, Paula decided she liked the way she looked. The suit was crisp and businesslike without being overly severe and was therefore perfect for the store; it was also chic enough to go to lunch at an elegant restaurant. And no doubt they would be going somewhere smart. Michael always took her to the best places.

The staff elevator carried her rapidly down to the main floor.

Paula crossed the jewellery department and headed in the direction of cosmetics and perfumery, looking about as she did.

The store was crowded this morning.

But then it was generally thronged with shoppers from the moment it opened its doors at ten until it closed them at six. Over the decades it had become a famous landmark in London, and people from all over the world flocked through its great portals, to walk around its renowned halls and simply *look* as well as to buy the merchandise.

Paula loved the bustle, the activity, the crowds, the high-pitched buzz of the voices, so many of them foreign, the excitement that seemed to hang in the air. She usually experienced a small thrill when she returned after an absence, however short it had been, and this morning was no exception. The Yorkshire shops were important entities in the chain, just as those in Paris and New York were, but this was the flagship, and the one she loved the most.

Emma Harte had opened it in 1921.

In three months they would be celebrating its sixtieth anniversary. And what a celebration she had planned. It would be a tribute to her grandmother, one of the greatest merchant princes who had ever lived, as well as a salute to sixty years of superlative retailing and a record unchallenged by any department store, in any city, in any country in the world. Harte's of Knightsbridge was the best. The only one of its kind. A legend.

A sense of exhilaration at being back on this very special territory, her favourite bit of turf, brought an extra spring to her step as she walked into perfumery and drew to a stop.

Eagle-eyed as always, she stood seeking out imperfections but found none. This pleased her. The area had recently been redesigned under her close supervision and even though she said so herself, the results were smashing.

Glass panels etched in the manner of Lalique, many mirrors, masses of chrome and silver accents, crystal chandeliers and wall sconces ... all these elements combined to create a shimmering effect that was stunning. The scheme made the perfect backdrop for the eyecatching displays of cosmetics, perfumes and beauty products. Opulent, glamorous, inviting, the department was designed to lure women into spending tons of money, and it had succeeded brilliantly, just as she had known it would when it was still on the drawing board.

Good merchandising and marketing, that's what it's all about, Paula thought, moving on briskly, making a detour through lingerie on the way to the Rayne-Delman shoe salon. She was revelling in her morning walk through her store ... the finest department store in the world. It was the seat of her power, her strong citadel, her pride and joy. In fact, it was everything to her.

2

For the second time that morning the portrait of Emma hanging in Paula's office was undergoing a close and fixed scrutiny.

The man who had just drawn to a standstill in front of it was in his late thirties, fair-haired with light blue eyes and a summer tan. He stood about five feet eight, but appeared taller because of his lean, trim build. Also, his clothes added to the illusion of height. He wore a white shirt and a burgundy silk tie, and his dark blue suit, made of the finest imported raw silk, was so flawlessly cut, so unerringly tailored, it hung on him perfectly, was obviously a work of art from Savile Row.

His name was Michael Kallinski and he stood examining the alluring face captured in oils on the life-sized canvas, his eyes narrowed in concentration as he ruminated on the formidable Emma Harte.

It suddenly struck him as quite curious that a woman who had been dead for over a decade – eleven years to this very day to be exact – was always spoken about as if she were still alive, and by most people at that, not merely her immediate family. He supposed that someone of Emma's charisma and brilliance, who had made such a vivid and powerful impact in her lifetime, *would* be on the short list for immortality. After all, the dent she had made on the world – in her personal relationships, in international business and through her many philanthropies – was enormous.

Michael stepped back, tilted his head to one side, trying to ascertain how old Emma had been when she had sat for this portrait. Most probably in her late thirties, he decided. With her chiselled features, flawless complexion, reddish-gold hair and those extraordinary green eyes, she had been a great beauty as a young woman: there was no doubt about that whatsoever.

Little wonder his own grandfather had been madly in love with her those many years ago, and ready and willing to leave his wife and children for her – according to Kallinski family gossip, at any rate. And from what he understood from his father, David Kallinski had not been the only man to fall under her mesmeric spell. Blackie O'Neill had apparently been bewitched by her, too, in their youth.

The Three Musketeers. That's what Emma had called them – his grandfather, Blackie and herself. In their early days together, at the turn of the century, they had been considered an unlikely trio . . . a Jew, an Irish Catholic and a Protestant. Seemingly they had not paid much attention to what people thought of them or their friendship, and they had remained close, almost inseparable, throughout their long lives. And what an unbeatable trio they had proven to be. They had founded three impressive financial empires which straddled half the world and three powerful family dynasties which only went from strength to strength with the passing of time.

But it had been Emma who had been the real mover, the doer and the shaker, always pushing ahead with vision and enterprise, the two men following her lead. Anyway, that was the way his father told it, and he had no reason to disbelieve him. And he knew from his own experience of her that Emma had been absolutely unique. As far as the younger members of the three clans were concerned, she had certainly left her imprint on each one of them, himself included. Her indelible stamp, his father called it.

Michael smiled to himself, remembering exactly how Emma had been thirty-odd years ago ... rounding them up as children and carting them off to Heron's Nest for the spring and summer holidays. They had called her 'The General' behind her back, and the house in Scarborough had been affection-ately referred to as 'the army camp'. She had put them through their paces and instilled in them her own philosophy of life, had taught them the meaning of honour and integrity, the importance of the team spirit and playing the game. And all through the years of their growing up she had given unstintingly of her love and understanding and friendship; they were better people now for having known her then.

A look of love washed over his face, and he touched his hand to his forehead, gave the portrait a small salute. She had been the very best ... just as her granddaughters were the best. A rare breed, the Harte women, all of them, and most especially Paula.

The sound of the door opening prompted him to swing around quickly.

His face lit up at the sight of Paula.

'I'm sorry to have kept you waiting!' she exclaimed, looking apologetic, hurrying forward to greet him.

'You didn't, I was early,' he replied, going to meet her in the centre of the floor. He gave her a huge bear hug, then held her away, stared down into her face. 'You're looking wonderful.' He glanced over his shoulder at the portrait, then brought his gaze back to hers. 'And you're beginning to resemble *that* legendary lady more than ever.'

Paula groaned, gave him a look of mock horror as they drew apart.

'Oh God, Michael, not you too! *Please.* There are enough people who call me the Clone behind my back without *you* giving voice to the idea.' She shook her head. 'That's all I need from a dear friend ...'

He burst out laughing. 'I sometimes think you're all clones, actually. The lot of you ... Emily and Amanda, as well as you.' He swivelled to face the portrait. 'And when was that painted, by the way?'

'In 1929. Why?'

'I'd been trying to figure out how old Emma was when she sat for it.'

'Thirty-nine. It was started and finished just before her fortieth birthday.'

'Mmmm. I guessed as much. And she *was* beautiful then, wasn't she?' Not giving Paula a chance to reply, he went on, with a small grin, 'Do you realize that you and I would have been related if David *had* left my grandmother Rebecca and run off with Emma?'

'Let's not get into all that old history today,' she said with a light laugh, moved rapidly towards the desk, sat down and added, 'Anyway, I feel as if we are, don't you? Related, I mean.'

'Yes.'

He followed her across the room and seated himself in the chair facing her.

There was a brief silence, then he remarked quietly, 'Blood might *not* be thicker than water as far as some families are concerned, but it is when it comes to the three clans. Our grandparents would've killed for each other, and I think their kind of loyalty has been passed down to our generation, hasn't it?'

'I should say so –' She cut herself short when the phone rang and reached to answer it. After saying hello and listening for a second she put her slim, tapering hand over the receiver, explained, 'It's the manager of the Harrogate store, I'll only be a minute.'

He nodded, sat back in the chair, waiting for her to finish her call, quietly studying her as he had studied the painting only a few minutes before.

Michael Kallinski had not seen Paula for over two months, and because he had been away her uncanny resemblance to Emma had struck him more forcibly than ever when she walked in. Her colouring was different from Emma's, of course. Paula had hair as black as pitch and eyes of the deepest darkest blue. She had inherited Emma's clear, finely wrought features, though, and the famous widow's peak, which was extremely dramatic above those large eyes set wide apart. With the passing of time the two women seemed to merge more and more, to become identical, to him at least. Perhaps it had something to do with the expression in Paula's eyes these days, her mannerisms, her pithiness, the way she moved – swiftly, always in a hurry – and the habit she had of laughing at her misfortunes. These characteristics reminded him of Emma Harte, just as her attitude in business did.

He had known Paula his entire life and yet, oddly enough, he had not really known her until they were both in their thirties.

When they had been children he had not liked her one little bit, had considered her to be cold, standoffish and indifferent to them all, except for her cousin Emily, that roly-poly pudding of a child whom she had forever mothered, and Shane O'Neill, of course, whom she had always striven to please.

Privately, Michael had called her Miss Goody Two Shoes, because she had been just that, a child who appeared to have no faults whatsoever, one who was always being clucked over, praised and held up as an example to them by their respective parents. His brother Mark had had his own name for her . . . Paragon of Virtue. He and Mark had secretly laughed at her, made fun of her behind her back, but then again, they had scoffed at *all* the girls from the clans, had never wanted to spend time with them, had preferred to be roistering around with the other boys. They had banded together with Philip, Winston, Alexander, Shane and Jonathan, who had been their boon companions in those days.

It was only in the last six years that he had come to know Paula and he had discovered that this shrewd, hardworking and brilliant woman hid a deep emotional side behind her cool air and her inbred refinement. The aloof manner was merely an outward manifestation of her shyness and natural reserve, those traits he had so misunderstood in childhood.

Discovering that Paula was quite different than he had believed her to be had come as something of a shock to him. To his astonishment, he found she was so very, very human. She was vulnerable, warm, loving, fiercely loyal, and devoted to her family and friends. Terrible things had happened to her over the past ten years, devastating things which would have felled most other people, perhaps even destroyed them. But not Paula. She had suffered deeply, yet had found strength from adversity, had become a most compassionate woman.

Since they had been working together they had drawn closer, and she was his staunch supporter in business and an ally in every way, whenever he needed one. It occurred to Michael now that he would not have been able to cope with his messy divorce and his dreadful personal problems without Paula's friendship. She was always willing to listen to his woes at the end of the phone, or make herself available for a drink or a meal when the going really got tough. She had cornered a special place in his life, and he would be forever grateful that she had.

For all her success and sophistication and self-confidence, there was something about Paula – an endearing little-girl quality – which tugged at his heart, made him want to do things for her, want to please her. Frequently he went out of his way to accomplish this, as he had in New York recently. He wished the interminable phone call from the Harrogate store would come to an end so that he could impart his news.

Paula put down the receiver, made a little moue.

'Sorry about that,' she apologized. Leaning back in the chair, she went on, in an affectionate tone, 'It's lovely to see you Michael . . . and how was New York?'

'*Terrific. Hectic.* I was up to my neck with work, since our business is going well over there right now. Still, I also managed to enjoy myself, even had a few weekends out in the Hamptons.' He leaned closer to the desk. 'Paula –'

'Yes, Michael?' she cut in, eyeing him astutely, alerted by the urgency in his voice.

'I think I may have found it . . . what you've been looking for in the States.'

Excitement flew onto her face. She sat forward slightly, her eagerness only too apparent. 'Private or public?'

'Private.'

'Is it for sale?'

'Isn't everything – if the price is right.' There was a hint of mischief on his face as he held her eyes.

'Come on, don't tease me!' she exclaimed. 'Is it actually *on* the market?'

'No, it isn't. But what does that mean in this day and age of the takeover? The owners can be approached . . . it doesn't cost anything to do that.'

'What's the name of the company? Where is it? How big is it?'

Michael chuckled. 'Hey, steady on, I can only answer one question at a time. The company is called Peale and Doone and it's in the midwest. It's not big, only seven stores . . . suburban stores. In Illinois and Ohio. But it's an old company, Paula, founded in the 1920s by a couple of Scotsmen who settled in the States and at first dealt only in Scottish imports. You know, woollen goods, tartans and plaids, cashmeres and the like. They extended their inventory during the 'forties and 'fifties. But the merchandise is supposedly stodgy and the company's in the doldrums, management-wise that is. Quite solid financially, or so I've been led to understand.'

'How did you hear about Peale and Doone?'

'Through a lawyer friend who's with a Wall Street law firm. I'd asked him

516

to be on the look-out for a chain and he heard about this company through a colleague in Chicago. My chap thinks they're ripe for a takeover.'

Paula nodded. 'Who holds the stock?'

'The heirs to Mr Peale and Mr Doone.'

'There's no guarantee they'd sell, Michael.'

'Correct. On the other hand, often stockholders don't *know* they want to sell until they're actually approached to do so.'

'That's true, and it's worth investigating further.'

'You bet it is, and although this chain is small, it might well be perfect for you, Paula.'

'It's just a pity the stores are in the boondocks,' she murmured, and with a grimace, thinking out loud, 'Big cities like Chicago and Cleveland would be more my speed.'

Michael gave her a sharp stare. 'Look here, with your flair and expertise you can easily put your own special cachet on any store *anywhere*, and you *know* that. Besides, what's wrong with the boondocks? There's plenty of money to be made out there.'

'Yes, you're quite right,' she answered quickly, suddenly realizing she may have sounded ungrateful after the effort he had made on her behalf. 'Can you get some more information, please, Michael?'

'I'll ring my friend in New York later in the day and ask him to pursue this further.'

'Does he know you were inquiring about retail chains for *me*?'

'No, but I can tell him if you like.'

Paula said very briskly and firmly, 'No. I think not. At least not for the moment, if you don't mind. It's better no one knows. The mention of my name could send the price skyrocketing. *If* there's going to be a price, that is.'

'Point well taken. I'll keep Harvey in the dark for the time being.'

'Please . . . and thank you, Michael, for going to all this trouble for me.' Her smile was warm, sincere, as she added, 'I really do appreciate it.'

'I'll do anything for you Paula, anything at all,' he replied, his eyes filling with affection for her. Then he glanced down at his watch. 'Oh, it's getting late! We'd better be going. I hope you don't mind, but the old man's invited himself to lunch.'

'Of course I don't mind,' she said, her voice rising slightly. 'You know I adore Uncle Ronnie.'

'And the feeling is mutual, I can assure you.' He threw her an amused look. 'The old man dotes on you . . . he thinks the sun shines out of you.'

She picked up her black patent bag and moved across the room. 'Come on then, let's go. We don't want to keep him waiting, do we?'

Michael took her arm, escorted her out of the office.

As they went down in the elevator he could not help thinking about his father and Paula, and their special relationship which had developed over the past few years. The old man treated her like a beloved daughter, whilst she seemed to revere him. Certainly she behaved as if he were the shrewdest man alive, which, of course, he was. Dad's become her rabbi, Michael thought suddenly with an inner smile, and a substitute for her grandmother. Not surprising that some people considered their friendship peculiar and were jealous. Personally, he applauded it. Paula filled a void in his father's life. Perhaps he did in hers.

3

Sir Ronald Kallinski, chairman of the board of Kallinski Industries, walked across the impressive marble lobby of Kallinski House at a leisurely pace.

Tall, slender, a man of dominating presence, he had black wavy hair, heavily frosted with white, and a saturnine face. He had inherited the eyes of his father David and his grandmother Janessa Kallinski; they were of the brightest cornflower blue and seemed all the more startling because of his weatherbeaten complexion.

Renowned for never appearing ruffled or dishevelled, no matter what the circumstances, he was always perfectly groomed and elegantly attired. This morning he was wearing a charcoal grey three-piece suit with an impeccable white shirt and a pearl-grey silk tie. Although he was almost seventy, he was in such robust health and was so vigorous for his age he looked like a much younger man.

As he strolled through the vast entrance foyer, he nodded graciously to several people who recognized him, and paused to admire the Henry Moore reclining figure in the centre, which he had commissioned from the great English sculptor who also happened to be a Yorkshireman born and bred. Sir Ronald was as proud of his north-country origins as he was of his Jewish heritage.

After a brief moment of contemplation in front of the imposing piece of bronze, he continued on his way, pushed through the swing doors and stepped out into the street. He drew to an abrupt halt after taking only two steps, recoiling as the intense heat hit him. He had not realized how hot the day had become.

Sir Ronald could not abide heat of any kind. Upstairs in his executive suite, a series of handsomely-furnished rooms spanning the entire top floor of the giant office complex bearing his name, the atmosphere was icy cold, thanks to the air conditioning that was permanently turned up high and the well-shaded windows. This area of Kallinski House was generally referred to as 'Antarctica' by those who occupied it with him. Doris, his secretary of twelve years, had grown used to the freezing temperature by now, as had other executives who had been with him for more than a year or two, and none of them bothered to complain any more. They counteracted the chill simply by wearing warm sweaters in their offices. Even in winter, Sir Ronald kept the executive suite and his various homes as cold as he possibly dared without eliciting violent protests from staff, family and friends.

Earlier that morning he had contemplated walking to the Connaught Hotel; now he was relieved he had changed his mind and had ordered his car up

518

from the garage. It was sizzling out here, and oppressive, hardly the kind of weather for sauntering through the busy streets of Mayfair.

His chauffeur had spotted him the instant he had emerged from the building and was already standing stiffly to attention next to the back passenger door.

'Sir Ronald,' he said, inclining his head respectfully, and opened the door wider.

'Thank you, Pearson,' Sir Ronald responded with a half smile, stepping into the burgundy coloured Rolls-Royce. 'The Connaught, please.'

The car pulled away from the kerb and he settled back against the seat and stared absently ahead. He was looking forward to lunching with Paula and Michael. He had not seen her for several weeks and his son had been in New York for over two months and he had missed them both . . . in different ways.

His son was his good right hand, his alter ego, his heir apparent, and his favourite. He loved his younger son, Mark, very much; but Michael had a special hold on his heart. He was never quite sure why this was so. How could one explain these things? Sometimes he thought it was because his son was very much like his own father had been. Not that Michael *looked* anything at all like David Kallinski, being so much more Anglo-Saxon in appearance with his fair complexion and blondish hair. It had to do with a similarity of character and personality, and just as Sir Ronald had enjoyed a marvellous camaraderie with his father until the day of David's death, so did he now with his son. It had been thus ever since the boy's childhood, in fact, and he noticed Michael's absences most acutely these days, was frequently lonely when his first born was travelling.

As for Paula, she was the daughter he had never had, or rather, the surrogate for the daughter who had not lived through her childhood. Miriam, their second child, born after Michael and before Mark, would have been thirty-four this year, if she had not died of encephalitis at the age of five. How they had grieved, he and Helen; they had not understood why she had been taken from them at such a tender age. 'God works in mysterious ways, His wonders to perform,' his mother had said to them at the time, and only in old age had he come to terms with *that* extraordinary belief.

Paula was the smartest woman he had ever known, except for Emma, and he appreciated her sharp and clever mind, her quickness, her business acumen. But she could also be very female at times and he missed her femininity as much as he relished his role as her sounding board and, on occasion, her adviser. He had a lot of admiration for Paula. She was a good mother as well as a successful executive. Hers was a hard road and she trod it most adroitly, rarely ever stumbled.

He wished his daughter-in-law were half as practical and down to earth as she was. The trouble with Valentine was that she lived in another world. She was airy fairy, a bit flighty, and forever discontented. Nothing was ever *enough* for her, or ever *right*, and he understood only too well Michael's feelings. His son's frustration had grown to monumental proportions over the years and the inevitable explosion, when it had come, had been violent. He had not been surprised. He had never approved of Valentine as a wife for Michael, not because she was a *shiksa* – differences in religion scarcely mattered to him – but because she was so shallow, unworthy really. He had always known this, but how did one tell such a thing to a young man in love? In any event, the divorce agreement had been concluded finally, after much bitter wrangling and the exchange of vast amounts of money. Michael, most fortunately, had succeeded in getting what he wanted – a decree *nisi* and joint custody of his three children, the boy, Julian, and the two younger girls, Arielle and Jessica.

A smile softened Sir Ronald's stern face as he thought of his little grand-daughters. If only Helen had lived to see them, it would have made her so happy. But his wife had died eight years ago. He had never stopped missing her, and when he had been given his knighthood by Harold Wilson in 1976 his joy had been tempered by sadness because Helen was no longer with him.

This singular honour had come as a genuine surprise to him. He had never asked for nor sought a title, nor had he tried to buy one by making heavy donations to charity. He *was* philanthropic, and he had his favourite causes, had contributed generously to medical research and the arts, but this had been done discreetly and without fanfare.

To be on the Prime Minister's honours list was flattering, and especially since everyone knew the title had been earned and was therefore deserved. Kallinski Industries was one of the largest and most successful conglomerates in Great Britain, and as such it not only provided much-needed jobs for thousands but was a major exporter of British goods abroad. Ronald Kallinski had devoted his life to bringing the company to its present dominant position, and he was proud of his accomplishments. So was his country apparently, since this was the reason the knighthood had been bestowed upon him.

Sir Ronald was not the first Yorkshire Jew to be knighted; others had been singled out by grateful prime ministers over the years . . . men like Montague Burton, and Rudolph Lyons. But nevertheless he prized the honour, as if he *had* been the first, and most especially when he contemplated the Kallinski family's early history, thought of his grandfather Abraham fleeing Russia and the pogroms in the last century, settling in the ghetto in Leeds, and eventually opening his tailoring shop in North Street. That little factory turning out piecework for the John Barran company – the first readymade clothiers to start in Leeds after Singer invented the sewing machine – had been the beginning, the nucleus of the billion-pound empire that Kallinski Industries was today.

On the morning of his investiture his one regret had been that Helen, Abraham, his father David, Emma and Blackie had not been present to share his pride and happiness. The four old-timers in particular would have appreci-ated the significance of the ceremony at Buckingham Palace, truly understand-ing how far the Kallinskis had risen since Abraham, the young refugee from Kiev, had first set foot on English soil at Hull in 1880.

The Rolls-Royce came to a sudden stop in Carlos Place.

Sir Ronald shook off his thoughts, leaned forward, addressed his chauffeur: 'Please pick me up around two-thirty, Pearson,' he said as the uniformed doorman outside the Connaught Hotel stepped up to the car, opened the door for him, helped him alight.

They 'Sir Ronalded' him to death as he went from the front steps to the dining room, and a faint smile touched his eyes as he was shown to the table his son had reserved. Five years ago he had wondered how he would ever get used to being addressed by his title. But he had – and in no time at all.

After he had ordered a dry sherry, he took a sip of the iced water a waiter had placed before him, then sat back to wait for Paula and Michael.

Sir Ronald did a double take.

Paula and his son were heading across the restaurant in his direction, and she looked so much like Emma that it was quite amazing.

He realized, as she drew closer, that she was sporting a new hairdo, and that it was this which underscored her already-pronounced similarity to her grandmother. Her dark glossy hair had been cut short in a sort of sleek bob. It was chic and obviously of the moment, and yet to him it had the look of the 1930s. It brought to mind the film stars of his youth . . . and the elegant Emma he had known and admired as a boy.

He rose, took Paula's outstretched hand in both of his, shared her broad and loving smile, kissed her cheek. They exchanged affectionate greetings, seated themselves next to each other, and at once started chatting animatedly.

Michael went to the other side of the table, took a chair, motioned to the waiter. After Paula and he had ordered aperitifs, he asked for the menus.

Turning to Paula, he said, 'You're always in such a hurry, so let's order . . . then we can relax.'

'Why not?' she laughed and took the menu from the headwaiter.

The latter hovered next to the table, explaining the specialities of the day, and making his own recommendations. After a cursory glance at their menus, Paula and the Kallinskis followed his advice. All three asked for the cold poached salmon and cucumber salad, and Michael ordered a bottle of Sancerre.

The aperitifs had materialized in front of Paula and Michael whilst they had been ordering lunch, and once the waiters had disappeared, Sir Ronald raised his glass. He looked directly at Paula. 'To the memory of your grandmother.'

'To Emma,' Michael toasted.

Paula smiled at them both. 'Yes, to Grandy.'

They clinked glasses, sipped their drinks.

After a moment, Paula said, 'I thought you'd remember what day it is today, Uncle Ronnie.'

'We both remembered!' Michael exclaimed.

Sir Ronald remarked, 'How could anyone forget the passing of such a great woman. And she'd be so proud of you, my dear. You've never let her down, and you've held her dream wonderfully well.'

'I hope so, Uncle Ronnie . . . I've certainly endeavoured to guard everything she built . . . and make it stronger.'

'And you have,' Sir Ronald said, regarding her warmly. 'You're as much of a genius at retailing as Emma ever was. You've displayed a great deal of vision over the years, and I can only commend you on everything you've done with the stores.'

'Thanks, Uncle Ronnie,' Paula said, smiling, enjoying his approval.

'And I second everything Dad says,' Michael declared emphatically. He took a sip of his Cinzano Bianco, then winked at her over the rim of his glass.

Paula's violet-blue eyes filled with laughter. 'You're prejudiced, Michael. Actually, you both are.'

Sir Ronald settled back in his chair, said in a more confidential tone, 'One of the reasons I invited myself to lunch is to seek your advice, my dear.'

Paula's curiosity was instantly piqued, and she quickly asked, 'But how can I possibly advise *you*? Why, you're the wisest person I know, Uncle Ronnie.'

He made no response to this remark. It was almost as if he had not heard it. A preoccupied expression invaded his face; he took a sip of his sherry, then gave her a long and careful look. 'Ah, but you can advise me, Paula. About Alexander. Or, to be more precise, you can give me an opinion.' Sir Ronald briefly paused, before asking, 'Do you think Sandy would sell Lady Hamilton Clothes to Kallinski Industries?'

This was the last thing Paula had expected to hear, and she was taken aback. She stared at Sir Ronald without speaking for a moment. 'I'm quite sure he wouldn't,' she said at last in a surprised voice. 'That division is far too important to Harte Enterprises. And to Harte stores, for that matter.'

'Yes, it has great value to Sandy, and to you too, of course, since the Lady Hamilton line is made exclusively for Harte's,' Sir Ronald said.

Michael interjected, 'He may want to unload it, Paula – for the right price, and to the right people. Let's face it, Sandy has been terribly overburdened ever since that family débâcle, when he fired Jonathan and Sarah. He and Emily really have their hands full, and they have to work awfully hard running Harte Enterprises –'

'Oh, I don't know,' she cut in swiftly, 'they seem to manage quite well, Michael.'

'In any case, we'd be prepared to pay top money for that division,' Michael added, determined to get his point across.

'I'm sure you would,' Paula replied evenly, 'and I'm just as sure Sandy wouldn't even consider it, no matter what you offered.' She looked from the younger Kallinski to the older, rapidly and with quickening interest. '*Why* do you want to buy Lady Hamilton Clothes, Uncle Ronnie?'

'We'd like to have our own women's fashion division,' Sir Ronald explained. 'And to supply your stores with women's ready to wear in much the same way we supply your men's clothing, and to sell to your boutiques in the hotels. Just as importantly, we wish to start and to build up a strong export line.'

Paula nodded slowly. 'I see.'

'Obviously, we wouldn't sell the women's fashions in countries where you own retail stores,' Michael pointed out. 'We're thinking of trading only in common market countries –'

'Excluding France,' Sir Ronald interrupted, 'since you have a store in Paris.'

'Oh I know you'd never do anything to damage my business, that goes without saying,' Paula murmured. 'And I can see why you'd like the acquisition, Uncle Ronnie, it makes a lot of sense.'

She glanced at Michael. 'But *you* know how conservative Sandy is; and bound by tradition. Those are just two of the reasons Grandy gave him control of Harte Enterprises. She knew it would be safe in his hands because he would never do anything to *weaken* its basic structure. Such as selling off a very, *very* profitable division,' she finished dryly, but her mouth twitched with sudden amusement.

Both men laughed.

'*Touché*,' Sir Ronald said.

'Yes, I do know *exactly* what kind of person Sandy is,' Michael acknowledged, shifting in his chair. 'And that's why I suggested to Dad that we got your reading on the matter first.'

At this moment the waiter arrived with the food, and Michael changed the subject. The three of them chatted about inconsequential things for the next few minutes, and once they had been served, the *sommelier* poured the chilled white wine for Michael. After tasting it, he nodded approvingly.

Sir Ronald and Paula sipped their wine and both of them commented on its fresh dry taste and lightness, and then Sir Ronald put his goblet down. '*Bon appétit*,' he said, and picked up his fork and cut into the poached salmon.

'*Bon appétit*,' Paula and Michael responded almost in unison.

They ate in silence for a while, but at one moment Paula swung her gaze between the two Kallinski men, and asked curiously, 'Uncle Ronnie, Michael, why don't you simply start your own women's clothing division? Certainly you've got all the necessary resources.'

'We thought of that, my dear,' Sir Ronald admitted. 'But quite frankly we'd prefer to buy a well-established brand. So much easier, you know. And it would save us an enormous amount of time – and money, of course, in advertising and promoting a new product.'

'And surely there must be lots of manufacturers who would jump at the chance to sell to Kallinski Industries!' she exclaimed.

'I'm perfectly certain there are.' Sir Ronald gave her a pointed look. 'But I'm interested in Lady Hamilton Clothes because it was founded by Emma and my father all those years ago. He had a soft spot for the company long after he sold his shares to your grandmother, and so do I.' Sir Ronald smiled wryly, and finished, 'I must admit, I do feel rather sentimental about it.'

Paula placed an elegant, beautifully manicured hand on Sir Ronald's arm, squeezed it affectionately. 'But Alexander has no reason to sell that division ... at least, not one *I* can think of, Uncle Ronnie. His sister's been running it successfully for a number of years now.' Her arched black brows drew together in a small frown. 'Besides, what would she *do* if he sold Lady Hamilton? Amanda would be out of a job, and Sandy would always take that into consideration. You know how he fusses about her.'

'She need not necessarily be out of a job,' Michael was quick to announce. 'Amanda's terrific at what she does. She'd remain with the company and run it for us.'

Paula made no comment. She toyed with the cucumber salad on her plate, suddenly acknowledging to herself that if Lady Hamilton were ever up for grabs Sandy ought to sell it to the Kallinskis. In a way they were entitled to it.

Sir Ronald dabbed his mouth with his napkin and ventured, 'I'd like to pose a hypothetical question, Paula.'

'Of course.' She looked at him alertly, wondering what was on his mind now.

He said, 'Let us just suppose that Alexander did want to sell Lady Hamilton, was anxious to do so, in fact. *Could he?* Or would he have to go to the other shareholders, get their agreement?'

'Oh no. There's only Emily, and she would go along with anything her brother wanted to do. She always has, you know.'

Puzzlment flickered in Sir Ronald's eyes and he leaned back in his chair, regarding Paula thoughtfully. After a second, he said slowly, *'Only Emily*... But surely you told me several years ago that Sarah and Jonathan still owned their shares in Harte Enterprises, even though they were thrown out of the company because of their shoddy behaviour.'

'That's perfectly true, they do. They draw their dividends, receive the company reports and balance sheets, but they have no power whatsoever. But then, neither does Emily, now that I think about it.'

Sir Ronald appeared to be more baffled than ever.

Recognizing this, Paula said, 'Let me clarify things for you, Uncle Ronnie, and for you too, Michael.'

Father and son nodded and Sir Ronald said, 'Please do, my dear.'

'My grandmother left fifty-two per cent of Harte Enter prises to Sandy. The remaining forty-eight per cent was split three ways between Emily, Jonathan and Sarah, who each received sixteen per cent. As chairman of the board and majority stockholder, Sandy can do virtually anything he wishes in the company, or with it, for that matter. This is the way Grandy set it up. Whilst she wanted all four of them to draw income from the company, she knew Sandy must have absolute power to prevent any bickering between the four cousins. She felt Sandy had earned, and also deserved, the bulk of the shares in her privately owned company. She gave total control to him because she knew that he would always abide by her wishes.'

'Ah, yes, I can see the sense in everything your grandmother did.' Sir Ronald never failed to be impressed by the late Emma Harte's clever strategy. He went on, 'As usual, Emma was shrewd – and most prudent, I might add. Certainly Sandy has guided Harte Enterprises through some rough periods and done admirably well in the past few years.'

Quickly Michael said, 'Look, Paula, I know you're adamant about Sandy not being interested in selling, and perhaps you're right. At least about his attitude at present. But he may well change his mind and decide to pare down Harte Enterprises ... one day in the future ...' Michael paused. There was a speculative expression on his face as he added, *'No?'*

Paula could not help smiling at his dogged persistance. 'So you'd like to talk to him anyway, explain that Kallinski Industries are standing in the wings, if ever he decides to get rid of Lady Hamilton Clothes. Is that what you're trying to say?' she asked with a laugh.

Michael nodded. 'That's exactly it. You wouldn't object if Dad did have a word with him, would you, Paula?'

'No, of course not. There's no harm in letting Alexander know about your interest in the division.' She swung to the older man. 'Are you going to Yorkshire this weekend, Uncle Ronnie?'

'Yes, I am, my dear.'

'Then why don't you drive over to Nutton Priory, and have a chat with him. He's always much more relaxed when he's in the country.'

'I think I shall do that,' Sir Ronald said. 'And my thanks to you, Paula, you've been most helpful.'

Michael flashed her one of his engaging smiles. 'Yes, thanks, we really do appreciate your input.' He sipped his wine and his light blue eyes grew thoughtful and after a moment he asked, 'By the way, just out of curiosity, is Sarah Lowther still married to that French painter? Or don't you hear anything about her any more?'

'Obviously not directly, since I kicked her out of the family along with Jonathan,' Paula murmured, the gaiety on her face instantly fading. 'But there was a piece on Yves Pascal in a French magazine about six months ago . . . *Paris Match*, I believe. Anyway, amongst the many photographs was one of Sarah and Yves and their five-year-old daughter, Chloe. Seemingly they live in Mougins in the Alpes-Maritimes. They own an old farmhouse; that's where he has his studio. He's known as the *enfant terrible* of French art, and he's become very big, immensely successful.'

Michael said, 'He's a damned good painter actually, although his work's not my cup of tea. Having been raised on the school of French Impressionist painting, all this ultra-modern stuff leaves me utterly unmoved. Give me Monet, Manet, Sisley and van Gogh any day of the week.'

'Absolutely,' Paula agreed.

'And talking of Sarah, whatever happened to her partner in crime, Jonathan Ainsley?' Michael stared at Paula, frowning. 'Is he still lurking in the Far East?'

'I believe so, but not even Sandy knows for sure,' Paula said, her voice low and unemotional. 'Friends of Emily's reported seeing him in Hong Kong, and then Singapore on another occasion. Jonathan's dividends and the balance sheets of Harte Enterprises go to a firm of accountants here in London who handle his business seemingly.' She made a sour face. 'Just so long as he doesn't show up in England, that's all that matters to me. As Emma would have said, *good riddance to bad rubbish.*'

'Christ, yes!' Michael began to shake his head wonderingly. 'I've never been able to understand why he did what he did. He was such a fool – bloody stupid if you ask me. He had everything going for himself and he threw it all away.'

'Perhaps he believed he would never get caught,' Sir Ronald ventured to Michael. 'But then I'm sure he hadn't bargained for this one here.' He glanced at Paula through the corner of his eye, patted her arm and finished with a chuckle, 'He met his match in you, my dear, no doubt about that whatsoever.'

Paula attempted to laugh with him but it came out sounding forced and artificial, and for a moment she did not trust herself to speak. She was hating this discussion about Jonathan Ainsley, her cousin, her deadly enemy of long ago.

Michael pressed, 'And so nobody in the family knows what he's doing for a living?'

Paula stared at Michael through eyes grown bleak and flat. She gave him a long and careful look, and pursed her lips, a habit she had picked up from her grandmother years before. After a split second, she said with a certain pithiness, 'Jonathan Ainsley doesn't have to *earn* a living, since he receives a very sizeable income from Harte Enterprises.' There was a small pause before she thought to add, 'And nobody's ever bothered to find out about his personal or business life ... because none of us *care* what's happened to him.' Now frowning in perplexity, and pinning Michael with her vivid blue gaze, Paula asked testily, 'Why the sudden preoccupation with Jonathan anyway?'

'I don't know, I haven't thought about him in years, and now, unexpectedly, I'm riddled with curiosity,' Michael admitted with a rueful grin.

'I'm not.' Despite the warmth of the Connaught dining room, Paula shivered. She had never forgotten the last words Jonathan had spoken to her ... *I'll get you for this, Paula Fairley. Sebastian and I will bloody well get you*, he had screamed, shaking his fist at her in the most ridiculous way, like the villain in a Victorian novel. Well, Sebastian Cross could not 'get her' since *he* was dead. But Jonathan would if he could. Sometimes she had nightmares about her cousin, nightmares in which he did her terrible harm. He was certainly capable of it. Capable of almost anything. She knew that from their childhood. Once, a few years ago, she had confided her fears in Sandy, who had laughed and had told her to dismiss Jonathan from her mind. Sandy had reminded her that Jonathan was a bully and, like all bullies, a coward. This was true; nevertheless, she had never been able to expunge the memory of the day Sandy had fired him. It was only too easy to recall the baleful look in Jonathan's eyes, the mask of hatred contorting his face and instinctively, ever since then, she had known he would always remain her enemy until the day they buried him. Ten years had passed and she had not set eyes on him again, none of them had, in fact, and yet deep down inside her was this small kernel of fear.

Suddenly becoming aware that Michael and Sir Ronald were watching her, were waiting for her to say something, she turned towards Michael. Adopting the lightest of tones, she said, 'Master Ainsley turned out to be a bad penny, and the least said about *him* the better.'

'Quite so, my dear, quite so!' Sir Ronald muttered. He had grown conscious of the change in her demeanour whilst they had been discussing Ainsley and he decided it would be wise to change the subject. And so he said with a rush of genuine enthusiasm, 'I received your invitation to the dinner dance you're giving for the sixtieth anniversary of the store, Paula, and I'm looking forward to it immensely. Now, tell me more about the other celebrations you've planned.'

'Oh I'd love to, Uncle Ronnie, I have some really special things coming up –' She cut herself off as the waiter drew to a standstill at the table. 'But perhaps we should order dessert first,' she went on, accepting one of the menus being thrust at her.

'Splendid idea, and I do recommend the sorbets,' Sir Ronald said. 'It's really far too hot for anything else, isn't it?'

Paula nodded. 'I think that's what I'll have.' She glanced at the waiter, half smiled. 'A lemon sorbet for me, please.'

'You can make that two,' Sir Ronald said. 'And what about you Michael, will you join us?'

'Oh, no.' Michael threw his father a look of mock horror and grimaced. 'Only coffee for me.'

As the waiter went off with their order, Michael's eyes swept over Paula appreciatively. He grinned as he remarked, 'It seems to me *you* can eat anything and never put on an ounce ... I'm afraid I have to watch myself these days.'

Paula shook her head and laughed with him. 'Oh, I don't know, you're trim enough, Michael.'

Swivelling to face his father, she now picked up the conversation where they had left off a moment ago, and launched into a recital about the forthcoming events to be held at the Knightsbridge store later that year.

Michael had settled back in his chair, toying with his wine glass. He was only vaguely listening to Paula.

His mind remained focused on Lady Hamilton Clothes and the endless possibilities the company held for them, *if* they were lucky enough to buy it back from Harte Enterprises. Amanda Linde, Sandy's half sister, had been creating the line for a number of years now, and in his opinion she was a far better designer than Sarah Lowther had ever been. Her clothes were easy and comfortable to wear, and yet they had a special kind of elegance because she always managed to give them a touch of the Harte class. Her designs would sell as well in other Continental countries as they did in France, of that he was quite certain.

Michael's mind turned on business matters.

Sir Ronald and Paula continued to chat about her celebratory plans for the store's anniversary. Their voices were a faint murmur, barely audible against the buzz of the lunchtime crowd in the busy restaurant.

The waiter came back and served the dessert, poured the coffee.

Michael picked up his cup, further ruminating on the talented Amanda. If they bought Lady Hamilton, whether now or in the future, she would have to remain as head fashion designer and managing director. That was an imperative. If she was in any way reluctant to stay on, to work for them, he would have to come up with some special inducements –

Paula's sudden laughter reverberated on the warm air, cut into his myriad thoughts. It was a full, throaty, curiously sexual laugh and it caused Michael to lift his head swiftly.

He glanced across the table at her. She was spooning sorbet into her mouth. A small glob of it clung to her upper lip and she licked it off with the tip of her tongue and went on eating. He watched her, fascinated, and as he did he experienced the most extraordinary physical attraction to her. His reaction unnerved him. Michael held himself perfectly still in the chair, dropped his eyes and stared into his coffee cup.

When he eventually looked up she had finished the sorbet and her face was averted as she responded to something his father had just said. He blinked, not understanding himself at all. He must be mad to think of Paula in this way.

Brilliant sunshine was pouring in through the window immediately behind her and it encircled her with shimmering light, brought her into focus as if she were under a pinspot on a stage. Her colouring appeared to be more vivid than ever ... the black hair, the violet eyes, the incomparable skin touched with a faint tan like the golden bloom on a summer peach. How vibrantly alive she was at this moment ... and how very sexual.

Michael, who had never felt anything but fraternal affection for Paula, was filled with a fierce desire to make love to her. He took a steely hold of his feelings, which had flared so suddenly, and lowered his head, fearful that something would show in his face, that his eyes would betray his lust for her. *Why?* he asked himself. Why do I want to take her to bed *now* after knowing her for so many years? He gazed intently at the small vase of flowers in the centre of the table, his face unreadable as he endeavoured to quell his emotions.

Sir Ronald was saying, 'And I shall be in Paris next weekend, Paula, en route to Biarritz. If you're going to be over there, visiting the Paris store, perhaps we could dine together.'

'No, I won't be in Paris next weekend –' Paula began, and came to an abrupt halt. 'Oh damn!' she exclaimed, sitting up jerkily in her seat, frowning, remembering the note on her desk. She had forgotten to cancel the Paris airline reservation which had been made for her for later in the day.

'Is something wrong?' Sir Ronald asked in concern.

'No, no, it's nothing,' Paula assured him, making a mental note to telephone British Airways the minute she returned to her office. 'I forgot to do something before lunch, but there's no problem, really there isn't, Uncle Ronnie.'

Michael, who had managed to extinguish his erotic thoughts about Paula, gave his father a puzzled look. 'Why are you going to Biarritz at this time of year, Dad? The season's over.'

'Yes, I know it is ... but I'm going to look at an Imperial Russian Easter Egg by Fabergé,' Sir Ronald announced with obvious pleasure.

He beamed at them both. 'My art dealer in Paris has a client in Biarritz. A very old lady. A White Russian lady. She is apparently ready to sell her jewelled egg at long last. And, quite naturally, I want to get there first, before the American publisher Malcolm Forbes or any other serious collector hears about it and snaps it up before I do. You know how extremely rare the Fabergé eggs have become.' Sir Ronald peered at his watch, clucked to himself, and before Michael had a chance to comment, he rapidly went on, 'And that reminds me, I have an appointment at Wartski's in fifteen minutes. Kenneth Snowman recently acquired a cigarette box which belonged to Czar Nicholas the Second. It's by Perchin, one of the greatest of the Fabergé designers, and I promised I would pop in to see it this afternoon.'

'I'm delighted for you, Dad, and I hope that you manage to get both items,' Michael said with real sincerity, knowing how important collecting these beautiful objects had become to his father. What had begun as a vague hobby had turned into a grand passion. The Kallinski Fabergé Collection was renowned, and was frequently on exhibition with the Sandringham Collection, which had been started by King Edward VII and Queen Alexandra, sister of the Czarina Marie Feodorovna, later added to by Queen Mary and now owned by Queen Elizabeth II.

Michael smiled at his father. 'Since you're in a hurry, I'd better get the bill, Dad,' he said, and motioned to their waiter.

Sir Ronald glanced at Paula. 'If you wouldn't mind dropping me off at Wartski's first, my car can then take you back to the store, my dear.'

'Thanks, Uncle Ronnie, that'll be lovely.'

'Michael, can I give you a lift too?'

'Oh no,' Michael said, suddenly having no wish to be around Paula any longer than was necessary today. 'Thanks anyway, Dad, but I prefer to walk.'

528

4

She went to Paris after all.

It was a sudden decision, made when she returned to the store at three o'clock. She had picked up the phone and begun to dial British Airways, ready to cancel her reservation, when she had changed her mind and let the receiver drop back into its cradle.

It had been a scramble then to finish her work and stuff several silk dresses into the garment bag and get out to Heathrow to catch the six o'clock plane. She had made it with ten minutes to spare and the flight had been smooth and fast with the wind behind them, and exactly one hour and five minutes after take-off they had landed serenely at Charles de Gaulle Airport.

Her luggage had come through without much delay and she had passed customs quickly and with no fuss. Now she sat comfortably in the back of the chauffeur-driven car he had sent to meet her, being whizzed towards Paris and her rendezvous.

For the first time since lunch at the Connaught with the Kallinskis earlier in the day, Paula began to unwind. And as she did she realized that it had not been such a sudden decision to come here ... she had known from the first moment she had read his note that she would go to him, hadn't she? Hadn't it been a *fait accompli* even then? Of course it had, but, very simply, she had not wanted to admit this to herself and so she had clouded the issue with thoughts of duty and responsibility.

Paula leaned into the corner of the seat and crossed her long and shapely legs; a smile flitted across her face as she recalled something her grandmother had said to her many, many years before. 'When the right man beckons a woman will always go running to him, no matter who she is, no matter what her responsibilities are. And no doubt you'll fall into that same trap one day, just as I did when I met your grandfather. You mark my words, Paula,' Grandy had remarked in her knowing way. As usual, Emma had been correct.

The smile lingered on Paula's face as she turned her head to glance out of the window. With the hour's difference in time between London and Paris it was now nearly nine and already growing dark.

The car was leaving the Boulevard de Courcelles at a good clip, following the other traffic through the Etoile without slowing and as it whirled at a dizzying speed around the Arc de Triomphe, that giant monument to a nation's valour, Paula cringed. She wondered how all these fast-moving automobiles, being driven as if they were in a miniature Grand Prix, would make it safely without crashing into each other and creating a major disaster. That seemed to be almost an impossibility.

But suddenly their car was free of the traffic jam, jostling bumpers, screeching tyres and madly hooting horns, and was pulling onto the Champs-Elysées.

She caught her breath in delight as she usually did upon seeing this glittering avenue.

Whenever she returned to Paris she remembered the very first time she had come here and all the other times after that, and there was always something of those times caught up in her feeling for it. Memory and nostalgia were woven into her love for the City of Light, her favourite city, the most beautiful city in the world. It was full of evocations of the past and of all those who had been with her who had made those occasions so very special: Grandy, her mother and father, her brother Philip, Tessa, and her cousin Emily, who had been her dearest companion on so many trips when they had been girls.

He was very much bound up with her remembrances of Paris, too, and in a short while she would be seeing him; she made up her mind not to spoil the weekend by worrying about the children or having regrets that she had changed her plans to be with him instead of them. That would not be fair, and anyway, she had always considered regrets to be pointless and a waste of valuable time.

They were on the Rond-Point now and ahead she could see the Egyptian obelisk built in the reign of Ramses II and transported from Luxor to rest in the immense rectangle of floodlit stone that was the Place de la Concorde. How spectacular the sight was . . . a breathtaking scene that was forever etched in her mind. She felt a sudden thrill of pleasure at being back here and she was glad she had told the chauffeur to take the longer route to the hotel.

But within a matter of minutes they were entering the Place Vendôme, that quiet gracious square of perfectly-proportioned buildings designed in the reign of Louis XIV, and coming to a standstill in front of the Ritz, and Paula was alighting and thanking the chauffeur and asking him to deal with the luggage.

She moved rather swiftly through the grand and elegant lobby and down the seemingly endless gallery filled with display cases from Paris shops, making for the Rue Cambon section of the hotel – known as *côté Cambon*, just as the other side where she had entered was called *côté Vendôme*. When she reached the smaller lobby she took the lift to the seventh floor and ran the length of the corridor to his suite. She found she was taut with excitement when she reached the door. It was slightly ajar, in anticipation of her arrival, and she pushed it open, went in, closed it softly, and leaned against it, catching her breath.

He was standing behind the desk, his jacket off, the sleeves of his white shirt rolled up, his dark tie dangling loose around his neck. He was talking on the telephone and he lifted a sunburned hand in greeting, his face lighting up at the sight of her. He paused in what he was saying into the receiver, listened carefully to his caller and finally said in a low rapid tone, '*Merci, Jean-Claude, à demain*,' and hung up.

They moved towards each other at precisely the same moment.

As she passed the small Louis XV table holding a bucket of champagne and two crystal glasses she gaily twirled the bottle resting in the ice and said in a light voice, '*You* were sure of yourself, sure I'd come, weren't you?'

'Of course,' he laughed, 'I'm irresistible.'

'And so terribly modest.'

They met in the middle of the room, stood facing each other for a split second.

Quickly she said, 'I almost didn't . . . I was worried . . . worried about the children . . . they need me –'

'Madam,' he said, 'your husband needs you too,' and reaching out he pulled her into his arms. He bent down and kissed her deeply on the mouth and she returned his kiss, clung to him, and he held her hard and very tightly for the longest moment after they stopped kissing.

'Oh, Shane,' she said at last against his chest, 'you have me.'

'Yes, I know I do,' he answered. And then with a deep chuckle he drew away from her, held her by the shoulders, and looked down into her face upturned to his. He shook his head slowly.

'But you're always surrounded,' he continued, the residue of laughter clinging to his voice, 'by children and relatives and secretaries and staff, and I can never seem to get you alone for very long, or have you entirely to myself for a while these days. And that's why I decided early this morning, when I was flying up to Paris for a meeting with Jean-Claude, that we were going to have this weekend together. *Without* our usual encumbrances. A bit of private time for us, before you leave for New York. We're entitled to that, aren't we?'

'Yes, we most certainly are.' Paula gave him a small, rueful smile. 'Coming in from the airport I vowed I wouldn't say anything about the children, and I've only been here a few minutes and already I've –'

Shane gently placed his hand over her mouth. '*Sssh*! I know how much you wanted to see the kids before going away, and you shall.'

'What do you mean?' she asked, giving him a puzzled look.

'Tonight and Saturday belong to us, and then on Sunday morning Kevin will fly us down to the Riviera to spend Sunday and Monday at the villa with the brood. You'll have to go to New York one day later, that's all. On Wednesday instead of Tuesday. Okay?'

'Oh darling, yes, of course! What a marvellous idea and how lovely of you to think of it, to think of pleasing them as well as us,' she exclaimed.

He grinned at her. 'They're my kids, too, you know.'

'But you've been coping alone with them for the last two weeks and you must have had your fill of them by now.'

'Only too true . . . in some ways. On the other hand, they've really been looking forward to seeing you, and I don't want them to be disappointed, or you to think I'm an *entirely* selfish sod. So, I'm prepared to share you with our offspring . . . after all, you are going to be gone from us for five or six weeks.'

Paula gazed up to him, loving him. 'Yes, I am . . .' She paused, hesitated, then asked softly, almost tentatively, 'How's Patrick? Is he all right, Shane?' A worried frown knotted her dark brows together and her clear blue eyes turned cloudy and apprehensive.

'He's wonderful, Paula, and as happy as a sandboy, enjoying every minute of the day and having lots of fun,' Shane reassured her, his tone very positive. 'Please, darling, don't *worry* so much.' He put his hand under her chin, tilted her face to his and added, 'Patrick manages very well, really he does.'

'I'm sorry, Shane, I know I fuss about him, but he's such a little boy and so diffident . . . and different. And the others can be so boisterous at times, and I'm always afraid he'll get hurt when he's out of his usual environment . . .'

She let her sentence trail off, not wanting to express the thought that anything might ever happen to their first-born child. Patrick, who was seven, was slow, retarded, and she could not help being concerned about him when he was not under her sharp and watchful eyes.

Although Shane was equally protective of their son, he was constantly – if gently – chastising her for being overly anxious. Deep down, she knew Shane was right and so she tried very hard to control her anxiety, to treat Patrick as if he were perfectly normal, like his five-year-old sister, Linnet, and his half-brother and half-sister, Lorne and Tessa, the twelve-year-old twins fathered by Jim Fairley.

Shane, observing her carefully, fully understanding her complex feelings about Patrick, said with a confiding smile, 'I haven't mentioned this to you before, but Linnet's become a real little mother while we've all been down at the villa. She's taken Patrick under her very small but very loving wing and, actually, without you around, she's even turned a bit bossy. And you know how Lorne is with Patrick ... he adores him. So all is well, my darling, and –' Shane broke off at the sound of knocking, exclaimed '*Entrez*,' and, moving away from Paula, he went hurrying to the door as it was being pushed open in response to his command.

A genial-looking porter came in carrying her garment bag and small suitcase, and Shane dealt with him briskly, showed him through into the bedroom, told him where to put the luggage and tipped him.

Once they were alone again, Shane strode over to the table, began to peel the metal paper off the champagne cork.

'Listen,' he said, 'enough of the kids. They're absolutely fine with Emily and Winston.'

'Yes, of course they are, darling.'

A moment before, Paula's thoughts had swung to their youngest child, and now she started to chuckle and her eyes crinkled up at the corners in amusement. 'So Linnet's *true* character has finally emerged, has it? I always suspected that that daughter of ours had inherited a bit of Emma's imperiousness, that she also had the makings of a general in her.'

Shane glanced up, pulled a face, rolled his eyes heavenward. 'Another general in the family! Oh my God, I don't think I can stand it! Oh well, I suppose *all* of my women compensate for their bossiness by being so easy on the eye.' Winking at her, he said, 'And by the way, Emily sends her love. When I rang her earlier this evening, to tell her I'd side-tracked you to Paris, that we wouldn't be at the villa until Sunday, she was tickled to death about our weekend alone together. She thought it was a smashing idea, and she says you're not to be concerned about a thing. Now, how about a glass of this marvellous stuff, before we get ready for dinner?'

'That'd be lovely, darling.'

Paula had seated herself on the sofa whilst he had been dealing with the porter, and she kicked off her shoes, curled her legs under her and sat back, watching him.

It did not matter whether they had been apart for four days or a fortnight, she was always a little startled when she saw Shane after an absence and overwhelmed by the sheer physical presence of him. It had much to do with the force of his personality – that extraordinary charisma he possessed – as well as his height and build and natural dark good looks. Sixteen years ago, at his twenty-fourth birthday party, Emma Harte had said that Shane O'Neill had an intense glamour, and this had never been more true than it was today. He was the most dazzling of men.

Shane had celebrated his fortieth birthday this past June: he was in his prime and looked it. He had a powerful physique with a broad back and massive shoulders, and he had stayed lithe and trim; his sojourn in the sun with the children had given him a deep tan. There was a touch of grey at his temples now, but, curiously, this did not age him. Rather, in combination with his bronzed complexion, the grey seemed to underscore the youthfulness of his strong and virile face. And in contrast to his hair, there was not a strand of grey in his moustache which was as coal black as it had always been.

I've known him all of my life and it's never changed, this extraordinary feeling I have for him, Paula thought, continuing to quietly observe him. He's the only man I've ever loved. The only man I will ever want . . . for the rest of my life . . . my husband, my lover, my closest friend.

'Hey, Beanstalk,' he said, using his childhood nickname for her as he walked across the room. 'You're a million miles away.' He handed her the glass of champagne, sat down next to her on the sofa and gave her a quick quizzical glance.

'Just daydreaming,' she replied, clinking her glass to his when he held it out.

He leaned into her and fastened his eyes on her face. 'Emma would've approved of this weekend of ours . . . she was a thorough-going romantic, just as I am.'

'Yes, that's very true.'

'She was on my mind earlier today and for the obvious reasons,' Shane went on, 'and it suddenly struck me how quickly the time has passed since her death. It's frightening, really, the way the years have sped by. It seems like only yesterday that she was ordering all of us around –'

'I was thinking *exactly* the same thing when I was at the cemetery this morning!'

Their eyes met. They exchanged slightly startled glances and then smiled knowingly at each other. This frequently happened, the shared thought when they were apart, or, when they were together, the sudden voicing by one of them of a sentiment that the other had been about to express.

As a small child, Paula had believed Shane had the ability to read her mind and that he knew her every thought, and she still believed this. But it no longer surprised her; they were too much a part of each other now and she took their closeness for granted and considered it perfectly natural that they were on the same wavelength.

Looking across at him, she said in a voice that rose slightly, as if she were suddenly surprised, 'It doesn't seem possible that we'll have been married for ten years in November, does it?'

'No . . .' He lifted his hand and touched her cheek lightly. 'But we have, and every single day I've been your husband has been meaningful to me, and I wouldn't have missed one of them, not even the really bad days. Better to be with you, no matter what the circumstances, than without you.'

'Yes, I feel the same way,' she said and her eyes signalled her deep and abiding love to him.

Shane returned Paula's unwavering gaze and the expression in his brilliant black eyes echoed the one in hers.

A silence fell between them.

It was a compatible and harmonious silence, one of those quiet interludes they often shared when they discovered words were not necessary to communicate their feelings.

Paula sat back and sipped her drink and unexpectedly thought of what it would be like to be without him, and she felt herself shrivelling inside, appalled at the idea. It was Shane who gave true meaning to her existence. He was the substance of her life, her rock; he was always there for her, just as she was for him. She was glad he had devised this weekend, that they had this bit of special time together before she went off on her business trip to the States and Australia. She smiled inwardly, thinking of the clever and masterful way he had planned the interlude for them, adoring him for it.

Shane, studying her, became aware that the tensions of the day were slowly ebbing out of her face, and this gladdened his heart. He frequently worried about her, knowing how hard she worked, but he never interfered. She was far too much like Emma to be any different, and protesting about her unremitting schedule would only be a waste of *his* breath and an irritant to *her*.

He eased his large frame into the corner of the blue velvet Louis XVI sofa, settled back to enjoy his drink; he, too, was finally able to relax, to let go for the first time since leaving the villa that morning. From the moment he had stepped off the O'Neill corporate jet, until Paula's arrival in the suite, he had been busy with Jean-Claude Soissons, the head of O'Neill Hotels International in France. But he had no intention of letting business intrude any further, either tonight or tomorrow, which was why they were not staying at the hotel he owned in Paris. Whenever he wanted Paula to himself, to spend some quiet private time with her, he always took a deluxe suite at the Ritz where he knew no one would disturb him.

Now, as Paula had done a moment before, he turned his gaze inward, contemplating the next thirty-six hours and the joy they would derive from being together – and completely alone.

There was something very special between these two.

It had always been there, even as children, this spiritual oneness, this closeness, this bonding together, and what had begun in infancy had come to full flower with their sexual union as adults.

For a period of time, during Paula's disastrous marriage to Jim Fairley, Shane had been at odds with her, but the bond between them had never *really* been broken. When they had patched up their friendship and had subsequently become lovers at long last, they had been profoundly shaken by the strength and force of their physical passion for each other. But they had recognized how right it was, knew they had always been meant to be together in this way, and they felt whole and complete for the first time in their lives.

Shane realized how utterly worthless his liaisons with countless other women

534

had been, and at once understood that without Paula his life would be meaningless; Paula finally knew that Shane was the only man she had ever loved, saw how empty and loveless her marriage to Jim was, and acknowledged that to continue to live this lie would be like killing herself. And she accepted that she must end the marriage if she was to save her life – and keep her self-respect and sanity.

Expecting to meet opposition from Jim as she had, Paula, nevertheless, had been staggered by his vituperativeness and the spiteful way he had behaved once he knew she wanted a divorce. They had battled, locked horns, reached an impasse.

In the middle of one of their worst crises, Jim had done a bolt to Chamonix for a winter holiday with her parents at their rented chalet, and she had been furious with him for going skiing with the family at such a crucial time in their lives. And then he had been fatally struck down on Mont Blanc by the avalanche that had decimated the family, and she did not have to worry about getting a divorce any more because she was suddenly a widow at the age of twenty-six.

Jim's death had come between Paula and Shane and she had sent him away out of her great and terrible guilt. But eventually she had come to her senses and had found her true self again, and had gone to him, had told him she wanted to spend the rest of her life with him, and they had been reconciled immediately, for Shane O'Neill had never stopped loving her.

Two months later, with Emily and Winston Harte as their witnesses, they had been married at Caxton Hall registry office in London.

And they both knew deep in the innermost recesses of their hearts that they had finally fulfilled their destiny.

The antique ormolu clock on the white marble mantelpiece began to chime loudly.

Paula and Shane both started in surprise and glanced across at it, and Shane exclaimed, 'Good Lord, it's nine-thirty already, and I booked a table at the Espadon for quarter to ten. Can you get ready in fifteen minutes, darling?'

'Yes, of course,' Paula said, putting down her glass, stretching, then smothering a yawn behind her hand.

Shane stared hard at her and scowled. 'You're terribly tired,' he said in concern. 'How thoughtless of me to expect you to go downstairs to the restaurant. It's a hot bath for you, my girl, and immediately. We'll have a snack from room service tonight.'

'Don't be silly, I'm fine,' Paula began and paused, yawning again. 'Well, to tell you the truth, it has been a long day,' she admitted. 'Perhaps you're right about eating in the suite.'

'I know I am.'

As he spoke, Shane stood up, reached down, took her hands in his and pulled her to her feet. He laid his arm around her shoulders and propelled her towards the bedroom door. 'I wish I'd cancelled Kevin's weekend off and sent him with the plane to collect you this evening –'

'I'm jolly glad you didn't cancel it!' Paula cried, giving him a sharp, almost reproving look. She was fond of Kevin Reardon and was aware that the pilot's devotion to them frequently caused him to neglect his personal life. 'Kevin's been looking forward to his girlfriend's birthday party tomorrow night for weeks now. Anyway, he made a good messenger, didn't he? It *was* Kevin who delivered your note to the store this morning, wasn't it?'

'Yes, it was.' Shane grinned as he proceeded to bundle her into the bedroom. 'Come on, get undressed and take a hot bath, and whilst you're relaxing I shall order supper. What do you fancy?'

'Oh anything you like . . . I'll leave it to you, darling.'

'How about a picnic . . . with some of your favourite things? And another bottle of bubbly.'

Paula laughed gaily. She said, 'If I drink any more champagne I might *just* pass out.'

'That's permissible,' Shane shot back, 'you have your husband here to look after you.'

'True. And a very special husband at that.' She stood on tiptoe, kissed his cheek.

Shane's arms went around her and he caught her to him for a moment, tightening his grip, kissing the top of her dark head, and then he suddenly let go of her abruptly, stepped away from her.

'I'd better be a good boy and go and order supper, otherwise you never know *what* might happen. After all, I have been deprived of you for two whole weeks, and I don't mind telling you, I've missed you like bloody hell, my love . . .'

'Oh Shane darling,' she said slowly, very softly. 'Yes . . . I know what you mean . . .'

It was the inflection in her voice, the sudden longing on her face that made him instantly take a step forward.

She reached out her hand to him.

He took it.

Their clasped hands tightened and they moved into each other's arms swiftly. He bent his face to hers, seeking her mouth, and felt the sudden hotness of her cheeks, and the knowledge that she always wanted him as much as he always wanted her aroused him, made his heart begin to clatter erratically. They kissed, a long deep kiss, and he let his tongue explore her mouth, and they shared a feeling of the most profound intimacy.

Paula was suddenly trembling in his arms and together they swayed on their feet as if they were intoxicated, and of course they were – with each other – and then they half-stumbled, half-walked in the direction of the bed, their arms still wrapped around one another.

Shane stripped her of her clothes.

She went and lay down on the bed, waiting for him, and her eyes never once left his face as he flung off his own clothes. As she watched him intently she was hardly able to contain herself, wanting him so much, and when she saw how excited he was she felt a shiver trickle down her spine.

As Shane stared back into those violet eyes turning inky black with longing for him, he was possessed by such a violent desire for her it sent the blood rushing to his head and made his heart begin to pound against his rib cage. He felt dizzy and lightheaded as he walked across to the bed and stretched out beside her.

Pushing himself up on one elbow, he bent over her, looked down into her face.

She gazed up at him.

Their eyes locked and held for the longest moment of the most intense and adoring communion, and then he touched her cheek with two fingers, moving their tips across her brows, her eyelids, her nose and onto her mouth; slowly he traced the outline of her lips and parted them and rested his fingertips against her tongue. She sucked on them and the sensuality of this little act inflamed him, made the fire leap through him. Immediately, he crushed his mouth to hers. It was hard and insistent and their teeth grazed as he kissed her with mounting passion, and as he did he moved his fingers away from her lips, slid them along the elongated line of her lovely throat. They did not linger there, but moved on to fondle her voluptuous breasts, then slipped further down to flutter lightly across her flat stomach until they were finally resting between her thighs.

Shane began to stroke her lovingly, languorously, in slow motion, and with such tenderness he seemed hardly to be touching her at all. But he could feel the velvet softness of her increasing and he continued to stroke, to explore, until his fingertips came to nestle against that precious core of her that was the fountainhead of her womanhood.

Instantly, Paula twisted herself into him, bringing her body closer to his, her slender hand reaching out for him, and she began to caress him as delicately as he was her. Shane felt his hardness growing as she unexpectedly moved her hand with greater rapidity and he had to bite back a cry as he began to throb under her touch. He grasped her wrist, stilled her hand, and then he intensified the pressure of his fingertips and she tensed, and held her body rigid. He explored further, slipped deeper into the velvet folds of her, and as he did he heard a strangled cry in her throat.

He leaned over her satin-smooth breasts, very taut and upright, and savoured the hard, erect nipples with his mouth, first one and then the other. She started to gently undulate under his expert fingers, his loving mouth, and she sighed and murmured his name softly, over and over. Now her hands went out to him again, were strong and hard on the nape of his neck and in his thick hair, and they suddenly moved on to grasp his wide shoulders as her excitement accelerated.

Paula stiffened and gasped. She was filling with an exquisite warmth. His touch quickened, became ever more nimble and deft, and she cried out in her excitement, 'Shane, oh Shane, my darling husband, I love you so much!' And he said against her throat, in a voice thickened by desire, 'You're my true love, Paula, my own true love. Come to me, my darling, so that I can take you to me.' And she gasped again and said, 'Yes, oh yes,' and gripped his shoulders more tenaciously than ever.

Shane thought he was going to explode as she opened up to him like an exotic flower unfolding soft lush petals, moaning his name and shuddering. He was unable to contain himself, and he moved onto her, took possession of her swiftly, raging with the same kind of molten heat that was suffusing her.

She held him to her, as he pushed his hands under her body and lifted her to him and they cleaved together, were joined, became one.

As Shane thrust deeper, lost himself completely in her and in the joy of her, he suddenly thought: *I want to make her pregnant tonight. I want another child.*

This idea, unexpected as it was, sent such thrills surging through him he moved against her violently and she responded with unbridled ardour, matching his passion equally, and they quickly found their own rhythm as they had all through the years of their marriage. But for Shane, tonight was suddenly like the first time they had ever made love and in an instant the years fell away. He was back in Connecticut, in the barn he had once owned, taking her to him as he had yearned to take her during the years of her marriage to another man, loving her as he had never loved any other woman, as only he and she were meant to love.

And then he was reaching up . . . reaching into the light . . . the light was surrounding him . . . she was at the centre of the light . . . waiting for him . . . his dreamlike child of his childhood dreams. And she was his now. Nothing, no one, could ever separate them again. They belonged together for all time, into eternity. He felt weightless . . . he was soaring higher and higher . . . rising up into that timeless light . . . floating into infinity. And he was carrying her with him, holding the world in his arms, calling her name, just as she called his.

And together they crested on waves of ecstasy in the golden shimmering light . . . were blinded by it and then could see . . . and oh the blessed peace of it . . .

Shane woke up abruptly.

He moved his head to the right and looked at the bedside clock. In the dim light he could see that it was almost five.

Paula slept soundlessly by his side.

He braced himself on one elbow, bent over her, touched her face lovingly, but very lightly, so as not to awaken her from her exhausted sleep, and lifted a strand of hair away from her eyes. Then he settled down again, stretched out on his back and closed his eyes, but before many minutes had passed he decided he was not going to fall off again quite so easily, or as quickly as he had just imagined he would. He was suddenly wide awake. Still, he had slept very deeply for the past few hours, as he always did when he was with Paula, as if he were more content and at peace when she was in his bed. Well, of course he was.

He turned over onto his side, made an arc of his body around hers. She was his whole life, and now, lying next to her in the darkness, adoring her in the silence of his heart, he wondered if he had made her pregnant? Weeks ago they had agreed she should stop taking the pill.

Tonight he had planted his seed in her and he prayed that the seed had taken hold and would come to flower as a child . . . a true love child conceived at the height of passion and spiritual joining. He stifled a sigh, thinking of Patrick. He loved his little boy with a deeply tender and protective love, but he could not help being sad that their first born was not normal. He dare not let Paula perceive his feelings, for fear of underscoring her own pain, but they were never far from the surface and yet, somehow, he always managed to conceal his sorrow from her.

Instinctively, Shane lifted his right arm, put it around her, drew closer, burrowed his face in her fragrant hair, overflowing with his love for her. He closed his eyes again, let himself drift into sleep. Yes, he thought, now is the time for our next child. And he wondered, as he finally dozed off, if that was the real reason he had side-tracked her to Paris.

5

The Villa Faviola was situated in the town of Roquebrune-Cap Martin, approximately halfway between Monte Carlo and Menton.

It stood in its own small park at the end of the little peninsula of Cap Martin, sheltered by pines at its back, with its many tall windows facing out towards the sea.

Built in the 1920s, it was a lovely old house, sprawling, airy and gracious, with a curving driveway bordered by pines, spacious green lawns that swept down from the terrace past the swimming pool, up to the edge of the rocky promontory and the glittering Mediterranean Sea beyond.

Its exterior walls were painted a soft melon, but in a tone so pale it was almost sand, and the canvas awnings shading the windows were of a deeper melon, were partnered with shutters of pristine white.

A wide terrace stretched along the side of the house facing the sea and was made of white stone and marble, and it appeared to float gracefully above the verdant gardens where flowers grew in riotous colour and fountains sparkled in the shimmering sunlight. Scattered along the terrace were several round white-metal tables topped by melon-coloured parasols; matching white chairs, swing-sofas with sunawnings, and chaises all had cushions of cream, and because only these soft integrated tones had been used nothing jarred the harmonious flow of pale colour across the lovely front façade.

The Villa Faviola had been purchased by Emma Harte in the late 1940s, just after the end of the Second World War, and it was she who had originally created the gardens surrounding the house and intersecting the lawns. But in recent years, Paula had enlarged the flower beds and borders and had planted a wide variety of small flowering trees and shrubs and exotic plants, cultivating the entire park to its present beauty – and a magnificence that was renowned along the Côte d'Azur.

Inside Faviola its cool, lofty rooms were filled with lovely filtered sunlight and furnished with a simple yet distinctive elegance. Charming old French Provincial pieces made of dark woods or bleached oak were mingled with vast sofas and comfortable chairs and there were chaises and ottomans, and occasional tables held small pots of African violets and pink and white cyclamen and the latest magazines and books.

Floors of highly polished parquet and rose-veined cream marble were either bare or were covered here and there by old Aubussons and plain rugs of cream wool, and throughout the house colours were pale and cool. Cream, vanilla and white predominated, flowed over the walls, were repeated in the fabrics that fell at the windows and covered sofas and chairs, and accent colours were variations of melon and peach and sand, and there were touches of *café-au-lait*, that lovely milky brown that was so typically French.

Spilling vivid colour into these monochromatic-toned rooms were romantic, lyrical paintings by such noted contemporary French artists as Epko, Taurelle and Bouyssou and huge Baccarat crystal urns overflowing with a great abundance of flowers and foliage from the gardens.

But none of the rooms were so imposing or so grand that guests and children were intimidated and felt they were in a museum and therefore hardly dare breathe. On the contrary, Emma had designed the house as a vacation home, one to be lived in and enjoyed to the fullest, and it had a great deal of comfort and an easy grace that was all its own. It also happened to be one of those houses that had always had a warm, welcoming and happy atmosphere, and there was a lovely serenity about its calm, sun-drenched rooms and the inviting pine-shaded park with its glorious gardens.

Alexander Barkstone owned Faviola, having inherited it from Emma along with its contents – with the exception of the Impressionist art, which his grand-mother had bequeathed to Philip in Australia. But Sandy rarely came to the villa, preferring his country estate in Yorkshire, and it was mostly used by his sister Emily and her family, his cousins Paula O'Neill and Anthony Dunvale and their respective spouses and children, and occasionally his mother, Elizabeth, and her French husband, Marc Deboyne, who came down from Paris for long weekends, usually when the season was over.

But of all of them, it was Emily who loved Faviola the most – and with an enduring passion.

As a little girl some of the happiest times of her childhood had been spent at the villa with her beloved Gran, and she had always believed it to be an enchanted and magical place. She knew every cranny and every corner of every room on every floor, and every inch of the park and the garden and the beach below the rocky promontory. After she had married her cousin, Winston Harte, in June of 1970, they had flown down to the Riviera for their honeymoon and the first two weeks of their life as man and wife had been spent at the villa. The lovely carefree days and romantic evenings were so blissful, Emily's deep feelings for Faviola were only intensified, and ever since then the villa had been her haven which she could escape to at odd times during the spring and winter, either alone or with Winston, and always in the summer months with their children, Toby, Gideon and Natalie. And she had never grown tired of it and she knew she never would, and she thought of the villa as the most perfect place in the world to be.

But in contrast, Sandy's visits to the house had grown fewer and fewer after his wife's death; in 1973, recognizing how much Emily loved the place, he had asked her to take over from him, to supervise its general management. He had been relieved and happy when she had promptly and enthusiastically agreed.

Inevitably, Emily had put her individual stamp on Faviola over the years, but she had not tried to turn it into a replica of an English country house. Instead she had retained its Gallic flavour in every possible way, and if anything she had even enhanced the predominantly Provençal feeling with her inimitable touches. But as involved with it as she had become in the last eight years, Emily never considered the villa to be her own, never once forgot that it was the property of her brother. And yet it *was* hers in a certain sense, because of the time and the care and the great love she constantly lavished on it, and certainly everyone thought of Emily as *la grande châtelaine* of the Villa Faviola.

When Emma Harte was living, the day-to-day running of the villa had been in the capable hands of a local woman from Roquebrune, one Madame Paulette Renard. Engaged by Emma in 1950, she had moved into the pleasant and roomy caretaker's house in the private park – known as *la petite maison* – and had looked after the Harte family with unfailing care for the next twenty years.

But with Emma's death in 1970, Madame Paulette had decided the time had come for her to retire and she had handed over her responsibilities and her keys to her daughter, Solange Brivet, who wished to leave her job as the housekeeper at a hotel in Beaulieu. Madame Paulette was a widow, and the Brivets and their children had been living with her in *la petite maison* for a number of years, and so there had been no great upheavals or sad goodbyes. And since it was only a short walk across the vegetable garden to the villa, Madame Paulette was always on hand to give her expert advice or air her considerable knowledge, and she was delighted she was still able to participate in life at the villa.

Over the past eleven years, the management and running of Faviola had become something of a Brivet family affair. Solange's husband, Marcel, was the chef, two of their three daughters, Sylvie and Marie, were the maids, and their son, Henri, was the butler and, as Emily put it, 'our general factotum *par excellence*', while Marcel's nephews, Pierre and Maurice, were the gardeners. These two drove over from Roquebrune in their little Renault every morning, bringing with them another Brivet, Cousin Odile, who worked in the kitchen as assistant to Marcel, and it was Odile who carried with her the huge basket of breads from her mother's *boulangerie*. . . fresh *croissants* and *brioche*, which Marcel served warm for the family's breakfast, and *baguettes*, those long French loaves with a hard crust which the children especially loved.

Madame Solange, as she was called by everyone, had been trained at the Hôtel de Paris in nearby Monte Carlo, and she ran the villa in the grand Riviera style, rather in the manner of a great hotel, with efficiency, meticulous attention to detail, and with the same kind of loving devotion her mother had expended before her. And in all the years she had been employed, she and Emily had worked together in harmony, with rarely, if ever, a cross word; to Emily the brisk, bustling, but very motherly Frenchwoman was indispensable.

The phrase, 'Thank God for Solange,' was forever on Emily's lips, and she was muttering it under her breath on this August Monday morning as she hurried into the kitchen, stood in the centre of the floor, glanced around, and nodded to herself, looking pleased.

They had had their annual, end-of-the-summer dinner party last night, but no one would have known it from the look of the large, old-fashioned kitchen. As usual, the hanging pots and pans sparkled, the wood counter tops were scrubbed to gleaming white, the terracotta tile floor shone and everything else was spotless and back in its given place.

Solange must have really cracked the whip to get everything so ship-shape for this morning, Emily thought, recalling the mess in the kitchen the night before, after the last of their guests had finally departed. Smiling to herself, she took a glass from the cupboard, went to the refrigerator, poured herself some Vichy water, and carrying the glass she walked back through the pantry, across the dining room and out of the French doors onto the terrace, the clicking of her sandals the only sound on the warm, still air.

Emily was always the first one to be up and about every morning, sometimes as early as dawn.

She treasured this private time before the family awakened and the staff started to arrive. She liked being entirely alone to enjoy the gentle quiescence of the silent slumbering house, to savour the early morning smells and colours of the Mediterranean landscape.

It was also her hour for reviewing the paperwork she invariably brought with her, making notes for her secretary in London, whom she phoned several times a week, working out the day's menus and planning activities for the children. But frequently she just sat quietly on the terrace, glad to have a few moments of solitude and introspection before the excitement of the day began and a horde of children descended on her, dragging a kind of chaos in their wake.

It was not so bad when she had only her own three to cope with, but when Paula's four and Anthony's three children were at Faviola, often bringing with them a number of young guests, it was rather like having an unruly juvenile football team underfoot. But Emily had her own system and she managed to control them far better than anyone else. It was not for nothing the children called her 'The Sergeant Major' behind her back.

Now, taking sips of Vichy as she walked, Emily went up to the edge of the terrace and leaned against the balustrade, looked out across the gardens to the sea. It was a dark metallic blue and choppy, and the sky that surged above it was a curdled cloudy grey that seemed ominous.

She hoped the weather was not going to change again, as it had last week when the mistral, that dry north wind that blew down out of the Rhône Valley, had brought several days of mean weather with it. Without exception, all of the children had been restive and moody and difficult, and Solange had immediately blamed the mistral, reminding Emily that this wind usually disturbed everyone's equilibrium, and Emily had agreed, and they had both been relieved when it had finally blown out to sea. The weather had changed for the better – and so had the children. They were much calmer, almost their normal selves again, and even Emily felt more at ease. She had been edgy and irritable during those dull and incredibly windy days, and she now had to admit there was probably a lot of truth in what Solange – and the locals – said about the mistral and its peculiar effect on people. She glanced at her watch. It was only twenty minutes past six and by nine o'clock the sky would be a perfect cerulean blue, the sun would be out and the sea would be as still as a pond, she decided, as always the eternal optimist, as her grandmother had been before her.

Turning away from the balustrade, she stepped up to the table where she had laid out her papers a few minutes earlier, and sat down. As far as work was concerned, her immediate priority was her impending trip to Hong Kong to buy merchandise for Genret, the import-export trading company she ran for Harte Enterprises. She opened her diary and glanced at the dates in September she had tentatively selected some weeks ago. She flipped the pages backward and forward several times, carefully studied her schedule, pencilled in the changes she now wished to make, and began to scribble a note for Janice, her secretary in London, outlining her new itinerary.

A few minutes later, Emily almost jumped out of her skin as a strong cool hand came to rest firmly on her shoulders, and she started up in her chair and swung her head swiftly, her eyes wide with astonishment. 'My God, Winston! You mustn't creep up on me like that! *So silently*. You scared me!' she cried.

'Oh, sorry, darling,' he apologized and bent over and kissed her cheek. 'Good morning,' he added as he walked across the terrace and leaned against the balustrade, where he stood regarding her lovingly for a moment before proffering her a warm smile.

Emily smiled back. 'And tell me, what are *you* doing up so early? You're usually dead to the world until ten o'clock at the earliest.'

Winston shrugged his bare shoulders, put the towel he was holding on the balustrade. 'I couldn't sleep this morning. But it's always the same with me, isn't it, Em? I mean, on our last few days here I seem to want to cram everything in, enjoy every single second, just like the kids.'

'And as I do, too.'

'Yes, that's true ... you do love this place so. But then it loves *you*, Emily ... why you're positively blooming.'

'Thank you, kind sir,' she said.

He eyed the glass in front of her. 'I suppose that's water you're drinking ... aren't you going to make coffee?'

Emily shook her head. 'No, Winston, I'm not,' she said very adamantly. 'Because if I do, I'll also make some toast and I'll butter the toast and put jam on it and then I'll eat it, and when Odile arrives at seven, with all that scrumptious stuff from the bakery, I'll have another breakfast, a *second* breakfast, and you know perfectly well that I've got to watch my weight.'

'You look pretty terrific to me, Mrs Harte,' he said with a chuckle and leered at her. 'I don't half fancy you.'

'Honestly, Winston, at this hour!'

'What's wrong with this hour? It's still very early ... come on darling, let's go back to bed.'

'Oh don't be so silly, I've a thousand things to do this morning.'

'So do I,' he remarked lightly, giving her a pointed look. Then his face changed suddenly, and he levelled a swift appraising glance at her, liking what he saw. Emily was now thirty-four and one of the prettiest women alive, in his opinion. She was blonder than ever and brown from the sun and her brilliant green eyes, so identical in colour to his own, sparkled with a vivid intelligence and a *joie de vivre* that were uniquely hers. She was wearing a lime-green-and-pink cotton shift over her bikini and looked impossibly young, fresh and delectable this morning.

'Winston, you're staring. And very *rudely*. What's wrong?'

'Nothing. Just admiring you, that's all. And thinking that you look like a delicious ice cream . . . and good enough to eat.'

'Oh pooh!' Emily laughed, but her neck turned bright pink and she dropped her head, stared at her engagement book intently.

There was a tiny silence.

Winston swallowed a smile, both amused and pleased that he could still make her blush after eleven years of marriage, but then that was his Emily and he adored her for her girlishness and her femininity and her softness. Odd, he thought, that she can be so tough in business and yet she has such a soft edge to her in her personal life. Like Paula, of course, and Aunt Emma, when she was alive; it was just this dichotomy in their natures that made the Harte women so original. He had known that for a long time.

Emily raised her head. At once, she saw the contemplative expression on her husband's face and asked, 'And what are you thinking about *now*?'

'I was just wondering what all this is in aid of this morning?' Winston murmured, strolling over to join her at the table. He flopped down in the chair opposite and held her eyes as she looked across at him.

'What do you mean?' she asked, puzzled.

'Why are you going at the work hammer and tongs today, when you'll be back in London at the end of the week? It hardly seems worth it, love.'

'I'm not working, actually, I'm trying to figure out the dates for my buying trip to Hong Kong and Mainland China,' Emily explained. 'If I leave on the tenth of September, instead of the sixth as I'd planned, I'd still be there when Paula breaks her return journey back to the States from Sydney. We were talking about it yesterday afternoon, and decided it would be nice to have a couple of days in Hong Kong. Relaxing . . . doing our Christmas shopping . . . and then we could fly on to New York together, spend a day or two there before taking the Concorde home to England. What do you think?'

'It sounds good to me, if that's what you feel like doing. I've certainly no objections, I don't have to be in Canada until the first week of October. Presumably you'd be back in England before I left?'

'Yes, of course I would. I've taken your Canadian trip into consideration and planned around it.'

'Then it's fine, darling,' Winston answered with a smile and stood up, went to get his towel. 'Well, if you're not going to take pity on your poor husband and make him a cup of coffee, I think I'll go for a swim before that tribe of fiendish little monsters invades the area and ploughs down everything in sight.'

Emily couldn't help laughing at the expression on his face. 'Oh I don't know, darling, they're not *so* bad,' she protested, feeling the sudden need to defend the younger generation.

'Oh yes they are!' he retorted. 'They're bloody awful most of the time!' A lopsided grin glanced across his face. 'But I must admit, I do love 'em . . . especially the three that are mine.' He kissed her quickly and loped off in the direction of the swimming pool without another word, nonchalantly swinging the towel and whistling merrily.

Emily watched him go, thinking how fit and healthy he looked with his tanned body and face and his reddish hair turned to gold by the Riviera sun. The summer here had done him good. He worked extremely hard running the

Yorkshire Consolidated Newspaper Company and its Canadian subsidiaries, and she was always after him to slow down a bit. But he paid not the slightest attention to her, merely commented that they *all* worked like demons, which was true, of course. It was the way her Gran had brought them up. Emma had only disdained slackers, so naturally they had all become over-achievers.

How lucky I am to have Winston, Emily mused, settling back in the chair, idly drifting with her thoughts, putting off preparing the menus for that day's meals for a few moments longer.

Sometimes, when she turned her gaze back into the past, she realized she had managed to catch him by the skin of her teeth, understood how easily she might have lost him to another woman.

Emily had been in love with Winston since she was sixteen. They were third cousins. His grandfather and namesake, Winston Harte, had been her grandmother's brother. Although Winston was five years older than she, they had been bosom pals as children, but once he had grown up he had hardly noticed her again, at least not as an attractive young woman with whom he might become romantically involved.

He had gone off to Oxford with his best friend, Shane, and the two of them had rapidly acquired reputations as terrible womanizers. Almost everyone had been scandalized by their disreputable antics. *She* had ached with a mixture of jealousy and longing, wishing *she* were one of the girls Winston chased and bedded. Only her Gran had been sanguine. Emma had simply laughed, had said they were merely young bucks sowing their wild oats. But then neither Winston or Shane could do much wrong in Emma Harte's eyes and she had had a special fondness for them both.

And so Emily had worshipped Winston from afar, hoping that one day his glance would fall on her again. But it hadn't, and much to her profound dismay he suddenly became seriously involved with a local girl, Alison Ridley. At the beginning of 1969 the gossip going around the three clans was that he was about to get engaged to Alison. Emily had thought her heart was going to break.

Then everything had changed. Quite miraculously, Winston had noticed her at the christening of Paula and Jim Fairley's twins in March of that same year. And all because of an incident with Shane which had upset her grandmother. She and Winston had been called into the library at Pennistone Royal and had been grilled by Emma about Shane's feelings for Paula. When they had finally escaped, they had gone for a walk in the gardens to recover from their gruelling ordeal, and for some reason Winston had been prompted to kiss her. This action on his part had been as sudden as it was unexpected, and Emily, loving him though she did, had been as stunned as he by their intense physical reaction to each other as they had sat on the bench by the lily pond, entwined in each other's arms. The world had turned dizzily and wonderfully upside down for them both.

Winston, in typical Harte fashion, had wasted little time. The moment their affair had begun he had broken off with Alison, and shortly thereafter he had asked Emily's grandmother if they could become engaged. Emma had given her consent, thoroughly approving of the match between her granddaughter and her great nephew. And one year later, when her Gran had returned from

Australia, they had been married in the quaint old church in Pennistone village, and Gran had given the most beautiful wedding reception for them in the gardens of Pennistone Royal; her life as Winston's wife had begun . . . and it was the best life any woman could ever want . . .

Emily sighed with contentment, brought her thoughts back to the present, picked up her pen and began to write out the menu for lunch. When she finished, she started on the one for dinner, but stopped abruptly as an idea occurred to her. Tonight, she and Winston, Paula and Shane, would drive over to Reaulieu and have dinner at La Reserve. Just the four of them. Without the tribe. That would be much more peaceful. Not to mention romantic. Winston will approve, she thought, and smiled a small secret smile.

6

'You clot! You unbelievably stupid clot! Look what you've *done*! You've splashed my beautiful painting and ruined it!' Tessa Fairley yelled at the top of her lungs, glaring at Lorne, adopting an angry stance, waving the paintbrush in the air.

'The side of the swimming pool is hardly the proper place to set up an easel and start painting,' Lorne rejoined loftily, returning her glare. 'Especially when everyone's leaping in and out of the pool. It's your own fault the watercolour's been splashed, not mine. And one more thing – I'm *not* a stupid clot.'

'No, you're a stupid CRETIN,' his twelve-year-old twin shot back, then sucked in her breath with a horrified gasp. 'Don't do that, Lorne Fairley! Don't shake yourself like that! Oh! Oh! you *rotten* thing. You've spoiled my other pictures. Oh, God, you've made them all *trickly*.' She had the sudden murderous urge to bash her brother in the head, to do him some kind of bodily harm, but instantly suppressed it because of her mother's presence this morning. 'Mummy . . . *Mummy*. . . tell Lorne to stay away from my paintings drying on the grass,' she wailed.

'I want this hat,' Linnet announced matter-of-factly and snatched Tessa's large yellow sun hat from the chaise near the easel, placed it on top of her bright red curls and happily marched off, dragging a rubber duck on a string behind her and pushing the hat up as it kept sliding down over her eyes.

'Bring my hat back at once, you naughty girl!'

When her five-year-old sister paid not a blind bit of notice, Tessa exclaimed to no one in particular, 'Did you see that? She took my hat without my permission. Well! *Her* behaviour certainly leaves a lot to be desired. Mummy . . . *Mummy*. . . that child's spoiled rotten. You and Daddy have ruined her. There's no hope –'

'Pompous, pompous, Tessa's being pompous, just like Lornie, she's parroting Forlornie,' Gideon Harte taunted in a sing-song tone from the relative safety of the pool.

'I won't dignify *that* ridiculous remark,' Lorne sniffed with hauteur and lowered himself onto a mattress, picked up his copy of Homer's *Iliad* and buried his face in the book.

'Bring my hat back!' Tessa screamed, stamping her foot.

'Oh for God's sake, leave her alone,' a faintly disembodied voice admonished from the pool, and Toby Harte's reddish-gold head bobbed up over the side. The ten-year-old grinned at Tessa, who was his favourite girl cousin, and then hauled himself out of the water, being careful not to splash her or her paintings, having no wish to incur her wrath. Reaching for a towel, he added, 'After all, she's only a little itty bitty *baby*, and how could she –'

'*Not* a baby,' a muffled voice informed them from underneath the large sun hat.

'– possibly damage it,' continued Toby, towelling himself dry. 'And why do you care so much, Tess? It's only a stupid old hat you bought in Nice market . . . a cheap bit of rag.'

'It's not a bit of rag! It's *beautiful*. And it cost me a whole week's pocket money, Toby Harte!'

'More fool you,' called out Gideon, and with this inflammatory comment the eight-year-old paddled swiftly to the centre of the pool, flipped over, floated on his back, and began to make faces at her.

'What do you know about anything, Gideon Harte! You're a CRETIN like my brother.'

'Is that the only *stupid* word you know, *Stupid*?' Gideon shouted back and stuck his tongue out at her.

'Brat! Brat!' Tessa yelled at him. 'You're a spoiled brat, too!'

'Oh shut up both of you,' Toby admonished in a bored voice. 'Listen, Tess, can I borrow one of your old Beatles' albums?'

'Which one?' Tessa asked, suddenly wary, squinting up at him in the bright sunlight, moving a strand of fair hair away from her face.

'Sergeant Pepper's Lonely Hearts Club Band.'

'Oh no, I can't possibly lend you that one! It's er . . . er . . . it's become a . . . *classic*. When Auntie Amanda gave it to me, she told me it'd be very, *very* valuable one day, 'cos it's an early one . . . she'd had it since before *we* were even born. But . . . Well . . . all right, because it's *you* I'll make an exception, so –'

'Gosh, thanks, Tess,' Toby cut in, his freckled face lighting up.

'– you can rent it if you want, it's ten pence an hour,' Tessa finished, sounding as magnanimous as she now looked.

'*Ten pence an hour*! That's highway robbery!' Toby spluttered, his expression indignant. 'No thanks, Tessa, I'm not going to help you become a capitalist.'

'In this family, everybody's a capitalist,' Tessa declared smugly, with a small smirk.

'Forget it, I'll play my new Bee-Gees.'

'Suit yourself.'

'Aunt Paula. *Aunt Paula*. . . your daughter's turned into a really nasty little sharpie this summer,' Toby exclaimed scathingly and threw a disgusted look in Tessa's direction.

'Mummy . . . I'm taking my knickers off, they're all wet,' Linnet cried from the depths of the sun hat.

'You see what I mean about her behaviour, Mummy,' Tessa sniggered. 'She's the only five-year-old *I* know who still wee-wees in her pants.'

'I don't! I didn't, Mummy!' a clear voice shrilled as the hat was pushed back and Linnet's round flushed face appeared.

'Auntie Paula, may I have one of these ginger snaps, please?' three-year-old Natalie Harte asked and promptly took one and crunched on it before she was forbidden to do so.

'Mummy! Look at her now! She's *dragging* my gorgeous sun hat in the puddles. Stop it, you little monster. *Stop it!* Mummy, make her stop. *Mother*. . . you're not listening. If you throw that hat into the pool, I'll kill you, Linnet O'Neill! Gideon! Get my hat! Quick, before it sinks!'

'Okay, I will, but it'll cost you plenty.'

Tessa ignored this threat. 'Wait until I catch you, Linnet,' she screamed after the small, plump figure retreating swiftly in the direction of the pool house.

'Mother . . . *Mother*. . . will you *please* tell Tessa to stop screeching like a banshee? I'm getting a frightful headache,' Lorne murmured languidly from the mattress where he lay reading.

'Auntie Paula, Natalie's eaten *all* of the ginger snaps,' India Standish gasped and, turning to her cousin, she added in the most dire tone a seven-year-old could summon, '*You're* going to be *sick*. Horribly, horribly sick, and it serves you right, you greedy little girl.'

'Have this, India,' Natalie said with a winning smile, pulling a half-eaten chocolate out of the pocket of her sundress, dusting it off and offering it to the older girl, whom she adored.

'Ugh! *No thanks*. It looks icky!' India pulled a face. 'It's covered in sand. And *fluff*. Ugh!'

'Auntie Paula, there's a dead *something* at the bottom of the pool,' Gideon shouted, coming up for air with a splash, triumphantly holding the sodden sun hat aloft.

'Oh my God, my beautiful *gorgeous* new sun hat has been ruined! Mummy, she's ruined my *expensive* hat. *Who's* going to buy me a new one? *Mummy*, did you hear what I just said?'

'Where's the dead *something*?' Patrick asked, throwing himself flat on the ground, dangling his dark head over the pool, craning his neck so that he could peer down into the depths. 'Can't see it, Gid.'

'I've got to dive for it,' Gideon explained, running his hands through his wet blond hair, taking a deep breath and instantly plunging underwater again like an agile little dolphin.

'Patrick, don't lean over the edge,' Linnet warned from the door of the pool house. 'You'll fall in.'

'*Won't* fall.'

'Will you take five pence an hour for Sergeant Pepper's Lonely Hearts Club Band?' Toby negotiated hopefully.

'Eight pence . . . *perhaps*.'

'No thanks, Miss Sharpie. You can go and shove it up your . . . jumper.'

'Oh Mummy, Mummy, look! A bird. *Dead*,' Patrick cried. 'Oh poor birdie. Funeral. Can we have a funeral?'

548

'Auntie Paula, please make Gideon get rid of that foul, disgusting, revolting object,' eleven-year-old Jeremy Standish exclaimed. 'It pongs to high heaven and it's contaminating the air.'

'No, it *isn't*!' Gideon glared at his cousin. 'We're going to bury it, like Patrick wants, aren't we, Auntie Paula? Auntie Paula, cooee! *Auntie Paula*, we *can* bury it, can't we?'

'*Mummy*, can birdie have a funeral?'

'*Mummy*, I want some dry knickers.'

'*Mother*, look at Linnet now. She's waving her knickers in the air. She's a disgusting child. Just look at her, Mummy. *Mummy*. MOTHER!'

'For Christ's sake, Tessa, stop screaming,' Lorne shouted. 'How can I concentrate on my Homer with you bellowing in my ears. I'll be jolly glad to get back to school next week and away from you. Far, far away. There's never a minute's bloody peace when you're around. You're a bloody little pest, a bloody nuisance.'

'If Daddy hears you swearing, you'll catch it.'

'And who's going to tell him, Miss Tattle Tale?'

'I've never split on you yet, you MORON.'

'If I'm a moron, then so are you, TWIN!'

'Don't bring that frightful smelly disgusting *thing* anywhere near me, Gideon, or I'll punch you on the nose,' Jeremy threatened. '*Auntie Paula*, please make him stop waving that beastly dead bird in my face.'

'Auntie Paula! Auntie Paula! Natalie's being sick! I *knew* she would be. Look, over there by the tree. *Auntie Paula*, did you hear me?'

'Gideon Harte, I'm *warning* you. Keep your distance or I'll thump you!'

'Stop it, Gid, stop being childish,' Toby ordered loudly.

'*I'm* not. *He* is. Sissy! Sissy! Lord Jeremy Standish's a sissy!'

'I'm going to really *thump* you for that!' Jeremy cried, jumping up.

'Gideon, give me that dead bird,' Toby shouted, racing after his brother, catching him by the top of his wet bathing trunks.

'*Auntie Paula*, tell Toby to let go of me!' Gideon screamed. 'He's *hurting* me.'

'And it's *my* turn next,' Jeremy threatened with sudden manic glee.

'Mummy, *Mummy*, make the boys stop fighting,' Linnet shrieked.

Paula threw down her book and angrily leaped to her feet.

She began to chastise them loudly and vociferously, but they heard nothing. Her voice was drowned out by a series of strange booming echoes that reverberated on the warm air, and as the echoes died away, Paula was able to ask, in a tone that rose slightly, 'What on earth was *that*?'

'The gong,' Linnet said.

'*Gong*,' Paula repeated in perplexity, and it instantly struck her how chastened the children seemed and she stared at them sharply through narrowed eyes. 'What gong? Whose gong?'

Lorne explained, 'Auntie Emily's gong . . . she bought it –'

'From the house up the mountain,' Tessa quickly interjected, then volunteered to her still-baffled mother, 'The old lady who owned the house died, and there was a sale. Two weeks ago, just after you left, the last time you were here, Mummy. And we all went with Aunt Emily, she thought we might find some bargains.'

'But all we found was the gong,' Jeremy muttered.

'And where does Aunt Emily keep this gong?' Paula inquired, her eyes flicking over each one of them with considerable interest.

'Up there in the gazebo,' India replied.

'But why did Emily buy the gong?' Paula wondered out loud.

Toby supplied the answer, when he said quietly, 'Mummy uses it to signal us. One strike means that breakfast's ready, two is for lunch, three is to summon us inside, to get ready for dinner, and –'

'When she bangs and bangs and *bangs*, like just now, it means we're going to *catch* it,' Linnet confided and grimaced. 'For being *bad*. For something *terrible* we've done.'

'I see,' Paula said and her shrewd eyes swept over the group of youngsters yet again. It was more apparent to her than ever that each child was suitably intimidated – even the most recalcitrant of them. She turned away to hide a smile, thinking how terribly clever Emily was.

'We're definitely in for it. Because of the unholy row we've been making,' Lorne muttered, jumping up, edging away.

'You're right,' Toby agreed. 'Come on, Troops, let's skedaddle before my mother gets here and starts giving us stupid chores to do, or worse still, starts thinking up idiotic activities to keep us properly occupied.'

Within the space of seconds, the older children had raced after Lorne and Toby, as always the ringleaders, who were heading at breakneck speed for the steps that led down to the beach below the promontory. Only Patrick, Linnet and Natalie remained with Paula in the pool area.

Silence finally reigned.

Paula sank gratefully into her chair, delighted to have peace and quiet for the first time that morning. She had done her utmost to ignore them, had remained aloof from their endless bickering – as she had learned to do over the years – at least until Toby and Gideon had started fighting and Jeremy had seemed about to join in the *mêlée*. She couldn't permit that to happen. Anthony and Sally Dunvale's eldest son had not been well, and the last thing his father had said, before leaving for Ireland earlier that morning, was for them to make sure the boy did not overtax himself for the rest of his stay at the villa. Paula knew that if Jeremy went home to Clonloughlin looking as if he had been scrapping with the boys, she and Emily would never hear the end of it from his mother. Their cousin Sally fussed a great deal about her first born, the heir to the Dunvale title, lands and fortune.

Paula took a deep breath, and was about to give her small daughter a stern lecture about removing her underclothing in public, when she saw Emily hurrying down the path between the lawns.

'Cooee! Cooee!' Emily called, waving.

Paula waved back.

A moment later, Emily drew to a stop and she and Paula exchanged looks. They began to laugh.

Emily said, 'I know it's noisy, but it's *very* effective.'

'And *how*,' Paula agreed. 'I've never seen them silenced quite so quickly. *Never*. It was an inspired buy on your part.'

'Yes,' Emily chuckled, 'so it's proved. My God, they were kicking up such a racket, I'm surprised you don't have a splitting headache by now. I know I could hardly hear myself think when I was in the kitchen, talking to Marcel about the meals for today.'

'Mummy, I've been sick,' Natalie announced, going over to Emily, tugging at her shift. 'I frowed up.'

'Don't talk like a baby, you're a big girl. And it's *threw* up,' Emily corrected. She looked down at her youngest child, frowning, and put a hand on her forehead in concern. 'Are you feeling all right? Are you better now, angel?'

'I don't know, Mummy.'

'It's because she ate *all* the ginger snaps,' Linnet said.

'Now, now, Linnet, you know it's wrong to tell tales out of school!' Paula reprimanded sharply, scowling at her daughter. 'And let's not forget that you've been very naughty this morning. First, flinging Tessa's sun hat in the pool, and then taking your knickers off in public. I'm terribly cross with you, and ashamed of you, Linnet.' Paula shook her head, trying hard to look appropriately angry without much success, but nevertheless, she added, 'You've disgraced yourself, and the only reason you haven't been punished *yet* is because I'm still trying to think of a *suitable* punishment.'

Linnet bit her lip, adopted a sorrowful expression, and wisely said nothing.

Emily looked from her daughter to her niece and then glanced at Paula. She exclaimed, 'Why do I do such stupid things? Such as letting both nannies have the same day off, so they can go up to Grasse to buy perfume. And today of all days – the last chance you have to get a bit of rest before you go to New York on Wednesday. I'm sorry, Paula.'

'It's all right, really it is, lovey.'

Sighing under her breath, Emily now took hold of Natalie's hand. 'Come along, let's go inside and get something to settle your tummy. And you'd better come along, too, Linnet, for a pair of clean underpants.'

'Oh thanks, Emily,' Paula murmured, settling back in her chair.

'Lunch is at one,' Emily said, 'and I've booked a table at La Reserve for dinner tonight. Just the four of us.'

'I should jolly well hope so,' Paula laughed. 'And it sounds absolutely lovely. It's ages since we've been over there . . . it's one of my favourite places.'

'Yes, I know,' Emily replied, looking pleased as she turned away. She took a couple of steps, stopped, and said over her shoulder to Paula, 'Oh by the way, I've got to go into Monte Carlo this afternoon, to pick up a repair from my antique porcelain man. Do you want to drive in with me? I'll only be a few minutes with Jules, and then we could take a stroll around the town and have tea at the Hôtel de Paris . . . watch the world go by for a while, like we used to with Gran.'

'What a nice idea, Emily, yes, I'd like that.'

Emily gave her a sunny smile, then bustled her charges forward, half bending down, talking to them as they made for the villa.

Paula watched the three of them go up the path together, the two little girls walking on either side of Emily, clinging to her hands. Linnet and Natalie bore a strong resemblance to each other, could easily be mistaken for sisters since they had both inherited the famous Harte colouring – Emma's red hair and vivid green eyes and English rose complexion. They were beautiful. Dazzling children, really. A couple of Botticellis.

Patrick now came to Paula, stood by her chair, touched her arm, stared deeply into her face. 'Mummy . . .'

'What is it, darling?'

'Mummy . . . poor birdie. Gid took it. No funeral now.' The child shook his head and looked sad.

'Of course we'll have a funeral,' Paula said gently, taking his small, rather grubby hand in hers, looking into his angelic face. His black O'Neill eyes were bright and lively for once, not devoid of expression and vacant as they so frequently were. Her heart lifted with joy to see such life in them today.

She gave her son a reassuring smile, and went on, 'I know Gideon will bring the little bird back, and we'll ask Madame Solange for one of her old tin biscuit boxes to put the birdie in, and then after lunch we'll have the funeral. I promise, darling.'

Patrick put his head on one side and studied her carefully. 'Bury it in the garden?' he asked, and gave her a slow, tentative smile.

'Yes, that's *exactly* what we'll do. Oh darling, *look* who's coming!'

Patrick swung his head and when he saw Shane approaching his face lit up and he extracted his hand from his mother's and ran to meet his father.

Paula called out worriedly, 'Patrick, do be careful. Don't fall.'

Patrick did not answer. He sped ahead as fast as his little legs would carry him, shouting, 'Daddy! Daddy! Daddy!'

Shane caught his son in his arms and swung him up high in the air, then placed him on his shoulders, and the two of them laughed merrily as Patrick rode Shane back to the pool area, crying, 'Gee-up, gee-up. Nice horsey. Gee-up, gee-up.'

'I'm going to take him for a swim. Is that okay, darling?' Shane called. He knelt down and carefully lowered Patrick to the ground.

'Yes, of course,' Paula called back.

She sat up straighter, so that she could see the two of them better, shading her eyes with her hand.

Shane jumped into the shallow end of the pool, holding Patrick tightly in his arms, and immediately they began to frolic in the water, still laughing, and shouting with glee, and Patrick's face was bright with excitement and happiness and so was Shane's.

From this distance, her son seemed like any normal seven-year-old; the problem was that he would always have the mind of a seven-year-old. His body would grow and age, but his mental capacities would remain as they were now for the rest of his life. He would never be any different; they had given up hope of that. When they had first discovered Patrick was retarded, Paula had blamed herself, believing she carried some flaw in her genes which had been inherited from her grandfather. Paul McGill had had a legitimate son, Howard, by his legal wife, Constance, in Australia, and the boy, who had been dead now for a number of years, had been retarded. She had so convinced herself that this was the case, she had told Shane she dare not risk having any more children. But Shane had immediately pooh-poohed her theory, and he had insisted they see Professor Charles Hallingby, a leading geneticist.

They had both been tested and the results had proved conclusively that neither she nor Shane had passed on any kind of deficiency to their son. Patrick's condition was inexplicable, simply a terrible fluke of nature. Professor Hallingby, having studied their family histories, had pointed out to Paula that her grandfather's son may well have suffered prenatal damage because of Constance McGill's heavy drinking during her pregnancy, a possibility her mother, Daisy, had mentioned innumerable times. She had finally conceded that the professor and her mother could be right. Not unnaturally, the knowledge that Professor Hallingby had imparted had helped to ease her mind. Shortly after, she had conceived again, and when Linnet was born she was a perfectly normal baby.

Paula loved her children equally, and tried not to have a favourite, but deep down in the innermost regions of her heart she was aware that Patrick was special to her, that he had a unique place in her affections. There was a terrible fierceness about her love for her afflicted child, perhaps, in part, *because* of his affliction, which made him so vulnerable and dependent.

His siblings also loved him dearly, were patient, and took great care with him, and for this she was thankful. Often she thought how heartbreaking it would have been if they had despised him or treated him badly or shunned him, as sometimes happened in families where there was a retarded child. But Lorne, Tessa, and even little Linnet, were as protective of Patrick as she and Shane were and, in fact, so were his many cousins. Not one single child in the family had ever made Patrick feel that he was in any way different to them. It was an awful tragedy that her little Patrick had not been born a perfect child, that he was damaged in the way he was. But Paula recognized that his inherent sweetness, his gentle nature, and his loving disposition compensated for so many things and endeared him to the family, and certainly he brought out the best in all of them.

An afflicted child is like a bruise on the heart, one never quite gets rid of the aching pain, Paula thought, and she sighed under her breath and held herself very still, pressing down on her sadness, continuing to watch the two dark heads bobbing around in the water. Her husband, her son. Oh how she loved them both, and with a love that was heartstopping at times.

It did her good to see how much they were enjoying their nautical games. Shane could be very gentle and tender with Patrick, or roughhouse with him, as he was doing now, and from the joyous shrieks and the whoops of delight filling the air, she knew the little boy was having the best time with the father whom he worshipped. A great rush of happiness filled her to the brim, displaced the sorrow she had felt a moment ago.

Paula lay back and closed her eyes, feeling a measure of contentment, but she lifted her lids almost immediately and sat up at the sound of Winston's voice.

He walked into the pool area carrying a large tray of plastic tumblers, and trotting dutifully behind him was his nephew, Giles Standish, second son of his sister Sally, the Countess of Dunvale. Giles was carefully holding a large jug of lemonade with both hands.

'*Bonjour, Tante Paula. Voilà! Ici citron pressé pour toi,*' the nine-year-old Giles said, showing off his little bit of French, as he had been doing all through the summer. He was having special tutoring in the language and made a point of speaking it whenever he could, much to the irritation of the other children, who were not as fluent as he was becoming. But their constant ribbing rolled off his back; he was independent by nature, so he paid no attention and went on speaking French whenever he felt like it.

Giles put the jug down on one of the tables in the shade, and politely stood aside to make way for his uncle.

'How delicious it looks, Giles dear,' Paula said. 'Just what I need, I'm getting quite parched from this heat. Did your parents get off all right?'

'Yes, but Nice airport was jammed, wasn't it, Uncle Winston?' Giles said, reverting to English.

'It was bloody awful, Paula,' Winston asserted, pouring lemonade into a tumbler and bringing it to her. 'Chaotic. I've never seen so many people. Sally and Anthony were thankful they were returning on Shane's private jet, and I must say, that plane's turned out to be a real godsend. I'm certainly glad Emily and I will be able to use it to get the mob back home at the end of the week. Now, Giles, do you want a glass of this?'

'No, thank you very much.' Giles glanced around. 'Where are Jeremy and India, Auntie Paula?'

'I believe your brother and sister decamped to the beach. With the rest of the troops.'

'Oh goody! I bet they're all fishing or looking for *oursins*. I'm going down there too!' Giles squealed excitedly. 'Please excuse me, Auntie Paula, Uncle Winston,' and so saying he took off, leaping across the grass in great bounds, making for the long flight of steps.

Winston stared after him, and said to Paula, 'That kid's got the best manners of the whole bunch of them. If only some of the others – mine in particular – would borrow even *half* a page from his book I'd be happy.' He lowered himself onto a nearby chair, took a long swallow of lemonade, and continued, 'Emily told me every single one of them was raising hell earlier, driving you crazy.'

'It did start to get a bit out of hand, actually, Winston. But Emily finally put a stop to their bickering with that wonderfully effective gong.' She glanced at her cousin through the corner of her eye, and chuckled. 'Trust Emily to come up with something ridiculous like that. Still, it really works and I must admit, I wish I had a handle on them the way she does.'

Winston grinned. 'Don't we all.'

7

'I adore old-fashioned hotels, especially when they're in the *belle époque* style and have a grandiose splendour,' Emily said to Paula as they turned into the Place Casino in Monte Carlo later that afternoon. 'You know, like the Hôtel de Paris here, the Negresco in Nice, the Ritz in Paris and the Imperial in Vienna.'

'Not to mention the Grand in Scarborough,' Paula said, laughing, tucking her arm through Emily's companionably. 'I can well recall how attached you were to that place when we were little. You never stopped pestering me to take you there for afternoon tea, and you couldn't wait to stuff your fat little face with cucumber sandwiches and cream puffs and scones with strawberry jam and clotted cream,' she teased, her violet eyes dancing merrily.

Emily shuddered at the remembrance and made a gruesome face. 'My God, all those fattening things! No wonder I've had to work so hard to keep my weight down ever since. Too much ballast as a child, methinks!' She grinned at Paula. 'You shouldn't have let me eat like that.'

'How could I stop you! I tried very hard to keep you out of the Grand Hotel, using every kind of ruse, even pretending I didn't have any money on me. But you always had an answer for everything, even for that . . . "scribble on the bill like Grandma does," you used to tell me. You were a very enterprising child, you know.'

'And so were you.'

They both stopped at precisely the same moment and automatically swung to face each other and they shared a smile, thinking of those lighthearted happy days when they were growing up together in Yorkshire and London. There was a brief and loving silence before Emily said, 'We *were* lucky, weren't we, Paula? We had such a wonderful childhood, and especially when we were with our Gran.'

'Yes, it was the *best*,' Paula agreed. 'And she was the *best*.'

They started walking again, lost in their own thoughts as they crossed the pleasant square, heading in the direction of the Hôtel de Paris, which was situated in the far corner, opposite the renowned Casino de Monte Carlo.

It was a lovely afternoon, filled with dappled sunlight and soft white clouds scudding across the azure-blue sky, and there was a refreshing breeze blowing up from the sea; it ruffled the skirts of their summer dresses and puffed them out like tulip bells, and made the white sails on the boats in the harbour billow about and the brightly-coloured flags on the masts ripple and dance gaily.

Emily had driven them down to Monte Carlo in her powder-blue Jaguar, after a family luncheon on the terrace at the villa, and the burial of the dead bird in the garden afterwards, which everyone had attended, much to Patrick's satisfaction.

Once they had arrived in the Principality of Monaco they had parked the car and gone to *Jules et Cie*, the antique shop where Emily frequently bought old porcelain, to pick up a Limoges plate Jules had repaired for her. The charming old man had chatted to them at length about antique china and glass, and had shown them his private collection of rare items, and they had browsed for a while before leaving the *antiquaire's* to stroll around the main streets and window shop on their way to the famous hotel for afternoon tea.

'It's impossibly grand, even a bit gingerbready, but it's irresistible, at least to me,' Emily said, pausing on the pavement outside the Hôtel de Paris, looking up at it, beginning to laugh at herself as they climbed the front steps. Almost instantly the laughter died in her throat, and she grabbed Paula's arm so tightly her cousin winced and followed her gaze.

Heading towards them down the steps was a tall woman with an abundance of flaming red hair and the kind of elegance that was indisputably French. She wore a white silk dress, very chic and severely tailored, with a black silk rose pinned to one shoulder, black-and-white high-heeled shoes, a matching bag, and white gloves. She carried a black straw picture hat, and she was holding the hand of a little girl of about three years, also dressed entirely in white, who had the same natural, bright red hair. The woman was bending over the child, saying something to her as they moved forward, and she had not seen them.

'Christ Almighty! It's Sarah!' Emily gasped and squeezed Paula's arm again.

Paula sucked in her breath, but she had no chance to make any response, nor could she and Emily turn around and hurry away.

A split second later their cousin had drawn level with them. The three women were standing on the same step, gaping at each other, and they were so stunned they were utterly speechless, rooted to the spot.

It was Paula who finally broke the uncomfortable silence.

'Hello, Sarah,' she said, very quietly, in a soft voice. 'You're looking well.' She stopped, took a deep breath. 'And this must be your daughter ... Chloe, isn't it?' she added, forcing a smile, looking down at the child, whose upturned face was solemn and filled with enormous curiosity. And Paula saw, on closer inspection, that this was a true offspring of Emma Harte.

Sarah had regained her self-possession, and she gave Paula a look that was deadly. 'How dare you speak to me!' she cried, not bothering to sheathe her hostility and loathing. 'How dare *you* attempt to make a friendly gesture towards *me*.' Leaning closer, she hissed in Paula's face, 'You have a bloody nerve, behaving as if nothing happened between us, Paula O'Neill, and after what you did to me, you rotten bitch!'

The angry words, spoken so violently, the undisguised hatred on Sarah's face, and her threatening manner, made Paula recoil in shock and dismay.

'You'd better stay away from me and mine!' Sarah exclaimed, her face turning brilliant red. She looked almost choleric, and her voice was unnecessarily loud and shrill. 'And you too, Emily Harte, you're no better than she is,' she scoffed, her scarlet lips curling in scorn. 'You two turned Grandmother against me, and then you cheated me of what was rightfully mine! You're both *thieves*. Now, get out of my way! Both of you!'

Tightening her grip on the child's hand, Sarah pushed between Paula and Emily, almost knocking Paula over as she did. And she swept on grandly down the remainder of the steps without a backward glance, the child hurrying and stumbling to keep up with her mother, exclaiming, '*Maman, Maman, attendez*!'

Paula had gone cold all over, despite the heat of the day, and there was a queasy feeling in the pit of her stomach. She was momentarily paralysed, powerless to move. Then suddenly she grew conscious of Emily taking hold of her arm.

Emily said, '*Phew*! That was awful. She's not changed, has she?'

'No, she hasn't,' Paula agreed, rousing herself. 'Let's go in, Emily, people are staring at us.' Paula extricated herself, flew up the steps and through the doors of the hotel, wanting to put distance between herself and those passersby who had witnessed the scene. She was mortified and still shaking inside.

Emily ran after her and found her cousin waiting inside the door, striving to calm herself. She slipped her arm through Paula's and drew her forward into the hotel, saying, 'At least we didn't *know* any of those people who were listening and gawping at us, darling, so forget it. Come on, let's go and have a nice cup of tea. It'll do us both good.'

Once they had been shown to a secluded table in the lounge area of the vast lobby, and had settled down and ordered a pot of tea, Emily sat back and expelled a great sigh. 'What a nasty performance that was,' she said.

'Yes. Ugly. And embarrassing. I could hardly believe my ears when she started to shout at us like a fish wife, not to mention the ghastly things she was saying.'

Emily nodded and gave Paula a careful look. 'Why on earth did you speak to her in the first place?'

'I didn't know what else to do. We were eyeball to eyeball. It was terribly awkward, you know that, Emily,' Paula replied, and paused. A contemplative expression settled on her face and she shook her head slowly. 'I suppose I've always felt a bit sorry for Sarah ... deep down. She *was* Jonathan's pawn, and his victim, in a certain sense. He duped her, used her and her money. I've never really considered her to be wicked like Jonathan. Just rather stupid.'

'I agree with you – about her stupidity, but I don't feel sorry for her, and neither should you,' Emily exclaimed. She drew closer, continued, 'Look here, Paula, you're far too nice always trying to be fairminded and compassionate, and seeing everyone else's point of view. That's all very well, when you're dealing with people who deserve your concern, but I don't think Sarah does. Stupid or not, she knew it was wrong to back Jonathan, to put up money for his private company. That truly was going against Harte Enterprises – and the family.'

'Yes, it was,' Paula admitted. 'But I still think that in some ways she's more dense than anything else, and I'm sure Jonathan pulled the wool over her eyes.'

Emily said, 'Maybe he did.' She sat back, crossed her legs, and went on, 'Don't you think it's odd that we haven't run across Sarah before now. I mean after all, she's been living up the coast near Cannes for about five years, according to that story we saw in *Paris Match*, and Mougins isn't that far away.'

Paula was silent.

After a moment she levelled her steady gaze at Emily, and murmured, 'What's also kind of odd is that for the first time in years Michael Kallinski was talking about Sarah and Jonathan on Friday and –'

'Why?' Emily cut in peremptorily, arching a blonde brow. 'No special reason, other than his own curiosity. We'd been talking about Lady Hamilton Clothes for a good half hour, as I told you yesterday, so I suppose it was natural for him to inquire about Sarah's whereabouts. Still . . .' Paula broke off, shook her head.

'Still *what?*' Emily pressed.

'I was just thinking that his talking about them was almost prophetic.' Paula gave a curious, rather nervous little laugh as she stared pointedly at Emily.

'Gosh, it was! And I hope to God we don't run into Jonathan next. I'm not sure I could survive an encounter with *him* quite as coolly as the one with Sarah.'

'I know I couldn't.' As she spoke Paula shivered involuntarily, and she felt the hackles rise on the back of her neck and goose flesh speckle her arms. She sat back in the chair, biting her inner lip, wishing the mention of Jonathan's name did not upset her in the way that it did.

Fortunately, the waiter arrived with the laden tea tray, and Paula was glad for the distraction as he started to place the cups and saucers on the table in front of them and speak in rapid French to Emily, whom he apparently knew by sight. He departed, almost instantly returned with the pot of tea and a jug of hot water, went away and came back again, this time pushing a four-tier trolley in front of him. Paula declined the many delicious pastries being offered, and stole a surreptitious glance at Emily, wondering if her cousin would succumb to temptation.

Emily looked longingly at the cakes, but she also shook her head, and as Paula poured the tea, she said, 'Don't think I didn't want one of *everything*, because I did. I could have cheerfully made a meal out of the chocolate eclairs and the vanilla slices, but you saw how I resisted. All for the benefit of my figure. And Winston. He likes me to be svelte, so I've developed a will of iron when it comes to nasty fattening things like cream buns. You should be very proud of me,' she finished, irrepressible laughter bubbling up in her.

'And so should Winston,' Paula said, also laughing. Their sudden gaiety helped to dissipate the unpleasantness of the scene with Sarah, which still lingered in their thoughts, and it changed their mood, brought them back to normal. Almost at once they began to talk about spending a few days in Hong Kong together next month, and made their plans.

At one moment, between sips of tea, Paula said, 'You and Shane are right, Emily. I think I will take Madelana to Australia with me.'

'Oh, I am glad you agree with us, darling. If the boutiques really are in a mess, she'll be of tremendous help.'

'Yes, that's true, and I think she'll be thrilled to come with me, don't you?'

'Who wouldn't be – it's a marvellous trip, and anyway she's devoted to you.'

'She is. It was a smart move on my part, promoting her to be my assistant a year ago. She's proved herself to be invaluable.' Paula glanced at her watch. 'It's five o'clock . . . eleven in the morning in New York. I'll give her a ring later, explain that I want her to come with me. She'll have her hands full this week, clearing the decks in order to leave with me on Saturday, so the sooner she knows, the better.'

'You could call her from here, if you wanted to, Paula,' Emily suggested, never the one to waste any time if she could help it.

'No, no, that's all right. I can do it when we get home to Faviola. The six-hour time difference gives me plenty of leeway.'

Emily nodded, and then right out of the blue, she said, 'I bet you anything that dress she was wearing was a Givenchy.'

'I've no doubt it was. Sarah always did have a flair for clothes.'

'Mmmm.' Emily turned thoughtful, sat looking into the distance for a few moments. Finally, she asked Paula, 'Do you think she ever hears from Jonathan?'

'I can't even hazard a guess.'

'I wonder what did happen to him, Paula? Where he's living?' Emily said softly, thinking out loud.

'I'd prefer not to know. Or to talk about him, if you don't mind, Emily. You know very well that Jonathan Ainsley's not my favourite subject,' Paula answered sharply.

'Oh gosh, sorry, darling,' Emily said, suddenly regretful that she had started talking about their cousins again. Changing the subject, she said quickly, 'Well, I'd better pay and we'll get off home, so you can call Madelana at Harte's in New York.'

'Yes, let's go,' Paula agreed.

8

She was the kind of woman that men looked at twice. And women, too, for that matter.

It was not that Madelana O'Shea was very beautiful. She was not. But she had what the French call *je ne sais quoi*, that indefinable something that made her special and different and caused heads to turn wherever she went.

Tonight was no exception.

She stood outside Harte's department store on Fifth Avenue, patiently waiting for the radio cab she had ordered from her office a short while before. It was eight o'clock on a Thursday and the store was still open. Everyone who hurried in and out stole a glance at her, obviously wondering who she was, for she had style and there was a touch of regality in her bearing.

A tall young woman of about five feet eight, and slender, she had a willowy figure and legs that were long and shapely. Her thick, chestnut-brown hair was shoulder length, worn full and loose around her heart-shaped face. This was a little too bony to be called pretty, but the smooth forehead and high, slanting cheekbones, sharp as blades, gave her the look of a thoroughbred, as did the finely drawn aristocratic nose sprinkled faintly with freckles. She had a wide Irish mouth, with a full, somewhat voluptuous bottom lip, and a lovely smile that filled her face with radiance, but it was her eyes that fascinated and compelled. They were large, widely set, and of an unusual pale grey the colour of chalcedony, their marvellous transparency emphasized by the dark brows arched above them. They were highly intelligent eyes, and filled with a determination that could turn steely at times, but there was also laughter in them and sometimes a hidden recklessness.

Madelana had a flair for clothes and wore them well. She looked smart in anything she put on, gave it her own cachet; it might be the way she knotted a scarf, snapped down the brim of a hat, wrapped a length of Oriental silk into a unique cummerbund or twisted antique beads around her long and slender neck. And it was this great personal chic in combination with her svelte good looks that made her appearance so arresting.

The evening was stifling, humid as only New York in the middle of summer can be, and everyone seemed worn down and wilted in the oppressive weather as they toiled up Fifth, or stood at the edge of the sidewalk, looking for a yellow cab or waiting to cross to the other side.

But not Madelana O'Shea. Her tailored cream silk tunic, with its simple round neckline and three-quarter length sleeves, worn over a straight black silk skirt, was as crisp as it had been when she had set out for work that morning, and she looked cool and untouched by the heat, and as elegant as usual.

The burgundy radio cab pulled up in front of the store, and she hurried forward with an ease and lightness of movement that bespoke her childhood ballet and tap lessons. She was limber, and had the agile grace of a dancer, and this, too, was part of her immense appeal.

After opening the taxi door, she put the large Harte's shopping bag on the seat and slid in next to it.

'West Twenty-Fourth Street, right, miss?' the driver said, moving off down Fifth.

'Yes, between Seventh and Eighth, in the middle of the block, please.'

'Okay, miss.'

Madelana sat back, rested her hands on the black patent bag in her lap, her mind racing as it almost always did, no matter where she was or what she was doing.

Ever since Monday afternoon, when Paula had called from the south of France to tell her she was going to Australia, she had felt as if she had been running in a marathon. She had had to complete her current work, cancel her business appointments for the next few weeks, along with the few personal dates she had made, plan ahead for a possibly protracted absence from the store, and select appropriate clothes and accessories for the trip.

And then Paula had arrived in New York on the Concorde, early on Wednesday morning, and had come directly to the store. The two of them had worked like demons for two solid days, but they *had* accomplished miracles, and they would have a relatively normal business day tomorrow, before leaving on Saturday on the first leg of their journey. Tonight she would go over the files of papers she had stacked in the shopping bag and finish working on them, and tomorrow night she would pack.

I'm ahead of the game, Madelana thought with sudden relief, and nodded to herself, feeling gratified. She glanced out of the window, hardly noticing the tawdry glitter and squalor of Times Square with its hustlers and peddlers and drug addicts and pushers and undercover cops and hookers on the make. As the cab slid swiftly through this clamouring rinky-tink wedge of real estate and headed on downtown towards Chelsea, her mind focused on the trip to the other side of the world.

They were going first to Sydney, then on to Melbourne and perhaps even to Adelaide after that, before returning to Sydney where they would spend most of their time. From what Paula had told her, they had a lot of work to do, and it would be a gruelling two or three weeks. But the prospect did not daunt her. She and Paula O'Neill worked well together, had always seemed to understand each other right from the beginning, and they were compatible.

It struck her, and not for the first time, how strange it was that she, a poor Irish-American Catholic girl from the South, and an aristocratic Englishwoman, heiress to one of the world's great fortunes and a noted international business tycoon, could have so many things in common, could be so similar, and in so many ways. They were both workaholics and had boundless energy, were sticklers for detail, disciplined, dedicated and driven, and extremely well organized. In consequence, they did not grate on each other's nerves, or create problems for each other, and they seemed always to be in step. It's like dancing with Fred Astaire or Gene Kelly, she thought and smiled inwardly, liking her analogy.

In the year she had been Paula's personal assistant, she had not put a foot wrong and she did not intend to, not ever, and especially not on their forthcoming trip to Australia. Paula was the key to her future. Her goal was to become President of Harte's store in New York one day, and with Paula's help she would achieve it.

Ambition. She was loaded with it, she knew this only too well, and she was pleased that she was. She considered it to be a plus not a minus. It had goaded her on, helped her to arrive where she was today. Her father had occasionally complained that she was too ambitious. But her mother had merely smiled her lovely Irish smile at him, and behind his back had winked at her and nodded maternal approval and encouraged her at every opportunity.

She wished her parents were still alive. And her little sister, Kerry Anne, who had died when she was four. And Joe and Lonnie. Her two brothers had been killed in Vietnam. She missed them so very much, just as she missed her baby sister and her parents, and at times she felt as though she had no roots, no centre to her life, with all of them gone from her. They had been close knit as a family, and very loving of each other. She considered her losses over the past few years, thought of her sorrow, and her heart clenched. Resolutely, she pushed the pain away.

Madelana took several deep breaths, keeping absolute control of herself and her emotions, as she had taught herself to do after her father had been buried four years ago. Only when he was lying in the ground did her sense of aloneness truly overwhelm her, and only then did she fully comprehend that she no longer had any family left, except for Aunt Agnes, her father's sister, who lived in California and whom she hardly knew.

The cab drew up outside the Residence Jeanne D'Arc. She took the receipt from the driver, said goodnight, grabbed her shopping bag and alighted. She ran swiftly up the steps and into the building.

The minute she walked inside, Madelana felt herself relaxing.

This place was so familiar and cosy and welcoming . . . she had lived here in one of the rooms when she had first come to New York, had stayed for three years. It had been her home. She still thought of it as home, even though she now had her own apartment uptown in the East Eighties.

She crossed the small entrance foyer and turned right, heading for the office.

'Hello, Sister Mairéad,' Madelana said to the nun behind the counter, who was in charge of the office this evening. 'How are you?'

'Why, Madelana, it's nice to see you, and I'm just fine, very fine indeed,' the sister replied, the faint Irish lilt echoing softly in her voice, her rose-apple cheeks dimpling with pleasure. The sister had had a soft spot for Madelana when she had lived here, and she was always delighted to see this lovely young woman who was such a credit to her parents, God rest their souls, and who in every way exemplified her good Catholic upbringing.

'Sister Bronagh's expecting me,' Madelana said with a smile, and put the large Harte's bag on the counter, took out a gift-wrapped package and looked at the sister. 'Can I leave my shopping bag with you, please?'

'Of course you can, Madelana.'

'It's full of my papers from work, so please put it somewhere safe, won't you? It'd be more than a disaster if it got mislaid.'

'Now don't you be fretting yourself about it, I'll keep it safe, and you know there's no need to be worrying about anything you leave here. Sister Bronagh said for you to go to the garden. She'll be up to join you in a few minutes. I'll let her know you've arrived.' Sister Mairéad beamed and nodded to herself and picked up the phone, began to dial.

'Thank you, Sister,' Madelana murmured, and swung around, heading for the small, box-like elevator that would take her up to the fifth floor and the stairs that led to the roof of the building.

Surprisingly, the roof garden was empty.

Usually in the summer, on pleasant evenings, some of the girls who lived at the residency came up here to chat and socialize with each other, and with the sisters, to share a drink of wine or juice, or read a book or simply be alone.

It was a charming spot, planted with rambling ivy, and there were vines, growing on trellis panels, and window boxes of bright red and pink geraniums, and pots of yellow and peach begonias, and the sisters grew vegetables up here. Scattered about were chairs and several small tables, and the atmosphere was inviting and suggested conviviality.

She paused to look at the statue of the Blessed Virgin, surrounded by masses of flowers as it generally was in the summer, recalling how often she had tended the flowers when she had been living here. She had always thought of this spot as a little oasis, a lovely patch of green-growing things in the middle of the concrete canyons of Manhattan, and it had given her a feeling of wellbeing, had nourished her soul.

Gliding forward, she went to one of the tables, put down the gift and her handbag, and seated herself in one of the chairs facing uptown. Straight ahead of her, in her direct angle of vision, were the Empire State and the Chrysler Buildings thrusting up above the higgledy-piggledy roofs and chimney pots of Chelsea and the less-distinguished skyscrapers of the city.

Dusk was already falling, and the lavender-and-grey tinted sky was changing as a deep cobalt blue seeped in like ink and slowly extinguished these paler hues. The lights that washed over the towers of the two dominating buildings had been turned on, but the grandeur of the architecture would not be properly visible until the sky was pitch black. Then these towers would be thrown into relief, would shimmer magnificently against the dark velvet backdrop of the sky, and it was a sight that never failed to make her catch her breath in delight.

Even in winter, Madelana had enjoyed coming up here when she had lived at the residency. Wrapped in warm clothes, she had huddled in a sheltered corner, admiring these two extraordinary edifices and a skyline that stunned with its unique beauty.

The Chrysler, with its Art Deco sunburst motif on its elegant tapering tower, was only ever flooded with clear white light that gave it a pristine beauty and underscored the purity of its design, whereas the Empire State changed its colours to suit the season and the holidays. At Thanksgiving, the two tiers and the slender tower above were flooded with amber, gold and orange; at Christmas with red and green. The lights changed to blue and white for Chanukah and other Jewish holidays, became yellow at Easter, green on St Patrick's Day, and red, white and blue for the fourth of July. And if the Chrysler Building really was the more beautiful of the two, then certainly the Empire State was the most eyecatching when it blazed with a celebratory selection of its rainbow colours.

'Good evening, Madelana,' Sister Bronagh called as she walked across to the table, carrying two glasses of white wine.

Madelana sprang up at the sound of her voice.

'Hello, Sister.' She hurried forward, smiling, and took the glass being offered to her, and the two women clasped hands affectionately, before sitting down together at the table.

'You're looking extremely well,' Sister Bronagh said, peering at her in the gathering dusk.

'Thank you, I feel good.'

They touched glasses and sipped their drinks.

'This is for you, Sister,' Madelana said, after a moment, and slid the gift across the table.

'For me?' Sister Bronagh glanced at it, raised a brow, her warm hazel eyes suddenly twinkling merrily behind her spectacles, her face wreathed in smiles.

'That's why I came tonight . . . to bring you the present and to say goodbye. I won't be able to come to your farewell party next week. I'll be in Australia by then.'

'Australia! My goodness, so far away, Madelana. But exciting, I think, for you. I'm so sorry you won't be at the party . . . your absence will be noticed. It always has been, when you haven't been able to make one of our little get togethers. And thank you for the gift, it was thoughtful of you.'

'You're quite welcome.'

'May I open it now?'

'Of course,' Madelana said, laughing, enjoying her obvious delight in the small token she had brought.

Sister Bronagh untied the yellow ribbon, dispensed with the wrapping paper and lifted the lid of the Harte's silver cardboard box. Underneath the layers of tissue paper were three different-sized toilet bags made of deep blue silk and trimmed with a lighter blue welting.

'Oh, how lovely they are!' Sister Bronagh exclaimed, taking one out, turning it over in her hands, opening the zip, looking inside. Her small, birdlike face was bright with sudden happiness and she took Madelana's hand resting on the table and squeezed it. 'Thank you so much, my dear, they're just what I need.'

'I'm glad you like them. I wanted to get you something that was pretty but also useful.' Madelana grinned at her. 'I *know* you . . . how practical you are. Anyway, I thought these would be perfect for travelling.' She rested her elbows on the table. Her fingers toyed with the glass of wine. 'When *do* you leave for Rome?'

'On the tenth of September, and I'm becoming excited about going. It'll be a challenge, helping to run the residency over there. It's situated not very far away from the Vatican, and that's an added joy for me, being so close to the Holy See.' There was a lovely glow about her as she continued, 'I must confess to you, Madelana, I was thrilled when Sister Marie-Theresa picked me to be the one to go.'

Madelana nodded. 'Everyone here at the residency is going to miss you, though, me included.'

'Oh and I shall miss you, too, Madelana, and the other old girls who still come to see me, and the ones living here now, and the sisters.' There was a brief pause. A fleeting sadness touched Sister Bronagh's eyes, and they grew moist, and then she cleared her throat quickly, sat up, straightened the collar of her white blouse. She gave Madelana a warm smile. 'Tell me about your trip to Australia. It's rather sudden, isn't it?'

'Yes. I'm going on business with my boss, Paula O'Neill. We're leaving for Los Angeles on Saturday morning, and we'll spend the night there, since she thinks we'll both be in better shape if we break the trip instead of flying direct. We take the Qantas flight to Sydney at ten o'clock on Sunday night.'

'And how long will you be gone?'

'Two or three weeks, perhaps even four. Paula may have to leave me behind to follow through for her. We're going out there because of the boutiques in the hotels. She's concerned they're not being run properly. The manager has been sick, and her assistant seems to either panic or flounder on alternate days.'

'You've done well at Harte's, Madelana, I'm proud of you.'

'Thank you. Anyway, my career's very important to me, as you know . . .' Madelana stopped, and there was a hesitation in her manner, and she looked down at her hands resting on the table. Shortly, she went on in a more muted, thoughtful tone, 'But working so hard these past few years has also helped me to keep grief at bay, to come to grips with my losses . . .' Her voice suddenly trailed off.

The sister reached out, took Madelana's hand in hers, and there was a sense of comfort in this gesture. 'Yes, I know it has. But then so has your great faith, Madelana. Always remember that God has His reasons, and that He never gives us a burden that is too heavy to carry.'

'Yes, you've told me that many times before.' Madelana tightened her grip on Sister Bronagh's hand. There was a short silence between them. She lifted her head then, and smiled faintly at this devout and gentle middle-aged woman who had been so warm and loving to her when she had lived here, who had singled her out for special attention.

'I couldn't let you leave for Rome without coming to see you, Sister Bronagh, to thank you from the bottom of my heart for helping me to get through so much pain and sorrow, for making me feel so welcome when I first arrived. You gave me courage.'

'No, no, I didn't, Madelana,' the sister said swiftly. 'The courage was within you, already part of you then. As it is now. And as it will always be. If I did anything at all, it was simply to show you that it *was* there, to make you understand that all you needed to do was to reach inside of yourself, and to draw on it.'

'Yes . . . But I'll never be able to thank you enough for all you've done for me. And for all you've taught me – especially about myself.'

'You were always very special to me, my child,' Sister Bronagh replied in a soft voice. 'If I had not chosen this way of life, had not chosen to be in service to God, to do His work, and if I had married and had had a daughter, I would have wanted her to be exactly like you.'

'Oh Sister Bronagh, what a beautiful thing to say, thank you, thank you so much!' Madelana experienced a sudden rush of emotion as her genuine feeling for this woman rose up in her and there was the unexpected sting of tears behind her eyes and she blinked them away, not wanting to break down. She realized how much she would miss Sister Bronagh after the nun had departed for her new job in Rome.

Now Madelana said, 'Your belief in me has been so important, Sister, it's mirrored the belief my mother had in me. She encouraged me the way you have. I'll try never to let you down.'

The sweetest of smiles brushed across Sister Bronagh's pale mouth and she said slowly, to give greater emphasis to her words, 'The important thing is never to let yourself down, Madelana.'

9

It was a long, hot ride uptown from the Residence Jeanne D'Arc to East Eighty-Fourth Street, and for the first time that day Madelana felt uncomfortably warm and damp when she finally alighted in front of the small apartment building where she lived.

'Hi, Alex,' she said, greeting the doorman breezily as he helped her out of the cab.

The doorman responded in kind, and there was an admiring look in his eyes as he watched her walk rapidly across the sidewalk with her usual ease of movement and gracefulness. She swung into the building before he could rush to open the door for her, and appeared to float across the lobby, her feet hardly seeming to touch the marble as she sped ahead.

She stopped to collect her mail and then took the elevator to the seventeenth floor. The phone was ringing inside her apartment when she put the key in the lock. It stuck, and she struggled with it, muttering under her breath, but finally she managed to get the door open and hurried in, and the phone continued its strident shrilling in the cool silence of the empty apartment.

Snapping on the light in the minuscule, almost non-existent entrance hall, she dumped her things unceremoniously on the floor and ran to pick up the nearest extension.

This was on the desk in the yellow-and-white living room, which opened directly off the tiny entrance hall, and snatching the receiver, she exclaimed, 'Hello,' only to discover that there was no one at the other end. All she could hear was the faint burring of the dialling tone; the caller had obviously disconnected a split second before she had reached the phone.

Oh well, she thought, whoever it is will call back, if it's important, and she dropped the receiver into the cradle with a shrug of her elegant shoulders.

Blinking in the shadowy half light that flowed in from the entrance hall, she switched on the desk lamp and swung around, making to leave the room, then hesitated, pivoted to look at the phone. She was on the verge of picking it up again, wondering if it had been Paula calling her, concerned with some last minute bit of business. Or about something they had forgotten. It was hardly likely, since it was almost ten o'clock. She immediately dismissed the idea of calling her boss at her Fifth Avenue apartment. That would be an unwarranted intrusion, and anyway, Paula always went to bed early when she first arrived in New York, in an effort to counteract jet lag.

Madelana shivered, becoming aware of the chilly temperature. The air conditioning had been running at its highest all day, and the apartment was like a freezer. But her body would soon adjust, and she welcomed the coolness after the humidity of the stuffy, airless streets of Manhattan.

She went to retrieve her things, and carried them back to the living room, sat down on the yellow-velvet sofa, and glanced at her mail. There was nothing of any importance and she put it on the glass-and-brass coffee table, rose, and went into the adjoining bedroom to change her clothes.

A second or two later she emerged, barefooted and wearing a long pink cotton caftan, and hurried into the kitchen to prepare a light supper for herself, before digging into the work she had brought home from the store.

The kitchen in her small apartment was long and narrow; it had reminded Madelana of a ship's galley the first time she had seen it, just a year ago this month. And for this reason she had decorated it in various shades of blue with lots of white and dashes of brilliant red. She had covered the walls with nautical prints, ranging from Boston whalers, nineteenth-century sailing ships and Mississippi riverboats to ocean-going liners and modern yachts. All were framed in brass, and there were other touches of brass in small accessories; and copper moulds hung above the stove and the sink, and these added their own sparkle.

At one end, near the window, she had placed a small, dropleaf table and two bentwood chairs, an ideal spot for a snack. A small window box on the sill was filled with feathery spider ferns, and the kitchen had a gaiety and charm which owed more to her ingenuity and flair than to the amount of money she had spent.

One of the colourful yachting prints caught Madelana's eye, and she smiled to herself, thinking of her friend, Patsy Smith. Patsy was a Boston girl who had lived at the residency at the same time that she had, and two years ago Patsy had invited her to the Smiths' summer home in Nantucket for the long Fourth of July weekend. They had done a lot of sailing over those four glorious days, and Madelana had loved every moment she had been on the water. It had been a new and exhilarating experience for her, and much to her amazement she had discovered she had a great affinity for boats and the sea.

Perhaps one day I'll do it again, she thought, turning to the refrigerator, taking out the ingredients for a salad.

The telephone on the wall behind her rang. She reached for it. 'Hello?'

'So, you're finally home.'

'Oh Jack, hi. Yes, I was –'

'You cancelled our date in order to work, or so you said,' he interrupted rudely, sourness curling around the edge of his beautiful, resonant voice. 'But you ain't been home, kiddo, I've been calling you all night.'

Madelana felt herself stiffening at his tone, and she resented the fact that he had obviously been checking up on her. But she took a deep breath, managed to muster a reasonable tone, to say evenly, 'I had to go down to the residency. To see Sister Bronagh.'

'I suppose that's as good an excuse as any.'

'But it's *true*, and please don't take this attitude with me. I don't like it, Jack.'

'You don't expect me to believe that's where you *really* were, do you? Visiting a nun?' He laughed hollowly. 'Come on, babe –'

'I'm not a liar,' she cut in, bristling with anger. Her voice rose, and she added coldly, 'Nor do I appreciate being called one.'

He ignored this remark. 'Why won't you tell me *who* you were with tonight?'

'I *have*. I was with Sister Bronagh.' She tightened her grip on the phone to steady herself. Her exasperation was running high, her patience growing thin.

He laughed again, this time more sardonically. 'Sister Bronagh indeed! That's a laugh. Come on, babe, don't start getting holier than thou with me. It's Jack you're talking to. *Me. Jack.* Jack your lover, Jack the big man in your life. But is he the *only* man in your life? That's the question.'

She realized then that not only had he been drinking again, but that he was, in fact, quite drunk. Although there was no slurring of his speech, she could recognize the signs these days. He became sarcastic, argumentative, aggressive and suspicious of her, and all of his insecurities started to show. And of course he enjoyed baiting her, which only infuriated her further. Jack was a bad drunk. In the last few months she had learned that firmness was the only way in which to deal with him, and that if she adopted the stern posture of a school teacher she could somehow get the upper hand. But she didn't want the upper hand with Jack. She wanted an equal partnership, a balanced relationship in which neither one of them was manipulating or controlling the other.

Sounding crisp and cool, she said, 'Good night, Jack. Go to bed. I'll call you in the morning.'

There was a sudden silence at the other end of the phone.

567

She heard him suck in his breath, as if he were taken aback that she was about to hang up on him.

She said again, her voice firm and colder than ever, '*Good night.*'

'Hey, wait a minute, Madelana, how about dinner tomorrow night? A quick, quiet little dinner. At my place. Or yours. Or somewhere in your neighbourhood. Come on, say yes, honey,' he cajoled, unexpectedly much less hostile, almost contrite.

'You know I can't, Jack. I explained earlier in the week that I have to pack on Friday night. In case it's slipped your mind, I'm going to Australia on Saturday morning.'

'*That*' *right*! *Of course*! I keep forgetting that you're the little career girl dedicated heart and soul to work. Or should I say *big* career girl. Much more appropriate, no? And yes, indeedy, *big* career. *Big* job. *Big* ambitions. But tell me one more thing, babe, is work going to keep you warm in bed on cold nights?' He laughed thinly. 'I doubt it. You don't need a *big* career, babe. You need a *big* man. Like me. Listen, I've got a great idea. Why don't I come over right now and –'

'Y'all've had too much to drink, Jack Miller! Why you're drunker than a skunk that's been suckling at the moonshine barrel!' she cried, inadvertently slipping into the idiom of her Southern childhood, as she sometimes did when she was angry or overly excited. 'Go to bed,' she instructed fiercely, 'I'll call y'all in the morning.' She replaced the receiver quietly, even though she felt like slamming it down hard. She was humiliated by his attitude towards her, and resentful and angry.

I hate the way he makes me feel these days, she said under her breath, opening the cupboard, taking out a small metal strainer. Furiously, she tore the lettuce apart, dropped it in the strainer standing in the sink, let the tap water run on the broken leaves.

She stared morosely at the wall, her mind intently fixed on Jack Miller.

He's a jerk, she thought, and I'm a bigger jerk for continuing to see him. I've known for weeks that the two of us are not making it together. We're going no place fast. I can't tolerate his possessiveness, jealousy and accusations, and the drunken scenes he's been creating lately are insupportable.

She ran her hand through her hair distractedly. I can't cope any longer. I just know I can't. He makes me madder than a wet hen in a thunderstorm. Damn it, why do I take this from him? Well, I'm not going to, and I'm not going to aid and abet him in his own self-destruction!

Opening a drawer, she took out a sharp chopping knife, began to slice the tomato. But her hands were shaking so much she put the knife down, for fear of cutting herself.

Leaning against the sink for the longest moment, she endeavoured to still her fulminating anger.

It's all over between us.

As this unexpected thought penetrated her brain like an arrow hitting its given mark, she felt her tension lessen. And very slowly she shaking began to subside.

It was true. There was nothing left. At least, not for her. Even her sexual desire for him had diminished. His bad behaviour was turning her off ever more frequently. I'll break up with him when I get back from Australia, she decided. There's no point in wasting my time with him. I must get on with my own life. I can't baby-sit Jack Miller, which is what I've been doing for several months now. No, I'd better tell him tomorrow. That'll be much kinder than waiting until I come back. Now, why am I trying to be kind to *him*? That dude's led me a real merry dance of late.

Madelana expelled a wearisome sigh. Jack seemed to want to punish her these days. Or was it someone else he was punishing? Himself, perhaps? He had been out of work for several months, and that was proving extremely hard on him. When he worked he was a different man. A whole man. He stopped carousing in bars with his friends and never touched a drop of liquor.

Poor Jack, she thought, the anger unexpectedly falling away. He has so much. Good looks and charm, talent and even brilliance. But he's wasting it all, letting it drain away down the neck of a bottle. It was the boozing that troubled her; and it was the boozing that had come between them. Invariably, he was full of chagrin afterwards, and apologetic, but this did not take the sting out of the way he had behaved, the hurt he had inflicted.

It struck her then that he needed her pity more than anything else. Broadway actor, almost but not quite Star, he was a virtuoso performer who could have made it very, very big if he had wanted, gone to Hollywood, conquered the silver screen as he had the legitimate theatre, which was his *forte*. His clean-cut handsomeness and silver-gilt hair and those marvellous baby blues were arresting and made him impossibly photogenic. And he even had movie star charisma – when he wished to exercise it. He could have been another Paul Newman, or so his peers constantly informed her. It was always on the tip of her tongue to ask, 'Then why isn't he?', but she never did. Yes, his friends were most admiring of Jack Miller . . . he was an actor's actor, they said. The best. In the same class as Al Pacino and Jack Nicholson. But to her way of thinking, there was something missing in him, something gone askew in his character. If only he were different of temperament.

It seemed to her that Jack wasn't driven, and certainly he wasn't ambitious enough. Maybe that was the reason he was always jabbing at her, why he resented her career . . . because she had an over-abundance of ambition, while he had none. Maybe he had had it once, but he didn't any more.

Madelana let out a knowing laugh. Jack resented her career because at heart he was a male chauvinist. In his own rather oblique way, he had told her that more than once, hadn't he?

She picked up the knife and began to slice a tomato, and she was gratified to see that her hands no longer shook.

Later, after Madelana had eaten her chicken salad, she sat drinking a glass of iced lemon tea in the living room, aimlessly staring at the television set, not really seeing the mindless movie that was playing, and certainly not listening to it.

Lolling back against the cushions, she realized that she was much lighter in spirit. The constricted feeling in her chest had dissipated, and she had to admit that she was full of relief and felt better because she had finally resolved to terminate her relationship with Jack Miller.

Also in the last half hour, she had come to understand that this decision had not been quite so quick or so sudden as she had previously imagined. She had wanted to cut the umbilical cord between them for some time, but she had simply not had the guts to do so before.

She wondered why, wondered if she had stayed with Jack these last months out of loneliness – and the fear of being absolutely alone once more?

Patsy Smith had gone back to Boston to live, and Madelana didn't have too many other close friends in New York. Then again, because she worked so hard and kept such long hours, she had hardly any time for socializing with the few women she knew and liked.

But Jack was a different matter.

Since he was in the theatre, his leisure hours started after the ten o'clock curtain had dropped. Their odd time schedules had somehow dovetailed neatly.

Several times a week she had stayed late at the store, or taken papers home with her and worked there, until she had met him at Joe Allen's or Sardi's for supper at eleven. And on other nights he had often come up to her apartment after the show, and she had cooked for him, and he had stayed over; and they usually spent Sundays together at his place on East 79th Street.

But when he was not in a play, like now, he wanted to see her every night, regardless of her work. That wasn't possible, and she religiously stuck to her own schedule, refusing to be budged by him, and that's when the trouble started. He loved acting with a passion; in a way, it was the centre of his life. Yet he couldn't seem to grasp that her work was just as important to her as his was to him. And thus there was conflict between them.

Patsy had introduced them. She had known him for two years now, and she *had* loved him, and he *was* the one person she had grown truly close to in the time she had lived in Manhattan. In a way, he was almost like family, and perhaps that was why she had continued to cling to him when her deepest instincts had told her to run for her life.

Family, she thought again, turning the word over in her mind, then she swung her head and looked at the framed colour photograph on the end table. They were all in it . . . her brothers, Young Joe and Lonnie, herself with baby Kerry Anne sitting on her knee, and her mommy and her daddy. How young they looked, even her parents, and there was such joy and love on their sweet and shining faces. Her family would have been charmed by Jack Miller, would have found him entertaining and likeable, because he *was* those things, but they wouldn't have approved of him. Not as a boyfriend for her, at any rate.

Her parents and her siblings had considered her to be unique and great things had been expected of her, especially by her mother, and for as far back as she could remember. 'You're the one who's going to go out and do it, mavourneen,' her mommy would tell her in that lovely lilting voice that had never lost its beguiling Irish brogue. 'You're the clever one, Maddy, the one who's been blessed . . . kissed by the gods, to be sure, me darlin'. Why, you're one of the golden girls. Maddy.'

Madelana became motionless, as if turned to stone on the sofa, suddenly hearing their voices echoing in her inner ear, every voice so clear and distinct and individualistic ... Joe ... Lonnie ... Kerry Anne ... her mommy ... and her daddy ...

They were dead, yet she still felt very close to them.

Each one of them had left little pieces of themselves behind in her; they were deeply embedded in her heart and very much a part of her, and they were with her all the time. She had the memories to cherish, and they sustained her and gave her enormous strength.

For a time she drifted off, as if in a trance, travelling back into the past in her mind, but after a short while she roused herself and stood up. She turned off the television, went and got her guitar and brought it back to the sofa.

Tucking her bare feet under her, she played a few chords, tuned it, then began to strum lightly, thinking of her family, reliving those happy times they had spent together. Each of the O'Sheas had been musically gifted, and they had enjoyed many lovely evenings over the years, playing their different instruments, harmonizing together or singing solo.

And now, quietly, almost to herself, Madelana started to hum one of the old folk ballads which she and her brothers had sung, and when she finally got the feel of it, found the exact beat she wanted, her voice rang out clear and true and pure in the quiet apartment.

'*On top of old Smoky, all covered with snow, I lost my true lover, come a-courtin' too slow. A-courtin's a pleasure, a-flirtin's a grief, a falsehearted lover, is worse than a thief. For a thief he will rob you, and take what you have, but a falsehearted lover will send you to your grave. On top of old Smoky, all covered with snow, I lost my true lover, a-courtin' too slow.*'

10

She had arrived in New York shaking the dust of Kentucky off the heels of her silver kid boots.

That was in the autumn of 1977, when she was twenty-three years old. It was probably her wry sense of humour that made her characterize herself as 'just a poor country girl, a hillbilly who knows nothing much about anything', since, in point of fact, she was neither.

Her full name was Madelana Mary Elizabeth O'Shea, and she had been born just outside Lexington, in the very heart of bluegrass country, in July of 1954.

She was the first daughter of Fiona and Joe O'Shea and she had been adored from the moment she had opened her eyes to the world. She had two older brothers, Joseph Francis Xavier Jr, so named after his father, and Lonnie Michael Paul; Joe was eleven at the time of her birth, and Lonnie was then seven. Both boys fell in love with their beautiful baby sister, and it was a love that never dimmed during the boys' short lives.

Everyone petted and indulged her throughout her childhood, and it was a miracle that Madelana grew up to be so unaffected and unspoiled, and this was due in no small measure to her own strength of character and sweetness of nature.

Her father was third-generation Irish-American, and a Kentuckian through and through, but her mother had been born in Ireland, and had come to America in 1940, at the age of seventeen. Fiona Quinn had been dispatched by her older sister and brother to stay with cousins in Lexington, in order to escape the war in Europe. 'I'm an evacuee from the old sod,' she would say with a bright smile, her green eyes sparkling, enjoying being something of a novelty amongst her cousins and their friends.

Joe O'Shea was twenty-three in 1940, and an engineer who worked for his father in their small family construction business, and he was the best friend of Liam Quinn, Fiona's cousin. It was at Liam's house that Joe first met Fiona, and he had immediately fallen in love with the tall, lissome girl from County Cork. He thought she had the prettiest of faces and the most dazzling of smiles it had ever been his great good fortune to see. They had started courting, and to Joe's delight, Fiona soon confessed that she reciprocated his feelings and they were married in 1941.

After their honeymoon in Louisville, they set up house in Lexington, and in 1943 their first son was born, just a few weeks after his father had embarked for England to fight the war in Europe.

Joe, who was in the US 1st Infantry Division, was initially stationed in England, and later his unit was part of the Omaha Beach Assault Force that landed in Normandy on D-Day, the sixth of June, 1944. He was lucky and survived this and other Allied offensives in the European theatre of war, and came home safely at the end of 1945, proudly wearing a Purple Heart pinned to his battledress.

Once he had settled down to civilian life in Kentucky, Joe had again gone to work in his father's small business, and slowly life for the O'Sheas had returned to normal. In 1947, Lonnie was born, and with the addition of Maddy seven years later, Fiona and Joe decided it might be wisest not to have any more children, wanting to give as much as they could to the three they already had. Most especially, they were thinking of the cost of college educations for the two boys and Maddy. Joe's father had retired, and Joe had taken over the little family business and was making a decent living. Whilst they were not poor, they were not rich either. 'Middlin' comfortable,' was the way Joe would put it, and he would always add, 'But that's no cause for celebratin', or for bein' extravagant.'

Joe O'Shea was a good husband and father, Fiona a tender, loving wife, and the proudest of mothers, and they were a happy family, unusually devoted to each other, and caring.

Young Joe, Lonnie and Maddy were inseparable – 'the terrible trio,' Fiona called them.

Madelana was something of a tomboy when she was growing up and wanted to do everything her brothers did; she swam and fished in the creeks with them, went hunting and trekking in the hills, always tagging along on any expedition, but invariably holding her own.

Riding was her favourite sport and at this she excelled. She became an accomplished equestrian at an early age, being fortunate enough to work out at various horse farms in and around Lexington where thoroughbreds were trained, and where her father did jobs from time to time.

She loved horses, had an understanding of them, and like her father and her brothers, she was keen on racing, and her greatest thrill was to accompany them to Churchill Downs in Louisville when the Kentucky Derby ran. And it was she who cheered loudest of all when a horse they favoured won.

From a young age, Maddy was determined never to be outstripped by her brothers, and they, so adoring of her and immensely proud of her good looks, intelligence, independence and derring-do, forever encouraged her. But their mother was constantly shaking her head at the blue jeans and plaid work shirts, and the boyish, boisterous antics, and she tried to instil in her more ladylike ways.

'Whatever's going to become of you, Maddy O'Shea?' Fiona would demand, clucking with exasperation under her breath. 'Just look at you ... why, to be sure, anybody could be mistakin' you for a stable lad in that get up, and your friends so bonny and feminine in their pretty dresses. You won't be finding a nice young man to go a-courtin' with, no, not looking like that, you will not, me girl. I aim to enrol you in Miss Sue Ellen's dancing class if it's the last thing I do, so you can be learnin' a bit about deportment and gracefulness and femininity. I swear I will, Maddy O'Shea. Be warned, me girl.'

Maddy would respond with a vibrant laugh and a jaunty toss of her chestnut head, for this was an old threat. And she would hug her mother tightly then, and promise to mend her ways, and they would sit down at the kitchen table for a cup of hot, steaming chocolate, and talk and talk their hearts away, and they were never anything but the best of friends.

And eventually, just to please her mother, Madelana did attend Miss Sue Ellen's School for Dancing and Deportment in Lexington, taking ballet and tap. As it happened, she discovered she had a natural aptitude for dance, and she enjoyed her lessons, and it was here that she quickly learned to move with lightness and elegance, where she acquired the dancer's agile grace that she would never lose.

In later years, when she looked back, Madelana took comfort from the fact that she and her brothers had had such a marvellous childhood. There had been large doses of the Catholic religion rammed down them by their mother, and a good deal of discipline from their father, and they had had to work hard at school and to do chores in the house and yard, but it had been one of the happiest times of her life, and it had made her all the things she was.

Nobody was more surprised than Fiona when, towards the end of 1964, she learned that she was pregnant again, and the following year, at the age of forty-one, she gave birth to Kerry Anne.

Although the child had been unexpected, she was loved, and her christening was a happy affair. The only thing that slightly marred their joy that day was Young Joe's imminent departure for his tour of duty in Vietnam. He was a private in the US Army and just twenty-two years old.

Sometimes tragedy strikes a family many times in quick succession, and it is so incomprehensible, so inexplicable, it defies belief. So it was with the O'Sheas.

Young Joe was killed at Da Nang in 1966, one year after he had shipped out to Indochina. Lonnie, who had joined the marines and was also serving in Vietnam, lost his life during the Tet offensive in 1968. He was twenty-one.

And then to their further horror and heartbreak, little Kerry Anne died of complications following a tonsillectomy, shortly before her fifth birthday in 1970.

Reeling from shock and stunned by their enormous grief, Fiona, Joe and Maddy cleaved to each other, were barely able to handle their anguish and the pain of their sudden and terrible losses over five short and fatal years. It seemed to them that each new blow was more ferocious than the one before, and it was a suffering they found unendurable.

Fiona was never really to recover, remained forever after bereft and grieving, but despite this, and even though she needed her only living child by her side, she insisted Madelana continue her higher education at Loyola University in New Orleans, when she became eighteen.

Madelana had set her heart on going there some years before, and her parents had approved of this small college run by the Jesuits. Even so, she was reluctant to leave her parents, her mother in particular, who was so dependent on her, and she was more than willing to change her plans.

But Fiona would have none of it, since it had been a long-cherished dream of hers that Madelana attend college. She knew by this time that she was suffering from cancer, as did Joe, but they scrupulously kept this devastating news from their daughter.

However, four years later, towards the end, Fiona became so debilitated it was no longer possible to hide the medical facts from Maddy, who struggled through her last few months at Loyola fighting despair and endeavouring to hold sorrow at arm's length. The only thing that kept her going during this excruciatingly painful time was the determination not to let her mother down.

Fiona lived long enough to see Maddy graduate with a bachelor's degree in Business Administration in the summer of 1976. She died two months later.

'Kerry Anne's going was the last nail in your mommy's coffin,' Joe kept saying all through the winter of that year, until the words began to sound like a dreadful litany to her.

Or he would sit and stare at Maddy, then ask, with tears welling in his eyes, 'Wasn't one son enough to give to my country? Why did Lonnie have to get massacred too? For what?' And before she could say anything in response, he would add with anger and bitterness: 'For *nothing*, that's what, Maddy. Young Joe and Lonnie both died for *nothing*.'

Madelana would take his hand and try to comfort him the best way she could, whenever he talked like this, but she never had any answers for her father, and certainly she had none for herself either. Like the majority of Americans, she had scant understanding of the war they were fighting in Vietnam.

After graduating from Loyola, Madelana had found herself a job in the offices of Shilito's department store in Lexington.

Despite her hoydenish ways and lack of interest in feminine things as a child, she had fallen in love with clothes in her late teens, and had recognized that she had a great deal of flair when it came to fashion. Retailing attracted her, and when she had been attending college she had decided she wanted to carve out a career for herself in this field.

Madelana's job in the marketing department at Shilito's had proved to be challenging, and she had found it both stimulating and absorbing as well. She had thrown herself into the work, and divided her time between the store and the family home, where she had continued to live with her father.

Joe had begun to worry her considerably in the early part of 1977, for he had grown more morose than ever and apathetic since her mother's death, and, unlike her mother, he seemed unable to draw solace from his religion. He still continued to mutter to Maddy that his sons had died in vain, and she would frequently find him staring at their photographs on the mantelpiece in the living room, his eyes filled with hurt and bafflement, his face grown painfully thin, and ravaged by emotional suffering.

Maddy's heart ached for him, and she did everything possible in her power to take him out of himself, to cheer him, to give him a reason to go on living, but it was to no avail.

By the spring of that year, Joe O'Shea had become a shadow of the handsome, outgoing, jocular man he had once been, and when he died suddenly of a heart attack in May, Maddy realized, in the midst of her searing grief, that she was not really so surprised. It was as if he had willed himself to die, as if he had desperately wanted to join Fiona in the grave.

Once she had buried her father, Madelana had begun to sort out and settle his business affairs. He had left everything neat and orderly, and so this task was relatively easy for her to do.

His small construction company had been in the black for a number of years, and she was able to sell the equipment, the materials and the 'goodwill' to Pete Andrews, who had been her father's right-hand man and wanted to keep the business going for himself and the handful of old employees. And though it was wrenching for her, she had also sold the house where she had grown up, along with most of her mother's furniture, and moved into an apartment in Lexington.

It was not very long after this that she had started to understand just how difficult living in Lexington was going to be for her from now on. As much as her beloved bluegrass country was part of her, in her blood, each day grew increasingly painful. Wherever she went, wherever she looked, she saw their faces . . . her parents, Kerry Anne, Young Joe and Lonnie. She yearned for them and for the past, and for the way things once were.

Her father's passing had opened up her old grief for the others who had died before him.

She knew she had to get away. Perhaps she could come back one day in the future and rejoice in the past. But now she had to put distance between herself and this place. The heartbreak was too fresh, too potent in her, and her emotions were far too near the surface for her to draw any kind of solace from the memories of her family at this particular moment.

Only through the passing of time would her pain lessen, and only then would she be able to draw a measure of comfort from her remembrances, and find peace in them.

And so Madelana made the decision to move to the North, to go to New York City, to start a whole new life.

She was very brave.

She had no job, knew no one, had no contacts, but at least she had a roof over her head when she arrived in Manhattan. This had already been arranged for her before she had left Lexington.

The Sisters of Divine Providence, a teaching order of nuns from Kentucky, and one of the first such orders to be founded in America, maintained a residency in New York. Rooms could be rented at a nominal charge, and were available to Catholic girls and young women from all over the world.

And it was to this residency, the Jeanne D'Arc, that Maddy went in October of 1977.

Within a week of her arrival at West Twenty-Fourth Street she had settled in, and was beginning to get her bearings.

The sisters were warm and helpful, the girls friendly, and the residency itself was pleasant, convenient, and well run. It had five floors of rooms, with showers and bathrooms on each floor. There was a small but rather beautiful chapel, where the young residents and the sisters could pray or meditate, and close by were the common rooms – a library and a television-parlour. Other facilities included a kitchen and a canteen in the basement, for the cooking and serving of meals, plus a laundry room, and lockers for the storage of personal belongings.

One of the first things Maddy had done was to put her nest-egg of forty thousand dollars in the bank, opening both current and saving accounts. After this she had had her own phone installed in her room on the fourth floor. Patsy Smith, who lived across the corridor from her, had recommended that she do so, explaining that it would simplify her life, make it much easier.

She had then gone looking for a job.

Ever since she had decided to make a career for herself in retailing, Maddy's role model had been the late Emma Harte, one of the greatest merchant princes of all time, in her opinion. In the past few years she had read everything about the renowned Emma that she could lay her hands on, and Harte's in New York was the only store where she wanted to work. But she quickly discovered there were no vacancies when she went for an interview. The personnel manager had been impressed with her, however, and had promised to be in touch if something suitable came up. Her résumé and application had been duly filed for future reference.

By the end of her third week in the city, Maddy had managed to find employment in the business offices of Saks Fifth Avenue.

Exactly one year later there was finally an opening at Harte's and she had grabbed it immediately, filled with enthusiasm at the opportunity to work there, and within six months she had made her mark.

And she had come to the attention of Paula O'Neill.

Paula had spotted her in the marketing department, had been struck by her great personal style, pleasant demeanour, efficiency, and vivid intelligence. Thereafter, Paula had constantly singled her out, given her a variety of special assignments, and had ultimately moved her to work in the executive offices. A year after this, in July of 1980, Paula had promoted Maddy to be her personal assistant, in effect, actually creating this job for her.

With this big promotion and a sizeable increase in salary, Madelana had at last felt reasonably secure enough to look for her own apartment. She had found one she liked in the Upper East Eighties, and had had her furniture and other possessions shipped up from the storage warehouse in Kentucky. And she had finally left the residency, feeling a little pang as she had said goodbye to Sister Bronagh and Sister Mairéad.

The first meal she had cooked at the new apartment had been for Jack and Patsy one Sunday night, just before Patsy had gone back to Boston to live.

It had been a lovely evening, very celebratory, and Jack had kept them amused and laughing. But she and Patsy had grown a bit sad towards the end, knowing they would be living in different cities soon. They had promised faithfully not to grow apart, to stay in touch, and they had corresponded on a fairly regular basis ever since.

With her new promotion, Madelana's life had changed in other ways, and a whole new world had been opened up to her. Paula had brought her over to London so that she would understand the inner workings of the famed Knightsbridge store, and she had visited the Harte stores in Yorkshire and Paris. And twice Paula had taken her to Texas, although this had been on Sitex business rather than Harte's. She had discovered how much she enjoyed travelling, going to new places, and meeting new people.

Her first year as Paula's assistant had fled by, filled with excitement, challenges and continuing successes, and very quickly Maddy had begun to recognize that she had found her niche in life. It was at Harte's of New York, where she was a star.

11

Playing some of her favourite old folk songs had soothed Madelana. She was feeling at ease with herself at last.

Earlier in the evening, she had half-expected Jack Miller to call her back, had been dreading that he would. But he had not. Now, at last, she was filled with a peacefulness, and she was completely calm. She got up, put the guitar to one side, and went over to the desk near the window.

The files she had brought home with her from the store were stacked and waiting for her attention. She sat down, glanced at the clock, saw that it was almost midnight. But that did not matter to her. She was wide awake and full of energy. Stamina had always been one of her strong suits, and she knew she could complete the work quite easily within two or three hours.

Picking up her pen, she sat back in the chair, staring at the wall, thinking for a moment.

The needlepoint sampler which hung there, and which her mother had made for her when she had been a little girl, suddenly held her attention. It had hung above her bed in her room in Lexington, and it was one of the things she had brought with her when she had first moved to New York.

'*If your day is hemmed with prayer it is less likely to unravel*' her mother had stitched in royal blue wool against the beige background, and she had bordered the sampler with tiny flowers in brilliant primary colours.

Madelana smiled inwardly, seeing Fiona's lovely image in her mind's eye. I think she'd be proud of me, proud of what I've made of my life, and of where I am today. I know she wouldn't approve of Jack, of course. I don't believe I do, either. Not for me. Not any more. I'll call him in the morning, ask him to have lunch, and I'll end it face to face, she added to herself, reiterating her decision of earlier in her mind. That's the only decent thing to do. I can't tell him over the phone.

She put down the pen and began to shuffle through her files, looking for the one which held her notes and the material for the fashion exhibit.

Each of these folders pertained to the forthcoming celebrations for Harte's sixtieth anniversary. Paula's theme was simple, but clever in its simplicity: sixty years of stylish retailing from the jazz age to the space age.

Paula had put her in charge of the anniversary programme at the New York store, and she was responsible for the overall planning of different events and shows, and telexes had been flying back and forth across the Atlantic for many, many months. Ideas had been approved of, or knocked down, by Paula, and merchandise ordered, campaigns put in work, advertising art completed, brochures and invitations printed. The files represented endless hours of work and thought and dedication, and she must complete the last few memorandums about each event and campaign tonight.

Maddy's own special projects included Fragrance Month; a stylish art show in the art gallery of the store, highlighting decorative objects from the Art Deco period; an exhibit of real and costume jewellery from the Art Deco period to the present, featuring some of the world's greatest jewellery designers. These included Verdura, Jeanne Toussaint of Cartier, and Renée Puissant of Van Cleef and Arpels, and their work from decades past; Alain Boucheron and David Webb were two of the designers of the present who would be showcased. At the other end of the price scale, she had decided to highlight the unique costume jewellery and fabulous fakes designed by Kenneth Jay Lane, along with a collection of paste pieces from the nineteen-thirties.

Her hands came to rest on the fashion folder at last. This held information and details of the fashion exhibition which Paula planned to hold at the London store next spring. Maddy had convinced her to bring it over to New York in the late summer of 1982. Having agreed, Paula had then suggested she try to expand the exhibit, by adding clothes borrowed from American women who had either been on the best dressed list at some time or other, or who owned a garment by a top couturier, whether living or dead. And this she had done – with great success.

The nucleus of the couture exhibition were clothes which had once belonged to Emma Harte, and which she had kept in good condition for years before her death. Paula had carefully preserved these clothes again, after they had been in the Fashion Fantasia exhibition at the London store some ten or eleven years ago.

Emma's clothing in the show dated as far back as the early twenties, and included a Paquin evening coat of brown velvet trimmed with a huge fox collar, a short evening dress with a big bow on the back, designed in 1926 by Poiret, and a blue-and-green beaded evening gown by Vionnet. This was apparently in extraordinary condition, and looked stunning in the photograph the London marketing department had sent over; it seemed hardly dated at all to Madelana.

Sifting through the other drawings and photographs, she pored over Emma's Chanel suits from the twenties, a huge collection of her hats by French and English couturiers, outfits by Lanvin, Balmain and Balenciaga, two Fortuny pleated silk evening gowns, evening pyjamas by Molyneux, and an exquisitely-cut coat by Pauline Trigère, designed in the fifties but as chic now as it had been then. There were other modern outfits by Dior, Givenchy, Yves Saint Laurent, Bill Blass and Hardy Amies.

Maddy began to make her notes, creating the exact order in which she wanted the drawings and photographs to appear in the catalogue. She had already put this into work with the art department, and they were pressuring her for these illustrations.

One of Maddy's favourites was a charmeuse evening dress by Mainbocher, which according to Paula her grandfather Paul McGill had bought for Emma in New York in 1935. It was trimmed with clustered silk flowers stitched as epaulets on the shoulders, and worn with a matching muff made of the same clustered silk flowers.

Picking up a photograph of Emma wearing the dress, Madelana studied it for a moment. God, what a beautiful woman she was, she murmured to herself, and decided to lead off with this particular picture.

After she had finished with the fashion exhibit file, she dealt with the information required for the Fragrance Month, and then tackled the Art Deco show, leaving the final details of the jewellery exhibit until last. She worked relentlessly for another hour and a half, making sure there could be no mistakes whatsoever while she was in Australia.

At two in the morning she stood in her little kitchen waiting for the kettle to boil for a cup of instant coffee. And as she carried this back into the living room a moment later, she braced herself for another hour of work at least.

Well, Maddy thought, seating herself at the desk, if Emma Harte could work around the clock, then so can I. After all, she has been my inspiration and my idol for years, and I want to emulate her in every way I possibly can.

12

'How did you manage to complete everything?' Paula asked, eyeing the files on her desk which she had just read, then glancing across at Madelana.

'I stayed up until three-thirty this morning.'

'Oh Maddy, you didn't have to do that. We could have finished the files together on the plane, and telexed our final instructions from Australia.' As Paula spoke, she could not help feeling slightly relieved that they would not have to do this.

'But it's better this way, isn't it, Paula?' Madelana asked swiftly. 'We'll have free minds, and we'll be able to concentrate that much more keenly on the boutiques with this stuff out of the way.'

'That's perfectly true,' Paula agreed. 'And I must say, your hard work, what you've accomplished, is very commendable.' Paula's violet eyes narrowed and she studied the other woman closely, then began to laugh. 'And what's even more remarkable is that burning the midnight oil doesn't show on your face.'

'Doesn't it?' Madelana laughed with her boss, whom she not only admired and respected, but genuinely cared for. 'Thank you, it's nice of you to say so.'

Paula tapped the folders. 'I like the way you've managed to tie in so many different products and merchandise. By pulling everything together in the way you have, you've also strengthened my theme considerably. To be truthful, when I came up with the idea of calling our sixtieth celebration *From The Jazz Age To The Space Age*, I wondered if I was making it far too broad to be effective. But you've helped to prove yet again that I wasn't, and frankly you've even gone a step further than Marketing has in London. That's what has been so exciting for me this last hour as I've read your memos.'

Paula was a firm believer in giving credit where it was due, and now she added, 'Congratulations. Some of the things you've thought of are quite brilliant, and your ideas are most innovative. I'm delighted with your efforts.'

Madelana filled with satisfaction and her face was wreathed in smiles. 'Thanks, Paula, but don't let's forget that your theme *was* clever, and very challenging. And everything was already there really, just waiting to be pulled out of the reference books and the research files.'

'Not to mention your clever little head!' Paula exclaimed. She picked up the folder marked FRAGRANCE PROMOTION and opened it, took out the top sheet.

After glancing at the paper again, she said, 'Some of this stuff's really fascinating. For instance, I never knew that Chanel actually considered the number five to be her lucky number, and that that was the reason she called her first perfume *Chanel No. 5*. Nor was I aware that Jean Patou created *Joy* in 1931, and that Jeanne Lanvin brought out *Arpège* in 1927. Here we have three of the world's greatest perfumes, which are still enormously popular today, and they are actually fifty years old.'

'Quality always lasts, doesn't it,' Madelana said. 'And I thought some of those odd little items were kind of interesting, too. Perhaps we can use them somewhere in our promotional material, or in our advertisements.'

'Absolutely. That's a terrific idea. And you might tell the art department to make up display cards featuring a few of the items, for the counters in Perfumery.'

'Okay. Talking about displays, could you spare me a minute, please? I'd like you to see a piece of artwork which I had created, hopefully for use here in the store. If you approve.'

'Let's go and look at it then.' Paula jumped up, followed Madelana into the adjoining office.

An easel had been placed in one corner, near the window which looked out onto Fifth Avenue. Madelana picked up a large display card and put it on the easel. She said, 'I'd like to use this on silk banners throughout the store, and if I could get a yea or a nay from you now, I'd appreciate it. The banners have to be ordered today, at the *latest* on Monday, if they're going to be ready for the commencement of the celebrations in December.'

'I understand. So come on, let's see it.'

Madelana flipped the tracing paper that protected the hardboard card, and then stepped aside.

Paula stood staring at the bold lettering, which read: FROM THE JAZZ AGE TO THE SPACE AGE: 1921 TO 1981.

Underneath the giant-sized slogan was a smaller subheading, and this said: SIXTY YEARS OF STYLE AND ELEGANCE AT HARTE'S.

Paula continued to study it.

This was her slogan, the words she had written down over a year ago, when she had first started to plan the anniversary celebrations and special events. The only thing which made this suggested banner different to the ones created by the marketing department in London was a portrait of Emma Harte etched in shadowy form behind the lettering.

Paula said nothing. Her eyes grew thoughtful.

Watching her intently, and anxiously, waiting for her reaction, Madelana held her breath. When Paula remained silent, she said worriedly, 'You don't like it, do you?'

'I'm not sure, to be honest,' Paula murmured, then hesitated. She moved around the office, looking at the board from different angles. 'Yes . . . yes . . . I think I do,' she finally said, her voice more positive. 'But I wouldn't want to use my grandmother's image on *every* banner in the store. I think that would be in poor taste, and overkill, really. And I certainly don't want to go over the top. But the more I look at this, I think we *could* use it, in a *limited* way . . . in some of the big halls in the London and Paris stores, and on the first floor here. Oh, and in the Leeds store, too! That's a *must*, I suppose, since that's where it all began.'

'Are you really sure? You still sound a bit uncertain.'

'No, I'm positive. You can order the banners, and why don't you get enough for the other stores. We might as well have them made in New York. They can be shipped out air express to London and Paris when they're ready.'

'Good idea. And I'm glad you approve of the things we've done. Everyone's going to be thrilled that you're so pleased, and that we can now go forward with these plans.'

Paula half-smiled. 'Well, I suppose that's about it, as far as the special events are concerned. Come back to my office for a moment, though, would you, Madelana, there's something I wish to discuss with you.'

'Yes,' Maddy said, hurrying after her, wondering what this was all about. All of a sudden there had been an anxious note in Paula's voice, which was unusual for her, and therefore disconcerting.

Paula walked around her desk and sat down.

Madelana took the chair facing her, perched on the edge, and looked across at her boss, asking herself if trouble was brewing.

Paula sat back, steepled her fingers, and contemplated the tips of them for a moment. Then she said, 'I want to take you into my confidence about something, Madelana, but I must stress that it *is* confidential. I haven't mentioned it to Shane or Emily yet, although actually that's really because I haven't had the right opportunity. However, since you work so closely with me, I thought you should know immediately.'

'You have my confidentiality, Paula. I'd never divulge anything you told me, or discuss your business with anyone. That's not my way.'

'I'm aware of that, Madelana.'

Paula sat back, her eyes serious. She said carefully, 'I've had several phone calls from a Harvey Rawson during the past few days, which I'm sure you know, since you put a couple of those calls through to me.'

Madelana nodded.

Paula continued, 'He's a lawyer with a Wall Street firm, and a friend of Michael Kallinski's. He's been doing some work for me. Private work.'

'You don't have a legal problem, do you?'

'No, no, Maddy. For a long time I've wanted to go into an expansion programme in the United States ... I've wanted to take Harte stores right across the country, and I've been looking for an existing chain to buy, with that purpose in mind. Michael's known about this, and he put the word out some time ago, without mentioning my name, of course. Last week he heard about a small suburban chain through Harvey Rawson. Before I left for New York, I spoke to Michael, and told him he could tell Harvey I was the one interested in the chain and to get in touch with me directly.'

'So Harvey Rawson's actually representing you in the buy out,' Madelana asserted, sitting up straighter in the chair, pinning her eyes on her boss.

'It's not a buy out yet. But yes, he is representing me, in as much as he's approaching the chain, but without saying I'm the interested party.'

'Yes, I understand. That would jack up the price, and then some, if they knew it was you. But I think this is a wonderful move you're making, Paula, and very visionary.' Madelana's excitement was reflected on her face and she leaned forward with eagerness. 'What's the name of the chain? Where are the stores located?'

'The chain is called Peale and Doone, and there are seven stores altogether, in Illinois and Ohio,' Paula explained. 'This is not the type of chain I was originally looking for – I'd prefer my stores to be in big cities like Chicago, Los Angeles, San Francisco and Boston. Still, Peale and Doone would be a beginning, a step in the right direction.'

'Are they a public company?'

'No, private. And next week Harvey will ascertain whether or not the stock-holders are interested in selling, and then we'll take it from there. He'll be in touch with me, and with Michael, and they both have the Australian itinerary, at least the part of it that's planned,' she finished, sitting back in her chair.

Standing up, recognizing that Paula had just brought this conversation to a close, Madelana said, 'Thanks for telling me about your plans, Paula, for sharing with me. I'm flattered, and I'm looking forward to working with you on the expansion programme.'

'Good. I hoped you would be. I want you to be very involved with me in this, Maddy.' Paula also stood. Lifting the stack of files off her desk, she brought them to Madelana.

Together the two women walked across the room, paused at the door to Madelana's office, turned to face each other.

Paula remarked, 'You seem to be finished, so there's no reason for you to come back after lunch, if you don't want to. I don't need you for the rest of the day, and I'm sure you've plenty to do between now and tomorrow morning.'

'Oh thank you, that's nice of you, Paula, but I'm sure I'll be back, and anyway, I want to pick up a couple of track suits in Active Sportswear. Didn't you say that was the only way to fly? To Australia, I mean.'

Paula laughed. 'It is, and I'm afraid the suit is not very elegant, but it *is* very practical. And don't forget your Reeboks or a pair of tennis shoes. Los Angeles-Sydney is around thirteen to fourteen hours' flying time, depending on the winds, and every part of the body seems to swell up. Not only that, I find that I sleep much better and more comfortably when I'm dressed in a track suit.'

'Then I'll be sure to get myself properly outfitted after I've had lunch with Jack –' Madelana broke off, and her face instantly changed, grew taut with anxiety.

Paula did not miss this. She frowned, asked softly, in concern, 'Is something wrong?'

Maddy shook her head. 'Not really,' she began and again stopped abruptly. There was a closeness between Paula and herself, and they had always been open and forthright with each other. 'I shouldn't say that, Paula, because it's not true. Things are pretty lousy between Jack and me, and I'm going to break off with him. I want to get it out of the way before I leave. That's why I'm having lunch with him.'

'I am sorry,' Paula murmured, giving her a small, sympathetic smile, touching her arm lightly. 'I thought everything was working well between the two of you. At least that's the impression you gave, the last time we spoke about him when you were in London.'

'It was then, and he's a nice guy in many ways. But there's such a lot of conflict between us. I think he resents me these days, and resents my career.' Madelana shook her head. 'There's no future in it as far as I can see.'

Paula was silent, remembering words of Emma's, words uttered at a time when she had been where Madelana was today. She said quietly, 'Many years ago, when I was having great difficulties in my first marriage, my grandmother gave me a bit of advice that I've never forgotten. She said, "If something's not working, then don't be afraid to end it whilst you're still young enough to start again, to find happiness with someone else." Grandy was a very wise woman. And I can only reiterate those words of hers to you, Maddy, and add that you must trust your own instincts. From what I know of you, they've never let you down yet.'

Paula paused, gave her a quick, penetrating look, went on, 'Personally, I think you're about to do the right thing. The best thing for you.'

'I know I am. And thanks for caring, Paula. I'll break up with Jack today, make it clean and swift. And then I want to concentrate on my career.'

13

It rose up against the azure sky like some great monolith, an immense, unyielding structure of black glass and steel. It was a statement of wealth and privilege, prestige and power, and a glittering monument to the founding fathers of a gargantuan business empire.

The McGill Tower was its name, and it dominated the skyline of Sydney.

The man who had conceived this extraordinary and quite beautiful edifice, and caused it to be built, occupied the tower in the manner of a great magnate from a time long past, completely in control, overseeing and operating all that he owned from this stylish, modern command post, and doing so with a shrewdness, wisdom and fairness that went far beyond his years.

The black glass tower was his true domain.

He worked there from early morning until late at night, and during the business week he frequently lived there. His executive offices and his penthouse flat were situated one above the other, and occupied the entire two top floors of the building.

Late on this Monday afternoon, the man stood with his back to the immense sweep of plate glass which formed the window-wall at one end of his private office, and which offered a panoramic view of Sydney Harbour and the city. With his head tilted to one side, his eyes narrowed in concentration, he was listening attentively to his visitor, a young American businessman.

Always the most handsome of Emma Harte's grandsons, at thirty-five Philip McGill Amory was in his prime and at his full power. He had magnetism and a mystique in international business circles, and with the press and to many people he was something of an enigma. Like his mother and his sister, he had inherited Paul McGill's colouring. His hair was the same glossy black and his eyes were that uncanny blue which was almost violet, and he possessed the vitality and virile looks and height which had made his grandfather such an arresting man.

Today he was wearing a stone-coloured light gabardine suit that was fashionably-cut, and he was perfectly groomed from the collar of his deep-blue shirt to the tip of his dark brown loafers that gleamed like highly-polished glass.

'And so,' his visitor was saying, 'that's the story. And before I put up a couple of million dollars – US dollars that is – I thought I'd better high-tail it over here and get your advice. Shane told me, before I left London, that if I felt the need, I *should* come and talk things over with you, because you know more about opal mining than anybody else.'

Philip let out a deep chuckle.

'Not quite, Mr Carlson. I'm afraid my brother-in-law tends to exaggerate, but I'm fairly knowledgeable, yes. We've been mining opals for years – among other things. One of our subsidiaries, McGill Mining, was founded by my great-grandfather in 1906, a few years after the famous black opal field at Lightning Ridge was discovered around 1903. But to get back to your situation, from what you've told me so far, I don't believe you've been getting the best guidance. If I were you, I'd move with some caution, think twice before putting your money into this syndicate you've been telling me about.'

Steve Carlson sat up straighter, gave Philip a questioning look. 'You don't think it's some sort of scam, do you?' he asked, his voice rising nervously, sudden anxiety filling his eyes.

Philip shook his head. 'No, no, not at all,' he answered swiftly and emphatically. 'But we've heard of Jarvis Lanner, and whilst he's honest enough, as far as we've been able to ascertain, he's hardly the right man to be advising you about opal mining in the outback.'

'That's not the way he presents himself, and –'

'Maybe not. But he's a pommy Jackeroo, for God's sake!'

Carlson looked baffled. '*Pommy jackeroo*. What's that?'

Philip tried, unsuccessfully, to smother a laugh. 'Sorry, I shouldn't be confusing you by using Australian slang. It means an English immigrant who's a greenhorn.'

'Oh, I see.' Carlson nodded. 'It did strike me, a few days ago, that Jarvis Lanner didn't know as much as he professed, that's why I came running to you, I guess.'

Philip made no comment. He strolled over to his desk, stood behind it, regarding the young man for a moment, feeling sorry for him. Now here was a jackeroo, if ever he'd seen one. Wanting to help him, and also to bring the meeting to a close, Philip now said, 'I think the best thing I can do for you, Mr Carlson, is to put you in touch with a couple of reputable mining experts and some leading geologists. They'll be able to steer you in the right direction. Would you like me to do that?'

'Well, gee, yes, I guess so, and I really appreciate that you've taken the time and trouble to see me. But just as a matter of interest, what's *your* opinion of Queensland, as far as opals are concerned? Don't you think it offers as much as I've been led to believe?'

'I wouldn't say that, no.'

Philip sat down, pulled a pad towards him, reached for his gold pen. 'A lot of prospectors and miners will tell you that the Queensland fields still have a lot to offer, and I suppose that's true, in certain ways. But I doubt you'll find much precious opal there. That's very rare. Plenty of common opal, of course, in the Queensland fields. Jarvis Lanner was not lying to you, when he told you that. But I do stress *common* opal. You indicated to me that you want to mine *quality* stones.'

'Yes.' Carlson got up off the sofa, meandered over to the desk, took the chair facing it. 'Where do *you* think I should do my mining, Mr Amory?'

'There are any number of places,' Philip responded with a light shrug of his shoulders, not wanting to be drawn on this one, or held responsible for making a recommendation that might turn out to be the wrong one for young Carlson. But he had no wish to appear discourteous either, and so he said, 'Our company's still mining at Lightning Ridge in New South Wales, and also at Coober Pedy. That's actually Australia's largest opal centre where we get our exquisite light opal from. Then there's Mintabie, in South Australia. Prospectors have been mining there very successfully since about 1976.'

'So it's a new field.'

'No, it was discovered in 1931, but lack of water, very harsh conditions, and bloody awful equipment made it hard to coax the opal out of the ground, prevented proper mining for many, many years. Today's modern machinery has opened it up pretty good. In any case, let me give you the names and phone numbers of the experts I mentioned. Go and talk to them. I'm confident they'll put you on the right track. They'll also be able to tell you whether or not you should invest in the syndicate Lanner recommended to you.'

'Do you think that group might be A-Okay then?'

'I never said there was anything wrong with the syndicate, merely that you should think twice about investing your money with it,' Philip was swift to remind the other man. 'And I pointed out that you'd not received the best advice from Lanner.' Philip smiled faintly, and not giving Carlson a chance to say anything, he murmured, 'Excuse me,' picked up the gold pen for the second time, and began to write in his neat, rapid hand.

'Sure, go ahead,' Steve Carlson said, somewhat after the fact, and sat back in the chair, his scrutiny keen. He was impressed with this man who had agreed to see him so quickly and without fuss. Admittedly, he'd had the best introduction. On the other hand, tycoons of Amory's calibre and power were hard to get to personally, even when members of the family opened the door. They were usually too busy, up to their eyeballs in high finance and balance sheets, to be bothered with strangers wanting advice. Invariably they had assistants stand in for them. But not this cowboy, who seemed like a decent enough guy, unaffected, with no bullshit about him. He'd been struck dumb when he'd first met him an hour ago. Philip McGill Amory was so goddamned good looking he ought to be in front of a movie camera in Hollywood, for God's sake, not behind a desk. That handsome face, those mesmerizing blue eyes, the gleaming teeth, and the very deep tan had to be seen to be believed. And what about the fabulous suit he was wearing and the custom-made voile shirt, not to mention the sapphire cuff links? Why, this guy was larger than life, more like a superstar than a businessman. He hadn't expected Amory to have a moustache though. He decided it was dashing, gave the tycoon the look of a riverboat gambler . . . no, a buccaneer.

Steve Carlson suppressed the laughter rising in his throat, thinking that there were surely plenty of pirates around these days – all sailing the waters of Big

Business. But Amory didn't have the reputation for being a predator, one of those modern-day corporate raiders who swooped down on other companies and commandeered them for their own ends. Amory didn't need to raid anybody, did he? Not with a conglomerate the size of The McGill Corporation to play with, and keep him busy. It was worth millions, no, billions.

Carlson shifted in his chair, gave Philip a glance that was full of speculation. I bet this cowboy has one helluva private life, a real ball, the young American thought with a stab of envy tinged with admiration. With his physique and looks, all that power, all that dough, women probably drool all over him. Boy, oh boy, what I wouldn't give to be in that pair of handmade Italian loafers just for one night.

Philip flipped the intercom. 'Maggie?'

'Yes?'

'Mr Carlson is about to leave. I'm giving him a list of names. Please affix the appropriate telephone numbers, will you?'

'Certainly.'

Philip strode around the desk.

Carlson jumped up, took the sheet of paper being offered, walked with him to the door.

Philip shook the young man's hand firmly. 'Lots of luck, Mr Carlson. I'm certain it'll all pan out.'

'Gee, thanks, Mr Amory. I sure am grateful for your time, and the advice you've given me.'

'My pleasure,' Philip answered, and motioned to his secretary, who was standing waiting near her desk. 'Look after Mr Carlson, would you please, Maggie?' he added before stepping back into his inner sanctum and closing the door firmly behind him.

Alone at last, and glad to be, Philip ambled over to the plate glass window-wall and looked out towards the harbour. It was the beginning of spring and the weather had been glorious all day. Any number of sailboats were out there on the bright water, racing in front of the wind, their multi-coloured spinnakers billowing straight out, the mainsails set out wide over the sides, catching every bit of the wind following behind them.

What a beautiful sight it was ... Sydney Harbour Bridge so majestic in the distance, the white racing yachts and their colourful spinnakers, the glittering, sunlit sea, and, off to the side, the Opera House with its unique roof of curved white demi-domes that from this angle looked like the giant sails of a galleon set against the edge of the sea and the powder-blue sky.

A smile touched Philip's eyes. He had loved this city since he was a boy, and to him there was no sight in the world quite like Sydney Harbour. It never failed to give him pleasure, especially when he surveyed it from this vantage point.

As he turned away from the window, he made a mental note to have the spinnaker on his own racing yacht checked. The big parachute was made of gossamer-thin nylon and attention had to be paid to it and to the other sails. He smiled wryly to himself. Yacht racing was an expensive hobby these days. A full suit of sails, ranging from the light-weather spinnaker to heavyweight Kevlar for a storm mainsail, cost just under a million Australian dollars.

There was a knock on the door. It opened, and Barry Graves, his personal assistant, poked his head around it, grinning. 'Can I come in?'

'Sure,' Philip said, walking over to his desk.

'Got kangaroos in his top paddock then, has he?' Barry asked, a brow lifting eloquently.

The two men exchanged knowing looks and then they both started to laugh.

'No,' Philip said, 'he's not crazy. Carlson's just young and inexperienced. He's been bitten by the adventure bug, I guess. Apparently he heard somewhere that Australia supplies ninety-five per cent of the world's opals, and he decided to come over here, try his luck, and invest his inheritance in opal mining.'

'Another jackeroo,' Barry sighed. 'Poor sod. Oh, well, I guess there's one born every minute. What's he to Shane?'

'Nothing really. Carlson's brother-in-law is one of Shane's top executives at O'Neill International in New York, and Shane was just trying to do the guy a favour. The kid went to see him in London and Shane told him to check with me before he did anything wild.'

'Good thing he did, too.' Barry hovered at the side of the desk, went on rapidly. 'I just came in to say goodnight, Philip. If you don't need me for anything else, I'd like to push off. Committee meeting at the tennis club tonight.'

'Go ahead, Barry.'

'Thanks. Oh, there's just one thing – do you want me to send a car to pick Paula up at the airport tomorrow morning?'

'No, thanks anyway, but it's not necessary. My mother's taking care of that.'

'Good-o.' Barry headed for the door. He paused as he went out, swung to face Philip. 'Don't stay too late tonight.'

'I won't. I'm driving out to Rose Bay in a little while, to have dinner with my mother.'

'Give Daisy my best.'

'I will.'

'See you tomorrow, Philip.'

Philip nodded, turned to the papers on his desk and began to work. Just before six o'clock he buzzed Maggie on the intercom and told her to go home.

'Thanks, Philip.'

'Oh, and Maggie, please call down to the garage and tell Ken to have the car outside at seven.'

'I will. Good night.'

'Good night, Maggie.' He flipped off the intercom, and went on working on his papers with the diligence and dedication that had been instilled in him by his grandmother years before.

From the moment he had taken his first breath, in June of 1946, it had been understood by his mother and father, and everyone else in the family, that Philip McGill Amory would be raised and groomed to run The McGill Corporation in Australia.

Before he had killed himself in 1939, after being partially paralysed in a near-fatal car crash, Paul McGill had drawn a new will. In it he had bequeathed everything he owned to Emma Harte, his common-law wife of sixteen years.

His immense personal fortune, personal real estate and other personal possessions in Australia, England and America he left directly to Emma, to do with as she wished. But the business empire in Australia and his big block of shares in Sitex Oil of America, the company he had founded in Texas, were to be held in trust by Emma for Daisy, the only child they had had together, and any offspring Daisy herself might one day have.

From 1939 until 1969, Emma herself had run The McGill Corporation, both at close range in Sydney, and long distance from London. She had managed to do this successfully with the help of trusted appointees, some of whom had worked for Paul McGill until his death. These men, the managing directors of the various companies within the conglomerate, carried out her instructions and were responsible for the day-to-day running of their divisions. These were diverse, ranged from the mining of opals and minerals to coal fields, land development, and commercial real estate, and included the family sheep station at Coonamble.

The McGill family's vast business enterprises, which were now the responsibility of Philip, had begun with that sheep station, one of the largest in New South Wales. Called Dunoon, it had been founded in 1852 by Philip's great-great-grandfather, Andrew McGill, a Scottish sea captain, who was a free settler in the Antipodes. The McGill Corporation, as such, had been created by his great-grandfather, Bruce McGill, and later expanded to become one of the most important companies in the world by his grandfather, Paul.

When he was still only a very little boy, Emma had begun to talk to Philip about Australia, telling him of the wonders and beauty and riches of that extraordinary land. And she had filled his head with adventurous yarns about his grandfather, speaking to him about Paul so beautifully, so vividly and with such an enduring love she had brought the man to life for the small child. Certainly Philip sometimes felt as though he had actually known his grandfather.

As he grew older, Emma had explained that one day Paul's mighty empire, which took *her* so frequently to Australia, would belong to him and Paula, but that he would run it, as she herself was doing on behalf of their mother and them.

Philip had been six years old when Emma had first taken him out to Sydney with his parents, Daisy and David Amory, and his sister, and he had fallen in love with it from the first moment he had set foot on Australian ground. That love had never waned.

Philip had been educated in England, attending Wellington, his grandfather's old school, but at seventeen he had rebelled, had told Emma and his parents that he wanted to leave school, that he had no intention of going to university. He had explained, and in no uncertain terms, that the time had come for him to start learning about the business he was supposed to run when he was old enough.

Eventually his father had given in, had shrugged philosophically, knowing he was not going to win the day.

Emma's attitude had been somewhat similar. She had brought Philip to work

589

with her, hiding a smile on that first day, knowing that her grandson had not the slightest idea of what was in store for him. And so it had begun – Emma's relentless training programme which demanded complete dedication. She was stern, exacting, and the hardest taskmaster he had ever met. She insisted on excellence in all things, and diligence and concentration, and his life was hers until the time came when he had absorbed the precepts of her business ethos.

But Emma was eminently fair, and Philip had eventually come to understand that his grandmother's unremitting pounding on himself, his sister, and his cousins was merely her way of ensuring they would be able to hold their own when they were out on their own, and when she was no longer there to guide or protect them.

During the years of his training, Philip travelled constantly to Australia with Emma, and whenever possible he spent his holidays there, invariably going up to Dunoon at Coonamble, wanting to learn as much as he could about their sheep station. Sometimes Emma went with him, and he enjoyed it even more when she did, because she would reminisce about the old days, the times she had spent there with Paul, and he was always captivated by her stories.

In 1966, when he was twenty, Emma sent Philip to live permanently in Australia.

She wanted him to learn at first hand about the business empire he would operate and control as chief executive officer and chairman of the board.

At the end of three years, Philip had proved himself to be worthy of Emma's belief in him.

She had not been unduly surprised, since she knew he had inherited her astuteness, her canny Yorkshire ways, her instinct for making money, and that he had the ability to turn situations to his own advantage, as she had done all her life. Also, quite aside from being the spitting image of his grandfather, Emma was aware that Philip was blessed with Paul's acumen and financial genius.

Philip was soon well entrenched professionally and socially in Sydney, and he made a good life for himself in Australia. The country of his McGill fore-fathers, which had so fascinated and intrigued him since those childhood visits, became his true home. He had not the slightest desire to live anywhere else in the world.

Two of Emma's appointees, Neal Clarke and Tom Patterson, had been instrumental in Philip's training in Australia, and they had earned his genuine respect and affection. However, it was usually Emma to whom Philip turned for guidance and counsel when he was uncertain, or when he faced a crisis. After his grandmother's death in 1970, his father took her place, in as much as he became his confidant and sounding board whenever Philip deemed it necessary to seek advice outside his own organization. David Amory's untimely death in the avalanche at Chamonix in January of 1971 had robbed Philip not only of his beloved father, but of a wise counsellor and guiding hand.

When Philip had returned to Sydney in March of that year, fully recovered from the minor injuries he had suffered on the mountain that fateful day, he had been an extremely troubled young man of twenty-five. He was not only grieving for his father, but filled with anxiety and concern about the future.

He had a mighty business to run, enormous responsibilities to shoulder, and he was entirely alone with Emma and his father now dead.

Paula, never anything but devoted and loyal, had her own problems to contend with, and he could not inflict his terrible worries on her.

His mother, Daisy, who had returned to Australia with him at Paula's urging, was crushed by sorrow at the loss of her husband. And although The McGill Corporation was hers, technically speaking, she had never been involved in business, and he knew she could be no help whatsoever. In fact, he was aware that she was looking to him for strength and support.

But quite apart from these problems, Philip was grappling with another emotion at this particular point in his life: *Survivor guilt.*

Few people would be left unaffected after surviving an avalanche in which other members of the family had been killed, and Philip was no exception. He had floundered, been unable to come to grips with himself. Why had *he* been singled out to live when the others had died? This question had dominated his thoughts, jostled for prominence in his mind.

He had no ready answer.

However, gradually, he had recognized that he must get over the traumatic experience, put it behind him, and if at all possible, somehow turn it to a positive. His mother and sister needed him and he had the conglomerate to run, he repeatedly reminded himself in the ensuing months. And so he focused on the future, and hoped that perhaps the reason for his survival, the purpose of it, would one day be revealed to him.

With the blood of Emma Harte and Paul McGill coursing through his veins, Philip was nothing if not a hard and dedicated worker, and as he began to marshal his turbulent emotions he directed his full energies into The McGill Corporation. Work blocked out problems and worries, and, as far as he was concerned, it was also the most satisfying way to lead his life, to fill his days and nights.

And so it was that by 1981 Philip McGill Amory had become one of Australia's leading industrialists, an important man in his own right, and one to be reckoned with.

The conglomerate had had its ups and downs in the eleven years since Emma's death. But he had held the helm firmly, kept it steady, and steered the company ahead. He had divested himself of losing divisions, diversified his holdings, purchased other companies which mined iron ore and harnessed natural resources, and he had branched out into communications with the acquisition of newspapers and magazines, radio and television stations.

Under Philip's aegis, the company founded and brought to prominence by his forefathers, and immeasurably strengthened by Emma during the years of her trusteeship, had moved forward into the 1980s with greater power and financial growth than it had ever known in the past.

The phone on Philip's desk buzzed several times. He picked it up.

'Yes?' he asked, glancing at his watch.

'It's Ken, Mr Amory, I have the car waiting.'

'Thanks, Ken, I'll be right down.' Philip replaced the receiver, put a pile of financial statements, other documents and the *Asian Wall Street Journal* in his briefcase, snapped it shut, and left his private office.

His wine-coloured Rolls-Royce stood outside the McGill Tower on Bridge Street, and Ken, his driver of the last five years, leaned against the hood.

''Evening, Mr Amory,' Ken said, straightening up, opening the back door for him.

'Hello, Ken,' Philip replied and stepped into the car. A second later they were pulling away from the kerb, and he instructed, 'Rose Bay, please, Ken. Mrs Rickards' house.'

'Right you are, sir.'

Philip settled back into the soft, beige-leather upholstery, trying to shed the general preoccupations of the business day.

He closed his eyes, relaxing, letting the tension ease out of him. He thought of Paula and experienced a small rush of happiness, knowing she would be arriving in Sydney in the morning. He missed her. So did their mother. Philip's mind swung instantly to Daisy. He had not seen her for the past week, since she had been in Perth with her husband, Jason Rickards, and had only returned to the city late last night. But he had no doubt she was hardly able to contain herself, impatiently waiting for Paula's arrival.

He was well aware that the only thing casting a faint shadow across their mother's happiness these days was being so far away from her daughter and grandchildren. But she did have Jason, and for that he was extremely thankful.

What a vital role timing plays in life, Philip suddenly reflected. He had introduced his mother to the Perth industrialist in 1975, when Jason had finally recovered from his messy divorce of three years earlier, and when his mother was at last ready to enter into a relationship with another man. Despite their busy lives and their many commitments, both Daisy and Jason had been lonely, and they had welcomed the introduction. And then, lo and behold, much to everyone's surprise but his, these two had fallen in love and had married a year later.

Seemingly it was a good marriage. Jason had a permanent smile on his rugged face and his mother never looked anything less than radiant these days, and she had put her sorrow truly behind her. But then his mother was a wise woman.

In the years immediately following his father's death, she had done her level best to make the most of her new life in Australia. She had acted as Philip's hostess, had then gone on to create her own social circle, and she had eventually thrown herself into charity work with a great deal of zeal and dedication to her chosen causes, mostly do with the welfare of children. This had given her tremendous satisfaction, added purpose to her existence.

As the only child of Paul McGill, who had been one of the richest men in Australia, heiress to his great fortune, and half Australian herself, Daisy believed that doing good works was her duty, the responsibility of wealth and privilege such as hers. She had created the McGill Foundation, had endowed millions to medical research, children's hospitals and education. Yes, living in

Sydney had been good for his mother, just as she, in her way, had been good for Sydney.

Jason Rickards was an added bonus in her life, in all of their lives, really. He was well liked by everyone, was very much a part of the family. Childless, Jason had thrown himself heart and soul into being an adopted grandfather, and Paula's children adored him.

Yes, timing *was* on their side, Philip thought. *And luck... lots of it.*

He opened his eyes, pulled himself upright on the seat, smiled ruefully. *His* timing was invariably wrong and *he* never had any luck when it came to women. Just the opposite. But he didn't really care. He had no desire to get married, much preferred the life of a bachelor. There were, after all, worse fates.

14

The balmy night air drifting in through the open French doors was fragrant with a variety of mingled scents . . . honeysuckle, wisteria, rambling roses and eucalyptus, and inside the room there was a faint hint of *Joy*, Daisy's favourite perfume, the one she invariably wore.

A Chopin *étude* played softly on the stereo in the background, and silk-shaded lamps added their mellow glow to the gracious drawing room, where peach, white and pale green predominated, and where a certain gentle calm prevailed.

Philip sat facing his mother across the antique Chinese coffee table made of hand-carved ebony, enjoying a snifter of cognac after the delicious dinner they had just shared. Fernando, the Filipino chef, had prepared Barramundi, his favourite fish, and Daisy had made an English trifle, which had always been a special treat when he was a child, and now he was feeling well satisfied, replete with good food and vintage wine, and completely spoiled as he relaxed on the comfortable sofa.

He brought the brandy balloon up to his nose and sniffed, appreciating the strong, almost harsh bouquet of the alcohol. He took a swallow, savoured it, then sat back, nursed the balloon in his hands, nodding from time to time as he listened to her softly modulated voice, giving her his entire attention.

'And since Jason will be back from Perth on Thursday, I thought it would be nice to take Paula up to Dunoon for the weekend. Don't you, darling? And you will come with us, won't you?'

Philip put the balloon down on the end table and frowned.

'Do you honestly think she'll want to start travelling the minute she gets here, after she's flown half way across the world?' He shook his head. 'I doubt it, Mother.' Instantly a grin surfaced, replaced his frown. 'Besides, if I know *my* sister, *your* daughter, she'll have her nose to the grindstone on Saturday, trying to bring order to the boutique at the Sydney-O'Neill. That's why she's flying out here, remember.'

'Oh but she's coming to see us as well!' Daisy asserted, giving him a sharp look. She wondered if either of her children ever thought about anything else except business. She doubted it. They took after her mother.

Daisy's face changed, became reflective, and after a moment she said, 'But perhaps you're right, Philip. It is *rushing* her a bit, I suppose. Maybe we can go up to the sheep station the following weekend.'

'Yes, why not, Mother,' he agreed, humouring her.

The smile flicked into Daisy's vivid blue eyes again, and she leaned forward, her face full of enthusiasm and eagerness. 'Jason and I have decided to spend an extra month in England, Philip. We're leaving at the beginning of November instead of December, and we won't be back until January. Three months . . . and I'm *so* looking forward to them, to being in London and at Pennistone Royal. Christmas in Yorkshire with Paula, Shane and the grandchildren, and the rest of the family as well, is my idea of sheer bliss. It's going to be like old times . . . when Mummy was alive.'

'Yes,' Philip said. A brow lifted as he next asked, 'Can Jason afford to be away so long though?'

'Of course. And it's one of the reasons he's been spending so much time in Perth these last few weeks, making sure everything will run smoothly during his absence. And in any case, he has every confidence in his staff, just as you do.' She smiled at him. 'You're coming too, aren't you? To England for Christmas, I mean.'

'Well, I'm not sure,' he began, and stopped abruptly when he saw his mother's expression. Her face had dropped.

'I hope I can get away, darling,' he muttered noncommitally, having no desire to make a decision about Christmas so far in advance, or to promise her anything. She would hold him to it.

'Oh Philip, you must! You *promised* Paula! Have you forgotten about the sixtieth anniversary of Harte's? You *have* to be at the dinner dance she's giving on New Year's Eve. Everyone's going to be there, and it will look simply awful if you're not.'

'I'll do my damnedest, Mother, okay?'

'Yes, all right,' she responded quietly, leaning back against the big pillows on the sofa, smoothing the skirt of her silk dress, sighing under her breath. After a moment, Daisy raised her eyes, studied Philip, trying to gauge his mood, wondering if she dare mention his current girlfriend. He could be touchy at times, and especially when it came to his private life.

Deciding to take a chance, she said in her low, even tone, 'If you do come to England, I think it might be rather nice if you bring Veronica with you. She's such a lovely young woman.'

Philip started to laugh and gave his mother an odd look.

Daisy stared back at him in surprise, perplexity flitting across her face. 'What is it?'

Still chuckling and catching his breath, Philip finally managed to say, 'Honestly, Mother, you *are* behind the times. I broke up with Veronica Marsden weeks and weeks ago. It's over . . . finished . . . kaput.'

'You didn't tell me,' Daisy replied, sounding reproachful. She filled with dismay. 'Oh darling, I *am* sorry. As I said, she is a lovely person, and, frankly, I thought the two of you were quite serious about each other. But never mind, I expect you know best, Pip,' she murmured, using the diminutive of his childhood.

Her look became quizzical when she ventured, 'Perhaps you'd like to bring the current favourite?'

'There isn't a current favourite, Mother. And please stop trying to get me married off!' he exclaimed crossly. At once conscious of the hurt invading her eyes, he softened his harsh tone, added, with a light laugh, 'You just want to get me hitched so that you can have lots of grandchildren to fuss over here in Australia.'

'Yes, there's some truth in that,' Daisy admitted.

She lifted her cup, took a sip of the lemon tea, and fell silent, slipping down into her thoughts. And she asked herself why her son continually broke off with suitable young women at the most crucial time in his relationship with them. She remembered Selena, his girlfriend before Veronica, who had come to see her after she and Philip had parted company last year. Selena had confided that Philip had the need to end a relationship the moment it became serious, or rather, became *threatening* was the way Selena had put it. Daisy wondered if the girl had been correct. She stifled another sigh. Her son was as baffling to *her* as he was to many other people. There were those who said he was an enigma, and wasn't that the absolute truth?

Philip, watching her closely, said, 'Hey, Ma, what are you cooking up in that head of yours? I can almost see your mind working.'

'Nothing, nothing at all, darling.' Then Daisy gave a little laugh, and went on confidingly, 'Actually, I was asking myself if you would ever marry.'

'I have the reputation of being the biggest playboy in the western world. I aim to keep the title.' Lifting the brandy balloon to his mouth, he winked at her over its rim, his expression mischievous.

'Hardly a playboy, not the way you work, Philip. That's an exaggeration, and merely the press pinning a label on you, because you're so eligible.'

Now Daisy shifted on the sofa, crossed her long legs, and a new seriousness entered her voice, as she continued, 'But I can't bear to think of you being alone later in your life, Philip. That's a terrible prospect for you, and not a very comforting one for me to envisage either. And I certainly don't want you to become a crusty old bachelor.'

Daisy paused, gave him a penetrating stare, hoping her words would sink in. 'Not like poor John Crawford,' she finished, thinking of her solicitor in London. He had once had a crush on her, had wanted to marry her after David's death. But she had harboured only friendship for John, nothing deeper than that.

'Yes, poor John indeed,' Philip agreed. 'He is a bit of a sorry case these days. Yearning after you, Ma, I do suspect. But me *crusty*? Never. The ladies will keep *me* young and merry into my old age.' He gave her a cheeky grin. 'You know what they say . . . variety's the spice of life, and so I shall always make sure I have a pretty girl on my arm, even in my dotage.'

'I don't doubt it,' Daisy conceded, laughing with him. But privately she wondered if these fleeting liaisons with countless women were ever going to be enough for her son in the final analysis. If that was what he wanted then she supposed they would be. On the other hand, he was missing so much, not being married. She longed to continue the conversation, to speak to him very seriously about his personal life, his future, and the future of The McGill Corporation if he did not produce heirs. But instinct, and her better judgement, told her to keep quiet. After all, Philip was thirty-five and answerable to no one but himself, and he might easily resent her probing.

The phone trilled in the adjoining library, and a second later Daisy's Filipino houseman, Rao, appeared in the arched doorway to the living room. 'Excuse me, madam, it's Mr Rickards.'

'Thank you, Rao,' Daisy said, and glanced across at her son. 'I won't be a moment, darling.'

There was a faint swish of silk, a whiff of *Joy*, as Daisy rose and hurried out.

Philip's eyes followed her.

He could not help thinking how young his mother looked tonight. She had celebrated her fifty-sixth birthday in May, but she appeared to be years younger. She had a slim, almost girlish figure, and her lovely face was quite unlined, and because she had stayed out of the sun most of her life, she had preserved her flawless English complexion. There was a freshness, a youthfulness about her still, and even the few strands of grey streaking her black hair did nothing to age her. She was remarkable; but then Emma had been well-preserved too.

Philip was finishing the last of his cognac when Daisy returned to the living room.

She said, 'Jason sends his love, Pip. I told him what you said about dragging Paula to Coonamble, and he tends to agree with you that it wouldn't be fair. Perhaps we'll have a little dinner party for her on Saturday. Is that all right with you? You will come, won't you?'

'Of course! I wouldn't miss being with old Beanstalk for anything. Listen, Mother, I'd really like you to take a look at the financial statements and balance sheets I brought with me. I want to go over them –'

'You know very well that's not necessary, Philip,' Daisy interrupted. 'I don't know a blessed thing about business, yet you constantly force these papers on me.'

'But The McGill Corporation is *your* company, Mother.'

'Oh fiddlesticks, Philip, it's yours and Paula's, except in name, and you know that. And obviously I trust you implicitly. Good Lord, darling, my mother trained you all those years ago to do the job properly. *She* had immense faith in your judgement and business acumen, and so do I.'

'Thanks for that lovely vote of confidence, Ma, but I insist you look at the papers. Let me go and get them.' As he was speaking he hurried out to the foyer and returned at once with his briefcase.

Reluctantly, Daisy took the papers he offered and, settling back on the sofa, she began to read them slowly, although she only did so to please her son.

For his part, Philip sat observing her quietly, thinking that she looked stunning in the silk dress she was wearing. It was a peculiar bluish-purple, like the wisteria growing in her garden, and it underscored the blueness of her eyes. So did the sapphires on her ears and at her throat, a recent gift from Jason, she had told him over dinner. Jason Rickards is a lucky man, Philip thought, and then as his mother lifted her dark head, looked across at him, he smiled and handed her a second sheaf of papers.

'Oh God, not more of them,' Daisy groaned, making a face. 'This is a pointless exercise, you know, they're double Dutch to me.'

Philip merely grinned. This was now an old story between them.

'Here, let me explain,' he said, and went to join her on the sofa. For the next half hour he patiently walked her through the balance sheets, striving hard to explain everything in the simplest of terms, as he had been doing for years.

He did not return to the city that night.

He went instead to his house at Point Piper. Earlier he had phoned, and had told his housekeeper he would be arriving later, but not to wait up for him. She and the rest of the staff were in their own quarters when the car dropped him off at eleven.

He went straight to his den, laid his briefcase on the sofa and strode over to the bar, where he poured himself a brandy. Carrying it out to the terrace, he stood leaning against the balustrade, sipping the drink and staring out at the ocean, dark as pitch now under a dark and moonless sky.

His mother's words reverberated in his head.

She wanted him to get married because she did not want him to end up a lonely man. That was a belly laugh. Being married didn't necessarily prevent loneliness. Sometimes it even underscored one's very aloneness. He'd never been married, but he had lived with a woman at one point in his life, and he was well aware that the company of another person did not change a damn thing. Certainly it did not chase the devils away.

He had had an unconventional private life for years now, and it worried Daisy, and he fully understood why. But there was nothing he could do about changing it. He sighed. Too many women over too short a period lately, and too damn many even for me, he thought, filling with sudden distaste.

As he examined his life with a new objectivity, he saw that it was as arid as the Great Sandy Desert. A meaningful relationship with a woman *had* eluded him. It would *always* elude him. But did that really matter? Long ago he had decided it was simpler to settle for sex. A physical relationship was reasonably uncomplicated. Anyway, he was a loner by nature. At least he could live comfortably with himself.

As he swallowed the last drop of brandy, swung around and walked back into the house, Philip McGill Amory had no way of knowing that his life was about to change, for better and for worse. And forever.

15

'I want to sell the Sitex stock.'

Paula's words fell like an exploding bomb into the quiescence of her mother's beautiful peach drawing room, and she realized she had startled herself as much as she had her mother and her brother.

Daisy and Philip were obviously flabbergasted, and neither of them spoke; they simply stared at her for the longest moment.

Paula glanced from one to the other. She had not meant to tell them tonight, nor had she meant to be so blunt about it, but since she could not take the words back, she might as well finish what she had started.

She took a deep breath, but before she could continue, her mother broke the short, uncomfortable silence.

Daisy said, 'I don't understand, Paula. Why do you want to sell the stock all of a sudden?'

'Any number of reasons, Mummy, but mainly because oil prices have dropped considerably, and since there's currently a glut of oil on the world market, I feel they're going to drop even lower. And anyway, you know that Sitex has been a pain in the neck to me for years now, so I think we ought to get out, once and for all. Sell our entire forty per cent and be done with it.'

'I see,' Daisy murmured, puckering her eyebrows. She swung her head, stared at Philip.

Philip returned his mother's questioning glance, but remained silent.

He rose, walked over to the French doors, stood gazing out across Rose Bay to the lights of Sydney glittering in the distance. The McGill Tower, soaring up into the starlit sky, dominated the cityscape even at night.

Paula's unexpected announcement puzzled him, and he wondered what was *really* behind it. He turned slowly, his eyes sweeping over her as he returned to his chair. Despite her tan, she looked drawn and tired, and he thought she ought to be in bed, not discussing business at this hour. However, her eyes told him she was waiting for some sort of comment from him.

'The situation's bound to change, Paula, it usually does,' Philip said at last. 'Oil prices have always fluctuated, sometimes even wildly, and in my opinion, if we're going to sell, it should be at a more auspicious time than now, when we can get the most for the stock, don't you think? When oil is at a premium and prices are high, for instance.'

'And when will that be, Philip? I just told you, there's an over-abundance of oil in the world today, but you know that as well as I do.' Paula sighed, shook her head wearily. 'Hundreds of thousands of barrels are being stored up, yet the world demand for oil has dropped by fifteen per cent – ever since those artificially high prices were imposed by the cartels in 1979. I honestly believe the demand for oil will continue to fall. It'll go down, down, *down*.

598

You'll see, this current trend will go on for several years . . . in my estimation until 1985.'

Philip laughed. 'Come on, darling, your outlook is awfully bleak.'

Paula said nothing. She sat back on the sofa, rubbed her neck, feeling very tired, once more wishing she had not begun this.

Daisy, whose blue eyes were still troubled, turned to her daughter and said, 'But I promised my mother I'd never sell our Sitex stock, Paula, just as she promised the same thing to Paul all those years ago. My father told her to hang on to it, insisted that she never let it go, no matter what, and – '

Cutting in, Paula muttered, 'Times have changed, Mummy.'

'Yes, they have, and I'm the first to acknowledge that. On the other hand, I would feel very funny about selling our interest in Sitex. Uncomfortable really.'

Paula gave Daisy a pointed look. 'I bet if Grandy were alive today, she'd agree with *me*,' she asserted, and stifled a yawn. She felt dizzy, woozy actually, and the room seemed suddenly to swim before her eyes, and she thought that if she didn't lie down soon she would collapse right there on the peach sofa. But Philip had started to say something else, so she tried to focus on him, to listen to his words.

He was saying, 'What does it matter if the shares bring in lower dividends for a year or two, or even three or four. Mother doesn't need the additional income.'

'That's absolutely true, I don't,' Daisy concurred. 'In any case, Paula darling, I really don't think we should be discussing this matter right now. You look exhausted and seem about ready to keel over. I'm not a bit surprised either – as usual, you've done far too much since you arrived yesterday,' she chastised gently.

Paula blinked again. 'Too true, Mother, and the jet lag generally hits me hard on the second night, doesn't it?' She was struggling to keep her eyes open as waves of exhaustion washed over her, almost engulfed her. 'I think I do have to go to bed. Right now. I'm so sorry, I shouldn't have brought this up . . . we'll have to finish our chat about Sitex another day.'

Pushing herself to her feet, Paula went and kissed her mother goodnight.

Philip, who had risen at the same time, put his arm around her and walked her across the drawing room and out into the entrance foyer.

They stood together at the bottom of the staircase.

'Shall I help you upstairs, Beanstalk?' he asked, his eyes kind, full of brotherly affection.

Paula shook her head. 'Don't be daft, Pip, I'm not *so* decrepit that I can't make it to my bedroom.' She covered her mouth with her hand and yawned several times, then grasped the banister, put a foot on the first step. 'Oh dear, I *think* I can make it . . . I shouldn't have had the wine with dinner.'

'It'll make you sleep like a top.'

'Gosh, I don't need anything to do that,' she murmured, leaned forward and kissed his cheek. 'Goodnight, love.'

''Night, Paula darling, and let's have lunch tomorrow. I'll meet you in the Orchid Room at twelve-thirty. Okay?'

'You're on, brother o'mine.'

When she got to her room, Paula was so bone tired she hardly had the strength to undress and take off her makeup. But she managed somehow, and within minutes she was pulling a silk nightgown over her head and gratefully sliding into bed.

As her head touched the pillow she admitted to herself that she had made a tactical error, *had* picked the wrong time to discuss Sitex. With a sudden flash of insight, she knew her mother would never agree to sell the stock, no matter what *she* said, and that this would drastically interfere with her plans.

Or would it? Her last thought, before she fell asleep, was of her grandmother. 'There's more than one way to skin a cat,' Emma had been fond of saying. Remembering this, Paula smiled to herself in the dark before her eyelids fluttered and closed.

Silence reigned in the back office of the Harte Boutique in the Sydney-O'Neill Hotel the following morning.

Paula and Madelana sat facing each other across the large desk, their heads bent and close together as they pored over two ledgers.

It was Madelana who looked up first.

'I can't imagine how Callie Rivers managed to make such a mess,' she said to Paula, shaking her head, her face a picture of disbelief. 'It took some sort of perverse genius to create a muddle of these proportions.'

Paula raised her eyes, looked at Madelana, and grimaced. 'Either she's totally dense and my judgement was haywire when I hired her, or her illness debilitated her to such an extent she just hasn't known what she was doing these past few months.'

'It had to be her illness, not you, Paula. You're far too smart not to spot a dud the minute you see one,' Madelana said confidently, and closed the ledger in front of her with a degree of finality. 'I've checked these figures three times now . . . twice with the calculator and once by hand. You're right, I'm afraid. We are in the red here . . . and the red is *very* red.'

Paula took a deep breath, expelled it, stood up and began to pace for a few seconds, her face reflective. Returning to the desk, she took the ledgers, put them in the filing cabinet and locked it, then dropped the key in the pocket of her grey linen jacket.

'Come on, Maddy, let's go back to the stock room and try to make some sense there.'

'Good idea,' Madelana answered, rising immediately, following Paula out of the office and into the main area of the three-level boutique.

'We'll be downstairs, Mavis,' Paula informed the assistant manager, and swept on across the floor without pausing, making for the heavy glass doors which opened into the hotel lobby.

'Yes, Mrs O'Neill,' Mavis answered quietly, staring after Paula, her gloomy face reflecting her worry.

Madelana merely nodded to the young woman.

But once she and Paula were crossing the dark-green marble lobby, she confided, 'I think Mavis is all right basically, Paula. Just out of her depth. Callie Rivers should never have made her the assistant manager. She doesn't have what it takes to run a boutique of this size and importance, and she's not very imaginative or creative either. Still, she *is* honest, and that counts for a lot, I guess.'

'Everything you say is quite true,' Paula agreed, walking briskly into the empty elevator as the door opened, pushing the button for the floor below. 'Callie left her a mess to cope with, and she didn't know what to do to correct it, I realize that now.' Paula glanced at Madelana through the corner of her eye. 'I don't hold Mavis responsible, you know. I just wish she'd had the sense to tell me everything. She knew she could phone me, or telex me, any time she wished.'

The two women stepped out of the elevator, and Paula went on, 'Let's face it, if the hotel manager hadn't mentioned it to Shane on the phone a few weeks ago, I still wouldn't be any the wiser.'

'Yes, it was a good thing he found out there were problems, and that Mavis was in a panic and floundering. I think we just got here in time to avert a real disaster.'

'You can say that again,' Paula muttered.

The stock room which belonged to the Harte Boutique was located on the mezzanine floor of the hotel, and was actually a series of rooms. These included an office with filing cabinets, a desk, chairs and telephones in the entrance, and several large storage rooms behind this. Racks of clothes were kept there, along with chests of accessories ranging from costume jewellery, scarves, hats and belts to handbags and shoes.

Madelana grimaced as she and Paula paced along the lines of bulging racks, looking at the stock for the second time since their arrival, but only now doing their first proper assessment. Groaning, she eyed her boss. 'We're going to have one hell of a job making inroads into this lot. It's worse than I realized yesterday.'

'Don't I know it,' Paula responded grimly. 'And I dread to think what awful secrets those chests over there hold.' She shook her head, and her annoyance and dismay rose to the surface yet again. 'This is partially my fault. I shouldn't have let Callie persuade me to carry several less expensive lines, as well as the Lady Hamilton Clothes. But she convinced me she knew this market better than I did, and fool that I was I gave her a good deal of leeway. And so here we are today, looking at clothes she bought from other manufacturers and which haven't moved.'

'I think we do have to have a sale, like you suggested yesterday,' Madelana volunteered.

'Yes. We must get rid of the old merchandise, including the remainder of the Lady Hamilton line from last season. A clean sweep, that's the only thing to do – and then we can start again from scratch. I'll telex Amanda this afternoon, instructing her to send as much Lady Hamilton stock as she has available. She can air freight it out to us. We need spring and summer merchandise, of course, since Australia's heading into those seasons now.' She broke off, stood with her hand resting on the rack, staring at the clothes hanging there, a look of anxiety settling on her face.

'What's wrong?' Madelana asked, as always quick to sense any change in Paula's demeanour.

'I hope we *can* move these clothes in a sale, and make *something* on them, however little that is.'

Madelana exclaimed, 'Oh I'm sure we will, Paula, and I've got an idea ... why not make it a Grand Sale. Capital G, capital S, and advertise it as being comparable only to the one at Harte's of Knightsbridge. That's the world's most famous sale – so let's cash in on it. Surely the agency here in Sydney can come up with some clever copy for the newspaper advertisements.' Maddy thought for a moment, and when she continued it was with a rush of enthusiasm. 'I think the message we want to convey to the public goes something like this ... *you don't have to fly to London to go to the Harte's sale of the year. It's right here on your own doorstep.* Well, what do you think?'

For the first time that morning, a genuine smile flickered on Paula's mouth. 'Brilliant, Maddy, I'll put a call into Janet Shiff at the ad agency this afternoon, and have her start working up some of her snappy copy. Now come on, let's sort through these clothes, and pick out as much as we can for the sale.'

Madelana needed no further encouragement. She dashed over to one of the other racks, and began her own ruthless process of selection and elimination.

The Orchid Room of the Sydney-O'Neill Hotel was considered to be one of the most beautiful places to lunch or dine in the city. It was also a very *in* spot where people went to be seen and to see, and so it had acquired a certain cachet in local society.

Situated on the top floor of the hotel, two of its walls were made entirely of plate glass running floor to ceiling, and thus it appeared to float, as though suspended between the blue sky and the sea far below, and offered a sweeping view for miles around.

Breathtaking giant-sized murals of handpainted white, yellow, pink and cerise orchids covered the other two walls, and there were real orchids everywhere ... arranged in tall cylindrical glass vases, planted in Chinese porcelain pots, and clustered in bowls on every table.

Paula was particularly proud of the room, since Shane had conceived it and had taken an active part in its planning with the architects, at the time the hotel was being designed and constructed. He liked to use animals, birds or flowers endemic to a country as the motif for a lobby, a dining room or a bar in his foreign hotels, and since orchids grew in such profusion in the forests, heaths and woodlands of Australia, this species had seemed appropriate to him. Also, because of the orchid's various shapes and sizes, and lovely vibrant colours, the flower lent itself to any number of artistic effects and decorative themes.

Paula sat in the elegant, sun-filled restaurant, sipping a mineral water before lunch, and she glanced around admiringly, realizing she had forgotten how truly magnificent the real orchids were, and how brilliantly the hotel florist arranged them in the room, so that they were shown off to their best advantage. Talented gardener that she was, she could not help wishing she could grow these exotic blooms in England.

'Penny for your thoughts,' Philip said, peering at her across the table.

'Oh sorry, I didn't mean to drift off like that ... I was just thinking about the possibility of growing orchids at Pennistone Royal, but I don't think it's feasible.'

'Of course it is. You could have a greenhouse built in which to cultivate them . . . you know, like growing tomatoes.' He chuckled and there was mischief in his bright blue eyes as he went on teasingly, 'After all, *you* have so much free time on your hands these days.'

Paula smiled at him. 'If only I did . . . gardening is very relaxing for me though. And why not a greenhouse? That's a very good thought of yours.'

'Oh Lord, what have I done now?' her brother groaned in mock horror at himself. 'Shane'll kill me.'

'No, he won't, he loves me to garden, to grow things, and he's always giving me new seed catalogues, and packets of seeds and bulbs, and similar stuff. I shall tell him I want an orchid greenhouse for Christmas. How about that?' she finished, laughing, her eyes as merry as her brother's.

'If *he* doesn't give it to you, *I* will.' Philip sat back in his chair, went on, 'By the way, Mother phoned me just before I left the office. She's thrilled you're spending the weekend at Dunoon. But you proved *me* wrong, you know.'

'What do you mean?'

'When Ma told me she wanted you to go up there, I said you wouldn't be interested, not after stepping off a fourteen-hour flight from LA.' He studied Paula for a moment. 'And I must admit, I was a bit surprised that you agreed to go. And so readily, she said. I thought you'd be hard at it in the boutique on Saturday. Don't tell me that you've already sorted out the mess there?' This came out sounding like a question and he raised his brows.

'Not completely, Philip, but I'm on my way to doing so.'

'Good for you! So come on, tell me the real story, Beanstalk.'

Paula quickly filled him in, then explained, 'And after I've had the sale next week, I'll do new window displays with the Lady Hamilton stock I'm bringing in from London in a hurry, and I'll back the merchandise with a fresh advertising campaign. With the spring-summer season ahead of me here, I think I can turn the boutique around again, in a relatively short period of time.'

Philip nodded. 'You're one terrific retailer. If you can't do it, no one can, darling. And what about your manager? You're not having her back, are you?'

'I can't, Pip, even though I do believe that some of the mistakes she made were because she wasn't in good health. Obviously I've lost my faith in her, and I know I'd be worried to death if I put her in charge again.'

'I can't say I blame you. What's happening at the boutiques in the hotels in Melbourne and Adelaide? They're not affected are they?'

'Fortunately not. They seem to be all right, from what the managers told me yesterday. Callie was no longer involved in them, thank God. If you remember, I set up a new system some time ago, made each manager autonomous, answerable only to me. Hence, since I am here in Australia, I'm going to fly down there later next week, just to make sure all is well.'

'Good idea. And you shouldn't have too many problems finding a new manager for the Sydney boutique. There are plenty of excellent people around.'

'Yes, so I understand. I hope to start interviewing on Monday, and if I haven't found anybody suitable before I leave in a couple of weeks, Madelana O'Shea will follow through for me. In any case, she's staying on for a while, to work with the advertising agency, and get the Sydney boutique organized and running properly. I trust her judgement, and I've every confidence in her.'

'So you've said before. I'm looking forward to meeting her sometime.'

'It'll be this weekend, Pip. I've invited her to Coonamble. Are you flying up with us tomorrow night?'

'No, I can't. You'll be going with Mother in Jason's plane, and I'll come in on Saturday morning. I'm glad we're going to have the weekend together, and it'll do you good. You can have two days' complete rest, and lots of fresh air.'

Paula smiled faintly, and leaned across the table, pinning her gaze on her brother. There was a slightly different nuance in her voice, when she asked, 'Do you think Mummy will change her mind about the Sitex stock?'

'No, I don't,' Philip was swift to reply. 'Ma's attitude about the stock is all tied up with her emotions about her father. You know as well as I do that she worshipped him, and she just can't bring herself to go against his wishes. And she believes that is what she *would* be doing if she sold the stock. It may sound far-fetched, but it happens to be the truth.'

'But those were Paul's wishes over forty years ago, for God's sake!' Paula cried vehemently. 'His view of the situation would be quite different today, just as Grandy's would be.'

'Maybe so, but I know Mother won't budge.' Philip gave Paula a searching look. 'Anyway, why *do* you want her to sell the stock. *Why* are you so anxious about it?'

Paula hesitated fractionally, wondering whether to tell her brother the truth, but decided against it. 'I gave you the reasons last night,' she said, keeping her voice neutral. 'Although I do have to admit I'm also rather fed up with Marriott Watson and his cronies on the board. They do everything they can to obstruct me, to make my life as difficult as possible.'

Philip gave her a curious look. 'But Paula, they always have – that's nothing new, is it? Furthermore, they were always at loggerheads with Grandy.' He paused, scowling, and rubbed his hand over his chin, was reflective for a moment. 'Still, if their behaviour is beginning to get to you, perhaps I should explain this to Ma, and –'

'No, no, don't do that,' Paula cut in rapidly. 'Look, let's forget about selling the Sitex stock. I'll cope with Marriott Watson and the board.'

'Yes, I know you will,' Philip said. 'You always have. You're very much like me. It's impossible for you not to do your duty – it goes against the grain.' He flashed her a loving smile. 'Now come on, let's order lunch.'

16

Sunlight filtering through the shaded windows awakened Madelana.

Blinking, she sat up abruptly in the antique four-poster bed, feeling at once both startled and disoriented, wondering where she was. And then she adjusted her eyes to the gentle, hazy light and looked around, took in the details of the lovely room, and remembered that she was at Dunoon, the McGill sheep station near Coonamble.

She turned her head, glanced at the little carriage clock on the taffeta-skirted bedside table, saw that it was early, only six o'clock. But that did not matter; she was accustomed to rising at the crack of dawn. Anyway, last night Daisy had told her she could get up whenever she wished, that she should make herself at home, explaining that she would find the housekeeper in the kitchen after six-fifteen. From that time on, such things as freshly-squeezed juice, coffee, tea, toast and fruit were always set out in the breakfast room; after seven, when one of the two cooks arrived, she could order a hot breakfast if she wanted, Daisy had added.

Throwing back the sheets, Madelana leapt out of bed, and hurried into the adjoining bathroom to shower.

Ten minutes later she emerged, wrapped in her white towelling bathrobe, and went over to the windows. She pushed up the shades on both of them, stood for a moment looking down into the gardens below. They were brilliantly green, filled with an abundance of vivid flowers planted in spectacular herbaceous borders, and in huge central flower beds cut into the rolling lawns. It was a radiant day, very sunny, with a bright blue sky scattered with billowing white clouds that looked like handfuls of cotton candy.

The excitement and anticipation she had experienced on arriving the night before flowed through her again, and she could hardly wait to go outside and investigate her immediate surroundings. Most especially she wanted to walk through those inviting gardens, which she knew Paula had had a hand in creating some years earlier.

Seating herself at the kidney-shaped dressing table positioned between the two soaring windows, Madelana began to brush her thick chestnut hair before applying her makeup, and as she wielded her brush her thoughts centred on this unique place where she had come with Paula, and Daisy and Jason Rickards, to spend the weekend.

Dunoon was unlike anything Madelana had expected, or had imagined it to be.

It was approximately five hundred and seventy kilometres from Sydney, situated in the North West plains region of New South Wales, and the flight in Jason Rickards's corporate jet had been short and fast. They had left Sydney at five yesterday afternoon and had landed on the private airfield at Dunoon just after six o'clock.

Tim Willen, the station manager, had met them, greeting them jovially, and laughing and joking with them as he had helped the pilot and the steward load their luggage into the vintage station wagon.

Ten minutes later, when they were driving off the airfield, Madelana had been startled to see several different types of planes resting in the huge hangars they passed, as well as two helicopters parked on the nearby helipad.

She had voiced her surprise to Daisy, who had explained that it was easier to use air power to get around Dunoon, especially if there was some kind of sudden emergency. On the flight up, Daisy had told her that their fully-operating sheep station covered thousands upon thousands of acres, and from the air it had looked like a small kingdom. Seeing the planes and the helicopters had only confirmed this sense of vastness to Madelana.

The main house was five miles away from the airfield, and on the way there Madelana had sat with her nose pressed to the window, frequently feeling awestruck by the things she was seeing. Daisy had been her guide last evening, had pointed out a variety of interesting sights as the station wagon rolled along the wide tarmac road, which cut through the huge property and also encircled it.

At one point they had passed a cluster of buildings which resembled a small village, and Madelana had learned from her hostess that these included sheep-shearing sheds, barns for storing the raw wool shorn from the Merino sheep bred and raised on Dunoon, sheep pens, a smithy, a small abattoir for slaughtering the livestock used for consumption on the station, a small freezer plant for preserving the sides of lamb, mutton and beef, and a series of other large barns where feed, havy and grain were stored. There was also a water tower off to one side, and a generator which provided the sheep station with its own electrical power.

A short distance beyond these buildings were several fenced-in paddocks shaded in parts by beautiful golden elm trees and willows. Here cattle and horses grazed contentedly in the luxuriant grass, and overlooking the bucolic paddocks was a compound of attractive houses built on a slight rise against a backdrop of elms and thick old oaks.

Tim had slowed down so that she could see everything better. He had told her that he and his wife lived there, as did the station hands and some of the indoor staff from the main house; adjoining the compound were tennis courts and a swimming pool for the sole use of the staff and their families.

A quarter of a mile farther along the main road, they drove past indoor and outdoor riding rings, where the horses were trained, and close by were large stables.

These buildings had captivated Madelana. Low, rambling and very rustic in appearance, they were made of dark grey and black stone, and were partially covered in creeper. They seemed very old to her, and she had mentioned this to Daisy, who had explained that the stables dated back to the 1920s and had been built by her father, Paul McGill.

The landscape had made a deep impression on Madelana during the drive from the airfield to the house. Somehow, she had not expected the countryside to be so beautiful, had not anticipated such green lushness in Australia. Until she had arrived here, she had always pictured the continent as being arid and dry, and composed almost entirely of scrub-laden Outback once the great coastal cities had been left behind.

But Dunoon was glorious, set amidst lovely, undulating hill country, where gentle slopes fell down into verdant valleys, wide paddocks, and wooded areas. It was truly a pastoral landscape, with the Castlereagh River running through its dark rich earth, where everything seemed to flourish.

The driveway leading up to the main residence, known simply as the manor, was half a mile long, and the minute they had pulled into it Daisy had rolled down one of the windows. Instantly the station wagon had filled with the all-pervasive scent of lemon. 'It's the Eucalyptus *citriodora*,' Daisy had explained, gesturing to the trees towering up above them and bordering the drive on both sides. 'They stretch all the way to the house, and they're very aromatic.' And Paula had added, 'When I smell lemons, no matter where I am in the world, I immediately think of Dunoon.' Madelana had nodded. 'I can understand why,' she had murmured, breathing in the lovely sharp fragrance of citrus.

The manor had blazed with lights to welcome them in the dimming light of gloaming, and when Madelana had alighted from the station wagon and had looked up at the house, she had been momentarily dazzled, transported back to her beloved bluegrass country. Instantaneously filling with nostalgia and a flock of memories, she had had to blink back sudden, incipient tears. The manor at Dunoon was built in a classical style reminiscent of the great plantation houses of the American South, somewhat antebellum in feeling.

Its front façade was mainly of white-painted wood, with sections of very dark red brick. Wide verandahs swept around its four sides, shaded the walls in summer but allowed the sun to reach them during the winter months. Standing at the edge of the front verandah were eight elegant white columns, four on each side of the front door made of polished mahogany. These columns were tall, stately, and soared up past the first two storeys to support a terrace that encircled the entire third floor.

The green foliage of wisteria growing against the manor's white paintwork contributed greatly to the feeling of cool serenity, as did the many leafy trees shading the graceful house in the back. Lawns bordered with huge pink and white azalea bushes sloped away from the gravel driveway, and the flower gardens were situated beyond these smooth and spacious greens.

Once inside the manor, Madelana had discovered that the interiors did justice to the exterior architecture. The rooms were furnished with choice antiques, crystal chandeliers, fine old carpets and marvellous paintings, many of them French Impressionists. Later she learned that the collection had been Emma Harte's and included works by Monet, Van Gogh, Gauguin, Cézanne and Degas.

Paula had brought her upstairs to this charming bedroom located next door to hers. Decorated in delicate shades of apricot, lime and pale blue, it was large and airy, with a high ceiling, a white marble fireplace and watercolours of Dunoon hanging on the walls. The antique four poster took pride of place, and there was a loveseat and two chairs arranged in a grouping in front of the fireplace.

Fresh flowers in vases had been placed everywhere and they permeated the room with the mingled scents of the gardens outside. The flowers were potent this morning, but Madelana did not mind.

She peered at herself in the dressing-table mirror, smoothed the brush over her hair again, and then went over to the armoire, took out tailored, grey-flannel slacks, a white silk shirt and a hand knitted jacket of a bluish-grey mohair.

After she had dressed in these clothes, she slipped her feet into a pair of brown leather moccasins, put on her gold watch and a pair of gold Tiffany shrimp earrings, and left the bedroom.

It was just after six-thirty when she pushed open to the door of the breakfast room and looked inside.

The housekeeper, Mrs Carr, whom she had met last night, was nowhere in sight, but Madelana's nose twitched at the tantalizing aromas of coffee and warm bread and ripe fruit. She noticed that these were set out on the table placed against the far wall underneath a painting of a circus clown. The round table in the middle of the octagonal-shaped room was covered with a fresh white organdy cloth and had been set with pretty floral china for four people.

Madelana went over and poured herself a cup of black coffee. She stared at the painting of the clown. Oh, it's a Picasso, she thought, as she turned away, not at all surprised. Nothing about Dunoon could surprise her anymore. It was a magical place.

She carried her cup of coffee outside, sat down on the steps of the back verandah, and drank it slowly, enjoying the smell of the grass and green-growing things, the lemony tang of the eucalyptus trees pervading the air, listening to the stillness of nature. The silence was broken only by the twittering of the small birds and the faint rustling of the leaves under the soft breeze.

How peaceful it was here. It was the kind of peace which was only ever found in the country, and she had forgotten it existed. It's such a luxury, she thought, and closed her eyes, allowing the peace to penetrate her bones, to settle deep inside her. And she realized, quite suddenly, that she had not known a peace like this since her childhood.

A little later, Madelana went back into the house, deposited her cup and saucer in the breakfast room, and then wandered out to the main entrance hall. Earlier, when she had been doing her makeup, she had intended to take a stroll through the gardens in front of the house, but now she hesitated.

Opening off the other end of the foyer was the gallery. Paula had pointed it out last night on their way upstairs; they had not had time to go in then, since they were in a hurry to change for dinner. As they had mounted the grand, curving staircase together, Paula had said: 'The gallery is hung with portraits of our McGill ancestors, but there's also an extraordinary painting of Emma in there, which you must see, Maddy, before you leave Dunoon.'

Her curiosity of last night was aroused again, and Madelana decided to take a peek at Emma's portrait. She would go for her walk afterwards.

The gallery was much longer than she had envisioned, with a high ceiling and a huge window at one end. The polished wood floor was bare, the walls were painted white, and a dark oak refectory table stood in the middle. A Chinese porcelain horse, quite large in size, had been placed on the table, and this appeared to be yet another priceless antique to Madelana.

She hurried down the length of the gallery, barely glancing at the portraits of the McGills, mainly interested in finding the one of Emma Harte.

When finally she stood in front of it, she caught her breath. It was extraordinary, just as Paula had said, so very lifelike, and so much better than any of those she had seen in the Harte Stores, even superior to the one at Pennistone Royal in Yorkshire.

She gazed at it for the longest time, marvelling at the vividness of the painting, and the exceptional brushwork. It had obviously been painted in the 1930s; the evening gown Emma wore was of the period and made of white satin, and

Madelana felt that if she reached out to touch the painting, her fingers would rest against the real fabric. Emeralds blazed around Emma's throat, at her ears and wrists, and there was a square-cut emerald on her left hand; the stones echoed the colour of her radiant eyes.

What small hands she had, Madelana thought, stepping closer, peering at the picture. Why, they're so tiny, they're almost a child's hands.

The portrait which hung next to Emma's was of a darkly handsome man, elegant in a white tie and tails. He had the most piercing blue eyes she had ever seen, a strong, very arresting face, a black moustache, and a deep cleft in his chin. Clark Gable, Maddy thought, and then smiled to herself, knowing it could not possibly be the late movie star. It was undoubtedly Paul McGill.

Tilting her head to one side, she studied the painting carefully, thoughtfully, wondering what kind of man he had been. A match for Emma Harte, she had no doubt.

Philip came running downstairs as the grandfather clock in the entrance foyer was striking seven.

He crossed the vast hall, heading in the direction of the breakfast room, when he noticed that the double mahogany doors leading into the gallery were slightly ajar. He walked over, intending to close them, and immediately saw the young woman inside. She stood at the far end, leaning towards the painting of his grandfather, studying it, and he realized she must be Paula's American assistant.

As if she sensed his presence, she swung around swiftly. When she saw him in the doorway her eyes opened very wide and a look of astonishment crossed her face. She stared at him intently.

And in that instant his life changed.

It seemed to Philip that all about her was the light. Not simply the bright sunlight pouring in through the big window, but the light which emanated from within her. She was an incandescent being.

He knew at once that he wanted her, and that he would have her. Philip could not comprehend how he knew this, but it flashed through his brain like a bolt of lightning striking, and he accepted it as the undeniable truth.

Slowly he began to walk forward, his riding boots clattering loudly against the wood, and the noise was overwhelming to him, a dreadful intrusion on the perfect stillness enveloping her. She stood there waiting for him, not moving, appearing hardly to breathe, still watching him intently. And his eyes did not leave her face.

She was a stranger, yet entirely familiar to him, and he experienced a deep sense of predestination – of fate – as he finally drew to a standstill in front of her.

Looking up into his face, she smiled a slow, tentative smile, and he was aware that something stupendous was happening to him, and what startled him the most was that it was happening here, in his own home, in the one place he truly loved on this planet. She continued to smile up at him, and he felt as though a burden was lifting from his shoulders, and there was the total cessation of pain; a sense of peace flowed through him.

Dimly, as though from faraway, he heard his own voice. 'I'm Philip, Paula's brother,' he was saying, and he was surprised he sounded so normal.

'I'm Madelana O'Shea.'

'So I'd guessed.'

She put her hand in his, and he clasped it firmly; he knew he had been waiting for her all his life.

17

It was a great effort for Philip to let go of Madelana's hand, but he did so – with some reluctance.

Immediately, Madelana slipped it into her pocket quickly. The feel of his strong fingers lingered, as though their imprint had been permanently burned onto hers. She shifted on her feet, and glanced away. Philip McGill Amory unnerved her.

Philip, watching her closely, said, 'You looked surprised when I appeared in the doorway. I'm sorry, I didn't mean to startle you.'

'I thought for a minute that Paul McGill had suddenly sprung to life –'

His vibrant laughter cut into her sentence, echoed around the quiet gallery, and he glanced at the painting but made no comment.

'Also,' she went on, 'Paula said you wouldn't be arriving from Sydney until around noon today.'

'I changed my mind, decided to fly up last night. I got in at eleven-thirty, but everyone was already in bed.'

She nodded, said nothing, stared up at him.

'You were studying my grandfather's portrait very closely.' He gave her a lopsided grin and his bright blue eyes were full of laughter, danced teasingly. 'Did it reveal anything to you? Secrets of his character, perhaps?'

'I was thinking that he must have been very special, a true man, to have won Emma Harte and to have married her.'

'From what my grandmother told me about him, Paul McGill was everything you or I could ever imagine him to have been. And *more*, I suspect,' Philip said. There was a slight pause, before he went on in a softer tone, 'But they were never married, actually . . . his wife wouldn't divorce him. So they took matters into their own hands, flouted convention and lived together for about sixteen or seventeen years. Until his death in 1939, in fact. I suppose what they did was considered quite scandalous in those days, but they didn't care.' Philip shrugged. 'They were madly in love, wildly happy, and apparently they never regretted a thing. And naturally they adored their only child, my mother.' There was another pause, then Philip said, 'She's illegitimate, of course.'

Madelana was taken aback. 'I didn't know that, or any of the things you've just told me. Paula has never said anything about your grandmother's personal life. And what I've heard or read has been to do with her business achievements.'

'Yes, she had quite a success story, didn't she? She was so far ahead of her time. A brilliant and truly emancipated woman who showed a lot of other women the way ... into big business and the corporate world. And I'm glad she did. I for one don't know what I'd do without the women executives in our company.'

Philip chuckled, suddenly looked amused again. 'But I'm sure everybody's forgotten about Emma's private life by now. It's old history. After all, it happened so long ago. Anyway, she has become something of a mythical figure. A legend. And there are any number of keepers of the flame around, both in the family and out ... who don't want her image tarnished in any way.' He pursed his lips, shook his head. 'Of course, as far as I'm concerned, nothing could tarnish Emma's image, least of all living out of wedlock with a man she truly loved – and with all her heart.'

'I agree with you. But *why* wouldn't she divorce him? His wife, I mean.'

'Her religion got in the way, and rather conveniently, *I* think. Constance McGill was a Roman Catholic, and *I* feel she simply hid behind the church and its teachings in order to frustrate Paul. She didn't want him, but she didn't want anyone else to have him. And she didn't want him to be happy, that's an *absolute* certainty. So, she put a bunch of priests and a lot of ridiculous religious mumbo-jumbo in the middle of their marital affairs, merely to confuse the issue, in my opinion.'

'Oh –'

Philip was acutely aware of Madelana, and he immediately saw the oddest look entering her eyes. Shrewd, sensitive, he knew instinctively that he had blundered. 'I've offended you ... you're a Roman Catholic, aren't you?'

'Yes, I am, but you haven't offended me. Honestly.'

'I'm so sorry.'

'It's all right, really Philip ...' Her voice trailed off. She glanced up at him.

Their eyes met and held. Neither of them could look away. The silence between them deepened.

As he stared into her luminous eyes, silvery, curiously transparent, Philip understood that it *was* all right. She meant exactly what she said, and would always mean it. For there was no guile in her. She was open and honest, and this pleased him. Once more, he had that peculiar feeling of familiarity. It was as if he had known her long ago, had been separated from her, and had found her again. He felt natural with her, comfortable as he had never been with any other woman, and completely at ease. *I want her*, he thought for the second time that morning. *And I aim to have her*. But go slowly, go very slowly, a voice inside him cautioned.

Madelana, held by his mesmeric blue gaze, was also filled with strange feelings, ones she had hitherto never experienced. Her throat was constricted and dry, she had a tight pain in her chest, and she was shaking inside. She was reacting strongly to Philip, physically and emotionally, and in a way she never had in her entire life, not even with Jack Miller. But then Philip McGill Amory was unique ... she had never met anyone like him before. He was so masculine, so potent, and there was all that charm. Fatal charm. He threw her off balance. And, worse still, he frightened her.

Inexplicably, Madelana thought she was about to burst into tears. She averted

611

her head swiftly, broke the eye contact between them. She had begun to tremble, and, afraid that he would notice, she walked to the other side of the gallery.

Clearing her throat, she said, without looking back at him, 'And which ancestor is this?'

Philip followed her across the room.

He stood directly behind her, breathing in the fragrance of her hair, her perfume. It was something spicy, musky almost, and he found it provocative. He had the sudden urge to put his arms around her, and he had to exercise enormous constraint not to do so.

In a tightly controlled voice, he said, 'Oh, that's Andrew, the Scottish sea captain, who came to Australia as a free settler in 1852, and that's his wife, Tessa, in the portrait next to his. Andrew was the founding father, settling here on this land, starting the sheep station, and putting down the original foundations of this house, which he called Dunoon, after the place he came from in Scotland.'

'It's a very beautiful house,' Madelana murmured in a husky voice, so conscious of Philip's proximity she could barely speak.

'Thank you . . . I think so, too. But actually, it was Andrew's son, Bruce, my great-grandfather, who gave the manor its feeling of the American Old South in the early 1900s, after a trip to America. He built the new façade, added the pillars, and superimposed the look of the plantations of Georgia and Virginia.'

'And Kentucky . . . it reminds me of home.'

Philip walked around her so that he was able to see her face, and his dark brows lifted in surprise. 'You come from bluegrass country?'

Madelana nodded.

'But you don't sound at all southern.'

'And you don't sound particularly Australian,' she said, and then she laughed for the first time since meeting him, and this eased the tension which had been building inside her. 'I was born and raised in Lexington.'

'Then you must have grown up around horses. You *did*, didn't you? And you *do* ride, don't you?'

'Yes.'

His eyes lit up, and his voice was buoyant as he exclaimed spontaneously, 'Come riding with me! *Now*. I want to show you the land, take you over the station . . . you can't have seen very much last night, especially in the dusk.' He glanced at her clothes. 'I'm sure we have breeches and boots to fit you.'

'I brought my own riding things,' Madelana said, then explained, 'Before we left New York, Paula told me we'd probably be coming here for a weekend, and to be prepared. In fact, she told me exactly which clothes to bring.'

'Smart girl, my sister,' he said, the lopsided grin sliding onto his mouth again. 'Come on then, what are we waiting for!'

Philip grabbed hold of her hand, hurried her out of the gallery and into the hall, adding, 'I'll have a quick cup of coffee in the breakfast room while you're changing. I'll be waiting for you in there.'

'I'll only be a few minutes,' she said quietly, swept up by the power and magnetism of this man.

612

True to her word, she arrived in the breakfast room within the space of ten minutes.

When she appeared in the doorway so quickly, he was surprised, but pleasantly so. Women who fussed about their hair and their makeup, and dawdled, and kept him waiting had always been an irritant to him. He was accustomed to the Harte women, who rarely primped but always looked smart, and he was glad Madelana fitted into this mould.

As he rose and went over to her, admiration flickered in his eyes. He liked the way she was dressed. She was obviously a genuine horsewoman, not an amateur who merely fancied herself in the get-up, and did not take riding seriously. Her clothes announced this to him. Her man-tailored, red-and-purple plaid wool shirt and cream breeches were in good condition, but by no means new, and her black boots, as highly polished as his own, were well worn and obviously a few years old.

Smiling broadly, taking her elbow, he led her out of the house and across the back courtyard to the garage.

As they walked past the collection of vintage cars lined up against the wall of the roofed-in walkway, he asked, 'Which way did you drive to the manor from the airfield last night?'

'Tim Willen brought us on the main road,' Madelana answered. 'I saw quite a lot of the station – the sheep pens, the shearing sheds, and that whole area of work buildings, as well as the compound.'

'Good-o . . . then we can get out to the countryside immediately, go for a *real* ride, instead of just puttering around,' he announced, helping her into his dark blue Maserati.

Philip had phoned through to the stables while she was changing, and when they arrived at the old buildings which she had so admired the night before, their horses were already saddled.

The head groom was waiting for them, and after Philip had introduced her to Matt, he took her over to the stalls. 'This is Gilda,' he said, opening the stall gate, leading out the roan mare. Handing Madelana the reins, he went on, 'She's all yours. You'll find she's gentle, but with enough spirit not to be too boring for you.'

Philip stepped away from the horse, and resisted the temptation to help Madelana mount.

'Thanks, she's beautiful,' Madelana said, looking at the roan appreciatively. She began to stroke and fondle the young mare's nose and head, and nuzzle her, then she whispered in her ear, endeavouring to make friends, as the grooms in Kentucky had taught her always to do with a strange horse. After a couple of minutes of this play, Madelana felt that they knew each other well enough, and she put her left foot in the stirrup, swung herself up into the saddle.

Philip had watched her performance with Gilda, nodding to himself at her expertise, and smiling inwardly. Now he mounted Black Opal, his glossy ebony-coloured stallion, and led the way out of the cobbled stable yard, across the main road, and down a dirt track that sloped towards a small copse.

They trotted single file along the narrow track overhung with golden elms and willows, and soon came out into a wide meadow where the green grass rippled under the light breeze. For a while they cantered side by side, and then unexpectedly Philip broke into a gallop, spurring Black Opal forward, leaving Madelana behind.

'Come on, Gilda girl, come on mah honey,' Madelana cooed, leaning forward on the mare's neck, rising slightly out of the saddle, standing as she broke into a gallop and streaked after Philip.

She caught up with him, and they galloped together through several adjoining meadows, jumping fences, racing neck and neck, until Philip finally slowed and reined-in Black Opal.

Madelana instantly followed suit, knowing that she must take his lead, since she was on strange ground and in unfamiliar surroundings.

As they caught their breath, they looked at each other.

'That was great. You're terrific,' Philip said. 'But we've got to cool it now, we're coming to the sheep and cattle grazing fields.'

'Yes, I understand,' she said.

They wandered at a gentle pace through the beautiful pastoral countryside, passing herds of cattle and flocks of sheep roaming the meadows and the lower slopes. They skirted copses filled with the ever-present golden elms and eucalyptus, and travelled along a deep and lovely valley, following the winding, silver thread of the river Castlereagh for a short way, and finally they went slowly up into the green hills of Dunoon.

They spoke intermittently.

Madelana asked the odd question now and again, and occasionally Philip volunteered bits of information, but for the most part they were quiet.

This pleased Philip. He did not always wish to talk, was frequently introspective and preoccupied and women who chattered nonstop got on his nerves. Her silence was like a balm. He was conscious of her in every respect, yet she was not an intrusion on him or his inbred sense of privacy, and there was no awkwardness between them, at least as far as he was concerned. In fact, just simply riding along with her like this made him feel lighter, happier than he had in years.

Madelana was having similar feelings.

The anxiety and tension she had experienced in the portrait gallery had lessened when she was in her room changing her clothes, had dissipated almost entirely during the time she had been out here in the open air with him.

Although New South Wales was as far away from Kentucky as anyone could get, she felt closer to home than she had since leaving her beloved bluegrass country four years ago. The stillness of the gardens, which had struck her so forcibly earlier that morning, was even more pronounced in this vast landscape, and the overwhelming peacefulness was filling her with a sense of tranquillity. And because she was relaxed, she was unexpectedly at ease with herself and with Philip.

They rode together across his land for almost two hours.

At last they came to the place he had been heading for since they had left the stables. It was the highest point on Dunoon, and Philip led the way up the steep incline. When he reached the top of the hill, he jumped down off Black Opal, stood waiting by the side of the horse for Madelana, who was only a short distance behind him.

She came up onto the crest, handling the roan beautifully and with the skill of a seasoned equestrian. Nevertheless, he wanted to help her dismount, but once again he refrained. He was afraid to touch her.

As she swung out of the saddle, dropped lightly to the grass, he strolled over to the huge oak that spread its ancient branches across the hilltop like a giant parasol of lacy green.

Madelana joined him, and he told her, 'My great-great-grandfather planted this oak over a hundred years ago, and this is my favourite spot. It was Emma who first brought me up here when I was a little boy – she loved it, too. You can see for miles around. Just look!' he exclaimed, flinging his arm out in a sudden sweeping gesture. Then he shaded his eyes with his hand, gazed out across the undulating terrain, and there was pride and love in his voice, when he said 'There's nowhere in the world like it, at least not for me.'

'It is staggeringly beautiful,' Madelana replied, meaning her words. Everything seemed more vivid to her at Dunoon . . . the sky looked infinitely bluer, the clouds whiter, the grass and trees greener, the flowers more colourful. It was a paradise, as he had said earlier when they were riding through the valley. She took several deep breaths. The air was crystal clear up here, and so pure and bracing.

Philip took off his wide brimmed hat, threw it down, ran his hand through his thick black hair. 'Let's take a rest before heading back,' he suggested, motioned to the ground, and sat down.

Madelana nodded, also seated herself, enjoying the dark-green coolness under the shady tree after their long ride in the sun.

They were both silent for a short while, and then Philip said, 'It must have been wonderful to feel the way they did, don't you think?'

'Yes,' Madelana said, understanding immediately that he was referring to Paul and Emma.

'Have you ever been in love like that?' Philip asked.

'No, have you?'

'No.' He immediately fell silent, slipped down into his thoughts, and Madelana was quiet.

'Are you married?' he asked suddenly.

'No, I'm not . . . nor have I ever been.'

Philip gave her a sidelong glance. He wanted to ask her if she was involved with anyone special but he did not dare. Already the conversation had been more breathtakingly personal than he had intended.

As if aware that he was studying her surreptitiously, she turned her head, gave him a long look through those quiet, unwavering grey eyes.

He smiled at her.

She smiled back. Then she pulled her knees up to her chest, rested her chin on them, sat staring out into the blue-and-white haze of sky and cumulus clouds, drifting.

Philip leaned back, rested his head against the gnarled tree trunk. Intuitively, he knew that she knew about his reputation as a playboy. He stifled a sigh. It had never bothered him in the past. Now it did. He wondered how he was going to overcome this with her.

18

The evening had turned suddenly cool, and a strong wind was blowing down from the hills above Dunoon, ruffling the curtains, making them billow about wildly, and chilling the air in her bedroom.

Paula shivered, rose from the dressing table, and went to close the window. Once seated again, she picked up her pearl choker, fastened it around her neck, put on the *mabé* pearl-and-diamond earrings, and then sat back, staring at her reflection in the mirror. Not bad, she thought, for an overworked executive and harassed wife and mother of four who's knocking thirty-seven.

She turned her head, glanced at the colour photograph on the dressing table. It was of Shane and her with Lorne, Tessa, Patrick and Linnet, taken by Emily on the terrace of Pennistone Royal in the spring. Her heart tightened imperceptibly when she thought of her two youngest children; in their different ways they were both so vulnerable, and they needed her.

They had been in bed and fast asleep when she had phoned Shane earlier that morning. With the difference in time between Australia and England she was actually one day ahead, and it had been almost midnight on Friday when she had reached him at Pennistone Royal. He had just returned from dinner with Winston at Beck House; Emily had already left for Hong Kong, on her buying trip for Genret, and apparently the two best friends had enjoyed a rare bachelor evening together.

It had been wonderful to hear his loving and reassuring voice, to know that all was well at home. Lorne and Tessa were now properly settled in at their respective boarding schools, and Nanny Pat was back from her week's holiday in the Lake District, and was once again in command of the nursery and her young charges.

'No problems, darling,' Shane had said, sounding so close he might have been in the next room. 'I'll spend the weekend here with the kids, then push off to London on Sunday night. And listen, angel, I heard from Dad today. He phoned to tell me he and Mother are definitely coming for Christmas, and so young Laura will be with us too, and Merry and Elliot have also accepted. It looks as if we're going to have quite a mob with us up here in Yorkshire . . . it'll be like the old days when Blackie and Emma were alive. We'll have a wonderful time.'

His news had delighted her, and they had chatted for another half hour about the Christmas plans, the children, and other family matters, and Shane had promised to ring her in a couple of days. She had felt much better when she had hung up. She missed him and the children enormously when she was travelling, was never completely at ease when she was separated from her family. She tried not to worry, but invariably she did, and she suspected she would never change. Her nature, after all, was her nature.

Paula glanced at her watch, saw that she had ten minutes to spare before going downstairs for drinks. Rising, smoothing down the skirt of her silk cocktail dress, she walked across to the writing desk where she began to sort through the papers strewn there. Among them were the Christmas lists she had started in Sydney earlier in the week. Shane's family were marked down for major gifts, but not for stocking stuffers and tree presents. She must add their names, now that they were coming to Yorkshire, along with ideas for suitable little tokens, since she planned to do all of her Christmas shopping in Hong Kong when she met Emily there in ten days.

Paula's thoughts focused on Shane's parents as she leaned over the desk, rapidly making notes for herself. She was truly thrilled that Bryan and Geraldine were coming to England in December; they had been ambivalent about it for a number of weeks. Ever since Bryan's heart attack five years ago they had been living in Barbados. Bryan kept an eye on the other O'Neill hotels in the Caribbean, but for the most part he took it easy these days, and was semi-retired at Shane's insistence.

She missed them, and there had been a void in all their lives since the O'Neills had lived abroad. She missed Miranda, too. She and Shane's sister had been close friends from childhood, and although they managed to see each other in New York, they were forever grumbling that they never had enough time together these days. As head of O'Neill Hotels International in the United States, Merry was a busy executive, and now that she was married to the noted American architect, Elliot James, she wanted to spend any free time she had with him at their homes in Manhattan and Connecticut. In consequence, Merry had not been to England much lately, and even her business trips were brief. 'Hit and runs,' Merry laughingly called them.

For once all the O'Neills would be under one roof at the same time, along with the Hartes. Sir Ronald and Michael Kallinski had already accepted to come for Christmas dinner, so the three clans would be represented for the first time in years. This thought made Paula smile with pleasure.

Clipping the sheaf of papers together, she slipped them into her briefcase for safe keeping. When she had another free moment, either later tonight or tomorrow morning, she would make a few more notes, allocate bedrooms at Pennistone Royal, do the menus for the holiday period, and start the guest lists for the parties she wanted to give. Christmas was three months away, but that was not really very long, not with the schedule she had, and all she had to accomplish. Planning ahead, being well organized, was the only way she knew how to cope with everything. That was how she had been brought up by her grandmother, and sometimes she wondered if this was indeed the secret of her success.

Paula believed herself to be the first one downstairs when she stood in the doorway of the living room a few minutes later. It was so hushed, so still.

But then Jason Rickards stepped into the room from the verandah, closed the French windows, locked them firmly, and swung around. His tanned, craggy face lit up when he saw her.

'Hi there, sweet'art,' he said, striding across the floor towards her.

Lean and rangy, Jason had the gait of a man who had spent years on a horse, a weatherbeaten complexion from being constantly outdoors, and dark hair silvered at the sides. He was in his early sixties, but looked younger. Tonight he wore a navy-blue cashmere jacket and dark-grey trousers, with a white shirt and a navy tie, and was as impeccable as he generally was, but to Paula he seemed to be uncomfortable when he was dressed up for the evening. It was as if more formal clothes constrained him, and she couldn't help thinking that Jason would much prefer to be in blue jeans, riding boots and an open-necked shirt.

Coming to a standstill, he caught one of her hands in his, twirled her around. 'My, you look pretty, Paula. Red suits you as much as it does your mother.'

'Thank you, Jason.' Paula smiled up into his face, tucked her arm through his, and walked with him to the fireplace. 'Where is Mummy, anyway?'

'Upstairs, finishing dressing. She'll be down in a minute. Now, me darlin', let's have a drink together. What would you like?'

'If that's a bottle of champagne I spy over there in the silver bucket, then that's what I'll have, please.'

'Good-o.' He loped over to the console, where a tray of liquor, glasses, a bucket of ice, and the champagne stood, and proceeded to open the bottle of Louis Roederer Crystal.

Paula watched him, her eyes full of warmth. She thoroughly approved of Jason, had grown very fond of him, admired his down-to-earth attitude towards life. Her respect for him was immense, not only because of his brilliance as a businessman, but for his personal qualities as well. He was kind, thoughtful, caring. Like Philip, she was overjoyed that her mother had become his wife. Despite the disparities in their backgrounds, they got along beautifully and he was a devoted husband. A self-made man, Jason had married late for the first time, and had lost his wife from cancer after only seven years; he had then had a very brief, very disastrous second marriage. 'Third time lucky,' was his favourite expression these days, and he was most adoring of Daisy, as she was of him. Sometimes they reminded Paula of a couple of young lovers, and this pleased her.

Pouring champagne into a Baccarat crystal flute, then mixing a scotch and soda for himself, Jason remarked, 'It's damn windy out there tonight, Paula. I bet you there's one helluva damn storm down in Sydney.'

'I hope it doesn't hit here,' she said, accepting the glass from him when he brought it to her.

'I doubt it will, and if it does, it'll soon blow over. We always get a drop of rain in the spring, you know. And we'll have a nice sunny day tomorrow, never fear.' He clinked his glass to hers. 'Cheers, darlin'.'

'Cheers, Jason.'

They stood together in front of the fire, perfectly at ease, full of affection for each other.

Suddenly Jason eyed her speculatively. 'There you go again, Paula, smilin' quietly, and looking mighty damn pleased with yourself.' He chuckled. 'As your mother would say, you look like the cat that's swallowed the canary.'

Paula could not help laughing. Jason had adopted many of her mother's expressions, almost all of which had originated with her grandmother, but they did not sound quite the same without Emma's pithy delivery.

She said, 'I'm thrilled about the way Christmas is shaping up, Jason, that's all. It's going to be the biggest get-together we've had in years, now that Shane's parents and sisters are coming.'

'Your mother's worried that –'

'What am I worried about?' Daisy asked from the doorway, and floated into the living room on a cloud of *joy* perfume and a swirl of purple silk.

'Sweet'art, you look gorgeous!' Jason exclaimed, his dark brown eyes glowing with love and admiration. He hurried to Daisy, took her arm, ushered her over to the fireplace. 'What can I get for you, sweet'art? Champagne, or a vodka tonic?'

'Champagne, please, Jason darling.'

'Jason's right, you *do* look fabulous tonight, Mummy,' Paula said. 'I've not seen you in purple for years. It's a great colour for you, and simply marvellous with those exquisite opals. Are they new?'

'Thank you, dear, and yes, they are. Jason gave them to me on Thursday night. They're from his mine in Coober Pedy.'

'Lightning Ridge,' Jason corrected, grinning, bringing her the drink. 'They're very rare black opals, Paula.'

'Thanks,' Daisy said, taking the glass. She repeated, 'And what am I worried about, Jason?'

'Philip.'

Daisy frowned, sat down on the sofa, raised her flute. 'Cheers.'

'Cheers,' Paula and Jason said in unison.

Daisy took a sip of the champagne, peered quizzically at her husband over the rim. 'And *why* am I worried about him?'

'Because he's so reluctant to commit himself . . . about coming to England with us for Christmas,' Jason explained. 'Paula was just remarking how thrilled she is about the big family reunion and I was on the verge of telling her that her brother was undecided about his plans.'

'Oh I think he'll come now,' Daisy murmured with a small, but knowing smile.

'You *do*?' Jason sounded surprised and he stared hard at Daisy. 'What's happened to make you change your mind, sweet'art? You were pretty damn adamant about it when I got back from Perth on Thursday night, and that's only two days ago.'

'At lunch today Paula invited Madelana to go to London for Harte's sixtieth anniversary dinner and dance at the Ritz, and she also invited her to spend Christmas with us in Yorkshire. And Madelana accepted, didn't she, Paula?'

'Well, yes, she did, Mummy.' Paula seemed slightly baffled, and she frowned. 'But what's that got to do with anything?'

Daisy sat back, beamed first at her daughter, and then at her husband, and said, 'It has everything to do with Philip coming to England in December.'

Both Jason and Paula gaped at her, but neither of them said a word.

'Haven't you noticed how Philip looks at Madelana?' Daisy asked softly. 'When he thinks no one else is watching, of course. And haven't you also noticed how he was behaving around her today . . . at the pool, during lunch, and at tea time? *So very solicitous*. And they were out riding *all* morning, you know, Paula. For about four hours or so.'

'Oh Mummy, honestly, you're such a romantic!' Paula exclaimed. 'He was merely being a good host. After all, you brought him up to be well mannered. He's a gentleman.' Paula laughed dismissively. 'He's only known her for *one* day! Not even that, for heaven's sake!'

'So what?' Daisy said, and took another sip of champagne.

Paula frowned at her mother, then looked at Jason, raising a brow.

Jason let out an amused chortle. 'I'd only known your mother for one hour when I realized I wanted to marry her, and I was hell bent on getting her, I don't mind telling you, Paula. I think a man and a woman *know* immediately if they've clicked in a special way, *know* how they truly feel about each other. It's kind of . . . well, it's kind of an instinctive thing. And *time*, as such, doesn't make a helluva lot of difference. You can know a person for years, yet never really know them, feel nothing for them. Or you can suddenly meet someone, and *bang*! That's it!' He glanced across at Daisy. 'What's that French expression, sweet'art?'

'*Coup de foudre*. . . a clap of thunder, an unexpected blow . . . meaning love at first sight,' Daisy replied. 'And you're absolutely right, Jason, I agree with everything you say.' She smiled at him lovingly.

'*Madelana and Philip*,' Paula muttered. 'Oh no!' Her heart sank. She adored her brother, but the last thing she wanted was for him to become involved with Madelana. For Madelana's sake. She did not want her to get hurt. Also, she had her own plans for her assistant in the future.

Paula said slowly, 'He might be interested in her, Mother, but you know full well what he's like with women. He thinks they're a dime a dozen. Why, he's told me that so many times, and *you* also know better than *anyone* that he breaks off with them the minute the relationship starts developing into something more meaningful than a romp in the hay.' She shook her head. 'I hate to say this about him, but Philip is actually only interested in one-night stands.'

'Really, Paula, how can you make a statement like that! He went out with Veronica Marsden for almost three months,' Daisy exclaimed vehemently, although she kept her voice low and muted.

Paula groaned wearily. 'Yes, that *is* about the duration of his affairs, isn't it? *Three months*. I sincerely hope he *doesn't* get involved with Maddy, because he'll only cause her heartache, and that I couldn't bear. She's had too much pain in her life already. Please don't encourage him, Ma. Promise me.'

Daisy's face dropped. 'Yes, I suppose you're right, as usual, Paula.' She let out a heavy sigh. 'Oh, dear, and I do like her so much. I was so happy today, when I saw how keen he seemed to be . . .' Her voice tapered off lamely.

Paula insisted, 'Mummy, please promise me you won't encourage Philip. I'm very *serious* about this.'

Daisy nodded swiftly. 'Oh, I do, dear, I do.' She instantly noticed Paula's stern, almost forbidding expression, and added, '*I promise*.' Daisy recognized that her daughter was only reiterating what she herself had been thinking earlier in the week, and dismay lodged in the pit of her stomach. She could not bear to think that her son was destined to be a playboy for the rest of his life. What an empty and shallow existence that would be for him.

Jason said, 'I think we'd better get off this subject mighty damn sharpish. I'm sure they'll both be down any minute.'

'Of course, Jason,' Daisy was quick to agree. 'And it really isn't very nice, talking about them in this way, is it?'

'No,' Paula muttered, still feeling disturbed, and wondering why *she* hadn't noticed Philip's behaviour around Madelana, the attention he had supposedly paid to her. Renowned in the family for being eagle-eyed, for never missing a trick, she suddenly asked herself if she was slipping.

Jason strolled over to the console, refilled his glass, and remarked, 'By the way, Paula, when are you planning to go to Hong Kong?'

'Not for about ten days or so. It really depends on what I find in Melbourne and Adelaide. Madelana and I are flying down there on Wednesday, once we've got the Sydney boutique organized for the sale. But why do you ask, Jason?'

'One of my executives, Don Metcalfe, has to go over to the crown colony around that time. It occurred to me that you might like a lift on the corporate jet.'

'Gosh, Jason, that would be wonderful,' Paula exclaimed, smiling at him. 'If our dates coincide, of course.'

'Don can leave any time around the twenty-first, the twenty-second or even the twenty-third of September, whichever suits you, darlin'.'

'Thanks so much, I'll let you know.'

'You never did say why you're going to Hong Kong, dear,' Daisy murmured, giving Paula a questioning look.

'To meet Emily, Mummy. She's there now, on one of her buying trips for General Retail Trading, and we thought it would be fun to have a few days together, relaxing, doing our Christmas shopping. Then we'll continue on to New York, spend a day or two there, return to London on the Concorde.'

Daisy smiled somewhat ruefully. 'I don't know, Paula, here you are, the head of one of the greatest department stores in the world, and you have to do your shopping in Hong Kong.' She shook her head, looking a trifle perplexed. 'It doesn't make sense to me.'

Paula grinned at her mother. 'It's much more fun shopping in foreign places –' She cut her sentence off when Madelana appeared in the doorway. 'There you are, Maddy! I was thinking of sending out a search party,' Paula teased, her expression affectionate.

In view of the previous discussion, three pairs of alert and curious eyes automatically fastened on Madelana as she glided across the floor with her usual gracefulness, her stylish, elegant and beautifully-cut dress moving with fluidity around her long legs.

'Forgive me for being so late,' Madelana apologized. 'I decided to have a rest earlier, and promptly fell asleep. It must be all the fresh air I've had today . . . and the riding. I haven't been on a horse in a coon's age.'

'Then you'll feel it tomorrow,' Jason warned. 'You'll have damn sore muscles. Take a very hot bath filled with Epsom salts tonight, that'll help a bit. I know Mrs Carr has plenty of salts in the kitchen. We'll get a box or two for you before you go to bed. Now, what can I get you to drink? A glass of champagne?'

'Thanks, Jason, but I'd prefer a mineral water for the moment,' Madelana murmured, and joined Paula in front of the fireplace.

Paula eyed Madelana's cocktail dress. It was a superb piece of clothing, made of cut velvet on silk chiffon, and was a light grey colour that emphasized the silvery lights in her eyes. Paula said, 'That dress is perfection on you, Maddy. It's a Trigère, isn't it?'

'Yes, it is, and thank you very much.' Madelana smiled at her boss. 'You're pretty elegant yourself . . . that's a Christina Crowther.'

'Yes, but an old one which I left here a couple of years ago. Still, it's not a bit dated is it? Like Pauline Trigère's clothes, Christina's have a wonderful timelessness.'

Daisy was smiling approvingly at Madelana. 'Paula just took the words right out of my mouth, Maddy, you *do* look particularly lovely tonight.' Patting the sofa, she added, 'Come, six next to me, dear.'

Madelana did so, and the two of them immediately fell into a conversation about clothes, and the merits of various fashion designers in New York, Paris and London.

Paula continued to hover in front of the fire, only half listening to Daisy and Maddy. She had the distinct feeling that her mother *would* encourage Philip in his pursuit of Madelana, if indeed he *was* interested, despite Daisy's promise to her to the contrary. Her mother was desperate for him to get married, and it was patently obvious she thought Madelana was the perfect candidate for daughter-in-law.

Jason brought Madelana a Perrier water, carrying the champagne bottle in his other hand. He topped up Paula's glass, then Daisy's, and as he walked back to the console, he said over his shoulder, 'Philip's late coming down, Paula. I hope everything's all right on the station. That wind is damn strong, more like a gale, if you ask me.'

Paula said, 'I'm sure there's nothing wrong, Jason. Oh, here he comes now.'

Philip sauntered into the living room a split second later, looking nonchalant, without a care. He apologized for being late, adding, 'Tim Willen kept me on the phone longer than I expected.'

'Any problems with the weather?' Jason asked.

'None at all,' Philip assured him. 'And how about fixing your old cobber a scotch on the rocks, since you're standing right next to the bottle, Jason?'

19

The cautionary voice inside his head had warned Philip to go slow with Madelana. But on this Wednesday night, ten days after meeting her at Dunoon, he was asking himself if he had perhaps gone *too* slowly.

He walked across the living room of his penthouse atop the McGill Tower and stood looking out of the window absently, for once not seeing the magnificent view of the harbour which he so loved. He was thoroughly preoccupied with his interior meanderings.

Instinctively, he had known not to rush Madelana, had recognized that he had his reputation as a womanizer to overcome with her. If she had thought she was merely going to be another notch on his belt, she would have undoubtedly fled from him. But she was rarely if ever out of his thoughts. He was obsessed with her, and his longing to know her more intimately had created the most enormous tension within him; there had been times lately when he had felt as though he was about to explode.

I *should* have made my moves before, he thought dismally, regretting the way he had delayed, acknowledging that time was running out on him. She would be leaving soon for the States. On the other hand, even if he had decided to go more quickly with her, it would have been difficult to do so with Paula around.

His sister had become Madelana's self-appointed chaperone during the weekend at Dunoon. She had not left them alone for one minute on the Sunday. Wherever they went, she went too, and then she had spirited Madelana off to Melbourne and Adelaide for most of the following week, and the two of them had not returned to Sydney until Friday evening.

In their absence, he had hit on the idea of showing Madelana the sights of Sydney, thinking that at least he would get to know her *better*, if not more intimately. But Paula had accompanied them on their jaunts around the city, and, whilst it had been fun, it had not been what he had originally planned. Although seduction had not been his intent, he had thought a bit of mild flirting would enable him to test the waters. But once they were a threesome this was impossible.

A wry smile touched Philip's mouth as he reflected on the past few days. Just as Paula had striven hard never to leave them alone together, so his mother had done everything in her power to push him towards Madelana. Without appearing to do so, of course. But he had seen through Daisy's discreet little ploys. Sadly, none of them had worked, because of Paula's vigilance.

Finally, his sister had left this morning for Hong Kong.

He had driven her to the airport himself, and on the way there he had told her that he intended to invite Madelana out for dinner that evening.

'Yes, I suspected you would,' Paula had said. There had been a small silence between them, before he had exclaimed, 'She's twenty-seven, Paula, and a grown woman. Not to mention extremely intelligent, and quite capable of making her own decisions. You shouldn't have done her thinking for her, nor should you have interfered ... you haven't been fair to me, or to her. And that's so unlike you, darling.'

At once, his sister had apologized, had admitted that he was absolutely right, and she had tried to explain her protectiveness. 'I care about Madelana,' Paula had said. 'She's one of the most special women I've ever met, and I couldn't bear it if you, of all people, did anything to cause her grief.' She had then gone on to tell him something about Madelana's past, the tragedies that had befallen her family, her dreadful losses, and he had been profoundly touched. He had promised Paula he would do nothing to hurt her assistant, and he intended to keep his promise.

Philip glanced down at his watch. It was seven-forty and time to go. Turning away from the floor-to-ceiling window, he hurried across the huge, modern living room decorated entirely in shades of white and cream, and went on through the marble foyer at the same rapid pace. He was going to be alone with Madelana at last and he could not wait to get to her.

As he rode down in his private elevator, it suddenly struck him that he had no idea whether Madelana was interested in him or not. Her behaviour had not revealed her thoughts or her feelings; her calm grey eyes had told him nothing. In fact, the only certain thing was the way he felt about her. It was quite possible that she would consider his overtures repugnant and so reject him.

The same wry smile flickered in the cool blue eyes. He would soon find out exactly where he stood with her . . . if anywhere at all.

Madelana's suite at the Sydney-O'Neill was on the thirtieth floor of the hotel. It covered a corner of the building, and the L-shaped expanse of windows in the sitting room offered panoramic vistas.

She stood at one of the windows, looking out towards the Opera House on Bennelong Point and the Sydney Harbour Bridge beyond. It was almost eight o'clock, and the night sky was aglow with stars and the myriad lights of the city.

The spectacular view was familiar to her by now, and she was beginning to feel at home here, had become enamoured of Sydney and its people. She had quickly discovered she liked the Australians, who were down to earth, open, friendly, and she had come to understand, through Philip, that their sardonic humour was simply an insurance against pomposity and pretentiousness. 'It goes way back, to the early settlers, the Cockneys in particular,' he had explained.

Walking over to the sofa, Madelana sat down. Spread out on the coffee table were the photographs which had been taken last weekend on their sight-seeing tour of the city. She began to sort through them, selecting the best for the album she had bought that afternoon.

Memories of the weekend brought a smile to her face. Here was one of Paula and herself at Taronga Park Zoo. They were standing next to a kangaroo with a joey in its pouch, and again it struck her how much the roo reminded her of a deer with its narrow, sensitive face and tender, soulful eyes. She had not realized they were such gentle animals until her visit to the zoo on Saturday morning. The photo was good and she put it on one side to include in the album later.

Picking up a shot of Philip and Paula, which she had taken in the rainforest aviary at Taronga, she marvelled again at the jewel-coloured parrots and other brilliant, exotic birds shown in the background. This was another must for the album. Next she reached for the small stack of pictures taken on Philip's boat, the *Saraband*. He owned two yachts. The one called *Dunoon*, after the sheep station, was used solely for racing; the *Saraband* was for cruising and entertaining. Magnificently decorated and appointed, it slept six, and had a permanent crew.

To Madelana, Sunday had been the best day of the weekend. Certainly she had revelled in their jaunt up the coastline, past Philip's house at Point Piper, and Daisy's and Jason's at Rose Bay. Loving the sea as much as she did, the excursion on the water had been wonderful for her. Deciding that the yachting trip should take pride of place in the album, she selected a handful of snaps of the three of them on board the *Saraband*, and fanned them out in front of her.

A shot of Philip caught her eye, and she picked it up, studied it for a moment.

Paula had not told her very much about him before they had left New York, and what little she did know had been gleaned from various magazines, where she had also seen pictures of him from time to time. Now, staring at the snap in her hand, she realized that nothing could have prepared her for Philip McGill Amory. His presence overwhelmed her. There was something about him, something within him, that reached out to her, moved her in a way she had never been moved before by any other human being. Her reaction to him had been intense from the first moment she had set eyes on him at Dunoon. She felt unsteady when she was with him, and breathless, almost as if she had been punched in the stomach.

Peering closer at the picture, she could not help thinking how debonair and dashing he looked, standing there on the deck of the beautiful *Saraband*. His sailing whites emphasized his tan, his vivid colouring. It had been windy on Sunday, and his black hair was ruffled, his laughing blue eyes screwed up against the glare of brilliant sunlight and glittering sea. How irresistible he seemed.

She was most powerfully drawn to him, and this disturbed and worried her for a number of reasons. He was her boss's brother, but quite aside from this, he was hardly likely to be interested in her. He was immensely powerful, immensely rich, and devastatingly attractive, and therefore he could have any woman in the world he wanted. His reputation as a playboy only verified this as a fact. A career girl like herself, who was not a member of the international social circles he moved in, was hardly a candidate for one of his romantic interludes. Nor did she care to be. The last thing she wanted was a quick fling. She was not cut out for one-night stands or brief encounters. No, Philip McGill Amory was not the kind of man a woman like her should *ever* become involved with. He was too dangerous, guaranteed to wreak havoc and heartbreak.

I don't need any more problems with beautiful, difficult men, she thought, remembering her recent experiences with Jack Miller. Her career was her priority now. And in any case, she would be leaving Sydney in ten days, and that would be that. She and Paula had fortunately found a manager for the boutique yesterday. The young woman met all of Paula's requirements, and had already started working on a week's trial. Providing all went well, she would soon be winging her way back to New York . . . far, far away from Mr Amory.

The telephone on the writing desk shrilled and she went to answer it. 'Hello?'

'It's Philip,' he said, 'I'm in the lobby.'

'I'll be right down,' she said, and replaced the receiver. Picking up her bag, her silk shawl, and the doorkey, she left the suite.

Going down in the elevator, she wondered what the evening would be like. She had accepted his invitation against her better judgement, and only because he had been so charming and gracious, just a little bit insistent on the phone that morning. Also, being who he was, she had not wanted to offend him. But this was the first time she was going to be alone with him since they had gone riding at the sheep station, and sudden nervousness invaded her.

She saw him the moment she stepped out of the elevator.

He wore a dark-blue blazer, a pale-blue shirt and tie, and grey slacks. He dominated the lobby with his height and his arresting looks, his inbred self-confidence, and his commanding air of authority.

When he saw her he raised a hand in greeting, and strode towards her.

She instantly tensed up in the way she had when she had met him in the portrait gallery, and she almost missed a step as she walked across the marble floor. Then she took hold of herself, and pushed a bright smile onto her face, and as they came together in the middle of the lobby, she extended her hand, still smiling.

Philip took it, gave it a small squeeze, instantly released it. Looking down at her, he returned her smile, and said, 'It's nice to see you, Madelana, you look lovely, as usual.' He glanced approvingly at her full, black wool skirt and the tailored, white silk shirt.

'Thank you. You did say to dress simply.'

'Yes,' he murmured, escorting her across the lobby, then explained, 'I've booked a table at Doyle's . . . it's a fish restaurant on the beach. Very casual, lots of fun, and they have the best fish and chips in Sydney, not to mention the most wonderful view of the city skyline from there.'

'It sounds terrific.'

They went out into the street. His wine-coloured Rolls-Royce was parked immediately in front of the hotel, and after helping her inside, Philip strode around to the driver's side, got in, turned on the ignition, and pulled away from the kerb.

'Doyle's is out at Watson's Bay,' he informed her. 'It'll take us about half an hour. So sit back, relax, and enjoy the music.' As he spoke he turned on the tape in the dashboard and the voice of Mel Tormé singing *Moonlight in Vermont* filled the interior of the car.

Madelana tried to do as he suggested, not even attempting to make conversation. She could think of nothing to say to him. Unexpected panic choked her, made her throat dry. She did not know how she would manage to get through the evening. Sitting here next to him, in such close proximity, she was filled with some awful kind of terror, and she fervently wished she had not accepted his invitation.

'Relax,' he said, as if reading her mind.

She looked at him through the corner of her eye, and laughed nervously.

'I am relaxed.'

'No, I don't think so.'

She was silent. She bit her inner lip.

Now it was his turn to laugh, and he sounded as nervous as she had.

Eventually, he murmured in a low voice, 'We both work too hard, I suspect, and I suppose you've had as rough a day as I have. It takes a while to unwind . . . and I haven't been very thoughtful. I should have taken you for a drink at the bar in the hotel first.'

'No, I'm fine,' she told him, and realized that this was partially true. The feeling of panic was easing somewhat. Anyway, she was being silly, wasn't she? He had no way of knowing how attracted she was to him. Thank God. She had cultivated a bland face for the past few days, worn an inscrutable expression especially for him. Anyway, he was obviously only being polite, taking care of her for Paula. Undoubtedly, it was her boss who had asked him to take her out. Paula was always so thoughtful, so solicitous of her welfare.

The exterior architecture of Doyle's had lovely Victorian mannerisms. Made of red brick and beige stone, the building was two storeys high, and its upstairs balconies were decorated with fancy, pierced-wood valances painted white, which were repeated around the edge of the front portico. The rooms inside were bright and cheerful, simply furnished, and without pretension; there was a pub-like atmosphere.

It was busy when they arrived, but Philip was quickly shown to a table in a quiet, windowed corner overlooking the beach and the dark sea curling away to the edge of a dim horizon. He insisted Madelana take the chair facing towards the city, and, just as he had said earlier, the view of Sydney from Watson's Bay was breathtaking, with the McGill Tower dominating the skyline.

He ordered a bottle of Pouilly Fuissé, dry and cold and refreshing, and as they sipped it he asked her about the new manager, and how the grand sale was going at the boutique. She felt on safe ground, talking about business, and as they chatted she began to relax further, and so did he. He answered her questions about their opal mines at Coober Pedy and Lightning Ridge, told her about opal mining in general, and he talked at length about the various divisions of the giant conglomerate he ran. The McGill Corporation fascinated her, and she gave him her entire attention, as always intrigued by big business. Before either of them realized it almost an hour had passed.

'I think we'd better order,' Philip said, when the waitress appeared at their table for the third time.

'I'll have the same as you, please,' Madelana murmured, after a quick glance at the menu.

He grinned. 'Fried fish and chips . . . how does that sound?'

'Just great. Thanks.'

Once he had ordered dinner, he asked her exactly what she did for Paula at Harte's in New York, and she told him a little about her work, how she had been planning and organizing the special events for the sixtieth anniversary of the stores.

When she finished, he laughed, shook his head. 'And I thought Paula was a workaholic! My God, you're as bad as she is!'

'I guess I am,' Madelana agreed, also laughing, enjoying being alone with him; her apprehension of earlier had entirely dissipated.

'And tell me, how do you manage to have a private life, working the way you do? Doesn't your boyfriend object?'

'I don't have one.'

'Oh.' A black brow lifted. 'A girl like you . . . so beautiful . . . so bright . . .' He did not finish, merely stared at her intently, puzzlement flickering.

Ignoring his compliments, she said softly, 'I just broke up with someone.'

'I'm sorry.'

'You don't have to be. It was for the best . . . I'd made an error in judgement.' Now the black brows drew together in a frown. 'What do you mean?'

'I mistook personality for character.'

'Ah, I *see*,' he said, liking the shrewdness of this observation. He was suddenly eaten up with curiosity about the man she had so recently been involved with, and he couldn't help probing. 'What does he do? You know, for a living?'

'He's an actor. A rather brilliant one, too. On the Broadway stage.'

'Famous? Would I know him?'

'Possibly . . . probably. Jack Miller.'

'Oh sure, I saw him in something a couple of years ago when I was in New York. A Eugene O'Neill play, I think.'

Madelana nodded.

'What went wrong between the two of you?'

Madelana bit her inner lip, glanced away.

But after a brief moment, she brought her eyes back to his, smiled faintly. 'Mah daddy used to say there's nothing worse than the ole moonshine for killin' a romance and curin' a woman of fanciful ideas she might be havin' about a dude. Ah doan know that a truer word has ever been spoken.'

Philip smiled, loving the sudden, Southern intonation in her voice. It was soft, beguiling, very feminine. 'Now you really sound as though you come from Kentucky,' he said. 'And I must admit, I agree with your daddy . . . about a drinking man.'

'It wasn't just the booze,' she now said in her New York voice. 'Jack was always a bit odd with me . . . about my work, I mean. He is a male chauvinist, by his own admission, and he resented my career. Anyway –'

At this moment the waitress arrived with their food, and Madelana changed the subject by asking him about yacht racing. Since this was Philip's favourite sport and his only genuine hobby, he was happy to discuss it with her. And when he finally paused, she told him how much she loved the sea, and how she had first gone sailing with the Smiths at Nantucket.

'I met Patsy Smith the first day I arrived at the residence, and we became friends instantly. And we're still close, even though she's gone back to Boston.'

'What's the residence?' Philip asked, between mouthfuls of fish.

'It's a place in Manhattan where Catholic girls and young women can live comfortably for very little money. It's run by the Sisters of Divine Providence, a teaching order of nuns from Kentucky.' She proceeded to tell him about Sister Bronagh, the other nuns, what life had been like at the residence, and her early days in New York.

Philip listened carefully, nodding from time to time, occasionally laughing at her anecdotes. But he did not interrupt her once. She was opening up to him tonight, revealing a great deal about herself for the first time, and he wanted to encourage this. He needed to know everything there was to know about this woman. She was under his skin.

628

It was later, over coffee, that Philip suddenly said, 'I thought you might like to come up to Dunoon this weekend, Madelana. It'll do you good after all your running around with Paula, all your hard work. And it *is* your last chance, since you're leaving at the end of next week. Aren't you?'

'Yes, I am.' She lifted her cup, took a sip of the coffee.

He waited a moment, then pressed her. 'Say you'll come, Madelana. I want you to . . . so very much.'

An odd nuance in his voice made her glance at him more closely, and she saw there was a curious expression in his eyes, one she could not quite fathom. And then intuitively she knew he was interested in her, and she felt a sudden tightening in her chest. She found it impossible to speak. Her throat went tight and dry again. She instantly understood that to go to Dunoon with him would be playing with fire. Therefore she must refuse his invitation. To protect herself. That was the only wise thing to do.

She said, 'Yes, I'd love to come. Thank you very much, Philip.' As these words left her mouth, she sat back in the chair, surprised at herself, and at her perversity. You fool, she thought. You're just asking for trouble.

Philip was beaming at her and saying, 'We can fly up tomorrow afternoon.'

'No, no, I can't go then,' she exclaimed quickly, staring at him. 'I've got to be at the boutique. I couldn't possibly come until Saturday.'

'Friday,' he insisted, holding her with his eyes. 'You can come up Friday morning. Everything will be all right at the boutique. Don't worry so much.'

She swallowed hard, wondering why she had ever accepted. 'I must go into the boutique for a couple of hours at least,' she compromised.

'Okay, if you say so,' Philip agreed. 'But Ken will collect you there at eleven, drive you out to the airport. My plane will be waiting, and if you leave Sydney at noon, you'll get to the station in time for lunch.' Philip smiled deeply into her eyes, reached out, took her hand, held it in both of his.

Madelana nodded, not trusting herself to speak.

20

Philip took off his soaking wet sweater and shirt, and threw them to one side. Hooking his right foot into the boot jack, he pushed off one riding boot, and then the other, stripped down to his underpants, and hurried through into the bathroom, feeling chilled to the bone.

He took a very hot shower, letting the steaming water sluice down over his body for a few minutes, until his blood was tingling and he felt warmer. Stepping out of the shower stall, he dried himself, pulled on his towelling robe and walked over to the washbasin. He stood in front of the mirror, combing his wet hair, slapping on cologne, and thinking of Madelana.

What a pity the thunderstorm had blown up when it had, so suddenly, about an hour ago. It had curtailed their ride. They had been up in the hills above Dunoon, and he had begun to sense a lessening of the tension in her out there in the peaceful countryside. Certainly she appeared to be more at ease with him today. When she had arrived yesterday at lunchtime, she had been very quiet, and so taut he thought at one moment that she might snap in half, and she had remained tense for the rest of the day. She had seemed a bit better in the evening though, had evidently enjoyed their dinner with Tim and Anne Willen.

By the time they had gone riding this afternoon she had been lighthearted, almost gay, and she was opening up to him once more; he knew he was gaining her confidence. So much so, he had been on the verge of telling her how strongly he felt about her when the weather had changed abruptly. The sky had grown overcast and dark. Heavy torrential rain had started to fall, and they had mounted their horses and galloped back to the stables at top speed. Even so, it had taken them a good twenty minutes to get there. Matt had been waiting for them with one of the other grooms, and they had led Gilda and Black Opal off to the tack room; he had driven Madelana up to the manor in the Maserati, the two of them drenched to the skin and shivering. She had become very white, her teeth chattering uncontrollably as they had dashed into the house, and now, as he went through into his bedroom, Philip hoped that she had not caught a cold.

He stood warming himself in front of the fire for a few minutes, before crossing to the black lacquer Chinese cabinet, which contained a small, fully stocked bar. He poured two cognacs into small brandy balloons, gulped one down, then went to dress, pulling on a thick Fair Isle sweater and socks, and heavy grey flannels. He slipped his feet into a pair of brown loafers, collected the other brandy balloon, and left the room with it.

A second later he stood in front of Madelana's door. He was about to knock, but hesitated fractionally, wondering if he had given her enough time to shed her wet riding clothes, shower and change. Deciding that he had, he rapped softly.

'Come in,' she called.

He did so, stood hovering on the threshold.

She was huddled in front of the fire, seated on the floor with her back to the sofa, dressed in a track suit and thick socks, sipping the tea he had asked Mrs Carr to have sent up to her a short while before.

'I thought you might want this,' he said, holding out the brandy balloon. 'It'll warm you through.'

'Thank you.' She put the cup she was holding back in its saucer on the end table. 'Yes, I'd like it, Philip.' There was a pause. 'Thank you,' she said again.

He pushed the door closed with his foot, walked over to her, handed her the glass. She took it from him, and as she did their fingers grazed. She jumped slightly, as if surprised, drew back, pushed herself harder against the sofa. Then she lifted her eyes to his.

It was still raining outside, and sombre; she had not turned on the lamps, and in the shadows of the dim room she looked ethereal, illuminated as she was by the blazing fire. Her face shimmered with an incandescent, fragile beauty, and her eyes were huge, transparent and shining.

He found it impossible to look away.

They continued to gaze at each other. For a split second Philip thought he was looking deep into her soul. Finally he dropped his eyes. He did not trust himself with her, and he swung around without a word, walked back to the door, intending to leave her alone until dinner. But he could not help turning to glance at her before he went out, his eyes irresistibly drawn to hers once more.

She returned his long, penetrating stare steadily, solemnly. Her face was infinitely quiet. She did not move, nor did she speak. The air was hushed, very still between them.

He took a step forward, then another. 'I want to be with you,' he said in a voice that was unexpectedly hoarse. 'Please don't send me away.'

'I'm not going to.'

At first he thought he had not heard her correctly, and he looked at her swiftly, through narrowed eyes.

She put down the brandy glass, lifted her arm, held out her hand to him.

He hurried back to her, took the slender hand in his, brought it to his mouth, brushed his lips over her long fingers. Then he knelt down on the floor by her side.

'Oh Maddy,' he said, using the diminutive of her name for the first time. 'Oh Maddy.'

'Philip,' she whispered in a voice so low it was hardly audible.

He pulled her forward. She was in his arms, clinging to him, saying his name over and over, and he held her close to his body, tightening his grip. With one hand he stroked her hair. His mouth found hers, and he kissed her as he had wanted to kiss her from the very first day, deeply, fiercely, passionately, his tongue thrusting as if he was taking possession of her with his mouth. She returned his kisses, and her tongue grazed his; he realized that her ardour for him matched his own for her. This knowledge sent a thrill searing through him.

There was no going back, he knew that. They must make love at once, now, here. There was no time to waste . . . too much time had been wasted already. He pulled her down under him, slid his hand under her loose top. When his fingers closed around one of her breasts she let out a long sigh; he stroked her gently, smoothed the tips of his fingers across her nipple, caressed it lovingly. Almost instantly, he felt it harden under his fondling, and this inflamed him even more. He tugged at her top, wanting to lift it over her head.

She sat up, pulled it off. He tore at his own clothes, flung them to one side. Suddenly they were stretched out next to each other on the rug, completely naked. They began to kiss again, frantically, more urgently than ever, and they could not keep their hands off each other. They reached out hungrily, longingly, to touch, to explore, to caress, to excite. The urgency between them grew and intensified as they became more and more aroused.

There was a violence in his desire for her, and he sensed the same turbulent emotion in her. She wanted him as desperately as he wanted her, and she was making that quite clear. And so he fell across her, slid into her. As he did he felt her tense, gasp, and then relax.

He braced his hands on either side of her, rose up above her, looked down into her face. It was full of yearning and desire, and the wild expression that blazed in her eyes mirrored exactly what he was feeling. His breath caught in his throat in surprise and pleasure.

Philip began to move against her, very slowly, expertly, and she thrust her body forward to meet his, cleaving to him.

Their rhythm grew faster and the urgency of their passion spiralled up into total abandonment, and they were on a dizzying climb, rising higher and higher together, out of control. He had fantasized about her for days. Now his fantasy had become his reality, and he was unable to hold back. He flowed into her, gave himself to her, and then his mouth was on hers, devouring hers. And she was flying with him on that dizzying flight, and she cried his name suddenly and stiffened, and they began a slow slide down over the edge, down into scorching white heat.

Her arms and legs were woven around him, binding him in their silken vice. He was welded to her, part of her, and she was part of him, and the miracle was that they had become one single being . . .

Entirely spent, they lay still, locked in each other's arms. There was no sound except for their laboured breathing, the crackling of the logs on the fire, the faint ticking of a clock somewhere in the background.

Philip stirred first. He buried his face in the mass of her chestnut hair, murmured against her neck, 'I've wanted you since I first saw you downstairs in the portrait gallery, Maddy.'

When she made no comment, he asked, 'Didn't you know that?'

'No, I didn't,' she whispered. With a small smile, she confessed, 'I wanted you too.'

'You certainly hid it very well,' he exclaimed quietly.

She said, 'And so did you.'

They both laughed, but fell silent immediately, caught in the webs of their own thoughts. After a short while, Philip released his hold on her, got up, took her hands in his, pulled her to her feet. He slipped an arm around her, and they stood together in front of the fire, gazing at each other as though mesmerized. He tilted her chin, bent down, kissed her on the mouth, lightly, gently, and then reached for the brandy balloon. He offered it to her. She shook her head. He took several swallows, placed the glass on the table, and as he led her over to the large four-poster bed, he said, 'I do hope you don't think that I'm a drinking man, too . . .'

Madelana laughed, said nothing, slid under the bed-clothes. Philip joined her, wrapped his arms around her. She curved her body into his, relaxing her shoulders against his broad chest, filled with a rare joy. It had as much to do with the pleasure she had given Philip as the fulfilment and release he had brought to her. The tension which had been building in her for days had disappeared. She felt as though she were wrapped in a cocoon of peace and contentment and happiness. And she knew it was because of him, all the things he was. He was a very special kind of man.

Philip continued to hold her close to him, nuzzling his face into the nape of her neck, her hair, the space between her shoulder blades. To his surprise he was suddenly at full arousal again. He threw the bedclothes to one side, pushed himself up on one elbow, looked down at her.

Madelana smiled up at him. Her face was radiant.

He smiled back, lifted one hand, began to stroke her cheek, his eyes spilling with emotion. The truth was, he loved her. He had fallen in love with her that very first day. He was glad it had happened at Dunoon, and that they had first made love here. It seemed very right to him that something as important as this had taken place in his home. He knew that he would always love her. This was not a passing thing. There could be no other woman in his life now. Never, ever again.

'You look thoughtful,' she said, her eyes quizzical.

He leaned over her, answered in a low voice, 'It was too quick, Maddy. I'm sorry . . . anxiety on my part, I'm afraid.' He laughed lightly, ruefully. 'But I'd ached for you for days . . . fantasized about you.'

'You were wonderful.'

'Perhaps you're prejudiced, darling.'

He brought his mouth down on her breasts, began to kiss them, whilst stroking her body, running his hands all over her. Her skin felt like satin to him, and in the firelight it had a lovely roseate cast to it. He marvelled at the beauty of her lithe body, so slender, so delicately formed, her long legs, the heavy, voluptuous breasts, taut now under his touch.

Lifting his head, he brought his mouth to her mouth, kissed her deeply, traced a line down her stomach with one finger, until his hand came to rest between her thighs. He caressed her lightly, adeptly, and she reached out for him, began to stroke him. As he felt her tense and spasm, he pushed her hand away from him, entered her, and again they were instantly swept away by the intensity and urgency of their passion for each other.

They were together for a long time, and then he got up and left the bed. He strode over to the fireplace where he had discarded his clothes earlier, began to dress.

She watched him as he moved around in front of the fire, thinking what a beautiful man he was. He had a wonderful body. He was over six feet and broad shouldered, and there was not an ounce of extra flesh on him; he was tanned from being constantly in the sun.

Madelana had the sudden curious feeling that she had known him before . . . long ago. There was something so very familiar about him to her that it was startling. And yet they *were* strangers . . . albeit *intimate* strangers now

He came back to her, sat down on the edge of the bed, moved a strand of hair away from her eyes. Bending over her, he kissed her lightly, said, 'This is just the beginning, Maddy darling.'

'It's the beginning of the end –' She stopped abruptly, stared up at him, her eyes wide with surprise at her words.

He scowled. 'What an odd thing to say. What do you mean?'

'I don't know,' she exclaimed. 'It was a thought that flashed through my head, and I said it without thinking.'

'I'm not going to talk about the *end* of anything.' He laughed dismissively, and pulled her into his arms, hugged her tightly. Then he let her go, stood up. 'I'll see you downstairs shortly. Dress casually, darling, it's just the two of us.'

'Yes,' she said.

She lay there for a while after he had gone. There was an indentation on the pillow next to her, where his head had been, and she reached out to touch the spot, slithered to his side of the bed, buried her face in the pillow. It smelled of him . . . of his hair and his cologne. She began to weep.

An enormous sense of loss overwhelmed her and she was afraid.

21

Hong Kong glittered. It was all colour and light and movement and noise.

From the moment Jason Rickards's private jet had thundered down the runway at Kai Tak airport five days ago, and Paula had alighted, she had been caught in the spell of the British Crown Colony.

She had not been there for fourteen years, and she had forgotten what it was really like. It overpowered in every sense.

Visually it reminded her of Manhattan, with its towering skyscrapers, air-conditioned shopping emporiums, boutiques, banks and businesses, stylish restaurants and elegant hotels. Yet withal, Hong Kong had a rhythm that was uniquely its own, a tempo that was rapid, pulsating, full of excitement and tumult.

Paula felt movement all around her. Wherever she looked she saw perpetual motion. Great jets soared up into the misty blue skies above Victoria Peak; sailing boats and sampans, yachts and junks, hydrofoils and ferries ploughed the busy harbour waters around Central and Kowloon; automobiles, trams, buses, and rickshaws surged through the streets; and people jostled each other in swarming crowds as they rushed about their business. It was over-populated. Space was at a premium, on land and sea, and there was so much teeming life and deafening noise Paula had begun to feel slightly battered by it.

Yet in contrast, there were lovely little pockets of calm and tranquillity that caught her by surprise . . . the quiet hills of the New Territories, that rural area between Kowloon and mainland China . . . the temples and shrines . . . and even a spot down near the Star Ferry Pier, where every morning a group of Chinese men performed the slow, meditative movements of tai chi.

To Paula, it was the many contrasts which so startled, and which made the deepest impression on her.

Nowhere on earth was there such limitless wealth and grinding poverty within the same few miles, such breathtaking beauty rubbing shoulders with sickening squalor. Ritzy high life was perilously juxtaposed against dangerous low life. Grand and ancient families lived in close proximity to desperate refugees. Hong Kong was a place of old money and tai-pans, over one-hundred-and-forty years of British rule and colonial traditions, newly-made fortunes, stunning success stories, and mind-boggling business bonanzas. It also had one of the highest suicide rates in the world.

It had captivated Paula, and she fully understood its extraordinary allure for residents and visitors alike.

Until Paula's arrival, Emily had been ensconced in the Peninsula in Tsimshatsui on Kowloon side. This was the hotel where she invariably stayed on her buying trips. It was convenient for her business dealings with mainland China, since she had ready access to the factories which manufactured the varied products she purchased for Genret.

The night before Paula had flown in with Don Metcalfe of Rickards International on the company plane, Emily had moved Hong Kong side. She had checked into the vast and beautiful suite she had booked in the famous Mandarin Hotel in the heart of the Central District.

'I've finished all my business, and Central's much more convenient for us, and what we want to do,' Emily had explained to Paula when she was settling in after her arrival. 'It's the shopping Mecca of Asia, and anyway, I think it's much more interesting for you to be on Hong Kong Island itself.' Paula had nodded and agreed. 'Whatever you say, Emily. You're in charge. And I love this hotel. It's just beautiful.'

Emily had planned a programme which hardly left them a moment to breathe. Nevertheless, Paula had been enthusiastic about doing everything, and tremendously energized by the sightseeing, the shopping, the visits to different restaurants and several of the other smart hotels, not to mention their tour of night clubs in Wanchai.

The first evening she was there, Emily had taken her to Gaddi's for dinner. It was considered to be the finest European restaurant in Hong Kong, and Rolf Heiniger, the renowned maître d'hôtel, had lived up to his reputation for knowledge and attentiveness, had suggested the most delicious dishes and the finest wines.

The following morning they had gone browsing and shopping in Emily's favourite boutiques, shops, markets and galleries. 'Don't forget, I'm an old China hand,' she had confided to Paula with a grin. 'Trust me and you'll get the best bargains. Quality merchandise at the right prices.'

Paula had laughed, had exclaimed, 'Oh, I trust you all right, Emily. You had a sharp eye even as a child. I think that's one of the reasons Grandy gave you Genret to run.'

In the course of several hectic days they did all of their Christmas shopping, buying important gifts as well as stocking-fillers and tree presents. They purchased pearls, jade jewellery, cufflinks for the men in the family, embroidered silks and brocades, Chinese evening jackets and cheongsams, beaded evening bags, unusual wooden toys, cloisonné, hand-embroidered linens, trinkets and knick-knacks.

Emily had suggested they pay a visit to Hollywood Road, just above Central, explaining that this was an imperative, and Paula quickly discovered that she was right. Many of the more important antique shops and art galleries were located here, and as they had gone on the rounds Paula had been enchanted by the artifacts on display. She had bagged an ancient nefrite vase for Jason, who collected Oriental art, and a beautiful antique jade necklace for her mother.

And in between the shopping expeditions and all manner of exotic meals in unique restaurants, Emily had arranged a few other fascinating excursions. She had taken Paula to Aberdeen Harbour, where thousands of Boat People lived and worked on junks and sampans; they had made a trip to the New Territories on Kowloon side; had driven up to the top of misty Victoria Peak to see the spectacular view; and visited various temples and shrines.

On the flight from Sydney, Paula's travelling companion, Don Metcalfe, had said he would like to take her and Emily out to dinner before they left for New York. And this he had done the previous night. They had gone with him on the hydrofoil to Macau, the Portuguese enclave at the entrance to the Pearl River, just fifty minutes away, where they had dined in an elaborate restaurant before visiting some of the famous gambling casinos. It had been a memorable evening. They had enjoyed themselves tremendously with Don, who had kept them laughing and highly entertained; Emily, in particular, had been excited by the trip to Macau, where she had never been and had always wanted to go.

In the early hours of the morning, when Paula had finally fallen into bed exhausted, it struck her that they had packed in more in a few days than she had imagined possible. Every minute of her stay in Hong Kong had been enjoyable, and being alone with Emily had been an added bonus. It reminded her of the trips they had taken together as girls, and she felt young again, lighthearted, almost carefree.

Today was their last day in Hong Kong; they were taking the night flight to New York. Emily had been determined that she see the beautiful Regent hotel in Kowloon, and the unparalleled view of Hong Kong Island from this vantage point. And so they had gone there for lunch. She had had to get up very early to do her packing first, but it had been worth making the effort. The lunch and the view would linger in her mind and memory for a long time.

Immediately after lunch, they had caught the Star Ferry back to Central. Emily had made for the hotel to finish her suitcases; Paula had returned to the jewellery shop where she had seen a pair of exquisite earrings, which she wanted to buy as a Christmas gift for Emily.

Once inside the shop, Paula had bargained in the way she had seen Emily doing it for the last few days. Much to her surprise and enormous delight, she had won the earrings at a far better price than she had expected. And now, as she walked the short distance to the hotel, she was filled with a great sense of satisfaction at this small success.

Hurrying across the lobby of the Mandarin, Paula realized she was twenty minutes late to meet her cousin for tea. And so she headed straight for their point of rendezvous, the Clipper Lounge, which floated like a gallery above the lobby on the mezzanine floor, and ran lightly up the steps.

Emily saw her, raised her hand in greeting.

Paula waved back.

A moment later she was sitting down in one of the comfortable chairs facing Emily.

'Sorry I'm late. The last hour just flew by,' Paula said with an apologetic smile.

'It's all right. I've not been here long, and you know I love this place. I feel as if I'm on a boat, what with the brass portholes and all this mahogany. Oh, and before I forget –' Emily opened her handbag, fished around, handed Paula two small envelopes, and finished, 'These were in the suite waiting for you when I got back after lunch.'

'Oh telexes! Thanks, darling.' Paula took them, opened the first, scanned it quickly, then read the second. She pursed her lips, filling with disappointment. One was from Michael Kallinski in London, the other from Harvey Rawson in New York, and both effectively said the same thing: Peale and Doone, the small chain of stores in the Midwest, had been sold right under their noses to another buyer. Too bad, she thought, the chain would have been a good beginning for my expansion programme. On the other hand, she had never been quite as enthusiastic as Michael about the locations of the shops. This thought consoled her a little.

Emily was watching Paula closely. She said, 'Is something wrong at home?'

'No, no, nothing like that,' Paula responded quickly, reassuringly. 'These are business telexes.'

'Oh. Who from?' Emily probed, as usual inquisitive.

'One's from Michael, the other from a Wall Street lawyer who was doing some work for me.' Paula smiled faintly. 'A deal we wanted didn't come off. Now, let's order. I think I'm going to have the mulberry tea again. I've grown rather partial to it.'

'Yes, I'll have the same.' Emily swung her blonde head, caught the attention of the waiter, motioned to him.

Once she had given the order, she leaned across the table, levelled her shrewd green eyes at her cousin. 'What kind of deal didn't come off?' When Paula did not immediately answer, Emily remarked, 'It must have been something important to you. I noticed how put out you looked.'

Paula nodded. 'Actually, I *was* disappointed, Emily. I was hoping to buy a small chain of stores in the States. Unfortunately, we missed getting them by a hair's breadth.'

'Why do you want to buy more stores?' Emily was perplexed, and she frowned.

'I've been wanting to expand Harte's in America. Buying an existing chain seems to be the best way to go about it to me, Emily.'

'One store in America was enough for Gran. Why would *you* want more?'

'Times have changed radically. You know that as well as I do. I must expand, darling, it's the only way to survive as a retailer today.'

Emily said, in her blunt way, 'I think you're biting off more than you can chew, if you ask me.'

Paula laughed. 'Now how many times did our grandmother tell us that everyone said *that* to her, and throughout her life, too, and *she* never paid a blind bit of notice.'

Ignoring this comment, Emily said strongly, 'I bet Shane agrees with me. What does *he* think about this expansion idea of yours?'

'Well, very frankly, Emily, I haven't had a chance to tell him yet. This summer the south of France was so hectic, and there seemed no point in bringing it up until there was a chain available. And the week we were together, before I left for Australia, was so rushed, you know.'

'I don't think he'll like it, Paula. You've enough to keep you pretty busy, what with Harte's in London, Paris and Yorkshire, Sitex Oil, and the boutiques in the hotels.'

'Grandy used to tell us that organization was the key to everything, and that an organized woman had the world by the balls.'

'That's true, she did say that. Nevertheless, Shane *won't* be happy. And there's something else, Paula. I don't think Gran would approve of this idea of yours if she were alive.'

'Nonsense! Of course she would! She'd see the wisdom behind my plans,' Paula cried spiritedly, sounding confident. She drew closer to Emily, and began to outline her plans for the future of the Harte stores in the United States.

Emily listened attentively, nodding from time to time.

Both women were so absorbed in their conversation neither of them saw the man who was regarding them intently from the stairs leading up to the Clipper Lounge.

He was stunned at the sight of the two women, and was momentarily rooted to the spot. Recovering himself rapidly, he pivoted, ran down the steps, sped across the lobby, and went out through the front door.

The blood rushed to the man's head, and he filled with a fulminating rage as he raced back to Pedder Street, dodging in and out, pushing past people almost violently in his haste and anxiousness to put distance between himself and the Mandarin.

Exactly two minutes after leaving the hotel, he was standing in the elevator, riding up to the top floor of the skyscraper where his company, Janus and Janus Holdings Ltd, was housed. Avoiding the front entrance, and in so doing bypassing the large outer offices where his staff worked, he hurried down the long corridor, let himself in through the private door.

This opened into a foyer, handsomely furnished with Chinese antiques, which in turn led through double mahogany doors to his inner sanctum, luxuriously appointed, with a stunning view of Victoria Harbour visible through a wall of plate glass.

Going straight to the small mirrored bar, he poured himself a straight vodka. To his annoyance his hand shook as he lifted the glass to his mouth. He downed the drink, strode over to his desk, flipped on the intercom.

'Yes, sir?' his English secretary said.

'Please have Lin Wu bring the Daimler around to the front, Peggy, I'm leaving early today. And I'll sign my letters now.'

'Yes, sir, I'll be right in with them.'

He arranged a suitably inscrutable expression on his face, and sat down, willing his anger to subside.

22

His rage lingered.

He carried it with him in the Daimler on the drive up the Peak to his home. It was still with him now as he sat in the library of his elegant duplex apartment, going through his personal mail. The rage was of a kind he had not experienced for the longest time, and the fact that he had reacted so strongly when he had seen the two women had unnerved him. He seethed inside, and with good reason. However, he knew he must bring the anger under control. He dare not allow emotion to cloud his vision or flaw his judgement.

He put the half dozen or so social invitations, various thank-you notes, and personal letters to one side, pushed the carved rosewood chair away from the antique rosewood desk, went out into the gallery.

It was from this long and spacious hallway that the other rooms in the apartment flowed; a staircase at one end led up to the second floor. He crossed the flowing space, walking in the direction of the drawing room, thinking how restful the gallery was after the busy activity of his offices. It never failed to give him pleasure. The floor was stained ebony and highly polished, the walls white and hung with his collection of very fine Chinese paintings by past masters, dating from the fifteenth century to the present.

Drawing to a standstill in front of an ink-on-paper painting by Sun Kehong, dated 1582, he straightened it, then stood back, regarded it for a prolonged moment, smiling, nodding to himself in appreciation of its refinement, elegance and simple beauty.

Moving slowly, he continued along the gallery, admiring the art he had so lovingly assembled. The gallery was sparse, the only piece of furniture a console table made of ebony upon which rested a carved celadon vase with a cover from the Qianlong period, balanced by two white nefrite rams carved in the Song spirit. At the far end, against a short wall, glass shelves suspended on brass chains from the ceiling appeared to float, held his prized collection of rare Ming bronzes.

Recessed ceiling spots, discreet, strategically placed, illuminated the art; these were the only lights and this area of the apartment was dim, shadowy, tranquil. He lingered, allowed the peacefulness to penetrate his bones, calm his turbulent spirit, in the way he had learned to do over these many years.

After a short while, he entered the drawing room, and his face changed, lit up, and so lost some of its tightness. He hovered in the doorway.

It was early evening, and the mist was rolling down the Peak. Outside the long wall of window, the sweeping view of Hong Kong, Victoria Harbour and Kowloon across the water was slightly obscured. Familiar images were smudged, indistinct, wrapped in a haze of greyed blues and whites, the colour combination reminding him of the faded glaze on a piece of ancient Chinese porcelain. Ah Qom, the Chinese amah who had looked after him and his home since the beginning, had turned on the silk-shaded carved jade lamps and lighted the fire, and this airy graceful room of perfect proportions was bathed in warm and mellow light. It welcomed him.

Huge overstuffed sofas and chairs, covered in pale blue and lavender and grey Thai silks by Jim Thompson, were balanced by Chinese cabinets, chests, and tables of varying sizes and shapes made of black or dark-red lacquered wood. Wherever he looked, his eyes rested on an object of rare beauty. His possessions were meaningful to him. They gave him great satisfaction, nourished him, helped to restore his mood when he was feeling out of sorts.

He felt this lightening now, and a return to normal, and he moved forward across the antique Chinese silk carpet, sat down on the sofa. He knew that in a moment, Ah Qom's niece, Mee Seen, would bring his jasmine tea, as she usually did half an hour after he had been home, no matter what time he returned from the office. It was a ritual, as so many things were a ritual here.

This thought had no sooner passed through his head, when the pretty, delicately-formed Chinese girl in her black silk cheongsam came hurrying in with the tray.

Smiling and bowing, she placed it on the low table in front of him.

He thanked her graciously, inclining his head.

Smiling and bowing, she departed.

He poured the fragrant tea into the small, paper-thin porcelain bowl, drank it quickly, poured another, sipped this more slowly, let his mind relax and empty itself of all thoughts. After savouring a third bowl, he placed it on the dark-red lacquer tray, leaned his head against the sofa, and closed his eyes.

Gradually the last shreds of his anger drifted away.

He had been half dozing, awakened with a start, when the antique chiming clock on the mantelpiece struck the hour of six.

Sitting up, stretching his long frame, he realized he must go upstairs to shower and change for Lady Susan Sorrell's dinner party at her house in Recluse Bay.

Immediately pushing himself to his feet, he walked swiftly across the drawing room, but stopped suddenly in front of the long console next to the coromandel screen. The silverframed photographs arranged there glittered brilliantly in the light from the adjacent lamp. He stared at the photograph of his father, then let his glance wander to the smaller picture of the woman.

His hatred for her had never dimmed. It rose up in him again. Impatiently, he shoved it away. Nothing must impinge on his new-found calmness, or ruin the evening ahead, which he had been anticipating for several days.

He had never intended to keep a photograph of *her* in his home, where every single object was perfect, chosen by him, the perfectionist, for its very perfection. But his better judgement had triumphed over emotion when he had unexpectedly found the picture amongst a trunk full of old possessions years ago. He had been on the verge of throwing it away when he had recognized its great usefulness.

Hong Kong was a place of status, of keeping face. Both were of paramount importance. And so it did him no harm whatsoever to be known as the grandson of that late great international tycoon, Emma Harte. However, tonight he could not bear to see that diabolical old woman's face, and he pushed her picture behind the larger one of his father standing outside the Commons. Being the son of Robin Ainsley, respected Labour politician, Member of Parliament and former Cabinet Minister, had done him no harm either. His family ties had made him eminently acceptable, had propelled him into the highest echelons of local society.

Returning to the library, Jonathan Ainsley seated himself at the desk, took a ring of keys from his jacket pocket, opened the bottom drawer. He lifted out the folder marked HARTE'S and opened it, let his eyes scan the top sheet covered with several columns of meticulous figures in his own neat handwriting.

A smile of triumph brought a lift to his mouth, and he chuckled quietly. He generally laughed when he reviewed this list, reminded himself exactly how much stock in the stores he now owned. Harte's shares were traded on the London Stock Exchange, and for years he had been buying shares through nominees: his Swiss bank and other financial institutions. Today he was a major shareholder in the Harte department store chain, although only he knew this.

Closing the folder, he set it down on the desk, leaned back in the chair, and steepled his fingers, gloating to himself. Paula O'Neill would make a mistake one day. No one was infallible. Not even her. And then he would strike.

Jonathan reached down into the drawer for another folder, this one unidentified, and slipped out a sheaf of papers. They were detailed reports from the London detective agency he had been employing for a number of years.

Since 1971, Jonathan had had his cousin Paula O'Neill watched on a regular basis. Nothing scurrilous about her had ever been turned up, and he had not expected it to be. On the other hand, it suited his purpose to know as much as possible about her and her life, her family, her friends, and any business moves she made.

From time to time, he had had Alexander Barkstone and Emily Harte watched and reported on as well. Like Paula, they were pristine. In any case, he was not particularly interested in them. As long as his cousins continued to run Harte Enterprises on a profitable basis, and he continued to get his large dividend cheque every quarter, that was all that mattered to him. After all, it was Paula O'Neill who was his target.

He glanced at the last report which had come in from the agency in London. It placed her at the Villa Faviola in late August. He supposed that was why he had been so startled to see her in the Clipper Lounge of the Mandarin Hotel earlier. Obviously she was either on her way to Australia, or going back to England from there.

Damn her, he thought. He returned the folders to the drawer, locked it, and hurried out, climbed the stairs to his bedroom, having no wish to become enraged again. Thinking about that bitch made his blood boil.

He paused on the landing, breathing deeply, cleansing his mind of her infuriating image.

As he went into his room, Jonathan expected to see his valet, and was surprised to find the room empty. Tai Ling was nowhere in sight, although his pleated dress shirt, black tie, and black silk socks had been laid out on the bed. Undoubtedly Tai Ling was downstairs in the laundry, steaming his dinner jacket, and would reappear at any moment. Humming to himself, he strolled over to a Ming chest, emptied his pockets of keys, credit-card wallet and money, and began to undress.

Like the other rooms in his home, the bedroom was furnished in excellent taste, with the emphasis on all things Chinese and unique Oriental objects of art. It was understated, masculine in feeling, a trifle cold and austere, and the women who were brought by him to his bed soon discovered that the ambience reflected something in Jonathan's nature.

Taking a dark blue Chinese silk robe from the armoire and slipping it on, he went into the adjoining bathroom, wondering who it was that Susan had invited to the dinner party especially to meet him. She had sounded mysterious on the phone the other day, but it was bound to be an interesting woman. Susan knew his taste very well.

He sighed, thinking yet again how much he missed the arrangement they had had for almost a year. It had been purely sexual, a relationship convenient for them both. Although they had also enjoyed each other on an intellectual level, there had been no emotional involvement to spoil things. Just sex and intelligent talk. Perfect, to his way of thinking.

Three months ago, when she had told him her husband was suspicious of her, that they must end their affair, he had believed her, had immediately agreed to do as she wished. He had not realized at the time that there would be such a void in his life when she was no longer available to him. It was not particularly the sex he missed, even though she was very good in bed, since sex was an easy commodity to find anywhere in the world these days. Rather, he missed their conversations, their repartee, their shared English upbringings and backgrounds.

But he had not tried to pursue Susan, or reinstitute the affair. The last thing he wanted was to be cited as corespondent in a messy divorce, or spotlighted as one of the chief players in a nasty little scandal in the Crown Colony. After all, he was a man of great standing here, and it was his home.

He stared at himself in the mirror over the washbasin, ran his hand over his chin. He had risen very early to play squash before a business breakfast at seven, and there was a hint of blond stubble on his chin. The electric razor was handy, and he plugged it in, ran it over his jawline. As he did, he thought of his cousins, Paula O'Neill and Emily Harte, but fleetingly. And with a sudden rush of pride he congratulated himself on all that he had accomplished in eleven years. He had come a long way.

When Jonathan Ainsley had alighted in Hong Kong in 1970 he knew at once that he had found his natural habitat and his spiritual home.

The air was full of excitement, mystery, adventure and intrigue. Anything – and everything – seemed possible. Furthermore, he smelled money. Vast amounts of it.

He had come to the Far East licking his wounds, after being ignominiously kicked out of Harte Enterprises, where he had been head of the real estate division. Alexander had fired him; Paula had banished him from the family.

642

And forever after he had blamed her for everything, believing that Alexander did not have the guts to stand up to him without her encouragement and support.

Before he had left England, Jonathan had done three things. He had dissolved his partnership with Sebastian Cross; sold his interest in Stonewall Properties to Sebastian for an excellent price; put his real estate holdings in London and Yorkshire on the block, and had made a tidy profit in the process.

When he had set out on his travels he had had two overriding goals – to amass a great fortune and to wreak revenge on his cousin Paula, whom he loathed.

Jonathan had been attracted to the Eastern world ever since his youth. Its religions, philosophies, and customs fascinated him; he drew aesthetic pleasure from its art, decorative objects and furniture. And so he decided to do a tour of this part of the world before settling in Hong Kong, which he had concluded was the most logical place to set up in business. For the first six weeks of his self-imposed exile, he had wandered around, sightseeing and enjoying being a tourist. He had stopped off in Nepal and Kashmir, gone hunting in Afghanistan, made a leisurely trip through Thailand, before proceeding to Hong Kong.

Before leaving London, he had taken the precaution of collecting letters of introduction from friends in the City and in real estate. Within a few days of arriving at the Mandarin Hotel, he had begun to call on those to whom the letters were addressed. At the end of his second week he had met a dozen or more bankers, businessmen, owners of land and construction companies, as well as a number of wheeler-dealers whom he considered to be dubious and not worth pursuing.

Two of the men he was particularly drawn to were a fellow Englishman and a Chinese. Separately, they had decided to help Jonathan get started, for their own reasons and to suit their own ends, and they were to prove invaluable to him. The Englishman, Martin Easton, was a real estate developer; the Chinese was a highly respected banker by the name of Wan Chin Chiu. Both were highly influential in their own circles, professionally and socially, but it was Jonathan who brought them together.

Exactly four weeks after he had landed at Kai Tak airport, he had set himself up in business. With the help of his new associates he had found small but attractive offices in Central, had hired a small staff consisting of an English secretary, a Chinese expert in land and construction, and a Chinese book-keeper, and had formed his own company, Janus and Janus Holdings Ltd. In Greek mythology Janus was the god of portals and the patron of beginnings and endings, and Jonathan had selected the name with relish – tongue in cheek – deeming it highly appropriate under the circumstances.

Luck was on his side when he started out in Hong Kong. It was to hold for over a decade.

This extraordinary luck, and the guidance and patronage of his two very powerful friends and backers, were the keys to his immense success. And timing played an important role.

It just so happened that when Jonathan arrived in the Crown Colony in 1970, land and construction were on the upswing. Since his expertise was in real estate, he knew he had accidentally landed on his feet. Shrewd enough to recognize a grand opportunity when he saw it, he plunged into local business with a gambler's instinct for the main chance, and a certain amount of courage, in that he was risking almost everything he had, plus the money invested in Janus and Janus by Martin Easton and Wan Chin Chiu.

Afterwards he was to realize that he had been unable to throw the dice wrong once. His number always came up.

He made a considerable profit in the first six months, and in 1971, when the really big boom in property and land hit Hong Kong, he was well positioned. Suddenly there was a great deal of activity on the Hang Seng Index, the major index for the Hong Kong Stock Market. Like many others, Jonathan took advantage of the market activity. He cashed in quickly by taking his company public.

His two advisers, who had been guiding him all along, but independently of each other, warned him to start easing off a few months later. He continued to do a considerable amount of wheeling and dealing through the end of 1971 and 1972, but he had reduced his investments in the Hong Kong Stock Market by the beginning of 1973. Wan Chin Chiu, who had his ear to the ground and seemed to know everything, had been more cautionary than Easton, and wisely Jonathan had followed his advice scrupulously.

In any case, he had already made a killing, and was on his way to parlaying those profits into a huge personal fortune. He never looked back from this moment on.

By 1981 he had become a force to be reckoned with in Hong Kong and the world of Far East Asian business. He was a millionaire many times over, owned the skyscraper where his offices were located, the duplex on the Peak, several expensive cars, and a string of thoroughbreds which he raced at the Happy Valley race track in Hong Kong.

Some years earlier, he had bought out Martin Easton, who had decided to retire to Switzerland, but he had remained closely associated with Wan Chin Chiu until his death two months ago. Tony Chiu, the American-educated son of the banker, had taken his father's place, and Jonathan's association with the bank continued to flourish. His personal outside investments were secure, and Janus and Janus Holdings was rock solid.

Business aside, he was socially prominent, one of the most eligible European bachelors in the community, and considered to be something of a catch. Except that no woman had managed to get anywhere near catching him.

Jonathan sometimes wondered about his own elusiveness, asked himself if he was far too fastidious, too much of a perfectionist when it came to the kind of woman he wanted to marry. Maybe no such woman existed. Yet he had discovered he was unable to alter his disposition.

Perfect, Jonathan suddenly thought, remembering the word Susan Sorrell had used to describe the young woman who was to be his dinner partner tonight.

'She's just the girl for you, Jonny darling,' Susan had said, sounding sincere. 'She's divine. Simply *perfect*.' He had laughed, had pressed for more information, but Susan had merely murmured, 'No, no, I won't tell you anything at all. Not even her name. You must wait and see for yourself.' Well, he would *see* very shortly.

Now he stepped back from the full length mirror on the door of the armoire, took a last look at himself. He adjusted his bow tie, straightened the black silk handkerchief in the breast pocket of his white dinner jacket, and shot down his cuffs.

At thirty-five, Jonathan bore a strong resemblance to his grandfather, Arthur Ainsley, who had been Emma's second husband. He had inherited Arthur's blond hair and colouring, his light eyes, his polished, rather refined good looks, and like Arthur he was tall, slender, extremely English in his appearance. If anything, he looked better than he ever had. He had aged well and knew it.

But fair and handsome though he was, Jonathan's character had changed little in the decade that had passed. He was as devious and as manipulative as ever, and despite his unquestioned success he was profoundly bitter about his ousting from Harte Enterprises. Nevertheless, he was able to camouflage his innermost feelings behind a façade that was a combination of his own natural blandness, an inscrutability learned from his Chinese friends, and a manner that was insouciant and charming.

He glanced at the paper-thin Patek Philippe watch on his wrist. It was not quite seven. He had to leave in a few minutes. But within half an hour he would be arriving at Susan's house in Recluse Bay. And, finally, meeting the mysterious lady she had found for him.

As he hurried out of the bedroom and ran down the stairs he grinned. He hoped she lived up to Susan's description, hoped she was indeed perfect. But if she was not, no matter. He would date her a couple of times anyway, and see what happened. Besides, she was obviously a newcomer to Hong Kong. *A stranger.* And strangers were always fascinating, weren't they?

23

He spotted her at once.

She stood at the far end of the living room, just near the French doors leading out to the terrace, talking to Elwin Sorrell, Susan's American banker husband.

He hesitated on the threshold for a moment before going in, scrutinizing her intently. Her face was in profile and in the shadows, and it was difficult to ascertain whether she was beautiful or not.

And then suddenly Susan saw him and glided over to greet him, and he thought again, as he had so often in the past, how beautiful *she* was. Her red hair was like an aureole of bright amber light around her lovely tranquil face, and her eyes were vividly blue tonight, full of her irrepressible laughter.

'Jonny darling,' she exclaimed as she closed in on him, 'I was just beginning to wonder where you were.'

She lifted her face to be kissed. He pecked her cheek quickly, perfunctorily, but squeezed her arm in a more intimate fashion. 'I'm only a few minutes late,' he said. Dropping his voice, he whispered, 'Can't you find a way to meet me one afternoon at the flat? Or at my office? We can be just as private there. I've missed you.'

She shook her head rapidly, looked around the room, smiling brightly. 'I daren't,' she muttered as she brought her gaze back to him. Tucking her arm through his, she laughed gaily, said in her normal voice, 'By the way, Jonathan, I forgot to mention that Elwin and I are going to San Francisco the day after tomorrow. For a couple of months. That's the real reason for tonight's dinner party. A sort of farewell get together with a few of our favourite people.'

'We'll all miss you,' Jonathan said, following her cue, aware that several of the other guests were looking across at them.

One of the Chinese houseboys came up to him with a tray of champagne, and he took a glass, murmured his thanks, turned to Susan. 'Cheers,' he said as he took a sip. 'Now, tell me about the mystery lady. That's her, isn't it, talking to Elwin in the doorway?'

'Yes, but I can't tell you much, because I don't know her well. I've only met her once, at Betsy Androtti's house last week. I was instantly struck by her. She's extremely attractive, charming, well turned out, and intelligent. Naturally I thought of you immediately.'

'You used the word *perfect* on the phone.'

'I think she *is* perfect. For you at any rate. There's something about her that will appeal to you tremendously.' Susan paused, gave him an appraising stare. 'I *do* know you very well, you know, Jonny.'

His mouth twitched with sudden hidden laughter, and he asked, 'Didn't Betsy give you *any* information about her?'

'Betsy doesn't know her either. She came to the dinner with some visiting banker. German, I think. And seemingly *he* met her last summer in the south of France. Or was it Sardinia? Oh dear, I'm not sure.'

'So she's truly the mystery lady, eh?'

Susan laughed. 'I suppose she is. On the other hand, that makes it more fun, doesn't it? And anyway, a stranger in our tight little group is always rather fascinating, elicits a great deal of curiosity, wouldn't you say?' She eyed him knowingly, and not giving him a chance to respond, rushed on, 'Some of the single men are bound to be interested in her. That's why I wanted to nab her at once for this dinner. And for my darling Jonny.'

'How very thoughtful of you.' He stared at her speculatively for a split second, then murmured sotto voce, 'I'd much rather have you though.'

'But I'm married, Jonny,' she shot back softly, her tone as low as his had been. 'To Elwin. And I always shall be married to him.'

'I wasn't proposing to you. Merely propositioning you, my love.'

Looking highly amused at his retort, she shook her head, but did not comment.

Jonathan went on, 'Anyway, what's the mystery lady doing in Hong Kong? Seeing the sights? Or what?'

'She's living here now. She told me she's opened a small antique shop and gallery on Hollywood Road.'

'Oh really!' he exclaimed, pricking up his ears, looking at Susan alertly. 'What kind of antiques?'

'Jade, I think. I got the impression she's an expert. That's another reason I thought the two of you would hit it off. So come along, my darling, don't let's loiter here in the doorway. Let me take you over to meet her. After all, that's why I invited her to this dinner in the first place. For you. Before any of the other young blades could scoop her up and carry her off.'

'Lead the way,' he said, following his hostess – and former lover – across the room.

Elwin Sorrell's face lit up at the sight of Jonathan. They were good friends and Jonathan was convinced the American had never ever once suspected him of a dalliance with his wife.

The two men greeted each other warmly, and then Susan said, 'Arabella, I'd like to introduce Jonathan Ainsley. Jonathan, this is Arabella Sutton.'

'Hello,' she said, stretching out her hand. 'I'm so pleased to meet you.'

He took her hand, shook it, half smiled. 'I'm delighted to meet you, too, Arabella.' He paused, then added, 'You're English.'

'Yes.'

They stared at each other, weighing each other up.

She had silver-gilt hair, parted in the centre, that was absolutely straight and fell in smooth fluid folds around her face and down her back to the top of her shoulder blades. Her face was extremely pale, without a spot of colour in the cheeks. It looked carved from alabaster, the features cleanly defined. She had a narrow nose, high cheekbones, a rounded chin with a cleft, and her mouth, wide, sensual, was painted brilliant red. At first glance this was startling in the very white face, yet somehow it was right on her. A young woman of medium height, and slender, she was dressed in an elegant white silk dress that screamed Paris and haute couture to his discerning eye.

Thirty, thirty-two, or thereabouts, Jonathan thought, and decided her looks were more interesting than beautiful. It was her eyes that held him. They were large, curiously elongated, almost, but not quite, almond shaped. Dark as pitch, they seemed bottomless.

Arabella was studying Jonathan as intently as he was her.

She had heard a lot about him, knew he was from a famous family, the grandson of the legendary Emma Harte. She had not expected him to be so prepossessing though. His blond good looks were arresting. He was well groomed, expensively dressed, and he had an air about him – something special yet indefinable. And then she realized that it *was* definable. He had the air of a man who was accustomed to authority and power and money, and the things money bought.

She liked what she saw.

So did Jonathan.

Susan said, 'Why don't you two get better acquainted? Come along, Elwin, let's mingle with our other guests.'

Suddenly Arabella and Jonathan found themselves standing alone. He put one hand under her elbow and guided her out to the empty terrace. He said, 'That's the most extraordinary piece you're wearing, Arabella.'

She looked down at the large carved jade pendant hanging on a string of carved jade beads. 'It's of the Daoguang period,' she told him. 'Very, very old.'

'I realize that. Susan told me you have an antique shop, that you're a dealer in jade.'

'Yes, jadite jewellery and nefrite carved pieces.'

He smiled inwardly, immediately noting the way she had made the distinction between the two types of jade, something only a real expert would do. He said, 'Where do you find your jade? Do you buy it here in Hong Kong from other dealers? Or on the mainland?'

'Both. I've been finding some wonderful things in Shanghai, especially jade jewellery like this piece –' She paused briefly, fingered the pendant. '– And snuff bottles and vases. I came across some old nefrite belt buckles from the Qing period last week, and I've started to collect the multi-coloured Beijing glass. Mostly the deep yellow.'

'Very clever of you, buying the glass, I mean. It's become highly prized because it's so difficult to craft. I'm interested in those nefrite belt buckles, by the way. I'd like to come over to your shop to look at them. Tomorrow perhaps?'

'Oh, but I haven't actually opened yet! I've been busy buying, collecting stock. My official opening is a week from this coming Monday.' Noticing the disappointment registering on his face, she added, 'Do come tomorrow. It's still a bit of a mess, but I'd love to show you some of the truly rare objects of art I've managed to find in the last couple of months.'

'I'd enjoy that, Arabella. Would you care to dine with me afterwards?'

There was only the merest hesitation on her part before she said, 'Why yes, Jonathan. Thank you very much.'

He nodded. 'Give me the address later, and I'll be there about six.' He shifted slightly on his feet, looked down at her. 'I understand from Susan that you're an expert in Chinese jades and antiques. Where did you actually study?'

'Oh, I didn't – I mean everything I know I sort of taught myself, and I've read a great deal. I also took several courses at Sotheby's in London, at different times during the past three years.' She shook her head, laughing. 'But I'm hardly an expert. Just knowledgeable. And I hope I learn more here in Hong Kong.'

'Oh you will. Indeed you will,' he murmured, and averted his face.

'Susan told me you have quite a collection of Chinese antiques yourself, Jonathan, including some marvellous bronzes.'

'Yes, I do. Would you like to see them? We could go to my flat for drinks before dinner tomorrow. Would you enjoy that?'

'It would be nice. Thanks.'

'Where do you come from, Arabella?' he asked suddenly, changing the subject.

'Hampshire. My father's a doctor. And you're from Yorkshire, aren't you?'

'Among other places.' Jonathan smiled thinly, put his hand under her elbow and ushered her into the living room. 'I think we'd better join the others now, don't you? I've not said hello to any of my friends yet. Besides, I mustn't monopolize you.'

Arabella smiled up at him, thinking how easy this had been, much easier than she had anticipated. She felt a rush of success, allowed her eyes to linger on him for a brief moment. And then she drifted off to talk to Vance and

Marion Campbell, whom she vaguely knew, and who had given her a lift to the dinner party. She was determined to leave with them at the end of the evening.

Susan had placed Arabella opposite Jonathan at the table, and he was able to study her surreptitiously throughout the dinner.

He was seated between Susan, who was at the head of the table to his left, and Marion Campbell, on his right. He paid enough attention to them both so as not to appear rude.

Mostly, though, he watched Arabella Sutton, and listened to her, and he was impressed in a variety of ways. He was captivated by her voice. It was husky, very beguiling. And her presence was hypnotic. Elwin seemed entranced, and so did Andy Jones, seated on her other side.

Jonathan noted how poised she was, and she was articulate, well informed on many subjects, not just Chinese art. He liked her intelligence, her sophistication. She had obviously travelled extensively, had done a good bit of living, and this pleased him. He did not care for women who were gauche or inexperienced whether in bed or out of it. He preferred women to be his equals. To match him.

The more Jonathan studied her the more he realized that she *was* beautiful. It was an unusual kind of beauty, different, intriguing. In the candlelight her face had become oddly mysterious, and highly sexual.

It was the perfect curve of the rounded cheek, the depth of the sloe eyes, the lusciousness of the full mouth, the silken sheen of the silver gold hair that made her such a sensual-looking woman. To him there was something exceedingly erotic about her, and the sexuality was not only visible in her face, and in the seemingly perfect body under the white gown, but was even apparent in her hands.

Jonathan had never seen hands like hers before. They were extraordinary. Slender, very white, with tapering fingers, and the long, perfect nails were painted brilliant red to match her inviting mouth.

He wanted those hands on him, wanted her. But thinking about seducing her was too tantalizing, anticipation too dangerous a game. And then, before he could switch gears in his head, he was aroused. Getting an erection at a dinner table had not happened to him since he had been a schoolboy. How remarkable, he thought, feeling hot under the collar.

Shifting his gaze from the fascinating – and potent – Arabella, he brought his attention to Andy Jones, and began to talk to him about sport.

'Why do you do it?' Jonathan whispered in Susan's ear as they strolled across the living room after dinner. They came to a stop near the fireplace, stood waiting for the Filipino butler to serve the coffee.

'Do what?' she asked, her eyes swivelling around the room, making sure Elwin was fully occupied elsewhere for a few minutes.

'Procure for me,' Jonathan replied, and surreptitiously ran his hand down her back, let it rest in the hollow above her buttocks.

'Don't do that, Jonny, someone might see you,' she whispered.

'Come on, confess. It turns you on, doesn't it?'

'Of course not!' she hissed. Sudden anger made her swing to face him. Then catching herself swiftly, she adopted a bland expression, took a deep breath, said in a steady voice, 'Perhaps it's because I still feel guilty about ending our affair the way I did. I want to make it up to you, Jonny. You've always been very special to me, and you were such a wonderful lover. The best I've ever had. Besides, this is the first time I've procured for you, as you so crudely put it. *I* prefer the word *introduce*.'

He grinned, said nothing, wondering what it would be like to take the two of them to bed together. Arabella and Susan would be quite an interesting and exciting combination. But he knew neither of them would go for it. English women were not a bit adventurous when it came to sex. And especially these two – the daughters of an earl and a doctor. No way.

Susan was saying, 'I was right though, wasn't I, Jonny? Arabella is perfect, isn't she?'

'Outwardly, yes.' He waited for a second, eyed her carefully, continued softly, suggestively, 'However, I can't really give you an assessment, a truthful answer, until I've stripped off those elegant clothes and bedded her.'

His gaze had not left Susan's face and he saw the sudden flicker, the expression at the back of her eyes. Jealousy? Anger? Or a mixture of both, perhaps? The idea that he might have hurt her, if only ever so slightly, pleased him. He had not wished to become involved in a marital scandal, but deep down it rankled that she had dumped him the way she had.

There was a painful silence.

Eventually she said in an amused voice, 'What a pity I won't be in Hong Kong to hear your report.'

'You probably will be.'

'Oh.' Now her eyes were surprised.

'I'm going to see Arabella's antique shop tomorrow. In the late afternoon. And then I'm taking her to my flat for drinks: before dinner . . . an intimate little dinner at home. And perhaps we'll get down to something even *more* intimate later in the evening. I have high hopes. I really do.'

'Bastard,' she muttered under her breath, but loud enough for him to hear.

'But my love, you started all this,' he retorted, grinning, now understanding that he was glad she had. Arabella Sutton was a challenge. He had not had a challenge for a long time.

Much later that evening, Jonathan sat near the window in his bedroom, brooding and still, his eyes focused on the cloudless night sky sprinkled with countless stars. The room was in total darkness, the only illumination coming from the very bright full moon that cast a silvery sheen over everything.

He held a pebble of mutton-fat jade in his hands, turning it over and over, rubbing it between his fingers occasionally. It was his talisman, his lucky piece, and he had owned it since he had first come to the British Crown Colony.

He was contemplative for a long while, considering the two women he had encountered today.

His cousin, Paula O'Neill.

The stranger, Arabella Sutton.

In their different ways they haunted him now. He separated the images in his head, and as he did he made two promises to himself.

The first woman he would destroy.

The second he would conquer and own.

The vows made, he sighed deeply, filled with a curious sense of satisfaction. Rising, he slipped off his blue silk Chinese robe, walked slowly over to the bed, and he could not resist smiling to himself. There was not the slightest doubt in his mind that he would succeed.

It was only a question of time.

PART TWO

Saints & Sinners

A lure more strong, a wish more faint,
Makes one a monster, one a saint.

WALTER LEARNED

'Tis the eye of childhood that fears a painted devil.

WILLIAM SHAKESPEARE

Riches and power are but gifts of blind fate, whereas
goodness is the result of one's own merits.

HÉLOISE

24

Success was in the air.

From the moment the dance had begun, Paula had known the evening was going to be magical.

Everything was exactly right.

The grand ballroom at Claridges had been decorated by the design staff of Harte's to her specific instructions, and it was stunning. Extraordinary, really. Forsaking the staid, the traditional, she had had them create a colour scheme of silver and white crystal, developed with silver lamé tablescloths, white candles in silver sticks, crystal bowls filled with mixed white flowers. More white flowers – lilies, orchids, chrysanthemums and carnations – were banked around the room in great masses, and spilled out of huge urns standing in various corners.

To Paula the ballroom looked like a winter ice palace, all silvery and glittering, yet it had a neutrality that made a splendid backdrop for the guests in their finery – the women in their colourful, stylish evening gowns and fabulous jewels, the men in their impeccable, well-cut black dinner jackets.

She was delighted that everyone she had invited had come to this very special party. In attendance were a mixture of family and close friends, executives from the Harte stores and Harte Enterprises, honoured guests and celebrities.

Glancing about yet again, she could not help thinking that in particular the women in the family looked especially beautiful tonight.

Her cousin Sally, the Countess of Dunvale, lovely in delphinium-blue taffeta and the famous Dunvale sapphires that exactly matched her eyes ... Emily, a vision in dark ruby silk and a superb ruby-and-diamond necklace and earrings Winston had given her for Christmas ... Emily's half sisters, the twins Amanda and Francesca, pert and pretty in magenta chiffon and scarlet brocade respectively ... her vivacious red-haired sister-in-law, Miranda, a law unto herself when it came to fashion, striking in a russet-satin column, stark, simple, strapless, worn with a long matching stole and an antique topaz-and-diamond necklace that fell down from her neck in a lacy cobweb of a bib.

Paula's gaze shifted over to the three sisters.

They were sitting at a nearby table, talking amongst themselves. Her mother, Daisy, dramatic in dark-green chiffon and the magnificent McGill emeralds that Paul had bought for Emma almost half a century ago ... Aunt Edwina, the Dowager Countess of Dunvale, in her seventies, white-haired, frail, yet regally elegant in black lace and the Fairley diamond necklace, presented to her by Emma the last Christmas she had been alive.

These two, the youngest and the eldest daughters of Emma Harte, both born on the wrong side of the blanket, bonded together, more than likely, by similar circumstances of birth, and by her mother's deep compassion for the older woman. And seated between them, the legitimate daughter, the middle one ... Aunt Elizabeth. Still a raven-haired beauty and looking half her age, she was positively stunning in silver lamé and a king's ransom of rubies, diamonds and emeralds.

The three sisters were the only children of Emma Harte who were present tonight. Paula had not invited Emma's two sons, Kit Lowther and Robin Ainsley, and their wives. They had been *persona non grata* for years because of their treachery to Emma, and the treachery of their children, Sarah and Jonathan.

A nest of vipers, she thought, remembering something her grandmother had said to her once. How horribly true that statement had turned out to be. Paula pulled her thoughts away from those despicable family members and lifted her glass, took a sip of champagne.

The evening was drawing to a close, and it suddenly struck her that this dinner dance, the first of the celebrations she had planned to mark the sixtieth anniversary of the opening of the Knightsbridge store, was going to be the talk of the town tomorrow. The newspapers would be full of it. The stunning backdrop, the delicious food, the fine wines, the designer clothes and fabulous jewels, the celebrity guests, Lester Lannin and his orchestra . . . all added up to glamour with a capital G, something the press and the public could not resist.

Paula was pleased. Good publicity was a tremendous boost for the store. She smiled inwardly. It was New Year's Eve. The end of 1981. The beginning of a New Year. And, she hoped, the beginning of a new and brilliant era of retailing for the chain stores founded by her grandmother.

Leaning back in the chair, she silently made a new year's resolution: *the stores were going to be greater than ever in the coming decade.* She owed that to her grandmother, who had had such faith in her, and to her own daughters, who would one day inherit the chain from her.

Shane, who had been chatting to Jason Rickards and Sir Ronald Kallinski, cut in to her thoughts, when he suddenly turned to her, murmured, 'You look as though you're miles away, darling.' He took hold of her hand, leaned closer. 'You can relax. The evening's an assured success, and everyone's having a wonderful time. It's a smashing party, Paula.'

She gave her husband a radiant smile. 'Yes, it is, isn't it! And I'm so glad I decided on the ballroom at Claridges, rather than a series of private rooms at the Ritz. This has worked so much better.'

Shane nodded. Then he half groaned, half laughed, and exclaimed, 'Oho! Here comes Michael! Obviously I'm about to lose you again, and you only just sat down a few minutes ago.'

'They are keeping me busy tonight, aren't they? Actually, it's a bit exhausting, but I *am* the hostess, Shane, and I have my duty to do.' Her mouth curved up with laughter. 'I'm doing enough dancing to last me for the whole of 1982. I hope this is it, that we won't be going to any more dances for a long time. Remind me not to plan any, darling.' Despite these words, her face was still covered with smiles and her eyes were sparkling.

Shane gazed at her, loving her. Admiration flooded his face. He thought she had never looked more ravishing than she did tonight in all the years he had known her. She wore an elegant evening gown of midnight blue velvet, beautifully cut, but understated with long sleeves, a round neckline and a straight skirt. It had been designed by Christina Crowther especially for her, and it was flattering, emphasized her height and her slenderness. Pinned to one shoulder was the large pansy brooch he had commissioned Alain Boucheron, the Paris jeweller, to make for her. Composed entirely of sapphires, it echoed the bright blue of her eyes, as did the matching sapphire earrings. He had given the set to her on Christmas Eve, had known from the look on her face how much she liked them, how thrilled she was, even though she protested he had been overly extravagant. 'After all, you had the orchid greenhouse built for me. That is enough,' she had said. He had grinned, had told her the greenhouse was a present from the kids as well. 'They all chipped in, darling,' he had explained.

Michael drew to a standstill next to Paula's chair. 'Come on, shake a leg, Paula . . . you promised me the first slow number, and I have a feeling this one's it. Possibly for the rest of the evening.' He grabbed Shane's shoulder. 'You don't mind, do you?'

'Not half I don't,' Shane shot back swiftly, but in a jocular tone. 'However, since it's you, okay.'

'Philip's wife is a beautiful woman,' Michael said as he steered Paula around the ballroom floor. 'He's a lucky chap.'

'Yes, he is,' Paula agreed.

'But his gain is your loss.'

Paula laughed. 'Too true, Michael, in some ways.' She looked over his shoulder, focusing on Philip and his new bride gliding ahead of them to the strains of *Strangers in the Night*. 'But I've never seen him so happy. He adores her. As she does him. I may have lost the best personal assistant I've ever had, but I've gained a lovely and very loving sister-in-law.'

'Mmmm,' Michael murmured, moving nearer to Paula. Instantly he checked himself, pulled back, realizing that he was taking chances, holding her in such an intimate way. Her presence continued to inflame him, and being entwined on the dance floor was dangerous. Physically dangerous, for him at least. Their proximity was far too close. Also, it might cause tongues to wag. And besides, joke though Shane might, his eyes seemed to have been on *him* all evening. If Shane suspected him of being enamoured of Paula, *she* certainly did not. She was blithely unaware of his romantic interest in her, continued to treat him like an old shoe, the childhood friend, familiar, dependable, trustworthy. And that was the way he wanted it.

Paula was saying, 'Anyway, Maddy's going to continue working when they return to Sydney. I've made her the managing director of the Australian division of Harte's. She'll be supervising the running of the boutiques in Shane's hotels out there. But I *will* miss her in New York, no two ways about that, Michael. On the other hand, their happiness is so important to me . . . it must come first.' Leaning away from him, she smiled into his face, finished, 'Those two are madly in love, you know.'

'That's patently obvious.'

They danced in silence for a few minutes.

Michael grimaced to himself. He wished he had the same kind of private life and personal happiness as Philip Amory. But he had not been so fortunate. Valentine had been a strike-out as a wife, and he had never found anyone else who had the necessary attributes. He wondered then if he was in love with Paula, or merely turned on by her. There was no doubt in his mind that he was sexually attracted to her, and would like to take her to bed. But love? He wasn't sure.

Immediately squashing this thought, clearing his throat, he said, 'Daisy seems to be over the moon about Philip and Madelana.'

'She is. Of course, she was disappointed they got married in New York at the beginning of December, and only told the family after the fact. We all were, actually. But Mummy's relief at knowing her wayward, playboy son is finally hitched has cancelled out the disappointment, I'm absolutely sure of that.'

'I wanted to give a dinner party for them, but Philip was telling me earlier that they're leaving in a couple of days. Off on their honeymoon.'

'Yes. To Vienna, West Berlin, and then down to the south of France and the Villa Faviola.'

'Pretty coolish in those places right now. I would have thought they'd have chosen somewhere warm. Like Shane's hotel in Barbados, for instance.'

'Philip's always loved the Imperial in Vienna, ever since Grandy took us there when we were children. He and Emily think it's one of the greatest hotels in the world, and he wanted Madelana to see it. They're going to be staying in the Royal Suite, which is quite magnificent. It was Maddy who suggested that they then go on to Berlin, ending up at Faviola. She's heard a lot about it from me and Emily. Anyway, Maddy seems to have an obsession about Grandy, is wildly curious about every blessed home she owned. So naturally Faviola is a *must*.'

Michael laughed, fully understanding why Madelana was obsessed with Emma Harte. So many people had been, throughout her life, and after her death, which was why she was a legendary lady. Unexpectedly, he felt an easing of the tension within himself. 'I haven't had a chance to tell you, Paula, but I think you've done Aunt Emma proud tonight,' he said. 'This is a fabulous party, one of the best I've been to in the longest time, and –'

'Mind if I take over, old chap?' Anthony said with a huge grin.

'Every time I dance with you, one of your male relatives cuts in,' Michael grumbled, relinquishing her to the Earl of Dunvale. 'No doubt about it, Paula, you're the belle of the ball tonight.'

Paula laughed, winked at him mischievously.

Michael stepped to one side, ambled off, went in search of young Amanda.

Anthony took Paula in his arms and whirled her into the middle of the floor. After a couple of seconds, he said against her hair, 'Any chance of talking you and Shane into coming over to Ireland for a long weekend soon? It's been ages since you've visited Clonloughlin, and Sally and I would love to have you. You could bring Patrick and Linnet with you.'

'What a lovely idea, Anthony, and thanks for asking us. Perhaps we *can* make it . . . at the end of January. I'll talk to Shane. As far as I know, neither one of us is planning any foreign trips.'

'What a change that is!' Anthony answered in an amused voice. 'You two are worse than a couple of gypsies these days, forever trotting off around the world, wheeling and dealing. I can hardly keep track of you both.'

Before she had an opportunity to answer, Alexander was tapping Anthony on the shoulder, exclaiming, 'You're monopolizing the lady. It's my turn, Cousin.'

So saying, Sandy manoeuvred her into his arms and they swept away from Anthony. The latter stood gaping at them, a surprised look settling on his face.

They danced without speaking at first, enjoying being together on the floor. As children they had favoured each other as dancing partners. They had been in step then, as they were now.

Eventually, Alexander murmured quietly, 'Thanks so much, Paula.'

She looked up at him in puzzlement. 'What for, Sandy?'

'Christmas at Pennistone Royal, and this evening. For a short while you've turned the clock back for me, brought back so many lovely memories . . . of the past . . . of people whom I truly loved. Gran . . . my darling Maggie . . . your father . . .'

'Oh Sandy, you sound so sad!' Paula exclaimed. 'And I wanted the Christmas holidays and tonight to be happy occasions for all of us. I didn't –'

'And you succeeded admirably, Paula! They have been wonderful. And I'm not a bit sad. Quite the contrary, in fact.'

'Are you sure?' she asked in concern.

'Positive,' he lied smoothly, smiling at her.

Paula offered him a warm and loving smile in return, moved closer into his arms, gave his shoulder a squeeze. Her cousin Sandy had always been very special to her, and she was determined not to neglect him in the future. He needed her as much as he needed his sister, Emily. He was quite lonely, really. She realized that more than ever.

Sandy stared ahead, glad that they were on the floor, which was dim and crowded, since he was no longer able to keep the bleak look out of his eyes, the grim expression from his mouth. But Paula could not see his face, and everyone else was too preoccupied to notice, and for these small mercies he was thankful. They finished the dance, and, to his relief, not once did his step falter.

Sandy was a devastated man, and it was only a matter of weeks before the others knew this. They would have to know. He had no alternative but to tell them. He dreaded the day.

'Well, Paula, what do *you* think? Can the modern woman have it all?' Sir Ronald asked, looking at her quizzically, his eyes twinkling. 'You know – career, marriage and children.'

'Only if she's one of Emma Harte's granddaughters,' Paula quipped with a wicked grin.

Sir Ronald and the others seated at the table chuckled, and then Paula went on, 'But seriously, Grandy did teach us to be well organized, and that's my secret, and Emily's too. So, my answer is *yes*, the modern woman can have it all, provided she plans her life properly, and is a master of organization.'

'There are many who would differ with you, Paula,' Sir Ronald countered, 'who say you can have *two* of those things, but not all three. However, don't get me wrong, my dear, I applaud the way you and Emily run your lives. You're both quite remarkable, quite remarkable indeed.'

Paula said, 'Let's ask Maddy what she thinks . . . here she comes now . . . and if anyone personifies the modern woman of the eighties, then she certainly does.'

Several pairs of eyes focused on Madelana and Philip, who were approaching the table. She was glowing and radiant in a Pauline Trigère evening gown of deep purple chiffon overpatterned with swirls of purple cut velvet. With it she wore a magnificent diamond-and-pearl choker and matching chandelier earrings which had been wedding presents from Philip. Her hair was upswept, and, if anything, she was more striking than ever. Added to her natural gracefulness and poise was a new and lovely serenity.

She clung to her husband's arm as if never to let him go, and Philip looked equally possessive, proud of her, as they drew to a standstill at the table.

'Join us,' Paula said, beaming at them.

They did so, and Philip said, 'Congratulations, darling. This has been a smashing evening, truly remarkable, and it was an inspiration on your part to fly Lester Lannin in from the States.'

'Thanks, Pip.' Turning to Madelana, Paula went on, 'Listen, Maddy dear, Uncle Ronnie just asked me if the modern woman can have it all . . . marriage, career, babies. And I said who better to answer that than you . . . the career girl newly married.'

'I *hope* I can have it *all*,' Madelana laughed, glancing at Philip out of the corner of her eye. 'Philip wants me to continue working, to have a career, and I think I'd like to do so even after I have a child.'

'Anything that makes my wife happy is perfectly all right by me,' Philip announced, endorsing her words. He reached for her left hand on which she wore a platinum wedding band and a thirty-carat diamond that was flawless and blazed in the candlelight.

Madelana returned Philip's squeeze, looked from Paula to Sir Ronald, said quietly, 'I think it's a terrible waste for an educated woman with a career to stop working when she has a baby. I believe one can do both . . . it's all a question of juggling. And of course it depends on the woman, to a certain extent.'

Shane exclaimed, 'This is it! The last waltz!'

He sprang up, walked around the table, took hold of Paula's arm. Leading her off, he said, 'I wasn't going to let anyone else grab you for this one, my love.'

'I would have refused anyone who asked.'

They moved into each other's arms, and Shane held her tightly as they waltzed. Paula relaxed against his body, feeling safe and content with him, as she had since childhood. They were lucky, she and Shane. They had so much together. Their deep and abiding love. Their children. Shared interests. A common background. And he understood her so well, understood her immense need to fulfil her destiny as Emma Harte's heir. She wished she had pointed out to Sir Ronald a few seconds ago that a woman could only *really* have it all if she were married to the right man. She was. And he was a very special man. He had been a wonderful father to her children by Jim Fairley, treating them as though they were his own, loving them as though he were their natural father.

She thought of Jim then, but in the most fleeting way. He had become a dim figure in her mind, and her memories of him were fragmented, blurred by events that had taken place since his death, by those whom she loved, those who now peopled her life, by time passing. It seemed to her that she could not remember when she had not been Shane's wife. But the years *had* flown by since their marriage. This sudden thought made her draw away, look up at him.

He stared down at her, his black brows knitting together.

'What's the matter?'

'Nothing, darling. I was just thinking that very soon a new year will begin, and I expect that it, too, will disappear in a flash, like all the others have.'

'Too true, my love. On the other hand, look at it this way – 1982 is only the *first* of the next fifty years we're going to spend together.'

'Oh Shane, what a lovely thing to say, and it's a beautiful thought with which to start the new year.'

He brushed her cheek with his mouth, tightened his arm around her, swirled her around several times, and moved her out into the middle of the ballroom. Paula smiled inside, loving him so very much. Then she peered around the ballroom, seeking members of the family, her closest friends. It truly was a gathering of the clans ... the Hartes, the O'Neills and the Kallinskis were all represented tonight.

She spotted her mother dancing with Jason, looking as much in love as Madelana, who dreamily floated by in Philip's arms. Her father-in-law, Bryan, was leading Shane's mother in a sweeping, old-fashioned waltz, and Geraldine winked at her as they went sailing grandly past. Emily and Winston were coming onto the floor, followed closely by Michael and Amanda. She saw her Aunt Elizabeth gazing into the face of her French husband, Marc Deboyne, who was obviously enjoying himself tremendously tonight; even her old Aunt Edwina was on her feet making an effort, being solicitously shepherded around by a gallant Sir Ronald.

The music stopped abruptly, and Lester Lannin was saying into the microphone, 'Ladies and gentlemen ... it's almost midnight. We have BBC radio on the hotel's relay system. Here it comes ... here's Big Ben ... the countdown to midnight ...'

Everyone had stopped dancing to listen to the orchestra leader, and the ballroom was quiet, perfectly still. The chimes of the great clock in Westminster boomed out again and again. When the last stroke finally reverberated there was a resounding drumroll, and Shane was hugging Paula, kissing her, wishing her a happy new year, to be followed by Philip, then Madelana, doing the same thing.

Paula returned Madelana's affectionate embrace.

'Let me say it again, Maddy ... welcome to the family. And may this be the first of many happy years for you and Philip.'

Maddy was touched by Paula's lovely words, but before she had a chance to respond the orchestra struck up *Auld Lang Syne*.

Paula and Philip grabbed hold of her hands, pulled her forward as they began to sing.

Encircled by her new family, Maddy felt their love flowing out to her, and she wondered how *she* had ever been so lucky to become one of *them*. But she had, and she would be forever grateful. For years she had had nothing but sadness and loss. Now at last everything had changed.

25

Madelana lay with her head resting on Philip's shoulder.

The bedroom was shadow-filled, quiet except for the sound of his even breathing as he dozed, the faint rustling of the silk curtains, the ticking of the ormolu clock on the antique French Provincial chest.

The weather was somewhat mild for January, spring-like almost, and earlier Philip had opened the tall window. Now the night air blowing in was fresh and cool, laden with the tangy salt smell of the Mediterranean, the freshness of green-growing things in the sprawling gardens of Faviola.

She slipped out of bed, glided over to the window, leaned against the sill, looked out at the grounds, enjoying the gentle silence that pervaded the landscape at this late hour. She lifted her eyes. The sky was a deep pavonian blue that was nearly black, and resembled a canopy of velvet, high-flung like a great arc above the earth, filled with brilliant stars. Earlier, clouds had obscured the moon, but they had drifted away, and she saw that it was full tonight, a perfect sphere, and clear.

A long sigh of contentment trickled through her. They had been at the villa for ten days, relaxing, taking it easy after their trips to Vienna and Berlin. They had done very little since they had been here, except love each other, sleep late, go for walks in the gardens and on the beach, and take leisurely drives along the coast. They had spent most of their time at the villa, where Solange fussed over them like a mother hen, and Marcel cooked imaginative and delicious meals, and was forever thinking up some new dish with which to tempt them.

They read and listened to music, and sometimes she played her guitar for Philip, and sang her favourite Southern folk songs. He listened enraptured, and Madelana was pleased and flattered that he found her music entertaining. 'It's been ten days of absolute bliss, doing nothing in particular, having you all to myself,' Philip had said to her that morning, and she had told him she felt exactly the same way.

A tranquillity abounded here at Faviola, just as it did at Dunoon, and she drew enormous strength, as well as pleasure, from the quietness and the natural beauty of both places. *Dunoon*. It was her home now, just as the penthouse atop the McGill Tower in Sydney was her home. But it was the house on the sheep station at Coonamble that she loved the most. She had fallen in love with it at first sight. As she had with Philip. And he with her.

Madelana shivered and goose bumps speckled her arms, as she remembered the first time they had made love. She had lain in bed, weeping into his pillow after he had left the room, because when she had tried to envision the future with him she had seen no future. How foolish she had been that day . . . and how wrong. She *did* have a future with Philip McGill Amory. She was his wife. And, as Paula had said, 1982 was only the first of many happy years to come. They had a lifetime together stretching out before them.

She loved him . . . loved him so much it seemed almost unbearable at times. When he was absent from her she felt an enormous sense of loss, and experienced genuine physical pain, a tightness across her chest that only went away when he returned. Fortunately they had not been apart much since he had followed her to New York last October. He had suddenly arrived without warning, two weeks after she had left Sydney, had breezily walked into her office at Harte's on Fifth Avenue, unannounced, grinning from ear to ear. But his eyes had been anxious, she had noticed that immediately.

He had swept her off to lunch at '21', then taken her to dinner at Le Cirque, and it had been wonderful to be with him again. The minute she had left him at the airport in Sydney, she had suddenly known how much she cared. And on the long flight home there was a yearning for him in her heart that she knew would never go away. Never, not as long as she lived. The love she felt for Philip superseded everything in her life, even her career, if she had been asked to choose.

Later that same night, as they lay enfolded in each other's arms, after making love in the privacy of her apartment, he had asked her to marry him. She had not hesitated, had accepted his proposal at once.

They had talked well into the night, making their plans for the future. He had insisted they keep their engagement a secret. 'But only because I don't want a big fuss,' he had carefully explained. Equally as strong willed as he in certain ways, she had tried to persuade him to tell Paula. 'Because she will have to find a replacement for me. I can't – I won't – leave her in the lurch, Philip. She's been far too good to me. Besides, that's not my way of doing things. I have a responsibility to her, and to myself.'

Philip had understood her sentiments. Nevertheless he had pointed out that she could find a replacement without informing Paula, and he had been so tough with her about it she had had no option but to agree. And, oddly enough, she had not had to look far in the end. Cynthia Adamson, who worked in Marketing, had been a protégée of hers and a favourite of Paula's for some time. The young woman showed extraordinary promise, was quick, intelligent, diligent, and devoted to Paula and Harte's.

Maddy had realized that Cynthia could handle most of her work when she left, had the necessary potential to become Paula's personal assistant eventually. This had put her mind at ease to some extent, and she had made a point of bringing Cynthia into her orbit for the remainder of her time at the store.

Philip had stayed on until the end of the month, had then gone back to Australia for two weeks to attend to certain business matters, and had finally returned to New York at the end of November.

The minute he had arrived, he had announced that they were going to get married immediately. To have a big wedding, with his family in attendance, would have meant too much of a delay for him, he had explained. And far too much excitement. 'But we ought to give them a chance to come over. And we ought at least to inform your mother. And Paula,' Maddy had pointed out, filled with discomfort about excluding them.

He had been adamant. 'No, I won't wait for them to make their endless plans, to take over. It's got to be now.' He had laughed then, had said lightly, 'I'm afraid of losing you, don't you see? I must marry you at once.' Despite that laughing face, the carefree tone of voice, she had noticed the anxiety dwelling there once more, clouding his clear blue eyes. She had agreed to do anything he wished . . . just to make that panic-stricken look go away. She could not bear to see him troubled or upset.

And so they were married quietly at the beginning of December, in a Roman Catholic ceremony at St Patrick's Cathedral on Fifth Avenue, with only her Boston friend, Patsy Smith, and Miranda O'Neill and her husband Elliot James present. She had worn an elegant winter-white wool dress with a matching coat by Trigère, and had carried a trailing spray of pink and yellow orchids, and afterwards Philip had taken them all to lunch at La Grenouille.

'I think we'd better consummate this marriage at once,' he had said teasingly later in the day, when they had returned to their vast suite at the Pierre Hotel. And only after they had made love did he finally agree that they could telephone his family in England.

They had spoken first to Daisy, who was staying at Pennistone Royal in Yorkshire, and then to Paula, who was at the house in Belgrave Square. His mother and his sister had not sounded particularly surprised, and they had been overjoyed at the news, if somewhat disappointed to have missed the actual wedding. Both of them had welcomed her warmly into the family, and she had felt their sincerity and love coming across the transatlantic wire as they had reached out to her.

And then it had begun . . . a whole new life for her.

Philip loved her as deeply, as desperately, as she loved him. This not only manifested itself in his physical passion for her, his tenderness and kindness, but in the way in which he showered gifts on her, spoiled her outrageously. The flawless, pure white diamond engagement ring, the pearl-and-diamond choker and chandelier earrings, had been only the first of many valuable jewels he presented to her. There had been other gifts as well . . . furs, Hermès bags, and couture clothes. But he was just as likely to show up with a pair of gloves, a silk scarf, a favourite book or tape he wished to share with her, a bottle of perfume, a bunch of violets, or some other such small yet meaningful token.

But the most important aspect of her new life was her husband. Philip filled the empty spaces of her heart, and he gave her a sense of security and of belonging; she no longer felt so alone.

There were times when she had to pinch herself to make sure this was not all a dream. That it was real, that he was real . . .

She did not hear Philip get out of bed, and she started in surprise when he wrapped his arms around her. She looked up at him.

He kissed the top of her head. 'What are you doing, standing here at the window? You'll catch cold, darling.'

Madelana turned around within the circle of his arms so that she was facing him. She reached up to touch his cheek. 'I couldn't sleep, so I got up to look at the gardens. They're so beautiful in the moonlight. And then I started thinking –'

'What about?' he interrupted, gazing down at her.

'Everything that's happened in the last few months. It's like a dream, Philip. And sometimes I have the awful feeling I'm going to wake up and discover none of it is true, and that you're not real.'

'Oh, but I am very real, my darling, and this is not a dream. It's reality. *Our reality*.' He drew her closer to him, held her tightly against his bare chest, stroked her hair. There was a long moment of silence between them, before he said, 'I've never known peace like this. Or such love. I cherish you, my lovely Maddy. And I want you to know I will always be constant. There will never be another woman in my life, not ever again.'

'I know that, Philip. Oh darling . . . I do love you so . . .'

'Thank God for that! And I love you, too.'

He bent down, kissed her gently on the lips.

She clung to him.

He found himself involuntarily sliding his hands down her back, over her lovely, small, rounded buttocks. The satin of her nightdress was smooth and cool and curiously erotic to him. He pressed his body closer to his wife's and in an instant he was aroused.

Madelana began to tremble, wanting him again, as she knew he suddenly wanted her, even though they had made love only a short while before. They were always like this, reaching out to each other, unable to keep their hands off each other. She had never known this kind of aching, all-consuming physical desire, this overwhelming passion, this constant need to possess and be possessed. The depth and strength of her feelings for him were unlike anything she had ever experienced in her life.

The heat was flowing through her, rising from her thighs, from the very core of her, spreading through her body up into her neck and face. Her cheeks were flaming. She kissed his chest, then put her arms around him tightly. Her fingers pressed against his shoulder blades, smoothed down over his broad back.

Philip was conscious of the heat from her body, and it seemed to scorch him. He reached for one of her breasts, began to caress it, and as he did he kissed her neck, then brought his mouth to hers once more. Their kisses were deep, sensual, and they stood in front of the window, locked in a fierce embrace, welded together as if never to be separated. And then finally, unable to contain himself any longer, he lifted her in his arms and carried her over to the bed.

They slipped out of their nightclothes, and he ran his strong but gentle hands over her slender body, marvelling at its beauty. Moonlight was flooding the room, and in its soft and muted light her skin was taking on a silvery sheen; she looked ethereal, of another world.

He bent over her, kissed the cleft between her breasts, trailed his mouth down her stomach, and she shivered and reached for him. And quickly, with little preamble, he took her to him, joined himself to her, and they loved each other for a long time.

She told him two days later.

It was a radiant day, bright and hard as a diamond. The sky was a sharp azure blue and cloudless, the glittering Mediterranean Sea the colour of lapis, the sun a golden orb, but without any warmth. Despite the beauty of the day there was a nip in the air, a hint of snow coming down from the Alps.

They were sitting on the terrace overlooking the vast sunfilled gardens of Faviola, bundled up in thick sweaters and warm coats. Earlier they had gone for a walk, and now they were sipping an aperitif before lunch. Philip had been talking about their travel plans for the next few weeks. Maddy had listened, said little, even though he had given her the opening she'd been looking for, and a small silence had fallen between them.

She broke it, when she said, 'I don't think we should go on to Rome, Philip. I think it would be better if we returned to London.'

He looked at her swiftly, struck by the odd note of tension in her voice, a nuance that had been absent for weeks. A black brow arched. 'Why, darling?'

Madelana cleared her throat, said softly. 'There's something I've been wanting to say for a few days ... I have a strange feeling ...' She stopped, cleared her throat, and after a slight hesitation, finished quietly, 'I think I'm pregnant.'

He looked startled for a moment, taken aback, and then a smile broke through and his blue eyes sparkled with joy. His excited voice echoed the expression on his face, when he exclaimed, 'Maddy, this is the most wonderful news! The best I've had since you said you'd marry me.'

Reaching for her, he brought her into his arms, kissed her tenderly, then pressed her head close to his chest, stroked her hair.

After a moment, he murmured, 'But you said *think*. Aren't you sure, darling?'

Drawing away from him, she looked up into his face and nodded. 'Pretty sure. All the signs are there, and when I see a doctor I know he'll confirm it. That's the reason I'd like to go back to London instead of continuing on to Italy.'

'Absolutely, darling. You're right. That's what we must do. Oh Maddy, this is just marvellous.'

'Then you're happy about it?' Her voice was low.

'Thrilled.' He gave her a puzzled glance, frowned. 'Aren't you?'

'Of course ... I just thought you might think it's a bit too soon.'

'To have a son and heir! You must be kidding. I'm elated, angel.'

'It might be a girl ...'

'Then she'll be a daughter and heir. Let's not forget, I'm the grandson of Emma Harte, and she never drew distinctions between men and women when it came to heirs. And neither did my grandfather Paul. He made my mother his heir, you know.'

Madelana nodded, half smiled.

But there was a quietness about her that gave Philip reason to pause for a moment. He studied her, then asked, 'What's wrong, darling?'

'Nothing. Truly, Philip.'

He was not so sure about this. He said, 'Are you worried about your career? About running Harte's in Australia?'

'No, I'm not.'

Still unconvinced, he went on quickly, 'Because if you are, you mustn't be. You'll have no problems with me about working. My grandmother went to business when she was pregnant. So did Paula and Emily, and neither Shane nor Winston objected. That's the way the men are in this family, since we were raised and trained by the famous matriarch.'

'I know all that, darling.'

'So what's wrong? You seem so quiet, deflated.'

Reaching out, she took hold of his hand, held it very tightly. 'I've been worrying about telling you for days, worrying that you would think the timing was wrong, that it was too soon in our marriage, that we needed more time alone together, to get to know each other better before a child came along. I suppose I thought you might be annoyed, think I'd been careless.'

'It takes two to tango,' he murmured.

'Yes.' She paused, smiled at him tremulously. 'I love you so much, Philip . . . you're everything in the world to me. And I want you to be happy with me . . . I want to please you . . . always.'

He saw the sudden glitter of tears in her lovely grey eyes, and his heart twisted inside. He brought his hand to her cheek, stroked it lovingly. 'You *do* please me. In every way. And you make me very happy. You're my life, Maddy. And the baby will be my life.'

Unexpectedly, he threw back his head and began to laugh, entirely changing the mood between them.

Baffled, she looked at him curiously. 'What is it?'

'To think that the dyed-in-the-wool international playboy is now very much a married man and an expectant father! Who would have believed it?' he said, eyeing her merrily, chuckling again.

Maddy laughed with him. He always managed to assuage her worries, to lift her spirits.

He jumped up, took her hand in his, pulled her to her feet. 'Come on, love. Let's go inside. I want to make some phone calls.'

'To whom, darling?'

'The family, of course.'

'All right.'

They walked along the terrace towards the French doors, their arms wrapped around each other.

Abruptly, Madelana stopped, turned to Philip.

'Once I've seen the gynaecologist in London, and we've spent a few days in Yorkshire with your mother, as we promised, I'd like to go home, Philip . . . home to Australia. Home to Dunoon.'

He hugged her to him, loving her more than ever for saying this. 'Yes, my darling, we'll go home,' he said, 'and make ready for our first child . . .'

Half an hour later he was still on the phone in the library.

He had spoken first to Daisy and Jason in Yorkshire, then to Paula at the store in London, passing along the news about her pregnancy. And each time he had brought her to the phone to have a word.

There had been many congratulations, and lots of love sent, and Daisy, in particular, had been ecstatic, knowing she was to become a grandmother again.

Now Philip was talking to his cousin Anthony at Clonloughlin in Ireland.

She had not anticipated this, had not expected him to shout their news to the world in this way. Philip was such a private man when it came to his personal life, and after all, he had insisted on a secret engagement and marriage. Maddy knew then, with a sudden flash of insight, why he had excluded his family from their wedding. It had been for her, to save her from undue heartache, to balance the situation. He had a vast family; every member of hers was dead.

How painful her wedding day might have been . . . Philip would have been surrounded by his loved ones, she would have been alone, with no one from her side to witness that very special and important day in her life. And she would have longed for her parents and little Kerry Anne, for Young Joe and Lonnie.

Philip had understood all this. Of course he had. Everything was suddenly very clear to her.

Madelana curled up on the big, comfortable sofa, listening to him speaking, watching him, thinking what an extraordinary man he was. Shrewd, brilliant, tough in business, yet so sensitive and loving when it came to his feelings for her.

She blinked, sat back, held her head on one side, trying to visualize him objectively for a split second. What a handsome man he was. It was his colouring that so startled her at times – the dark glossy hair, the black moustache, the tanned face, the eyes so supernaturally blue. He seemed larger than life. And he was so wonderfully alive and vital; he positively glowed with well being at this moment.

He must always be like this, the way he is today, she thought. Full of laughter and life and joyousness. And I must never be the one to cause him pain.

26

There was no question in Arabella's mind that Sarah considered her to be a usurper of sorts.

No, that's too strong a word, she thought, impatiently throwing down the magazine she had been reading, unable to concentrate. I'm the . . . *interloper*. Yes, that's the right word. Until I strolled into his life Sarah had him all to herself whenever he came to Europe. The woman enjoys being the centre of attraction. That was only too apparent at lunch today.

Arabella rose, glided across the sitting room of the guest suite of the farmhouse in Mougins, stood looking out of the window for a moment.

It had been a glorious day, but now dusk was falling, and the gardens below were bosky, mysterious, almost eerie in the dimming light. A faint, vaporous mist shrouded everything in a mantle of grey and opal tints, and the trees in the apple orchard beyond the white fence were inchoate, illusory.

She shivered, filling with melancholy, feeling unexpectedly sad. She shrugged these feelings away before they took hold. She had no reasons to be sad. She had everything. Arabella smiled a small, secret smile. Well, not *everything*. But she was getting there.

Swinging around, she returned to the fireside, settled herself on the sofa once more, enjoying the warmth and cheerfulness of the blazing logs. She liked a fire. There was something comforting about it ... perhaps because it reminded her of her childhood in Hampshire, the big old house where she had grown up.

After a few moments' reflection and several adjustments to her plans for the next few weeks, she glanced around for the umpteenth time since they had arrived that morning, admiring the room again.

Here, and in the adjoining bedroom, ancient, dark wood ceiling beams, white, half-timbered walls and old brick fireplaces had been left intact. In combination with the slightly slanting ceiling, they gave this top floor under the eaves a cosiness, and character. Thick wool carpet stretched wall to wall, and its *café-au-lait* beige was the perfect backdrop for the lovely English chintzes on the huge sofa and the chairs, the French Provençal country furniture made of ripe woods polished to a mellow gleam. The same coffee-coloured carpet flowed through into the bedroom, where fine Porthault linens dressed the bed, upholstered the antique headboard and hung as curtains at the mullioned windows.

The suite was as fresh as a flower garden, overflowing with diverse floral patterns that somehow blended well together, and it was infinitely comfortable. A fortune had been spent on the entire farmhouse, and all of the rooms had been put together with taste, discernment and an eye to colour and design.

Whatever else Sarah Lowther Pascal might be, she is certainly a clever homemaker, Arabella decided. She had done wonders with the sprawling old farm perched on a hillside high above Cannes, had decorated it with flair, given it undeniable cachet and charm. And in the grounds outside she had turned a series of decrepit old barns into one huge, superb studio for Yves, had covered the central section with a roof of glass to let in the maximum amount of light.

Yves Pascal's paintings hung everywhere in the farm. They were bold, modern, not to Arabella's taste at all, which ran to Old Masters and the traditional. But the artist was a powerhouse in the international art world, and his paintings were in great demand; apparently others liked his works, even if she did not. These days they were commanding huge prices.

On the other hand, she had really taken to the small, wiry Frenchman from the moment she had met him. He was a bit of a peacock, a strutter, an egocentric. But nonetheless, he was the possessor of an inordinate amount of Gallic charm. She did not quite understand his relationship with Sarah. They seemed to be poles apart. Yet he adored his wife and their child, Chloe; she had noticed that immediately.

Jonathan had told her that the little girl had his grandmother's looks and colouring. He had not volunteered much about the legendary Emma Harte in the four months she had known him, but from a remark Sarah had made at lunch, she had gathered that the two of them were at loggerheads with their cousin, Paula O'Neill. After lunch, later that afternoon, she had asked Jonathan why there was a feud in the family, and he had muttered something about Paula turning their grandmother against them, persuading her to make certain changes in her will. He had seemed suddenly upset, even angry, and after murmuring a few sympathetic words, she had wisely let the matter drop. She had not wanted to underscore his unprecedented agitation. She had never seen him like that before.

Her thoughts centred on Jonathan.

She had been led to believe he would be difficult to ensnare. But this had not proved to be the case. He had immediately fallen for her, and heavily so, had courted her assiduously in Hong Kong. She had withheld herself in every way in the beginning. Then slowly she had opened up, both mentally and physically. She had let him see her intelligence, her inquiring mind, her knowledge about art and antiques, her sophistication; and she had tempted him with her body. Their fraternal good night kisses had led to deeper kissing, then petting and increasingly intimate touching, until she had finally succumbed to his potent sexuality, had allowed him to take her to bed.

All along she had never pretended to be a virgin, had let him know there had been other men before him. But she had carefully pointed out that she was discriminating, not promiscuous, and wanted to be certain of her feelings, his feelings, before they embarked on an affair. He had applauded her candour, and had confided he was only interested in women who were as experienced and worldlywise as he. And he had shown patience with her.

A knowing look slid into Arabella's pitch-black eyes. She had expertise. She knew how to give him pleasure in countless ways . . . ways he had no comprehension of as yet. She did not want him to know just how experienced she was in the art of sex. She wanted him to become totally besotted with her, to fall truly in love with her first. Only then would she take him to heights he had never dreamed of, as only she knew how.

And so she continued to lead him along gently, and little by little it was all happening . . . every day he became more committed to her. There was a new warmth in him, and he could not get enough of her. In bed and out of it. He wanted her with him all the time.

Arabella looked down at the plain gold wedding band on the third finger of her left hand. It was gleaming brightly in the firelight. Jonathan had wanted to give her a circle of diamonds. She had asked for this plain, old-fashioned gold ring, telling him that it was more symbolic. He had been surprised, yet obviously touched, by her sentiments.

How thunderstruck Tony had been when Jonathan had married her so quickly in Hong Kong just before Christmas, then swept her off to Europe on their honeymoon. He had been startled to discover she was suddenly going to be out of reach for several months. Very put out, in actuality. And she had taken great satisfaction in being able to ruffle Tony's infuriating equanimity for once.

Her new husband had wanted to take her to Paris. But there was so much of her past in that city, so much sadness to be recalled, she was not excited about honeymooning there. Nor did she particularly want to take the chance of running into someone who had known her in the old days. She did not need to deal with friends long since departed from her life, nor confront memories gone stale and cold. And so she convinced Jonathan they would enjoy Rome more, had suggested they then go on to Mougins in the south of France, to visit his cousin Sarah, whom he had spoken about so warmly. This had delighted him, and he had readily agreed to her travel plans.

Rome had been fun. Since she knew the city like a native, she had been able to take him sightseeing, and to the choicest restaurants and clubs, which were well off the usual tourist track, patronized by local society and the international jet set.

And she had been very loving, sexually pliable, catering to his desires, more than ready to please him, and this had made him extremely happy.

It was in Rome that he had bought her yet another wedding gift, an extraordinary necklace which he had presented to her as a surprise on their last night in the Eternal City, before they had left for France. Composed of a single strand of large black pearls, it had a cream-coloured, teardrop pearl hanging from a ten-carat diamond in the centre of the strand.

Although she had some nice jewellery of her own, the black pearl necklace was not only rare but surpassed everything in her possession. Except, of course, for the huge Burmese ruby-and-diamond ring Jonathan had given her when they had become engaged.

The chimes of the little carriage clock brought Arabella out of her reverie. She glanced at it, surprised to see it was seven. Jonathan, who had gone to Cannes with Yves, had said he would be back by seven-thirty. She must be ready for him.

Rising, she hurried into the bedroom, took a sheer, black chiffon nightgown trimmed with coffee-coloured lace out of the armoire, then went into the bathroom to undress and freshen up.

A few minutes later, wearing the glamorous nightgown and a matching black chiffon peignoir that floated around her in a cloud, Arabella seated herself at the dressing table. She had worn her silver-gilt hair in a severe chignon all day; now she pulled out the pins and let it fall around her face and down her back. She brushed it until it gleamed.

Leaning forward, she peered at herself in the glass. Sometimes she was startled by her own beauty, by the lack of lines around her eyes and other tell-tale signs of ageing, by the suppleness of her skin, the flawlessness of her complexion. Life had left hardly any marks on her face, and nothing seemed to mar its youth and beauty. Even when she was ill with a cold, or some other minor complaint, she appeared to be in blooming health. How lucky she was. She looked much younger than her thirty-four years.

After scrubbing off her bright red lipstick with a tissue, she toned down her flushed face with creamy foundation and transparent powder until she was very pale, almost wan looking. She added extra eyeliner to her lids, emphasizing their natural almond shape. Smoothing on black shadow, she then highlighted the bones under the brows with touches of purple and silver, and instantly her eyes stood out like huge, dark coals in her face. Once she had blotted her lips, she smeared on colourless salve, and sprayed herself generously with the musky perfume Jonathan preferred. She then lifted the black pearl necklace out of its leather case and clasped it around her neck. Jonathan liked her to wear jewellery in bed. It was a fetish of his.

Hurrying now, she stepped over to the armoire, opened it, stared at herself in the full-length mirror, approving of her reflection. She looked so young, like a girl of sixteen, her face full of innocence – and promise. Yet in contrast, her body was the body of an alluring woman, shapely, sensual, and provocative in the revealing nightgown.

The black chiffon was taut across her breasts. Her nipples and their dark aureoles were faintly visible through the filmy chiffon and lace. She had had the nightgown made in Hong Kong, and the seamstress had cut it to fit her body perfectly; it clung to her in all the right places. And in the most tantalizing way, she decided.

Stepping into a pair of high-heeled, black-satin mules, she went through into the sitting room where she stood for a moment warming herself in front of the fire. And then she stretched out on the Chesterfield sofa to wait for her husband.

As the minutes ticked by, Arabella began to realize she was anxious for Jonathan to return, looked forward to seeing him, even though he had only been gone for a couple of hours. She hoped he would want to make love before they went down to dinner.

Started by these thoughts, she sat upon the sofa with a jolt, frowned, reached for a cigarette, lit it.

As she smoked, her mind turned over at a rapid pace, and it dawned on her how much she liked Jonathan's blond good looks, his lovely manners, the finesse with which he did things, his very Englishness. It was such a change, such a relief, to be with an Englishman after the foreigners she had known. She also enjoyed the avid attention he paid to her, his passion for her, his sexual prowess. Jonathan Ainsley, her husband, was as good a lover as she had ever had, if not, indeed, the very best.

She suddenly suspected she was falling in love with him, and she was further surprised at herself.

Fifteen minutes later Jonathan hurried into the sitting room. It was dimly lit, but the logs blazing in the hearth cast a roseate glow throughout.

Arabella was standing in front of the fireplace, and he thought she looked quite extraordinary tonight. This brought him to a standstill.

He paused in the centre of the floor, staring at her, appreciating her beauty, her sensuality. How inviting she was in the black-chiffon negligée. He could faintly make out parts of her body through the delicate fabric . . . the high, full breasts, the slender waist, the blonde mound of Venus below. Black was a colour that suited her well. It brought out the creaminess of her incomparable skin, the silver lights in the cascade of glorious, shimmering hair.

She held out her arms to him, half smiling.

Her black eyes seemed to burn right through him, and they held an expression he had never seen reflected there before. But curiously enough, whatever the expression meant, it excited him. As he moved forward he felt his desire for her stirring.

'I've missed you, darling,' she murmured in her low, husky voice as he came to a stop next to her.

'I've not been all *that* long,' he replied. Nevertheless he was pleased. He reached for her, took her in his arms, kissed her on the mouth. When they finally drew apart, he held her away from him, gripping her shoulders firmly with both hands, gazing deeply into her face.

'What is it?' she asked at last.

'You are so very, *very* beautiful tonight, Arabella. More beautiful than I have ever seen you, I do believe.'

'Oh Jonathan . . .'

He leaned into her, kissed the hollow in her throat, and as he did he slipped the peignoir off her shoulders. It slid to the floor. Next he pulled at the narrow nightgown straps tied in bows, and as they came undone this garment, too, fell in a swirl of chiffon at her feet.

She stood before him naked except for the black pearls encircling her slender throat.

Jonathan stepped back. Of all the women he had ever had, she was the most experienced sexually, and therefore the most exciting, the most desirable . . . Of all the objects of art in his collection, she was the most beautiful thing, the biggest prize of all . . . His greatest possession. She was perfection itself. And he owned her. Owned every part of her. No, that was not quite true. She was still withholding. This continued to surprise him. But soon she would give herself up to him completely, abandon herself fully. He was confident of his powers . . . and his power over her.

Arabella said slowly, 'Jonathan, is something wrong? You're looking at me oddly.'

'No, of course there's nothing wrong,' he replied. 'I'm just admiring you, thinking how lovely you look . . . wearing only my black pearls. How white your body is in contrast.' As he spoke, he reached out, ran a finger down one of her breasts.

He thought he would explode. The blood rushed to his face, and he trembled as he moved closer to her, put his hands around her neck, unclasped the necklace.

'There, that's much better,' he said, slipping it into his pocket. 'You need no adornment, Arabella. You are perfect as you are . . . like a Grecian statue exquisitely chiselled out of the finest alabaster.'

He removed his sports jacket, threw it on a chair. Then, taking hold of her hand, he led her towards the sofa. 'Come let us lie here together for a while. Let us love each other, enjoy each other,' he said. 'I want to know you more intimately than I already do, possess even more of you. And then more . . . and more. Will you let me, Arabella?'

'Yes,' she whispered huskily. 'If you will do the same.'

'Ah Arabella, we are so alike, you and I, in every conceivable way.' He chuckled softly. 'A couple of sinners, I do believe.'

Jonathan held her with his eyes. A knowing look crossed his face. He pressed her down onto the cushions with one hand. With the other he began to unbutton his shirt.

27

'I'm not quite sure how to tell you this,' Alexander began, looking from his sister, Emily, to his cousins, Paula O'Neill and Anthony Standish, the Earl of Dunvale.

The three of them were seated on the two sofas in front of the fire, sipping the drinks he had poured for them a short while before.

'In fact,' Alexander went on, 'I've racked my brains for weeks now, seeking the right words, the best way of explaining –'

Breaking off, he rose from his chair, walked across the drawing room, stood at the huge, bow-shaped window that soared to the ceiling, overlooked the small garden behind his Mayfair house.

He suddenly wished that he hadn't asked them to come over, that he didn't have to tell them ... *fervently* wished that he could simply ... let it happen. But that would be unthinkable. Unfair of him. And besides, there were too many things to be decided, too many legalities involved.

Alexander was tense, held himself stiffly, his shoulders hunched underneath his jacket. He took a deep breath, summoning his courage. This was perhaps the most difficult thing he had ever had to do in his entire life.

Emily, watching him intently, had detected the strained note in his voice when she had first arrived at the house. And now she noticed how taut he was. They had been unusually close throughout their lives, and she knew him as well as she knew herself. Intuitively she felt that something was radically wrong.

Pressing back her alarm, she said, 'You sound awfully serious, Sandy.'

'Yes,' he responded, continuing to stare out of the window, wondering how to begin. In the gathering dusk of this January evening, the patch of garden looked sad and bereft with its blackened skeletal trees, empty flower beds frosted with old snow turned grey by London soot. It seemed to him that this bit of earth echoed his bleak mood.

The three cousins were waiting for Alexander to continue, to explain why he had invited them here, had actually *insisted* they come tonight. And they exchanged concerned glances behind his back.

Paula swung her head, focused on Anthony, lifted a brow questioningly.

The Earl shrugged, half-raised his hands in a helpless gesture, indicating his own considerable bafflement.

Paula peered at Emily on the sofa opposite. Emily tightened her lips, shook her head rapidly, expressing her own puzzlement. 'I don't know what this is all about either,' Emily mouthed silently to Paula. After a moment, she cleared her throat, ventured aloud, 'Sandy dear ... Gran always said that if a person had something difficult to explain, or unpleasant to say, the best thing to do was simply to blurt it out. Why don't you do that?'

'That's not as easy as it sounds,' her brother answered quietly.

'Whatever problems you have, you know you have our full support,' Anthony volunteered in his most reassuring voice.

Alexander pivoted on his heels, stood with his back to the great window, regarding the three of them thoughtfully, 'Yes, I do know that, Anthony, and thanks,' he said at last. A faint wavering smile touched his mouth, then faded instantly.

Paula, studying him alertly, saw something strange in the back of his light blue eyes, the emptiest of expressions, and it made her heart tighten. 'There's something awfully wrong ... it's ... it's bad, isn't it, Sandy?'

He nodded. 'I've always prided myself on being able to handle anything, Paula. But this ...' He discovered he was unable to finish his sentence.

Paula remembered then, remembered the telephone conversation she had had with him at the end of August last year. She had sensed he had a problem that particular morning, had then dismissed it as being merely her vivid imagination at work. But she had been right after all, she was sure of that. She clasped her hands together tightly, feeling unaccountably nervous and filling, unexpectedly, with apprehension.

Alexander said slowly, 'I asked the three of you to come round this evening ... because of our closeness over the years, the special relationship I have with each one of you.' He waited, took a breath. 'I do have certain problems. I thought we could discuss them rationally, and that perhaps you would help me to come to a few decisions.'

'Of course we will,' Anthony said. His cousin was behaving out of character and he was desperately worried. He fixed his clear, steady gaze on the other man, wanting to convey his affection and devotion. They had helped each other over some rough terrain in the past, and would no doubt do so again.

Leaning forward with a degree of urgency, Anthony asked, 'Is it to do with business? Or is it a family matter?'

'Personal really,' Alexander answered.

He moved away from the window, walked slowly across the elegant, period drawing room, lowered himself into the chair he had vacated a short while before. He knew there was no point in putting it off any longer. They simply had to be told.

Alexander let out a deeply weary sigh. He said, in a controlled voice, 'I'm very ill ... I'm dying, actually.'

Emily, Paula and Anthony gaped at him. None of them had expected to hear anything as devastating as this. They were stunned.

Alexander went on hurriedly, 'I'm sorry to have told you in such a blunt manner, but I took Emily's advice. And Gran *was* right, you know. It *is* the only way ... best to blurt it out, get it said without too much preamble.'

Paula was so shaken she was unable to respond. Blindly, she groped for Anthony's hand.

He took it, enfolded it in his comfortingly. He was as stupefied as she, at a complete loss. There were no words. Anything he said to Sandy would be cold comfort. A great sadness flowed through him. What an appalling thing to happen to poor Sandy, who was in his prime. Sandy had been such a good friend, a source of strength during his own travails over the years. And most especially at the time Min had been found drowned in the lake at Clonloughlin.

Anthony reached for his glass of scotch-and-soda on the end table. He suddenly needed a drink.

Emily was ashen with shock.

She sat perfectly still, staring at her brother in disbelief, her eyes dark with sudden pain. She felt as though all blood had drained out of her. Then taking hold of herself, she got to her feet a bit shakily, and went to him. Kneeling down next to his chair, she took his hand in hers, clung to it.

'Sandy, it's not true! It can't be!' she cried in a low but vehement tone. 'Oh please say it isn't . . .' Emily's voice quavered, came to a stop, and her green eyes brimmed. 'Not you, Sandy, oh please, not *you*.'

'I'm afraid so,' he said in the steadiest voice imaginable, 'and there's not much I can do to change this one, Dumpling. It's out of my hands.'

His use of her old nickname made her choke, and long forgotten memories came rushing back unbidden, evoked their childhood years together; she remembered how he had protected her, looked after her, and her throat suddenly ached and her heart felt as if it was being squeezed in a vice. She closed her eyes for a split second, striving to come to grips with her brother's tragic and frightening news.

'You say you're d-d-dying.' She stumbled on this last word, had to take several deep breaths before continuing, 'But of what? What's wrong with you, Sandy? You seem perfectly well to me. What are you suffering from?'

'I have leukaemia . . . it's known as acute granulocytic leukaemia.'

'Surely that can be treated!' Anthony exclaimed, sudden hope leaping onto his worried face. 'Tremendous strides have been made in medicine today, especially in the treatment of cancer, and perhaps –'

'There is no cure,' Alexander interrupted.

'But what actually is it?' Emily demanded, anxiety making her voice rise, giving it a shrillness abnormal for her. 'What on earth *causes* it?'

'A malignant change in cells that produce granulocytes, one of the types of white blood cells made in the bone marrow,' he explained, so well educated about his disease the details were now readily on the tip of his tongue. 'They multiply and survive longer than normal cells. Very simply put, they destroy. As their numbers increase, they invade the bone marrow, enter the bloodstream and eventually attack the organs and tissue.'

'Oh God, Sandy –' Paula began, and came to a halt. Her feelings got the better of her. The words she had been about to say strangled in her throat. She steadied herself; somehow she managed to hang onto her self-possession. After a few moments, she went on, 'I'm so sorry, so very sorry, darling. I'm here for you, we're all here for you, whenever you need us, day or night.'

'Yes,' he said, 'I know you are. I'm counting on it, actually, Paula.'

'Isn't there any chance of at least *arresting* the leukaemia?' Paula probed, her manner gentle, her sympathy and compassion reflected in her eyes.

'There really isn't,' Alexander replied.

With sudden fierceness, Emily said, 'I realize you must have been to the best doctors in London, but we must go farther afield. We really must. What about the States? Sloan-Kettering in New York, for instance? We can't just stand by and *allow* this to happen, Sandy. We must do *something*.'

'I agree with you, Emily,' Anthony said. 'There has to be some sort of advanced treatment in this day and age. *Somewhere*. I can't accept this either, Sandy. I won't.' He averted his face, struggling with his feelings.

Alexander shook his head, and it was with a finality that was unmistakable. 'I understand how the three of you feel. I was exactly the same as you in the beginning. Looking for a cure, full of hope, but the hope rapidly changed to frustration, then anger, and finally to *acceptance*. You see . . .' He stopped, took several deep breaths, continued slowly, 'There is absolutely nothing that can be done for me. And believe me, I *have* been to the very best specialists in London, New York and Zurich. What I'm suffering from *is* fatal. I'm having treatment, of course, but there has been hardly any remission.'

A grim silence settled in the drawing room.

Alexander sat back in his chair, relieved at last to have finally told them. He had resigned himself to his fate some time ago, but he had worried greatly about the family and how they would take it, most especially Emily.

For their parts, his sister and his cousins were trying to come to grips with the heartbreaking news he had just imparted, striving to absorb it, and to get a hold of their emotions as well. They each, in their different ways, loved Alexander, and although they did not know it, they were sharing the same thought at this precise moment. All were asking themselves why it had to be Alexander who had been stricken in this manner. He was the finest, the kindest, the most loving and understanding of men. The very best. He had always been there for them, whenever they had needed him, no matter what the problem, and that was how he had been since childhood. The three cousins believed him to be the one truly *good* man they knew. If anyone was a saint, it was Alexander.

Paula eventually spoke. 'You've known for some months, haven't you?'

Alexander nodded, then picked up his glass of white wine, took a sip.

'Was it the end of August last year when you found out you were ill?' she asked.

'No, it was October. But you're close enough, Paula.' He gave her an odd look. 'How did you know?'

Paula's grave face was infinitely still. 'I didn't. Not really. But I did have a queer feeling things were not right with you, when you phoned me from Leeds – the day we missed each other at Fairley. There was such a peculiar note in your voice, it prompted me to ask you if there was a problem, and, if you recall, you said no. So I dismissed it, I thought it was my imagination getting the better of me.'

'You were very perceptive that morning,' Alexander murmured. 'I felt uneasy, wanted to talk to you. I was already starting to have symptoms. I was becoming fatigued quickly, and it worried me, and I discovered I bruised and bled very easily . . . if I merely knocked myself against something.'

Alexander got up, went to fetch the bottle of wine, refilled Paula's and Emily's glasses, and his own, took the bottle back to the silver ice bucket on the console.

The others waited in silence, dreading what else he had to say to them.

He went on, as he sat down, 'I was doing a lot of work on the estate at Nutton Priory in late September, and I was baffled. I wondered if I'd become a haemophiliac overnight – if that was possible. Then early in October I developed the most frightful ulcers in my mouth. I was growing more alarmed than ever, and that's why I cancelled our lunch date, Paula. I finally went to see my doctor. He immediately sent me to a specialist in Harley Street. The tests and the bone marrow biopsy were quite conclusive.'

'You say you're having treatment,' Anthony said. 'It must be doing you some good, Sandy, having some effect. You don't look as though you're dreadfully ill. You're a trifle pale perhaps, thinner, but –'

'All it's doing is keeping me going for the moment,' Alexander interjected.

Emily looked at her brother closely. 'What sort of treatment is it?'

'Transfusions of red blood cells, and platelets when I need them. I also take antibiotics from time to time, to help reduce the chances of my getting infections.'

'I see.' Emily bit her inner lip nervously. 'You just said the treatment is keeping you going ... for ... for ... how long?' she asked in a voice that shook. She was filled with fear for her brother.

'Four to five months at the outside, I think. Not many people last much longer than a year, after this type of leukaemia has been diagnosed.'

Emily's mouth trembled. 'I can't bear it. Not *you*. It's just not fair. Oh Sandy, you can't be dying!' She tried to push back the tears, knowing he wanted her to be strong, to face this with the same kind of courage he was displaying. She was unable to do so.

She jumped up, hurried out of the drawing room, aware that she was about to break down completely.

28

Emily stood at the bottom of the staircase in the entrance hall, holding the banister, filled with an internal shaking. Slowly the tears slid down her cheeks unchecked as she quietly wept for her brother. He was only thirty-seven. Her mind balked at the thought of his imminent death. It was unacceptable to her.

After only a matter of seconds, the drawing room door opened and closed softly. Emily felt Alexander's arms encircling her. He turned her around to face him, took a handkerchief out of his pocket, wiped the tears from her face.

'Come on, Dumpling, try to hang in there. For me,' he said. 'I can't stand to see you so upset. It doesn't help me. I realize this has been a ghastly shock for you, on the other hand there is no *easy* way to break this kind of news. How *do* you tell your loved ones that you're dying?'

Emily was incapable of responding. Her eyes welled again, and she buried her face against his chest, held onto him tightly.

He said, very softly, 'I'm glad you reminded me of Gran's attitude ... you know, about just blurting it out. It *did* help me to screw up my courage and get it said. I'd been putting it off for weeks.'

Alexander smoothed his hand over her hair, and there was a pause before he remarked, 'I've hidden my illness from you for a very long time, old thing.

However, it is going to start showing very soon. So you *had* to be told. And there are a lot of things which must be properly dealt with. *Now*. They can't be put off any longer . . . time does go so *quickly*, especially when one is trying to hold onto it.'

Emily swallowed hard, wanting to be strong, but finding it difficult. She stood very still, snapping her eyes shut.

After a moment, when she had regained a little of her self-possession, she said, 'Nothing will ever be the same again, Sandy, not when you're . . . gone. Whatever will we all do? Whatever will *I* do?' As the words left her mouth she realized how selfish she was being, but she could not take them back. It was too late, they had been said, and to apologize to him would only make matters worse.

He said softly, in a confident tone, 'You'll be all right, Emily. You'll keep going, and with the strength and courage you've always had . . . Gran's kind of fortitude. She taught you how to soldier on when you were a little girl. And you have Winston and your family.' A long sigh trickled through Alexander, and as if thinking aloud he murmured against her hair, 'Francesca's all right too, now that she's married to Oliver, but I do worry about Amanda. She's such a vulnerable young woman, so impressionable, really. You will keep an eye on her, won't you?' For the first time Alexander's voice held a slight tremor. He glanced away, hid his face from her, then coughed behind his hand.

Emily said, 'You know I will, darling.'

They stood together for a few minutes longer.

Alexander held her closer, gathering as much of his diminished strength as possible, aware that he had a great deal to say in the next half hour. He was not looking forward to it. But it had to be done, and the best way, he had decided earlier, was to be very businesslike about everything.

Emily could feel Sandy's bones through his clothes, and she realized how thin he had grown. She drew away, stole a quick glance at him, took note of his pallor, the faint purplish smudges under his eyes, and her heart sank. She could not understand why she had not noticed signs that he was ill before now, and she cursed herself angrily for not having paid more attention in the last few months.

Alexander finally released her, and taking out his handkerchief once more he blotted her damp cheeks. A fleeting smile touched his eyes. How blonde and small and dainty she was. She had always reminded him of a fragile piece of Dresden china. Yet she had a backbone of steel, and there was an indomitability about her that reminded him of their grandmother. And he knew that as distressed as she was now, in the long run she would be strong for everyone. He could count on his sister. Like Emma Harte before her, she had grit.

Emily was acutely aware of Alexander's intense scrutiny. She returned it, said, 'I'll be fine, Sandy,' as though she had read his mind.

Alexander smiled at her, nodded.

There was a brief silence before Emily went on slowly, in a low voice, 'You've not only been a wonderful brother to me, but mother, father, best friend as well. You've been . . . everything to me, Sandy. I've never *really* told you before how I feel, but I do want you to know that I –'

'I'm very aware of how you feel,' he interrupted swiftly, unable to deal with any more emotion at this time. 'And I love you too, Emily. Now we'd better go back to the drawing room, join the others, don't you think? There are arrangements to be made. For the future.'

'I'd like to talk about business first. About Harte Enterprises to be specific,' Alexander said, once they were all gathered around the fire again.

'Yes, of course, anything you wish,' Paula answered. Her eyes were red and watery, betrayed her, despite her air of calmness. It was obvious that she had wept whilst her cousins had been out of the room, but she now appeared to be in total control of herself.

'I've had time to think things out,' Alexander began, 'and I'd like to share some of my thoughts with you before I come to my final decisions. I suppose I'm looking for your input before I put my plans into motion.'

'But I'm not involved in any of the family businesses,' Anthony immediately reminded him. 'Are you sure I'm not in the way?' His expression turned quizzical.

'No, you're not. And anyway, you're the eldest of Emma Harte's grand-children, and you ought to –'

'Paula's the head of the family though,' Anthony countered. 'And thank God she is, too. It's not a job I'd relish, I don't mind telling you.'

Alexander smiled with a certain wryness. 'I know what you mean. But to continue, you're my closest male friend, and very simply put, I want you here. Let's just say for moral support shall we, old chap?'

The Earl nodded, got up, strode over to the console where he refreshed his scotch and soda. He glanced across at Paula and Emily. 'Do either of you want another drink?'

Both women shook their heads.

'How about you, Sandy?'

'I'm fine right now, thanks.'

Alexander waited until Anthony had returned to the sofa before he turned to Emily, and went on, 'I'm sorry I called this meeting when Winston is in Canada, but I had to have it this week because I'm going into hospital tomorrow for treatment. He ought to have been here, of course, as head of the Yorkshire Consolidated Newspaper Company and our Canadian papers. On the other hand, the divisions he runs are not actually relevant to this discussion.'

'He'll understand, Sandy.' Emily leaned forward, pinned her brother with her green eyes. 'How long are you going to be in hospital?' she asked, her worry instantly showing.

'Only a few days, and don't be concerned about it. The treatment does help me. Now, I would like to move along. Look, I know what I'm going to talk about is upsetting. But please, *don't be upset*. It must all be said, and I want my affairs to be in order . . . a Harte family trait, I believe.'

Alexander's gaze swept over the three of them, and he went on to explain in a thoughtful tone, 'I've analysed Harte Enterprises in every conceivable way over the past couple of weeks, trying to decide what to do with the company. I considered selling it, knowing it would fetch hundreds of millions of pounds which we could reinvest in the market. Then I thought of selling off only certain divisions, keeping others. And then it struck me how unfair I was being to you, Emily.'

Before she had a chance to say anything, he rushed on, 'After all, you run Genret, which is one of our biggest money-making divisions, and you're the only other shareholder –'

'Except for Jonathan and Sarah,' Emily cut in, 'and I don't suppose they're of any consequence.'

'No, they're not,' Alexander agreed. 'In any event, Emily, I realized it was rather imperious of me to make decisions without consulting you. And it was certainly wrong of me to assume, as I did initially, that you might not want to run Harte Enterprises yourself. A few days ago, yet another thought occurred to me . . . what would Grandy have wanted us to do with Harte Enterprises in view of my illness? I instantly concluded that she would not want us to sell it. The company is too solid, too rich, too important to the family as a whole for us to relinquish it. Don't you agree?'

'Yes,' Emily managed, more aware than ever of what the future without her brother would actually mean.

'Paula, what is your opinion?' Alexander asked.

'You're absolutely right about everything,' Paula said, striving to sound normal. 'Grandy did have very strong feelings about Harte Enterprises. She would want Emily to continue in your stead. That *is* what you have in mind, isn't it?'

'Yes, I think Emily should become chairman of the board and chief executive officer within the next few weeks. That way we can make a smooth transfer of power in the company and I can step down. Fairly soon, too, I hope.'

'I suppose you'll want Amanda to run Genret,' Emily ventured.

'With your agreement. And the one division I think we should sell is Lady Hamilton Clothes.'

'To the Kallinskis presumably,' Paula interjected.

'Yes.' Alexander cleared his throat, reached for his glass, took a sip of wine. 'If anyone is entitled to buy Lady Hamilton Clothes it's Uncle Ronnie. For sentimental reasons, and because of our long involvement with the family for over seventy years. I say let's keep everything in the three clans. As you both know –' He looked from Emily to Paula, continued, 'Uncle Ronnie is prepared to meet our price. I'm not worried about that aspect. My only real concern is that you're comfortable with the deal, Paula. Whilst you're not involved with the running of Harte Enterprises, Lady Hamilton does supply the Harte stores and the boutiques.'

'Uncle Ronnie assured me they would continue to do so, and on an exclusive basis, when we discussed the idea of Kallinski Industries buying the fashion division last August,' Paula told him.

'Well, Emily?' Alexander peered across at her, lifted a brow.

'Yes, it's all right with me. But what about Amanda? She loves her division, Sandy.'

'I know she does. But under these unexpected circumstances I'm sure she'll understand the necessity for making certain changes, for streamlining the company to an extent. Grandy's philosophy was that we must be loyal to the company as a whole, not just to our own divisions. I believe that, too, as you and

Amanda are aware. Anyway, Genret will be a challenge to Amanda, just as it was to you when you took over from Len Harvey twelve years ago.'

'That's true . . . yes . . .'

'What's the matter, Emily?' Alexander asked, frowning at her. 'You look and sound rather hesitant.'

'I'm not really. It's just that I'm not terribly well informed about the real estate division of Harte Enterprises. And that worries me.'

'There's not *really* a problem, darling. Thomas Lorring is my right hand in that division, and he's been virtually running it for several years. And you *know* that he has, Emily.' He levelled a long, very direct look at her. 'He'll do the same for you, when you take over from me . . . and you *will*, won't you?'

'Of course I will.' Emily sat back on the sofa jerkily, wishing she did not have to step into her brother's shoes. If only things could suddenly be the way they were yesterday. She longed suddenly for Winston, regretted her husband was not here, that he would not be returning to England for another week. The thought plunged her into deeper dismay.

Paula said, 'You've made some very sound judgements, Sandy.'

He rose, paced to the window, glanced out at the garden almost absently. He said, without turning around, 'I think they're the most logical moves, given the situation.' He remained motionless in front of the bay for a few seconds longer.

No one said a word.

Finally Alexander returned to the fireplace, where he stood with his back to the blazing logs, warming himself.

And then, without any preamble, he announced in a brisk and businesslike voice. 'About my will. I intend to leave this house to Francesca, and Nutton Priory to Amanda. Naturally the Villa Faviola is yours, Emily.'

'Oh Sandy –' She stopped abruptly. She could not speak. Her throat closed on her. She blinked back sudden tears.

He hurried on relentlessly, 'Fifty per cent of my personal wealth will be divided between the three of you, Emily, and the other fifty per cent will go to the children in the family. And not just my nephews and nieces, but to your children, Paula, and yours, Anthony.'

They both nodded their understanding.

Anthony looked away, not wanting Alexander to see the anguish flickering onto his face. He stared fiercely at the painting on the opposite wall.

Paula twisted her wedding ring nervously, gazed down at her hands, thinking how uncertain life was. Only that afternoon she had been congratulating herself on so many things accomplished lately, and she had been happy. Now, without warning, she was miserable, filled with worry and concern, and facing the untimely death of a beloved cousin, who was also a dear friend. The implications of Sandy's fatal illness were manifold.

'Now, Emily,' Alexander proceeded, determined to be done with everything tonight, so that there would be no need for this kind of discussion again. 'Next we come to my holdings in Harte Enterprises. To be precise, the fifty-two per cent of the shares Grandy left me. I am going to give thirty-two per cent to you, and twenty per cent to Amanda. I am not leaving any of my shares to Francesca since she does not work for the company.'

'Yes, I see . . . thank you,' Emily said in the steadiest voice she could muster. 'But I'm just wondering . . . is that quite fair to Amanda, darling?' She asked this softly, not wishing to argue with him, but at the same time wanting her half-sister to be fully involved and totally committed to Harte Enterprises. After all, it would be just the two of them running it eventually.

'I believe it is *eminently* fair,' Alexander was quick to respond. 'Grandmother insisted that one person had control of this particular company, to prevent any dissension between us, and that is how I want it, why I have divided my shares in the way I have. You will be the majority shareholder and head of Harte Enterprises, as I am now.' His tone was unusually firm and uncompromising and it left no room for doubt about his feelings or for further conversation on the matter.

Emily made no comment, directed her gaze to the fire, grappling with her overwhelming sadness, still finding it difficult to comprehend that her brother would not be with them for much longer, that next year at this time he would be dead. Her heart was heavy, and once more she longed for her husband and his comforting presence, the emotional security Winston gave her.

Anthony now spoke up at last. He said, 'When you've finished your treatment, I want you to come and stay with us at Clonloughlin, Sandy. And for as long as you can.'

'Yes, I *would* like that. It'll do me good to be with you all. And then afterwards, Emily, I'll work with you for a few weeks, take you through every aspect of the job. Mind you, I do believe you'll be capable of doing it blindfolded.'

Emily bit her lip, nodded rapidly, glanced at Paula, her eyes full of mute appeal.

Paula quickly bridged this tense moment, when she said in a warm and cheerful voice, 'Is there anything I can do, Sandy? Anything that will make things easier for you?'

'Not really, Paula, thanks anyway. Oh wait! Yes, there is one thing you can *all* do for me!' His intelligent, light blue eyes roamed over them, and he shifted on his feet, slightly changed his stance in front of the fire. 'I'd like you to keep the news of my illness quiet, if you don't mind. I really don't wish it to become a topic for discussion in the family. And I certainly don't want to have to cope with sadness and sympathy, or be surrounded by a lot of long, gloomy faces.'

A stricken expression settled in Emily's eyes. 'I appreciate your feelings,' she said, and paused. Her voice wavered as she went on, 'I'll try not to tell Winston, but I think it'll be ever so hard for me . . .'

'Oh but of course you must tell *him*!' her brother exclaimed. He looked at Paula and Anthony. 'And naturally you must tell Shane and Sally. I didn't mean you to exclude them, only your children. And yours, Emily, and our half sisters. I don't want Amanda and Francesca to know – at least not just yet.'

'What about Mummy?' Emily asked, worry flaring. 'Has she got to be kept in the dark, too?'

Alexander inclined his head. 'Oh yes, very much so. It's better Mother doesn't know anything at all. She has a tendency to become hysterical about the slightest thing. She would only upset me.'

Striding over to the Georgian console table, Alexander picked up the bottle of white wine, brought it to Paula and Emily. 'Well, that's about it,' he said, as he refilled their crystal goblets. 'I've covered everything, I think. Incidentally, Emily, John Crawford knows about the situation. Obviously, as my solicitor, he had to be told, and he'll help you with any and all legalities after I'm ... er ... when I'm no longer around.'

'Yes,' she said in the smallest of voices, and she clenched her hands together in her lap, wishing he would not keep alluding to his impending death.

'This has been a terrible burden for you to carry alone, Sandy,' Anthony said a short while later.

Emily and Paula had left together, and the two men were finishing their drinks in the drawing room before going out to dinner.

Looking across at his cousin intently, the Earl added, 'You ought to have told me before, you know.'

'Perhaps I should have,' Alexander admitted. 'But to be honest, *I* had to come to grips with my illness first. As I explained earlier, I went through any number of different emotions – disbelief, anger, frustration, and acceptance. Then the fury came back, and the frustration, and the sense of total *helplessness*. I was on an emotional see-saw for the longest time, and naturally it was impossible for me to confide in anyone until I could handle myself properly. And, of course, I did want to pursue every avenue, look for a cure, if there was one to be found. I soon discovered there was absolutely nothing I could do except take the treatment, and seize a bit of borrowed time.'

Alexander smiled faintly, shrugged. 'I am resigned to it now, Anthony, and completely in control. That is why I was finally able to tell you tonight. And now that that ordeal is over, I can relax, get on with my life for the next few months. I aim to make the most of it ...'

'Yes,' Anthony said, then discovered he could not go on. He took a quick sip of his scotch. What a bloody waste, he thought. A waste of a rare and special man. And such a young man. Anthony asked himself if he would have been able to handle himself with the same kind of courage and grace his cousin was displaying if he had been in similar circumstances. He was not sure. It took an awful lot of character to cope with one's own imminent death with such extraordinary stoicism.

Alexander said, 'Come on, Anthony, don't look so morose. And please don't start getting maudlin on me. I couldn't cope ... I had a difficult time dealing with Emily's emotion this evening. I realize how rough it is on all of you ... but it's not quite as rough as it is on me.'

'So sorry. Do forgive me, old chap.'

'Nothing to forgive ... I want everything to be as normal as possible. That makes it so much easier for me. I must now endeavour to ignore my illness, go about my business as best I can, and in the most controlled manner. Otherwise it'll be pure hell.'

'You will come to Clonloughlin, won't you?'

'Yes, in about two weeks' time.'

'Marvellous. Sally and I will enjoy having you. How long do you think you can stay?'

'Ten days, two weeks perhaps.' Alexander swallowed the last of his wine, put the glass down on the end table near the fireplace. 'I've booked a table at Mark's Club for nine o'clock. Perhaps we should stroll down there shortly, have a drink in the bar –'

Alexander rose at the sound of the phone ringing in the library which adjoined the drawing room. 'Excuse me,' he said as he hurried to answer it. He returned a second later. 'It's for you, Anthony . . . Sally calling from Ireland.'

'Oh yes, I expected to hear from her. Thanks.'

'Don't tell her anything now. About my illness, I mean. Not over the phone,' Sandy instructed.

'I wouldn't dream of it,' Anthony reassured him as he strode across the floor, went through the double mahogany doors and into the library.

Left alone, Alexander sat down on one of the sofas and closed his eyes.

The last couple of hours had been trying, had vitiated his energy. Even though the others had striven hard not to display their feelings, to be brave, they *had* been terribly upset. As he had known they would be. That was why he had so dreaded telling them. He had only managed to get through the ordeal of breaking his bad news by being utterly detached and matter of fact.

He accepted his death with equanimity now, had come to terms with his fate. There was little else he could do. And in so doing he had been able to confide in those closest to him, because he could help *them* to do exactly the same thing. It was going to be hardest on Emily, of course. They had been as close as two peas in a pod when they were growing up. They had relied on each other in a certain sense. Their mother had been so flighty in those days, running from man to man, and marrying all sorts of disreputable characters. And their sweet but weak-willed father, crushed by the burden of his broken heart, had scarcely seemed aware of their existence. Alexander sighed under his breath. What a catastrophe his father's life had been. And his mother's, too. But wasn't life itself a catastrophe?

Alexander instantly let go of this thought, not wanting to sink into deep philosophical ruminations this evening, as he had been so wont to do of late. Grandy wouldn't approve, he said to himself, and smiled, remembering Emma Harte. How invincible *she* had been, and right up to the end. Life for her had been a triumph. So much for *his* theories . . . but then perhaps life *was* rooted in doom and tragedy for some.

Opening his eyes, Alexander glanced around the room blinking. It looked beautiful tonight in the glow of the lamps and the warming firelight. Maggie had decorated this room just after their marriage, and he always thought of it as a bit of English spring, whatever the time of year, with its primrose and daffodil yellows, pale blues and greens. Whenever it needed redoing he simply had the scheme repeated. He had been doing so since her death . . .

His cousin interrupted his musings when he said, 'I say, Sandy, are you all right?' Anthony hovered over him, looking concerned.

Alexander pushed himself upright on the sofa. 'Yes, I'm fine. I was recouping . . . the last few hours have been a little wearing.'

'Of course they have. Come on, let's go to Mark's.'

Within the space of ten minutes the two cousins were leaving Alexander's house in Chesterfield Hill and heading for Charles Street where the club was located.

It was a chilly night and windy, and Alexander hunched further into his overcoat, shoved his hands in his pockets, shivering slightly. 'Anyway, how was Sally?' he asked, falling into step with Anthony.

'Wonderful, as usual. She sends her love. I told her you were coming to stay . . . but that's all I said.'

'Quite.'

They walked on in silence. Suddenly Anthony remarked, as if to himself, 'There was something odd though . . .'

'Oh, in what sense?' Alexander asked, looking at him curiously.

'Sally told me that Bridget has been pestering her . . . wanting to know when I'm returning to Clonloughlin. According to Sally she seems rather anxious to talk to me, has something on her mind, no doubt. In fact, Sally said she seemed a trifle agitated today.'

'That *is* odd. On the other hand, I have always found your housekeeper to be somewhat eccentric, if you don't mind me saying so.'

'Have you really? Mmmm. Perhaps she is . . . and a bit fey too, like most of the Irish. Well, it can't be anything important,' Anthony finished as they crossed Charles Street in the direction of the club.

But he was wrong. Events that had happened a decade ago were about to come back to haunt him.

29

It was raining at Clonloughlin the first morning Anthony was back, and there was a faint mist that softened the dark skeletal trees and the tall chimneys of the house etched so starkly against the leaden sky.

As he walked up the central path carved out between wide lawns he thought how lovely it looked even on this bleak winter's day, with its symmetrical, harmonious proportions, soaring windows, and the four white Palladian pillars supporting the front portico. Georgian in origin, it was a stately mansion situated on a small rise in the middle of a splendid park, with excellent views from its many windows. There were three hundred and sixty-five of them altogether, one for each day of the year, a fine madness on the part of his ancestor who had built the house in the eighteenth century. But it was a madness that Anthony had always secretly applauded. The many windows were unique, gave the exteriors a certain gracefulness, opened up the interiors to the pastoral landscape, filled those beautiful rooms with light and air the whole year round, and hazy sunshine in the summer months.

Anthony loved Clonloughlin with a fierce and abiding passion. It was his ancestral home and the only place he had ever wanted to live. He had been born here forty-five years ago and he would die here when his time came. And his son Jeremy would continue in his place, the Standish line unbroken as it had been for centuries.

His mind swung to Alexander and a rush of sadness engulfed him as it had last night when he had been talking to Sally. Although she had met him at Cork Airport he had resisted giving her the grave news about Sandy on their drive home. He had not even told her when they finally reached Clonloughlin, had waited instead until they were in the privacy of their bedroom suite.

Sally had been dreadfully upset once she had heard the stark facts about Sandy's illness; she had wept, and he had comforted her. And then to cheer themselves up and trying to be as positive as possible, they had made extensive plans for Sandy's stay with them after he left the hospital. But later, when Sally had fallen asleep in his arms, her cheeks had been tear-stained once again. She and her brother Winston had grown up in Yorkshire with Sandy and Emily, and they had been unusually close; Sandy was one of the godfathers to Giles, their nine-year-old son.

Anthony now veered to the left as he drew nearer to the house, and went around to the other side, entered through the back door. Inside the small indoor porch he shed his barbour and tweed cap, which were both drenched with rain, hanging the oilskin and the hat on the coatstand to drip. Seating himself on the wooden chair, he pulled off his green Wellington boots, slipped into a pair of brown loafers, then hurried down the back passageway to the library.

The house was very quiet.

It was early, only seven, and Sally was still asleep, as were the younger children. Settling himself at the desk near the window, he pulled a pile of correspondence towards him, began to sort through the mail that had accumulated in the week he had been in London on business.

He did not hear the housekeeper come into the room until she spoke.

'Good morning, your lordship,' said Bridget O'Donnell. 'I didn't expect you to be up so early after your late arrival last night. Excuse me for not having the fire going in here.'

'Ah, good morning, Bridget,' Anthony said with a quick smile as he looked up. 'No problem. I'm not cold.'

'The kettle's boiling. I'll just be putting a match to the fire, and then I'll be back with your pot of tea and toast.'

'Thank you,' he murmured, glanced down at the papers, wondering whether to ask her what it was she wished to discuss with him, then decided against it. Far better to wait until he had been fortified by his light breakfast. Bridget had a tendency to be garrulous at times, which required an enormous amount of patience on his part. He was not in the mood for her this morning.

He heard matches being struck, a faint *whoosh* as the paper and wood chips ignited and flames flew up the wide chimney back. Then there was the sound of bellows being pumped, the scraping of metal against stone as she placed the guard around the fire, and finally departed to the kitchen.

Anthony reached for the letter addressed to him in his son's handwriting. Jeremy had only just returned to prep school after the Christmas holidays, and as he slit open the envelope he wondered what his eldest son and heir had to say to him. There would be a request for cash, no doubt. Eleven-year-old schoolboys were forever hard up. He smiled. Jeremy was exactly like he had been at the same age. But the boy worried him at times. Jem was not strong physically, did not have the robust health of his brother Giles and his sister India, and Anthony had to resist the temptation to mollycoddle him, as did Sally.

Anthony scanned the letter quickly. It was, as usual, a sketchy, imprecise report of Jeremy's activities over the last few days since he had been back at school, with a postscript, underscored, to *please send money urgently, please, daddy, please.*

Bridget came sailing in with the breakfast tray sooner than he had expected, and Anthony put the letter down as she approached.

'Where would you like this, your lordship?'

'You can put it here on the desk,' he answered her, pushing aside the papers he had been perusing a moment before.

She did so, then went around to the other side of the large partners' desk, stood looking at him.

Lifting the teapot, he poured tea into the oversized breakfast cup, added milk, then glanced at her. 'Yes, what is it, Bridget?'

'I've got to talk to you, Lord Dunvale. About something important.'

'*Now?*'

'Yes, sir, I think so . . . I'd like to get it out of the way . . . this morning.'

Anthony smothered a sigh. 'All right.' He spread his favourite thick-cut Frank Cooper marmalade onto the buttered toast, crunched on it, took a sip of tea. When the housekeeper was silent, he said, 'Go on, Bridget, get it off your chest. And don't hover there, you know I detest people doing that. Please, do sit down.'

She lowered herself into the chair, sat facing him, twisted her hands together nervously in her lap, focused her dark blue eyes on him.

The Earl finished his slice of toast as he waited for her to begin. Finally he raised a brow.

Bridget said slowly, 'I'm not quite sure how to tell you this,' and stopped abruptly mid-sentence.

Anthony, who had his cup halfway to his mouth, put it down with a clatter, stared at her in alarm. This was the second time in the space of several days that someone had begun a sentence with those words. First Sandy, and now Bridget, and it seemed like a bad omen. 'You really ought to be able to tell me anything, Bridget. After all, we've known each other since we were children.'

The housekeeper nodded. 'Well, your lordship . . . what I have to say . . . Well, it is about Lady Dunvale.'

'*Oh.*' He sounded surprised and his eyes narrowed.

'Not this Lady Dunvale. The first one.'

'My mother?'

'No, no, not the Dowager Countess. Your first wife . . . that's who I mean . . . the Lady Minerva, sir.'

Startled, Anthony sat back in his chair and gave Bridget a long, probing look. 'What *about* the late Lady Dunvale?' he asked at last.

'It's . . . er . . . er . . . about her death.'

For a moment he could not speak or move. Instinctively, he knew that something awful was about to be said, and he braced himself before muttering, 'Is it important to discuss her death now . . . so long after the event?'

'Yes,' Bridget said tersely.

'Why?' he probed, unable to resist the question, yet, conversely, not wanting to hear a word she had to say.

'Because I don't want it on my conscience any more,' Bridget replied. 'I have to tell you what really happened . . . it's been a burden for me to carry, a nightmare still, even after all these years.'

His mouth had gone very dry. 'Tell me.'

'It wasn't suicide like they said it was at the inquest.'

He frowned, at first uncomprehending, not fully understanding her meaning. 'Are you trying to tell me that Lady Dunvale fell into the lake, that she had an *accident* as I've always maintained? That she didn't take her own life?'

'No, she didn't, she –' Bridget cut herself off, pursed her lips, then muttered, 'She was *put there*.'

'By whom?' His voice was barely audible.

'Michael Lamont. They had a quarrel that fateful Saturday night, those two did, and he struck her. She fell, hit her face on the brass fender in his living room. If you remember, she did have a bruise on her face. The pathologist and Doctor Brennan mentioned it at the inquest. Well anyway, Lamont couldn't revive her. She appeared to be unconscious. Within seconds he realized she was actually dead. He said she'd had a heart attack or something. All that liquor she had drunk continually through the afternoon and evening, the tranquillizers she was forever swallowing . . . the combination killed her, he said. So Lamont took her and put her in the lake to cover everything up, and the next morning he drove past, pretended to have found her body . . . then he came up to the mansion to tell you there had been an accident, and he sent for the police and no one ever suspected *him* of being involved in any way. But they did suspect *you* though. At least, Sergeant McNamara did.'

Events that had happened over a decade ago came rushing back to hit Anthony between the eyes, and he remembered every tiny detail with great vividness and clarity. He felt as if he had been kicked several times in the stomach, and he began to tremble all over, clasped his hands together to stop them shaking, took several deep steadying breaths. He said at last, 'And how do you know all this, Bridget?'

'I had seen her ladyship that afternoon, when she had driven over to Clonloughlin from Waterford. You know she came to the estate quite a lot, even though you had forbidden her to do so and were in the middle of the divorce. But Lady Min couldn't stay away, she loved Clonloughlin so much. She often came to see me. And *him*. We had tea together that afternoon, and she drove off around five, told me she was going down to the lake . . . she'd always been drawn to the lough, even when she was a small girl. Don't you remember the picnics the three of us used to have there when we were children? In any case, sir, you saw her little red car at the edge of the lake, after your Land-Rover had stalled, and you'd decided to walk home, taking the long way round in order to avoid her. And her ladyship also took a walk . . . over to Michael Lamont's house. She'd told me she was going to have dinner with him, but explained that she wouldn't be staying the night. You see, your lordship, they were –'

Bridget took a gulp of air, rushed on in breathless haste, the words pouring out of her, 'They were having an affair. Lady Min had told me she would come by the kitchen at ten-thirty to say goodnight to me. She never *ever* left Clonloughlin without doing that. When she hadn't arrived by eleven-thirty I got worried, so I went down to Lamont's house looking for her.'

Bridget paused and her face crumpled and she almost broke down. She was suddenly thinking of their childhood, remembering how close they had been . . . she and Lady Minerva Glendenning, daughter of the Earl of Rothmerrion and the young Lord Anthony Standish, now the Earl of Dunvale. So long ago. And yet those days were as clear to her as yesterday, and they had been the best part of her life.

Watching her, Anthony saw the distress on Bridget's face, the anguish in her eyes, and he was about to make a sympathetic gesture towards her, but inexplicably changed his mind. He said, a trifle harshly, 'Continue, Bridget, tell me everything. *I must know.'*

She nodded, swallowed. 'When I got to Lamont's door it was locked and the curtains were drawn, but I could hear them. Screaming at each other like banshees they were, saying horrible things, vile they were, and her ladyship . . . well, she sounded very drunk. Out of control. And then suddenly everything was quiet. There was absolute silence. I was frightened. I banged hard on the door, called out that it was me, and Michael let me in. He had no option, did he. Besides, he knew how close I was to Lady Min. When I saw her lying on the floor my heart stopped. I ran to her, tried to revive her. But she was gone. It was then that Lamont dreamed up the idea of putting her in the lake, so as to make it look as if she had drowned herself. You see, he didn't want you to know that he'd been sleeping with Lady Min for all those years. He was afraid you'd sack him if you found out. He couldn't afford to lose his job. And even though he hadn't had a hand in Lady Min's death, it might have *looked* as if he had. That's what he said to me, your lordship. And he kept repeating it, over and over again, and he told me that circumstantial evidence can be very damning.'

Anthony was appalled and outraged. 'Why in God's name didn't you come up to the mansion to get me?' he demanded furiously, his voice rising in anger and disgust. 'Why did you go along with Lamont?'

Bridget compressed her lips, said nothing.

He saw the stubborn set of her jaw, the defiance in the ice-blue eyes and he knew he was wasting his breath. She had been independent and difficult as a child; she had changed little over the years. If she did not want to confide her reasons for her silence at the time of Min's death, and for so many years after, then nothing could drag it out of her.

Sitting back in the chair, he studied her thoughtfully, trying to still his rage, the urge to shake her violently. And then suddenly a terrible thought occurred to him, one so unacceptable he tried to squash it, was barely able to face it. But he found himself saying carefully, and with great deliberation, 'Why were you so sure Lady Min was actually dead?' He leaned forward, fixed his probing, steely eyes on her. 'Lady Min may only have been *unconscious*, Bridget. In which case, Michael Lamont did murder her if he put her in the lough whilst she was still alive.'

'No, no, she was dead, I know she was dead!' Bridget cried excitedly, her eyes wide and flaring. 'I know she was dead!' she insisted, verging on hysteria.

'Do you not recall the pathologist's report? Doctor Kenmarr said that when he did the autopsy he discovered an excessive amount of alcohol and barbiturates in her blood-stream and a quantity of water in her lungs. This led him to conclude that her death had been by drowning. And since her lungs were full of water she could not have been dead when she was placed in the lake. I don't believe a dead body can take in water.'

As the implications of his words sank in, Bridget paled. She had loved Minerva like a sister, had mothered her from the first moment she had set eyes on her as a child.

'No!' Bridget shouted. 'She wasn't alive. She was dead. I would never have harmed *her*. I loved her. I loved her. You know I did. The water must have somehow seeped into her lungs afterwards.'

Anthony wondered if this was actually possible. He decided it might be, depending on the length of time Min had been dead before she had been submerged in the lake. He rubbed his forehead wearily, looked across at the housekeeper, asked in a quiet, very controlled voice, 'Was her body still warm when Lamont took her out to the lake?'

Bridget nodded, not able to speak, shaken by the Earl's horrifying suggestion.

'Rigor mortis doesn't set in for about two to four hours after death. I suppose she might have been able to take water into her lungs for a short time after she died. Maybe for half an hour. But no longer, I'm absolutely sure of that. Still, only a pathologist could give me a truly accurate answer,' Anthony said softly, almost to himself, as if thinking aloud.

Bridget stared at him, twisted her hands in her lap.

There was a long and deadly silence. The strain between them was a most palpable thing, hung heavy in the air.

Eventually the Earl spoke. Pinning his eyes on the housekeeper, he said, 'Why did you suddenly decide to speak up, to confide in me now, after so many years? Tell me that, Bridget O'Donnell.'

Bridget cried, 'But I already told you . . . I couldn't have it on my conscience any longer . . . I mean about you not knowing the truth, not knowing the real circumstances of Lady Min's death. I realized how much it troubled you . . . the idea that she had committed suicide while the balance of her mind was disturbed. You'd blamed yourself for years, blamed her death on your decision to leave her and get a divorce. And I was sure you believed your relationship with your cousin Miss Sally Harte had been a contributing factor in your wife's death.'

Anthony flinched. There was a certain truth in all this.

Bridget gave Anthony a hard stare. 'I wanted to put your mind at rest, your lordship,' she finished.

Like hell you did, Anthony thought, not for one moment believing her. And then, in a flash of sudden insight, he understood. There was no question in his mind that Bridget had been having an affair with Michael Lamont. But Lamont was leaving Clonloughlin in a few days. He was going away and he was never coming back. He was going to America to work for Mrs Alma Berringer, the young American widow who had recently returned to her horse farm in Virginia after renting Rothmerrion Lodge for the past year. Lamont and Mrs Berringer had been friendly, but Anthony had not realized just how intimate they had become until Lamont had given his notice a month ago, announced that he was moving to the States.

Anthony rose, walked over to the huge stone fireplace, picked up the poker and stirred the logs. His expression was ruminative. He was convinced he was right. Slowly he spun around, stood facing Bridget, studying her with infinite care. Never really pretty, she had, however, been very arresting when she was younger, with her blazing red hair and milk white skin and cornflower blue eyes. Her striking colouring and long legs and lissome figure had always caught men's attention. But sadly she had not aged well. The red hair was a faded salt-and-pepper auburn rapidly turning grey, her figure had lost its willowy appeal. Only those bright blue eyes remained unchanged, vivid and youthful. And very calculating, he decided. Yes, Bridget O'Donnell was always manipulative and devious even when she was a child. And oh how she had dominated poor Min. Odd that he had never realized this until now.

'There's an old saying, Bridget,' Anthony remarked in an icy, contained voice. 'Hell hath no fury like a woman scorned.'

'I'm sorry, sir, but I'm not following you.'

'You're in love with him. You've always loved him since the first day he came to run the estate for me. That's why you helped him, protected him since my wife's death. And after she was dead, *you* became involved with him. And now, because he's leaving you, going off, chasing after another woman, you want your revenge. You're sticking the knife between Michael Lamont's shoulder blades with a real vengeance, aren't you? That's what all this is about, isn't it?'

She stared him down. 'No,' she said flatly. 'It isn't. I simply wanted to put your mind at rest. I didn't want you to blame yourself for Lady Min's death.'

'But I don't,' Anthony said coldly, in all truthfulness, 'and I haven't for years. You're pointing a finger at Lamont because he's found somebody younger and prettier than you. Let's face it, Bridget, your lover has passed you over.'

At these words she flushed deeply, looked down at her hands.

Anthony knew his words had struck home.

After a moment, she asked in a low, subdued voice, 'What are you going to do about Michael Lamont? Are you going to have it out with him?'

Anthony looked at her with steadiness for several seconds, then slowly walked across the floor, resumed his position behind his desk. He leaned over it, looked deeply into those blue eyes so warily returning his penetrating gaze.

'Obviously I shall confront Lamont. The facts you have given me cannot be ignored. As you know they cannot. That's why you told me in the first place.' There was a small pause before he said, 'However, I may also go to the police, open up the investigation into my wife's death again. And I wonder, Bridget, if it's ever occurred to you that you helped to tamper with evidence in a sudden and questionable death.

And that you perjured yourself under oath. Also, if my first wife *was* alive when Michael Lamont put her in the lake, then you are also an accessory after the fact. *An accessory to murder.*'

Once Bridget had returned to the kitchen to go about her duties for the day, Anthony made a telephone call to Cork. It lasted for ten minutes and mostly he listened. When he quietly put the receiver back in the cradle his face was white and his expression was grim.

Glancing at the clock on the mantel, he rose to his feet, left the library and went down the passageway to the indoor porch. After putting on his wellingtons and his barbour, he took his tweed cap off the coat stand and went outside.

He looked up. It had stopped raining but the sky was still overcast and a light mist persisted. Walking at a brisk pace, he took the path which led to Michael Lamont's house. It was just a few yards away from the lake, set back against a copse of trees next to a field. When he reached the front door he barged inside without knocking, strode through the hall, across the living room and into the adjoining office.

Lamont, a dark-haired, heavy-set but good-looking man, was seated behind the desk, entering figures in a large estate ledger. He looked up in surprise as the door was flung open unceremoniously and a gust of air caused the papers on his desk to flutter and lift.

'Good morning, Lord Dunvale,' he said pleasantly, his weatherbeaten face breaking into a smile. And then the smile vanished as he became aware of Anthony's dire expression, his angry stance.

'Is something wrong?' Lamont asked, rising.

Anthony did not at first reply. He stepped into the room, closed the heavy oak door behind him firmly, leaned against it. He studied the estate manager through icy eyes. Lamont had worked for him for almost twenty years, and he suddenly wondered what in God's name made him tick. Anthony had always believed he knew Lamont inside out; apparently he had not known him at all. He had considered him to be a trustworthy and devoted employee and a good friend. Now he was filled with loathing for him.

At last Anthony said, 'Bridget had rather a strange tale to tell earlier this morning. About the late Lady Dunvale's death.'

Taken by surprise, off guard, Lamont gaped at him, opened his mouth to speak, then closed it. He walked away from the desk swiftly, hovered near the fireplace, wanting to put distance between himself and Anthony. Reaching for a cigarette, he lit it, then pivoted to look at the Earl.

Lamont's expression was one of uncertainty and his dark brown eyes flickered with apprehension. 'What exactly are you getting at?' he asked finally.

'Bridget told me everything, confided every little detail about what happened here in this house that tragic evening.' Anthony stepped forward, drew closer to the estate manager, let his eyes rest on him for the longest moment.

Lamont flinched under this intense and unwavering scrutiny. Blinking, he eventually glanced away, took a long drag on his cigarette, inhaling deeply.

'How could you be so certain Min was dead after she collapsed?' Anthony demanded in a hard voice. 'You're not a doctor, Lamont.'

Lamont's face turned brilliant red and he cried out angrily, 'She *was* dead!

I'm telling you she was dead!' Unexpectedly he began to cough, and it took him a few minutes to recover. When he finally caught his breath, he added, 'I might not be a doctor, but I do know when somebody has stopped breathing.' He puffed on the cigarette again with nervous intensity, then exclaimed in a shaky voice, 'I tried to revive her, to breathe life into her with mouth-to-mouth resuscitation, but she was gone. I loved Min. Which is more than you ever did.'

Anthony took another step forward. His hands were clenched tightly at his sides, his knuckles shining white in the pale morning light. He wanted to ram his fist into Lamont's red, boozy face, smash it to a pulp until it was unrecognizable. But he resisted the impulse, hung onto his self-possession with a masterful control.

'You don't know the meaning of the word *love*, Lamont. You're a philandering, double-dealing bastard, and a menace to any decent woman.'

'*You* talk to *me* about philandering. What about you!' Lamont snorted. 'Certainly you drove Minerva into my arms with your constant womanizing and years of neglect.'

Anthony held himself very taut. He was once more afraid that he might do Lamont bodily harm. He said slowly, 'Why didn't you come for me when my wife collapsed? Or at least call a doctor? Why did you take matters into your own hands? Your behaviour was unconscionable and nothing short of reckless.'

Michael Lamont was not blessed with great intelligence, but he had sufficient native shrewdness to recognize that Bridget O'Donnell had done her work well. He decided there was no point in lying, and so he spoke the absolute truth when he mumbled, 'I was afraid. Afraid that once you knew what had been going on between us you'd get rid of me. I couldn't lose my job. It also occurred to me that you might blame me for her death. Circumstantial evidence has condemned more than one innocent man. Don't you see,' he finished in a whining tone, 'I had no choice, I *had* to cover everything up.'

Disgust and revulsion swamped Anthony as he continued to observe the estate manager with a steely gaze. 'I wonder how you've been able to look me in the eye all these years, knowing the terrible things you did, knowing how you lied to everyone to protect your own skin. You're despicable, Lamont. Monstrous.'

Lamont did not respond. How stupid he had been not to leave Clonloughlin years ago. He had stayed because of Bridget O'Donnell, the terrible hold she had over him. He had never really trusted her. Apparently he had been right not to do so. When their long relationship had ended by mutual consent, he had believed himself to be finally free of her. There had been no rancorous feelings on her part, or so he had thought. He had been wrong. The minute he had taken up with another woman she had struck out at him like a viper, wanting to destroy him. She had succeeded.

'I ache to give you the biggest thrashing of your life,' Anthony was saying. 'But I'm not going to lay a finger on you. I shall let the law do my work for me.'

Lamont started, drawn out of his thoughts. He peered at Anthony. '*What*? What are you saying?'

'I fully intend to reopen the investigation into my wife's death. I believe you killed Lady Dunvale. And I aim to see that you pay for it,' Anthony said with cold deliberation.

'You're mad, stark raving mad!' Lamont shouted, his dark eyes popping out of his face, his expression one of sudden fear. 'You don't know what you're talking about, Dunvale. Min poisoned her system with all that muck she was forever swallowing. She died within a few minutes of collapsing.'

'That's where you're quite wrong,' Anthony said in a voice that was murderously soft. 'She was in a deeply unconscious state, which was indeed induced by excessive amounts of alcohol and barbiturates. But when you placed her in the lake she was very much alive, and – '

'I don't believe you! You're lying! Inventing all this!'

'I *am not!*' Anthony shot back with ferocity. 'When Bridget confided in me this morning I was not absolutely sure about certain medical facts! So I telephoned Forensic at the hospital in Cork, where I located Doctor Stephen Kenmarr. The pathologist who did the autopsy on Min's body, who discovered her lungs were full of water and testified at the inquest that she had died of drowning.'

Anthony paused, finished emphatically, and very slowly, as if to give added weight to his words, 'Doctor Kenmarr confirmed to me what I already suspected ... *that water cannot be inhaled by a person who is dead.* Therefore, Min was alive when you placed her in the lake. You drowned her.'

Michael Lamont felt his hackles rising, and he was so shocked, so stunned by Anthony's dreadful accusation he could barely stand. He swayed slightly on his feet, reached out, supported himself against the mantelpiece. The idea that he might have actually caused Min's death struck horror in him. Over the years he had suffered greatly, had been haunted by his deceit, the lies he had told, the cover up he had wrought, and he had never stopped wrestling with his guilt and his conscience.

Now he cried out in protest, 'No, Dunvale, no! She had no pulse, no heartbeat!' He choked on his words and tears came into his eyes and he broke down completely. 'I could not have done anything to hurt her,' he sobbed. 'I loved her. Talk to Bridget again. *Please. Please.* She'll verify that I'm telling the truth. Min was dead ... and Bridget O'Donnell knows that she was.'

'*She was alive, Lamont!*'

'No! No!' Demented, Lamont rushed at Anthony, his arms flailing in the air, his face apoplectic. He felt a sudden and excruciating pain shoot across his temple and along the side of his face, but he did not let it slow him down. He lunged at Anthony. As he did another searing pain blinded him. The blood rushed to his head and everything went black. He fell sprawling to the floor, and then was still.

Startled, Anthony stood looking down at him, momentarily rooted to the spot, unable to move. He had noticed the sudden and dreadful change when Lamont had rushed towards him, had instantly realized that the other man was having some sort of seizure.

Pulling himself together, Anthony bent down, felt Lamont's pulse. It was erratic, faint, but it *was* there.

Hurrying to the telephone, Anthony dialled the cottage hospital in the village of Clonloughlin.

'Dunvale here,' he said to the duty nurse when she answered. 'Could you please send an ambulance immediately. To the estate manager's house. Michael Lamont has just had a stroke, I think. But he's still alive. If you hurry we can probably save him.'

To see justice done, Anthony thought, as he hung up.

<h1 style="text-align:center">30</h1>

'I've really got to take it over!' Paula exclaimed, tightening her grip on Michael Kallinski's arm. 'It would be nothing short of criminal if I let it slip through my fingers.'

'Yes, I know it would.' Michael looked at her through the corner of his eye. 'Six hundred and fifty million dollars is a hell of a lot of money, though.'

'That's true, it is. On the other hand, it isn't *really*, not if you consider what I'm actually buying. A chain of department stores that has a fine reputation, great prestige, with invaluable real estate assets, and a balance sheet that's in the black. And it's a perfect chain for me, Michael, as you well know. That's why you brought it to my attention in the first place.' She leaned closer, added in an emphatic tone tinged with excitement, 'Larson's locations couldn't be better for me if I'd hand picked them myself. Westchester, Philadelphia and Boston cover the Eastern Seaboard. Chicago and Detroit the Midwest. Los Angeles and San Francisco the West Coast. It's a deal made in heaven, as far as I'm concerned.'

'If you make a deal.'

Paula gave him a hard stare. 'Is there a chance I might not?' she asked, her voice instantly changing, rising slightly in sudden concern.

'I suppose there's always that chance, Paula. But I don't think you have too much to worry about in this particular situation. As far as I know, there's no one else after the company, and I understand from Harvey in New York that the chairman of the board is willing to start talking, to open negotiations whenever you're ready. And what Millard Larson says goes, since he's the majority stockholder as well as CEO. If I were you, I'd make plans to fly to New York as soon as possible.'

'I agree with you, and I want to go. But I can't . . . at least not for two weeks. Lorne and Tessa are both coming home from their schools tomorrow. It's the Easter break, in case you'd forgotten. I just can't be away right now.'

'Oh God, I *had* forgotten about Easter! I have the same problem as you I'm afraid, so I'll have to stay put, too.'

'Oh.' Puzzled, she frowned, asked, 'Are you planning a trip to the States, Michael?'

'I thought I should be there in case you need me,' he explained, his voice vibrant with enthusiasm, his face lighting up. 'After all, I'm the one who introduced you to Harvey Rawson, found the Larson chain for you, set everything in motion.' He gave her a small, confiding smile. 'Besides, I have to be in New

696

York on business sometime this month, and if I go when you're going I can kill two birds with one stone, so to speak.' When she did not initially respond, he asked, 'What do you think?'

'Well . . . yes . . . I suppose so.' She realized how hesitant she sounded and rapidly nodded her head. 'Yes, yes, why not,' she added in a more positive tone.

'Good, it's settled then,' he exclaimed, looking delighted, congratulating himself on his adroit little manoeuvre. The thought of being alone with her in New York excited him. But he said in the most neutral voice, 'Now we'd better concentrate on Dad's exhibition. He's been giving us peculiar looks for the last ten minutes. I have a feeling he's a bit miffed.'

Paula laughed. 'I'm sure he is. We *have* been rather rude, standing here in the middle of the floor deep in conversation. Not only ignoring him and everyone else, but all these priceless art treasures as well. Come on, we must go and join him at once. He wants to show me around the exhibition himself, tell me about each piece of Fabergé he owns. And I must admit, I am rather staggered by all this. His collection is much larger than I ever imagined it to be.'

'Not every piece on display belongs to him,' Michael was quick to point out. 'The Queen and the Queen Mum have loaned some of their Fabergé objects, and so has Kenneth Snowman, the great British expert on Peter Carl Fabergé, and Malcolm Forbes, the American publisher, who's another avid collector, like Dad.'

'I know. Your father explained. Still, he does have a superb collection.'

'I'll say. Not only that, it's given him a truly consuming interest other than business these last few years.'

They moved together down the long salon, one of two in the Royal Academy of Arts at Burlington House where the reception for the opening of the Fabergé exhibition was in full swing on this April evening. The event had been organized by Sir Ronald Kallinski to benefit one of his favourite charities, and the gallery was packed.

A waiter drew to a standstill in front of them.

Michael took two glasses of champagne from the silver tray being proffered, murmured his thanks, and handed a flute of Dom Perignon to Paula.

When Sir Ronald spotted them coming towards him, he extricated himself from a small group of people and hurried to meet them.

'I know you two are committed to business and rarely think of anything else, but do you really have to have a confab during my reception?' he asked, obviously quite put out. But then his eyes became warm with affection and twinkled brightly as he took Paula's arm and led her along the gallery, his irritation instantly forgotten.

'Now, my dear,' he said, 'let me take you around. I have many new acquisitions, none of which you have seen. Neither have you, Michael,' he added, glancing over his shoulder at his son.

'I've been looking forward to this for weeks,' Michael replied in all sincerity. 'And I'm sorry we got caught up with our business discussion the way we did. My apologies, Dad.'

'Accepted, accepted, my boy,' Sir Ronald answered briskly, striding down the salon with Paula, Michael dutifully in tow. Suddenly he came to a stop in front of a display case.

Turning to Paula, he said, 'This is not one of my pieces. Sadly, I might add. It was graciously lent for the exhibition by Her Majesty The Queen. And it happens to be a particular favourite of mine. It's called the Mosaic Egg, and I think it's perhaps the most poignant of all the Imperial Easter Eggs. It was presented to Czarina Alexandra Feodorovna by Nicholas II on Easter morning of 1914. As you can see, it's a gossamer platinum shell which has been "embroidered" with flowers made of precious stones . . . rubies, sapphires, diamonds and emeralds, the whole encircled with bands of pearls. And look, there on the little gold stand are the miniature sepia profiles of the Imperial children.'

'It's exquisite,' Paula said admiringly, leaning forward, peering at the egg. 'And the stand is concealed inside the egg, isn't it, when not on display?'

'Correct.' Sir Ronald took her arm, and the three of them progressed down the gallery slowly, pausing to admire other treasures in the show. 'That's the beauty and genius of the Fabergé *objets*,' he went on, 'those extraordinary, and very often magical, surprises contained within the egg itself. Like that dazzling little golden chanticleer which emerges from the translucent blue enamelled Imperial Easter Egg your grandmother once owned,' Sir Ronald reminded her, smiling.

Paula smiled back at him. 'Oh yes, that egg is the most beautiful – at least that's what I think, Uncle Ronnie. And I'm glad it's in your collection, that you won it at the auction. At least it's still in the clans.'

He chuckled. 'I don't think I'll ever forget that day at Sotheby's. There was such competitive bidding for the egg. But it was exciting. And gratifying when I suddenly realized *I* owned it. Naturally it's on display tonight. Let's go and have a look at it, and then we can go through into the other salon. There are more breathtaking examples of Fabergé masterpieces, which were made for the Imperial family before the Romanov dynasty came to its tragic end . . .'

'I didn't know Amanda was coming to the exhibition!' Michael exclaimed in surprise a short while later when he spotted her standing in the doorway, glancing around, obviously looking for them.

'Oh, I forgot to tell you,' Paula murmured. 'I sent her a ticket and she said she would do her best to make it.'

'I'll go and get her, bring her over to join us,' Michael said, hurrying across the room.

Paula's eyes followed him and she smiled to herself, then looked at his father and winked.

Sir Ronald regarded her closely for a moment, then said slowly, 'I'm not wrong in thinking you're playing *shadchan* am I, Paula? *Matchmaking?*'

'And why not?' she answered, laughing. 'Anyway, she has such a crush on him . . . wouldn't it be lovely if Michael reciprocated her feelings, Uncle Ronnie?'

Sir Ronald seemed initially startled, then suddenly pleased, and he nodded. 'It would indeed. Amanda's a lovely young woman. Clever, too. Emily and

Alexander have trained her well. She's certainly made our takeover of Lady Hamilton Clothes very smooth. But of course you know that, my dear. As I was telling Emily the other day, my people are terribly impressed with her. We're all sorry she won't be staying on to run the company for us. Emily explained she's needed at Harte Enterprises and I do understand that. Still –' He cut himself short, and a look of infinite sadness crossed his face fleetingly.

Paula, aware that he was thinking of Alexander, experienced a little rush of sadness herself. Sandy had retired at the beginning of March, and now Emily was chairman of the board and chief executive officer. Amanda had moved over to become head of Genret, whilst Winston continued to run his own division, the Yorkshire Consolidated Newspaper Company and its subsidiaries, of which he was a part owner. They had become a close-knit triumvirate and Harte Enterprises was running as efficiently as it always had, but Paula knew that Alexander was terribly missed by them. She missed him herself now that he was living quietly at Nutton Priory, although they did speak a lot on the telephone.

'Hello, darling,' Paula said, greeting Amanda warmly as she and Michael joined them. 'You look stunning.'

'Thank you, Paula,' Amanda said, smiling at her cousin, pecking her on the cheek. 'Hello, Uncle Ronnie. Sorry I'm late, but the traffic was ghastly tonight.'

'No problem, my dear,' Sir Ronald said, taking her hand in his, giving her a quick kiss. 'Now, Michael, do the honours, my boy, and get a glass of champagne for Amanda, would you please?'

'I certainly will. Be back in a jiffy.'

Amanda turned to Paula, began to say something about her twin, Francesca, and it gave Sir Ronald a chance to study her surreptitiously, appraisingly, for a brief moment. Tall, slender and blonde, Amanda was a lovely looking young woman who bore a strong resemblance to her half-sister, Emily. Tonight she was wearing a smartly tailored red silk suit with a diamond Victorian bow brooch pinned onto one lapel and antique diamond earrings. Chic but discreet, Sir Ronald thought, and very well bred. Suddenly he saw her through new eyes. As a potential daughter-in-law. The idea strongly appealed to him. Amanda was perfect for Michael, an intelligent, charming and outgoing girl with perfect manners, like all of Emma's granddaughters. Just the sort of wife his son needed. The possibility that the Kallinski and Harte clans might finally be united in marriage thrilled him. He would encourage this friendship, as apparently Paula was intending to do. Yes, Amanda and Michael must become husband and wife. He would have a long chat to Paula later, together they would map out a plan of action. Michael needed to be gently guided into this relationship. His son tended to vacillate when it came to women. And he had been single far too long since his divorce.

31

The garden was still her most magical place.

Ever since childhood Paula had found satisfaction and reward in planting and weeding, pruning and hoeing, and working outdoors was therapeutic, soothing to her, never failed to put her in the best of moods.

Also, she had discovered long ago that she often did her best thinking in her gardens at Pennistone Royal, and today was no exception. It was a bright April afternoon, just after Easter, sunny and brisk with a light breeze, and a powder-blue sky that was cool and cloudless.

As she worked on the new rockery she was creating, she focused her thoughts on business, in particular the Larson chain in the United States. The deal was already in the first stage of negotiation, and Millard Larson was expecting her in New York next week, when they would sit down at the conference table and hammer out the terms and conditions of the sale.

When she had first had the idea of expanding her operations in the States, long before the possibility of Larson's had come up, she had made the decision to purchase any new retailing company that caught her eye with her own money.

Six hundred and fifty million dollars, she thought now, mulling the figure over in her mind whilst concentrating on the alpine plants she was sorting through. It *was* a lot of money, no doubt about that, and she had been wondering for several days which financial combination would work best for her.

Paula sighed under her breath. If her mother had agreed to sell the Sitex stock last year her problem would have been solved. Under the terms and conditions of her grandfather's will, she and her brother Philip would automatically have received one third of the proceeds of that sale – hundreds of millions of dollars each. But her mother had refused to sell the oil stock and continued to be quite adamant about not doing so. Paula had acknowledged months ago that she would have to raise the necessary cash another way, once she found the right department store chain to buy.

She ran several possibilities through her mind, then dismissed each one as convoluted and complex, went back to her original idea. To her way of thinking, the best solution was to sell ten per cent of her Harte shares which Emma had left her. They would realize between two hundred and three hundred million dollars on the market, but without making much of a dent in her holdings. She would still be the majority stockholder with forty-one per cent, as well as chairman and chief executive officer of the Harte chain. The remainder of the money she could easily raise from the banks, by borrowing against the retail chain she was acquiring, pledging its assets, in particular its real estate holdings which were valuable.

Suddenly, after days of indecision, she made up her mind. She *would* go that route. And she would put everything in motion at once. First thing on

Monday morning when she got to her office in the Leeds store she would speak to her stockbroker.

A bright smile broke through, expunging the worried and preoccupied expression she had worn all day, and she continued to smile to herself as she finished planting the small alpine species in the narrow crevices of the rocks.

'Mummy! Mummy!'

Paula lifted her head alertly at the sound of Patrick's voice. He and his sister, Linnet, were running as fast as their legs would carry them along the gravel path that sloped down from the long terrace at the back of Pennistone Royal.

They both wore sweaters and jeans under their duffel coats and mufflers, and she could not help thinking how healthy and fit they both looked today. Especially Patrick. That vacant expression which so often dulled his eyes was absent, as it had been for some weeks. This pleased her, raised her hopes that he was improving mentally, if only ever so slightly. She loved her sensitive, damaged and beautiful child so very much.

'Patrick! Do be careful! You're going to fall!' She called out. 'And you too, Linnet! Do slow down, both of you! I'm not going anywhere, you know.' She rose as she spoke, picked up the basket full of her gardening tools and carefully climbed down from the top of the clustered rocks.

Patrick hurled himself against her body, clinging to her, panting hard and trying to catch his breath.

She pushed his dark hair away from his temple and clucked quietly. 'Dear, dear, you are a one, aren't you? Running so hard, I –'

'Puffed, Mummy,' he interrupted her, raising his solemn little face to hers. 'Linnet puffed too.'

'I'm *not*!' Linnet protested fiercely, glaring.

Ignoring her, Patrick went on, 'Horsey, Mummy. Patrick wants horsey.'

Puzzled, Paula swung her eyes to her six-year-old daughter, as she so often did when Patrick spoke in riddles and she wanted edification. She gave Linnet a questioning stare.

Linnet explained, 'The horse in the attic, Mummy. That's what Patrick wants. I said he couldn't take it, not without asking Daddy. And Daddy said to ask you.'

'*Horse in the attic*. What on earth are you talking about, darling?'

'The cresel horse ... the one that goes round and round and round and round. To the music, Mummy.'

'The carousel, the horse on the carousel. Now I understand.' Paula smiled at them both. 'But I don't remember there being a carousel in the attic. I suppose it must be, since you've apparently seen it.'

'It's in a trunk,' Linnet rushed on excitedly. 'We saw it just now. Daddy let us play in the attic after our walk this afternoon.'

'Did he now.' Paula pulled off her gardening gloves, threw them on top of the basket, and taking a small hand in each of hers, she led her children back to the house.

A short while later the three of them were rummaging in the old trunks which had been stored in the attics of Pennistone Royal for many years. Patrick had already taken possession of the carousel, which Paula had immediately given to him, and he was turning the small key, making it work in the way she had shown him.

The horses on the merry-go-round were moving up and down to the strains of the *Carousel Waltz*, and the little boy was fascinated, his happy, eager face a pleasure for Paula to witness.

Linnet and Paula left him to play with the carousel on his own, and they soon had their heads and their hands in another trunk which Paula had pulled out and opened.

Busily they sorted through the toys that brimmed to the top, taking out a large, painted wooden soldier, a box of bricks, a scruffy teddy bear with one arm and no eyes, several stuffed animals, various jig-saw puzzles, a box of tin soldiers and various rag toys.

Paula's hands finally came to rest on a beautiful china baby doll at the bottom of the trunk, and lifting it out she caught her breath in surprise and pleasure. She remembered it very well. Her grandmother had given it to her, and she had taken great care of it, had loved this doll more than any of her other possessions. Years ago she had packed it carefully away when she had moved from Long Meadow to Pennistone Royal after Jim's death. She had meant to give the doll to Tessa but had somehow forgotten all about it during the troubled year after the avalanche.

Sitting back on her haunches, she held the doll up, smoothed its golden curls, straightened its dainty ecru-coloured lace dress. She was amazed that the doll was in such good condition.

Linnet was watching her closely, her eyes lingering with longing on the doll. 'Was it yours, Mummy?' she asked at last.

'Yes, darling, it was. My grandmother gave it to me when I was your age.'

'You mean Grandy Emma?'

Paula nodded.

'So you wouldn't want to give that doll to anybody then, would you? Not if *Grandy Emma* gave it to you,' Linnet said gravely, her eyes still fastened on the doll.

Paula laughed. 'Well, perhaps I would give it to a girl whom I knew would look after it, would take good care of it, as I did.'

'Tessa,' Linnet said a trifle sadly in a small and quiet voice.

'No. I think her name's Linnet.'

'Oh Mummy! Mummy!'

'Here you are, my darling, it's for you.' Paula held out the doll. 'I used to call her Florabelle.'

'Then I shall, too.' Linnet struggled to her feet, took the doll, her eyes shining, her smile brilliant.

'Thank you, Mummy, oh thank you.' Hugging the doll tightly in her arms, she leaned into Paula, nuzzled her nose against her cheek. 'I love you, Mummy,' she whispered. 'Oh you do smell nice. Like a bunch of flowers.' Linnet put her head on one side and observed Paula thoughtfully. Then she reached out, touched Paula's cheek gently with her small hand. 'You won't get lost, will you, Mummy?' she asked, her voice unexpectedly wistful, almost fretful.

Paula's brows puckered together into a jagged line. 'What do you mean, lovey?'

'Sometimes when we're waiting for you to come home, Daddy says, "I think your mother must have got lost. I don't know *where* she can be." And then he goes to the window and looks out. And I worry 'til you get home and so does Patrick. Well, I think he does.'

'Oh darling, it's merely a *saying*. It doesn't mean that I'm really lost,' Paula said, and smiled at her daughter reassuringly.

'Are you sure, Mummy?'

'Of course I am.'

'Oh. That's all right then.'

Paula smoothed a hand over her daughter's red-gold hair, and sat back on the floor, watching her as she played with the doll. How easy it is to please children, she thought at one moment. As long as they receive love and care and kindness and discipline that's all that really counts. Their needs are really very simple. If only adults could be the same . . .

'So this is where you're all hiding!' Shane exclaimed from the doorway, making the three of them start in surprise.

Paula pushed herself to her feet. 'We've been finding all sorts of lovely treasures in the trunks,' she explained, hurrying over to him. 'A carousel for Patrick, and my old doll Florabelle for Linnet.'

Shane nodded, put his arm around his wife. 'But now I think you have to come downstairs . . . Nanny has tea waiting in the nursery . . . for all of us.'

'That was such fun, and the kids thoroughly enjoyed it too,' Shane said to Paula that evening as they were dressing for dinner. 'It's ages since we've had a nursery tea with them. We must do it more often.'

'You're absolutely right, darling,' Paula agreed, leaning forward, looking into the mirror of her dressing table, smoothing the silver brush over her sleek black hair. Putting the brush down, she outlined her mouth with bright red lipstick, then sprayed on Christina Crowther's *Blue Gardenia* perfume, one of her favourites. 'And I'm really thrilled with Patrick, the progress he's making, aren't you?' She half-turned to look at Shane.

'I am indeed. He's so much better in every way, and there's been a vast improvement in his understanding of things. It's the new tutor. Mark is doing wonders for the boy.'

'Yes, he is,' Paula said.

Shane slipped into a dark blue blazer, adjusted his tie, walked across the floor. He stood behind Paula with his hands resting lightly on her shoulders, smiling at her in the mirror.

'You look beautiful, Beanstalk,' he said, his lopsided grin surfacing briefly. 'So stop titivating yourself. Come on, let's go into the upstairs parlour. I put a couple of bottles of champagne on ice earlier, and we can have a quiet drink together before Emily and Winston arrive for dinner.'

'That's a lovely idea,' Paula exclaimed, pushing back the dressing table stool, rising to her feet, reaching up, kissing him on the cheek. 'But then *you* usually *do* have the best ideas.'

She tucked her arm through his and together they walked across the floor into the adjoining room.

The upstairs parlour at Pennistone Royal had been Emma Harte's favourite room in the great old house in Yorkshire, and Paula loved it as much as her grandmother had. Its impressive architectural details and splendid furnishings belied the name *parlour*, but for some reason it had never been called anything else. The soaring dimensions gave it a singular grandeur and its high ceiling was Jacobean in style, decorated with elaborate plasterwork. Tall, leaded windows flanked an unusual oriel window, and there was a carved fireplace of bleached oak and the floor was of parquet. Emma had years ago balanced its imposing detail and size with a mellow charm, intimacy, and comfort, as well as her own brand of understated elegance.

Paula had never felt the need to change the room, even thought it would be sacrilege to do so, and the décor was the same as it had been for nigh on fifty years. Since the day Emma had bought it in the 1930s, in fact. The primrose coloured walls were repainted every year to the same shade, and new slipcovers and draperies were made when they were required, otherwise it was exactly the way it had been throughout Emma's lifetime.

The priceless Turner landscape filled with misty blues and greens hung above the mantelpiece, and the only other paintings in the parlour were excellent portraits of a young nobleman and his wife by Sir Joshua Reynolds. The three oils were in perfect harmony with the Georgian antiques, the Savonnerie carpet and the rare Rose Medallion china in the Chippendale cabinet. Brightly patterned yellow chintz fabric covered the two huge sofas in the centre of the room, which faced each other across a mahogany butler's tray table, and the antique porcelain lamps were shaded in cream silk; everywhere there was the gleam of silver and crystal.

The lamps had been turned on and a huge fire blazed in the hearth; the warmth had opened up the narcissi, daffodils and hyacinths planted in bowls, and the air was fragrant with their mingled scents.

As she moved towards one of the sofas and sat down, Paula thought the parlour had never looked more beautiful than it did this evening. It was dusk and the light was changing. Outside the great soaring windows, the sky was turning to navy-blue tinged with lilac bleeding into amethyst and deeper purple. A strong wind had blown up, was rustling the trees, and distant thunder heralded a storm.

But here in the gracious room there was a sense of peacefulness and tranquillity. To Paula, the parlour had a timeless quality, never changing. It was full of her past, her entire life really, and so many cherished memories . . . memories of her childhood, her youth, the days of her growing into womanhood. And there were memories of the most special people in her life . . . those dead and living . . . her father and Grandy . . . her mother . . . Philip . . . the special friends of her youth . . . and her cousins Emily, Winston and Alexander. And Shane, too, was caught up in the memories which were held captive in this room. *Home*, she thought. The parlour represents home to me, and my roots, just as it did to my grandmother. And that's why I could never be happy living anywhere else . . .

'Penny for your thoughts,' Shane said, looming over her, making her jump. He handed her the crystal glass brimming with icy, sparkling champagne.

'Oh darling, thank you,' she said, taking the glass from him. 'I was just thinking how lovely this room is, and it's truly filled with the past, isn't it?'

'All the days of our lives actually,' he said, touching his champagne flute to hers. 'Since we were very little.'

They smiled into each other's eyes, loving each other, and then Shane moved across to the other sofa, where he sat down, settled into the plump chintz cushions, relaxing.

Paula leaned forward, focused her violet eyes on him. 'Talking of the past – I've been thinking of the *future* in the last few days, Shane, and I'm definitely going to go ahead and buy the Larson chain in the States.'

Shane looked at her sharply. The expression in his black Irish eyes changed slightly, became anxious, but he said in the same even, well-controlled voice, 'If that's what you want, then I'm glad you've made the decision to go ahead, darling.' Privately he believed she may well be taking on too much responsibility, but he never interfered in her business, remained neutral and uninvolved. It was one of the reasons their marriage was so solid.

She said slowly, 'Six hundred and fifty million dollars is a fair price for the chain, I think.' She raised a shapely brow. 'No?'

He nodded. 'Yes, I agree with you. It is.'

'Well, anyway . . . I've decided to buy it myself, with my own money,' she added, giving him a direct look.

For a fraction of a second he was quite floored and gaped at her in astonishment, but once again his tone was even, steady, as he said, 'Have you now. And what are you going to sell to raise the necessary cash to pay for it?'

'I'll borrow from the banks, take out a mortgage on the Larson real estate, pledge some of the chain's other assets. I'll probably be able to borrow about three hundred million dollars or so. And to raise the other half of the money I need I intend to sell ten per cent of my Harte shares.'

'Paula!' he cried, askance. 'Do you really think you should?' Holding her gaze with his eyes, he asked swiftly, 'Isn't that rather foolish – and *risky*? Far be it from me to interfere in your business, darling, but those Harte shares are a great weapon – and your security – in as much as they give you absolute power in the company. If you sell ten per cent of your fifty-one per cent you're reducing your holdings in the company. You're leaving yourself wide open to challenge.'

'Don't be silly, Shane. Whoever's going to challenge me!' she laughed. 'I have the full support of my board and my shareholders. They're behind me. Good Lord, the store is *mine*. Nobody would ever dream of going against me, neither the board members nor stockholders. I *am* Harte's, just as Emma was.'

'Well . . . I don't know . . .' Shane began and stopped. He had finally broken the rule he had made the day he had married her. He had promised himself he would never give her any business advice, and he never had. She was far too much like Emma Harte to take it anyway. Paula was stubborn and independent. And usually infallible in her judgements, like her grandmother had been before her. He took a deep breath, resisted arguing against this planned move on her part.

'I can see from your face that you've made up your mind to do things your way,' he said carefully. 'You're confident, determined, and your attitude is admirable, the only one you *should* have when you embark on a venture like this.' Shane smiled at her, and he meant every word when he added, 'I'm behind you all the way, Paula.'

'Oh Shane darling, thank you . . . thank you for believing in me. That means such a lot. I was only saying so to Michael the other day.'

'Were you?'

She nodded. 'I told him I hoped you'd approve of what I'm doing. By the way, he'll be in New York next week when I'm there.'

'That's a coincidence . . . or is it?' He gazed at her intently, his dark eyes narrowing.

'No, darling, it's not. Michael does have to be in New York some time this month, but he has made his plans to dovetail with mine. He thinks he should be there to give me any help I might need with the Larson takeover.'

Stiffening, Shane held himself rigid on the sofa, and for a moment he did not respond. Then he cleared his throat. 'You've never needed help with deals in the past. Not from anyone. Why *now* all of a sudden?'

She shrugged, laughed. 'I don't need any help, but Michael introduced me to Harvey Rawson, found me the Larson chain, as you know. *He* thinks he ought to be there, and I don't want to hurt his feelings by telling him not to come over specially for me.'

'I see.'

Shane sprang to his feet, strode over to the console, not wanting her to see his sudden anger. He poured himself another glass of Dom Perignon, pushed back the jealousy he was feeling, endeavoured to arrange a suitably unconcerned expression on his face. Michael was irritating him of late. He had an instinctive, gut feeling that the other man was interested in his wife in a more personal way than she realized. He trusted Paula implicitly, knew that she loved him with all her heart, and would always be true. But he was no longer certain that he trusted Michael Kallinski. Certainly he did not want Paula to be placed in an awkward or embarrassing situation when she was in New York, and that might possibly happen. Or was he being unfair to Michael? After all, his old friend was a gentleman, wasn't he?

Shane made a snap decision, and pivoted to face his wife, flashed her a brilliant smile. 'I was keeping this as a little surprise, but I might as well tell you. I'm going to be in New York too next week, Paula darling,' he improvised. 'Miranda needs me to go over there. I know we try not to be away at the same time, for the sake of the children, but this trip is unavoidable. I do have some pressing problems to deal with.'

'But how marvellous!' Paula cried, her face filling with happiness. 'And Patrick and Linnet will be perfectly all right with Nanny and Mark . . .' Paula stopped, chuckled quietly. 'It just so happens that Amanda is going to be in the States as well, on a buying trip for Genret. I plan to give a few dinner parties for her . . . and Michael. You see, Shane, Amanda's quite potty about him, and Uncle Ronnie and I think they would make a perfect couple.'

'I'm not so sure that Michael is interested in matrimony at the moment,' Shane remarked as he strolled back to the sofa and sat down. 'Not after that débâcle with Valentine. Still, I'm rather inclined to agree with you and Uncle Ronnie about Amanda being ideal for him.' Shane leaned back on the sofa, feeling a curious sense of relief. He added, as an afterthought, 'I think we'd better fly separately though, as we usually do.'

'Yes, of course, that is wisest. Anyway, Shane –' Paula stopped mid-sentence as the door opened and her daughter, Tessa, came into the room.

'Goodnight, Mummy, Daddy.' She hovered in the doorway, blew them kisses. 'I'm off to Melanie's party now. Her brother's just arrived to drive me over there.'

'You're not going looking like that!' Paula exclaimed, and stood up.

Tessa frowned. 'What do you mean, Mummy?'

'You know very well what I mean.' Paula beckoned with one finger. 'Come over here, Tessa, I want to look at you.'

'It's only a bit of blush-on,' Tessa muttered, throwing her mother a hostile look, not budging from the door. 'Everybody wears it these days.'

'I'd hardly say that. Please come over to the fire, Tessa.'

Reluctantly the girl did as her mother asked. Paula took hold of her shoulders and gently turned her into the light emanating from the lamps on the tables on either side of the fireplace. She shook her head, grimaced. 'Just a little blush-on, you said. But you're wearing mascara and lipstick as well.'

'It's a very *pale* pink lipstick,' Tessa protested.

'You're only *thirteen*!' Paula shook her head in dismay. 'I can't allow you to wear cosmetics. Now run up to your room and wash your face, please.'

'No! I won't! I'm not going to take it off! You're just old-fashioned! That's what's wrong with you!' Tessa cried angrily, and she glared at Paula, then tossed her head.

'Steady on, Tessa!' Shane warned, sitting up straighter on the sofa, throwing the girl a cautionary glance. 'Don't speak to your mother in that way. You're being extremely rude. I will not have it.'

'She *is* old-fashioned, Daddy. Out of date. All the girls in my class wear makeup after school.'

'I sincerely doubt that.' Paula took a step backward, regarded her daughter through freshly objective eyes. My God, she thought, Tessa could easily pass for seventeen. She's grown up all of a sudden. Whatever's happened to the years? It seems like only yesterday that she was a baby in her pram.

Adopting a conciliatory manner, softening her voice, Paula now murmured, 'Please do as I say, darling.'

Tessa compressed her lips in a stubborn line and her silver-grey eyes became defiant. 'I won't go to the party if you make me take my makeup off. I'll look childish, ridiculous. The other girls will be made up, and they'll laugh at me.'

'Mother, and daughter stared at each other.

Paula shook her head slowly. 'No, they won't.'

'Mother, please . . . you're being stupid!' Tessa wailed.

'No, I'm not. And as long as you live in this house and are supported by us, you will live by our rules,' Paula said quietly, but with great firmness.

Tessa looked down at her feet, thinking hard. She admitted to herself that her mother had the upper hand; nevertheless, she was quite determined to get her own way. She took another approach when she said, 'I'll make a deal with you. I'll –'

'*No negotiating*,' Paula shot back.

707

'But the ability to negotiate is often the secret of business success,' Tessa pointed out, quoting Paula to Paula.

Her mother swallowed a smile and glanced away to hide the merriment unexpectedly brimming in her eyes. Shane was less successful at concealing his amusement, and he burst out laughing.

Paula looked over at him and shook her head, then she turned to Tessa. 'All right, you can wear the blush-on. But that's all. And for this concession on my part you must promise to spend an extra hour practising the piano. You've been neglecting it lately.'

'Okay, I promise. But please let me keep the mascara on. My eyelashes are so pale. I look awful. Bleached out. I'll double my piano practice, and . . . and . . . I'll take Linnet off your hands on Nanny's day off.'

'That's tomorrow, you know,' Paula pointed out, and relenting, she added, 'All right, it's a deal. But no lipstick. *Understood*?'

'Yes. Thanks, Mums.' Laughter touched Tessa's face and she danced lightly across the room, pirouetting until she reached the door.

'And don't be late,' Paula instructed.

'I won't. 'Bye.'

The door slammed behind her with such a crash Paula grimaced, then winced as the Rose Medallion china trembled in the Chippendale cabinet. She murmured, 'Tess looks older than thirteen, doesn't she, Shane?'

'Yes, she's suddenly becoming quite the young lady. She's growing up a little too fast for my liking. I think it's time we considered taking her out of Harrogate College, Paula, sending her to Heathfield, as we've always intended.'

'I'll get in touch with the headmistress next week. I agree that the sooner Tess goes there the better.'

'I told you years ago that she was a maverick, Paula. She and Lorne are very different, even though they're twins. She's going to need a strong hand in the next few years.'

Paula nodded, recognizing the truth in everything Shane said. She fell into her thoughts. Her daughter was headstrong, wilful, reckless, and even defiant at times. She was a loving girl, warm, outgoing, and she was bright, clever at school. Yet she could be temperamental, and to Paula this was a negative. Her daughter was very much a Fairley, had inherited many of their characteristics, not the least of which were the personal vanity, preoccupation with clothes and with self that had always been Fairley flaws. There's not a great deal of Harte in her, Paula thought with a little stab of dismay. She even looks like her great-great-grandmother Adele Fairley, with her pale blonde hair and those silvery, enigmatic eyes. Paula shivered unexpectedly, and gazed into the fire.

'You've got the oddest look on your face, Paula,' Shane said. 'Is something wrong, darling?'

'No, no, of course not,' she exclaimed, rousing herself from her ruminations. 'Can I have another glass of champagne, please?'

'I *was* right, wasn't I?' Emily said, glancing from Paula to Winston. 'Now come on, the two of you, have the good grace to admit it.'

'You were right about *everything*,' Paula acknowledged. 'And I'm sorry I pooh-poohed your theories all those years ago.' She lifted her wine glass, took a swallow of the claret. 'Is that good enough for you, Dumpling?'

Emily grinned.

Winston said, 'I apologize for ever thinking you were slightly bonkers when you kept on insisting that Min had not committed suicide.'

'Apologies accepted.' Emily smiled at her husband and then at her cousin, picked up her knife and fork, cut into the slice of spring lamb on her dinner plate, and ate a mouthful.

Shane, sipping his wine thoughtfully, said, 'You always suspected it was murder, didn't you, Emily?'

'Yes.'

'Why?' Shane probed curiously.

'It was the missing five hours that troubled me, Shane.' Emily put down her cutlery, sat back in the chair. 'I simply couldn't understand where Min had been from about six o'clock, when Anthony first saw her at the lake, until the time she died around eleven. Her car had remained at the lake, so I was sure she had been visiting someone . . . either in the village of Clonloughlin or on the estate. I even thought of a lover . . . but I was unable to figure it all out . . . it was a great mystery to me.'

'One that has been solved at long last,' Winston added. 'And my sister, for one, is vastly relieved. For years poor Sally has believed that she and Anthony somehow drove Min to her death. Thank God that's finally been cleared up. A cloud has been lifted from the Dunvale family.'

'Did Anthony explain why Michael Lamont suddenly confessed to accidentally killing Min?' Shane asked, levelling his eyes at Winston.

'Anthony told us that Lamont couldn't go on, that his conscience was troubling him so much it was making him ill,' Winston said. 'Apparently he went to Anthony, told him the truth about that night. When Anthony pointed out that a dead person couldn't take water into the lungs, and therefore Min had to have been alive when he put her in the lake, Lamont went berserk, was so shocked, so devastated, he had the stroke.'

'At least Lamont's subsequent death enabled Anthony to bury the whole matter with him,' Paula murmured. 'It would have been ghastly for the family if Anthony had been obliged to reopen the case. Not to mention for Lamont, who would have been standing trial for murder, I've no doubt.'

'I always felt that Bridget O'Donnell knew more than she was admitting,' Emily remarked. 'But when Anthony was here last week I asked him about her, and he looked at me in the most peculiar way. He told me Bridget had known nothing about Min's death, that she had been suffering from a migraine in her room that night, just as she had said at the inquest, when she also gave Anthony his alibi. Still –'

'Excuse me, Mrs O'Neill,' the housekeeper said, coming into the dining room. 'I'm sorry to interrupt you during dinner, but there's an important telephone call for you.'

'Thank you, Mary,' Paula said, pushing back her chair, rising. 'Excuse me, chaps, I won't be a moment.'

Paula hurried out to the Stone Hall and the nearest telephone, wondering who could be calling her at this hour on a Saturday night. Lifting the receiver, she said, 'Hello?'

'Mrs O'Neill, it's Ursula Hood here.'

Paula tightened her grip on the receiver at the sound of Mrs Hood's voice. She was Alexander's housekeeper at Nutton Priory, and all of Paula's senses were instantly alerted to trouble. Her throat was slightly dry when she said, 'Good evening, Mrs Hood. How can I help you?'

'Mrs O'Neill . . . I'm calling because . . . well, something dreadful has happened.' The woman's voice cracked. She was unable to go on, and there was a small silence before she continued quietly, 'Mr Barkstone went out hunting in the woods early this evening. He . . . he . . . accidentally shot himself.'

The hackles rose on the back of Paula's neck and she began to tremble. She asked shakily, 'Is he badly injured, Mrs Hood?'

Mrs Hood cleared her throat. 'Oh Mrs O'Neill . . . he's . . . he's . . . Mr Barkstone's dead. I'm so sorry. So very sorry.'

'Oh God, no!' Paula cried and steadied herself against the oak table, trying to absorb the shock, blinking back the tears that had sprung into her eyes.

Mrs Hood said softly, 'I can't believe he's gone . . . Such a lovely man.' The housekeeper broke down again, but managed to get a grip on herself, to explain, 'I'm ringing *you* because I don't have the heart to get in touch with his sisters . . . I just wouldn't know how to tell Mrs Harte, or Miss Amanda and Miss Francesca . . . I wouldn't . . .'

Paula said slowly, 'It's all right, Mrs Hood, I understand. And Mrs Harte is here for dinner this evening. I'll break the news to her, and to her sisters. But please . . . can you tell me . . . a little more about . . . what happened?'

'Not really I can't, Mrs O'Neill. When Mr Barkstone didn't come down for dinner this evening, I sent the butler up to his bedroom. Mr Barkstone wasn't there. It seemed that no one in the house had seen him return from the woods. The butler, the houseman and the chauffeur then went out to look for him . . .' Mrs Hood blew her nose, finished, 'They found him lying under one of the big oaks, the gun by his side. He was already dead.'

'Thank you, Mrs Hood,' Paula managed to say, striving hard to control her feelings, to contain them as best she could. 'I'll handle things here, and my husband and I will drive up to Nutton Priory within the hour. I'm sure Mr and Mrs Harte will come with us.'

'I'll be waiting for you, Mrs O'Neill, and thank you.'

Paula put the receiver back in the cradle and stood for a moment longer in the Stone Hall thinking of her cousin. Oh Sandy, Sandy, why did you have to die like that? All alone in the woods. Her heart clenched. And then a most terrible and unacceptable thought flashed through her mind, stunning her. Had he taken his own life? No. Never. He wouldn't do that, she told herself. Sandy wanted so much to live. He fought so hard to keep going. Every minute was precious to him. He told me that so many times lately. She dismissed the idea of suicide, blocked it out of her mind.

Taking several deep breaths, Paula walked slowly back to the dining room, bracing herself to break the shocking news to Emily.

32

It was a bleak day for April.

Great clouds, curdled and grey, rolled with gathering speed across the lowering sky which merged into the grim and blackened Yorkshire moors. Lonely and implacable, their daunting aspects appalled the eye, cast dark shadows over Fairley this morning. There was not a drop of sunlight to soften those savage windswept reaches, the cold bracing air held a strong hint of rain and a thunderstorm seemed imminent.

Along the moorland road that cut through this great Pennine Chain of hills a line of cars moved slowly, following the funeral cortège. Soon the cortège left the moors, began its slow descent into the village, and within fifteen minutes it was coming to a stop in front of the lovely little Norman church. Here the new vicar, the Reverend Eric Clarke, was waiting to greet the family and friends of the deceased on the ancient porch.

There were six pallbearers to carry Alexander's coffin. Anthony Standish, the Earl of Dunvale, and Winston Harte, his cousins; Shane O'Neill and Michael Kallinski, and two of his friends from school. They had known him most of their lives and so it was fitting that they were with him at the end, had brought him to his last resting place in this old churchyard.

The six men lifted Alexander's coffin, shouldered it lightly, carried it through the lych-gate into the cemetery, moving at a slow and dignified pace down the flagged path. Their hearts were heavy and their sorrow was etched on their grieving faces. In their different ways, they had cared deeply about this man they had come to bury.

The pallbearers brought the coffin to the graveside where the vicar was now standing with Alexander's sorrowing sisters, Emily, Amanda and Francesca, and his distraught and weeping mother, Elizabeth, who was being physically supported by her French husband, Marc Deboyne. At the other side of the grave stood the rest of the family and many friends, all of them dressed in mourning.

Anthony looked burdened down, his face morose and stark as he walked over to join his wife, Sally, and Paula, who was next to her. He hunched further into his black overcoat, shivering in the gusting wind blowing down from the moors. It was making the new leaves on the trees rustle, and ruffling the flowers in the wreaths. Anthony stared at them. They were a reminder that it *was* spring ... tender blossoms, so colourful against the dark earth ... the vivid yellow and purple of jonquil and crocuses, the transparent white of pale narcissi ... the dark blood-red of tulips. He was barely listening as the vicar began the burial ceremony, his mind awash with troubling thoughts.

Sandy's funeral was evoking memories of the one he had attended only a few weeks ago in Ireland. He was still disturbed about the way Michael Lamont had keeled over on that dreadful morning in Clonloughlin, when he had confronted him about Min's death. Lamont had died in the cottage hospital several days later, the victim of a massive stroke. He would have been a vegetable if he had lived. In a curious way, Anthony felt somehow responsible for the death of the estate manager. On the other hand, as Sally kept pointing out, Lamont had been saved the shame, agony and disgrace of a trial, which, she insisted, he would never have survived anyway. Perhaps she was right. He tried to erase Lamont from his mind, partially succeeded.

A long sigh trickled through Anthony, and he turned his head, looked at Sally, gave her a faint smile as she slipped her arm through his, drew nearer to him. It was as if she understood everything. She did, of course. They were very close, as close as two people could ever be.

He stole a glance at his mother, Edwina, the Dowager Countess, wishing she had not insisted on coming over from Ireland with them for Sandy's funeral. She had not been well lately, and how frail she *did* look, a white-haired old lady, in her seventies. She was the first born child of Emma Harte, the daughter of Edwin Fairley.

There is so much history in this graveyard, it's awesome, Anthony thought all of a sudden, his eyes roaming over the gravestones. The ground was full of Hartes and Fairleys. Generations of them. He was both Harte and Fairley, as well as part Standish. It struck him then that it had all begun here in the quaint little church looming up behind him . . . begun with Emma Harte when she had been christened here in April of 1889. Almost a hundred years ago. Good Lord, his grandmother would have been ninety-three at the end of this month, if she had lived. He continued to miss her even after all these years.

An image of Emma slipped into his mind. What an exceptional, brilliant woman she had been. She had loved each one of her grandchildren, but he was aware she had had a special sort of relationship with Alexander. But then they all had, hadn't they? And Sandy had managed to bring out the best in them. Yes, they *were* better people for having known him.

Now his thoughts swung back to his cousin. The letter was in the inside breast pocket of his jacket. He had kept it on him ever since he had received it the day after Sandy's death. He already knew that Sandy was dead before the letter came in the morning post, because Paula had telephoned him from Nutton Priory the night before to tell him and Sally. Nonetheless, the letter had been a shock at first. Until he had understood, and had accepted the words.

He had reread it so many times by now, much of it was committed to memory. He felt as if it were engraved on his mind. It was not a long letter, and it was level-headed, matter-of-fact, really, so like Sandy, and Sandy had meant it only for his eyes. That was why he had not shared it with his wife, close as they were, or with Paula, who, after all, was head of the family. But there was no need for them to see it.

Closing his eyes, he saw Sandy's handwriting in his mind's eye . . . and that particular fragment of the letter which had so moved him.

'*I wanted you to understand why I am doing this, Anthony,*' Sandy had written in his careful script. '*Mostly it is for myself, of course. A chance to go at last. But it will save everyone the agony of my protracted dying. I know none of you could bear*

to see me suffer. And so before I take my life, I say goodbye dear cousin and friend.
Know that I am happy to shed my mortal coil . . . I escape . . . I am free . . .'

And Sandy had scribbled a postscript. *'You have been such a good friend to me,*
Anthony. You have helped me through my private hells more than once, perhaps
without even knowing it. I thank you. God bless you and yours.'

Anthony realized it would be unwise to keep the letter, yet he had been
incapable of destroying it. But he *must* do so. Today. After the funeral, in fact,
when he returned to Pennistone Royal. He would go to the bathroom in their
suite of rooms and burn it, then flush the charred pieces down the toilet. Only
he knew that Sandy had carefully planned his death, had gone out into the
woods hunting, and after bagging several rabbits and hares, had shot himself
but rigged it to look like an accident. He would never reveal Sandy's secret to
anyone. There had been an inquest, of course, and the coroner had returned
a verdict of accidental death, exactly as Alexander had intended. No one suspected the truth.

So be it, Anthony said under his breath, looking out towards the distant
moors, continuing to dwell on Sandy, so many memories seizing him . . .
carrying him backwards in time for a few more moments longer.

Unexpectedly, brilliant sunshine burst through the dark clouds with such
suddenness the leaden, sombre sky was filled with a most marvellous radiance
that seemed to emanate from below the smudged horizon. Anthony caught his
breath at the sudden beauty and raised his eyes to the heavens, and smiled
inwardly. In the quietness of his gentle, loving heart he said farewell to Sandy.
His pain is over, Anthony thought. He's at peace at last. Gone to his beloved
Maggie.

The brief ceremony was coming to an end.

The coffin was being lowered into the rich Yorkshire earth where Sandy's
ancestors lay, and Anthony turned away from the grave as the vicar closed his
prayer book.

He took Sally's arm. 'Let's go back to Pennistone Royal for a drink, and
lunch,' he said.

Sally nodded. 'Yes, we do need something to warm us up. It's freezing this
morning.'

Paula, walking with them, shivered, looked from Shane to Anthony, and
muttered, 'I detest these hearty meals after funerals. They're barbaric.'

'No,' Anthony said in a muted voice. 'They're not.' He linked arms with her
as they fell in step, went down the flagged path to the lych-gate and the waiting
cars. 'The lunch today gives us a chance to be together for a while, to console
each other . . . and to remember Sandy as he was. To take comfort from having
known him, and known his love. And to celebrate his life.'

Paula was to remember those words.

They were still echoing in her ears a week later, on the morning she was
being driven out to Heathrow to take the Concorde to New York.

Amanda sat next to her on the back seat of the Rolls-Royce, sad and with-
drawn, hardy speaking. A few minutes before they arrived at the airport, Paula
reached out, took her cousin's hand in hers, squeezed it.

Swinging her head, Amanda frowned slightly, and then she returned the pressure of Paula's hand.

Paula said, 'You're thinking of Sandy, aren't you?'

'Yes,' Amanda whispered.

Patting her hand lovingly, Paula murmured, 'Grieve for him by all means, and get the grief out. That's so very necessary . . . part of the healing process. But also take comfort from your lovely memories of Sandy, the years you had with him when you were growing up. Be glad he was your brother, that he gave you so much love, so much of himself.'

'You're very wise, Paula. I will try . . .' Amanda's lip trembled. 'But I miss him so much.'

'Of course you do, it's only natural. And you will – for the longest time. But I also think you should take solace from the fact that Sandy is out of his suffering now.' Paula paused, then added softly, 'Let him go, darling, let him rest.'

It was difficult for Amanda to speak, and she simply nodded several times, swung her head, stared out of the car window. She felt too emotional to respond coherently, and she knew that Paula would understand and respect her silence.

But a short while later, when they were sitting in the Concorde lounge, sipping coffee before the flight, Amanda suddenly leaned closer to Paula, said in a low voice, 'Thanks for being such a good friend. I do appreciate it.' She looked off into the distance, before murmuring softly, 'How uncertain life is, isn't it, Paula? None of us know what might happen to us next . . . people's lives can change in the flicker of an eyelash . . .'

'Yes . . . life *is* tenuous. But it's also quite marvellous, you know. And life is for the living. We must get on with it.'

'Grandy always said that!' Amanda brought her gaze to Paula's and a smile broke through. 'I had the most amazing phone call from Francesca last night . . . she's pregnant.'

'That *is* lovely news! We'll have to do some shopping for baby clothes in New York.' Paula picked up her cup, took a swallow of coffee, and eyed Amanda thoughtfully over the rim. Placing the cup in its saucer, she said carefully, 'Forgive me for prying, but you're rather keen on Michael Kallinski, aren't you?'

Amanda looked at her, surprise flashing in her light green eyes. A faint blush tinged her neck, swept up into her pale cheeks. 'Is it *so* apparent?'

'Only to me. Don't forget, I've known you since the day you were born.'

'*He's* not interested in *me*, though,' Amanda asserted.

'We'll see about that.'

'What do you mean?'

'Michael's spent a great deal of time with you lately, but always on business, dealing with their takeover of Lady Hamilton Clothes. Now he ought to see you in a different light, in social situations, with other men flocking around you . . . which they generally *do*, so don't shake your head in that way. Whilst you're both in New York, Shane and I are going to be giving a few dinners and cocktail parties . . . I want to make certain Michael gets to know you even better. And in a more personal way.'

'Oh,' was the only thing Amanda could think of to say.

'Trust me. Your future looks very bright you know, from my vantage point.'

'And so does yours,' Amanda was swift to say. 'I feel certain you're going to get the Larson chain.'

'I sincerely hope you're right,' Paula said, and crossed her fingers.

As the British Airways Concorde flight took off for New York, a Qantas flight from Hong Kong was simultaneously landing at Heathrow.

Within an hour the passengers had disembarked, the luggage had come down on the carousel, and Jonathan Ainsley, looking like the prosperous business tycoon he was, walked through customs and out into the arrival hall.

His eyes scanned those people waiting near the barrier, and he raised his hand in greeting when he saw the flaming red hair and beaming face of his smartly-dressed cousin, Sarah Lowther Pascal.

Sarah waved back, and a moment later they were embracing affectionately.

'Welcome home, Jonny,' Sarah said as they drew apart, looked each other over appraisingly and with mutual approval.

'It's nice to be back. It's been ages.' He grinned at her, motioned to the porter to follow with his luggage, and grabbing Sarah's arm, led her out to the car park.

'I *am* glad your trip to London coincided with mine,' Jonathan was saying some ten minutes later as they rolled comfortably towards London in the large chauffeur-driven limousine Sarah had hired to meet him.

'So am I,' she said. 'Yves wanted me to come to see the gallery that represents him here, and I had some business of my own to attend to this week. So it was perfect timing, Jonny.'

'And how is Yves?' Jonathan asked.

'Extremely well,' Sarah answered, her voice full of enthusiasm. 'Painting with great brilliance at the moment.'

'And selling very well too,' Jonathan murmured, and glanced across at her. 'Not stinting you, I see, if the jewellery is anything to go by . . . and that *is* a Givenchy suit, isn't it?'

Sarah nodded, smiled with pleasure at his compliments. 'He's very generous, but my own investments have been paying good dividends . . .' She gave Jonathan a sidelong glance. 'And how is Arabella?'

'Wonderful!' Jonathan's face instantly lit up, and he began to talk about Arabella and their life in Hong Kong in great detail, hardly drawing breath.

Sarah wished she had never brought up the woman's name. She hated her cousin's wife.

Settling back against the butter-soft, wine-coloured leather of the car, she appeared to give her attention to Jonathan, nodding from time to time, looking as if she was absorbing every word he uttered, but, in point of fact, she was not listening to one single thing he was saying.

She's innocence, all innocence, Sarah thought, her mind focused on Arabella. But I spotted her type the minute I met her. She's clever and crafty and out for the main chance. And she's got a past, that one. I'm sure of it. I just wish I could warn him about her, but I daren't. She found it hard to believe that Jonathan had been taken in by Arabella Sutton. Even Yves, usually uninterested in other women, had appeared to be bewitched by her when Jonathan had brought her to stay at Mougins earlier in the year. Of course, she *was* charming. And beautiful. All that silver hair, the sloe eyes, the sensational figure. A sexpot, I bet, Sarah thought disparagingly, loathing her, irrationally. What did it matter to her whom her cousin married. Except that she cared about Jonny, cared about his well being.

She had her own family now, an adoring husband, an angelic and gifted child. But Jonathan represented her past, her ties in England. Her parents were alive and so were Jonny's, her Aunt Valerie and Uncle Robin. But somehow Jonathan was the one she loved the most, even though he was mostly responsible for her estrangement from their other cousins, and aunts and uncles. The rift in the Harte family had so distressed her. Although she harboured dislike for some of them, she nonetheless felt the sting of banishment, minded that she was no longer a member of that distinguished clan.

Arabella fascinated Jonny, that was quite obvious. Sarah hated competing for his attention. She had had to do that when Sebastian Cross was alive. Bosom chums they had been, Jonathan and Sebastian, from their days at Eton. And they had stayed close. She used to wonder why. Sebastian had not been very nice. Sleazy, in her opinion. And he had had such a strange fixation about Jonny. If she had not known otherwise, she would have sworn Sebastian was gay. But his reputation as a womanizer had preceded him. Now she wondered if that had actually meant anything. Sebastian had been such an odd bird. He had died of an accidental overdose of cocaine. He had had nothing but bad luck after Jonathan left England, had made nothing but disastrous business deals. She had heard that he died flat broke.

Jonathan touched her arm, exclaimed crossly, 'You seem far away, Sarah, haven't you been listening to me?' He peered into her face, his pale eyes narrowing shrewdly.

'Yes, yes, of course I have,' she protested, now truly giving him her fullest attention, not wishing to displease him. Jonny had quite a temper, was easily provoked.

'Is something bothering you?' Jonathan pressed, as usual attuned to her, as if he could read her mind. He had always managed to unnerve Sarah because of this ability.

'Actually, I was just thinking about Sebastian Cross,' Sarah admitted. 'It was odd the way he died, wasn't it?'

Jonathan was quiet for a fraction of a second.

'Yes,' he said at last. 'Very odd indeed.' There was another pause, before he volunteered quietly, 'He was bi-sexual. I didn't know, of course.' He looked Sarah fully in the face, confided, 'He only admitted that to me when he flew out to Hong Kong to see me, the first year I was there . . . he confessed that I was . . . er . . . er . . . well, the object of his passion, shall we say?'

'Oh dear,' Sarah said, not particularly surprised by this sudden revelation. 'How frightful for you.'

Jonathan smiled narrowly. 'In all truth, it was, Sarah. But he took my rejection of him very well indeed. Or so I believed at the time.'

Sarah said not a word, watched him acutely.

716

He asked eventually, 'Do you think that's why he died, Sarah? Do you think that the overdose was intentional . . . you know, an *accident on purpose?*'

'It has occurred to me from time to time.'

'Sad really.'

'Yes.'

'How rude of me, darling, I forgot to ask after that adorable child of yours. How is little Chloe?' Jonathan abruptly changed the subject, not wishing to dwell on Sebastian Cross, to rake over the past. He was only interested in the future, which he had been looking at very closely of late.

'Chloe is simply wonderful,' Sarah said, glowing as she launched into a recital about her daughter, one of her two favourite subjects, the other being her husband. 'She fell in love with her Uncle Jonny . . . and before I left France earlier this week she made me promise I'd bring you back to Mougins for the weekend. You will come, won't you?'

'I'll certainly try.'

'Good,' Sarah half turned in her seat, gave him a long and searching look. 'What did you mean when you phoned me from Hong Kong and said our day would come, that we'd soon get our own back on Paula?'

Jonathan leaned closer. A wicked and knowing smirk spread across his bland face. 'I believe that no one is infallible, that even the smartest tycoons can make flawed judgement calls at times. And I have always known, deep down, that Paula O'Neill would make a mistake one day. I've been waiting . . . and watching . . . and my gut instinct tells me she's about to do something foolish. The odds are there, you see, she's had too good and too long a run for her money. And when she makes her fatal error I shall be there. Ready to pounce.'

Sarah gave him a penetrating stare, her green eyes quickening. 'What do you mean? How do you know? Tell me, Jonny, tell me more!'

'Later,' he said, squeezing her arm in the very intimate way he had with her. 'Let's wait until we're in the privacy of my suite at Claridge's . . . and then I shall explain how I aim to destroy Paula O'Neill.'

Sarah shivered with pleasure and anticipation at the thought of Paula's downfall. 'I can't wait to hear your plan. I'm sure it's brilliant . . . and how I've longed to get *my* revenge on that cold, frigid, thieving bitch. She stole Shane from me, quite aside from everything else.'

'Of course she did,' Jonathan concurred, fanning Sarah's festering hatred of Paula, as he had for years, needing an ally in his scheming, if only for moral support.

He put his hand in his jacket pocket, and his fingers curled around the pebble of mutton-fat jade. His talisman. It had brought him great good luck in the past. He had no reason to doubt that it would do so again.

PART THREE

Winners & Losers

Unnatural deeds do breed unnatural troubles.

Macbeth: WILLIAM SHAKESPEARE

One must therefore be a fox to recognize traps, and a lion to frighten wolves.

The Prince: MACHIAVELLI

All or nothing.

Brand: HENRIK IBSEN

33

'You really are the best thing that ever happened to Philip,' Daisy said, filled with love and respect for the young American woman who was her daughter-in-law.

Madelana's face lit up, and she laughed lightly as she settled herself more comfortably on the sofa. 'Thank you. That's a lovely thing to know.'

They were sitting in the drawing room of the house at Point Piper in Sydney, which Philip had owned for a number of years, and where he and Maddy now lived for most of the week when they were not at Dunoon. It was August and a lovely afternoon, even though it was still the winter season in Australia, and earlier Madelana had opened the French doors leading out to the terrace and the garden beyond. A soft breeze drifted in, made the silk draperies flutter and whisper, carried with it the mixed scents of honeysuckle and eucalyptus and the salt tang of the sea.

After a moment, Madelana smiled at her mother-in-law and added, 'Anyway, I have to say the same thing about your son, Daisy. He's made me a whole person again, chased all my sorrow and gloom away, and given me so much love that there are times when I think I might just burst with happiness.'

Daisy nodded, understanding exactly what she meant. It had always pleased her that Maddy was so open, without guile, and readily able to articulate her feelings. Also, it was gratifying to know that her son was such a good husband, had adjusted to being a married man after years of playing around, and that he and Maddy were so blissfully happy.

'When a marriage truly works there's nothing else like it in the world, nothing that can take its place,' Daisy said with great feeling. 'And it's pure joy to have a relationship with a man who gives so much of himself . . . as both Philip and Jason do.'

Daisy paused, quickly glanced to her left, stared at the various photographs of David, her late husband, taken with Philip, Paula and her twins, Lorne and Tessa, and with she herself. Happy, loving family pictures which Philip kept grouped on a small side table near the fireplace. She was thoughtful for a moment, remembering her life with David, and when she swung her head and smiled across at Maddy it was with a certain ruefulness.

'When David was killed in the avalanche I thought the world had come to an end for me. And of course it had in so many ways,' Daisy confided, speaking to Maddy about her first husband in a more intimate way than she ever had before.

'You see, Maddy, I'd shared a perfect marriage with my darling David . . . ever since I'd married him at eighteen. I believed it could never be repeated or recaptured with another man, and it couldn't. For the simple reason that no two men are the same, no two women either, for that matter, and every relationship is different, has its own strengths and weaknesses. Leaving England, coming out here, helped me to start over again, and my charity work for sick and needy children especially helped to give me a purpose. But it was Jason who made me come alive again as a woman. *He* made *me* whole, Maddy.'

'He's a very special man,' Maddy acknowledged in all sincerity, thinking of the gruff Australian's many kindnesses and loving gestures to her over the past few months. 'We both lucked out, finding ourselves a couple of genuine forty-carat dudes.'

'I'll say we did!' Daisy exclaimed, laughing, as usual highly amused by Madelana's quaint expressions. She couldn't wait to tell Jason of Maddy's assessment of him, which, she decided, was absolutely spot on. Daisy leaned forward, picked up her cup of tea, took a sip of it.

A compatible silence fell between these two women who sprang from such different echelons of society, from such different worlds, yet who had grown to care deeply for each other in the year they had known each other. Their great common bond was the love they both felt for Philip and Paula, and Maddy's obsessional admiration of Emma Harte. Daisy was devoted to the memory of her mother, and she enjoyed answering Maddy's never-ending questions, speaking about Emma, recounting anecdotes about the legendary tycoon; she had a rapt and enthralled listener in her daughter-in-law. And finally there was the bond created by the child Madelana was carrying. Philip's child . . . and the heir to the McGill empire Daisy had longed for.

Daisy thought of the baby now as she sipped her tea and quietly studied Madelana. She wished the baby would arrive. It was nearly two weeks late, and everyone was growing more impatient by the day: except for Maddy, who was tranquil and healthy . . . and somewhat amused by their constant fussing.

'I'm glad you didn't have the amniocentesis test after all,' Daisy said, breaking the silence, 'even though I can't wait to know whether I have a grandson or a granddaughter inside that tummy of yours.'

Madelana grinned. 'I don't think I've ever wanted to know . . . I prefer to be surprised.' She placed her hands over her stomach, feeling the baby, the gesture protective, and then she started to laugh. 'However, I have a peculiar feeling that she's a girl, Daisy.'

'Do you really?'

Maddy nodded, leaned forward, announced, 'And if it's a girl we're going to call her Fiona Daisy Harte McGill. Rather a long name, isn't it? But we did want to name her after my mother and you, and include the surnames of her great-grandparents.'

'I'm touched and honoured – and terribly flattered,' Daisy responded, pleasure lighting up her vividly blue McGill eyes, which were so like her father's.

Madelana shifted her weight on the sofa, pushed herself into the pile of cushions, seeking a more comfortable position. She felt awkward and ungainly, slightly cramped all of a sudden.

'Are you all right?' Daisy asked, noticing Maddy's grimacing, her pained expression.

'I'm fine, just a bit stiff today. But to tell you the truth, I, too, wish the baby would come now. I feel like a giant-sized, over-ripe watermelon that's about to go plop! And I'm lumbering around after Philip as if I'm a fish out of water . . . a huge beached whale, or something of the sort!'

Daisy burst out laughing. 'You do have the most colourful expressions, darling. And what if you have a boy? Have you chosen a name yet?'

'Paul McGill. After your father.'

'Oh, Maddy, how lovely of you and Philip. I'm delighted.'

Daisy got to her feet, walked across to the console where she had left her handbag when she had arrived earlier in the afternoon. She opened it, took out a small leather box, brought it over to Madelana. Handing it to her, she said, 'This is for you.'

Madelana looked up at her mother-in-law in surprise, then brought her eyes down to the jewel box in her hands. The leather was worn and scratched, the gilt-embossed edge faded by time. She lifted the lid and caught her breath when she saw the emerald bow lying on the black velvet.

'Why, Daisy, it's simply beautiful. *Gorgeous*. Thank you, thank you so much. It's old, isn't it?'

Daisy, who had seated herself next to Madelana on the sofa, nodded. 'It dates back to the 1920s. I've wanted to give you something very special for the longest time, and I finally –'

'But you have!' Madelana interrupted. 'I've had so many extraordinary gifts from you and Jason, as well as from Philip. You all spoil me.'

'We love you, Maddy. But as I was saying, I wanted to give you something that would be truly meaningful to you at this particular time . . . and so I picked the emerald bow from my collection. Not only because it's exquisite and will suit you admirably, but also because it belonged to my mother. I felt you'd appreciate that, appreciate the sentimental value attached to the brooch more than anything else.'

'I do. But I can't take it after all, Daisy . . . why, it's a family heirloom.'

'And what are *you*, if not family? Darling, you're Philip's *wife*,' Daisy said softly but emphatically. She took the brooch out of the box and together they looked at it, admiring the exquisite workmanship, the beauty of the design, the lustre and depth of colour of the emeralds.

Presently, Daisy said, 'There's a lovely story about this piece of jewellery . . . would you like to hear it?'

'Oh yes, I would.'

Daisy smiled to herself as she laid the brooch in the velvet-padded box, and settled back on the sofa. She was thinking of her mother, seeing her as a little girl at the turn of the century, as she had so frequently done in the past, forever marvelling at her extraordinary character.

'The story actually began in 1904,' Daisy explained. 'Emma was a servant girl in service at Fairley Hall in Yorkshire, where she had worked since she was twelve. One Sunday afternoon in March of that year, her best friend Blackie O'Neill arrived to see her. He had bought her a green-glass brooch shaped like a bow for her fifteenth birthday at the end of April. He was going away, you see, and he wanted her to have something from him before he left. Anyway, Blackie explained to Emma that when he had noticed the bow in the window of a shop in Leeds the stones had reminded him of her emerald eyes. Naturally, young Emma was enchanted with the brooch, cheap as it was, because she had never had anything like it. She thought it was the most beautiful thing in the world. And that afternoon, Blackie made a promise to her . . . he

723

told her that one day, when he was rich, he would buy her a replica of the brooch, and that it would be made of emeralds. He was true to his word. Many years later he gave her this . . . *this* is Blackie's emerald bow,' Daisy finished. She thought to add, 'When my mother died she left the brooch to me, along with her collection of emeralds which my father had given her over the years.'

'What a lovely story, and the bow is beautiful, but as I just said, I'm not sure I should accept it, Daisy. Ought it not to go to Paula in view of its history?'

'No, no, she and I want you to have it!' Daisy insisted, reaching out, squeezing Madelana's hand affectionately. 'I've spoken to Paula, and she thinks it's a most fitting gift for you. As I do. And I know that if my mother was alive she would want you to have it, too.'

Madelana realized there was no point in protesting further, that it would be even ungracious to do so, and she murmured her thanks again, permitted her mother-in-law to pin the emerald bow to her maternity smock. Then, pushing herself up, she went to the mirror over the fireplace, looked at herself. The bow was an extraordinary piece, and she was greatly moved because Daisy had given her something which had once belonged to Emma Harte.

Madelana went back to the sofa, and after a moment Daisy leaned back against the cushions. 'Speaking of my daughter, do you think she's made a mistake buying the Larson chain in the States?'

'Of course not!' Madelana cried, sitting up straighter on the sofa, returning Daisy's penetrating gaze. 'She's a brilliant businesswoman and I've never known her to make a wrong move yet.'

'I just wish she'd told me *why* she wanted me to sell the Sitex stock when she suggested I do so last year. Or at least given me the chance to let her have the additional money she needed for the takeover of Larson's.' Daisy sighed heavily. 'Paula can be awfully stubborn and she's determined to do everything her own way. She's so like my mother. Oh dear, I don't know . . . business does baffle me most of the time.'

Daisy rose, moved to the fireplace, stood with one hand resting on the mantel. 'And I don't understand Shane, if the truth be known. I can't imagine why he didn't tell me or Philip about her plans long ago. And why on earth didn't he advise her? After what he said last night, I think he should have, don't you?'

'I'm not sure anyone can advise Paula. She's so confident and self-assured. And so brilliant in business she doesn't need advice from anyone. Besides, Shane would never interfere. He would remain aloof . . . that would be the wisest course for anyone to take, as I'm sure he realizes by now.'

Daisy frowned. 'I was surprised by some of the things I heard over dinner last night, weren't you?'

'Not really,' Madelana answered truthfully. 'Don't forget, I was Paula's assistant at the New York store, and she has been after an American chain for a long time. In any event, as I said before, I trust her judgement implicitly. And so should you. I know Philip does, and from what Shane said at dinner, he does too.' Madelana gave Daisy a look she hoped was reassuring. 'There's one more thing I'd like to add. Hasn't it ever occurred to you that Paula might want to own something of her own?'

'But she does, Maddy dear,' Daisy exclaimed in a startled tone. 'The Harte chain, not to mention –'

'But that was founded by Emma,' Madelana was quick to point out. 'In fact, everything Paula runs she inherited from her grandmother. Perhaps emotionally she has the need to . . . to . . . well, to *create* and *build* something of her very own and with her own money.'

'Is that what she indicated to you when you worked together in New York?'

'No, it's just a feeling I have, knowing her as well as I do.'

Daisy looked further surprised and fell silent, ruminating on her daughter-in-law's words. Eventually, she said, 'Perhaps you're right, Maddy dear. I hadn't looked at it quite like that. Nevertheless, apart from anything else, I do think she has taken on an enormous amount of responsibility in addition to everything else she has to do.'

Maddy said in a loving voice, 'Try not to worry about Paula and her expansion programme in the States. She'll be fine, it'll be fine. Philip believes she's a chip off the old block, and you said only a few minutes ago that she's like your mother. Being another Emma Harte can't be all that bad, can it?' Maddy finished on a teasing note, raising a brow.

Daisy had the good grace to laugh. 'No, it can't,' she said.

34

Later, after her mother-in-law had left to return to her house in Rose Bay, Madelana put on a thick, white wool cape and went outside. She walked slowly through the gardens as she did twice a day, enjoying the exercise and the air.

Although the wind had dropped, it had turned cold; dusk was falling, and in that lovely half light, neither day nor night but hovering somewhere in between, everything appeared to be softer, gentler.

The pristine sky of earlier had lost its sharp, icy blue-and-white tints, was slowly darkening, and its rim at the edge of the horizon was streaked with flaring ribbons of amber and rose as the sun sank into the sea. And in those hushed and silent gardens, where not a single thing stirred, the only sound was the lapping of the waves against the rocks of the jutting headland on which the mansion was built.

When she reached the end of the wide path, Madelana stood for a moment gazing out across the endless stretch of inky water. It looked cold, forbidding, bottomless, and she shivered despite the warmth of her cape. Turning swiftly on her heels, she hurried back up to the house. She could see that lamps were being turned on in some of the rooms, and narrow corridors of light were streaming out from the windows, illuminating her way.

How warm and welcoming her home looked in contrast to the daunting sea behind her. She increased her pace, wanting suddenly to be inside. Within minutes she was closing the French doors of the library, walking through the room and out into the foyer, still shivering slightly.

As she hung her cape in the hall cupboard she heard the chatter of voices coming from the kitchen area of the house. It was the two maids, Alice and Peggy, and Mrs Ordens, the housekeeper, twittering away together like a flock of chirpy sparrows. The three women took care of them exceptionally well, eased the burden of running two homes in Sydney – the house out here at Point Piper and the penthouse atop the McGill Tower. She took a step towards the door, then decided to change her clothes in readiness for the evening before going in to speak to them.

A little sigh of happiness trickled through Madelana as she climbed the staircase leading to the upper floors. She had been experiencing a lovely sense of contentment in the last few days. It was Philip's love and the baby she was carrying that filled her with such abundant joyousness. Soon they would be three instead of two. She could hardly wait . . . longed to hold her child in her arms.

The rosy glow of the fire greeted her when she pushed open the door of their bedroom and went in. This was one of the two rooms in the house she had redecorated after her marriage; she had used a mixture of soft greens and a striking white chintz splashed with pink peonies, scarlet roses, yellow lilies and dark green leaves. The play of greens in the overall scheme and the airy chintz, lavishly used, served to endorse the spaciousness of the bedroom. There was a sweeping bay window overlooking the gardens and the sea, a curving, cushioned window seat underneath, and a huge four-poster bed.

A small antique writing desk was positioned in a corner near the fireplace, and Maddy went and sat down, picked up the letter she had been writing to Sister Bronagh in Rome when Daisy had arrived for tea earlier than expected.

She read it quickly, added a last sentence and her love, then signed it. After sealing it in an envelope and addressing it, she propped it up with the others going to Sister Mairéad in New York, Patsy Smith in Boston and Paula in London. Maddy was a diligent correspondent, regularly penned entertaining epistles with her latest news to her four favourites. After lunch today she had decided to get the letters written before she went into hospital to have the baby; she was positive their child would be born this week.

Leaning back in the chair, Maddy began to ruminate on the past year. How extraordinary it had been. *Wondrous*. That truly was the only word to describe it. But it's not even a year, she suddenly thought, I didn't meet Philip until September, and it's only August. What a lot has happened in that short span of time. She rested her hands on her lap, linked her fingers under her large stomach, thinking again of the baby, making endless plans for the future.

Eventually she lifted her eyes, let them rest on the little sampler she had owned since childhood. It had been shipped out to Australia with her other possessions and it hung on the wall above her desk.

'If your day is hemmed with prayer it is less likely to unravel,' her mother had stitched so meticulously in bright blue wool all those years ago.

Oh Mom, she thought, everything did turn out beautifully for me, just as you said it would when I was little. I *am* your Golden Girl after all. I *have* been blessed.

Maddy turned her eyes to the photographs framed in silver standing on her desk . . . her parents, Kerry Anne, Young Joe and Lonnie. You've been gone from me for a long time now, but I carry each one of you in my heart and I always will, she whispered to herself.

As she continued to gaze at her family she realized her memories were much sweeter, far less painful than they had ever been. This was surely because she was a fulfilled and happy woman who no longer felt lonely or alone. At last her keen sense of loss was muted if not totally eradicated.

Maddy left the bedroom half an hour later, freshly madeup and immaculately groomed, dressed in a well-cut navy blue silk tunic over loose, pyjama-style pants of the same dark silk. Emma's emerald bow was pinned to one shoulder. With it she wore a strand of perfectly matched pearls, large pearl earrings, and her wedding and engagement rings. On her arm was a navy-blue shawl of heavy jacquard silk, thickly fringed, and she carried a navy silk evening purse into which she had just popped her letters. She would mail them later at the Sydney-O'Neill Hotel.

Before going downstairs she paused at a door a little further along the corridor, turned the handle and went inside. Switching on the nearest lamp, she beamed with pleasure as she looked around the former guest room, now transformed into the nursery. Philip and she had decorated it together. It was done in a cheerful combination of yellow and white, with shocking pink as a lively accent colour. They had decided on this particular scheme since it was neither feminine nor masculine, and therefore suitable for a girl or a boy.

Lovingly she smoothed one hand along the edge of the crib, went over to the window wall to straighten a slightly crooked nursery rhyme print, moving around the large and pleasant room slowly, checking everything for the umpteenth time. Then she turned off the lamp, closed the door behind her as she went out, smiling beatifically, satisfied that everything was perfect, in total readiness for their child.

Maddy ran into Mrs Ordens in the entrance hall.

'Oh there you are, Mrs Amory,' the housekeeper said, giving her a warm smile. 'I was just coming up to tell you Ken has arrived with the car to take you into Sydney.'

'Thanks, Mrs Ordens,' Maddy said, smiling back. 'But there's plenty of time, let's go into the kitchen for a minute. I'd like to go over a few things with you before I leave.'

Shane decided that he had never seen Madelana looking more beautiful than she did tonight. She was obviously more head-over-heels in love with Philip than ever, and he with her; their happiness was reflected in everything they did and said. Not unnaturally it showed in their glowing rapturous faces.

The first thing he had noticed when he had arrived in Sydney several days ago was the way her face had filled out since he had last seen her in Yorkshire in January. It was no longer quite so bony, and the extra bit of weight suited her. Her cheeks were slightly flushed, her large grey eyes filled with sparkling lights, and there was a special radiance about her which he found utterly breathtaking. She seemed lit from within. No wonder some of the other people in the restaurant kept glancing in their direction. But then Philip was a handsome son-of-a-gun, very distinguished looking, and his face was well-known in Australia. That might also explain the numerous surreptitious looks. These two made a striking couple, had an aura of glamour about them.

It had been a merry evening from the outset.

The three of them had laughed a lot over dinner in the Orchid Room of the hotel. In fact, from the moment she had arrived at Shane's suite, where Philip was having an aperitif with him, hilarity had been in the air. Philip had fussed over Madelana, pressed her into a comfortable chair, poured cool Evian water for her, and generally behaved like a man besotted, which he was. And she had been warm and loving, somewhat placid in her general demeanour, the beatific smile intact. Shane was happy for them, knowing full well what a good marriage meant. They were as lucky as he and Paula.

Philip was saying, 'Anyway, Shane, we're not going to Dunoon this weekend. The baby is *so* overdue now, Doctor Hardcastle wants us to stay in Sydney. He's positive the birth is imminent, and so is Maddy, for that matter, and he thinks it's best we stay put.'

'He's absolutely right, too,' Shane said. 'And from a strictly selfish point of view, I'm glad you'll be in the city. Perhaps I'll come out to Point Piper on Sunday, spend the day with you both, if you'll have me, and if the little scallywag still hasn't budged, of course.'

Madelana burst out laughing.

Philip grinned, then explained, 'That's what we had in mind, although we hoped you'd come for the whole weekend. You could drive out with me on Friday evening. It'll give you a chance to relax, get away from the hotel and its problems.'

'That's a splendid idea, I'll do that. It'll be nice being with you, taking it easy, doing nothing much except read and listen to music. I don't seem to have had a minute's peace since I arrived.'

Maddy exclaimed, 'Oh I am glad you're going to stay with us, Shane. And Mrs Ordens is a wonderful cook. She'll make all your favourite dishes if you tell me what you'd like.'

Shane laughed, shook his head. 'No fancy meals, darling girl. Paula's put me on a strict diet. She seems to think I gained weight in the south of France this summer. Mind you, Beanstalk's always been so bone thin I suppose anyone looks fat next to her.' He eyed Madelana, his expression merry and teasing. 'You're pretty skinny yourself – when you're not pregnant.'

'Yes,' she agreed, 'I think Paula and I both burn off pounds when we're working. It's all that nervous energy being expended, I guess.'

'Talking of work, are you still planning to run Harte's-Australia after the baby's born?' Shane asked curiously.

'Oh yes, I think so,' Maddy told him. 'I plan to have a month or two off with the baby, since I can do paperwork and phoning from the house or the penthouse until I start keeping regular business hours again . . . nine to five and all that.'

'Actually, I'm having a suite decorated for Maddy, next to my office in the McGill Tower,' Philip said. 'That way, she's only one flight down from the nursery we've designed in the flat upstairs.'

'Paula has often hauled one of ours into the office with her . . . and so has

Emily,' Shane laughed. 'It's a trait of the Harte women, I do believe. You might as well join the club, Maddy!'

She gave him a huge smile, which turned into a languorous yawn. She tried to stifle it without much success, brought her hand to her mouth, yawned again several times.

Philip did not fail to miss this. 'I'd better get my lady home to bed,' he announced, instantly rising, helping Maddy to her feet. 'I hope you don't mind having an early evening, Shane, but I do think we should be making tracks.'

'Of course I don't mind.' Shane also pushed back his chair, stood. 'I'll come down with you, and anyway it won't do me any harm to get to bed at a reasonable hour for once.'

Shane escorted them through the Orchid Room, down in the elevator, across the dark-green marble lobby to the front doors. 'There's Ken with the car,' he said as they stepped out into the street. He kissed Maddy goodnight, embraced his brother-in-law, and slammed the back door firmly shut when they were inside, waved them off.

As the Rolls-Royce pulled away from the kerb, Philip put his arm around Madelana, drew her close to him on the back seat. 'Are you feeling all right, sweetheart?'

'Yes, I'm fine, Philip. Very tired, that's all.' She rested her head against his body. 'It just suddenly hit me . . . the feeling of total and absolute exhaustion, I mean.'

'Do you think the baby's coming? Do you have any labour pains?'

'Not a one.' She smiled against his chest, slipped her arm inside his jacket and around his back, wanting to be even closer to him. 'I'll let you know, and in no uncertain terms, the minute I get the slightest twinge,' she promised.

He stroked her chestnut hair, brought his face down, kissed the top of her head. 'Oh God, I love you so much, Maddy. I don't believe I can ever tell you exactly how much you mean to me.'

'Mmmmm, that's lovely,' she said, smiling again, then stifling another series of long yawns. 'I love you, too . . . I'll be glad when we get home . . . I can't wait to put my head on the pillow.' Her eyelids felt so heavy she could hardly keep them open. They drooped and finally closed, and she dozed intermittently all the way to the Point Piper house.

After breakfast the following morning, Philip went back upstairs to say goodbye to Maddy.

But she was still fast asleep in the great four-poster bed, her chestnut hair tumbled across the pillow. In repose her face was tranquil, relaxed, devoid of the quickness and mobility that gave it such vivacity when she was awake.

How beautiful my wife is, he thought, bending over her, kissing her lightly on the cheek. He did not have the heart to awaken her. She had been almost speechless with fatigue the night before and she needed her rest this morning. He moved a strand of hair away from her face, kissed her again, crept out of the bedroom quietly.

Ken was waiting in the driveway with the Rolls when Philip walked out of the house just before seven o'clock, and within seconds they were en route for

Sydney. Philip opened his briefcase, went over the most urgent documents he had collected from his desk last night, preparing himself for the day's business as he usually did during the half hour drive into the city. He made a number of quick notations on his pad; studied a detailed memorandum from Tom Patterson, head of their mining division and one of the world's great opal experts; perused other communications from various executives who worked for the McGill Corporation, eventually returned all the documents to his case. He sat back, mulling over everything he had read for the remainder of the drive.

When he strode into the executive offices of the McGill Corporation atop the McGill Tower it was exactly seven-thirty. His personal assistant, Barry Graves, and his secretary, Maggie Bolton, were both waiting for him. After greeting each other affably, the three of them went into Philip's inner sanctum for their usual early morning confab.

Lowering himself into the chair behind his desk, Philip said, 'The most important meeting on our agenda today is going to be the one with Tom Patterson. Presumably he got in all right from Lightning Ridge last night?'

'He did,' Barry said. 'He phoned about ten minutes ago and I confirmed that we were expecting him around eleven-thirty this morning, and that lunch would be with you in your private dining room here.'

'Good-o!' Philip said. 'I'm looking forward to seeing my old cobber, talking to him. It's been months since Tom's been to Sydney. He had a lot of pertinent things to say in his memo. I went over it again in the car on the way in, and I want him to elaborate on a number of points he's raised. But better not to go into that right now.' Philip glanced over at Maggie, sitting at the other side of the desk, her pad in her hand, her pencil poised.

'Anything special in the post today?' he asked, dropping his eyes to the pile of papers in front of him, then looking at her again.

'Nothing of any great consequence, mostly personal letters, a few invitations, charity requests, the usual daily stuff. Oh, and a cheery note from Steve Carlson. He's still in Coober Pedy. And doing quite well,' Maggie finished with a small grin.

Philip couldn't help grinning with her. 'So much for *my* assessment of him! The jackeroo seems to have turned out to be quite smart.'

The three of them exchanged knowing glances, chuckling, remembering the young American they had characterized as a greenhorn, when he had come seeking Philip's advice about opal mining a year ago.

Barry said, with a touch of acerbity, 'Beginner's luck, that's all it is. You mark my words, he'll come a cropper yet.' He opened one of the folders he was holding, went on briskly, 'I now have all the information you require on the newspaper chain in Queensland. The boss man over there seems to be interested in selling. I've prepared a fact sheet, Philip, with all the salient details. Also, Gregory Cordovian phoned just a few minutes after you left the office last night. He wants to set up a meeting with you.'

'Does he now!' Philip exclaimed, surprise echoing in his voice. He eyed Barry quizzically. 'Could it be that he finally wants to call a truce?'

'Hard to say. He's a cagey sod, that one is. But I kinda got the feeling he was receptive to having a friendly little natter with you. More so than he's ever been in the past. Could be that he even wants to sell the television stations in Victoria. And listen Philip, *he* called *us*, didn't he? I take that as a good sign.'

'It is. And you may well be right – about the television stations.'

Barry nodded, tapped the other folder he was holding. 'Reports here about our natural energy companies, our Sydney real estate, and our other mining interests. You'll have to go over most of them before next Thursday week, when we have that series of meetings with the executives of these companies.'

'I will. Leave the folders with me, Barry. Anything else from you, Maggie?'

His secretary flipped back to a previous page on her pad. 'Ian MacDonald called late yesterday afternoon. He has a full suit of sails for you, including the spinnaker and the Kevlar for the storm mainsail. He wants to know when you can get out to see him? Wonders if you'd like to lunch with him at the yard?'

'Tomorrow or Friday . . . I am free, aren't I?'

'Tomorrow you are, yes. But not on Friday. You have a meeting with your mother and the board of trustees of the Daisy McGill Amory Foundation. A working lunch here at the Tower in the private dining room.'

'Oh that's right, I'd totally forgotten.' Philip pondered a moment. 'Perhaps you'd better make a date with Ian for next week sometime. That'll be more convenient.'

'All right.' Maggie stood up. 'That's it for me, I'll leave you two alone. Buzz me if you want a cup of coffee, Philip.'

'Thanks, I will.'

Barry strode over to the desk. 'I don't have anything else either at the moment. I want to get back to my office, dig into the report I'm preparing for you on your mother's foreign holdings. I'm still behind on it.'

'Okay, go ahead, Barry, do what you have to do. In any case, I have enough to keep me busy with that lot,' he said, gesturing to the folders Barry had just placed on his desk. 'I'll see you at the meeting with Tom. Let me know the minute he arrives.'

'Sure thing, Philip.'

Left alone, Philip turned his attention to the two reports on their iron ore mining interests. Settling back in his chair, he began to read the first one, which consisted of fifteen typed pages. He was still reading the second, and making copious notes, an hour later when Maggie brought him a cup of coffee, and he did not start on the report about their Sydney real estate until ten o'clock. He was half way through this when Maggie's voice came over the intercom.

'Philip . . .'

'Yes, Maggie?'

'Sorry to disturb you, but I have your housekeeper on the phone. She says it's urgent.'

'Oh . . . Okay, put her through.' The phone on his left immediately began to ring. He picked it up. 'Yes, Mrs Ordens?'

'Something's the matter with Mrs Amory,' the housekeeper said, getting straight to the point, her anxiety and concern echoing down the wire.

'What do you mean?' Philip demanded sharply, instantly alarmed. He sat up straighter, gripped the phone hard.

'I can't wake her. I looked in on her at nine-thirty, as you told me to, but she was sleeping so soundly I decided to leave her be for a while. I just brought her breakfast tray up, and I've tried for the past ten minutes to rouse her, but it's no good, Mr Amory. I think she might be unconscious.'

'Oh my God!' Philip sprang to his feet, alarm signals going off in his head. 'I'll be right there!' he exclaimed. 'No, no, that won't help. We must get her into hospital. The emergency room at St Vincent's. I'll send an ambulance. You must go with her. I'll meet you there with Doctor Hardcastle, but I'll call you back in a few minutes. Are you in the bedroom now?'

'Yes.'

'Then stay there until the ambulance comes. And don't leave my wife alone for one moment.'

'No, I won't. But please hurry, Mr Amory. I know there's something terribly wrong.'

35

A private ambulance transported Madelana to St Vincent's Hospital in Darlinghurst, about fifteen minutes away from the Point Piper house. It was the hospital closest to the Eastern suburbs of Sydney.

Mrs Ordens rode with her in the ambulance, holding onto her limp hand, watching over her as she had promised Philip she would. Not an eyelash flickered against that wan face, but Madelana's breathing was even, and for this, at least, Mrs Ordens was thankful.

The moment the ambulance arrived at the hospital Madelana was rushed straight into Emergency, and Mrs Ordens was shown into a private office which had been made available at the request of the patient's doctor.

Rosita Ordens sat down to wait for Philip Amory. He was on his way from the McGill Tower with Malcolm Hardcastle, the noted Sydney gynaecologist, who had been a close friend of Philip's for several years.

Clasping her hands together, Rosita Ordens focused her eyes on the door expectantly. She wished her boss would arrive. He was a brilliant man, always in command. He would soon find out exactly what was wrong with his wife. One thing was certain – she had not liked the peculiar looks exchanged by the two ambulance men when they had first seen Madelana Amory.

Rosita bowed her head. She focused her thoughts on the lovely young American woman, who she had grown so fond of in the last eight months, *willing* her to be all right, to open her eyes, to speak to the doctors now examining her.

A Catholic, like Maddy, Rosita began to pray under her breath. 'Hail Mary, full of grace, the Lord is with thee, blessed art thou amongst women, and blessed is the fruit of thy womb, Jesus ... Hail Mary, full of grace, the Lord is with thee, blessed art thou ... Hail Mary, full of grace ... Hail Mary ...' She went on repeating these words over and over again. Praying helped Rosita, gave her solace in times of trouble. Moreover, she was devout, believed her prayers would be answered by her merciful God.

Suddenly she lifted her head with a start as the door was flung open. 'Oh Mr Amory, thank goodness you're here!' she cried at the sight of Philip, jumping up, going over to him.

Philip took hold of her hand. 'Thanks for phoning me when you did, Mrs Ordens, and for acting so promptly. I'm grateful.'

'Have you seen Mrs Amory yet?'

'Very briefly, with Doctor Hardcastle. He's examining her himself. Naturally, he's concerned about the baby. And after he's conferred with the doctors in Emergency, I'm sure he'll be able to tell me what has caused her condition.'

'She is unconscious then?'

'I'm afraid so.'

Rosita Ordens sucked in her breath quickly. 'I do wish I'd tried to waken her earlier, that I –'

'Don't blame yourself, Mrs Ordens,' Philip interrupted swiftly. 'That serves no purpose, and you did what you believed was right. After all, she did appear to be merely in a deep sleep. I also thought that myself.'

Rosita Ordens nodded glumly. Her worry knew no bounds.

Philip went on, 'Ken's outside with the car. He'll drive you back to the house. I'll phone you the minute I have more news.'

'Please do, Mr Amory. I'll be anxious until I hear from you. So will Alice and Peggy.'

'I know.' He escorted the housekeeper over to the door. 'Ken's parked in front of the main entrance . . . he's waiting for you.'

'Thanks, Mr Amory.' Rosita slipped out of the office, knowing her employer wished to be alone.

Philip sat down, sank at once into his troubled thoughts. His mind raced, seeking answers. It was not natural for anyone to fall into unconsciousness in the way Maddy had. Something serious had induced this state in her, he was convinced of that. Radical action was needed. He would bring in a team of specialists, send his private jet to get them if necessary, wherever they were. Yes, he would do it immediately. *Now.* Suddenly he stood up, then sat down again, his nerves on edge. He pushed back the awful panic swarming over him once more. He must stay calm, handle things with cool intelligence. Yet he could hardly contain himself. He wanted to rush back to Emergency to be with Maddy, to look after her, to stay with her until she was her normal self. But there was no point, not at this moment. He was helpless, could do nothing. And she was in the best hands for now. Philip believed in allowing the experts to do their jobs. He was not going to play doctor. That was a dangerous game.

After what seemed like an eternity to Philip, but was, in reality, only twenty minutes, Malcolm Hardcastle entered the office.

Philip was on his feet immediately, striding across the floor. He stared sharply at the gynaecologist, searching his face, his own anxious and full of questions. Urgently he asked, 'What caused Maddy's condition, Malcolm?'

Taking hold of Philip's arm, the doctor led him back to the group of chairs. 'Let's sit down for a minute.'

Philip was astute, and when Malcolm did not give him a direct reply he was instantly alerted to trouble. Fear for Maddy gripped him. 'What do you think happened to my wife between last night and this morning?' he asked fiercely, his blue eyes flaring.

Malcolm did not know how to break the news. After a split-second's hesitation, he said, very quietly, 'We're fairly certain that Maddy's had a brain haemorrhage.'

'Oh my God no!' Philip gaped at the doctor. He was stunned, shocked. 'It can't be so . . . it just can't be!'

'I'm so sorry, Philip, but I'm afraid all the signs are there. Two very respected brain surgeons have now seen Maddy since she was admitted. I've just consulted with them, and –'

'I want a second opinion! Specialists brought in!' Philip interjected, his voice rising harshly.

'I guessed you would. I asked Doctor Litman to try and contact Alan Stimpson. As I'm sure you know, he's Australia's most renowned brain surgeon, and considered to be one of the best in the world. Thankfully he lives in Sydney.' Malcolm put his hand on Philip's arm, added in a most reassuring tone, 'And even more fortunately for us, he happened to be at St Margaret's Hospital out here in Darlinghurst this morning. Doctor Litman managed to catch him just as he was leaving to go back to the city. He should be joining us in a matter of seconds.'

'Thanks, Malcolm,' Philip said, calming down somewhat. 'And excuse me for being snappish. I'm fraught with worry.'

'That's understandable, and you don't have to apologize to me, Philip, I know the strain you're under.'

There was a knock, and the door opened to admit a tall, slender, sandy-haired man with a freckled face and sympathetic grey eyes.

Malcolm Hardcastle leapt to his feet. 'That was fast, Alan. Thanks for coming. I'd like to introduce Philip McGill Amory. Philip, this is Doctor Alan Stimpson, whom I was just speaking to you about.'

Philip, who had also risen, greeted the renowned surgeon. They shook hands, and then the three of them sat down together.

Alan Stimpson was a direct man who believed in getting to the crux of the matter at once. 'I've just spoken to Doctor Litman, Mr Amory, and I will examine your wife in a moment.' His gaze was steady, level, as he went on, 'However, I hadn't realized the baby's birth was so imminent, that the child is actually now two weeks overdue.' He glanced at Malcolm. 'Have you explained to Mr Amory how dangerous a brain scan would be to the unborn child?'

Malcolm shook his head. 'No, I haven't. I was waiting for you.'

'Could you elucidate further, please?' Philip said to Alan Stimpson, his alarm increasing. He clasped his hands together to stop them trembling.

'There would be danger of radiation from a brain scan, Mr Amory. It would most probably injure the unborn child.'

Philip was silent briefly. Then he asked, 'Do you have to do a brain scan on my wife?'

'It would enable us to ascertain the true extent of the cerebral damage.'

'I see.'

Doctor Stimpson continued in the same gentle tone, 'However, before we make a decision about that, I must give Mrs Amory a very thorough physical examination. I will then consult with my colleagues, and we'll decide on the best course of medical action to take.'

'I understand,' Philip said. 'But I hope some fairly fast decisions are going to be made. Surely time is of the essence?'

'It is,' Alan Stimpson replied. He stood. 'Please excuse me.' When the brain surgeon reached the door, he glanced back at the gynaecologist. 'I'd like you to be at this examination, Malcolm, and consult with us, in view of your patient's pregnancy.'

Malcolm jumped up. 'Of course, Alan.' He turned to Philip. 'Hang in there . . . and try to stay calm . . . take it easy.'

'I will,' Philip muttered, but he knew that this was the last thing he would be able to do. His gaze turned inward as he dropped his head into his hands, worrying about Maddy, becoming more anxious than ever for her. He was reeling from the shock. He could not believe this horrendous thing had happened. She had been so well last night. He felt as if he was living in some horrifying nightmare to which there was no end.

Ten minutes later Philip jerked his head up, found himself looking at the worried face of his brother-in-law, Shane O'Neill, who stood framed in the doorway.

Shane exclaimed, 'I came as soon as I heard! I was out of the hotel. Barry tracked me down. He said to tell you he hasn't been able to contact Daisy yet.'

'Thanks for coming,' Philip murmured, relieved to see him.

'Barry told me the housekeeper found Maddy unconscious this morning. What happened, Philip? What's wrong with her?'

'The doctors think she's had a brain haemorrhage.'

'Oh Jesus!' Shane was aghast. He stood staring at Philip, disbelief washing over his face.

'It occurred during the night most probably,' Philip thought to add. His voice was hardly audible.

Shane took the next chair. 'But she seemed perfectly normal last evening at dinner! Do they *know* what caused the haemorrhage?'

Philip shook his head. 'Not yet. But Doctor Stimpson is examining her right now. He's one of the world's foremost brain surgeons. We're damned lucky he wasn't abroad, and that he was actually out here at a nearby hospital in Darlinghurst this morning.'

'I've heard of Alan Stimpson,' Shane said. 'He has an extraordinary record, has performed some miraculous brain operations. From what I've read about him, there's nobody better.'

'Yes, he *is* brilliant.' Philip turned to Shane. 'I don't know what I'll do if anything happens to Maddy,' he blurted out shakily. 'She's the most important thing in my life . . .' He bit off the end of the sentence, unable to continue, averted his head so that Shane would not see the sudden tears glittering in his eyes.

'Maddy's going to be all right,' Shane asserted, his voice confident, strong. 'Let's not dwell on the worst, but think of the best instead. We've got to take a positive attitude, Philip. And you're not going to lose her. We must hold that thought.'

'Yes . . . I'm glad you're here, Shane. It does help.'

Shane nodded.

A silence developed between the two men.

All of Philip's thoughts and his mind and his heart were with his wife in Emergency. He kept seeing her face. It had been pale, still, devoid of expression when he had seen her a short while before. He could not forget the limpness of her hand when he had held it in his. There had been something so lifeless about Maddy. His mind balked at the idea that she might slip away from him. He refused to contemplate this.

From time to time, Shane looked at Philip. His heart went out to his brother-in-law. But he did not say a word, not wishing to intrude on Philip's privacy. It was obvious that he wanted to be quiet, to be left alone. He was faraway, his handsome face ringed with worry, and his bright blue eyes, so like Paula's, were troubled, filled with growing anxiety.

Shane sat back. Silently he offered up a prayer for Maddy.

When Daisy came into the office a little later, Shane was on his feet and across the room to her immediately. She was white, and there was a stricken expression on her face. Shane put his arm around her protectively.

She looked up at him questioningly. 'What has happened to Maddy?' she asked tremulously, clutching at him.

Shane explained in a muted voice, 'It looks as if she may have had a brain haemorrhage.'

'Oh no! Not Maddy! Philip –' She flew across the room to her son, sat down in the chair Shane had just vacated, reached out her hand to him, wanting to give him comfort.

'I'm all right, Ma,' Philip said, taking her hand in his, squeezing it. 'The doctors are with Maddy now . . . Malcolm Hardcastle, two doctors from the hospital, and Alan Stimpson, the famous brain surgeon.'

'He's wonderful,' Daisy said, relieved to hear that this man was in charge medically. Her hopes for Maddy soared. 'I've met him several times through the Foundation . . . he's the very best. You could not ask for a finer doctor to take care of Maddy.'

'I know, Ma.'

Daisy swung her eyes to Shane, hovering nearby. 'Barry is very anxious . . . he hasn't heard from either of you. You must call him, Shane, let him know what's going on. He can then get in touch with Jason, who went to Perth last night.'

'Oh God, yes, I did forget to phone him,' Philip muttered. 'I'll do so now, and I'll call Mrs Ordens at the house. She and the maids are as concerned as we are.'

'I'm sorry, Mr Amory, but there is little question that your wife has suffered a cerebral haemorrhage,' Doctor Stimpson told Philip forty minutes later. 'Her condition is very grave.'

Philip, who was standing near the window, thought his legs were going to give way under him. He sat down heavily in the nearest chair. He was unable to speak.

Shane had been introduced to the two doctors by Daisy a moment before, and he took charge, addressed the brain surgeon. 'What's your recommendation, Doctor Stimpson?'

'I would like to do the brain scan as soon as possible, and then trepan her skull. That operation would at least relieve the pressure of the blood clot on her brain. Also, I should point out that without the trepanning of her skull she might never regain consciousness. She could be in a coma for the rest of her life.'

Philip stifled an anguished cry. He clenched his hands, digging his nails into his palms. *Maddy never to be conscious again.* The thought of this was so appalling, so terrifying, he could not – would not – countenance it.

Alan Stimpson, compassionate, caring, saw the agony on Philip's face, the mixture of pain and apprehension now flickering in those blue eyes. He was silent, waiting for the other man to marshal his swimming senses.

At last Philip whispered, 'Please go on, Doctor Stimpson.'

'There is the complication for the baby, Mr Amory. If your wife were only a few weeks or even a few months pregnant, I would recommend aborting the child. Obviously that is not possible at this late stage of the pregnancy. And . . . well, she could go into labour at any moment. Therefore, the child must be delivered by caesarian section. I recommend that this be done without further delay.'

'I can perform the caesarian immediately,' Malcolm said.

'Will that endanger my wife's life?' Philip asked quickly.

It was Alan Stimpson who answered him. 'Quite the contrary . . . I'd say she could be in more danger if Malcolm doesn't perform the caesarian. Also, in another sense it would be very helpful, in that I could perform the scan and the operation without fear of doing injury to the unborn baby.'

'Then go ahead with the caesarian. Now,' Philip answered rapidly, wanting no further procrastination. 'But I would like Maddy sent to a private hospital . . . if she can be moved, of course.'

'We can arrange to transfer Mrs Amory to St Vincent's private wing next door,' the surgeon said.

'Then let's do that.' Philip rose to his feet. 'I want to go to my wife now, to be with her. And I'll accompany her next door.'

36

At a few minutes past two o'clock that afternoon, Malcolm Hardcastle performed a caesarian section on Madelana Amory.

The child he delivered was perfect. But the mother did not know this. She remained in a coma.

Malcolm brought the news to Philip.

He was waiting impatiently with Shane and Daisy in a private room adjacent to the one he had taken for Maddy.

'You have a baby girl. A daughter, Philip,' Malcolm announced.

Philip was pacing the floor.

He stopped, pivoted to face the gynaecologist. 'Is Maddy all right? Did she come through it all right?' he demanded, his wife his first priority.

'Yes, she did. And her condition is the same as it was when she was brought to St Vincent's this morning. I'm afraid she still hasn't regained consciousness; on the other hand, she has not taken a turn for the worse.'

'Is that a good sign? Hopeful?' Shane probed.

'Yes . . . she seems . . . quite stable.'

'Can I see her?' Philip asked.

'Not just yet . . . she's in Recovery.'

'*But when*?' he asked again in the same soft yet demanding tone.

'In an hour. Now, about your daughter . . . she's perfect, just beautiful, and she weighs seven pounds ten ounces.'

Philip remembered his manners. He grasped Malcolm's hand tightly. 'Thanks for everything you've done, Malcolm. I'm grateful to you, relieved that the baby's all right.'

'Can we at least see the child?' Daisy looked at Malcolm, then shifted her gaze to her son standing next to him. 'I'd like to welcome my granddaughter into the world.'

'Of course you can see her, Mrs Rickards.'

The four of them left the room together, walked down the corridor to the glass-windowed hygienically-controlled nursery where new babies were taken immediately following their births.

'There she is!' Malcolm was exclaiming a few seconds later. A duty nurse, catching sight of the noted gynaecologist, had already lifted a baby from a crib and was bringing her over to the window for them to see her.

'Oh Philip, she is beautiful,' Daisy murmured, her eyes lighting up. 'And look, she's got a little tuft of reddish-blonde fluff on top of her head. I think we're going to have another redhead in the family.'

'Yes,' her son responded laconically, staring at the baby through the glass. He wished he could be more enthusiastic about the child. But he was so sick at heart about his wife nothing else seemed to matter to him.

Eventually, he brought his gaze away from the nursery window, drew Malcolm to one side. 'What happens next? When is Stimpson going to do the brain scan?'

'Shortly. Now, why don't you go outside and get some air? Or take your mother and brother-in-law for a cup of tea or coffee.'

'I won't leave the hospital! I won't leave Maddy!' Philip exclaimed. 'Perhaps I can persuade them to go. But not me, oh no. Again, thanks for everything you've done for my wife and my child, Malcolm,' he said as he turned away.

Later, when they had returned to the room in the private wing of the hospital, Philip suggested to Shane that he accompany Daisy to the Point Piper house, to relax and take some sort of refreshment. 'You don't have to keep vigil with me,' he muttered, throwing himself into a chair.

'We do,' Shane shot back quickly. 'We're not going to let you go through this alone.'

'We're staying, Philip, and that's flat!' Daisy said in a voice that was as resolute as her mother's had ever been. 'My God, Shane and I couldn't stand it, being away from you, and from Maddy. We're worried enough as it is without being isolated at the Point Piper house, not knowing what's going on.'

Philip did not have the energy to respond, never mind argue with Daisy or Shane.

For a time he nervously paced the floor, then the corridor outside, his agitation increasing. In an effort to stem his spiralling anxiety, he returned to the room, phoned his offices in the McGill Tower, spoke to his secretary, Maggie, and to Barry, his assistant. He made the occasional comment to his mother and Shane, but for the most part he was silent, stood staring morosely out of the window, burdened down.

He was accustomed to being in control and master of his own fate. All his adult life he had been a man of action, a decision-maker, a mover, a doer. He was not used to standing idly by in an emergency, no matter what the emergency was. But at this moment, perhaps the most crucial in his life, he had no alternative. He was not a doctor, and therefore he could do nothing to help the woman he loved beyond all reason. His frustration mounted, drew level with his fear.

Just before three o'clock he was permitted to see Maddy in Recovery. She was unresponsive, unaware of his presence, still in a coma. He returned to the private room filled with fresh anguish and distress and a burgeoning despair.

Daisy and Shane tried to comfort him, to reassure him, but they were not very successful.

'I know there is no wisdom at a time like this,' Daisy said, going to Philip, taking hold of his arm, filled with compassion for her son, and concern for her daughter-in-law's well being. 'But we must try to be brave, and have hope, darling. Maddy is strong; if anyone can pull through this, she can.'

He looked down at Daisy and nodded, then turned away from her so that she would not see the pain and heartache flooding his face.

Alan Stimpson arrived at four and quietly told them he had performed the brain scan on Madelana.

'Your wife did have a massive brain haemorrhage, as I originally thought when I first examined her, but I wanted to be absolutely positive,' he reported.

Philip swallowed. His worst fears had been confirmed. His voice shook slightly when he asked, 'Have you any idea what might have caused the haemorrhage?'

Alan Stimpson was silent for a split second. 'It may very well have developed because of her pregnancy. There have been similar cases.'

Appalled, Philip had no words.

'I want to operate, to trepan her skull now, Mr Amory. I thought you would wish to see her before she is prepared for surgery.'

'Yes, I do.' Philip glanced at his mother. 'We ought to have sent for Father Ryan. Maddy would have wanted her priest here, no matter what the outcome of the operation. Could you call him for me, Mother?'

Unnerved though she was by this sudden request, which underscored her own considerable fears for Maddy, Daisy nodded. 'Yes,' she said as steadily as possible, 'I'll do it now, darling.'

'There is every chance the operation will be successful,' Alan Stimpson said confidently, looking with swiftness from Daisy to Philip. 'And I will do everything in my power to save her life.'

'I know you will,' Philip said.

The two men were silent as they walked down the corridor together. The brain surgeon showed Philip into the anteroom, which was a few steps away from the operating theatre, and closed the door softly behind him.

Philip walked over to Maddy.

He stood gazing down at her, loving her with all his heart. How small and defenceless she looked, lying there on the narrow hospital bed. Her face was chalk white, the colour of the sheets. Earlier, Alan Stimpson had told him they would have to shave off her hair. That beautiful chestnut hair. He did not care as long as they saved her life. It was fanned out on the pillow around her face. He touched it, feeling its silkiness, and then he bent, kissed a strand.

Seating himself on the chair, he took her hand in his. It was listless. He brought his face close to hers, kissed her cheek. Against her hair, he whispered, 'Don't leave me, Maddy. Please don't leave me. Fight. Fight for your life, my darling.'

Lifting his head, he stared at her for the longest moment, hoping and praying for a flicker of understanding, a sign that she had heard him.

He knew she had not. She was so very still.

He kissed her again and left. He felt as if his heart was cracking in half.

'My watch has stopped,' Daisy said to Shane. 'What time is it?'

Shane glanced at his wrist. 'Almost six. Shall I go and rustle up a pot of tea?'

'Yes, I think I could use a cup. What about you, Father Ryan?'

Maddy's priest, who had arrived a little while ago, lifted his eyes from the prayer book in his hand. 'Thank you Mrs Rickards, that's very kind. I'll join you.'

'Philip?'

'I'd prefer a cup of coffee, Ma, if –' he began, and stopped short when Alan Stimpson entered the room.

The surgeon closed the door behind him, leaned against it. He was dressed in his green cotton surgical gown and pants, had obviously come straight from the operating theatre. He remained standing by the door, not speaking, his eyes on Philip.

Philip stared back at him. There was such an odd expression on the surgeon's face, one he could not quite fathom . . .

Alan Stimpson said, 'I'm sorry, so very, very sorry, Mr Amory. I did everything within my skill to save your wife . . . but I'm afraid she just died on the operating table. I'm so sorry.'

'No,' Philip said. 'No.'

He reached for the chair he was standing behind, gripped it to steady himself.

The knuckles of his tanned hands turned white. He swayed slightly. He was devastated. '*No*,' he repeated.

Father Ryan rose, helped Daisy to her feet. Tears had sprung into her eyes and she clamped a hand over her mouth to hold back the sob rising in her throat. She moved towards Philip, followed by Shane and Father Ryan.

Daisy's heart was breaking for her son. She dare not contemplate the effect Maddy's death would have on him. He had worshipped his wife. Life is not fair, Daisy thought, her eyes brimming. Maddy was too young to leave us.

Philip side-stepped his mother, Shane, and the concerned priest, shaking his head violently from side to side, as though denying the surgeon's words. His blue eyes were stunned, uncomprehending. He got hold of Alan Stimpson's arm. 'Take me to my wife,' he rasped.

Stimpson led him back to the small ante-room near the operating theatre where he left him alone with Maddy.

Once more Philip stood gazing down at her. How peaceful she looked in death. There was not a trace of pain or suffering on her face. He knelt beside the bed, took hold of her hand. It was icy. Irrationally, he tried to warm it.

'Maddy! Maddy!' he suddenly cried in a low voice raw with agony. 'Why did you have to die? I have nothing without you. Nothing at all . . . Oh Maddy, Maddy . . .'

He bent his head and his scalding tears fell on his fingers which were tightly holding hers. He stayed there with her for a long time until Shane came and led him away.

37

He took her back to Dunoon.

After a short private service at St Mary's Roman Catholic Cathedral in Sydney he flew her body to the sheep station at Coonamble. He sat next to her coffin the entire way. Shane accompanied him.

His mother and Jason followed in Jason's corporate jet, bringing with them Father Ryan and Barry Graves.

Once Philip's plane had landed, he had her coffin driven up to the manor where it was placed in the long gallery amidst the portraits of his ancestors. It rested there overnight.

The following morning dawned bright and clear with a sky vividly blue and spotless, and in the brilliant, shimmering sunlight the gardens and grounds of Dunoon looked magnificent. But Philip saw nothing. He was numb with shock, doing the things he had to do automatically, by rote, and, for the most part, he was oblivious to those around him.

To carry her coffin on the last stage of its journey he chose as the pallbearers Shane, Jason, Barry, Tim, the station manager, and Matt and Joe, the grooms, who had become devoted to her in the brief time she had lived there.

At exactly ten o'clock on Saturday morning, the six men shouldered her coffin and carried it out of the manor. They followed Father Ryan down the winding path that cut through the spacious lawns and flower gardens and led to the little private cemetery beyond. It was in a sheltered glade surrounded by trees and enclosed by an old stone wall. Here Andrew McGill, the founding father, was buried along with his wife, Tessa, and all of the other Australian McGills who were descended from them, their graves marked by simple marble headstones.

Philip had chosen the plot next to Paul for his wife.

The first day he had ever set eyes on Madelana O'Shea she had been gazing at Paul's portrait, had later said that she thought it was the great man himself suddenly sprung to life when she had seen *him* hovering in the doorway of the gallery. Maddy had often teasingly remarked that he looked like a riverboat gambler, just as his grandfather had, and she had been as fascinated by Paul McGill as she had been by Emma Harte.

And so he thought it appropriate, very fitting, that her final resting place was with his grandfather. In the most curious way, it was oddly comforting to him to know that they lay close together in this patch of earth.

The priest and Philip and the pallbearers finally came to a standstill by the open grave. It was in a corner of the cemetery, shaded by the lovely golden elms and lemonscented eucalyptus trees she had come to love, just as she had come to love Dunoon and the glorious land upon which it stood, and which had so reminded her of her native Kentucky.

Daisy was waiting with Mrs Carr, the housekeeper, the household staff, and the other men and women who worked on the sheep station, their spouses and their children. Everyone was dressed in black, or wore black armbands on their most sombre clothes, and the women and children carried sprays of flowers or held single blooms in their hands. And as they stood with their heads bowed, listening to Father Ryan conduct the Roman Catholic burial service, they openly wept for Madelana, whom they had held in great affection, and who had lived with them at Dunoon for far too short a time.

Philip's grief had turned inward.

It was frozen inside him, and he was dry eyed throughout the ceremony. He stood stiffly, his body rigid, his hands clenched at his sides. There was a grim moroseness about him, and his vivid, cornflower eyes were hollow, empty, his handsome face thinner, wiped clean of all expression. He was a forbidding figure, and there was an aloofness about him that held everyone at bay.

When the final prayer for Maddy's soul had been offered up by Father Ryan, and her coffin had been lowered into the earth, he accepted the whispered, heartfelt condolences of his employees, then strode swiftly back to the manor.

Shane and Daisy hurried after him. He spoke not at all until they were inside the house. Turning to them in the great hall, he muttered, 'I can't stay here. I'm going, Ma. I have to be by myself.'

Daisy looked up at her son. Her face was drawn, white, her eyes red from crying. She touched his arm gently. 'Please don't let it be like it was when your father was killed in the avalanche, Philip. You must get the pain out, you must grieve for your Maddy. Only then will you be able to function properly again, go on living.'

He looked at Daisy as if not seeing her. His eyes pierced right through her, focused on some distant image that was visible only to him. 'I don't want to live. Not without Maddy.'

'Don't say such a thing! You're a young man!' Daisy cried.

'You don't understand, Mother. I've lost everything.'

'But there's the baby, your daughter, Maddy's daughter,' Daisy said swiftly. She was wretched, heartsick, and her feelings were only too apparent on her troubled face.

Once more Philip stared right through his mother. He made no comment, swung around, crossed the entrance hall and left the manor without a backward glance.

Daisy watched him go, filled with the most enormous pain for her son. She began to weep quietly, turned to Shane. There was a dreadful helplessness about her. She did not know what to do.

Shane put his arm around her, led her into the drawing room. 'Philip will be all right,' he assured her. 'He's in shock right now, not thinking straight.'

'Yes, I know that, Shane, but I'm so afraid for him. So is Paula,' Daisy said tearfully. 'She told me so yesterday when she phoned from London. She said, "He mustn't let his grief fester inside him like he did when Daddy died. If he does, he'll never recover from Maddy's death." I know exactly what she means. And she's right of course.'

Daisy sat down on the sofa, fished around in her bag for her handkerchief, wiped her eyes, blew her nose. She glanced at Shane standing by the fireplace, added pointedly, 'Perhaps we made a terrible mistake, stopping Paula from flying out here.'

'No, Daisy, we *didn't*! It's much too long a trip for her to make for only three or four days! Philip was the first one to say so. He was quite adamant that she stayed in England.'

'She might have been able to help him. They've always been close, Shane, you *know* that.'

'True, she might,' Shane agreed, softening his tone. 'On the other hand, I don't think that even *her* presence would have diminished the shock, eased his suffering. It's the terrible suddenness, the unexpectedness, that has so thrown him, quite aside from his awful pain. And that's perfectly understandable, when you consider that less than a week ago Maddy was in blooming health, awaiting the birth of their child. Everything was wonderful for them, and they were so much in love. And then *wham*! Overnight she's dead. He's been hit between the eyes, he's literally staggering from this tragedy, Daisy. But he *will* recoup. He has to . . . he's no alternative. We just have to give him time.'

'I don't know,' Daisy said doubtfully, 'he worshipped Maddy.'

'That he did,' Jason said, striding into the drawing room, hurrying to be at Daisy's side. 'And he'll suffer for a very long period. But Shane *is* correct, darlin', Philip will recover. *Eventually*. Somehow we all do, don't we?'

'Yes,' Daisy whispered, remembering David.

Jason seated himself next to her, placed an arm around her comfortingly. 'Now, sweet'art,' he went on, 'try not to worry about him.'

'I can't help it.' She looked at Shane. 'Where do you think he's gone?'

'Most likely to Sydney . . . to be by himself. Like an animal in pain he wants to lick his wounds in private.'

Jason volunteered, 'Philip has a huge conglomerate to run and he's very conscientious, Daisy. You'll see, he'll be at the helm on Monday, as usual, and if I know him as well as I think I do, he'll throw himself into business with a vengeance.'

'And the work will be his salvation,' Shane interjected quietly. 'He'll use it as an antidote to grief yet again, as he did when David was killed, and it'll help him to keep going until the healing process starts.'

'I hope he will come to grips with his sorrow, and that he'll make some sort of life for himself in the future,' Daisy said.

She looked from her husband to her son-in-law with a worried frown. 'Philip can be so odd. He's been an enigma to many people for years, including me at times.' She sighed, and then unexpectedly her eyes filled again. 'Poor Maddy, I loved that girl so very much. But then we all did, didn't we? She was like a second daughter to me. Why did *she* have to die?' Daisy shook her head, and before either man could comment, she continued softly, 'But it's always the good ones who go, isn't it? It's all so unfair ... *so unfair*. Life's cruel ...' Tears spilled from Daisy's eyes, trickled down her cheeks.

Jason drew her into his arms. 'Ah me darlin', me darlin',' he murmured, wanting to soothe her, to calm her. He was at a loss, had no words. He knew only too well that words were cold comfort at a time like this.

After a moment or two, Daisy took hold of herself, sat up straighter, blew her nose, patted her eyes. Her expression was one of sudden resolve, and she said in her bravest voice, 'We must be as strong as we possibly can to help Philip pull through this tragedy.'

'He knows we're here for him,' Shane said, giving Daisy his most cheerful smile, trying to be as reassuring as he could. 'Take heart.'

'Yes, yes, I will.' She turned to face Jason. 'Where is Father Ryan?'

'He's in the library with Tim and his wife, and some of the others. Mrs Carr is serving coffee and cake, and drinks for those who prefer something stronger.'

'How rude of us! We should be there!' Daisy announced, immediately rising. 'We must stand in for Philip.' She hurried out.

Jason followed on her heels with Shane in his wake.

Privately, Shane was desperately worried about Philip, despite his encouraging words to Daisy a moment before. He could not wait to leave Dunoon on Monday morning. He was impatient to get back to Sydney, wanted to be close to Philip, to keep a watchful eye on him.

No one ever knew where Philip had gone that weekend after he left Dunoon with such abruptness on the day of Maddy's funeral.

When Shane had tried to reach him later that night at the Point Piper house, Mrs Ordens had said he was not there. Nor was he at the penthouse in the McGill Tower, according to José, the Filipino houseman.

Whether or not these two were lying on behalf of their employer, Shane could not quite determine; he did not even try very hard, knowing that if Philip wanted to hide behind the domestic help he would do so. He could be as stubborn as Paula. It was a family trait inherited from their grandmother, Emma Harte.

And then, on Monday morning, Philip had walked into his suite of offices in the McGill Tower as he always did at seven-thirty precisely, and called Maggie and Barry into his inner sanctum for their usual early morning confab.

There was an air of such cold containment about him, and he appeared to be so formidable in his iron-clad grief, that both Maggie and Barry were intimidated, dare not make a consoling gesture towards him, or venture any kind of personal comment.

As Jason had predicted, Philip threw himself into work, with a fury that defied description. As the days passed his hours grew longer and longer. He rarely went upstairs to the penthouse before nine or nine-thirty in the evening, where he ate a light supper prepared by the Filipino houseman. He then retired to his bedroom, rose the following morning at six, was back in his office at seven-thirty, never once deviating from this relentless schedule. He had no social life, no contact with any persons other than his employees. In fact, he shunned everyone who was not directly involved with him in business, including his mother and Shane, to whom he was the closest. They became increasingly troubled by his behaviour, but were helpless to do anything.

Barry Graves, who was with Philip most of the time during business hours, kept expecting him to make some sort of reference to Maddy, or to her death, or to the child, but he never did. And, to Barry, he appeared to become colder and more introverted as time passed. There was a sheathed anger in him that Barry knew would have to erupt in some form or another before very long.

Finally, in desperation, Barry called Daisy at her Rose Bay house one afternoon, and spoke to her confidentially, and at length, about her son and his concern for him.

The minute she hung up on Barry, Daisy telephoned Shane, who had just returned from a two-day trip to Melbourne and Adelaide, where he had been visiting the O'Neill hotels.

'I have to come into Sydney today . . . in a short while, in fact. May I pop in to see you, Shane?' Daisy asked.

'Of course,' he said. 'That'll be fine.' He glanced at the clock on his desk. It was exactly five minutes past three. 'Come by in about an hour. We'll have tea together and a nice chat, Daisy dear.'

'Thanks, Shane, I appreciate it.'

Promptly at four, his secretary showed his mother-in-law into his private office in the Sydney-O'Neill Hotel. Shane rose, went around the desk to greet her.

After kissing her on the cheek, he held her away, eyed her closely. 'You look lovely, as usual, Daisy. But troubled,' he said. 'About Philip,' he added, leading her over to the sofa in front of the wall of plate glass overlooking Sydney Harbour.

Daisy made no comment.

They sat down together. She reached out, took hold of his hand, stared into his face. She had known him all his life, since the day he was born, and she loved him like a child of her own.

She said, after a moment, 'You've always been such a good friend to me,

Shane, not to mention a wonderful son-in-law. You were a great comfort to me when Mother died, and I don't think I'll ever forget how caring you were, and supportive, at that most awful time in my life – when David was killed. You've been a rock for me, and for Paula, too. Now, yet again, I must ask you to help me, to do something else for me.'

'You know I'll do anything I can, Daisy.'

'Go to Philip,' she said, leaning closer to Shane with some urgency. 'Talk to him. Try to get through to him. Make him see that he'll become ill if he goes on like this.'

'But he won't see me!' Shane exclaimed. 'It takes me all my time to get through to him on the phone! You know I ring him every day. Maggie literally has to force him to take my calls. It's one hell of a tussle, I don't mind telling you. And when I ask to see him, beg almost, he hides behind pressure of work, business meetings, and the like.'

'Oh yes, I know, I'm having the same problems with him myself. And encountering the same type of resistance. But I believe you're one of the two people who *can* get through to Philip. The other is Paula, but she's not here. So it has to be you. Please, please do this for me, and for Philip. Help him to help himself,' she pleaded, her desperation surfacing.

Shane was silent, ruminative.

Daisy said swiftly, 'Go over to the penthouse tonight! Force your way in! Actually, that won't be necessary. I'll phone José, alert him that you're coming. He'll let you in, and once you're inside the penthouse, Philip will see you, I'm sure of that.'

'All right,' he agreed. 'I'll go. I'll do my best.'

'Thank you, Shane.' She tried to smile without success. 'Barry's been helpful,' Daisy now explained. 'But there's only so far he can go with Philip. He's awfully worried about him. He says Philip's full of anger. Rage, really. Rage that Maddy died. He doesn't seem able to accept it, or place her death in any kind of perspective.'

'It's been the worst shock to him . . . a very severe shock.'

Daisy opened her mouth, closed it, bit her inner lip. Then she said softly, 'Oh Shane, he hasn't even been to see the baby since Jason and I brought her to our house from the hospital, or asked me about her either.'

Shane was not altogether surprised to hear this. 'Give him time on that one,' he said, and paused thoughtfully. He chose his words with care when he added, 'He may well blame the baby for Maddy's death, and therefore himself, since he is the father of the child. Remember what Alan Stimpson said – that Maddy's pregnancy might have caused her to have the brain haemorrhage. I haven't forgotten how appalled Philip looked.'

Daisy nodded. 'Neither have I, and I'd thought of that, too. Blaming himself, I mean.' She sighed heavily. 'Barry says Philip sinks into the most awful depressions. Maddy's death is a terrible scar on his heart, one that will take months to heal.'

If it ever does, Shane thought gloomily, although he did not voice this opinion to his mother-in-law, seeing no reason to worry her unduly. Instead, he said, 'Now, tell me about the baby, Daisy.'

Instantly her face changed, lit up. 'Oh Shane, she's the most adorable little thing. Actually she reminds me of your Linnet and Emily's Natalie. She's definitely going to be another Botticelli redhead ... she's a real little Harte through and through.'

Shane smiled and nodded and listened, giving Daisy every ounce of his attention. He knew how important it was for her to speak about her new granddaughter, the long-awaited heiress to the great McGill empire. Poor kid, he thought suddenly at one moment, she's come into this world under a cloud and carrying a rotten burden ... her mother's death. Shane knew then that he had to do everything within his power to make Philip accept and love the baby. For both of their sakes. The father needed the daughter just as much as the daughter needed him.

After Daisy finally left, Shane waded through an enormous amount of paperwork that had been accumulating over the past week. He then penned a quick but loving note to Paula, and wrote postcards to Lorne, Tessa, Patrick and Linnet. He finished just before six o'clock, when he went into a meeting with Graham Johnson, managing director of the O'Neill hotel chain in Australia, and three of the other top executives in the company. The main subject on the agenda was the new O'Neill hotel currently under construction in Perth.

At seven-thirty Shane brought the meeting to a close, and he and Graham walked over to the Wentworth for dinner. When Shane was in Sydney he always made it a point to visit other hotels in the city. He liked to take stock of the décor, food, drink, service and conditions in general, in order to make comparisons between the competition and his own hotel. He had always liked the Wentworth, and he and Graham spent a pleasant couple of hours together over a delicious meal of roast baby lamb with the most succulent vegetables, and a bottle of local red wine that was excellent. For the most part they spoke about business, covering various aspects of the new hotel in Perth. Shane agreed to fly out to Western Australia with Graham the following week, before returning to London.

It was ten o'clock when the two men exited the hotel. Graham took a taxi home, and Shane strode off in the direction of Bridge Street where the McGill Tower was located. He needed the walk and the fresh air, after being cooped up in the executive offices of the hotel all day; also, he wanted to be certain Philip had finished dinner and was relaxing when he arrived at the penthouse. Daisy had suggested that he get there around ten-thirty and he had taken her advice.

A little while later, as he approached the black-glass skyscraper, Shane steeled himself for the impending encounter with his brother-in-law. He knew it was going to be difficult – painful, emotional and upsetting. Riding up in the elevator he asked himself what kind of wisdom he could offer Philip in his pain and sorrow, and he realized that he had none. All he could do was talk to the other man with compassion, give him his understanding, his support and his love.

As prearranged by Daisy, the houseman, José, let Shane into the apartment immediately he rang the doorbell.

The Filipino showed him into the beautiful cream-and-white living room that floated high over the city. It was dimly lit tonight, permitting the spectacular view to dominate. Bowing politely, the houseman said, 'I tell Mr Amory you here, sir.'

'Thank you, José.' Shane strolled over to a chair and sat down.

A split second later José was back, bowing again. 'Mr Amory says please wait.'

'Yes, all right. Thanks again.'

The Filipino smiled and bowed and hurried out on silent feet.

After fifteen minutes had elapsed, Shane grew restless, wondering what was keeping Philip. He got to his feet, walked over to the bar set against the far wall, poured himself a small cognac. He carried this back to the chair, where once more he sat down to wait. Sipping the drink, he mentally prepared himself for Philip, seeking the right words to use, the proper approach to take with him. One thing was vital. No matter what else he accomplished tonight, he must persuade Philip to go to Daisy's house with him tomorrow. To see the baby. He had made that promise to Daisy, and he himself knew how important it was that Philip put aside any feeling of blame, all guilt. Shane was convinced the baby was the key to Philip's well being. Once he accepted her he would love her, and only then would he begin to recover from his grief for Maddy, the loss of her.

It was another fifteen minutes before Philip finally emerged from his study. He stood hovering in the entrance to the living room, silently staring at Shane, his demeanour morose.

Shane rose at once, took a step forward, then stopped abruptly with a quick intake of breath. It took all of his self-control not to exclaim in concern when he saw his brother-in-law's appearance. Philip had lost weight, and there was an air of exhaustion about him, but it was his face that so appalled. It was ravaged. The cheeks were hollow, gaunt, the bright blue eyes dulled and red-rimmed, the purplish shadows beneath resembling dark bruises. The most startling thing of all, perhaps, was his black hair. It had turned pure white on either side of his temples.

There had never been any question in Shane's mind that Philip had taken Maddy's death badly; he had merely miscalculated the extent of his agony. The man was lacerated inside, suffering more horribly than even Shane had imagined. He understood then that whatever exterior equanimity Philip may display to the world it was utterly fraudulent. His cold containment and aloofness, so described by Barry, were his only defences against total collapse. All this instantly became clear to Shane as he regarded Philip, and his heart went out to him.

Shane moved forward, and the two men clasped hands.

Philip said, 'I almost sent you away.' He let go of Shane's hand, shrugged wearily, walked to the bar where he poured himself a large vodka, added ice cubes from the silver bucket.

'But there was no point, I suddenly realized that,' he went on without turning around. 'I knew you'd be back tomorrow or the day after, and that my mother

748

would come. And Jason. And then it occurred to me that one of you might have the insane idea of dragging Paula out here, so I decided I'd better see you . . .' Philip did not bother to finish his sentence. His voice was drained. He was worn out from lack of sleep, and his tiredness became apparent as he lethargically ambled over to the sofa and sat down. His usual vitality had fled.

Shane observed him quietly for a moment, then murmured, 'It's been three weeks since Maddy was buried, and in that time you've seen me only once, Daisy only once. Your mother is worried about you, Philip, and so am I, for that matter.'

'Don't be! I'm okay!' Philip said snappishly, with more spirit than he had displayed thus far.

'That's not true! You're not okay!' Shane shot back.

'Oh for God's sake, I'm fine.'

'*I* don't think you are. And, very frankly, you need your family around you at a time like this. You need me and Daisy and Jason. Don't shun us, please. We want to help you, Philip, to comfort you as best we can.'

'There is no comfort for me. I'll survive, everyone survives, I suspect. But the sorrow will stay with me forever . . . she was so young, don't you see? One expects old people to die . . . that's the life cycle. When we bury the old, time heals the pain eventually. But when we bury the young, the pain never, ever goes away.'

'It will, please believe me, it will,' Shane answered in his most compassionate voice. 'And Maddy wouldn't want you to be like this. She would want you to take strength from –'

'I don't want you to make one religious statement to me, Shane!' Philip exclaimed with a flash of irritation.

'I wasn't going to,' Shane replied gently.

Philip let out a long wearisome sigh, leaned back against the sofa, closed his eyes.

A silence drifted between the two men for a short while.

Suddenly, Philip got to his feet, went over to the bar, plopped more ice into his glass. He gave Shane a most penetrating stare, said in the bleakest of voices, 'I can't remember anything about the past year, Shane. That's the most horrendous thing. It's . . . it's . . . *blank*. She's gone as if she never existed in my life.' His voice broke, and he said hoarsely, 'I can't remember *her*. . . I can't remember Maddy.'

'That's the shock,' Shane was quick to say, speaking with assurance, knowing this was the truth. 'Really, it's only the shock, Philip. She'll come back to you.'

Philip shook his head with vehemence. 'No, she won't. I know she won't.'

'The body is dead, but you have the spirit,' Shane told him. 'She's alive in you. Her spirit is in you, and in the child. Only her body's gone. Please believe that. Maddy is in your heart and in your memories, and she will be with you always. And there is the child.'

Philip made no response.

He moved away from the bar, slowly crossed the room to the window, moving like an old man. He stood looking out. He had listened carefully to Shane, had absorbed his words. Now he was trying to come to terms with them, to

749

accept them. Were they true? Was Maddy's spirit in him? Would she be with him always?

He sighed. He found no solace in anything Shane had just said to him. He had acknowledged the finality of death days ago, had acknowledged that his Maddy was gone from him forever. She had meant everything to him. She had been his life. Maddy had made the pain inside him stop, and just thinking about her had warmed his heart. Now he could not even recall her face in his mind's eye. He had to look at a photograph to remember her. He did not understand why this was so. He had loved her so very much.

He snapped his eyes tightly shut, resting his aching head against the glass. He had killed her. He had killed the woman he loved more than life itself through the very act of love . . .

Shane said something, and Philip opened his eyes, but he did not answer. He had not been listening to his brother-in-law.

He stared at the night sky. How magnificent it was tonight, a deep midnight blue, velvet smooth, cloudless, filled with diamond stars and the bright, winking lights of the city's many skyscrapers. And off towards the eastern suburbs the sky was a curious amethyst spreading into the most vibrant of golds and a warm, glowing red.

It will be a beautiful day tomorrow, Philip thought absently. *Red sky at night, shepherd's delight, red sky at morning, shepherd's warning.* How many times had his grandmother said that to him when he was a little boy growing up. Emma had always been fascinated by skies and the light in them. Unexpectedly, the beauty of this evening's sky brought a lump to his throat and he did not comprehend exactly why. And then he remembered. Maddy, too, had forever commented about the clarity of light, cloud formations, the changing colours of the day as it moved into night.

Suddenly Philip stiffened, stepped closer to the window, frowning, his eyes focused on a dark cloud mass moving up above the skyscrapers several blocks away. How odd it looked. He couldn't quite make out what it was. 'Oh my God!' he exclaimed a split second later. 'Oh my God!'

Shane was on his feet, hurrying over to him. 'What's wrong? Don't you feel well?'

Philip swung around, grabbed Shane's arm, pulled him over to the window. 'Look! Over there! The black smoke billowing up, the red glow. Oh Christ, Shane, you've got a fire! The Sydney-O'Neill is on fire!'

Shane tensed. The breath caught in his throat as he followed Philip's gaze. He did not know the Sydney skyline as well as his brother-in-law, and it took him a moment to distinguish the smoke, find its source. He knew at once that it *was* his hotel going up in flames. He had just located the huge expanse of glass window-wall that fronted his famous Orchid Room.

Without a word he pivoted, shot across the floor.

Philip followed fast on his heels.

Together they took the elevator down, staring at each other speechlessly. As the elevator doors slid open both men hit the lobby simultaneously, raced out into Bridge Street.

They began to run in the direction of the Sydney-O'Neill, the sound of their pounding feet drowned out by the screaming sirens of the three fire engines hurtling past them at breakneck speed.

<h1 style="text-align:center">38</h1>

As Shane ran on, heading for the hotel, he was not sure what to expect when he got there. Disaster, obviously, but to what extent and degree he was uncertain.

Only a hotelier understood the true horror of a hotel fire and its nightmarish consequences. All of Shane's senses were alerted for the greatest possible danger. There would be distress, panic, fear, chaos, every type of injury. Smoke inhalation, burns, broken bones, trauma, shock. And death.

Rounding the corner of the street, he came into full view of the Sydney-O'Neill, his pride and joy, his favourite hotel in the international chain. What he saw brought him to a complete standstill. 'Oh God! No! No!' he gasped. He was stunned, rooted to the spot.

His hotel was an inferno.

Flames, black smoke, heat confronted him. Helicopters circled and hovered over the top of the burning building, lifting people off the roof. Fire engines were in full operation with swarms of fire-fighters manning hoses from the ground and from ladders; others were using ropes and ladders to rescue those trapped on some of the high floors.

There were ambulances and police cars parked at various strategic points. Doctors, paramedics and the police were doing everything in their power to help those in need. Three ambulances carrying the injured sped past him, their sirens wailing as they headed to the nearest hospital.

Shane pulled his handkerchief out of his pocket, wiped his damp face. He was sweating profusely from running, the sudden intense heat, and fear for those who might still be trapped in the hotel. The scene before him was appalling. Everywhere there was broken glass, debris on the ground, blinding smoke that was lethal, the raised voices of police and hotel staff shouting orders, the sounds of crying and moaning from those in distress. A group of hotel guests, many of them in their night clothes, looked unnerved and frightened as they huddled together near a police car. Shane was about to go over to them when he saw two of the hotel's porters assisting them. They were taken over to the ambulance set up as a first-aid unit; here they would be treated for minor injuries, shock and trauma.

Covering his mouth with his handkerchief, Shane pushed his way through the people milling around – hotel staff and security guards, police officers, paramedics and ambulance drivers. He had to get closer to the hotel, knew he must take command of the situation immediately.

A policeman stopped him. 'You can't go any nearer than this, sir. It could be dangerous.'

'Thanks, officer, for your warning. But I'm Shane O'Neill, the owner of the hotel. I must get through, do what I can to help.'

'Go right ahead, Mr O'Neill,' the officer said, suddenly recognizing him.

He gave Shane a sympathetic look as he let him pass through the wooden barricade that had been erected.

Almost at once Shane spotted Peter Wood, the night duty manager. He grabbed his arm.

Wood swung around almost violently. A look of relief spread across his grimy face when he saw it was Shane. 'Mr O'Neill! Thank God you're okay! We tried to ring you when the first alarm went off around eleven o'clock. We realized you weren't in your suite. But we didn't know whether you were somewhere else in the hotel. We've been as worried as hell, keeping our eyes peeled for you.'

'I was out of the hotel,' Shane said. 'Do you know how many casualties there have been?'

Peter Wood shook his head. 'Not exactly. But I'd say about fifteen people injured.' He paused, dropped his voice. 'And four dead I think.'

'Oh Jesus!' Shane drew Wood to one side as several guests were being shepherded to safety by a hotel security guard. When they were out of earshot, he asked, 'Do we know what started this?'

'No, but I have my own ideas.'

Shane peered at him swiftly, frowning. 'You're not suggesting arson?'

'No, no. Why would anyone want to set the hotel on fire?'

'A disgruntled employee, perhaps? One who'd been sacked recently?'

Wood said very firmly, 'No, Mr O'Neill, I'm sure it's nothing like that. If you want my opinion, I believe it was an accident.'

'I see. Where did it start, Peter?'

'On the thirty-fourth floor.' Wood gave Shane a pointed look. 'You were lucky, Mr O'Neill. You had a narrow escape.'

Shane stared at Wood, the full impact of the manager's words suddenly hitting him. His own suite was on that floor, along with a number of other private apartments leased out on a permanent basis. There were rooms and suites for hotel guests on the thirty-fifth floor, and situated on the thirty-sixth floor, at the very top of the building, was the famous Orchid Room.

Shane exclaimed, 'I can only thank God that I closed the entire thirty-fifth floor and the Orchid Room for redecoration last week. Otherwise this disaster would have been ten times worse if we'd had guests on the thirty-fifth floor, not to mention two hundred people dining and dancing in the restaurant tonight.'

'Yes, we've all been saying the same thing.'

'I presume most of the guests have been evacuated to emergency facilities in other hotels?'

Wood nodded. 'To the Hilton and the Wentworth. We're lucky in another sense, sir. The O'Neill was not filled to capacity this week.'

Philip ran up to them at this moment. He was out of breath, perspiring. 'I've been looking for you,' he said to Shane, then turned, nodded to Peter Wood, went on, 'What can I do to help?'

'Not very much,' Shane replied. 'From what I can see, the actions of my staff and the various agencies called to the scene have been tremendous. It *looked* like chaos when I arrived a few minutes ago, but it's not. They seem to have things under control.' He glanced towards the hotel, his expression pained. Two of the middle floors were still burning, but reinforcements had been brought in; additional fire-fighters were tackling the blaze with renewed energy, would soon have it put out.

Philip said, 'Perhaps I can –'

Neither Shane nor Peter Wood heard what he said next. His voice was drowned out by a thunderous explosion that sounded like several huge kegs of dynamite going off. It rent the air, made all of them jump. They swung to stare at the hotel. Shock and apprehension flooded their faces.

'What the bloody hell was that?' Philip cried.

'Windows blowing out from the intense heat within the shell of the hotel,' Shane said, shuddering. He dreaded to think that there might be more casualties.

'But I don't see any broken glass falling,' Philip muttered, looking baffled.

'Neither do I,' Shane said. 'But I'm sure that's what it was.'

Peter Wood volunteered, 'It's probably the windows on the other side of the building, Mr Amory, the rooms facing Sydney Harbour.'

A young woman wearing a dressing gown, her face streaked with dirt, hurried up to them. She appeared distracted, afraid. 'Please help me,' she said, tugging at Philip's arm. 'Please, please help me. I can't find my little girl. She's lost. I can't find her. I know we got her out. I know we did.' The woman's face crumpled. She began to weep hysterically.

Philip put his arm around her. 'I'm sure she's in a safe spot. Come along, I'll help you to find your child.'

'She's only four,' the woman sobbed. 'A baby, just a baby.'

Philip attempted to comfort her as he led her off. His own agony, his all-consuming grief were forgotten in the horrendous tragedy of the hotel fire.

By four o'clock in the morning the fire was out.

All of the injured, numbering some twenty-five, had been taken to the emergency room at St Vincent's Hospital and to other hospitals in the city. The dead, totalling nine men and women, had been taken to the morgue.

Fire-fighters, police, and hotel staff were bringing complete order to the area. Shane had been in command for several hours, handling everything with cool authority and decisiveness.

The Sydney-O'Neill was a smouldering ruin, blackened by smoke, a burnt-out hulk against the skyline. Shane and Philip stood together in the rubble as dawn broke, looking up at it, both of their faces grim.

'What a horrible tragedy,' Shane murmured, turning to his brother-in-law. 'So many injured and dead. It should never have happened. All I can think about are the families of those who have lost loved ones.' He sighed heavily. 'Well, I'm glad you were able to help that young woman. She was quite demented. Where *did* you find her little girl?'

'In one of the ambulances, being looked after by a paramedic. She wasn't injured, thankfully. Just scared, after becoming separated from her mother.' Philip took hold of Shane's arm, wanting to console him. 'I'm sorry this disaster had to happen to you, Shane. You're suffering terribly because of the loss of lives, and for those who have been injured. But quite aside from that, I know how much you prided yourself on your safety systems.'

When Shane was silent, Philip added, 'I understand what this particular hotel meant to you. I'm so very sorry. I'll do anything I can to help you.'

'Thanks, Philip.' Shane rubbed his tired face, shook his head with weariness. So much for Blackie's dream, he thought, remembering how excited his grandfather had been about building the Sydney-O'Neill. It was he who had found and bought the land on a visit to Sydney with Emma years before; he who had decided it would be the flagship hotel in the Antipodes. Blackie had not lived to see it constructed, but he had approved of the first architectural blueprints before he died. Now his dream had gone up in smoke in the space of a few hours.

'I'll build it again,' Shane said, as if making a promise to his grandfather.

'I know you will,' Philip answered. 'Now, come on back with me to the penthouse to clean up. You're going to need clothes and the like. It's a good thing we're about the same size.'

Later that morning, showered, shaved and wearing his brother-in-law's clothes, an exhausted Shane set up headquarters in the board room of The McGill Corporation.

It was here that he held his first meeting, began the investigation into the cause of the fire at his hotel. With him were Peter Wood, the night manager who had been on duty when the fire broke out; Lewis Bingley, the general manager; Graham Johnson, managing director of the O'Neill hotel chain in Australia, various executives from the Sydney-O'Neill, and Fire Chief Don Arnold, who had been in charge of the fire-fighters the night before.

Once introductions had been made, greetings exchanged, Shane went straight to the heart of the matter. 'We're looking to you for information at this moment, I'm afraid, Chief Arnold,' he said. 'I understand that you and your men have talked at length to many members of the hotel staff. Have you any idea how the fire started?'

'Through carelessness on the part of someone staying in the hotel,' the chief said. 'From what we found on the thirty-fourth floor, where it began, and from what we've since discovered, we're certain it was started by a cigarette. One that most probably fell into a sofa in a suite on that floor. One of the private jobs you lease out. In this instance, the suite leased to the Jaty Corporation.'

'Could you go into a few more details, please, Chief Arnold?' Shane asked.

'Sure thing. One of the room service waiters came forward in the early hours of this morning. He told me that he remembered noticing an ashtray perched on the arm of a sofa in that particular suite. That was when he went to remove the dinner trolley around eight o'clock. I believe that the ashtray remained on the arm of the settee, that it was used several times before the couple occupying the suite went to bed. The ashtray later fell into the sofa, and a cigarette, which was not quite out, set light to the sofa. More than likely, it smouldered for a couple of hours until it actually burst into flames. Only seconds after waking, the two people in that private suite were dead.'

'How do you know that?' Shane asked quietly.

'Two of my firemen found them huddled in the bedroom. They were not burnt. They were poisoned by the fumes from the foam stuffing in the sofa.

It's so highly flammable that within seconds it creates the kind of inferno you had in your hotel last night. And those flames are so hot, so intense they can punch a hole in a wall or a ceiling, and shatter windows. The foam also gives off the most fatal fumes, chiefly cyanide and carbon monoxide.'

Shane was horrified. He looked at Lewis Bingley, and exclaimed sharply, 'Discussions about the use of foam in furniture have been going on for ages. I've had foam banned in all my hotels for the past year. How come it was used here?'

Lewis Bingley shook his head. 'We followed your instructions, Mr O'Neill, we really did. There's *no* foam in any of the furniture used in the hotel. You know we replaced all the furniture.'

'But you just heard what Chief Arnold said! That sofa in the Jaty Corporation suite was filled with foam!'

The general manager pursed his lips nervously. 'I can only think that it crept past us. *Somehow.* You see, Mr O'Neill, the president of the Jaty Corporation used his own interior decorators, and they furnished the suite for him.'

'Were they told of our new regulations?' Shane demanded.

'Oh yes. But they apparently ignored them,' Bingley muttered.

'That is outrageous!' Shane exploded. 'And in any case, we were remiss for not going back, checking that the decorators had heeded our warning about the foam.' He tried to quiet his boiling anger, turned to the fire chief. 'Who were the couple who died in the suite? Have they been identified yet?'

'The son and daughter-in-law of the president of the Jaty Corporation.'

Shane shook his head sadly. His face was grave, troubled. 'That's your analysis of how the fire began. But what happened next, Chief Arnold?'

'I think the sequence of events went like this.' Don Arnold then explained, 'To quickly recap, the cigarette set the sofa alight. The foam smouldered, eventually burst into flames. That would have been around ten forty-five, ten-fifty, in my estimation. The flames had such intensity they blew out the windows within seconds. The sudden, new supply of oxygen created a wall of fire that burned right through the doors of the suite. Fuelled by the oxygen, the fire gained murderous force as it roared along the corridor of the thirty-fourth floor. It all happened in the space of minutes. Ten or fifteen, I'd say. Fire travels with the speed of light.'

Shane nodded his understanding. He was unable to speak for a moment. He was shocked by what he had just heard. Negligence, he thought. First on the part of the decorators, and then on the part of my management. They should have had that private suite checked once it was furnished. This tragedy might well have been avoided if they had. He sighed. He had to hold Lewis Bingley accountable.

'One thing's for sure, Mr O'Neill,' Chief Arnold was saying. 'Your safety systems are the very best. The smoke-detectors, the fire doors and the sprinklers all worked like clockwork. If the hotel hadn't been as perfectly maintained for safety as it was, you would have had an even worse disaster on your hands.'

Jason said, 'This places gives me the joes.'

Shane stared at him. 'What do you mean?'

'It makes me depressed. It's so damn gloomy, the shades drawn, the lamps turned low.' Jason eyed the half-empty bottle of scotch on the coffee table. 'And drinking in the middle of the afternoon, that's not you, Shane. Come on, mate, the booze ain't going to get you anywhere.'

'I'm stone cold sober. But frankly, I feel like getting drunk. Bloody pissed to the gills, if you want to know the truth.'

Jason shook his head. 'You've had kronk mozzle, Shane, real bad luck. But you ain't no jackeroo. You know things like this can happen.'

'I can't believe the hotel burned to the ground,' Shane began and stopped. He sprang up, began pacing the floor as he had been doing off and on for days.

'*Negligence*! *Sheer bloody negligence*!' he fumed. 'If I'm not breathing down their necks every minute of the day, things start to go wrong –'

'You shouldn't be in business if you don't want the aggro. And aggravation *is* the key word these days, mate. Still, I know what you mean. The fire's been a bleedin' horrible tragedy. I can well understand why you're angry.'

Shane exclaimed, 'I pay the best wages, big bonuses, they get all kinds of benefits and God knows what else, and they can't check out the furniture in a bloody private suite. It's criminal, Jason. Criminal. You know as well as I do that the fire would never have happened if they'd been on top of the situation. Those poor people would not have died or been injured, if my managers had done their jobs properly. That's what makes my blood boil. So much pain and suffering for all those concerned. And I'm going to be up to my eyeballs in lawsuits and lawyers, not to mention insurance company investigators. Now they're about to start their own investigation into the fire.'

'Well, that's to be expected, Shane,' Jason was quick to point out. 'And you *know* that. Anyway, they're going to come to the same conclusions as the Fire Chief, I'm sure. And look, there's no reason why you can't start making plans for the rebuilding of the Sydney-O'Neill, get the architects working on the blueprints already.'

'I don't think I'm going to rebuild.'

Jason was shocked. 'You have to build a new hotel, Shane! You owe it to your grandfather. More importantly, you owe it to yourself.'

Shane made no response. He sat down heavily on the sofa, dropped his head in his hands, full of weariness and despair.

Jason looked down at him, suddenly worried. He had never seen Shane like this, so dishevelled and unshaven, still wearing his pyjamas and dressing gown in the middle of the afternoon. What was wrong with these young guys? Didn't they have any balls? First Philip had fallen apart after Maddy's death, and now Shane looked as if he was about to go to pieces, too.

Jason cleared his throat. 'You were so abrupt with Daisy on the phone earlier, she asked me to come over to see what was going on here. She wants you to come out to Rose Bay for dinner tonight.'

Shane lifted his head, shook it. 'I have to work.' He shoved the pile of folders on the coffee table in front of him. 'I have all this paperwork about the fire to deal with.'

'It's Saturday. You've got to take a break sometime. And by the way, where's Philip?'

'I honestly don't know, Jason. And if you'll forgive me, I really can't worry about him right now. Frankly, I've got enough problems of my own to contend with.'

'Yes, I know. That's why Daisy and I want you to come over for dinner. It'll do you good to get out, to be with people.'

'No, I want to be alone. And really, it's best that I am. I've a lot to do. And a lot of thinking to do.'

'You know you can come over any time, if you change your mind.'

'Yes. Thanks, Jason.'

Shane picked up the bottle of scotch and poured himself another drink.

Jason shook his head sadly as he left the study, crossed the foyer and quietly let himself out of the penthouse.

39

Alone, he rode across his land.

He was mounted on Black Opal, his ebony-coloured stallion. Keeping pace at his side was a riderless horse. It was Gilda, the roan he had given Maddy after their marriage. Before leaving the stables he had strapped on Maddy's favourite silver-chased saddle, and turned the stirrups backwards to symbolize that her owner would never ride her again.

It was the first time he had been back to Dunoon since he had buried Maddy here four weeks ago.

When he had arrived on Friday night, Tim and everyone else on the sheep station had welcomed him warmly, and it was apparent they were glad that he had at last returned. So was he.

Maddy's death had torn him apart, and he was filled with an unendurable sorrow. He had been afraid that it would be too painful to come here. They had been so happy together at Dunoon. But now, as he rode through the lovely, pastoral countryside on this Sunday afternoon, he felt a certain kind of peace settling over him. He knew that in part it was due to the tranquillity, the gentleness, the stillness that abounded here.

He followed the Castlereagh River for a long time, then branched off, crossed several meadows, and took the winding track that led through the green hills of Dunoon. When he reached the crest of the steep incline, he dismounted, walked over to the great oak, stood gazing out across the extraordinary landscape.

How beautiful it looked after two days of rain. Everything was green and shimmering. It was the end of August, almost the end of winter. In a few weeks it would be spring; already the weather was superb, mild for this time of year. Philip lifted his eyes. The sky was a bright, polished blue, radiant with sunlight.

The very perfection of the day seemed to underscore his sadness. It was a day to share ... with someone ...

Philip turned away, went and sat down under the oak, propped himself against its ancient trunk. Taking off his flat-brimmed hat, he threw it to one side, trying to relax. His thoughts were scattered, chaotic still, his mind fogged by pain. But perhaps here he would be able to find a little ease.

This was his special place; it always had been since his childhood. Maddy, too, had grown to love it up here on this high land. She had said it was like being part of the sky. He smiled to himself at the remembrance, then recalled the morning he had met her in the portrait gallery, not quite a year ago.

They had ridden out here, had sat for a while under this leafy old tree. He had said some extremely personal things to her, things which had even startled him at the time. But she had not seemed to mind. She had looked at him for the longest moment, her lovely, intelligent grey eyes so quiet and unwavering, but she had made no comment. And at that precise moment he had known he would marry her.

Madelana had been the most remarkable woman he had ever met. Right from the outset of their relationship there had been a strange familiarity about her. It was as if he had known her, been separated from her, then reunited with her again. He realized now that he had felt this way because he had been looking for someone like her all his life, that she was the woman he had idealized in his mind. He had found her finally, only to lose her ... so quickly.

Maddy had had such inner grace. That, perhaps, had been the source of her radiance ... she had been an incandescent being. A fragment of a poem by Rupert Brooke flashed through his mind ... *All about you was the light That dims the greying end of night ... And, in the flowing of your dress, Undiscerning Tenderness*.

Philip sighed and closed his eyes, allowed himself to drift with his myriad thoughts, and slowly the memories came flooding back. He began to remember every little thing about their relationship ... every single moment he had ever spent with her was suddenly crystal clear. He recalled the hours, the days, the weeks, the months. Each and every detail was precise and exactly in place, as if a reel of film was being projected before his eyes. And on that hillside, where he had been taken by Emma Harte as a boy, he found his Maddy again. He saw her as she had been the instant he had first set eyes on her in the gallery, her image intact. He smelled the fragrance of her hair, heard the laughter and joyousness in her voice, felt the gentle touch of her hand on his. And the tears came then, and he wept for her, and he remained on the hillside until the light began to fade.

And as he rode back to the manor, down through the green hills of Dunoon, the riderless horse at his side, he felt her presence everywhere, and he knew he would never lose his Maddy ever again. She was in his heart, and she would be a part of him for as long as he lived. Shane *had* been right. Her spirit *was* in him.

He flew back to Sydney late that night. Early on Monday morning he went out to Rose Bay.

His mother was startled to see him standing in the middle of her living room, and her surprise showed as she hurried to greet him.

Cool sunlight was pouring in through the windows, illuminating Philip's face most painfully. Daisy felt herself flinching inside and her heart shrivelled. He looked as if he hadn't slept for weeks. His face was a study in desolation.

There was a haggardness about him that startled her, as did the streaks of white in his black hair. It seemed to Daisy that he was a shadow of the man he had once been, his looks gone, his vigour and energy vitiated completely.

She wanted to take her son in her arms and comfort him, but she did not dare. He had pushed her away, held her at arm's length since Maddy's death, and she had respected his wishes, had had no alternative but to leave him alone in his sorrow.

And so she was further surprised when he took a step forward, wrapped his arms around her. He held onto her tightly, as he had done when he was a small boy needing consolation, and she clung to him, loving him with all her heart. Neither spoke. This long embrace was enough; words were not needed. And Daisy understood deep within herself that the healing process had started for him. And she thanked God.

Eventually he released her, and said, 'Well, Mother, I thought I'd better come out to see you . . .'

'I'm so glad you did, Philip.'

'I'm sorry for the way I've behaved, Ma. I realize I've been impossible, difficult with you, and with everyone else for that matter. But, very simply, I couldn't help myself.'

'Oh darling . . . I understand, truly I do. You've been suffering so very much.'

'Yes.' He hesitated a moment, then continued slowly, 'Seeing Maddy's young life cut tragically short has been so heartbreaking for me, and I honestly thought I would never be able to sustain the loss of her. It's been pure hell, Ma. But then last night, flying back from Dunoon, I began to realize there was also a degree of self-pity in my grief. I was not only mourning for Maddy, but mourning for myself as well . . . and mourning for the life we'll never have together now.'

'That's only natural,' Daisy murmured softly, her vivid blue eyes filling with sympathy and understanding.

'Yes, I suppose it is.' He moved away from her, edged towards the door, then swung to face her suddenly. There was a little pause before he blurted out, 'I've come to get the baby.'

Daisy looked at him swiftly. Her heart lifted. 'Fiona's with the nanny. The young Englishwoman Maddy engaged before she –' Daisy cut herself off, looked at Philip uneasily.

'Don't be afraid to mention Maddy's death, Ma. I've accepted it.'

Daisy could only nod. She was reluctant to speak in case her voice trembled. She led the way upstairs. 'This is Mr Amory. My son,' Daisy said to the nanny as they entered the room.

'Yes, I know, Mrs Rickards. We met when I went for the interview with Mrs Amory.'

Philip shook the nanny's hand, murmured a greeting, then strode over to the crib in the corner of the bedroom which was serving as a nursery.

He stood staring down at the baby.

He had not seen her since the day she was born. She was already a month old After a few seconds, he bent down, reached into the crib, picked her up somewhat tentatively, as though he thought she might break in half.

Holding her away from him, he gazed into her small face. A pair of solemn grey eyes stared back at him unwaveringly. Maddy's eyes, he thought. Bringing the baby to his chest, he held her tightly in his arms, close to his heart, one hand on her head protectively. This was Maddy's child. His child. A wave of love for the baby swept through him.

Slowly, Philip walked across the floor, still holding Fiona in his arms. He paused at the door, swung around.

'I'm taking my daughter home,' he said. He glanced at Daisy. 'Don't look so worried, Ma. It's all right. I'm all right.' A small smile glanced across his mouth. 'And *we're* going to be all right. We have each other.'

40

'I tried to stop you coming over, Emily,' Paula said as her cousin hurried into the study of the house in Belgrave Square. 'But I was too late. Your housekeeper told me you'd just left.'

Emily paused in the middle of the antique Aubusson carpet. She squinted across at Paula, who was sitting on the sofa in a pool of September sunlight. 'Don't you want me to go with you to Heathrow after all?'

Paula shook her head, looking regretful. 'I just hung up on Shane a short while ago. He doesn't want me to fly out to Sydney. So I've cancelled my trip.'

Emily was amazed. 'But why doesn't he want you to join him? You said he was all for it the other day, when you suggested it, urging you to come, in fact.'

'He was, and *I* believe I *should* be with him at a time like this, but he now says he can handle things by himself, insists he's over the shock of the fire. Anyway, he thinks I ought to be here with the children. You know he's always had a bee in his bonnet about one of us being at home for their sakes.'

'Winston feels the same way. But then so do we,' Emily reminded her. She eyed Paula carefully. 'Let's not forget that Grandy taught us to be responsible parents. She said that when we had children we should put them first, consider their needs above all else. In fact, she was adamant about it, most probably because she so frequently neglected her own.'

'Emily! That's not a nice thing to say!'

'But it's true. And Grandy said so herself. She was so busy empire building, her kids took second place. Except for your mother. Aunt Daisy was the lucky one. Probably because Gran had made it by the time she was born.'

Paula had the good grace to laugh. 'Yes, you're right, as usual, Emily.' She let out a long sigh. 'As much as I really want to be with Shane, I'm afraid it has to be his decision.' A wry little smile touched her mouth. 'Still, I can't help wishing I'd missed his phone call this morning. You see, I do think he needs me, despite what he says, if only for moral support.'

'Then why not just *go*,' Emily suggested.

'And incur Shane's wrath! Come on, Dumpling, you ought to know better than that!' Paula laughed hollowly. 'Shane would be furious with me – you know how bossy and dictatorial he is – and the trip would then serve no purpose whatsoever.'

'I suppose you'd better do what he says,' Emily agreed, knowing how difficult Shane could be at times. She sat down in the chair opposite Paula, glanced at the breakfast tray on the antique Georgian coffee table positioned between them, saw that it was set for two. 'It was jolly nice of you to include a cup for me,' she said, smiling at her cousin. As she lifted the teapot and poured, she contemplated the basket of fancy French breakfast rolls. 'You don't want that brioche, do you?'

'No, I seem to have put on weight in the past week. But you shouldn't eat it either,' Paula warned.

'I know I shouldn't,' Emily said, and promptly reached for it. She looked thoughtful as she munched on the brioche. After a sip of tea, she sat back, said slowly, 'Look here, Paula, perhaps Winston ought to go to Sydney. At least he would be able to keep Shane company, and I'm certain he could be very helpful, in innumerable ways. He's leaving Toronto this afternoon and he'll be in New York tonight. Instead of going to Rochester to look at that printing plant, he could fly to LA. From there he could continue on to Sydney, take that night flight you always rave about. I'll phone him right now.'

'It's four o'clock in the morning in Canada!'

'So what. This is an emergency.'

'No, it isn't, Emily, not any more. Besides, I don't think Winston should go. Shane will be fine, he's a very strong person. He was just badly shaken up by the fire. And quite frankly, who wouldn't be? He was devastated that so many people were killed and injured. He kept repeating that every time he called, and you know he's hardly been off the phone to me since it happened. I think he went into depression for several days, at least, that's the impression Mummy gave me. But he's pulled out of it now, I can tell by the tone of his voice. As I said, I'd prefer to go, to be with him, but I must do what *he* thinks is best.'

'Yes,' Emily said slowly, then she added, 'And of course he does have a lot of strength, you're correct there. If anyone can cope, it's Shane.'

'I *know* he can, Dumps. And remember, it's not as if he's alone. There's my mother and Jason, and Philip, of course.'

'Is Philip better then?' Emily asked.

'Yes, I'm glad to report. Shane told me Philip went over to my mother's the other day and took the baby home with him at long last.'

'Thank goodness for that! I was getting a bit worried, I must admit. I had visions of Aunt Daisy and Jason having to raise Fiona. Imagine, at their ages!'

Paula smiled faintly at this remark. 'Shane believes the disastrous fire and all it entailed shocked Philip out of his frozen state, brought him back to reality.'

'I'm sure he's right. Shane's got a lot of insight into people, knows what makes them tick.' She shook her head sadly. 'Poor Maddy . . . dying in that way, so suddenly. It's been hard for me to accept.'

'I know what you mean.' Paula fell silent, thinking of Maddy. There was a dull ache in her heart for her sister-in-law. She missed her terribly, and her own grief had still not entirely abated. There were times when her eyes would fill up, even at work, and she had to excuse herself if she was with people, hurry away to be alone, to regain her composure. Maddy had been a most unusual woman and she had affected all of their lives; it would not be the same without her.

Paula settled herself against the cushions, gazed off into the distance. Her eyes held a faraway look.

Emily watched her, but said nothing, not wishing to intrude on her at this moment. She knew Paula was thinking of Madelana, whose death had so shocked her, upset her so badly.

Out of the blue, Paula murmured in a voice suddenly turned gloomy, 'I'm beginning to think there's a curse on this family.'

Struck by the seriousness of her tone, Emily sat up in the chair and gaped at her. 'Paula! How superstitious of you! You sound positively Celtic . . . some of Shane's Irishness must be rubbing off on you!'

'Well, just consider the past year, Emily. There's been the regurgitation of that old deception in Ireland, which ultimately led to the death of the estate manager. It was all very upsetting for Anthony and Sally, having to relive Min's death. And Anthony's felt responsible for Michael Lamont's stroke ever since it happened.'

'It's better Michael Lamont keeled over from a stroke and died, than face trial for murder.'

'Good God, Emily! You fair take my breath away at times, some of the things you say!'

'But it's true, and I'm not a hypocrite.'

'I know that, but you're so *blunt*.'

'Like Gran.'

'Yes, like Gran,' Paula agreed. There was a short pause before she continued softly, 'Then there was Sandy's fatal illness, his shooting accident, followed by Maddy's brain haemorrhage and death, and last week the Sydney-O'Neill went up in smoke. Surely that's enough to make anybody think there's some sort of curse on them. Anyway, look at the terrible things that happened to Grandy throughout her lifetime. And what about the avalanche that killed Daddy, Jim and Maggie? And there's my little Patrick, who was born retarded.' Paula gave Emily a pointed stare. 'It's as if we're being punished for something.'

Not wishing to encourage Paula in these sudden, dire thoughts, Emily exclaimed dismissively. 'Oh pooh! I don't believe that! We're a big, sprawling family – like the Kennedys. All sorts of awful things happen to people during their lives, but when there are a lot of you, as in our case, disasters only appear to be so much more numerous than in a small family. And despite everything, *I* happen to think we've been lucky . . . and in so many ways.'

'Granted, we're all successful, and rich, but we've had more than our fair share of tragedies.'

'And I suppose we'll have many more.'

'My God, Emily, you sound like Job's comforter.'

'Oh sorry, darling, I don't mean to, nor do I mean to make light of the dreadful things that have recently happened in Australia. But I won't subscribe to superstition, and I'm surprised at you. Cursed indeed.' Emily grinned, shook her head as if highly amused. 'I can tell you this – if our Gran were alive, she'd have a real belly laugh.'

'What do you mean?'

'She'd pooh-pooh you, too. She often said that we write our own scripts, live in what we ourselves create, and that we're ultimately responsible for everything that happens to us.'

'*I* don't ever remember hearing her say that.' Paula stared at Emily, frowning. Her eyes were puzzled. 'Are you sure it was Grandy who said it?'

'Oh yes.'

Paula nodded, and then she changed the subject.

But later that night she was to recall those words, and as she acknowledged their basic truth she did so with growing apprehension.

Paula spent the rest of the morning and most of the afternoon out on the floor of the store in Knightsbridge.

As she walked back into her private office, just after three-thirty, her private line began to shrill. Hurrying to the desk, she leaned across it, snatched up the phone, half expecting it to be Shane. Sydney was ten hours ahead of London, and he frequently rang her before going to sleep.

Her voice was therefore light, cheerful, as she said, 'Paula O'Neill here,' and clutching the phone to her ear she walked briskly around the desk.

'It's Charles Rossiter, Paula.'

'Hello, Charles! How are you?' She was disappointed but she kept her voice gay.

'Er . . . I'm fine, thank you.'

'You got my message then?'

'Message?' he sounded vague, slightly impatient.

'I telephoned you this morning, to let you know I'm not going to Sydney after all. So we can still have lunch on Friday, as we'd originally planned.'

'Oh yes, of course I received it –'

There was a sudden pause, a hesitation on the part of her banker, and Paula said, 'That *is* why you're calling, isn't it? To confirm our lunch?'

'No, actually, it's not.'

She caught an odd note in his voice. 'Is there some kind of problem, Charles?'

'I'm afraid so.'

'But I thought those new documents were in order, and that –'

'It's nothing to do with your usual banking business with us, Paula,' Charles interrupted. 'Something very urgent has come up. I think you must come down to the bank for a meeting this afternoon. Say at five o'clock.'

'Why, Charles? What's going on? You sound very mysterious.'

'I received a telephone call a bit earlier this afternoon from Sir Logan Curtis. I'm sure you've heard of him, and of Blair, Curtis, Somerset and Lomax.'

'Of course. They're a very prestigious firm of solicitors, and Sir Logan is distinguished as one of the foremost legal brains in the country.'

'Quite. Sir Logan requested a meeting today. Here at the bank with me. He wishes you to be present.'

'Why?' she asked, surprised.

'Seemingly he represents your cousin, Jonathan Ainsley. The latter is visiting London from Hong Kong, where he has apparently lived for the past ten or twelve years. According to Sir Logan, it is actually Ainsley who wants the meeting with us. To discuss a matter of business he has with you.'

Paula was so startled she almost dropped the receiver. She was speechless for a moment, before exclaiming, 'I have no business dealings with Jonathan Ainsley! As you are well aware, Charles. You've been my banker for years, as your Uncle Henry was before you, when my grandmother was alive. My cousin draws dividends from Harte Enterprises, of course, but that is his sole involvement with the family. And with any of our businesses.'

'Not according to Sir Logan.'

'But you know otherwise!' she cried, her voice rising shrilly. 'Sir Logan has been misinformed.'

'I don't believe so.'

'Charles, what on earth do you mean?' Aghast, she sat down in the chair.

'Look here, Paula, I'd really prefer not to go into it any further over the telephone. Quite aside from the confidentiality of the matter, I just stepped out of our annual board meeting to phone you, after I'd made the decision to accede to Sir Logan's request for a meeting. I'm very pressed. I must go back to the board room at once. However, I will say this, it is *imperative* that you are present.'

'*I don't understand.*'

'Whatever Jonathan Ainsley's business is with you, seemingly it could affect this bank, the other banks you deal with in the City, and the Harte stores.'

'I'm more puzzled than ever! You must explain in greater detail!'

'I'm afraid I can't, Paula,' Charles exclaimed, trying to keep his voice down. 'I'm not being evasive. Please believe me, I'm not. Sir Logan gave me only the broadest outlines. He, too, did not wish to have a protracted conversation about confidential business over the phone. However, he did stress the importance of the matter to all of us. That's why I'm agreeing to the meeting. It sounds critical. Furthermore, I deem your presence to be crucial.'

'I'll be there, Charles. At five sharp.'

'Good. One more thing . . . I must forewarn you, Paula. Jonathan Ainsley will be in attendance this afternoon.'

'I see,' she answered grimly.

After she had said goodbye and hung up, Paula leaned back in the chair, pressed her fingers to her eyes. She was so stunned it took her a few minutes to gather her scattered thoughts, to get her mind working properly again.

She focused her concentration on her cousin. *Jonathan Ainsley*, she thought. *Why has he come back? What does he want?* She had no answers for herself. But she did remember the threat he had made against her years before, and her blood ran cold.

41

It was exactly five minutes to five when Paula walked into the Rossiter Merchant Bank in the City of London.

Charles Rossiter's private secretary was waiting for her in the reception area and took her into Charles's office at once.

The chairman of the bank, an old family friend, hurried to greet her, kissed her on the cheek.

'Have they arrived?' Paula asked as they drew apart, stood regarding each other worriedly in the middle of the room.

'Yes, about fifteen minutes ago. They're waiting for us in the board room.'

'Do you know more about all this now, Charles?'

'A little. Sir Logan discussed it with me briefly.'

'Jonathan Ainsley owns shares in Harte's, doesn't he?'

Charles nodded.

'He bought some, or all, of my ten per cent, which I put on the market recently, didn't he?'

'Yes. *All of it.*'

'I thought so. I figured that much out on the way here,' Paula murmured, giving the banker a bleak little smile.

'He wants a seat on Harte's board of directors.'

'He can't ask that! Owning ten per cent of the shares doesn't give him the right to ask that! He can go to hell!'

'He's demanding it, Paula. And in my estimation he's out to make trouble for you.'

'Obviously, Charles. Otherwise he wouldn't have bothered to come all the way from Hong Kong. Now, shall we go in? Get it over with?'

'Yes, let's do that,' Charles agreed, escorting her across the room. He opened the side door which led directly into the oak-panelled board room of the bank.

Sir Logan Curtis, small, grey-haired, younger looking than she had expected, came forward as they walked in.

'Mrs O'Neill, I'm Logan Curtis,' he announced before Charles had a chance to make the introduction. He smiled as he offered her his hand.

Paula took it. 'How do you do,' she said in a businesslike tone. Out of the corner of her eye she could see Jonathan seated at the conference table. He did not rise, neither did he greet her, and she did not acknowledge him.

Sir Logan said, 'Your cousin wishes to speak with you privately, Mrs O'Neill. We will withdraw, leave you alone together.' He glanced pointedly at Charles Rossiter as he walked over to the door.

The banker, who did not appreciate being pushed around in his own board room, was seething inside. He turned to Paula. 'Is that all right with you?' he asked, his expression one of concern for her.

'Yes, of course, Charles,' she responded evenly.

Charles Rossiter could not help admiring her coolness, her extraordinary poise under the circumstances. Nevertheless, he felt bound to add reassuringly, 'I'll be next door in my office, if you should need me, Paula.'

'Thanks, Charles, you're most considerate.' She smiled at him as he slipped out and closed the door quietly behind him.

Alone in the room with her cousin, she turned slowly, walked towards the conference table.

Jonathan's eyes did not leave her face. He was elated, knowing he had the upper hand, enjoyed playing cat and mouse with her. He had waited a long time to get his revenge on Paula O'Neill, and now at last it was within his grasp. Earlier, he had resolved not to get up or ask her to sit down. He was not going to pay tribute to this cold, calculating bitch, who was the reincarnation of his diabolical grandmother, Emma Harte.

Paula came to a stop a few feet away from the table. She returned his stare unflinchingly. Her blue eyes were cold, steely.

Jonathan spoke first. He said in his smoothest voice, 'It's been a long time since we faced each other across a conference table. I do believe the last time was twelve years ago, when the saintly Alexander gave me the sack, and you kicked me out of the family.'

'I'm perfectly certain this meeting wasn't arranged in order that you and I could reminisce about old times,' Paula snapped. 'So let's get to the point, shall we?'

'The point is that I have –'

'I know you hold shares in Harte stores,' she said sharply, cutting him off. 'Ten per cent. I also know that you think you're entitled to a seat on the board. The answer is *no*, you're not. And now that you have my answer, I will leave.'

Paula pivoted, walked back to the door. Her intelligence and shrewdness told her that he had more up his sleeve, so she was not surprised, or perturbed, when he said, 'I haven't finished with you, Paula. I have something else to say to you.'

She paused, turned to look at him. 'What is it?'

'Over these many years I've been purchasing Harte shares through various nominees. Altogether, I now hold twenty-six per cent.'

Although this startled her, she managed not to show it. She kept her face still, her eyes steady, decided to make no comment. She watched him alertly. Instinctively, her guard went up.

Jonathan went on, 'Furthermore, I also have the voting power over another twenty per cent –' He paused for dramatic effect, and a smug smile slowly spread itself across his face. 'Just think, Paula, forty-six per cent in my hands! And you only have forty-one per cent now.' He laughed triumphantly. 'I actually control more shares in the Harte stores than you do!' A gloating expression slid into his eyes.

'How unwise of you to put yourself in such a vulnerable position . . . just to buy the Larson chain in the States.'

The shock Paula felt was so enormous she thought her legs were going to give way under her. But she managed to keep herself upright and steady, despite the tremors running through her whole body. She dare not allow any reaction to show.

Keeping her voice low, composed, she remarked, 'And whose twenty per cent do you control?'

'The shares left to James and Cynthia Weston, by their grandfather, the late Samuel Weston.'

'They are minors. Those shares are in the control of their solicitors, executors of their grandfather's estate. And traditionally Jackson, Coombe and Barbour have always voted those shares with me, as Sam Weston did when Emma Harte was alive.'

'Allegiances can change, Paula.'

'I find it hard to believe that Jackson, Coombe and Barbour would involve themselves with you.'

'Believe it . . . it's true.'

'You're bluffing.'

'Not at all.' He rose, strolled down the other side of the room. Half way to the door he stopped, swung around. 'It's only going to take me a week or two to buy the five per cent I need to get control of Harte's. You'd better start packing your things, lady, and clear out of your office. I'm moving in.' He gave her a cold, penetrating stare, his bitter loathing for her surfacing. 'I'm putting you on notice. I am going to make a takeover bid for Harte's. And I promise you, I will succeed. I will be the winner this time! And *you* are going to be the loser, Paula O'Neill!'

She did not deign to answer him.

He slammed the door behind him as he left the board room.

Paula sank into the nearest chair.

She was filled with an internal shaking, and she clutched her bag in her lap to keep her hands from trembling. It seemed to her that all her strength had drained away.

Charles Rossiter appeared in the doorway. He rushed across the room to her, his face as white as hers, his expression grave, his eyes reflecting his apprehension.

'I knew we had trouble brewing this afternoon, when I received that phone call. But I didn't anticipate that it was going to be this bad,' he cried. 'Sir Logan Curtis just briefed me fully on Ainsley's intentions. I'm flabbergasted.'

Paula nodded, unable to speak for a moment. Her composure was shattered.

Charles peered at her. 'Let me get you a brandy. You look awful.'

'Thanks, but not brandy, Charles. I don't like it. Do you have vodka?'

'Yes, I'll go and get it. I need a drink myself.'

He returned in a moment with a bottle and two glasses from the bar in his private office. He poured, handed her a glass. 'Just knock it back. It'll do the trick.'

She did as he said, felt the sting of the alcohol in her throat, then a warm sensation. After a moment, she said slowly, wonderingly, 'I find it difficult to believe that a staid, old-fashioned firm of solicitors like Jackson, Coombe and Barbour have done this. Thrown their lot in with Jonathan. *Could* he be bluffing, Charles?'

'I doubt it. Anyway, why *would* he? Besides, having Sir Logan Curtis at his

767

side was a manoeuvre on his part to show you – *to show me* – that he is absolutely above board, very legitimate, and that everything he is trying to do is perfectly legal. Sir Logan told me he is rich, a tycoon in his own right, head of a big company, Janus and Janus Holdings, in Hong Kong. He and his wife have been staying at Claridge's for some time. No, Paula, I am afraid this is no bluff.'

She exclaimed irately, 'But why would Arthur Jackson go against me? Agree to vote those shares he controls with Jonathan's?'

'There is no question in my mind that Ainsley has offered Jackson a fabulous inducement to vote with him, something beneficial to those children. Ainsley must have some sort of agreement with the law firm, Paula. He wouldn't have come here today if he hadn't been holding all the cards.'

She nodded miserably, knowing he was correct.

Charles continued, 'He wanted to undermine your reputation as CEO of Harte's with our bank, of course, shake our confidence in you. That's why he asked for the meeting to be held here. Clever devil, isn't he? However, I just want to say this . . . I am behind you, Paula. This *bank* is behind you. As we were always behind your grandmother.'

'Thank you, Charles.' She stared at him morosely. 'I'm in a mess.'

'Yes, you are.' He paused thoughtfully, added, 'The mere *rumour* of a takeover bid for Harte's could be disastrous for you.'

'I know.' Abruptly, she jumped up.

Charles was taken aback. 'Where are you going?'

'I have to get some air. I'm going back to the store.'

'But surely you want to talk with me further, work out some sort of strategy, Paula.'

'I'd prefer to do that tomorrow, Charles, if you don't mind. I feel the need to be alone right now, if you'll excuse me.'

She sat at her desk in her office at Harte's in Knightsbridge, the world's most famous department store, her special territory, her strong citadel.

She was unable to move or think or focus on anything except the terrible problems facing her. She felt as if she had been bludgeoned about her head and her body. Her brain was still reeling, and, from time to time, waves of panic swept through her, blocking all rational thought.

For the first time in her life, Paula O'Neill was afraid.

She was frightened of Jonathan Ainsley, of the power he had over her, so suddenly, so unexpectedly. His spectre loomed like a black cloud. And she detested the feelings of helplessness, of powerlessness . . .

He has me cornered, she thought, trying to quell the nausea rising in her again, as it had been doing off and on for the past hour. *He's going to ruin me, as he threatened he would all those years ago. And I've no one to blame but myself.*

The queasy feeling intensified and she ran into the bathroom in the adjoining dressing area. Leaning over the washbasin, she retched and retched until she thought there was nothing left inside her. When she finally straightened, looked at herself in the mirror, she saw that her face was the colour of putty; her eyes were red, watery, her cheeks streaked with mascara. After cleaning them with a damp tissue, she filled a glass with cold water, drank it gratefully. The vodka made me sick, she told herself, all the while knowing this was not so. It was nerves and fear and panic that were having such a dire effect on her system.

Returning to her office, she moved quickly towards the desk, then came to a halt in the centre of the room. The portrait of her grandmother hanging over the fireplace caught her attention, brought into focus as it was by the picture light on top of the frame. Aside from the lamp on her desk, this was the only illumination in the shadow-filled room. Consequently, the portrait stood out in bold relief. Walking over to it, she stood staring up at the beloved face of Emma Harte, captured with such life-like precision in oils.

Oh Grandy, what have I done? How could I have been so stupid? I've jeopardized all that you built, put myself in jeopardy. You asked me once to hold your dream, and I've done just the opposite. I've let you down. I have made the most terrible error. Oh Gran, whatever am I going to do? How can I retrieve the situation? Regain the advantage to prevent the stores from falling into the wrong hands?

The beautiful face in the portrait gazed back. The smile was benign, but the green eyes were watchful and shrewd.

If only she were alive, Paula thought. Tears came into her eyes. She felt so alone.

Patting her eyes with her handkerchief, she sat down on the sofa, continuing to study her grandmother's face. She began to twist the hankie in her hands fretfully, asking herself how the brilliant Emma Harte would have extricated herself from such an appalling situation.

But no sudden insights or clever solutions came to Paula, and in her anxiety she began to shred the lace hankie into tiny pieces. Her nerves were taut, she was paralysed by apprehension. She leaned back against the sofa, closed her eyes, trying to compose herself, hoping to bring some order to her turbulent and disturbing thoughts.

The chiming of the hour made Paula sit up swiftly. She glanced at the clock on the chimney piece. To her astonishment it was nine o'clock. Where had the time gone? Had she dozed? She realized she had been sitting on the sofa for over an hour.

Rising, she went to the desk, picked up the phone, instantly dropped the receiver back into the cradle. There was no point in calling Shane now. He had enough to cope with. Her news would only distress him. Far better to wait until tomorrow, or the day after, to tell him, when she had worked out some sort of strategy. And she would most certainly have to do that, find a way to block Jonathan Ainsley's takeover bid for Harte's. *She could not let it happen.*

The feeling of claustrophobia she had experienced in the board room of the Rossiter Merchant Bank gripped her again. She felt as if she was suffocating, had the sudden pressing need to escape this room, to be outside, to breathe in fresh air.

Snatching up her bag, she flew out of the office, took the staff elevator down to the ground floor. And with a brisk goodnight to the security guard on duty, she left the store.

The air was crisp on this Wednesday evening, rather chilly for September. But Paula welcomed the coolness, found it refreshing. Certainly it seemed to revive her as she hurried away from the main thoroughfare of Knightsbridge, headed in the direction of her house in Belgrave Square.

Ever since she had left the bank in the City she had felt dazed, unnerved, and panicked. But slowly, as she walked, these negative feelings were starting to lift. She had no idea what she would do, how she would proceed with Jonathan Ainsley, but she did know it was going to be an all-out war between them. And she was determined now to fight him with everything she had, do everything in her power to win. She could not afford to lose. Her cousin would be a cool, calculating and devious adversary, she had no doubt about that. His threat had not been an idle one. He was in deadly earnest, would stop at nothing. He wanted the Harte stores. Equally as important, he wanted – no, needed – to ruin her. Manifold emotions were tangled up in his drives. And not the least of them was his overwhelming jealousy of her which he had harboured since their childhood.

Unexpectedly, it occurred to her there were several possible ways to out-manoeuvre Jonathan. But would they work? Were they viable? She wondered if one of them was even legal. She was not sure. She would have to check Harte's papers of incorporation tomorrow. She made a mental note to call John Crawford, her solicitor, when she got home. She was obviously going to need legal counsel.

Her brain was functioning again. This realization gave her a great sense of relief. Her mind began to race, and so intent was she on her mental machinations that she was unaware she had bypassed her house until she found herself crossing Eaton Square.

She knew at once exactly where she was going. To see Sir Ronald Kallinski. Her Uncle Ronnie, her wise rabbi. He was the only one who could help her, guide her as Emma Harte would have guided her had she been alive.

42

Wilberson, Sir Ronald Kallinski's butler, opened the door of the Eaton Square house a few seconds after Paula rang the bell.

A look of surprise crossed his face when he saw her standing on the front steps. 'Why, Mrs O'Neill, good evening,' he said, inclining his head politely.

'Is Sir Ronald at home, Wilberson? I must see him urgently.'

'But he's entertaining guests this evening, Mrs O'Neill. A dinner party is in progress.'

'This is an emergency, Wilberson. Please tell Sir Ronald I'm here.' Before the butler could stop her, she walked right past him into the marble entrance hall hung with antique French tapestries. 'I'll wait in here,' she said firmly, pushing open the door of the library.

'Yes, Mrs O'Neill,' Wilberson said, sheathing his annoyance, but looking pained as he hurried across the vast foyer and knocked on the dining-room door.

It was only a matter of seconds before Sir Ronald hurried into the library to join her. Paula's unannounced arrival at nine-thirty in the evening had startled him. But his surprised expression changed to one of concern when he saw her face.

'You look frightful, Paula! Deathly pale. What on earth is wrong? Are you ill?'

'No, I'm not, Uncle Ronnie. And I do apologize for bursting in on you like this. But something awful has happened. I'm in serious trouble and I need your help. There could be a takeover bid for Harte's. I could lose the stores.'

Sir Ronald was thunderstruck. He understood at once that she was not exaggerating. It was not in her character to do so. 'Excuse me for a moment, Paula. Let me explain to my dinner guests that I have an emergency, and ask Michael to hold the fort for a while, I'll be right back.'

'Thank you, Uncle Ronnie,' she said, and sat down on the leather Chesterfield sofa.

When he returned almost immediately he took a seat opposite her. 'Begin at the beginning, Paula, and don't leave anything out,' he instructed.

Slowly, precisely, with her usual attention to detail she told him everything that had happened that day. She had a prodigious memory, was able to repeat every conversation verbatim. She started with Charles Rossiter's phone call to her, and finished with her confrontation with Jonathan Ainsley at the bank.

Sir Ronald had been listening to her attentively, his chin resting on his hand, nodding from time to time. When she had finally finished, given him all the facts, he exclaimed angrily, 'My father had a name for a man like Jonathan Ainsley!' He paused, levelled his gaze at her, pronounced with contempt, 'A *gonif*.'

'Yes, he *is* the biggest thief alive.' Paula cleared her throat. 'But actually, I've only got myself to blame. I set myself up for the likes of him.' She sighed, shook her head. 'I forgot that Harte's is a public company, forgot that I had stockholders. I believed it was mine, believed that no one would ever challenge me. I was over-confident. Relaxed in too many ways. And that's always when the sharp knives come out, isn't it?'

He gave a slight nod, sat scrutinizing her closely. He loved her like a daughter, admired and respected her more than anyone he knew. She was daring, brilliant and intuitive in business. It had taken a lot of guts to say what she had just said, to admit her mistakes. Nevertheless, he had been stunned at the outset of their conversation, when she had told him she had liquidated some of her Harte stock. It had been an error of the worst magnitude.

'I'll never understand why you sold that ten per cent, Paula,' he found himself saying sharply. 'Never, as long as I live. Very flawed judgement on your part.'

She looked down at her hands, fiddled with her wedding ring. When she finally looked up at him, she gave him a faint smile of chagrin. 'I know. But I wanted to buy a chain of stores with my own money . . . So that it would really be mine.'

'Your ego got in the way.'

'That's true.'

Sir Ronald exhaled heavily, adopted a softer tone. 'But then nobody's infallible, Paula, least of all business executives like us. People seem to think that we're cut from a different cloth, that we're a special breed, with immunity from human frailties. They think we must be hard-headed, passionless, without any weaknesses, to be able to wheel and deal, make fortunes the way we do. But none of it's true.' He shook his head, finished, 'In your case, some sort of genuine emotional need got in your way. And it distracted you.'

'I think I had to prove something to myself.'

A costly way of doing it, he thought, but said, 'Recriminations and regrets are a waste of valuable time. We must turn disadvantage to advantage, make certain you come out the winner. Let's examine your options.'

She nodded. His words reinforced her own attitude, which had grown more positive since she had been with him. 'I could go and see Arthur Jackson, at Jackson, Coombe and Barbour, appeal to his better instincts, get him to reverse his decision to vote the shares he controls with Jonathan's,' she said. 'I might even be able to find out what inducement Jonathan used, come up with a –'

'Telephone Jackson by all means,' Sir Ronald interrupted. 'But don't be surprised if he turns a deaf ear. He's not beholden to you, and he doesn't have to tell you anything.'

'Uncle Ronnie, he's behaved unethically!'

'It may seem that way, but it's not necessarily so. Arthur Jackson is the executor of Sam Weston's estate. He has only one obligation. To those children whose interests he protects. If he can strike a lucrative deal, or make additional income for them, he will.'

'I think that's what he's done with Jonathan, don't you?'

'Most likely. Ainsley's always been a shrewd operator. He's probably offered to pay a big cash dividend out of his own pocket to the Weston estate, as long as the law firm vote the stock they control with his.' Sir Ronald rubbed his chin, pursed his lips, ruminated. Then he added, 'I'll do a little fishing tomorrow. I have ways and means of finding things out. There are no secrets in our world, you know. Hold off on your phone call to Arthur Jackson for the moment.'

'Yes, I will. Thanks, Uncle Ronnie.' She leaned forward eagerly. 'Is there any reason why I can't launch a bid to take Harte's private? Buy out my stockholders?'

'Yes, one very good reason. I won't let you.'

'But it *would* be legal?'

'It would. But to take your company private, you would have to offer money publicly, in the open market, to your stockholders. And you would immediately expose yourself to every predator and corporate raider in the City and in Wall Street.' He shook his head with great vehemence. 'No, no, I won't permit you to do that, Paula. There would be other takeover bids, possibly hostile ones. And anyway why should your stockholders take your money? They may prefer to take Sir Jimmy Goldsmith's money or Sir James Hanson's or Carl Icahn's or Tiny Rowland's . . . or *Jonathan Ainsley's*. You'd all be bidding against each other, accomplishing nothing except pushing up the price of the shares.'

Her face changed ever so slightly and she glanced away, biting her lip. After a moment she looked at him and asked in a tired voice, 'Then what *can* I do, Uncle Ronnie?'

'You can start looking for a few small stockholders who between them hold ten per cent of the Harte shares. Perhaps four or five, maybe even as many as twelve. Track them down, buy them out – at a premium, if necessary. You've already got forty-one per cent. You only need fifty-one to have control.'

'God, I'm so stupid, Uncle Ronnie! What's wrong with me tonight? I keep losing sight of things. Obviously I'm not thinking straight.'

'That's understandable, you've had a nasty shock. Also –' He paused thoughtfully before saying, 'I think there's one other thing you *must* do, my dear.'

'What's that?'

'You must dispose of Jonathan Ainsley.'

She looked at him. '*How?*'

'I don't know at this moment.' Sir Ronald pushed himself to his feet, walked over to the window, stood staring out into Eaton Square, his analytical mind examining various possibilities. Eventually he swung around. 'What do we know about this *gonif?*'

'Not much, I'm afraid, since he left England and went to live in Hong Kong.'

'*Hong Kong!* So that's where he ended up after Alexander turfed him out. A very *interesting* place, Hong Kong. Now, tell me what little you do know.'

Paula did as he asked, repeating the information Charles Rossiter had given her, which he, in turn, had learned from Sir Logan Curtis.

'Start digging, Paula,' Sir Ronald told her, 'And dig deep. Do you have a particular private investigating firm you use for business matters? If you don't, I can recommend one.'

'No, that's all right, thanks. I use Figg International, and have for years. They handle all of my security at the stores, provide guards, you know, the usual thing. They happen to have a private investigating division with offices and agents all over the world.'

'Good. Hire them immediately. A *momzer* like Jonathan Ainsley must have more than one skeleton in his closet –' Sir Ronald bit off the end of his sentence when the library door flew open.

Michael walked in, and when he saw Paula he exclaimed, with a laugh, 'Oho, so *you're* the emergency!' Instantly, he realized how serious Paula and his father were, and continued in a more sober tone, 'From the way you both look, it *must* be an emergency.' His eyes rested on Paula. He took in her extreme pallor, her tired eyes. 'What's wrong? It's not something to do with the fire in Sydney, Paula, is it?'

'No, Michael, it's not,' Paula said quietly, then glanced across at his father.

Sir Ronald said, 'Jonathan Ainsley has returned; he's in London. To make trouble for Paula.'

'How can he do that?' Michael demanded, turning to her, frowning, his eyes full of puzzlement.

'Uncle Ronnie will explain.'

Once his father had acquainted him with the facts, Michael went to sit next to Paula on the sofa. He took hold of her hand affectionately. 'Dad's made some excellent suggestions, but what can *I* do to help you?' he asked. He was full of sympathy and worry for her.

'I honestly don't know, Michael, but thanks for offering. Right now I'm going back to the store. I must start checking the records, go over the computer printouts. I must find those crucial stockholders. And as fast as possible.'

'I'm coming with you, to help you,' Michael announced.

'Oh, you don't have to, honestly. Uncle Ronnie has guests. I've interrupted your dinner party.'

'You can't do a job like that alone,' Michael protested fiercely. 'It's endless. You'll be at it all night.'

'I was going to phone Emily.'

'Good idea. Let's call her from here. We'll meet her at Harte's. The three of us can handle it together.'

'But –'

'Do let Michael go with you, my dear,' Sir Ronald interjected. '*I* will feel better, knowing he's at the store with you.'

'All right.' Paula rose, kissed him on the cheek. He hugged her to him, and she murmured, 'I can't thank you enough, Uncle Ronnie.'

He smiled down at her. 'We're *mishpocheh*,' he said.

43

'*Know thine enemy*,' Paula said. 'That's what this is all about, Jack, why I asked you here.'

Jack Figg, managing director of Figg International, nodded quickly. 'I get the picture. And this Jonathan Ainsley chap is also your cousin, is he?'

'Correct. And a very troublesome one at that. The situation is critical. I wouldn't have dragged you to the store at eleven-thirty at night otherwise.'

'That's no problem. I'd come out at any time for you, Paula. I've always valued our friendship, as well as our longstanding business relationship.'

'Thanks.' She gave a warm smile. 'I feel the same way.'

Jack Figg, who ran the biggest and most successful security and private investigating company in Britain, sat back in the chair facing her. He pulled an Asprey leather jotting pad out of his sports jacket, said, 'All right, Paula, *shoot*. Give me as many facts as you can.'

'That's just it, I don't have very many. However, it's my understanding that Jonathan Ainsley has lived in Hong Kong for about twelve years. That's when he left England. He owns a company called Janus and Janus Holdings. More than likely it's to do with real estate, that's always been his area of expertise. He's married, but I don't know to whom. Charles Rossiter told me that they're presently staying at Claridge's; oh, and he mentioned that the wife is pregnant.' Paula lifted her shoulders in a shrug. 'I can't tell you more than that.'

'Hong Kong is obviously our jumping off point. But I'll also have him watched here, so we know what he's up to.'

'That's a good idea, and, as I just said, the situation is *critical*.'

'I understand. And no doubt you needed the information yesterday.'

'No, five years ago, if the truth be known,' Paula answered quietly.

Jack Figg gave her a knowing look. 'I get the picture. But actually, how long *do* I have?'

'Five days – at the most. I'd like your report on my desk by Monday.'

'Good God, Paula! You're asking for miracles! I can't deliver in that short a time!'

'Jack, you have to, otherwise the information will be worthless to me. It'll be too late.' She leaned across the desk, her face tense, her blue eyes focused intently on him. 'I don't care how many agents you put on. It can be a hundred, if necessary –'

'If I do that, it's going to cost you a lot of money,' Jack interjected.

'Have I ever haggled with you, Jack?'

'No, of course you haven't, it's not your style. But digging deep, doing a complete profile of this nature can become very expensive. Very quickly. Especially when there's a time element involved. To gather the kind of information you want, I have to turn Ainsley inside out. I *will* have to put a lot of operatives on. It'll also be necessary to move a number of my agents from other Far East countries into Hong Kong. That in itself will send the costs skyrocketing. Then there'll be all kinds of payoffs, bribes –'

Paula cut in, 'I don't need to know the details, Jack. Just do it. *Please.* Get me as much information on Jonathan Ainsley as you can. I need ammunition against him, in order to defend myself. There've got to be some skeletons in his closet.'

'Maybe not, Paula. He might be as clean as a whistle.'

She was silent, knowing this was true.

'But I hope he's not,' Jack added swiftly, 'for your sake.

And look, I'll try to get back to you on Monday. However, it could be Tuesday.'

'Do your very best, Jack.'

'I'll get to it tonight,' he promised, impatient to start working the telephones and the telex machine. He stood up. 'The Far East is already open for business.'

After Paula had walked Jack Figg to the staff lift and thanked him once again, she hurried into the office where Emily and Michael were working on the records of Harte's shareholders.

'Any luck yet?' she asked from the doorway.

'Not yet,' Emily answered. 'But never fear, we're bound to come up with some names before too long. How did it go with Jack Figg? Is he on the job?'

'He is. And I have a lot of confidence in him. If there's anything to find, Jack will find it.'

'Oh I'm sure there's *sleaze* in Jonathan Ainsley's life!' Emily exclaimed. 'He always was weird and mixed with a strange bunch when he lived here. Like that awful Sebastian Cross.'

Paula felt a cold little shiver run through her. 'I'd rather not think about *him*, if you don't mind.'

'Why should *he* bother you! He's dead. Anyway, don't stand there looking like a sucking duck. Come and help us.'

'Of course.' Paula joined them.

Emily gave her a batch of computer printouts. 'Start on these, but before you really dig in, let me get you a cup of coffee, and one of the sandwiches I brought with me. You haven't eaten all night, Paula.'

'I'm not hungry, darling. But I will have a cup of coffee. Thanks, Dumps.'

Paula concentrated on the top sheet, running her eyes quickly down the page of names. Harte's had hundreds of small stockholders who held nominal amounts of shares, as well as those others who had acquired larger blocks over the years. Suddenly, her heart sank. This *was* an endless task, as Michael had said earlier. It might even take longer than one night, several days perhaps, to find the people they needed. She was conscious of time, felt the pressure. Jonathan had boasted he was quickly going to buy up the five per cent he needed. But it was not a boast. She knew he fully intended to do exactly that.

'I bet Jonathan has his stockbrokers and all kinds of flunkies skittering around, trying to buy Harte shares!' she exclaimed, looking at Michael.

He returned her glance. 'I'm sure he has. But you have the advantage, Paula. You have the inside information – these records.'

'Yes,' she said dully, and dropped her eyes to the printout, starting to read again.

Emily brought coffee for the three of them, sat down next to Paula. 'Cheer up, lovey. We'll get the results soon. As Gran used to say, many hands make light work. But, oh boy, do I wish Winston and Shane were here to help us.'

'Oh so do I, Emily. I miss Shane so much. I can't wait for him to get back from Australia. I feel as if half of me is missing when he's not here.'

'Are you going to phone him tomorrow, tell him about this?' Emily inquired.

'I think I have to, he'd be hurt if I didn't. I only hope it doesn't upset him too much. I couldn't bear that. Poor darling, he's had too much to contend with lately.'

It was the gentle tone, the loving nuances, the look of longing in her eyes that stabbed at Michael. *She worships Shane*, he thought. *He is her life.* At that precise moment Michael knew what a fool he had been to think she would ever entertain any advances from him. The mere thought of what he might have done in a foolish moment caused him acute embarrassment.

He dropped his head, pretended to concentrate on the sheet of names to hide his sudden discomfiture. His sexual desire for her had not waned in the past year. He had constantly fantasized about her, but how ridiculous he had been, he saw that now. She was happily married to his friend. How could he have ever thought that she would be interested in him, or any other man for that matter. It had always been Shane since their childhood.

Michael felt as if a veil had been lifted. He saw everything with sudden clarity. He understood then what she had been doing earlier in the year . . . she had been persistently pushing Amanda at him. He ought to have recognized that months ago in New York, known that Paula was out of his range. But he had been so caught up in the fantasy in his own head, he had been blind to many things, most especially reality.

'Here it is!' Emily shrieked. 'I've found a shareholder with quite a substantial number of shares.'

'How many?' Paula asked, hardly daring to breathe.

'*Four* per cent. Gosh, she must be a fairly wealthy woman.'

'Who is she?' Paula asked excitedly, her voice echoing Emily's enthusiasm.

'A Mrs Iris Rumford of –' Emily traced her finger across the printout. '– Bowden Ghyll House, Ilkley!'

'A Yorkshire woman,' Michael said quietly. 'Perhaps this is a good omen, Paula.'

On Saturday morning at ten o'clock, Paula sat opposite Mrs Iris Rumford in the handsome drawing room of her lovely old manor house in Ilkley.

It was obvious to Paula that Mrs Rumford was a woman of considerable means, and she had been graciously received and offered coffee on her arrival minutes before.

Paula had accepted a cup, and the two women had exchanged pleasantries, discussed the weather. Now, as she finished her coffee, Paula said, 'It was very kind of you to see me, Mrs Rumford. As my assistant told you, I wanted to talk to you about your shares in Harte's stores.'

'Yes. And it's my pleasure, Mrs O'Neill. Anyway, it was the least I could do, in that I had tea with your cousin, Jonathan Ainsley, on Thursday.'

Paula almost dropped the coffee cup. She put it down carefully on the end table. This was the last thing she had expected to hear, and she gave Iris Rumford a sharp look. 'He also came to see you about your shares in Harte's presumably?'

'Yes, Mrs O'Neill. He did. He offered me an excellent price for them, went very high actually.'

Paula felt her throat tighten, and she swallowed several times before saying, 'And did you accept his offer, Mrs Rumford?'

'No, as a matter of fact, I didn't.'

Paula relaxed. She smiled at the older woman. 'Then I can make you an offer for them, can't I?'

'You could, yes.'

'Name your price, Mrs Rumford.'

'I don't have a price.'

'But you must know how much you want for your shares.'

'No, I don't. You see, I'm not all that keen to sell them. My late husband bought them for me in 1959.' She gave a funny little laugh. 'I'm sort of sentimentally attached to them. Harte's is my favourite shop in Leeds. I've always patronized it.'

Paula held herself still, pressing back her annoyance. She had obviously come here on a wild goose chase. But she could not afford to antagonize this woman; she needed her too badly. Paula said, 'Well, of course I'm glad you like the store, that you're a satisfied customer. But look here, I do wish you would consider my offer. I will purchase your shares at the same price Mr Ainsley quoted to you.'

Iris Rumford studied her for a moment, frowning slightly, as if she were trying to make up her mind about something. Then she said, 'Is there going to be one of those big battles? The kind I read about in the financial pages of the *Sunday Times?*'

'I sincerely hope not,' Paula exclaimed.

Unexpectedly, Iris Rumford pushed herself to her feet.

Paula also rose, realizing the conversation was suddenly at an end.

'I'm sorry, Mrs O'Neill,' Mrs Rumford murmured. 'Perhaps I should not have let you come to see me. I've wasted your time, I'm afraid. You see, I thought that I might sell my shares, but now I've changed my mind.'

'I'm truly sorry to hear that.' Paula stretched out her hand, trying to be cordial, courteous to her.

Iris Rumford shook it. 'I can see you're angry. And I can't say I blame you. Forgive my vacillation. And please excuse the indecisiveness of an old lady.'

Paula said, 'It's all right, really it is. But if you should change your mind again, please ring me.'

All the way back to Leeds, Paula fumed.

She was baffled and irritated by the woman's odd behaviour, as well as being disappointed. Had Iris Rumford just wanted to be important for a brief moment in her life? Or was it a case of simple curiosity on the part of a lonely old woman? Had she merely wanted to meet Jonathan and herself? Paula wondered how Jonathan Ainsley had found Iris Rumford, how *he* knew that she owned a block of Harte shares. Obviously, he had his ways and his means.

She sighed with exasperation as she pressed her foot hard on the accelerator, and headed the Aston Martin in the direction of Leeds. Going to see Iris Rumford *had* been a waste of time.

Paula spent most of the day working in her office at the Leeds store.

Several times she went out onto the floor, but mostly she kept herself busy with paperwork. And she strove hard not to think about Jonathan Ainsley, the possible takeover bid on his part, or dwell on the frightening prospect of losing the stores to him.

When she did become tense, she reminded herself that in the last forty-eight hours her stockbrokers and Charles Rossiter had between them managed to acquire another seven per cent of Harte shares on her behalf. They had bought them from nine small stockholders Emily and Michael had pinpointed on the computer printouts.

Only three per cent, that's all I need now, she kept saying under her breath whenever she needed to lift her sagging spirits. The words consoled her.

At four o'clock she placed a pile of papers in her briefcase, locked her office and left the store. She usually stayed until six, even on Saturdays. But Emily was coming over to Pennistone Royal for dinner that evening, and Paula wanted to spend an hour with Patrick and Linnet before she arrived.

It was a lovely September afternoon, very sunny, and Leeds had been busy all day. The traffic was heavy on Chapeltown Road as shoppers returned to the outskirts after a day in town. But Paula was an excellent driver; she dodged in and out between the other cars, was soon on the open road going to Harrogate.

She was approaching the roundabout in Alwoodley when the Cellnet phone in her car rang. Reaching for it, she said, 'Hello?' half expecting it to be Emily.

'Mrs O'Neill, it's Doris at the store.'

'Yes, Doris?'

'I have a Mrs Rumford of Ilkley on another line,' the switchboard operator said. 'She insists it's very urgent she speaks to you. Apparently you have her phone number.'

'I do, Doris. But it's in my briefcase. Please give her the car number, ask her to phone me at once. And thank you.'

Only a few minutes after Paula had hung up, the car phone rang again. It was Iris Rumford, and she got straight to the point. 'I wonder if you could come and see me tomorrow? To discuss those shares again.'

'I really can't, Mrs Rumford. I have to drive to London tomorrow. In any case, since you don't want to sell, there doesn't really seem to be much point, does there?'

'I might reconsider your offer, Mrs O'Neill.'

'Then why don't I drive over now?'

'All right,' Iris Rumford agreed.

'You don't know who I am, do you?' Iris Rumford was saying to Paula an hour later.

Paula shook her head. 'Should I? Do I know you?' Her brows knitted together in perplexity. She fixed her gaze intently on the other woman. Iris Rumford was thin but sprightly, with silver hair and a ruddy complexion; she looked to be in her seventies. Paula was certain she did not know her. 'Have we met?' she asked with another frown.

Iris Rumford sat back and returned Paula's penetrating stare. At last, she said slowly, 'No, we haven't met. But you knew my brother. Or at least, you were acquainted with him.'

'Oh,' Paula said, lifting a black brow. 'What was his name?'

'John Cross.'

This name so startled Paula she almost exclaimed out loud. She managed to say in a normal tone, 'We met when he owned Cross Communications.' As she spoke Paula thought of his late son, Sebastian, once her deadly enemy and Jonathan's best friend. She realized immediately how Jonathan knew about Iris Rumford and the stock she owned in Harte's.

'You were very kind and courteous to my brother at the end of his life,' Iris Rumford continued. 'He told me about you when he was dying. He respected you, thought you were very fair. It was your other cousin, Mr Alexander Barkstone, that I met briefly, when my brother was in St James's Hospital in Leeds.' Iris Rumford looked into the fire. There was a short pause. 'You and Mr Barkstone . . . well, you're different from Jonathan Ainsley . . .' She brought her eyes to Paula, half smiled.

Paula waited, wondering what was coming next. When Mrs Rumford made no further comment, she said, 'Yes, I do believe we are. I hope so. But sadly, Mr Barkstone is now dead.'

'I'm sorry to hear that.' The old lady gazed into the flames again. She muttered, 'It's funny, isn't it, how people in families can differ so very much. He was wicked, evil, my nephew, Sebastian. I never had much time for him. John, of course, idolized him, the only son, the only child. But he killed my brother, drove him into his grave with all that wickedness. And Jonathan Ainsley

779

was just as wicked. *He* hammered quite a few nails into my poor brother's coffin. Bad lot, Sebastian and your cousin.'

Suddenly, Iris swung her silver head, focused her eyes on Paula once more. 'I wanted to meet you, Mrs O'Neill, to judge for myself what kind of person you are. That's why I asked you to come this morning. You're a sincere woman, I can tell that from your eyes. Anyway, I've never heard anything bad about you hereabouts. Mostly they say you're like Emma Harte. She was a good woman. I'm glad you take after her.'

Paula had no words. She held her breath.

'And so, if it will help you personally, I *will* sell you my Harte shares.'

For a moment Paula thought she might burst into tears. 'Thank you, Mrs Rumford. It would help me, very much so. I would be most grateful if you sold them to me and not to my cousin.'

'Oh I never intended to sell them to him. I just wanted . . . well, wanted to look him over again, satisfy myself that I'd always been right in my judgement. Also, I got a bit of satisfaction from dangling the carrot in front of him and then snatching it away.' She shook her head. There was a shrewd glint in her wise old eyes. 'When you both phoned me about selling the shares, I got a feeling he was out to make trouble for you. Well, never mind, he'll get his comeuppance one day.'

'Yes.' Paula leaned forward, said, 'I told you this morning I would purchase the shares at the price Jonathan Ainsley had offered. That still stands, of course.'

'Good Lord, that doesn't matter! I wouldn't dream of holding you up, Mrs O'Neill.'

44

Paula stood in front of the fireplace in her office at Harte's in Knightsbridge, below the portrait of Emma. It was three-fifteen on Tuesday afternoon, and she was waiting for Jonathan Ainsley.

Generally she wore black to work. Today she had chosen a bright red wool dress, simply tailored with long sleeves. She thought the colour was appropriate. It was strong, defiant, bold, and it echoed the way she felt.

She had turned disadvantage to advantage. She had the upper hand. She was about to demolish her enemy.

But when Jonathan appeared a few minutes later, she realized that he misguidedly believed *she* was going to capitulate to *him*. Everything about him indicated this. He sauntered in, his step jaunty, his demeanour arrogant, his smile superior.

He halted in the middle of the floor.

Adversaries, they did not greet each other.

He said, 'You sent a message. I'm here. You have something to say to me?'

'You've lost!'

He laughed in her face. 'I never lose!'

'Then this is a first for you.' She lifted her head slightly, the gesture one of confidence and pride. 'I've acquired additional Harte stock . . .' She paused for effect. 'I now hold fifty-two per cent.'

This information threw him. He recovered himself. Displaying no emotion whatsoever, he sneered, 'So what. I have forty-six per cent. I'm the *second* largest stockholder, and entirely within my rights in demanding a seat on the board. I shall do so formally today. Through my solicitors. I also fully intend to proceed with my takeover bid.' His eyes swept over her coldly. 'This will be my office in the not too distant future.'

'I doubt it!' she shot back. 'Furthermore, you don't have forty-six per cent. Only twenty-six.'

'Have you forgotten that I control the shares held in trust by Arthur Jackson for the Weston children?'

'I forget nothing. And I am absolutely certain Arthur Jackson will not be doing business with you after today.'

'Don't be so ridiculous!' His expression turned smug. 'I have an agreement with him, with the law firm. A written agreement.'

Paula took a step forward, reached for a manila envelope on the coffee table, stood holding it in her hands. She tapped it with a bright red fingernail. 'When Arthur Jackson finishes reading this report, which was delivered to him an hour ago, I feel quite confident he will be shredding the agreement.'

'What report is that?' he asked, his expression now one of disdain.

'An investigation into your life in Hong Kong.'

He threw her a look of contempt, said with scorn, 'You have nothing on me. I'm clean.'

Paula studied him thoughtfully. 'Funnily enough,' she said after a short pause, 'I'm inclined to believe you. But nobody else will.'

'What are you implying?'

Ignoring this question, she continued, 'You have a partner in Hong Kong, a silent partner, one Tony Chiu, son of Wan Chin Chiu, who died last year. The man was your mentor, your adviser, and your silent partner from the moment you arrived in the Crown Colony. Pity the son's not as honourable, reliable and honest as the father.'

'My life and my business in Hong Kong have nothing to do with you!' he spluttered. He was irate, trying to hold himself in check.

'Oh yes it does. It has a great deal to do with me when you are trying to take over Harte's.'

'And I will take it over!'

'*No, you won't!*' Her eyes narrowed, and she proceeded in a soft but deadly voice, 'It was very interesting to discover that Tony Chiu has a sideline. A very profitable sideline. *Drugs*. He's alleged to be the biggest dealer of opium in the Golden Triangle, with a huge network spreading through Laos and Thailand. Convenient, isn't it, that he can apparently launder the drug money through Janus and Janus Holdings without anyone being the wiser about what he's up to. What a wonderful front for him. But I wonder how the Hong Kong Government and the Hong Kong police would react, what they would do about it – if they knew the real facts.'

He gaped at her. 'You're lying!' he screamed. 'That report you're clinging onto for dear life is a pack of lies! Tony Chiu is not a drug dealer, he's a respectable, and *respected* banker. And he certainly has not been using my company to launder drug money. I would know about it. He could not do a thing like that and hide it from me.'

She smiled sardonically. 'Don't be naive. You have Chinese employees who are his men, placed there by him even when his father was alive. He hand-picked them in readiness for the future, for the time he would take over his father's banking concerns. And those men are his spies in your organization.'

'*Bullshit!*'

'Your wife, Arabella, knows all about it. She is his business partner, has been for years. And he's financed many of her businesses at various times, including the antique shop she now owns in Hong Kong. She, too, is his spy. That's why she married you. To spy on you.'

Jonathan was livid with rage, unable to speak coherently. He wanted to hit Paula O'Neill in the face for saying such unspeakable things about Arabella. He took several deep breaths, gasped angrily, 'Someone with a vivid imagination has written a piece of fiction for you. *It's all lies, lies, lies!*' His breathing was ragged as he finished, 'He is my silent partner, we are never seen together. My wife does not even know Tony Chiu.'

'Why don't you ask her?'

His lip curled and his pale eyes filled with hatred for her. He shifted his gaze to the portrait of Emma Harte above her head, and his loathing for the two of them intensified. 'You bloody bitch!' he hissed. 'You're just like that old cow used to be! I piss on her grave. I piss on yours!' he cursed.

His words denigrating her grandmother incensed Paula. She went in for the kill. With meticulous care, she said, 'The beautiful Arabella Sutton, doctor's daughter from Hampshire, is not quite what she seems to be. No doubt you are aware she lived in Paris for years. But did you know she was a "Claude girl"?' Paula laughed coldly, taunted, 'Don't tell me a sophisticated man like you doesn't know all about Madame Claude. She ran the most successful, indeed the finest, sex operation ever known in Paris. And until 1977.'

Jonathan gaped at her. He was dumbfounded.

'Arabella Sutton, *your wife*, was one of Madame Claude's call girls. She went by the name Francine.'

'I do not believe you,' he shouted. 'Arabella is –'

'Believe it,' she shouted back. She flung the envelope at him. It landed at his feet. 'The report and copies of certain official documents attached to it will make interesting reading for you.'

Jonathan saw it out of the corner of his eye but he made no move to pick it up.

Paula said in an icy voice, 'Instead of trying to knock my house down, go and put your own in order.'

He opened his mouth to say something, then closed it. He glanced at the envelope at his feet. He longed to show her what he thought about her report by walking away from it. But he could not. His overriding desire, his consuming need, to see the official documents she had just alluded to got the better of him. He bent down, picked it up, swung around and strode to the door.

'I've won!' Paula called after him. 'And don't you ever forget it!'

He halted, looked back at her. 'We'll see about that,' he said.

Paula walked back to her desk. She sat thinking for a while. There was one more thing she had to do to ensure complete success, but it required her to be utterly ruthless, more ruthless than Emma Harte had ever been. She was still balking at the idea. She glanced over at the portrait of her grandmother, then brought her eyes back to the photograph in the silver frame on her desk. It was of Shane and the children. They, too, were Emma's heirs. She had to protect Harte's for them, no matter what it took.

Without any further hesitation, she reached for her private phone, dialled Sir Ronald on his direct line.

He picked up the phone after two rings. 'Kallinski here.'

'Uncle Ronnie, it's me again. Sorry to keep bothering you today.'

'You're not, my dear.' There was a slight pause. 'Has he left?'

'Yes. Shaken, but not conceding anything. In fact, he was obviously determined to keep on fighting me. And so I will dispose of him in the way we discussed. A copy of the report will go to the authorities in Hong Kong. But honestly, Uncle Ronnie, I –'

'No regrets, I hope, Paula.'

'It's such a ruthless thing to do. It makes me far more ruthless than Grandy ever was.'

'That's not true, my dear. Emma could be *extremely* ruthless, too, when there was something for her to be ruthless about . . . such as Harte's, the business empire she built from nothing, and those she loved.'

'Perhaps you're right.'

'I know I am,' Sir Ronald murmured, speaking in a softer voice. 'I told you last night that Jonathan Ainsley will never leave you alone, never be off your back. He'll always keep trying to get the stores. That's the nature of the man.'

When she remained silent at the other end of the phone, Sir Ronald added, 'You have no option but to stop him now. To protect yourself.'

'Yes, I realize that, Uncle Ronnie.'

He sat in the corner of Claridge's foyer, where afternoon tea was being served. But he scarcely heard the rattle of tea cups, the violins, or the varied background noises. He was reading far too intently to notice anything.

Jonathan had read the report twice.

At first he had wanted to dismiss it as pure invention, a vindictive interpretation of the facts on someone else's part, and especially the sections about Tony Chiu. But now he was finding this difficult to do. There was too much genuine information included to dismiss the entire thing as bogus. He had been amazed to read a whole page about his affair with Lady Susan Sorrell. That had been such a clandestine relationship he could hardly believe his eyes when he had come across her name. He was convinced Susan would not have talked about their sexual relationship when it was in progress. Or after it finished. She was terrified of gossip and of invoking her husband's wrath. Divorce from her rich banker was the last thing she wanted.

He came out as clean as he had insisted he was to Paula O'Neill, despite the information about Tony, which disturbed and alarmed him. If it *was* actually true, then he could be implicated in something he knew nothing about. Janus and Janus could be in jeopardy, as he might be himself. It could turn out to be serious. He would have to fly back to Hong Kong as soon as possible, start his own investigation there.

The thing which truly distressed him, however, was the detailed account of Arabella's past. This was backed up with photostats of documents relating to her years in Paris. Her whole life in France had been tracked and meticulously recorded in these pages of typescript. There was no longer any question in his mind that she had used the name Francine, and that she had been one of Madame Claude's girls. Quite aside from the documentation, there were so many other things which made him give credence to the report. There was her sexual expertise and knowledge, her overall attitude towards a man, which smacked of the courtesan's trade, her sophistication, her worldliness, her elegance . . . Madame Claude's girls had all been like her.

Carefully sliding the papers back into the envelope, he got to his feet, hurried out to the lift. There was nothing productive he could do about Hong Kong at this moment, but he could go upstairs and confront the woman he was married to.

As he rode up in the lift to the tenth floor, his suppressed anger bubbled up in him, spiralled into a terrible fury. He was ashen faced and shaking inside when he entered the suite. He went in quietly, but she heard him and came out into the foyer, smiling.

'Jonathan darling, how did it go?' she asked, coming over to him, kissing him on the cheek.

Jonathan was devastated by what he had just read about his wife, and he could hardly bear her to touch him. He had to hold himself rigid in order not to react to her kiss, or strike her.

He had loved her, had considered her to be his most perfect possession. She was imperfect now, soiled, damaged, worthless.

Again she said, 'How did the meeting go at Harte's?'

'So-so,' he muttered noncommittally, controlling himself even though the rage boiled inside him.

Arabella looked at him oddly, detecting a sudden coldness in him, then she immediately dismissed this as irritation with Paula O'Neill, his *bête noire*.

Turning, she walked back into the sitting room where she had been reading, settled herself on the sofa. Her knitting bag was next to her, and she opened it, took out the baby's jacket she was making, began to ply the needles.

Jonathan walked in after her, put the envelope down on an end table, went over to the bar, where he poured himself a neat vodka.

He stood sipping it, regarding her, thinking how heavy with child she looked this afternoon. The baby was due any moment, and as much as he wanted to confront Arabella head on, he knew he must restrain himself. He did not want her any more, and he would divorce her as quickly as possible, but he certainly wanted his child . . . his son and heir.

He said, conversationally, 'Did you ever know a man in Hong Kong called Tony Chiu?'

If Arabella was startled by this question, she did not show it. 'No, why do you ask?' she murmured, all calm contentment.

'No special reason. His name happened to come up at lunch with my solicitors today. I thought you might have run across him in your travels, know something about him.'

'I'm afraid I don't, darling.'

He finished the vodka, reached for the envelope and crossed the room. Taking the chair facing her, he said, 'You lived in Paris for years . . . but you never want to go there. Why is that?'

'It's never been my favourite place,' she said, lifting her eyes from the knitting, smiling at him lovingly.

'Then why did you live there for almost eight years?'

'My work was there. You know I was a model. And why all these questions about Paris, Jonny darling?'

He said slowly, 'Are you afraid to go to Paris?'

'Of course not. And why are *you* being so strange? I don't understand you.'

'Are you afraid you'll run into some of your old . . . paramours, is that what it's all about, *Francine?*'

Arabella gazed at him. Her pitch-black eyes were full of innocence. 'I don't know what you're getting at, or why you're calling me Francine.' She laughed lightly, shook her head.

'Because that's the name you used when you were a call girl.'

'What on earth are you saying?' she cried.

'Don't deny it! The documentation is all here, courtesy of Paula O'Neill. You can read it for yourself,' he said, pinning her with his eyes. 'It's an investigation into my life, and they've done quite a number on yours, too.'

Arabella had no alternative but to take the documents he was thrusting at her.

'*Read them.*'

She was suddenly terrified. She saw the dark gleam in his eyes, the cold implacability on his face. He could be cruel, dangerous when crossed, she knew that, knew all about his temper. She did as he said, scanning the pages swiftly, not wanting to read, knowing the papers were damning. But words jumped out at her; she took in the general contents, and her heart tightened in her chest.

She handed them back to him. Her face was the colour of chalk. Tears glittered in her eyes. 'Darling, please, you don't understand. Let me explain. Please. My past has nothing to do with today, with now, with you, with us. It happened so long ago. I was very young. Only a child, really. Only nineteen. I left that life behind me long ago, Jonny darling.'

'I'm going to ask you one more time,' he said. 'Do you know Tony Chiu?'

'Yes,' she whispered.

'Did he back your antique jade business in Hong Kong?'

'Yes.'

'Why?'

'We've been in business before at different times. He's a bit of an entrepreneur.'

'And he put you on to me, didn't he? Set me up as a target for you. He wanted you to ensnare me, to marry me so you could keep an eye on me. For him.'

'No, no, that's not true. Oh Jonny, I fell in love with you! I did! You know I did.'

'Admit you set me up. I know everything,' he railed at her.

She began to shake. Floundering, she cried, 'Yes, I did try to ensnare you, that night at Susan Sorrell's, when we first met. But very soon after that I became involved with you. I didn't want to do anything but love you. *Truly*. You must know that from our time at Mougins, from our extraordinary intimacy there, the way we became almost one person.'

'I can't believe anything you say,' he exclaimed, going to pour another drink.

She watched him go, return to the chair. Once he was seated again, she said, 'I told Tony I couldn't give him any information about you. *That I wouldn't*. And that decision was reinforced more strongly than ever when I became pregnant with our child ... I love you,' she repeated, meaning this, her eyes riveted to his face.

'And are you involved in the drugs with him?'

'I don't know what you mean,' she cried, truly baffled.

'For God's sake, don't keep denying things,' he shouted. Something in him snapped. He jumped up, took hold of her shoulders, shook her violently. 'Whore,' he yelled at her, 'tart, *putain*. I loved you, no, adored you. I thought you were the most perfect thing, the most beautiful woman in the world, without blemish. But you're nothing ... dirt.'

Arabella began to weep uncontrollably. 'You've got to believe me, Jonny. I love you with all my heart, and I've told him nothing –'

'Liar!' he screamed at her.

She reached out to him, grabbed his coat sleeve.

He shook her hands off him, his face filling with contempt and hatred. 'Don't touch me.'

Suddenly Arabella's face twisted and she brought her hands to her stomach. 'The baby! I think the baby's coming. I'm having a contraction. Oh please help me ... help me, Jonny. Get me to the hospital. *Please*,' she begged.

Arabella was in labour by the time he got her to the London Clinic. She was taken to the delivery room immediately.

Jonathan went to wait in the lounge reserved for expectant fathers in the famous private clinic. An hour and a half later his son was born. A nurse came to inform him of this, explaining that he could see his wife and child shortly.

He did not care about his wife. His only interest was in his son. The heir he had always wanted. He would take the child away from her as soon as he could. Women like Arabella – whores – were not interested in children. The boy would be brought up as an English gentleman. Suddenly his mind turned to schools. He would send the boy to Eton, where he had gone, and then to Cambridge.

Settling into his thoughts, he sat quietly, waiting patiently to see his child. He realized he was excited, that he looked forward to holding the baby in his arms. His father and mother would be happy. This was their first grandchild. Perhaps he would call the boy Robin. After the christening, the reception would be held at the House of Commons. As a leading politician and Member of Parliament, his father could easily arrange that.

He switched gears, contemplated Paula O'Neill, considered the problem of the Harte stores. More than ever he was determined to go through with his plans to wrest control of the chain from her. He must. There was his son and heir to consider now.

A nurse came to fetch him sooner than he expected. He followed her down the corridor to the private suite he had booked for Arabella a month ago. The nurse showed him in, disappeared, murmuring she was going to get the baby.

Arabella was in bed, propped up against the pillows. She looked pale, exhausted.

'Jonny,' she began, reaching out her hand to him. Her eyes were imploring. 'Please don't be like this with me. Give me another chance, for the sake of our child. I've never done anything to hurt you. Never. I love you, darling.'

'I don't want to talk to you,' he snapped.

'But Jonny –' She broke off as the door opened. The same nurse walked in, this time carrying the baby wrapped in blankets and a lacy cashmere shawl.

He hurried over to the bed as the nurse placed the baby in Arabella's outstretched arms. They looked down at their child together.

Jonathan stiffened. The first thing he saw was the epicanthic fold of the eye, that little bit of skin covering the inner corner that was unmistakably Oriental.

The shock on his face mirrored the stunned expression on hers. Arabella looked up at him speechlessly.

'This is not my child!' Jonathan shouted, his rage exploding. 'It's Tony Chiu's! Or some other Chinaman's, you bloody whore!'

He pushed past the incredulous nurse, half stumbled, half ran out of the suite, wanting to put as much distance between himself and Arabella as he could.

The uniformed chauffeur turned on the ignition and the stately, silver-grey Rolls-Royce pulled noiselessly away from Claridge's, rolled off on its way to London airport.

Jonathan leaned back, sank into the glove-soft leather of the seat. His rage was monumental, would not abate. He could not get over the shock of Arabella's past, her duplicity, her treachery, and the knowledge that she had been sleeping with another man whilst married to him. An Oriental man. There was no way she could ever deny that. The baby was living proof. *Tony Chiu*, Jonathan thought for the umpteenth time. Her old friend and benefactor was the most likely candidate.

He glanced at his briefcase next to him on the back seat, and his mind zeroed in yet again on the report. He was not sure how much truth there was in the information it contained about Tony Chiu's activities. But if the man was laundering money through Janus and Janus, he was going to put a stop to it. Immediately. And somehow he would find a way to even the score with his Chinese partner.

Jonathan could not wait to get back to Hong Kong. He glanced at his watch, saw that it was only nine-thirty. He had plenty of time to catch the midnight flight that would take him to the British Crown Colony.

Slipping his hand into his pocket, he automatically curled his fingers around the pebble of mutton-fat jade. He brought it out, stared at it in the dim light of the car. His eyes narrowed thoughtfully. It no longer looked the same. Somehow it had lost its luminosity, its lustre. But it was his talisman. He laughed hollowly to himself. Some talisman. It had brought him no luck recently. Only bad joss. Very bad joss.

Rolling down the window, Jonathan flung the pebble out into the street, watched it roll away into the gutter.

The car sped on. He sat back, smiled to himself. He was glad to be rid of the jade piece. Now, perhaps, his luck would change.

EPILOGUE

We are each the authors of our own lives . . .
there is no way to shift the blame and no-one
else to accept the accolades.

PAUL McGILL, in *A Woman of Substance*

EPILOGUE

They sat together on the rocks at the Top of the World.

It was a glorious Saturday afternoon in late September. The sky was the colour of speedwells and glittering with sunlight, and below them the implacable moors were softened by wave upon wave of purple heather. Somewhere in the distance there was the sound of rushing water as a stream tumbled down over rocky crags, and on the lucent air there was the smell of heather and bracken and bilberry.

They had been silent for a while, lost in their own thoughts, enjoying being together again, being up here where it was so peaceful.

All of a sudden Shane put his arms around Paula, held her close to him. 'It's wonderful to be home, to be with you,' he said. 'I'm lost when we're apart.'

She turned her head, smiled at him. 'I feel the same.'

'I'm glad we came up to the moors today,' Shane went on. 'There's nowhere like them in the whole world.'

'Grandy's moors,' Paula said. 'She loved them, too.'

'Especially up here, at the Top of the World.'

'Grandy once said that the secret of life is to endure,' Paula murmured and looked at him quizzically. 'I hope *I* will.'

'Of course you will, my darling. *You have.* In fact, you've not only endured, you've prevailed. She'd be very proud of you. Emma always wanted you to be the best. And you are.'

'You're prejudiced.'

'I am indeed. But that doesn't make my statement any less true.'

'I almost lost Harte's, Shane,' she whispered.

'But you didn't. And that's what counts, Paula.'

He jumped off the rocks, took hold of her hands, helped her down. 'Come on, we'd better get back. I promised Patrick and Linnet we'd have nursery tea with them.'

They walked through the heather, holding hands, buffeted forward by the wind as they headed for the car parked on the dirt road. Paula stole a look at him, loving him, relieved and happy that he had returned from Australia. He had arrived in Yorkshire last night, and he had not stopped talking since, full of his plans for rebuilding the Sydney-O'Neill Hotel.

Paula came to a sudden halt.

Shane also stopped, turned to look at her. 'What is it?' he asked. 'Is there something wrong?'

'I hope not,' she replied, starting to laugh. Her eyes were bright with happiness. 'I've wanted to tell you since last night, but you haven't given me the chance –'

'Tell me what?' he probed.

She leaned into him, looked up into his face, that face she had known and loved all her life. 'We're going to have another baby. I'm almost three months pregnant.'

He pulled her into his arms and hugged her, then held her away. 'That's the best welcome home present I've ever had,' Shane said, smiling at her.

And he continued to smile all the way back to Pennistone Royal.